To all my good

Penny Louise

Tipper John

John

Flip

Archie and Ed

Tippy

Spots

Emily

Ajax

Molly

Gus

Homer and JJ

DIANA GABALDON

AN ECHO
IN THE BONE

A NOVEL

An Orion paperback

First published in Great Britain in 2010
by Orion
This paperback edition published in 2010
by Orion Books Ltd,
Orion House, 5 Upper St Martin's Lane,
London WC2H 9EA

An Hachette UK company

1 3 5 7 9 10 8 6 4 2

A CIP catalogue record for this book is available
from the British Library.

ISBN 978-1-4091-0373-8

Printed and bound in Great Britain by CPI Mackays, Chatham ME5 8TD

The Orion Publishing Group's policy is to use papers that
are natural, renewable and recyclable products and
made from wood grown in sustainable forests. The logging
and manufacturing processes are expected to conform to
the environmental regulations of the country of origin.

'The White Swan', taken from *Carmina Gadelica*.
Reproduced by kind permission of Floris Books.

www.orionbooks.co.uk

Used as Grey was to the swift brutality of army surgeons, Mrs. Fraser's preparations seemed laborious in the extreme: she swabbed Henry's belly repeatedly with an alcoholic solution she had concocted, talking to him through her highwayman's mask in a low, soothing voice. She rinsed her hands – and made Hunter and Mrs. Woodcock do the same – and her instruments, so that the whole room reeked like a distillery of low quality.

Her motions were in fact quite brisk, he realized after a moment. But her hands moved with such sureness and . . . yes, grace, that was the only word . . . that they gave the illusion of gliding like a pair of gulls upon the air. No frantic flapping, only a sure, serene, and almost mystic movement. He found himself quieting as he watched them, becoming entranced and half forgetting the ultimate purpose of this quiet dance of hands.

She moved to the head of the bed, bending low to speak to Henry, smooth the hair away from his brow, and Grey saw the hawk's eyes soften momentarily into gold. Henry's body relaxed slowly under her touch; Grey saw his clenched, rigid hands uncurl. She had yet another mask, he saw, this one a stiff thing made of basket withes lined with layers of soft cotton cloth. She fitted this gently to Henry's face and, saying something inaudible to him, took up her dropping bottle.

The air filled at once with a pungent, sweet aroma that clung to the back of Grey's throat and made his head swim slightly. He blinked, shaking his head to dispel the giddiness, and realized that Mrs. Fraser had said something to him.

'I beg your pardon?' He looked up at her, a great white bird with yellow eyes – and a gleaming talon that sprouted suddenly from her hand.

'I said,' she repeated calmly through her mask, 'you might want to sit back a little farther. It's going to be rather messy.'

Diana Gabaldon is the *New York Times* bestselling author of the wildly popular Outlander novels – *Outlander, Dragonfly in Amber, Voyager, Drums of Autumn, The Fiery Cross,* and *A Breath of Snow and Ashes* – and one work of non-fiction, *The Outlandish Companion,* as well as the bestselling series featuring Lord John Grey, an important character from the original series. She lives with her family and a lot of other assorted wildlife in Scottsdale, Arizona. Visit her website at www.dianagabaldon.com.

ACKNOWLEDGMENTS

It takes me a good three years to write one of these books, during which time I constantly ask people questions, and during which time helpful people offer me fascinating bits of information that I didn't think to ask for. I'll never remember them all, but think of them all with enormous gratitude.

In addition, I wish to offer grateful thanks to . . .

. . . John Flicker and Bill Massey, my editors, both gentlemen of gall and kidney, who coped nobly with a book written in pieces (lots of pieces), and an author who lives dangerously.

. . . Danny Baror and Russell Galen, my literary agents, two gentlemen literally worth their weight in gold—which is saying something in these recessionary days.

. . . Kathy Lord, heroic copy editor, and Virginia Norey, book designer (aka "the book goddess"), who are jointly responsible for the beauty and readability of this book.

. . . Vincent La Scala and the other cruelly used members of the production crew, who succeeded in getting this book into print on time against looooong odds.

. . . Steven Lopata for his vivid description of being chased overland by a cottonmouth—as well as the poetic description of what they smell like ("A combination of that snakehouse smell from the zoo and rotten cucumbers").

. . . Catherine MacGregor and Catherine-Ann MacPhee for *Gàidhlig* translations and help in the subtleties of Gaelic usage. Also Katie Beggs and various unsung but much appreciated members of the International Gaelic Mafia.

. . . Tess Jones the nurse, Dr. Amarilis Iscold, Sarah Meir (Certified Nurse Midwife), and a number of other helpful medical professionals, for advice on matters medical, picturesque maladies, and horrifying surgical details.

. . . Janet McConnaughey for *OEDILF* (Omnificant English Dictionary in Limerick Form) entries, being the Muse of Bloody Axes, and drawing my attention to exploding cypress trees.

. . . Larry Tuohy (and others) for telling me what a Spitfire pilot's flight jacket looked like.

. . . Ron Parker, Helen, Esmé and Lesley, for 'elp with the 'airy ape.

. . . Beth and Matthew Shope and Jo Bourne for useful information regarding the Religious Society of Friends. Any inaccuracies are definitely my fault.

. . . Jari Backman, for his detailed time lines and excerpt listings, and for help with the night sky and which stars are visible in Inverness and Fraser's Ridge.

. . . Katrina Stibohar for her exquisitely detailed lists of who was born when and What Happened to Everybody then. Also to the hordes of kindly trivia freaks who are always on hand to tell me how old someone is, or whether Lord John met Fergus when he had the measles.

. . . Pamela Patchet Hamilton (and Buddy) for a nose-wrenchingly vivid description of a close-range skunking.

. . . Karen Henry, Czarina of Traffic, who keeps my folder in the Compuserve Books and Writers Community tidy and the inhabitants diplomatically herded. (http://community.compuserve.com/n/pfx/forum.aspx?nav=start&webtag =ws-books)

. . . Nikki Rowe and her daughter Caitlin, for the wonderful YouTube channel they created for me (http://www.youtube.com/user/voyagesof theartemis—for those who want to see whether I really do sound like Donald Duck when I talk).

. . . Rosana Madrid Gatti, my web-mistress, for prompt and faithful updates and imaginative design.

. . . Susan Butler, for constant logistic support, dog sleepovers, keeping me supplied with black-ink cartridges, and for her brilliant suggestion regarding Jem.

. . . Allene Edwards, Catherine MacGregor, and Susan Butler, for proofreading and Extremely Helpful (if eyeball-numbing) nitpicking.

. . . Shirley Williams for the Moravian cookies and vistas of New Bern.

. . . Becky Morgan for the historical cookbooks.

. . . my great-grandfather, Stanley Sykes, for Jamie's line about marksmanship.

. . . Bev LaFrance, Carol Krenz, and many others for help with French. Also Florence the translator, Peter Berndt, and Gilbert Sureau for the nice distinctions between the French Lord's Prayer of 1966 (*accorde-lui*) versus the earlier, more formal version (*accordez-lui*).

. . . John S. Kruszka, for the proper spelling and pronunciation of "Kościuszko" (it's "kohs-CHOOSH-koh," in case you wondered; nobody in the Revolution could pronounce it, either—they really did all call him "Kos").

. . . the Ladies of Lallybroch, for continuous support and Really Interesting Gifts.

. . . my husband, because he knows fine what a man is for, too.

. . . Alex Krislov, Janet McConnaughey, and Margaret Campbell, sysops of the Compuserve Books and Writers Community, and the many, many, many helpful people who roam through the site daily, offering observations, information, and general entertainment.

. . . Alfred Publishing for permission to quote from the lyrics to "Tighten Up," by Archie Bell and the Drells.

"The White Swan," taken from *Carmina Gadelica,* is reproduced by kind permission of Floris Books.

"The Hippopotamus Song" (referenced briefly in Claire's thoughts on page 114) was written (1959) by Michael Flanders, of the famous comic duo Flanders and Swann.

CONTENTS

PART THREE
Privateer

PART FOUR
Conjunction

PART FIVE

To the Precipice

PART SIX
Coming Home

PART SEVEN
Reap the Whirlwind

PROLOGUE

THE BODY IS amazingly plastic. The spirit, even more so. But there are some things you don't come back from.

Say ye so, *a nighean*? True, the body's easily maimed, and the spirit can be crippled—yet there's that in a man that is never destroyed.

PART ONE

A Troubling of the Waters

SOMETIMES
THEY'RE REALLY DEAD

Wilmington, colony of North Carolina
July 1776

THE PIRATE'S HEAD had disappeared. William heard the speculations from a group of idlers on the quay nearby, wondering whether it would be seen again.

"Na, him be gone for good," said a ragged man of mixed blood, shaking his head. "De ally-gator don' take him, de water will."

A backwoodsman shifted his tobacco and spat into the water in disagreement.

"No, he's good for another day—two, maybe. Them gristly bits what holds the head on, they dry out in the sun. Tighten up like iron. Seen it many a time with deer carcasses."

William saw Mrs. MacKenzie glance quickly at the harbor, then away. She looked pale, he thought, and maneuvered himself slightly so as to block her view of the men and the brown flood of high tide, though since it *was* high, the corpse tied to its stake was naturally not visible. The stake was, though—a stark reminder of the price of crime. The pirate had been staked to drown on the mudflats several days before, the persistence of his decaying corpse an ongoing topic of public conversation.

"Jem!" Mr. MacKenzie called sharply, and lunged past William in pursuit of his son. The little boy, red-haired like his mother, had wandered away to listen to the men's talk, and was now leaning perilously out over the water, clinging to a bollard in an attempt to see the dead pirate.

Mr. MacKenzie snatched the boy by the collar, pulled him in, and swept him up in his arms, though the boy struggled, craning back toward the swampish harbor.

"I want to see the wallygator eat the pirate, Daddy!"

The idlers laughed, and even MacKenzie smiled a little, though the smile disappeared when he glanced at his wife. He was at her side in an instant, one hand beneath her elbow.

"I think we must be going," MacKenzie said, shifting his son's weight in order better to support his wife, whose distress was apparent. "Lieutenant Ransom—Lord Ellesmere, I mean"—he corrected with an apologetic smile at William—"will have other engagements, I'm sure."

This was true; William was engaged to meet his father for supper. Still, his father had arranged to meet him at the tavern just across the quay; there was no risk of missing him. William said as much, and urged them to stay, for he was enjoying their company—Mrs. MacKenzie's, particularly—but she smiled regretfully, though her color was better, and patted the capped head of the baby in her arms.

"No, we do have to be going." She glanced at her son, still struggling to get down, and William saw her eyes flicker toward the harbor and the stark pole that stood above the flood. She resolutely looked away, fixing her eyes upon William's face instead. "The baby's waking up; she'll be wanting food. It was so lovely to meet you, though. I wish we might talk longer." She said this with the greatest sincerity, and touched his arm lightly, giving him a pleasant sensation in the pit of the stomach.

The idlers were now placing wagers on the reappearance of the drowned pirate, though by the looks of things, none of them had two groats to rub together.

"Two to one he's still there when the tide goes out."

"Five to one the body's still there, but the head's gone. I don't care what you say about the gristly bits, Lem, that there head was just a-hangin' by a thread when this last tide come in. Next un'll take it, sure."

Hoping to drown this conversation out, William embarked on an elaborate farewell, going so far as to kiss Mrs. MacKenzie's hand with his best court manner—and, seized by inspiration, kissed the baby girl's hand, too, making them all laugh. Mr. MacKenzie gave him rather an odd look, but didn't seem offended, and shook his hand in a most republican manner—playing out the joke by setting down his son and making the little boy shake hands as well.

"Have you kilt anybody?" the boy inquired with interest, looking at William's dress sword.

"No, not yet," William replied, smiling.

"My grandsire's kilt two dozen men!"

"Jemmy!" Both parents spoke at once, and the little boy's shoulders went up around his ears.

"Well, he *has*!"

"I'm sure he is a bold and bloody man, your grandsire," William assured the little boy gravely. "The King always has need of such men."

"My grandda says the King can kiss his arse," the boy replied matter-of-factly.

"JEMMY!"

Mr. MacKenzie clapped a hand over his outspoken offspring's mouth.

"You *know* your grandda didn't say that!" Mrs. MacKenzie said. The little boy nodded agreeably, and his father removed the muffling hand.

"No. Grannie did, though."

"Well, that's somewhat more likely," Mr. MacKenzie murmured, obviously trying not to laugh. "But we still don't say things like that to soldiers—they work for the King."

"Oh," said Jemmy, clearly losing interest. "Is the tide going out now?" he asked hopefully, craning his neck toward the harbor once more.

"No," Mr. MacKenzie said firmly. "Not for hours. You'll be in bed."

Mrs. MacKenzie smiled at William in apology, her cheeks charmingly flushed with embarrassment, and the family took its leave with some haste, leaving William struggling between laughter and dismay.

"Oy, Ransom!"

He turned at his name, to find Harry Dobson and Colin Osborn, two second lieutenants from his regiment, evidently escaped from duty and eager to sample the fleshpots of Wilmington—such as they were.

"Who's that?" Dobson looked after the departing group, interested.

"A Mr. and Mrs. MacKenzie. Friends of my father's."

"Oh, married, is she?" Dobson sucked in his cheeks, still watching the woman. "Well, make it a bit harder, I suppose, but what's life without a challenge?"

"Challenge?" William gave his diminutive friend a jaundiced look. "Her husband's roughly three times your size, if you hadn't noticed."

Osborn laughed, going red in the face.

"She's *twice* his size! She'd crush you, Dobby."

"And what makes you think I mean to be on the bottom?" Dobson inquired with dignity. Osborn hooted.

"What's this obsession of yours with giantesses?" William demanded. He glanced at the little family, now nearly out of sight at the end of the street. "That woman's nearly as tall as I am!"

"Oh, rub it in, why don't you?" Osborn, who was taller than Dobson's five feet, but still a head shorter than William, aimed a mock kick at his knee. William dodged it and cuffed Osborn, who ducked and shoved him into Dobson.

"Gennelmen!" The menacing cockney tones of Sergeant Cutter brought them up sharp. They might outrank the sergeant, but not one of them would have the nerve to point this out. The entire battalion went in fear of Sergeant Cutter, who was older than God and approximately Dobson's height, but who contained within his diminutive physique the sheer fury of a full-sized volcano on the boil.

"Sergeant!" Lieutenant William Ransom, Earl of Ellesmere and senior of the group, drew himself up straight, chin pressed back into his stock. Osborn and Dobson hastily followed his lead, quaking in their boots.

Cutter strode back and forth in front of them, in the manner of a stalking leopard. You could just see the lashing tail and the preliminary licking of chops, William thought. Waiting for the bite was almost worse than getting it in the arse.

"And where's your troops, then?" Cutter snarled. *"Sirs?"*

Osborn and Dobson at once began sputtering explanations, but Lieutenant Ransom—for once—walked on the side of the angels.

"My men are guarding the Governor's Palace, under Lieutenant Colson. I'm given leave, Sergeant, to dine with my father," he said respectfully. "By Sir Peter."

Sir Peter Packer's was a name to conjure with, and Cutter abated in midspew. Rather to William's surprise, though, it wasn't Sir Peter's name that had produced this reaction.

"Your father?" Cutter said, squinting. "That's Lord John Grey, is it?"

"Er . . . yes," William replied cautiously. "Do you . . . know him?"

Before Cutter could reply, the door of a nearby tavern opened, and William's father came out. William smiled in delight at this timely appearance, but quickly erased the smile as the sergeant's gimlet gaze fixed on him.

"Don't you be a-grinnin' at *me* like an 'airy ape," the sergeant began, in dangerous tones, but was interrupted by Lord John's clapping him familiarly on the shoulder—something none of the three young lieutenants would have done if offered significant money.

"Cutter!" Lord John said, smiling warmly. "I heard those dulcet tones and said to myself, why damn me if it isn't Sergeant Aloysius Cutter! There can't be another man alive who sounds so much like a bulldog that's swallowed a cat and lived to tell about it."

"*Aloysius?*" Dobson mouthed at William, but William merely grunted briefly in response, unable to shrug, as his father had now turned his attention in his direction.

"William," he said, with a cordial nod. "How very punctual you are. My apologies for being so late; I was detained." Before William could say anything or introduce the others, though, Lord John had embarked upon a lengthy reminiscence with Sergeant Cutter, reliving high old times on the Plains of Abraham with General Wolfe.

This allowed the three young officers to relax slightly, which, in Dobson's case, meant a return to his earlier train of thought.

"You said that red-haired poppet's a friend of your father's?" he whispered to William. "Find out from him where she's staying, eh?"

"Idiot," hissed Osborn. "She isn't even pretty! She's long-nosed as—as—as Willie!"

"Didn't see as high as her face," Dobson said, smirking. "Her tits were right at eye-level, though, and *those...*"

"Ass!"

"Shh!" Osborn stamped on Dobson's foot to shut him up as Lord John turned back to the young men.

"Will you introduce me to your friends, William?" Lord John inquired politely. Rather red in the face—he had reason to know that his father had acute hearing, despite his artillery experiences—William did so, and Osborn and Dobson both bowed, looking rather awed. They hadn't realized who his father was, and William was at once proud that they were impressed, and mildly dismayed that they'd discovered Lord John's identity—it would be all over the battalion before supper tomorrow. Not that Sir Peter didn't know, of course, but—

He gathered his wits, realizing that his father was taking leave for them both, and returned Sergeant Cutter's salute, hastily but in good form, before hurrying after his father, leaving Dobby and Osborn to their fate.

"I saw you speaking to Mr. and Mrs. MacKenzie," Lord John said casually. "I trust they are well?" He glanced down the quay, but the MacKenzies had long since disappeared from view.

"Seemed so," Willie said. He was *not* going to ask where they stayed, but the impression the young woman had made on him lingered. He couldn't say if she was pretty or not; her eyes had struck him, though—a wonderful deep blue with long auburn lashes, and fixed on him with a flattering intensity that had warmed the cockles of his heart. Grotesquely tall, of course, but—what was he thinking? The woman was married—with children! And red-haired, to boot.

"You've—er—known them long?" he asked, thinking of the startlingly perverse political sentiments that evidently flourished in the family.

"Quite some time. She is the daughter of one of my oldest friends, Mr. James Fraser. Do you recall him, by chance?"

William frowned, not placing the name—his father had thousands of friends, how should he . . .

"Oh!" he said. "Not an English friend, you don't mean. Was it not a Mr. Fraser that we visited in the mountains, that time when you fell sick of the— of the measle?" The bottom of his stomach dropped a little, remembering the sheer terror of that time. He had traveled through the mountains in a daze of misery; his mother had died only a month before. Then Lord John had caught the measle, and William had been sure that his father was about to die likewise, leaving him completely alone in the wilderness. There hadn't been room for anything in his mind but fear and grief, and he retained only a jumble of confused impressions from the visit. He had some dim recollection that Mr. Fraser had taken him fishing and been kind to him.

"Yes," his father said, with a sidelong smile. "I'm touched, Willie. I should have thought you might recall that visit more because of your own misadventure than mine."

"Mis—" Memory rushed over him, succeeded by a flood of heat, hotter than the humid summer air. "Thanks very much! I'd managed to expunge that from my memory, until you mentioned it!"

His father was laughing, and making no attempt to hide it. In fact, he was convulsed.

"I'm sorry, Willie," he said, gasping and wiping his eyes with a corner of his handkerchief. "I can't help it; it was the most—the most—oh, God, I'll never forget what you looked like when we pulled you out of that privy!"

"You *know* it was an accident," William said stiffly. His cheeks burned with remembered mortification. At least Fraser's daughter hadn't been present to witness his humiliation at the time.

"Yes, of course. But—" His father pressed the handkerchief to his mouth, his shoulders shaking silently.

"Feel free to stop cackling at any point," William said coldly. "Where the devil are we going, anyway?" They'd reached the end of the quay, and his father was leading them—still snorting like a grampus—into one of the quiet, tree-lined streets, away from the taverns and inns near the harbor.

"We're dining with a Captain Richardson," his father said, controlling himself with an obvious effort. He coughed, blew his nose, and put away the handkerchief. "At the house of a Mr. Bell."

Mr. Bell's house was whitewashed, neat, and prosperous, without being ostentatious. Captain Richardson gave much the same sort of impression: of middle age, well-groomed and well-tailored, but without any notable style, and with a face you couldn't pick out of a crowd two minutes after seeing it.

The two Misses Bell made a much stronger impression, particularly the younger, Miriam, who had honey-colored curls peeping out of her cap, and big, round eyes that remained fixed on William throughout dinner. She was seated too far away for him to be able to converse with her directly, but he fancied that the language of the eyes was sufficient to indicate to her that the fascination was mutual, and if an opportunity for more personal communication should offer later . . . ? A smile, and a demure lowering of honey-colored lashes, followed by a quick glance toward a door that stood open to the side porch, for air. He smiled back.

"Do you think so, William?" his father said, loudly enough to indicate that it was the second time of asking.

"Oh, certainly. Um . . . think what?" he asked, since it was after all Papa, and not his commander. His father gave him the look that meant he would have rolled his eyes had they not been in public, but replied patiently.

"Mr. Bell was asking whether Sir Peter intends to remain long in Wilmington." Mr. Bell, at the head of the table, bowed graciously—though William observed a certain narrowing of his eyes in Miriam's direction. Perhaps he'd best come back to call tomorrow, he thought, when Mr. Bell might be at his place of business.

"Oh. I believe we'll remain here for only a short time, sir," he said respectfully to Mr. Bell. "I collect that the chief trouble is in the backcountry, and so we will no doubt move to suppress it without delay."

Mr. Bell looked pleased, though from the corner of his eye, William saw Miriam pout prettily at the suggestion of his imminent departure.

"Good, good," Bell said jovially. "No doubt hundreds of Loyalists will flock to join you along your march."

"Doubtless so, sir," William murmured, taking another spoonful of soup. He doubted that Mr. Bell would be among them. Not really the marching type, to look at. And not that the assistance of a lot of untrained provincials armed with shovels would be helpful in any case, but he could hardly say so.

William, trying to see Miriam without looking directly at her, instead intercepted the flicker of a glance that traveled between his father and Captain Richardson, and for the first time, began to wonder. His father had distinctly said they were dining with Captain Richardson—meaning that a meeting with the captain was the point of the evening. Why?

Then he caught a look from Miss Lillian Bell, who was seated across from him, next his father, and ceased thinking about Captain Richardson. Dark-eyed, taller and more slender than her sister—but really quite a handsome girl, now he noticed.

Still, when Mrs. Bell and her daughters rose and the men retired to the porch after dinner, William was not surprised to find himself at one end with Captain Richardson, while his father engaged Mr. Bell at the other in a spirited discussion of tar prices. Papa could talk to anyone about anything.

"I have a proposition to put before you, Lieutenant," Richardson said, after the usual cordialities had been exchanged.

"Yes, sir," William said respectfully. His curiosity had begun to rise. Richardson was a captain of light dragoons, but not presently with his regiment; that much he had revealed over dinner, saying casually that he was on detached duty. Detached to do what?

"I do not know how much your father has told you regarding my mission?"

"Nothing, sir."

"Ah. I am charged with the gathering of intelligence in the Southern Department. Not that I am in command of such operations, you understand"—the captain smiled modestly—"but a small part of them."

"I . . . appreciate the great value of such operations, sir," William said, groping for diplomacy, "but I—for myself, that is to say—"

"You have no interest in spying. No, of course not." It was dark on the porch, but the dryness of the captain's tone was evident. "Few men who regard themselves as soldiers do."

"I meant no offense, sir."

"None taken. I am not, however, recruiting you as a spy—that is a delicate occupation, and one involving some danger—but rather as a messenger. Though should you find opportunity to act the intelligencer along your way . . . well, that would be an additional contribution, and much appreciated."

William felt the blood rise in his face at the implication that he was capable neither of delicacy nor danger, but kept his temper, saying only, "Oh?"

The captain, it seemed, had gathered significant information regarding local conditions in the Carolinas, and now required to send this to the commander of the Northern Department—General Howe, presently in Halifax.

"I will of course be sending more than one messenger," Richardson said. "It is naturally somewhat quicker by ship—but I desire to have at least one messenger travel overland, both for safety's sake and for the sake of making observations *en route*. Your father speaks very highly of your abilities, Lieutenant"—did he detect a hint of amusement in that dry-as-sawdust voice?—"and I collect that you have traveled extensively in North Carolina and Virginia. That is a valuable attribute. You will appreciate that I do not wish my messenger to disappear into the Dismal Swamp, never to be seen again."

"Ha-ha," said William, politely, perceiving this to be meant as a jest. Clearly, Captain Richardson had never been near the Great Dismal; William had, though he didn't think anyone in his right mind would go that way a-purpose, save to hunt.

He also had severe doubts regarding Richardson's suggestion—though even as he told himself that he shouldn't consider leaving his men, his regiment . . . he was already seeing a romantic vision of himself, alone in the vast wilderness, bearing important news through storm and danger.

More of a consideration, though, was what he might expect at the other end of the journey.

Richardson anticipated his question, answering before he could speak.

"Once in the north, you would—it being agreeable—join General Howe's staff."

Well, now, he thought. Here was the apple, and a juicy red one, too. He was aware that Richardson meant "it being agreeable" to General Howe, rather than to William—but he had some confidence in his own capabilities, and rather thought he might prove himself useful.

He had been in North Carolina only a few days, but that was quite long enough for him to have made an accurate assessment of the relative chances for advancement between the Northern Department and the Southern. The entire Continental army was with Washington in the north; the southern rebellion appeared to consist of troublesome pockets of backwoodsmen and impromptu militia—hardly a threat. And as for the relative status of Sir Peter and General Howe as commanders...

"I would like to think on your offer, if I might, Captain," he said, hoping eagerness didn't show in his voice. "May I give my answer tomorrow?"

"Certainly. I imagine you will wish to discuss the prospects with your father—you may do so."

The captain then deliberately changed the subject, and within a few moments, Lord John and Mr. Bell had joined them, the conversation becoming general.

William paid little heed to what was said, his own attention distracted by the sight of two slender white figures that hovered ghostlike among the bushes at the outer edge of the yard. Two capped white heads drew together, then apart. Now and then, one turned briefly toward the porch in what looked like speculation.

" 'And for his vesture, they cast lots,' " his father murmured, shaking his head.

"Eh?"

"Never mind." His father smiled, and turned toward Captain Richardson, who had just said something about the weather.

Fireflies lit the yard, drifting like green sparks among the damp, lush growth of plants. It was good to see fireflies again; he had missed them, in England—and that peculiar softness of the southern air that molded his linen to his body and made the blood throb in his fingertips. Crickets were chirping all around them, and for an instant, their song seemed to drown out everything save the sound of his pulse.

"Coffee's ready, gen'mun." The soft voice of the Bells' slave cut through the small ferment of his blood, though, and he went in with the other men, with no more than a glance toward the yard. The white figures had disappeared, but a sense of promise lingered in the soft, warm air.

An hour later, he found himself walking back toward his billet, thoughts in a pleasant muddle, his father strolling silent by his side.

Miss Lillian Bell had granted him a kiss among the fireflies at the end of the evening, chaste and fleeting, but upon the lips, and the thick summer air seemed to taste of coffee and ripe strawberries, despite the pervasive dank smell of the harbor.

"Captain Richardson told me of the proposal he made to you," Lord John said casually. "Are you inclined?"

"Don't know," William replied, with equal casualness. "I should miss my men, of course, but..." Mrs. Bell had pressed him to come to tea, later in the week.

"Little permanence in a military life," his father said, with a brief shake of the head. "I did warn you."

William gave a brief grunt of assent, not really listening.

"A good opportunity for advancement," his father was saying, adding offhandedly, "though of course there is some danger to the proposition."

"What?" William scoffed, hearing this. "Riding from Wilmington to take ship at New York? There's a road, nearly all the way!"

"And quite a number of Continentals on it," Lord John pointed out. "General Washington's entire army lies this side of Philadelphia, if the news I hear be correct."

William shrugged.

"Richardson said he wanted me because I knew the country. I can make my way well enough without roads."

"Are you sure? You have not been in Virginia for nearly four years."

The dubious tone of this annoyed William.

"Do you think me incapable of finding my way?"

"No, not at all," his father said, still with that note of doubt in his voice. "But there is no little *risk* to this proposition; I should not like to see you undertake it without due thought."

"Well, I *have* thought," said William, stung. "I'll do it."

Lord John walked in silence for a few steps, then nodded, reluctantly.

"It's your decision, Willie," he said softly. "I should be personally obliged if you would take care, though."

William's annoyance melted at once.

"Course I will," he said gruffly. They walked on beneath the dark canopy of maple and hickory, not talking, close enough that their shoulders brushed now and then.

At the inn, William bade Lord John good night, but didn't return at once to his own lodgings. Instead, he wandered out along the quay, restless, unready for sleep.

The tide had turned and was well out, he saw; the smell of dead fish and decaying seaweed was stronger, though a smooth sheet of water still covered the mudflats, quiet in the light of a quarter-moon.

It took a moment to locate the stake. For an instant, he thought it had gone, but no—there it was, a thin dark line against the glimmer of the water. Empty.

The stake no longer stood upright, but leaned sharply, as though about to fall, and a thin loop of rope trailed from it, floating like a hangman's noose on the waning tide. William was conscious of some visceral uneasiness; the tide alone would not have taken the whole body. Some said there were crocodiles or alligators here, though he had not yet seen one himself. He glanced down involuntarily, as though one of these reptiles might suddenly lunge from the water at his feet. The air was still warm, but a small shiver went through him.

He shook this off, and turned away toward his lodgings. There would be a day or two before he must go, he thought, and wondered whether he might see the blue-eyed Mrs. MacKenzie again before he left.

LORD JOHN LINGERED for a moment on the porch of the inn, watching his son vanish into the shadows under the trees. He had some qualms; the matter had been arranged with more haste than he would have liked—but he did have confidence in William's abilities. And while the arrangement clearly had its risks, that was the nature of a soldier's life. Some situations were riskier than others, though.

He hesitated, hearing the buzz of talk from the taproom inside, but he had had enough of company for the night, and the thought of tossing to and fro under the low ceiling of his room, stifling in the day's trapped heat, determined him to walk about until bodily exhaustion should ensure sleep.

It wasn't just the heat, he reflected, stepping off the porch and setting off in the opposite direction to the one Willie had taken. He knew himself well enough to realize that even the apparent success of his plan would not prevent his lying awake, worrying at it like a dog with a bone, testing for weaknesses, seeking for ways of improvement. After all, William would not depart immediately; there was a little time to consider, to make alterations, should that be necessary.

General Howe, for instance. Had that been the best choice? Perhaps Clinton . . . but no. Henry Clinton was a fussy old woman, unwilling to stir a foot without orders in triplicate.

The Howe brothers—one a general, one an admiral—were famously uncouth, both having the manners, aspect, and general aroma of boars in rut. Neither of them was stupid, though—God knew they weren't timid—and Grey thought Willie fully capable of surviving rough manners and harsh words. And a commander given to spitting on the floor—Richard Howe had once spat on Grey himself, though this was largely accidental, the wind having changed unexpectedly—was possibly easier for a young subaltern to deal with than the quirks of some other military gentlemen of Grey's acquaintance.

Though even the most peculiar of the brotherhood of the blade was preferable to the diplomats. He wondered idly what the term of venery might be for a collection of diplomats. If writers formed the brotherhood of the quill, and a group of foxes be termed a skulk . . . a stab of diplomats, perhaps? Brothers of the stiletto? No, he decided. Much too direct. An opiate of diplomats, more like. Brotherhood of the boring. Though the ones who were not boring could be dangerous, on occasion.

Sir George Germain was one of the rarer sorts: boring *and* dangerous.

He walked up and down the streets of the town for some time, in hopes of exhausting himself before going back to his small, stuffy room. The sky was low and sullen, with heat lightning flickering among the clouds, and the atmosphere was damp as a bath sponge. He should have been in Albany by now—no less humid and bug-ridden, but somewhat cooler, and near the sweet dark forests of the Adirondacks.

Still, he didn't regret his hasty journey to Wilmington. Willie was sorted; that was the important thing. And Willie's sister, Brianna—he stopped dead for a moment, eyes closed, reliving the moment of transcendence and heartbreak he had experienced that afternoon, seeing the two of them together for what would be their only meeting, ever. He'd scarcely been able to breathe, his eyes fixed on the two tall figures, those handsome, bold faces, so alike—and both so like the man who had stood beside him, unmoving, but by contrast with Grey, taking in great tearing gulps of air, as though he feared he might never breathe again.

Grey rubbed idly at his left ring finger, not yet accustomed to finding it bare. He and Jamie Fraser had done the best they could to safeguard those they loved, and despite his melancholy, he was comforted at the thought that they were united in that kinship of responsibility.

Would he ever meet Brianna Fraser MacKenzie again? he wondered. She had said not—and seemed as saddened by that fact as he was.

"God bless you, child," he murmured, shaking his head as he turned back toward the harbor. He would miss her very much—but as with Willie, his relief that she would soon be out of Wilmington and out of danger overwhelmed his personal sense of loss.

He glanced involuntarily at the water as he came out onto the quay, and drew a deep sigh of relief at seeing the empty stake, aslant in the tide. He hadn't understood her reasons for doing what she'd done, but he'd known her father—and her brother, for that matter—far too long to mistake the stubborn conviction he'd seen in those catlike blue eyes. So he'd got her the small boat she'd asked for, and stood on the quay with his heart in his throat, ready to create a distraction if needed, as her husband had rowed her out toward the bound pirate.

He'd seen men die in great numbers, usually unwillingly, occasionally with resignation. He'd never seen one go with such passionate gratitude in his eyes. Grey had no more than a passing acquaintance with Roger MacKenzie, but suspected him to be a remarkable man, having not only survived marriage to that fabulous and dangerous creature but actually having sired children upon her.

He shook his head and turned, heading back toward the inn. He could safely wait another two weeks, he thought, before replying to Germain's letter—which he had deftly magicked out of the diplomatic pouch when he'd seen William's name upon it—at which time he could truthfully say that, alas, by the time the letter had been received, Lord Ellesmere was somewhere in the wilderness between North Carolina and New York, and thus could not be informed that he was recalled to England, though he (Grey) was positive that Ellesmere would greatly regret the loss of his opportunity to join Sir George's staff, when he learned of it—several months hence. Too bad.

He began to whistle "Lillibulero," and strode back to the inn in good spirits.

He paused in the taproom, and asked for a bottle of wine to be sent up—only to be informed by the barmaid that "the gentleman" had already taken a bottle upstairs with him.

"And two glasses," she added, dimpling at him. "So I don't s'pose he meant to drink it all himself."

Grey felt something like a centipede skitter up his spine.

"I beg your pardon," he said. "Did you say that there is a gentleman in my room?"

"Yes, sir," she assured him. "He said as he's an old friend of yours. . . . Now, he did tell me his name . . ." Her brow furrowed for an instant, then cleared. "Bow-shaw, he said, or summat of the kind. Frenchy kind of name," she clarified. "And a Frenchy kind of gentleman, too. Will you be wanting food at all, sir?"

"No, I thank you." He waved her off, and went up the stairs, thinking rapidly whether he had left anything in his room that he shouldn't have.

A Frenchman, named Bow-shaw . . . *Beauchamp.* The name flashed in his mind like the flicker of heat lightning. He stopped dead for an instant in the middle of the staircase, then resumed his climb, more slowly.

Surely not . . . but who else might it be? When he had ceased active service, some years before, he had begun diplomatic life as a member of England's Black Chamber, that shadowy organization of persons charged with the interception and decoding of official diplomatic mail—and much less official messages—that flowed between the governments of Europe. Every one of those governments possessed its own Black Chamber, and it was not unusual for the inhabitants of one such chamber to be aware of their opposite numbers—never met, but known by their signatures, their initials, their unsigned marginal notes.

Beauchamp had been one of the most active French agents; Grey had run across his trail several times in the intervening years, even though his own days in the Black Chamber were well behind him. If he knew Beauchamp by name, it was entirely reasonable that the man knew him as well—but their invisible association had been years ago. They had never met in person, and for such a meeting to occur *here* . . . He touched the secret pocket in his coat, and was reassured by the muffled crackle of paper.

He hesitated at the top of the stair, but there was no point in furtiveness; clearly, he was expected. With a firm step, he walked down the hall and turned the white china knob of his door, the porcelain smooth and cool beneath his fingers.

A wave of heat engulfed him and he gasped for air, involuntarily. Just as well, as it prevented his uttering the blasphemy that had sprung to his lips.

The gentleman occupying the room's only chair was indeed "Frenchy"—his very well-cut suit set off by cascades of snowy lace at throat and cuff, his shoes buckled with a silver that matched the hair at his temples.

"Mr. Beauchamp," Grey said, and slowly closed the door behind him. His damp linen clung to him, and he could feel his pulse thumping in his own temples. "I fear you take me at something of a disadvantage."

Perseverance Wainwright smiled, very slightly.

"I'm glad to see you, John," he said.

———————

GREY BIT HIS TONGUE to forestall anything injudicious—which description covered just about anything he might say, he thought, with the exception of "Good evening."

"Good evening," he said. He lifted an eyebrow in question. "*Monsieur* Beauchamp?"

"Oh, yes." Percy got his feet under him, making to rise, but Grey waved him back and turned to fetch a stool, hoping the seconds gained by the movement would allow him to regain his composure. Finding that they didn't, he took another moment to open the window, and stood for a couple of lungfuls of the thick, dank air, before turning back and taking his own seat.

"How did that happen?" he asked, affecting casualness. "Beauchamp, I mean. Or is it merely a *nom de guerre?*"

"Oh, no." Percy took up his lace-trimmed handkerchief and dabbed sweat delicately from his hairline—which was beginning to recede, Grey noted. "I married one of the sisters of the Baron Amandine. The family name is Beauchamp; I adopted it. The relationship provided a certain *entrée* to political circles, from which . . ." He shrugged charmingly and made a graceful gesture that encompassed his career in the Black Chamber—and doubtless elsewhere, Grey thought grimly.

"My congratulations on your marriage," Grey said, not bothering to keep the irony out of his voice. "Which one are you sleeping with, the baron or his sister?"

Percy looked amused.

"Both, on occasion."

"Together?"

The smile widened. His teeth were still good, Grey saw, though somewhat stained by wine.

"Occasionally. Though Cecile—my wife—really prefers the attentions of her cousin Lucianne, and I myself prefer the attentions of the sub-gardener. Lovely man named Emile; he reminds me of you . . . in your younger years. Slender, blond, muscular, and brutal."

To his dismay, Grey found that he wanted to laugh.

"It sounds extremely French," he said dryly, instead. "I'm sure it suits you. What do you want?"

"More a matter of what *you* want, I think." Percy had not yet drunk any of the wine; he took up the bottle and poured carefully, red liquid purling dark against the glasses. "Or perhaps I should say—what England wants." He held out a glass to Grey, smiling. "For one can hardly separate your interests from those of your country, can one? In fact, I confess that you have always seemed to me to *be* England, John."

Grey wished to forbid him the use of his Christian name, but to do so would merely emphasize the memory of their intimacy—which was, of course, what Percy intended. He chose to ignore it, and took a sip of his wine, which was good. He wondered whether he was paying for it—and if so, how.

"What England wants," he repeated, skeptical. "And what is your impression of what England wants?"

Percy took a swallow of the wine and held it in his mouth, evidently savoring it, before finally swallowing.

"Hardly a secret, my dear, is it?"

Grey sighed, and stared pointedly at him.

"You've seen this 'Declaration of Independency' issued by the so-called Continental Congress?" Percy asked. He turned and, reaching into a leather bag he had slung over the back of the chair, withdrew a folded sheaf of papers, which he handed to Grey.

Grey had not in fact seen the document in question, though he'd certainly heard about it. It had been printed only two weeks previous, in Philadelphia, yet copies had spread like wind-borne weeds through the Colonies. Raising a brow at Percy, he unfolded the paper and skimmed it rapidly.

"The King is a tyrant?" he said, half-laughing at the outrageousness of some of the document's more extreme sentiments. He folded the sheets back together and tossed them on the table.

"And if I am England, I suppose you are the embodiment of France, for the purposes of this conversation?"

"I represent certain interests there," Percy replied blandly. "And in Canada."

That rang small alarm bells. Grey had fought in Canada with Wolfe, and was well aware that while the French had lost much of their North American holdings in that war, they remained ferociously entrenched in the northern regions, from the Ohio Valley to Quebec. Close enough to cause trouble now? He thought not—but wouldn't put anything past the French. Or Percy.

"England wants a quick end to this nonsense, plainly." A long, knob-jointed hand waved toward the paper. "The Continental army—so-called—is a flimsy association of men with no experience and conflicting notions. What if I were prepared to provide you with information that might be used to . . . separate one of Washington's chief officers from his allegiance?"

"What if you were?" Grey replied, making no effort to conceal the skepticism in his voice. "How would this benefit France—or your own interests, which I take leave to think are possibly not entirely identical?"

"I see that time has not softened your natural cynicism, John. One of your less attractive traits—I don't know whether I ever mentioned that to you."

Grey widened his stare slightly, and Percy sighed.

"Land, then," he said. "The Northwest Territory. We want it back."

Grey uttered a short laugh.

"I daresay you do." The territory in question, a large tract northwest of the Ohio River Valley, had been ceded to Great Britain from France at the end of the French and Indian War. Britain had not occupied the territory, though, and had prevented the colonists' expansion into it, owing to armed resistance from the natives and the ongoing negotiation of treaties with them. The colonists weren't pleased about it, he understood. Grey had encountered some of said natives himself, and was inclined to think the British government's position both reasonable and honorable.

"French traders had extensive ties with the aboriginals in that area; you have none."

"The fur-trading merchants being some of the . . . interests . . . you represent?"

Percy smiled openly at that.

"Not the major interests. But some."

Grey didn't bother asking why Percy was approaching him—an ostensibly retired diplomat of no particular influence—in the matter. Percy knew the power of Grey's family and connections from the days of their personal association—and "Monsieur Beauchamp" knew a great deal more about his present personal connections from the nexus of information that fed the Black Chambers of Europe. Grey could not act in the matter, of course. But he was well placed to bring the offer quietly to the attention of those who could.

He felt as though every hair on his body was standing on end like an insect's antennae, alert for danger.

"We would require something more than the suggestion, of course," he said, very cool. "The name of the officer in question, for example."

"Not mine to share, at the moment. But once a negotiation in good faith is opened..."

Grey was already wondering to whom he should take this offer. *Not* Sir George Germain. Lord North's office? That could wait, though.

"And your personal interests?" he asked, with an edge. He knew Percy Wainwright well enough to know that there would be some aspect of the affair to Percy's personal benefit.

"Ah, that." Percy sipped at his wine, then lowered the glass and gazed limpidly at Grey across it. "Very simple, really. I am commissioned to find a man. Do you know a Scottish gentleman named James Fraser?"

Grey felt the stem of his glass crack. He went on holding it, though, and sipped the wine carefully, thanking God, firstly, that he had never told Percy Jamie Fraser's name and, secondly, that Fraser had left Wilmington that afternoon.

"No," he said calmly. "What do you want with this Mr. Fraser?"

Percy shrugged, and smiled.

"Only a question or two."

Grey could feel blood seeping from his lacerated palm. Holding the cracked glass carefully together, he drank the rest of his wine. Percy was quiet, drinking with him.

"My condolences upon the loss of your wife," Percy said quietly. "I know that she—"

"You know nothing," Grey said roughly. He leaned over and set the broken glass on the table; the bowl rolled crazily, the lees of wine washing the glass. "Not one thing. About my wife, *or* about me."

Percy lifted his shoulders in the faintest of Gallic shrugs. *As you like,* it said. And yet his eyes—they were still beautiful, damn him, dark and soft—rested on Grey with what seemed a genuine sympathy.

Grey sighed. Doubtless it *was* genuine. Percy could not be trusted—not ever—but what he'd done had been done from weakness, not from malice, or even lack of feeling.

"What do you want?" he repeated.

"Your son—" Percy began, and Grey turned suddenly on him. He gripped Percy's shoulder, hard enough that the man gave a little gasp and stiffened. Grey leaned down, looking into Wainwright's—sorry, *Beauchamp's*—face, so close that he felt the warmth of the man's breath on his cheek and smelled his cologne. He was getting blood on Wainwright's coat.

"The last time I saw you," Grey said, very quietly, "I came within an inch of putting a bullet through your head. Don't give me cause to regret my restraint."

He let go and stood up.

"Stay away from my son—stay away from me. And if you will take a well-meant bit of advice—go back to France. Quickly."

Turning on his heel, he went out, shutting the door firmly behind him. He was halfway down the street before he realized that he had left Percy in his own room.

"The devil with it," he muttered, and stamped off to beg a billet for the night from Sergeant Cutter. In the morning, he would make sure that the Fraser family and William were all safely out of Wilmington.

AND SOMETIMES THEY AREN'T

Lallybroch
Inverness-shire, Scotland
September 1980

W E ARE ALIVE," Brianna MacKenzie repeated, her voice tremulous. She looked up at Roger, the paper pressed to her chest with both hands. Her face streamed with tears, but a glorious light glowed in her blue eyes. "Alive!"

"Let me see." His heart was hammering so hard in his chest that he could barely hear his own words. He reached out a hand, and reluctantly she surrendered the paper to him, coming at once to press herself against him, clinging to his arm as he read, unable to take her eyes off the bit of ancient paper.

It was pleasantly rough under his fingers, handmade paper with the ghosts of leaves and flowers pressed into its fibers. Yellowed with age, but still tough and surprisingly flexible. Bree had made it herself—more than two hundred years before.

Roger became aware that his hands were trembling, the paper shaking so that the sprawling, difficult hand was hard to read, faded as the ink was.

December 31, 1776

My dear daughter,

As you will see if ever you receive this, we are alive . . .

His own eyes blurred, and he wiped the back of his hand across them, even as he told himself that it didn't matter, for they were surely dead now, Jamie Fraser and his wife, Claire—but he felt such joy at those words on the page that it was as though the two of them stood smiling before him.

It *was* the two of them, too, he discovered. While the letter began in Jamie's hand—and voice—the second page took up in Claire's crisply slanted writing.

Your father's hand won't stand much more. And it's a bloody long story. He's been chopping wood all day, and can barely uncurl his fingers—but he insisted on telling you himself that we haven't—yet— been burnt to ashes. Not but what we may be at any moment; there are fourteen people crammed into the old cabin, and I'm writing this more or less sitting in the hearth, with old Grannie MacLeod wheezing away on her pallet by my feet so that if she suddenly begins to die, I can pour more whisky down her throat.

"My God, I can *hear* her," he said, amazed.

"So can I." Tears were still coursing down Bree's face, but it was a sun-shower; she wiped at them, laughing and sniffing. "Read more. Why are they in our cabin? What's happened to the Big House?"

Roger ran his finger down the page to find his place and resumed reading. "Oh, Jesus!" he said.

You recall that idiot, Donner?

Gooseflesh ran up his arms at the name. A time-traveler, Donner. And one of the most feckless individuals he'd ever met or heard of—but nonetheless dangerous for that.

Well, he surpassed himself by getting together a gang of thugs from Brownsville to come and steal the treasure in gems he'd convinced them we had. Only we hadn't, of course.

They hadn't—because he, Brianna, Jemmy, and Amanda had taken the small hoard of remaining gemstones to safeguard their flight through the stones.

They held us hostage and rubbished the house, damn them— breaking, amongst other things, the carboy of ether in my surgery. The fumes nearly gassed all of us on the spot . . .

He read rapidly through the rest of the letter, Brianna peering over his shoulder and making small squeaks of alarm and dismay. Finished, he laid the pages down and turned to her, his insides quivering.

"So *you* did it," he said, aware that he shouldn't say it, but unable not to, unable not to snort with laughter. "You and your bloody matches—*you* burned the house down!"

Her face was a study, features shifting between horror, indignation—and, yes, a hysterical hilarity that matched his own.

"Oh, it was not! It was Mama's ether. Any kind of spark could have set off the explosion—"

"But it wasn't any kind of spark," Roger pointed out. "Your cousin Ian lit one of your matches."

"Well, so it was Ian's fault, then!"

"No, it was you and your mother. Scientific women," Roger said, shaking his head. "The eighteenth century is lucky to have survived you."

She huffed a little.

"Well, the whole thing would never have happened if it weren't for that bozo Donner!"

"True," Roger conceded. "But he was a troublemaker from the future, too, wasn't he? Though admittedly neither a woman nor very scientific."

"Hmph." She took the letter, handling it gently, but unable to forbear rubbing the pages between her fingers. "Well, *he* didn't survive the eighteenth century, did he?" Her eyes were downcast, their lids still reddened.

"You aren't feeling *sorry* for him, are you?" Roger demanded, incredulous.

She shook her head, but her fingers still moved lightly over the thick, soft page.

"Not ... *him,* so much. It's just—the idea of anybody dying like that. Alone, I mean. So far from home."

No, it wasn't Donner she was thinking of. He put an arm round her and laid his head against her own. She smelled of Prell shampoo and fresh cabbages; she'd been in the kailyard. The words on the page faded and strengthened with the dip of the pen that had written them, but nonetheless were sharp and clear—a surgeon's writing.

"She isn't alone," he whispered, and putting out a finger, traced the postscript, again in Jamie's sprawling hand. "Neither of them is. And whether they've a roof above their heads or not—both of them are home."

I PUT BY THE LETTER. Time enough to finish it later, I thought. I'd been working on it as time allowed over the last few days; not as though there was any rush to catch the outgoing mail, after all. I smiled a little at that, and folded the sheets carefully, putting them in my new workbag for safekeeping. I wiped the quill and put it aside, then rubbed my aching fingers, savoring for a little longer the sweet sense of connection the writing gave me. I could write much more easily than Jamie could, but flesh and blood had its limits, and it had been a very long day.

I looked over at the pallet on the far side of the fire, as I had been doing every few minutes, but she was still quiet. I could hear her breath, a wheezing gurgle that came at intervals so long that I could swear she had died between each one. She hadn't, though, and from my estimation wouldn't for a while. I was hoping that she would, before my limited supply of laudanum gave out.

I didn't know how old she was; she looked a hundred or so, but might be younger than I. Her two grandsons, boys in their teens, had brought her in two days before. They had been traveling down from the mountains, meaning to take their grandmother to relatives in Cross Creek before heading to Wilmington to join the militia there, but the grandmother had "been took bad," as they put it, and someone had told them there was a conjure-woman on the Ridge nearby. So they had brought her to me.

Grannie MacLeod—I had no other name for her; the boys had not thought to tell me before departing, and she was in no condition to do so herself—almost certainly was in the terminal stages of a cancer of some kind.

Her flesh had wasted, her face pinched with pain even while unconscious, and I could see it in the grayness of her skin.

The fire was burning low; I should stir it, and add another stick of pine. Jamie's head was resting against my knee, though. Could I reach the wood-pile without disturbing him? I put a light hand on his shoulder for balance and stretched, just getting my fingers on the end of a small log. I wiggled this gently free, teeth set in my lower lip, and managed by leaning to poke it into the hearth, breaking up the drifts of red-black embers and raising clouds of sparks.

Jamie stirred under my hand and murmured something unintelligible, but when I thrust the log into the freshened fire and sat back in my chair, he sighed, resettled himself, and fell back into sleep.

I glanced at the door, listening, but heard nothing save the rustle of trees in the wind. Of course, I thought, I *would* hear nothing, given that it was Young Ian I was waiting for.

He and Jamie had been taking it in turns to watch, hiding in the trees above the burnt ruins of the Big House. Ian had been out for more than two hours; it was nearly time for him to come in for food and a turn at the fire.

"Someone's been trying to kill the white sow," he'd announced at breakfast three days ago, looking bemused.

"What?" I handed him a bowl of porridge, garnished with a lump of melting butter and a drizzle of honey—luckily my kegs of honey and boxes of honeycomb had been in the springhouse when the fire happened. "Are you sure?"

He nodded, taking the bowl and inhaling its steam in beatific fashion.

"Aye, she's got a slash in her flank. Not deep, and it's healing, Auntie," he added, with a nod in my direction, evidently feeling that I would regard the sow's medical well-being with the same interest as that of any other resident of the Ridge.

"Oh? Good," I said—though there was precious little I could have done if she weren't healing. I could—and did—doctor horses, cows, goats, stoats, and even the occasional non-laying chicken, but that particular pig was on her own.

Amy Higgins crossed herself at mention of the sow.

"Likely 'twas a bear," she said. "Nothing else would dare. Aidan, mind what Mr. Ian says, here! Dinna be wandering far from the place, and mind your brother outside."

"Bears sleep in winter, Mam," Aidan said absently. His attention was fixed on a new top that Bobby, his new stepfather, had carved for him, and which he hadn't yet got to spin properly. Giving it a cross-eyed glare, he set it gingerly on the table, held the string for a breathless moment, and yanked. The top shot across the table, ricocheted off the honey jar with a sharp *crack!*, and headed for the milk at a high rate of speed.

Ian reached out and snatched the top in the nick of time. Chewing toast, he motioned to Aidan for the string, rewound it, and with a practiced flick of the wrist, sent the top whizzing straight down the center of the table. Aidan watched it, openmouthed, then dived under the table as the top fell off the end.

"No, it wasna an animal," Ian said, finally succeeding in swallowing. "It was a clean slash. Someone went for her wi' a knife or a sword."

Jamie looked up from the burnt piece of toast he had been examining.

"Did ye find his body?"

Ian grinned briefly, but shook his head.

"Nay, if she killed him, she ate him—and I didna find any leavings."

"Pigs are messy eaters," Jamie observed. He essayed a cautious bite of the burnt toast, grimaced, and ate it anyway.

"An Indian, d'ye think?" Bobby asked. Little Orrie was struggling to get down from Bobby's lap; his new stepfather obligingly set him down in his favorite spot under the table.

Jamie and Ian exchanged glances, and I felt a slight stirring of the hair at the back of my neck.

"No," Ian answered. "The Cherokee near here all ken her weel, and wouldna touch her with a ten-foot pole. They think she's a demon, aye?"

"And traveling Indians from the north would have arrows or tomahawks," Jamie finished.

"Ye're sure it wasna a panther?" Amy asked, dubious. "They hunt in the winter, no?"

"They do," Jamie assured her. "I saw pug-marks up by the Green Spring yesterday. D'ye hear me there?" he said, bending to speak to the boys under the table. "Go canny, aye?

"But no," he added, straightening up. "Ian kens the difference between claw marks and a knife slash, I think." He gave Ian a grin. Ian politely refrained from rolling his eyes, and merely nodded, eyes fixed dubiously on the toast basket.

No one suggested that any resident of the Ridge or from Brownsville might have been hunting the white sow. The local Presbyterians would not have seen eye-to-eye with the Cherokee on any other spiritual matter you might name, but they were in decided agreement on the sow's demonic character.

Personally, I wasn't sure they weren't right. The thing had survived even the burning of the Big House unscathed, emerging from her den beneath its foundations amid a shower of burnt wood, followed by her latest litter of half-grown piglets.

"Moby Dick!" I now said aloud, inspired.

Rollo raised his head with a startled "Wuff?," gave me a yellow-eyed look and laid it down again, sighing.

"Dick who?" said Jamie, drowsy. He sat up, stretching and groaning, then rubbed a hand over his face and blinked at me.

"I just thought what it is that sow reminds me of," I explained. "Long story. About a whale. I'll tell you tomorrow."

"If I live that long," he said, with a yawn that nearly dislocated his jaw. "Where's the whisky—or d'ye need it for yon poor woman?" He nodded at Grannie MacLeod's blanket-wrapped form.

"Not yet. Here." I bent and rummaged in the basket beneath my chair, coming up with a corked bottle.

He pulled the cork and drank, the color gradually coming back to his face.

Between spending his days hunting or chopping wood and half the nights lurking in a freezing forest, even Jamie's great vitality was showing signs of flagging.

"How long will you keep this up?" I asked, low-voiced so as not to rouse the Higginses—Bobby, Amy, the two little boys, and Amy's two sisters-in-law from her first marriage, who had come for the wedding held a few days before, accompanied by a total of five children under the age of ten—all asleep in the small bedroom. The departure of the MacLeod boys had eased the congestion in the cabin slightly, but with Jamie, me, Ian, Ian's dog, Rollo, and the old woman sleeping on the floor of the main room, and such possessions as we had managed to salvage from the fire stacked round the walls, I sometimes felt a distinct surge of claustrophobia. Little wonder if Jamie and Ian were patrolling the woods, as much to get a breath of air as from a conviction that there was something out there.

"No much longer," he assured me, shuddering slightly as a large swallow of whisky went down. "If we dinna see anything tonight, we'll—" He broke off, his head turning abruptly toward the door.

I hadn't heard anything, but saw the latch move, and an instant later, a freezing gust of air rolled into the room, poking frigid fingers under my skirts and stirring up a shower of sparks from the fire.

I hastily seized a rag and beat these out before they could set Grannie MacLeod's hair or bedding on fire. By the time I had the fire back under control, Jamie was putting pistol, shot bag, and powder horn on his belt, talking low-voiced with Ian by the door. Ian himself was red-cheeked with cold and clearly excited about something. Rollo was up, too, nosing at Ian's legs, tail wagging in anticipation of an icy adventure.

"Best ye stay, *a choin*," Ian told him, rubbing his ears with cold fingers. *"Sheas."*

Rollo made a disgruntled noise in his throat and tried to push past Ian, but was deftly blocked by a leg. Jamie turned, shrugging on his coat, bent, and kissed me hastily.

"Bolt the door, *a nighean*," he whispered. "Dinna open to anyone save me or Ian."

"What—" I began, but they were gone.

THE NIGHT WAS COLD and pure. Jamie breathed deep and shivered, letting the cold enter him, strip away the warmth of wife, the smoke and smell of his hearth. Ice crystals shimmered in his lungs, sharp in his blood. He turned his head to and fro like a wolf scenting, breathing the night. There was little wind, but the air moved from the east, bringing the bitter smell of ashes from the ruins of the Big House . . . and a faint tang he thought was blood.

He looked to his nephew, question in the cock of his head, and saw Ian nod, dark against the lavender glow of the sky.

"There's a dead pig, just beyond Auntie's garden," the lad said, low-voiced.

"Oh, aye? Not the white sow, ye don't mean?" His heart misgave him for an instant at the thought, and he wondered whether he'd mourn the thing or dance on its bones. But no. Ian shook his head, the movement felt rather than seen.

"Nay, not that wily beast. A young one, maybe last year's farrowing. Someone's butchered it, but taken nay more than a collop or two from the haunch. And a good bit of what they *did* take, they scattered in chunks down the trail."

Jamie glanced round, surprised.

"What?"

Ian shrugged.

"Aye. One more thing, Uncle. 'Twas killed and butchered with an ax."

The ice crystals in his blood solidified with a suddenness that nearly stopped his heart.

"Jesus," he said, but it was not so much shock as it was unwilling admission of something he had known for a long time. "It's him, then."

"Aye." Both of them had known it, though neither one had been willing to speak of it. Without consultation, they moved away from the cabin, into the trees.

"Aye, well." Jamie took a long, deep breath and sighed, the mist of it white in the darkness. He'd hoped the man had taken his gold and his wife and left the Ridge—but it had never been more than a hope. Arch Bug was a Grant by blood, and clan Grant were a vengeful lot.

The Frasers of Glenhelm had caught Arch Bug on their lands some fifty years before, and given him the choice: lose an eye or the first two fingers of his right hand. The man had come to terms with his crippled hand, turning from the bow he could no longer draw to the use of an ax, which he wielded and threw with a skill equal to any Mohawk's, despite his age.

What he had not come to terms with was the loss of the Stuart cause and the loss of the Jacobite gold, sent too late from France, rescued—or stolen, depending on your view of things—by Hector Cameron, who had brought one third of it to North Carolina, this share then stolen—or retrieved—from Cameron's widow in turn by Arch Bug.

Nor had Arch Bug come to terms with Jamie Fraser.

"Is it threat, d'ye think?" Ian asked. They had moved away from the cabin, but kept to the trees, circling the large clearing where the Big House had been. The chimney and half a wall still stood, charred and bleak against the dirty snow.

"I canna think so. If it was threat he meant, why wait until now?" Still, he gave silent thanks that his daughter and her weans were safely gone. There were worse threats than a dead pig, and he thought Arch Bug would not hesitate to make them.

"Perhaps he left," Ian suggested. "To see his wife settled, and he's only now come back."

It was a reasonable thought—if there was one thing in the world Arch Bug loved, it was his wife, Murdina, his helpmate of more than fifty years.

"Perhaps," Jamie said. *And yet*...And yet he'd felt eyes on his back more than once in the weeks since the Bugs had left. Felt silence in the forest that was not the silence of the trees and rocks.

He didn't ask whether Ian had looked for the ax-wielder's track; if one could be found, Ian would have found it. But it hadn't snowed in more than a week, and what was left on the ground was patchy and trodden by the feet of innumerable people. He looked up at the sky; snow again, and soon.

He made his way up a small outcrop, careful among the ice; the snow was melting in the day, but the water froze again at night, hanging from the cabin's eaves and from every branch in glittering icicles that filled the forest with the light of blue dawn, then dripped gold and diamonds in the rising sun. Now they were colorless, tinkling like glass as his sleeve brushed the twigs of an ice-covered bush. He stopped, crouching at the top of the outcrop, looking down across the clearing.

All right. The certainty that Arch Bug was here had set off a chain of half-conscious deductions, the conclusion of which now floated to the top of his mind.

"He'd come again for one of two reasons," he said to Ian. "To do me harm—or to get the gold. All of it."

He'd given Bug a chunk of gold when he'd sent the man and his wife away, upon the discovery of the Bugs' treachery. Half a French ingot, it would have allowed an elderly couple to live the rest of their lives in modest comfort. But Arch Bug was not a modest man. He'd once been tacksman to the Grant of Grant, and while he'd hidden his pride for a time, it was not the nature of pride to stay buried.

Ian glanced at him, interested.

"All of it," he repeated. "So ye think he hid it here—but somewhere he couldna get it easily when ye made him go."

Jamie lifted one shoulder, watching the clearing. With the house now gone, he could see the steep trail that led up behind it, toward the place where his wife's garden had once stood, safe behind its deer-proof palisades. Some of the palisades still stood, black against the patchy snow. He would make her a new garden one day, God willing.

"If his purpose was only harm, he's had the chance." He could see the butchered pig from here, a dark shape on the path, shadowed by a wide pool of blood.

He pushed away a sudden thought of Malva Christie, and forced himself back to his reasoning.

"Aye, he's hidden it here," he repeated, more confident now. "If he had it all, he'd be long gone. He's been waiting, trying for a way to get to it. But he hasna been able to do it secretly—so now he's trying something else."

"Aye, but what? That—" Ian nodded toward the amorphous shape on the path. "I thought it might be a snare or a trap of some kind, but it's not. I looked."

"A lure, maybe?" The smell of blood was evident even to him; it would be a plain call to any predator. Even as he thought this, his eye caught movement near the pig, and he put a hand on Ian's arm.

A tentative flicker of movement, then a small, sinuous shape darted in, disappearing behind the pig's body.

"Fox," both men said together, then laughed, quietly.

"There's that panther in the wood above the Green Spring," Ian said dubiously. "I saw the tracks yesterday. Can he mean to draw it wi' the pig, in hopes that we should rush out to deal with it and he could reach the gold whilst we were occupied?"

Jamie frowned at that, and glanced toward the cabin. True, a panther might draw the men out—but not the women and children. And where might he have put the gold in such a densely inhabited space? His eye fell on the long, humped shape of Brianna's kiln, lying some way from the cabin, unused since her departure, and a spurt of excitement drew him upright. That would be—but no; Arch had stolen the gold from Jocasta Cameron one bar at a time, conveying it secretly to the Ridge, and had begun his theft long before Brianna had gone. But maybe . . .

Ian stiffened suddenly, and Jamie turned his head sharp to see what the matter was. He couldn't see anything, but then caught the sound that Ian had heard. A deep, piggish grunt, a rustle, a crack. Then there was a visible stirring among the blackened timbers of the ruined house, and a great light dawned.

"Jesus!" he said, and gripped Ian's arm so tightly that his nephew yelped, startled. "It's under the Big House!"

The white sow emerged from her den beneath the ruins, a massive cream-colored blotch upon the night, and stood swaying her head to and fro, scenting the air. Then she began to move, a ponderous menace surging purposefully up the hill.

Jamie wanted to laugh at the sheer beauty of it.

Arch Bug had cannily hidden his gold beneath the foundations of the Big House, choosing his times when the sow was out about her business. No one would have dreamed of invading the sow's domain; she was the perfect guardian—and doubtless he'd meant to retrieve the gold in the same way when he was ready to go: carefully, one ingot at a time.

But then the house had burned, the timbers collapsing into the foundation, rendering the gold unreachable without a great deal of work and trouble—which would certainly draw attention. It was only now, when the men had cleared away most of the rubble—and spread soot and charcoal all over the clearing in the process—that anyone might be able to reach something hidden under it without attracting notice.

But it was winter, and the white sow, while not hibernating like a bear, kept strictly to her cozy den—save when there was something to eat.

Ian made a small exclamation of disgust, hearing slobbering and crunching from the path.

"Pigs havena got much delicacy of feeling," Jamie murmured. "If it's dead, they'll eat it."

"Aye, but it's likely her own offspring!"

"She eats her young alive now and then; I doubt she'd boggle at eating them dead."

"Hst!"

He hushed at once, eyes fixed on the blackened smear that had once been the finest house in the county. Sure enough, a dark figure emerged from behind the springhouse, sidling cautiously on the slippery path. The pig, busy with her grisly feast, ignored the man, who seemed to be clad in a dark cloak and carrying something like a sack.

———

I DIDN'T BOLT THE DOOR at once, but stepped out to breathe fresh air for a moment, shutting Rollo in behind me. Within moments, Jamie and Ian had vanished into the trees. I glanced uneasily round the clearing, looked across to the black mass of the forest, but could see nothing amiss. Nothing moved, and the night was soundless; I wondered what Ian might have found. Unfamiliar tracks, perhaps? That would account for his sense of urgency; it was clearly about to snow.

No moon was visible, but the sky was a deep pinkish gray, and the ground, though trodden and patchy, was still covered with old snow. The result was a strange, milky glow in which objects seemed to float as though painted on glass, dimensionless and dim. The burnt remains of the Big House stood at the far side of the clearing, no more at this distance than a smudge, as though a giant, sooty thumb had pressed down there. I could feel the heaviness of impending snow in the air, hear it in the muffled sough of the pines.

The MacLeod boys had come over the mountain with their grandmother; they'd said it was very hard going through the high passes. Another big storm would likely seal us in until March or even April.

Thus reminded of my patient, I took one last look round the clearing and set my hand on the latch. Rollo was whining, scratching at the door, and I pushed a knee unceremoniously into his face as I opened it.

"Stay, dog," I said. "Don't worry, they'll be back soon." He made a high, anxious noise in his throat, and cast to and fro, nudging at my legs, seeking to get out.

"No," I said, pushing him away in order to bolt the door. The bolt dropped into place with a reassuring *thunk,* and I turned toward the fire, rubbing my hands. Rollo put back his head and gave a low, mournful howl that raised the hair on the back of my neck.

"What?" I said, alarmed. "Hush!" The noise had made one of the small children in the bedroom wake and cry; I heard rustling bedclothes and sleepy maternal murmurs, and I knelt quickly and grabbed Rollo's muzzle before he could howl again.

"Shhhhh," I said, and looked to see whether the sound had disturbed Grannie MacLeod. She lay still, waxen-faced, her eyes closed. I waited, automatically counting the seconds before the next shallow rise of her chest.

...*six*...*seven*..."Oh, bloody hell," I said, realizing.

Hastily crossing myself, I shuffled over to her on my knees, but closer inspection told me nothing I hadn't seen already. Self-effacing to the last, she had seized my moment of distraction to die inconspicuously.

Rollo was shifting to and fro, no longer howling, but uneasy. I laid a hand gently on the sunken chest. Not seeking diagnosis or offering aid, not any longer. Just . . . a necessary acknowledgment of the passing of a woman whose first name I didn't know.

"Well . . . God rest your soul, poor thing," I said softly, and sat back on my heels, trying to think what to do next.

Proper Highland protocol held that the door must be opened at once after a death, to allow the soul to leave. I rubbed a knuckle dubiously over my lips; might the soul have made a quick dash when I opened the door to come in? Probably not.

One would think that in a climate as inhospitable as Scotland's, there would be a bit of climatological leeway in such matters, but I knew that wasn't the case. Rain, snow, sleet, wind—Highlanders always *did* open the door and leave it open for hours, both eager to free the departing soul and anxious lest the spirit, impeded in its exit, might turn and take up permanent residence as a ghost. Most crofts were too small to make that a tolerable prospect.

Little Orrie was awake now; I could hear him singing happily to himself, a song consisting of his stepfather's name.

"Baaaaah-by, baaah-by, BAAAH-by . . ."

I heard a low, sleepy chuckle, and Bobby's murmur in reply.

"There's my wee man. You need the pot, *acooshla*?" The Gaelic endearment—*a chuisle*, "my heart's blood"—made me smile, both at the word and at the oddness of it in Bobby's Dorset accent. Rollo made an uneasy noise in his throat, though, bringing back to me the need for some action.

If the Higginses and in-laws rose in a few hours to discover a corpse on the floor, they'd all be disturbed, their sense of rightness affronted—and agitated at thought of a dead stranger possibly clinging to their hearth. A very bad omen for the new marriage and the new year. At the same time, her presence was undeniably agitating Rollo, and the prospect of his rousing them all in the next few moments was agitating me.

"Right," I said under my breath. "Come on, dog." There were, as always, bits of harness needing mending on a peg near the door. I disentangled a sound length of rein and fashioned a makeshift come-along with which I lassoed Rollo. He was more than happy to go outside with me, lunging ahead as I opened the door, though somewhat less delighted to be dragged to the lean-to pantry, where I wrapped the makeshift leash hastily round a shelf upright, before returning to the cabin for Grannie MacLeod's body.

I looked about carefully before venturing out again, Jamie's admonitions in mind, but the night was as still as a church; even the trees had fallen silent.

The poor woman couldn't weigh more than seventy pounds, I thought; her collarbones poked through her skin, and her fingers were frail as dried twigs. Still, seventy pounds of literal dead weight was a bit more than I could manage to lift, and I was obliged to unfold the blanket wrapped round her and use it as an impromptu sledge, on which I dragged her outside, murmuring mingled prayers and apologies under my breath.

Despite the cold, I was panting and damp with sweat by the time I'd got her into the pantry.

"Well, at least your soul's had plenty of time to make a getaway," I muttered, kneeling to check the body before resettling it in its hasty shroud. "And I shouldn't imagine you want to hang about haunting a pantry, in any case."

Her eyelids were not quite closed, a sliver of white showing, as though she had tried to open them for one last glimpse of the world—or perhaps in search of a familiar face.

"*Benedicite,*" I whispered, and gently shut her eyes, wondering as I did so whether one day some stranger might do the same for me. The odds of it were good. Unless . . .

Jamie had declared his intention to return to Scotland, fetch his printing press, and then come back to fight. *But what,* said a small, cowardly voice inside me, *if we didn't come back?* What if we went to Lallybroch and stayed there?

Even as I thought of that prospect—with its rosy visions of being enfolded by family, able to live in peace, to grow slowly old without the constant fear of disruption, starvation, and violence—I knew it wouldn't work.

I didn't know whether Thomas Wolfe had been right about not being able to go home again—well, I *wouldn't* know about that, I thought, a little bitterly; I hadn't had one to go back to—but I did know Jamie. Idealism quite aside—and he did have some, though of a very pragmatic sort—the simple fact was that he was a proper man, and thus required to have proper work. Not just labor; not just making a living. Work. I understood the difference.

And while I was sure that Jamie's family would receive him with joy—the nature of my own reception was in somewhat more doubt, but I supposed they wouldn't actually call the priest and try to have me exorcised—the fact was that Jamie was no longer laird of Lallybroch, and never would be.

" '. . . and his place shall know him no more,' " I murmured, wiping the old woman's intimate parts—surprisingly unwithered; perhaps she had been younger than I thought—with a damp cloth. She hadn't eaten anything in days; even the relaxation of death hadn't had much effect—but anyone deserved to go clean to their grave.

I paused. That was a thought. Would we be able to bury her? Or might she just rest peacefully under the huckleberry jam and the sacks of dried beans until spring?

I tidied her clothes, breathing out, openmouthed, trying to judge the temperature from the steam of my breath. This would be only the second major snowfall of the winter, and we had not yet had a really hard freeze; that usually happened in mid to late January. If the ground had not yet frozen, we could probably bury her—provided the men were willing to shovel away the snow.

Rollo had lain down, resigned, while I went about my business, but at this point, his head jerked upright, ears pointed.

"What?" I said, startled, and turned round on my knees to look out the open pantry door. "What's happening?"

"SHALL WE TAKE HIM NOW?" Ian murmured. He had his bow over one shoulder; he let his arm fall, and the bow dropped silently into his hand, ready.

"No. Let him find it first." Jamie spoke slowly, trying to make up his mind what was right to do with the man, so suddenly reappeared before him.

Not kill him; he and his wife had made a good deal of trouble with their treachery, aye, but hadn't intended harm to his family—not to start, at least. Was Arch Bug even truly a thief, by his own lights? Surely Jamie's aunt Jocasta had no greater—if no lesser—claim to the gold than he did.

He sighed and put a hand to his belt, where his dirk and pistol hung. Still, he couldn't allow Bug to make off with the gold, nor could he merely drive him off and leave him free to make more trouble. As to what in God's name to do with him once caught . . . it would be like having a snake in a sack. But naught to do now save catch him, and worry later what to do with the sack. Perhaps some bargain might be struck . . .

The figure had reached the black smear of the foundations and was climbing awkwardly among the stones and the charred timbers that remained, the dark cloak lifting and billowing as the air shifted.

Snow began to fall, sudden and silent, big, lazy flakes that seemed not so much to fall from the sky as simply to appear, whirling out of the air. They brushed his face and stuck thick in his lashes; he wiped them away, and motioned to Ian.

"Go behind," he whispered. "If he runs, send a shaft past his nose to stop him. And keep well back, aye?"

"*You* keep well back, Uncle," Ian whispered back. "If ye get within decent pistol shot o' the man, he can brain ye with his ax. And I'm no going to explain *that* to Auntie Claire."

Jamie snorted briefly and nudged Ian away. He loaded and primed his pistol, then walked firmly out through the falling snow toward the ruin of his house.

He'd seen Arch fell a turkey with his ax at twenty feet. And it was true that most pistols weren't accurate at much more than that. But he didn't mean to shoot the man, after all. He drew the pistol, holding it clear in his hand.

"Arch!" he called. The figure had its back to him, bent over as it rooted about in the ashes. At his call, it seemed to stiffen, still crouched.

"Arch Bug!" he shouted. "Come out o' there, man. I'd speak with ye!"

In answer, the figure drew itself up abruptly, turned, and a spurt of flame lit the falling snow. In the same instant, the flame seared his thigh, and he staggered.

He was conscious mostly of surprise; he'd never known Arch Bug to use a pistol, and was impressed that he could aim so well with his left—

He'd gone to one knee in the snow, but even as he brought his own weapon up to bear, he realized two things: the black figure was aiming a second pistol at him—but not with the left hand. Which meant—

"Jesus! Ian!" But Ian had seen him fall, and seen the second pistol, too. Jamie didn't hear the arrow's flight, above the rush of wind and snow; it appeared as though by magic, stuck in the figure's back. The figure went straight and stiff, then fell in a heap. Almost before it hit the ground, he was running, hobbling, his right leg buckling under him with every step.

"God, no, God, no," he was saying, and it sounded like someone else's voice.

A voice came through snow and night, calling out in desperation. Then Rollo was bounding past him, a blur—who had let him out?—and a rifle cracked from the trees. Ian bellowed, somewhere near, calling the dog, but Jamie had no time to look, was scrambling heedless over the blackened stones, slipping on the skim of fresh snow, stumbling, his leg was cold and hot at once, but no matter, oh, *God,* please, no ...

He reached the black figure and flung himself on his knees beside it, grappling. He knew at once; he'd known from the moment he realized the pistol had been held in her right hand. Arch, with his missing fingers, couldn't fire a pistol right-handed. But, oh, God, no ...

He'd got her over, feeling the short, heavy body limp and unwieldy as a fresh-killed deer. Pushed back the hood of the cloak, and passed his hand, gentle, helpless, over the soft round face of Murdina Bug. She breathed against his hand—perhaps ... but he felt the shaft of the arrow, too, against his hand. It had come through her neck, and her breath bubbled wet; his hand was wet, too, and warm.

"Arch?" she said hoarsely. "I want Arch." And died.

LIFE FOR LIFE

I TOOK JAMIE into the pantry. It was dark, and cold, particularly for a man with no breeches on, but I didn't want to risk any of the Higginses being wakened. God, not now. They'd all erupt from their sanctum like a flight of panicked quail—and I quailed myself at thought of having to deal with them before I had to. It would be sufficiently horrible to tell them what had happened by daylight; I couldn't face the prospect now.

For lack of any better alternative, Jamie and Ian had laid Mrs. Bug in the pantry alongside Grannie MacLeod, tucked under the lowest shelf, her cloak drawn up over her face. I could see her feet sticking out, with their cracked, worn boots and striped stockings. I had a sudden vision of the Wicked Witch of the West, and clapped a hand to my mouth before anything truly hysterical could escape.

Jamie turned his head toward me, but his gaze was inward, his face haggard, deep-lined in the glow of the candle he carried.

"Eh?" he said vaguely.

"Nothing," I said, my voice trembling. "Nothing at all. Sit—sit down." I put down the stool and my medical kit, took the candle and tin of hot water from him, and tried to think of absolutely nothing but the job before me. Not feet. Not, for God's sake, Arch Bug.

Jamie had a blanket wrapped round his shoulders, but his legs were necessarily bare, and I could feel the hairs bristling with gooseflesh as my hand brushed them. The bottom of his shirt was soaked with half-dried blood; it stuck to his leg, but he made no sound when I pulled it loose and nudged his legs apart.

He had been moving like a man in a bad dream, but the approach of a lighted candle to his balls roused him.

"Ye'll take care wi' that candle, Sassenach, aye?" he said, putting a protective hand over his genitals.

Seeing his point, I gave him the candle to hold, and with a brief admonition to beware of dripping hot wax, returned to my inspection.

The wound was oozing blood, but plainly minor, and I plunged a cloth into the hot water and began to work. His flesh was chilled, and the cold damped even the pungent odors of the pantry, but I could still smell him, his usual dry musk tainted with blood and frantic sweat.

It was a deep gouge that ran four inches through the flesh of his thigh, high up. Clean, though.

"A John Wayne special," I said, trying for a light, dry tone. Jamie's eyes, which had been fixed on the candle flame, changed focus and fixed on me.

"What?" he said hoarsely.

"Nothing serious," I said. "The ball just grazed you. You may walk a little oddly for a day or two, but the hero lives to fight another day." The ball had in fact gone between his legs, deeply creasing the inside of his thigh, near both to his testicles and his femoral artery. One inch to the right, and he'd be dead. One inch higher . . .

"Not a great help, Sassenach," he said, but the ghost of a smile touched his eyes.

"No," I agreed. "But some?"

"Some," he said, and briefly touched my face. His hand was very cold, and trembled; hot wax ran over the knuckles of his other hand, but he didn't seem to feel it. I took the candlestick gently from him and set it on the shelf.

I could feel the grief and self-reproach coming off him in waves, and fought to keep it at bay. I couldn't help him if I gave in to the enormity of the situation. I wasn't sure I could help him in any case, but I'd try.

"Oh, Jesus," he said, so softly I barely heard him. "Why did I not let him take it? What did it matter?" He struck a fist on his knee, soundless. "*God*, why did I not just let him take it!?"

"You didn't know who it was, or what they meant to do," I said, just as softly, putting a hand on his shoulder. "It was an accident." His muscles were bunched, hard with anguish. I felt it, too, a hard knot of protest and denial— *No, it* can't *be true, it can't have happened!*—in my throat, but there was work to be done. I'd deal with the inescapable later.

He put a hand over his face, shaking his head slowly to and fro, and neither spoke nor moved while I finished the cleaning and bandaging of the wound.

"Can ye do aught for Ian?" he said, when I'd finished. He took his hand away and looked up at me as I stood, his face drawn in exhausted misery, but calm again. "He's . . ." He swallowed, and glanced at the door. "He's badly, Sassenach."

I glanced at the whisky I'd brought: a quarter of a bottle. Jamie followed the direction of my gaze and shook his head.

"Not enough."

"You drink it, then." He shook his head, but I put the bottle in his hand and pressed his fingers round it.

"Orders," I said, soft but very firm. "Shock." He resisted, made to put the bottle back, and I tightened my hand on his.

"I *know*," I said. "Jamie—I know. But you can't give in. Not now."

He looked up at me for a moment, but then he nodded, accepting it because he had to, the muscles of his arm relaxing. My own fingers were stiff, chilled from water and frigid air, but still warmer than his. I folded both hands round his free one, and held it, hard.

"There's a reason why the hero never dies, you know," I said, and attempted a smile, though my face felt stiff and false. "When the worst happens, someone still has to decide what to do. Go into the house now, and get warm." I glanced out at the night, lavender-skied and wild with swirling snow. "I'll... find Ian."

WHERE WOULD HE have gone? Not far, not in this weather. Given his state of mind when he and Jamie had come back with Mrs. Bug's body, he *might*, I thought, simply have walked off into the woods, not caring where he went or what happened to him—but he'd had the dog with him. No matter what he felt like, he wouldn't take Rollo off into a howling blizzard.

And a blizzard was what it was shaping up to be. I made my way slowly uphill toward the outbuildings, sheltering my lantern under a fold of my cloak. It came to me suddenly to wonder whether Arch Bug might have taken shelter in the springhouse or the smoke shed. And... oh, God—did he *know*? I stopped dead on the path for an instant, letting the thickly falling snow settle like a veil on my head and shoulders.

I had been so shocked by what had happened that I hadn't thought to wonder whether Arch Bug knew that his wife was dead. Jamie said that he had called out, called for Arch to come, as soon as he realized—but there had been no answer. Perhaps Arch had suspected a trick; perhaps he had simply fled, seeing Jamie and Ian and assuming that they would certainly not harm his wife. In which case...

"Oh, *bloody* hell," I said under my breath, appalled. But there was nothing I could do about that. I hoped there was something I could do about Ian. I rubbed a forearm over my face, blinked snow from my lashes, and went on, slowly, the light from the lantern swallowed in the vortex of whirling snow. Were I to find Arch... My fingers clenched on the lantern's handle. I'd have to tell him, bring him back to the cabin, let him see... Oh, dear. If I came back with Arch, could Jamie and Ian occupy him long enough for me to remove Mrs. Bug from the pantry and display her in more seemly fashion? I hadn't had time to remove the jutting arrow or lay out the body decently. I dug the fingernails of my free hand into the palm, trying to get a grip of myself.

"Jesus, don't let me find him," I said under my breath. "Please don't let me find him."

But springhouse, smoke shed, and corncrib were all—thank God—empty, and no one could have hidden in the chicken coop without the chickens making a fuss about it; they were silent, sleeping out the storm. The sight of the coop brought Mrs. Bug suddenly to mind, though—the vision of her scattering corn from her apron, crooning to the silly things. She'd named them all. I didn't bloody care whether we were eating Isobeaìl or Alasdair for supper, but just at the moment, the fact that no one now would ever be able to tell one from another, or rejoice in the fact that Elspeth had hatched ten chicks, seemed unspeakably heartrending.

I found Ian at last in the barn, a dark form huddled in the straw by the feet of Clarence the mule, whose ears pricked up at my appearance. He brayed ecstatically at the prospect of more company, and the goats blatted hysterically, thinking I was a wolf. The horses, surprised, tossed their heads, snorting and nickering in question. Rollo, nestled in the hay next to his master, gave a short, sharp bark of displeasure at the racket.

"Ruddy Noah's Ark in here," I remarked, shaking snow off my cloak and hanging the lantern on a hook. "All we need is a pair of elephants. Hush, Clarence!"

Ian turned his face toward me, but I could see from his blank expression that he hadn't taken in what I'd said.

I squatted next to him and cupped a hand round his cheek; it was cold, bristled with young beard.

"It wasn't your fault," I said gently.

"I know," he said, and swallowed. "But I dinna see how I can live." He wasn't dramatic about it at all; his voice was simply bewildered. Rollo licked his hand, and his fingers sank into the dog's ruff, as though for support.

"What can I do, Auntie?" He looked at me, helpless. "There's nothing, is there? I canna take it back, or undo it. And yet I keep looking for some way that I can. Something I can do to make things right. But there's . . . nothing."

I sat down in the hay next to him and put an arm round his shoulder, pressing his head toward me. He came, reluctantly, though I felt small constant shudders of exhaustion and grief running through him like a chill.

"I loved her," he said, so low I could barely hear him. "She was like my grandmother. And I—"

"She loved you," I whispered. "She wouldn't blame you." I had been holding on to my own emotions like grim death, in order to do what had to be done. But now . . . Ian was right. There was nothing, and in sheer helplessness, tears began to roll down my face. I wasn't crying. Grief and shock simply overflowed; I could not contain them.

Whether he felt the tears on his skin or only the vibrations of my grief, I couldn't tell, but quite suddenly Ian gave way as well, and he wept in my arms, shaking.

I wished with all my heart that he was a small boy, and that the storm of grief could wash away his guilt and leave him cleansed, at peace. But he was far beyond such simple things; all I could do was hold him, and stroke his back, making small, helpless noises myself. Then Clarence offered his own support, breathing heavily on Ian's head and nibbling thoughtfully on a lock of his hair. Ian jerked away, slapping at the mule's nose.

"Och, awa' wi' ye!"

He choked, laughed in a shocked way, wept a little more, and then straightened up and wiped his nose on his sleeve. He sat still for a little while, gathering the pieces of himself, and I let him be.

"When I killed that man in Edinburgh," he said at last, his voice thick but controlled, "Uncle Jamie took me to confession, and told me the prayer that ye say when ye've killed someone. To commend them to God. Will ye say it with me, Auntie?"

I hadn't thought of—let alone said—"Soul Leading" in many years, and stumbled awkwardly through the words. Ian spoke it without hesitation, though, and I wondered how often he had used it through those years.

The words seemed puny and powerless, swallowed among the sounds of hay rustling and beasts chewing. But I felt a tiny bit of comfort for having said them. Perhaps it was only that the sense of reaching out to something larger than yourself gives you some feeling that there *is* something larger—and there really has to be, because plainly *you* aren't sufficient to the situation. I surely wasn't.

Ian sat for a time, eyes closed. Finally, he opened them and looked at me, his eyes black with knowledge, face very pale under the stubble of his beard.

"And then, he said, ye live with it," he said softly.

He rubbed a hand across his face.

"But I dinna think I can." It was a simple statement of fact, and scared me badly. I had no more tears, but felt as though I looked into a black, bottomless hole—and couldn't look away.

I drew a deep breath, trying to think of something to say, then pulled a handkerchief from my pocket and gave it to him.

"Are you breathing, Ian?"

His mouth twitched a little.

"Aye, I think so."

"That's all you have to do, for now." I got up, brushed hay from my skirts, and held out a hand to him. "Come along. We need to go back to the cabin before we're snowed in here."

The snow was thicker now, and a gust of wind put out the candle in my lantern. It didn't matter; I could have found the cabin blindfolded. Ian went ahead of me without comment, breaking a trail through the fresh-fallen snow. His head was bent against the storm, his narrow shoulders hunched.

I hoped the prayer had helped him, at least a little, and wondered whether the Mohawk had any better means of dealing with unjust death than did the Catholic Church.

Then I realized that I knew exactly what the Mohawk would do in such a case. So did Ian; he'd done it. I pulled the cloak tighter round me, feeling as though I had swallowed a large ball of ice.

NOT YET AWHILE

FTER A GOOD DEAL of discussion, the two corpses were carried gently outside and laid at the edge of the porch. There simply was no room to lay them out properly inside, and given the circumstances...

"We canna let auld Arch be in doubt any longer than he must," Jamie had said, putting an end to the arguments. "If the body's in plain sight, maybe he'll come out and maybe he'll not—but he'll ken his wife's dead."

"He will," Bobby Higgins said, with an uneasy look toward the trees. "And what d'ye think he'll do then?"

Jamie stood for a moment, looking toward the wood, then shook his head.

"Grieve," he said quietly. "And in the morning, we'll see what's to do."

It wasn't the normal sort of wake, but it was conducted with what ceremony we could manage. Amy had donated her own shroud—made after her first wedding, and carefully kept by—for Mrs. Bug, and Grannie MacLeod was clad in the remnants of my spare chemise and a couple of aprons, hastily stitched up into respectability. They were laid one on either side of the porch, foot to foot, with a small saucer of salt and a slice of bread on the chest of each corpse, though no sin-eater was available. I had packed a small clay firepot with coals and set this near the bodies, and it was agreed that we would all take it in turns through the night to sit over the deceased, as the porch would hold no more than two or three people.

"The moon on the breast of the new-fallen snow/Gave the lustre of mid-day to objects below," I said softly. It did; the storm had blown over and the three-quarter moon cast a pure, cold light that made each snow-covered tree stand out, stark and delicate as a painting in Japanese ink. And in the distant ruins of the Big House, the jackstraw of charred timbers hid whatever lay below.

Jamie and I were taking the first watch. No one had argued when Jamie announced this. No one spoke of it, but the image of Arch Bug, lurking alone in the forest, was in everyone's mind.

"You think he's there?" I asked Jamie, low-voiced. I nodded toward the dark trees, peaceful in their own soft shrouds.

"If it were you lying here, *a nighean,*" Jamie said, looking down at the still white figures at the edge of the porch, "I should be beside ye, alive or dead. Come sit down."

I sat down beside him, the firepot close to our cloak-wrapped knees.

"Poor things," I said, after a bit. "It's a long way from Scotland."

"It is," he said, and took my hand. His fingers were no warmer than my own, but the size and strength of them were a comfort, nonetheless. "But they'll be buried amongst folk who ken their ways, if not among their own kin."

"True." Should Grannie MacLeod's grandsons ever come back, at least they would find a marker for her grave and know she had been treated with kindness. Mrs. Bug hadn't any kin, save Arch—no one to come and look for the grave marker. But she would be among people who'd known and loved her. What about Arch, though? If he had kin in Scotland, he'd never mentioned it. His wife had been everything to him, as he to her.

"You, um, don't think that Arch might . . . do away with himself?" I asked delicately. "Once he knows?"

Jamie shook his head, definite.

"No," he said. "It's not in him."

On one level, I was relieved to hear this. On a lower and less compassionate level, I couldn't help wondering uneasily just what a man of Arch's passions might do, stricken by this mortal blow, now bereft of the woman who had been his anchor and safe harbor for most of his life.

What *would* such a man do? I wondered. Run before the wind until he hit a reef and sank? Or tie his life to the makeshift anchor of fury, and take revenge as his new compass? I'd seen the guilt Jamie and Ian were bearing; how much more was Arch carrying? Could any man bear such guilt? Or must he turn it outward, as a matter of simple survival?

Jamie had said nothing about his own speculations, but I'd noticed that he had both pistol and dirk in his belt—and the pistol was loaded and primed; I could smell the whiff of black powder under the resinous breath of spruce and fir. Of course, it *might* be for driving off a roving wolf or foxes . . .

We sat in silence for a little while, watching the shifting glow of the coals in the firepot and the flicker of light in the folds of the shrouds.

"Ought we to pray, do you think?" I whispered.

"I havena given over praying since it happened, Sassenach."

"I know what you mean." I did—the passionate prayer that it might not be, and the desperate prayer for guidance thereafter; the need to do something, when nothing, really, could be done. And, of course, prayer for the repose of the recently departed. At least Grannie MacLeod had expected death—and welcomed it, I thought. Mrs. Bug, on the other hand, must have been terribly startled at being so suddenly dead. I had a disconcerting vision of her standing in the snow just off the porch, glaring at her corpse, hands on stout hips, lips pursed in annoyance at having been so rudely disembodied.

"It *was* rather a shock," I said apologetically to her shade.

"Aye, it was that."

Jamie reached into his cloak and drew out his flask. Uncorking this, he leaned forward and carefully poured a few drops of whisky on the head of each of the dead women, then lifted the flask in silent toast to Grannie MacLeod, then to Mrs. Bug.

"Murdina, wife of Archibald, ye were a great cook," he said simply. "I'll recall your biscuits all my life, and think of ye wi' my morning parritch."

"Amen," I said, my voice trembling between laughter and tears. I accepted the flask and took a sip; the whisky burned through the thickness in my throat, and I coughed.

"I know her receipt for piccalilli. That shouldn't be lost; I'll write it down."

The thought of writing reminded me quite suddenly of the unfinished letter, still folded up in my workbag. Jamie felt the slight stiffening of my posture and turned his head toward me in question.

"I was only thinking of that letter," I said, clearing my throat. "I mean, in spite of Roger and Bree knowing the house has burnt down, they'll be happy to hear that we're still alive—always supposing they do eventually get it."

Aware both of the precarious times and of the uncertain survival of historical documents, Jamie and Roger had worked out several schemes for the passage of information, ranging from the publication of coded messages in various newspapers to something elaborate involving the Church of Scotland and the Bank of England. All of these, of course, relied upon the basic fact of the MacKenzie family having made the passage through the stones safely and arrived in more or less the right time—but I was obliged for my own peace of mind to assume that they had.

"But I don't want to end it by having to tell them—about this." I nodded toward the shrouded figures. "They loved Mrs. Bug—and Bree would be so upset for Ian."

"Aye, ye're right," Jamie said thoughtfully. "And chances are that Roger Mac would think it all through and realize about Arch. Knowing, and not able to do anything about it . . . aye, they'd be worrit, 'til they found another letter telling them how it's all come out—and God knows how long it may be before it *has* all come out."

"And if they didn't *get* the next letter . . ." *Or if we didn't survive long enough to write it,* I thought.

"Aye, best not tell them. Not yet awhile."

I moved closer, leaning against him, and he put his arm round me. We sat quiet for a bit, still troubled and sorrowful, but comforted at thought of Roger, Bree, and the children.

I could hear sounds from the cabin behind me; everyone had been quiet, shocked—but normality was fast reasserting itself. Children couldn't be kept quiet long, and I could hear high-pitched questions, demands for food, the chatter of little ones excited at being up so late, their voices threading through the clanging and thumps of food preparation. There would be bannocks and pasties for the next part of the wake; Mrs. Bug would be pleased. A sudden shower of sparks flew from the chimney and fell all round the porch like falling stars, brilliant against the dark night and the white, fresh snow.

Jamie's arm tightened round me, and he made a small sound of pleasure at the sight.

"That—what ye said about the breast o' the new-fallen snow"—the word emerged as "breest" in his soft Highland lilt—"that's a poem, is it?"

"It is. Not really appropriate to a wake—it's a comic Christmas poem called 'A Visit from Saint Nicholas.' "

Jamie snorted, his breath white.

"I dinna think the word 'appropriate' has much to do wi' a proper wake, Sassenach. Give the mourners enough drink, and they'll be singing '*O thoir a-nall am Botul*' and the weans dancing ring-a-round-a-rosy in the dooryard by moonlight."

I didn't quite laugh, but could envision it, all too easily. There *was* enough to drink, too; there was a fresh tub of beer just brewed in the pantry, and Bobby had fetched down the emergency keg of whisky from its hiding place in the barn. I lifted Jamie's hand and kissed the cold knuckles. The shock and sense of dislocation had begun to fade with the growing awareness of the pulse of life behind us. The cabin was a small, vibrant island of life, afloat in the cold of the black and white night.

"*No man is an island, entire of itself,*" Jamie said softly, picking up my unspoken thought.

"Now, that one *is* appropriate," I said, a little dryly. "Maybe too appropriate."

"Aye? How so?"

"*Never send to know for whom the bell tolls, it tolls for thee?* I never hear *No man is an island* without that last line tolling right behind it."

"Mmphm. Ken the whole of it, do ye?" Not waiting for my reply, he leaned forward and stirred the coals with a stick, sending up a tiny drift of silent sparks. "It isna really a poem, ken—or the man didna mean it to be one."

"No?" I said, surprised. "What is it? Or was it?"

"A meditation—something atwixt a sermon and a prayer. John Donne wrote it as part of his 'Devotions upon Emergent Occasions.' That's sufficiently appropriate, no?" he added, with a hint of wry humor.

"They don't get much more emergent than this, no. What am I missing, then?"

"Mmm." He pulled me closer, and bent his head to rest on mine. "Let me call what I can to mind. I'll not have all of it, but there are bits that struck me, so I remember those." I could hear his breathing, slow and easy, concentrating.

"*All mankind is of one author,*" he said slowly, "*and is one volume. When one man dies, one chapter is not torn out of the book, but translated into a better language; and every chapter must be so translated.* Then there are bits I havena got by heart, but I liked this one: *The bell doth toll for him that thinks it doth*"— and his hand squeezed mine gently—"*and though it intermit again, yet from that minute that that occasion wrought upon him, he is united to God.*"

"Hmm." I thought about that for a bit. "You're right; that's less poetic, but a bit more . . . hopeful?"

I felt him smile.

"I've always found it so, aye."

"Where did you get that?"

"John Grey lent me a wee book of Donne's writing, when I was prisoner at Helwater. That was in it."

"A very literate gentleman," I said, somewhat piqued at this reminder of the substantial chunk of Jamie's life that John Grey had shared and I had not—but grudgingly glad that he had had a friend through that time of trial. How often, I wondered suddenly, had Jamie heard that tolling bell?

I sat up, reached for the flask, and took a cleansing swallow. The smell of baking, of onion and simmered meat, was seeping through the door, and my stomach rumbled in an unseemly manner. Jamie didn't notice; he was squinting thoughtfully off toward the west, where the bulk of the mountain lay hidden by cloud.

"The MacLeod lads said the passes were already hip-deep in snow when they came down," he said. "If there's a foot of new snow on the ground here, there are three in the high passes. We're going nowhere 'til the spring thaw, Sassenach. Time enough to carve proper grave markers, at least," he added, with a glance at our quiet guests.

"You do still mean to go to Scotland, then?" He'd said so, after the Big House burned, but hadn't mentioned it since then. I wasn't sure whether he'd meant it or had merely been reacting to the pressure of events at the time.

"Aye, I do. We canna be staying here, I think," he said, with some regret. "Come the spring, the backcountry will be boiling again. We've come close enough to the fire." He lifted his chin in the direction of the Big House's charred remains. "I've no mind to be roasted, next time."

"Well . . . yes." He was right, I knew. We could build another house—but it was unlikely we would be allowed to live peaceably in it. Among other things, Jamie was—or at least had been—a colonel of militia. Short of physical incapacity or simple absence, he couldn't relinquish that responsibility. And sentiment in the mountains was by no means all in favor of rebellion. I knew a number of people who had been beaten, burnt out, and driven into the woods or swamps, or killed outright as the direct result of injudiciously expressed political sentiments.

The weather prevented our leaving, but it also put a stopper on the movement of militias—or roving bands of brigands. The thought of that sent a sudden bolt of cold through me, and I shivered.

"Shall ye go in, *a nighean?*" Jamie asked, noticing. "I can bear watch alone for a bit."

"Right. And we'll come out with the bannocks and honey and find you stretched out beside the old ladies with an ax in your head. I'm fine." I took another sip of whisky, and handed him the flask.

"We wouldn't necessarily have to go to Scotland, though," I said, watching him drink. "We could go to New Bern. You could join Fergus in the printing business there." That's what he'd said he meant to do: go to Scotland, fetch the printing press he had left in Edinburgh, then come back to join the fight, armed with lead in the form of type slugs, rather than musket balls. I wasn't sure which method might be the more dangerous.

"Ye dinna suppose your presence would stop Arch trying to brain me, if that's what he's got in mind?" Jamie smiled briefly at that, slanted eyes creasing into triangles. "No—Fergus has a right to put himself in danger, and he wants to. But I've no right to drag him and his family into my own."

"Which tells me all I need to know about what sort of printing you have in mind to do. And my presence might not stop Arch going for you, but I could at least shout 'Look out!' if I saw him creeping up behind you."

"I should always want ye at my back, Sassenach," he assured me gravely. "Ye kent already what I mean to do, surely?"

"Yes," I said with a sigh. "Occasionally I have the vain hope that I'm wrong about you—but I never am."

That made him laugh outright.

"No, ye're not," he agreed. "But ye're still here, aye?" He lifted the flask in salute to me, and drank from it. "Good to know someone will miss me, when I fall."

"I did not miss that 'when,' rather than 'if,' " I said coldly.

"It's always been 'when,' Sassenach," he said gently. "*Every chapter must be so translated*. Aye?"

I took a deep breath and watched it drift out in a plume of mist.

"I sincerely hope I'm not going to have to do it," I said, "but should the question arise—would you want to be buried here? Or taken back to Scotland?" I was thinking of a granite marriage stone in the graveyard at St. Kilda, with his name on it, and mine, too. The bloody thing had nearly given me heart failure when I saw it, and I wasn't sure I had forgiven Frank for it, even though it had accomplished what he'd meant it to.

Jamie made a small snorting noise, not quite a laugh.

"I shall be lucky to be buried at all, Sassenach. Much more likely I shall be drowned, burnt, or left to rot on some battlefield. Dinna fash yourself. If ye've got to dispose of my carcass, just leave it out for the crows."

"I'll make a note of that," I said.

"Will ye mind going to Scotland?" he asked, eyebrows raised.

I sighed. Despite my knowing that he wasn't going to lie under that particular gravestone, I couldn't quite rid myself of the notion that he would at some point die there.

"No. I'll mind leaving the mountains. I'll mind watching you turn green and puke your guts out on the ship, and I may well mind whatever happens on the way *to* said ship, but ... Edinburgh and printing presses aside, you want to go to Lallybroch, don't you?"

He nodded, eyes on the glowing coals. The light from the firepot was faint but warm on the ruddy arch of his brows, a line of gilding down the long, straight bridge of his nose.

"I promised, aye?" he said simply. "I said I'd bring Young Ian back to his mother. And after this ... best he goes."

I nodded silently. Three thousand miles of ocean might not be enough for Ian to escape his memories—but it couldn't hurt. And perhaps the joy of seeing his parents, his brothers and sisters, the Highlands ... perhaps it would help heal him.

Jamie coughed, and rubbed a knuckle over his lips.

"There's the one other thing," he said, a little shy. "Another promise, ye might say."

"What's that?"

He turned his head then, and met my eyes, his own dark and serious.

"I've sworn to myself," he said, "that I shallna ever face my son across the barrel of a gun."

I took a deep breath and nodded. After a moment's silence, I looked up from my contemplation of the shrouded women.

"You didn't ask what I want done with *my* body." I'd meant it at least half in jest, to lighten his mood, but his fingers curled so abruptly over mine that I gasped.

"No," he said softly. "And I never will." He wasn't looking at me but at the whiteness before us. "I canna think of ye dead, Claire. Anything else—but not that. I can't."

He stood abruptly. The rattle of wood, the clang of a falling pewter dish, and voices raised in adjuration inside saved me from reply. I simply nodded and let him lift me to my feet, as the door opened, spilling light.

THE MORNING DAWNED clear and bright, with a scant foot of fresh snow on the ground. By noon, the icicles that hung from the cabin's eaves had begun to loose their hold, dropping like random daggers with muffled, intermittent *thunks*. Jamie and Ian had gone up the hill to the small burying ground, with spades, to see whether the ground might be dug deep enough for two decent graves.

"Take Aidan and one or two of the other boys with you," I'd said at breakfast. "They need to be gotten out from underfoot." Jamie had given me a sharp glance, but nodded. He knew very well what I was thinking. If Arch Bug *didn't* yet know that his wife was dead, he'd certainly start drawing conclusions if he saw a grave being dug.

"Best if he'll come and speak to me," Jamie had said quietly to me, under cover of the noise made by the boys readying themselves to go, their mothers packing lunch to be taken up the hill, and the smaller children playing ring-a-round-a-rosy in the back room.

"Yes," I said, "and the boys won't stop him doing that. But if he *doesn't* choose to come out and speak to you . . ." Ian had told me that he'd heard a rifle fired during the encounter the night before; Arch Bug was no particular marksman, though, and would presumably hesitate to fire on a group that included young children.

Jamie had nodded, silent, and sent Aidan to fetch his two eldest cousins.

Bobby and Clarence the mule had gone up with the grave-digging party. There was a stock of freshly sawn pine boards at the site higher up on the mountainside, where Jamie had declared our new house would one day rise; if graves could be dug, Bobby would bring back some of the boards to make coffins.

From my viewpoint on the front porch, I could see Clarence now, heavily laden, but mincing downhill with ballerina grace, ears pointed delicately to either side as though to aid his balance. I caught a glimpse of Bobby walking on the far side of the mule, reaching up now and then to keep the load from slipping; he saw me and waved, smiling. The M branded on his cheek was visible even at this distance, livid against the cold-chapped ruddiness of his skin.

I waved back and turned in to the house, to tell the women that we would indeed have a funeral.

WE MADE OUR WAY up the winding trail to the small graveyard next morning. The two old ladies, unlikely companions in death, lay side by side in their coffins on a sledge, pulled by Clarence and one of the McCallum women's mules, a little black jenny called Puddin'.

We were not dressed in our best; no one *had* a "best," with the exception of Amy McCallum Higgins, who had worn her lace-trimmed wedding kerchief as a sign of respect. We were mostly clean, though, and the adults at least were sober in aspect, and watchful. Very watchful.

"Which will be the new guardian, Mam?" Aidan asked his mother, eyeing the two coffins as the sledge creaked slowly uphill ahead of us. "Which died first?"

"Why . . . I dinna ken, Aidan," Amy replied, looking mildly taken aback. She frowned at the coffins, then glanced at me. "D'ye know that, Mrs. Fraser?"

The question hit me like a thrown pebble, and I blinked. I did know, of course, but—with some effort, I refrained from glancing into the trees that lined the trail. I had no idea exactly where Arch Bug was, but he was near; I had no doubt of that at all. And if he were near enough to overhear this conversation . . .

Highland superstition held that the last person to be buried in a graveyard became the guardian and must defend the souls who rested there from any evil, until another should die and take the guardian's place—whereupon the earlier guardian was released and might go on to heaven. I didn't think Arch would be at all happy about the notion of his wife trapped on earth to guard the graves of Presbyterians and sinners like Malva Christie.

I felt a small chill in the heart at thought of Malva—who was, now I thought of it, presumably the graveyard's present guardian. "Presumably," because while other people had died on the Ridge since her own death, she was the last to have been buried in the graveyard proper. Her brother, Allan, was buried nearby, a little way into the forest, in a secret, unmarked grave; I didn't know whether that was near enough to count. And her father . . .

I coughed into my fist, and clearing my throat said, "Oh, Mrs. MacLeod. She was dead when we came back to the cabin with Mrs. Bug." Which was strictly true; the fact that she'd been dead when I *left* the cabin seemed better suppressed.

I had been looking at Amy when I spoke. I turned my head back to the trail, and there he was, right in front of me. Arch Bug, in his rusty black cloak, white head bared and bent, following the sledge through the snow, slow as an earthbound raven. A faint shudder ran through the mourners.

He turned his head then, and saw me.

"Will ye sing, Mrs. Fraser?" he asked, his voice quiet and courtly. "I'd have her taken to her rest wi' the proper observances."

"I—yes, of course." Enormously flustered, I groped for something suitable. I simply wasn't up to the challenge of composing a proper *caithris*, a lament for the dead—let alone providing the formal wailing that a truly first-class Highland funeral would have.

I settled hastily for a Gaelic psalm that Roger had taught me, *"Is e Dia fèin a's buachaill dhomh.*" It was a line chant, each line meant to be sung by a pre-centor, then echoed line by line by the congregation. It was simple, though, and while my voice seemed thin and insubstantial on the mountainside, those around me were able to take it up, and by the time we reached the burying ground, we had achieved a respectable level of fervor and volume.

The sledge stopped at the edge of the pine-circled clearing. A few wooden crosses and cairns were visible through the half-melted snow, and the two fresh graves gaped in the center, muddy and brutal. The sight of them stopped the singing as abruptly as a pail of cold water.

The sun shone pale and bright through the trees, and there was a gang of nuthatches conversing in the branches at the edge of the clearing, incongru-ously cheerful. Jamie had been leading the mules, and had not glanced back at Arch's appearance. Now, though, he turned to Arch and with a small ges-ture at the nearer coffin, asked in a low voice, "Will ye look upon your wife once more?"

It was only as Arch nodded and moved to the side of the sledge, that I re-alized that while the men had nailed down the lid of Mrs. MacLeod's coffin, they had left Mrs. Bug's lying loose. Bobby and Ian lifted it off, their eyes on the ground.

Arch had unbound his hair as a sign of grief; I had never seen it loose be-fore. It was thin, pure white, and wavered about his face like wisps of smoke as he bent and gently lifted the shroud from Murdina's face.

I swallowed hard, clenching my hands. I'd removed the arrow—not a pleasant business—and had then wrapped her throat carefully in a clean ban-dage before combing her hair. She looked all right, though terribly unfamil-iar; I didn't think I'd ever seen her without her cap, and the bandage across her full throat gave her the sternly formal air of a Presbyterian minister. I saw Arch flinch, just slightly, and his own throat move. He got control of his face almost at once, but I saw the lines that ran from nose to chin like gullies through wet clay, and the way in which he opened and closed his hands, over and over, seeking a grip on something that wasn't there.

He gazed into the coffin for a long moment, then reached into his sporran and drew out something. I saw when he put back his cloak that his belt was empty; he had come without weapons.

The thing in his hand was small and glittering. He leaned down and tried to fix it to the shroud, but could not, with his missing fingers. He fumbled, said something under his breath in Gaelic, then looked up at me, with some-thing near panic in his eyes. I went at once to him, and took the thing from his hand.

It was a brooch, a small, beautifully made thing in the shape of a flying swallow. Made of gold, and very new-looking. I took it from him and, turn-ing back the shroud, pinned it to Mrs. Bug's kerchief. I'd never seen the brooch before, either on Mrs. Bug or among her things, and it came to me that Arch had likely had it made from the gold he had taken from Jocasta Cameron—perhaps when he began to take the ingots, one by one; perhaps later. A promise made to his wife—that their years of penury and dependence were over. Well . . . indeed they were. I glanced at Arch, and at his nod, pulled the shroud gently up over his wife's cold face.

I put out a hand impulsively to touch him, take his arm, but he drew away and stood back, watching impassively as Bobby nailed down the lid. At one point, his gaze rose and passed slowly over Jamie, then Ian, in turn.

I pressed my lips tight, glancing at Jamie as I came back to his side, seeing the trouble etched so plainly on his face. So much guilt! Not that there wasn't enough and to spare—and plainly enough, Arch felt his own. Did it not occur to any of them that Mrs. Bug had had something to do with this, herself? Had she not fired at Jamie . . . but people didn't always behave intelligently, or well, and did the fact that someone had contributed to their own demise lessen the tragedy of it?

I caught sight of the small boulder that marked the grave of Malva and her son, only the top of it visible through the snow—rounded, wet, and dark, like the crowning of a baby's head at birth.

Rest in peace, I thought, and felt a small easing of the tension I'd been under for the last two days. *You can go now.*

It occurred to me that whatever I'd told Amy and Aidan, it didn't alter the truth of which woman really *had* died first. Still, considering Mrs. Bug's personality, I rather thought she might enjoy being in charge, clucking and fussing after the resident souls like her flock of much-loved chickens, banishing evil spirits with a sharp word and a brandished sausage.

That thought got me through the brief reading from the Bible, the prayers, the tears—from the women and the children, most of whom had no idea why they were crying—the removal of the coffins from the sledge, and a rather disjoint recitation of the Lord's Prayer. I missed Roger very much—his sense of calm order and genuine compassion in the conducting of a funeral. And he would, perhaps, have known what to say in eulogy of Murdina Bug. As it was, no one spoke when the prayer concluded, and there was a long, awkward pause, people shifting uneasily from foot to foot—we were standing in a foot of snow, and the women's petticoats were wet to the knee.

I saw Jamie shift his shoulders, as though his coat was too tight, and glance at the sledge, where the shovels lay under a blanket. Before he could signal Ian and Bobby, though, Ian drew a deep, gasping breath and stepped forward.

He came to the side of Mrs. Bug's waiting coffin, opposite the bereaved husband, and stopped, plainly wanting to speak. Arch ignored him for a long moment, staring down into the hole, but finally raised his face, impassive. Waiting.

"It was by my hand that this"—Ian swallowed—"that this woman of great worth has died. I didna take her life by malice, or of purpose, and it is sorrow to me. But she died by my hand."

Rollo whined softly by Ian's side, feeling his master's distress, but Ian laid a hand on his head, and he stilled. Ian drew the knife from his belt and laid it on the coffin in front of Arch Bug, then straightened and looked him in the eye.

"Ye swore once to my uncle, in a time of great wrong, and offered life for life, for this woman. I swear by my iron, and I offer the same." His lips pressed together for an instant, and his throat moved, his eyes dark and sober. "I think ye maybe didna mean it, sir—but I do."

I found that I was holding my breath, and forced myself to breathe. Was this Jamie's plan? I wondered. Ian plainly meant what he said. Still, the chances of Arch accepting that offer on the spot and cutting Ian's throat in front of a dozen witnesses were slim, no matter how exigent his feelings. But if he publicly declined the offer—then the possibility of a more formal and less bloody recompense was opened, yet young Ian would be relieved of at least a measure of his guilt. Bloody Highlander, I thought, glancing up at Jamie— not without a certain admiration.

I could feel small jolts of energy running through him, though, every few seconds, each one suppressed. He wouldn't interfere with Ian's attempt at atonement—but neither would he see him injured, if by chance old Arch *did* opt for blood. And evidently he thought it a possibility. I glanced at Arch, and thought so, too.

The old man looked at Ian for a moment, heavy brows wild with curling iron-gray old-man hairs—and the eyes beneath them iron-gray, too, and cold as steel.

"Too easy, boy," he said at last, in a voice like rusty iron.

He looked down at Rollo, who was standing next to Ian, ears pricked and wolf eyes wary.

"Will ye give me your hound to kill?"

Ian's mask broke in an instant, shock and horror making him suddenly young. I heard him gulp air and steady himself, but his voice was cracked in reply.

"No," he said. "He's done nothing. It's my—my crime, not his."

Arch smiled then, very slightly, though it did not touch his eyes.

"Aye. Ye see, then. And he's no but a flea-ridden beast. Not a wife."

"Wife" was spoken in barely a whisper. His throat worked as he cleared it. Then he looked carefully from Ian to Jamie, and then at me.

"Not a wife," he said softly. I'd thought my blood ran cold already; that froze my heart.

In no hurry, Arch turned his gaze deliberately upon each man in turn; Jamie, then Ian, whom he regarded for an instant that seemed a lifetime.

"When you've something worth taking, boy—you'll see me again," he said quietly, then turned upon his heel and walked into the trees.

5

MORALITY FOR TIME-TRAVELERS

THERE WAS AN electric desk lamp in his study, but Roger often preferred to work by candlelight in the evening. He took a match from the box, and struck it with one soft scratch. After Claire's letter, he didn't think he'd ever light a match again without thinking of her story of the burning of the Big House. God, he wished he'd been there.

The match flame shrank as he touched it to the wick, and the translucent wax of the candle went a dim, unearthly blue for an instant, then brightened into its normal glow. He glanced at Mandy, singing to a collection of stuffed toys on the sofa; she'd had her bath and was meant to be keeping out of trouble while Jem had his. Keeping one eye on her, he sat down at his desk and opened his notebook.

He'd begun it half as a joke. The other half as the only thing he could think of to combat paralyzing fear.

"You can teach kids not to cross the street alone," Bree had pointed out. "Surely you can teach them to stay the heck away from standing stones."

He'd agreed, but with substantial mental reservations. Small kids, yes; you could brainwash them into not sticking forks in the electric outlets. But as they became teenagers, with all that inchoate yearning for self-discovery and things unknown? He recalled his own teenaged self much too vividly. Tell a teenaged boy not to stick forks in the outlet, and he'd be off rifling the silverware drawer the minute your back was turned. Girls might be different, but he doubted it.

He glanced again at the sofa, where Amanda was now lying on her back, legs thrust into the air and a large, ratty-looking stuffed bear balanced on her feet, to which she was singing "Frère Jacques." Mandy had been so young that she wouldn't remember. Jem would. He did; Roger could tell, when the little boy woke up from nightmares, eyes huge and staring at nothing, and could not describe his dream. Thank God, it didn't happen often.

He still broke out in a cold sweat whenever he remembered it himself. That last passage. He'd clutched Jemmy to his chest and stepped into... God, there was no name for it, because humanity at large had never experienced it, and lucky for them they hadn't. It wasn't even *like* anything to which it could be compared.

None of the senses worked there—and at the same time, all of them did, in such a state of hypersensitivity that you'd die of it if it lasted any longer than it did. A howling void, where sound seemed to batter you, pulsing through your body, trying to separate each cell from the next. Absolute blindness, but the blindness of looking into the sun. And the impact of... bodies? Ghosts? Unseen others who brushed past like moth wings or seemed to hurtle right through you in a colliding thump of entangling bones. A constant sense of screaming.

Did it smell? He paused, frowning, trying to remember. Yes, it damned well did. And oddly enough, it was a describable smell: the scent of air burnt by lightning—ozone.

It smells strongly of ozone, he wrote, feeling remarkably relieved to have even this small foothold of reference to the normal world.

This relief disappeared in the next instant, as he returned to the struggle of memory.

He'd felt as though nothing save his own will held them together, nothing but raw determination to survive held *him* together. Knowing what to expect hadn't helped in the slightest; it was different—and much worse—than his previous experiences.

He did know not to look at them. The ghosts, if that's what they were. "Look" wasn't the right word . . . pay attention to them? Again, there wasn't a word, and he sighed in exasperation.

"Sonnez les matines, sonnez les matines . . ."

"Din dan don," he sang softly with her chorus. *"Din dan don."*

He tapped the pen on the paper for a minute, thinking, then shook his head and bent over the paper again, trying to explain his first attempt, the occasion on which he'd come within . . . moments? inches? Some unthinkably small degree of separation of meeting his father—and destruction.

I think you cannot cross your own lifeline, he wrote slowly. Both Bree and Claire—the scientific women—had assured him that two objects cannot exist in the same space, whether said objects were subatomic particles or elephants. That being true, it would explain why one couldn't exist twice in the same time period, he supposed.

He assumed it was that phenomenon that had come so close to killing him on his first attempt. He had been thinking of his father when he entered the stones, and—presumably—of his father as he, Roger, had known him. Which was, of course, during the period of his own life.

He tapped the pen on the page again, thinking, but could not bring himself just now to write about that encounter. Later. Instead, he flipped back to the rudimentary outline in the front of the book.

A Practical Guide for Time-Travelers

I. *Physical Phenomena*

    A. *Known Locations (Ley Lines?)*

    B. *Genetic Inheritance*

    C. *Mortality*

    D. *The Influence and Properties of Gemstones*

    E. *Blood?*

He'd scratched through that last one, but hesitated, looking at it. Did he have an obligation to tell everything he knew, believed, or suspected? Claire thought that the notion of a blood sacrifice being required or useful was nonsense—a pagan superstition without real validity. She might be right; she was the scientist, after all. But he had the uneasy memory of the night Geillis Duncan had gone through the stones.

Long blond hair, flying in the rising wind of a fire, the whipping locks silhouetted for an instant against the face of a standing stone. The gagging scent of petrol mingled with roasting flesh, and the log that was not a log lying charred in the center of the circle. And Geillis Duncan had gone too far.

"It's always two hundred years, in the old fairy tales," Claire had told him. Literal fairy tales; stories of people stolen by the fairies, "taken through the stones" of faerie hills. *It was a time, two hundred years ago,* such tales often began. Or the people were returned to their own place—but two hundred years past the time they had left. Two hundred years.

Claire, Bree, himself—each time they had traveled, the span of time was the same: two hundred and two years, close enough to the two hundred years of the ancient tales. But Geillis Duncan had gone too far.

With great reluctance, he slowly wrote *Blood* again, and added a parenthetical *(Fire??)*, but nothing beneath it. Not now; later.

For reassurance, he glanced at the spot on the bookshelf where the letter lay, weighted down by a small snake carved of cherrywood. *We are alive....*

He wanted suddenly to go and fetch the wooden box, pull out the other letters, rip them open and read. Curiosity, sure, but something more—wanting to touch them, Claire and Jamie, press the evidence of their lives against his face, his heart, erase the space and time between them.

He forced back the impulse, though. They'd decided—or rather, Bree had, and they were her parents.

"I don't want to read them all at once," she'd said, turning over the contents of the box with long, gentle fingers. "It's . . . it's like once I've read them all, then they'll be . . . *really* gone."

He'd understood. As long as one letter remained unread, they *were* alive. In spite of his historian's curiosity, he shared her sentiment. Besides . . .

Brianna's parents had not written those letters as journal entries, meant for the eventual eyes of a vaguely imagined posterity. They'd been written with the definite and specific intent of communication—with Bree, with *him*. Which meant that they might well contain unsettling things; both his in-laws had a talent for such revelation.

Despite himself, he rose, took down the letter and unfolded it, and read the postscript once more, just to assure himself he hadn't been imagining it.

He hadn't. With the word "blood" ringing faintly in his ears, he sat back down. *An Italian gentleman.* That was Charles Stuart; couldn't be anyone else. Christ. After staring off into space for a bit—Mandy had now started in on "Jingle Bells"—he shook himself, flipped over a few pages and started in again, doggedly.

II. Morality

A. Murder and Wrongful Death

Naturally, we assume that the killing of someone for any reason short of self-defense, the protection of another, or the legitimate use of force in wartime is completely indefensible.

He looked at that for a moment, muttered, "Pompous ass," and ripped the page out of the notebook, crumpling it.

Ignoring Mandy's warbling rendition of *"Gingle bells, Bamman smells, Wobin waid enegg!"* he scooped up the notebook and stomped across the hall to Brianna's study.

"Who am I to be gassing on about morality?" he demanded. She looked up from a sheet showing the disassembled components of a hydroelectric turbine, with the rather blank look that indicated she was aware of being spoken to, but had not detached her mind sufficiently from the subject matter as to realize who was speaking or what they were saying. Familiar with this phenomenon, he waited with mild impatience for her mind to let go of the turbine and focus on him.

" . . . gassing on . . . ?" she said, frowning. She blinked at him and her gaze sharpened. "Who are you gassing on to?"

"Well . . ." He lifted the scribbled notebook, feeling suddenly shy. "The kids, sort of."

"You're supposed to gas on to your kids about morality," she said reasonably. "You're their father; it's your job."

"Oh," he said, rather at a loss. "But—I've *done* a lot of the things I'm telling them not to." *Blood*. Yeah, maybe it was protection of another. Maybe it wasn't.

She raised a thick, ruddy brow at him.

"You never heard of benign hypocrisy? I thought they teach you stuff like that when you go to minister school. Since you mention gassing away about morality. That's a minister's job, too, isn't it?"

She stared at him, blue-eyed and waiting. He took a good, deep breath. Trust Bree, he thought wryly, to walk straight up to the elephant in the room and grab it by the trunk. She hadn't said a word since their return about his near-ordination, or what he proposed to do now about his calling. Not a word, during their year in America, Mandy's surgery, their decision to move to Scotland, the months of renovation after they'd bought Lallybroch—not until he'd opened the door. Once opened, of course, she'd walked straight through it, knocked him over, and planted a foot on his chest.

"Yeah," he said evenly. "It is," and stared back.

"Okay." She smiled, very gently, at him. "So what's the problem?"

"Bree," he said, and felt his heart stick in his scarred throat. "If I knew, I'd tell you."

She stood up then and put her hand on his arm, but before either of them could say more, the thump of small, bare feet came hop-skipping down the hall, and Jem's voice came from the door of Roger's study, saying, "Daddy?"

"Here, pal," he called back, but Brianna was already moving toward the door. Following, he found Jem—in his blue Superman pajamas, wet hair standing up in spikes—standing by his desk, examining the letter with interest.

"What's this?" he asked.

"Wassis?" Mandy echoed faithfully, rushing over and scrambling up on the chair to see.

"It's a letter from your grandda," Brianna replied, not missing a beat. She put a hand casually on the letter, obscuring most of the postscript, and pointed with the other at the last paragraph. "He sent you a kiss. See there?"

A huge smile lighted Jem's face.

"He said he wouldn't forget," he said, contented.

"Kissy, Grandda," Mandy exclaimed, and bending forward so her mass of black curls fell over her face, planted a loud, "MWAH!" on the letter.

Caught between horror and laughter, Bree snatched it up and wiped the moisture off it—but the paper, old as it was, was tough. "No harm done," she said, and handed the letter casually to Roger. "Come on, what story are we reading tonight?"

"Aminal Nursy Tales!"

"An-i-mal," Jem said, bending down to speak distinctly into his sister's face. "An-i-mal Nur-ser-y Tales."

"Okay," she said amiably. "Me first!" and scampered madly out the door, giggling, followed by her brother in hot pursuit. Brianna took three seconds to seize Roger by the ears and kiss him firmly on the mouth, then released him and set off after their offspring.

Feeling happier, he sat down, listening to the uproar of toothbrushing and face-washing above. Sighing, he put the notebook back in the drawer. Plenty of time, he thought. Years before it might be needed. Years and years.

He folded up the letter with care, and standing on tiptoe, put it on the highest shelf of the bookcase, moving the little snake to guard it. He blew out the candle then, and went to join his family.

———

Postscriptum: I see I am to have the last Word—a rare Treat to a Man living in a House that contains (at last count) eight Women. We propose to leave the Ridge so soon as the Climate thaws, and to go to Scotland, there to procure my printing Press, and return with it. Travel in these times is uncertain, and I cannot predict when—or if—it will be possible to write again. (Nor do I know whether you will receive this Letter at all, but I proceed in necessary Faith that you will.)

I wished to tell you of the Disposition of the Property which was once held in trust by the Camerons for an Italian Gentleman. I think it unwise to carry this with us, and have therefore removed it to a Place of safety. Jem knows the Place. If you should at some Time have need of this Property, tell him the Spaniard guards it. If so, be sure to have it blessed by a Priest; there is Blood upon it.

Sometimes I wish that I might see the Future; much more often, I give thanks to God that I cannot. But I will always see your Faces. Kiss the Children for me.

Your loving father,
JF

———

THE CHILDREN WASHED, toothbrushed, kissed, and put to bed, their parents returned to the library, a dram of whisky, and the letter.

"An Italian gentleman?" Bree looked at Roger, one brow raised in a way that brought Jamie Fraser so immediately to mind that Roger glanced involuntarily at the sheet of paper. "Does he mean—"

"Charles Stuart? He can't mean anyone else."

She picked the letter up and read the postscript for perhaps the dozenth time.

"And if he *does* mean Charles Stuart, then the property..."

"He's found the gold. And Jem knows where it is?" Roger couldn't help this last taking on the tone of a question, as he cast his eyes toward the ceiling, above which his children were presumably asleep, wrapped in virtue and cartoon pajamas.

Bree frowned.

"Does he? That isn't exactly what Da said—and if he *did* know . . . that's an awfully big secret to ask an eight-year-old boy to keep."

"True." Eight or not, Jem was very good at keeping secrets, Roger thought. But Bree was right—her father would never burden anyone with dangerous information, let alone his beloved grandson. Certainly not without a good reason, and his postscript made it clear that this information was provided only as a contingency in case of need.

"You're right. Jem doesn't know anything about the gold—just about this Spaniard, whatever that may be. He's never mentioned anything like that to you?"

She shook her head, then turned as a sudden puff of wind from the open window blew through the curtains, breathing immanent rain. Bree got up and went hastily to close it, then trotted upstairs to close the windows there, waving at Roger to see to those on the ground floor. Lallybroch was a large house, and unusually well provided with windows—the children kept trying to count them, but never came up with the same number twice.

Roger supposed he could go and count them himself one day and settle the matter, but was reluctant to do this. The house, like most old houses, had a distinct personality. Lallybroch was welcoming, all right; large and gracious, comfortably rather than grandly built, with the echoes of generations murmuring in its walls. But it was a place that had its secrets, too, no doubt of that. And hiding the number of its windows was quite in keeping with the sense he had of the house as being rather playful.

The windows in the kitchen—now equipped with modern refrigerator, Aga cooker, and decent plumbing, but still with its ancient granite counters stained with the juice of currants, the blood of game and poultry—were all closed, but he went through it nonetheless, and through the scullery. The light in the back hall was off, but he could see the grating in the floor near the wall that gave air to the priest's hole below.

His father-in-law had hidden there briefly, during the days after the Rising, before being imprisoned at Ardsmuir. Roger had gone down there once—also briefly—when they had bought the house, and had come up out of the dank, fetid little space with a complete understanding of why Jamie Fraser had chosen to live in a wilderness on a remote mountaintop, where there was no constraint in any direction.

Years of hiding, of duress, of imprisonment . . . Jamie Fraser was not a political creature, and he knew better than most what the true cost of war was, whatever its presumed purpose. But Roger had seen his father-in-law now and then rub absently at his wrists, where the marks of fetters had long since faded—but the memory of their weight had not. Roger had not the slightest doubt that Jamie Fraser would live free, or die. And wished for an instant, with a longing that gnawed his bones, that he might be there, to fight by his father-in-law's side.

The rain had started; he could hear the patter of it on the slate roofs of the outbuildings, then the rush as it came on in earnest, wrapping the house in mist and water.

"For ourselves... and our posterity," he said aloud, but quietly.

It was a bargain made between men—unspoken, but understood completely. Nothing mattered but that the family be preserved, the children protected. And whether the cost of it was paid in blood, sweat, or soul—it would be paid.

"Oidche mhath," he said, with a brief nod in the direction of the priest's hole. Good night, then.

He stood a moment longer in the old kitchen, though, feeling the embrace of the house, its solid protection against the storm. The kitchen had always been the heart of the house, he thought, and found the warmth of the cooker as much a comfort as the fire on the now-empty hearth had once been.

He met Brianna at the foot of the stairs; she'd changed for bed—as opposed to sleep. The air in the house was always cool, and the temperature had dropped several degrees with the onset of rain. She wasn't wearing her woolies, though; rather, a thin nightgown of white cotton, deceptively innocent-looking, with a small red ribbon threaded through it. The white cloth clung to the shape of her breasts like cloud to a mountain peak.

He said as much, and she laughed—but made no objection when he cupped his hands around them, her nipples against his palms round as beach pebbles through the thin cloth.

"Upstairs?" she whispered, and leaning in, ran the tip of her tongue along his lower lip.

"No," he said, and kissed her solidly, quelling the tickle of the touch. "In the kitchen. We haven't done it there, yet."

He had her, bent over the ancient counter with its mysterious stains, the sound of her small grunts a punctuation to the rush of wind and rain on the ancient shutters. Felt her shiver and liquefy and let go, too, his knees trembling with it, so he fell slowly forward, clutched her by the shoulders, his face pressed into the shampoo-fragrant waves of her hair, the old granite smooth and cool beneath his cheek. His heart was beating slow and hard, steady as a bass drum.

He was naked, and a cold draft from somewhere raised gooseflesh down his back and legs. Brianna felt him shiver and turned her face to his.

"Cold?" she whispered. She wasn't; she glowed like a live coal, and he wanted nothing more than to slide into bed beside her and ride out the storm in snug warmth.

"I'm fine." He bent and scooped up the clothes he had thrown on the floor. "Let's go to bed."

The rain was louder upstairs.

"Oh, the animals went in two by two," Bree sang softly, as they climbed the stairs, *"the elephants and the kangaroos..."*

Roger smiled. You *could* imagine the house an ark, floating on a roaring world of water—but all snug within. Two by two—two parents, two kids... maybe more, someday. There was plenty of room, after all.

With the lamp put out and the beating of rain on the shutters, Roger lingered on the edge of sleep, reluctant to surrender the pleasure of the moment.

"We won't ask him, will we?" Bree whispered. Her voice was drowsy, her soft weight warm all down the side of his body. "Jem?"

"Oh? No. Of course not. No need."

He felt the prick of curiosity—who was the Spaniard? And the notion of buried treasure was always a lure—but they didn't need it; they had enough money for the present. Always assuming the gold was still wherever Jamie had put it, which was a long shot in itself.

Nor had he forgotten the last injunction of Jamie's postscript.

Have it blessed by a priest; there is blood upon it. The words melted as he thought them, and what he saw on the inside of his eyelids was not gold ingots but the old granite counter in the kitchen, dark stains sunk so far into the stone as to have become part of it, ineradicable by the most vigorous scrubbing, let alone an invocation.

But it didn't matter. The Spaniard, whoever he was, could keep his gold. The family was safe.

PART TWO

Blood, Sweat, and Pickles

LONG ISLAND

ON JULY 4, 1776, the Declaration of Independence was signed in Philadelphia.

ON JULY 24, Lieutenant General Sir William Howe arrived on Staten Island, where he set up field headquarters at the Rose and Crown Tavern in New Dorp.

ON AUGUST 13, Lieutenant General George Washington arrived in New York to reinforce the fortifications of the city, which the Americans held.

ON AUGUST 21, William Ransom, Lieutenant Lord Ellesmere, arrived at the Rose and Crown in New Dorp, reporting—somewhat late—for duty as the newest and most junior member of General Howe's staff.

ON AUGUST 22 . . .

L IEUTENANT EDWARD MARKHAM, Marquis of Clarewell, peered searchingly into William's face, offering him an unappetizingly close view of a juicy pimple—just ready to burst—on the former's forehead.

"You all right, Ellesmere?"

"Fine." William managed the word between clenched teeth.

"Only, you look rather . . . green." Clarewell, looking concerned, reached into his pocket. "Want a suck of my pickle?"

William just about made it to the rail in time. There was a certain amount of jocularity going on behind him regarding Clarewell's pickle, who might suck it, and how much its owner would be obliged to pay for said service. This, interspersed with Clarewell's protestations that his aged grandmother swore by a sour pickle for the prevention of seasickness, and plainly it worked, for look at him, solid as a rock . . .

William blinked watering eyes and fixed his vision on the approaching shore. The water wasn't particularly rough, though the weather was brewing, no doubt about it. It didn't matter, though; even the gentlest of up-and-down motions on water, the briefest of journeys, and his stomach promptly tried to turn itself inside out. Every damned time!

It was still trying, but as there was nothing left in it, he could pretend it wasn't. He wiped his mouth, feeling clammy despite the heat of the day, and straightened his shoulders.

They would drop anchor any minute; time he was going below and badgering the companies under his command into some kind of order before they went into the boats. He risked a brief glance over the rail, and saw the *River* and the *Phoenix* just astern. The *Phoenix* was Admiral Howe's flagship, and his brother the general was aboard. Would they have to wait, bobbing like corks on the increasingly choppy waves, until General Howe and Captain Pickering, his aide-de-camp, got ashore? God, he hoped not.

In the event, the men were allowed to disembark at once. "With ALL POSSIBLE SPEED, gennelmun!" Sergeant Cutter informed them at the top of his voice. "We're going to catch the rebel whoresons on the 'op, so we are! And WOE BETIDE any man what I see lollygaggin'! YOU, there...!" He strode off, forceful as a plug of black tobacco, to apply the spurs to a delinquent second lieutenant, leaving William feeling somewhat better. Surely nothing truly terrible could happen in a world containing Sergeant Cutter.

He followed his men down the ladder and into the boats, forgetting his stomach entirely in the rush of excitement. His first real battle was waiting to be fought, somewhere on the plains of Long Island.

EIGHTY-EIGHT FRIGATES. That's what he'd heard Admiral Howe had brought, and he didn't doubt it. A forest of sails filled Gravesend Bay, and the water was choked with small boats, ferrying troops ashore. William was half choked himself, with anticipation. He could feel it gathering among the men, as the corporals collected their companies from the boats and marched off in good order, making room for the next wave of arrivals.

The officers' horses were being swum ashore, rather than rowed, the distance not being great. William ducked aside as one big bay surged up out of the surf nearby and shook himself in a shower of salt spray that drenched everyone within ten feet. The stable-lad clinging to his bridle looked like a drowned rat, but shook himself off likewise and grinned at William, his face blanched with cold but vivid with excitement.

William had a horse, too—somewhere. Captain Griswold, a senior member of Howe's staff, was lending him a mount, there having been no time to organize anything else. He supposed whoever was minding the horse would find him, though he didn't see how.

Organized confusion reigned. The shore here was a tidal flat, and coveys of red coats swarmed amongst the sea wrack like flocks of shorebirds, the bellowing of sergeants a counterpoint to the shrieking of gulls overhead.

With some difficulty, as he'd been introduced to the corporals only that morning and did not have their faces firmly fixed in memory yet, William located his four companies and marched them up the shore into sand dunes thick with some sort of wiry grass. It was a hot day, sweltering in heavy uniform and full equipment, and he let the men take their ease, drink water or beer from their canteens, eat a bit of cheese and biscuit. They'd be on the move soon.

Where? That was the question preying on his mind at the moment. A hasty staff meeting the night before—his first—had reiterated the basics of the invasion plan. From Gravesend Bay, half the army would march inland, turning north toward the Brooklyn Heights, where the rebel forces were thought to be entrenched. The remainder of the troops would spread outward along the shore to Montauk, forming a line of defense that could move inward across Long Island, forcing the rebels back into a net, if necessary.

William wanted, with an intensity that knotted his spine, to be in the vanguard, attacking. Realistically, he knew it wasn't likely. He was completely unfamiliar with his troops, and not impressed with their looks. No sensible commander would put such companies in the front line—unless to serve as cannon fodder. That thought gave him pause for a moment, but only a moment.

Howe wasn't a waster of men; he was known to be cautious, sometimes to a fault. His father had told him that. Lord John hadn't mentioned that that consideration was the major reason for his consent to William's joining Howe's staff, but William knew it anyway. He didn't care; he'd calculated that his chances of seeing significant action were still a great deal better with Howe than fiddling about in the North Carolina swamps with Sir Peter Packer.

And after all . . . he turned slowly, side to side. The sea was a mass of British ships, the land before him crawling with soldiers. He would never have admitted aloud to being impressed by the sight—but his stock was tight across his throat. He realized he was holding his breath and consciously let it go.

The artillery was coming ashore, floating perilously on flat-bottomed barges, manned by swearing soldiers. The limbers, the caissons, and the draft horses and oxen needed to drag them were splashing up the beach in a thrashing, sand-spattered herd, neighing and lowing in protest, having come ashore farther south. It was the biggest army he had ever seen.

"Sir, sir!" He looked down to see a short private soldier, perhaps no older than William himself, plump-cheeked and anxious.

"Yes?"

"Your spontoon, sir. And your horse has come," the private added, gesturing at the rangy light bay gelding whose reins he held. "Captain Griswold's compliments, sir."

William took the spontoon, seven feet long, its burnished steel head gleaming dully even under the clouded sky, and felt the weight of it thrill through his arm.

"Thank you. And you are . . . ?"

"Oh. Perkins, sir." The private hastily knuckled his brow in salute. "Third company, sir; the Hackers, they call us."

"Do they? Well, we will hope to give you plenty of opportunity to justify your name." Perkins looked blank.

"Thank you, Perkins," William said, gesturing the private off.

He took the bridle of the horse, joy rising in his heart. It was the biggest army he'd ever seen. And he was part of it.

HE WAS LUCKIER THAN he'd thought he might be, if not as lucky as he'd hoped. His companies were to be in the second wave, following up the vanguard of foot, guarding the artillery. Not a guarantee of action, but a good chance nonetheless, if the Americans were half the fighters they were reputed to be.

It was past noon before he lifted his spontoon into the air and shouted, "Forward, march!" The brewing weather had broken in a spattering rain, a welcome relief from the heat.

Beyond the shore, a fringe of woods gave way to a broad and beautiful plain. Waving grasses lay before them, flecked with wildflowers, the colors rich in the dim, rainy light. Far ahead, he could see flights of birds—doves? quail? too far to see—rising into the air despite the rain, as the marching soldiers drove them from their cover.

His own companies marched close to the center of the advancing line, snaking in orderly columns behind him, and he directed a grateful thought toward General Howe. As a junior staff officer, he should by rights have been delegated to messenger duty, scampering to and fro among the companies on the field, relaying orders from Howe's headquarters, carrying information to and from the two other generals, Sir Henry Clinton and Lord Cornwallis.

Given his late arrival, though, he knew none of the other officers or the army's disposition; he was completely ignorant of who was who, let alone where they should be at any moment. He would be useless as a messenger. General Howe, somehow finding a moment in the bustle of the oncoming invasion, had not only welcomed him with great courtesy but had offered him the choice: accompany Captain Griswold, serving in such manner as the captain might direct—or take command of a few companies orphaned of their own lieutenant, who had fallen ill of the ague.

He had jumped at the chance, and now sat proud in his saddle, his spontoon resting in its loop, leading men to war. He shifted a little, enjoying the feel of the new red wool coat on his shoulders, the orderly club of the queued pigtail on his neck, the stiff leather stock about his throat, and the small weight of his officer's gorget, that tiny silver remnant of Roman armor. He'd not worn uniform for nearly two months and, rain-damp or not, felt its resumption to be a glorious apotheosis.

A company of light horse traveled near them; he heard the shout of their officer and saw them draw ahead and turn toward a distant copse of wood. Had they seen something?

No. A tremendous cloud of blackbirds exploded from the copse, in a chatter so great that many of the horses shied and spooked. The horse soldiers foraged about, weaving through the trees with sabers drawn, slashing at branches, but just for show. If anyone had been hiding there, they had gone, and the light horse rode back to rejoin the advance, catcalling each other.

He relaxed back into his saddle, releasing his grip on the spontoon.

No Americans in sight—but they wouldn't be. He'd seen and heard enough in his intelligencing to know that only real Continentals were likely to fight in an organized fashion. He'd seen militia drilling in village squares, shared food with men who belonged to such militias. None of them were soldiers—seen in groups drilling, they were laughable, barely able to march in a line, let alone in step—but nearly all were skilled hunters, and he'd seen too many of them shoot wild geese and turkey on the fly to share the common contempt of most British soldiers.

No, if there were Americans nearby, the first warning of it was likely to be men falling dead. He signaled to Perkins, had him convey orders to the corporals, to keep the men alert, weapons loaded and primed. He saw one corporal's shoulders stiffen at receipt of this message, which he plainly considered an insult—but the man did it nonetheless, and William's sense of tension eased a bit.

His thoughts returned to his recent journey, and he wondered when—and where—he might meet with Captain Richardson, to turn over the results of his intelligencing.

He had committed most of his observations to memory while on the road, writing down only what he must, and that coded in a small copy of the New Testament that his grandmother had given him. It was still in the pocket of his civilian coat, back on Staten Island. Now that he was safely returned to the bosom of the army, perhaps he ought to write up his observations, in proper reports? He could—

Something raised him in his stirrups, just in time to catch the flash and crack of musket fire from the woods on the left.

"Hold!" he shouted, seeing his men start to lower their weapons. "Wait!"

It was too far, and there was another column of infantry, closer to the wood. These swung into firing order and loosed a volley into the woods; the first rank knelt and the second fired over their heads. Return fire came from the wood; he saw one or two men fall, others stagger, but the line pulled together.

Another two volleys, the sparks of returning fire, but more sporadic—from the corner of his eye, he saw movement and whirled in his saddle, to see a gang of woodsmen in hunting shirts running from the far side of the copse.

The company in front of him saw them, too. A shout from their sergeant, and they fixed bayonets and ran, though it was plain to William that they'd never catch the fleeing woodsmen.

This sort of random skirmishing kept up all afternoon, as the army pressed on. The fallen were picked up and carried to the rear, but they were few. One of William's companies was fired upon at one point, and he felt godlike as he gave the order to attack and they poured into the wood like a stream of angry hornets, bayonets fixed, managing to kill one rebel, whose body they dragged out onto the plain. The corporal suggested hanging it from a tree as discouragement to the other rebels, but William firmly declined this suggestion as not honorable and made them lay the man at the edge of the wood, where he could be found by his friends.

Toward evening, orders came along the line of march, from General Clinton. They would not stop to make camp. A brief pause for cold rations, and then press on.

There were murmurs of surprise in the ranks, but no grumbling. They'd come to fight, and the march resumed with a greater sense of urgency.

It was raining sporadically, and the harassment from skirmishers faded with the sullen light. It was not cold, and despite the growing soddenness of his garments, William preferred the chill and damp to the sultry oppression of the day before. At least the rain dampened the spirits of his horse, which was a good thing; it was a nervous, skittish creature, and he had cause to doubt Captain Griswold's goodwill in lending it to him. Worn down by the long day, though, the gelding ceased shying at windblown branches and jerking at the reins, and plodded onward with its ears falling sideways in tired resignation.

It wasn't bad for the first several hours of the night march. After midnight, though, the strain of exertion and sleeplessness began to tell on the men. Soldiers began to stumble and slow, and a sense of the vast expanse of dark and effort between themselves and dawn settled upon them.

William called Perkins up beside him. The soft-cheeked private showed up yawning and blinking, and paced beside him, a hand on William's stirrup leather as William explained what he wanted.

"Sing?" Perkins said doubtfully. "Well, I s'pose I can sing, yes, sir. Nobbut hymns, though."

"Not quite what I had in mind," William said. "Go and ask Sergeant... Millikin, is it? The Irishman? Anything he likes, so long as it's loud and lively." After all, they weren't trying to hide their presence; the Americans knew exactly where they were.

"Yes, sir," Perkins said dubiously, and let go the stirrup, fading at once into the night. William rode for some minutes, then heard Patrick Millikin's very loud Irish voice lifted in a very bawdy song. There was a ripple of laughter through the men, and by the time he reached the first chorus, a few had joined in. Two more verses and they were all roaring lustily along, William included.

They couldn't keep it up for hours while marching at speed with full equipment, of course, but by the time they had exhausted their favorite songs and grown breathless, everyone was awake and optimistic once more.

Just before dawn, William smelled the sea and the rank mud scent of a marsh in the rain. The men, already wet, began to splash through a number of tiny tidal inlets and creeks.

A few minutes later, the boom of cannon broke the night, and marsh birds rose into the lightening sky with shrieks of alarm.

OVER THE COURSE OF the next two days, William never had any idea where he was. Names such as "Jamaica Pass," "Flatbush," and "Gowanus Creek" occurred now and then in the dispatches and hasty messages that passed through the army, but they might as well have said "Jupiter" or "the backside of the moon" for all the meaning they had.

He did see Continentals, at last. Hordes of them, swarming out of the marshes. The first few clashes were fierce, but William's companies were held to the rear, supporting; only once were they close enough to fire, in order to repulse an oncoming group of Americans.

Nonetheless, he was in a constant state of excitement, trying to hear and see everything at once, intoxicated by the smell of powder smoke, even as his flesh quivered at the report of cannon. When the firing ceased at sunset, he took a little biscuit and cheese, but without tasting it, and slept only briefly, from sheer exhaustion.

In late afternoon of the second day, they found themselves some little way behind a large stone farmhouse that the British and some Hessian troops had taken over as an artillery emplacement; the barrels of cannon protruded from the upper windows, shining wet with the constant rain.

Wet powder was a problem now; the cartridges were all right, but if the powder poured into priming pans was left more than a few minutes, it began to cake and go dead. The order to load, then, had to be delayed until the last possible moment before firing; William found himself grinding his teeth in anxiety as to when the order should be given.

On the other hand, sometimes there was no doubt at all. With hoarse shouts, a number of Americans charged out of the trees near the front of the house and made for the doors and windows. Musket fire from the troops inside got several of them, but some made it as far as the house itself, where they began to clamber into the shattered windows. William automatically reined up and rode to the right, far enough to get a look at the rear of the house. Sure enough, a larger group was already at it, a number of them climbing the wall by means of the ivy that covered the back of the house.

"That way!" he bellowed, wheeling his horse around and waving his spontoon. "Olson, Jeffries, the back! Load and fire as soon as you're in range!"

Two of his companies ran, ripping the ends of cartridges with their teeth, but a party of green-coated Hessians was there before him, seizing Americans by the legs and pulling them from the ivy to club them on the ground.

He reined round and dashed the other way, to see what was happening in front, and came in sight just in time to see a British artilleryman fly out of one of the open upper windows. The man landed on the ground, one leg bent under him, and lay screaming. One of William's men, close enough, darted forward and grabbed the man's shoulders, only to be shot by someone within the house. He crumpled and fell, his hat rolling off into the bushes.

They spent the rest of that day at the stone farmhouse; four times, the Americans made forays—twice, they succeeded in overcoming the inhabitants and briefly seizing the guns, but both times were overrun by fresh waves of British troops and evicted or killed. William never got closer than two hundred yards or so to the house itself, but once managed to interpose one of his companies between the house and a surge of desperate Americans dressed like Indians and yelling like banshees. One of them raised a long rifle and fired directly at him, but missed. He drew his sword, intending to ride the man down, but a shot from somewhere struck the man and sent him rolling down the face of a small hillock.

William urged his mount closer, to see whether the man was dead or not—the man's companions had already fled round the far corner of the house, pursued by British troops. The gelding wasn't having any; trained to the sound of musket fire, it found artillery unnerving, and the cannon happening to speak at this particular moment, the gelding laid its ears flat back and bolted.

William had his sword still in hand, the reins loosely wrapped round his other hand; the sudden jolt unseated him, and the horse whipped to the left, jerking his right foot from the stirrup and pitching him off. He had barely presence of mind to let go of the sword as he fell, and landed on one shoulder, rolling.

Simultaneously thanking God that his left foot hadn't been trapped in its stirrup and cursing the horse, he scrambled up onto hands and knees, smeared with grass and mud, heart in his mouth.

The guns in the house had stopped; the Americans must be in there again, engaged in hand-to-hand fighting with the gun crews. He spat out mud, and began to make a cautious withdrawal; he thought he was in range of the upper windows.

To his left, though, he caught sight of the American who had tried to shoot him, still lying in the wet grass. With a wary glance at the house, he crawled to the man, who was lying on his face, unmoving. He wanted to see the man's face, for what reason he couldn't have said. He rose on his knees and took the man by both shoulders, pulling him over.

The man was clearly dead, shot through the head. Mouth and eyes sagged half open and his body felt strange, heavy and flopping. He wore a militia uniform of sorts; William saw the wooden buttons, with "PUT" burnt into them. That meant something, but his dazed mind made no sense of it. Gently laying the man back in the grass, he rose and went to fetch his sword. His knees felt peculiar.

Halfway to the spot where his sword lay, he stopped, turned round, and came back. Kneeling down, cold-fingered and hollow-bellied, he closed the man's dead eyes against the rain.

THEY MADE CAMP that night, to the pleasure of the men. Camp kitchens were dug, the cook wagons brought up, and the scent of roasting meat and fresh bread filled the damp air. William had just sat down to eat when Perkins, that harbinger of doom, appeared apologetically at his side with a message: report to General Howe's field headquarters at once. Snatching a loaf of bread and a steaming chunk of roast pork to put in it, he went, chewing.

He found the three generals and all of their staff officers gathered together, deep in a discussion of the day's results. The generals sat at a small table thick with dispatches and hastily drawn maps. William found a place among the staff officers, standing respectfully back against the walls of the big tent.

Sir Henry was arguing for an attack on the Brooklyn Heights, come morning.

"We could dislodge them easily," Clinton said, waving a hand at the dispatches. "They've lost half their men, if not more—and weren't such a lot of 'em to start with."

"Not easily," said my lord Cornwallis, pursing fat lips. "You saw them fight. Yes, we could get them out of there—but at some cost. What say you, sir?" he added, turning deferentially to Howe.

Howe's lips all but disappeared, only a white line marking their former existence.

"I can't afford another victory like the last one," he snapped. "Or if I could, I don't want it." His eyes left the table and passed over the juniors standing against the wall. "I lost every man on my staff at that damned hill in Boston," he said, more quietly. "Twenty-eight of them. Every one." His eyes lingered on William, the youngest of the junior officers present, and he shook his head, as though to himself, and turned back to Sir Henry.

"Stop the fighting," he said.

Sir Henry wasn't pleased, William could see that, but he merely nodded.

"Offer them terms?"

"No," Howe said shortly. "They've lost nearly half their men, as you said. No one but a madman would go on fighting without cause. They—you, sir. Did you have an observation to make?"

With a start, William realized that Howe was addressing this remark to him; those round eyes were boring into his chest like bird shot.

"I—" he began, but then caught himself and drew up straight. "Yes, sir. It's General Putnam in command. There at the creek. He's . . . perhaps not a madman, sir," he added carefully, "but he has the name of a stubborn man."

Howe paused, eyes narrowed.

"A stubborn man," he repeated. "Yes. I should say he is."

"He was one of the commanders at Breed's Hill, wasn't he?" objected Lord Cornwallis. "The Americans ran fast enough away from *there*."

"Yes, but—" William stopped dead, paralyzed by the fixed joint stares of three generals. Howe motioned him impatiently to go on.

"With respect, my lord," he said, and was glad that his voice didn't shake, "I . . . hear that the Americans did not run in Boston until they had exhausted every scrap of ammunition. I think . . . that is not the case, here. And with regard to General Putnam—there was no one behind him at Breed's Hill."

"And you think that there is now." It wasn't a question.

"Yes, sir." William tried not to look pointedly at the stack of dispatches on Sir William's table. "I'm sure of it, sir. I think nearly all of the Continentals are on the island, sir." He tried not to make that sound like a question; he'd heard as much from a passing major the day before, but it might not be true. "If Putnam's in command here—"

"How do you know it's Putnam, Lieutenant?" Clinton interrupted, giving William the fish-eye.

"I am lately come from an—an intelligencing expedition, sir, which took me through Connecticut. I heard there, from many people, that militia were gathering to accompany General Putnam, who was to join with General Washington's forces near New York. And I saw a button on one of the rebel dead near the creek this afternoon, sir, with 'PUT' carved on it. That's what they call him, sir—General Putnam: 'Old Put.' "

General Howe straightened himself before Clinton or Cornwallis could interject anything further.

"A stubborn man," he repeated. "Well, perhaps he is. Nonetheless . . . suspend the fighting. He is in an untenable position, and must know it. Give him a chance to think it over—to consult with Washington if he likes.

Washington is perhaps a more sensible commander. And if we might gain the surrender of the whole Continental army without further bloodshed . . . I think it worth the risk, gentlemen. But we will not offer terms."

Which meant that if the Americans saw sense, it would be an unconditional surrender. And if they didn't? William had heard stories about the fight at Breed's Hill—granted, stories told by Americans, and therefore he took them with several grains of salt. But by account, the rebels there had taken the nails from the fencing of their fortifications—from the very heels of their shoes— and fired them at the British when their shot ran out. They had retreated only when reduced to throwing stones.

"But if Putnam's expecting reinforcement from Washington, he'll only sit and wait," Clinton said, frowning. "And then we'll have the whole boiling of them. Had we best not—"

"That's not what he meant," Howe interruputed. "Was it, Ellesmere? When you said there was no one behind him at Breed's Hill?"

"No, sir," William said, grateful. "I meant . . . he has something to protect. Behind him. I don't think he's waiting for the rest of the army to come to his aid. I think he's covering their retreat."

Lord Cornwallis's hooped brows shot up at that. Clinton scowled at William, who recalled too late that Clinton had been the field commander at the Pyrrhic victory of Breed's Hill and was likely sensitive on the subject of Israel Putnam.

"And why are we soliciting the advice of a boy still wet behind the—have you ever even seen combat, sir?" he demanded of William, who flushed hotly.

"I'd be fighting now, sir," he said, "were I not detained here!"

Lord Cornwallis laughed, and a brief smile flitted across Howe's face.

"We shall make certain to have you properly blooded, Lieutenant," he said dryly. "But not today. Captain Ramsay?" He motioned to one of the senior staff, a short man with very square shoulders, who stepped forward and saluted. "Take Ellesmere here and have him tell you the results of his . . . intelligencing. Convey to me anything which strikes you as being of interest. In the meantime"—he turned back to his two generals—"suspend hostilities until further notice."

WILLIAM HEARD NO MORE of the generals' deliberations, he being led away by Captain Ramsay.

Had he spoken too much out of turn? he wondered. Granted, General Howe had asked him a direct question; he had had to answer. But to put forward his paltry month's intelligencing, against the combined knowledge of so many experienced senior officers . . .

He said something of his doubts to Captain Ramsay, who seemed a quiet sort but friendly enough.

"Oh, you hadn't any choice but to speak up," Ramsay assured him. "Still . . ."

William dodged round a pile of mule droppings in order to keep up with Ramsay.

"Still?" he asked.

Ramsay didn't answer for a bit, but led the way through the encampment, down neat aisles of canvas tents, waving now and then at men round a fire who called out to him.

At last, they arrived at Ramsay's own tent, and he held back the flap for William, gesturing him in.

"Heard of a lady called Cassandra?" Ramsay said at last. "Some sort of Greek, I think. Not very popular."

THE ARMY SLEPT SOUNDLY after its exertions, and so did William.

"Your tea, sir?"

He blinked, disoriented and still wrapped in dreams of walking through the Duke of Devonshire's private zoo, hand in hand with an orangutan. But it was Private Perkins's round and anxious face, rather than the orangutan's, that greeted him.

"What?" he said stupidly. Perkins seemed to swim in a sort of haze, but this was not dispelled by blinking, and when he sat up to take the steaming cup, he discovered the cause of it was that the air itself was permeated with a heavy mist.

All sound was muffled; while the normal noises of a camp rising were to be heard, they sounded far away, subdued. No surprise, then, when he poked his head out of his tent a few minutes later, to find the ground blanketed with a drifting fog that had crept in from the marshes.

It didn't matter much. The army was going nowhere. A dispatch from Howe's headquarters had made the suspension of hostilities official; there was nothing to do but wait for the Americans to see sense and surrender.

The army stretched, yawned, and sought distraction. William was engaged in a hot game of hazard with Corporals Yarnell and Jeffries when Perkins came up again, breathless.

"Colonel Spencer's compliments, sir, and you're to report to General Clinton."

"Yes? What for?" William demanded. Perkins looked baffled; it hadn't occurred to him to ask the messenger what for.

"Just...I suppose he wants you," he said, in an effort to be helpful.

"Thank you very much, Private Perkins," William said, with a sarcasm wasted on Perkins, who beamed in relief and retired without being dismissed.

"Perkins!" he bellowed, and the private turned, round face startled. "Which way?"

"What? Er...what, sir, I mean?"

"In which direction does General Clinton's headquarters lie?" William asked, with elaborate patience.

"Oh! The hussar...he came from..." Perkins rotated slowly, like a weather vane, frowning in concentration. "That way!" He pointed. "I could see that bit of hillock behind him." The fog was still thick near the ground, but the crests of hills and tall trees were now and then visible, and William had no difficulty in spotting the hillock to which Perkins referred; it had an odd lumpy look to it.

"Thank you, Perkins. Dismissed," he added quickly, before Perkins could make off again. He watched the private disappear into the shifting mass of fog and bodies, then shook his head and went to hand command over to Corporal Evans.

The gelding didn't like the fog. William didn't like it, either. Fog gave him an uneasy feeling, as though someone was breathing on the back of his neck.

This was a sea fog, though: heavy, dank, and cold, but not smothering. It thinned and thickened, with a sense of movement to it. He could see a few feet before him, and could just make out the dim shape of the hillock Perkins had indicated, though the top kept appearing and disappearing like some fantastic conjuration in a fairy tale.

What might Sir Henry want with him? he wondered. And was it only he who'd been sent for, or was this a meeting called to apprise the line officers of some change of strategy?

Maybe Putnam's men had surrendered. They should, certainly; they had no hope of victory in the circumstances, and that must be plain to them.

But he supposed Putnam would need, perhaps, to consult with Washington. During the fighting at the old stone farmhouse, he'd seen a small group of horsemen on the crest of a distant hill, an unfamiliar flag fluttering amongst them; someone at the time had pointed at it and said, "That's him there, Washington. Shame we've not got a twenty-four in place—teach him to gawk!" and laughed.

Sense said they'd surrender. But he had an uneasy feeling that had nothing to do with the fog. During his month on the road, he'd had occasion to listen to a good many Americans. Most were uneasy themselves, not wanting conflict with England, particularly not wanting to be anywhere near armed strife—a very sensible conclusion. But the ones who *were* decided on revolt...were very decided indeed.

Maybe Ramsay had conveyed some of this to the generals; he hadn't seemed at all impressed by any of William's information, let alone his opinions, but perhaps—

The horse stumbled, and he lurched in his saddle, accidentally jerking the reins. The horse, annoyed, whipped round its head and bit him, big teeth scraping on his boot.

"Bastard!" He smacked the horse across the nose with the ends of the reins, and hauled the gelding's head round forcibly, until the rolling eyes and curled lip were nearly in his lap. Then, his point made, he slowly released the pressure. The horse snorted and shook his mane violently, but resumed progress without further argument.

He seemed to have been riding for some time. But time as well as distance was deceiving in fog. He glanced up at the hillock that was his goal, only to discover that it had vanished again. Well, doubtless it would come back.

Only it didn't.

The fog continued to shift around him, and he heard the dripping of moisture from the leaves of the trees that seemed to come suddenly out of the mist at him and as suddenly retreat again. But the hillock stayed stubbornly invisible.

It occurred to him that he hadn't heard any sounds of men for some time now.

He should have.

If he were approaching Clinton's headquarters, he should not only be hearing all the normal camp sounds, he should have encountered any number of men, horses, campfires, wagons, tents . . .

There was no noise anywhere near him, save the rushing of water. He'd bloody bypassed the camp.

"Damn you, Perkins," he said under his breath.

He drew up for a moment and checked the priming of his pistol, sniffing at the powder in the pan; it smelled different when the damp got at it. Still all right, he thought; it smelled hot and nose-prickling, not so much of the rotten-egg scent of sulfur as wet powder had.

He kept the pistol in his hand, though so far he'd seen nothing threatening. The fog was too heavy to see more than a few feet in front of him, though; someone could come out of it suddenly, and he'd have to decide on the instant whether to shoot them or not.

It was quiet; their own artillery was silent; there was no random musket fire like the day before. The enemy was in retreat; no doubt about that. But if he should stumble across a stray Continental, lost in the fog like himself, ought he to shoot? The thought made his hands sweat, but he thought he must; the Continental would likely have no hesitation about shooting *him*, the instant he saw the red uniform.

He was somewhat more worried about the humiliation of being shot by his own troops than about the actual prospect of death, but was not entirely oblivious to the risk of that, either.

The bloody fog had got thicker, if anything. He looked in vain for the sun, to give some sense of direction, but the sky was invisible.

He fought back the small quiver of panic that tickled his tailbone. Right, there were 34,000 British troops on this bloody island; he had to be within pistol shot of any number of them at this moment. *And you only need be in pistol shot of one American,* he reminded himself, grimly pushing through a growth of larches.

He heard rustlings and the cracking of branches nearby; the wood was inhabited, no doubt about it. But by whom?

The British troops wouldn't be moving in this fog, that was one thing. Curse Perkins! If he heard movement, then, as of a body of men, he'd stop and stay hidden. And otherwise . . . all he could hope to do was to run across a body of troops, or to hear something unmistakably military in nature—shouted orders, perhaps . . .

He rode on slowly for some time, and finally put the pistol away, finding the weight of it wearisome. God, how long had he been out? An hour? Two? Ought he to turn around? But he had no way of knowing what "around" was—he might be traveling in circles; the ground all looked the same, a gray blur of trees and rocks and grasses. Yesterday, he'd spent every minute keyed to fever pitch, ready for the attack. Today, his enthusiasm for fighting had ebbed substantially.

Someone stepped out in front of him and the horse reared, so abruptly that William had only the vaguest impression of the man. Enough to know he wasn't wearing a British uniform, though, and he would have snatched his pistol out, were both hands not occupied in trying to control the horse.

The horse, having given way to hysteria, crow-hopped in mad circles, jarring William to the spine with each landing. His surroundings spun past in a blur of gray and green, but he was half conscious of voices, whooping in what might be either derision or encouragement.

After what seemed an age, but must be only half a minute or so, William succeeded in bringing the bloody creature to a standstill, panting and blowing, still flinging its head around, the whites of its eyes showing, gleaming wet.

"You fucking piece of cat's meat!" William said to it, hauling its head round. The horse's breath sank damp and hot through the doeskin of his breeches, and its sides heaved under him.

"Not the best-tempered horse I ever seen," a voice agreed, and a hand came up, seizing the bridle. "Healthy-looking, though."

William got a glimpse of a man in hunting dress, stout and swarthy—and then someone else seized him round the waist from behind and hauled him bodily off the horse.

He hit the ground hard and flat on his back, knocking out his wind, but tried valiantly to get to his pistol. A knee pressed into his chest, and a large hand wrestled the pistol out of his grip. A bearded face grinned down at him.

"Not very sociable," the man said, reproving. "Thought you-all was meant to be civilized, you British."

"You let him get up and at you, Harry, I imagine he'd civilize you, all right." This was another man, shorter and slightly built, with a soft, educated voice like a schoolmaster, who peered over the shoulder of the man kneeling on William's chest. "You could let him breathe, though, I suppose."

The pressure on William's chest relaxed, and he got a whisper of air into his lungs. This was promptly driven out again when the man who had held him down punched him in the stomach. Hands promptly began to rifle his pockets, and his gorget was jerked off over his head, painfully scraping the underside of his nose. Someone reached round him and unbuckled his belt, neatly removing it with a whistle of pleasure at the equipment attached.

"Very nice," said the second man, approving. He glanced down at William, lying on the ground and gasping like a landed fish. "I thank you, sir; we're much obliged. All right, Allan?" he called, turning toward the man holding the horse.

"Aye, I've got 'im," said a nasal Scottish voice. "Let's be off!"

The men moved away, and for an instant, William thought they had left. Then a meaty hand seized his shoulder and flipped him over. He writhed up onto his knees by sheer will, and the same hand seized his pigtail and jerked his head back, exposing his throat. He caught the gleam of a knife, and the man's broad grin, but had neither breath nor time for prayers or curses.

The knife slashed down, and he felt a yank at the back of his head that brought water to his eyes. The man grunted, displeased, and hacked twice more, finally coming away triumphant, William's pigtail held up in a ham-sized hand.

"Souvenir," he said to William, grinning, and whirling on his heel, made off after his friends. The horse's whinny drifted back to William through the fog, mocking.

HE WISHED, URGENTLY, that he had managed to kill at least one of them. But they'd taken him as easily as a child, plucked him like a goose and left him lying on the ground like a fucking turd! His rage was so overwhelming that he had to stop and punch a tree trunk. The pain of that left him gasping, still murderous but breathless.

He clutched the injured hand between his thighs, hissing between his teeth until the pain abated. Shock was mingling with fury; he felt more disoriented than ever, his head spinning. Chest heaving, he reached behind his head with his sound hand, feeling the bristly stumpage left there—and overcome with fresh rage, kicked the tree with all his strength.

He limped round in circles, swearing, then finally collapsed onto a rock and put his head down on his knees, panting.

Gradually, his breath slowed, and his ability to think rationally began to return.

Right. He was still lost in the wilds of Long Island, only now minus horse, food, or weapons. Or hair. *That* made him sit up straight, fists clenched, and he fought back the fury, with some difficulty. Right. He hadn't time to be angry now. If he ever laid eyes on Harry, Allan, or the little man with the educated voice . . . well, time enough for that when it happened.

For now, the important thing was to locate some part of the army. His impulse was to desert on the spot, take ship to France, and never come back, leaving the army to presume that he'd been killed. But he couldn't do that for assorted reasons, not least his father—who'd probably prefer that he *was* killed than run cravenly away.

No help for it. He rose resignedly to his feet, trying to feel grateful that the bandits had at least left him his coat. The fog was lifting a little here and there, but still lay damp and chilly on the ground. Not that he was troubled by that; his own blood was still boiling.

He glared round at the shadowy shapes of rocks and trees. They looked just like all the other fucking rocks and trees he'd encountered in the course of this misbegotten day.

"Right," he said aloud, and stabbed a finger into the air, turning as he did so. "Eeny-meeny-miney-mo, catch a Frenchy by the toe, if he's squealing—oh, the hell with it."

Limping slightly, he set off. He had no idea where he was going, but he had to move, or burst.

He entertained himself for some little time in reimagining the recent encounter, with satisfying visions of himself seizing the fat man named Harry and wringing his nose into bloody pulp before smashing his head on a rock.

Grabbing the knife away from him and gutting that supercilious little bastard ... ripping his lungs out ... there was a thing called the "blood eagle" that the savage German tribes used to do, slitting a man's back and dragging out his lungs through the slits, so they flapped like wings as he died ...

Gradually, he grew calmer, only because it was impossible to sustain such a level of fury.

His foot felt better; his knuckles were skinned, but not throbbing as much, and his fantasies of revenge began to seem faintly absurd to him. Was that what the fury of battle was like? he wondered. Did you want not just to shoot and stab because it was your duty to kill, but did you *like* it? Want it like wanting a woman? And did you feel like a fool after doing it?

He'd thought about killing in battle. Not all the time, but on and off. He'd made a great effort to visualize it when he'd made up his mind to join the army. And he did realize that there might be regret attached to the act.

His father had told him, baldly and with no effort at self-justification, about the circumstances under which he had killed his first man. Not in battle, but following one. The point-blank execution of a Scot, wounded and left on the field at Culloden.

"Under orders," his father had said. "No quarter to be given; those were our written orders, signed by Cumberland." His father's eyes had been fixed on his bookshelves during the telling, but at this point he'd looked at William directly.

"Orders," he repeated. "You follow orders, of course; you have to. But there will be times when you have no orders, or find yourself in a situation which has changed suddenly. And there will be times—there *will* be times, William—when your own honor dictates that you cannot follow an order. In such circumstances, you must follow your own judgment, and be prepared to live with the consequences."

William had nodded, solemn. He'd just brought his commission papers for his father to look over, Lord John's signature being required as his guardian. He'd regarded the signing as a mere formality, though; he hadn't been expecting either a confession or a sermon—if that's what this was.

"I shouldn't have done it," his father had said abruptly. "I shouldn't have shot him."

"But—your orders—"

"They didn't affect me, not directly. I hadn't yet got my commission; I'd gone with my brother on campaign, but I wasn't a soldier yet; I wasn't under the army's authority. I could have refused."

"If you had, wouldn't someone else have shot him?" William asked practically.

His father smiled, but without humor.

"Yes, they would. But that's not the point. And it's true that it never occurred to me that I had a choice in the matter—but that *is* the point. You always have a choice, William. Do remember that, will you?"

Without waiting for an answer, he'd leaned forward and plucked a quill from the blue-and-white Chinese jar on his desk, and flipped open his rock-crystal inkwell.

"You're sure?" he'd said, looking seriously at William, and at the latter's nod, signed his name with a flourish. Then had looked up and smiled.

"I'm proud of you, William," he'd said quietly. "I always will be."

William sighed. He didn't doubt that his father would always love him, but as for making him proud . . . this particular expedition did not seem likely to cover him in glory. He'd be lucky to get back to his own troops before someone noticed how long he'd been gone and raised the alarm. God, how ignominious, to get lost and robbed, as his first notable act!

Still, better than having his first notable act being killed by bandits.

He continued to make his way cautiously through the fog-draped woods. The footing wasn't bad, though there were boggy places where the rain had pooled in low spots. Once, he heard the ragged crack of musket fire and hurried toward it, but it stopped before he came in sight of whoever had been firing.

He trudged grimly along, wondering just how long it might take to traverse the whole of the bloody island on foot, and how close he was to having done so? The ground had risen sharply; he was climbing now, sweat running freely down his face. He fancied the fog was thinning as he climbed, and sure enough, at one point he emerged onto a small rocky promontory and had a brief glimpse of the ground below—completely covered in swirling gray fog. The sight gave him vertigo, and he was obliged to sit down on a rock for a few moments with his eyes closed before continuing.

Twice, he heard the sound of men and horses, but the sound was subtly wrong; the voices didn't have the rhythms of the army, and he turned away, edging cautiously in the opposite direction.

He found the ground change abruptly, becoming a sort of scrub forest, full of stunted trees poking from a light-colored soil that scrunched under his boots. Then he heard water—waves lapping on a beach. The sea! Well, thank God for that, he thought, and hastened his steps toward the sound.

As he made his way toward the sound of the waves, though, he suddenly perceived other sounds.

Boats. The grating of hulls—more than one—on gravel, the clank of oarlocks, splashing. And voices. Hushed voices, but agitated. Bloody hell! He ducked under the limb of a runty pine, hoping for a break in the drifting fog.

A sudden movement sent him lunging sideways, hand reaching for his pistol. He barely remembered that the pistol was gone, before realizing that his adversary was a great blue heron, which eyed him with a yellow glare before launching itself skyward in a clatter of affront. A cry of alarm came from the bushes, no more than ten feet away, together with the boom of a musket, and the heron exploded in a shower of feathers, directly over his head. He felt drops of the bird's blood, much warmer than the cold sweat on his face, and sat down very suddenly, black spots dizzy before his eyes.

He didn't dare move, let alone call out. There was a whisper of voices from the bushes, but not loud enough that he could make out any words. After a few moments, though, he heard a stealthy rustling that moved gradually away. Making as little noise as possible, he rolled onto hands and knees and crawled for some distance in the other direction, until he felt it safe to rise to his feet again.

He thought he still heard voices. He crept closer, moving slowly, his heart thumping. He smelled tobacco, and froze.

Nothing moved near him, though—he could still hear the voices, but they were a good way distant. He sniffed, cautiously, but the scent had vanished; perhaps he was imagining things. He moved on, toward the sounds.

He could hear them clearly now. Urgent, low-voiced calls, the rattle of oarlocks and the splash of feet in the surf. The shuffle and murmur of men, blending—almost—with the susurrus of sea and grass. He cast one last desperate glance at the sky, but the sun was still invisible. He *had* to be on the western side of the island; he was sure of it. Almost sure of it. And if he was . . .

If he was, the sounds he was hearing had to be those of American troops, fleeing the island for Manhattan.

"Don't. Stir." The whisper behind him coincided exactly with the pressure of a gun's barrel, jammed hard enough into his kidney as to freeze him where he stood. It withdrew for an instant and returned, rammed home with a force that blurred his eyes. He made a guttural sound and arched his back, but before he could speak, someone with horny hands had seized his wrists and jerked them back.

"No need," said the voice, deep, cracked, and querulous. "Stand aside and I'll shoot him."

"No, 'ee won't," said another, just as deep but less annoyed. " 'e's nobbut a youngun. And pretty, too." One of the horny hands stroked his cheek and he stiffened, but whoever it was had already bound his hands tight.

"And if 'ee meant to shoot 'im, you'm 've done it already, sister," the voice added. "Turn y'self, boy."

Slowly, he turned round, to see that he had been captured by a pair of old women, short and squat as trolls. One of them, the one with the gun, was smoking a pipe; it was her tobacco he'd smelled. Seeing the shock and disgust on his features, she lifted one corner of a seamed mouth while keeping a firm grip on the pipestem with the stumps of brown-stained teeth.

" 'andsome is as 'andsome does," she observed, looking him up and down. "Still, no need to waste shot."

"Madam," he said, collecting himself and trying for charm. "I believe you mistake me. I am a soldier of the King, and—"

Both of them burst into laughter, creaking like a pair of rusty hinges.

"Wouldn't never've guessed," the pipe-smoker said, grinning round the stem of her pipe. "Thought 'ee was a jakesman, sure!"

"Hush up, sonny," her sister interrupted his further attempt to speak. "We bain't going to harm 'ee, so long as 'ee stands still and keeps mum." She eyed him, taking in the damage.

"Been in the wars, have 'ee?" she said, not without sympathy. Not waiting for an answer, she pushed him down onto a rock, this liberally crusted with mussels and dripping weed, from which he deduced his closeness to the shore.

He didn't speak. Not for fear of the old women, but because there was nothing to say.

He sat, listening to the sounds of the exodus. No idea how many men might be involved, as he had no notion how long it had been going on.

Nothing useful was said; there were only the breathless half-heard exchanges of men working, the mutter of waiting, here and there the sort of muffled laughter born of nervousness.

The fog was lifting off the water. He could see them now—not more than a hundred yards away, a tiny fleet of rowboats, dories, here and there a fishing ketch, moving slowly to and fro across water smooth as glass—and a steadily dwindling crowd of men on shore, keeping their hands on their guns, glancing continually over their shoulders, alert for pursuit.

Little did they know, he reflected bitterly.

At the moment, he had no concern for his own future; the humiliation of being an impotent witness as the entire American army escaped under his nose—and the further thought of being obliged to return and recount this occurrence to General Howe—was so galling that he didn't care whether the old women had it in mind to cook and eat him.

Focused as he was on the scene on the beach, it didn't occur to him at once that if he could now see the Americans, he was himself visible to them. In fact, so intent were the Continentals and militiamen on their retreat that none of them *did* notice him, until one man turned away from the retreat, seeming to search the upper reaches of the shore for something.

The man stiffened, then, with a brief glance back at his oblivious companions, came purposefully up across the shingle, eyes fixed on William.

"What's this, Mother?" he asked. He was dressed in the uniform of a Continental officer, built short and wide, much like the two women, but a good deal bigger, and while his face was outwardly calm, there were calculations going on behind his bloodshot eyes.

"Been fishing," said the pipe-smoker. "Caught this wee redfish, but we think we'll throw 'im back."

"Aye? Maybe not just yet."

William had stiffened with the man's appearance, and stared up at him, keeping his own face as grim as possible.

The man glanced up at the shredding fog behind William.

"More like you at home, are there, boy?"

William sat silent. The man sighed, drew back his fist, and hit William in the stomach. He doubled up, fell off the rock, and lay retching on the sand. The man grasped him by the collar and hauled him up, as though he weighed nothing.

"Answer me, lad. I haven't much time, and 'ee don't want me to be hasty in my asking." He spoke mildly, but touched the knife at his belt.

William wiped his mouth, as well as he could, on his shoulder and faced the man, eyes burning. *All right,* he thought, and felt a certain calmness descend on him. *If this is where I die, at least I'll die for something.* The thought was almost a relief.

The pipe-smoker's sister put paid to the dramatics, though, poking his interrogator in the ribs with her musket.

"If there was more, sister and I'd'a heard 'em long since," she said, mildly disgusted. "They ain't quiet, sojers."

"True, that," the pipe-smoker agreed, and paused to remove her pipe long enough to spit. "This 'un's only lost, 'ee can see as much. 'Ee can see he

won't talk to 'ee, either." She grinned familiarly at William, displaying one remaining yellow dogtooth. "Rather die than speak, eh, lad?"

William inclined his head a stiff inch, and the women giggled. No other
word for it: they *giggled* at him.

"Get on with 'ee," the aunt told the man, waving a hand at the beach behind him. "They'll leave without 'ee."

The man didn't look at her—didn't take his eyes off William's. After a moment, though, he nodded briefly and turned on his heel.

William felt one of the women behind him; something sharp touched his
wrist, and the twine they'd bound him with parted. He wanted to rub his
wrists, but didn't.

"Go, boy," the pipe-smoker said, almost gently. "Before someun else sees
'ee and gets ideas."

He left.

At the top of the beach, he paused and looked back. The old women had
vanished, but the man was sitting in the stern of a rowboat, drawing rapidly
away from the shore, now nearly empty. The man was staring at him.

William turned away. The sun was finally visible, a pale orange circle burning through the haze. It was coming down the sky now, early afternoon. He
turned inland and struck southwest, but felt eyes on his back for a long time
after the shore had fallen out of sight behind him.

His stomach was sore, and the only thought in his mind was what Captain
Ramsay had said to him. *Heard of a lady called Cassandra?*

AN UNCERTAIN FUTURE

Lallybroch
Inverness-shire, Scotland
September 1980

NOT ALL OF the letters were dated, but some were. Bree sorted
gingerly through the half-dozen on top, and with a sense of being poised at the top of a roller coaster, chose one with *2 March,*
A.D. *1777* written across the flap.

"I think this one's next." She had trouble taking a full breath. "It's—thin.
Short."

It was, no more than a page and a half, but the reason for its brevity was
clear; her father had written the whole of it. His awkward, determined writing wrung her heart.

"We are never letting a teacher try to make Jemmy write with his right hand," she said fiercely to Roger. "Never!"

"Right," he said, surprised and a little amused at her outburst. "Or left, if you prefer."

2 March, Anno Domini 1777
Fraser's Ridge, colony of North Carolina

My dearest daughter—

We prepare now to remove to Scotland. Not forever, or even for long. My Life—our Lives—lie here in America. And in all Honesty, I should greatly prefer to be stung to Death by Hornets than set foot on board another Ship; I try not to dwell upon the Prospect. But there are two chief Concerns which compel me to this Decision.

Had I not the Gift of Knowledge that you and your Mother and Roger Mac have brought me, I would likely think—as the great Majority of People in the Colony do think—that the Continental Congress will not last six Months, and Washington's Army less than that. I have spoken myself with a man from Cross Creek, who was discharged (honourably) from the Continental army on account of a festering Wound in the Arm—your Mother has of course dealt with this; he screamed a great Deal and I was pressed into service to sit upon him—who tells me that Washington has no more than a few thousand regular Soldiers, all very poor in Equipment, Clothes, and Arms, and all owed Money, which they are unlikely to receive. Most of his men are Militia, enlisted on short Contracts of two or three Months, and already melting away, needing to return Home for the Planting.

But I do know. At the same Time, I cannot be sure how the Things that I know will come about. Am I meant to be in some Way Part of this? Should I hold back, will that somehow damage or prevent the Success of our Desires? I often wish I could discuss these Questions with your Husband, though Presbyterian that he is, I think he would find them even more unsettling than I do. And in the end, it does not matter. I am what God has made me, and must deal with the Times in which He has placed me.

While I have not yet lost the Faculties of Sight or Hearing, nor even Control of my Bowels, I am not a young Man. I have a Sword, and a Rifle, and can use them both—but I also have a printing Press, and can use that to much greater Effect; it does not escape me that one can wield Sword or Musket only upon one Enemy at a time, while Words may be employed upon any Number.

Your Mother—doubtless contemplating the Prospect of my being seasick for several Weeks in her immediate Vicinity—suggests that I might enter Business with Fergus, making use of L'Oignon's Press, rather than travel to Scotland to retrieve my own.

I considered this, but I cannot in Conscience expose Fergus and his

Family to Danger by making use of their Press for such Purposes as I intend. Theirs is one of only a few Presses in operation between Charleston and Norfolk; even were I to do my Printing with the utmost Secrecy, Suspicion would focus upon them in short order—New Bern is a Hotbed of Loyalist Sentiment, and the Origins of my pamphleteering would become known almost immediately.

Beyond Consideration for Fergus and his Family, I think there may be some Benefit in visiting Edinburgh in order to retrieve my own Press. I had a varied Acquaintance there; some may have escaped Prison or the Noose.

The second—and most important—Consideration that compels me to Scotland, though, is your Cousin Ian. Years ago, I swore to his Mother—upon the Memory of our own Mother—that I would bring him Home to her, and this I mean to do, though the Man I bring back to Lallybroch is not the Lad who left there. God alone knows what they will make of each other, Ian and Lallybroch—and God has a most peculiar Sense of Humor. But if he is to go back at all, it must be now.

The Snow is melting; Water drips from the Eaves all Day, and Icicles reach from the Roof of the Cabin nearly to the Ground by Morning. Within a few Weeks, the Roads will be clear enough for Travel. It seems strange to ask that you pray for the Safety of a Voyage which will have been long completed by the Time you learn of it—for good or ill—but I ask it, nonetheless. Tell Roger Mac that I think God takes no account of Time. And kiss the Children for me.

> *Your most affectionate Father,*
> *JF*

Roger sat back a little, eyebrows raised, and glanced at her.

"The French Connection, you think?"

"The *what?*" She frowned over his shoulder, saw where his finger marked the text. "Where he's talking about his friends in Edinburgh?"

"Aye. Were not a good many of his Edinburgh acquaintances smugglers?"

"That's what Mama said."

"Hence the remark about nooses. And where were they smuggling things *from*, mostly?"

Her stomach gave a small hop.

"Oh, you're kidding. You think he's planning to mess with French smugglers?"

"Well, not smugglers, necessarily; he apparently knew a good many seditionists, thieves, and prostitutes, too." Roger smiled briefly, but then grew serious again.

"But I told him as much as I knew about the shape of the Revolution—admittedly, not a lot of detail, it not being my period—and I certainly told him how important France would be to the Americans. I'm just thinking"—he paused, a little awkwardly, then looked up at her—"he isn't going to Scotland to avoid the fighting; he's pretty clear about that."

"So you think he might be looking for political connections?" she asked slowly. "Not just grabbing his printing press, dropping Ian off at Lallybroch, and beating it back to America?"

She found the idea something of a relief. The notion of her parents intriguing in Edinburgh and Paris was much less hair-raising than her visions of them in the midst of explosions and battlefields. And it *would* be both of them, she realized. Where her father went, her mother would be, too.

Roger shrugged.

"That offhand remark about being what God made him. Ye ken what he means by that?"

"A bloody man," she said softly, and moved closer to Roger, putting a hand on his shoulder as though to ensure that he wouldn't suddenly vanish. "He told me he was a bloody man. That he'd seldom chosen to fight, but knew he was born to do it."

"Aye, that," Roger said, just as softly. "But he's no longer the young laird who took up his sword and led thirty crofters to a doomed battle—and took them home again. He knows a lot more now, about what one man can do. I think he means to do it."

"I think so, too." Her throat felt tight, but as much with pride as fear.

Roger reached up and put his hand over hers, squeezing.

"I remember..." he said slowly. "A thing your mother said, telling us about—about when she came back, and how she became a doctor. A thing your—Frank—that he said to her. Something about it being bloody inconvenient to the people round her, but a great blessing that she knew what it was she was meant to be. He was right about that, I think. And Jamie does know."

She nodded. She probably shouldn't say it, she thought. But she couldn't hold the words back any longer.

"Do *you* know?"

He was silent for a long time, looking at the pages on the table, but at last shook his head, the motion so small that she felt rather than saw it.

"I used to," he said quietly, and let go of her hand.

HER FIRST IMPULSE WAS to punch him in the back of the neck; her second was to seize him by the shoulders, bend down with her eyeballs an inch from his, and say—calmly, but distinctly—"What the hell do you mean by *that?*"

She refrained from doing either, only because both were likely to lead to a prolonged conversation of a sort deeply inappropriate for children, and both the kids were in the hall a few feet from the study door; she could hear them talking.

"See that?" Jemmy was saying.

"Un-huh."

"Bad people came here, a long time ago, looking for Grandda. Bad *English* people. They did that."

Roger's head turned as he caught what Jemmy was saying, and he caught Brianna's eye, with a half smile.

"Bad Engwish!" Mandy repeated obligingly. "Make 'em cwean it up!"

In spite of her annoyance, Brianna couldn't help sharing Roger's smile, though she felt a small shimmer in the pit of her stomach, recalling her uncle Ian—so calm, so kind a man—showing her the saber slashes in the wooden paneling of the hall and telling her, "We keep it so, to show the children—and tell them, this is what the English are." There had been steel in his voice—and hearing a faint, absurdly childish echo of it in Jemmy's voice, she had her first doubts regarding the wisdom of keeping this particular family tradition.

"Did you tell him about it?" she asked Roger, as the children's voices moved away toward the kitchen. "I didn't."

"Annie'd told him part of it; I thought I'd best tell him the rest." He raised his eyebrows. "Should I have told him to ask you?"

"Oh. No. No," she repeated, dubiously. "But—should we be teaching him to hate English people?"

Roger smiled at that.

" 'Hate' might be pitching it a bit strong. And he did say *bad* English people. They *were* bad English people who did that. Besides, if he's going to grow up in the Highlands, he'll likely hear a few barbed remarks regarding Sassenachs—he'll balance those against his memories of your mother; your da always called her 'Sassenach,' after all."

He glanced at the letter on the table, caught a glimpse of the wall clock, and rose abruptly.

"Christ, I'm late. I'll stop at the bank whilst I'm in town—need anything from the Farm and Household?"

"Yes," she said dryly, "a new pump for the milk separator."

"Right," he said, and kissing her hastily, went out, one arm already into his jacket.

She opened her mouth to call after him that she'd been joking, but on second thought closed it. The Farm and Household Stores just *might* have a pump for a milk separator. A large, bewilderingly crowded building on the edge of Inverness, the Farm and Household supplied just about anything a farm might need, including pitchforks, rubber fire buckets, baling wire, and washing machines, as well as crockery, jars for canning, and not a few mysterious implements whose use she could only guess at.

She stuck her head into the corridor, but the kids were in the kitchen with Annie MacDonald, the hired girl; laughter and the wire *clong!* of the ancient toaster—it had come with the house—floated past the ratty green baize door, along with the enticing scent of hot buttered toast. The smell and the laughter drew her like a magnet, and the warmth of home flowed over her, golden as honey.

She paused to fold up the letter, though, before going to join them, and the memory of Roger's last remark tightened her mouth.

"I used to."

Snorting ferociously, she tucked the letter back into the box and went out into the hall, only to be arrested by sight of a large envelope on the table near the door, where the daily mail—and the contents of Roger's and Jemmy's pockets—were daily unloaded. She grabbed the envelope out of the pile of circulars, pebbles, pencil stubs, links of bicycle chain, and . . . was that a dead mouse? It was; flattened and dried, but adorned with a stiff loop of pink tail. She picked it up gingerly and, with the envelope clasped against her breast, made her way toward tea and toast.

In all honesty, she thought, Roger wasn't the only one keeping things to himself. The difference was, she planned to tell him what she was thinking—once it was settled.

SPRING THAW

Fraser's Ridge, colony of North Carolina
March 1777

O NE THING ABOUT a devastating fire, I reflected. It did make packing easier. At present, I owned one gown, one shift, three petticoats—one woolen, two muslin—two pairs of stockings (I'd been wearing one pair when the house burned; the other had been carelessly left drying on a bush a few weeks before the fire and was discovered later, weathered but still wearable), a shawl, and a pair of shoes. Jamie had procured a horrible cloak for me somewhere—I didn't know where, and didn't want to ask. Made of thick wool the color of leprosy, it smelled as though someone had died in it and lain undiscovered for a couple of days. I'd boiled it with lye soap, but the ghost of its previous occupant lingered.

Still, I wouldn't freeze.

My medical kit was nearly as simple to pack. With a regretful sigh for the ashes of my beautiful apothecary's chest, with its elegant tools and numerous bottles, I turned over the pile of salvaged remnants from my surgery. The dented barrel of my microscope. Three singed ceramic jars, one missing its lid, one cracked. A large tin of goose grease mixed with camphor—now nearly empty after a winter of catarrhs and coughs. A handful of singed pages, ripped from the casebook started by Daniel Rawlings and continued by myself—though my spirits were lifted a bit by the discovery that the salvaged pages included one bearing Dr. Rawlings's special receipt for Bowel-Bind.

It was the only one of his receipts I'd found effective, and while I'd long since committed the actual formula to memory, having it to hand kept my sense of him alive. I'd never met Daniel Rawlings in life, but he'd been my friend since the day Jamie gave me his chest and casebook. I folded the paper carefully and tucked it into my pocket.

Most of my herbs and compounded medications had perished in the flames, along with the earthenware jars, the glass vials, the large bowls in which I incubated penicillin broth, and my surgical saws. I still had one scalpel and the darkened blade of a small amputation saw; the handle had been charred, but Jamie could make me a new one.

The residents of the Ridge had been generous—as generous as people who had virtually nothing themselves could be at the tail end of winter. We had food for the journey, and many of the women had brought me bits of their household simples; I had small jars of lavender, rosemary, comfrey, and mustard seed, two precious steel needles, a small skein of silk thread to use for sutures and dental floss (though I didn't mention that last use to the ladies, who would have been deeply affronted by the notion), and a very small stock of bandages and gauze for dressings.

One thing I had in abundance, though, was alcohol. The corncrib had been spared from the flames, and so had the still. Since there was more than enough grain for both animals and household, Jamie had thriftily transformed the rest into a very raw—but potent—liquor, which we would take along to trade for necessary goods along the way. One small cask had been kept for my especial use, though; I'd carefully painted the legend *Sauerkraut* on the side, to discourage theft on the road.

"And what if we should be set upon by illiterate banditti?" Jamie had asked, amused by this.

"Thought of that," I informed him, displaying a small corked bottle full of cloudy liquid. "*Eau de sauerkraut.* I'll pour it on the cask at first sight of anyone suspicious."

"I suppose we'd best hope they're not German bandits, then."

"Have you ever met a German bandit?" I asked. With the exception of the occasional drunkard or wife-beater, almost all the Germans we knew were honest, hardworking, and virtuous to a fault. Not all that surprising, given that so many of them had come to the colony as part of a religious movement.

"Not as such," he admitted. "But ye mind the Muellers, aye? And what they did to your friends. They wouldna have called themselves bandits, but the Tuscarora likely didna make the same distinction."

That was no more than the truth, and a cold thumb pressed the base of my skull. The Muellers, German neighbors, had had a beloved daughter and her newborn child die of measles, and had blamed the nearby Indians for the infection. Deranged by grief, old *Herr* Mueller had led a party of his sons and sons-in-law to take revenge—and scalps. My viscera still remembered the shock of seeing my friend Nayawenne's white-streaked hair spill out of a bundle into my lap.

"Is my hair turning white, do you think?" I said abruptly. He raised his eyebrows, but bent forward and peered at the top of my head, fingering gently through my hair.

"There's maybe one hair in fifty that's gone white. One in five-and-twenty is silver. Why?"

"I suppose I have a little time, then. Nayawenne . . ." I hadn't spoken her name aloud in several years, and found an odd comfort in the speaking, as though it had conjured her. "She told me that I'd come into my full power when my hair turned white."

"Now there's a fearsome thought," he said, grinning.

"No doubt. Since it hasn't happened yet, though, I suppose if we stumble into a nest of sauerkraut thieves on the road, I'll have to defend my cask with my scalpel," I said.

He gave me a slightly queer look at this, but then laughed and shook his head.

His own packing was a little more involved. He and Young Ian had removed the gold from the house's foundation the night after Mrs. Bug's funeral—a delicate process preceded by my putting out a large slop basin of stale bread soaked in corn liquor, then calling "Sooo-eeee!" at the top of my lungs from the head of the garden path.

A moment of silence, and then the white sow emerged from her den, a pale blotch against the smoke-stained rocks of the foundation. I knew exactly what she was, but the sight of that white, rapidly moving form still made the hairs stand up on the back of my neck. It had come on to snow—one of the reasons for Jamie's decision to act at once—and she came through the whirl of big, soft flakes with a velocity that made her seem like the spirit of the storm itself, leading the wind.

For an instant, I thought she was going to charge me; I saw her head swing toward me and caught the loud snuff as she took my scent—but she scented the food as well, and swerved away. An instant later, the ungodly sounds of a pig in ecstasy floated through the hush of the snow, and Jamie and Ian hurried out of the trees to begin their work.

It took more than two weeks to move the gold; they worked only at night, and only when fresh snow was either falling or about to fall, to cover their tracks. Meantime, they took it in turn to guard the remains of the Big House, keeping an eye peeled for any sign of Arch Bug.

"Do you think he still cares about the gold?" I'd asked Jamie in the midst of this endeavor, chafing his hands to get enough heat into them for him to hold his spoon. He'd come in for breakfast, frozen and exhausted after a long night spent walking round and round the burnt house to keep his blood flowing.

"He's no much else left to care about, has he?" He spoke softly, to avoid waking the Higgins family. "Other than Ian."

I shivered, as much from thought of old Arch, living wraithlike in the forest, surviving on the heat of his hatred, as from the cold that had come in with Jamie. He'd let his beard grow for warmth—all the men did in winter, on the mountain—and ice glimmered in his whiskers and frosted his brows.

"You look like Old Man Winter himself," I whispered, bringing him a bowl of hot porridge.

"I feel like it," he replied hoarsely. He passed the bowl under his nose, inhaling the steam and closing his eyes beatifically. "Pass the whisky, aye?"

"You're proposing to pour it on your porridge? It's got butter and salt on, already." Nonetheless, I passed him the bottle from its shelf over the hearth.

"Nay, I'm going to thaw my wame enough to eat it. I'm solid ice from the neck down."

No one had seen hide nor hair of Arch Bug—not even an errant track in the snow—since his appearance at the funeral. He might be denned up for the winter, snug in some refuge. He might have gone away to the Indian villages. He might be dead, and I rather hoped he was, uncharitable as the thought might be.

I mentioned this, and Jamie shook his head. The ice in his hair had melted now, and the firelight glimmered like diamonds on the water droplets in his beard.

"If he's dead, and we never learn of it, Ian willna have a moment's peace—ever. D'ye want him to be looking over his shoulder at his wedding, afraid of a bullet through his wife's heart as she speaks her vows? Or wed with a family, fearing each day to leave his house and his bairns, for fear of what he might come back to?"

"I'm impressed at the scope and morbidity of your imagination—but you're right. All right, I don't hope he's dead—not unless we find his body."

But no one did find his body, and the gold was moved, bit by bit, to its new hiding place.

That had taken a bit of thought and considerable private discussion between Jamie and Ian. Not the whisky cave. Very few people knew about that—but some did. Joseph Wemyss, his daughter, Lizzie, and her two husbands—I marveled, rather, that I'd got to the point where I could think about Lizzie and the Beardsleys without boggling—all knew, of necessity, and Bobby and Amy Higgins would need to be shown its location before we left, as they would be making whisky themselves in our absence. Arch Bug had not been told of the cave's location—but very likely knew it.

Jamie was adamant that no one should know even of the gold's existence on the Ridge, let alone its location.

"Let even a rumor of it get out, and everyone here is in danger," he'd said. "Ye ken what happened when yon Donner told folk we had jewels here."

I kent, all right. I still woke up in the midst of nightmares, hearing the muffled *whumph!* of exploding ether fumes, hearing the crash of glass and smashing wood as the raiders wrecked the house.

In some of these dreams, I ran fruitlessly to and fro, trying to rescue someone—who?—but met always by locked doors, blank walls, or rooms engulfed in flame. In others, I stood rooted, unable to move a muscle, as fire crawled up the walls, fed with delicate greed on the clothes of bodies at my feet, burst through a corpse's hair, caught in my skirts and swarmed upward, wrapping my legs in a blazing web.

I still felt overpowering sadness—and a deep, cleansing rage—when I looked at the sooty smudge in the clearing that had once been my home, but I always had to go out in the morning after one of these dreams and look at it nonetheless: walk round the cold ruins and smell the taint of dead ash, in order to quench the flames that burned behind my eyes.

"Right," I said, and pulled my shawl tighter round me. We were standing by the springhouse, looking down on the ruins as we talked, and the chill was seeping into my bones. "So . . . where, then?"

"The Spaniard's Cave," he said, and I blinked at him.

"The what?"

"I'll show ye, *a nighean*," he said, grinning at me. "When the snow melts."

SPRING HAD SPRUNG, and the creek was rising. Swelled by melting snow and fed by hundreds of tiny waterfalls that trickled and leapt down the mountain's face, it roared past my feet, exuberant with spray. I could feel it cold on my face, and knew that I'd be wet to the knees within minutes, but it didn't matter. The fresh green of arrowhead and pickerelweed rimmed the banks, some plants dragged out of the soil by the rising water and whirled downstream, more hanging on by their roots for dear life, leaves trailing in the racing wash. Dark mats of cress swirled under the water, close by the sheltering banks. And fresh greens were what I wanted.

My gathering basket was half full of fiddleheads and ramp shoots. A nice big lot of tender new cress, crisp and cold from the stream, would top off the winter's vitamin C deficiency very well. I took off my shoes and stockings, and after a moment's hesitation, took off my gown and shawl as well and hung them over a tree branch. The air was chilly in the shade of the silver birches that overhung the creek here, and I shivered a bit but ignored the cold, kirtling up my shift before wading into the stream.

That cold was harder to ignore. I gasped, and nearly dropped the basket, but found my footing among the slippery rocks and made my way toward the nearest mat of tempting dark green. Within seconds, my legs were numb, and I'd lost any sense of cold in the enthusiasm of forager's frenzy and salad hunger.

A good deal of our stored food had been saved from the fire, as it was kept in the outbuildings: the springhouse, corncrib, and smoking shed. The root cellar had been destroyed, though, and with it not only the carrots, onions, garlic, and potatoes but most of my carefully gathered stock of dried apples and wild yams, and the big hanging clusters of raisins, all meant to keep us from the ravages of scurvy. The herbs, of course, had gone up in smoke, along with the rest of my surgery. True, a large quantity of pumpkins and squashes had escaped, these having been piled in the barn, but one grows tired of squash pie and succotash after a couple of months—well, after a couple of days, speaking personally.

Not for the first time, I mourned Mrs. Bug's abilities as a cook, though of course I did miss her for her own sake. Amy McCallum Higgins had been raised in a crofter's cottage in the Highlands of Scotland and was, as she put it, "a good plain cook." Essentially, that meant she could bake bannocks, boil porridge, and fry fish simultaneously, without burning any of it. No mean feat, but a trifle monotonous, in terms of diet.

My own pièce de résistance was stew—which, lacking onions, garlic, carrots, and potatoes, had devolved into a sort of pottage consisting of venison or turkey stewed with cracked corn, barley, and possibly chunks of stale bread. Ian, surprisingly, had turned out to be a passable cook; the succotash and squash pie were his contributions to the communal menu. I did wonder who had taught him to make them, but thought it wiser not to ask.

So far no one had starved, nor yet lost any teeth, but by mid-March, I would have been willing to wade neck-deep in freezing torrents in order to acquire something both edible and green.

Ian had, thank goodness, gone on breathing. And after a week or so had ceased acting quite so shell-shocked, eventually regaining something like his normal manner. But I noticed Jamie's eyes follow him now and then, and Rollo had taken to sleeping with his head on Ian's chest, a new habit. I wondered whether he really sensed the pain in Ian's heart, or whether it was simply a response to the cramped sleeping conditions in the cabin.

I stretched my back, hearing the small pops between my vertebrae. Now that the snowmelt had come, I could hardly wait for our departure. I would miss the Ridge and everyone on it—well, almost everyone. Possibly not Hiram Crombie, so much. Or the Chisholms, or—I short-circuited this list before it became uncharitable.

"On the *other* hand," I said firmly to myself, "think of beds."

Granted, we would be spending a good many nights on the road, sleeping rough—but eventually we would reach civilization. Inns. With food. And beds. I closed my eyes momentarily, envisioning the absolute bliss of a mattress. I didn't even aspire to a feather bed; anything that promised more than an inch of padding between myself and the floor would be paradise. And, of course, if it came with a modicum of privacy—even better.

Jamie and I had not been completely celibate since December. Lust aside—and it wasn't—we needed the comfort and warmth of each other's body. Still, covert congress under a quilt, with Rollo's yellow eyes fixed upon us from two feet away, was less than ideal, even assuming that Young Ian was invariably asleep, which I didn't think he was, though he was sufficiently tactful as to pretend.

A hideous shriek split the air, and I jerked, dropping the basket. I flung myself after it, barely snatching the handle before it was whirled away on the flood, and stood up dripping and trembling, heart hammering as I waited to see whether the scream would be repeated.

It was—followed in short order by an equally piercing screech, but one deeper in timbre and recognizable to my well-trained ears as the sort of noise made by a Scottish Highlander suddenly immersed in freezing water. Fainter, higher-pitched shrieks, and a breathless "Fook!" spoken in a Dorset accent indicated that the gentlemen of the household were taking their spring bath.

I wrang out the hem of my shift and, snatching my shawl from the branch where I'd left it, slipped on my shoes and made my way in the direction of the bellowing.

There are few things more enjoyable than sitting in relative warmth and comfort while watching fellow human beings soused in cold water. If said human beings present a complete review of the nude male form, so much the better. I threaded my way through a small growth of fresh-budding river willows, found a conveniently screened rock in the sun, and spread out the damp skirt of my shift, enjoying the warmth on my shoulders, the sharp scent of the fuzzy catkins, and the sight before me.

Jamie was standing in the pool, nearly shoulder-deep, his hair slicked back like a russet seal. Bobby stood on the bank, and picking up Aidan with a grunt, threw him to Jamie in a pinwheel of flailing limbs and piercing shrieks of delighted fright.

"Me-me-me-*me*!" Orrie was dancing around his stepfather's legs, his chubby bottom bouncing up and down among the reeds like a little pink balloon.

Bobby laughed, bent, and hoisted him up, holding him for a moment high overhead as he squealed like a seared pig, then flung him in a shallow arc out over the pool.

He hit the water with a tremendous splash and Jamie grabbed him, laughing, and pulled him to the surface, whence he emerged with a look of openmouthed stupefaction that made them all hoot like gibbons. Aidan and Rollo were both dog-paddling round in circles by now, shouting and barking.

I looked across to the opposite side of the pool and saw Ian rush naked down the small hill and leap like a salmon into the pool, uttering one of his best Mohawk war cries. This was cut off abruptly by the cold water, and he vanished with scarcely a splash.

I waited—as did the others—for him to pop back up, but he didn't. Jamie looked suspiciously behind him, in case of a sneak attack, but an instant later Ian shot out of the water directly in front of Bobby with a bloodcurdling yell, grabbed him by the leg, and yanked him in.

Matters thereafter became generally chaotic, with a great deal of promiscuous splashing, yelling, hooting, and jumping off of rocks, which gave me the opportunity to reflect on just how delightful naked men are. Not that I hadn't seen a good many of them in my time, but aside from Frank and Jamie, most men I'd seen undressed usually had been either ill or injured, and were encountered in such circumstances as to prevent a leisurely appreciation of their finer attributes.

From Orrie's chubbiness and Aidan's spidery winter-white limbs to Bobby's skinny, pale torso and neat little flat behind, the McCallum-Higginses were as entertaining to watch as a cageful of monkeys.

Ian and Jamie were something different—baboons, perhaps, or mandrills. They didn't really resemble each other in any attribute other than height, and yet were plainly cut from the same cloth. Watching Jamie squatting on a rock above the pool, thighs tensing for a leap, I could easily see him preparing to attack a leopard, while Ian stretched himself glistening in the sun, warming his dangly bits while keeping an alert watch for intruders. All they needed were purple bottoms, and they could have walked straight onto the African veldt, no questions asked.

They were all lovely, in their wildly various ways, but it was Jamie my gaze returned to, over and over again. He was battered and scarred, his muscles roped and knotted, and age had grooved the hollows between them. The thick welt of the bayonet scar writhed up his thigh, wide and ugly, while the thinner white line of the scar left by a rattlesnake's bite was nearly invisible, clouded by the thick fuzz of his body hair, this beginning to dry now and stand out from his skin in a cloud of reddish-gold. The scimitar-shaped sword cut across his ribs had healed well, too, no more than a hair-thin white line by now.

He turned round and bent to pick up a cake of soap from the rock, and my insides turned over. It wasn't purple but could not otherwise have been improved on, being high, round, delicately dusted with red-gold, and with a delightful muscular concavity to the sides. His balls, just visible from behind, *were* purple with the cold, and gave me a strong urge to creep up behind him and cup them in my rock-warmed hands.

I wondered whether the resultant standing broad-jump would enable him to clear the pool.

I had not, in fact, seen him naked—or even substantially undressed—in several months.

But now...I threw back my head, closing my eyes against the brilliant spring sun, enjoying the tickle of my own fresh-washed hair against my shoulder blades. The snow was gone, the weather was good—and the whole outdoors beckoned invitingly, filled with places where privacy could be assured, bar the odd skunk.

I LEFT THE MEN dripping and sunning themselves on the rocks, and went to retrieve my clothes. I didn't put these on, though. Instead, I went quickly up to the springhouse, where I submerged my basket of greens in the cool water—if I took it to the cabin, Amy would seize them and boil them into submission—and left my gown, stays, and stockings rolled up on the shelf where the cheeses were stacked. Then I went back toward the stream.

The splashing and shouting had ceased. Instead, I heard low-voiced singing, coming along the trail. It was Bobby, carrying Orrie, sound asleep after his exertions. Aidan, groggy with cleanliness and warmth, ambled slowly beside his stepfather, dark head tilting to and fro to the rhythm of the song.

It was a lovely Gaelic lullaby; Amy must have taught it to Bobby. I did wonder if she'd told him what the words meant.

> *S'iomadh oidhche fhliuch is thioram*
> *Sìde nan seachd sian*
> *Gheibheadh Griogal dhomhsa creagan*
> *Ris an gabhainn dìon.*

> *(Many a night, wet and dry*
> *Even in the worst of weather*
> *Gregor would find a little rock for me*
> *Beside which I could shelter.)*

> *Òbhan, òbhan òbhan ìri*
> *Òbhan ìri ò!*
> *Òbhan, òbhan òbhan ìri*
> *'S mòr mo mhulad 's mòr.*

> *(Woe is me, woe is me*
> *Woe is me, great indeed is my sorrow.)*

I smiled to see them, though with a catch in my throat. I remembered Jamie carrying Jem back from swimming, the summer before, and Roger singing to Mandy in the night, his harsh, cracked voice little more than a whisper—but music, all the same.

I nodded to Bobby, who smiled and nodded back, though without interrupting his song. He raised his brows and jerked a thumb over his shoulder and uphill, presumably indicating where Jamie had gone. He betrayed no surprise at seeing me in shift and shawl—doubtless he thought I was bound for the stream to wash, as well, inspired by the singular warmth of the day.

> *Eudail mhòir a shluagh an domhain*
> *Dhòirt iad d' fhuil an dè*
> *'S chuir iad do cheann air stob daraich*
> *Tacan beag bhod chrè.*

> *(Great sweetheart of all people of the world*
> *They poured your blood yesterday*
> *And they put your head on an oak stick*
> *A short distance from your body.)*

> *Òbhan, òbhan òbhan ìri*
> *Òbhan ìri ò!*
> *Òbhan, òbhan òbhan ìri*
> *'S mòr mo mhulad 's mòr.*

> *(Woe is me, woe is me*
> *Woe is me, great indeed is my sorrow.)*

I waved briefly and turned up the side trail that led to the upper clearing. "New House," everyone called it, though the only indications that there might someday *be* a house there were a stack of felled logs and a number of pegs driven into the ground, with strings tied between them. These were meant to mark the placement and dimensions of the house Jamie intended to build in replacement of the Big House—when we came back.

He'd been moving the pegs, I saw. The wide front room was now wider, and the back room intended for my surgery had developed a growth of some sort, perhaps a separate stillroom.

The architect was sitting on a log, surveying his kingdom, stark naked.

"Expecting me, were you?" I asked, taking off my shawl and hanging it on a convenient branch.

"I was." He smiled, and scratched his chest. "I thought the sight of my naked backside would likely inflame ye. Or was it maybe Bobby's?"

"Bobby hasn't got one. Do you know, you haven't got a single gray hair below the neck? Why is that, I wonder?"

He glanced down, inspecting himself, but it was true. There were only a few strands of silver among the fiery mass of his hair, though his beard—the winter growth tediously and painfully removed a few days before—was heavily frosted with white. But the hair on his chest was still a dark auburn, and that below a fluffy mass of vivid ginger.

He combed his fingers thoughtfully through the exuberant foliage, looking down.

"I think it's hiding," he remarked, and glanced up at me, one eyebrow raised. "Want to come and help me hunt for it?"

I came round in front of him and obligingly knelt down. The object in question was in fact quite visible, though admittedly looking rather shell-shocked by the recent immersion, and a most interesting shade of pale blue.

"Well," I said, after a moment's contemplation. "Great oaks from tiny acorns grow. Or so I'm told."

A shiver ran through him at the warmth of my mouth and I lifted my hands involuntarily, cradling his balls.

"Holy God," he said, and his hands rested lightly on my head in benediction.

"What did ye say?" he asked, a moment later.

"I said," I said, coming up momentarily for air, "I find the gooseflesh rather erotic."

"There's more where that came from," he assured me. "Take your shift off, Sassenach. I havena seen ye naked in nearly four months."

"Well . . . no, you haven't," I agreed, hesitating. "And I'm not sure I want you to."

One eyebrow went up.

"Whyever not?"

"Because I've been indoors for weeks on end without sun or exercise to speak of. I probably look like one of those grubs you find under rocks—fat, white, and squidgy."

"Squidgy?" he repeated, breaking into a grin.

"Squidgy," I said with dignity, wrapping my arms around myself.

He pursed his lips and exhaled slowly, eyeing me with his head on one side.

"I like it when ye're fat, but I ken quite well that ye're not," he said, "because I've felt your ribs when I put my arms about you, each night since the end of January. As for white—ye've been white all the time I've known ye; it's no likely to come a great shock to me. As for the squidgy part"—he extended one hand and wiggled the fingers beckoningly at me—"I think I might enjoy that."

"Hmm," I said, still hesitant. He sighed.

"Sassenach," he said, "I said I havena seen ye naked in four months. That means if ye take your shift off now, ye'll be the best thing I've seen in four months. And at my age, I dinna think I remember farther back than that."

I laughed, and without further ado, stood up and pulled the ribbon tie at the neck of my shift. Wriggling, I let it fall in a puddle round my feet.

He closed his eyes. Then breathed deep and opened them again.

"I'm blinded," he said softly, and held out a hand to me.

"Blinded as in sun bouncing off a vast expanse of snow?" I asked dubiously. "Or as in coming face to face with a gorgon?"

"Seeing a gorgon turns ye to stone, not strikes ye blind," he informed me. "Though come to think"—he prodded himself with an experimental forefinger—"I may turn to stone yet. Will ye come here, for God's sake?"

I came.

I FELL ASLEEP IN the warmth of Jamie's body, and woke some time later, snugly wrapped in his plaid. I stretched, alarming a squirrel overhead, who ran out on a limb to get a better view. Evidently he didn't like what he saw, and began scolding and chattering.

"Oh, hush," I said, yawning, and sat up. The squirrel took exception to this gesture and began having hysterics, but I ignored him. To my surprise, Jamie was gone.

I thought he'd likely just stepped into the wood to relieve himself, but a quick glance round didn't discover him, and when I scrambled to my feet, the plaid clutched to me, I saw no sign of him.

I hadn't heard anything; surely if someone had come, I would have wakened—or Jamie would have wakened me. I listened carefully, but—the squirrel having now gone about its own business—heard nothing beyond the normal sounds of a forest waking to spring: the murmur and rush of wind through new-leafed trees, punctuated by the occasional crack of a falling branch, or the rattle of last year's pinecones and chestnut hulls bouncing through the canopy; the call of a distant jay, the conversation of a gang of pygmy nuthatches foraging in the long grass nearby, the rustle of a hungry vole in the winter's dead leaves.

The jay was still calling; another had joined it now, shrill with alarm. Perhaps that was where Jamie had gone.

I unwound myself from the plaid and pulled on my shift and shoes. It was getting on for evening; we—or I, at least—had slept a long time. It was still warm in the sun, but the shadows under the trees were cold, and I put on my shawl and bundled up Jamie's plaid into my arms—likely he'd want it.

I followed the calling of the jays uphill, away from the clearing. There was a pair nesting near the White Spring; I'd seen them building the nest only two days before.

It wasn't far from the house site at all, though that particular spring always had the air of being remote from everything. It lay in the center of a small grove of white ash and hemlock, and was shielded on the east by a jagged outcropping of lichen-covered rock. All water has a sense of life about it, and a mountain spring carries a particular sense of quiet joy, rising pure from the heart of the earth. The White Spring, so called for the big pale boulder that stood guardian over its pool, had something more—a sense of inviolate peace.

The closer I came to it, the surer I was that that was where I'd find Jamie.

"There's something there that listens," he'd told Brianna once, quite casually. "Ye see such pools in the Highlands; they're called saints' pools—folk say the saint lives by the pool and listens to their prayers."

"And what saint lives by the White Spring?" she'd asked, cynical. "Saint Killian?"

"Why him?"

"Patron saint of gout, rheumatism, and whitewashers."

He'd laughed at that, shaking his head.

"Whatever it is that lives in such water is older than the notion of saints," he assured her. "But it listens."

I walked softly, approaching the spring. The jays had fallen silent now.

He was there, sitting on a rock by the water, wearing only his shirt. I saw why the jays had gone about their business—he was still as the white boulder itself, his eyes closed, hands turned upward on his knees, loosely cupped, inviting grace.

I stopped at once when I saw him. I had seen him pray here once before—when he'd asked Dougal MacKenzie for help in battle. I didn't know who he was talking to just now, but it wasn't a conversation I wished to intrude upon.

I ought to leave, I supposed—but aside from the fear that I might disturb him by an inadvertent noise, I didn't want to go. Most of the spring lay in shadow, but fingers of light came down through the trees, stroking him. The air was thick with pollen, and the light was filled with motes of gold. It struck answering glints from the crown of his head, the smooth high arch of his foot, the blade of his nose, the bones of his face. He might have grown there, part of earth and stone and water, might have been himself the spirit of the spring.

I didn't feel unwelcome. The peace of the place reached out to touch me gently, slow my heart.

Was that what he sought here? I wondered. Was he drawing the peace of the mountain into himself, to remember, to sustain him during the months—the years, perhaps—of coming exile?

I would remember.

The light began to go, brightness falling from the air. He stirred, finally, lifting his head a little.

"Let me be enough," he said quietly.

I started at the sound of his voice, but he hadn't been speaking to me.

He opened his eyes and rose then, quiet as he'd sat, and came past the stream, long feet bare and silent on the layers of damp leaves. As he came past the outcropping of rock, he saw me and smiled, reaching out to take the plaid I held out to him, wordless. He said nothing, but took my cold hand in his large warm one and we turned toward home, walking together in the mountain's peace.

A FEW DAYS LATER, he came to find me. I was foraging along the creek bank for leeches, which had begun to emerge from their winter's hibernation, ravenous for blood. They were simple to catch; I merely waded slowly through the water near shore.

At first, the thought of acting as live bait for the leeches was repellent, but after all, that was how I usually obtained leeches—by letting Jamie, Ian, Bobby, or any of a dozen young males wade through the streams and pick them off. And once you got used to the sight of the creatures, slowly engorging with your blood, it wasn't all that bad.

"I have to let them have enough blood to sustain themselves," I explained, grimacing as I eased a thumbnail under the sucker of a leech in order to dislodge it, "but not enough that they'll be comatose, or they won't be of any use."

"A matter of nice judgment," Jamie agreed, as I dropped the leech into a jar filled with water and duckweed. "When ye've done feeding your wee pets, then, come along and I'll show ye the Spaniard's Cave."

It was no little distance. Perhaps four miles from the Ridge, through cold, muddy creeks and up steep slopes, then through a crack in a granite cliff face that made me feel as though I were being entombed alive, only to emerge into a wilderness of jutting boulders, smothered in nets of wild grape.

"We found it, Jem and I, out hunting one day," Jamie explained, lifting a curtain of leaves for me to pass beneath. The vines snaked over the rocks, thick as a man's forearm and knotted with age, the rusty-green leaves of spring not yet quite covering them. "It was a secret between us. We agreed we'd tell no one else—not even his parents."

"Nor me," I said, but wasn't offended. I heard the loss in his voice at the mention of Jem.

The entrance to the cave was a crack in the ground, over which Jamie had pushed a large, flat rock. He slid this back with some effort, and I bent over cautiously, experiencing a brief clench of the innards at the faint sound of moving air through the fissure. The surface air was warm, though; the cave was drawing, not blowing.

I remembered all too well the cave at Abandawe, that had seemed to breathe around us, and it took some force of will to follow Jamie as he disappeared into the earth. There was a rough wooden ladder—new, I saw, but replacing a much older one that had fallen to pieces; some bits of rotted wood were still in place, dangling from the rock on rusted iron spikes.

It could have been no more than ten or twelve feet to the bottom, but the neck of the cave was narrow, and the descent seemed endless. At last I reached the bottom, though, and saw that the cave had opened out, like the bottom of a flask. Jamie was crouched to one side; I saw him draw out a small bottle and smelled the sharp scent of turpentine.

He'd brought a torch, a pine knot with a head dipped in tar and wrapped with a rag. He soaked the rag with turpentine, then drew the fire-starter Bree had made for him. A shower of sparks lit his face, intent and ruddy. Twice more, and the torch caught, the flame bursting through the flammable cloth and catching the tar.

He lifted the torch, and gestured toward the floor behind me. I turned and nearly jumped out of my skin.

The Spaniard leaned against the wall, bony legs stretched out, skull fallen forward as if in a doze. Tufts of reddish, faded hair still clung here and there, but the skin had gone entirely. His hands and feet were mostly gone, too, the small bones carried away by rodents. No large animals had been able to get at him, though, and while the torso and long bones showed signs of nibbling, they were largely intact; the swell of the rib cage poked through a tissue of cloth so faded that there was no telling what color it had ever been.

He *was* a Spaniard, too. A crested metal helmet, red with rust, lay by him, along with an iron breastplate and a knife.

"Jesus H. Roosevelt Christ," I whispered. Jamie crossed himself, and knelt by the skeleton.

"I've no notion how long he's been here," he said, also low-voiced. "We didna find anything with him save the armor and that." He pointed to the gravel just in front of the pelvis. I leaned closer to look; a small crucifix, probably silver, now tarnished black, and a few inches away, a tiny triangular shape, also black.

"A rosary?" I asked, and Jamie nodded.

"I expect he was wearing it about his neck. It must have been made of wood and string, and when it rotted, the metal bits fell. That"—his finger gently touched the little triangle—"says *Nr. Sra. Ang.* on the one side— *Nuestra Señora de los Angeles,* I think it means, 'Our Lady of the Angels.' There's a wee picture of the Blessed Virgin on the other side."

I crossed myself by reflex.

"Was Jemmy scared?" I asked, after a moment's respectful silence.

"I was," Jamie said dryly. "It was dark when I came down the shaft, and I nearly stepped on this fellow. I thought he was alive, and the shock of it liked to stop my heart."

He'd cried out in alarm, and Jemmy, left aboveground with strict instructions not to move from the spot, had promptly scrambled into the hole, losing his grip of the broken ladder halfway down and landing feetfirst on his grandfather.

"I heard him scrabbling and looked up, just in time to have him plunge out of the heavens and strike me in the breast like a cannonball." Jamie rubbed the left side of his chest with rueful amusement. "If I hadn't looked up, he'd have broken my neck—and he'd never have got out, by himself."

And we'd never have known what happened to either one of you. I swallowed, dry-mouthed at the thought. And yet . . . on any given day, something just as random might happen. To anyone.

"A wonder neither one of you broke anything," I said instead, and gestured toward the skeleton. "What do you think happened to this gentleman?" *His people never knew.*

Jamie shook his head.

"I dinna ken. He wasna expecting an enemy, because he wasna wearing his armor."

"You don't think he fell in and couldn't get out?" I squatted by the skeleton, tracing the tibia of the left leg. The bone was dried and cracked, gnawed at the end by small sharp teeth—but I could see what might be a greenstick fracture of the bone. Or might just be the cracking of age.

Jamie shrugged, glancing up.

"I shouldna think so. He was a good bit shorter than I am, but I think the original ladder must have been here when he died—for if someone built the ladder later, why would they leave this gentleman here at the bottom of it? And even with a broken leg, he should have been able to climb it."

"Hmm. He might have died of a fever, I suppose. That would account for his taking off his breastplate and helmet." Though I personally would have taken them off at the first opportunity; depending on the season, he must either have been boiled alive or suffered severely from mildew, semi-enclosed in metal.

"Mmphm."

I glanced up at this sound, which indicated dubious acceptance of my reasoning but disagreement with my conclusion.

"You think he was killed?"

He shrugged.

"He has armor—but nay weapon save a wee knife. And ye can see he was right-handed, but the knife's lying to his left."

The skeleton *had* been right-handed; the bones of the right arm were noticeably thicker, even by the flicker of torchlight. Possibly a swordsman? I wondered.

"I kent a good many Spanish soldiers in the Indies, Sassenach. All of them fair bristled wi' swords and spears and pistols. If this man died of a fever, his companions might take his arms—but they'd take the armor, too, *and* the knife. Why leave it?"

"But by that token," I objected, "why did whoever killed him—if he was killed—leave the armor and the knife?"

"As for the armor—they didna want it. It wouldna be particularly useful to anyone other than a soldier. As for the knife—because it was sticking in him?" Jamie suggested. "And it's no a very good knife to begin with."

"Very logical," I said, swallowing again. "Putting aside the question of how he died—what in God's name was he doing in the mountains of North Carolina in the first place?"

"The Spanish sent explorers up as far as Virginia, fifty or sixty years ago," he informed me. "The swamps discouraged them, though."

"I can see why. But why . . . *this*?" I stood up, waving a hand to encompass the cave and its ladder. He didn't reply, but took my arm and lifted his torch, turning me to the side of the cave opposite the ladder. Well above my head, I saw another small fissure in the rock, black in the torchlight, barely wide enough for a man to wriggle through.

"There's a smaller cave through there," he said, nodding upward. "And when I put Jem up to look, he told me there were marks in the dust—square marks, as though heavy boxes had sat there."

Which is why, when the need to hide treasure had occurred to him, so had thought of the Spaniard's Cave.

"We'll bring the last of the gold tonight," he said, "and pile rocks to hide the opening up there. Then we'll leave the *señor* here to his rest."

I was obliged to admit that the cave made as suitable a resting place as any. And the Spanish soldier's presence would likely discourage anyone who stumbled on the cave from further investigation, both Indians and settlers having a distinct aversion to ghosts. For that matter, so did Highlanders, and I turned curiously to Jamie.

"You and Jem—you weren't troubled about being haunted by him?"

"Nay, we said the proper prayer for the repose of his soul, when I sealed the cave, and scattered salt around it."

That made me smile.

"You know the proper prayer for every occasion, don't you?"

He smiled faintly in return, and rubbed the head of the torch in the damp gravel to extinguish it. A faint shaft of light from above glowed on the crown of his head.

"There's always a prayer, *a nighean*, even if it's only *A Dhia, cuidich mi.*" *Oh, God—help me.*

9

A KNIFE THAT
KNOWS MY HAND

NOT ALL THE GOLD rested with the Spaniard. Two of my petticoats had an extra turnup in the hem, with shavings of gold evenly distributed in tiny pockets, and my large pocket itself had several ounces of gold stitched into the seam at the bottom. Jamie and Ian each carried a small amount in his sporran. And each of them would carry two substantial shot pouches on his belt. We had retired, the three of us, to the New House clearing, to make the shot in private.

"Now, ye'll no forget which side to load from, aye?" Jamie dropped a fresh musket ball out of the mold, glowing like a miniature sunrise, into the pot of grease and soot.

"As long as ye dinna take my shot bag in mistake, no," Ian said caustically. He was making lead shot, dropping the hot fresh balls into a hollow lined with moist leaves, where they smoked and steamed in the crisp spring evening.

Rollo, lying nearby, sneezed as a wisp of smoke drifted past his nose, and snorted explosively. Ian glanced at him with a smile.

"Will ye like chasing the red deer through the heather, *a choin*?" he asked. "Ye'll need to keep off the sheep, though, or someone's like to shoot ye for a wolf."

Rollo sighed and let his eyes go to drowsy slits.

"Thinking what ye'll say to your mam when ye see her?" Jamie asked, squinting against the smoke of the fire as he held the ladle of gold shavings over the flame.

"Tryin' not to think too much," Ian replied frankly. "I get a queer feeling in my wame when I think of Lallybroch."

"Good queer or bad queer?" I asked, gingerly scooping the cooled gold balls out of the grease with a wooden spoon and dropping them into the shot pouches.

Ian frowned, eyes fixed on his ladle as the lead went suddenly from crumpled blobs to a quivering puddle.

"Both, I think. Brianna told me once about a book she'd read in school that said ye can't go home again. I think that's maybe true—but I want to," he added softly, eyes still on his work. The melted lead hissed into the mold.

I looked away from the wistfulness in his face, and found Jamie looking at me, his gaze quizzical, eyes soft with sympathy. I looked away from him, too, and rose to my feet, groaning slightly as my knee joint cracked.

"Yes, well," I said briskly. "I suppose it depends on what you think home is, doesn't it? It isn't always a place, you know."

"Aye, that's true." Ian held the bullet mold for an instant, letting it cool. "But even when it's a person—ye can't always go back, aye? Or maybe ye can," he added, his mouth quirking a little as he glanced up at Jamie, and then at me.

"I think ye'll find your parents much as ye left them," Jamie said dryly, choosing to ignore Ian's reference. "You may come as a greater shock to them."

Ian glanced down at himself and smiled.

"Got a bit taller," he said.

I gave a brief snort of amusement. He'd been fifteen when he'd left Scotland—a tall, scrawny gowk of a boy. He *was* a couple of inches taller now. He was also lean and hard as a strip of dried rawhide, and normally tanned to much the same color, though the winter had bleached him, making the tattooed dots that ran in semicircles across his cheekbones stand out more vividly.

"You remember that other line I told you?" I asked him. "When we came back to Lallybroch from Edinburgh, after I...found Jamie again. *Home is where, when you have to go there, they have to take you in.*"

Ian raised a brow, looked from me to Jamie, and shook his head.

"Nay wonder ye're sae fond of her, Uncle. She must be a rare comfort to ye."

"Well," Jamie said, his eyes fixed on his work, "she keeps takin' me in—so I suppose she must be home."

THE WORK FINISHED, Ian and Rollo took the filled shot pouches back to the cabin, while Jamie stamped out the fire and I packed up the paraphernalia of bullet-making. It was growing late, and the air—already so fresh it tickled the lungs—acquired that extra edge of cool liveliness that caressed the skin as well, the breath of spring moving restless over the earth.

I stood for a moment, enjoying it. The work had been close, and hot, despite being done in the open, and the cold breeze that lifted the hair off my neck was delightful.

"Have ye got a penny, *a nighean?*" said Jamie, next to me.

"A what?"

"Well, any sort of money will do."

"I don't *think* so, but..." I rummaged in the pocket tied at my waist, which by this point in our preparations held nearly as large a collection of improbabilities as did Jamie's sporran. Among hanks of thread, twists of paper containing seeds or dried herbs, needles stuck through bits of leather, a small jar full of sutures, a woodpecker's black-and-white-spotted feather, a chunk of white chalk, and half a biscuit, which I had evidently been interrupted while eating, I did in fact discover a grubby half-shilling, covered in lint and biscuit crumbs.

"That do you?" I asked, wiping it off and handing it over.

"It will," he said, and held out something toward me. My hand closed automatically over what turned out to be the handle of a knife, and I nearly dropped it in surprise.

"Ye must always give money for a new blade," he explained, half smiling. "So it kens ye for its owner, and willna turn on ye."

"Its owner?" The sun was touching the edge of the Ridge, but there was still plenty of light, and I looked at my new acquisition. It was a slender blade, but sturdy, single-edged and beautifully honed; the cutting edge shone silver in the dying sun. The hilt was made from a deer's antler, smooth and warm in my hand—and had been carved with two small depressions, these just fitting my grip. Plainly it was my knife.

"Thank you," I said, admiring it. "But—"

"Ye'll feel safer if ye have it by you," he said, matter-of-fact. "Oh—just the one more thing. Give it here."

I handed it back, puzzled, and was startled to see him draw the blade lightly across the ball of his thumb. Blood welled up from the shallow cut, and he wiped it on his breeches and stuck his thumb in his mouth, handing me back the knife.

"Ye blood a blade, so it knows its purpose," he explained, taking the wounded digit out of his mouth.

The hilt of the knife was still warm in my hand, but a small chill went through me. With rare exceptions, Jamie wasn't given to purely romantic gestures. If he gave me a knife, he thought I'd need it. And not for digging up roots and hacking tree bark, either. Know its purpose, indeed.

"It fits my hand," I said, looking down and stroking the small groove that fit my thumb. "How did you know to make it so exactly?"

He laughed at that.

"I've had your hand round my cock often enough to know the measure of your grip, Sassenach," he assured me.

I snorted briefly in response to this, but turned the blade and pricked the end of my own thumb with the point. It was amazingly sharp; I scarcely felt it, but a bead of dark-red blood welled up at once. I put the knife into my belt, took his hand, and pressed my thumb to his.

"Blood of my blood," I said.

I didn't make romantic gestures, either.

10

FIRESHIP

New York
August 1776

I N FACT, WILLIAM'S news of the Americans' escape was received much better than he had expected. With the intoxicating feeling that they had the enemy cornered, Howe's army moved with remarkable speed. The admiral's fleet was still in Gravesend Bay; within a day, thousands of men were marched hastily to the shore and reembarked for the quick crossing to Manhattan; by sunset of the next day, armed companies began the attack upon New York—only to discover the trenches empty, the fortifications abandoned.

While something of a disappointment to William, who had hoped for a chance of direct and physical revenge, this development pleased General Howe inordinately. He moved, with his staff, into a large mansion called Beekman House and set about solidifying his hold upon the colony. There was a certain amount of chafing among senior officers in favor of running the Americans to ground—certainly William favored that notion—but General Howe was of the opinion that defeat and attrition would shred Washington's remaining forces, and the winter would finish them off.

"And meanwhile," said Lieutenant Anthony Fortnum, looking round the stifling attic to which the three most junior staff officers had been consigned, "we are an army of occupation. Which means, I think, that we are entitled to the pleasures of the post, are we not?"

"And what would those be?" William inquired, looking in vain for a spot in which to put the weathered portmanteau that presently contained most of his worldly goods.

"Well, women," Fortnum said consideringly. "Certainly women. And surely New York has fleshpots?"

"I didn't see any on the way in," Ralph Jocelyn said dubiously. "And I looked!"

"Not hard enough," Fortnum said firmly. "I feel sure there must be flesh-pots."

"There's beer," William suggested. "Decent public house called Fraunces Tavern, just off Water Street. I had a good pint there on the way in."

"Has to be something closer than that," Jocelyn objected. "I'm not walking miles in this heat!" Beekman House had a pleasant situation, with spacious grounds and clean air—but was a good way outside the city.

"Seek and ye shall find, my brothers." Fortnum twisted a side-curl into place and slung his coat over one shoulder. "Coming, Ellesmere?"

"No, not just now. I've letters to write. If you find any fleshpots, I shall expect a written report. In triplicate, mind."

Left momentarily to his own devices, he dropped his bag on the floor and took out the small sheaf of letters Captain Griswold had handed him.

There were five of them; three with his stepfather's smiling half-moon seal—Lord John wrote to him promptly on the fifteenth of every month, though at other times, as well—one from his uncle Hal, and he grinned at sight of that; Uncle Hal's missives were occasionally confusing, but invariably entertaining—and one in an unfamiliar but feminine-looking hand, with a plain seal.

Curious, he broke the seal and opened the letter to discover two closely written sheets from his cousin Dottie. His eyebrows went up at that; Dottie had never written to him before.

They stayed up as he perused the letter.

"I will be damned," he said aloud.

"Why?" asked Fortnum, who had come back to retrieve his hat. "Bad news from home?"

"What? Oh. No. No," he repeated, returning to the first page of the letter. "Just . . . interesting."

Folding up the letter, he put it inside his coat, safely away from Fortnum's interested gaze, and took up Uncle Hal's note, with its crested ducal seal. Fortnum's eyes widened at sight of that, but he said nothing.

William coughed and broke the seal. As usual, the note occupied less than a page and included neither salutation nor closing, Uncle Hal's opinion being that since the letter had a direction upon it, the intended recipient was obvious, the seal indicated plainly who had written it, and he did not waste his time in writing to fools.

> *Adam is posted to New York under Sir Henry Clinton. Minnie has given him some obnoxiously cumbersome Things for you. Dottie sends her Love, which takes up much less room.*
> *John says you are doing something for Captain Richardson. I know Richardson and I think you shouldn't.*
> *Give Colonel Spencer my regards, and don't play Cards with him.*

Uncle Hal, William reflected, could cram more information—cryptic as it often was—into fewer words than anyone he knew. He did wonder whether Colonel Spencer cheated at cards or was simply very good or very lucky. Uncle Hal had doubtless omitted purposely to say, because if it had been one of the latter alternatives, William would have been tempted to try his skill—dangerous as he knew it was to win consistently against a superior officer. Once or twice, though . . . No, Uncle Hal was a very good cardsman himself, and if he was warning William off, prudence suggested he take the warning. Perhaps Colonel Spencer was both honest and an indifferent player but a man to take offense—and revenge—if beaten too often.

Uncle Hal was a cunning old devil, William thought, not without admiration.

Which was what worried him, rather, about that second paragraph. *I know Richardson . . .* In this instance, he understood quite well why Uncle Hal had omitted the particulars; mail might be read by anyone, and a letter with the

Duke of Pardloe's crest might attract attention. Granted, the seal didn't seem to have been tampered with, but he'd seen his own father remove and replace seals with the greatest dexterity and a hot knife, and was under no illusions on that score.

That didn't stop him from wondering just *what* Uncle Hal knew about Captain Richardson and why he was suggesting that William stop his intelligencing—for evidently Papa had told Uncle Hal what he was doing.

Further food for thought—if Papa had told his brother what William was doing, then Uncle Hal would have told Papa what he knew about Captain Richardson, if there was anything to the captain's discredit. And if he had done that—

He put by Uncle Hal's note and ripped open the first of his father's letters. No, nothing about Richardson.... The second? Again no. In the third, a veiled reference to intelligencing, but only a wish for his safety and an oblique remark about his posture.

A tall man is always notable in company; the more so if his glance be direct and his dress neat.

William smiled at that. Westminster, where he'd gone to school, held its classes in one large room, this divided by a hanging curtain into the upper and lower classes, but there were boys of all ages being taught together, and William had quickly learned when—and how—to be either inconspicuous or outstanding, depending upon the immediate company.

Well, then. Whatever Uncle Hal knew about Richardson, it wasn't something that troubled Papa. Of course, he reminded himself, it needn't be anything discreditable. The Duke of Pardloe was fearless on his own behalf, but tended to excessive caution with regard to his family. Perhaps he only thought Richardson reckless; if that was the case, Papa would presumably trust to William's own good sense, and thus not mention it.

The attic was stifling; sweat was running down William's face and wilting his shirt. Fortnum had gone out again, leaving the end of his cot tilted up at an absurd angle over his protruding trunk. It did leave just enough floor space vacant as to allow William to stand up and walk to the door, though, and he made his escape into the outer air with a sense of relief. The air outside was hot and humid, but at least it was moving. He put his hat on his head and set off to find out just where his cousin Adam was billeted. *Obnoxiously cumbersome* sounded promising.

As he pressed through a crowd of farm wives headed for the market square, though, he felt the crackle of the letter in his coat, and remembered Adam's sister.

Dottie sends her love, which takes up much less room. Uncle Hal was cunning, William thought, but the cunningest of devils has the occasional blind spot.

———

OBNOXIOUSLY CUMBERSOME fulfilled its promise: a book, a bottle of excellent Spanish sherry, a quart of olives to accompany it, and three pairs of new silk stockings.

"I am awash in stockings," his cousin Adam assured William, when the latter tried to share this bounty. "Mother buys them by the gross and dispatches them by every carrier, I think. You're lucky she didn't think to send you fresh drawers; I get a pair in every diplomatic pouch, and if you don't think *that's* an awkward thing to explain to Sir Henry . . . Wouldn't say no to a glass of your sherry, though."

William was not entirely sure his cousin was joking about the drawers; Adam had a grave mien that served him well in relations with senior officers, and had also the Grey family trick of saying the most outrageous things with a perfectly straight face. William laughed, nonetheless, and called downstairs for a pair of glasses.

One of Adam's friends brought three, helpfully staying to assist with disposal of the sherry. Another friend appeared, apparently out of the woodwork—it was very good sherry—and produced a half bottle of porter from his chest to add to the festivities. With the inevitability of such gatherings, both bottles and friends multiplied, until every surface in Adam's room—admittedly a small one—was occupied by one or the other.

William had generously made free with his olives, as well as the sherry, and toward the bottom of the bottle raised a glass to his aunt for her generous gifts, not omitting to mention the silk stockings.

"Though I rather think your mother was not responsible for the book?" he said to Adam, lowering his empty glass with an explosion of breath.

Adam broke into a fit of the giggles, his usual gravity quite dissolved in a quart of rum punch.

"No," he said, "nor Papa, neither. That was my own contribution to the cause of cutlural, culshural, I mean, advanshment in the colonies."

"A signal service to the sensibilities of civilized man," William assured him gravely, showing off his own ability to hold his liquor and manage his tongue, no matter how many slippery esses might throw themselves in his way.

A general cry of "What book? What book? Let us see this famous book!" resulting, he was obliged to produce the prize of his collection of gifts—a copy of Mr. Harris's famous *List of Covent Garden Ladies,* this being a lavishly descriptive catalog of the charms, specialities, price, and availability of the best whores to be found in London.

Its appearance was greeted with cries of rapture, and following a brief struggle over possession of the volume, William rescued it before it should be torn to pieces, but allowed himself to be induced to read some of the passages aloud, his dramatic rendering being greeted by wolflike howls of enthusiasm and hails of olive pits.

Reading is of course dry work, and further refreshment was called for and consumed. He could not have said who first suggested that the party should constitute itself an expeditionary force for the purpose of compiling a similar list for New York. Whoever first bruited the suggestion, though, was roundly seconded and hailed in bumpers of rum punch—the bottles having all been drained by now.

And so it fell out that he found himself wandering in a spirituous haze through narrow streets whose darkness was punctuated by the pinpricks of candlelit windows and the occasional hanging lantern at a crossroad. No one appeared to have any direction in mind, and yet the whole body advanced insensibly as one, drawn by some subtle emanation.

"Like dogs following a bitch in heat," he observed, and was surprised to receive a buffet and shout of approbation from one of Adam's friends—he hadn't realized that he'd spoken aloud. And yet he had been correct, for eventually they came to an alley down which two or three lanterns hung, sheathed in red muslin so the light spilled in a bloody glow across the doorways—all welcomingly ajar. Whoops greeted the sight, and the body of would-be investigators advanced a-purpose, pausing only for a brief argument in the center of the street regarding the choice of establishment in which to begin their researches.

William himself took little part in the argument; the air was close, muggy, and fetid with the stench of cattle and sewage, and he was suddenly aware that one of the olives he had consumed had quite possibly been a wrong 'un. He was sweating heavily and unctuously, and his wet linen clung to him with a clasping insistence that terrified him with the thought that he might not be able to get his breeches down in time, should his inward disturbance move suddenly southward.

He forced a smile, and with a vague swing of the arm, indicated to Adam that he might proceed as he liked—William would venture a bit farther.

This he did, leaving the moil of riotous young officers behind him, and staggered past the last of the red lanterns. He was looking rather desperately for some semblance of seclusion in which to be sick, but finding nothing to his purpose, at length stumbled to a halt and vomited profusely in a doorway—whereupon, to his horror, the door swung open, revealing a highly indignant householder, who did not wait for explanations, apologies, or offers of recompense, but seized a cudgel of some kind from behind his door and, bellowing incomprehensible oaths in what might be German, chased William down the alleyway.

What with one thing and another, it was some time of wandering through pig yards, shacks, and ill-smelling wharves before he found his way back to the proper district, there to find his cousin Adam going up and down the street, banging on doors and hallooing loudly in search of him.

"Don't knock on that one!" he said in alarm, seeing Adam about to attack the door of the cudgel-wielding German. Adam swung about in relieved surprise.

"There you are! All right, old man?"

"Oh, yes. Fine." He felt somewhat pale and clammy, despite the sweltering heat of the summer night, but the acute inner distress had purged itself, and had the salutary side effect of sobering him in the process.

"Thought you'd been robbed or murdered in an alleyway. I'd never be able to look Uncle John in the face, was I to have to tell him I'd got you done in."

They were walking down the alley, back toward the red lanterns. All of the young men had disappeared into one or another of the establishments, though the sounds of revelry and banging from within suggested that their high spirits had not abated, but merely been relocated.

"Did you find yourself decently accommodated?" Adam asked. He jerked his chin in the direction from which William had come.

"Oh, fine. You?"

"Well, she wouldn't rate more nor a paragraph in Harris, but not bad for a sinkhole like New York," Adam said judiciously. His stock was hanging loose round his neck, and as they passed the faint glow of a window, William saw that one of the silver buttons of his cousin's coat was missing. "Swear I've seen a couple of these whores in camp, though."

"Sir Henry send you out to make a census, did he? Or do you just spend so much time with the camp followers you know them all by—"

He was interrupted by a change in the noise coming from one of the houses down the street. Shouting, but not of the genially drunken sort evident heretofore. This was ugly shouting, a male voice in a rage and the shrieks of a woman.

The cousins exchanged glances, then started as one toward the racket.

This had increased as they hurried toward its source, and as they came even with the farthest house, a number of half-dressed soldiers spilled out into the alleyway, followed by a burly lieutenant to whom William had been introduced during the party in Adam's room, but whose name he did not recall, dragging a half-naked whore by one arm.

The lieutenant had lost both coat and wig; his dark hair was polled close and grew low on his brow, which, together with his thick-shouldered build, gave him the look of a bull about to charge. In fact, he did, turning and ramming a shoulder into the woman he'd dragged out, slamming her into the wall of the house. He was roaring drunk, and bellowing incoherent profanities.

"Fireship."

William didn't see who'd spoken the word, but it was taken up in excited murmurs, and something ugly ran through the men in the alley.

"Fireship! She's a fireship!"

Several women had gathered in the doorway. The light behind them was too dim to show their faces, but they were clearly frightened, huddling together. One called out, tentative, stretching out an arm, but the others pulled her back. The black-haired lieutenant took no notice; he was battering the whore, punching her repeatedly in the stomach and breasts.

"Hoy, fellow!"

William started forward, shouting, but several hands grasped his arms, preventing him.

"Fireship!" The men were beginning to chant it, with each blow of the lieutenant's fists.

A fireship was a poxed whore, and as the lieutenant left off his bashing and hauled the woman under the light of the red lantern, William could see that indeed she was; the rash across her face was plain.

"Rodham! Rodham!" Adam was shouting the lieutenant's name, trying to break through the crush of men, but they moved together, pushing him back, and the chant of "Fireship!" got louder.

Shrieks came from the whores in the doorway, and they crammed back as Rodham flung the woman down on the doorstep. William lunged and succeeded in breaking through the press, but before he could reach the lieutenant, Rodham had seized the lantern and, dashing it against the front of the house, flung blazing oil over the whore.

He fell back then, panting, eyes wide and staring as though in disbelief, as the woman leapt to her feet, arms windmilling in panic as the flames caught her hair, her gauzy shift. Within seconds, she was wrapped in fire, screaming in a high, thin voice that cut through the confusion of noise in the street and ran straight into William's brain.

The men fell back as she staggered toward them, lurching, hands reaching—whether in a futile plea for help or in the desire to immolate them as well, he couldn't tell. He stood rooted to the spot, his body clenched with the need to do something, the impossibility of doing anything, the overwhelming sense of disaster. An insistent pain in his arm made him glance mechanically aside, to find Adam beside him, fingers digging hard into the muscle of his forearm.

"Let's go," Adam whispered, his face white and sweating. "For God's sake, let's go!"

The door of the whorehouse had slammed shut. The burning woman fell against it, hands pressed against the wood. The appetizing smell of roasting meat filled the close, hot confines of the alley, and William felt his gorge rise once more.

"God curse you! May your goddamned pricks all rot and fall off!" The scream came from a window above; William's head jerked up and he saw a woman shaking a fist at the men below. There was a rumble from the men, and one shouted something foul in reply; another bent and seized a cobblestone and rising, flung it hard. It bounced against the front of the house below the window, and fell back, striking one of the soldiers, who cursed and shoved the man who'd thrown it.

The burning woman had sunk down by the door; the flames had made a charred spot on it. She was still making a faint keening noise, but had ceased to move.

Suddenly William lost his mind and, grabbing the man who had thrown the stone, took him by the neck and cracked his head against the doorpost of the house. The man stiffened and slumped, his knees giving way, and sat in the street, moaning.

"Get out!" William bellowed. "All of you! Leave!" Fists clenched, he turned on the black-haired lieutenant, who, his rage all vanished, was standing motionless, staring at the woman on the stoop. Her skirts had vanished; a pair of blackened legs twitched feebly in the shadow.

William reached the man in one stride and took him by the front of his shirt, yanking him round.

"Go," he said, in a dangerous voice. "Leave. Now!"

He released the man, who blinked, swallowed, and, turning, walked like an automaton into the dark.

Panting, William turned on the rest of them, but they had lost the thirst for violence as quickly as it had come upon them. There were a few glances toward the woman—she had gone still now—and shufflings, incoherent murmurs. None of them would meet another's eye.

He was vaguely conscious of Adam by his side, trembling with shock but solidly beside him. He put a hand on his smaller cousin's shoulder and held on, trembling himself, as the men melted away. The man sitting in the street got slowly to his hands and feet, half-rose, and lurched after his companions, caroming off the fronts of houses as he made his way into the dark.

The alley fell quiet. The fire had gone out. The other red lanterns in the street had been extinguished. He felt as though he had grown to the spot, would stand in this hateful place forever—but Adam moved a little, and his hand fell from his cousin's shoulder and he found that his feet would carry him.

They turned away, and walked in silence back through the dark streets. They came by a sentry point, where soldiers on guard were standing round a fire, keeping casual watch. They were to keep order in the occupied city, the guards. The sentries glanced at them, but did not stop them.

In the light of the fire, he saw the tracks of wetness on Adam's face and realized that his cousin was crying.

So was he.

11

TRANSVERSE LIE

Fraser's Ridge
March 1777

THE WORLD WAS DRIPPING. Freshets leapt down the mountain, grass and leaves were wet with dew, and the shingles steamed in the morning sun. Our preparations were made and the passes were clear. There remained only one more thing to do before we could leave.

"Today, d'ye think?" Jamie asked hopefully. He was not a man made for peaceful contemplation; once a course of action was decided upon, he wanted to be acting. Babies, unfortunately, are completely indifferent to both convenience and impatience.

"Maybe," I said, trying to keep a grip on my own patience. "Maybe not."

"I saw her last week, and she looked then as though she was goin' to explode any minute, Auntie," Ian remarked, handing Rollo the last bite of his muffin. "Ken those mushrooms? The big round ones? Ye touch one and *poof!*" He flicked his fingers, scattering muffin crumbs. "Like that."

"She's only having the one, no?" Jamie asked me, frowning.

"I told you—six times so far—I think so. I bloody *hope* so," I added, repressing an urge to cross myself. "But you can't always tell."

"Twins run in families," Ian put in helpfully.

Jamie did cross himself.

"I've heard only one heartbeat," I said, keeping a grip on my temper, "and I've been listening for months."

"Can ye not count the bits that stick out?" Ian inquired. "If it seemed to have six legs, I mean . . ."

"Easier said than done." I could, of course, make out the general aspect of the child—a head was reasonably easy to feel, and so were buttocks; arms and legs a bit more problematical. That was what was disturbing me at the moment.

I'd been checking Lizzie once a week for the past month—and had been going up to her cabin every other day for the last week, though it was a long walk. The child—and I did *think* there was only one—seemed very large; the fundus of the uterus was a good bit higher than I thought it should be. And while babies frequently changed position in the weeks prior to birth, this one had remained in a transverse lie—wedged sideways—for a worryingly long time.

The fact was that without a hospital, operating facilities, or anesthesia, my ability to deal with an unorthodox delivery was severely limited. *Sans* surgical intervention, with a transverse lie, a midwife had four alternatives: let the woman die after days of agonizing labor; let the woman die after doing a cesarean section without benefit of anesthesia or asepsis—but possibly save the baby; possibly save the mother by killing the child in the womb and then removing it in bits (Daniel Rawlings had had several pages in his book— illustrated—describing this procedure) or attempt an internal inversion, trying to turn the baby into a position in which it might be delivered.

While superficially the most attractive option, that last one could easily be as dangerous as the others, resulting in the deaths of mother *and* child.

I'd tried an external version the week before, and managed—with difficulty—to induce the child to turn head-down. Two days later, it had turned right back, evidently liking its supine position. It might turn again by itself before labor started—and it might not.

Experience being what it was, I normally managed to distinguish between intelligent planning for contingencies and useless worrying over things that might not happen, thus allowing myself to sleep at night. I'd lain awake into the small hours every night for the last week, though, envisioning the possibility that the child wouldn't turn in time, and running through that short, grim list of alternatives in futile search for one more choice.

If I had ether . . . but what I'd had had gone when the house burned.

Kill Lizzie, in order to save the new child? No. If it came to that, better to kill the child *in utero,* and leave Rodney with a mother, Jo and Kezzie with their wife. But the thought of crushing the skull of a full-term child, healthy, ready to be born . . . or decapitating it with a loop of sharp wire—

"Are ye no hungry this morning, Auntie?"

"Er . . . no. Thank you, Ian."

"Ye look a bit pale, Sassenach. Are ye sickening for something?"

"No!" I got up hastily before they could ask any more questions—there was absolutely no point in anyone but me being terrorized by what I was thinking—and went out to fetch a bucket of water from the well.

Amy was outside; she had started a fire going under the big laundry kettle, and was chivying Aidan and Orrie, who were scrambling round to fetch wood, pausing periodically to throw mud at each other.

"Are ye wanting water, *a bhana-mhaighstir*?" she asked, seeing the bucket in my hand. "Aidan will fetch it down for ye."

"No, that's all right," I assured her. "I wanted a bit of air. It's so nice out in the mornings now." It was; still chilly until the sun got high, but fresh, and dizzy with the scents of grass, resin-fat buds, and early catkins.

I took my bucket up to the well, filled it, and made my way down the path again, slowly, looking at things as you do when you know you might not see them again for a long time. If ever.

Things had changed drastically on the Ridge already, with the coming of violence, the disruptions of the war, the destruction of the Big House. They'd change a great deal more, with Jamie and me both gone.

Who would be the natural leader? Hiram Crombie was the *de facto* head of the Presbyterian fisher-folk who had come from Thurso—but he was a rigid, humorless man, much more likely to cause friction with the rest of the community than to maintain order and foster cooperation.

Bobby? After considerable thought, Jamie had appointed him factor, with the responsibility of overseeing our property—or what was left of it. But aside from his natural capabilities or lack thereof, Bobby was a young man. He— along with many of the other men on the Ridge—could so easily be swept up in the coming storm, taken away and obliged to serve in one of the militias. Not the Crown's forces, though; he had been a British soldier, stationed in Boston seven years before, where he and several of his fellows had been menaced by a mob of several hundred irate Bostonians. In fear for their lives, the soldiers had loaded their muskets and leveled them at the crowd. Stones and clubs were thrown, shots were fired—by whom, no one could establish; I had never asked Bobby—and men had died.

Bobby's life had been spared at the subsequent trial, but he bore a brand on his cheek—"M," for "Murder." I had no idea of his politics—he never spoke of such things—but he would never fight with the British army again.

I pushed open the door to the cabin, my equanimity somewhat restored.

Jamie and Ian were now arguing as to whether the new child would be a sister or brother to little Rodney or a half sibling.

"Well, no way of telling, is there?" Ian said. "Nobody kens whether Jo or Kezzie fathered wee Rodney, and the same for this bairn. If Jo is Rodney's father, and Kezzie this one's—"

"It doesn't really matter," I interrupted, pouring water from the bucket into the cauldron. "Jo and Kezzie are identical twins. That means their ... er ... their sperm is identical, as well." That was oversimplifying matters, but it was much too early in the day to try to explain reproductive meiosis and recombinant DNA. "If the mother is the same—and she is—and the father is genetically the same—and they are—any children born would be full sisters or brothers to each other."

"Their spunk's the same, too?" Ian demanded, incredulous. "How can ye tell? Did ye *look*?" he added, giving me a look of horrified curiosity.

"I did not," I said severely. "I didn't have to. I know these things."

"Oh, aye," he said, nodding with respect. "Of course ye would. I forget sometimes what ye are, Auntie Claire."

I wasn't sure what he meant by that, exactly, but it didn't seem necessary either to inquire or to explain that my knowledge of the Beardsleys' intimate processes was academic, rather than supernatural.

"But it *is* Kezzie that's this one's father, no?" Jamie put in, frowning. "I sent Jo away; it's Kezzie she's been living with this past year."

Ian gave him a pitying look.

"Ye think he went? Jo?"

"I've not seen him," Jamie said, but the thick red brows drew together.

"Well, ye wouldn't," Ian conceded. "They'll ha' been gey careful about it, not wantin' to cross ye. Ye never do see more than one of them—at a time," he added, offhanded.

We both stared at him. He looked up from the chunk of bacon in his hand and raised his brows.

"I ken these things, aye?" he said blandly.

AFTER SUPPER, the household shifted and settled for the night. All the Higginses retired to the back bedroom, where they shared the single bedstead.

Obsessively, I opened my midwifery bundle and laid out the kit, checking everything over once more. Scissors, white thread for the cord. Clean cloths, rinsed many times to remove all trace of lye soap, scalded and dried. A large square of waxed canvas, to waterproof the mattress. A small bottle of alcohol, diluted fifty percent with sterile water. A small bag containing several twists of washed—but not boiled—wool. A rolled-up sheet of parchment, to serve in lieu of my stethoscope, which had perished in the fire. A knife. And a length of thin wire, sharpened at one end, coiled up like a snake.

I hadn't eaten much at dinner—or all day—but had a constant sense of rising bile at the back of my throat. I swallowed and wrapped the kit up again, tying the twine firmly round it.

I felt Jamie's eyes on me and looked up. He said nothing, but smiled a little, warmth in his eyes, and I felt a momentary easing—then a fresh clenching, as I wondered what he would think, if worst came to worst, and I had to—but he'd seen that twist of fear in my face. With his eyes still on mine, he quietly took his rosary from his sporran, and began silently to tell the beads, the worn wood sliding slowly through his fingers.

TWO NIGHTS LATER, I came instantly awake at the sound of feet on the path outside and was on my own feet, pulling on my clothes, before Jo's knock sounded on the door. Jamie let him in; I heard them murmuring together as I burrowed under the settle for my kit. Jo sounded excited, a little worried—but not panicked. That was good; if Lizzie had been frightened or in serious trouble, he would have sensed it at once—the twins were nearly as sensitive to her moods and welfare as they were to each other's.

"Shall I come?" Jamie whispered, looming up beside me.

"No," I whispered back, touching him for strength. "Go back to sleep. I'll send, if I need you."

He was tousled from sleep, the embers of the fire making shadows in his hair, but his eyes were alert. He nodded and kissed my forehead, but instead of stepping back, he laid his hand on my head and whispered, "O blessed Michael of the Red Domain..." in Gaelic, then touched my cheek in farewell.

"I'll see ye in the morning then, Sassenach," he said, and pushed me gently toward the door.

To my surprise, it was snowing outside. The sky was gray and full of light and the air alive with huge, whirling flakes that brushed my face, melting instantly on my skin. It was a spring storm; I could see the flakes settle briefly on the grass stems, then vanish. There would likely be no trace of snow by morning, but the night was filled with its mystery. I turned to look back, but could not see the cabin behind us—only the shapes of trees half shrouded, uncertain in the pearl-gray light. The path before us looked likewise unreal, the trace disappearing into strange trees and unknown shadows.

I felt weirdly disembodied, caught between past and future, nothing visible save the whirling white silence that surrounded me. And yet I felt calmer than I had in many days. I felt the weight of Jamie's hand on my head, with its whispered blessing. *O blessed Michael of the Red Domain...*

It was the blessing given to a warrior going out to battle. I had given it to him, more than once. He'd never done such a thing before, and I had no idea what had made him do it now—but the words glowed in my heart, a small shield against the dangers ahead.

The snow covered the ground now in a thin blanket that hid dark earth and sprouting growth. Jo's feet left crisp black prints that I followed upward, the needles of fir and balsam brushing cold and fragrant against my skirt, as I listened to a vibrant silence that rang like a bell.

If ever there were a night when angels walked, I prayed it might be this one.

IT WAS NEARLY an hour's walk to the Beardsley cabin, in daylight and good weather. Fear hastened my footsteps, though, and Jo—I thought it was Jo, by his voice—was hard-pressed to keep up with me.

"How long has she been at it?" I asked. You could never tell, but Lizzie's first labor had been fast; she'd delivered little Rodney quite alone and without incident. I didn't think we were going to be that lucky tonight, though my mind couldn't help hopefully envisioning an arrival at the cabin to find Lizzie already holding the new baby, safely popped out without difficulty.

"Not long," he panted. "Her waters came all of a sudden, when we were all abed, and she said I best come fetch you at once."

I tried not to notice that "all abed"—after all, he and/or Kezzie might have slept on the floor—but the Beardsley *ménage* was the literal personification of double entendre; nobody who knew the truth could think of them without thinking of...

I didn't bother asking how long he and Kezzie had both been living at the cabin; from what Ian had said, they'd likely both been there all the time. Given the normal conditions of life in the backcountry, no one would have blinked at the notion of a man and his wife living with his brother. And so far as the general population of the Ridge was aware, Lizzie was married to Kezzie. She was. She was also married to Jo, as the result of a set of machinations that still caused me to marvel, but the Bearsdley household kept that fact quiet, on Jamie's orders.

"Her pap'll be there," Jo said, breath pluming white as he pulled alongside me where the trail opened out. "And Auntie Monika. Kezzie went to fetch 'em."

"You left Lizzie *alone*?"

His shoulders hunched defensively, uncomfortable.

"She said to," he said simply.

I didn't bother replying, but hastened my step, until a stitch in my side made me slow a little. If Lizzie hadn't already given birth and hemorrhaged or had some other disaster while alone, it might be a help to have "Auntie Monika"—Mr. Wemyss's second wife—to hand. Monika Berrisch Wemyss was a German lady, of limited and eccentric English but boundless courage and common sense.

Mr. Wemyss had his share of courage, too, though it was a quiet sort. He was waiting for us on the porch, with Kezzie, and it was clear that Mr. Wemyss was supporting his son-in-law, rather than the reverse. Kezzie was openly wringing his hands and jigging from foot to foot, while Mr. Wemyss's slight figure bent consolingly toward him, a hand on his arm. I caught low murmurs, and then they saw us and turned toward us, sudden hope in the straightening of their bodies.

A long, low howl came from the cabin, and all the men stiffened as though it had been a wolf springing out of the dark at them.

"Well, she sounds all right," I said mildly, and all of them exhaled at once, audibly. I wanted to laugh, but thought better not, and pushed open the door.

"Ugh," said Lizzie, looking up from the bed. "Oh, it's you, ma'am. Thank the Lord!"

"*Gott bedanket*, aye," agreed Auntie Monika, tranquilly. She was on her hands and knees, sponging the floor with a wad of cloth. "Not so long now, I hope."

"I hope not, too," said Lizzie, grimacing. "GAAAAARRRRRGH!" Her face convulsed into a rictus and went bright red, and her swollen body arched backward. She looked more like someone in the grip of tetanus than an expectant mother, but luckily the spasm was short-lived, and she collaped into a limp heap, panting.

"It wasna like this, last time," she complained, opening one eye as I palpated her abdomen.

"It's never the same," I said absently. One quick glance had made my heart leap; the child was no longer sideways. On the other hand . . . it wasn't neatly head-down, either. It wasn't moving—babies generally didn't, during labor—and while I thought I had located the head up under Lizzie's ribs, I wasn't at all sure of the disposition of the rest.

"Let me just have a look here . . ." She was naked, wrapped in a quilt. Her wet shift was hanging over the back of a chair, steaming in front of the fire. The bed wasn't soaked, though, and I deduced that she'd felt the rupturing of her membranes and made it to a standing position before her water broke.

I'd been afraid to look, and let my breath out in audible relief. The chief fear with a breech presentation was that part of the umbilical cord would prolapse when the membranes ruptured, the loop then being squeezed between the pelvis and some part of the fetus. All clear, though, and a quick feel indicated that the cervix was very nearly effaced.

The only thing to do now was to wait and see what came out first. I undid my bundle, and—shoving the coil of sharpened wire hastily under a packet of cloths—spread out the waxed canvas, hoicking Lizzie onto it with Auntie Monika's help.

Monika blinked and glanced at the trundle where little Rodney was snoring when Lizzie let out another of those unearthly howls. She looked to me for reassurance that nothing was wrong, then took hold of Lizzie's hands, murmuring softly to her in German while she grunted and wheezed.

The door creaked gently, and I looked round to see one of the Beardsleys peering in, his face showing a mixture of fear and hope.

"Is it here?" he whispered hoarsely.

"NO!" bellowed Lizzie, sitting bolt upright. "Get your neb out of my sight, or I'll twist your wee ballocks off! All four o' them!"

The door promptly closed, and Lizzie subsided, puffing.

"I hate them," she said through clenched teeth. "I want them to die!"

"Mmm-hmm," I said sympathetically. "Well, I'm sure they're suffering, at least."

"Good." She went from fury to pathos in a split second, tears welling in her eyes. "Am I going to die?"

"No," I said, as reassuringly as possible.

"EEEAAAAARRRRRRGGGGG!"

"Großer Gott," Auntie Monika said, crossing herself. *"Ist das gut?"*

"Ja," I said, still reassuring. "I don't suppose there are any scissors . . . ?"

"Oh, *ja,*" she replied, reaching for her bag. She produced a tiny pair of very worn but once-gilded embroidery scissors. "Dese you need?"

"Danke."

"BLOOOOOORRRRRGGGG!"

Monika and I both looked at Lizzie.

"Don't overdo it," I said. "They're frightened, but they aren't idiots. Besides, you'll scare your father. *And* Rodney," I added, with a glance at the little heap of bedclothes in the trundle bed.

She subsided, panting, but managed a nod and the ghost of a smile.

Matters proceeded fairly rapidly thereafter; she *was* fast. I checked her pulse, then her cervix, and felt my own heart rate double as I touched what was plainly a tiny foot, on its way out. Could I get the other one?

I glanced at Monika, with an eye to size and strength. She was tough as whipcord, I knew, but not that large. Lizzie, on the other hand, was the size of—well, Ian had not been exaggerating when he thought it might be twins.

The creeping thought that it still *might* be twins made the hair on the back of my neck stand up, despite the humid warmth of the cabin.

No, I said firmly to myself. *It isn't; you know it isn't. One is going to be bad enough.*

"We're going to need one of the men, to help hold her shoulders up," I said to Monika. "Get one of the twins, will you?"

"Both," Lizzie gasped, as Monika turned toward the door.

"One will be—"

"Both! Nnnnnngggggg..."

"Both," I said to Monika, who nodded in a matter-of-fact manner.

The twins came in on a rush of cold air, their faces identical ruddy masks of alarm and excitement. Without my saying anything to them, they came at once to Lizzie, like a pair of iron filings to a magnet. She had struggled into a sitting position, and one of them knelt behind her, his hands gently kneading her shoulders as they relaxed from the last spasm. His brother sat beside her, a supportive arm round what used to be her waist, his other hand smoothing back the sweat-soaked hair from her brow.

I tried to arrange the quilt round her, over her protruding belly, but she pushed it away, hot and fretful. The cabin was filled with moist heat, from the steaming cauldron and the sweat of effort. Well, presumably the twins were somewhat more familiar with her anatomy than I was, I reflected, and handed the wadded quilt to Auntie Monika. Modesty had no place in childbirth.

I knelt in front of her, scissors in hand, and snipped the episiotomy quickly, feeling a tiny spray of warm blood across my hand. I seldom needed to do one for a routine birth, but for this, I was going to need room to maneuver. I pressed one of my clean cloths to the cut, but the amount of bleeding was negligible, and the insides of her thighs were streaked with bloody show in any case.

It *was* a foot; I could see the toes, long ones, like a frog's, and glanced automatically at Lizzie's bare feet, planted solidly on the floor to either side of me. No, hers were short and compact; it must be the twins' influence.

The humid, swampish scent of birth waters, sweat, and blood rose like fog from Lizzie's body, and I felt my own sweat running down my sides. I groped upward, hooked a finger round the heel, and brought the foot down, feeling the life in the child move in its flesh, though the baby itself was not moving, helpless in the grip of birth.

The other one, I needed the other one. Feeling urgently through the belly wall between one contraction and the next, I slid my other hand up the emergent leg, found the tiny curve of the buttock. Switched hands hastily and, with my eyes closed, found the curve of the flexed thigh. Bloody hell, it seemed to have its knee tucked up under its chin... felt the yielding stiffness of tiny, cartilaginous bones, solid in the squish of fluid, the stretch of muscle

. . . got a finger, two fingers, circling the other ankle, and—snarling, "Brace her! Hold her!" as Lizzie's back arched and her bottom scooted toward me—brought the second foot down.

I sat back, eyes open and breathing hard, though it hadn't been a physical strain. The little froggy feet twitched once, then drooped, as the legs came into view with the next push.

"Once more, sweetheart," I whispered, a hand on Lizzie's straining thigh. "Give us one more like that."

A growl from the depths of the earth as Lizzie reached that point where a woman no longer cares whether she lives, dies, or splits apart, and the child's lower body slid slowly into view, the umbilicus pulsing like a thick purple worm looped across the belly. My eyes were fixed on that, thinking, *Thank God, thank God,* when I became aware of Auntie Monika, peering intently over my shoulder.

"*Sind das* balls?" she said, puzzled, pointing at the child's genitals.

I hadn't spared time to look, concerned as I was with the cord, but I glanced down and smiled.

"No. *Es ist ein Mädchen,*" I said. The baby's sex was edematous; it did look much like a little boy's equipment, the clitoris protruding from swollen labia, but wasn't.

"What? What is it?" One of the Beardsleys was asking, leaning down to look.

"You haff a leedle girl," Auntie Monika told him, beaming up.

"A girl?" the other Beardsley gasped. "Lizzie, we have a daughter!"

"Will you fucking *shut up*?!?" Lizzie snarled. "NNNNNNNGGGGG!"

At this point, Rodney woke up and sat bolt upright, openmouthed and wide-eyed. Auntie Monika was on her feet at once, scooping him out of his bed before he could start to scream.

Rodney's sister was inching reluctantly into the world, shoved by each contraction. I was counting in my head, *One hippopotamus, two hippopotamus* . . . From the appearance of the umbilicus to successful delivery of the mouth and the first breath, we could afford no more than four minutes before brain damage from lack of oxygen began to occur. But I couldn't pull and risk damage to the neck and head.

"Push, sweetheart," I said, bracing my hands on both Lizzie's knees, my voice calm. "Hard, now."

Thirty-four hippopotamus, thirty-five . . .

All we needed now was for the chin to hang up on the pelvic bone. When the contraction eased, I slid my fingers hastily up onto the child's face, and got two fingers over the upper maxilla. I felt the next contraction coming, and gritted my teeth as the force of it crushed my hand between the bones of the pelvis and the baby's skull, but didn't pull back, fearful of losing my traction.

Sixty-two hippopotamus . . .

Relaxation, and I drew down, slowly, slowly, pulling the child's head forward, easing the chin past the rim of the pelvis . . .

Eighty-nine hippopotamus, ninety hippopotamus . . .

The child was hanging from Lizzie's body, bloody-blue and shining in the firelight, swaying in the shadow of her thighs like the clapper of a bell—or a body from a gibbet, and I pushed that thought away . . .

"Should not we take...?" Auntie Monika whispered to me, Rodney clutched to her breast.

One hundred.

"No," I said. "Don't touch it—her. Not yet." Gravity was slowly helping the delivery. Pulling would injure the neck, and if the head were to stick...

One hundred ten hippo—that was a lot of hippopotami, I thought, abstractedly envisaging herds of them marching down to the hollow, there they will wallow, in mud, glooooorious...

"Now," I said, poised to swab the mouth and nose as they emerged—but Lizzie hadn't waited for prompting, and with a long deep sigh and an audible *pop!,* the head delivered all at once, and the baby fell into my hands like a ripe fruit.

I DIPPED A LITTLE more water from the steaming cauldron into the washing bowl and added cold water from the bucket. The warmth of it stung my hands; the skin between my knuckles was cracked from the long winter and the constant use of dilute alcohol for sterilization. I'd just finished stitching Lizzie up and cleaning her, and the blood floated away from my hands, dark swirls in the water.

Behind me, Lizzie was tucked up neatly in bed, clad in one of the twins' shirts, her own shift being not yet dried. She was laughing with the euphoria of birth and survival, the twins on either side of her, fussing over her, murmuring admiration and relief, one tucking back her loose, damp fair hair, the other softly kissing her neck.

"Are you fevered, my lover?" one asked, a tinge of concern in his voice. That made me turn round to look; Lizzie suffered from malaria, and while she hadn't had an attack in some time, perhaps the stress of birth...

"No," she said, and kissed Jo or Kezzie on the forehead. "I'm only flushed from bein' happy." Kezzie or Jo beamed at her in adoration, while his brother took up the neck-kissing duties on the other side.

Auntie Monika coughed. She'd wiped down the baby with a damp cloth and some wisps of the wool I'd brought—soft and oily with lanolin—and had it now swaddled in a blanket. Rodney had got bored with the proceedings long since and gone to sleep on the floor by the wood-basket, a thumb in his mouth.

"Your *Vater,* Lizzie," she said, a slight hint of reproof in her voice. "He vill cold begetting. *Und die Kleine* he vant see, *mit* you, but maybe not so much *mit den beiden*..." She managed to incline her head toward the bed, while simultaneously modestly averting her eyes from the frolicsome trio on it. Mr. Wemyss and his sons-in-law had had a gingerly reconciliation after the birth of Rodney, but best not to press things.

Her words galvanized the twins, who hopped to their feet, one stooping to scoop up Rodney, whom he handled with casual affection, the other rushing for the door to retrieve Mr. Wemyss, forgotten on the porch in the excitement.

While slightly blue round the edges, relief made his thin face glow as though lit from within. He smiled with heartfelt joy at Monika, sparing a brief glance and a ginger pat for the swaddled bundle—but his attention was all for Lizzie, and hers for him.

"Your hands are frozen, Da," she said, giggling a little, but tightening her grip as he made to pull away. "No, stay; I'm warm enough. Come sit by me and say good e'en to your wee granddaughter." Her voice rang with a shy pride, as she reached out a hand to Auntie Monika.

Monika set the baby gently in Lizzie's arms, and stood with a hand on Mr. Wemyss's shoulder, her own weathered face soft with something much deeper than affection. Not for the first time, I was surprised—and vaguely abashed that I should be surprised—by the depth of her love for the frail, quiet little man.

"Oh," Mr. Wemyss said softly. His finger touched the baby's cheek; I could hear her making small smacking noises. She'd been shocked by the trauma of birth and not interested in the breast at first, but plainly was beginning to change her mind.

"She'll be hungry." A rustle of bedclothes as Lizzie took up the baby and put her to the breast with practiced hands.

"What will ye call her, *a leannan?*" Mr. Wemyss asked.

"I hadna really thought of a girl's name," Lizzie answered. "She was so big, I thought sure she was a—ow!" She laughed, a low, sweet sound. "I'd forgot how greedy a newborn wean is. Ooh! There, *a chuisle,* aye, that's better..."

I reached for the sack of wool, to rub my own raw hands with one of the soft, oily wisps, and happened to see the twins, standing back out of the way, side by side, their eyes fixed on Lizzie and their daughter, and each wearing a look that echoed Auntie Monika's. Not taking his eyes away, the Beardsley holding little Rodney bent his head and kissed the top of the little boy's round head.

So much love in one small place. I turned away, my own eyes misty. Did it matter, really, how unorthodox the marriage at the center of this odd family was? Well, it would to Hiram Crombie, I reflected. The leader of the rock-ribbed Presbyterian immigrants from Thurso, he'd want Lizzie, Jo, and Kezzie stoned, at the least—together with the sinful fruit of their loins.

No chance of that happening, so long as Jamie was on the Ridge—but with him gone? I slowly cleaned blood from under my nails, hoping that Ian was right about the Beardsleys' capacity for discretion—and deception.

Distracted by these musings, I hadn't noticed Auntie Monika, who had come quietly up beside me.

"*Danke,*" she said softly, laying a gnarled hand on my arm.

"*Gern geschehen.*" I put my hand over hers and squeezed gently. "You were a great help—thank you."

She still smiled, but a line of worry bisected her forehead.

"Not so much. But I am afraid, *ja?*" She glanced over her shoulder at the bed, then back at me. "What happens, next time, you are not *hier?* Dey don't stop, you know," she added, discreetly making a circle of thumb and forefinger and running the middle finger of the other hand into it in a most indiscreet illustration of exactly what she meant.

I converted a laugh hastily into a coughing fit, which fortunately went ignored by the relevant parties, though Mr. Wemyss glanced over his shoulder in mild concern.

"You'll be here," I told her, recovering. She looked horrified.

"Me? *Nein*," she said, shaking her head. "*Das reicht nicht.* Me—" She poked herself in her meager chest, seeing that I hadn't understood. "I . . . am not enough."

I took a deep breath, knowing that she was right. And yet . . .

"You'll have to be," I said, very softly.

She blinked once, her large, wise brown eyes fixed on mine. Then slowly nodded, accepting.

"*Mein Gott, hilf mir,*" she said.

JAMIE HADN'T BEEN ABLE to go back to sleep. He had trouble sleeping these days, in any case, and often lay awake late, watching the fading glow of embers in the hearth and turning things over in his mind, or seeking wisdom in the shadows of the rafters overhead. If he did fall asleep easily, he often came awake later, sudden and sweating. He knew what caused that, though, and what to do about it.

Most of his strategies for reaching slumber involved Claire—talking to her, making love to her—or only looking at her while she slept, finding solace in the solid long curve of her collarbone, or the heartbreaking shape of her closed eyelids, letting sleep steal upon him from her peaceful warmth.

But Claire, of course, was gone.

Half an hour of saying the rosary convinced him that he had done as much in that direction as was necessary or desirable for the sake of Lizzie and her impending child. Saying the rosary for penance—aye, he saw the point of that, particularly if you had to say it on your knees. Or to quiet one's mind, fortify the soul, or seek the insight of meditation on sacred topics, aye, that, too. But not for petition. If he were God, or even the Blessed Virgin, who was renowned for patience, he thought he would find it tedious to listen to more than a decade or so of someone saying please about something over and over, and surely there was no point to boring a person whose aid you sought?

Now, the Gaelic prayers seemed much more useful to the purpose, being as they were concentrated upon a specific request or blessing, and more pleasing both in rhythm and variety. If you asked him, not that anyone was likely to.

> *Moire gheal is Bhride;*
> *Mar a rug Anna Moire,*
> *Mar a rug Moire Criosda,*
> *Mar a rug Eile Eoin Baistidh*
> *Gun mhar-bhith dha dhi,*
> *Cuidich i na 'h asaid,*
> *Cuidich i a Bhride!*

Mar a gheineadh Criosd am Moire
Comhliont air gach laimh,
Cobhair mise, mhoime,
An gein a thoir bho 'n chnaimh;
'S mar a chomhn thu Oigh an t-solais,
Gun or, gun odh, gun ni,
Comhn i 's mor a th' othrais,
Comhn i a Bhride!

he murmured as he climbed.

Mary fair and Bride;
As Anna bore Mary,
As Mary bore Christ,
As Eile bore John the Baptist
Without flaw in him,
Aid thou her in her unbearing,
Aid her, O Bride!

As Christ was conceived of Mary
Full perfect on every hand,
Assist thou me, foster mother,
The conception to bring from the bone;
And as thou didst aid the Virgin of joy,
Without gold, without corn, without kine,
Aid thou her, great is her sickness,
Aid her, O Bride!

He'd left the cabin, unable to bear its smothering confines, and wandered in a contemplative fashion through the Ridge in the falling snow, ticking through mental lists. But the fact was that all his preparation was done, bar the packing of the horses and mules, and without really thinking about it, he found that he was making his way up the trail toward the Beardsley place. The snow had ceased to fall now, but the sky stretched gray and gentle overhead, and cold white lay calm upon the trees and stilled the rush of wind.

Sanctuary, he thought. It wasn't, of course—there was no safe place in time of war—but the feel of the mountain night reminded him of the feel of churches: a great peace, waiting.

Notre Dame in Paris . . . St. Giles' in Edinburgh. Tiny stone churches in the Highlands, where he'd sometimes gone in his years of hiding, when he thought it safe. He crossed himself, remembering that; the plain stones, often nothing more than a wooden altar inside—and yet the relief of entering, sitting on the floor if there was no bench, just sitting, and knowing himself to be not alone. Sanctuary.

Whether the thought of churches or of Claire reminded him, he remembered another church—the one they had married in, and he grinned to himself at the memory of that. Not a peaceful waiting, no. He could still feel the thunder of his heart against his ribs as he'd stepped inside, the reek of his sweat—he'd smelled like a rutting goat, and hoped she didn't notice—the inability to draw a full breath. And the feel of her hand in his, her fingers small and freezing cold, clutching at him for support.

Sanctuary. They'd been that for each other then—and were so now. *Blood of my blood.* The tiny cut had healed, but he rubbed the ball of his thumb, smiling at the matter-of-fact way she'd said it.

He came in sight of the cabin, and saw Joseph Wemyss waiting on the porch, hunched and stamping his feet against the cold. He was about to hail Joseph, when the door suddenly opened and one of the Beardsley twins—Christ, what were *they* doing in there?—reached out and seized his father-in-law by the arm, nearly pulling him off his feet in his excitement.

It *was* excitement, too, not grief or alarm; he'd seen the boy's face clearly in the glow of the firelight. He let out the breath he hadn't realized he was holding, white in the dark. The child was come, then, and both it and Lizzie had survived.

He relaxed against a tree, touching the rosary around his neck.

"Moran taing," he said softly, in brief but heartfelt thanks. Someone in the cabin had put more wood on the fire; a shower of sparks flew up from the chimney, lighting the snow in red and gold and hissing black where cinders fell.

Yet man is born to trouble, as the sparks fly upward. He'd read that line of Job many times in prison, and made no great sense of it. Upward-flying sparks caused no trouble, by and large, unless you had very dry shingles; it was the ones that spat straight out of the hearth that might set your house on fire. Or if the writer had meant only that it was the nature of man to be in trouble—as plainly it was, if his own experience was aught to go by—then he was making a comparison of inevitability, saying that sparks always flew upward—which anyone who'd ever watched a fire for long could tell you they didn't.

Still, who was he to be criticizing the Bible's logic, when he ought to be repeating psalms of praise and gratitude? He tried to think of one, but was too content to think of more than odd bits and pieces.

He realized with a small shock that he was entirely happy. The safe birth of the child was a great thing in itself, to be sure—but it also meant that Claire had come safe through her trial, and that he and she were now free. They might leave the Ridge, knowing they had done all that could be done for the folk who remained.

Aye, there was always a sadness in leaving home—but in this case, it might be argued that their home had left *them*, when the house burned, and in any case, it was overbalanced by his rising sense of anticipation. Free and away, Claire by his side, no daily chores to do, no petty squabbles to settle, no widows and orphans to provide for—well, that was an unworthy thought, doubtless, and yet . . .

War was a terrible thing, and this one would be, too—but it was undeniably exciting, and the blood stirred in him from scalp to soles.

"Moran taing," he said again, in heartfelt gratitude.

A short time later, the door of the cabin opened again, spilling light, and

Claire came out, pulling up the hood of her cloak, her basket over her arm. Voices followed her, and bodies crowded the door. She turned to wave farewell to them, and he heard her laugh; the sound of it sent a small thrill of pleasure through him.

The door closed and she came down the path in the gray-lit dark; he could see that she staggered just a little, from weariness, and yet there was an air of something about her—he thought it might be the same euphoria that lifted him.

"Like the sparks that fly upward," he murmured to himself, and smiling, stepped out to greet her.

She wasn't startled, but turned at once and came toward him, seeming almost to float on the snow.

"It's well, then," he said, and she sighed and came into his arms, solid and warm within the cold folds of her cloak. He reached inside it, drew her close, inside the wool of his own big cloak.

"I need you, please," she whispered, her mouth against his, and without reply he took her up in his arms—Christ, she was right, that cloak stank of dead meat; had the man who sold it to him used it to haul a butchered deer in from the forest?—and kissed her deep, then put her down and led her down the hill, the light snow seeming to melt away from their feet as they walked.

It seemed to take no time at all to reach the barn; they spoke a little on the trail, but he could not have said what they talked about. It only mattered to be with each other.

It wasn't precisely cozy inside the barn, but not freezing, either. Welcoming, he thought, with the pleasant warm smell of the beasts in the dark. The weird gray light of the sky filtered in, just a bit, so you could see the hunched shapes of horses and mules dozing in their stalls. And there was dry straw to lie on, for all it was old and a trifle musty.

It was too cold to undress, but he laid his cloak in the straw, her upon it, and lay upon her, both of them shivering as they kissed, so their teeth clacked together and they drew back, snorting.

"This is silly," she said, "I can see my breath—*and* yours. It's cold enough to blow smoke rings. We'll freeze."

"No, we won't. Ken the way the Indians make fire?"

"What, rubbing a dry stick on a . . ."

"Aye, friction." He'd got her petticoats up; her thigh was smooth and cold under his hand. "I see it's no going to be dry, though—Christ, Sassenach, what have ye been about?" He had her firmly in the palm of his hand, warm and soft and juicy, and she squealed at the chill of his touch, loud enough that one of the mules let out a startled wheeze. She wriggled, just enough to make him take his hand out from between her legs and insert something else, quick.

"Ye're going to rouse the whole barn," he observed, breathless. God, the enveloping shock of the heat of her made him giddy.

She ran her cold hands up under his shirt and pinched both his nipples, hard, and he yelped, then laughed.

"Do that again," he said, and bending, stuck his tongue in her cold ear for the pleasure of hearing her shriek. She wriggled and arched her back, but didn't—he noticed—actually turn her head away. He took her earlobe gently between his teeth and began to worry it, rogering her slowly and laughing to himself at the noises she made.

It had been a long time of making silent love.

Her hands were busy at his back; he'd only let down the flap of his breeks and pulled his shirttail up out of the way, but she'd got the shirt out at the back now, and shoved both hands down his breeks and got his hurdies in a good two-handed grip. She pulled him in tight, digging in her nails, and he took her meaning. He let go her ear, rose on his hands, and rode her solid, the straw a-rustle round them like the crackle of burning.

He wanted simply to let go at once, spill himself and fall on her, hold her to his body and smell her hair in a doze of warmth and joy. A dim sense of obligation reminded him that she'd asked him for this; she'd needed it. He couldn't go and leave her wanting.

He closed his eyes and slowed himself, lowered himself onto her so her body strained and rose along his length, the cloth of their clothes rasping and bunching up between them. He got a hand down under her, cupped her bare bum, and slid his fingers into the straining warm crease of her buttocks. Slid one a little farther, and she gasped. Her hips rose, trying to get away, but he laughed deep in his throat and didn't let her. Wiggled the finger.

"Do that again," he whispered in her ear. "Make that noise again for me."

She made a better one, one he'd never heard before, and jerked under him, quivering and whimpering.

He pulled out the finger and guddled her, light and quick, all along the slick deep parts, feeling his own cock under his fingers, big and slippery, stretching her . . .

He made a terrible noise himself—like a dying cow—but was too happy to be shamed.

"Ye're no verra peaceful, Sassenach," he murmured a moment later, breathing in the smell of musk and new life. "But I like ye fine."

12

ENOUGH

I TOOK MY LEAVE, starting from the springhouse. Stood inside for a moment, listening to the trickle of the water in its stone channel, breathing the cold, fresh smell of the place, with its faint sweet scents of milk and butter. Coming out, I turned left, passing the weathered palisades of my garden, covered with the tattered, rattling remnants of gourd vines. I paused, hesitating; I hadn't set foot in the garden since the day that Malva and her child had died there. I set my hands on two of the wooden stakes, leaning to look between them.

I was glad I hadn't looked before; I couldn't have borne to see it in its winter desolation, the ragged stems blackened and stiff, the rags of leaves rotted into the ground. It was still a sight to strike a pang to a gardener's heart, but no longer desolate. Fresh green sprouted everywhere, spangled with tiny flowers; the kindness of spring laying garlands over winter's bones. Granted, half the green things growing were grass and weeds; by summer, the woods would have reclaimed the garden, smothering the stunted sproutings of cabbages and onions. Amy had made a new vegetable patch near the old cabin; neither she nor anyone else on the Ridge would set foot here.

Something stirred in the grass, and I saw a small gopher snake slide through, hunting. The sight of something live comforted me, little as I cared for snakes, and I smiled as I lifted my eyes and saw that bees were humming to and fro from one of the old bee gums that still stood at the foot of the garden.

I looked last at the spot where I had planted salad greens; that's where she had died. In memory, I'd always seen the spreading blood, imagined it still there, a permanent stain soaked dark into the earth among the churned wreckage of uprooted lettuces and wilting leaves. But it was gone; nothing marked the spot save a fairy ring of mushrooms, tiny white heads poking out of the wild grass.

"I will arise and go now," I said softly, *"and go to Innisfree, and a small cabin build there, of clay and wattles made; nine bean rows will I have there, a hive for the honeybee, and live alone in the bee-loud glade."* I paused for a moment, and as I turned away, added in a whisper, *"And I shall have some peace there, for peace comes dropping slow."*

I made my way briskly down the path then; no need to apostrophize the ruins of the house, nor yet the white sow. I'd remember *them* without effort. As for the corncrib and hen coop—if you've seen one, you've seen them all.

I could see the little gathering of horses, mules, and people moving in the slow chaos of imminent departure in front of the cabin. I wasn't quite ready yet for goodbyes, though, and stepped into the wood to pull myself together.

The grass was long beside the trail, soft and feathery against the hem of my weighted skirts. Something heavier than grass brushed them, and I looked down to see Adso. I'd been looking for him most of yesterday; typical of him to show up at the last minute.

"So there you are," I said, accusing. He looked at me with his huge calm eyes of celadon green, and licked a paw. On impulse, I scooped him up and held him against me, feeling the rumble of his purr and the soft, thick fur of his silvery belly.

He'd be all right; I knew that. The woods were his private game preserve, and Amy Higgins liked him and had promised me to see him right for milk and a warm spot by the fire in bad weather. I knew that.

"Go on, then," I said, and set him on the ground. He stood for a moment, tail waving slowly, head raised in search of food or interesting smells, then stepped into the grass and vanished.

I bent, very slowly, arms crossed, and shook, weeping silently, violently.

I cried until my throat hurt and I couldn't breathe, then sat in the grass, curled into myself like a dried leaf, tears that I couldn't stop dropping on my knees like the first fat drops of a coming storm. Oh, God. It was only the beginning.

I rubbed my hands hard over my eyes, smearing the wetness, trying to scrub away grief. A soft cloth touched my face, and I looked up, sniffing, to find Jamie kneeling in front of me, handkerchief in hand.

"I'm sorry," he said, very softly.

"It's not—don't worry, I'm . . . He's only a cat," I said, and a small fresh grief tightened like a band round my chest.

"Aye, I know." He moved beside me and put an arm round my shoulders, pulling my head to his chest, while he gently wiped my face. "But ye couldna weep for the bairns. Or the house. Or your wee garden. Or the poor dead lass and her bairn. But if ye weep for your cheetie, ye know ye can stop."

"How do you know that?" My voice was thick, but the band round my chest was not quite so tight.

He made a small, rueful sound.

"Because I canna weep for those things, either, Sassenach. And I havena got a cat."

I sniffled, wiped my face one last time, and blew my nose before giving him back the handkerchief, which he stuffed into his sporran without grimace or thought.

Lord, he'd said. *Let me be enough.* That prayer had lodged in my heart like an arrow when I'd heard it and thought he asked for help in doing what had to be done. But that wasn't what he'd meant at all—and the realization of what he *had* meant split my heart in two.

I took his face between my hands, and wished so much that I had his own gift, the ability to say what lay in my heart, in such a way that he would know. But I hadn't.

"Jamie," I said at last. "Oh, Jamie. You're . . . everything. Always."

An hour later, we left the Ridge.

13

UNREST

IAN LAY DOWN WITH a sack of rice under his head for a pillow. It was hard, but he liked the whisper of the small grains when he turned his head and the faint starched smell of it. Rollo rooted under the plaid with his snout, snorting as he worked his way close against Ian's body, ending with his nose cozily buried in Ian's armpit. Ian scratched the dog's ears gently, then lay back, watching the stars.

It was a sliver moon, thin as a nail paring, and the stars were big and brilliant in the purple-black of the sky. He traced the constellations overhead. Would he see the same stars in Scotland? he wondered. He'd not paid much mind to the stars when he was home in the Highlands, and you couldn't see stars at all in Edinburgh, for the smoke of the reeking lums.

His aunt and uncle lay on the other side of the smoored fire, close enough together as to look like one log, sharing warmth. He saw the blankets twitch, settle, twitch again, and then a stillness, waiting. He heard a whisper, too low to make out the words but the intent behind them clear enough.

He kept his breathing regular, a little louder than usual. A moment, and then the stealthy movements began again. It was hard to fool Uncle Jamie, but there are times when a man wants to be fooled.

His hand rested gently on the dog's head, and Rollo sighed, the huge body going limp, warm and heavy against him. If not for the dog, he would never be able to sleep out of doors. Not that he ever slept soundly, or for long—but at least he could surrender now and then to bodily need, trusting that Rollo would hear any footstep long before he did.

"Ye're safe enough," his uncle Jamie had told him, their first night on the road. He'd been unable to fall asleep then for nerviness, even with Rollo's head on his chest, and had got up to sit by the fire, poking sticks into the embers until the flames rose up into the night, pure and vivid.

He was well aware that he was perfectly visible to anyone who might be watching, but there was nothing to be done about that. And if he had a target painted on his chest, lighting it up wouldn't make a deal of difference.

Rollo, lying watchful beside the growing fire, had lifted his big head suddenly, but only turned it toward a faint sound in the dark. That meant someone familiar, and Ian wasn't bothered, nor yet surprised when his uncle came out of the wood where he'd gone to relieve himself and sat down beside him.

"He doesna want ye dead, ken," Uncle Jamie had said without preamble. "You're safe enough."

"I dinna ken if I want to be safe," he'd blurted, and his uncle had glanced at him, his face troubled—but not surprised. Uncle Jamie had only nodded, though.

He knew what his uncle meant; Arch Bug didn't want him to die, because that would end his guilt, and thus his suffering. Ian had looked into those ancient eyes, the whites of them yellowed and threaded with red, watering with cold and grief, and seen something there that had frozen the core of his soul. No, Arch Bug wouldn't kill him—yet.

His uncle was staring into the fire, the light of it warm on the broad bones of his face, and the sight gave Ian both comfort and panic.

Does it not occur to you? he'd thought, anguished, but did not say. *He said he'd take what I love. And there ye sit beside me, clear as day.*

The first time the thought had come to him, he'd pushed it away; old Arch owed Uncle Jamie, for what he'd done for the Bugs, and he was a man to acknowledge a debt—though perhaps more ready to claim one. And he had nay doubt Bug respected his uncle as a man, too. For a time, that had seemed to settle the matter.

But other thoughts had come to him, uneasy, many-legged things that crept out of the sleepless nights since he'd killed Murdina Bug.

Arch was an old man. Tough as a fire-hardened spear, and twice as dangerous—but old. He'd fought at Sheriffmuir; he had to be rising eighty. Revenge might keep him alive for a time, but all flesh came to an end. He might well think that he hadn't time to wait for Ian to acquire "something worth taking." If he meant to keep his threat, he'd need to act soon.

Ian could hear the subtle shifts and rustlings from the other side of the fire, and swallowed, his mouth dry. Old Arch might try to take his aunt, for surely Ian loved her, and she would be much easier to kill than Uncle Jamie. But no—Arch might be half crazed with grief and rage, but he wasn't insane. He'd know that to touch Auntie Claire—without killing Uncle Jamie at the same time—would be suicide.

Maybe he wouldn't care. That was another thought that walked over his belly with small, cold feet.

He should leave them; he knew that. He'd meant to—he still meant to. Wait 'til they'd fallen asleep, then rise and steal away. They'd be safe then.

But his heart had failed him, that first night. He'd been trying to gather his courage, there by the fire, to go—but his uncle had forestalled him, coming out of the wood and sitting by him, silent but companionable, until Ian had felt able to lie down again.

Tomorrow, he'd thought. After all, there was no sign of Arch Bug; hadn't been, since his wife's funeral. *And maybe he's dead.* He *was* an old man, and alone.

And there was the consideration that if he left without a word, Uncle Jamie would come after him. He'd made it clear that Ian was going back to Scotland, whether he did it willingly or tied in a sack. Ian grinned, despite his thoughts, and Rollo made a small grunt as the chest under him moved in a silent laugh.

He'd barely spared a thought for Scotland and what might await him there.

Perhaps it was the noises from the other side of the fire that made him think it—a sudden high-pitched intake of breath and the deep twin sighs that followed it, his familiarity providing a vivid physical memory of the action that had caused that sigh—but he wondered suddenly whether he might find a wife in Scotland.

He couldn't. Could he? Would Bug be able to follow him so far? *Maybe he's already dead,* he thought again, and shifted a bit. Rollo grumbled in his throat but, recognizing the signs, shuffled off him and curled up a little distance away.

His family would be there. Surrounded by the Murrays, surely he—and a wife—would be safe. It was simple to lurk and steal through the dense woods here in the mountains—not nearly so simple in the Highlands, where every eye was sharp and no stranger passed unnoticed.

He didn't know quite what his mother would do when she saw him—but once she got used to it, maybe she could think of a girl who wouldn't be too frightened of him.

A suck of breath and a sound not quite a moan from his uncle—he did that when she put her mouth on his nipple; Ian had seen her do it once or twice, by the glow of embers from the cabin's hearth, her eyes closed, a quick wet gleam of teeth, and her hair falling back from naked shoulders in a cloud of light and shadow.

He put a hand on his cock, tempted. He had a private collection of images that he cherished for the purpose—and not a few of them were of his cousin, though it shamed him a little. She was Roger Mac's wife, after all. But he'd thought at one point that he'd need to marry her himself, and while terrified at the prospect—he'd been only seventeen and she considerably older—had been emboldened at the thought of having her to bed.

He'd watched her close for several days, seeing her arse round and solid, the dark shadow of her red-haired quim under the thin muslin of her shift when she went to bathe, imagining the thrill of seeing it plain on the night when she'd lie down and open her legs for him.

What was he doing? He couldn't be thinking of Brianna like that, not lying a dozen feet from her father!

He grimaced and squinched his eyes tight shut, hand slowing as he summoned up a different image from his private library. Not the witch—not tonight. Her memory aroused him with great urgency, often painfully, but was tinged with a sense of helplessness. Malva . . . No, he was afraid to summon her; he often thought her spirit was not yet so very far away.

Wee Mary. Aye, her. His hand settled at once into its rhythm and he sighed, escaping with relief to the small pink breasts and encouraging smile of the first lass he'd ever lain with.

Hovering moments later on the edge of a dream of a wee blond girl who was his wife, he thought drowsily, *Aye, maybe he's already dead.*

Rollo made a deep, dissentient noise in his throat, and rolled over with his paws in the air.

14

DELICATE MATTERS

London
November 1776

T HERE WERE MANY compensations to growing older, Lord
John thought. Wisdom, perspective, position in life, the sense of ac-
complishment, of time well spent, a richness of affection for friends
and family . . . and the fact that he needn't keep his back pressed against a wall
when talking to Lord George Germain. While both his looking glass and his
valet assured him that he continued to be presentable, he was at least twenty
years too old to appeal to the secretary of state, who liked them young and
tender-skinned.

The clerk who had shown him in met this description, being equipped also
with long dark lashes and a soft pout. Grey spared him no more than a glance;
his own tastes were harder-edged.

It was not early—knowing Germain's habits, he had waited until one
o'clock—but the man still showed the effects of a long night. Deep blue
pouches cupped eyes like soft-boiled eggs, which surveyed Grey with a distinct lack of enthusiasm. Still, Germain made an effort at courtesy, bidding
Grey sit and sending the doe-eyed clerk for brandy and biscuits.

Grey seldom took strong drink before teatime, and wanted a clear head
now. He therefore barely sipped his own brandy, excellent though it was, but
Germain dipped the famous Sackville nose—sharply protrusive as a letter
opener—into his glass, inhaled deeply, then drained it and poured another.
The liquid appeared to have some restorative effect, for he emerged from his
second glass looking somewhat happier and inquired of Grey how he did.

"Very well, I thank you," Grey said politely. "I have recently returned from
America, and have brought you several letters from mutual acquaintances
there."

"Oh, have you?" Germain brightened a bit. "Kind of you, Grey. Decent
voyage, was it?"

"Tolerable." In fact, it had been miserable; they had run a gauntlet of
storms across the Atlantic, pitching and yawing without cease for days on end,
to the point that Grey had wished fervently for the ship to sink, just to put an
end to it all. But he did not want to waste time on trivial chat.

"I had a rather remarkable encounter, just before leaving the colony of
North Carolina," he said, judging that Germain was now sufficiently alert as
to listen. "Allow me to tell you about it."

Germain was both vain and petty, and had brought the art of political vagueness to a fine point—but could apply himself to a matter when he wished, which was largely when he perceived some benefit to himself in a situation. The mention of the Northwest Territory focused his attention admirably.

"You did not speak to this Beauchamp further?" A third glass of brandy sat by Germain's elbow, half drunk.

"No. He had delivered his message; there was nothing to be gained by further conversation, as plainly he has no power to act upon his own. And had he intended to divulge the identity of his principals, he would have done so."

Germain picked up his glass, but did not drink, instead turning it in his hands as an aid to thought. It was plain, not faceted, and smeared with fingerprints and the smudges of Germain's mouth.

"Is the man familiar to you? Why did he seek you out, in particular?" *No, not stupid,* Grey thought.

"I had encountered him many years ago," he replied equably. "In the course of my work with Colonel Bowles."

Nothing on earth would compel Grey to reveal Percy's true identity to Germain; Percy had been—well, still *was*—stepbrother to himself and Hal, and only good fortune and Grey's own determination had prevented an almighty scandal at the time of Percy's presumed death. Some scandals dimmed with time—that one wouldn't.

Germain's plucked eyebrow flickered at mention of Bowles, who had headed England's Black Chamber for many years.

"A spy?" Mild distaste showed in his voice; spies were vulgar necessities; not something a gentleman would touch with his bare hands.

"At one time, perhaps. Apparently he has risen in the world." He picked up his own glass, took a healthy mouthful—it was very good brandy, after all—then set it down and stood up to take his leave. He knew better than to prod Germain. Leave the matter in the secretary's lap, and trust to his own self-interest to pursue it.

Grey left Germain sitting back in his chair, staring contemplatively into his empty glass, and took his cloak from the soft-lipped clerk, whose hand brushed his in passing.

NOT, HE REFLECTED, pulling the cloak around him and tugging down his hat against the rising wind, that he proposed to leave the matter to Germain's capricious sense of responsibility. Germain was secretary of state for America, true—but this was not a matter that concerned only America. There were two other secretaries of state in Lord North's cabinet—one for the Northern Department, that being all of Europe, and another for the Southern Department, this constituting the rest of the world. He would have preferred not to deal with Lord Germain at all. However, both protocol and politics prevented him from going straight to Lord North, which had been his first impulse. He'd give Germain a day's head start, then call upon the Southern secretary, Thomas Thynne, Viscount Weymouth, with the invidious Mr. Beauchamp's proposal. The Southern secretary was charged with dealing with the Catholic countries of Europe, thus matters with a French connection were his concern as well.

If both men chose to take up the matter, it would certainly come to Lord North's attention—and North, or one of his ministers, would come to Grey.

A storm was rolling up the Thames; he could see billows of black cloud, fuming as though to unleash their fury directly upon the Houses of Parliament.

"A bit of thunder and lightning would do them good," he murmured balefully, and hailed a cab, as the first thick drops began to fall.

The rain was pelting down in sheets by the time he arrived at the Beefsteak, and he was nearly drenched in the three paces from curb to doorway.

Mr. Bodley, the elderly steward, received him as though he had come in the day before, rather than some eighteen months.

"Turtle soup with sherry tonight, my lord," he informed Grey, gesturing to a minion to take Grey's damp hat and cloak. "Very warming to the stomach. Followed by a nice lamb cutlet with new potatoes?"

"The very thing, Mr. Bodley," Grey replied, smiling. He took his place in the dining room, soothed by its good fire and cool white napery. As he leaned back to allow Mr. Bodley to tuck the napkin under his chin, though, he noted a new addition to the room's decoration.

"Who is that?" he asked, startled. The painting, prominently displayed upon the wall opposite, showed a stately Indian, festooned in ostrich plumes and embroidered draperies. It looked distinctly odd, set as it was among the staid portraits of several distinguished—and mostly deceased—members.

"Oh, that is Mr. Brant, of course," Mr. Bodley said, with an air of mild reproof. "Mr. Joseph Brant. Mr. Pitt brought him to dine last year, when he was in London."

"Brant?"

Mr. Bodley's brows rose. Like most Londoners, he assumed that everyone who had been in America must of necessity know every other person there.

"He is a Mohawk chief, I believe," he said, pronouncing the word "Mohawk" carefully. "He has been to visit the King, you know!"

"Indeed," Grey murmured. He wondered whether the King or the Indian had been more impressed.

Mr. Bodley withdrew, presumably to fetch the soup, but returned within moments to lay a letter upon the cloth before Grey.

"This was sent for you in care of the secretary, sir."

"Oh? Thank you, Mr. Bodley." Grey took it up, recognizing his son's hand immediately, and suffering a mild drop of the stomach in consequence. What had Willie not wanted to send in care either of his grandmother or of Hal?

Something he didn't want to risk either of them reading. His mind supplied the logical answer at once, and he took up his fish knife to open the letter with due trepidation.

Was it Richardson? Hal disliked the man, and hadn't approved at all of William's working for him, though he had nothing concrete to adduce against him. Perhaps he should have been more cautious about setting William on that particular path, knowing what he did about the black world of intelligencing. Still, it had been imperative to get Willie away from North

Carolina, before he came face-to-face with either Jamie Fraser or Percy so-called Beauchamp.

And you did have to let a son go, to make his own way in the world, no matter what it cost you; Hal had told him that, more than once. Three times, to be exact, he thought with a smile—every time one of Hal's boys had taken up his commission.

He unfolded the letter with caution, as though it might explode. It was penned with a care that he found instantly sinister; Willie was normally legible, but not above the odd blot.

> *To Lord John Grey*
> *The Society for Appreciation of the English Beefsteak*
> *From Lieutenant William Lord Ellesmere*
> *7 September, 1776*
> *Long Island*
> *The Royal Colony of New York*
>
> *Dear Father,*
> *I have a Matter of some delicacy to confide.*

Well, there was a sentence to chill the blood of any parent, Grey thought. Had Willie got a young woman with child, gambled and lost substantial property, contracted a venereal complaint, challenged someone or been challenged to a duel? Or—had he encountered something sinister in the course of his intelligencing, on his way to General Howe? He reached for the wine, and took a prophylactic swallow before returning, thus braced, to the letter. Nothing could have prepared him for the next sentence, though.

> *I am in love with Lady Dorothea.*

Grey choked, spluttering wine over his hand, but waved off the steward hastening toward him with a towel, instead wiping his hand on his breeches as he hastily scanned the rest of the page.

> *We have both been conscious of a growing Attraction for some time, but I hesitated to make any Declaration, knowing that I was soon to depart for America. However, we discovered ourselves unexpectedly alone in the Garden at Lady Belvedere's Ball, the Week before I left, and the beauty of the Setting, the romantic sense of the Evening, and the intoxicating nearness of the Lady overpowered my Judgment.*

"Oh, Jesus," Lord John said aloud. "Tell me you didn't deflower her under a bush, for God's sake!"

He caught the interested gaze of a nearby diner, and with a brief cough, returned to the letter.

> *I blush with Shame to admit that my Feelings overcame me, to an Extent that I hesitate to commit to Paper. I apologized, of course, not*

that there could be any sufficient Apology for such dishonourable Conduct. Lady Dorothea was both generous in her Forgiveness and vehement in her Insistence that I must not—as I was at first inclined—to go at once to her Father.

"Very sensible of you, Dottie," Grey murmured, envisioning all too well the response of his brother to any such revelation. He could only hope that Willie was blushing over some indiscretion a good deal short of . . .

I intended to ask you to speak to Uncle Hal for me next Year, when I should return Home and be able to formally request Lady Dorothea's Hand in Marriage. However, I have just learned that she has received another Offer, from Viscount Maxwell, and that Uncle Hal is seriously considering this.

I would not besmirch the lady's Honour in any Way, but under the Circumstances, clearly she cannot marry Maxwell.

You mean Maxwell would discover that she's not a virgin, Grey thought grimly, *and come barreling round the morning after the wedding night to tell Hal so.* He rubbed a hand hard over his face and went on.

Words cannot convey my Remorse at my actions, Father, and I cannot bring myself to ask a Forgiveness I do not deserve, for so grievously disappointing you. Not for my Sake, but for hers, I beg that you will speak to the Duke. I hope that he can be persuaded to entertain my Suit and allow us to be affianced, without the Necessity of making such explicit Discoveries to him as might distress the Lady.

> *Your most humble Prodigal,*
> *William*

He sank back in the chair and closed his eyes. The first shock was beginning to dissipate, and his mind come to grips with the problem.

It should be possible. There would be no bar to a marriage between William and Dottie. While titularly cousins, there were no blood ties between them; William was his son in all ways that mattered, but not by blood. And while Maxwell was young, wealthy, and very suitable, William was an earl in his own right, as well as heir to Dunsany's baronetcy, and far from poor.

No, that part was all right. And Minnie liked William very much. Hal and the boys . . . well, provided they never got wind of William's behavior, they should be agreeable. On the other hand, should any of them discover it, William would be lucky to escape with being horsewhipped and having every bone in his body broken. So would Grey.

Hal would be very much surprised, of course—the cousins had seen a good deal of each other during Willie's time in London, but William had never spoken of Dottie in a way that would have indicated . . .

He picked up the letter and read it over again. And again. Set it down and gazed at it for several minutes with narrowed eyes, thinking.

"I'm damned if I believe it," he said aloud, at last. "What the devil are you up to, Willie?"

He crumpled the letter, and taking a candlestick from a nearby table with a nod of apology, set fire to the missive. The steward, observing this, instantly produced a small china dish, into which Grey dropped the flaming paper, and together they watched the writing blacken into ash.

"Your soup, my lord," said Mr. Bodley, and waving the smoke of conflagration gently away with a napkin, placed a steaming plate before him.

WILLIAM BEING OUT of reach, the obvious course of action must be to go and confront his partner in crime—whatever sort of crime it was. The more he considered, the more convinced he became that whatever complicity lay between William, Ninth Earl of Ellesmere, and Lady Dorothea Jacqueline Benedicta Grey, it was not the complicity either of love or guilty passion.

How was he to speak to Dottie, though, without exciting the notice of either of her parents? He could not hang about in the street until both Hal and Minnie went somewhere, hopefully leaving Dottie alone. Even if he managed to catch her somehow alone at home and interview her privately, the servants would certainly mention that he had done so, and Hal—who had a sense of protective alertness regarding his daughter akin to that of a large mastiff regarding its favorite bone—would be round promptly to find out why.

He declined the doorman's offer to secure him a carriage, and walked back to his mother's house, pondering ways and means. He could invite Dottie to dine with him . . . but it would be very unusual for such an invitation not to include Minnie. Likewise, were he to invite her to a play or opera; he often escorted the women, as Hal could not sit still long enough to hear an entire opera, and considered most plays to be tedious twaddle.

His way lay through Covent Garden, and he skipped nimbly out of the way of a swash of water, flung from a bucket to wash the slimy cabbage leaves and rotten apples from the cobbles by a fruiterer's stall. In summer, wilted blooms littered the pavement; before dawn, the fresh flowers would come in by cart from the countryside, and fill the square with scent and freshness. In autumn, the place held a ripely decadent smell of squashed fruit, decaying meat, and broken vegetables that was the signature to the changing of the guard in Covent Garden.

During the day, vendors shouted their wares, haggled, fought pitched battles with one another, fought off thieves and pickpockets, and shambled off at nightfall to spend half their profits in the taverns in Tavistock and Brydges streets. With the shades of evening drawing nigh, the whores claimed the Garden for their own.

The sight of a couple of these, arrived early and trolling hopefully for customers among the home-going vendors, distracted him momentarily from his familial quandary and returned his thoughts to the earlier events of his day.

The entrance to Brydges Street lay before him; he could just see the genteel house that stood near the far end, set back a little in elegant discretion.

That was a thought; whores knew a great deal—and could find out more, with suitable inducement. He was tempted to go and call upon Nessie now, if only for the pleasure her company gave him. But no—not yet.

He needed to find out what was already known about Percy Beauchamp in more official circles, before he started his own hounds in pursuit of that rabbit. And before he saw Hal.

It was too late in the day to make official calls. He'd send a note, though, making an appointment—and in the morning, would visit the Black Chamber.

15

THE BLACK CHAMBER

GREY WONDERED what romantic soul had originally christened the Black Chamber—or whether it was in fact a romantic designation. Perhaps the spies of an earlier day had been consigned to a windowless hole under the stairs at Whitehall, and the name was purely descriptive. These days, the Black Chamber designated a class of employment rather than a specific location.

All the capitals of Europe—and not a few lesser cities—had Black Chambers, these being the centers wherein mail intercepted *en route* or by spies or simply removed from diplomatic pouches was inspected, decoded with varying degrees of success, and then sent to whichever person or agency had need of the information thus derived. England's Black Chamber had employed four gentlemen—not counting clerks and office boys—when Grey had labored there. There were more of them now, distributed in random holes and corners in the buildings down Pall Mall, but the main center of such operations was still in Buckingham Palace.

Not in any of the beautifully equipped areas that served the Royal Family or their secretaries, ladies' maids, housekeepers, butlers, or other upper servants—but still, within the palace precincts.

Grey passed the guard at the back gate with a nod—he'd worn his uniform, with the lieutenant-colonel's insignia, to facilitate entry—and made his way down a shabby, ill-lit corridor whose scent of ancient floor polish and ghosts of boiled cabbage and burnt tea cake gave him a pleasant *frisson* of nostalgia. The third door on the left stood ajar, and he entered without knocking.

He was expected. Arthur Norrington greeted him without rising, and motioned him to a chair.

He'd known Norrington for years, though they were not particular friends, and found it comforting that the man seemed not to have changed at all in the years since their last meeting. Arthur was a large, soft man, whose large, slightly protruding eyes and thick lips gave him the mien of a turbot on ice: dignified and faintly reproachful.

"I appreciate your help, Arthur," Grey said, and as he sat, deposited on the corner of the desk a small wrapped parcel. "A small token of that appreciation," he added, waving a hand at it.

Norrington raised one thin brow and took the package, which he unwrapped with greedy fingers.

"Oh!" he said, with unfeigned delight. He turned the tiny ivory carving over gently in his large, soft hands, bringing it close to his face to see the details, entranced. "Tsuji?"

Grey shrugged, pleased with the effect of his gift. He knew nothing of *netsuke* himself, but knew a man who dealt in ivory miniatures from China and Japan. He had been surprised at the delicacy and artistry of the tiny thing, which showed a half-clothed woman engaged in a very athletic form of sexual congress with a naked obese gentleman with his hair in a topknot.

"I'm afraid it has no provenance," he said apologetically, but Norrington waved that aside, eyes still fixed on the new treasure. After a moment, he sighed happily, then tucked the thing away in the inner pocket of his coat.

"Thank you, my lord," he said. "As for the subject of your own inquiry, I am afraid that we have relatively little material available regarding your mysterious Mr. Beauchamp." He nodded at the desk, where a battered, anonymous leather folder reposed. Grey could see that there was something bulky inside—something not paper; the folder was pierced, and a small piece of twine ran through it, fastening the object in place.

"You surprise me, Mr. Norrington," he said politely, and reached for the folder. "Still, let me see what you do have, and perhaps—"

Norrington pressed his fingers flat against the file and frowned for a moment, trying to convey the impression that official secrets could not be imparted to just *anyone*. Grey smiled at him.

"Come off it, Arthur," he said. "If you want to know what *I* know about our mysterious Mr. Beauchamp—and I assure you, you do—you'll show me every word you have about him."

Norrington relaxed a little, letting his fingers slide back—though still with a show of reluctance. Cocking one eyebrow, Grey picked up the leather folder and opened it. The bulky object was revealed to be a small cloth bag; beyond that, there were only a few sheets of paper. Grey sighed.

"Poor protocol, Arthur," he said reprovingly. "There are snowdrifts of paper involving Beauchamp—cross-referenced to that name, too. Granted, he hasn't been active in years, but someone ought to have looked."

"We did," Norrington said, an odd note in his voice that made Grey look sharply up. "Old Crabbot remembered the name, and we looked. The files are gone."

The skin across Grey's shoulders tightened, as though he'd been struck with a lash.

"That *is* odd," he said calmly. "Well, then . . ." He bent his head over the folder, though it took a moment to subdue his racing thoughts enough to see what he was looking at. No sooner had his eyes focused on the page than the name "Fraser" leapt out of it, nearly stopping his heart.

Not Jamie Fraser, though. He breathed slowly, turned the page, read the next, turned back. There were four letters in all, only one completely decoded, though another had been started; it bore someone's tentative notes in the margin. His lips tightened; he had been a good decoder in his day, but had been absent from the field of battle far too long to have any notion of the current common idioms in use by the French, let alone the idiosyncratic terms an individual spy might use—and these letters were the work of at least two different hands; so much was clear.

"I've looked them over," Norrington said, and Grey looked up to find Arthur's protruding hazel eyes fixed on him like a toad eyeing a juicy fly. "I haven't *officially* decoded them yet, but I've a good general idea what they say."

Well, he'd already decided that it had to be done, and he'd come prepared to tell Arthur, who was the most discreet of his old Black Chamber contacts.

"Beauchamp is one Percival Wainwright," he said bluntly, wondering even as he said it, why he kept the secret of Percival's real name. "He's a British subject—was an army officer, arrested for the crime of sodomy but never tried. It was thought that he'd died in Newgate awaiting trial, but"—he smoothed the letters and closed the folder over them—"evidently not."

Arthur's plump lips rounded in a soundless "O."

Grey wondered for an instant if he could leave it there—but no. Arthur was persistent as a dachshund digging into a badger sett, and if he discovered the rest of it on his own, he would at once suspect Grey of withholding much more.

"He's also my stepbrother," Grey said, as casually as possible, and laid the folder on Arthur's desk. "I saw him in North Carolina."

Arthur's mouth sagged for an instant. He firmed it up at once, blinking.

"I see," he said. "Well, then . . . I see."

"Yes, you do," Grey said dryly. "You see exactly why I must know the contents of these letters"—he nodded at the folder—"as soon as possible."

Arthur nodded, compressing his lips, and settled himself, taking the letters into his hands. Once determined to be serious, there was no nonsense about him.

"Most of what I could decode seems to deal with matters of shipping," he said. "Contacts in the West Indies, cargoes to be delivered—simple smuggling, though on a fairly large scale. One reference to a banker in Edinburgh; I couldn't make out his connection exactly. But three of the letters mentioned the same name *en clair*—you will have seen that, of course."

Grey didn't bother denying it.

"Someone in France wants very much to find a man named Claudel Fraser," Arthur said, and raised one brow. "Any idea who that is?"

"No," Grey said, though he certainly had the glimmer of an idea. "Any idea *who* it is that wants to find him—or why?"

Norrington shook his head.

"No idea why," he said frankly. "As to who, though—I think it may be a

French nobleman." He opened the folder again and, from the little bag attached to it, carefully removed two wax seals, one cracked almost in half, the other largely intact. Both showed a martlet against a rising sun.

"Haven't found anyone yet who recognized it," Norrington said, poking one of the seals gently with a podgy forefinger. "Do you, by chance?"

"No," Grey said, his throat gone suddenly dry. "But you might look into one Baron Amandine. Wainwright mentioned that name to me as—a personal connexion of his."

"Amandine?" Norrington looked puzzled. "Never heard of him."

"Neither has anyone else." Grey sighed and rose to his feet. "I begin to wonder whether he exists."

HE WAS STILL WONDERING, as he made his way to Hal's house. The Baron Amandine might or might not exist; if he did, he might be only a front, disguising the interest of someone much more prominent. If he didn't . . . matters became simultaneously more confusing and simpler of approach; with no way of knowing who was behind the matter, Percy Wainwright was the only possible avenue of approach.

None of Norrington's letters had mentioned the Northwest Territory nor held any hint of the proposition Percy had put before him. That was not surprising, though; it would have been extremely dangerous to put such information on paper, though he had certainly known spies do such things before. If Amandine did exist, and was directly involved, apparently he was both sensible and cautious.

Well, Hal would have to be told about Percy, in any case. Perhaps he would know something regarding Amandine, or could find out; Hal had a number of friends in France.

The thought of what Hal must be told reminded him abruptly of William's letter, which he had nearly forgotten in the intrigues of the morning. He breathed strongly through his nose at the thought. No. He wasn't mentioning *that* to his brother until he'd had a chance to speak to Dottie, alone. Perhaps he could contrive a private word with her, arrange to meet later.

Dottie proved not to be at home, though, when Grey arrived at Argus House.

"She's at one of Miss Brierley's musical afternoons," his sister-in-law Minnie informed him, when he inquired politely how his niece and goddaughter did. "She's very sociable these days. She'll be sorry to have missed you, though." She stood on tiptoe and kissed him, beaming. "It's good to see you again, John."

"And you, Minnie," he said, meaning it. "Is Hal at home?"

She rolled her eyes expressively at the ceiling.

"He's been at home for a week, with the gout. Another week, and I shall put poison in his soup."

"Ah." That reinforced his decision not to speak to Hal of William's letter. Hal in good spirits was a prospect that daunted hardened soldiers and lifetime politicians; Hal in ill health . . . Presumably that was why Dottie had had the good sense to absent herself.

Well, it wasn't as though his news would improve Hal's mood in any case, he thought. He pushed open the door to Hal's study with due caution, though; his brother had been known to throw things when peevish—and nothing peeved him more than bodily indisposition.

As it was, Hal was asleep, slumped in his chair before the fire, his bandaged foot on a stool. The smell of some strong and acrid medicine floated in the air, overlying the scents of burning wood, melted tallow, and stale bread. A congealed plate of soup sat upon a tray at Hal's side, untasted. Perhaps Minnie had made her threat explicit, Grey thought with a smile. Aside from himself and their mother, Minnie was likely the only other person in the world who was never afraid of Hal.

He sat down quietly, wondering whether to wake his brother. Hal looked ill and tired, much thinner than usual—and Hal was normally lean to start with. He could not look less than elegant, even clad in breeches and a worn linen shirt, bare-legged, and with a ratty shawl draped about his shoulders, but the lines of a life spent fighting were eloquent in his face.

Grey's heart contracted with a sudden, unexpected tenderness, and he wondered whether, after all, he should trouble Hal with his news. But he couldn't risk Hal being confronted unexpectedly with the tidings of Percy's untimely resurrection; he would have to be warned.

Before he could make up his mind whether to go away and come back, though, Hal's eyes opened abruptly. They were clear and alert, the same light blue as Grey's own, with no sign of drowsiness or distraction.

"You're back," Hal said, and smiled with great affection. "Pour me a brandy."

"Minnie says you have the gout," Grey said, with a glance at Hal's foot. "Don't the quacks say you ought not to take strong drink, with the gout?" Nonetheless, he rose to his feet.

"They do," Hal said, pulling himself upright in his chair and grimacing as the movement jarred his foot. "But from the look of you, you're about to tell me something that means I'll need it. Best bring the decanter."

IT WAS SEVERAL HOURS before he left Argus House—declining Minnie's invitation to stay for supper—and the weather had deteriorated substantially. There was autumn chill in the air; a gusty wind was getting up, and he could taste salt in the air—the traces of sea fog drifting toward shore. It would be a good night to stay indoors.

Minnie had apologized for not being able to offer her coach, as Dottie had gone off to her afternoon *salon* in it. He had assured her that walking suited him, assisting him to think. It did, but the whoosh of wind flapping the skirts of his coat and threatening to carry away his hat was a distraction, and he was beginning to regret the coach, when he suddenly saw the equipage itself, waiting in the drive of one of the big houses near the Alexandra Gate, the horses blanketed against the wind.

He turned in at the gate and, hearing a cry of "Uncle John!", looked toward the house and was in time to see his niece, Dottie, bearing down on him like a ship under full sail—literally. She wore a plum silk mantua and a rose-pink cloak and, with the wind behind her, billowed alarmingly. In fact, she scudded toward him with such velocity that he was obliged to catch her in his arms in order to halt her forward progress.

"Are you a virgin?" he demanded without preamble.

Her eyes widened, and without the least hesitation, she wrested one arm free and slapped his cheek.

"What?" she said.

"My apologies. That was a trifle abrupt, wasn't it?" He glanced at her waiting coach—and the driver, looking rigidly ahead—and, calling to the driver to wait, took her by the arm and turned her in the direction of the park.

"Where are we going?"

"Just for a little walk. I have a few questions to ask you, and they aren't the sort that I wish to have overheard—nor do you, I assure you."

Her eyes widened still further, but she didn't argue; merely clapped a hand to her saucy little hat and came with him, her skirts foaming in the wind.

Weather and passersby prevented his asking any of the questions he had in mind until after they had made their way well into the park and found themselves in a more or less deserted path that led through a small topiary garden, where evergreen bushes and trees had been clipped into fanciful shapes.

The wind had dropped momentarily, though the sky was darkening. Dottie pulled to a halt in the shelter of a topiary lion and said, "Uncle John. *What* is this taradiddle about?"

Dottie had her mother's autumn-leaf coloring, with hair the color of ripened wheat and cheeks with the perpetual faint flush of rose hips. But where Minnie's face was pretty and gently appealing, Dottie's was underlain by Hal's fine bones and embroidered with his dark lashes; her beauty had a dangerous edge to it.

The edge was uppermost in the look she turned on her uncle, and he thought that, in fact, if Willie *was* enamored of her, it was perhaps not surprising. *If* he was.

"I had a letter from William, intimating that he had—if not actually forced his attentions upon you—behaved in a manner unbecoming a gentleman. Is it true?"

Her mouth fell open in undissimulated horror.

"He told you *what?*"

Well, that relieved his mind of one burden. She was likely still a virgin, and he needn't have William shipped off to China to avoid her brothers.

"It was, as I say, an intimation. He didn't provide me with details. Come, let us walk before we freeze." He took her by the arm and guided her up one of the paths that led to a small oratory. Here they took shelter in the vestibule, overlooked only by a stained-glass window of St. Barbara, carrying her severed breasts on a platter. Grey affected to study this elevating image, allowing Dottie a moment to settle her wind-flustered garments—and decide what she was going to tell him.

"Well," she began, turning to him with her chin raised, "it's true that we— well, that I let him kiss me."

"Oh? Where? I mean"—he added hastily, seeing the momentary shock in her eye—and *that* was interesting, for would a completely inexperienced young lady realize that it was possible to be kissed elsewhere than on lips or hand?—"in what geographical location?"

The flush in her cheeks deepened, for she realized as well as he what she had just given away, but she met his eye directly.

"In Lady Windermere's garden. We'd both come to her musicale, and the supper wasn't ready, so William invited me to walk outside with him for a bit, and—I did. It was *such* a beautiful evening," she added ingenuously.

"Yes, he noted that, as well. I had not previously realized the intoxicant properties of good weather."

She gave him a slight glare.

"Well, anyway, we're in love! Did he say *that*, at least?"

"Yes, he did," Grey replied. "He began with a statement to that effect, in fact, before going on to make his scandalous confessions regarding your virtue."

Her eyes widened.

"He—what, exactly, did he say?" she demanded.

"Enough to persuade me—he hoped—to go at once to your father and put before him the desirability of William's suit for your hand."

"Oh." She drew a deep breath at that, as though relieved, and looked away for a moment. "Well. Are you going to, then?" she asked, swiveling big blue eyes back in his direction. "Or have you already?" she added, with an air of hopefulness.

"No, I have said nothing to your father regarding William's letter. For one thing, I thought I had best speak to *you* first, and see whether you were in such agreement with William's sentiments as he appears to think."

She blinked, then gave him one of her radiant smiles.

"That was *very* considerate of you, Uncle John. Many men wouldn't bother with the woman's opinion of the situation—but you've always been *so* thoughtful. Mother cannot say enough good things about your kindness."

"Don't over-egg the pudding, Dottie," he said tolerantly. "So you say that you are willing to marry William?"

"Willing?" she cried. "Why, I desire it more than anything!"

He gave her a long, level look, and while she continued to meet his eye, the blood rose precipitously in her throat and cheeks.

"Oh, yes?" he said, allowing all the skepticism he felt to show in his voice. "Why?"

She blinked twice, very fast.

"Why?"

"Why?" he repeated patiently. "What is there in William's character—or appearance, I suppose," he added fairly, for young women had no great reputation as judges of character, "that so attracts you as to desire marriage to him? And hasty marriage at that."

He could just about see one or both of them developing an attraction—but what was the hurry? Even if William feared Hal's deciding to allow Viscount Maxwell's suit, Dottie herself could not possibly be under the illusion that her doting father would force her to marry anyone she did not want to.

"Well, we are in love, of course!" she said, though with a rather uncertain note in her voice for such a theoretically fervent declaration. "As for his—his *character* ... why, Uncle, you are his own father; surely you cannot be in ignorance of his ... his ... intelligence!" She came up with the word triumphantly. "His kindness, his good humor ..." she was picking up speed now, "... his gentleness ..."

Now it was Lord John's turn to blink. William was undoubtedly intelligent, good-humored, and reasonably kind, but "gentle" was not the word that sprang immediately to mind with regard to him. On the other hand, the hole in the paneling of his mother's dining room, through which William had inadvertently thrown a companion during a tea party, had still not been repaired, and this image was fresh in Grey's mind. Probably Willie behaved more circumspectly in Dottie's company, but still ...

"He is the very model of a gentleman!" she declaimed with enthusiasm, having now got the bit well between her teeth. "And his appearance—well, of course he is admired by every woman I know! So tall, so imposing a figure ..."

He noticed, with an air of clinical detachment, that while she touched on several of William's notable characteristics, she did not at any point mention his eyes. Aside from his height—which could scarcely escape notice—his eyes were probably his most striking feature, being a deep and brilliant blue, and unusually shaped, with a catlike slant. They were, in fact, Jamie Fraser's eyes, and they gave John a faint, passing clench of the heart whenever Willie looked at him with a certain expression.

Willie knew the effect his eyes had on young women excellently well—and had no hesitation in making the most of it. Had he been gazing longingly into Dottie's own eyes, she would have been transfixed, whether she loved him or not. And that touching account of rapture in the garden ... Following a musicale, or during a ball, and at Lady Belvedere's or at Lady Windermere's ...

He had been so occupied by his own thoughts that he did not realize for a moment that she had stopped talking.

"I beg your pardon," he said, with great courtesy. "And I thank you for the encomia regarding William's character, which cannot fail to warm a father's heart. Still—what is the urgency in arranging a marriage? William will be sent home in a year or two, surely."

"He might be killed!" she said, and there was in her voice a sudden note of real fear, so real that his attention sharpened. She swallowed visibly, a hand going to her throat.

"I couldn't bear it," she said, her voice suddenly small. "If he were killed, and we'd never ... never had a chance to ..." She looked up at him, her eyes brilliant with emotion, and put her hand pleadingly on his arm.

"I have to," she said. "Really, Uncle John. I must, and I cannot wait. I want to go to America and be married."

His mouth fell open. Wanting to be married was one thing, but *this* ...!

"You cannot possibly be serious," he said. "You cannot think that your parents—your father, in particular—would ever countenance such a thing."

"He would," she countered. "If *you* put the matter to him properly. He values your opinion more than anyone's," she went on persuasively, squeezing a little. "And you, of all people, must understand the horror I feel at the thought that something might . . . happen to William before I see him again."

Indeed, he thought, the only thing weighing in her favor was the feeling of desolation that the mention of William's possible death caused in his own heart. Yes, he *could* be killed. Any man might be, in time of war, and most particularly a soldier. That was one of the risks you took—and he could not in conscience have prevented William taking it, even though the mere thought of William blown to pieces by cannon fire or shot through the head or dying in agony of the flux . . .

He swallowed, dry-mouthed, and with some effort shoved those pusillanimous images firmly back into the locked mental closet in which he normally kept them confined.

He took a long breath.

"Dorothea," he said firmly. "I *will* discover what you're up to."

She looked at him for a long, thoughtful moment, as though estimating the chances. The corner of her mouth rose insensibly as her eyes narrowed, and he saw the response on her face, as clearly as if she'd said it aloud.

No. I don't think so.

The expression was no more than a flicker, though, and her face resumed its air of indignation mingled with pleading.

"Uncle John! How dare you accuse me and William—your own son!—of, of . . . what *are* you accusing us of?"

"I don't know," he admitted.

"Well, then! *Will* you speak to Papa for us? For me? Please? Today?"

Dottie was a born flirt; as she spoke, she leaned toward him, so that he could smell the fragrance of violets in her hair, and twined her fingers charmingly in the lapels of his coat.

"I can't," he said, striving to extricate himself. "Not just now. I've already given him one bad shock today; another might finish him off."

"Tomorrow, then," she coaxed.

"Dottie." He took her hands in his, and was rather touched to find them cold and trembling. She *did* mean it—or mean something, at least.

"Dottie," he repeated, more gently. "Even if your father were disposed to send you to America to be married—and I cannot think that anything less exigent than your being with child would compel it—there is no possibility of sailing before April. There is therefore no need to harry Hal into an early grave by telling him any of this, at least not until he has recovered from his current indisposition."

She wasn't pleased, but was obliged to admit the force of his reasoning.

"Besides," he added, letting go of her hands, "campaigning ceases in winter; you know that. The fighting will stop soon, and William will be relatively safe. You need have no fears for him." *Other than accident, flux, ague, blood poisoning, griping belly, tavern brawls, and ten or fifteen other life-threatening possibilities,* he added privately to himself.

"But—" she began, but stopped, and sighed. "Yes, I suppose you're right. But . . . you *will* speak to Papa soon, won't you, Uncle John?"

He sighed in turn, but smiled at her nonetheless.

"I will, if that is what you truly desire." A gust of wind hit the oratory and the stained-glass image of St. Barbara shivered in its leaded frame. A rush of sudden rain rattled across the roof slates, and he drew his cloak around him.

"Stay here," he advised his niece. "I'll fetch the coach round to the road."

As he made his way against the wind, one hand on his hat to prevent it taking flight, he recalled with some unease his own words to her: *I cannot think that anything less exigent than your being with child would compel it.*

She wouldn't. Would she? No, he assured himself. Become pregnant by someone in order to convince her father to allow her to marry someone else? Fat chance; Hal would have her married to the guilty party before she could say "cat." Unless, of course, she chose someone impossible to do the deed: a married man, say, or—But this was nonsense! What would William say, were she to arrive in America, pregnant by another man?

No. Not even Brianna Fraser MacKenzie—the most hair-raisingly pragmatic woman he had ever known—would have done something like that. He smiled a little to himself at thought of the formidable Mrs. MacKenzie, recalling her attempt at blackmailing *him* into marriage—while pregnant by someone who was definitely not him. He'd always wondered if the child was in fact her husband's. Perhaps *she* would. But not Dottie.

Surely not.

16

UNARMED CONFLICT

Inverness, Scotland
October 1980

THE OLD HIGH CHURCH of St. Stephen's stood serene on the bank of the Ness, the weathered stones in its kirkyard a testament to righteous peace. Roger was aware of the serenity—but none of it was for him.

His blood was still throbbing in his temples, and the collar of his shirt was damp from exertion, chilly though the day was. He'd walked from the High Street car park, at a ferocious pace that seemed to eat the distance in seconds.

She'd called him a coward, by God. She'd called him a lot of other things, too, but that was the one that stung—and she knew it.

The fight had started after supper the day before, when she'd put a crusted pot into the old stone sink, turned to him, drawn a deep breath, and informed him that she had an interview for a job at the North of Scotland Hydro Electric Board.

"Job?" he'd said stupidly.

"Job," she'd repeated, narrowing her eyes at him.

He *had* been swift enough to suppress the automatic "But you've got a job" that had sprung to his lips, substituting a rather mild—he thought—"Why?"

Never one for quiet diplomacy, she'd fixed him with a stare and said, "Because one of us needs to work, and if it isn't going to be you, it'll have to be me."

"What do you mean, 'needs to work'?" he'd asked—damn it, she was right, he *was* a coward, because he knew goddamned well what she meant by it. "We've money enough for a time."

"For a time," she agreed. "A year or two—maybe more, if we're careful. And you think we should just sit on our asses until the money runs out, and then what? *Then* you start thinking about what you ought to be doing?"

"I've been thinking," he said through his teeth. True, that; he'd been doing little else for months. There was the book, of course; he was writing down all the songs he'd committed to memory in the eighteenth century with commentary—but that was hardly a job in itself, nor would it earn much money. Mostly thinking.

"Yeah? So have I." She turned her back on him, turning on the tap, either to drown out whatever he might say next, or just in order to get a grip on herself. The water ceased, and she turned round again.

"Look," she said, trying to sound reasonable. "I can't wait much longer. I can't stay out of the field for years and years and just walk back into it anytime. It's been nearly a year since the last consulting job I did—I can't wait any longer."

"You never said you meant to go back to work full-time." She'd done a couple of small jobs in Boston—brief consulting projects, once Mandy was out of the hospital and all right. Joe Abernathy had got them for her.

"Look, man," Joe had said confidentially to Roger, "she's antsy. I know that girl; she needs to *move*. She's been focused on the baby day and night, probably since she was born, been cooped up with doctors, hospitals, clingy kids for weeks now. She's gotta get out of her own head."

And I don't? Roger had thought—but couldn't say so.

An elderly man in a flat cap was weeding round one of the gravestones, a limp mass of uprooted greenery lying on the ground beside him. He'd been watching Roger as he hesitated near the wall, and nodded to him in a friendly way, but didn't speak.

She was a mother, he'd wanted to say. Wanted to say something about the closeness between her and the kids, the way they needed her, like they needed air and food and water. He was now and then jealous over not being needed in the same primal way; how could she deny that gift?

Well, he'd *tried* to say something of the kind. The result had been what might be expected by lighting a match in a mine filled with gas.

He turned abruptly and walked out of the kirkyard. He couldn't speak to the rector right this minute—couldn't speak at all, come to that; he'd have to cool down first, get his voice back.

He turned left and went down along Huntly Street, seeing the facade of St. Mary's across the river from the corner of his eye; the only Catholic church in Inverness.

During one of the earlier, more rational parts of the fight, she'd made an effort. Asked if it was her fault.

"Is it me?" she'd asked seriously. "Being a Catholic, I mean. I know— I know that makes it more complicated." Her lips twitched. "Jem told me about Mrs. Ogilvy."

He hadn't felt at all like laughing, but couldn't help a brief smile at the memory. He'd been out by the barn, shoveling well-rotted manure into a wheelbarrow to spread on the kailyard, Jem assisting with his own small spade.

"Sixteen tons and what do you get?" Roger had sung—if the sort of hoarse croaking he produced could be called that.

"Another day older and deeper in shit!" Jem bellowed, doing his best to pitch his voice down into Tennessee Ernie Ford range, but then losing control in a glissando of giggles.

It was at this unfortunate moment that he'd turned round to find that they had visitors: Mrs. Ogilvy and Mrs. MacNeil, pillars of the Ladies' Altar and Tea Society at the Free North Church in Inverness. He knew them—and he knew just what they were doing here, too.

"We've come to call upon your good wife, Mr. MacKenzie," Mrs. MacNeil said, smiling with pursed lips. He wasn't sure whether the expression was meant to indicate inner reservations, or whether it was merely that she feared her ill-fitting false teeth might fall out if she opened her mouth more than a quarter of an inch.

"Ah. She'll be away to the town just now, I'm afraid." He'd wiped his hand on his jeans, thinking to offer it, but looked at it, thought better of it, and nodded to them instead. "But please to come in. Will I have the girl make tea?"

They shook their heads in unison.

"We havena seen your wife in kirk as yet, Mr. MacKenzie." Mrs. Ogilvy fixed him with a fishy eye.

Well, he'd been expecting that one. He could buy a little time by saying, ach, the baby'd been ailing—but no point; the nettle would have to be grasped sooner or later.

"No," he said pleasantly, though his shoulders stiffened by reflex. "She's a Catholic. She'll be to the Mass at St. Mary's of a Sunday."

Mrs. Ogilvy's square face sagged into a momentary oval of astonishment.

"Your wife's a Papist?" she said, giving him a chance to correct the clearly insane thing he'd just said.

"She is, aye. Born one." He shrugged lightly.

There had been relatively little conversation following this revelation. Just a glance at Jem, a sharp question about whether he went to Sunday school, an intake of breath at the answer, and a gimlet-eyed stare at Roger before they took their leave.

Do you want me to convert? Bree had demanded, in the course of the argument. And it had been a demand, not an offer.

He'd wanted suddenly and fiercely to ask her to do just that—only to see if she would, for love of him. But religious conscience would never let him do such a thing; still less, his conscience as her lover. Her husband.

Huntly Street turned suddenly into Bank Street, and the foot traffic of the shopping precinct disappeared. He passed the small memorial garden, put up to commemorate the service of nurses during World War II, and thought—as he always did—of Claire, though this time with less than the usual admiration he had for her.

And what would you *say?* he thought. He knew damned well what she'd say—or at least, whose side she'd be on, in this. *She* hadn't hung about being a full-time mum, had she? She'd gone to medical school when Bree was seven. And Bree's dad, Frank Randall, had taken up the slack, whether he wanted to or not. He slowed his step briefly, realizing. No wonder, then, if Bree was thinking . . .

He passed the Free North Church and half-smiled at it, thinking of Mrs. Ogilvy and Mrs. MacNeil. They'd be back, he knew, if he didn't do something about it. He knew their brand of determined kindliness. Dear God, if they heard that Bree had gone to work and—to their way of thinking—abandoned him with two small children, they'd be running shepherd's pies and hot stovies out to him in relays. That mightn't be such a bad thing, he thought, meditatively licking his lips—save that they'd stay to poke their noses into the workings of his household, and letting them into Brianna's kitchen would be not merely playing with dynamite but deliberately throwing a bottle of nitroglycerin into the midst of his marriage.

"Catholics don't believe in divorce," Bree had informed him once. "We *do* believe in murder. There's always Confession, after all."

On the far shore was the only Anglican church in Inverness, St. Andrew's. One Catholic church, one Anglican church—and no fewer than six Presbyterian churches, all standing foursquare by the river, in the space of less than a quarter mile. Tell you all you needed to know, he thought, about the basic character of Inverness. And he *had* told Bree—though without, he admitted, mentioning his own crisis of faith.

She hadn't asked. He'd give her that. He'd come within a hair of ordination in North Carolina—and in the traumatic aftermath of that interruption, with Mandy's birth, the disintegration of the Ridge's community, the decision to risk the passage through the stones . . . no one had mentioned it. Likewise, when they'd come back, the immediate demands of taking care of Mandy's heart and then assembling some kind of life . . . the question of his ministry had been ignored.

He thought Brianna hadn't mentioned it because she wasn't sure how he meant to handle it and didn't want to seem to push him in either direction— if her being a Catholic made his being a Presbyterian minister in Inverness more complicated, he couldn't ignore the fact that his being a minister would cause major complications in her life, and she'd know that.

The upshot was that neither of them had talked about it when working out the details of their return.

They'd worked out the practicalities as best they could. He couldn't go back to Oxford—not without a truly elaborate cover story.

"You just can't drop in and out of academia," he'd explained to Bree and to Joe Abernathy, the doctor who had been Claire's longtime friend before her own departure to the past. "You can go on a sabbatical, true—or even an extended leave. But you have to have a stated purpose and something to show for your absence when you come back, in terms of published research."

"You could write a killer book about the Regulation, though," Joe Abernathy had observed. "Or the run-up to the Revolution in the South."

"I could," he admitted. "But not a respectable scholarly one." He'd smiled wryly, feeling a slight itch in the joints of his fingers. He *could* write a book—one that no one else could write. But not as a historian.

"No sources," he'd explained, with a nod at the shelves in Joe's study, where they were holding the first of several councils of war. "If I wrote a book as a historian, I'd need to provide sources for all the information—and for most of the unique situations I could describe, I'm sure nothing was ever recorded. 'Eyewitness testimony of author' wouldn't go over well with a university press, I assure you. I'd have to do it as a novel." That idea actually held some small appeal—but wouldn't impress the colleges of Oxford.

Scotland, though . . .

People didn't appear in Inverness—or anywhere else in the Highlands—unremarked. But Roger wasn't an "incomer." He'd grown up in the manse in Inverness, and there were still a good many people who had known him as an adult. And with an American wife and children to explain his absence . . .

"See, folk there don't really care what it is you were doing when you were away," he explained. "They only care about what you do when you're there."

He'd reached the Islands of the Ness by now. A small, quiet park set on small islets that lay only a few feet off the river's bank, it had packed-dirt paths, big trees, and little traffic at this time of day. He wandered the paths, trying to empty his mind, let it be filled only with the sound of the rushing water, the quietness of the overcast sky.

He reached the end of the island and stood for a time, half-seeing the debris left in the branches of the bushes that edged the water—wodges of dead leaves, birds' feathers, fish bones, the odd cigarette packet, deposited by the passage of high water.

He had, of course, been thinking of himself. What *he'd* be doing, what folk would think about *him*. Why had it never occurred to him to wonder what Brianna intended doing, if they went to Scotland?

Well, that was obvious—if stupid—in retrospect. On the Ridge, Bree had done . . . well, a bit more than the usual woman there did, true—one couldn't overlook the buffalo-hunting, turkey-shooting, goddess–huntress, pirate-killing side of her—but also what the usual woman did. Mind her family, feed, clothe, comfort—or occasionally smack—them. And with Mandy sick, and Brianna grieving the loss of her parents, the question of working at anything had been irrelevant. Nothing could have separated her from her daughter.

But Mandy was well now—hair-raisingly healthy, as the trail of destruction that followed her testified. The painstaking details of reestablishing their identities in the twentieth century had been accomplished, the purchase of Lallybroch made from the bank that owned it, the physical removal to Scotland accomplished, Jem settled—more or less—into the village school nearby, and a nice girl from the same village engaged to come clear up and help look after Mandy.

And now Brianna was going to work.

Roger was going to hell. Metaphorically, if not literally.

BRIANNA COULDN'T SAY she hadn't been warned. It was a man's world she was walking into.

A rough job it had been, a tough undertaking—the toughest, digging the tunnels that carried the miles of cable from the turbines of the hydroelectric plants. "Tunnel tigers," they'd called the men who dug them, many of them Polish and Irish immigrants who'd come for a job in the 1950s.

She'd read about them, seen pictures of them, grimy-faced and white-eyed as coal miners, in the Hydro Electric authority office—the walls were covered with them, documentation of Scotland's proudest modern achievement. *What had been Scotland's proudest ancient achievement?* she wondered. *The kilt?* She'd suppressed a laugh at the thought, but evidently it made her look pleasant, because Mr. Campbell, the personnel manager, had smiled kindly at her.

"You're in luck, lass; we've an opening at Pitlochry, starting in a month," he'd said.

"That's wonderful." She had a folder in her lap, containing her credentials. He didn't ask to see it, which rather surprised her, but she set it on the desk before him, flipping it open. "Here are my ... er ... ?" He was staring at the curriculum vitae on top, his mouth hanging open far enough for her to see the steel fillings in his back teeth.

He shut his mouth, glanced up at her in astonishment, then looked back at the folder, slowly lifting the CV as though afraid there might be something even more shocking underneath.

"I think I have all the qualifications," she said, restraining the nervous urge to clench her fingers in the fabric of her skirt. "To be a plant inspector, I mean." She knew damned well she did. She had the qualifications to *build* a freaking hydroelectric station, let alone inspect one.

"Inspector ..." he said faintly. Then he coughed, and flushed a bit. Heavy smoker; she could smell the fug of tobacco that clung to his clothes.

"I'm afraid there's been a bit of a misunderstanding, my dear," he said. "It's a secretary we're needing at Pitlochry."

"Perhaps you do," she said, giving in to the cloth-clenching urge. "But the advertisement I replied to was for plant inspector, and that's the position I'm applying for."

"But ... my dear ..." He was shaking his head, clearly appalled. "You're a woman!"

"I am," she said, and any of a hundred men who'd known her father would have picked up the ring of steel in her voice and given in on the spot. Mr. Campbell unfortunately hadn't known Jamie Fraser—but was about to be enlightened. "Would you care to explain to me exactly which aspects of plant inspection require a penis?"

His eyes bulged and he turned the shade of a turkey's wattles in courting season.

"That—you—that is—" With evident effort, he mastered himself enough to speak courteously, though the shock was still plain on his blunt features.

"Mrs. MacKenzie. I'm not unfamiliar with the notion of women's liberation, aye? I've daughters of my own." *And none of them would have said something like* that *to me,* his raised brow said. "It's not that I think ye'd be incompetent." He glanced at the open folder, raised both brows briefly, then shut it firmly. "It's the—the work environment. It wouldn't be suitable for a woman."

"Why not?"

He was recovering his aplomb by now.

"The conditions are often physically rough—and to be honest, Mrs. MacKenzie, so are the men you would encounter. The company cannot in good conscience—or as a matter of good business—risk your safety."

"You employ men who would be likely to assault a woman?"

"No! We—"

"You have plants that are physically dangerous? Then you *do* need an inspector, don't you?"

"The legalities—"

"I'm well up on the regulations pertaining to hydroelectric plants," she said firmly, and reaching into her bag, produced the printed booklet of regulations—obviously well thumbed—supplied by the Highlands and Islands Development Board. "I can spot problems, and I can tell you how to rectify them promptly—and as economically as possible."

Mr. Campbell was looking deeply unhappy.

"And I hear that you haven't had many applicants for this position," she finished. "None, to be exact."

"The men . . ."

"Men?" she said, and allowed the smallest edge of amusement to tinge the word. "I've worked with men before. I get on with them well."

She looked at him, not saying anything. *I know what it's like to kill a man,* she thought. *I know just how easy it is. And you don't.* She was not aware of having changed expression, but Campbell lost a bit of his high color and looked away. She wondered for a split second whether Roger would look away, if he saw that knowledge in her eyes. But this was no time to think of things like that.

"Why don't you show me one of the work sites?" she said gently. "Then we'll talk some more."

IN THE EIGHTEENTH CENTURY, St. Stephen's had been used as a temporary prison for captured Jacobites. Two of them had been executed in the graveyard, by some accounts. It wasn't the worst thing to have as your last sight of earth, he supposed: the wide river and the vast sky, both flowing to the sea. They carried an abiding sense of peace, wind and cloud and water did, despite their constant movement.

"If ever you find yourself in the midst of paradox, you can be sure you stand on the edge of truth," his adoptive father had told him once. *"You may not know what it is, mind,"* he'd added with a smile. *"But it's there."*

The rector at St. Stephen's, Dr. Weatherspoon, had had a few aphorisms to share, too.

"When God closes a door, he opens a window." Yeah. The problem was that this particular window opened off the tenth story, and he wasn't so sure God supplied parachutes.

"Do You?" he asked, looking up at the drifting sky over Inverness.

"Beg pardon?" said the startled sexton, popping up from the gravestone behind which he'd been working.

"Sorry." Roger flapped a hand, embarrassed. "Just . . . talking to myself."

The elderly man nodded understandingly. "Aye, aye. Nay bother, then. It's when ye start getting answers ye should worry." Chuckling hoarsely, he descended back out of sight.

Roger made his way down from the high graveyard to street level, walking slowly back to the car park. Well, he'd taken the first step. Well past the time he should have done—Bree was right, to a degree; he *had* been a coward—but he had done it.

The difficulty wasn't resolved as yet, but it had been a great comfort, only being able to lay it out for someone who understood and sympathized.

"I'll pray for you," Dr. Weatherspoon had said, shaking his hand in parting. That was a comfort, too.

He started up the dank concrete steps of the car park, fumbling in his pocket for the keys. Couldn't say he was entirely at peace with himself, just yet—but he felt a lot more peaceable toward Bree. Now he could go home and tell her . . .

No, damn it. He couldn't, not yet. He had to check.

He didn't have to check; he knew he was right. But he had to have it in his hands, had to be able to show Bree.

Turning abruptly on his heel, he strode past a puzzled car-park attendant coming up behind him, took the stairs two at a time, and walked up Huntly Street as though he trod on red-hot coals. He stopped briefly at the Fox, digging in his pocket for coins, and rang through from the call box to Lallybroch. Annie answered the phone with her customary rudeness, saying "Yiss?" with such abruptness that it emerged as little more than an interrogatory hiss.

He didn't bother rebuking her phone manners.

"It's Roger. Tell the Missus I'm going down to Oxford to look something up. I'll spend the night."

"Mmphm," she said, and hung up.

SHE WANTED TO HIT Roger over the head with a blunt object. Something like a champagne bottle, maybe.

"He went *where?*" she asked, though she'd heard Annie MacDonald clearly. Annie lifted both narrow shoulders to the level of her ears, indicating that she understood the rhetorical nature of the question.

"To Oxford," she said. "To *England.*" The tone of her voice underlined the sheer outrageousness of Roger's action. He hadn't simply gone to look up something in an old book—which would have been strange enough, though to be sure himself was a scholar and they'd do anything—but had abandoned his wife and children without notice and hied away to a foreign country!

"Himself did say as he'd come home tomorrow," Annie added, with great dubiousness. She picked up the bottle of champagne in its carrier bag, gingerly, as though it might explode. "Ought I put this to the ice, d'ye think?"

"To the—oh, no, don't put it in the freezer. Just in the fridge. Thank you, Annie."

Annie disappeared into the kitchen, and Brianna stood in the drafty hall for a moment, trying to get her feelings firmly under control before going to find Jem and Mandy. Kids being kids, they had ultra-sensitive radar concerning their parents. They already knew something was the matter between her and Roger; having their father suddenly disappear was *not* calculated to give them a feeling of cozy security. Had he even said goodbye to them? Assured *them* he'd be back? No, of course not.

"Bloody selfish, self-centered . . ." she muttered. Unable to find a satisfying noun with which to complete this, she said, "rat-fink *bastard!*" and then snorted with reluctant laughter. Not merely at the silliness of the insult, but with a wry acknowledgment that she'd got what she wanted. Both ways.

Granted, he couldn't have stopped her going for the job—and once he got past the dislocations involved, she thought he'd be all right with it.

"Men hate things to change," her mother had once casually told her. *"Unless it's their idea, of course. But you can make them think it* is *their idea, sometimes."*

Maybe she should have been less direct about it; tried to get Roger to feel that at least he had something to say about her going to work, even if not to think it was his idea—*that* would have been pushing it. She'd been in no mood to be devious, though. Or even diplomatic.

As for what she'd done to *him* . . . well, she'd put up with his immobility for as long as she could, and then she'd pushed him off a cliff. Deliberately.

"And I don't feel the least bit guilty about it!" she said to the coatrack.

She hung up her coat slowly, taking a little extra time to check the pockets for used tissues and crumpled receipts.

So, had he gone off out of pique—to get back at her for going back to work? Or out of anger at her having called him a coward? He hadn't liked that one bit; his eyes had gone dark and he'd nearly lost his voice—strong emotion choked him, quite literally, freezing his larynx. She'd done it on purpose, though. She knew where Roger's soft spots were—just as he knew hers.

Her lips tightened at that, just as her fingers closed on something hard in the inner pocket of her jacket. A weathered shell, turreted and smooth, worn white by sun and water. Roger had picked it up on the shingle by Loch Ness and handed it to her.

"To live in," he'd said, smiling, but given away by the gruffness of his damaged voice. "When ye need a hiding place."

She closed her fingers gently over the shell, and sighed.

Roger wasn't petty. Ever. He wouldn't go off to Oxford—a reluctant bubble of amusement floated up at the thought of Annie's shocked description: *to England!*—just to worry her.

So he'd gone for some specific reason, doubtless something jarred loose by their fight—and *that* worried her a bit.

He'd been wrestling with things since they came back. So had she, of course: Mandy's illness, decisions about where to live, all the petty details of relocating a family in both space and time—they'd done all that together. But there were things he wrestled with alone.

She'd grown up an only child, just as he had; she knew how it was, how you live in your own head a lot. But damn him, whatever he was living with in his head was eating him up before her eyes, and if he wouldn't tell her what it was, it was either something he considered too private to share—which bugged her, but she could live with it—or it was something he thought too disturbing or too dangerous to share, and she wasn't bloody *having* that.

Her fingers had clenched round the shell, and she deliberately loosened them, trying to calm down.

She could hear the kids upstairs, in Jem's room. He was reading something to Mandy—*The Gingerbread Man,* she thought. She couldn't hear the words, but could tell by the rhythm, counterpointed by Mandy's excited shouts of "Wun! Wun!"

No point in interrupting them. Time enough later to tell them Daddy'd be away overnight. Maybe they wouldn't be bothered, if she was matter-of-fact about it; he'd never left them since they'd come back, but when they lived on the Ridge, he was often gone with Jamie or Ian, hunting. Mandy wouldn't remember that, but Jem . . .

She'd meant to go into her study, but found herself drifting across the hall, through the open door to Roger's. It was the old speak-a-word room of the house; the room where her uncle Ian had run the affairs of the estate for years—her father for a short time before that, and her grandfather before him.

And now it was Roger's. He'd asked if she wanted the room, but she'd said no. She liked the little sitting room across the hall, with its sunny window and the shadows of the ancient yellow rose that flagged that side of the house with its color and scent. Aside from that, though, she just felt that this room was a man's place, with its clean, scuffed wooden floor and comfortably battered shelves.

Roger had managed to find one of the old farm ledgers, from 1776; it sat on an upper shelf, its worn cloth binding sheltering the patient, careful minutiae of life on a Highland farm: *one-quarter pound of silver fir seed, a he-goat for breeding, six rabbits, thirty-weight of seed potatoes . . .* had her uncle written it? She didn't know, had never seen a sample of his writing.

She wondered, with an odd little quiver of the insides, if her parents had made it back to Scotland—back *here.* Had seen Ian and Jenny again; if her father had sat—*would* sit?—here in this room, at home once more, talking over the matters of Lallybroch with Ian. And her mother? From the little Claire had said about it, she hadn't parted from Jenny on the best of terms, and Brianna knew her mother felt sad about that; once, they had been close friends. Maybe things could be mended—maybe they *had* been mended.

She glanced at the wooden box, safe on its high shelf beside the ledger, the little cherrywood snake curved in front of it. On impulse, she took the snake down, finding some comfort in the sleek curve of the body and the comical look of its face, peering back over its nonexistent shoulder. She smiled back at it, involuntarily.

"Thanks, Uncle Willie," she said softly, out loud, and felt an extraordinary shiver run through her. Not fear, or cold—a kind of delight, but a quiet kind. Recognition.

She'd seen that snake so often—on the Ridge, and now here, where it had first been made—that she never thought of its maker, her father's older brother, dead at the age of eleven. But he was here, too, in the work of his hands, in the rooms that had known him. When she'd visited Lallybroch before—in the eighteenth century—there had been a painting of him on the upstairs landing, a small, sturdy red-haired boy, standing with a hand on the shoulder of his baby brother, blue-eyed and serious.

Where is that now? she wondered. And the other paintings done by her grandmother? There was the one self-portrait, which had made it somehow to the National Portrait Gallery—she must be sure to take the kids down to London to see it, when they were a little older—but the others? There had been one of a very young Jenny Murray, feeding a tame pheasant, who had her uncle Ian's soft brown eyes, and she smiled at the memory.

It had been the right thing. Coming here, bringing the kids . . . home. It didn't matter if it took a little doing for her and Roger to find their places. Though maybe she shouldn't speak for Roger, she thought with a grimace.

She looked up at the box again. She wished her parents were here—either of them—so she could tell them about Roger, ask their opinion. Not that she wanted advice, so much. . . . What she wanted, if she was honest, she thought, was a reassurance that she'd done the right thing.

With a heightened flush in her cheeks, she reached up with both hands and brought down the box, feeling guilty for not waiting to share the next letter with Roger. But . . . she wanted her mother just now. She took the first letter on top that bore her mother's writing on the outside.

> *Offices of L'Oignon, New Bern, North Carolina*
> *April 12, 1777*

> *Dear Bree (and Roger and Jem and Mandy, of course),*

> *We've made it to New Bern, without major incident.* Yes, *I hear you thinking,* Major? *And it is true that we were held up by a pair of would-be bandits on the road south of Boone. Given that they were probably nine and eleven respectively, and armed solely with an ancient wheel-lock musket that would have blown them both to bits had they been able to fire it, though, we weren't in any marked danger.*

> *Rollo leapt out of the wagon and knocked one of them flat, whereupon his brother dropped the gun and legged it. Your cousin Ian ran him down, though, hauling him back by the scruff of the neck.*

> *It took your father some time to get anything sensible out of them,*

but a little food worked wonders. They said their names are Herman and—no, really—Vermin. Their parents died during the winter—their father went hunting and didn't come back, the mother died giving birth, and the baby died a day later, as the two boys had no way to feed it. They know of no people on their father's side, but they said their mother's family name was Kuykendall. Luckily, your father knows a Kuykendall family, near Bailey Camp, and so Ian took the little vagabonds off to find the Kuykendalls and see if they could be settled. If not, I suppose he'll bring them along to New Bern, and we'll try to apprentice them somewhere, or perhaps take them with us to Wilmington and find them a berth as cabin boys.

Fergus and Marsali and the children seem all to be doing very well, both physically—bar a family tendency to enlarged adenoids and the biggest wart I've ever seen on Germain's left elbow—and financially.

Aside from the Wilmington Gazette, L'Oignon *is the only regular newspaper in the colony, and Fergus thus gets a great deal of business. Add in the printing and sale of books and pamphlets, and he's doing very well indeed. The family now owns two milch goats, a flock of chickens, a pig, and* three *mules, counting Clarence, whom we are bequeathing to them on our way to Scotland.*

*Conditions and uncertainties being what they are [*meaning, Brianna thought, *that you don't know who might read this letter, or when] I'd better not be specific about* what *he's printing, besides newspapers.* L'Oignon *itself is carefully evenhanded, printing rabid denunciations by both Loyalists and those less loyal, and publishing satirical poetry by our good friend "Anonymous," lampooning both sides of the present political conflict. I've seldom seen Fergus so happy.*

War agrees with some men, and Fergus, rather oddly, is one of them. Your cousin Ian is another, though in his case, I think perhaps it keeps him from thinking too much.

I do wonder what his mother will make of him. But knowing her as I do, my guess is that after the first shock has passed, she'll begin the work of finding him a wife. Jenny is a very perceptive woman, all things said—and just as stubborn as your father. I do hope he remembers that.

Speaking of your father, he's out and about a good deal with Fergus, doing bits of "business" (unspecified, which means he's probably doing something that would turn my hair white—or whiter—to know about) and inquiring among the merchants for a possible ship—though I think our chances of finding one will be better in Wilmington, where we'll go as soon as Ian joins us.

Meanwhile, I've set up my shingle—literally. It's tacked to the front of Fergus's printshop, and says, TEETH PULLED, RASHES, PHLEGM, AND THE AGUE CURED, *this being Marsali's work. She wanted to add a line about the pox, but both Fergus and I dissuaded her—he from a fear that it would lower the tone of his establishment, self from a certain morbid attachment to truth in advertising, as there is in fact nothing I can presently do about any condition they call the pox. Phlegm . . . well, there's always something you can do about phlegm, even if it's nothing more than a cup of hot tea (these days, that's hot water over sassafras root, catnip, or lemon balm) with a dram in it.*

I called on Dr. Fentiman in Cross Creek on our way, and was able to buy several necessary instruments and a few medicines from him to refurbish my kit (this at the cost of a bottle of whisky and of being forced to admire the latest addition to his ghastly collection of pickled curiosities—no, you don't want to know; you really don't. A good thing he can't see Germain's wart, or he'd be down to New Bern in a flash, sneaking round the printshop with an amputation saw).

I still lack a pair of good surgical scissors, but Fergus knows a silversmith called Stephen Moray in Wilmington who he says could make a pair to my specifications. For the moment, I occupy myself largely in the pulling of teeth, as the barber who used to do it was drowned last November, having fallen into the harbor while drunk.

> *With all my love,*
> *Mama*

P.S. Speaking of the Wilmington Gazette, *your father has it in mind to call there and see if he can find out just who left that blasted notice about the fire. Though I suppose I oughtn't to complain; if you hadn't found it, you might never have come back. And while there are a lot of things I wish hadn't happened as a result of your coming—I can't ever regret that you know your father, and he you.*

 17

WEE DEMONS

IT WASN'T MUCH DIFFERENT than any of the deer trails they'd come across; in fact, it had doubtless begun as one of them. But there was something about this particular trace that said "people" to Ian, and he'd been so long accustomed to such judgments that he seldom registered them consciously. He didn't now, but gave Clarence's leading rein a twitch, turning his own horse's head aside.

"Why're we stoppin'?" Herman asked suspiciously. "Ain't nothin' here."

"There's someone living up there." Ian jerked his chin toward the wooded slope. "The trail's not wide enough for horses; we'll tie up here, and walk."

Herman and Vermin exchanged a wordless glance of deep skepticism, but slid off the mule and trudged after Ian, up the trail.

He was beginning to have his doubts; no one he'd spoken to in the last week knew of any Kuykendalls in the area, and he couldn't take too much more time about the matter. He might have to bring the wee savages down to New Bern with him, after all, and he had no notion how they'd take to the suggestion.

He had no notion how they took much of anything, come to that. They were not so much shy as secretive, whispering together behind him as they rode, then shutting up like clams the minute he looked at them, regarding him with carefully bland faces, behind which he plainly saw any amount of reckoning going on. What the devil were they plotting?

If they meant to run from him, he thought he might not make any monstrous great effort to chase them down. If, on the other hand, they meant to steal Clarence and the horse while he slept, that was another matter.

The cabin was there, a curl of smoke coming from its chimney; Herman turned a look of surprise on him, and he smiled at the boy.

"Told ye," he said, and hallooed.

The door creaked open, and the barrel of a musket poked out of it. This was not an uncommon response to strangers in the far backcountry, and Ian was not put off by it. He raised his voice and stated his business, pushing Herman and Vermin in front of him as evidence of his *bona fides*.

The gun wasn't withdrawn, but lifted in a significant manner. Obeying instinct, Ian flung himself flat, yanking the boys down with him, as the shot roared overhead. A woman's voice yelled something strident in a foreign tongue. He didn't understand the words, but took the meaning clearly, and pulling the little boys to their feet, ushered them hastily back down the trail.

"Ain't gonna live with *her*," Vermin informed him, focusing a narrow glare of dislike over his shoulder. "Tell you that for free."

"No, ye're not," Ian agreed. "Keep moving, aye?" For Vermin had stopped dead.

"Gotta shit."

"Oh, aye? Well, be quick about it." He turned away, having discovered early on that the boys had an exaggerated requirement for privacy in such matters.

Herman had gone on already; the tangled mess of his dirty-blond hair was just visible, some twenty yards down the slope. Ian had suggested that the boys might cut, if not comb, their hair, and maybe wash their faces, as a gesture of civility toward any relations who might be faced with the prospect of taking them in, but this suggestion had been rejected with vehemence. Fortunately he was not responsible for forcing the wee buggers to wash—and to be fair, he thought washing would make little difference to their smell, given the state of their clothes, which they had plainly been living in for some months. He did make them sleep on the other side of the fire from himself and Rollo at night, in hopes of limiting his exposure to the lice both of them crawled with.

Could the notable infestation he sported possibly be where the younger boy's parents had acquired his name? he wondered. Or had they no notion of its meaning and had only picked it to rhyme with his elder brother's?

Clarence's earsplitting bray pulled him abruptly from his thoughts. He lengthened his stride, berating himself for having left his own gun in its saddle loop. He hadn't wanted to approach the house armed, but—

A shriek from below sent him dodging off the path, into the trees. Another shriek was cut off suddenly, and he scrambled down the slope, as quickly as he might without making a racket. Panther? A bear? Nay, Clarence would be bellowing like a grampus, if it was that; instead, he was gurgling and wheezing like he did when he spotted—

Someone he knew.

Ian stopped dead, behind a screen of poplars, his heart cold in his chest.

Arch Bug turned his head, hearing the noise, faint as it was.

"Come on out, lad," he called. "I see ye there."

Plainly he did; the ancient eyes were looking straight at him, and Ian came slowly out of the trees.

Arch had taken the gun from the horse; it was slung across his shoulder. He had an arm crooked round Herman's throat, and the little boy's face was bright red from the choking; his feet kicked like a dying rabbit's, a few inches off the ground.

"Where's the gold?" Arch said, without preamble. His white hair was neatly bound up, and he seemed, so far as Ian could see, to have taken no harm from the winter. Must have found folk to bide with. *Where?* he wondered. *Brownsville, maybe?* Bloody dangerous, if he'd told the Browns about the gold—but he thought old Arch was too downy a bird to talk in such company.

"Where ye'll never find it," Ian said bluntly. He was thinking furiously. He'd a knife in his belt—but it was a good deal too far to throw it, and if he missed . . .

"What d'ye want wi' that wean?" he asked, moving a little closer. "He's naught to do wi' you."

"No, but he seems somewhat to do wi' *you*." Herman was making rasping squeaks, and his feet, while still kicking, were slowing.

"No, he's naught to me, either," Ian said, striving for casualness. "I'm only helping him to find his people. Ye plan to cut his throat if I dinna tell ye where the gold is? Go ahead; I'm no telling ye."

He didn't see Arch pull the knife, but it was there, suddenly, in his right hand, held awkwardly because of the missing fingers, but doubtless useful enough.

"All right," Arch said calmly, and put the point of the knife under Herman's chin.

A scream burst from behind Ian, and Vermin half-ran, half-fell down the last few feet of the trail. Arch Bug looked up, startled, and Ian crouched to rush him, but was forestalled by Vermin.

The little boy rushed at Arch Bug and gave him a tremendous kick in the shin, shouting, "You bad old man! You let her go right now!"

Arch seemed as startled by the speech as by the kick, but didn't let go.

"Her?" he said, and looked down at the child in his grasp, who promptly turned her—her?—head and bit him fiercely in the wrist. Ian, seizing the moment, lunged at him, but was impeded by Vermin, who had now seized Arch by the thigh and was clinging like grim death, trying to punch the old man in the balls with one small clenched fist.

With a ferocious grunt, Arch jerked the little girl—if that's what she was—up and flung her staggering into Ian. He then brought one big fist down on top of Vermin's head, stunning him. He shook the child off his leg, kicked the boy in the ribs as he staggered back, then turned and ran.

"Trudy, Trudy!" Herman ran for his—no, her—brother, who was lying in the leaf mold, mouth opening and closing like a landed trout.

Ian hesitated, wanting to pursue Arch, worried that Vermin might be badly hurt—but Arch was already gone, vanished into the wood. Gritting his teeth, he crouched and passed his hands rapidly over Vermin. No blood, and the wean was getting back his breath now, gulping and wheezing like a leaky bellows.

"Trudy?" Ian said to Herman, who was clinging tightly to Vermin's neck. Not waiting for an answer, he pulled up Vermin's ragged shirt, pulled out the waistband of his too-big breeches, and peeked inside. He let go hastily.

Herman leapt up, eyes bugged and hands clasped protectively over her—yes, her!—crotch.

"No!" she said. "I won't let you stick your nasty prick in me!"

"Ye couldna pay me to," Ian assured her. "If this is Trudy"—he nodded at Vermin, who had rolled up onto his—no, her—hands and knees and was vomiting into the grass—"what the devil's *your* name?"

"Hermione," the lassie said, sullen. "She's Ermintrude."

Ian ran a hand over his face, trying to adjust to this information. Now he looked . . . well, no, they still looked like filthy wee demons rather than little girls, their slitted eyes burning through the greasy, matted underbrush of their hair. They'd have to have their heads shaved, he supposed, and hoped he was nowhere in the neighborhood when it was done.

"Aye," he said, for lack of anything sensible. "Well, then."

"You've got gold?" said Ermintrude, having stopped her retching. She sat up, wiped a small hand over her mouth, and spat expertly. "Where?"

"If I wouldna tell him, why would I tell you? And ye can just forget *that* notion right now," he assured her, seeing her eyes dart to the knife in his belt.

Damn. What was he to do now? He pushed away the shock of Arch Bug's appearance—time to think of that later—and ran a hand slowly through his hair, considering. The fact that they were girls didn't change anything, really, but the fact that they knew he had gold hidden did. He didn't dare leave them with anyone now, because if he did . . .

"If you leave us, we'll tell about the gold," Hermione said promptly. "We don't want to live in a stinky cabin. We want to go to London."

"What?" He stared at her, incredulous. "What d'ye ken of London, for God's sake?"

"Our mam came from there," Herman—no, Hermione—said, and bit her lip to stop it trembling at mention of her mother. It was the first time she *had* spoken of her mother, Ian noted with interest. Let alone displayed any sign of vulnerability. "She told us about it."

"Mmphm. And why would I no just kill ye myself?" he demanded, exasperated. To his astonishment, Herman smiled at him, the first halfway-pleasant expression he'd ever seen on her face.

"The dog likes you," she said. "He wouldn't like you if you killed people."

"That's all you know," he muttered, and stood up. Rollo, who had been off about his own business, chose this opportune moment to saunter out of the underbrush, sniffing busily.

"And where were *you* when I needed ye?" Ian demanded. Rollo smelled carefully round the spot where Arch Bug had stood, then lifted his leg and urinated on a bush.

"Would that bad old man have killed Hermie?" the little one asked suddenly, as he boosted her onto the mule behind her sister.

"No," he said, with certainty. But as he swung up into his own saddle, he wondered. He had the very uncomfortable feeling that Arch Bug understood the nature of guilt much too well. Enough to kill an innocent child, only because her death would make Ian feel guilty for it? And Ian would; Arch knew that.

"No," he repeated more strongly. Arch Bug was both vengeful and vindictive—and had a right to be, he'd admit that. But Ian had nay grounds to think the man a monster.

Still, he made the little girls ride in front of him, until they made camp that night.

THERE WAS NO further sign of Arch Bug, though Ian felt now and then the crawling sensation of being watched, when they camped. Was the man following him? Very likely he was, Ian thought—for surely it wasn't accident that had made him appear so suddenly.

So. He'd gone back to the ruins of the Big House, then, thinking to retrieve the gold after Uncle Jamie had left, only to find it gone. He wondered briefly whether Arch had managed to kill the white sow, but dismissed that notion; his uncle said the creature was plainly from the infernal regions and thus indestructible, and he was himself inclined to believe it.

He glanced at Rollo, who was dozing by his feet, but the dog gave no sign that anyone was near, though his ears were half cocked. Ian relaxed a little, though he kept the knife on his person, even while sleeping.

Not entirely in respect of Arch Bug, marauders, or wild beasts, either. He looked across the fire, to where Hermione and Trudy lay rolled up together in his blank—only they weren't. The blanket was cunningly wadded so as to appear to contain bodies, but a gust of wind had pulled a corner loose, and he could see that it lay flat.

He closed his eyes in exasperation, then opened them and glanced down at the dog.

"Why did ye no say something?" he demanded. "Surely ye saw them leave!"

"We ain't gone," said a gruff, small voice behind him, and he whirled to find the two of them crouched on either side of his open saddlebag, busily rifling it for food.

"We 'uz hungry," said Trudy, matter-of-factly stuffing the remains of a journeycake into her face.

"I fed ye!" He'd shot a few quail and baked them in mud. Granted, it wasn't a feast, but—

"We's *still* hungry," Hermione said, with impeccable logic. She licked her fingers and burped.

"Have ye drunk all the beer?" he demanded, snatching up a stone bottle rolling near her feet.

"Mmm-hmm," she said dreamily, and sat down, quite suddenly.

"Ye canna be thieving food," he said severely, taking the depleted saddle-bag from Trudy. "If ye eat it all now, we'll be starving before I get ye to—wherever we're going," he ended, rather weakly.

"If we don't eat it, we'll starve now," Trudy said logically. "Best starve later."

"Where *are* we going?" Hermione was swaying gently to and fro, like a small filthy flower in the wind.

"To Cross Creek," he said. "It's the first good-sized town we'll come to, and I ken folk there." Whether he knew anyone who might be of help in this present circumstance . . . too bad about his great-auntie Jocasta. Were she still at River Run, he could easily have left the girls there, but as it was, Jocasta and her husband, Duncan, had emigrated to Nova Scotia. There was Jocasta's body slave, Phaedre . . . He thought she was employed as a barmaid in Wilmington. But, no, she couldn't—

"Is it as big as London?" Hermione collapsed gently onto her back and lay with her arms spread out. Rollo got up and came and sniffed her; she giggled—the first innocent sound he'd heard from her.

"You all right, Hermie?" Trudy scampered over to her sister and squatted next to her in concern. Rollo, having smelled Hermione thoroughly, turned his attention to Trudy, who merely pushed aside his inquisitive nose. Hermione was now humming tunelessly to herself.

"She's fine," Ian said, after a quick glance. "She's no but a bit drunk. It'll pass."

"Oh." Reassured, Trudy sat down next to her sister, hugging her knees. "Pap used to get drunk. He hollered and broke things, though."

"Did he?"

"Uh-huh. He broke my mam's nose once."

"Oh," Ian said, having no idea how to answer this. "Too bad."

"You think he's dead?"

"I hope so."

"Me, too," she said, satisfied. She yawned hugely—he could smell her rotting teeth from where he sat—and then curled herself on the ground, cuddling close to Hermione.

Sighing, Ian got up and fetched the blanket, and covered them both, tucking it gently round their small, limp bodies.

Now what? he wondered. The recent exchange was the closest thing he'd had yet to an actual conversation with the girls, and he was under no illusions that their brief foray into amiability would last past daylight. Where would he find someone willing and able to deal with them?

A tiny snore, like the buzzing of a bee's wings, came from the blanket, and he smiled involuntarily. Wee Mandy, Bree's daughter, had made a noise like that when she slept.

He'd held Mandy, sleeping, now and then—once for more than an hour, not wanting to surrender the tiny, warm weight, watching the flicker of the pulse in her throat. Imagining, with longing and a pain tempered by distance, his own daughter. Stillborn, her face a mystery to him. Yeksa'a, the Mohawk had called her—"little girl," too young to have a name. But she did have a name. Iseabail. That's what he'd called her.

He wrapped himself in the ragged plaid Uncle Jamie had given him when he'd chosen to be a Mohawk and lay down by the fire.

Pray. That's what his uncle, his parents, would have advised. He was unsure who to pray to, really, or what to say. Should he speak to Christ, or His mother, or perhaps one of the saints? The spirit of the red cedar that stood sentinel beyond the fire, or the life that moved in the wood, whispering on the night breeze?

"A Dhia," he whispered at last to the open sky, *"cuidich mi,"* and slept.

Whether it was God or the night itself who answered him, at dawn he woke with a notion.

HE'D BEEN EXPECTING the walleyed maid, but Mrs. Sylvie came to the door herself. She recalled him; he saw a flicker of recognition and—he thought—pleasure in her eyes, though it didn't go so far as a smile, of course.

"Mr. Murray," she said, cool and calm. She looked down then, and lost a trifle of her composure. She pushed the wire-rimmed spectacles up on her nose for a better look at what accompanied him, then raised her head and fixed him with suspicion.

"What's this?"

He'd been expecting this reaction and was ready for it. Without answering, he held up the fat wee pouch he'd made ready and shook it, so she could hear the metal clink inside.

Her face changed at that, and she stood back to let them in, though she went on looking wary.

Not so wary as the little heathens—he still had trouble thinking of them as girls—who hung back until he took them each by a scrawny neck and propelled them firmly into Mrs. Sylvie's parlor. They sat—under compulsion—but looked as though they had something in mind, and he kept a beady gaze on them, even as he talked with the proprietor of the establishment.

"Maids?" she said, in open disbelief, looking at the girls. He'd washed them *in* their clothes—forcibly, and had several bites to show for it, though luckily none had festered yet—but there had been nothing to do about their hair save chop it off, and he wasn't about to come near either one with a knife, for fear of injuring them or himself in the subsequent struggle. They sat and glared through the mats of their hair like gargoyles, red-eyed and malignant.

"Well, they dinna want to be whores," he said mildly. "And I dinna want them to be, either. Not that I've any objection to the profession personally," he added for the sake of politeness.

A muscle twitched by her mouth and she shot him a sharp glance—tinged with amusement—through her spectacles.

"I'm glad to hear it," she said dryly. And dropped her eyes to his feet and raised them slowly, almost appraisingly, up the length of his body in a way that made him feel suddenly as though he'd been dipped in hot water. The eyes came to rest on his face again, and the look of amusement had intensified considerably.

He coughed, recollecting—with a mixture of embarrassment and lust—a number of interesting images from their encounter more than two years before. Outwardly, she was a plain woman past thirty, her face and manner much more those of an autocratic nun than a whore. Beneath the unassuming calico gown and muslin apron, though . . . she gave fair value, did Mistress Sylvie.

"I'm no asking as a favor, aye?" he said, and nodded at the pouch, which he had put down on the table by his chair. "I had it in mind to apprentice them, maybe?"

"Apprentice girls. In a brothel." She didn't make it a question, but her mouth twitched again.

"Ye could start them as maids—surely ye've cleaning to be done? Chamber pots to be emptied, and the like? And then if they should be clever enough"—he shot them a narrow glance of his own, and Hermione stuck out her tongue at him—"ye could maybe train them up to be cooks. Or sempstresses. Ye must need a deal of mending done, aye? Torn sheets and the like?"

"Torn shifts, more like," she said, very dryly. Her eyes flickered toward the ceiling, where a sound of rhythmic squeaking indicated the presence of a paying customer.

The girls had sidled off their stools and were prowling the parlor like wild cats, nosing things and bristling with caution. He realized suddenly that they'd never seen a town, let alone a civilized person's house.

Mrs. Sylvie leaned forward and picked up the pouch, her eyes widening in surprise at the weight of it. She opened it and poured a handful of greasy black shot into her hand, glancing sharply up from it to him. He didn't speak, but smiled and, reaching forward, took one of the balls from the palm of her hand, dug his thumbnail hard into it, and dropped it back into her hand, the scored line glinting bright gold amid the darkness.

She pursed her lips, weighing the bag again.

"All of it?" It was, he'd estimated, more than fifty pounds' worth of gold: half what he'd been carrying.

He made a long reach and took a china ornament out of Hermione's hands. "It'll no be an easy job," he said. "Ye'll earn it, I think."

"I think so, too," she said, watching Trudy, who—with extreme nonchalance—had lowered her breeches and was relieving herself in a corner of the hearth. The secret of their sex revealed, the girls had quite abandoned their requirements of privacy.

Mrs. Sylvie rang her silver bell, and both girls turned toward the sound in surprise.

"Why me?" she asked.

"I couldna think of anyone else who might be able to deal with them," Ian said simply.

"I'm *very* flattered."

"Ye should be," he said, smiling. "Have we a bargain, then?"

She drew a deep breath, eyeing the girls, who had their heads together, whispering, as they viewed her with the deepest suspicion. She let it out again, shaking her head.

"I think it's likely a bad bargain—but times are hard."

"What, in your business? I should think the demand must be fairly constant." He'd meant to joke, but she rounded on him, eyes narrowing.

"Oh, the customers are ready enough to knock on my door, no matter what," she said. "But they've no money these days—no one does. I'll take a chicken or a flitch of bacon—but half of them haven't got so much as that. They'll pay with proclamation money, or Continentals, or scrip from a militia unit—want to guess how much any of those are worth in the market?"

"Aye, I—" But she was steaming like a kettle, and turned on him, hissing.

"Or they don't pay at all. When times are fair, so are men, mostly. But pinch them a bit, and they stop seeing just why they need to pay for their pleasure—after all, what does it cost *me*? And I cannot refuse, or they will simply take what they want and then burn my house or hurt us for my temerity. You see that, I suppose?"

The bitterness in her voice stung like a nettle, and he abruptly abandoned a half-formed impulse to propose that they seal their bargain in a personal way.

"I see that," he replied, as evenly as he could. "Is such a thing not always a risk of your profession, though? And ye've prospered so far, aye?"

Her mouth compressed for an instant.

"I had a . . . patron. A gentleman who offered me protection."

"In return for . . . ?"

A hot flush rose in her thin cheeks.

"None of your business, sir."

"Is it not?" He nodded at the pouch in her hand. "If I'm placing my— these—well, them"—he gestured at the girls, now fingering the fabric of a curtain—"with you, surely I am entitled to ask whether I might be placing them in danger by doing so?"

"They're girls," she replied briefly. "They were born in danger and will live their lives in that condition, regardless of circumstance." But her hand had tightened on the pouch, knuckles white. He was that bit impressed that she was so honest, given that she plainly did need the money badly. In spite of her bitterness, though, he was rather enjoying the joust.

"D'ye think life's no dangerous for a man, then?" he asked, and without pausing, "What happened to your pimp?"

The blood washed abruptly from her face, leaving it white as bleached bone. Her eyes flashed in it like sparks.

"He was my brother," she said, and her voice dropped to a furious whisper. "The Sons of Liberty tarred and feathered him and left him on my doorstep to die. Now, sir—have you any further questions regarding my affairs, or is our business *done*?"

Before he could make shift to find any response at all to this, the door opened and a young woman came in. He felt a visceral shock at seeing her, and the edges of his vision went white. Then the room steadied round him and he found he could draw breath again.

It wasn't Emily. The young woman—looking curiously from him to the little savages wrapped in the curtains—was part-Indian, small and gracefully built, with Emily's long, thick, raven's-wing hair flowing loose down her back. With Emily's broad cheekbones and delicate round chin. But she wasn't Emily.

Thank God, he thought, but at the same time suffered a hollowness of the wame. He felt as though the sight of her had been a cannonball that had struck him and, having passed straight through his body, left a gaping hole in its wake.

Mrs. Sylvie was giving the Indian girl brisk instructions, pointing at Hermione and Trudy. The girl's black brows rose briefly, but she nodded, and smiling at the girls, invited them to accompany her to the kitchen for some food.

The little girls promptly disentangled themselves from the curtains; it had been a long time since breakfast, and he'd had nothing for them then save a bit of drammach and some jerked bear meat, hard as shoe leather.

They followed the Indian girl to the door of the room, sparing him not a glance. At the door, though, Hermione turned, and hitching up her baggy-seated breeches, fixed him with a glare and pointed a long, skinny finger of accusation at him.

"If we turns out to be whores after all, you fucker, I'm gonna hunt you down, cut your balls off, and stuff 'em up your arse."

He took his leave with what dignity he could, the peals of Mrs. Sylvie's laughter ringing in his ears.

18

PULLING TEETH

New Bern, colony of North Carolina
April 1777

I HATED PULLING TEETH. The figure of speech that likens something of extreme difficulty to pulling teeth is not hyperbole. Even in the best of situations—a large person with a big mouth and a placid temperament, the affected tooth one of those toward the front of the mouth and in the upper jaw (less in the way of roots and much easier of access)—it was a messy, slippery, bone-crack business. And underlying the sheer physical unpleasantness of the job was usually an inescapable feeling of depression at the probable outcome.

It was necessary—beyond the pain of an abscessed tooth, a bad abscess could release bacteria into the bloodstream, causing septicemia and even death—but to remove a tooth, with no good means of replacing it, was to compromise not merely the patient's appearance but also the function and structure of the mouth. A missing tooth allowed all those near it to shift out of place, altering the bite and making chewing much less efficient. Which in turn affected the patient's nutrition, general health, and prospects for a long and happy life.

Not, I reflected grimly, changing position yet again in hopes of gaining a view of the tooth I was after, that even the removal of several teeth would greatly damage the dentition of the poor little girl whose mouth I was working on.

She couldn't be more than eight or nine, with a narrow jaw and a pronounced overbite. Her canine baby teeth had not fallen out on time, and the permanent ones had come in behind them, giving her a sinister double-fanged appearance. This was aggravated by the unusual narrowness of her upper jaw, which had forced the two emergent front incisors to buckle inward, turning toward each other in such a way that the front surfaces of each tooth almost touched each other.

I touched the abscessed upper molar and she jerked against the straps that bound her to the chair, letting out a shriek that ran under my fingernails like a bamboo splinter.

"Give her a bit more, please, Ian." I straightened up, feeling as though my lower back had been squeezed in a vise; I'd been working for several hours in the front room of Fergus's printshop, and had a small bowl full of bloodstained teeth at my elbow and a rapt crowd outside the window to show for it.

Ian made a dubious Scottish noise, but picked up the bottle of whisky and made an encouraging clucking noise toward the little girl, who screamed again at sight of his tattooed face and clamped her mouth shut. The girl's mother, out of patience, slapped her briskly, snatched the bottle from Ian's hand, and inserting it into her daughter's mouth, upended it, pinching the girl's nose shut with the other hand.

The child's eyes went round as pennies and an explosion of whisky droplets sprayed from the corners of her mouth—but her scrawny little neck bobbed convulsively as she swallowed, nonetheless.

"I really think that's enough," I said, rather alarmed at the quantity of whisky the child was swallowing. It was very bad whisky, acquired locally, and while Jamie and Ian had both tasted it and, after some discussion, decided that it probably wouldn't make anyone go blind, I had reservations about using it in any great amount.

"Hmm," said the mother, examining her daughter critically, but not removing the bottle. "That'll do it, I suppose."

The child's eyes had rolled back in her head, and the straining little body suddenly relaxed, falling limp against the chair. The mother removed the whisky bottle, wiped the mouth of it tidily on her apron, and handed it back to Ian with a nod.

I hastily examined her pulse and breathing, but she seemed in reasonably good shape—so far, at least.

"*Carpe diem,*" I muttered, grabbing my tooth pliers. "Or perhaps I mean *carpe vinorum*? Watch to see she keeps breathing, Ian."

Ian laughed and tilted the bottle, wetting a tiny swab of clean cloth with whisky for the mopping up.

"I think ye'll have time to take more than the one tooth, Auntie, if ye want. Ye could likely pull every tooth in the poor lassie's head and she wouldna twitch."

"It's a thought," I said, turning the child's head. "Can you bring the mirror, Ian?"

I had a tiny square of looking glass which could, with luck, be used to direct sunlight into a patient's mouth. And there was sunlight streaming through the window in abundance, warm and bright. Unfortunately, there were any number of curious heads pressed against the window, too, which kept moving into the path of the sun, frustrating Ian's attempts to beam sunlight where I needed it.

"Marsali!" I called, a thumb on the girl's pulse, just in case.

"Aye?" She came through from the back room where she'd been cleaning—or, rather, dirtying—type, wiping inky hands on a rag. "D'ye need Henri-Christian again?"

"If you—or he—don't mind."

"Not him," she assured me. "Likes nothing better, the wee praise-hog. Joanie! Félicité! Come fetch the wean, will ye? He's wanted out front."

Félicité and Joan—aka the hell-kittens, as Jamie called them—came eagerly; they enjoyed Henri-Christian's performances nearly as much as he did.

"Come on, Bubbles!" Joanie called, holding open the door to the kitchen. Henri-Christian came scampering out, rolling from side to side on short, bowed legs, ruddy face beaming.

"Hoopla, hoopla, hoopla!" he shouted, making for the door.

"Put his hat on him!" Marsali called. "The wind will get in his ears."

It was a bright day, but *was* windy, and Henri-Christian had a tendency to ear infection. He had a woolen hat that tied under the chin, though, knitted in blue and white stripes and decorated with a row of red bobbles—Brianna had made it for him, and the sight of it squeezed my heart a little, warmth and pain together.

The girls each took him by a hand—Félicité stretching up at the last moment to grab an old slouch hat of her father's from the peg, to put out for coins—and went out, to cheers and whistles from the crowd. Through the window, I could see Joanie clearing the books displayed on the table outside, and Félicité hoisting Henri-Christian up in their stead. He spread his stubby, powerful arms, beaming, and bowed in accomplished fashion to one side and the other. Then he bent, put his hands on the tabletop, and, with a remarkable degree of controlled grace, stood on his head.

I didn't wait to watch the rest of his show—it was mostly simple dancing and kicks, interspersed with somersaults and headstands, but made enchanting by his dwarfed stature and vivid personality. He had shifted the crowd away from the window momentarily, though, which was what I wanted.

"Now, Ian," I said, and went back to work. With the flickering light from the mirror, it was a little easier to see what I was doing, and I got to grips with the tooth almost at once. This was the tricky part, though; the tooth was badly cracked, and there was a good chance that it might fracture when I twisted it, rather than draw cleanly. And if that should happen . . .

But it didn't. There was a small, muffled *crack!* as the roots of the tooth parted from the jawbone, and I was holding the tiny white thing, intact.

The child's mother, who had been watching intently, sighed and relaxed a little. The little girl sighed, too, and settled in the chair. I checked again, but her pulse was fine, though her breathing was shallow. She'd likely sleep for—

A thought struck me.

"You know," I said to the mother, a little hesitantly, "I *could* draw one or two more teeth without hurting her. See . . ." I moved aside, motioning her to look. "These"—I touched the overdue baby canines—"ought to be drawn at once, to let the teeth behind take their places. And you see these front teeth, of course. . . . Well, I've taken the upper bicuspid molar on the left; if I were to take the same tooth on the right, I *think* that perhaps her teeth would shift a bit, to fill the empty space. And if you could persuade her to press with her tongue against those front teeth, whenever she thought of it . . ." It wasn't orthodontia by any means, and it did carry some increased risk of infection, but I was sorely tempted. The poor child looked like a cannibal bat.

"Hmmmm," said the mother, frowning into her daughter's mouth. "How much will you give me for them?"

"How much . . . you want me to pay *you?*"

"They're fine, sound teeth," the mother replied promptly. "The tooth-drawer down to the harbor 'ud give me a shilling apiece. And Glory'll need the money for her dowry."

"Her dowry?" I repeated, surprised. The mother shrugged.

"No one's likely to take the poor creature for her looks, now, are they?"

I was obliged to admit that this was likely true; her deplorable dentition quite aside, calling the child homely would be a compliment.

"Marsali," I called. "Have you got four shillings?" The gold in my hem swung heavily round my feet, but I couldn't make use of it in this situation.

Marsali turned from the window, where she'd been keeping an eye on Henri-Christian and the girls, startled.

"Not cash money, no."

"It's all right, Auntie. I've some money." Ian put down the mirror and dug in his sporran, emerging with a handful of coins. "Mind," he said, fixing the woman with a hard eye, "ye'd no get more nor thruppence each for sound teeth—and likely no but a penny for a child's."

The woman, nothing daunted, looked down her nose at him.

"There speaks a grasping Scotchman," she said. "For all you're tattooed like a savage. Sixpence each, then, you penny-pinching miser!"

Ian grinned at her, displaying his own fine teeth, which, if not entirely straight, were in excellent condition.

"Going to carry the wean down to the quay and let yon butcher rip her mouth to shreds?" he inquired pleasantly. "She'll be awake by then, ken. And screaming. Three."

"Ian!" I said.

"Well, I'm no going to let her cheat ye, Auntie. Bad enough she's wantin' ye to draw the lassie's teeth for nothing, let alone pay for the honor!"

Emboldened by my intervention, the woman stuck out her chin and repeated, "Sixpence!"

Marsali, attracted by the altercation, came to peer into the girl's mouth.

"Ye'll not find that one a husband for less than ten pound," she informed the woman bluntly. "Not lookin' like that. A man would be feart of bein' bitten when he kissed her. Ian's right. In fact, ye should be payin' double for it."

"Ye agreed to pay when ye came in, no?" Ian pressed. "Tuppence to have the tooth drawn—and my aunt made ye a bargain at that, out of pity for the wean."

"Bloodsuckers!" the woman exclaimed. "It's true what they say—you Scots 'ud take the pennies from a dead man's eyes!"

Plainly this wasn't going to be settled in a hurry; I could feel both Ian and Marsali settling down to an enjoyable session of tag-team haggling. I sighed and took the mirror out of Ian's hand. I wouldn't need it for the canines, and perhaps by the time I got to the other bicuspid, he'd be paying attention again.

In fact, the canines were simple; baby teeth, almost without roots, and ready to fall—I could probably have tweaked them out with my fingers. One quick twist each and they were out, the gums barely bleeding. Pleased, I dabbed the sites with a whisky-soaked swab, then considered the bicuspid.

It was on the other side of the mouth, which meant that by tilting the girl's head back, I could get a bit of light without using the mirror. I took Ian's hand—he was so engaged in argument that he barely noticed—and put it on the girl's head to hold it back and steady, then carefully insinuated my pliers.

A shadow crossed my light, vanished—then came back, blocking it utterly. I turned in annoyance, to find a rather elegant-looking gentleman peering through the window, a look of interest on his face.

I scowled at him and motioned him aside. He blinked at me, but then nodded apology and stepped aside. Not waiting for any further interruption, I crouched, got hold of the tooth, and twisted it free with a lucky wrench.

Humming with satisfaction, I dribbled whisky over the bleeding hole, then tilted her head to the other side and pressed a swab gently over the gum, to help drain the abscess. Felt a sudden extra slackness in the wobbly little neck and froze.

Ian felt it, too; he broke off in the middle of a sentence and shot me a startled look.

"Untie her," I said. "Quick."

He had her loosed in an instant, and I seized her under the arms and laid her on the floor, her head flopping like a rag doll's. Ignoring startled exclamations from Marsali and the girl's mother, I tilted back her head, swiped the swab out of her mouth, and, pinching shut her nose with my fingers, sealed my mouth to hers and started resuscitation.

It was like blowing up a small, tough balloon: reluctance, resistance, then, finally, a rise of the chest. But chests don't yield like rubber; the blowing didn't get easier.

I had the fingers of my other hand on her neck, feeling desperately for a carotid pulse. There...Was it?...Yes, it was! Her heart was still beating, though faintly.

Breathe. Pause. Breathe. Pause...I felt the tiny gush of exhalation, and then the narrow chest moved by itself. I waited, blood pounding in my ears, but it didn't move again. Breathe. Pause. Breathe...

Again the chest moved, and this time continued to rise and fall under its own power. I sat up on my heels, my own breath coming fast and a cold sweat misting my face.

The girl's mother was staring down at me, her mouth half open. I noted dimly that her own dentition wasn't bad; God knew what her husband looked like.

"She's—is she...?" the woman asked, blinking and glancing back and forth between me and her daughter.

"She's fine," I said flatly. I stood up slowly, feeling light-headed. "She can't go until the whisky's worn off, though; I think she'll be all right, but she might stop breathing again. Someone needs to watch her 'til she wakes. Marsali...?"

"Aye, I'll put her in the trundle," Marsali said, coming to look. "Oh, there ye are, Joanie—will ye come and keep an eye on this poor wean for a bit? She needs to lie down on your bed."

The children had come in, red-cheeked and giggling, with a hatful of small coins and buttons, but seeing the girl on the floor, hurried over to look, too.

"Hoopla," Henri-Christian remarked, impressed.

"Is she deid?" Félicité asked, more practically.

"If she was, *Maman* wouldna be asking me to watch her," Joanie pointed out. "She's no going to sick up in my bed, is she?"

"I'll put a towel down," Marsali promised, squatting to scoop the little girl up. Ian beat her to it, lifting the child gently.

"We'll just charge ye tuppence, then," he said to the mother. "But we'll give ye all the teeth for free, aye?"

Looking stunned, she nodded, then followed the crowd into the back of the house. I heard the thunder of multiple feet going up the stairs, but didn't follow; my own legs had gone to water, and I sat down quite suddenly.

"Are you all right, *madame?*" I looked up to find the elegant stranger inside the shop, looking curiously at me.

I picked up the half-empty bottle of whisky and took a substantial swallow. It burned like brimstone and tasted like charred bones. I made wheezing noises and my eyes watered, but I didn't actually cough.

"Fine," I said hoarsely. "Perfectly fine." I cleared my throat and wiped my eyes on my sleeve. "Can I help you?"

A faint look of amusement crossed his features.

"I do not require to have a tooth drawn, which is probably good luck for both of us. However—may I?" He withdrew a slim silver flask from his pocket and handed it to me, then sat down. "I think it's perhaps a little more fortifying than ... that." He nodded at the uncorked whisky bottle, his nose wrinkling a little.

I uncorked the flask, and the full-bodied scent of very good brandy floated out like a genie.

"Thank you," I said briefly, and drank, closing my eyes. "Very much indeed," I added a moment later, opening them. Fortifying, indeed. Warmth collected in my center and purled like smoke through my limbs.

"My pleasure, *madame*," he said, and smiled. He was undeniably a dandy, and a rich one, too, with a good deal of lace about his person, gilt buttons on his waistcoat, a powdered wig, and two black silk beauty patches on his face—a star beside his left brow, and a rearing horse on his right cheek. Not a getup one saw often in North Carolina, especially not these days.

Despite the encrustations, he was a handsome man, I thought, perhaps forty or so, with soft dark eyes that glinted with humor, and a delicate, sensitive face. His English was very good, though it carried a distinct Parisian accent.

"Have I the honor of addressing Mrs. Fraser?" he asked. I saw his eyes pass over my scandalously bare head, but he politely made no comment.

"Well, you have," I said dubiously. "But I may not be the one you want. My daughter-in-law is Mrs. Fraser, too; she and her husband own this shop. So if you were wanting something printed—"

"Mrs. James Fraser?"

I paused instinctively, but there wasn't much alternative to answering.

"I am, yes. Is it my husband you want?" I asked warily. People wanted Jamie for a lot of things, and it wasn't always desirable that they find him.

He smiled, eyes crinkling pleasantly.

"It is indeed, Mrs. Fraser. The captain of my ship said that Mr. Fraser had come to speak with him this morning, seeking passage."

My heart gave a sharp leap at this.

"Oh! You have a ship, Mr. . . . ?"

"Beauchamp," he said, and, picking up my hand, kissed it gracefully. "Percival Beauchamp, at your service, *madame*. I do—she is called *Huntress*."

I actually thought my heart had stopped for a moment, but it hadn't, and resumed beating with a noticeable thump.

"Beauchamp," I said. "Beechum?" He'd pronounced it in the French way, but at this, he nodded, smile growing wider.

"Yes, the English say it that way. You said your daughter-in-law ... so the Mr. Fraser who owns this shop is your husband's son?"

"Yes," I said again, but automatically. *Don't be silly*, I scolded myself. *It isn't an uncommon name. Likely he hasn't anything at all to do with your family!* And yet—a French–English connection. I knew my father's family had come from France to England sometime in the eighteenth century—but that was all I knew about them. I stared at him in fascination. Was there anything familiar about his face, anything I could match with my faint recollections of my parents, the stronger ones of my uncle?

He had pale skin, like mine, but then, most upper-class people did, they taking great pains to shelter their faces from the sun. His eyes were much darker than mine, and beautiful, but shaped differently, rounder. The brows—had my uncle Lamb's brows had that shape, heavy near the nose, trailing off in a graceful arch . . . ?

Absorbed in this tantalizing puzzle, I'd missed what he was saying.

"I beg your pardon?"

"The little boy," he repeated, with a nod toward the door through which the children had disappeared. "He was shouting, 'Hoopla!' As French street performers do. Has the family a French connection of some kind?"

Belated alarms began to go off, and unease rippled the hairs on my fore-arms.

"No," I said, trying to iron my face into a politely quizzical expression. "Likely he's just heard it from someone. There was a small troupe of French acrobats who passed through the Carolinas last year."

"Ah, doubtless that's it." He leaned forward a little, dark eyes intent. "Did you see them yourself?"

"No. My husband and I . . . don't live here," I ended hurriedly. I'd been about to tell him where we *did* live, but I didn't know how much—if anything—he knew about Fergus's circumstances. He sat back, pursing his lips a little in disappointment.

"Ah, too bad. I thought perhaps the gentleman I am in search of might have belonged to this troupe. Though I suppose you would not have known their names, even had you seen them," he added as an afterthought.

"You're looking for someone? A Frenchman?" I lifted the bowl of blood-stained teeth and began to pick through it, affecting nonchalance.

"A man named Claudel. He was born in Paris—in a brothel," he added, with a faint air of apology for using such an indelicate term in my presence. "He would be in his early forties now—forty-one or -two, perhaps."

"Paris," I repeated, listening for Marsali's footfalls on the stair. "What leads you to suppose that he's in North Carolina?"

He lifted one shoulder in a graceful shrug.

"He may well not be. I do know that roughly thirty years ago, he was taken from the brothel by a Scotsman, and that this man was described as of strik-ing appearance, very tall, with brilliant red hair. Beyond that, I encountered a morass of possibilities . . ." He smiled wryly. "Fraser was described to me var-iously as a wine merchant, a Jacobite, a Loyalist, a traitor, a spy, an aristocrat, a farmer, an importer—or a smuggler; the terms are interchangeable—with connections reaching from a convent to the Royal court."

Which was, I thought, an extremely accurate portrait of Jamie. Though I could see why it hadn't been much help in finding him. On the other hand . . . here Beauchamp was.

"I did discover a wine merchant named Michael Murray, who, upon hear-ing this description, told me that it resembled his uncle, one James Fraser, who had emigrated to America more than ten years ago." The dark eyes were less humorous now, fixed intently upon me.

"When I inquired about the child Claudel, though, Monsieur Murray pro-fessed complete ignorance of such a person. In rather vehement terms."

"Oh?" I said, and picked up a large molar with serious caries, squinting at it. Jesus H. Roosevelt Christ. I knew Michael only by name; one of Young

Ian's elder brothers, he had been born after my departure and had already gone to France by the time I returned to Lallybroch—there to be educated and taken into the wine business with Jared Fraser, an elderly and childless cousin of Jamie's. Michael had, of course, grown up with Fergus at Lallybroch and knew bloody well what his original name was. And apparently had detected or suspected something in this stranger's demeanor that had alarmed him.

"Do you mean to say that you came all the way to America, knowing nothing except a man's name and that he has red hair?" I asked, trying to seem mildly incredulous. "Goodness—you must have considerable interest in finding this Claudel!"

"Oh, I do, *madame*." He looked at me, smiling faintly, head on one side. "Tell me, Mrs. Fraser—has your husband red hair?"

"Yes," I said. There was no point in denying it, since anyone in New Bern would tell him so—and likely had already, I reflected. "So do any number of his relations—and about half the population of the Scottish Highlands." This was a wild overstatement, but I was reasonably sure that Mr. Beauchamp hadn't been combing the Highlands personally, either.

I could hear voices upstairs; Marsali might be coming down any minute, and I didn't want her walking into the midst of this particular conversation.

"Well," I said, and got to my feet in a decided manner. "I'm sure you'll be wanting to talk to my husband—and he to you. He's gone on an errand, though, and won't be back until sometime tomorrow. Are you staying somewhere in the town?"

"The King's Inn," he said, rising, as well. "If you will tell your husband to find me there, *madame*? I thank you." Bending low, he took my hand and kissed it again, then smiled at me and backed out of the shop, leaving a scent of bergamot and hyssop mingled with the ghost of good brandy.

A GOOD MANY merchants and businessmen had left New Bern, owing to the chaotic state of politics; with no civil authority, public life had come to a standstill, bar the simplest of market transactions, and many people—of both Loyalist and rebel sympathies—had left the colony out of fear of violence. There were only two good inns in New Bern these days; the King's Inn was one, and the Wilsey Arms the other. Luckily, Jamie and I had a room in the latter.

"Will you go and talk to him?" I had just finished telling Jamie about the visit of Monsieur Beauchamp—an account that had left him with a deep crease of concern between his brows.

"Christ. How did he find out all that?"

"He must have begun with a knowledge that Fergus was at that brothel, and started his inquiries there. I imagine it wouldn't have been difficult to find someone who'd seen you there, or heard about the incident. You're rather memorable, after all." Despite my own agitation, I smiled at the memory of Jamie, aged twenty-five, who had taken temporary refuge in the brothel in question armed—quite coincidentally—with a large sausage, and then escaped through a window, accompanied by a ten-year-old pickpocket and sometime child-whore named Claudel.

He shrugged, looking mildly embarrassed.

"Well, aye, perhaps. But to discover quite so much . . ." He scratched his head, thinking. "As to speaking with him—not before I speak to Fergus. I think we might want to know a bit more about this Monsieur Beauchamp, before we make him a present of ourselves."

"I'd like to know a bit more about him, too," I said. "I did wonder whether . . . Well, it's a remote possibility, the name isn't all that uncommon— but I did wonder whether he might be connected in some way with a branch of my family. They *were* in France in the eighteenth century, I know that much. But not much more."

He smiled at me.

"And what would ye do, Sassenach, if I discover that he's really your six-times-great-grandfather?"

"I—" I stopped abruptly because, in fact, I didn't know *what* I'd do in such a circumstance. "Well . . . probably nothing," I admitted. "And we probably can't find that out for sure in any case, since I don't recall—if I ever knew—what my six-times-great-grandfather's first name was. I just—would be interested to know more, that's all," I finished, feeling mildly defensive.

"Well, of course ye would," he said, matter-of-fact. "But not if my asking might put Fergus in any danger, would ye?"

"Oh, no! Of course not. But do you—"

I was interrupted by a soft knock on the door that struck me dumb. I raised my brows at Jamie, who hesitated a moment, but then shrugged and went to open it.

Small as the room was, I could see the door from where I sat; to my surprise, it was filled with what appeared to be a deputation of women—the corridor was a sea of white caps, floating in the dimness like jellyfish.

"Mr. Fraser?" One of the caps bobbed briefly. "I am—my name is Abigail Bell. My daughters"—she turned, and I caught a glimpse of a strained white face—"Lillian and Miriam." The other two caps—yes, there were only three, after all—bobbed in turn. "Máy we speak with you?"

Jamie bowed and ushered them into the room, raising his eyebrows at me as he followed them in.

"My wife," he said, nodding as I rose, murmuring pleasantries. There was only the bed and one stool, so we all remained standing, awkwardly smiling and bobbing at one another.

Mrs. Bell was short and rather stout, and had probably once been as pretty as her daughters. Her once-plump cheeks now sagged, though, as though she had lost weight suddenly, and her skin was creased with worry. Her daughters looked worried, too; one was twisting her hands in her apron, and the other kept stealing glances at Jamie from downcast eyes, as though afraid he might do something violent if gazed at too directly.

"I beg your pardon, sir, for coming to you in this bold way." Mrs. Bell's lips were trembling; she had to stop and compress them briefly before continuing. "I—I hear that you are looking for a ship bound to Scotland."

Jamie nodded warily, plainly wondering where this woman had learned of it. He'd said everyone in the town would know within a day or two—evidently he'd been right about that.

"Do ye ken someone with such a voyage in view?" he asked politely.

"No. Not exactly. I . . . that is . . . perhaps—it is my husband," she blurted, but the speaking of the word made her voice break, and she clapped a handful of apron to her mouth. One of the daughters, a dark-haired girl, took her mother gently by the elbow and drew her aside, standing up bravely to face the fearsome Mr. Fraser herself.

"My father is in Scotland, Mr. Fraser," she said. "My mother is in hopes that you might find him, when you go there, and assist him to return to us."

"Ah," Jamie said. "And your father would be . . . ?"

"Oh! Mr. Richard Bell, sir, of Wilmington." She curtsied hastily, as though further politeness would help to make her case. "He is—he *was*—"

"He *is*!" her sister hissed, low-voiced but emphatic, and the first sister, the dark one, gave her a glare.

"My father was a merchant in Wilmington, Mr. Fraser. He had considerable business interests, and in the course of his business he . . . had reason to have contact with various British officers, who came to him for supplies. It was entirely a matter of business!" she assured him.

"But business in these dreadful times is never only business." Mrs. Bell had got hold of herself, and came to stand shoulder to shoulder with her daughter. "They said—my husband's enemies—they put it about that he was a Loyalist."

"Only because he was," put in the second sister. This one—fair-haired and blue-eyed—wasn't trembling; she faced Jamie with a lifted chin and blazing eyes. "My father was true to his King! I for one do not think that is something to be excused and apologized for! Nor do I think it right to pretend otherwise, only to get the help of a man who has broken every oath—"

"Oh, *Miriam*!" said her sister, exasperated. "Could you not keep quiet for one *second*? Now you've spoilt everything!"

"I haven't," Miriam snapped. "Or if I have, it wasn't ever going to work in the first place! Why should someone like him hel—"

"Yes, it would! Mr. Forbes said—"

"Oh, bother Mr. Forbes! What would *he* know?"

Mrs. Bell moaned softly into her apron.

"Why did your father go to Scotland?" Jamie asked, cutting through the confusion.

Taken by surprise, Miriam Bell actually answered him.

"He didn't *go* to Scotland. He was abducted in the street and thrust onto a ship bound for Southampton."

"By whom?" I asked, wiggling my way through the obstructing forest of skirts on my way to the door. "And why?"

I stuck my head out into the corridor and gestured to the boy cleaning boots on the landing that he should go down to the taproom and bring up a jug of wine. Given the apparent state of the Bells, I thought something to restore the social amenities might be a good idea.

I popped back inside in time to hear Miss Lillian Bell explaining that they didn't actually know who had abducted her father.

"Or not by name, at least," she said, face flushed with fury at the telling. "The villains wore hoods over their heads. But it was the Sons of Liberty, I know it!"

"Yes, it was," Miss Miriam said decidedly. "Father had had threats from them—notes pinned to the door, a dead fish wrapped in a bit of red flannel and left upon the porch to make a stink. That sort of thing."

The matter had gone beyond threats at the end of the previous August. Mr. Bell had been on his way to his warehouse, when a group of hooded men had rushed out from an alleyway, seized him, and carried him down the quay, then flung him bodily aboard a ship that had just cast off its hawser, sails filling as it drew slowly away.

I had heard of troublesome Loyalists being summarily "deported" in this manner, but hadn't run into an actual occurrence of the practice before.

"If the ship was bound for England," I inquired, "how did he end up in Scotland?"

There was a certain amount of confusion as all three Bells tried to explain at once what had happened, but Miriam won out once again.

"He arrived in England penniless, of course, with no more than the clothes on his back, and owing money for food and passage on the ship. But the ship's captain had befriended him, and took him from Southampton to London, where my father knew some men with whom he had done business in the past. One of these advanced him a sum to cover his indebtedness to the captain, and promised him passage to Georgia, if he would oversee the cargo on a voyage from Edinburgh to the Indies, thence to America.

"So he traveled to Edinburgh under the auspices of his patron, only to discover there that the intended cargo to be picked up in the Indies was a shipload of Negroes."

"My husband is an abolitionist, Mr. Fraser," Mrs. Bell put in, with timid pride. "He said he could not countenance slavery, nor assist in its practice, no matter what the cost to himself."

"And Mr. Forbes told us what you had done for that woman—Mrs. Cameron's body slave," Lillian put in, anxious-faced. "So we thought . . . even if you were . . ." She trailed off, embarrassed.

"An oath-breaking rebel, aye," Jamie said dryly. "I see. Mr. Forbes—this would be . . . Neil Forbes, the lawyer?" He sounded faintly incredulous, and with good reason.

Some years before, Forbes had been a suitor for Brianna's hand—encouraged by Jocasta Cameron, Jamie's aunt. Bree had rejected him, none too gently, and he had taken his revenge some time later by having her abducted by a notorious pirate. A very messy state of affairs had ensued, involving Jamie's reciprocal abduction of Forbes's elderly mother—the old lady had loved the adventure—and the cutting off of Forbes's ear by Young Ian. Time might have healed his external wounds, but I couldn't imagine anyone less likely to have been singing Jamie's praises.

"Yes," said Miriam, but I didn't miss the uncertain look that passed between Mrs. Bell and Lillian.

"What, exactly, did Mr. Forbes say about me?" Jamie asked. All three of them went pale, and his eyebrows went up.

"What?" he repeated, with a definite edge. He said it directly to Mrs. Bell, whom he had instantly identified as the weakest link in the family chain.

"He said what a good thing it was that you were dead," that lady replied faintly. Whereupon her eyes rolled up into her head and she slumped to the floor like a bag of barleycorn.

FORTUNATELY, I HAD got a bottle of spirits of ammonia from Dr. Fentiman. This roused Mrs. Bell promptly into a sneezing fit, and her daughters helped her, gasping and choking, onto the bed. The wine fortunately arriving at this juncture, I served liberal helpings to everyone in sight, reserving a sizable mugful for myself.

"Now, then," Jamie said, giving the women the sort of slow, penetrating look intended to cause miscreants to go weak in the knees and confess everything, "tell me where ye heard Mr. Forbes say about my being dead."

Miss Lillian, settled on the bed with a protective hand on her mother's shoulder, spoke up.

"I heard him. In Symond's ordinary. While we were still in Wilmington—before we came here to live with Aunt Burton. I'd gone to get a pitcher of hot cider—it was sometime in February; it was still very cold out. Anyway, the woman—Faydree, she's called—she works there, and went to draw and heat the cider for me. Mr. Forbes came in while I was there, and spoke to me. He knew about Father, and was sympathetic, asking how we were managing . . . then Faydree came out with the pitcher, and he saw her."

Forbes had, of course, recognized Phaedre, whom he'd seen many times at River Run, Jocasta's plantation. Expressing great surprise at her presence, he had inquired for an explanation and received a suitably modified version of the truth—in which Phaedre had apparently made much of Jamie's kindness in securing her freedom.

I gurgled briefly in my mug at this. Phaedre knew exactly what had happened to Neil Forbes's ear. She was a very quiet, soft-spoken person, Phaedre, but not above sticking pins in people she didn't like—and I knew she didn't like Neil Forbes.

"Mr. Forbes was rather flushed—perhaps it was from the cold," Lillian said tactfully, "and he said, yes, he understood that Mr. Fraser had always had a great regard for Negroes. . . . I'm afraid he said that rather nastily," she added, with an apologetic look at Jamie. "And then he laughed, though he tried to pretend he was coughing, and said what a pity it was that you and your family had all been burnt to cinders, and no doubt there would be great lamentations in the slave quarter."

Jamie, who had been taking a swallow of wine, choked.

"Why did he think that?" I demanded. "Did he say?"

Lillian nodded earnestly.

"Yes, ma'am. Faydree asked him that, too—I think she thought he was only saying it to upset her—and he said he'd read it in the newspaper."

"The *Wilmington Gazette*," Miriam put in, plainly not liking her sister to be hogging the limelight. "We don't read newspapers, of course, and since

Daddy . . . well, we seldom have callers anymore." She glanced down involuntarily, her hand automatically pulling her neat apron straight, to hide a large patch on her skirt. The Bells were tidy and well-groomed, and their clothes had originally been of good quality but were growing noticeably threadbare round the hems and sleeves. I imagined that Mr. Bell's business affairs must have been substantially impaired, both by his absence and by the interference of war.

"My daughter had told me about the meeting." Mrs. Bell had recovered herself so far as to sit up, her cup of wine clasped carefully in both hands. "So when my neighbor told me last night that he had met you by the docks . . . well, I didn't know quite what to think, but supposed there had been a stupid mistake of some kind—really, you cannot believe anything you read these days, the newspapers are grown quite wild. And my neighbor mentioned that you were seeking passage to Scotland. So we began to think . . ." Her voice trailed off, and she dipped her face toward her wine cup, embarrassed.

Jamie rubbed a finger down his nose, thinking.

"Aye, well," he said slowly. "It's true that I mean to go to Scotland. And of course I should be pleased to inquire after your husband and assist him if I can. But I've no immediate prospect of obtaining passage. The blockade—"

"But we can get you a ship!" Lillian interrupted eagerly. "That's the point!"

"We think we can get you *to* a ship," Miriam corrected. She gave Jamie a considering, narrow-eyed sort of look, judging his character. He smiled faintly at her, acknowledging the scrutiny, and after a moment she returned the smile, grudging.

"You remind me of someone," she said. Evidently, whoever it was, it was someone she liked, though, for she nodded to her mother, giving permission. Mrs. Bell sighed, her shoulders slumping a little in relief.

"I do still have friends," she said, with a tinge of defiance. "In spite of . . . everything."

Among these friends was a man named DeLancey Hall, who owned a fishing ketch, and—like half the town, probably—augmented his income with the odd bit of smuggling.

Hall had told Mrs. Bell that he expected the arrival of a ship from England, coming into Wilmington sometime within the next week or so—always assuming that it hadn't been seized or sunk *en route*. As both ship and cargo were the property of one of the local Sons of Liberty, it could not venture into the Wilmington harbor, where two British warships were still crouched. It would, therefore, lurk just outside the harbor, where assorted small local craft would make rendezvous with it, unloading the cargo for surreptitious transport to shore. After which, the ship would sail north to New Haven, there to retrieve a cargo.

"And then will sail for Edinburgh!" Lillian put in, her face bright with hope.

"My father's kinsman there is named Andrew Bell," Miriam put in, lifting her chin a little. "He is very well known, I believe. He is a printer, and—"

"Wee Andy Bell?" Jamie's face had lighted up. "Him who printed the great encyclopedia?"

"The very man," Mrs. Bell said, surprised. "You do not mean to say you know him, Mr. Fraser?"

Jamie actually laughed, startling the Bells.

"Many's the evening I've passed in a tavern wi' Andy Bell," he assured them. "In fact, he's the man I mean to see in Scotland, for he's got my printing press, safe in his shop. Or at least I hope he does," he added, though his cheerfulness was unimpaired.

This news—along with a fresh round of wine—heartened the Bell women to an amazing extent, and when they left us at last, they were flushed with animation and chattering amongst themselves like a flock of amiable magpies. I glanced out the window and saw them making their way down the street, clustered together in hopeful excitement, staggering into the street occasionally from the effects of wine and emotion.

"We don't only sing but we dance just as good as we walk," I murmured, watching them go.

Jamie gave me a startled look.

"Archie Bell and the Drells," I explained. "Never mind. Do you think it's safe? This ship?"

"God, no." He shuddered, and kissed the top of my head. "Put aside the question of storms, woodworm, bad caulking, warped timbers, and the like, there's the English warships in the harbor, privateers outside the harbor—"

"I didn't mean that," I interrupted. "That's more or less par for the course, isn't it? I meant the owner—and this DeLancey Hall. Mrs. Bell thinks she knows what their politics are, but . . ." But the thought of delivering ourselves—and our gold—so completely into the hands of unknown persons was unsettling.

"But," he agreed. "Aye, I mean to go and speak to Mr. Hall first thing tomorrow morning. And maybe Monsieur Beauchamp, as well. For now, though—" He ran a hand lightly down my back and cupped my bottom. "Ian and the dog willna be back for an hour, at least. Will ye have another glass of wine?"

HE LOOKED LIKE a Frenchman, Jamie thought. Which was to say, thoroughly out of place in New Bern. Beauchamp had just come out of Thorogood Northrup's warehouse and stood in casual conversation with Northrup himself, the breeze off the water fluttering the silk ribbon that tied back his dark hair. Elegant, Claire had described him as, and he was that: not—not quite—foppish, but dressed with taste and expense. A good deal of expense, he thought.

"He looks like a Frenchman," Fergus observed, echoing his thoughts. They were seated next to the window in the Whinbush, a middling tavern that catered to the needs of fishermen and warehouse laborers, and whose atmosphere was composed of equal parts beer, sweat, tobacco, tar, and aged fish guts.

"Is that his ship?" Fergus asked, a frown creasing his brow as he nodded toward the very trim black-and-yellow sloop that rocked gently at anchor, some distance out.

"It's the ship he travels in. Couldna say whether he owns it. Ye dinna ken his face, though?"

Fergus leaned into the window, nearly flattening his own face against the wavery panes in an attempt to get a better look at Monsieur Beauchamp.

Jamie, beer in hand, studied Fergus's face in turn. Despite having lived in Scotland since the age of ten, and in America for the last ten years or more, Fergus himself still looked French, he thought. It was something more than a matter of feature; something in the bone itself, perhaps.

The bones of Fergus's face were pronounced, with a jaw sharp enough to cut paper, an imperiously beaked nose, and eye sockets set deep under the ridges of a high brow. The thick dark hair brushed back from that brow was threaded with gray, and it gave Jamie a queer moment to see that; he carried within himself a permanent image of Fergus as the ten-year-old orphaned pickpocket he had rescued from a Paris brothel, and that image sat oddly on the gaunt, handsome face before him.

"No," Fergus said at last, sitting back on the bench and shaking his head. "I have never seen him."

Fergus's deep-set dark eyes were alive with interest and speculation. "No one else in the town knows him, either. Though I *have* heard that he had made inquiries for this Claudel Fraser"—his nostrils flared with amusement; Claudel was his own birth name, and the only one he had, though Jamie thought likely no one had ever used it outside Paris or anytime in the last thirty years—"in Halifax and Edenton, as well."

Jamie opened his mouth to observe that he hoped Fergus had been careful in his inquiries, but thought better of it, and drank his beer instead. Fergus hadn't been surviving as a printer in these troublous times by having a lack of discretion.

"Does he remind ye of anyone?" he asked instead. Fergus gave him a brief look of surprise, but returned to his neck-craning before settling back, shaking his head.

"No. Should he?"

"I dinna think so." He didn't, but was glad of Fergus's corroboration. Claire had told him her thought—that the man might be some relation of hers, perhaps a direct ancestor. She had tried to be casual about it, dismiss the idea even as she spoke it, but he'd seen the eager light in her eyes and been touched. The fact that she had no family or close kin in her own time had always struck him as a dreadful thing, even while he realized that it had much to do with her devotion to him.

He'd looked as carefully as he could, with that in mind, but saw nothing in Beauchamp's face or carriage that reminded him much of Claire—let alone Fergus.

He didn't think *that* thought—that Beauchamp might be some actual relation to himself—had crossed Fergus's mind. Jamie was reasonably sure that Fergus thought of the Frasers of Lallybroch as his only family, other than Marsali and the children, whom he loved with all the fervor of his passionate nature.

Beauchamp was taking his leave of Northrup now, with a very Parisian bow, accompanied by a graceful flutter of his silk handkerchief. Fortuitous that the man had happened to step out of the warehouse just in front of them, Jamie thought. They'd planned to go and have a keek at him later in the day, but his timely appearance saved them having to go and look for him.

"It's a good ship," Fergus observed, his attention deflected to the sloop called *Huntress*. He glanced back at Jamie, considering. "You're sure you do not wish to investigate the possibility of passage with Monsieur Beauchamp?"

"Aye, I'm sure," Jamie said dryly. "Put myself and my wife in the power of a man I dinna ken and whose motives are suspect, in a wee boat on a wide sea? Even a man who didna suffer from seasickness might boggle at that prospect, no?"

Fergus's face split in a grin.

"Milady proposes to stick you full of needles again?"

"She does," Jamie replied, rather crossly. He hated being stabbed repeatedly, and disliked being obliged to appear in public—even within the limited confines of a ship—bristling with spines like some outlandish porcupine. The only thing that would make him do it was the sure knowledge that if he didn't, he'd be puking his guts out for days on end.

Fergus didn't notice his discontent, though; he was leaning into the window again.

"*Nom d'nom...*" he said softly, with such an expression of apprehension that Jamie turned on the bench at once to look.

Beauchamp had proceeded some way down the street, but was still in sight. He had come to a stop, though, and appeared to be executing a sort of ungainly jig. This was sufficiently odd, but what was more disturbing was that Fergus's son Germain was crouched in the street directly in front of the man, and seemed to be hopping to and fro in the manner of an agitated toad.

These peculiar gyrations continued for a few seconds longer and then came to an end, Beauchamp now standing still, but waving his arms in expostulation, while Germain seemed to be groveling in front of the man. The boy stood up, though, tucking something into his shirt, and after a few moments' conversation, Beauchamp laughed and put out his hand. They exchanged a brief bow and handshake, and Germain came down the street toward the Whinbush while Beauchamp continued on his course.

Germain came in and, spotting them, slid onto the bench beside his father, looking pleased with himself.

"I've met that man," he said without preamble. "The man who wants Papa."

"Aye, we saw," Jamie said, brows raised. "What the devil were ye doing with him?"

"Well, I saw him coming, but I did not think he would stop and talk to me if I only shouted at him. So I tossed Simon and Peter into his path."

"Who—" Jamie began, but Germain was already groping within the depths of his shirt. Before Jamie could finish the sentence, the boy had produced two sizable frogs, one green and one a sort of vile yellow color, who huddled together on the bare boards of the table, goggling in a nervous manner.

Fergus cuffed Germain round the ear.

"Take those accursed creatures off the table, before we are thrown out of here. No wonder you are covered in warts, consorting with *les grenouilles!*"

"*Grandmère* told me to," Germain protested, nonetheless scooping up his pets and returning them to captivity.

"She did?" Jamie was not usually startled anymore by his wife's cures, but this seemed odd, even by her standards.

"Well, she said there was nothing to do for the wart on my elbow except rub it with a dead frog and bury it—the frog, I mean—at a crossroads at midnight."

"Oh. I think she might possibly have been being facetious. What did the Frenchman say to ye, then?"

Germain looked up, wide-eyed and interested.

"Oh, he's not a Frenchman, *Grandpère*."

A brief pulse of astonishment went through him.

"He's not? Ye're sure?"

"Oh, aye. He cursed most blasphemous when Simon landed on his shoe— but not the way Papa does." Germain aimed a bland look at his father, who looked disposed to cuff him again, but desisted at Jamie's gesture. "He is an Englishman. I'm sure."

"He cursed *in* English?" Jamie asked. It was true; Frenchmen often invoked vegetables when cursing, not infrequently mingled with sacred references. English cursing generally had nothing to do with saints, sacraments, or cucumbers, but dealt with God, whores, or excrement.

"He did. But I cannot say *what* he said, or Papa will be offended. He has very pure ears, Papa," Germain added, with a smirk at his father.

"Leave off deviling your father and tell me what else the man said."

"Aye, well," Germain said obligingly. "When he saw it was no but a pair o' wee froggies, he laughed and asked me was I taking them home for my dinner. I said no, they were my pets, and asked him was it his ship out there, because everyone said so and it was a bonny thing, no? I was making out to be simple, aye?" he explained, in case his grandfather might not have grasped the stratagem.

Jamie suppressed a smile.

"Verra clever," he said dryly. "What else?"

"He said no, the ship is not his but belongs to a great nobleman in France. And I of course said, oh, who was that? And he said it is the Baron Amandine."

Jamie exchanged looks with Fergus, who looked surprised and raised one shoulder in a shrug.

"I asked then how long he might remain, for I should like to bring my brother down to see the ship. And he says he will sail tomorrow on the evening tide, and asked me—but he was joking, I could tell—if I wished to come and be a cabin boy on the voyage. I told him no, my frogs suffer from seasickness—like my grandfather." He turned the smirk on Jamie, who eyed him severely.

"Has your father taught ye '*Ne petez pas plus haute que votre cul*'?"

"Mama will wash your mouth out with soap if you say things like that," Germain informed him virtuously. "Do you want me to pick his pocket? I saw him go into the inn on Cherry Street. I could—"

"You could not," Fergus said hastily. "And do not say such things where people can hear. Your mother will assassinate both of us."

Jamie felt a cold prickle at the back of his neck, and glanced hastily round to make sure that no one *had* heard.

"Ye've been teaching him to—"

Fergus looked mildly shifty.

"I thought it a pity that the skills should be lost. It is a family legacy, you might say. I do not let him steal things, of course. We put them back."

"We'll have a word in private later, I think," Jamie said, giving the pair of them a look full of menace. Christ, if Germain had been caught at it . . . He'd best put the fear of God into the two of them before they both ended up pilloried, if not hanged from a tree outright for theft.

"What about the man you were actually *sent* to find?" Fergus asked his son, seizing the chance of deflecting Jamie's ire.

"I found him," Germain said, and nodded toward the door. "There he is."

DELANCEY HALL WAS a small, neat man, with the quiet, nose-twitching manner of a church mouse. Anything less like a smuggler to look at could scarcely have been imagined—which, Jamie thought, was likely a valuable attribute in that line of business.

"A shipper of dry goods" was the way Hall discreetly described his business. "I facilitate the finding of ships for specific cargoes. Which is no easy matter these days, gentlemen, as you may well suppose."

"I do indeed." Jamie smiled at the man. "I have nay cargo to ship, but I am in hopes that ye might know of a situation that would suit. Myself, my wife, and my nephew seek passage to Edinburgh." His hand was under the table, in his sporran. He had taken some of the gold spheres and flattened them with a hammer, into irregular disks. He took three of these and, moving only slightly, placed them on Hall's lap.

The man didn't change expression in the slightest, but Jamie felt the hand dart out and seize the disks, weigh them for an instant, and then vanish into his pocket.

"I think that might be possible," he said blandly. "I know a captain departing from Wilmington in about two weeks' time, who might be induced to carry passengers—for a consideration."

Sometime later, they walked back toward the printshop, Jamie and Fergus together, discussing the probabilities of Hall's being able to produce a ship. Germain wandered dreamily in front of them, zigzagging to and fro in response to whatever was going on inside his remarkably fertile brain.

Jamie's own brain was more than occupied. Baron Amandine. He knew the name, but had no face to go with it, nor did he recall the context in *which* he knew it. Only that he had encountered it at some point, in Paris. But when? When he had attended the *université* there . . . or later, when he and Claire—yes. That was it; he'd heard the name at court. But no matter how he cudgeled his brain, it would give up no further information.

"D'ye want me to speak to this Beauchamp?" Jamie asked abruptly. "I could perhaps find out what he means toward you."

Fergus's mouth drew in a bit, then relaxed as he shook his head.

"No," he said. "I said I had heard this man had made inquiries concerning me in Edenton?"

"Ye're sure it *is* you?" Not that the ground in North Carolina crawled with Claudels, but still . . .

"I think so, yes." Fergus spoke very softly, with an eye on Germain, who had started emitting soft croaks, evidently conversing with the frogs in his shirt. "The person who told me of this said that man had not only a name, but a small information, of sorts. That the Claudel Fraser he sought had been taken from Paris by a tall red-haired Scotsman. Named James Fraser. So I think you cannot speak to him, no."

"Not without exciting his attention, no," Jamie agreed. "But . . . we dinna ken what his purpose is, but it may be something of great advantage to ye, aye? How likely is it that someone in France would go to the trouble and expense of sending someone like him to do ye harm, when they could be content just to leave ye be in America?" He hesitated. "Perhaps . . . the Baron Amandine is some relation to ye?"

The notion seemed the stuff of romances, and likely the sheerest moonshine. But at the same time, Jamie was at a loss to think of some sensible reason for a French nobleman to be hunting a brothel-born bastard across two continents.

Fergus nodded, but didn't reply at once. He was wearing his hook today, rather than the bran-stuffed glove he wore for formal occasions, and delicately scratched his nose with the tip before answering.

"For a long time," he said at last, "when I was small, I pretended to myself that I was the bastard of some great man. All orphans do this, I think," he added dispassionately. "It makes life easier to bear, to pretend that it will not always be as it is, that someone will come and restore you to your rightful place in the world."

He shrugged.

"Then I grew older, and knew this was not true. No one would come to rescue me. But then—" He turned his head and gave Jamie a smile of surpassing sweetness.

"Then I grew older still, and discovered that, after all, it was true. I *am* the son of a great man."

The hook touched Jamie's hand, hard and capable.

"I wish for nothing more."

19

AE FOND KISS

Wilmington, colony of North Carolina
April 18, 1777

THE HEADQUARTERS of the *Wilmington Gazette* were easy to find. The embers had cooled, but the all-too-familiar reek of burning was still thick in the air. A roughly dressed gentleman in a slouch hat was poking through the charred timbers in a dubious way, but left off at Jamie's hailing him and made his way out of the wreckage, lifting his feet high in ginger avoidance.

"Are ye the proprietor of the newspaper, sir?" Jamie asked, extending a hand to help him over a pile of half-burnt books that sprawled over the threshold. "My sympathies, if so."

"Oh, no," the man replied, wiping smudges of soot from his fingers onto a large, filthy handkerchief, which he then passed to Jamie. "Amos Crupp, he'd be the printer. He's gone, though—lit out when they burnt the shop. I'm Herbert Longfield; I own the land. Did own the shop," he added, with a rueful glance behind him. "You wouldn't be a salvor, would you? Got a nice lump of iron, there."

Fergus and Marsali's printing press was now evidently the sole press in operation between Charleston and Newport. The *Gazette*'s press stood twisted and blackened amid the wreckage: still recognizable, but beyond salvage as anything save scrap.

"How long ago did it happen?" I asked.

"Night before last. Just after midnight. It was well a-gone before the bucket brigade could get started."

"An accident with the furnace?" Jamie asked. He bent and picked up one of the scattered pamphlets.

Longfield laughed cynically.

"Not from around here, are you? You said you were looking for Amos?" He glanced warily from Jamie to me and back again. He wasn't likely to confide anything to strangers of unknown political affiliations.

"James Fraser," Jamie said, reaching out to shake his hand firmly. "My wife, Claire. Who was it? The Sons of Liberty?"

Longfield's eyebrows arched high.

"You really aren't from around here." He smiled, but not happily. "Amos was with the Sons. Not quite one of 'em, maybe, but of their mind. I told him to walk a narrow road with what he wrote and what he printed in the paper, and he mostly tried. But these days, it doesn't take much. A whisper of treason, and a man's beaten half to death in the street, tarred and feathered, burnt out—killed, even."

He eyed Jamie consideringly.

"So you didn't know Amos. May I ask what your business with him was?"

"I had a question regarding a bit of news that was published in the *Gazette*. Ye say Crupp's gone. D'ye ken where I might find him? I mean him nay ill," he added.

Mr. Longfield glanced thoughtfully at me, apparently gauging the prospects that a man bound on political violence would bring his wife along. I smiled, trying to look as respectably charming as possible, and he smiled uncertainly back. He had a long upper lip that gave him the aspect of a rather worried camel, this being substantially enhanced by his eccentric dentition.

"No, I don't," he said, turning back to Jamie with the air of a man making up his mind. "He did have a business partner, though, and a devil. Might be that one of them would know what you're looking for?"

Now it was Jamie's turn to size up Longfield. He made his own mind up in an instant, and handed the pamphlet to me.

"It might be. A small item of news regarding a house fire in the mountains was published last year. I wish to discover who might have given that item to the newspaper."

Longfield frowned, puzzled, and scratched at his long upper lip, leaving a smudge of soot.

"I don't recall that, myself. But then—well, I tell you what, sir. I was bound to see George Humphries—that's Amos's business partner—after looking over the premises . . ." He looked over his shoulder, grimacing. "Why don't you come along with me and ask your question?"

"That's most obliging of ye, sir." Jamie flicked an eyebrow at me, as a signal that I was no longer required for window dressing and thus might go about my own business. I wished Mr. Longfield good day, accordingly, and went to forage in the fleshpots of Wilmington.

Business here was somewhat better than it was in New Bern. Wilmington had a deepwater harbor, and while the English blockade had of necessity affected importing and exporting, local boats and coastal packets still came into the port. Wilmington also was substantially larger and still boasted a thriving market in the town square, where I spent a pleasant hour collecting herbs and picking up local gossip, before acquiring a cheese roll for my lunch, whereupon I wandered down to the harbor to eat it.

I strolled casually along, hoping to spot the vessel that might be carrying us to Scotland, but saw nothing at anchor that looked in any way large enough for such a voyage. But of course—DeLancey Hall had said that we would need to embark on a small ship, perhaps his own fishing ketch, and slip out of the harbor to rendezvous with the larger ship at sea.

I sat down on a bollard to eat, drawing a small crowd of interested seagulls, who floated down like overweight snowflakes to surround me.

"Think again, mate," I said, pointing a monitory finger at one particularly intransigent specimen, who was sidling toward my feet, eyeing my basket. "It's *my* lunch." I still had the half-burnt pamphlet Jamie had handed me; I flapped it vigorously at the gulls, who whirled up in a screech of alarm but then resettled round me, at a slightly more respectful distance, beady eyes all focused on the roll in my hand.

"Ha," I said to them, and moved the basket behind my feet, just in case. I kept a good grip on my roll and one eye on the gulls. The other was free to survey the harbor. A British man-of-war was anchored a little way out, and the sight of the Union Jack flying from its bow gave me a peculiarly paradoxical feeling of pride and unease.

The pride was reflexive. I'd been an Englishwoman all my life. I'd served Great Britain in hospitals, on battlefields—in duty and with honor—and I'd seen many of my countrymen and women fall in that same service. While the Union Jack I saw now was slightly different in design to the one I'd lived with, it was identifiably the same flag, and I felt the same instinctive lift of the heart at sight of it.

At the same time, I was all too aware of the menace that that flag now posed to me and mine. The ship's upper gunports were open; evidently some drill was being conducted, for I saw the cannon rolled rapidly in and out, in succession, blunt snouts poking out, then drawing in, like the heads of pugnacious gophers. There had been *two* men-of-war in the harbor the day before; the other had gone...where? On a particular mission—or merely cruising restlessly up and down outside the harbor mouth, ready to board, seize, fire upon, or sink any ship that looked suspicious?

I couldn't think of anything that would look more suspicious than the ship belonging to Mr. Hall's smuggling friend.

I thought again of the mysterious Mr. Beauchamp. France was still neutral; we would be a good deal safer in a ship flying French colors. Safer from the depredations of the British Navy, at least. As for Beauchamp's own motives... I reluctantly accepted Fergus's desire to have nothing to do with the man, but still wondered what on earth Beauchamp's interest in Fergus could be.

I also still wondered whether he might have any connection to my own family of Beauchamps, but there was no way of knowing; Uncle Lamb had done a rudimentary family genealogy, I knew—mostly for my sake—but I'd paid no attention to it. Where was it now? I wondered. He'd given it to me and Frank when we married, neatly typed up and put in a manila folder.

Perhaps I'd mention Mr. Beauchamp in my next letter to Brianna. She'd have all our old family records—the boxes of ancient income-tax forms, the collections of her own schoolwork and art projects.... I smiled at the memory of the clay dinosaur she'd made at the age of eight, a toothy creature leaning drunkenly to one side, a small cylindrical object hanging from its jaws.

"That's a mammal he's eating," she had informed me.

"What happened to the mammal's legs?" I'd asked.

"They fell off when the dinosaur stepped on it."

The memory had distracted me for a moment, and a bold gull swooped low and struck my hand, knocking the last remnant of my roll to the ground, where it was instantly engulfed by a shrieking crowd of its fellows.

I said a bad word—the gull had left a bleeding scratch across the back of my hand—and, picking up the pamphlet, flung it into the midst of the scrabbling birds. It hit one of them in the head, and the bird rolled over in a mad flutter of wings and pages that dispersed the mob, who all flapped off, yelling gull curses, leaving not a crumb behind.

"Ha," I said again, with a certain grim satisfaction. With some obscure twentieth-century inhibition against littering—certainly no such notions existed here—I retrieved the pamphlet, which had come apart into several pieces, and tidied them back into a rough rectangle.

An Examination of Mercy, it was titled, with a subtitle reading, *Thoughts upon the Nature of Divine Compassion, its Manifestation within the Human Bosom, and the Instruction of its Inspiration to the Improvement of the Individual and Mankind.* Possibly not one of Mr. Crupp's bestselling titles, I thought, stuffing it into the end of my basket.

Which led me to another thought. I wondered whether Roger would see it in an archive someday. I rather thought he might.

Did that mean that we—or I—ought to be doing things on purpose to ensure our appearance in said record? Given that most of the things that made the press in any era were war, crime, tragedy, and other hideous disasters, I rather thought not. My few brushes with notoriety had not been pleasant, and the last thing I wanted Roger to find was a report of my being hanged for bank robbery, executed for witchcraft, or having been pecked to death by vengeful gulls.

No, I concluded. I'd best just tell Bree about Mr. Beauchamp and the Beauchamp family genealogy, and if Roger wanted to poke about in *that,* well and good. Granted, I'd never know if he found Mr. Percival in the list, but if so, Jem and Mandy would have a little further knowledge of their family tree.

Now, where was it, that folder? The last time I'd seen it, it had been in Frank's office, sitting on his filing cabinet. I remembered it distinctly, because Uncle Lamb had rather whimsically drawn what I assumed to be the family coat of—

"I beg your pardon, madam," a deep voice said respectfully behind me. "I see that you—"

Jarred abruptly from my memory, I turned blankly toward the voice, thinking vaguely that I knew—

"Jesus H. Roosevelt Christ!" I blurted, leaping to my feet. "You!"

I took a step backward, stumbled over the basket, and nearly fell into the harbor, saved only by Tom Christie's instinctive grab for my arm.

He jerked me away from the edge of the quay and I fell against his chest. He recoiled as though I were made of molten metal, then seized me in his arms, pressed me hard against himself, and kissed me with passionate abandon.

He broke off, peered into my face, and gasped, "You're dead!"

"Well, no," I said, stunned into apology.

"I beg—I beg your pardon," he managed, letting his arms drop. "I—I—I—" He looked white as a ghost, and I rather thought *he* might fall into the harbor. I doubted that I looked much better, but I did at least have my feet under me.

"You'd better sit down," I said.

"I—not here," he said abruptly.

He was right. The quay was a *very* public place, and our little *rencontre* had attracted considerable notice. A couple of idlers were staring openly, nudging each other, and we were collecting slightly less-obvious glances from the traffic of merchants, seamen, and dock laborers going about their business. I was beginning to recover from the shock, enough to think.

"You have a room? Oh, no—that won't do, will it?" I could imagine all too well what sorts of stories would be flying round town within minutes of our leaving the docks; if we left and repaired to Mr. Christie's—I couldn't think of him presently as anything but "Mr. Christie"—room . . .

"The ordinary," I said firmly. "Come on."

IT WAS ONLY A FEW minutes' walk to Symonds' ordinary, and we passed those minutes in total silence. I stole occasional glances at him, though, both to assure myself that he *wasn't* a ghost and to assess his current situation.

The latter seemed tolerable; he was decently dressed in a dark gray suit, with clean linen, and if he was not fashionable—I bit my lip at the thought of Tom Christie being fashionable—he was at least not shabby.

Otherwise, he looked very much as I'd last seen him—well, no, I corrected myself. He actually looked much better. I'd last seen him in the extremity of exhausted grief, shredded by the tragedy of his daughter's death and its subsequent complications. My last sight of him had been on the *Cruizer,* the British ship on which Governor Martin had taken refuge when he was driven out of the colony, almost two years ago.

At that point, Mr. Christie had declared, first, his intent to confess to the murder of his daughter—of which I was accused—secondly, his love for me, and thirdly, his intent to be executed in my place. All of which made his sudden resurrection not merely surprising but more than slightly awkward.

Adding to the awkwardness was the question as to what—if anything—he knew about the fate of his son, Allan, who *had* been responsible for Malva Christie's death. The circumstances were nothing that any father ought to have to hear, and panic gripped me at the thought that I might have to tell him.

I glanced at him again. His face was deeply lined, but he was neither gaunt nor overtly haunted. He wore no wig, though his wiry salt-and-pepper hair was close-clipped as always, matching his neatly trimmed beard. My face tingled, and I barely kept myself from scrubbing my hand across my mouth to erase the feeling. He was clearly disturbed—well, so was I—but had got himself back under control, and opened the door of the ordinary for me with impeccable courtesy. Only the twitch of a muscle beside his left eye betrayed him.

I felt as though my entire body was twitching, but Phaedre, serving in the taproom, glanced at me with no more than mild interest and a cordial nod. Of course, she'd never met Thomas Christie, and while she'd doubtless heard about the scandal following my arrest, she wouldn't connect the gentleman accompanying me with it.

We found a table by the window in the dining room, and sat down.

"I thought you were dead," I said abruptly. "What did you mean, you thought *I* was dead?"

He opened his mouth to answer but was interrupted by Phaedre, who came to serve us, smiling pleasantly.

"I get you something, sir, ma'am? You wanting food? We've a nice ham to-day, roast taters, and Mrs. Symonds's special mustard 'n raisin sauce to go along of it."

"No," Mr. Christie said. "I—just a cup of cider, if ye please."

"Whisky," I said. "A lot of it."

Mr. Christie looked scandalized, but Phaedre only laughed and whisked off, the grace of her movement attracting the quiet admiration of most of the male patrons.

"Ye haven't changed," he observed. His eyes traveled over me, intense, taking in every detail of my appearance. "I ought to have known ye by your hair."

His voice was disapproving, but tinged with a reluctant amusement; he had always been vociferous in his disapproval of my refusal to wear a cap or otherwise restrain my hair. "Wanton," he'd called it.

"Yes, you should," I said, reaching up to smooth the hair in question, which was considerably the worse for recent encounters. "You didn't recognize me 'til I turned round, though, did you? What made you speak to me?"

He hesitated, but then nodded toward my basket, which I'd set on the floor beside my chair.

"I saw that ye had one of my tracts."

"What?" I said blankly, but looked where he was looking and saw the singed pamphlet on *Divine Compassion* sticking out from under a cabbage. I reached down and pulled it out, only now noticing the author: *by Mr. T. W. Christie, MA, University of Edinburgh.*

"What does the 'W' stand for?" I asked, laying it down.

He blinked.

"Warren," he replied rather gruffly. "Where in God's name did ye come from?"

"My father always claimed he'd found me under a cabbage leaf in the garden," I replied flippantly. "Or did you mean today? If so—the King's Arms."

He was beginning to look a little less shocked, his normal irritation at my lack of womanly decorum drawing his face back into its usual stern lines.

"Don't be facetious. I was told that ye were dead," he said, accusingly. "You and your entire family were burnt up in a fire."

Phaedre, delivering the drinks, glanced at me, eyebrows raised.

"She ain't looking too crispy round the edges, sir, if you pardon my mention of it."

"Thank ye for the observation," he said between his teeth. Phaedre exchanged a glance of amusement with me, and went off again, shaking her head.

"Who told you that?"

"A man named McCreary."

I must have looked blank, for he added, "from Brownsville. I met him

An Echo in the Bone 189

here—in Wilmington, I mean—in late January. He had just come down from the mountain, he said, and told me of the fire. *Was* there a fire?"

"Well, yes, there was," I said slowly, wondering whether—and how much—to tell him of the truth of *that*. Very little, in a public place, I decided. "Maybe it was Mr. McCreary, then, who placed the notice of the fire in the newspaper—but he can't have." The original notice had appeared in 1776, Roger had said—nearly a year before the fire.

"I placed it," Christie said. Now it was my turn to blink.

"You what? When?" I took a good-sized mouthful of whisky, feeling that I needed it more than ever.

"Directly I heard of it. Or—well, no," he corrected. "A few days thereafter. I . . . was very much distressed at the news," he added, lowering his eyes and looking away from me for the first time since we'd sat down.

"Ah. I'm sorry," I said, lowering my own voice, and feeling rather apologetic—though why I should feel apologetic for not having been burnt up . . .

He cleared his throat.

"Yes. Well. It, er, seemed to me that some . . . something should be done. Some formal observance of your—your passing." He looked up then, gray eyes direct. "I could not abide the thought that you—all of you," he added, but it was clearly an afterthought, "should simply vanish from the earth, with no formal marking of the—the event."

He took a deep breath, and a tentative sip of the cider.

"Even if a proper funeral had been held, there would be no point in my returning to Fraser's Ridge, even if I—well. I could not. So I thought I would at least make a record of the event here. After all," he added more softly, looking away again, "I could not lay flowers on your grave."

The whisky had steadied me a bit, but also rasped my throat and made it difficult to talk when hampered by emotion. I reached out and touched his hand briefly, then cleared my throat, finding momentarily neutral ground.

"Your hand," I said. "How is it?"

He looked up, surprised, but the taut lines of his face relaxed a bit.

"Very well, I thank you. See?" He turned over his right hand, displaying a large Z-shaped scar upon the palm, well healed but still pink.

"Let me see."

His hand was cold. With an assumption of casualness, I took it in mine, turning it, bending the fingers to assess their flexibility and degree of movement. He was right: it *was* doing well; the movement was nearly normal.

"I—did the exercises you set me," he blurted. "I do them every day."

I looked up to find him regarding me with a sort of anguished solemnity, his cheeks now flushed above his beard, and realized that this ground was not nearly so neutral as I'd thought. Before I could let go his hand, it turned in mine, covering my fingers—not tightly, but sufficiently that I couldn't free myself without a noticeable effort.

"Your husband." He stopped dead, having obviously not thought of Jamie at all to this point. "He is alive, too?"

"Er, yes."

To his credit, he didn't grimace at this news, but nodded, exhaling.

"I am—glad to hear it."

He sat in silence for a moment, looking at his undrunk cider. He was still holding my hand. Without looking up, he said in a low voice, "Does he . . . know? What I—how I—I did not tell him the reason for my confession. Did you?"

"You mean your"—I groped for some suitable way of putting it—"your, um, very gallant feelings toward me? Well, yes, he does; he was very sympathetic toward you. He knowing from experience what it's like to be in love with me, I mean," I added tartly.

He almost laughed at that, which gave me an opportunity to extricate my fingers. He did not, I noticed, inform me that he *wasn't* in love with me any longer. Oh, dear.

"Well, anyway, we aren't dead," I said, clearing my throat again. "What about you? Last time I saw you . . ."

"Ah." He looked less than happy, but gathered himself, changing gears, and nodded. "Your rather hasty departure from the *Cruizer* left Governor Martin without an amanuensis. Discovering that I was to some degree literate"—his mouth twisted a little—"and could write a fair hand, thanks to your ministrations, he had me removed from the brig."

I wasn't surprised at that. Driven completely out of his colony, Governor Martin was obliged to conduct his business from the tiny captain's cabin of the British ship on which he had taken refuge. Such business perforce consisted entirely of letters—all of which must be not only composed, drafted, and fair-copied but then reproduced several times each. A copy was required first for the governor's own official correspondence files, then for each person or entity having some interest in the subject of the letter, and, finally, several additional copies of any letters going to England or Europe must be made, because they would be sent by different ships, in hopes that at least one copy would make it through, should the others be sunk, seized by pirates or privateers, or otherwise lost in transit.

My hand ached at the mere memory of it. The exigencies of bureaucracy in a time before the magic of Xerox had kept me from rotting in a cell; no wonder they had freed Tom Christie from durance vile as well.

"You see?" I said, rather pleased. "If I hadn't fixed your hand, he'd likely have had you either executed on the spot or at least sent back to shore and immured in some dungeon."

"I am duly grateful," he said, with extreme dryness. "I was not, at the time."

Christie had spent several months as *de facto* secretary to the governor. In late November, though, a ship had arrived from England, bearing orders to the governor—essentially ordering him to subdue the colony, though offering no troops, armament, or useful suggestions as to how this might be managed—and an official secretary.

"At this point, the governor was faced with the prospect of disposing of me. We had . . . become acquainted, working in such close quarters . . ."

"And as you were no longer quite an anonymous murderer, he didn't want to yank the quill out of your hand and hang you from the yardarm," I finished for him. "Yes, he's actually rather a kind man."

"He is," Christie said thoughtfully. "He has not had an easy time of it, poor fellow."

I nodded. "He told you about his little boys?"

"Aye, he did." His lips compressed—not out of anger, but to control his own emotion. Martin and his wife had lost three small sons, one after another, to the plagues and fevers of the colony; small wonder if hearing of the governor's pain had reopened Tom Christie's own wounds. He shook his head a little, though, and returned to the subject of his deliverance.

"I had ... told him a bit about ... about my daughter." He picked up the barely touched cup of cider and drank half of it off at a swallow, as if dying of thirst. "I admitted privately to him that my confession had been false—though I stated also that I was certain of your innocence," he assured me. "And if you should ever be arrested again for the crime, my confession would stand."

"Thank you for that," I said, and wondered with still greater uneasiness whether he knew who *had* killed Malva. He had to have suspected, I thought—but that was a long way from having to know, let alone having to know why. And no one knew where Allan was now—save me, Jamie, and Young Ian.

Governor Martin had received this admission with some relief, and decided that the only thing to do in the circumstances was to put Christie ashore, there to be dealt with by the civil authorities.

"There *aren't* any civil authorities anymore," I said. "Are there?"

He shook his head.

"None capable of dealing with such a matter. There are still gaols and sheriffs, but neither courts nor magistrates. Under the circumstances"—he almost smiled, dour though the expression was—"I thought it a waste of time to try to find someone to whom to surrender myself."

"But you said you had sent a copy of your confession to the newspaper," I said. "Weren't you, er, received coldly by the people in New Bern?"

"By the grace of divine Providence, the newspaper there had ceased its operations before my confession was received by them, the printer being a Loyalist. I believe Mr. Ashe and his friends called upon him, and he wisely decided to find another mode of business."

"Very wise," I said dryly. John Ashe was a friend of Jamie's, a leading light of the local Sons of Liberty, and the man who had instigated the burning of Fort Johnston and effectively driven Governor Martin into the sea.

"There was some gossip," he said, looking away again, "but it was overwhelmed by the rush of public events. No one quite knew what had happened on Fraser's Ridge, and after a time it became fixed in everyone's mind simply that some personal tragedy had befallen me. People came to regard me with a sort of ... sympathy." His mouth twisted; he wasn't the sort to receive sympathy with any graciousness.

"You seem to be thriving," I said, with a nod at his suit. "Or at least you aren't sleeping in the gutter and living off discarded fish heads from the docks. I had no idea that the tract-writing business was profitable."

He'd gone back to his normal color during the previous conversation, but flushed up again at this—with annoyance, this time.

"It isn't," he snapped. "I take pupils. And I—I preach of a Sunday."

"I can't imagine anyone better for the job," I said, amused. "You've always had a talent for telling everyone what's wrong with them in Biblical terms. Have you become a clergyman, then?"

His color grew deeper, but he choked down his choler and answered me evenly.

"I was nearly destitute upon my arrival here. Fish heads, as you say—and the occasional bit of bread or soup given by a New Light congregation. I came in order to eat, but remained for the service out of courtesy. I thus heard a sermon given by the Reverend Peterson. It—remained with me. I sought him out, and we . . . spoke. One thing led to another." He glanced up at me, his eyes fierce. "The Lord does answer prayer, ye know."

"What had you prayed for?" I asked, intrigued.

That took him back a bit, though it had been an innocent question, asked from simple curiosity.

"I—I—" He broke off and stared at me, frowning. "You are a most uncomfortable woman!"

"You wouldn't be the first person to think so," I assured him. "And I don't mean to pry. I just . . . wondered."

I could see the urge to get up and leave warring with the compulsion to bear witness to whatever had happened to him. But he was a stubborn man, and he stayed put.

"I . . . asked why," he said at last, very evenly. "That's all."

"Well, it worked for Job," I observed. He looked startled, and I nearly laughed; he was always startled at the revelation that anyone other than himself had read the Bible. He got a grip, though, and glowered at me in something more like his usual fashion.

"And now you are here," he said, making it sound like an accusation. "I suppose your husband has formed a militia—or joined one. I have had enough of war. I am surprised that your husband has not."

"I don't think it's precisely a taste for war," I said. I spoke with an edge, but something in him compelled me to add, "It's that he feels he was born to it."

Something flickered deep in Tom Christie's eyes—surprise? Acknowledgment?

"He is," he said quietly. "But surely—" He didn't finish the thought, but instead asked abruptly, "What are you doing here, though? In Wilmington?"

"Looking for a ship," I said. "We're going to Scotland."

I'd always had a talent for startling him, but this one took the biscuit. He had lifted his mug to drink, but upon hearing my declaration, abruptly spewed cider across the table. The subsequent choking and wheezing attracted a good bit of attention, and I sat back, trying to look less conspicuous.

"Er . . . we'll be going to Edinburgh, for my husband's printing press," I said. "Is there anyone you'd like me to see for you? Deliver a message, I mean? You have a brother there, I think you said."

His head shot up and he glared at me, eyes streaming. I felt a spasm of horror at the sudden recollection and could have bitten my tongue off at the root. His brother had had an affair with Tom's wife while Tom was imprisoned in the Highlands after the Rising, and his wife had then poisoned his brother and subsequently been executed for witchcraft.

"I'm so sorry," I said, low-voiced. "Forgive me, please. I didn't—"

He seized my hand in both of his, so hard and so abruptly that I gasped, and a few heads turned curiously in our direction. He paid no attention, but leaned toward me across the table.

"Listen to me," he said, low and fierce. "I have loved three women. One was a witch and a whore, the second only a whore. Ye well may be a witch yourself, but it makes nay whit o' difference. The love of you has led me to my salvation, and to what I thought was my peace, once I thought ye dead."

He stared at me and shook his head slowly, his mouth going tight for a moment in the seam of his beard.

"And here you are."

"Er . . . yes." I felt once more as though I should apologize for not being dead, but didn't.

He drew a deep breath and let it out in a sigh.

"I shall have no peace while ye live, woman."

Then he lifted my hand and kissed it, stood up, and walked away.

"Mind," he said, turning at the door to look back at me over his shoulder, "I dinna say I regret it."

I picked up the glass of whisky and drained it.

I WENT ABOUT THE REST of my errands in a daze—not entirely induced by whisky. I hadn't any idea what to think of the resurrection of Tom Christie, but was thoroughly unsettled by it. Still, there seemed nothing, really, to *do* about him, and so I went on to the shop of Stephen Moray, a silversmith from Fife, to commission a pair of surgical scissors. Luckily, he proved an intelligent man, who appeared to understand both my specifications and the purpose behind them, and promised to have the scissors made within three days. Heartened by this, I ventured a slightly more problematic commission.

"Needles?" Moray knit his white brows in puzzlement. "Ye dinna require a silversmith for—"

"Not sewing needles. These are longer, quite thin, and without an eye. They have a medical purpose. And I should like you to make them from this."

His eyes went wide as I laid what appeared to be a gold nugget the size of a walnut on the counter. It was in fact a bit of one of the French ingots, hacked off and hammered into a lump, then rubbed with dirt by way of disguise.

"My husband won it in a card game," I said, with the tone of mingled pride and apology that seemed appropriate to such an admission. I didn't want anyone thinking that there was gold on Fraser's Ridge—in any form. Boosting Jamie's reputation as a card player wasn't likely to do any harm; he was already well known—if not quite notorious—for his abilities in that line.

Moray frowned a bit over the written specifications for the acupuncture needles, but agreed to make them. Luckily, he appeared never to have heard of voodoo dolls, or I might have had a bit more trouble.

With the visit to the silversmith and a quick trip through the market square for spring onions, cheese, peppermint leaves, and anything else available in the herbal line, it was late afternoon before I came back to the King's Arms.

Jamie was playing cards in the taproom, with Young Ian watching over his shoulder, but he saw me come in and, giving over his hand to Ian, came to take my basket, following me up the stairs to our room.

I turned round inside the door, but before I could speak, he said, "I know Tom Christie's alive. I met him in the street."

"He kissed me," I blurted.

"Aye, I heard," he said, eyeing me with what might have been amusement. For some reason, I found that very annoying. He saw *that*, and the amusement deepened.

"Like it, did ye?"

"It wasn't funny!"

The amusement didn't go away, but it retreated a bit.

"*Did* ye like it?" he repeated, but now there was curiosity in his voice, rather than teasing.

"No." I turned away abruptly. "That—I hadn't time to . . . to think about it."

Without warning, he put a hand behind my neck and kissed me briefly. And by simple reflex, I slapped him. Not hard—I'd tried to pull back even as I struck—and clearly I hadn't hurt him. I was as surprised and discomfited as though I'd knocked him flat.

"Doesna take much thought, does it?" he said lightly, and stepped back, surveying me with interest.

"I'm sorry," I said, feeling simultaneously mortified and angry—and angrier still in that I didn't understand why I *was* angry in the slightest. "I didn't mean to—I'm sorry."

He tilted his head to one side, eyeing me.

"Had I better go and kill him?"

"Oh, don't be ridiculous." I fidgeted, untying my pocket, not wanting to meet his eyes. I was prickly, discomfited, irritated—and the more discomfited by not really knowing *why*.

"It was an honest question, Sassenach," he said quietly. "Not a serious one, maybe—but honest. I think ye maybe owe me an honest answer."

"Of course I don't want you to kill him!"

"D'ye want me to tell you why ye slapped me, instead?"

"Why—" I stood with my mouth open for a second, then closed it. "Yes. I do."

"I touched ye against your will," he said, his eyes intent on mine. "Didn't I?"

"You did," I said, and breathed a little easier. "And so did Tom Christie. And, no, I *didn't* like it."

"But not on Tom's account," he finished. "Poor fellow."

"He wouldn't want your sympathy," I said tartly, and he smiled.

"He would not. But he's got it, nonetheless. Still, I'm glad of it," he added.

"Glad of what? That he's alive—or—surely not that he thinks he's in love with me?" I said, incredulous.

"Dinna belittle his feelings, Sassenach," he said, more quietly. "He's laid down his life for ye once. I'd trust him to do it again."

"I didn't want him to do it the first time!"

"You're bothered," he said, in a tone of clinical interest.

"Yes, I am bloody bothered!" I said. "And"—the thought struck me and I gave him a hard look—"so are you." I recalled suddenly that he'd said he'd met Tom Christie in the street. What had Tom said to him?

He tilted his head in mild negation, but didn't deny it.

"I willna say I *like* Thomas Christie," he said consideringly, "but I respect him. And I *am* verra much pleased to find him alive. Ye didna do wrong to grieve him, Sassenach," he said gently. "I did, too."

"I hadn't even thought of that." In the shock of seeing him, I hadn't remembered, but I'd wept for him—and for his children. "I don't regret it, though."

"Good. The thing about Tom Christie," he went on, "is that he wants ye. Badly. But he doesna ken a thing about you."

"And you do." I left it somewhere between question and challenge, and he smiled. He turned and shot the bolt on the door, then crossed the room and drew the calico curtain on the one small window, casting the room into a pleasant blue dimness.

"Oh, I've need and want in plenty—but I've knowing, too." He was standing very close, close enough that I had to look up to him. "I've never kissed ye without knowing who ye were—and that's a thing poor Tom will never know." God, what *had* Tom told him?

My pulse, which had been jumping up and down, settled down to a quick, light thump, discernible in my fingertips.

"You didn't know a thing about me when you married me."

His hand closed gently on my behind.

"No?"

"Besides that, I mean!"

He made a small Scottish sound in his throat, not quite a chuckle.

"Aye, well, it's a wise man who kens what he doesna know—and I learn fast, *a nighean*."

He drew me gently close then, and kissed me—with thought and tenderness, with knowing—and with my full consent. It didn't obliterate my memory of Tom Christie's impassioned, blundering embrace, and I thought it wasn't meant to; it was meant to show me the difference.

"You *can't* be jealous," I said, a moment later.

"I can," he said, not joking.

"You can't possibly think—"

"I don't."

"Well, then—"

"Well, then." His eyes were dark as seawater in the dimness, but the expression in them was entirely readable, and my heart beat faster. "I ken what ye feel for Tom Christie—and he told me plain what he feels for you. Surely ye ken that love's nothing to do wi' logic, Sassenach?"

Knowing a rhetorical question when I heard one, I didn't bother answering that, but instead reached out and tidily unbuttoned his shirt. There was nothing I could reasonably say about Tom Christie's feelings, but I had another language in which to express my own. His heart was beating fast; I could feel it as though I held it in my hand. Mine was, too, but I breathed deep and took comfort in the warm familiarity of his body, the soft crispness of the cinnamon-colored hairs of his chest, and the gooseflesh that raised them under my fingers. While I was thus engaged, he slid his fingers into my hair, separating a lock which he viewed appraisingly.

"It's not gone white yet. I suppose I've a little time, then, before ye get too dangerous for me to bed."

"Dangerous, forsooth," I said, setting to work on the buttons of his breeks. I wished he had on his kilt. "Exactly what do you think I might do to you in bed?"

He scratched his chest consideringly, and rubbed absently at the tiny knot of scar tissue where he'd cut Jack Randall's brand from his flesh.

"Well, so far, ye've clawed me, bitten me, stabbed me—more than once—and—"

"I have not stabbed you!"

"Ye did, too," he informed me. "Ye stabbed me in the backside wi' your nasty wee needle spikes—fifteen times! I counted—and then a dozen times or more in the leg with a rattlesnake's fang."

"I was saving your bloody life!"

"I didna say otherwise, did I? Ye're no going to deny ye enjoyed it, though, are ye?"

"Well . . . not the rattlesnake fang, so much. As for the hypodermic . . ." My mouth twitched, despite myself. "You deserved it."

He gave me a look of profound cynicism.

"Do nay harm, is it?"

"Besides, you were counting what I'd done to you in bed," I said, neatly returning to the point. "You can't count the shots."

"I was in bed!"

"I wasn't!"

"Aye, ye took unfair advantage," he said, nodding. "I wouldna hold that against ye, though."

He'd got my jacket off and was busily untying my laces, head bent in absorption.

"How'd you like it if *I* were jealous?" I asked the crown of his head.

"I'd like that fine," he replied, breath warm on my exposed flesh. "And ye were. Of Laoghaire." He looked up, grinning, eyebrow raised. "Maybe ye still are?"

I slapped him again, and this time I meant it. He could have stopped me but didn't.

"Aye, that's what I thought," he said, wiping a watering eye. "Will ye come to bed wi' me, then? It'll be just us," he added.

IT WAS LATE WHEN I woke; the room was dark, though a slice of fading sky showed at the top of the curtain. The fire hadn't yet been lit and the room was chilly, but it was warm and cozy under the quilts, snug against Jamie's body. He had turned onto his side, and I curled spoonlike against his back and put my arm over him, feeling the gentle rise and fall of his breath.

It *had* been just us. I'd worried, at the start, that the memory of Tom Christie and his awkward passion might fall between us—but Jamie, evidently thinking the same thing and determined to avoid any echo of Tom's embrace that might remind me, had started at the other end, kissing my toes.

Given the size of the room and the fact that the bed was jammed tightly into one end of it, he had been obliged to straddle me in order to do this, and the combination of having my feet nibbled and the view from directly behind and beneath a naked Scotsman had been sufficient to remove anything else from my head.

Warm, safe, and calm now, I could think about the earlier encounter without feeling threatened, though. And I *had* felt threatened. Jamie had seen that. *D'ye want me to tell you why ye slapped me?...I touched ye against your will.*

He was right; it was one of the minor aftereffects of what had happened to me when I had been abducted. Crowds of men made me nervous with no cause, and being grabbed unexpectedly made me recoil and jerk away in panic. Why hadn't I seen that?

Because I didn't want to think about it, that's why. I still didn't. What good would thinking do? Let things heal on their own, if they would.

But even things that heal leave scars. The evidence of that was literally in front of my face—pressed against it, in fact.

The scars on Jamie's back had faded into a pale spiderweb, with only a slight raised bit here or there, ridged under my fingers when we made love, like barbed wire beneath his skin. I remembered Tom Christie taunting him about them once, and my jaw tightened.

I laid a hand softly on his back, tracing one pale loop with my thumb. He twitched in his sleep and I stilled, hand flat.

What might be coming? I wondered. For him. For me. I heard Tom Christie's sarcastic voice: *I have had enough of war. I am surprised that your husband has not.*

"Well enough for *you*," I muttered under my breath. "Coward." Tom Christie had been imprisoned as a Jacobite—which he was, but not a soldier. He'd been a commissary supply officer in Charles Stuart's army. He'd risked his wealth and his position—and lost both—but not his life or body.

Still, Jamie did respect him—which meant something, Jamie being no mean judge of character. And I knew enough from watching Roger to realize that becoming a clergyman was not the easy path that some people thought it. Roger was not a coward, either, and I wondered how he would find his path in the future?

I turned over, restless. Supper was being prepared; I could smell the rich, saltwater smell of fried oysters from the kitchen below, borne on a wave of woodsmoke and roasting potatoes.

Jamie stirred a little and rolled onto his back, but didn't wake. Time enough. He was dreaming; I could see the movement of his eyes, twitching beneath sealed lids, and the momentary tightening of his lips.

His body tightened, too, suddenly hard beside me, and I jerked back, startled. He growled low in his throat, and his body arched with effort. He was making strangled noises, whether shouting or screaming in his dream I didn't know, and didn't wait to find out.

"Jamie—wake up!" I said sharply. I didn't touch him—I knew better than to do that while he was in the grip of a violent dream; he'd nearly broken my nose once or twice. "Wake up!"

He gasped, caught his breath, and opened unfocused eyes. Plainly he didn't know where he was, and I spoke to him more gently, repeating his name, reassuring him that he was all right. He blinked, swallowed heavily, then turned his head and saw me.

"Claire," I said helpfully, seeing him groping for my name.

"Good," he said hoarsely. He closed his eyes, shook his head, and then opened them again. "All right, Sassenach?"

"Yes. You?"

He nodded, closing his eyes again briefly.

"Aye, fine. I was dreaming about the house burning. Fighting." He sniffed. "Is something burning?"

"Supper, at a guess." The savory smells from below had in fact been interrupted by the acrid stench of smoke and scorched food. "I think the stewpot boiled over."

"Perhaps we'll eat elsewhere tonight."

"Phaedre said Mrs. Symonds had baked ham with mustard and raisin sauce at noon. There might be some left. Are you all right?" I asked again. The room was cold, but his face and breast were sheened with sweat.

"Oh, aye," he replied, sitting up and rubbing his hands vigorously through his hair. "That sort of dream, I can live with." He shoved his hair out of his face and smiled at me. "Ye look like a milkweed puff, Sassenach. Were ye sleeping restless, too?"

"No," I told him, getting up and pulling my shift on before groping for my hairbrush. "It was the restless part *before* we fell asleep. Or do you not remember that bit?"

He laughed, wiped his face, and got up to use the chamber pot, then pulled his shirt on.

"What about the other dreams?" I asked abruptly.

"What?" He emerged from the shirt, looking quizzical.

"You said, 'That sort of dream, I can live with.' What about the ones you can't live with?"

I saw the lines of his face shiver like the surface of water when you've thrown a pebble into it, and on impulse, reached out and clutched his wrist.

"Don't hide," I said softly. I held his eyes with mine, keeping him from raising his mask. "Trust me."

He did look away then, but only to gather himself; he didn't hide. When he glanced back at me, it was all still there in his eyes—confusion, embarrass-ment, humiliation, and the vestiges of a pain long suppressed.

"I dream...sometimes..." he said haltingly, "about things that were done to me against my will." He breathed through his nose, deep, exasper-ated. "And I wake from it with a cockstand and my balls throbbing and I want to go and kill someone, starting with myself," he ended in a rush, grimacing.

"It doesna happen often," he added, giving me a brief, direct look. "And I never...I would never turn to you in the wake of such a thing. Ye should know that."

I tightened my grip on his wrist. I wanted to say, "*You could—I wouldn't mind,*" for that was the truth, and once I would have said it without hesita-tion. But I knew a great deal more now, and had it been me, had I ever dreamed of Harley Boble or the heavy, soft-bodied man and wakened from it aroused—and thank *God* I never had—no, the last thing I would ever have done would be to take that feeling and turn to Jamie, or use his body to purge it.

"Thank you," I said instead, quietly. "For telling me," I added. "And for the knife."

He nodded, and turned to pick up his breeks.

"I like ham," he said.

20

I REGRET...

**Long Island, colony of New York
September 1776**

WILLIAM WISHED he could speak to his father. It wasn't, he assured himself, that he wanted Lord John to exert any influence; certainly not. He just wanted a bit of practical advice. Lord John had returned to England, though, and William was on his own.

Well, not precisely on his own. He was at the moment in charge of a de-tachment of soldiers guarding a customs checkpoint on the edge of Long Island. He slapped viciously at a mosquito that lighted on his wrist, and, for once, obliterated it. He wished he could do the same to Clarewell.

Lieutenant Edward Markham, Marquis of Clarewell. Otherwise known—to William and a couple of his more intimate friends—as Chinless Ned, or the Ponce. William swatted at a crawling sensation on his own prominent jaw, no-ticed that two of his men had momentarily disappeared, and stalked toward the wagon they had been inspecting, bellowing their names.

Private Welch appeared from behind the wagon like a jack-in-the-box, looking startled and wiping his mouth. William leaned forward, sniffed his breath, and said briefly, "Charges. Where's Launfal?"

In the wagon, hastily concluding a bargain with the wagon's owner for three bottles of the contraband brandywine that gentleman was seeking to illicitly import. William, grimly slapping at the man-eating hordes of mosquitoes that swarmed out of the nearby marshes, arrested the wagoneer, summoned the other three men of his detail, and told them off to escort the smuggler, Welch, and Launfal to the sergeant. He took up a musket then and stood in the middle of the road, alone and ferocious, his attitude daring anyone to try to pass.

Ironically, though the road had been busy all morning, no one did try for some time, giving him opportunity to refocus his bad temper on the thought of Clarewell.

Heir of a *very* influential family, and one with intimate ties to Lord North, Chinless Ned had arrived in New York a week before William and likewise been placed on Howe's staff, where he had nestled cozily into the woodwork, smarming round General Howe—who, to his credit, tended to blink and stare hard at the Ponce, as though trying to remember who the devil he was— and Captain Pickering, the general's chief aide-de-camp, a vain man, and one much more susceptible to Ned's enthusiastic arse-creeping.

As a result, Chinless had been routinely bagging the choicer assignments, riding with the general on short exploratory expeditions, attending him in meetings with Indian dignitaries and the like, while William and several other junior officers were left to shuffle papers and kick their heels. Hard cheese, after the freedoms and excitements of intelligencing.

He could have stood the constraints of life in quarters and army bureaucracy. His father had schooled him thoroughly in the necessity of restraint in trying circumstances, the withstanding of boredom, the handling of dolts, and the art of icy politeness as a weapon. Someone lacking William's strength of character, though, had snapped one day and, unable to resist the possibilities for caricature conjured up by a contemplation of Ned's profile, had drawn a cartoon of Captain Pickering with his breeches round his ankles, engaged in lecturing the junior staff and apparently ignorant of the Ponce, emergent headfirst and smirking from Pickering's arse.

William had not drawn this bit of diversion—though he rather wished he had—but had been discovered laughing at it by Ned himself, who—in a rare show of manliness—had punched William in the nose. The resultant brawl had cleared the junior officers' quarters, broken a few inconsequent items of furniture, and resulted in William, dripping blood onto his shirtfront, standing to attention in front of a cold-eyed Captain Pickering, the scurrilous cartoon laid out in evidence on the desk.

William had, of course, denied authorship of the thing but declined to identify the artist. He'd used the icy-politeness thing, which had worked to the extent that Pickering had not in fact sent William to the stockade. Merely to Long Island.

"Frigging fart-catcher," he muttered, glaring at an approaching milkmaid with such ferocity that she stopped dead, then edged past him, eyeing him with a wide-eyed alarm that suggested she thought he might explode. He bared his teeth at her, and she emitted a startled squeak and scuttled off so fast that some of her milk slopped out of the buckets she carried on a yoke across her shoulders.

That made him repentant; he wished he could follow her and apologize. But he couldn't; a pair of drovers were coming down the road toward him, bringing in a herd of pigs. William took one look at the oncoming mass of heaving, squealing, spotted hog flesh, tatter-eared and mud-besmeared, and hopped nimbly up onto the bucket that served as his command post. The drovers waved gaily at him, shouting what might be either greetings or insults—he wasn't sure they were even speaking English, and didn't care to find out.

The pigs passed, leaving him amid a sea of hoof-churned mud, liberally scattered with fresh droppings. He slapped at the cloud of mosquitoes that had regathered inquisitively round his head, and thought that he'd had just about enough. He'd been on Long Island for two weeks—which was thirteen and a half days too long. Not quite long enough yet to make him apologize to either Chinless or the captain, though.

"Lickspittle," he muttered.

He did have an alternative. And the longer he spent out here with the mosquitoes, the more attractive it began to look.

It was far too long a ride from his customs outpost to headquarters to make the journey twice each day. In consequence, he'd been temporarily billeted on a man called Culper and his two sisters. Culper wasn't best pleased; his left eye began to twitch whenever he saw William, but the two elderly ladies made much of him, and he returned the favor when he could, bringing them the odd confiscated ham or flask of cambric. He'd come in the night before with a flitch of good bacon, to have Miss Abigail Culper inform him in a whisper that he had a visitor.

"Out a-smoking in the yard," she'd said, inclining her bonneted head toward the side of the house. "Sister wouldn't let him smoke in the house, I'm afraid."

He'd expected to find one of his friends, come to bear him company or perhaps with news of an official pardon that would bring him back from exile on Long Island. Instead, he'd found Captain Richardson, pipe in hand, meditatively watching the Culpers' rooster tread a hen.

"Pleasures of a bucolic life," the captain remarked, as the rooster fell off backward. The cock staggered to his feet and crowed in disheveled triumph, while the hen shook her feathers into order and resumed pecking as though nothing had happened. "Very quiet out here, is it not?"

"Oh, yes," William said. "Your servant, sir."

In fact, it was not. Miss Beulah Culper kept a half-dozen goats, who blatted day and night, though Miss Beulah assured William that they served to keep thieves out of the corncrib. One of the creatures at this point gave a wild braying laugh from its pen, causing Captain Richardson to drop his tobacco pouch. Several more of the goats commenced to utter loud *mehs*, as though jeering.

William bent and picked the pouch up, keeping his face tactfully blank, though his heart was pounding. Richardson hadn't come all the way out to Long Island simply to pass the time.

"Christ," Richardson muttered, with a look at the goats. He shook his head, and gestured toward the road. "Will you walk a bit with me, Lieutenant?"

William would, gladly.

"I heard a bit regarding your present situation." Richardson smiled. "I'll have a word with Captain Pickering, if you like."

"That's very kind of you, sir," William said. "But I'm afraid I can't apologize for something I haven't done."

Richardson waved his pipe, dismissing it. "Pickering's got a short temper, but he doesn't hold a grudge. I'll see to it."

"Thank you, sir." *And what do you want in return?* William thought.

"There is a Captain Randall-Isaacs," Richardson said casually, "who is traveling within the month to Canada, where he has some military business to transact. While there, though, it is possible that he will meet with . . . a certain person who may provide the army with valuable information. I have some reason to suppose that this person has little English, though—and Captain Randall-Isaacs, alas, has no French. A traveling companion fluent in that language might be . . . useful."

William nodded, but asked no questions. Time enough for that, if he decided to accept Richardson's commission.

They exchanged commonplaces for the remainder of the walk back, whereupon Richardson politely declined Miss Beulah's invitation to take supper, and left with a reiterated promise to speak to Captain Pickering.

Should he do it? William wondered later, listening to Abel Culper's wheezing snores below. The moon was full, and while the loft had no windows, he could feel its pull; he never could sleep when the moon was full.

Ought he to hang on in New York, in hopes either of improving his position, or at least of eventually seeing some action? Or cut his losses and take Richardson's new commission?

His father would doubtless advise the former course of action; an officer's best chance of advancement and notice lay in distinguishing himself in battle, not in the shady—and vaguely disreputable—realm of intelligencing. Still . . . the routine and constraints of the army chafed, rather, after his weeks of freedom. And he *had* been useful, he knew.

What difference could one lieutenant make, buried under the crushing weight of the ranks above him, perhaps given command of his own companies but still obliged to follow orders, never allowed to act according to his own judgment. . . . He grinned up at the rafters, dimly visible a foot above his face, thinking what his uncle Hal might have to say regarding the judgment of junior officers.

But Uncle Hal was much more than simply a career soldier; he cared passionately for his regiment: its welfare, its honor, the men under his command. William had not really thought beyond the immediate future in terms of his own career with the army. The American campaign wouldn't last long; what next?

He was rich—or would be, when he achieved his majority, and that wasn't far off, though it seemed like one of those pictures his father was fond of, with a vanishing perspective that led the eye into an impossible infinity. But when he *did* have his money, he could buy a better commission where he liked—perhaps a captaincy in the Lancers. . . . It wouldn't matter whether he'd done anything to distinguish himself in New York.

His father—William could hear him now, and put the pillow over his face to drown him out—would tell him that reputation depended often on the smallest of actions, the daily decisions made with honor and responsibility, not the huge drama of heroic battles. William was not interested in daily responsibility.

It was, however, much too hot to stay under the pillow, and he threw it off onto the floor with an irritable grunt.

"No," he said aloud to Lord John. "I'm going to Canada," and flopped back into his damp and lumpy bed, shutting eyes and ears against any further wise counsel.

A WEEK LATER, the nights had grown chilly enough to make William welcome Miss Beulah's hearth and her oyster stew—and, thank God, cold enough to discourage the damned mosquitoes. The days were still very warm, though, and William found it almost a pleasure when his detail was told off to comb the shore in search of a supposed smuggler's cache that Captain Hanks had caught wind of.

"A cache of what?" Perkins asked, mouth hanging half open as usual.

"Lobsters," William answered flippantly, but relented at Perkins's look of confusion. "I don't know, but you'll probably recognize it if you find it. Don't drink it, though—come fetch me."

Smugglers' boats brought almost everything into Long Island, but the odds of the current rumor concerning a cache of bed linens or boxes of Dutch platters were low. Might be brandy, might be ale, but almost certainly something drinkable; liquor was by far the most profitable contraband. William sorted the men into pairs and sent them off, watching until they were a decent distance away before heaving a deep sigh and leaning back against a tree.

Such trees as grew near the shore here were runty twisted pines, but the sea wind moved pleasantly among their needles, soughing in his ears with a soothing rush. He sighed again, this time in pleasure, remembering just how much he liked solitude; he hadn't had any in a month. If he took Richardson's offer, though . . . Well, there'd be Randall-Isaacs, of course, but still—weeks on the road, free of the army constraints of duty and routine. Silence in which to think. No more Perkins!

He wondered idly whether he might be able to sneak into the junior officers' quarters and pound Chinless to a pulp before vanishing into the wilderness like a red Indian. Need he wear a disguise? Not if he waited 'til after dark, he decided. Ned might suspect, but couldn't prove anything if he couldn't see William's face. Was it cowardly to attack Ned in his sleep, though? Well, that was all right; he'd douse Chinless with the contents of his chamber pot to wake him up before setting in.

A tern swept by within inches of his head, startling him out of these enjoyable cogitations. His movement in turn startled the bird, which let out an indignant shriek at finding him not edible after all and sailed off over the water. He scooped up a pinecone and flung it at the bird, missing by a mile, but not caring. He'd send a note to Richardson this very evening, saying yes. The thought of it made his heart beat faster, and a sense of exhilaration filled him, buoyant as the tern's drift upon the air.

He rubbed sand off his fingers onto his breeches, then stiffened, seeing movement on the water. A sloop was tacking to and fro, just offshore. Then he relaxed, recognizing it—that villain Rogers.

"And what are *you* after, I should like to know?" he muttered. He stepped out onto the sandy edge of the shore and stood amid the marram grass, fists on his hips, letting his uniform be seen—just in case Rogers had somehow missed the sight of William's men strung all down the shore, reddish dots crawling over the sandy dunes like bedbugs. If Rogers had heard about the smuggler's cache, too, William meant to make sure Rogers knew that William's soldiers had rights over it.

Robert Rogers was a shady character who'd come slinking into New York a few months before and somehow wangled a major's commission from General Howe and a sloop from his brother, the admiral. Said he was an Indian fighter, and was fond of dressing up as an Indian himself. Effective, though: he'd recruited men enough to form ten companies of nattily uniformed rangers, but Rogers continued to prowl the coastline in his sloop with a small company of men as disreputable-looking as he was, looking for recruits, spies, smugglers, and—William was convinced—anything that wasn't nailed down.

The sloop came in a little closer, and he saw Rogers on deck: a darkskinned man in his late forties, seamed and battered-looking, with an evil cast to his brow. He spotted William, though, and waved genially. William raised a civil hand in reply; if his men found anything, he might need Rogers to carry the booty back to the New York side—accompanied by a guard to keep it from disappearing *en route*.

There were a lot of stories about Rogers—some plainly put about by Rogers himself. But so far as William knew, the man's chief qualification was that he had at one point attempted to pay his respects to General Washington, who not only declined to receive him but had him slung unceremoniously out of the Continentals' camp and refused further entry. William considered this evidence of good judgment on the part of the Virginian.

Now what? The sloop had dropped her sails, and was putting out a small boat. It was Rogers, rowing over on his own. William's wariness was roused at once. Still, he waded in and grabbed the gunwale, helping Rogers to drag the boat up onto the sand.

"Well met, Lieutenant!" Rogers grinned at him, gap-toothed but selfconfident. William saluted him briefly and formally.

"Major."

"Your fellows looking for a cache of French wine, by chance?"

Damn, he'd already found it!

"We had word of smuggling activities taking place in this vicinity," William said stiffly. "We are investigating."

"'Course you are," Rogers agreed amiably. "Save you a bit of time? Try up the other way . . ." He turned, lifting his chin toward a cluster of dilapidated fishing shacks a quarter mile in the distance. "It's—"

"We did," William interrupted.

"It's buried in the sand behind the shacks," Rogers finished, ignoring the interruption.

"Much obliged, Major," William said, with as much cordiality as he could manage.

"Saw two fellows a-burying it last evening," Rogers explained. "But I don't think they've come back for it yet."

"You're keeping an eye on this stretch of shore, I see," William observed. "Anything in particular you're looking for? Sir," he added.

Rogers smiled.

"Since you mention it, *sir*, I am. There's a fellow walking round asking questions of a damnable inquisitive sort, and I should very much like to talk to him. If might be as you or your men should spot the man . . . ?"

"Certainly, sir. Do you know his name, or his appearance?"

"Both, as it happens," Rogers replied promptly. "Tall fellow, with scars upon his face from a gunpowder explosion. You'd know him if you saw him. A rebel, from a rebel family in Connecticut—Hale is his name."

William experienced a sharp jolt to the midsection.

"Oh, you *have* seen him?" Rogers spoke mildly, but his dark eyes had sharpened. William felt a stab of annoyance that his face should be so readable, but inclined his head.

"He passed the customs point yesterday. Very voluble fellow," he added, trying to recall the details of the man. He'd noticed the scars: faded welts that mottled the man's cheeks and forehead. "Nervous; he was sweating and his voice shook—the private who stopped him thought he had tobacco or something else concealed, and made him turn out his pockets, but he hadn't any contraband." William closed his eyes, frowning in the effort of recall. "He had papers. . . . I saw them." He'd seen them, all right, but had not had the chance to examine them himself, as he'd been concerned with a merchant bringing in a cartload of cheeses, bound—he said—for the British commissary. By the time he'd done with that, the man had been waved on.

"The man who spoke with him . . ." Rogers was peering down the shore toward the desultory searchers in the distance. "Which is he?"

"A private soldier named Hudson. I'll call him for you if you like," William offered. "But I doubt he can tell you much about the papers; he can't read."

Rogers looked vexed at this, but nodded for William to call Hudson anyway. Thus summoned, Hudson verified William's account of the matter, but could recall nothing regarding the papers, save that one of the sheets had had some numbers written upon it. "And a drawing, I think," he added. "Didn't notice what it was, though, sir, I'm afraid."

"Numbers, eh? Good, good," Rogers said, all but rubbing his hands together. "And did he say whence he was bound?"

"To visit a friend, sir, as lived near Flushing." Hudson was respectful, but looked curiously at the ranger; Rogers was barefoot and dressed in a pair of ratty linen breeches with a short waistcoat made of muskrat fur. "I didn't ask the friend's name, sir. Didn't know as it might be important."

"Oh, I doubt it is, Private. Doubt the friend exists at all." Rogers chuckled, seeming delighted at the news. He stared into the hazy distance, eyes narrowed as though he might distinguish the spy among the dunes, and nodded slowly in satisfaction.

"Very good," he said softly, as though to himself, and was turning to go when William stopped him with a word.

"My thanks for the information regarding the smuggler's cache, sir." Perkins had overseen the digging whilst William and Rogers were interviewing Hudson, and was now chivying a small group of soldiers along, several sand-caked casks rolling bumpily down the dunes before them. One of the casks hit a hard spot in the sand, bounced into the air, and landed hard, rolling off at a crazy angle, pursued with whoops by the soldiers.

William flinched slightly, seeing this. If the wine survived its rescue, it wouldn't be drinkable for a fortnight. Not that that was likely to stop anyone trying.

"I should like to request permission to bring the seized contraband aboard your sloop for transport," he said formally to Rogers. "I will accompany and deliver it myself, of course."

"Oh, of course." Rogers seemed amused, but nodded agreement. He scratched his nose, considering something. "We shan't be sailing back until tomorrow—d'you want to come along of us tonight? You might be of help, as you've actually seen the fellow we're after."

William's heart leapt with excitement. Miss Beulah's stew paled in comparison with the prospect of hunting a dangerous spy. And being in at the capture could do nothing but good to his reputation, even if the major share of the credit was Rogers's.

"I should be more than pleased to assist you in any way, sir!"

Rogers grinned, then eyed him up and down.

"Good. But you can't go spy-catching like that, Lieutenant. Come aboard, and we'll fit you out proper."

WILLIAM PROVED TO BE six inches taller than the tallest of Rogers's crew, and thus ended up awkwardly attired in a flapping shirt of rough linen—the tails left out by necessity, to disguise the fact that the top buttons of his flies were left undone—and canvas breeches that threatened to emasculate him should he make any sudden moves. These could not be buckled, of course, and William elected to emulate Rogers and go barefoot, rather than suffer the indignity of striped stockings that left his knees and four inches of hairy shin exposed between stocking-top and breeches.

The sloop had sailed to Flushing, where Rogers, William, and four men disembarked. Rogers maintained an informal recruiting office here, in the back room of a merchant's shop in the high road of the village. He vanished into this establishment momentarily, returning with the satisfactory news that Hale had not been seen in Flushing and was likely therefore stopping at one of the two taverns to be found at Elmsford, two or three miles from the village.

The men accordingly walked in that direction, dividing for the sake of caution into smaller groups, so that William found himself walking with Rogers, a ragged shawl slung round his shoulders against the evening chill. He had not shaved, of course, and fancied that he looked a proper companion for the ranger, who had added a slouch hat with a dried flying fish stuck through the brim to his costume.

"Do we pose as oystermen, or carters, perhaps?" William asked. Rogers grunted in brief amusement and shook his head.

"You'd not pass for either, should anyone hear you talk. Nay, lad, keep your mouth shut, save to put something in it. The boys and I 'ull manage the business. All you need do is nod, if you spot Hale."

The wind had come onshore and blew the scent of cold marshes toward them, spiced with a distant hint of chimney smoke. No habitation was yet in sight, and the fading landscape was desolate around them. The cold, sandy dirt of the road was soothing to his bare feet, though, and he did not find the bleakness of their surroundings depressing in the least; he was too eager at thought of what lay ahead.

Rogers was silent for the most part, pacing with his head down against the cold breeze. After a bit, though, he said casually, "I carried Captain Richardson over from New York. And back."

William thought momentarily of saying, *"Captain Richardson?"* in tones of polite ignorance, but realized in time that this wouldn't do.

"Did you?" he said instead, and kept his own silence. Rogers laughed.

"Fly cove, aren't you? Perhaps he's right, then, choosing you."

"He told you that he had chosen me for . . . something?"

"Good lad. Never give anything away for free—but sometimes it pays to oil the wheels a bit. Nay, Richardson's a downy bird—he said not a word about you. But I know who he is, and what he does. And I know where I left him. He wasn't calling upon the Culpers, I'll warrant that."

William made an indeterminate sound of interest in his throat. Plainly, Rogers meant to say something. Let him say, then.

"How old are you, lad?"

"Nineteen," William said, with an edge. "Why?"

Rogers shrugged, his outline little more than a shadow among many in the gathering dusk.

"Old enough to risk your neck on purpose, then. But you might want to think twice before saying yes to whatever Richardson's suggesting to you."

"Assuming that he did indeed suggest something—again, why?"

Rogers touched his back, urging him forward.

"You're about to see that for yourself, lad. Come on."

THE WARM SMOKY LIGHT of the tavern and the smell of food embraced William. He had not been really conscious of cold, dark, or hunger, his mind intent on the adventure at hand. Now, though, he drew a long, lingering breath, filled with the scent of fresh bread and roast chicken, and felt like an insensible corpse, newly roused from the grave and restored to full life upon the day of Resurrection.

The next breath stopped dead in his throat, though, and his heart gave a tremendous squeeze that sent a surge of blood through his body. Rogers, next to him, made a low warning hum in his throat, and glanced casually round the room as he led the way to a table.

The man, the spy, was sitting near the fire, eating chicken and chatting with a couple of farmers. Most of the men in the tavern had glanced at the door when the newcomers appeared—more than one of them blinked at William—but the spy was so absorbed in his food and conversation that he didn't even look up.

William had taken little notice of the man when first seen, but would have known him again at once. He was not so tall as William himself, but several inches more than the average, and striking in appearance, with flax-blond hair and a high forehead, this displaying the flash-mark scars of the gunpowder accident Rogers had mentioned. He had a round, broad-brimmed hat, which lay on the table beside his plate, and wore an unremarkable plain brown suit.

Not in uniform . . . William swallowed heavily, not entirely in respect of his hunger and the smell of food.

Rogers sat down at the next table, motioning William to a stool across from him, and raised his brows in question. William nodded silently, but didn't look again in Hale's direction.

The landlord brought them food and beer, and William devoted himself to eating, glad that he was not required to join in conversation. Hale himself was relaxed and voluble, telling his companions that he was a Dutch schoolmaster from New York.

"Conditions there are so unsettled, though," he said, shaking his head, "that the majority of my students have gone—fled with their families to relatives in Connecticut or New Jersey. I might suppose similar—or perhaps worse—conditions obtain here?"

One of the men at his table merely grunted, but the other blew out his lips with a derisive sound.

"You might say so. Goddam lobsterbacks seize everything as hasn't been buried. Tory, Whig, or rebel, makes no goddam difference to those greedy bastards. Speak a word of protest, and you're like to be struck over the head or dragged off to the goddam stockade, so as to make it easier for 'em. Why, one hulking brute stopped me at the customs point last week, and took my whole load of apple cider and the goddam wagon to boot! He—"

William choked on a bite of bread, but didn't dare cough. Christ, he hadn't recognized the man—the man's back was to him—but he recalled the apple cider well enough. Hulking brute?

He reached for his beer and gulped, trying to dislodge the chunk of bread; it didn't work and he coughed silently, feeling his face go purple and seeing Rogers frowning at him in consternation. He gestured feebly at the cider farmer, struck himself in the chest, and, rising, made his way out of the room as quietly as possible. His disguise, excellent as it was, would in no way conceal his essential hulkingness, and if the man were to recognize him as a British soldier, bang went the whole enterprise.

He managed not to breathe until he was safely outside, where he coughed until he thought the bottom of his stomach might force its way out of his mouth. At last he stopped, though, and leaned against the side of the tavern, taking long, gasping breaths. He wished he'd had the presence of mind to bring some beer with him, instead of the chicken leg he held.

The last of Rogers's men had come along the road, and with a baffled glance at William, went inside. He wiped his mouth with the back of his hand and, straightening up, crept round the side of the building until he reached a window.

The new arrivals were taking up their own spot, near to Hale's table. Standing carefully to one side to save being spotted, he saw that Rogers had now insinuated himself into conversation with Hale and the two farmers, and appeared to be telling them a joke. The apple-cider fellow hooted and pounded the table at the end; Hale made an attempt at a grin, but looked frankly shocked; the jest must have been indelicate.

Rogers leaned back, casually including the whole table with the sweep of a hand, and said something that had them nodding and murmuring agreement. Then he leaned forward, intent, to ask Hale something.

William could catch only snatches of the conversation, above the general noise of the tavern and the whistling of the cold wind past his ears. So far as he could gather, Rogers was professing to be a rebel, his own men nodding agreement from their table, gathering closer to form a secretive knot of conversation about Hale. Hale looked intent, excited, and very earnest. He might easily have been a schoolmaster, William thought—though Rogers had said he was a captain in the Continental army. William shook his head; Hale didn't look any sort of a soldier.

At the same time, he hardly looked the part of a spy, either. He was noticeable, with his fair good looks, his flash-scarred face, his . . . height.

William felt a small, cold lump in the pit of his stomach. Christ. Was that what Rogers had meant? Saying that there was something William should be warned of, with regard to Captain Richardson's errands, and that he would see for himself, tonight?

William was quite accustomed both to his own height and to people's automatic responses to it; he quite liked being looked up to. But on his first errand for Captain Richardson, it had never struck him for a moment that folk might recall him on account of it—or that they could describe him with the greatest of ease. Hulking brute was no compliment, but it *was* unmistakable.

With a sense of incredulity, he heard Hale not only reveal his own name and the fact that he held rebel sympathies, but also confide that he was making observations regarding the strength of the British presence—this followed by an earnest inquiry as to whether the fellows he spoke with might have noticed any redcoated soldiers in the vicinity?

William was so shocked by this recklessness that he put his eye to the edge of the window frame, in time to see Rogers glance round the room in exaggerated caution before leaning in confidentially, tapping Hale upon the forearm, and saying, "Why, now, sir, I have, indeed I have, but you must be more wary of what you say in a public place. Why, anyone at all might hear you!"

"Pshaw," said Hale, laughing. "I am among friends here. Have we not all just drunk to General Washington and to the King's confusion?" Sobering, but still eager, he pushed his hat aside and waved to the landlord for more beer. "Come, have another, sir, and tell me what you have seen."

William had a sudden overwhelming impulse to shout, *"Shut your mouth, you ninnyhammer!"* or to throw something at Hale through the window. But it was far too late, even could he actually have done it. The chicken leg he had been eating was still in his hand; noticing, he tossed it away. His stomach was knotted, and there was a taste of sick at the back of his throat, though his blood still boiled with excitement.

Hale was making still more damaging admissions, to the admiring encouragements and patriotic shouts of Rogers's men, all of whom were playing out their parts admirably, he had to admit. How long would Rogers let it go on? Would they take him here, in the tavern? Probably not—some others of those present were doubtless rebel sympathizers, who might be moved to intervene on Hale's behalf, did Rogers go to arrest him in their midst.

Rogers appeared in no hurry. Nearly half an hour of tedious raillery followed, Rogers giving what appeared to be small admissions, Hale making much larger ones in return, his slab-sided cheeks glowing with beer and excitement over the information he was gaining. William's legs, feet, hands, and face were numb, and his shoulders ached with tension. A crunching sound nearby distracted him from his close attendance on the scene within, and he glanced down, suddenly aware of a penetrating aroma that had somehow insinuated itself without his cognizance.

"Christ!" He jerked back, nearly putting his elbow through the window, and fell into the wall of the tavern with a heavy thump. The skunk, disturbed in its enjoyment of the discarded chicken leg, instantly elevated its tail, the white stripe making the movement clearly visible. William froze.

"What was that?" someone said inside, and he heard the scrape of a bench being pushed back. Holding his breath, he edged one foot to the side, only to be frozen in place again by a faint thumping noise and the quivering of the white stripe. Damn, the thing was stamping its feet. An indication of imminent attack, he'd been told—and told by people whose sorry condition made it apparent that they spoke from experience.

Feet were coming toward the door, someone coming to investigate. Christ, if they found him eavesdropping outside . . . He gritted his teeth, nerving himself to what duty told him must be a self-sacrificial lunge out of sight—but if he did, what then? He could not rejoin Rogers and the others, reeking of skunk. But if—

The opening of the door put paid to all speculations. William lunged for the corner of the building by simple reflex. The skunk also acted by reflex—but, startled by the opening of the door, apparently adjusted its aim in consequence. William tripped over a branch and sprawled at full length into a heap of discarded rubbish, hearing a full-throated shriek behind him as the night was made hideous.

William coughed, choked, and tried to stop breathing long enough to get out of range. He gasped from necessity, though, and his lungs were filled with a substance that went so far beyond the concept of smell as to require a completely new sensory description. Gagging and spluttering, eyes burning and watering from the assault, he stumbled into the darkness on the other side of the road, from which vantage point he witnessed the skunk making off in a huff and the skunk's victim collapsed in a heap on the tavern's step, making noises of extreme distress.

William hoped it wasn't Hale. Beyond the practical difficulties involved in arresting and transporting a man who had suffered such an assault, simple humanity compelled one to think that hanging the victim would be adding insult to injury.

It wasn't Hale. He saw the flaxen hair shining in the torchlight among the heads that were thrust out in inquiry, only to be drawn hastily back again.

Voices reached him, discussing how best to proceed. Vinegar, it was agreed, was needed, and in quantity. The victim had by now sufficiently recovered himself as to crawl off into the weeds, from which the sounds of violent retching proceeded. This, added to the mephitis still tainting the atmosphere, caused a number of other gentlemen to vomit, as well, and William felt his own gorge rise, but controlled it by vicious nose-pinching.

He was nearly chilled through, though thankfully aired out, by the time the victim's friends saw him off—driving him like a cow along the road, as no one would touch him—and the tavern emptied, no one having further appetite for either food or drink in such an atmosphere. He could hear the landlord cursing to himself as he leaned out to take down the torch that burned beside the hanging sign and plunge it, sizzling, into the rain barrel.

Hale bade a general good night, his educated voice distinctive in the dark, and set off along the road toward Flushing, where doubtless he meant to seek a bed. Rogers—William knew him by the fur waistcoat, identifiable even by starlight—lingered near the road, silently collecting his men about him as the crowd departed. Only when everyone was out of sight did William venture to join them.

"Yes?" Rogers said, seeing him. "All present, then. Let's go." And they moved off, a silent pack coursing down the road, intent upon the track of their unknowing prey.

THEY SAW THE FLAMES from the water. The city was burning, mostly the district near the East River, but the wind was up, and the fire was spreading. There was much excited speculation among Rogers's men; had rebel sympathizers fired the city?

"Just as likely drunken soldiers," Rogers said, his voice grimly dispassionate. William felt queasy, seeing the red glow in the sky. The prisoner was silent.

They found General Howe—eventually—in his headquarters at Beekman House outside the city, red-eyed from smoke, lack of sleep, and a rage that was buried bone-deep. It stayed buried, though, for the moment. He summoned Rogers and the prisoner into the library where he had his office, and—after one brief, astonished look at William's attire—sent him to his bed.

Fortnum was in the attic, watching the city burn from the window. There was nothing to be done about it. William came to stand beside him. He felt strangely empty, somehow unreal. Chilled, though the floor was warm under his bare feet.

An occasional fountain of sparks shot up now and then, as the flames struck something particularly flammable, but from such a distance there was really little to be seen but the bloody glow against the sky.

"They'll blame us, you know," Fortnum said after a bit.

THE AIR WAS STILL THICK with smoke at noon the next day.

He couldn't take his eyes off Hale's hands. They had clenched involuntarily as a private soldier tied them, though he had put them behind his back with no protest. Now his fingers were clasped tight together, so hard that the knuckles had gone white.

Surely the flesh protested, William thought, even if the mind had resigned itself. His own flesh was protesting simply being here, his skin twitching like a horse plagued by flies, his bowels cramping and loosening in horrid sympathy—they said a hanged man's bowels gave way; would Hale's? Blood washed through his face at the thought, and he looked at the ground.

Voices made him look up again. Captain Moore had just asked Hale whether he wished to make any remarks. Hale nodded; evidently he had been prepared for this.

William felt that he should himself have been prepared by now; Hale had spent the last two hours in Captain Moore's tent, writing notes to be delivered to his family, while the men assembled for the hasty execution shifted their weight from foot to foot, waiting. He wasn't prepared at all.

Why was it different? He'd seen men die, some horribly. But this preliminary courtesy, this formality, this . . . obscene *civility*, all conducted with the certain knowledge of imminent and shameful death. Deliberation. The awful deliberation, that was it.

"At last!" Clarewell muttered in his ear. "Bloody get on with it; I'm starving."

A young black man named Billy Richmond, a private soldier whom William knew casually, was sent up the ladder to tie the rope to the tree. He came down now, nodding to the officer.

Now Hale was mounting the ladder, the sergeant major steadying him. The noose was round his neck, a thick rope, new-looking. Didn't they say new ropes stretched? But it was a high ladder . . .

William was sweating like a pig, though the day was mild. He mustn't close his eyes or look away. Not with Clarewell watching.

He tightened the muscles of his throat and concentrated again on Hale's hands. The fingers were twisting, helplessly, though the man's face was calm. They were leaving faint damp marks on the skirt of his coat.

A grunt of effort and a grating noise; the ladder was pulled away, and there was a startled *whoof!* from Hale as he dropped. Whether it was the newness of the rope or something else, his neck did not break cleanly.

He'd refused the hood, and so the spectators were obliged to watch his face for the quarter of an hour it took him to die. William stifled a horrific urge to laugh from pure nerves, seeing the pale blue eyes bulge to bursting point, the tongue thrust out. So surprised. He looked so surprised.

There was only a small group of men assembled for the execution. He saw Richardson a little way away, watching with a look of remote abstraction. As though aware of his glance, Richardson looked sharply up at him. William looked away.

THE MINISTER'S CAT

Lallybroch
October 1980

S HE WAS UP EARLY, before the children, though she knew this was foolish—whatever Roger had gone to Oxford for, it would take him a good seven or eight hours to drive there, and the same back. Even if he had left at dawn—and he might not be able to, if he hadn't arrived in time to do whatever it was the day before—he couldn't be home before midday at the earliest. But she'd slept restlessly, dreaming one of those monotonous and inescapably unpleasant dreams, this one featuring the sight and sound of the tide coming in, lapping wave by lapping wave by lapping . . . and wakened at first light feeling dizzy and unwell.

It had occurred to her for one nightmare instant that she might be pregnant—but she'd sat up abruptly in bed, and the world had settled at once into place around her. None of that sense of having shoved one foot through the looking glass that early pregnancy entails. She set one foot cautiously out of bed, and the world—and her stomach—stayed steady. Good, then.

Still, the feeling of unease—whether from the dream, Roger's absence, or the specter of pregnancy—stayed with her, and she went about the daily business of the household with a distracted mind.

She was sorting socks toward midday when she became aware that things were quiet. Quiet in a way that made the hair rise on the back of her neck.

"Jem?" she called. "Mandy?"

Total silence. She stepped out of the laundry, listening for the usual thumps, bangings, and screeches from above, but there was not the slightest sound of trampling feet, toppling blocks, or the high-pitched voices of sibling warfare.

"Jem!" she shouted. "Where are you?"

No reply. The last time this had happened, two days before, she'd discovered her alarm clock in the bottom of the bathtub, neatly disassembled into its component parts, and both children at the far end of the garden, glowing with unnatural innocence.

"*I* didn't do it!" Jem had declared virtuously, hauled into the house and faced with the evidence. "And Mandy's too little."

"Too widdle," Mandy had agreed, nodding her mop of black curls so ferociously as to obscure her face.

"Well, I don't think Daddy did it," Bree said, raising a stern brow. "And I'm sure it wasn't Annie Mac. Which doesn't leave very many suspects, does it?"

"Shussspects, shussspects," Mandy said happily, enchanted by the new word.

Jem shook his head in resigned fashion, viewing the scattered gears and dismembered hands.

"We must have got piskies, Mama."

"Pishkies, pishkies," Mandy chirped, pulling her skirt up over her head and yanking at her frilly underpants. "Needa go pishkie, Mama!"

In the midst of the urgency occasioned by this statement, Jem had faded artfully, not to be seen again until dinner, by which time the affair of the alarm clock had been superseded by the usual fierce rush of daily events, not to be recalled until bedtime, when Roger remarked the absence of the alarm clock.

"Jem doesn't usually lie," Roger had said thoughtfully, having been shown the small pottery bowl now containing the clock's remains.

Bree, brushing out her hair for bed, gave him a jaundiced look.

"Oh, you think we have pixies, too?"

"Piskies," he said absently, stirring the small pile of gears in the bowl with a finger.

"What? You mean they really are called 'piskies' here? I thought Jem was just mispronouncing it."

"Well, no—'pisky' is Cornish; they're called pixies in other parts of the West Country, though."

"What are they called in Scotland?"

"We haven't really got any. Scotland's got its fair share of the fairy folk," he said, scooping up a handful of clock innards and letting them tinkle musically back into the bowl. "But Scots tend toward the grimmer manifestations of the supernatural—water horses, *ban-sidhe*, blue hags, and the Nuckelavee, aye? Piskies are a wee bit frivolous for Scotland. We have got brownies, mind," he added, taking the brush from her hand, "but they're more of a household help, not mischief-makers like piskies. Can ye put the clock back together?"

"Sure—if the piskies didn't lose any of the parts. What on earth is a Nuckelavee?"

"It's from the Orkneys. Nothing ye want to hear about just before bed," he assured her. And, bending, breathed very softly on her neck, just below the earlobe.

The faint tingle engendered by the memory of what had happened after that momentarily overlaid her suspicions of what the children might be up to, but the sensation faded, to be replaced by increasing worry.

There was no sign of either Jem or Mandy anywhere in the house. Annie MacDonald didn't come on Saturdays, and the kitchen . . . At first glance, it seemed undisturbed, but she was familiar with Jem's methods.

Sure enough, the packet of chocolate biscuits was missing, as was a bottle of lemon squash, though everything else in the cupboard was in perfect order—and the cupboard was six feet off the ground. Jem showed great promise as a cat burglar, she thought. At least he'd have a career if he got chucked out of school for good one of these days after telling his classmates something especially picturesque he'd picked up in the eighteenth century.

The missing food allayed her uneasiness. If they'd taken a picnic, they were outside, and while they might be anywhere within a half mile of the house— Mandy wouldn't walk farther than that—chances were they wouldn't have gone far before sitting down to eat biscuits.

It was a beautiful fall day, and despite the need to track down her miscreants, she was glad to be out in the sun and breeze. Socks could wait. And so could turning the vegetable beds. And speaking to the plumber about the geyser in the upstairs bath. And . . .

"It doesna matter how many things ye do on a farm, there's always more than ye can do. A wonder the place doesna rise up about my ears and swallow me, like Jonah and the whale."

For an instant, she heard her father's voice, full of exasperated resignation at encountering another unexpected chore. She glanced round at him, smiling, then stopped, realization and longing sweeping over her in waves.

"Oh, Da," she said softly. She walked on, more slowly, suddenly seeing not the albatross of a big, semi-decayed house, but the living organism that was Lallybroch, and all those of her blood who had been part of it—who still were.

The Frasers and Murrays who had put their own sweat and blood and tears into its buildings and soil, woven their lives into its land. Uncle Ian, Aunt Jenny—the swarm of cousins she had known so briefly. Young Ian. All of them dead now . . . but, curiously enough, not gone.

"Not gone at all," she said aloud, and found comfort in the words. She'd reached the back gate of the kailyard and paused, glancing up the hill toward the ancient broch that gave the place its name; the burying ground was up on that same hill, most of its stones so weathered that the names and their dates were indecipherable, the stones themselves mostly obliterated by creeping gorse and heather. And amidst the splashes of gray, black-green, and deep purple were two small moving splotches of red and blue.

The pathway was badly overgrown; brambles ripped at her jeans. She found the children on hands and knees, following a trail of ants—who were in turn following a trail of cookie crumbs, carefully placed so as to lead the ants through an obstacle course of sticks and pebbles.

"Look, Mama!" Jem barely glanced up at her, absorbed in the sight before him. He pointed at the ground, where he had sunk an old teacup into the dirt and filled it with water. A black glob of ants, lured to their doom by chocolate crumbs, were struggling in the midst of it.

"Jem! That's mean! You mustn't drown ants—unless they're in the house," she added, with vivid memories of a recent infestation in the pantry.

"They're not drowning, Mama. Look—see what they do?"

She crouched beside him, looking closer, and saw that, in fact, the ants weren't drowning. Single ants that had fallen in struggled madly toward the center, where a large mass of ants clung together, making a ball that floated, barely denting the surface. The ants in the ball were moving, slowly, so that they changed places constantly, and while one or two near the edge of the mass were motionless, possibly dead, the majority were clearly in no immediate danger of drowning, supported by the bodies of their fellows. And the mass itself was gradually drawing closer to the rim of the cup, propelled by the movements of the ants in it.

"That's really cool," she said, fascinated, and sat beside him for some time, watching the ants, before finally decreeing mercy and making him scoop the ball of ants out on a leaf, where once laid on the ground, they scattered and at once went back to their business.

"Do you think they do it on purpose?" she asked Jem. "Cluster together like that, I mean. Or are they just looking for anything to hang on to?"

"Dinna ken," he said, shrugging. "I'll look in my ant book and see does it say."

She gathered up the remnants of the picnic, leaving one or two biscuit fragments for the ants, who had, she felt, earned them. Mandy had wandered off while she and Jem watched the ants in the teacup, and was presently squatting in the shade of a bush some way uphill, engaged in animated conversation with an invisible companion.

"Mandy wanted to talk to Grandda," Jem said matter-of-factly. "That's why we came up here."

"Oh?" she said slowly. "Why is here a good place to talk to him?"

Jem looked surprised, and glanced toward the weathered, tipsy stones of the burying ground.

"Isn't he here?"

Something much too powerful to be called a shiver shot up her spine. It was as much Jem's matter-of-factness as the possibility that it might be true that took her breath away.

"I—don't know," she said. "I suppose he could be." While she tried not to think too much about the fact that her parents were now dead, she had somehow vaguely assumed that they would have been buried in North Carolina—or somewhere else in the Colonies, if war had taken them away from the Ridge.

But she remembered the letters suddenly. He'd said he meant to come back to Scotland. And Jamie Fraser being a determined man, more than likely he'd done just that. Had he never left again? And if he hadn't—was her mother here, too?

Without really meaning to, she found herself making her way upward, past the foot of the old broch and through the stones of the burying ground. She'd come up here once, with her aunt Jenny. It had been early evening, with a breeze whispering in the grass, and an air of peace upon the hillside. Jenny had shown her the graves of her grandparents, Brian and Ellen, together under a marriage stone; yes, she could still make out the curve of it, overgrown and mossy as it was, the names weathered away. And the child who had died with Ellen was buried with her—her third son. Robert, Jenny said; her father, Brian, had insisted he be baptized, and her wee dead brother's name was Robert.

She was standing among the stones now; so many of them. A good many of the later ones were still readable, these with dates in the late 1800s.

Murrays and McLachlan's and McLean's, for the most part. Here and there the odd Fraser or MacKenzie.

The earlier ones, though, were all too weathered to read, no more than the shadows of letters showing through the black stains of lichen and the soft, obliterating moss. There, next to Ellen's grave, was the tiny square stone for Caitlin Maisri Murray, Jenny and Ian's sixth child, who had lived only a day or so. Jenny had shown Brianna the stone, stooping to run a gentle hand across the letters and laying a yellow rose from the path beside it. There had been a small cairn there, too—pebbles left by those who visited the grave. The cairn had been scattered long since, but Brianna stooped and found a pebble now and placed it by the little stone.

There was another, she saw, beside it. Another small stone, as for a child. Not quite as weathered, but plainly almost as old. Only two words on it, she thought, and, closing her eyes, ran her fingers slowly over the stone, feeling out the shallow, broken lines. There was an "E" in the first line. A "Y," she thought, in the second. And maybe a "K."

What sort of Highland name begins with "Y"? she thought, puzzled. *There's McKay, but that's in the wrong order . . .*

"You—er—don't know which grave might be Grandda's, do you?" she asked Jem hesitantly. She was almost afraid to hear the answer.

"No." He looked surprised, and glanced where she was looking, toward the assemblage of stones. Obviously he hadn't connected their presence with his grandfather. "He just said he'd like to be buried here, and if I came here, I should leave him a stane. So I did." His accent slid naturally into the word, and she heard her father's voice again, distinctly, but this time smiled a little.

"Where?"

"Up there. He likes to be up high, ken? Where he can see," Jem said casually, pointing up the hill. Just beyond the shadow of the broch, she could see the traces of something not quite a trail through a mass of gorse, heather, and broken rock. And poking out of the mass at the crest of the hill, a big, lumpy boulder, on whose shoulder sat a tiny pyramid of pebbles, barely visible.

"Did you leave all those today?"

"No, I put one whenever I come. That's what ye're meant to do, aye?"

There was a small lump in her throat, but she swallowed it and smiled. "Aye, it is. I'll go up and leave one, too."

Mandy was now sitting on one of the fallen gravestones, laying out burdock leaves as plates around the dirty teacup, which she had unearthed and set in the middle. She was chatting to the guests at her invisible tea party, politely animated. There was no need to disturb her, Brianna decided, and followed Jem up the rocky trail—the last of the journey accomplished on hands and knees, owing to the steepness.

It was windy, so near the crest of the hill. Damp with perspiration, she added her own pebble ceremoniously to the wee cairn, and sat down for a moment to enjoy the view. Most of Lallybroch was visible from here, as was the road that led to the highway. She looked that way, but no sign yet of Roger's bright-orange Morris Mini. She sighed and looked away.

It was nice, up so high. Quiet, with just the sigh of the cool wind and the buzz of bees busy working in the yellow blossoms. No wonder her father liked—

"Jem." He was slumped comfortably against the rock, looking out over the surrounding hills.

"Aye?"

She hesitated, but had to ask.

"You . . . can't *see* your grandda, can you?"

He shot her a startled blue look.

"No. He's dead."

"Oh," she said, at once relieved and slightly disappointed. "I know. I . . . just wondered."

"I think maybe Mandy can," Jem said, nodding toward his sister, a bright red blot on the landscape below. "But ye can't really tell. Babies talk to lots of people ye can't see," he added tolerantly. "Grannie says so."

She didn't know whether to wish he would stop referring to his grandparents in the present tense or not. It was more than slightly unnerving, but he had said he couldn't see Jamie. She didn't want to ask whether he could see Claire—she supposed not—but she felt her parents close, whenever Jem or Mandy mentioned them, and she certainly wanted Jem and Mandy to feel close to them, as well.

She and Roger had explained things to the kids as well as such things could be explained. And evidently her father had had his own private talk with Jem; a good thing, she thought. Jamie's blend of devout Catholicism and matter-of-fact Highland acceptance of life, death, and things not seen was probably a lot better suited to explaining things like how you could be dead on one side of the stones, but—

"He said he'd look after us. Grandda," he added, turning to look at her.

She bit her tongue. No, he was not reading her mind, she told herself firmly. They'd just been talking of Jamie, after all, and Jem had chosen this particular place in which to pay his respects. So it was only natural that his grandfather would be still in his mind.

"Of course he will," she said, and put a hand on his square shoulder, massaging the knobby bones at the base of his neck with her thumb. He giggled and ducked out from under her hand, then hopped suddenly down the trail, sliding on his bottom partway, to the detriment of his jeans.

She paused for a last look round before following him, and noticed the jumble of rock on top of a hill a quarter mile or so away. A jumble of rock was exactly what one might expect to see on any Highland hilltop—but there was something slightly different about this particular assortment of stones. She shaded her eyes with her hand, squinting. She might be wrong—but she was an engineer; she knew the look of a thing built by men.

An Iron Age fortress, maybe? she thought, intrigued. There were layered stones at the bottom of that heap, she'd swear it. A foundation, perhaps. She'd have to climb up there one of these days for a closer look—maybe tomorrow, if Roger . . . Again, she glanced at the road, and again found it empty.

Mandy had grown tired of her tea party and was ready to go home. Holding her daughter firmly by one hand and the teacup in the other,

Brianna made her way down the hill toward the big white-harled house, its windows fresh-washed and glinting companionably.

Had Annie done that? she wondered. She hadn't noticed, and surely window-washing on that scale would have entailed a good bit of fuss and bother. But then, she'd been distracted, what with the anticipations and apprehensions of the new job. Her heart gave a small hop at the thought that on Monday she would fit back one more piece of who she'd once been, one more stone in the foundation of who she now was.

"Maybe the piskies did it," she said aloud, and laughed.

"Piskies diddit," Mandy echoed happily.

Jem had nearly reached the bottom, and turned, impatient, waiting for them.

"Jem," she said, the thought occurring as they came even with him. "Do you know what a Nuckelavee is?"

Jem's eyes went huge, and he clapped his hands over Mandy's ears. Something with a hundred cold tiny feet skittered up Brianna's back.

"Aye," he said, his voice small and breathless.

"Who told you about it?" she asked, keeping her voice calm. She'd *kill* Annie MacDonald, she thought.

But Jem's eyes slid sideways, as he glanced involuntarily over her shoulder, up at the broch.

"He did," he whispered.

"He?" she said sharply, and grabbed Mandy by the arm as the little girl wiggled free and turned furiously on her brother. *"Don't* kick your brother, Mandy! Who do you mean, Jemmy?"

Jem's lower teeth caught his lip.

"Him," he blurted. "The Nuckelavee."

"THE CREATURE'S HOME *was in the sea, but it ventured upon land to feast upon humans. The Nuckelavee rode a horse on land, and its horse was sometimes indistinguishable from its own body. Its head was ten times larger than that of a man, and its mouth thrust out like a pig's, with a wide, gaping maw. The creature had no skin, and its yellow veins, muscle structure, and sinews could clearly be seen, covered in a red slimy film. The creature was armed with venomous breath and great strength. It did, however, have one weakness: an aversion to freshwater. The horse on which it rode is described as having one red eye, a mouth the size of a whale's, and flappers like fins around its forelegs."*

"Ick!" Brianna put down the book—one of Roger's collection of Scottish folklore—and stared at Jem. "You saw one of these? Up by the broch?"

Her son shifted from foot to foot. "Well, he said he was. He said if I didna clear straight off, he'd change into himself, and I didna want to see *that,* so I cleared."

"Neither would I." Brianna's heart began to slow down a little. All right. He'd met a man, then, not a monster. Not that she'd actually believed . . . but the fact that someone had been hanging around the broch was worrying enough.

"What did he look like, this man?"

"Well . . . big," Jem said dubiously. Given that Jem was not quite nine, most men would be.

"As big as Daddy?"

"Maybe."

Further catechism elicited relatively few details; Jem knew what a Nuckelavee was—he'd read most of the more sensational items in Roger's collection—and had been so terrified at meeting someone who might at any moment shed his skin and eat him that his impressions of the man were sparse. Tall, with a short beard, hair that wasn't very dark, and clothes "like Mr. MacNeil wears." Working clothes, then, like a farmer.

"Why didn't you tell me or Daddy about him?"

Jem looked about to cry.

"He said he'd come back and eat Mandy if I did."

"Oh." She put an arm around him and pulled him to her. "I see. Don't be afraid, honey. It's all right." He was trembling now, as much with relief as with memory, and she stroked his bright hair, soothing him. A tramp, most likely. Camping in the broch? Likely he was gone by now—so far as she could tell from Jem's story, it had been more than a week since he had seen the man—but . . .

"Jem," she said slowly. "Why did you and Mandy go up there today? Weren't you afraid the man would be there?"

He looked up at her, surprised, and shook his head, red hair flying.

"Nay, I cleared, but I hid and watched him. He went away to the west. That's where he lives."

"He said so?"

"No. But things like that all live in the west." He pointed at the book. "When they go away to the west, they dinna come back. And I've not seen him again; I watched, to be sure."

She nearly laughed, but was still too worried. It was true; a good many Highland fairy tales did end with some supernatural creature going away to the west, or into the rocks or the water where they lived. And of course they didn't come back, since the story was over.

"He was just a nasty tramp," she said firmly, and patted Jem's back before releasing him. "Don't worry about him."

"Sure?" he said, obviously wanting to believe her, but not quite ready to relax into security.

"Sure," she said firmly.

"Okay." He heaved a deep sigh and pushed away from her. "Besides," he added, looking happier, "Grandda wouldn't let him eat Mandy or me. I should have thought o' that."

IT WAS NEARLY SUNSET by the time she heard the chugging of Roger's car on the farm road. She rushed outside, and he'd barely got out of the car before she flung herself into his arms.

He didn't waste time with questions. He embraced her passionately and kissed her in a way that made it clear that their argument was over; the details of mutual apology could wait. For an instant, she allowed herself to let go of everything, feeling weightless in his arms, breathing the scents of petrol and dust and libraries full of old books that overlay his natural smell, that indefinable faint musk of sun-warmed skin, even when he hadn't been in the sun.

"They say women can't really identify their husbands by smell," she remarked, reluctantly coming back to earth. "I don't believe it. I could pick you out of King's Cross tube station in the pitch-dark."

"I did have a bath this morning, aye?"

"Yes, and you stayed in college, because I can smell the horrible industrial-strength soap they use there," she said, wrinkling her nose. "I'm surprised it doesn't take your skin off. And you had black pudding for your breakfast. With fried tomato."

"Right, Lassie," he said, smiling. "Or do I mean Rin-Tin-Tin? Saved any small children or tracked any robbers to their lairs today, have ye?"

"Well, yes. Sort of." She glanced up at the hill behind the house, where the broch's shadow had grown long and black. "But I thought I'd better wait until the sheriff came back from town before I went any further."

ARMED WITH A STOUT blackthorn walking stick and an electric torch, Roger approached the broch, angry but cautious. It wasn't likely the man was armed, if he was still there, but Brianna was at the kitchen door, the telephone—at the full stretch of its long cord—beside her, and two nines already dialed. She'd wanted to come with him, but he'd convinced her that one of them had to stay with the kids. Still, it would have been a comfort to have her at his back; she was a tall, muscular woman, and not one to shrink from physical violence.

The door of the broch hung askew; the ancient leather hinges had long since rotted away and been replaced with cheap iron, which had rusted in turn. The door was still attached to its frame, but barely. He lifted the latch and maneuvered the heavy, splintering wood inward, pulling it away from the floor so it swung without scraping.

There was still plenty of light outside; it wouldn't be full dark for half an hour yet. Inside the broch, though, it was black as a well. He shone his torch on the floor and saw fresh drag marks in the dirt that crusted the stone floor. Aye, someone had been here, then. Jem might be able to move the door, but the kids weren't allowed to go in the broch without an adult, and Jem swore he hadn't.

"Halloooo!" he shouted, and was answered by a startled movement somewhere far above. He gripped his stick in reflex, but recognized the flutter and rustle for what it was almost at once. Bats, hanging up under the conical roof. He flashed his light round the ground floor and saw a few stained and crumpled newspapers by the wall. He picked one up and smelled it: old, but the scent of fish and vinegar was still discernible.

He hadn't thought Jem was making up the Nuckelavee story, but this evidence of recent human occupation renewed his anger. That someone should not only come and lurk on his property, but threaten his son . . . He almost hoped the fellow was still here. He wanted a word.

He wasn't, though. No one with sense would have gone to the upper floors of the broch; the boards were half rotted, and as his eyes adjusted, he could see the gaping holes, a faint light coming through them from the slit windows higher up. Roger heard nothing, but an urge to be certain propelled him up the narrow stone stair that spiraled round the inside of the tower, testing each step for loose stones before trusting his weight to it.

He disturbed a quantity of pigeons on the top floor, who panicked and whirled round the inside of the tower like a feathery tornado, shedding down feathers and droppings, before finding their way out of the windows. He pressed himself against the wall, heart pounding as they battered blindly past his face. Something—a rat, a mouse, a vole—ran over his foot, and he jerked convulsively, nearly losing his torch.

The broch was alive, all right; the bats up above were shifting around, uneasy at all the racket below. But no sign of an intruder, human or not.

Coming down, he put his head out to signal to Bree that all was well, then closed the door and made his way down to the house, brushing dirt and pigeon feathers off his clothes.

"I'll put a new hasp and a padlock on that door," he told Brianna, lounging against the old stone sink as she started the supper. "Though I doubt he'll be back. Likely just a traveler."

"From the Orkneys, do you think?" She was reassured, he could tell, but there was still a line of worry between her brows. "You said that's where they have stories about the Nuckelavee."

He shrugged.

"Possible. But ye find the stories written down; the Nuckelavee's not so popular as kelpies or fairies, but anyone might come across him in print. What's that?" She had opened the refrigerator to get the butter out, and he'd glimpsed the bottle of champagne on the shelf, its foiled label gleaming.

"Oh, that." She looked at him, ready to smile, but with a certain apprehension in her eyes. "I, um, got the job. I thought we might . . . celebrate?" The tentative question smote him to the heart, and he smacked himself on the forehead.

"Christ, I forgot to ask! That's great, Bree! I knew ye would, mind," he said, smiling with every bit of warmth and conviction he could muster. "Never a doubt."

He could see the tension leave her body as her face lit up, and felt a certain peace descend on him, as well. This pleasant feeling lasted through the rib-cracking hug she gave him and the very nice kiss that followed, but was obliterated when she stepped back and, taking up a saucepan, asked with elaborate casualness, "So . . . did you find what you were looking for in Oxford?"

"Yeah." It came out in a gruff croak; he cleared his throat and tried again. "Yeah, more or less. Look—can the supper wait a bit, d'ye think? I think I'd have more appetite if I tell ye first."

"Sure," she said slowly, putting down the saucepan. Her eyes were fixed on him, interested, maybe a bit fearful. "I fed the kids before you got home. If you're not starving . . ."

He was; he hadn't stopped for lunch on the way back and his stomach was flapping, but it didn't matter. He reached out a hand to her.

"Come on out. The evening's fine." And if she took it badly, there were no saucepans out of doors.

"I WENT ROUND to Old St. Stephen's," he said abruptly, as soon as they'd left the house. "To talk to Dr. Weatherspoon; he's rector there. He was a friend of the Reverend's—he's known me since I was a lad."

Her hand had tightened on his arm as he spoke. He risked a glance at her and saw her looking anxious but hopeful.

"And . . . ?" she said, tentative.

"Well . . . the upshot of it is I've got a job, too." He smiled, self-conscious. "Assistant choirmaster."

That, of course, hadn't been what she was expecting at all, and she blinked. Then her eyes went to his throat. He knew fine what she was thinking.

"*Are you going to wear* that?" she had asked, hesitant, the first time they prepared to go into Inverness for shopping.

"*I was, aye. Why, have I got a spot?*" He'd craned to look over the shoulder of his white shirt. No surprise if he had. Mandy had rushed in from her play to greet him, plastering his legs with sandy hugs. He'd dusted her off a bit before lifting her for a proper kiss, but . . .

"*Not that,*" Bree had said, her lips compressing for a minute. "*It's just . . . What will you say about . . .*" She made a throat-cutting gesture.

His hand had gone to the open collar of his shirt, where the rope scar made a curving line, distinct to the touch, like a chain of tiny pebbles under the skin. It had faded somewhat, but was still very visible.

"*Nothing.*"

Her brows rose, and he'd given her a lopsided smile.

"*But what will they be thinking?*"

"*I suppose they'll just assume I'm into autoerotic asphyxiation and went a bit too far one day.*"

Familiar as he was with the rural Highlands, he imagined that was the least of what they would think. Externally proper his putative congregation might be—but no one could imagine more lurid depravity than a devout Scottish Presbyterian.

"Did . . . er . . . did you tell Dr. Weatherspoon . . . What *did* you tell him?" she asked now, after a moment's consideration. "I mean—he had to have noticed."

"Oh, aye. He noticed. I didn't say anything, though, and neither did he."

"*Look, Bree,*" he'd told her on that first day, "*it's a straight choice. We tell everyone the absolute truth, or we tell them nothing—or as close to nothing as possible—and let them think what they like. Concocting a story won't work, will it? Too many ways to trip up.*"

She hadn't liked it; he could still see the way her eyes had drawn down at the corners. But he was right, and she knew it. Decision had spread across her face, and she'd nodded, her shoulders squaring.

They'd had to do a certain amount of lying, of course, in order to legalize the existence of Jem and Mandy. But it was the late seventies; communes abounded in the States, and impromptu bands of "travelers," as they called themselves, drifted to and fro across Europe in cavalcades of rusted buses and clapped-out vans. They had brought very little through the stones with them, bar the children themselves—but among the tiny hoard Brianna had tucked into her pockets and down her stays were two handwritten birth certificates, attested by one Claire Beauchamp Randall, MD, attending physician.

"It's the proper form for a home birth," Claire had said, making the loops of her signature with care. *"And I* am—*or I was,"* she'd corrected, with a wry twist of the mouth, *"a registered physician, licensed by the Commonwealth of Massachusetts."*

"Assistant choirmaster," Bree said now, eyeing him.

He drew a deep breath; the evening air *was* fine, clear and soft, if beginning to be populated by midgies. He waved a cloud of them away from his face, and grasped the nettle.

"I didn't go for a job, mind. I went to . . . to get my mind clear. About being a minister."

She stopped dead at that.

"And . . . ?" she prompted.

"Come on." He pulled her gently into motion once more. "We'll be eaten alive if we stand here."

They strolled through the kailyard and out past the barn, walking along the path that led by the back pasture. He'd already milked the two cows, Milly and Blossom, and they'd settled for the night, big humped dark shapes in the grass, peacefully chewing their cuds.

"I told you about the Westminster Confession, aye?" This was the Presbyterian equivalent to the Catholics' Nicene Creed—their statement of officially accepted doctrine.

"Uh-huh."

"Well, see, to be a Presbyterian minister, I'd need to be able to swear that I accepted everything in the Westminster Confession. I did, when I—well, before." He'd come so close, he thought. He'd been on the eve of ordination as a minister when fate had intervened, in the person of Stephen Bonnet. Roger had been compelled to drop everything, to find and rescue Brianna from the pirate's lair on Ocracoke. Not that he regretted doing it, mind . . . She paced beside him, red and long-limbed, graceful as a tiger, and the thought that she might so easily have vanished from his life forever—and that he'd never have known his daughter . . .

He coughed and cleared his throat, abstractedly touching the scar.

"Maybe I still do. But I'm not sure. And I have to be."

"What changed?" she asked curiously. "What could you accept then that you can't now?"

What changed? he thought wryly. *Good question.*

"Predestination," he said. "In a manner of speaking." There was still enough light that he saw a look of mildly derisive amusement flicker across her face, though whether simply from the ironic juxtaposition of question and answer or from the concept itself, he didn't know. They'd never argued questions of faith—they were more than cautious with each other on *those* grounds—but they were at least familiar with the general shape of each other's beliefs.

He'd explained the idea of predestination in simple terms: not some inescapable fate ordained by God, nor yet the notion that God had laid out each person's life in great detail before his or her birth—though not a few Presbyterians saw it just that way. It had to do with salvation and the notion that God chose a pathway that led to that salvation.

"For some people," she'd said skeptically. "And He chooses to damn the rest?"

A lot of people thought *that*, too, and it had taken better minds than his to argue their way past that impression.

"There are whole books written about it, but the basic idea is that salvation's not just the result of our choice—God acts first. Extending the invitation, ye might say, and giving us an opportunity to respond. But we've still got free choice. And really," he added quickly, "the only thing that's not optional—to be a Presbyterian—is a belief in Jesus Christ. I've still got that."

"Good," she said. "But to be a minister . . . ?"

"Yeah, probably. And—well, here." He reached abruptly into his pocket and handed her the folded photocopy.

"I thought I'd best not steal the book," he said, trying for levity. "In case I *do* decide to be minister, I mean. Bad example for the flock."

"Ho-ho," she said absently, reading. She looked up, one eyebrow quirked.

"It's different, isn't it?" he said, the breathless feeling back beneath his diaphragm.

"It's . . ." Her eyes shot back to the document, and a frown creased her brow. She looked up at him a moment later, pale and swallowing. "Different. The date's different."

He felt a slight easing of the tension that had wound him up for the last twenty-four hours. He wasn't losing his mind, then. He put out a hand, and she gave him back the copy of the clipping from the *Wilmington Gazette*—the death notice for the Frasers of the Ridge.

"It's only the date," he said, running a thumb beneath the blurred type of the words. "The text—I think that's the same. Is it what you remember?" She'd found the same information, looking for her family in the past—it was what had propelled her through the stones, and him after her. *And that*, he thought, *has made all the difference. Thank you, Robert Frost.*

She'd pressed against him, to read it over again. Once, and twice, and once more for good measure, before she nodded.

"Only the date," she said, and he heard the same breathlessness in her voice. "It . . . changed."

"Good," he said, his voice sounding queer and gruff. "When I started wondering . . . I had to go and see, before I talked to you about it. Just to check—because the clipping I'd seen in a book, that couldn't be right."

She nodded, still a little pale.

"If I . . . if I went back to the archive in Boston where I found that newspaper—would it have changed, too, do you think?"

"Yeah, I do."

She was silent for a long moment, looking at the paper in his hand. Then she looked at him, intent.

"You said, when you started wondering. What made you start wondering?"

"Your mother."

IT HAD BEEN a couple of months before they left the Ridge. Unable to sleep one night, he'd gone out into the woods and, roaming restlessly to and fro, had encountered Claire, kneeling in a hollow full of white flowers, their shapes like a mist around her.

He'd just sat down then and watched her at her gathering, as she broke stems and stripped leaves into her basket. She wasn't touching the flowers, he saw, but pulling up something that grew beneath them.

"You need to gather these at night," she remarked to him after a little. "Preferably at the dark of the moon."

"I shouldn't have expected—" he began, but broke off abruptly.

She laughed, a small fizzing sound of amusement.

"You wouldn't have expected that I should put stock in such superstitions?" she asked. "Wait, young Roger. When you've lived as long as I, you may begin to regard superstitions yourself. As for this one..." Her hand moved, a pale blur in the darkness, and broke a stem with a soft, juicy snap. A pungent aroma suddenly filled the air, sharp and plangent through the softer aroma of the flowers.

"Insects come and lay their eggs on the leaves of some plants, do you see? The plants secrete certain rather strong-smelling substances in order to repel the bugs, and the concentration of these substances is highest when the need is greatest. As it happens, those insecticidal substances happen also to have quite powerful medicinal properties, and the chief thing that troubles this particular sort of plant"—she brushed a feathery stem under his nose, fresh and damp—"is the larvae of moths."

"Ergo, it has more of the substance late at night, because that's when the caterpillars feed?"

"Got it." The stem was withdrawn, the plant thrust into her bag with a rustle of muslin, and her head bent as she felt about for more. "And some plants are fertilized by moths. Those, of course..."

"Bloom at night."

"Most plants, though, are troubled by daylight insects, and so they begin to secrete their useful compounds at dawn; the concentration rises as the day waxes—but then, when the sun gets too hot, some of the oils will begin to vaporize from the leaves, and the plant will stop producing them. So most of the very aromatic plants, you pick in late morning. And so the shamans and the herbalists tell their apprentices to take one plant in the dark of the moon and another at midday—thus making it a superstition, hmm?" Her voice was rather dry, but still amused.

Roger sat back on his heels, watching her grope about. Now that his eyes were accustomed, he could make out her shape with ease, though the details of her face were still hidden.

She worked for a time, and then sat back on her heels and stretched; he heard the creak of her back.

"I saw him once, you know." Her voice was muffled; she had turned away from him, probing under the drooping branches of a rhododendron.

"Saw him? Who?"

"The King." She found something; he heard the rustle of leaves as she tugged at it, and the snap of the breaking stem.

"He came to Pembroke Hospital, to visit the soldiers there. He came and spoke separately to us—the nurses and doctors. He was a quiet man, very dignified, but warm in his manner. I couldn't tell you a thing that he said. But it was . . . remarkably inspiring. Just that he was there, you know."

"Mmphm." Was it the onset of war, he wondered, making her recall such things?

"A journalist asked the Queen if she would be taking her children and evacuating to the country—so many were, you know."

"I know." Roger saw suddenly in his mind's eye a pair of children: a boy and a girl, thin-faced and silent, huddling near each other beside a familiar hearth. "We had two of them—at our house in Inverness. How odd, I hadn't remembered them at all until just now."

She wasn't paying attention, though.

"She said—and I may not have the quote exactly right, but this is the gist of it—'Well, the children can't leave me, and I can't leave the King—and of course the King won't leave.' When was your father killed, Roger?"

Whatever he'd been expecting her to say, it wasn't that. For an instant, the question seemed so incongruous as not to be comprehensible.

"What?" But he *had* heard her, and shaking his head to dispel a feeling of surreality, he answered, "October 1941. I'm not sure I remember the exact date—no, I do, the Reverend had it written on his genealogy. The thirty-first of October, 1941. Why?" *"Why in God's name,"* he wanted to say, but he'd been trying to control the impulse toward casual blasphemy. He choked off the stronger impulse to escape into random thought and repeated, very calmly, "Why?"

"You said he'd been shot down in Germany, didn't you?"

"Over the Channel on his way to Germany. So I was told." He could just make out her features in the moonlight, but couldn't read her expression.

"Who told you? Do you remember?"

"The Reverend, I suppose. Or I suppose it might have been my mother." The sense of unreality was wearing off, and he was beginning to feel angry. "Does it matter?"

"Probably not. When we first met you—Frank and I, in Inverness—the Reverend said then that your father had been shot down over the Channel."

"Yes? Well . . ." *So what?* was unspoken, but she plainly picked it up, for there was a small snort of not-quite laughter from the rhododendrons.

"You're right, it doesn't matter. But—both you and the Reverend mentioned that he was a Spitfire pilot. Is that correct?"

"Yes." Roger wasn't sure why, but he was beginning to have an uneasy sense at the back of his neck, as though something might be standing behind him. He coughed, making an excuse to turn his head, but glimpsed nothing behind him but the black-and-white forest, smudged by moonlight.

"I do know that for sure," he said, feeling oddly defensive. "My mother had a photograph of him with his plane. *Rag Doll,* the plane was called; the name was painted on the nose, with a crude picture of a dolly in a red dress, with black curls." He did know that for sure. He'd slept with the picture under his pillow for a long time after his mother was killed—the studio portrait of his mother was too big, and he worried that someone would notice it missing.

"Rag Doll," he repeated, suddenly struck by something.

"What? What is it?"

He waved a hand, awkward.

"It—nothing. I—I just realized that 'Rag Doll' was probably what my father called my mother. A nickname, you know? I saw a few of his letters to her; they were usually addressed to *Dolly.* And just now, thinking of the black curls—my mother's portrait . . . Mandy. Mandy's got my mother's hair."

"Oh, good," Claire said dryly. "I'd hate to think I was entirely responsible for it. Do tell her that, when she's older, will you? Girls with very curly hair invariably hate it—at least in the early years, when they want to look like everyone else."

Despite his preoccupation, he heard the small note of desolation in her voice, and reached for her hand, disregarding the fact that she still held a plant in it.

"I'll tell her," he said softly. "I'll tell her everything. Don't ever think we'd let the kids forget you."

She squeezed his hand, hard, and the fragrant white flowers spilled over the darkness of her skirt.

"Thank you," she whispered. He heard her sniff a little, and she wiped the back of her other hand swiftly across her eyes.

"Thanks," she said again, more strongly, and straightened herself. "It *is* important. To remember. If I didn't know that, I wouldn't tell you."

"Tell me . . . what?"

Her hands, small and hard and smelling of medicine, wrapped his.

"I don't know what happened to your father," she said. "But it wasn't what they told you."

"I WAS *THERE,* ROGER," she repeated, patient. "I read the papers—I nursed airmen; I talked to them. I saw the planes. Spitfires were small, light planes, meant for defense. They never crossed the Channel; they hadn't the range to go from England into Europe and back, though they were used there later."

"But . . ." Whatever argument he'd meant to make—blown off course, miscalculation—faded. The hairs had risen on his forearms without his noticing.

"Of course, things happen," she said, as though able to read his thoughts. "Accounts get garbled, too, over time and distance. Whoever told your mother might have been mistaken; she might have said something that the Reverend misconstrued. All those things are possible. But during the War, I had letters from Frank—he wrote as often as he could, up until they recruited him into MI6. After that, I often wouldn't hear anything for months. But just before that, he wrote to me, and mentioned—just as casual chat, you know— that he'd run into something strange in the reports he was handling. A Spitfire had gone down, crashed—not shot down, they thought it must have been an engine failure—in Northumbria, and while it hadn't burned, for a wonder—there was no sign of the pilot. None. And he did mention the name of the pilot, because he thought Jeremiah rather an appropriately doomed sort of name."

"Jerry," Roger said, his lips feeling numb. "My mother always called him Jerry."

"Yes," she said softly. "And there are circles of standing stones scattered all over Northumbria."

"Near where the plane—"

"I don't know. " He saw the slight movement as she shrugged, helpless.

He closed his eyes and breathed deep, the air thick with the scent from the broken stems.

"And you're telling me now because we're going back," he said, very calmly.

"I've been arguing with myself for weeks," she said, sounding apologetic. "It was only a month or so ago that I remembered. I don't often think about the—my—past, but what with everything . . ." She waved a hand, encompass- ing their imminent departure and the intense discussions surrounding it. "I was just thinking of the War—I wonder if anyone who was in it ever thinks of it without a capital 'W'—and telling Jamie about it."

It was Jamie who had asked her about Frank. Wanted to know what role he had played in the war.

"He's curious about Frank," she said abruptly.

"I would be, too, under the circumstances," Roger had replied dryly. "Was Frank not curious about him?"

That seemed to unsettle her, and she'd not replied directly but had pulled the conversation firmly back on track—if you could use such a word for such a conversation, he thought.

"Anyway," she said, "it was that that reminded me of Frank's letters. And I was trying to recall the things he'd written me about, when suddenly I re- membered that one phrase—about Jeremiah being a name with a certain doom about it." He heard her sigh.

"I wasn't sure . . . but I talked to Jamie, and he said I should tell you. He says he thinks you've a right to know—and that you'd do the right thing with the knowledge."

"I'm flattered," he said. More like flattened.

"SO THAT'S IT." The evening stars had begun to come out, faint over the mountains. Not as brilliant as the stars had been on the Ridge, where the mountain night came down like black velvet. They'd come back to the house by now, but lingered in the dooryard, talking.

"I'd thought about it, now and again: how does the time-traveling fit into God's plan? Can things be changed? *Ought* they be changed? Your parents— they tried to change history, tried damned hard, and couldn't do it. I'd thought that was all there was to it—and from a Presbyterian point of view." He let a little humor show in his voice. "It was a comfort, almost, to think that it *couldn't* change. It shouldn't be able to be changed. Ye know: *God's in His heaven, all's right with the world* sort of thing."

"But." Bree was holding the folded photocopy; she waved it at a passing moth, a tiny white blur.

"But," he agreed. "Proof that things *can* be changed."

"I talked to Mama a little bit about it," Bree said, after a moment's thought. "She laughed."

"Did she?" Roger said dryly, and got the breath of a laugh from Bree in answer.

"Not like she thought it was funny," she assured him. "I'd asked her if she thought it was possible for a traveler to change things, change the future, and she told me it was, obviously—because she changed the future every time she kept someone from dying who would have died if she hadn't been there. Some of them went on to have children they wouldn't have had, and who knew what those children would do, that they wouldn't have done if they hadn't ... and *that* was when she laughed and said it was a good thing Catholics believed in Mystery and didn't insist on trying to figure out exactly *how* God worked, like Protestants do."

"Well, I don't know that I'd say—oh, was she talking about me?"

"Probably. I didn't ask."

Now it was his turn to laugh, though it hurt his throat to do it.

"Proof," she said thoughtfully. She was sitting on the bench near the front door, folding the photocopy in long, nervously deft fingers. "I don't know. *Is* it proof?"

"Maybe not up to your rigorous engineering standards," he said. "But I do remember—and so do you. If it was only me, then, yeah, I'd think it was just my mind going. But I've got a little more faith in *your* mental processes. Are you making a paper airplane out of that?"

"No, it's—whoa. Mandy." She was up and moving before he'd quite registered the wail from the nursery upstairs, and had vanished into the house a moment later, leaving him to lock up below. They didn't usually bother locking the doors—no one did, in the Highlands—but tonight ...

His heart rate surged as a long gray shadow shot out across the path in front of him. Then dropped as he smiled. Wee Adso, out for a prowl. A neighbor boy had come round with a basket of kittens a few months before, looking for homes for them, and Bree had taken the gray one, a green-eyed ringer for her mother's cat, and given it the same name. If they got a watchdog, would they name it Rollo? he wondered.

"*Cat a Mhinister ...*" he said. *The minister's cat is a hunting cat.*

"Good hunting, then," he added to the tail disappearing under the hydrangea bush, and bent to retrieve the half-folded paper from the path where Brianna had dropped it.

No, it wasn't a paper airplane. What was it? A paper hat? No telling, and he tucked it into his shirt pocket and went in.

He found Bree and Mandy in the front parlor, in front of a freshly made fire. Mandy, comforted and given milk, had half-dozed off again already in Bree's arms; she blinked sleepily at him, sucking on a thumb.

"Aye, what's the trouble, then, *a leannan?*" he asked her softly, pushing tumbled curls out of her eyes.

"Bad dream," Bree said, her voice carefully casual. "A naughty thing outside, trying to get in her window."

He and Brianna had been sitting below that very window at the time, but he glanced reflexively at the window beside him, which reflected only the domestic scene of which he was a part. The man in the glass looked wary, shoulders hunched in readiness to lunge at something. He got up and drew the curtains.

"Here," he said abruptly, sitting down and reaching for Mandy. She came into his arms with the slow amiability of a tree sloth, sticking her wet thumb in his ear in the process.

Bree went to fetch them cups of cocoa, returning with a rattle of crockery, the scent of hot milk and chocolate, and the look of someone who's been thinking what to say about a difficult matter.

"Did you ... I mean, given the nature of the, er, difficulty ... did you maybe think of asking God?" she said, diffident. "Directly?"

"Yeah, I did think of that," he assured her, torn between annoyance and amusement at the question. "And yes, I did ask—a number of times. Especially on the way to Oxford. Where I found that." He nodded at the bit of paper. "What is it, by the way? The shape, I mean."

"Oh." She picked it up and made the last few folds, quick and sure, then held it out on the palm of her hand. He frowned at it for a moment, then realized what it was. A Chinese fortune-teller, kids called them; there were four pockets showing, and you put your fingers in them and could open the thing in different combinations as questions were asked, so as to show the different answers—*Yes, No, Sometimes, Always*—written on the flaps inside.

"Very appropriate," he said.

They fell silent for a moment, drinking cocoa in a silence that balanced precariously on the edge of question.

"The Westminster Confession also says, *God alone is Lord of the conscience.* I'll make my peace with it," he said quietly, at last, "or I won't. I said to Dr. Weatherspoon that it seemed a bit odd, having an assistant choirmaster who couldn't sing—he just smiled and said he was wanting me to take the job so as to keep me in the fold while I thought things over, as he put it. Probably afraid I'd jump ship else, and go over to Rome," he added, as a feeble joke.

"That's good," she said softly, not looking up from the depths of the cocoa she wasn't drinking.

More silence. And the shade of Jerry MacKenzie, RAF, came and sat down by the fire in his fleece-lined leather flight jacket, watching the play of light in his granddaughter's ink-black hair.

"So you—" He could hear the little pop as her tongue parted from her dry mouth. "You're going to look? See if you can find out where your father went? Where he might . . . be?"

Where he might be. Here, there, then, now? His heart gave a sudden convulsive lurch, thinking of the tramp who'd stayed in the broch. God . . . no. It couldn't be. No reason to think it, none. Only wanting.

He'd thought about it a lot, on the way to Oxford, between the praying. What he'd say, what he'd ask, if he had the chance. He wanted to ask everything, say everything—but there really was only the one thing to say to his father, and that thing was snoring in his arms like a drunken bumblebee.

"No." Mandy squirmed in her sleep, emitted a small burp, and settled back against his chest. He didn't look up, but kept his eyes fixed in the dark labyrinth of her curls. "I couldn't risk my own kids losing their father." His voice had nearly disappeared; he felt his vocal cords grinding like gears to force the words out.

"It's too important. You don't forget having a dad."

Bree's eyes slid sideways, the blue of them no more than a spark in the firelight.

"I thought . . . you were so young. You do remember your father?"

Roger shook his head, the chambers of his heart clenching hard, grasping emptiness.

"No," he said softly, and bent his head, breathing in the scent of his daughter's hair. "I remember yours."

FLUTTERBY

Wilmington, colony of North Carolina
May 3, 1777

I COULD SEE AT ONCE that Jamie had been dreaming again. His face had an unfocused, inward look, as though he were seeing something other than the fried black pudding on his plate.

Seeing him like this gave me an urgent desire to ask what he had seen—quelled at once, for fear that if I asked too soon, he might lose some part of the dream. It also, truth be told, knotted me with envy. I would have given anything to see what he saw, whether it was real or not. That hardly mattered—it was connection, and the severed nerve ends that had joined me to my vanished family sparked and burned like shorted-out electrical cables when I saw that look on his face.

I couldn't stand not to know what he had dreamed, though in the usual manner of dreams, it was seldom straightforward.

"You've been dreaming of them, haven't you?" I said, when the serving maid had gone out. We'd risen late, tired from the long ride to Wilmington the day before, and were the only diners in the inn's small front room.

He glanced at me and nodded slowly, a small frown between his brows. *That* made me uneasy; the occasional dreams he had of Bree or the children normally left him peaceful and happy.

"What?" I demanded. "What happened?"

He shrugged, still frowning.

"Nothing, Sassenach. I saw Jem and the wee lass—" A smile came over his face at that. "God, she's a feisty wee baggage! She minds me o' you, Sassenach."

This was a dubious compliment as phrased, but I felt a deep glow at the thought. I'd spent hours looking at Mandy and Jem, memorizing every small feature and gesture, trying to extrapolate, imagine what they would look like as they grew—and I was almost sure that Mandy had my mouth. I knew for a fact that she had the shape of my eyes—and my hair, poor child, for all it was inky black.

"What were they doing?"

He rubbed a finger between his brows as though his forehead itched.

"They were outside," he said slowly. "Jem told her to do something and she kicked him in the shin and ran away from him, so he chased her. I think it was spring." He smiled, eyes fixed on whatever he'd seen in his dream. "I mind the wee flowers, caught in her hair, and lying in drifts across the stones."

"What stones?" I asked sharply.

"Oh. The gravestones," he answered, readily enough. "That's it—they were playing among the stones on the hill behind Lallybroch."

I sighed happily. This was the third dream that he'd had, seeing them at Lallybroch. It might be only wishful thinking, but I knew it made him as happy as it made me, to feel that they had made a home there.

"They could be," I said. "Roger went there—when we were looking for you. He said the place was standing vacant, for sale. Bree would have money; they might have bought it. They *could* be there!" I'd told him that before, but he nodded, pleased.

"Aye, they could be," he said, his eyes still soft with his memory of the children on the hill, chasing through the long grass and the worn gray stones that marked his family's rest.

"A flutterby came with them," he said suddenly. "I'd forgot that. A blue one."

"Blue? Are there blue butterflies in Scotland?" I frowned, trying to remember. Such butterflies as I'd ever noticed had tended to be white or yellow, I thought.

Jamie gave me a look of mild exasperation.

"It's a dream, Sassenach. I could have flutterbys wi' tartan wings, and I liked."

I laughed, but refused to be distracted.

"Right. What was it that bothered you, though?"

He glanced curiously at me.

"How did ye ken I was troubled?"

I looked at him down my nose—or as much down my nose as was possible, given the disparity of height.

"You may not have a glass face, but I *have* been married to you for thirty-odd years."

He let the fact that I hadn't actually been *with* him for twenty of those years pass without comment, and only smiled.

"Aye. Well, it wasna anything, really. Only that they went into the broch."

"The broch?" I said uncertainly. The ancient tower for which Lallybroch was named did stand on the hill behind the house, its shadow passing daily through the burying ground like the stately march of a giant sundial. Jamie and I had gone up there often of an evening in our early days at Lallybroch, to sit on the bench that stood against the broch's wall and be away from the hubbub of the house, enjoying the peaceful sight of the estate and its grounds spread white and green below us, soft with twilight.

The small frown was back between his brows.

"The broch," he repeated, and looked at me, helpless. "I dinna ken what it was. Only that I didna want them to go in. It . . . felt as though there was something inside. Waiting. And I didna like it at all."

PART THREE

Privateer

23

CORRESPONDENCE
FROM THE FRONT

October 3, 1776
Ellesmere
to Lady Dorothea Grey

Dear Coz—

I write in haste to catch the Courier. I am embarked upon a brief Journey in company with another Officer, on behalf of Captain Richardson, and do not know for certain what my Whereabouts may be for the immediate Future. You may write to me in care of your Brother Adam; I will endeavor to keep in Correspondence with him.

I have executed your Commission to the best of my Ability, and will persevere in your Service. Give my Father and yours my best Regards and Respects, as well as my continuing Affection, and do not omit to keep a large Part of this last Quantity for yourself.

Your most obedient,
William

October 3, 1776
Ellesmere to Lord John Grey

Dear Father,

After due Thought, I have decided to accept Captain Richardson's Proposal that I accompany a senior Officer on a Mission to Quebec, acting as Interpreter for him, my French being thought adequate to the Purpose. General Howe is agreeable.

I have not yet met Captain Randall-Isaacs, but will join him in Albany next Week. I do not know when we may return, and cannot say what Opportunities there may be to write, but I will do so when I can, and in the meantime beg that you will think fondly of

Your son,
William

Late October 1776
Quebec

WILLIAM WASN'T SURE quite what to make of Captain Denys Randall-Isaacs. On the surface, he was just the sort of genial, unremarkable fellow you found in any regiment: about thirty, decent with cards, ready with a joke, good-looking in a dark sort of way, open-faced, and reliable. He was a very pleasant traveling companion, too, with a fund of entertaining stories for the road and a thoroughgoing knowledge of bawdy songs and poems of the lower sort.

What he didn't do was talk about himself. Which, in William's experience, was what most people did best—or at least most frequently.

He'd tried a little tentative prodding, offering the rather dramatic story of his own birth, and receiving in turn a few spare facts: Randall-Isaacs's own father, an officer of dragoons, had died in the Highlands campaign before Denys's birth, and his mother had remarried a year later.

"My stepfather is a Jew," he'd told William. "A rich one," he'd added, with a wry smile.

William had nodded, amiable.

"Better than a poor one," he'd said, and left it at that. It wasn't much, as facts went, but it did go some way to explain why Randall-Isaacs was working for Richardson rather than pursuing fame and glory with the Lancers or the Welch Fusiliers. Money would buy a commission, but it would not ensure a warm reception in a regiment nor the sorts of opportunity that family connections and the influence spoken of delicately as "interest" would.

It occurred—fleetingly—to William to wonder just why he was turning his back on his own substantial connections and opportunities in order to engage in Captain Richardson's shadowy ventures, but he dismissed that consideration as a matter for later contemplation.

"Amazing," Denys murmured, looking up. They had reined in their horses on the road that led up from the bank of the St. Lawrence to the citadel of Quebec; from here, they could see the steep cliff face that Wolfe's troops had climbed, seventeen years before, to capture the citadel—and Quebec—from the French.

"My father made that climb," William said, trying to sound casual.

Randall-Isaacs's head swiveled toward him in astonishment. "He did? Lord John, you mean—he fought on the Plains of Abraham with Wolfe?"

"Yes." William eyed the cliff with respect. It was thick with saplings, but the underlying rock was crumbling shale; he could see the jagged dark fissures and quadrangular cracks through the leaves. The notion of scaling that height in the dark, and not only climbing it, but hauling all the artillery up the cliffside with them . . . !

"He said the battle was over almost as soon as it started—only the one great volley—but the climb to the battlefield was the worst thing he'd ever done."

Randall-Isaacs grunted respectfully, and paused for a moment before gathering his reins.

"You said your father knows Sir Guy?" he said. "Doubtless he'll appreciate hearing the story."

William glanced at his companion. Actually, he *hadn't* said that Lord John knew Sir Guy Carleton, the commander in chief for North America—though he did. His father knew everyone. And with that simple thought, he realized suddenly what his true function on this expedition was. He was Randall-Isaacs's calling card.

It was true that he spoke French very well—languages came easy to him—and that Randall-Isaacs's French was rudimentary. Richardson had likely been telling the truth about that bit; always best to have an interpreter you can trust. But while Randall-Isaacs had exhibited a flattering interest in William, William became aware *ex post facto* that Randall-Isaacs was much more specifically interested in Lord John: the highlights of his military career, where he had been posted, whom he had served with or under, who he knew.

It had happened twice already. They'd called upon the commanders of Fort Saint-Jean and Fort Chambly, and in both instances Randall-Isaacs had presented their credentials, mentioning casually that William was the son of Lord John Grey. Whereupon the official welcome had warmed at once into a long, late evening of reminiscence and conversation, fueled by good brandy. During which—William now realized—he and the commanders had done all the talking. And Randall-Isaacs had sat listening, his handsome, high-colored face aglow with a flattering interest.

Huh, William thought to himself. Having worked it out, he wasn't sure how he felt about it. On the one hand, he was pleased with himself for having smoked what was going on. On the other, he was less pleased to think that he was desirable mainly for his connections, rather than his own virtues.

Well, it was useful, if humbling, to know. What he *didn't* know was exactly what Randall-Isaacs's role was. Was he only gathering information for Richardson? Or had he other business, unspoken? Often enough, Randall-Isaacs had left him to his own devices, saying casually that he had a private errand for which he thought his own French adequate.

They were—according to the very limited instruction Captain Richardson had given him—assessing the sentiments of the French *habitants* and English settlers in Quebec, with an eye to future support in case of incursion by the American rebels or attempted threats and seductions by the Continental Congress.

These sentiments so far seemed clear, if not what he might have expected. The French settlers in the area were in sympathy with Sir Guy, who—as governor general of North America—had passed the Quebec Act, which legalized Catholicism and protected the French Catholics' trade. The English were disgruntled by the same act, for obvious reasons, and had declined *en masse* to answer Sir Guy's calls for militia assistance during the American attack on the city during the previous winter.

"They must have been insane," he remarked to Randall-Isaacs, as they crossed the open plain before the citadel. "The Americans who tried it on here last year, I mean."

They'd reached the top of the cliff now, and the citadel rose from the plain before them, peaceful and solid—very solid—in the autumn sun. The day was warm and beautiful, and the air was alive with the rich, earthy smells of the river and forest. He'd never seen such a forest. The trees that edged the plain and grew all along the banks of the St. Lawrence grew impenetrably thick, now blazing with gold and crimson. Seen against the darkness of the water and the impossible deep blue of the vast October sky, the whole of it gave him the dreamlike feeling of riding through a medieval painting, glowing with gold leaf and burning with a sense of otherworldly fervor.

But beyond the beauty of it, he felt the savagery of the place. Felt it with a clarity that made his bones feel transparent. The days were still warm, but the chill of winter was a sharp tooth that bit harder with each day's twilight, and it took very little imagination for him to see this plain as it would be a few weeks from now, cloaked in bitter ice, whitely inhospitable to all life. With a ride of two hundred miles behind him, and an immediate understanding of the problems of supply for two riders on the rugged journey north in *good* weather, combined with what he knew of the rigors of supplying an army in bad weather . . .

"If they weren't insane, they wouldn't be doing what they *are* doing." Randall-Isaacs interrupted his thoughts, he, too, drawing up for a moment to look over the prospect with a soldier's eye. "It was Colonel Arnold who led them here, though. That man is certainly insane. But a damned good soldier." Admiration showed in his voice, and William glanced curiously at him.

"Know him, do you?" he asked casually, and Randall-Isaacs laughed.

"Not to speak to," he replied. "Come on." He spurred up, and they turned toward the citadel gate. He wore an amused, half-contemptuous expression, though, as if dwelling on a memory, and after a few moments, he spoke again.

"He might have done it. Arnold, I mean; taken the city. Sir Guy hadn't any troops to speak of, and had Arnold got here when he planned to, and with the powder and shot he needed . . . well, it would have been a different story. But he chose the wrong man to ask directions of."

"What do you mean by that?"

Randall-Isaacs looked suddenly wary, but then seemed to shrug internally, as though to say, *"What does it matter?"* He was in good humor, already looking forward to a hot dinner, a soft bed, and clean linen, after weeks of camping in the dark forests.

"He couldn't make it overland," he said. "Seeking a way to carry an army and its necessities north by water, Arnold had gone looking for someone who had made the hazardous trip and knew the rivers and portages," Randall-Isaacs said. "He'd found one, too—Samuel Goodwin.

"But it never occurred to him that Goodwin might be a Loyalist." Randall-Isaacs shook his head at this naïveté. "Goodwin came to me and asked what he should do. So I told him, and he gave Arnold his maps—carefully rewritten to serve their purpose."

And serve their purpose they had. By misstating distances, removing landmarks, indicating passages where there were none, and providing maps that were pure figments of imagination, Mr. Goodwin's guidance succeeded in luring Arnold's force deep into the wilderness, obliging them to carry their ships and supplies overland for days on end, and eventually delaying them so badly that the winter caught them, well short of Quebec City.

Randall-Isaacs laughed, though there was a tinge of regret about it, William thought.

"I was amazed when they told me he'd made it after all. Aside from everything else, he'd been swindled by the carpenters who made his ships—I do believe that was sheer incompetence, not politics, though these days it's sometimes hard to tell. Made with green timbers and badly fitted. More than half of them came apart and sank within days of launching."

"It had to have been sheer hell," Randall-Isaacs said, as though to himself. He pulled himself up straight then, shaking his head.

"But they followed him. All his men. Only one company turned back. Starving, half naked, freezing . . . they followed him," he repeated, marveling. He glanced sideways at William, smiling. "Think your men would follow you, Lieutenant? In such conditions?"

"I hope I should have better sense than to lead them into such conditions," William replied dryly. "What happened to Arnold in the end? Was he captured?"

"No," Randall-Isaacs said thoughtfully, lifting a hand to wave at the guards by the citadel gate. "No, he wasn't. As to what's happened to him now, God only knows. Or God and Sir Guy. I'm hoping the latter can tell us."

24

JOYEUX NOËL

London
December 24, 1776

MOST PROSPEROUS MADAMS WERE stout creatures, Lord John reflected. Whether it was only the satisfaction of appetites denied in their early years, or was a shield against the possibility of a return to the lower stations of their trade, almost all of them were well armored in flesh.

Not Nessie. He could see the shadow of her body through the thin muslin of her shift—he had inadvertently roused her from her bed—as she stood before the fire to pull on her bed-sacque. She bore not an ounce more upon her scrawny frame than she had when he'd first met her, then aged—she'd said—fourteen, though he'd suspected at the time that she might be eleven.

That would make her thirty-odd. She still looked fourteen.

He smiled at the notion, and she smiled back, tying her gown. The smile aged her a bit, for there were gaps among her teeth, and the remainder showed black at the root. If she was not stout, it was because she lacked the capacity to become so; she adored sugar, and would eat an entire box of candied violets or Turkish Delight in minutes, compensating for the starvation of her youth in the Scottish Highlands. He'd brought her a pound of sugarplums.

"Think I'm that cheap, do ye?" she said, raising a brow as she took the prettily wrapped box from him.

"Never," he assured her. "That is merely by way of apology for having disturbed your rest." That was improvisation; he had in fact expected to find her at work, it being past ten o'clock at night.

"Aye, well, it *is* Christmas Eve," she said, answering his unasked question. "Any man wi' a home to go to's in it." She yawned, pulled off her nightcap, and fluffed her fingers through the wild mass of curly dark hair.

"Yet you seem to have some custom," he observed. Distant singing came from two floors below, and the parlor had seemed well populated when he passed.

"Och, aye. The desperate ones. I leave them to Maybelle to deal with; dinna like to see them, poor creatures. Pitiful. They dinna really want a woman, the ones who come on Christmas Eve—only a fire to sit by, and folk to sit with." She waved a hand and sat down, greedily pulling the bow from her present.

"Let me wish you a happy Christmas, then," he said, watching her with amused affection. She popped one of the sweetmeats into her mouth, closed her eyes, and sighed in ecstasy.

"Mmp," she said, not pausing to swallow before inserting and masticating another. From the cordial intonation of this remark, he assumed her to be returning the sentiment.

He'd known it was Christmas Eve, of course, but had somehow put the knowledge of it out of his head during the long, cold hours of the day. It had poured all day, driving needles of freezing rain, augmented now and then by irritable bursts of hail, and he'd been chilled through since just before dawn, when Minnie's footman had roused him with the summons to Argus House.

Nessie's room was small but elegant, and smelled comfortably of sleep. Her bed was vast, hung with woolen bed curtains done in the very fashionable pink and black "Queen Charlotte" checks. Tired, cold, and hungry as he was, he felt the pull of that warm, inviting cavern, with its mounds of goosedown pillows, quilts, and clean, soft sheets. What would she think, he wondered, if he asked to share her bed for the night?

"A fire to sit by, and folk to sit with." Well, he had that, at least for the moment.

Grey became aware of a low buzzing noise, something like a trapped bluebottle flinging itself against a windowpane. Glancing toward the sound, he perceived that what he had thought to be merely a heap of rumpled bedclothes in fact contained a body; the elaborately passementeried tassel of a nightcap trailed across the pillow.

"That's no but Rab," said an amused Scottish voice, and he turned to find her grinning at him. "Fancy it three ways, do ye?"

He realized, even as he blushed, that he liked her not only for herself, or for her skill as an intelligence agent, but because she had an unexcelled ability to disconcert him. He thought she did not know the shape of his own desires exactly, but she'd been a whore since childhood and likely had a shrewd apprehension of almost anyone's desires, whether conscious or not.

"Oh, I think not," he said politely. "I shouldn't wish to disturb your husband." He tried not to think of Rab MacNab's brutal hands and solid thighs; Rab had been a chairman, before his marriage to Nessie and the success of the brothel they owned. Surely he didn't also . . . ?

"Ye couldna wake yon wee oaf wi' cannon fire," she said, with an affectionate glance into the bed. She got up, though, and pulled the curtains across, muffling the snoring.

"Speak o' cannon," she added, bending to peer at Grey as she returned to her seat, "ye look as though ye've been in the wars yourself. Here, have a dram, and I'll ring for a bit of hot supper." She nodded at the decanter and glasses that stood on the elbow table and reached for the bell rope.

"No, I thank you. I haven't much time. But I will take a drop to keep the cold out, thank you."

The whisky—she drank nothing else, scorning gin as a beggar's drink and regarding wine as good but insufficient to its purpose—warmed him, and his wet coat had begun to steam in the fire's heat.

"Ye've not much time," she said. "Why's that, then?"

"I'm bound for France," he said. "In the morning."

Her eyebrows shot up, and she put another comfit in her mouth.

" 'Oo 'don me tkp Kismus wi' yrfmily?"

"Don't talk with your mouth full, my dear," he said, smiling nonetheless. "My brother suffered a bad attack last night. His heart, the quack says, but I doubt he really knows. The usual Christmas dinner is likely to be somewhat less of an occasion than usual, though."

"I'm that sorry to hear," Nessie said, more clearly. She wiped sugar from the corner of her mouth, brow puckered with a troubled frown. "His lordship's a fine man."

"Yes, he—" He stopped, staring at her. "You've *met* my brother?"

Nessie dimpled demurely at him.

"Discretion is a madam's most val-u-able stock in trade," she chanted, clearly parroting the wisdom of a former employer.

"Says the woman who's spying for me." He was trying to envision Hal . . . or perhaps *not* to envision Hal . . . for surely he wouldn't . . . to spare Minnie his demands, perhaps? But he'd thought . . .

"Aye, well, spying's no the same as idle gossip, now, is it? I want tea, even if you don't. Talking's thirsty work." She rang the bell for the porter, then turned back, one eyebrow raised. "Your brother's dying, and ye're goin' to France? Must be summat urgent, then."

"He's not dying," Grey said sharply. The thought of it split the carpet at his feet, a grinning abyss waiting to pull him in. He looked determinedly away from it.

"He . . . had a shock. Word was brought that his youngest son was wounded in America and has been captured."

Her eyes widened at that, and she clutched the dressing gown closer to her nonexistent breasts.

"The youngest. That would be . . . Henry, no?"

"It would. And how the *devil* do you know that?" he demanded, agitation making his voice harsh. A gap-toothed smile glimmered at him, but then went away as she saw the depth of his distress.

"One of his lordship's footmen is a regular," she said simply. "Thursdays; it's his night off."

"Oh." He sat still, hands on his knees, trying to bring his thoughts—and his feelings—under some kind of control. "It—I see."

"It's late in the year to be getting messages from America, no?" She glanced at the window, which was covered in layers of red velvet and lace that were unable to keep out the sound of lashing rain. "Did a late ship come in?"

"Yes. Blown off course and limped in to Brest with a wounded mainmast. The message was brought overland."

"And is it Brest ye're going to, then?"

"It is not."

A soft scratching came at the door before she could ask anything further, and she went to let in the porter, who had—without being asked, Grey noted—brought up a tray laden with tea things, including a thickly iced cake.

He turned it over in his mind. Could he tell her? But she hadn't been joking about discretion, he knew. In her own way, she kept secrets as much—and as well—as he did.

"It's about William," he said, as she shut the door and turned back to him.

HE KNEW DAWN WAS near, from the ache in his bones and the faint chime of his pocket watch. There was no sign of it in the sky. Clouds the color of chimney sweepings brushed the rooves of London, and the streets were blacker than they had been at midnight, all lanterns having been long since extinguished, all hearth fires burnt low.

He'd been up all night. There were things he must do; he ought to go home and sleep for a few hours before catching the Dover coach. He couldn't go without seeing Hal once more, though. Just to assure himself.

There were lights in the windows of Argus House. Even with the drapes drawn, a faint gleam showed on the wet cobbles outside. It was snowing thickly, but wasn't yet sticking to the ground. There was a good chance that the coach would be detained—was sure to be slow, bogged down on the miry roads.

Speaking of coaches—his heart gave a sickly leap at the sight of a battered-looking carriage standing in the porte cochere, which he thought belonged to the doctor.

His thump at the door was answered at once by a half-dressed footman, nightshirt tucked hastily into his breeches. The man's anxious face relaxed a little when he recognized Grey.

"The duke—"

"Took bad in the night, my lord, but easier now," the man—Arthur, that was his name—interrupted him, stepping back to let him in and taking the cloak from his shoulders, shaking off the snow.

He nodded and made for the stair, not waiting to be shown up. He met the doctor coming down—a thin gray man, marked by his black ill-smelling coat and the bag in his hand.

"How is he?" he demanded, seizing the man by the sleeve as he reached the landing. The doctor drew back, affronted, but then saw his face in the glow from the sconce and, recognizing his resemblance to Hal, settled his ruffled feathers.

"Somewhat better, my lord. I have let him blood, three ounces, and his breathing is grown easier."

Grey let go the sleeve and bounded up the stairs, his own chest tight. The door to Hal's suite of rooms stood open and he went in at once, startling a maid who was carrying out a chamber pot, lidded and then delicately draped with a cloth handsomely embroidered with large, brilliant flowers. He brushed past her with a nod of apology and went into Hal's bedroom.

Hal was sitting up against the bolster, pillows wedged behind him; he looked nearly dead. Minnie was beside him, her pleasant round face gaunt with anxiety and sleeplessness.

"I see you even shit with style, Your Grace," Grey remarked, sitting down on the other side of the bed.

Hal opened one gray lid and eyed him. The face might be that of a skeleton, but the pale, sharp eye was the living Hal, and Grey felt his chest flood with relief.

"Oh, the cloth?" Hal said, weakly but clearly. "That's Dottie. She will not go out, even though I assured her that if I thought I was going to die, I should certainly wait for her return to do it." He paused to breathe, with a faint wheezing note, then coughed and went on: "She is not the sort, thank God, to indulge in pieties, she has no musical talent, and her vitality is such that she is a menace to the kitchen staff. So Minnie set her to needlework, as some outlet for her formidable energies. She takes after Mother, you know."

"I *am* sorry, John," Minnie said apologetically to him. "I sent her to bed, but I saw that her candle is still lit. I believe she is at work this moment on a pair of carpet slippers for you."

Grey thought carpet slippers were likely innocuous, whatever motif she had chosen, and said so.

"So long as she isn't embroidering a pair of drawers for me. The knotwork, you know . . ."

That made Hal laugh, which in turn made him cough alarmingly, though it brought a little color back into his face.

"So you aren't dying?" Grey asked.

"No," Hal said shortly.

"Good," said Grey, smiling at his brother. "Don't."

Hal blinked, and then, recalling the occasion on which he had said exactly that to Grey, smiled back.

"Do my best," he said dryly, and then, turning, laid an affectionate hand on Minnie's. "My dear . . ."

"I'll have some tea brought up," she said, rising at once. "And a good hot breakfast," she added, after a scrutinizing look at Grey. She closed the door delicately behind her.

"What is it?" Hal hitched himself higher on the pillow, disregarding the bloodstained cloth wrapped round one forearm. "You have news?"

"Very little. But a great number of alarming questions."

The news of Henry's capture had been enclosed as a note for Hal inside a letter to himself, from one of his contacts in the intelligencing world, and carried an answer to his inquiries regarding the known French connections of one Percival Beauchamp. He hadn't wanted to discuss that with Hal until he'd seen Nessie, though—and Hal had been in no condition for such discussions, anyway.

"No known connections between Beauchamp and Vergennes"—naming the French foreign minister—"but he has been seen often in company with Beaumarchais."

That provoked another coughing fit.

"Little fucking wonder," Hal observed hoarsely, upon his recovery. "A mutual interest in hunting, no doubt?" That last was a sarcastic reference, both to Percy's disinclination for blood sports and to Beaumarchais's title of "Lieutenant General of Hunting," bestowed upon him some years previous by the late king.

"*And,*" Grey went on, ignoring this, "with one Silas Deane."

Hal frowned. "Who?"

"An American merchant. In Paris on behalf of the American Congress. He skulks round Beaumarchais, rather. And *he's* been seen speaking with Vergennes."

"Oh, him." Hal flapped a hand. "Heard of him. Vaguely."

"Have you heard of a business called *Rodrigue Hortalez et Cie*?"

"No. Sounds Spanish, doesn't it?"

"Or Portuguese. My informant had nothing but the name and a rumor that Beaumarchais has something to do with it."

Hal grunted and lay back.

"Beaumarchais has his fingers in any number of pies. Makes watches, for God's sake, as though writing plays weren't bad enough. Has Beauchamp anything to do with this company?"

"Not known. It's all vague associations at this point, nothing more. I asked for everything that could be turned up that had anything—anything not generally known, I mean—to do with Beauchamp or the Americans; this is what came back."

Hal's slender fingers played restless scales on the coverlet.

"Does your informant know what this Spanish company does?"

"Trade, what else?" Grey replied ironically, and Hal snorted.

"If they were bankers, as well, I'd think you might have something."

"I might, at that. But the only way to find out, I think, is to go and poke at things with a sharp stick. I'm taking the coach to Dover in"—he squinted at the carriage clock on the mantel, obscured by the gloom—"three hours."

"Ah."

The voice was noncommittal, but Grey knew his brother very well indeed.

"I'll be back from France by the end of March at the latest," he said, adding gently, "I shall be on the first ship that sails for the Colonies in the new year, Hal. And I'll bring Henry back." *Alive or dead.* Neither of them spoke the words; they didn't need to.

"I'll be here when you do," Hal said at last, quietly.

Grey put his hand over his brother's, which turned at once to take his. It might look frail, but he was heartened at the determined strength in Hal's grasp. They sat in silence, hands linked, until the door opened and Arthur— now fully dressed—sidled in with a tray the size of a card table, laden with bacon, sausages, kidneys, kippers, shirred eggs in butter, grilled mushrooms and tomatoes, toast, jam, marmalade, a huge pot of fragrantly steaming tea, bowls of sugar and milk—and a covered dish which he set ceremoniously before Hal, this proving to be filled with a sort of nasty thin gruel.

Arthur bowed and went out, leaving Grey wondering whether he was the footman who went to Nessie's house on Thursdays. He turned back to find Hal helping himself liberally to Grey's kidneys.

"Aren't you meant to be eating your slop?" Grey inquired.

"Don't tell me *you're* determined to hasten me into my grave, too," Hal said, closing his eyes in brief rapture as he chewed. "How the devil anyone expects me to recover, fed on things like rusks and gruel..." Huffing, he speared another kidney.

"Is it really your heart, do you think?" Grey asked.

Hal shook his head.

"I really don't think so," he said, his tone detached. "I listened to it, you know, after the first attack. Whanging away just as usual." He paused to prod himself experimentally in the chest, fork suspended in the air. "It doesn't hurt there. Surely it would, wouldn't it?"

Grey shrugged.

"What sort of attack was it, then?"

Hal swallowed the last of the kidney and reached for a slice of buttered toast, taking up the marmalade knife in his other hand.

"Couldn't breathe," he said casually. "Turned blue, that kind of thing."

"Oh. Well, then."

"I feel quite well, just now," Hal said, sounding mildly surprised.

"Do you?" Grey said, smiling. He had a moment's reservation, but after all...he was going abroad, and unexpected things not only could happen but often did. Best not leave the matter hanging, just in case something untoward befell either one of them before they met again.

"Well, then...if you're sure that a minor shock will not shuffle off your mortal coil, allow me to tell you something."

His news regarding the *tendresse* existing between Dottie and William made Hal blink and stop eating momentarily, but after a moment's contemplation he nodded and resumed chewing.

"All right," he said.

"All *right?*" Grey echoed. "You have no objections?"

"Hardly sit well with you if I did, would it?"

"If you expect me to believe that a concern for my feelings would in any way affect your own actions, your illness *has* severely damaged you."

Hal grinned briefly, and drank tea.

"No," he said, setting down the empty cup. "Not that. It's just—" He leaned back, hands clasped over his—very slightly—protruding belly, and gave Grey a straight look. "I *could* die. Don't mean to; don't think I will. But

I could. I'd die easier if I knew she was settled with someone who'd protect her and look after her properly."

"I'm flattered that you think William would," Grey said dryly, though he was in fact immensely pleased.

"Of course he would," Hal said, matter-of-fact. "He's your son, isn't he?"

A church bell began to ring, somewhere in the distance, reminding Grey.

"Oh!" he said. "Happy Christmas!"

Hal looked equally surprised, but then smiled.

"The same to you."

GREY WAS STILL FILLED with Christmas feeling when he set off for Dover—literally, as the pockets of his greatcoat were jammed with sweetmeats and small gifts and he carried under his arm a wrapped parcel containing the infamous carpet slippers, these lavishly embellished with lily pads and green frogs done in crewelwork. He had hugged Dottie when she gave them to him, managing to whisper in her ear that her job was done. She had kissed him with such vigor that he could still feel it on his cheek and rubbed absently at the spot.

He must write to William at once—though in fact there was no particular hurry, as a letter could not be carried any faster than he would go himself. He'd meant what he'd told Hal; as soon as a ship could set sail in the spring, he'd be on it. He only hoped he'd be in time.

And not only for Henry.

The roads were quite as bad as he'd expected, and the Calais ferry was worse, but he was oblivious to the cold and discomfort of the journey. With his anxiety for Hal somewhat allayed, he was free to think about what Nessie had told him—a bit of information he'd thought of mentioning to Hal but hadn't, not wanting to burden his brother's mind, in case it might hamper his recovery.

"Your Frenchman didn't come *here*," Nessie had told him, licking sugar off her fingers. "But he went to Jackson's regular, when he was in town. He's gone off now, though; back to France, they say."

"Jackson's," he'd said slowly, wondering. He didn't patronize bawdy houses himself—bar Nessie's establishment—but he certainly knew about Jackson's and had been there once or twice with friends. A flash house, offering music on the ground floor, gaming on the first floor, and more private diversions higher up. Very popular with mid-echelon army officers. But not, he was certain, a place catering to Percy Beauchamp's particular tastes.

"I see," he'd said, calmly drinking tea, feeling his heart beat in his ears. "And have you ever come across an officer named Randall-Isaacs?" That was the part of his letter he hadn't told Hal; Denys Randall-Isaacs was an army officer known to frequent Beauchamp's company, both in France and in London, his informant had said—and the name had gone straight through Grey's heart like an icicle.

It *might* be no more than coincidence that a man known to associate with Percy Beauchamp had taken William on an intelligencing expedition to Quebec—but damned if he thought it was.

Nessie had lifted her head abruptly at the name "Randall-Isaacs," like a dog hearing the rustle of something in the brush.

"Aye, I have," she said slowly. There was a blob of fine sugar on her lower lip; he wished to wipe it off for her, and in other circumstances would have. "Or heard of him. He's a Jew, they say."

"A Jew?" That startled him. "Surely not." A Jew would never be allowed to take a commission in the army or navy, no more than a Catholic.

Nessie arched a dark brow at him.

"Perhaps he doesna want anyone to know," she said, and, licking her lips like a cat, tidied away the blob of sugar. "But if not, he ought to stay awa' from kittle-hoosies, that's all I can say!" She laughed heartily, then sobered, hunching her bed-sacque over her shoulders and staring at him, dark-eyed in the firelight.

"He's got summat to do wi' your wee lad, the Frenchie, too," she said. "For it was a girl from Jackson's told me about the Jewish cove and what a shock it was to her when he took his breeches off. She said she wouldn't've, only his friend the Frenchie was there, too, wanting to watch, and when he— the Frenchie, I mean—saw she was put off, he offered her double, so she did it. She said when ye came right down to it"—and here she grinned lewdly at him, the tip of her tongue resting against the front teeth she still had—"it was nicer than some."

"Nicer than some," he muttered distractedly to himself, only half-noticing the wary glance cast toward him by the only other ferry passenger hardy enough to stay abovedecks. "Bloody *hell*!"

The snow was falling thickly over the Channel, and now swept nearly horizontal as the howling wind changed direction and the ship gave a sickening lurch. The other man shook himself and went below, leaving Grey to eat brandied peaches with his fingers from a jar in his pocket and stare bleakly at the oncoming coast of France, visible only in glimpses through low-lying clouds.

December 24, 1776
Quebec City

Dear Papa—
I write you from a Convent. Not, I hasten to explain, one of the Covent Garden variety, but a real Roman Convent, run by Ursuline Nuns.
Captain Randall-Isaacs and I arrived at the Citadel in late October, intending to call upon Sir Guy and discover his Opinion of the local Sympathies regarding the American Insurrection, only to be told that Sir Guy had marched to Fort Saint-Jean, to deal personally with an Outbreak of said Insurrection, this being a Sea Battle (or so I suppose I must call it), which took place upon Lake Champlain, this a narrow Body connecting with Lake George, which perhaps you will know from your own Time here.

I was much in favor of going to join Sir Guy, but Captain Randall-Isaacs was reluctant in consideration of the Distance involved and the Time of Year. In Fact his Judgment was proved sound, as the next Day brought freezing Rain, this giving way shortly to a howling Blizzard, so fierce as to darken the Sky so that you could not tell Day from Night, and which buried the World in Snow and Ice within Hours. Seeing this Spectacle of Nature, I will admit that my Disappointment at missing an Opportunity to join Sir Guy was substantially allayed.

As it was, I should have been too late in any Case, as the Engagement had already taken place, upon the 1st October. We did not learn the Particulars until mid-November, when some Hessian Officers from Baron von Riedesel's Regiment arrived at the Citadel with News of it. Most likely you will have heard more official and direct Descriptions of the Engagement by the Time you receive this Letter, but there may be some Details of interest omitted from the official Versions—and to be frank, the Composition of such an Account is the only Employment available to me at present, as I have declined a kind Invitation from the Mother Superior to attend the Mass they hold at midnight tonight in observance of Christmas. (The Bells of the city's Churches ring every quarter Hour, marking time through the Day and Night. The convent's Chapel lies directly beyond the Wall of the Guesthouse in which I am lodged upon the highest Floor, and the Bell is perhaps twenty Feet from my Head when I lie in Bed. I can thus inform you faithfully that it is now 9:15 p.m.)

To particulars, then: Sir Guy was alarmed by the attempted Invasion of Quebec last Year, even though it ended in abject Failure, and had thus determined to increase his Hold upon the upper Hudson, this being the only possible Avenue by which further Trouble could come, the Difficulties of land Travel being so exigent as to prevent any but the most determined (I have a small Jar of spirits of Wine with which to present you, this containing a Deerfly measuring nearly two Inches in Length, as well as a Quantity of very large Ticks, these removed from my Person with the assistance of Honey, which smothers them if applied liberally, causing them to loose their Grip).

While the Invasion of last Winter did not succeed, Colonel Arnold's Men determined to deny Sir Guy Access to the Lakes, and thus sank or burned all the Ships at Fort Saint-Jean as they withdrew, as well as burning the Sawmill and the Fort itself.

Sir Guy had therefore requisitioned collapsible Ships to be sent to him from England (I wish I had seen these!) and, ten of them arriving, went down to St. John to oversee their assembly upon the upper Richelieu River. Meanwhile, Colonel Arnold (who seems an amazing, industrious Fellow, if half what I hear of him is true) had been madly building his own Fleet of ramshackle Galleys and hog-beamed Sloops.

Not content with his Prodigies of collapsibility, Sir Guy also had the Indefatigable, *a Frigate of some 180 tonnes (some Argument between my informants as to the number of Guns she carries; after a second*

Bottle of the convent's Claret [the Nuns make it themselves, and from the Shade of the priest's Nose, no little of it gets consumed here, too], Consensus was reached, with "a bloody Lot, mate," always allowing for Errors of Translation, being the final Number), taken apart, hauled to the River, and there reassembled.

Colonel Arnold apparently decided that to wait any longer was to lose what Advantage of Initiative he might possess, and sallied out from his Hiding place at Valcour Island on 30 September. By Report, he had fifteen Craft, to Sir Guy's twenty-five, these former all hastily built, unseaworthy, and manned by Landsmen who did not know a Binnacle from a Bunion—the American Navy, in all its glory!

Still, I must not laugh too much. The more I hear of Colonel Arnold (and I hear a great Deal about him, here in Quebec), the more I think he must be a Gentleman of Gall and Kidney, as Grandpapa Sir George is wont to say; I should like to meet him one day.

There is Singing outside; the habitants *are coming to the Cathedral nearby. I don't know the Music, and it's too far to make out the Words, but I can see the Glow of Torches from my Eyrie. The Bells say it is ten o'clock.*

(The Mother Superior says that she knows you, by the way—Soeur Immaculata is her Name. I should scarcely have been startled by this; told her that you know the Archbishop of Canterbury and the Pope, by which she professed to be much impressed, and begs you will convey her most humble Obeisance to His Holiness when next you see him. She kindly asked me to Dinner, and told me Stories of the taking of the Citadel in '59, and how you quartered a number of Highlanders upon the Convent. How shocked the Sisters all were by their bare Legs, and sought a Requisition of Canvas that they might make the men Trousers. My Uniform has suffered noticeably through the last few Weeks of Travel, but I am still decently covered below the Waist, I am relieved to say. So was Mother Superior, no doubt!)

*I return to my Account of the Battle: Sir Guy's Fleet sailed south, intending to reach and recapture Crown Point, then Ticonderoga. As they passed Valcour Island, though, two of Arnold's Ships sprang out upon them, firing in challenge. These then attempted to withdraw, but one (*Royal Savage, *they said) could not make Way against the Headwinds, and ran aground. Several British Gunboats swarmed her and captured a few Men, but were forced to withdraw under heavy Fire from the Americans—though not omitting to set Fire to the* Royal Savage *as they did so.*

A great deal of Maneuvering then ensued in the Strait, and the Battle began in earnest about Midday, the Carleton *and* Inflexible *bearing most of the Brunt of the Action, along with the Gunboats. Arnold's* Revenge *and* Philadelphia *were badly hit by Broadsides, and the* Philadelphia *sank near Evening.*

The Carleton *continued firing until a fortunate Shot from the Americans severed the Line to her Anchor, causing her to drift. She was heavily attacked and a number of her Men killed or injured, the Butcher's Bill including her Captain, a Lieutenant James Dacres (I have an uneasy feeling that I have met him, perhaps at a Dance last Season) and the senior Officers. One of her Midshipmen took Command and carried her to Safety. They said it was Edward Pellew—and I know I have met him, once or twice, at Boodles with Uncle Harry.*

To resume: Another lucky Shot struck the Magazine of a Gunboat and blew it up, but meanwhile, the Inflexible *was finally brought into play and battered the American Boats with her heavy Guns. The smaller of Sir Guy's Craft landed Indians meanwhile upon the Shores of Valcour Island and the Shore of the Lake, thus cutting off this Avenue of Escape, and the Remnants of Arnold's Fleet were thus obliged to retreat down the Lake.*

They succeeded in slipping past Sir Guy, the Night being foggy, and took Refuge at Schuyler Island, some miles south. Sir Guy's Fleet pursued them, though, and was able to draw within Sight of them the next Day, Arnold's Boats being much hampered by Leakage, Damage, and the Weather, which had turned to heavy Rain and high Wind. The Washington *was caught, attacked, and forced to strike her Colors, her Crew of more than a hundred Men being captured. The rest of Arnold's Fleet, though, managed to get through to Buttonmold Bay, where, I understand, the Waters are too shallow to allow Sir Guy's Ships to follow.*

There Arnold beached, stripped, and set afire most of his Craft— their Flags still flying, as a Mark of Defiance, the Germans said; they were amused by this, but admired it. Colonel Arnold (or must we now call him Admiral Arnold?) personally set Fire to the Congress, *this being his Flagship, and set off Overland, narrowly escaping the Indians who had been set to prevent him. His troops did reach Crown Point, but did not linger there, pausing only to destroy the Fort before withdrawing to Ticonderoga.*

Sir Guy did not march his Prisoners back to Quebec, but returned them to Ticonderoga under a Flag of Truce—a very pretty Gesture, much admired by my Informants.

10:30. Did you see the aurora borealis *when you were here, or was it too early in the Year? It is a most remarkable Sight. Snow has fallen all Day, but ceased near Sunset and the Sky has cleared. From my Window, I see a northern Exposure, and there is presently an amazing shimmer that fills the whole Sky, waves of pale blue and some green—though I have seen it to be red sometimes—that swirl like Drops of Ink spilt in Water and stirred. I cannot hear it at present, because of the Singing— someone is Playing a Fiddle in the Distance; it is a very sweet and piercing Tune—but when I have seen the Phenomenon outside the City, in the Woods, there is often a most peculiar Sound, or Sounds, that accompany it. Sometimes a sort of faint Whistling, as of Wind around a Building, though there is no Movement of the Air; sometimes a strange, high, hissing Noise, interrupted now and then by a Fusillade of Clicks and Cracklings, as though a Horde of Crickets were advanc-*

ing upon the Listener through dry Leaves—though by the time the Aurora begins to be seen, the Cold has long since killed all Insects (and good riddance! We applied an Ointment used by the local Indians, which was of some help against stinging Flies and Mosquitoes, but does nothing to discourage the inquisitiveness of Lice, Roaches, and Spiders).

We had a Guide for our Journey between St. John and Quebec, a Man of mixed Blood (he had a most remarkable Head of Hair, thick and curly as Sheep's Wool and the color of Cinnamon Bark) who told us that some of the native People think that the Sky is a Dome, separating Earth from Heaven, but that there are Holes in the Dome, and that the Lights of the Aurora are the Torches of Heaven, sent out to guide the Spirits of the Dead through the Holes.

But I see I have yet to finish my Account, though it is only to add that following the Battle, Sir Guy withdrew to winter Quarters in St. John, and likely will not return to Quebec until the Spring.

So now I come to the true Point of my letter. I rose Yesterday to discover Captain Randall-Isaacs had decamped during the Night, leaving me with a brief Note stating that he had urgent Business, had enjoyed my Company and valuable Assistance, and that I was to remain here until either his Return or the arrival of new Orders.

The Snow is deep, more may come at any Moment, and Business must be urgent indeed which could compel a man to venture any Distance. I am of course somewhat disturbed at Captain Randall-Isaacs's abrupt Departure, curious as to what might have happened to cause it, and somewhat anxious as to his Welfare. This does not seem a Situation in which I would be justified in ignoring my Orders, however, and so . . . I wait.

11:30. I stopped writing for some little time, to stand and watch the Sky. The Lights of the Aurora come and go, but I think they have gone altogether now; the Sky is black, the Stars bright but tiny by contrast with the vanished brilliance of the Lights. There is a vast Emptiness in the Sky that one seldom senses in a City. Despite the Clangor of the Bells, the Bonfires in the Square, and the Singing of People—there is a Procession of some kind going on—I can feel the great Silence beyond it.

The Nuns are going in to their Chapel. I leaned out of my Window just now to watch them hurrying along, two by two like a marching Column, their dark Gowns and Cloaks making them look like small Pieces of the Night, drifting among the Stars of their Torches. (I have been writing a long Time, you must forgive the Fancies of an exhausted Brain.)

This is the first Christmas I have spent with no Sight of Home or Family. The First of many, no doubt.

I think of you often, Papa, and hope you are well and looking forward to roast Goose tomorrow with Grandmama and Grandpapa Sir George. Give my Love to them, please, and to Uncle Hal and his family. (And to my Dottie, especially.)

A very merry Christmas from your Son,
William

PostScriptum: 2:00 a.m. I went down after all, and stood at the
Back of the Chapel. It was somewhat Popish, and there was a great
Deal of Incense, but I said a Prayer for Mother Geneva and for Mama
Isobel. When I emerged from the Chapel, I saw that the Lights have
come back. Now they are blue.

 25

THE BOSOM OF THE DEEP

May 15, 1777

My dears,

I hate Boats. I despise them with the utmost Fiber of my Being. And
yet I find myself once more launched upon the dreadful Bosom of the
Sea, aboard a Craft known as the Tranquil Teal, *from which Absurdity*
you may deduce the grim Whimsy of her Captain. This Gentleman is a
Smuggler of mixed Race, evil Countenance, and low Humor, who tells
me, straight-faced, that his name is Trustworthy Roberts.

JAMIE PAUSED TO DIP his quill, glanced at the receding shore of North Carolina, and, observing it to rise and fall in an unsettling manner, fixed his eyes at once upon the page he had tacked to his lap desk to prevent its being borne away by the stiff breeze that filled the sails above his head.

We are in good Health, he wrote slowly. Putting aside the notion of seasickness, upon which he did not propose to dwell. Ought he to tell them about Fergus? he wondered.

"Feeling all right?"

He looked up to see Claire, bending to peer at him with that look of intent but cautious curiosity she reserved for people who might at any moment vomit, spurt blood, or die. He'd already done the first two, as a result of her having accidentally put one of her needles into a small blood vessel in his scalp, but hoped she didn't distinguish any further signs of his impending demise.

"Well enough." He didn't want even to think about his stomach, for fear of inciting it, and changed the subject in order to avoid further discussion. "Shall I tell Brianna and Roger Mac about Fergus?"

"How much ink have you got?" she asked, with a sidelong smile. "Yes, of course you should. They'll be very interested. And it will distract you," she added, squinting slightly at him. "You're still rather green."

"Aye, thanks."

She laughed with the cheerful callousness of the good sailor, kissed the top of his head—avoiding the four needles protruding from his forehead—and went to stand by the rail, watching the wavering land recede from view.

He averted his gaze from this distressing prospect, and returned to his letter.

> *Fergus and his family are also well, but I must tell you of a puzzling occurrence. A man who calls himself Percival Beauchamp...*

It took him most of a page to describe Beauchamp and his baffling interest. He glanced up at Claire, wondering whether he should also include the possibility of Beauchamp's relationship to her family, but decided against it. His daughter certainly knew her mother's maiden name and would notice it at once. He had no further useful information to provide in that respect—and his hand was beginning to ache.

Claire was still at the rail, one hand on it for balance, her face dreaming.

She had tied back the mass of her hair with ribbon, but the wind was whipping strands of it out, and with hair and skirts and shawl streaming back, the cloth of her gown molded to what was still a very fine bosom, he thought she looked like a ship's figurehead, graceful and fierce, a protective spirit against the dangers of the deep.

He found that thought obscurely comforting, and returned to his composition in better heart, despite the disturbing content he had now to confide.

> *Fergus elected not to speak with Monsieur Beauchamp, which I thought wise, and so we presumed this to be the end of the Matter.*
>
> *While we were in Wilmington, though, I went down to the Docks one Evening to meet Mr. DeLancey Hall, our Liaison with Captain Roberts. Owing to the Presence of an English Man-of-war in the Harbor, the Arrangement was that we should repair discreetly aboard Mr. Hall's fishing Ketch, which would transport us outwith the Harbor, whence we should rendezvous with the* Teal, *Captain Roberts disliking close Proximity to the British navy. (This is a fairly universal Response on the part of private and merchant Captains, owing both to the prevalence of Contraband aboard most Ships and to the Navy's rapacious Attitude toward the Ships' Crews, who are routinely abducted—pressed, they call it—and to all Intents and Purposes, enslaved for Life, save they are willing to risk Hanging for Desertion.)*
>
> *I had brought with me some minor Items of Luggage, intending under the Pretext of taking these aboard to inspect both the Ketch and Mr. Hall more closely before entrusting our Lives to either. The Ketch was not at Anchor, though, and Mr. Hall did not appear for some Time, so that I began to worry lest I had mistaken his Instructions or that he had run afoul either of His Majesty's Navy or some fellow Rapscallion or Privateer.*

*I waited until it had grown Dark, and was on the point of return-
ing to our Inn, when I saw a small Boat come into the Harbor with a
blue Lantern at its Tail. This was Mr. Hall's Signal, and the Boat was
his Ketch, which I assisted him to tie up to the Quay. He told me that he
had some News, and we repaired to a local Tavern, where he said that
he had been in New Bern the Day before, and there found the Town in
an Uproar, owing to an infamous Assault upon the Printer, Mr.
Fraser.*

*By report, he—Fergus—was making his Rounds of Delivery, and
had just got down from the Mule Cart when someone sprang upon him
from behind, thrusting a Sack over his Head, and someone else
attempted at the same Time to seize his Hands, presumably with the
Intent of binding them. Fergus naturally resisted these Attempts with
some Vigor, and according to Mr. Hall's Story, succeeded in wounding
one Assailant with his Hook, there being a certain Amount of Blood to
substantiate this Assumption. The wounded Man fell back with a
Scream and uttered loud Oaths (I should have been interested to know
the content of said Oaths, in order to know whether the Speaker might
be French or English, but this Information was not included), whereupon Clarence (who you will remember, I think) became excited and
apparently bit the second Assailant, this Man and Fergus having fallen
against the Mule in their Struggle. The second Man was discouraged by
this vigorous Intervention, but the first returned to the Fray at this
Point, and Fergus—still blinded by the Sack but bellowing for Help—
grappled with him, striking at him again with his Hook. Some Reports
(says Mr. Hall) claim that the Villain wrenched the Hook from Fergus's
Wrist, while others claim that Fergus succeeded in striking him again
but that the Hook became entangled in the Villain's Clothing and was
pulled off in the Struggle.*

*In any Event, people in Thompson's Ordinary heard the Stramash
and rushed out, whereupon the Villains fled, leaving Fergus somewhat
bruised and most indignant at the loss of his Hook, but otherwise
unharmed, for which God and St. Dismas (he being Fergus's particular
Patron) be thanked.*

*I questioned Mr. Hall as closely as I could, but there was little more
to be learned. He said that public Opinion was divided, with many saying that this was an attempted Deportation and the Sons of Liberty
were to blame for the attack, while some members of the Sons of Liberty
indignantly denied this Accusation, claiming that it was the work of
Loyalists incensed over Fergus's printing of a particularly inflamma-
tory Speech by Patrick Henry, and the Abduction was a Prelude to Tar
and Feathers. Apparently Fergus has been so successful in avoiding the
Appearance of taking Sides in the Conflict that both Sides are equally
likely to have taken Offense and decided to eliminate his Influence.*

*This is, of course, possible. But with the Presence and Behavior of
Monsieur Beauchamp in Mind, I think a third Explanation is more
likely. Fergus declined to speak with him, but it would not have
required a great deal of further Inquiry for him to learn that despite*

his Name and Scottish Wife, Fergus is a Frenchman. Surely most of the Inhabitants of New Bern know this, and someone could easily have told him.

I confess myself to be at a Loss as to why Beauchamp should wish to abduct Fergus, rather than simply come and confront him in Person to inquire whether he might be the Person for whom the Gentleman claimed to be searching. I must assume that he does not mean Fergus immediate Harm, for if he did, it would be a fairly simple Matter to have arranged to have him killed; there are a great many Men of no Attachment and mean Character drifting through the Colony these Days.

The Occurrence is worrying, but there is little I can do about it in my present abject Position. I have sent Fergus a Letter—ostensibly regarding the Specifications of a printing Job—which lets him know that I have placed a Sum with a Goldsmith in Wilmington, which he may draw upon in case of Need. I had discussed with him the Dangers of his present Position, not knowing at the Time how dangerous they might actually be, and he agreed that there might be some Advantage to his Family's Safety in his moving to a City where public Opinion is more strongly aligned with his own Inclinations. This latest Incident may compel his Decision, the more particularly as Proximity to ourselves is no longer a Consideration.

He had to stop again, as pain was radiating through his hand and up his wrist. He stretched the fingers, stifling a groan; a hot wire seemed to stab from his fourth finger up his forearm in brief electric jolts.

He was more than worried for Fergus and his family. If Beauchamp had tried once, he would try again. But why?

Perhaps the fact of Fergus's being French was not sufficient evidence that he was the Claudel Fraser that Beauchamp sought, and he proposed to satisfy himself upon this point in privacy, by whatever means came to hand? Possible, but that argued a coldness of purpose that disturbed Jamie more than he had wished to say in his letter.

And in fairness, he must admit that the notion of the attack having been executed by persons of inflamed political sensibility was a distinct possibility, and perhaps of a higher probability than the sinister designs of Monsieur Beauchamp, which were both romantical and theoretical to a high degree.

"But I havena lived this long without knowing the smell of a rat when I see one," he muttered, still rubbing his hand.

"Jesus H. Roosevelt Christ!" said his personal figurehead, appearing suddenly beside him with an expression of marked concern. "Your hand!"

"Aye?" He looked down at it, cross with discomfort. "What's amiss? All my fingers are still attached to it."

"That's the most that could be said for it. It looks like the Gordian knot." She knelt down beside him and took the hand into hers, massaging it in a forceful way that was doubtless helpful but so immediately painful that it made his eyes water. He closed them, breathing slowly through clenched teeth.

She was scolding him for writing too much at once. What was the hurry, after all?

"It will be days before we reach Connecticut, and then *months* on the way to Scotland. You could write one sentence per day and quote the whole Book of Psalms along the way."

"I wanted to," he said.

She said something derogatory under her breath, in which the words "Scot" and "pigheaded" featured, but he chose to take no notice. He *had* wanted to; it clarified his thoughts to put them down in black and white, and it was to some degree a relief to express them on paper, rather than to have the worry clogged up in his head like mud in mangrove roots.

And beyond that—not that he required an excuse, he thought, narrowing his eyes at the top of his wife's bent head—seeing the shore of North Carolina drop away had made him lonely for his daughter and Roger Mac, and he'd wanted the sense of connection that writing to them gave him.

"Do you think you will see them?" Fergus had asked him that, soon before they took leave of each other. *"Perhaps you will go to France."* So far as Fergus and Marsali and the folk on the Ridge were concerned, Brianna and Roger Mac had gone to France to escape the oncoming war.

"No," he'd said, hoping the bleakness of his heart didn't show in his voice. "I doubt we shall ever see them again."

Fergus's strong right hand had tightened on his forearm, then relaxed.

"Life is long," he said quietly.

"Aye," he'd answered, but thought, *No one's life is that long.*

His hand was growing easier now; while she still massaged it, the motion no longer hurt so much.

"I miss them, too," she said quietly, and kissed his knuckles. "Give me the letter; I'll finish it."

Your father's hand won't stand any more today. There is one notable thing about this ship, beyond the captain's name. I was down in the hold earlier in the day, and saw a good number of boxes, all stenciled with the name "Arnold" and "New Haven, Connecticut." I said to the hand (whose name is a very pedestrian John Smith, though no doubt to make up for this distressing lack of distinction he has three gold earrings in one ear and two in the other. He told me that each one represents his survival from the sinking of a ship. I am hoping that your father doesn't know this) that Mr. Arnold must be a very successful merchant. Mr. Smith laughed and said that, in fact, Mr. Benedict Arnold is a colonel in the Continental army, and a very gallant officer he is, too. The boxes are bound for delivery to his sister, Miss Hannah Arnold, who minds both his three small sons and his importing and dry-goods store in Connecticut, while he is about the business of the war.

I must say that a goose walked across my grave when I heard that. I've met men whose history I knew before—and at least one of those I knew to carry a doom with him. You don't get used to the feeling, though. I looked at those boxes and wondered—ought I to write to Miss Hannah? Get off the ship in New Haven and go to see her? And tell her what, exactly?

All our experience to date suggests that there is absolutely nothing I could do to alter what's going to happen. And looking at the situation objectively, I don't see any way . . . and yet. And yet!

And yet, I've come close to so many people whose actions have a noticeable effect, whether or not they end up making history as such. How can it not be so? your father says. Everyone's actions have some effect upon the future. And plainly he's right. And yet, to brush so close to a name like Benedict Arnold gives one a right turn, as Captain Roberts is fond of saying. (No doubt a situation that gave one a left turn would be very shocking indeed.)

Well. Returning tangentially to the original subject of this letter, the mysterious Monsieur Beauchamp. If your father's—Frank's, I mean— if you still have the boxes of papers and books from his home office, and a free moment, you might go through them and see if you find an old manila folder in there, with a coat of arms drawn on it in colored pencil. I think that it's azure and gold, and I recall that it has martlets on it. With luck, it still contains the Beauchamp family genealogy that my uncle Lamb wrote up for me, lo these many years ago.

You might just have a look and see whether the incumbent of the name in 1777 was perhaps a Percival. For the sake of curiosity.

The wind's come up a bit, and the water's getting rough. Your father has gone rather pale and clammy, like fish bait; I'll close and take him down below for a nice quiet vomit and a nap, I think.

All my love,
Mama

26

STAG AT BAY

ROGER BLEW THOUGHTFULLY ACROSS the mouth of an empty stout bottle, making a low, throaty moan. Close. A little deeper, though . . . and of course it lacked that hungry sound, that growling note. But the pitch . . . He got up and rummaged in the refrigerator, finding what he was looking for behind a heel of cheese and six margarine tubs full of God knew what; he'd lay odds it wasn't margarine.

There was no more than an inch or so of champagne left in the bottle—a remnant of their celebratory dinner the week before, in honor of Bree's new job. Someone had thriftily covered the neck of the bottle with tinfoil, but the wine had of course gone flat. He went to pour it out in the sink, but a lifetime of Scottish thrift was not so easily dismissed. With no more than an instant's hesitation, he drank the rest of the champagne, lowering the empty bottle to see Annie MacDonald holding Amanda by the hand and staring at him.

"Well, at least ye're no puttin' it on your cornflakes yet," she said, edging past him. "Here, pet, up ye go." She hoisted Mandy into her booster seat and went out, shaking her head over her employer's low moral character.

"Gimme, Daddy!" Mandy reached for the bottle, attracted by the shiny label. With the statutory parental pause as he mentally ran through potential scenarios of destruction, he instead gave her his glass of milk and hooted across the champagne bottle's fluted lip, producing a deep, melodious tone. Yes, that was it—something close to the F below middle C.

"Do again, Daddy!" Mandy was charmed. Feeling mildly self-conscious, he hooted again, making her fall about in a cascade of giggles. He picked up the stout bottle and blew across that one, then alternated, working up a two-note variation to the rhythm of "Mary Had a Little Lamb."

Attracted by the hooting and Mandy's ecstatic shrieks, Brianna appeared in the doorway, a bright blue plastic hard hat in her hand.

"Planning to start your own jug band?" she asked.

"Already got one," he replied, and having decided that the worst thing Mandy could do with the champagne bottle was drop it onto the rug, handed it to her and stepped out into the hall with Brianna, where he pulled her close and kissed her deeply, the baize door swinging shut with a cushioned *foosh*.

"Champagne for breakfast?" she broke the kiss long enough to ask, then returned for more, tasting him.

"Needed the bottle," he mumbled, tasting back. She'd had porridge with butter and honey for breakfast, and her mouth was sweet, turning the champagne bitter on the edges of his tongue. The hall was chilly, but she was warm as toast under her fleece jumper. His fingers lingered just under the edge of it, on the bare soft skin at the small of her back.

"Ye'll have a good day, aye?" he whispered. He fought the urge to slide his fingers down the back of her jeans; not respectful to be fingering the arse of a brand-new inspector of the North of Scotland Hydro Electric Board. "You're bringing the hat home, after?"

"Sure. Why?"

"Thought ye might wear it in bed." He took it from her hand and set it gently on her head. It made her eyes go navy blue. "Wear it, and I'll tell ye what I wanted with the champagne bottle."

"Oh, now there's an offer I can't re—" The navy-blue eyes slid suddenly sideways, and Roger glanced in that direction, to see Annie at the end of the hall, broom and dustpan in hand and an expression of deep interest on her narrow face.

"Yeah. Ah . . . have a good day," Roger said, letting go hastily.

"You, too." Face twitching, Brianna took him firmly by the shoulders and kissed him, before striding down the hall and past a round-eyed Annie, whom she airily wished good day in the Gaelic.

A sudden crash came from the kitchen. He turned automatically toward the baize door, though less than half his attention was on the incipient disaster. The greater part was focused on the sudden realization that his wife appeared to have departed for work wearing no knickers.

MANDY HAD, God knew how, managed to throw the champagne bottle through the window and was standing on the table, reaching for the jagged edge of the pane, when Roger rushed in.

"Mandy!" He grabbed her, swung her off the table, and in the same motion smacked her bottom once. She emitted an ear-piercing howl, and he carried her out under his arm, passing Annie Mac, who stood in the doorway with mouth and eyes all round as "O"s.

"See to the glass, aye?" he said.

He felt guilty as hell; what had he been thinking, handing her the bottle? Let alone leaving her by herself with it!

He also felt a certain irritation with Annie Mac—after all, she was employed to watch the children—but fairness made him admit that he ought to have made sure she'd come back to watch Mandy before he left. The irritation extended to Bree, as well, prancing off to her new job, expecting him to mind the household.

He recognized that the irritation was only his attempt to escape the guilt, though, and did his best to put it aside while soothing Mandy, having a wee chat about not standing on tables, not throwing things in the house, not touching sharp things, calling for a grown-up if she needed help—fat chance, he thought, with a wry inward smile; Mandy was the most independent three-year-old he'd ever seen. Which was saying something, considering that he'd also seen Jem at that age.

One thing about Amanda: she didn't hold a grudge. Five minutes after being smacked and scolded, she was giggling and begging him to play dollies with her.

"Daddy's got to work this morning," he said, but bent so she could scramble onto his shoulders. "Come on, we'll find Annie Mac; you and the dollies can maybe help her get the pantry sorted."

Leaving Mandy and Annie Mac happily working in the pantry, supervised by an assortment of scabby-looking dolls and grubby stuffed animals, he went back to his office and got out the notebook into which he was transcribing the songs he'd so painstakingly committed to memory. He had an appointment later in the week to talk with Siegfried MacLeod, the choirmaster at St. Stephen's, and had it in mind to present him with a copy of some of the rarer songs, by way of creating goodwill.

He thought he might need it. Dr. Weatherspoon had been reassuring, saying that MacLeod would be delighted to have help, especially with the children's choir, but Roger had spent enough time in academic circles, Masonic lodges, and eighteenth-century taverns to know how local politics worked. MacLeod might well resent having an outsider—so to speak—foisted on him without warning.

And there was the delicate issue of a choirmaster who couldn't sing. He touched his throat, with its pebbled scar.

He'd seen two specialists, one in Boston, another in London. Both of them had said the same thing. There was a possibility that surgery might improve his voice, by removing some of the scarring in his larynx. There was an equal possibility that the surgery might further damage—or completely destroy—his voice.

"Surgery on the vocal cords is a delicate business," one of the doctors had said to him, shaking his head. "Normally, we don't risk it unless there's a dire necessity, such as a cancerous growth, a congenital malformation that's preventing any useful speech—or a strong professional reason. A well-known singer with nodules, for instance; in that case, the desire to restore the voice might be sufficient motive to risk surgery—though in such cases, there usually isn't a major risk of rendering the person permanently mute. In your case . . ."

He pressed two fingers against his throat and hummed, feeling the reassuring vibration. No. He remembered all too well what it felt like to be unable to speak. He'd been convinced at the time that he'd never speak—let alone sing—again; the memory of that despair made him sweat. Never speak to his children, to Bree? No, he wasn't risking that.

Dr. Weatherspoon's eyes had lingered on his throat with interest, but he hadn't said anything. MacLeod might be less tactful.

Whom the Lord loveth, he chasteneth. Weatherspoon—to his credit—hadn't said that in the course of their discussion. It had, however, been the quotation chosen for that week's Bible group; it had been printed on their flyer, which was sitting on the rector's desk. And in Roger's hypersensitive frame of mind at the time, everything looked like a message.

"Well, if that's what Ye've got in mind, I appreciate the compliment," he said out loud. "Be all right with me if I wasn't Your favorite just this week, though."

It was said half jokingly, but there was no denying the anger behind it. Resentment at having to prove himself—*to* himself—one more time. He'd had to do it physically last time. Now to do it again, spiritually, in this slippery, less straightforward world? He'd been willing, hadn't he?

"You asked. Since when do Ye not take yes for an answer? Am I missing something here?"

Bree had thought so; the height of their quarrel came back to him now, making him flush with shame.

"You had—I *thought* you had," she'd corrected, "a vocation. Maybe that's not what Protestants call it, but that's what it *is*, isn't it? You told me that God spoke to you." Her eyes were intent on his, unswerving, and so penetrating that he wanted to look away—but didn't.

"Do you think God changes His mind?" she asked more quietly, and laid her hand on his arm, squeezing. "Or do you think you were mistaken?"

"No," he'd said, in instant reflex. "No, when something like that happens . . . well, when it *did* happen, I wasn't in any doubt."

"Are you now?"

"You sound like your mother. Making a diagnosis." He'd meant it as a joke, but it wasn't. Bree resembled her father physically to such a degree that he seldom saw Claire in her, but the calm ruthlessness in her questions was Claire Beauchamp to the life. So was the slight arch of one brow, waiting for an answer. He took a deep breath. "I don't know."

"Yes, you do."

Anger bubbled up, sudden and bright, and he'd jerked his arm away from her grasp.

"Where in hell do you get off telling me what I know?"

She widened her stare. "I'm *married* to you."

"You think that entitles you to try to read my mind?"

"I think that entitles me to worry about you!"

"Well, don't!"

They'd made it up, of course. Kissed—well, a bit more than that—and forgiven each other. Forgiving, of course, didn't mean forgetting.

"Yes, you do."

Did he know?

"Yes," he said defiantly to the broch, visible from his window. "Yes, I damned well do!" What to do about it: that was the difficulty.

Was he perhaps meant to be a minister but not a Presbyterian? Become a nondenominational, an evangelical . . . a *Catholic*? The thought was so disturbing, he was obliged to get up and walk to and fro for a bit. It wasn't that he had anything against Catholics—well, bar the reflexes inbred by a life spent as a Protestant in the Highlands—but he just couldn't see it. "Going over to Rome" was how Mrs. Ogilvy and Mrs. MacNeil and all the rest of them would see it ("Going straight to the Bad Place" being the unspoken implication); his defection would be discussed in tones of low horror for . . . well, for years. He grinned reluctantly at the thought.

Well, and besides, he couldn't be a Catholic priest, now, could he? Not with Bree and the kids. That made him feel a little calmer, and he sat down again. No. He'd have to trust that God—through the agency of Dr. Weatherspoon—proposed to show him the way through this particular thorny passage of his life. And if He did . . . well, was that not evidence of predestination in itself?

Roger groaned, thrust the whole thing out of his head, and immersed himself doggedly in his notebook.

Some of the songs and poems he'd written down were well-known: selections from his previous life, traditional songs he'd sung as a performer. Many of the rare ones, he'd acquired during the eighteenth century, from Scottish immigrants, travelers, peddlers, and seamen. And some he'd unearthed from the trove of boxes the Reverend had left behind. The garage of the old manse had been filled with them, and he and Bree had made no more than a dent in it. Pure luck that he'd run across the wooden box of letters so soon after their return.

He glanced up at it, tempted. He couldn't read the letters without Bree; that wouldn't be right. But the two books—they'd looked briefly at the books when they found the box, but had been concerned mostly with the letters and with finding out what had happened to Claire and Jamie. Feeling like Jem absconding with a packet of chocolate biscuits, he brought the box down carefully—it was very heavy—and set it on the desk, rummaging carefully down under the letters.

The books were small, the largest what was called a crown octavo volume, about five by seven inches. It was a common size, from a time when paper was expensive and difficult to get. The smaller was likely a crown sixteenmo, only about four by five inches. He smiled briefly, thinking of Ian Murray; Brianna had told him her cousin's scandalized response to her description of toilet paper. He might never wipe his arse again without a feeling of extravagance.

The small one was carefully bound in blue-dyed calfskin, with gilt-edged pages; an expensive, beautiful book. *Pocket Principles of Health,* it was entitled, by *C. E. B. R. Fraser, M.D.* A limited edition, produced by *A. Bell, Printer, Edinburgh.*

That gave him a small thrill. So they'd made it to Scotland, under the care of Captain Trustworthy Roberts. Or at least he supposed they must—though the scholar in him cautioned that this wasn't proof; it was always possible that the manuscript had somehow made it to Scotland, without necessarily being carried in person by the author.

Had they come here? he wondered. He looked around the worn, comfortable room, easily envisioning Jamie at the big old desk by the window, going through the farm ledgers with his brother-in-law. If the kitchen was the heart of the house—and it was—this room had likely always been its brain.

Moved by impulse, he opened the book and nearly choked. The frontispiece, in customary eighteenth-century style, showed an engraving of the author. A medical man, in a neat tiewig and black coat, with a high black stock. From above which his mother-in-law's face looked serenely out at him.

He laughed out loud, causing Annie Mac to peer cautiously in at him, in case he might be having a fit of some kind, as well as talking to himself. He waved her off and shut the door before returning to the book.

It was her, all right. The wide-spaced eyes under dark brows, the graceful firm bones of cheek, temple, and jaw. Whoever had done the engraving had not got her mouth quite right; it had a sterner shape here, and a good thing, too—no man had lips like hers.

How old...? He checked the date of printing: MDCCLXXVIII. 1778. Not much older than when he'd last seen her, then—and looking still a good deal younger than he knew her to be.

Was there a picture of Jamie in the other...? He seized it and flipped it open. Sure enough, another steel-point engraving, though this was a more homely drawing. His father-in-law sat in a wing chair, his hair tied simply back, a plaid draped over the chair behind him, and a book open upon his knee. He was reading to a small child sitting upon his other knee—a little girl with dark curly hair. She was turned away, absorbed in the story. Of course—the engraver couldn't have known what Mandy's face would look like.

Grandfather Tales, the book was titled, with the subtitle, "Stories from the Highlands of Scotland and the Backcountry of the Carolinas," by *James Alexander Malcolm MacKenzie Fraser.* Again, printed by *A. Bell, Edinburgh,* in the same year. The dedication said simply, *For my grandchildren.*

Claire's portrait had made him laugh; this one moved him almost to tears, and he closed the book gently.

Such faith they had had. To create, to hoard, to send these things, these fragile documents, down through the years, with only the hope that they would survive and reach those for whom they were intended. Faith that Mandy would be here to read them one day. He swallowed, the lump in his throat painful.

How had they managed it? Well, they did say faith moved mountains, even if his own seemed presently not adequate to flatten a molehill.

"Jesus," he muttered, not sure if this was simple frustration or a prayer for assistance.

A flicker of motion through the window distracted him from the paper, and he glanced up to see Jem coming out of the kitchen door at the far end of the house. He was red in the face, small shoulders hunched, and had a large string bag in one hand, through which Roger could see a bottle of lemon squash, a loaf of bread, and a few other foodlike bulges. Startled, Roger looked at the clock on the mantel, thinking he had lost complete track of time—but he hadn't. It was just on one o'clock.

"What the—" Shoving the paper aside, he got up and made for the back of the house, emerging just in time to see Jem's small figure, clad in wind-cheater and jeans—he wasn't allowed to wear jeans to school—making its way across the hayfield.

Roger could have caught him up easily, but instead slowed his pace, following at a distance.

Plainly Jem wasn't ill—so likely something drastic had happened at school. Had the school sent him home, or had he simply left on his own? No one had called, but it was just past the school's dinner hour; if Jem had seized the opportunity to run for it, it was possible they hadn't yet missed him. It was nearly two miles to walk, but that was nothing to Jem.

Jem had got to the stile in the drystone dyke that walled the field, hopped over, and was making determinedly across a pasture full of sheep. Where was he heading?

"And what the bloody hell did you do this time?" Roger muttered to himself.

Jem had been in the village school at Broch Mordha for only a couple of months—his first experience with twentieth-century education. After their return, Roger had tutored Jem at home in Boston, while Bree was with Mandy during her recovery from the surgery that had saved her life. With Mandy safe home again, they'd had to decide what to do next.

It was mostly Jem that had made them go to Scotland rather than stay in Boston, though Bree had wanted that anyway.

"It's their heritage," she'd argued. "Jem and Mandy are Scots on both sides, after all. I want to keep that for them." And the connection with their grandfather; that went without saying.

He'd agreed, and agreed also that Jem would likely be less conspicuous in Scotland—despite exposure to television and months in the United States, he still spoke with a strong Highland lilt that would make him a marked man in a Boston elementary school. On the other hand, as Roger observed privately, Jem was the sort of person who drew attention, no matter what.

Still, there was no question that life on Lallybroch and in a small Highland school were a great deal more like what Jem had been accustomed to in North Carolina—though given the natural flexibility of kids, he thought he'd adapt pretty well to wherever he found himself.

As to his own prospects in Scotland . . . he'd kept quiet about that.

Jem had reached the end of the pasture and shooed off a group of sheep that were blocking the gate that led to the road. A black ram lowered its head and menaced him, but Jem wasn't bothered about sheep; he shouted and swung his bag, and the ram, startled, backed up sharply, making Roger smile.

He had no qualms about Jem's intelligence—well, he did, but not about its lack. Much more about what kind of trouble it could lead him into. School wasn't simple for anyone, let alone a new school. And a school in which one stuck out, for any reason . . . Roger remembered his own school in Inverness, where he was peculiar first for having no real parents, and then as the minister's adopted son. After a few miserable weeks of being poked, taunted, and having his lunch stolen, he'd started hitting back. And while that had led to a certain amount of difficulty with the teachers, it had eventually taken care of the problem.

Had Jem been fighting? He hadn't seen any blood, but he might not have been close enough. He'd be surprised if it was that, though.

There'd been an incident the week before, when Jem had noticed a large rat scurrying into a hole under the school's foundation. He had brought a bit of twine with him next day, set a snare just before going in to the first lesson, and gone out at the recess to retrieve his prey, which he had then proceeded to skin in a businesslike manner, to the admiration of his male classmates and the horror of the girls. His teacher hadn't been best pleased, either; Miss Glendenning was a city woman from Aberdeen.

Still, it was a Highland village school, and most of the students came from the nearby farms and crofts. Their fathers fished and hunted—and they certainly understood about rats. The principal, Mr. Menzies, had congratulated Jem on his cunning, but told him not to do it again at school. He had let Jem keep the skin, though; Roger had nailed it ceremoniously to the door of the toolshed.

Jem didn't trouble opening the pasture gate; just ducked between the bars, dragging the bag after him.

Was he making for the main road, planning to hitchhike? Roger put on a bit of speed, dodging black sheep droppings and kneeing his way through a cluster of grazing ewes, who gave way in indignation, uttering sharp *baah*s.

No, Jem had turned the other way. Where the devil could he be going? The dirt lane that led to the main road in one direction led absolutely nowhere in the other—it petered out where the land rose into steep, rocky hills.

And that, evidently, was where Jem was headed—for the hills. He turned out of the lane and began climbing, his small form almost obscured by the luxuriant growth of bracken and the drooping branches of rowan trees on the lower slopes. Evidently he was taking to the heather, in the time-honored manner of Highland outlaws.

It was the thought of Highland outlaws that made the penny drop. Jem was heading for the Dunbonnet's cave.

Jamie Fraser had lived there for seven years after the catastrophe of Culloden, almost within sight of his home but hidden from Cumberland's soldiers—and protected by his tenants, who never used his name aloud but called him "the Dunbonnet," for the color of the knitted Highland bonnet he wore to conceal his fiery hair.

That same hair flashed like a beacon, halfway up the slope, before disappearing again behind a rock.

Realizing that, red hair or no, he could easily lose Jem in the rugged landscape, Roger lengthened his stride. Ought he to call out? He knew approximately where the cave was—Brianna had described its location to him—but he hadn't yet been up there himself. It occurred to him to wonder how Jem knew where it was. Perhaps he didn't and was searching for it.

Still, he didn't call, but started up the hill himself. Now he came to look, he could see the narrow path of a deer trail through the growth and the partial print of a small sneaker in the mud of it. He relaxed a little at the sight, and slowed down. He wouldn't lose Jem now.

It was quiet on the hillside, but the air was moving, restless in the rowan trees.

The heather was a haze of rich purple in the hollows of the soaring rock above him. He caught the tang of something on the wind and turned after it, curious. Another flash of red: a stag, splendidly antlered and reeking of rut, ten paces from him on the slope below. He froze, but the deer's head came up, wide black nostrils flaring to scent the air.

He realized suddenly that his hand was pressed against his belt, where he'd once carried a skinning knife, and his muscles were tensed, ready to rush down and cut the deer's throat, once the hunter's shot took it down. He could all but feel the tough hairy skin, the pop of the windpipe, and the gush of hot, reeking blood over his hands, see the long yellow teeth exposed, slimed with the green of the deer's last meal.

The stag belled, a guttural, echoing roar, his challenge to any other stag within hearing. For the space of a breath, Roger expected one of Ian's arrows to whir out of the rowans behind the deer or the echo of Jamie's rifle to crack the air. Then he shook himself back into his skin and, bending, picked up a stone to throw—but the deer had heard him and was off, with a crash that took it rattling into the dry bracken.

He stood still, smelling his own sweat, still dislocated. But it wasn't the North Carolina mountains, and the knife in his pocket was meant for cutting twine and opening beer bottles.

His heart was pounding, but he turned back to the trail, still fitting himself back into time and place. Surely it got easier with practice? They'd been back well more than a year now, and still he woke sometimes at night with no notion where or when he was—or, worse, stepped through some momentary wormhole into the past while still awake.

The kids, being kids, hadn't seemed to suffer much from that sense of being . . . otherwhere. Mandy, of course, had been too young and too sick to remember anything, either of her life in North Carolina or the trip through the stones. Jem remembered. But Jem—he'd taken one look at the automobiles on the road they'd reached half an hour after their emergence from the stones on Ocracoke and stood transfixed, a huge grin spreading across his face as the cars whizzed past him.

"Vroom," he'd said contentedly to himself, the trauma of separation and time travel—Roger had himself barely been able to walk, feeling that he had left a major and irretrievable piece of himself trapped in the stones— apparently forgotten.

A kindly motorist had stopped for them, sympathized with their story of a boating accident, and driven them to the village, where a collect phone call to Joe Abernathy had sorted out the immediate contingencies of money, clothes, a room, and food. Jem had sat on Roger's knee, gazing open-mouthed out the window as they drove up the narrow road, the wind from the open window fluttering his soft, bright hair.

Couldn't wait to do it again. And once they'd got settled at Lallybroch, had pestered Roger into letting him drive the Morris Mini round the farm tracks, sitting in Roger's lap, small hands clenching the steering wheel in glee.

Roger smiled wryly to himself; he supposed he was lucky Jem had decided to abscond on foot this time—another year or two, and he'd likely be tall enough to reach the pedals. He'd best start hiding the car keys.

He was high above the farm now, and slowed to look up the slope. Brianna had said the cave was on the south face of the hill, about forty feet above a large whitish boulder known locally as "Leap o' the Cask." So known because the Dunbonnet's servant, bringing ale to the hidden laird, had encountered a group of British soldiers and, refusing to give them the cask he carried, had had his hand cut off—

"Oh, Jesus," Roger whispered. "Fergus. Oh, God, Fergus." Could see at once the laughing, fine-boned face, dark eyes snapping with amusement as he lifted a flapping fish with the hook he wore in place of his missing left hand— and the vision of a small, limp hand, lying bloody on the path before him.

Because it was here. Right here. Turning, he saw the rock, big and rough, bearing silent, stolid witness to horror and despair—and to the sudden grip of the past that took him by the throat, fierce as the bite of a noose.

He coughed hard, trying to open his throat, and heard the hoarse eerie bell of another stag, close above him on the slope but still invisible.

He ducked off the trail, flattening himself against the rock. Surely to God he hadn't sounded bad enough that the stag had taken him for a rival? No— more likely it was coming down in challenge to the one he'd seen a few moments before.

Sure enough; an instant later a big stag came down from above, picking its way almost daintily through heather and rocks. It was a fine animal, but was already showing the strain of rutting season, its ribs shadowed under the thick coat and the flesh of its face sunk in, eyes red with sleeplessness and lust.

It saw him; the big head swiveled in his direction, and he saw the rolling, bloodshot eyes fix on him. It wasn't afraid of him, though; likely had no room in its brain for anything save fighting and copulation. It stretched its neck in his direction and belled at him, eyes showing white with the effort.

"Look, mate, you want her, you can have her." He backed slowly away, but the deer followed him, menacing him with lowered antlers. Alarmed, he spread his arms, waved and shouted at the deer; normally that would have sent it bounding away. Red deer in rut weren't normal; the thing lowered its head and charged him.

Roger dodged aside and threw himself flat at the base of the rock. He was wedged as tightly next the rock's face as he could get, in hopes of keeping the maddened stag from trampling him. It stumbled to a stop a few feet from him, thrashing at the heather with its antlers and breathing like a bellows—but then it heard the blatting of the challenger below, and jerked its head up.

Another roar from below, and the new stag turned on its haunches and bounded clear over the trail, the sound of its hell-bent passage down the slope marked by the crunch of breaking heather and the rattle of stones spurned by its hooves.

Roger scrambled to his feet, adrenaline running through his veins like quicksilver. He hadn't realized the red deer were at it up here, or he'd not have been wasting time strolling along maundering about the past. He needed to find Jem *now*, before the boy ran afoul of one of the things.

He could hear the roars and clashing of the two below, fighting it out for control of a harem of hinds, though they were out of sight from where he stood.

"Jem!" he bellowed, not caring whether he sounded like a rutting deer or a bull elephant. "Jem! Where are you? Answer me this minute!"

"I'm up here, Da." Jemmy's voice came from above him, a little tremulous, and he whirled to see Jem sitting on the Leap o' the Cask, string bag clutched to his chest.

"Right, you. Down. Now." Relief fought with annoyance but edged it out. He reached up, and Jem slid down the rock, landing heavily in his father's arms.

Roger grunted and set him down, then leaned down to pick up the string bag, which had fallen to the ground. In addition to bread and lemon squash, he saw, it held several apples, a large chunk of cheese, and a packet of chocolate biscuits.

"Planning to stay for a while, were ye?" he asked. Jemmy flushed and looked away.

Roger turned and looked up the slope.

"Up there, is it? Your grandda's cave?" He couldn't see a thing; the slope was a jumble of rock and heather, liberally splotched with scrubby gorse bushes and the odd sprout of rowan and alder.

"Aye. Just there." Jemmy pointed up the slope. "See, where that witch tree's leaning?"

He saw the rowan—a full-grown tree, gnarled with age; surely it couldn't have been there since Jamie's time, could it?—but still saw no sign of the cave's opening. The sounds of combat from below had ceased; he glanced round in case the loser should be coming back this way, but evidently not.

"Show me," he said.

Jem, who had been looking deeply uneasy, relaxed a little at this and, turning, scrambled up the slope, Roger at his heels.

You could be right next to the cave's opening and never see it. It was screened by an outcrop of rock and a heavy growth of gorse; you couldn't see the narrow opening at all unless you were standing in front of it.

A cool breath came out of the cave, moist on his face. He knelt down to peer in; couldn't see more than a few feet inside, but it wasn't inviting.

"Be cold to sleep in there," he said. He glanced at Jem, and motioned to a nearby rock.

"Want to sit down and tell me what happened at school?"

Jem swallowed and shifted from foot to foot.

"No."

"Sit down." He didn't raise his voice, but made it evident he expected to be obeyed. Jem didn't quite sit down but edged backward, leaning against the rocky outcrop that hid the cave mouth. He wouldn't look up.

"I got the strap," Jem muttered, chin buried in his chest.

"Oh?" Roger kept his voice casual. "Well, that's a bugger. I got it once or twice, when I was at school. Didn't like it."

Jem's head jerked up, eyes wide.

"Aye? What for, then?"

"Fighting, mostly," Roger said. He supposed he oughtn't to be telling the boy that—bad example—but it was the truth. And if fighting was Jem's problem . . .

"That what happened today?" He'd looked Jem over briefly when he sat down, and gave him a closer look now. Jem seemed undamaged, but when he turned his head away, Roger could see that something had happened to his ear. It was a deep crimson, the lobe of it nearly purple. He suppressed an exclamation at sight of it and merely repeated, "What happened?"

"Jacky McEnroe said if ye heard I'd got the strap, ye'd give me another whipping when I got home." Jem swallowed, but now looked at his father directly. "Will you?"

"I don't know. I hope I won't have to."

He'd tawsed Jemmy once—he'd had to—and neither of them wanted to repeat the experience. He reached out and touched Jem's flaming ear gently.

"Tell me what happened, son."

Jem took a deep breath, blowing out his cheeks, then deflated into resignation.

"Aye. Well, it started when Jimmy Glasscock said Mam and me and Mandy were all goin' to burn in hell."

"Yeah?" Roger wasn't all that surprised; Scottish Presbyterians weren't known for their religious flexibility, and the breed hadn't altered all that much in two hundred years. Manners might keep most of them from telling their papist acquaintance they were going straight to hell—but most of them likely thought it.

"Well, ye know what to do about that, though, don't you?" Jem had heard similar sentiments expressed on the Ridge—though generally more quietly, Jamie Fraser being who he was. Still, they'd talked about it, and Jem was well prepared to answer that particular conversational gambit.

"Oh, aye." Jem shrugged, looking down at his shoes again. "Just say, 'Aye, fine, I'll see ye there, then.' I did."

"And?"

Deep sigh.

"I said it in the *Gàidhlig.*"

Roger scratched behind his ear, puzzled. Gaelic was disappearing in the Highlands, but was still common enough that you heard it once in a while in the pub or the post office. No doubt a few of Jem's classmates had heard it from their grans, but even if they didn't understand what he'd said . . . ?

"And?" he repeated.

"And Miss Glendenning grabbed me by the ear and like to tore it off." A flush was rising in Jemmy's cheeks at the memory. "She shook me, Da!"

"By the ear?" Roger felt an answering flush in his own cheeks.

"Yes!" Tears of humiliation and anger were welling in Jem's eyes, but he dashed them away with a sleeve and pounded his fist on his leg. "She said, 'We—do—not—speak—like—THAT! We—speak—ENGLISH!'" His voice was some octaves higher than the redoubtable Miss Glendenning's, but his mimicry made the ferocity of her attack more than evident.

"And then she took a strap to you?" Roger asked incredulously.

Jem shook his head, and wiped his nose on his sleeve.

"No," he said. "That was Mr. Menzies."

"What? Why? Here." He handed Jem a crumpled paper handkerchief from his pocket, and waited while the boy blew his nose.

"Well . . . I was already fussed wi' Jimmy, and when she grabbed me like that, it hurt bad. And . . . well, my dander got up," he said, giving Roger a blue-eyed look of burning righteousness that was so much his grandfather that Roger nearly smiled, despite the situation.

"And ye said something else to her, did ye?"

"Aye." Jem dropped his eyes, rubbing the toe of his sneaker in the dirt. "Miss Glendenning doesna like the *Gàidhlig,* but she doesn't know any, either. Mr. Menzies does."

"Oh, God."

Drawn by the shouting, Mr. Menzies had emerged onto the play yard just in time to hear Jem giving Miss Glendenning the benefit of some of his grandfather's best Gaelic curses, at the top of his lungs.

"So he made me bend over a chair and gave me three good ones, then sent me to the cloakroom to stay 'til school was out."

"Only you didn't stay there."

Jem shook his head, bright hair flying.

Roger bent and picked up the string bag, fighting back outrage, dismay, laughter, and a throat-clutching sympathy. On second thought, he let a bit of the sympathy show.

"Running away from home, were ye?"

"No." Jem looked up at him, surprised. "I didna want to go to school tomorrow, though. Not and have Jimmy laugh at me. So I thought to stay up here 'til the weekend, and maybe by Monday, things would get sorted. Miss Glendenning might die," he added hopefully.

"And maybe your mam and I would be so worried by the time ye came down, ye'd get off without a second whipping?"

Jem's deep-blue eyes widened in surprise.

"Och, no. Mam would give me laldy if I just went off wi' no word. I put a note on my bed. Said I was living rough a day or two." He said this with perfect matter-of-factness. Then he wiggled his shoulders and stood up, sighing.

"Can we get it over and go home?" he asked, his voice trembling only a little. "I'm hungry."

"I'm not going to whip you," Roger assured him. He reached out an arm and gathered Jemmy to him. "Come here, pal."

Jemmy's brave facade gave way at that, and he melted into Roger's arms, crying a little in relief but letting himself be comforted, cuddling like a puppy against his father's shoulder, trusting Da to make it all right. *And his da bloody would,* Roger promised silently. No matter if he had to strangle Miss Glendenning with his bare hands.

"Why is it bad to speak *Gàidhlig,* Da?" he murmured, worn out by so much emotion. "I didna mean to do anything bad."

"It's not," Roger whispered, smoothing the silky hair behind Jem's ear. "Dinna fash yourself. Mam and I will get it sorted. I promise. And ye haven't got to go to school tomorrow."

Jem sighed at that, going inert as a bag of grain. Then he lifted his head and gave a small giggle.

"D'ye think Mam will give Mr. Menzies laldy?"

TUNNEL TIGERS

B RIANNA'S FIRST INTIMATION of disaster was the slice of light on the track, shrinking to nothing in the split second it took for the enormous doors to swing shut, echoing behind her with a boom that seemed to shiver the air in the tunnel.

She said something that she would have washed Jem's mouth out for saying, and said it with heartfelt fury—but said it also under her breath, having realized in the instant that it took the doors to close what was happening.

She couldn't see a thing save the swirls of color that were her retinas' response to sudden dark, but she was only ten feet or so inside the tunnel and could still hear the sound of the bolts sliding home; they were worked by big wheels on the outside of the steel doors and made a grinding sound like bones being chewed. She turned carefully, took five steps, and put out her hands. Yes, there were the doors; big, solid, made of steel, and now solidly locked. She could hear the sound of laughter outside.

Giggling, she thought with furious contempt. *Like little boys!*

Little boys, indeed. She took a few deep breaths, fighting off both anger and panic. Now that the dazzle of the darkness had faded, she could see the thin line of light that bisected the fifteen-foot doors. A man-height shadow interrupted the light but was jerked away, to the accompaniment of whispers and more giggling. Someone trying to peek in, the idiot. Good luck to him, seeing anything in *here*. Aside from the hair of light between the doors, the hydroelectric tunnel under Loch Errochty was dark as the pits of hell.

At least she could use that hair of light for orientation. Still breathing with deliberation, she made her way—stepping carefully; she didn't want to amuse the baboons outside any more than necessary by stumbling and falling noisily—to the metal box on the left wall where the power switches that controlled the tunnel lighting were located.

She found the box and was momentarily panicked to find it locked, before recalling that she had the key; it was on the big jangle of grubby keys that Mr. Campbell had given her, each one dangling a worn paper tag with its function written on. Of course, she couldn't *read* the bloody tags—and frigging Andy Davies had casually borrowed the flashlight that should have been in her belt, on the pretext of looking under the truck for an oil leak.

They'd planned it pretty well, she thought grimly, trying one key, then the next, fumbling and scratching to insert the tip in the tiny invisible slot. All three of them were clearly in on it: Andy, Craig McCarty, and Rob Cameron.

She was of an orderly mind, and when she'd tried each key in careful turn with no result, didn't try them again. She knew they'd thought of that one, too; Craig had taken the keys from her to unlock the toolbox in the panel truck, and returned them with a bow of exaggerated gallantry.

They'd stared at her—naturally—when she was introduced to them as the new safety inspector, though she supposed they'd already been informed she was that shocking thing, a woman. Rob Cameron, a handsome young man who clearly fancied himself, had looked her frankly up and down before extending his hand with a smile. She'd returned the slow up-and-down before taking it, and the other two had laughed. So had Rob, to his credit.

She hadn't sensed any hostility from them on the drive to Loch Errochty, and she thought she'd have seen it if it had been there. This was just a stupid joke. Probably.

In all honesty, the doors closing behind her had *not* been her first intimation that something was up, she thought grimly. She'd been a mother much too long to miss the looks of secretive delight or preternatural innocence that marked the face of a male up to mischief, and such looks had been all over the faces of her maintenance and repair team, if she'd spared the attention to look at them. Her mind had been only half on her job, though; the other half had been in the eighteenth century, worried for Fergus and Marsali, but encouraged by the vision of her parents and Ian safely bound at last for Scotland.

But whatever was going on—*had* gone on, she corrected herself firmly—in the past, she had other things to worry about in the here and now.

What did they expect her to do? she wondered. Scream? Cry? Beat on the doors and beg to be let out?

She walked quietly back to the door and pressed her ear to the crack, in time to hear the roar of the truck's engine starting up and the spurt of gravel from its wheels as it turned up the service road.

"You bloody *bastards*!" she said out loud. What did they mean by this?

Since she hadn't satisfied them by shrieking and crying, they'd decided simply to leave her entombed for a while? Come back later in hopes of finding her in shards—or, better yet, red-faced with fury? Or—more-sinister thought—did they mean to go back to the Hydro Electric Board office, innocent looks on their faces, and tell Mr. Campbell that his new inspector simply hadn't shown up for work this morning?

She breathed out through her nose, slow, deliberate.

Right. She'd eviscerate them when the opportunity offered. But what to do just now?

She turned away from the power box, looking into the utter black. She hadn't been in this particular tunnel before, though she'd seen one like it during her tour with Mr. Campbell. It was one of the original tunnels of the hydroelectric project, dug by hand with pick and shovel by the "hydro boys" back in the 1950s. It ran nearly a mile through the mountain and under part of the flooded valley that now held the greatly expanded Loch Errochty, and a toylike electric train ran on its track down the center of the tunnel.

Originally, the train had carried the workmen, the "tunnel tigers," to the work face and back; now reduced to only an engine, it served the occasional hydroelectric workers checking the huge cables that ran along the tunnel's walls or servicing the tremendous turbines at the foot of the dam, far off at the other end of the tunnel.

Which was, it occurred to her, what Rob, Andy, and Craig were meant to be doing. Lifting one of the massive turbines and replacing its damaged blade.

She pressed her back against the tunnel wall, hands flat on the rough rock, and thought. That's where they'd gone, then. It made no difference, but she closed her eyes to improve her concentration and summoned up the pages of the massive binder—presently on the seat of the vanished truck—that contained the structural and engineering details of all the hydroelectric stations under her purview.

She'd looked at the diagrams for this one last night and again, hastily, while brushing her teeth this morning. The tunnel led *to* the dam, and had obviously been used in the construction of the lower levels of that dam. How low? If the tunnel joined at the level of the turbine chamber itself, it would have been walled off. But if it joined at the level of the servicing chamber above—a huge room equipped with the multi-ton ceiling cranes needed to lift the turbines from their nests—then there would still be a door; there would have been no need to seal it off, with no water on the other side.

Try as she might, she couldn't bring the diagrams to mind in sufficient detail to be sure there was an opening into the dam at the far end of the tunnel—but it would be simple enough to find out.

SHE'D SEEN THE TRAIN, in that brief moment before the doors closed; it didn't take much fumbling round to get into the open cab of the tiny engine. Now, had those clowns taken the key to the engine, too? Ha. There was no key; it worked by a switch on the console. She flipped it, and a red button glowed with sudden triumph as she felt the hum of electricity run through the track beneath.

The train couldn't have been simpler to run. It had a single lever, which you pushed forward or back, depending on which direction you meant to go. She shoved it gently forward, and felt air move past her face as the train moved silently off into the bowels of the earth.

She had to go slowly. The tiny red button shed a comforting glow over her hands, but did nothing to pierce the darkness ahead, and she had no idea where or how much the track curved. Neither did she want to hit the end of the track at a high rate of speed and derail the engine. It felt as though she was inching through the dark, but it was much better than walking, feeling her way over a mile of tunnel lined with high-voltage cables.

It hit her in the dark. For a split second, she thought someone had laid a live cable on the track. In the next instant, a sound that wasn't a sound thrummed through her, plucking every nerve in her body, making her vision go white. And then her hand brushed rock and she realized that she had fallen across the console, was hanging halfway out of the tiny, trundling engine, was about to fall out into darkness.

Head spinning, she managed to grab the edge of the console and pull herself back into the cab. Flipped the switch with one shaking hand and half-fell to the floor, where she curled up, gripping her knees, her breath a whimpering in the dark.

"Holy God," she whispered. "Oh, Blessed Mother. Oh, Jesus."

She could feel it out there. Still feel it. It didn't make a sound now, but she felt its nearness and couldn't stop trembling.

She sat still for a long time, head on her knees, until rational thought began to come back.

She couldn't be mistaken. She'd passed through time twice, and *knew* the feeling. But this hadn't been nearly so shocking. Her skin still prickled and her nerves jumped and her inner ears rang as though she'd thrust her head into a hive of hornets—but she felt solid. She felt as though a red-hot wire had sliced her in two, but she hadn't had the horrible sense of being disassembled, turned physically inside out.

A terrible thought sent her surging to her feet, clinging to the console. Had she jumped? Was she somewhere—some*when*—else? But the metal console was cool and solid under her hands, the smell of damp rock and cable insulation unchanged.

"No," she whispered, and flicked the power light for reassurance. It came on, and the train, still in gear, gave a sudden lurch. Hastily, she throttled back the speed to less than a crawl.

She couldn't have jumped into the past. Small objects in direct contact with a traveler's person seemed to move with them, but an entire train and its track was surely pushing it. "Besides," she said out loud, "if you'd gone more than twenty-five years or so into the past, the tunnel wouldn't *be* here. You'd be inside . . . solid rock." Her gorge rose suddenly, and she threw up.

The sense of . . . it . . . was receding, though. It—whatever it was—was behind her. Well, that settled it, she thought, wiping her mouth with the back of her hand. There bloody well *had* to be a door at the far end, because there was no way she was going back the way she'd come.

There was a door. A plain, ordinary, industrial metal door. And a padlock, unlocked, hanging from an open hasp. She could smell WD-40; someone had oiled the hinges, very recently, and the door swung open easily when she turned the knob. She felt suddenly like Alice, after falling down the White Rabbit's hole. A really mad Alice.

A steep flight of steps lay on the other side of the door, dimly lit—and at the top was another metal door, edged with light. She could hear the rumble and the metallic whine of a ceiling crane in operation.

Her breath was coming fast, and not from the effort of climbing the stairs. What would she find on the other side? It was the servicing chamber inside the dam; she knew that much. But would she find Thursday on the other side? The *same* Thursday she'd had when the tunnel doors had closed behind her?

She gritted her teeth and opened the door. Rob Cameron was waiting, lounging back against the wall, lit cigarette in hand. He broke into an enormous grin at sight of her, dropped the butt, and stepped on it.

"Knew ye'd make it, hen," he said. Across the room, Andy and Craig turned from their work and applauded.

"Buy ye a pint after work, then, lass," Andy called.

"Two!" shouted Craig.

She could still taste bile at the back of her throat. She gave Rob Cameron the sort of look she'd given Mr. Campbell.

"Don't," she said evenly, "call me hen."

His good-looking face twitched and he tugged at his forelock with mock subservience.

"Anything you say, boss," he said.

28

HILLTOPS

I T WAS NEARLY SEVEN by the time he heard Brianna's car in the drive. The kids had had their supper, but came swarming out to her, clinging to her legs as though she'd just come back from darkest Africa or the North Pole.

It was some time before the kids were settled for the night and Bree had time to give her undivided attention to him. He didn't mind.

"Are you starving?" she said. "I can fix—"

He interrupted her, taking her by the hand and drawing her into his office, where he carefully closed and locked the door. She was standing there, hair half matted from her hard hat, grimy from spending the day in the bowels of the earth. She smelled of earth. Also engine grease, cigarette smoke, sweat, and . . . beer?

"I've a lot to tell you," he said. "And I know ye've a lot to tell me. But first . . . could ye just slip off your jeans, maybe, sit on the desk, and spread your legs?"

Her eyes went perfectly round.

"Yes," she said mildly. "I could do that."

ROGER HAD OFTEN WONDERED whether it was true what they said about redheaded people being more volatile than the usual—or whether it was just that their emotions showed so suddenly and alarmingly on their skins. Both, he thought.

Maybe he should have waited 'til she'd got her clothes on before telling her about Miss Glendenning. If he had, though, he'd have missed the remarkable sight of his wife, naked and flushed with fury from the navel upward.

"That bloody old besom! If she thinks she can get away with—"

"She can't," he interrupted firmly. "Of course she can't."

"You bet she can't! I'll go down there first thing tomorrow and—"

"Well, maybe not."

She stopped and looked at him, one eye narrowed.

"Maybe not *what*?"

"Maybe not you." He fastened his own jeans, and picked hers up. "I was thinking it might be best if I go."

She frowned, turning that one over.

"Not that I think ye'd lose your temper and set about the old bitch," he added, smiling, "but you have got your job to go to, aye?"

"Hmmm," she said, seeming skeptical of his ability to adequately impress Miss Glendenning with the magnitude of her crime.

"And if ye *did* lose the heid and nut the woman, I'd hate to have to explain to the kids why we were visiting Mummy in jail."

That made her laugh, and he relaxed a little. He really didn't *think* she'd resort to physical violence, but then, she hadn't seen Jemmy's ear right after he'd come home. He'd had a strong urge himself to go straight down to the school and show the woman what it felt like, but he was in better command of himself now.

"So what *do* you mean to say to her?" She fished her brassiere out from under the desk, giving him a succulent view of her rear aspect, as she hadn't put the jeans on yet.

"Nothing. I'll speak to the principal. *He* can have a word with her."

"Well, that might be better," she said slowly. "We don't want Miss Glendenning to take it out on Jemmy."

"Right." The beautiful flush was fading. Her hard hat had rolled off under the chair; he picked it up and set it on her head again. "So—how was work to-day? And why don't ye wear knickers to work?" he asked, suddenly remembering.

To his startlement, the flush roared back like a brushfire.

"I got out of the habit in the eighteenth century," she snapped, plainly tak-ing the huff. "I only wear knickers for ceremonial purposes anymore. What did you think, I was planning to seduce Mr. Campbell?"

"Well, not if he's anything like you described him, no," he said mildly. "I just noticed when ye left this morning, and wondered."

"Oh." She was still ruffled, he could see that and wondered why. He was about to ask again about her day when she took the hat off and eyed him speculatively.

"You said if I wore the hat, you'd tell me what you were doing with that champagne bottle. Other than giving it to Mandy to throw through the win-dow," she added, with a tinge of wifely censoriousness. "What were you *thinking*, Roger?"

"Well, in all honesty, I was thinking about your arse," he said. "But it never occurred to me that she'd throw the thing. Or that she *could* throw it like that."

"Did you ask her why she did it?"

He stopped, nonplused.

"It hadn't occurred to me that she'd have a reason," he confessed. "I snatched her off the table as she was about to pitch face-first into the broken window, and I was so frightened that I just picked her up and smacked her bum."

"I don't think she'd do something like that for no reason," Bree said med-itatively. She'd put aside the hard hat and was scooping herself into her brassiere, a spectacle Roger found diverting under just about any circum-stances.

It wasn't until they'd gone back to the kitchen for their own late supper that he remembered to ask again how her workday had gone.

"Not bad," she said, with a good assumption of casualness. Not so good as to convince him, but good enough that he thought better of prodding, and instead asked, "Ceremonial purposes?"

A broad grin spread across her face.

"You know. For you."

"Me?"

"Yes, you and your fetish for women's lacy underthings."

"What—you mean you only wear knickers for—"

"For you to take off, of course."

There was no telling where the conversation might have gone from this point, but it was interrupted by a loud wail from above, and Bree disappeared hastily in the direction of the stairs, leaving Roger to contemplate this latest revelation.

He'd got the bacon fried and the tinned beans simmering by the time she reappeared, a small frown between her brows.

"Bad dream," she said, in answer to his lifted brow. "The same one."

"The bad thing trying to get in her window again?"

She nodded and took the saucepan of beans he handed her, though she didn't move immediately to serve out the food.

"I asked her why she threw the bottle."

"Aye?"

Brianna took the bean spoon, holding it like a weapon.

"She said she saw him outside the window."

"Him? The—"

"The Nuckelavee."

IN THE MORNING, the broch was just as it had been the last time he'd looked. Dark. Quiet, save for the rustling of the doves overhead. He'd taken away the rubbish; no new fish papers had come. *Swept and garnished,* he thought. Waiting for the occupation of whatever roaming spirit might happen by?

He shook that thought off and closed the door firmly. He'd get new hinges and a padlock for it, next time he passed by the Farm and Household Stores.

Had Mandy really seen someone? And if she had, was it the same tramp who had frightened Jem? The idea of someone hanging round, spying on his family, made something hard and black curl through his chest, like a sharp-pointed iron spring. He stood for a moment, narrowly surveying the house, the grounds, for any trace of an intruder. Anywhere a man might hide. He'd already searched the barn and the other outbuildings.

The Dunbonnet's cave? The thought—with his memory of Jem standing right by the mouth of the cave—chilled him. Well, he'd soon find out, he thought grimly, and with a last glance at Annie MacDonald and Mandy, peacefully hanging out the family washing in the yard below, he set off.

He kept a sharp ear out today. He heard the echo of the red stags belling, still hard at it, and once saw a small herd of hinds in the distance, but luckily met no lust-crazed males. No lurking tramps, either.

It took him some time of casting about to find the cave's entrance, even though he'd been there only the day before. He made a good bit of noise, approaching, but stood outside and called, "Hallo, the cave!" just in case. No answer.

He approached the entrance from the side, pressing back the covering gorse with a forearm, ready in case the tramp might be lurking inside—but he could tell as soon as the damp breath of the place touched his face that it was unoccupied.

Nonetheless, he poked his head in, then swung himself down into the cave itself. It was dry, for a cave in the Highlands, which was not saying all that much. Cold as a tomb, though. It was no wonder Highlanders had a reputation for toughness; anyone who wasn't would have succumbed to starvation or pneumonia in short order.

Despite the chill of the place, he stood for a minute, imagining his father-in-law here. It was empty and cold, but oddly peaceful, he thought. No sense of foreboding. In fact, he felt . . . welcomed, and the notion made the hairs prickle on his arms.

"Grant, Lord, that they may be safe," he said quietly, his hand resting on the stone at the entrance. Then he climbed out, into the sun's warm benediction.

That strange sense of welcome, of having been somehow acknowledged, remained with him.

"Well, what now, *athair-céile*?" he said aloud, half joking. "Anyplace else I should look?"

Even as he said it, he realized that he *was* looking. On the top of the next small hill was the heap of stones Brianna had told him about. Human-made, she'd said, and thought it might be an Iron Age fort. There didn't look to be enough of whatever it was standing to offer shelter to anyone, but out of sheer restlessness, he made his way down through the tumble of rock and heather, splashed through a tiny burn that gurgled through the rock at the foot of the hill, and toiled his way up to the heap of ancient rubble.

It *was* ancient—but not as old as the Iron Age. What he found looked like the ruins of a small chapel; a stone on the ground had a cross chiseled crudely into it, and he saw what looked like the weathered fragments of a stone statue, scattered by the entrance. There was more of it than he'd thought from a distance; one wall still reached as high as his waist, and there were parts of two more. The roof had long since fallen in and disappeared, but a length of the rooftree was still there, the wood gone hard as metal.

Wiping sweat from the back of his neck, he stooped and picked up the statue's head. Very old. Celtic, Pictish? Not enough left to tell even the statue's intended gender.

He passed a thumb gently over the statue's sightless eyes, then set the head carefully atop the half wall; there was a depression there, as though there might once have been a niche in the wall.

"Okay," he said, feeling awkward. "See you later, then." And, turning, made his way down the rough hill toward home, still with that odd sense of being accompanied on his way.

The Bible says, "Seek, and ye shall find," he thought. And said aloud to the vibrant air, "But there's no guarantee about *what* you'll find, is there?"

CONVERSATION WITH A HEADMASTER

A FTER A PEACEFUL LUNCH with Mandy, who seemed to have forgotten all about her nightmares, he dressed with some care for his interview with the headmaster of Jem's school.

Mr. Menzies was a surprise; Roger hadn't thought to ask Bree what the man was like, and had been expecting something squat, middle-aged, and authoritarian, along the lines of his own headmaster at school. Instead, Menzies was close to Roger's own age, a slender, pale-skinned man with spectacles and what looked like a humorous eye behind them. Roger didn't miss the firm set of the mouth, though, and thought he'd been right to keep Bree from coming.

"Lionel Menzies," the headmaster said, smiling. He had a solid handshake and a friendly air, and Roger found himself revising his strategy.

"Roger MacKenzie." He let go and took the proffered seat, across the desk from Menzies. "Jem's—Jeremiah's—dad."

"Oh, aye, of course. I rather thought I might see you or your wife, when Jem didn't turn up at school this morning." Menzies leaned back a little, folding his hands. "Before we go very far . . . could I just ask exactly what Jem told ye about what happened?"

Roger's opinion of the man rose a grudging notch.

"He said that his teacher heard him say something to another lad in the Gaelic, whereupon she grabbed him by the ear and shook him. That made him mad and he called her names—also in Gaelic—for which you belted him." He'd spotted the strap itself, hung up inconspicuously—but still quite visible—on the wall beside a filing cabinet.

Menzies's eyebrows rose behind his spectacles.

"Is that not what happened?" Roger asked, wondering for the first time whether Jem had lied or omitted something even more horrible from his account.

"No, that's what happened," Menzies said. "I've just never heard a parent give such a concise account. Generally speaking, it's a half hour of prologue, dissociated trivia, contumely, and contradiction—that's if both parents come—and personal attacks before I can make out precisely what the trouble is. Thank you." He smiled, and quite involuntarily, Roger smiled back.

"I was sorry to have to do it," Menzies went on, not pausing for reply. "I like Jem. He's clever, hardworking—and really funny."

"He is that," Roger said. "But—"

"But I hadn't a choice, really," Menzies interrupted firmly. "If none of the other students had known what he was saying, we might have done with a simple apology. But—did he tell ye what it was he said?"

"Not in detail, no." Roger hadn't inquired; he'd heard Jamie Fraser curse someone in Gaelic only three or four times—but it was a memorable experience, and Jem had an excellent memory.

"Well, I won't, either, then, unless you insist. But the thing is, while only a few of the kids on the play yard likely understood him, they would tell—well, they have told, in fact—all their friends exactly what he said. And they know I understood it, too. I've got to support the authority of my teachers; if there's no respect for the staff, the whole place goes to hell. . . . Did your wife tell me ye'd taught yourself? At Oxford, I think she said? That's very impressive."

"That was some years ago, and I was only a junior don, but yes. And I hear what you're saying, though I unfortunately had to keep order and respect without the threat of physical force." Not that he wouldn't have loved to be able to punch one or two of his Oxford second-year students in the nose . . .

Menzies eyed him with a slight twinkle.

"I'd say your presence was likely adequate," he said. "And given that you're twice my size, I'm pleased to hear that you're not inclined to use force."

"Some of your other parents are?" Roger asked, raising his own brows.

"Well, none of the fathers has actually struck me, no, though it's been threatened once or twice. Did have one mother come in with the family shotgun, though." Menzies inclined his head at the wall behind him, and looking up, Roger saw a spray of black pockmarks in the plaster, mostly—but not entirely—covered by a framed map of Africa.

"Fired over your head, at least," Roger said dryly, and Menzies laughed.

"Well, no," he said, deprecating. "I asked her please to set it down carefully, and she did, but not carefully enough. Caught the trigger somehow and *blam!* The poor woman was really unnerved—though not quite as much as I was."

"You're bloody good, mate," Roger said, smiling in acknowledgment of Menzies's skill in handling difficult parents—including Roger—but leaning forward a little to indicate that he meant to take control of the conversation. "But I'm not—not yet, anyway—complaining about your belting Jem. It's what led to that."

Menzies drew breath and nodded, setting his elbows on the desk and steepling his hands.

"Aye, right."

"I understand the need to support your teachers," Roger said, and set his own hands on the desk. "But that woman nearly tore my son's ear off, and evidently for no crime greater than saying a few words—not cursing, just words—in the *Gàidhlig*."

Menzies eyes sharpened, catching the accent.

"Ah, you've got it, then. Wondered, ken, was it you or your wife had it."

"You make it sound like a disease. My wife's an American—surely ye noticed?"

Menzies gave him an amused look—no one failed to notice Brianna—but said only, "Aye, I noticed. She told me her da was Scots, though, and a Highlander. You speak it at home?"

"No, not much. Jem got it from his grandda. He's . . . no longer with us," he added.

Menzies nodded.

"Ah," he said softly. "Aye, I had it from my grandparents, as well—my mam's folk. Dead, too, now. They were from Skye." The usual implied question hovered, and Roger answered it.

"I was born in Kyle of Lochalsh, but I grew up mostly in Inverness. Picked up most of my own Gaelic on the fishing boats in the Minch." And in the mountains of North Carolina.

Menzies nodded again, for the first time looking down at his hands rather than at Roger.

"Been on a fishing boat in the last twenty years?"

"No, thank God."

Menzies smiled briefly, but didn't look up.

"No. You won't find much of the Gaelic there these days. Spanish, Polish, Estonian . . . quite a bit of those, but not the Gaelic. Your wife said ye'd spent a number of years in America, so you'll maybe not have noticed, but it's not much spoken in public anymore."

"To be honest, I hadn't paid it much mind—not 'til now."

Menzies nodded again, as though to himself, then took off his spectacles and rubbed at the marks they'd left on the bridge of his nose. His eyes were pale blue and seemed suddenly vulnerable, without the protection of his glasses.

"It's been on the decline for a number of years. Much more so for the last ten, fifteen years. The Highlands are suddenly part of the UK—or at least the rest of the UK says so—in a way they've never been before, and keeping a separate language is seen as not only old-fashioned but outright destructive.

"It's no what you'd call a written policy, to stamp it out, but the use of Gaelic is strongly . . . discouraged . . . in schools. Mind"—he raised a hand to forestall Roger's response—"they couldn't get away with that if the parents protested, but they don't. Most of them are eager for their kids to be part of the modern world, speak good English, get good jobs, fit in elsewhere, be able to leave the Highlands . . . Not so much for them here, is there, save the North Sea?"

"The parents . . ."

"If they've learnt the Gaelic from their own parents, they deliberately don't teach it to their kids. And if they haven't got it, they certainly make no effort to learn. It's seen as backward, ignorant. Very much a mark of the lower classes."

"Barbarous, in fact," Roger said, with an edge. "The barbarous Erse?"

Menzies recognized Samuel Johnson's dismissive description of the tongue spoken by his eighteenth-century Highland hosts, and the brief, rueful smile lit his face again.

"Exactly. There's a great deal of prejudice—much of it outspoken—against . . ."

"Teuchters?" "Teuchter" was a Lowland Scots term for someone in the Gaeltacht, the Gaelic-speaking Highlands, and in cultural terms the general equivalent of "hillbilly" or "trailer trash."

"Oh, ye do know, then."

"Something." It was true; even as recently as the sixties, Gaelic speakers had been viewed with a certain derision and public dismissiveness, but this . . . Roger cleared his throat.

"Regardless, Mr. Menzies," he said, coming down a bit on the "Mr.," "I object very much to my son's teacher not only disciplining him for speaking Gaelic but actually assaulting him for doing so."

"I share your concern, Mr. MacKenzie," Menzies said, looking up and meeting his eyes in a way that made it seem as though he truly did. "I've had a wee word with Miss Glendenning, and I think it won't happen again."

Roger held his gaze for a moment, wanting to say all sorts of things but realizing that Menzies was not responsible for most of them.

"If it does," he said evenly, "I won't come back with a shotgun—but I will come back with the sheriff. And a newspaper photographer, to document Miss Glendenning being taken off in handcuffs."

Menzies blinked once and put his spectacles back on.

"You're sure ye wouldn't rather send your wife round with the family shotgun?" he asked wistfully, and Roger laughed, despite himself.

"Fine, then." Menzies pushed back his chair and stood up. "I'll see ye out; I've got to lock up. We'll see Jem on the Monday, then, will we?"

"He'll be here. With or without handcuffs."

Menzies laughed.

"Well, he needn't worry about his reception. Since the Gaelic-speaking kids *did* tell their friends what it was he said, and he took his belting without a squeak, I think his entire form now regards him as Robin Hood or Billy Jack."

"Oh, God."

30

SHIPS THAT PASS IN THE NIGHT

May 19, 1777

T HE SHARK WAS EASILY twelve feet long, a dark, sinuous shape keeping pace with the ship, barely visible through the storm-stirred gray waters. It had appeared abruptly just before noon, startling me badly when I looked over the rail and saw its fin cut the surface.

"What's amiss with its head?" Jamie, appearing in response to my startled cry, frowned into the dark water. "It has a growth of some sort."

"I think it's what they call a hammerhead." I clung tight to the railing, slippery with spray. The head *did* look misshapen: a queer, clumsy, blunt thing at the end of such a sinisterly graceful body. As we watched, though, the shark came closer to the surface and rolled, bringing one fleshy stalk and its distant cold eye momentarily clear of the water.

Jamie made a sound of horrified disgust.

"They normally look like that," I informed him.

"Why?"

"I suppose God was feeling bored one day." That made him laugh, and I viewed him with approval. His color was high and healthy, and he'd eaten breakfast with such appetite that I'd felt I could dispense with the acupuncture needles.

"What's the strangest thing you've ever seen? An animal, I mean. A non-human animal," I added, thinking of Dr. Fentiman's ghastly collection of pickled deformities and "natural curiosities."

"Strange by itself? Not deformed, I mean, but as God meant it to be?" He squinted into the sea, thinking, then grinned. "The mandrill in Louis of France's zoo. Or . . . well, no. Maybe a rhinoceros, though I havena seen one of those in the flesh. Does that count?"

"Let's say something you've seen in the flesh," I said, thinking of a few pictorial animals I'd seen in this time that appeared to have been deeply affected by the artist's imagination. "You thought the mandrill was stranger than the orangutan?" I recalled his fascination with the orangutan, a solemn-faced young animal who had seemed equally fascinated by *him,* this leading to a number of jokes regarding the origins of red hair on the part of the Duc d'Orleans, who'd been present.

"Nay, I've seen a good many people who looked stranger than the orangutan," he said. The wind had shifted, yanking auburn lashings of hair out of his ribbon. He turned to face into the breeze and smoothed them back, sobering a little. "I felt sorry for the creature; it seemed to ken it was alone and might never see another of its kind again."

"Maybe it *did* think you were one of its kind," I suggested. "It seemed to like you."

"It was a sweet wee thing," he agreed. "When I gave it an orange, it took the fruit from my hand like a Christian, verra mannerly. Do ye suppose..." His voice died away, his eyes going vague.

"Do I suppose...?"

"Oh. I was only thinking"—he glanced quickly over his shoulder, but we were out of earshot of the sailors—"what Roger Mac said about France being important to the Revolution. I thought I should ask about, when we're in Edinburgh. See whether there might be any of the folk I knew who had fingers in France..." He lifted one shoulder.

"You aren't actually thinking of *going* to France, are you?" I asked, suddenly wary.

"No, no," he said hurriedly. "I only happened to think—if by some chance we did, might the orangutan still be there? It's been a great while, but I dinna ken how long they live."

"Not quite as long as people, I don't think, but they *can* live to a great age, if they're well cared for," I said dubiously. The doubt was not all on the orangutan's account. Go back to the French court? The mere thought made my stomach flip-flop.

"He's dead, ken," Jamie said quietly. He turned his head to look at me, eyes steady. "Louis."

"Is he?" I said blankly. "I...when?"

He ducked his head and made a small noise that might have been a laugh.

"He died three years ago, Sassenach," he said dryly. "It *was* in the papers. Though I grant ye, the *Wilmington Gazette* didna make a great deal of the matter."

"I didn't notice." I glanced down at the shark, still patiently keeping company with the ship. My heart, after the initial leap of surprise, had relaxed. My general reaction, in fact, was thankfulness—and that in itself surprised me, rather.

I'd come to terms with my memory of sharing Louis's bed—for the ten minutes it had taken—long since, and Jamie and I had long since come to terms with each other, turning to each other in the wake of the loss of our first daughter, Faith, and all the terrible things that had happened in France before the Rising.

It wasn't that hearing of Louis's death made any real difference at all—but still, I had a feeling of relief, as though some tiresome bit of music that had been playing in the far distance had finally come to a graceful end, and now the silence of peace sang to me in the wind.

"God rest his soul," I said, rather belatedly. Jamie smiled, and laid his hand over mine.

"*Fois shìorruidh thoir dha,*" he echoed. God rest his soul. "Makes ye wonder, ken? How it might be for a king, to come before God and answer for your life. Might it be a great deal worse, I mean, having to answer for all the folk under your care?"

"Do you think he would?" I asked, intrigued—and rather uneasy at the thought. I hadn't known Louis in any intimate way—bar the obvious, and that seemed less intimate than a handshake; he'd never even met my eyes—but he hadn't seemed like a man consumed by care for his subjects. "Can a person really be held to account for the welfare of a whole kingdom? Not just his own peccadilloes, you think?"

He considered that seriously, the stiff fingers of his right hand tapping slowly on the slippery rail.

"I think so," he said. "Ye'd answer for what ye'd done to your family, no? Say ye'd done ill by your children, abandoned them or left them to starve. Surely that would weigh against your soul, for you're responsible for them. If you're born a king, then ye're given responsibility for your subjects. If ye do ill by them, then—"

"Well, but where does that stop?" I protested. "Suppose you do well by one person and badly by another? Suppose you have people under your care—so to speak—and their needs are in opposition to one another? What do you say to that?"

He broke into a smile.

"I'd say I'm verra glad I'm not God and havena got to try to reckon such things."

I was silent for a moment, imagining Louis standing before God, trying to explain those ten minutes with me. I was sure he'd thought he had a right— kings, after all, were kings—but on the other hand, both the seventh and the ninth commandments were fairly explicit and didn't seem to have any clauses exempting royalty.

"If you were there," I said impulsively, "in heaven, watching that judgment—would you forgive him? I would."

"Who?" he said, surprised. "Louis?" I nodded, and he frowned, rubbing a finger slowly down the bridge of his nose. Then he sighed and nodded.

"Aye, I would. Wouldna mind watching him squirm a bit first, mind," he added, darkly. "A wee pitchfork in the arse would be fine."

I laughed at that, but before I could say anything further, we were interrupted by a shout of "Sail, ho!" from above. While we'd been alone the instant before, this advice caused sailors to pop out of hatches and companionways like weevils out of a ship's biscuit, swarming up into the rigging to see what was up.

I strained my eyes, but nothing was immediately visible. Young Ian, though, had gone aloft with the others, and now landed on the deck beside us with a thump. He was flushed with wind and excitement.

"A smallish ship, but she's got guns," he told Jamie. "And she's flying the Union flag."

"She's a naval cutter," said Captain Roberts, who had appeared on my other side and was peering grimly through his telescope. "Shit."

Jamie's hand went to his dirk, unconsciously checking, and he looked over the captain's shoulder, eyes narrowed against the wind. I could see the sail now, coming up rapidly to starboard.

"Can we outrun her, Cap'n?" The first mate had joined the crowd at the rail, watching the oncoming ship. She did have guns; six, that I could see—and there were men behind them.

The captain pondered, absently clicking his glass open and shut, then glanced up into the rigging, presumably estimating the chances of our putting on enough sail to outdistance the pursuer. The mainmast was cracked; he'd been intending to replace it in New Haven.

"No," he said gloomily. "The main'll be away, if there's any strain put on her." He shut the telescope with a decisive *click* and stowed it away in his pocket. "Have to brass it out, best we can."

I wondered just how much of Captain Roberts's cargo was contraband. His taciturn face didn't give anything away, but there was a distinct air of uneasiness among the hands, which grew noticeably as the cutter drew alongside, hailing.

Roberts gave the terse order to heave to, and the sails loosened, the ship slowing. I could see seamen at the guns and rail of the cutter; glancing sideways at Jamie, I saw that he was counting them and glanced back.

"I make it sixteen," Ian said, low-voiced.

"Undermanned, God damn it," said the captain. He looked at Ian, estimating his size, and shook his head. "They'll likely mean to press what they can out of us. Sorry, lad."

The rather formless alarm I'd felt at the cutter's approach sharpened abruptly at this—and sharpened still further as I saw Roberts glance appraisingly at Jamie.

"You don't think they—" I began.

"Shame you shaved this morning, Mr. Fraser," Roberts observed to Jamie, ignoring me. "Takes twenty years off your age. And you look a damned sight healthier than men half your age."

"I'm obliged to ye for the compliment, sir," Jamie replied dryly, one eye on the railing, where the cocked hat of the cutter's captain had suddenly poked up like an ill-omened mushroom. He unbuckled his belt, slid the dirk's scabbard free, and handed it to me.

"Keep that for me, Sassenach," he said under his breath, buckling his belt again.

The cutter's captain, a squat middle-aged man with a sullen brow and a pair of much-mended breeches, took a quick, piercing look around the deck when he came aboard, nodded to himself as though his worst suspicions had been confirmed, then shouted back over his shoulder for six men to follow.

"Search the hold," he said to his minions. "You know what to look for."

"What sort of way is this to carry on?" Captain Roberts demanded angrily. "You've no right to search my ship! What do you lot think you are, a raft of bloody pirates?"

"Do I look like a pirate?" The cutter's captain looked more pleased than insulted by the idea.

"Well, you can't be a naval captain, I'm sure," Roberts said coldly. "A nice, gentlemanlike set of individuals, I've always found His Majesty's navy. Not the sort to board a respectable merchant without leave, let alone without proper introduction."

The cutter's captain appeared to find this funny. He took off his hat and bowed—to me.

"Allow me, mum," he said. "Captain Worth Stebbings, your most humble." He straightened up, clapping on his hat, and nodded to his lieutenant. "Go through the holds like a dose of salts. And you—" He tapped Roberts on the chest with a forefinger. "Get all your men on deck, front and center, cully. *All* of them, mind. If I have to drag them up here, I won't be best pleased, I warn you."

Tremendous bangings and rumblings from below ensued, with seamen popping up periodically to relay news of their findings to Captain Stebbings, who lounged by the rail, watching as the men of the *Teal* were rounded up and herded together on deck—Ian and Jamie among them.

"Here, now!" Captain Roberts was game, I'd give him that. "Mr. Fraser and his nephew aren't crew; they're paying passengers! You've no call to molest free men, about their lawful business. And no right to press my crew, either!"

"They're British subjects," Stebbings informed him briefly. "I've every right. Or do you all claim to be *Americans*?" He leered briefly at that; if the ship could be considered a rebel vessel, he could simply take the whole thing as a prize, crew and all.

A mutter at this ran through the men on deck, and I saw more than one of the hands' eyes dart to the belaying pins along the rail. Stebbings saw it, too, and called over the rail for four more men to be brought aboard—with arms.

Sixteen minus six minus four is six, I thought, and edged a little closer to the rail to peer into the cutter rocking in the swell a little way below and tethered by a line to the *Teal. If the sixteen doesn't include Captain Stebbings. If it does...*

One man was at the helm, this being not a wheel but a sort of sticklike arrangement poking up through the deck. Two more were manning a gun, a long brass thing on the bow, pointed at the *Teal*'s side. Where were the others? Two on deck. The others perhaps below.

Captain Roberts was still haranguing Stebbings behind me, but the cutter's crew were bumping barrels and bundles over the deck, calling for a rope to lower away to the cutter. I looked back to find Stebbings walking along the row of crewmen, indicating his choices to four burly men who followed him. These jerked his choices out of line and set about tying them together, a line running from ankle to ankle. Three men had already been chosen, John Smith among them, looking white-faced and tense. My heart jumped at sight of him, then nearly stopped altogether as Stebbings came to Ian, who looked down at him impassively.

"Likely, likely," Stebbings said with approval. "A cross-grained son of a bitch, by the looks of you, but we'll soon knock sense into you. Take him!"

I saw the muscles swell in Ian's forearms as his fists clenched, but the press-gang was armed, two with pistols drawn, and he stepped forward, though with an evil look that would have given a wiser man pause. I had already observed that Captain Stebbings was not a wise man.

Stebbings took two more, then paused at Jamie, looking him up and down. Jamie's face was carefully blank. And slightly green; the wind was still up, and with no forward way on the ship, she was rising and falling heavily, with a lurch that would have disconcerted a much better sailor than he was.

"Nice big 'un, sir," said one of the press-gang, with approval.

"Trifle elderly," Stebbings said dubiously. "And I don't much like the look on his face."

"I dinna care much for the look of yours," Jamie said pleasantly. He straightened, squaring his shoulders, and looked down his long, straight nose at Stebbings. "If I didna ken ye for an arrant coward by your actions, sir, I should know ye for a fig-licker and a fopdoodle by your foolish wee face."

Stebbings's maligned face went blank with astonishment, then darkened with rage. One or two of the press-gang grinned behind his back, though hastily erasing these expressions as he whirled round.

"Take him," he growled to the press-gang, shouldering his way toward the booty collected by the rail. "And see that you drop him a few times on the way."

I was frozen in shock. Clearly Jamie couldn't let them press Ian and take him away, but surely he couldn't mean to abandon me in the middle of the Atlantic Ocean, either.

Not even with his dirk thrust into the pocket tied beneath my skirt, and my own knife in its sheath around my thigh.

Captain Roberts had watched this little performance openmouthed, though whether with respect or astonishment, I couldn't tell. He was a short man, rather tubby, and clearly not constructed for physical confrontation, but he set his jaw and stamped up to Stebbings, seizing him by the sleeve.

The crew ushered their captives over the rail.

There wasn't time to think of anything better.

I seized the rail and more or less rolled over it, skirts flying. I hung by my hands for a terrifying instant, feeling my fingers slide across the wet wood, groping with my toes for the rope ladder the cutter's crew had thrown over the rail. A roll of the ship threw me hard against the side, I lost my grip, plunged several feet, and caught the ladder, just above the cutter's deck.

The rope had burned through my right hand, and it felt as though I'd lost all the skin off my palm, but there was no time to trouble about that now. Any minute, one of the cutter's crew would see me, and—

Timing my jump to the next heave of the cutter's deck, I let go and landed like a bag of rocks. A sharp pain shot up the inside of my right knee, but I staggered to my feet, lurching to and fro with the roll of the deck, and lunged toward the companionway.

"Here! You! What you doing?" One of the gunners had seen me and was gaping at me, clearly unable to decide whether to come down and deal with me or stay with his gun. His partner looked over his shoulder at me and bellowed at the first man to stay put, it wasn't but monkey business of some sort, he said. *"Stay put, God damn your eyes!"*

I ignored them, my heart pounding so hard I could scarcely breathe. What now? What next? Jamie and Ian had disappeared.

"Jamie!" I shouted, as loudly as I could. "I'm here!" And then ran toward the line that held the cutter to the *Teal*, jerking up my skirt as I ran. I did this only because my skirts had twisted in my undignified descent, and I couldn't find the slit to reach through in order to get at the knife in its sheath on my thigh, but the action itself seemed to disconcert the helmsman, who had turned at my shout.

He gawped like a goldfish, but had sufficient presence of mind as to keep his hand on the tiller. I got my own hands on the line and dug my knife into the knot, using it to pry the tight coils loose.

Roberts and his crew, bless them, were making a terrible racket on the *Teal* above, quite drowning out the shouts of the helm and gunners. One of these, with a desperate glance toward the deck of the *Teal* above, finally made up his mind and came toward me, jumping down from the bow.

What wouldn't I give for a pistol just now? I thought grimly. But a knife was what I had, and I jerked it out of the half-loosened knot and drove it into the man's chest as hard as I could. His eyes went round, and I felt the knife strike bone and twist in my hand, skipping through the flesh. He shrieked and fell backward, landing on deck in a thump and nearly—but not quite—taking my knife with him.

"Sorry," I gasped, and, panting, resumed work on the knot, the fractious rope now smeared with blood. There were noises coming from the companionway now. Jamie and Ian might not be armed, but my guess was that that wouldn't matter a lot, in close quarters.

The rope slid reluctantly free. I jerked the last coil loose and it fell, slapping against the *Teal*'s side. At once, the current began to carry the boats apart, the smaller cutter sliding past the big sloop. We weren't moving quickly at all, but the optical illusion of speed made me stagger, gripping at the rail for balance.

The wounded gunner had got onto his feet and was advancing on me, staggering but furious. He was bleeding, but not heavily, and was by no means disabled. I stepped quickly sideways and glancing at the companionway, was relieved beyond measure to see Jamie coming out of it.

He reached me in three strides.

"Quick, my dirk!"

I stared blankly at him for a moment, but then remembered, and with no more than minimum fumbling, managed to get at my pocket. I jerked at the hilt of the dirk, but it was tangled in the fabric. Jamie seized it, ripped it free—tearing both the pocket and the waistband of my skirt in the process—whirled, and charged back into the bowels of the ship. Leaving me facing a wounded gunner, an unwounded gunner now making his way cautiously down from his station, and the helmsman, who was yelling hysterically for someone to do something to some sort of sail.

I swallowed and took a good hold on the knife.

"Stand back," I said, in as loud and commanding a voice as I could manage. Given my shortness of breath, the wind, and the prevailing noise, I doubt they heard me. On the other hand, I doubted that it would have made a difference if they had. I yanked my sagging skirt up with one hand, crouched, and lifted the knife in a determined manner, meant to indicate that I knew what to do with it. I did.

Waves of heat were going over my skin and I felt perspiration prickle my scalp, drying at once in the cold wind. The panic had gone, though; my mind felt very clear and very remote.

You aren't going to touch me was the only thing in my mind. The man I had wounded was cautious, hanging back. The other gunner saw nothing but a woman and didn't bother to arm himself, simply reaching for me with angry contempt. I saw the knife move upward, fast, and arc as though moving by itself, the shimmer of it dulled with blood as I slashed him across the forehead.

Blood poured down over his face, blinding him, and he gave a strangled yell of hurt and astonishment and backed away, both hands pressed to his face.

I hesitated for a moment, not quite sure what to do next, the blood still pounding through my temples. The ship was drifting, rising and falling on the waves; I felt the gold-laden hem of my skirt scrape across the boards, and jerked the torn waistband up again, feeling irritated.

Then I saw a belaying pin stuck into its hole in the railing, a line wrapped round it. I walked over and, poking the knife down the bodkin of my stays for lack of any better place to put it, took hold of the pin with both hands and jerked it free. Holding it like a short baseball bat, I shifted back on one heel and brought it down with as much force as I could on the head of the man whose face I'd slashed. The wooden pin bounced off his skull with a hollow ringing noise, and he staggered away, caroming off the mast.

The helmsman at this point had had enough. Leaving his helm to mind itself, he scrambled up out of his station and made for me like an angry monkey, all reaching limbs and bared teeth. I tried to hit him with the pin, but I'd lost my grip when I struck the gunner, and it slipped out of my hand, rolling away down the heaving deck as the helmsman flung himself on me.

He was small and thin, but his weight bore me back and we lurched together toward the rail; my back struck it and all my breath rushed out in a whoosh, the impact a solid bar of shock across my kidneys. This transformed within seconds to live agony, and I writhed under him, sliding downward. He came with me, grappling for my throat with a single-minded purpose. I flailed at him, my arms, my hands striking windmill-like at his head, the bones of his skull bruising me.

The wind was roaring in my ears; I heard nothing but breathless cursing, harsh gasps that might be mine or his, and then he knocked my hands away and grabbed me by the neck, one-handed, his thumb digging hard up under my jaw.

It hurt and I tried to knee him, but my legs were swaddled in my skirt and pinned beneath his weight. My vision went dark, with little bursts of gold light going off in the blackness, tiny fireworks heralding my death. Someone was making little mewling noises, and I realized dimly that it must be me. The grip on my neck tightened, and the flashing lights faded into black.

I WOKE WITH A confused sense of being simultaneously terrified and rocked in a cradle. My throat hurt, and when I tried to swallow, the resultant pain made me choke.

"Ye're all right, Sassenach." Jamie's soft voice came out of the surrounding gloom—where *was* I?—and his hand squeezed my forearm, reassuring.

"I'll . . . take your . . . word for it," I croaked, the effort making my eyes water. I coughed. It hurt, but seemed to help a little. "What . . . ?"

"Have a bit of water, *a nighean.*" A big hand cradled my head, lifting it a bit, and the mouth of a canteen pressed against my lip. Swallowing the water hurt, too, but I didn't care; my lips and throat were parched, and tasted of salt.

My eyes were beginning to accustom themselves to the darkness. I could see Jamie's form, hunched under a low ceiling, and the shape of rafters—no, timbers—overhead. A strong smell of tar and bilges. Ship. Of course, we were in a ship. But *which* ship?

"Where . . . ?" I whispered, waving a hand.

"I havena got the slightest idea," he said, sounding rather irritable. "The *Teal*'s people are managing the sails—I hope—and Ian's holding a pistol on one o' the naval folk to make him steer, but for all I ken, the man's taking us straight out to sea."

"I meant . . . what . . . ship." Though his remarks had made that clear enough; we must be on the naval cutter.

"They said the name of it's the *Pitt.*"

"How very appropriate." I looked glassily around the murky surroundings, and my sense of reality suffered another jolt as I saw a huge mottled bundle of some kind, apparently hanging in the dim air a few feet beyond Jamie. I sat up abruptly—or tried to, only at this point realizing that I was in a hammock.

Jamie seized me by the waist with a cry of alarm, in time to save me pitching out on my head, and as I steadied, clutching him, I realized that the thing I had taken as an enormous cocoon was in fact a man, lying in another hammock suspended from the rafters, but trussed up in it like a spider's dinner and gagged. His face pressed against the mesh, glaring at me.

"Jesus H. Roosevelt . . . ," I croaked, and lay back, breathing heavily.

"D'ye want to rest a bit, Sassenach, or shall I set ye on your feet?" Jamie asked, clearly edgy. "I dinna want to leave Ian on his own too long."

"No," I said, struggling upright once more. "Help me out, please." The room—cabin, whatever it was—spun round me, as well as heaving up and down, and I was obliged to cling to Jamie with my eyes closed for a moment, until my internal gyroscope took hold.

"Captain Roberts?" I asked. "The *Teal?*"

"God knows," Jamie said tersely. "We ran for it as quick as I could set the men to sailing this thing. For all I ken, they're on our tail, but I couldna see anything when I looked astern."

I was beginning to feel steadier, though the blood still throbbed painfully in my throat and temples with each heartbeat, and I could feel the tender patches of bruising on my elbows and shoulders, and a vivid band across my back, where I'd fallen against the rail.

"We've shut most of the crew up in the hold," Jamie said, with a nod at the man in the hammock, "save this fellow. I didna ken whether ye might want to look at him first. In the medical way, I mean," he added, seeing my momentary incomprehension. "Though I dinna think he's hurt badly."

I approached the fellow in the hammock and saw that it was the helmsman who had tried to throttle me. There was a large lump visible on his forehead, and he had the beginnings of a monstrous black eye, but from what I could see, leaning close in the dim light, his pupils were the same size and—allowing for the rag stuffed into his mouth—his breath was coming regularly. Probably not badly hurt, then. I stood for a moment staring at him. It was difficult to tell—the only light belowdecks came from a prism embedded in the deck above—but I thought that perhaps what I had taken for a glare was really just a look of desperation.

"Do you need to have a pee?" I inquired politely.

The man and Jamie made nearly identical noises, though in the first case it was a groan of need, and in Jamie's, of exasperation.

"For God's sake!" he said, grabbing my arm as I started to reach for the man. "I'll deal with him. Go upstairs." It was apparent from his much-tried tone that he had just about reached the last-straw stage, and there was no point in arguing with him. I left, making my ginger way up the companionway ladder to the accompaniment of a lot of Gaelic muttering that I didn't try to translate.

The belting wind above was enough to make me sway alarmingly as it caught my skirts, but I seized a line and held on, letting the fresh air clear my head before I felt steady enough to go aft. There I found Ian, as advertised, sitting on a barrel, a loaded pistol held negligently atop one knee, evidently engaged in amiable discourse with the sailor at the helm.

"Auntie Claire! All right, are ye?" he asked, jumping up and gesturing me toward his barrel.

"Fine," I said, taking it. I didn't think I had torn anything in my knee, but it felt a little wobbly. "Claire Fraser," I said, nodding politely to the gentleman at the helm, who was black and bore facial tattoos of an elaborate sort, though from the neck down he was dressed in ordinary sailor's slops.

"Guinea Dick," he said, with a broad grin that displayed—no doubt about it—filed teeth. "Youah sahvint, Mum!"

I regarded him openmouthed for a moment, but then regained some semblance of self-possession and smiled at him.

"I see His Majesty takes his seamen where he can get them," I murmured to Ian.

"He does for a fact. Mr. Dick here was pressed out of a Guinea pirate, who took him from a slave ship, who in turn took him from a barracoon on the

Guinea coast. I'm no so sure whether he thinks His Majesty's accommodations are an improvement—but he says he's got nay particular reservation about going along of us."

"Is your trust upon him?" I asked, in halting Gaelic.

Ian gave me a mildly scandalized look.

"Of course not," he replied in the same language. "And you will oblige me by not going too close to him, wife of my mother's brother. He says to me that he does not eat human flesh, but this is no surety that he is safe."

"Right," I said, returning to English. "What happened to—"

Before I could complete my question, a loud thump on deck made me turn, to see John Smith—he of the five gold earrings—who had dropped out of the rigging. He, too, smiled when he saw me, though his face was strained.

"Well enough so far," he said to Ian, and touched his forelock to me. "You all right, ma'am?"

"Yes." I looked aft, but saw nothing save tumbling waves. The same in all the other directions, as well. "Er . . . do you happen to know where we're going, Mr. Smith?"

He looked a trifle surprised at that.

"Why, no, ma'am. The captain hasn't said."

"The cap—"

"That would be Uncle Jamie," Ian said, sounding amused. "Puking his guts out below, is he?"

"Not when last seen." I began to have an uneasy feeling at the base of my spine. "Do you mean to tell me that *no* one aboard this ship has any idea where—or even which way—we're heading?"

An eloquent silence greeted this question.

I coughed.

"The, um, gunner. Not the one with the slashed forehead—the other one. Where is he, do you know?"

Ian turned and looked at the water.

"Oh," I said. There was a large splotch of blood on the deck where the man had fallen when I stabbed him. "Oh," I said again.

"Och, which reminds me, Auntie. I found this lyin' on the deck." Ian took my knife from his belt and handed it to me. It had been cleaned, I saw.

"Thank you." I slipped it back through the slit of my petticoats and found the scabbard, still fastened round my thigh, though someone had removed my torn skirt and pocket. With thought for the gold in the hem, I hoped it was Jamie. I felt rather peculiar, as though my bones were filled with air. I coughed and swallowed again, massaging my bruised throat, then returned to my earlier point.

"So *no* one knows which way we're heading?"

John Smith smiled a little.

"Well, we're not a-heading out to sea, ma'am, if that's what you were fearing."

"I was, actually. How do you know?"

All three of them smiled at that.

"Him sun over dere," Mr. Dick said, shrugging a shoulder at the object in question. He nodded in the same direction. "So him land over dere, too."

"Ah." Well, that was comforting, to be sure. And in fact, since "him sun" *was* over there—that is, sinking rapidly in the west—that meant we were in fact headed north.

Jamie joined the party at this point, looking pale.

"Captain Fraser," Smith said respectfully.

"Mister Smith."

"Orders, Cap'n?"

Jamie stared at him bleakly.

"I'll be pleased if we don't sink. Can ye manage that?"

Mr. Smith didn't bother hiding his grin.

"If we don't hit another ship or a whale, sir, I think we'll stay afloat."

"Good. Kindly don't." Jamie wiped the back of his hand across his mouth and straightened up. "Is there a port we might reach within the next day or so? The helmsman says there's food and water enough for three days, but the less of it we need, the happier I'll be."

Smith turned to squint toward the invisible land, the setting sun glinting off his earrings.

"Well, we're past Norfolk," he said, thoughtful. "The next big regular port would be New York."

Jamie gave him a jaundiced look.

"Is the British navy not anchored in New York?"

Mr. Smith coughed.

"I b'lieve they were, last I heard. 'Course, they might have moved."

"I was more in mind of a small port," Jamie said. "Verra small."

"Where the arrival of a royal naval cutter will make the maximum impression on the citizenry?" I inquired. I sympathized with his strong desire to set foot on land as soon as possible, but the question was—what then?

The enormity of our position was only now beginning to dawn on me. We had gone in the space of an hour from passengers on the way to Scotland to fugitives, on the way to God knew where.

Jamie closed his eyes and drew a long, deep breath. There was a heavy swell, and he was looking green again, I saw. And, with a pang of uneasiness, realized that I had lost my acupuncture needles, left behind in my hasty exodus from the *Teal*.

"What about Rhode Island, or New Haven, Connecticut?" I asked. "New Haven is where the *Teal* was going, anyway—and I think we're much less likely to run into Loyalists or British troops in either of those ports."

Jamie nodded, eyes still closed, grimacing at the movement.

"Aye, maybe."

"Not Rhode Island," Smith objected. "The British sailed into Newport in December, and the American navy—what there is of it—is blockaded inside Providence. They might not fire on us, if we come a-sailing into Newport with the British colors flying"—he gestured at the mast, where the Union Jack still fluttered—"but the reception once ashore might be warmer than we might find comfortable."

Jamie had cracked one eye open and was regarding Smith consideringly.

"I take it ye've no Loyalist leanings yourself, Mr. Smith? For if ye had, nothing simpler than to tell me to land at Newport; I'd not have known any better."

"No, sir." Smith tugged at one of his earrings. "Mind, I'm not a Separatist, neither. But I have got a marked disinclination to be sunk again. Reckon I've just about used up my luck in that direction."

Jamie nodded, looking ill.

"New Haven, then," he said, and I felt a small thump of uneasy excitement. Might I meet with Hannah Arnold, after all? Or—and there was an uneasier notion still—Colonel Arnold himself? I supposed he must visit his family once in a while.

A certain amount of technical discussion, involving a lot of shouting to and fro between deck and rigging, ensued, regarding navigation: Jamie knew how to use both a sextant and an astrolabe—the former was actually available—but had no idea how to apply the results to the sailing of a ship. The impressed hands from the *Teal* were more or less agreeable to sailing the ship wherever we cared to take her, as their only immediate alternative was being arrested, tried, and executed for involuntary piracy, but while all were good able seamen, none of them possessed anything in the way of navigational skills.

This left us with the alternative strategies of interviewing the captive seamen in the hold, discovering whether any of them could sail the ship, and if so, offering such inducements in the way of violence or gold as might compel him to do so, or sailing within sight of land and hugging the coast, which was slower, much more dangerous in terms of encountering either sandbanks or British men of war, and uncertain, insofar as none of the *Teal* hands presently with us had ever seen the port of New Haven before.

Having nothing useful to contribute to this discussion, I went to stand by the rail, watching the sun come down the sky and wondering how likely we were to run aground in the dark, without the sun to steer by?

The thought was cold, but the wind was colder. I had been wearing only a light jacket when I made my abrupt exit from the *Teal*, and without my woolen overskirt, the sea wind was cutting through my clothes like a knife. That unfortunate imagery reminded me of the dead gunner, and, steeling myself, I glanced over my shoulder toward the dark bloodstain on deck.

As I did so, my eye caught the flicker of a movement from the helm, and I opened my mouth to call out. I hadn't managed a sound, but Jamie happened to be looking in my direction and whatever was showing on my face was enough. He turned and threw himself without hesitation at Guinea Dick, who had produced a knife from somewhere about his person and was preparing to plunge it into Ian's negligently turned back.

Ian whirled round at the noise, saw what was up, and, thrusting the pistol into Mr. Smith's surprised hands, flung himself on the thrashing ball of humanity rolling round under the swinging helm. Fallen off her steerage, the ship slowed, her sails slackening, and she began to roll alarmingly.

I took two steps across the slanting deck and plucked the pistol neatly out of Mr. Smith's hand. He looked at me, blinking in bewilderment.

"It's not that I don't trust you," I said apologetically. "It's just that I can't take the chance. All things considered." Calmly—all things considered—I checked the pistol's priming—it was primed and cocked; a wonder it hadn't gone off by itself, with all this rough handling—and aimed it at the center of the melee, waiting to see who might emerge from it.

Mr. Smith looked back and forth, from me to the fight, and then backed slowly away, hands delicately raised.

"I'll . . . just . . . be up top," he said. "If wanted."

The outcome had been a foregone conclusion, but Mr. Dick had acquitted himself nobly as a British seaman. Ian rose slowly, swearing and pressing his forearm against his shirt, where a jagged wound left red blotches.

"The treacherous bugger *bit* me!" he said, furious. "Goddamned cannibal heathen!" He kicked his erstwhile foe, who grunted at the impact but remained inert, and then seized the swinging helm with an angry oath. He moved this slowly to and fro, seeking direction, and the ship steadied, her head turning into the wind as her sails filled again.

Jamie rolled off the supine body of Mr. Dick and sat on the deck beside him, head hanging, panting for breath. I lowered the gun and uncocked it.

"All right?" I asked him, for form's sake. I felt very calm, in a remote, strange sort of way.

"Tryin' to recall how many lives I've got left," he said, between gasps.

"Four, I think. Or five. Surely you don't consider this a near-miss, do you?" I glanced at Mr. Dick, whose face was considerably the worse for wear. Jamie himself had a large red patch down the side of his face that would undoubtedly be black and blue within hours, and was holding his middle, but seemed otherwise undamaged.

"Does nearly dyin' of seasickness count?"

"No." With a wary eye on the fallen helmsman, I squatted beside Jamie and peered at him. The red light of the sinking sun bathed the deck, making it impossible to judge his color, even had the color of his skin made this easy. Jamie held out a hand, and I gave him the pistol, which he tucked into his belt. Where, I saw, he had restored his dirk and its scabbard.

"Did you not have time to draw that?" I asked, nodding at it.

"Didna want to kill him. He's no dead, is he?" With a noticeable effort, he rolled onto hands and knees and breathed for a moment before thrusting himself to his feet.

"No. He'll come round in a minute or two." I looked toward Ian, whose face was averted but whose body language was eloquent. His stiff shoulders, suffused back of neck, and bulging forearms conveyed fury and shame, which were understandable, but there was a droop to his spine that spoke of desolation. I wondered at that last, until a thought occurred to me, and that odd sense of calm vanished abruptly in a burst of horror as I realized what must have made him drop his guard.

"Rollo!" I whispered, clutching Jamie's arm. He looked up, startled, saw Ian, and exchanged appalled glances with me.

"Oh, God," he said softly.

The acupuncture needles were not the only things of value left behind aboard the *Teal*.

Rollo had been Ian's closest companion for years. The immense byproduct of a casual encounter between an Irish wolfhound and a wolf, he terrified the hands on the *Teal* to such an extent that Ian had shut him in the cabin; otherwise, chances were that he would have taken the throat out of Captain Stebbings when the sailors seized Ian. What would he do when he realized that Ian was gone? And what would Captain Stebbings, his men, or the crew of the *Teal* do to him in response?

"Jesus. They'll shoot the dog and drop him overboard," Jamie said, voicing my thought, and crossed himself.

I thought of the hammerhead again, and a violent shudder ran through me. Jamie squeezed my hand tightly.

"Oh, God," he said again, very quietly. He stood thinking for a moment, then shook himself, rather like Rollo shaking water from his fur, and let go my hand.

"I'll have to speak to the crew, and we must feed them—and the sailors in the hold. Will ye go below, Sassenach, and see what ye can do wi' the galley? I'll just . . . have a word with Ian first." I saw his throat move as he glanced at Ian, standing stiff as a wooden Indian at the helm, the dying light harsh on his tearless face.

I nodded, and made my way unsteadily to the black, gaping hole of the companionway, and the descent into darkness.

THE GALLEY WAS NO more than a four-by-four space belowdecks at the end of the mess, with a sort of low brick altar containing the fire, several cupboards on the bulkhead, and a hanging rack of coppers, pot-lifters, rags, and other bits of kitchen impedimenta. No problem in spotting it; there was still a sullen red glow from the galley fire, where—thank God!—a few embers still lived.

There was a sandbox, a coal box, and a basket of kindling, tidied under the tiny countertop, and I set at once to coaxing the fire back into life. A cauldron hung over the fire; some of the contents had slopped over the side as a result of the ship's rolling, partially extinguishing the fire and leaving gummy streaks down the side of the cauldron. Luck again, I thought. Had the slop not put the fire mostly out, the contents of the pot would long since have boiled dry and burned, leaving me with the job of starting some kind of supper from scratch.

Perhaps literally from scratch. There were several stacked cages of chickens near the galley; they'd been dozing in the warm darkness but roused at my movement, fluttering, muttering, and jerking their silly heads to and fro in agitated inquiry, beady eyes blinking redly at me through the wooden lattice.

I wondered whether there might be other livestock aboard, but if there was, it wasn't living in the galley, thank goodness. I stirred the pot, which seemed to contain a glutinous sort of stew, and then began to look for bread. There would be some sort of farinaceous substance, I knew; sailors lived on either hardtack—the very aptly named unleavened ship's biscuit—or soft tack, this being any kind of leavened bread, though the term "soft" was often relative. Still, they would have bread. Where . . . ?

I found it at last: hard round brown loaves in a netting bag hung from a hook in a dark corner. To keep it from rats, I supposed, and glanced narrowly around the floor, just in case. There should be flour, as well, I thought—oh, of course. It would be in the hold, along with the other ship's stores. And the disgruntled remnants of the original crew. Well, we'd worry about them later. There was enough here to feed everyone aboard supper. I'd worry about breakfast later, too.

The exertion of building up the fire and searching the galley and mess warmed me and distracted me from my bruises. The sense of chilled disbelief that had attended me ever since I went over the *Teal*'s rail began to dissipate.

This wasn't entirely a good thing. As I began to emerge from my state of stunned shock, I also began to apprehend the true dimensions of the current situation. We were no longer headed for Scotland and the dangers of the Atlantic, but were under way to an unknown destination in an unfamiliar craft with an inexperienced, panic-stricken crew. And we had, in fact, just committed piracy on the high seas, as well as whatever crimes were involved in resisting impressment and assaulting His Majesty's navy. And murder. I swallowed, my throat still tender, and my skin prickled despite the warmth of the fire.

The jar of the knife hitting bone still reverberated in the bones of my own hand and forearm. How could I have killed him? I knew I hadn't penetrated his chest cavity, couldn't possibly have struck the large vessels of the neck. . . . Shock, of course . . . but could shock alone . . . ?

I couldn't think about the dead gunner just now, and pushed the thought of him firmly away. Later, I told myself. I would come to terms with it—it had been self-defense, after all—and I would pray for his soul, but later. Not now.

Not that the other things presenting themselves to me as I worked were much more appealing. Ian and Rollo—no, I couldn't think about that, either.

I scraped the bottom of the pot determinedly with a big wooden spoon. The stew was a little scorched at the bottom, but still edible. There were bones in it, and it was thick and gummy, with lumps. Gagging slightly, I filled a smaller pot from a water butt and hung it to boil.

Navigation. I settled on that as a topic for worry, on grounds that while it was deeply concerning, it lacked the emotional aspects of some of the other things on my mental agenda. How full was the moon? I tried to recall what it had looked like the night before, from the deck of the *Teal*. I hadn't really noticed, so it wasn't near the full; the full moon rising out of the sea is breathtaking, with that shining path across the water that makes you feel how simple it would be to step over the rail and walk straight on, into that peaceful radiance.

No, no peaceful radiance last night. I'd gone up to the ship's head, though, quite late, instead of using a chamber pot, because I'd wanted air. It had been dark on deck, and I'd paused for a moment by the rail, because there was phosphorescence in the long, rolling waves, a beautiful eerie glimmer of green light under the water, and the wake of the ship plowed a glowing furrow through the sea.

Dark moon, then, I decided, or a sliver, which would amount to the same thing. We couldn't come close into shore by night, then. I didn't know how far north we were—maybe John Smith did?—but was aware that the coastline of the Chesapeake involved all kinds of channels, sandbars, tide flats, and ship traffic. Wait, though, Smith had said we'd passed Norfolk . . .

"Well, bloody hell!" I said exasperated. "Where *is* Norfolk?" I knew where it was in relation to Highway I-64, but had no notion whatever what the blasted place looked like from the ocean.

And if we were obliged to stand far out from land during the night, what was to keep us from drifting *very* far out to sea?

"Well, on the good side, we needn't trouble about running out of gas," I said encouragingly to myself. Food and water . . . well, not yet, at least.

I seemed to be running out of good impersonal worrying material. What about Jamie's seasickness? Or any other medical catastrophe that might occur aboard? Yes, that was a good one. I had no herbs, no needles, no sutures, no bandages, no instruments—I was for the moment completely without any practical medicine at all, save boiling water and what skill might be contained in my two hands.

"I suppose I could reduce a dislocation or put my thumb on a spurting artery," I said aloud, "but that's about it."

"Uhh . . ." said a deeply uncertain voice behind me, and I spun round, inadvertently spattering stew from my ladle.

"Oh. Mr. Smith."

"Didn't mean to take you unawares, ma'am." He sidled into the light like a wary spider, keeping a cautious distance from me. " 'Specially not as I saw your nephew hand you back that knife of yours." He smiled a little, to indicate that this was a joke, but he was plainly uneasy. "You . . . um . . . were right handy with it, I must say."

"Yes," I said flatly, picking up a rag to mop the splatters. "I've had practice."

This led to a marked silence. After a moment or two, he coughed.

"Mr. Fraser sent me to ask—in a gingerly sort of way—whether there might be anything to eat soon?"

I gave a grudging snort of laughter at that.

"Was the 'gingerly' his idea or yours?"

"His," he replied promptly.

"You can tell him the food is ready, whenever anyone likes to come and eat it. Oh—Mr. Smith?"

He turned back at once, earrings swinging.

"I only wondered—what do the men . . . well, they must be very upset, of course, but what do the hands from the *Teal* feel about . . . er . . . recent developments? If you happen to know, that is," I added.

"I know. Mr. Fraser asked me that, not ten minutes ago," he said, looking mildly amused. "We been a-talking, up in the tops, as you may imagine, ma'am."

"Oh, I do."

"Well, we're much relieved not to be pressed, of course. Was that to happen, likely none of us would see home nor family again for years. To say nothing of being forced maybe to fight our own countrymen." He scratched at his chin; like all the men, he was becoming bristly and piratical-looking. "On t'other hand, though . . . well, you must allow of our situation at the moment being not all our friends might wish. Perilous, I mean to say, and us now minus our pay and our clothes, to boot."

"Yes, I can see that. From your point of view, what might be the most desirable outcome of our situation?"

"Make land as near to New Haven as we can get, but not in the harbor. Run her aground on a gravel bar and set her afire," he replied promptly. "Take her boat ashore, then run like the dickens."

"Would you burn the ship with the sailors in the hold?" I asked, as a matter of curiosity. To my relief, he appeared shocked at the suggestion.

"Oh, no, ma'am! Might be as Mr. Fraser would want to turn them over to the Continentals to use for exchange, maybe, but we wouldn't mind was they to be set free, either."

"That's very magnanimous of you," I assured him gravely. "And I'm sure Mr. Fraser is very grateful for your recommendations. Do you, er, know where the Continental army *is* just now?"

"Somewhere in New Jersey is what I heard," he replied, with a brief smile. "I don't suppose they'd be that hard to find, though, if you wanted 'em."

Aside from the royal navy, the last thing I personally wanted to see was the Continental army, even at a distance. New Jersey seemed safely remote, though.

I sent him to rummage the crew's quarters for utensils—each man would have his own mess kid and spoon—and set about the tricky task of lighting the two lamps that hung over the mess table, in hopes that we might see what we were eating.

Having got a closer look at the stew, I changed my mind about the desirability of more illumination, but considering how much trouble it had been to light the lamps, wasn't disposed to blow them out, either.

All in all, the meal wasn't bad. Though it likely wouldn't have mattered if I'd fed them raw grits and fish heads; the men were famished. They devoured the food like a horde of cheerful locusts, their spirits remarkably high, considering our situation. Not for the first time, I marveled at the ability of men to function capably in the midst of uncertainty and danger.

Part of it, of course, was Jamie. One couldn't overlook the irony of someone who hated the sea and ships as he did suddenly becoming the *de facto* captain of a naval cutter, but while he might loathe ships, he did in fact know more or less how one was run—and he had the knack of calm in the face of chaos, as well as a natural sense of command.

If you can keep your head when all about you are losing theirs and blaming it on you . . . I thought, watching him talk calmly and sensibly to the men.

Pure adrenaline had kept me going until now, but, now out of immediate danger, it was fading fast. Between fatigue, worry, and a bruised throat, I was able to eat only a bite or two of the stew. My other bruises had begun to throb, and my knee still felt tender. I was taking a morbid inventory of physical damage when I saw Jamie's eyes fixed on me.

"Ye need food, Sassenach," he said mildly. "Eat." I opened my mouth to say that I wasn't hungry, but thought better of it. The last thing he needed was to worry about me.

"Aye, aye, Captain," I said, and resignedly picked up my spoon.

A GUIDED TOUR THROUGH
THE CHAMBERS OF THE HEART

I SHOULD BE GOING to sleep. God knew I needed sleep. And there would be precious little of it until we reached New Haven. *If we ever do,* the back of my mind commented skeptically, but I ignored this remark as unhelpful to the current situation.

I longed to plunge into sleep, as much to escape the fears and uncertainties of my mind as to restore my much abused flesh. I was so tired, though, that mind and body had begun to separate.

It was a familiar phenomenon. Doctors, soldiers, and mothers encounter it routinely; I had, any number of times. Unable to respond to an immediate emergency while clouded by fatigue, the mind simply withdraws a little, separating itself fastidiously from the body's overwhelming self-centered needs. From this clinical distance, it can direct things, bypassing emotions, pain, and tiredness, making necessary decisions, cold-bloodedly overruling the mindless body's needs for food, water, sleep, love, grief, pushing it past its fail-safe points.

Why emotions? I wondered dimly. Surely emotion was a function of the mind. And yet it seemed so deeply rooted in the flesh that this abdication of the mind always suppressed emotion, too.

The body resents this abdication, I think. Ignored and abused, it will not easily let the mind return. Often, the separation persists until one is finally allowed to sleep. With the body absorbed in its quiet intensities of regeneration, the mind settles cautiously back into the turbulent flesh, feeling its delicate way through the twisting passages of dreams, making peace. And you wake once more whole.

But not yet. I had the feeling that something remained to be done but no idea what. I had fed the men, sent food to the prisoners, checked the wounded . . . reloaded all the pistols . . . cleaned the stewpot . . . My slowing mind went blank.

I set my hands on the table, fingertips feeling out the grain of the wood as though the tiny ridges, worn smooth by years of service, might be the map that would enable me to find my way to sleep.

I could see myself in the eye of the mind, sitting there. Slender, nearly scrawny; the edge of my radius showed sharp against the skin of my forearm. I'd got thinner than I realized, over the last few weeks of traveling. Round-shouldered with fatigue. Hair a bushy, tangled mass of writhing strands, streaked with silver and white, a dozen shades of dark and light. It reminded me of something Jamie had told me, some expression the Cherokee had...combing snakes from the hair, that was it. To relieve the mind of worry, anger, fear, possession by demons—that was to comb the snakes from your hair. Very apt.

I did not, of course, possess a comb at the moment. I'd had one in my pocket, but had lost it in the struggle.

My mind felt like a balloon, tugging stubbornly at its tether. I wouldn't let it go, though; I was suddenly and irrationally afraid that it might not come back at all.

Instead, I focused my attention fiercely on small physical details: the weight of the chicken stew and bread in my belly; the smell of the oil in the lamps, hot and fishy. The thump of feet on the deck above, and the song of the wind. The hiss of water down the sides of the ship.

The feel of a blade in flesh. Not the power of purpose, the guided destruction of surgery, damage done in order to heal. A panicked stab, the jump and stutter of a blade striking bone unexpected, the wild careen of an uncontrolled knife. And the wide dark stain on the deck, fresh-wet and smelling of iron.

"I didn't mean it," I whispered aloud. "Oh, God. I didn't mean it."

Quite without warning, I began to cry. No sobbing, no throat-gripping spasms. Water simply welled in my eyes and flowed down my cheeks, slow as cold honey. A quiet acknowledgment of despair as things spiraled slowly out of control.

"What is it, lass?" Jamie's voice came softly from the door.

"I'm so tired," I said thickly. "So tired."

The bench creaked under his weight as he sat beside me, and a filthy handkerchief dabbed gently at my cheeks. He put an arm round me and whispered to me in Gaelic, the soothing endearments one makes to a startled animal. I turned my cheek into his shirt and closed my eyes. The tears were still running down my face, but I was beginning to feel better; still weary unto death, but not utterly destroyed.

"I wish I hadn't killed that man," I whispered. His fingers had been smoothing the hair behind my ear; they paused for a moment, then resumed.

"Ye didna kill anyone," he said, sounding surprised. "Was that what's been troubling ye, Sassenach?"

"Among other things, yes." I sat up, wiping my nose on my sleeve, and stared at him. "I didn't kill the gunner? Are you sure?"

His mouth drew up in what might have been a smile, if it were a shade less grim.

"I'm sure. I killed him, *a nighean*."

"You—oh." I sniffed, and looked at him closely. "You aren't saying that to make me feel better."

"I am not." The smile faded. "I wish I hadna killed him, either. No much choice about it, though." He reached out and pushed a lock of hair behind my ear with a forefinger. "Dinna fash yourself about it, Sassenach. I can stand it."

I was crying again—but this time with feeling. I wept with pain and with sorrow, certainly with fear. But the pain and sorrow were for Jamie and the man he had no choice but to kill, and that made all the difference.

After a bit, the storm subsided, leaving me limp but whole. The buzzing sense of detachment had gone. Jamie had turned round on the bench, his back against the table as he held me on his lap, and we sat in peaceful silence for a bit, watching the glow of the fading coals in the galley fire and the wisps of steam rising from the cauldron of hot water. *I should put something on to cook through the night,* I thought drowsily. I glanced at the cages, where the chickens had settled themselves to sleep, with no more than an occasional brief cluck of startlement as one roused from whatever chickens dream about.

No, I couldn't bring myself to kill a hen tonight. The men would have to do with whatever came to hand in the morning.

Jamie had also noticed the chickens, though to different effect.

"D'ye recall Mrs. Bug's chickens?" he said, with a rueful humor. "Wee Jem and Roger Mac?"

"Oh, God. Poor Mrs. Bug."

Jem, aged five or so, had been entrusted with the daily chore of counting the hens to be sure they had all returned to their coop at night. After which, of course, the door was fastened securely, to keep out foxes, badgers, or other chicken-loving predators. Only Jem had forgotten. Just once, but once was enough. A fox had got into the hen coop, and the carnage had been terrible.

It's all rot to say that man is the only creature who kills for pleasure. Possibly they learned it from men, but all the dog family do it, too—foxes, wolves, and theoretically domesticated dogs, as well. The walls of the hen coop had been plastered with blood and feathers.

"Oh, my bairnies!" Mrs. Bug kept saying, tears rolling down her cheeks like beads. "Oh, my puir wee bairnies!"

Jem, called into the kitchen, couldn't look.

"I'm sorry," he whispered, eyes on the floor. "I'm really sorry."

"Well, and so ye should be," Roger had said to him. "But sorry's no going to help much, is it?"

Jemmy shook his head, mute, and tears welled in his eyes.

Roger cleared his throat, with a noise of gruff menace.

"Well, here it is, then. If ye're old enough to be trusted with a job, ye're old enough to take the consequences of breaking that trust. D'ye understand me?"

It was rather obvious that he didn't, but he bobbed his head earnestly, sniffling.

Roger took in a deep breath through his nose.

"I mean," he said, "I'm going to whip you."

Jem's small, round face went quite blank. He blinked and looked at his mother, openmouthed.

Brianna made a small movement toward him, but Jamie's hand closed on her arm, stopping her.

Without looking at Bree, Roger put a hand on Jem's shoulder and turned him firmly toward the door.

"Right, mate. Out." He pointed toward the door. "Up to the stable and wait for me."

Jemmy gulped audibly. He'd gone a sickly gray when Mrs. Bug brought in the first feathery corpse, and subsequent events had not improved his color.

I thought he might throw up, but he didn't. He'd stopped crying and didn't start again, but seemed to shrink into himself, shoulders hunching.

"Go," said Roger, and he went.

As Jemmy trudged out, head hanging, he looked so exactly like a prisoner headed for execution that I wasn't sure whether to laugh or cry. I caught Brianna's eye and saw that she was struggling with a similar feeling; she looked distressed, but her mouth twitched at the corner, and she looked hastily away.

Roger heaved an explosive sigh and made to follow, squaring his shoulders.

"Christ," he muttered.

Jamie had been standing silent in the corner, watching the exchange, though not without sympathy. He moved just slightly, and Roger glanced at him. He coughed.

"Mmphm. I ken it's the first time—but I think ye'd best make it hard," he said softly. "The poor wee lad feels terrible."

Brianna cut her eyes at him, surprised, but Roger nodded, the grim line of his mouth relaxing a little. He followed Jem out, unbuckling his belt as he left.

The four of us stood awkwardly round the kitchen, not quite sure what to do next. Brianna drew herself up with a sigh rather like Roger's, shook herself like a dog, and reached for one of the dead chickens.

"Can we eat them?"

I prodded one of the hens experimentally; the flesh moved under the skin, limp and wobbly, but the skin hadn't yet begun to separate. I picked the rooster up and sniffed; there was a sharp tang of dried blood and the musty scent of dribbled feces, but no sweet smell of rot.

"I think so, if they're thoroughly cooked. The feathers won't be much good, but we can stew some, and boil the rest for broth and fricassee."

Jamie went to fetch onions, garlic, and carrots from the root cellar, while Mrs. Bug retired to lie down and Brianna and I began the messy job of plucking and gutting the victims. We didn't say much, beyond brief murmured queries and answers about the job at hand. When Jamie came back, though, Bree looked up at him as he set the basket of vegetables on the table beside her.

"It will help?" she asked seriously. "Really?"

He'd nodded. "Ye feel badly when ye've done something wrong, and want to put it right, aye? But there's no means to put something like that right again." He gestured toward the pile of dead chickens. Flies were beginning to gather, crawling over the soft feathers.

"The best ye can do is feel ye've paid for it."

A faint shriek reached us through the window. Brianna had started instinctively at the sound, but then shook her head slightly and reached for a chicken, waving away the flies.

"I remember," I now said softly. "So does Jemmy, I'm sure."

Jamie made a small sound of amusement, then lapsed into silence. I could feel his heart beating against my back, slow and steady.

WE KEPT WATCH AT two-hour intervals all night, making sure that either Jamie, Ian, or myself was awake. John Smith seemed solid—but there was always the possibility that someone from the *Teal* might take it into his head to liberate the sailors in the hold, thinking that might save them from being hanged as pirates later.

I managed the midnight watch well enough, but rousing at dawn was a struggle. I fought my way up out of a deep well lined with soft black wool, an aching fatigue clinging to my bruised and creaking limbs.

Jamie had promptly fallen into the blanket-lined hammock, directly I was out of it, and despite the urgent reflexive desire to tip him out and climb back in myself, I smiled a little. Either he had complete trust in my ability to keep watch, or he was about to die from fatigue and seasickness. Or both, I reflected, picking up the sea officer's cloak he'd just discarded. That was one thing gained from the present situation: I'd left the horrid dead leper's cloak aboard the *Teal*. This one was a vast improvement, being made of new dark-blue thick wool, lined with scarlet silk, and still holding a good deal of Jamie's body heat.

I pulled it close around me, stroked his head to see if he would smile in his sleep—he did, just a twitch of the mouth—and made my way to the galley, yawning.

Another small benefit: a canister of good Darjeeling tea in the cupboard. I'd built up the fire under the cauldron of water when I came to bed; it was hot clear through now, and I dipped out a cup, using what was obviously the captain's private china, painted with violets.

I carried this above, and after an official stroll round the decks, eyeing the two hands on duty—Mr. Smith had the helm—I stood by the rail to drink my fragrant booty, watching the dawn come up out of the sea.

If one were in the mood to count blessings—and, oddly enough, I seemed to be—here was another one. I had seen dawnings in warm seas that came like the bloom of some tremendous flower, a great, slow unfurling of heat and light. This was a northern sunrise, like the slow opening of a bivalve's shell—cold and delicate, the sky shimmering nacre over a soft gray sea. There was something intimate about it, I thought, as though it presaged a day of secrets.

Just as I was getting well stuck into the poetic thoughts, they were interrupted by a shout of "Sail, ho!" from directly above me. Captain Stebbings's violet-painted china cup shattered on the deck, and I whirled to see the tip of a white triangle on the horizon behind us, growing larger by the second.

THE NEXT FEW MOMENTS were filled with low comedy, as I rushed into the captain's cabin so flustered and out of breath that I was unable to do more than gasp, "Ho!...s'l...Ho!" like a demented Santa Claus. Jamie, who could spring to instant wakefulness out of a deep sleep, did so. He also attempted to spring out of bed, forgetting in the stress of the moment that he was in a hammock. By the time he picked himself up, swearing, from the floor, feet were thundering on the deck as the rest of the *Teal*'s hands sprang more adroitly from their own hammocks and ran to see what was up.

"Is it the *Teal?*" I asked John Smith, straining my eyes to see. "Can you tell?"

"Yes," he said absently, squinting at the sail. "Or no, rather. I can tell, and she isn't. She's got three masts."

"I'll take your word for it." At this distance, the approaching ship looked like a wavering cloud scudding toward us over the water; I couldn't make out her hull at all yet.

"We don't need to run from her, do we?" I asked Jamie, who had rooted out a spyglass from Stebbings's desk and was examining our pursuer with a deep frown. He lowered the glass at this, shaking his head.

"It doesna matter whether we need to or not; we'd no stand a chance." He passed the glass to Smith, who clapped it to his eye, muttering, "Colors... she's got no colors flying—"

Jamie's head jerked sharply up and around at that, and I realized abruptly that the *Pitt* was still flying the Union Jack.

"That's good, don't you think?" I asked. "They won't trouble a naval ship, surely."

Jamie and John Smith both looked exceedingly dubious at this piece of logic.

"If they come within hailing distance, they'll likely notice something's fishy and it ain't a whale," Smith said. He glanced sideways at Jamie. "Still... would you maybe think of puttin' on the captain's coat? It might help—at a distance."

"If they get close enough for it to matter, it willna matter anyway," Jamie said, looking grim.

Still, he disappeared, pausing briefly to retch over the rail, and returned moments later looking splendid—if you stood well back and squinted—in Captain Stebbings's uniform. As Stebbings was perhaps a foot shorter than Jamie and a good deal larger round the middle, the coat strained across the shoulders and flapped around the waist, both sleeves and breeches showed a much greater expanse of shirtsleeve and stocking than was usual, and the breeches had been cinched up in folds with Jamie's sword belt in order not to fall off. He was now sporting the captain's sword, I saw, *and* a pair of loaded pistols, as well as his own dirk.

Ian's brows went up at sight of his uncle thus attired, but Jamie glared at him, and Ian said nothing, though his expression lightened for the first time since we had met the *Pitt*.

"Not so bad," Mr. Smith said, encouraging. "Might's well try to brass it out, eh? Nothing to be lost, after all."

"Mmphm."

"*The boy stood on the burning deck, whence all but he had fled,*" I said, causing Jamie to switch the glare to me.

Having seen Guinea Dick, I wasn't worried about Ian's passing muster as a hand in the royal navy, tattoos and all. The rest of the *Teal*'s hands were fairly unexceptional. We might just get away with it.

The oncoming ship was close enough now for me to see her figurehead, a black-haired female who seemed to be clutching a—

"Is that really a snake she's holding?" I asked dubiously. Ian leaned forward, squinting over my shoulder.

"It's got fangs."

"So's the ship, lad." John Smith nodded at the vessel, and at this point I saw that indeed it did: the long snouts of two small brass guns protruded from the bow, and as the wind drove her toward us at a slight angle, I could also see that she had gunports. They might or might not be real; merchantmen sometimes painted their sides with false gunports, to discourage interference.

The bow chasers were real, though. One of them fired, a puff of white smoke and a small ball that splashed into the water near us.

"Is that courteous?" Jamie asked dubiously. "Does he mean to signal us?"

Evidently not; both bow chasers spoke together, and a ball tore through one of the sails overhead, leaving a large hole with singed edges. We gaped at it.

"What does he think he's about, firing on a King's ship?" Smith demanded indignantly.

"He thinks he's a bloody privateer, and he means to take us, is what," Jamie said, recovering from his shock and hastily disrobing. "Strike the colors, for God's sake!"

Smith glanced uneasily between Jamie and the oncoming ship. Men were visible at the railings. Armed men.

"They have cannon and muskets, Mr. Smith," Jamie said, throwing his coat overboard with a heave that sent it spiraling out onto the waves. "I'm no going to try to fight them for His Majesty's ship. Run down that flag!"

Mr. Smith bolted, and began rooting among the myriad lines for the one connected to the Union Jack. Another boom came from the bow chasers, though this time a lucky roll of the sea carried us into a trough and both balls passed over us.

The colors came rattling down, to land in an ignominious heap on the deck. I had a moment's scandalized, reflexive impulse to rush over and pick them up, but stopped myself.

"Now what?" I asked, an uneasy eye on the ship. It was near enough that I could make out the shapes of the gunners, who were definitely reloading the brass bow chasers and re-aiming them. And the men at the railings behind them were indeed bristling with armament; I thought I made out swords and cutlasses, as well as muskets and pistols.

The gunners had paused; someone was pointing over the railing, turning to call to someone behind him. Shading my eyes with my hand, I saw the captain's coat, afloat on the rising swell. That appeared to have baffled the privateer; I saw a man hop up onto the bow and stare toward us.

What now? I wondered. Privateers could be anything from professional captains sailing under a letter of marque from one government or another to out-and-out pirates. If the vessel on our tail was the former, chances were that we would fare all right as passengers. If the latter, they could easily cut our throats and throw us into the sea.

The man in the bow shouted something to his men and hopped down. The ship had hauled her wind for a moment; now the bow turned and the sails filled with an audible thump of wind.

"She's going to ram us," Smith said, his tone one of blank disbelief.

I was sure he was right. The figurehead was close enough that I could see the snake grasped in the woman's hand, pressed against her bare breast. Such is the nature of shock that I was conscious of my mind idly considering whether the ship was more likely named *Cleopatra* or *Asp,* when it passed us in a foaming rush and the air shattered in a crash of searing metal.

The world dissolved and I was lying flat, my face pressed into ground that smelled of butchery, deafened and straining for my life to hear the scream of the next mortar round, the one that would strike us dead center.

Something heavy had fallen on me, and I struggled mindlessly to get out from under it, to get to my feet and run, run anywhere, anywhere away . . . away . . .

I gradually realized from the feel of my throat that I was making whimpering noises and that the surface under my flattened cheek was salt-sticky board, not blood-soaked mud. The weight on my back moved suddenly of its own volition, as Jamie rolled off, rising to his knees.

"Jesus *Christ*!" he shouted in fury. "What's *wrong* wi' you!?"

The only answer to this was a single boom, this coming evidently from a gun at the stern of the other ship, which had passed us.

I stood up, trembling, but so far past simple fright that I noticed with a purely detached sort of interest that there was a leg lying on the deck a few feet away. It was barefooted, clad in the torn-off leg of a pair of canvas breeches. There was a good deal of blood spattered here and there.

"Holy God, holy GOD," someone kept saying. I glanced incuriously to the side and saw Mr. Smith, staring upward with a look of horror.

I looked, too. The top of the single mast was gone, and the remains of sails and rigging sagged in a tattered, smoking mass over half the deck. Evidently the privateer's gunports were *not* just for show.

Dazed as I was, I hadn't even begun to ask myself why they'd done this. Jamie wasn't wasting any time asking questions, either. He seized Mr. Smith by the arm.

"Bloody hell! The wicked *nàmhaid* are comin' back!"

They were. The other ship had been moving too fast, I belatedly realized. She'd shot past as she unleashed her broadside, but likely only one of the heavy cannonballs had actually hit us, taking out the mast and the unfortunate Teal who'd been in the rigging.

The rest of the Teals were now on deck, shouting questions. The only answer was dealt by the privateer, who was now describing a wide circle, only too clearly meaning to come back and finish what she'd started.

I saw Ian glance sharply at the *Pitt*'s cannon—but that was plainly futile. Even if the *Teal*'s men included some with gunnery experience, there was no possibility of them being able to man the guns on the spur of the moment.

The privateer had completed her circle. She was coming back. All over the *Pitt*'s deck, men were shouting, waving their arms, crashing into one another as they stumbled toward the rail.

"We surrender, you filthy buggers!" one of them screamed. "Are you *deaf*?!"

Evidently so; a stray waft of wind brought me the sulfurous smell of slow match, and I could see muskets being brought to bear on us. A few of the men near me lost their heads and rushed belowdecks. I found myself thinking that perhaps that was not such a bad idea.

Jamie had been waving and shouting beside me. Suddenly he was gone, though, and I turned to see him running across the deck. He whipped his shirt off over his head and leapt up onto our bow chaser, a gleaming brass gun called a long nine.

He waved the shirt in a huge, fluttering white arc, his free hand clamped on Ian's shoulder for balance. That caused confusion for a moment; the crackle of firing stopped, though the sloop continued her deadly circle. Jamie waved the shirt again, to and fro. Surely they must see him!

The wind was toward us; I could hear the rumble of the guns running out again, and the blood froze in my chest.

"They're going to sink us!" Mr. Smith shrieked, and this was echoed in cries of terror from some of the other men.

The smell of black powder came to us on the wind, sharp and acrid. There were shouts from the men in the rigging, half of them now desperately waving their shirts, as well. I saw Jamie pause for an instant, swallow, then bend down and say something to Ian. He squeezed Ian's shoulder hard, then lowered himself on hands and knees to the gun.

Ian shot past me, nearly knocking me over in his haste.

"Where are you going?" I cried.

"To let the prisoners out! They'll drown if we sink!" he called over his shoulder, disappearing into the companionway.

I turned back to the oncoming ship, to find that Jamie had not come down off the gun, as I'd thought. Instead, he had scrambled round so his back was to the oncoming sloop.

Braced against the wind, arms spread for balance, and knees gripping the brass of the gun for all he was worth, he stretched to his full height, arms out, displaying his bare back—and the web of scars on it, these gone red with the blanching of his skin in the cold wind.

The oncoming ship had slowed, maneuvering to slide alongside us and blast us out of the water with a final broadside. I could see the heads of men poking up over her rail, leaning out from her rigging, all craning in curiosity. But not firing.

I suddenly felt my heart beating with huge, painful thumps, as though it had actually stopped for a minute and now, reminded of its duty, was trying to make up for lost time.

The side of the sloop loomed above us, and the deck fell into deep, cold shadow. So close, I could hear the talk of the gun crews, puzzled, questioning; hear the deep clink and rattle of shot in its racks, the creak of the gun carriages. I couldn't look up, didn't dare to move.

"Who *are* you?" said a nasal, very American voice from above. It sounded deeply suspicious and very annoyed.

"If ye mean the ship, she's called the *Pitt*." Jamie had got down from the gun and stood beside me, half naked and so pebbled with gooseflesh that the hairs stood out from his body like copper wires. He was shaking, though whether from terror, rage, or simply from cold, I didn't know. His voice didn't shake, though; it was filled with fury.

"If ye mean me, I am Colonel James Fraser, of the North Carolina militia."

A momentary silence, as the master of the privateer digested that.

"Where's Captain Stebbings?" the voice asked. The suspicion in it was undiminished, but the annoyance had waned a bit.

"It's a bloody long story," Jamie said, sounding cross. "But he's no aboard. If ye want to come over and look for him, do so. D'ye mind if I put my shirt back on?"

A pause, a murmur, and the clicks of hammers being eased. At this point, I unfroze enough to look up. The rail was a-bristle with the barrels of muskets and pistols, but most of these had been withdrawn and were now pointing harmlessly upward, while their owners pressed forward to gawk over the rail.

"Just a minute. Turn about," the voice said.

Jamie drew a deep breath in through his nose, but did so. He glanced at me, briefly, then stood with his head up, jaw clenched, and eyes fixed on the mast, around which the prisoners from the hold were now assembled, under Ian's eye. They looked completely baffled, gaping up at the privateer, then looking wildly round the deck before spotting Jamie, half naked and glaring like a basilisk. Had I not begun to worry that I was having a heart attack, I would have found it funny.

"Deserter from the British army, were you?" said the voice from the sloop, sounding interested. Jamie turned round, preserving the glare.

"I am not," he said shortly. "I am a free man—and always have been."

"Have you, then?" The voice was beginning to sound amused. "All right. Put your shirt on, and come aboard."

I could barely breathe and was bathed in cold sweat, but my heart began to beat more reasonably.

Jamie, now clothed, took my arm.

"My wife and nephew are coming with me," he called, and without waiting for assent from the sloop, seized me by the waist and lifted me to stand on the *Pitt*'s rail, from where I could grab the rope ladder that the sloop's crew had thrown down. He was taking no chances on being separated from either me or Ian again.

The ship was rolling in the swell, and I had to cling tightly to the ladder with my eyes closed for a moment, as dizziness swept over me. I felt nauseated as well as dizzy, but surely that was only a reaction to shock. With my eyes closed, my stomach settled a little, and I was able to set my foot on the next rung.

"Sail, ho!"

Tilting my head far back, I could just see the waving arm of the man above. I turned to look, the ladder twisting under me, and saw the sail approaching. On the deck above, the nasal voice was shouting orders, and bare feet drummed on the wood as the crew ran for their stations.

Jamie was on the rail of the *Pitt*, gripping me by the waist to save me falling.

"Jesus H. Roosevelt Christ," he said, in tones of utter astonishment, and I looked over my shoulder to see him turned to watch the oncoming ship. "It's the bloody *Teal.*"

A TALL, VERY THIN man with gray hair, a prominent Adam's apple, and piercing ice-blue eyes met us at the top of the ladder.

"Captain Asa Hickman," he barked at me, and then instantly switched his attention to Jamie. "What's that ship? And where's Stebbings?"

Ian scrambled over the rail behind me, looking anxiously back over his shoulder.

"I'd pull that ladder up if I were you," he said briefly to one of the sailors.

I glanced down at the deck of the *Pitt*, where a milling confusion of men was swarming toward the rail, pushing and shoving. There was a good deal of arm-waving and shouting, the naval seamen and the pressed men trying to put their cases, but Captain Hickman wasn't in the mood.

"Pull it up," he said to the sailor, and, "Come with me," to Jamie. He stalked off along the deck, not waiting for an answer and not turning to see whether he was followed. Jamie gave the sailors surrounding us a narrow look but apparently decided they were safe enough, and, with a terse "Look after your auntie" to Ian, went off after Hickman.

Ian was not paying attention to anything save the oncoming *Teal.*

"Jesus," he whispered, eyes fixed on the sail. "D'ye think he's all right?"

"Rollo? I certainly hope so." My face was cold; colder than just from the ocean spray; my lips had gone numb. And there were small flashing lights at the edges of my sight. "Ian," I said, as calmly as possible. "I think I'm going to faint."

The pressure in my chest seemed to rise, choking me. I forced a cough and felt a momentary easing. Dear God, *was* I having a heart attack? Pain in left arm? No. Pain in jaw? Yes, but I was clenching my teeth, no wonder. . . . I didn't feel myself fall, but felt the pressure of hands as someone caught and lowered me to the deck. My eyes were open, I thought, but I couldn't see anything. Dimly, it occurred to me that I might be dying, but I rejected that notion out of hand. No, I bloody *wasn't.* I couldn't. But there was an odd sort of gray swirling mist approaching me.

"Ian," I said—or thought I said. I felt very calm. "Ian, just in case—tell Jamie that I love him." Everything did not go black, rather to my surprise, but the mist reached me, and I felt gently enveloped in a peaceful gray cloud. All the pressure, the choking, the pain had eased. I could have floated, happily mindless, in the gray mist, save that I could not be sure I'd really spoken, and the need to convey the message niggled like a cocklebur in the sole of a foot.

"Tell Jamie," I kept saying to a misty Ian. "Tell Jamie that I love him."

"Open your eyes and tell me yourself, Sassenach," said a deep, urgent voice somewhere close.

I tried opening my eyes and found that I could. Apparently I had not died after all. I essayed a cautious breath and found that my chest moved easily. My hair was damp, and I was lying on something hard, covered by a blanket. Jamie's face swam above me, then steadied as I blinked.

"Tell me," he repeated, smiling a little, though anxiety creased the skin beside his eyes.

"Tell you . . . oh! I love you. Where . . . ?" Memory of recent events flooded in upon me, and I sat up abruptly. "The *Teal*? What—"

"I havena got the slightest idea. When did ye last have anything to eat, Sassenach?"

"I don't remember. Last night. What do you mean, you haven't the slightest idea? Is it still *there*?"

"Oh, aye," he said, with a certain grimness. "It is. It fired two shots at us a few minutes gone—though I suppose ye couldna hear them."

"It fired shots at—" I rubbed a hand over my face, pleased to find that I could now feel my lips, and that normal warmth had returned to my skin. "Do I look gray and sweaty?" I asked Jamie. "Are my lips blue?"

He looked startled at that, but bent to peer closely at my mouth.

"No," he said positively, straightening up after a thorough inspection. Then he bent and quickly kissed them, putting a seal on my state of pinkness. "I love ye, too," he whispered. "I'm glad ye're no dead. Yet," he added in a normal tone of voice, straightening up as an unmistakable cannon shot came from somewhere at a distance.

"I assume Captain Stebbings has taken over the *Teal*?" I asked. "Captain Roberts wouldn't be going around taking potshots at strange ships, I don't think. But why is Stebbings firing at us, I wonder? Why isn't he trying to board the *Pitt* and take her back? It's his for the taking now."

My symptoms had all but disappeared by now, and I felt quite clearheaded. Sitting up, I discovered that I had been laid out on a pair of large, flat-topped chests in what appeared to be a small hold; there was a latticed hatch cover overhead, through which I caught the fluttering shadows of moving sails, and the walls were stacked with a miscellaneous assortment of barrels, bundles, and boxes. The air was thick with the smells of tar, copper, cloth, gunpowder, and . . . coffee? I sniffed more deeply, feeling stronger by the moment. Yes, coffee!

The sound of another muffled cannon-shot came through the walls, muffled by distance, and a small visceral quiver ran through me. The notion of being trapped in the hold of a ship that might at any moment be sunk was enough to overcome even the smell of coffee.

Jamie had turned in response to the shot, too, half rising. Before I could stand and suggest that we go above, and quickly, there was a shift in the light, and a round, bristly head poked through the hatchway.

"Is the lady summat recovered?" a young boy asked politely. "Cap'n says if she's dead, you're no longer needed here, and he desires you to come above and speak to him prompt, sir."

"And if I'm not dead?" I inquired, trying to straighten out my petticoats, which were wet round the hems, damp through, and hopelessly rumpled. Drat. Now I had left my gold-weighted skirt and pocket aboard the *Pitt*. At this rate, I'd be lucky to arrive on dry land in my chemise and stays.

The boy—at second glance, he was likely twelve or so, though he looked much younger—smiled at this.

"In that case, he offered to come and drop you overboard himself, ma'am, in hopes of concentrating your husband's mind. Cap'n Hickman's a bit hasty in his speech," he added, with an apologetic grimace. "He doesn't mean much by it. Usually."

"I'll come with you." I stood up without losing my balance, but did accept Jamie's arm. We made our way through the ship, led by our new acquaintance, who helpfully informed me that his name was Abram Zenn ("My pa being a reading man, and much taken by Mr. Johnson's Dictionary, he was tickled by the thought of me being A through Zed, you see"), that he was the ship's boy (the ship's name *was* in fact *Asp,* which pleased me), and that the reason for Captain Hickman's present agitation was a long-standing grievance against the navy's Captain Stebbings: "which there's been more than one run-in betwixt the two, and Cap'n Hickman's sworn that there won't be but one more."

"I gather Captain Stebbings is of like mind?" Jamie asked dryly, to which Abram nodded vigorous assent.

"Fellow in a tavern in Roanoke told me Cap'n Stebbings was drinking there and said to the assembled as how he meant to hang Cap'n Hickman from his own yardarm, and leave him for the gulls to peck his eyes. They would, too," he added darkly, with a glance at the seabirds wheeling over the ocean nearby. "They're wicked buggers, gulls."

Further interesting tidbits were curtailed by our arrival in Captain Hickman's inner sanctum, a cramped stern cabin, as crammed with cargo as the hold had been. Ian was there, doing his impression of a captured Mohawk about to be burned at the stake, from which I deduced that he hadn't taken to Captain Hickman. The feeling seemed to be mutual, judging from the hectic patches of color burning in the latter's rawboned cheeks.

"Ah," Hickman said shortly, seeing us. "Glad to see you've not departed this life yet, ma'am. Be a sad loss to your husband, such a devoted woman." There was a sarcastic intonation to this last that made me wonder uncomfortably just how many times I'd told Ian to relay my love to Jamie and just how many people had heard me doing it, but Jamie simply ignored the comment, showing me to a seat on the captain's unmade bed before turning to deal with the man himself.

"I'm told that the *Teal* is firing at us," he observed mildly. "Does this occasion ye no concern, sir?"

"Not yet it doesn't." Hickman spared a negligent glance at his stern windows, half of them covered with deadlights, presumably because of broken glass; a good many of the panes were shattered. "He's just firing in hopes of a lucky shot. We've got the weather gauge on him, and will likely keep it for the next couple of hours."

"I see," said Jamie, with a convincing attitude of knowing what this meant.

"Captain Hickman is debating in his mind whether to engage the *Teal* in action, Uncle," Ian put in tactfully, "or whether to run. Having the weather gauge is a matter of maneuverability, and thus gives him somewhat more latitude in the matter than the *Teal* has presently, I think."

"Heard the one about *He who fights and runs away, lives to fight another day?*" Hickman said, giving Ian a glare. "If I can sink him, I will. If I can shoot

him on his own quarterdeck and take the ship, I'll like that better, but I'll settle for sending him to the bottom if I have to. But I won't let him sink *me*,
not today."

"Why not today?" I asked. "Rather than any other day, I mean?"

Hickman looked surprised; he had obviously assumed I was purely orna-
mental.

"Because I have an important cargo to deliver, ma'am. One that I daren't
risk. Not unless I could get my hands on that rat Stebbings without taking
any great chances," he added broodingly.

"I gather that your assumption that Captain Stebbings was aboard accounts for your most determined attempt to sink the *Pitt*?" Jamie asked. The
ceiling of the cabin was so low that he, Ian, and Hickman were all obliged to
converse in a crouching position, like a convention of chimpanzees. There
was really nowhere to sit other than the bed, and kneeling on the floor would
of course lack the requisite dignity for a meeting of gentlemen.

"It was, sir, and I'm obliged to you for stopping me in time. Perhaps we
may share a jar, when there's more leisure, and you can tell me what happened
to your back."

"Perhaps not," Jamie said politely. "I gather further that we are under sail.
Where is the *Pitt* presently?"

"Adrift, about two miles off the larboard quarter. If I *can* deal with
Stebbings," and Hickman's eyes fairly glowed red at the prospect, "I'll come
back and take her, too."

"If there's anyone left alive on board to sail her," Ian said. "There was a
fair-sized riot on her deck, when last I saw it. What might predispose ye to
take on the *Teal*, sir?" he asked, raising his voice. "My uncle and I can give ye
information regarding her guns and crew—and even if Stebbings has taken
the ship, I doubt but he'll have a job to fight her. He's got no more than ten
men of his own, and Captain Roberts and his crew will want nay part of an engagement, I'm sure."

Jamie gave Ian a narrow look.

"Ye ken they've likely killed him already."

Ian didn't resemble Jamie at all, but the look of implacable stubbornness
on his face was one I knew intimately.

"Aye, maybe. Would ye leave *me* behind, if ye only thought I *might* be
dead?"

I could see Jamie open his mouth to say, "*He's a dog.*" But he didn't. He
closed his eyes and sighed, obviously contemplating the prospect of instigat-
ing a sea battle—and incidentally risking all of our lives six ways from Sunday,
to say nothing of the lives of the men aboard the *Teal*—for the sake of an ag-
ing dog, who might be already dead, if not devoured by a shark. Then he
opened them and nodded.

"Aye, all right." He straightened, as much as was possible in the cramped
cabin, and turned to Hickman. "My nephew's particular friend is aboard the
Teal and likely in danger. I ken that's no concern of yours, but it explains our
own interest. As for yours...in addition to Captain Stebbings, there is a
cargo aboard the *Teal* in which ye may have an interest, as well—six cases of
rifles."

Ian and I both gasped. Hickman straightened up abruptly, cracking his head on a timber.

"Ow! Holy Moses. You're sure of that?"

"I am. And I imagine the Continental army might make use of them?"

I thought that was treading on dangerous ground; after all, the fact that Hickman had a strong animus toward Captain Stebbings didn't necessarily mean he was an American patriot. From the little I'd seen of him, Captain Stebbings looked entirely capable of inspiring purely personal animus, quite separate from any political considerations.

But Hickman made no denial; in fact, he'd barely noticed Jamie's remark, inflamed by mention of the rifles. Was it true? I wondered. But Jamie had spoken with complete certainty. I cast my mind back over the contents of the *Teal*'s hold, looking for anything . . .

"Jesus H. Roosevelt Christ," I said. "The boxes bound for New Haven?" I barely kept myself from blurting out Hannah Arnold's name, realizing just in time that *if* Hickman was indeed a patriot—for it did occur to me that he might merely be a businessman, as willing to sell to either side—he might well recognize the name and realize that these rifles were almost certainly already intended to reach the Continentals via Colonel Arnold.

Jamie nodded, watching Hickman, who was gazing at a small barometer on the wall as though it were a crystal ball. Whatever it told him seemed to be favorable, for Hickman nodded once, then dashed out of the cabin as though his breeches were on fire.

"Where's he gone?" Ian demanded, staring after him.

"To check the wind, I imagine," I said, proud of knowing something. "To make certain he still has the weather gauge."

Jamie was rifling Hickman's desk, and emerged at this point with a rather wizened apple, which he tossed into my lap. "Eat that, Sassenach. What the devil *is* a weather gauge?"

"Ah. Well, there you have me," I admitted. "But it has to do with wind, and it seems to be important." I sniffed the apple; it had plainly seen better days, but still held a faint, sweet smell that suddenly raised the ghost of my vanished appetite. I took a cautious bite and felt saliva flood my mouth. I ate it in two more bites, ravenous.

Captain Hickman's high nasal voice came piercingly from the deck. I couldn't hear what he said, but the response was immediate; feet thumped to and fro on deck, and the ship shifted suddenly, turning as her sails were adjusted. The chime and grunt of shot being lifted and the rumble of gun carriages echoed through the ship. Apparently, the weather gauge was still ours.

I could see a fierce excitement light Ian's face and rejoiced to see it, but couldn't help voicing a qualm or two.

"You haven't any hesitation about this?" I said to Jamie. "I mean—after all, he *is* a dog."

He gave me an eye and a moody shrug.

"Aye, well. I've known battles fought for worse reasons. And since this time yesterday, I've committed piracy, mutiny, and murder. I may as well add treason and make a day of it."

"Besides, Auntie," Ian said reprovingly, "he's a *good* dog."

WEATHER GAUGE OR NO, it took an endless time of cautious maneuvering before the ships drew within what seemed a dangerous distance of each other. The sun was no more than a handsbreadth above the horizon by now, the sails were beginning to glow a baleful red, and my chastely pristine dawn looked like ending in a wallowing sea of blood.

The *Teal* was cruising gently, no more than half her canvas set, less than half a mile away. Captain Hickman stood on the *Asp*'s deck, hands clenched on the rail as though it were Stebbings's throat, wearing the look of a greyhound just before the rabbit is released.

"Time you went below, ma'am," Hickman said, not looking at me. "Matters will be hotting up directly here." His hands flexed once in anticipation.

I didn't argue. The tension on deck was so thick I could smell it, testosterone spiced with brimstone and black powder. Men being the remarkable creatures that they are, everyone seemed cheerful.

I paused to kiss Jamie—a gesture he returned with a gusto that left my lower lip throbbing slightly—resolutely ignoring the possibility that the next time I saw him, it might be in separate pieces. I'd faced that possibility a number of times before, and while it didn't get less daunting with practice, I had got better at ignoring it.

Or at least I thought I had. Sitting in the main hold in near-total darkness, smelling the low-tide reek of the bilges and listening to what I was sure were rats rustling in the chains, I had a harder time ignoring the sounds from above: the rumbling of gun carriages. The *Asp* had only four guns to a side, but they were twelve-pounders: heavy armament for a coastal schooner. The *Teal*, equipped as an oceangoing merchantman who might have to fight off all manner of menace, fought eight to a side, sixteen-pounders, with two carronades on the upper deck, plus two bow chasers and a stern gun.

"She'd run from a man-o'-war," Abram explained to me, he having asked me to describe the *Teal*'s armament. "And she wouldn't be likely to try to seize or sink another vessel, so she wouldn't ship tremendous hardware, even was she built for it, and I doubt she is. Now, I doubt as well that Captain Stebbings can man even a whole side to good effect, though, so we mustn't be downhearted." He spoke with great confidence, which I found amusing and also oddly reassuring. He seemed to realize this, for he leaned forward and patted my hand gently.

"Now, you needn't fret, ma'am," he said. "Mr. Fraser said to me I must be sure to let no harm come to you, and I shall not—be sure of that."

"Thank you," I said gravely. Not wanting either to laugh or to cry, I cleared my throat instead and asked, "Do you know what caused the trouble between Captain Hickman and Captain Stebbings?"

"Oh, yes, ma'am," he replied promptly. "Captain Stebbings has been a plague on the district for some years, stopping ships what he hasn't any right to search, taking off legal goods what he says are contraband—and we take leave to doubt that any of it ever sees the inside of a Customs warehouse!" he added, obviously quoting something he'd heard more than once. "But it was what happened with the *Annabelle*, really."

The *Annabelle* was a large ketch, owned by Captain Hickman's brother. The *Pitt* had stopped her and attempted to press men from her crew. Theo Hickman had protested, resistance had broken out, and Stebbings had ordered his men to fire into the *Annabelle,* killing three crewmen—Theo Hickman among them.

There had been considerable public outcry over this, and an effort was made to bring Captain Stebbings to justice for his deeds. The captain had insisted that no local court had the right to try him for anything, though; if anyone wished to bring an action against him, it must be done in an English court. And the local justices had agreed with this.

"Was this before war was declared last year?" I asked curiously. "For if after—"

"Well before," young Zenn admitted. "Still," he added with righteous indignation, "they are cowardly dogs and ought be tarred and feathered, the lot of them, and Stebbings, too!"

"No doubt," I said. "Do you think—"

But I had no opportunity to explore his opinions further, for at this point the ship gave a violent lurch, throwing us both onto the damp floorboards, and the sound of a violent and prolonged explosion shattered the air around us.

I couldn't at first tell which ship had fired—but an instant later, the *Asp*'s guns spoke overhead, and I knew the first broadside had been from the *Teal*.

The *Asp*'s reply was ragged, the guns along her starboard side going off at more or less random intervals overhead, punctuated by the flat bangs of small-arms fire.

I resisted Abram's gallant attempts to throw his meager body protectively on top of mine and, rolling over, got up onto my hands and knees, listening intently. There was a lot of shouting, none of it comprehensible, though the shooting had stopped. We appeared not to be leaking water, so far as I could tell, so presumably we had not been struck below the waterline.

"They can't have given up, surely?" Abram said, scrambling to his feet. He sounded disappointed.

"I doubt it." I got to my own feet, bracing a hand against a large barrel. The main hold was quite as crowded as the forward one, though with bulkier items; there was barely room for Abram and me to worm our way between the netted bulk of crates and tiers of casks—some of which smelled strongly of beer. The ship was heeling to one side now. We must be coming about— probably to try again. The wheels of the gun carriages ground on the deck above; yes, they were reloading. Had anyone yet been hurt? I wondered. And what the devil was I going to do about it if they had?

The sound of a single cannon-shot came from overhead.

"The dog must be fleeing," Abram whispered. "We're chasing him down."

There was a long period of relative silence, during which I thought the ship was tacking but couldn't really tell. Maybe Hickman *was* pursuing the *Teal*.

Sudden yelling from overhead, with a sound of surprised alarm, and the ship heaved violently, flinging us to the floor once again. This time I landed on top. I delicately removed my knee from Abram's stomach and helped him to sit up, gasping like a landed fish.

"What—" he wheezed, but got no further. There was a hideous jolt that knocked us both flat again, followed at once by a grinding, rending noise of squealing timbers. It sounded as though the ship was coming apart around us, and I had no doubt that it was.

Shrieking like banshees and the thunder of feet on deck.

"We're being boarded!" I could hear Abram swallow, and my hand went to the slit in my petticoat, touching my knife for courage. If—

"No," I whispered, straining my eyes up into darkness as though that would help me hear better. "No. We're boarding *them*." For the pounding feet above had vanished.

THE YELLING HADN'T; EVEN muffled by distance, I could hear the note of insanity in it, the clear joy of the berserker. I thought I could make out Jamie's Highland screech, but that was likely imagination; they all sounded equally demented.

"Our Father, who art in heaven... Our Father, who art in heaven..." Abram was whispering to himself in the dark, but had stuck on the first line.

I clenched my fists and closed my eyes in reflex, screwing up my face as though by sheer force of will I could help.

Neither of us could.

It was an age of muffled noises, occasional shots, thuds and bangs, grunting and shouting. And then silence.

I could just see Abram's head turn toward me, questioning. I squeezed his hand.

And then a ship's gun went off with a crash that echoed across the deck above, and a shock wave thrummed through the air of the hold, hard enough that my ears popped. Another followed, I felt rather than heard a *thunk*, and then the floor heaved and tilted, and the ship's timbers reverberated with an odd, deep *bwong*. I shook my head hard, swallowing, trying to force air through my Eustachian tubes. They popped again, finally, and I heard feet on the side of the ship. More than one pair. Moving slowly.

I leapt to my feet, grabbed Abram, and hauled him bodily up, propelling him toward the ladder. I could hear water. Not racing along the ship's sides; a gushing noise, as of water gurgling into the hold.

The hatchway had been closed overhead but not battened down, and I knocked it loose with a desperate bang of both hands, nearly losing my balance and plunging into darkness but luckily sustained by Abram Zenn, who planted a small but solid shoulder under my buttocks by way of support.

"Thank you, Mr. Zenn," I said, and, reaching behind me, pulled him up the ladder into the light.

There was blood on the deck; that was the first thing I saw. Wounded men, too—but not Jamie. He was the second thing I saw, leaning heavily over the remains of a shattered rail with several other men. I hurried to see what they were looking at, and saw the *Teal* a few hundred yards away.

Her sails were fluttering wildly, and her masts seemed oddly tilted. Then I realized that the ship herself was tilted, the bow raised half out of the water.

"Rot me," said Abram, in tones of amazement. "She's run onto rocks."

"So have we, son, but not so bad," said Hickman, glancing aside at the cabin boy's voice. "Is there water in the hold, Abram?"

"There is," I replied before Abram, lost in contemplation of the wounded *Teal,* could gather his wits to answer. "Have you any medical instruments aboard, Captain Hickman?"

"Have I what?" he blinked at me, distracted. "This is no time for—why?"

"I'm a surgeon, sir," I said, "and you need me."

WITHIN A QUARTER HOUR, I found myself back in the small forward cargo hold where I had roused from my fainting spell a few hours earlier, this being now designated as the sick bay.

The *Asp* did not travel with a surgeon, but had a small store of medicinals: a half-full bottle of laudanum, a fleam and bleeding bowl, a large pair of tweezers, a jar of dead and desiccated leeches, two rusty amputation saws, a broken tenaculum, a bag of lint for packing wounds, and a huge jar of camphorated grease.

I was strongly tempted to drink the laudanum myself, but duty called. I tied back my hair and began poking about among the cargo, in search of anything useful. Mr. Smith and Ian had rowed across to the *Teal* in hopes of retrieving my own kit, but given the amount of damage I could see in the area where our cabin had been, I didn't have much hope. A lucky shot from the *Asp* had holed the *Teal* below the waterline; had she not run aground, she would likely have sunk sooner or later.

I'd done a rapid triage on deck; one man killed outright, several minor injuries, three serious but not instantly life-threatening. There were likely more on the *Teal;* from what the men said, the ships had exchanged broadsides at a distance of no more than a few yards. A quick and bloody little action.

A few minutes after the conclusion, the *Pitt* had limped into sight, her contentiously mixed crew having evidently come to a sufficient accommodation as to allow her to sail, and she was now occupied in ferrying the wounded. I heard the faint shout of her bosun's hail over the whine of the wind above.

"Incoming," I murmured, and, picking up the smaller of the amputation saws, prepared for my own quick and bloody action.

"YOU HAVE GUNS," I pointed out to Abram Zenn, who was rigging a couple of hanging lanterns for me, the sun having now almost set. "Presumably this means that Captain Hickman was prepared to use them. Didn't he think there might be a possibility of casualties?"

Abram shrugged apologetically.

"It's our first voyage as a letter of marque, ma'am. We'll do better next time, I'm sure."

"Your first? What sort of—how long has Captain Hickman been sailing?" I demanded. I was ruthlessly rummaging the cargo by now, and was pleased to find a chest that held lengths of printed calico.

Abram frowned at the wick he was trimming, thinking.

"Well," he said slowly, "he had a fishing boat for some time, out of Marblehead. Him—he, I mean—and his brother owned it together. But after his brother ran afoul of Captain Stebbings, he went to work for Emmanuel Bailey, as first mate on one of his—Mr. Bailey's, I mean—ships. Mr. Bailey's a Jew," he explained, seeing my raised eyebrow. "Owns a bank in Philadelphia and three ships as sail regularly to the West Indies. He owns this ship, too, and it's him who got the letter of marque from the Congress for Captain Hickman, when the war was announced."

"I see," I said, more than slightly taken aback. "But this is Captain Hickman's first cruise as captain of a sloop?"

"Yes, ma'am. But privateers don't usually have a supercargo, do you see," he said earnestly. "It would be the supercargo's job to provision the ship and see to such things as the medical supplies."

"And you know this because—how long have *you* been sailing?" I asked curiously, liberating a bottle of what looked like very expensive brandy, to use as antiseptic.

"Oh, since I was eight years old, ma'am," he said. He stood a-tiptoe to hang the lantern, which cast a warm, reassuring glow over my impromptu operating theater. "I've six elder brothers, and the oldest runs the farm, with his sons. The others . . . well, one's a shipwright in Newport News, and he got to talking with a captain one day and mentioned me, and next thing I know, I'm one of the cabin boys on the *Antioch,* her being an Indiaman. I went back with the captain to London, and we sailed to Calcutta the very day after." He came down onto his heels and smiled at me. "I've been a-sea ever since, ma'am. I find it suits me."

"That's very good," I said. "Your parents—are they still alive?"

"Oh, no, ma'am. My mother died birthing me, and my pa when I was seven." He seemed untroubled by this. But after all, I reflected, ripping calico into bandage lengths, that was half his lifetime ago.

"Well, I hope the sea will continue to suit you," I said. "Do you have any doubts, though—after today?"

He thought about that, his earnest young face furrowed in the lantern shadows.

"No," he said slowly, and looked up at me, his eyes serious—and not nearly so young as they had been a few hours ago. "I knew when I signed on with Captain Hickman that there might be fighting." His lips tightened, perhaps to keep them from quivering. "I don't mind killing a man, if I have to."

"Not now . . . you don't," said one of the wounded men, very softly. He was lying in the shadows, stretched across two crates of English china, breathing slowly.

"No, not now, you don't," I agreed dryly. "You might want to speak to my nephew or my husband about it, though, when things have settled a bit."

I thought that would be the end of it, but Abram followed me as I laid out my rudimentary tools and set about such sterilization as could be managed, splashing out brandy with abandon, 'til the hold smelled like a distillery—this to the scandalization of the wounded men, who thought it waste to use good drink so. The galley fire had been put out during the battle, though; it would be some time before I had hot water.

"Are you a patriot, ma'am? If you don't mind me asking," he added, blushing with awkwardness.

The question took me back a bit. The straightforward answer would be "Yes, of course." Jamie was, after all, a rebel, so declared by his own hand. And while he had made the original declaration out of simple necessity, I thought necessity had now become conviction. But me? Certainly I had been, once.

"Yes," I said—I couldn't very well say anything else. "Plainly you are, Abram. Why?"

"Why?" He seemed staggered that I would ask, and stood blinking at me over the top of the lantern he held.

"Tell me later," I suggested, taking the lantern. I'd done what I could on deck; the wounded who needed further attention were being brought down. It was no time for political discussion. Or so I thought.

Abram bravely settled down to help me and did fairly well, though he had to stop now and then to vomit into a bucket. After the second occurrence of this, he took to asking questions of the wounded—those in any condition to answer. I didn't know whether this was simple curiosity or an attempt to distract himself from what I was doing.

"What do you think of the Revolution, sir?" he earnestly asked one grizzled seaman from the *Pitt* with a crushed foot. The man gave him a distinctly jaundiced look but replied, probably in order to distract himself.

"Bloody waste of time," he said gruffly, digging his fingers into the edge of the chest he sat on. "Better to be fighting the frogs than Englishmen. What's to be gained by it? Dear Lord," he said under his breath, going pale.

"Give him something to bite on, Abram, will you?" I said, busy picking shattered bits of bone out of the wreckage and wondering whether he might do better with a swift amputation. Perhaps less risk of infection, and he would always walk with a painful limp in any case, but still, I hated to . . .

"No, that's all right, mum," he said, sucking in a breath. "What do *you* think of it, then, youngster?"

"I think it is right and necessary, sir," Abram replied stoutly. "The King is a tyrant, and tyranny must be resisted by all proper men."

"What?" said the seaman, shocked. "The King, a tyrant? Who says such a naughty thing?"

"Why . . . Mr. Jefferson. And—and all of us! We all think so," Abram said, taken aback at such vehement disagreement.

"Well, then, you're all a pack of bleedin' fools—saving your presence, mum," he added, with a nod to me. He got a look at his foot and swayed a bit, closing his eyes, but asked, "You don't think such a silly thing, do you, mum? You ought to talk sense into your boy here."

"Talk sense?" cried Abram, roused. "You think it sense that we may not speak or write as we wish?"

The seaman opened one eye.

"Of course that's sense," he said, with an evident attempt to be reasonable. "You get silly buggers—your pardon, mum—a-saying all kinds of things regardless, stirrin' folk up to no good end, and what's it lead to? Riot, that's what, and what you may call disorderliness, with folk having their houses burnt and being knocked down in the street. Ever hear of the Cutter riots, boy?"

Abram rather obviously had not, but countered with a vigorous denunciation of the Intolerable Acts, which caused Mr. Ormiston—we had got onto personal terms by now—to scoff loudly and recount the privations Londoners endured by comparison with the luxury enjoyed by the ungrateful colonists.

"Ungrateful!" Abram said, his face congested. "And what should we be grateful for, then? For having soldiers foisted upon us?"

"Oh, foisted, is it?" cried Mr. Ormiston in righteous indignation. "Such a word! And if it means what I think it does, young man, you should get down on your knees and thank God for such foistingness! Who do you think saved you all from being scalped by red Indians or overrun by the French? And who do you think paid for it all, eh?"

This shrewd riposte drew cheers—and not a few jeers—from the waiting men, who had all been drawn into the discussion by now.

"That is absolute . . . desolate . . . *stultiloquy*," began Abram, puffing up his insignificant chest like a scrawny pigeon, but he was interrupted by the entrance of Mr. Smith, a canvas bag in hand and an apologetic look on his face.

"I'm afraid your cabin was all ahoo, ma'am," he said. "But I picked up what bits was scattered on the floor, in case they—"

"Jonah Marsden!" Mr. Ormiston, on the verge of standing up, plumped back onto the chest, openmouthed. "Bless me if it isn't!"

"Who?" I asked, startled.

"Jonah—well, 'tisn't his real name, what was it . . . oh, Bill, I think it was, but we took to calling him Jonah, owing to him being sunk so many times."

"Now, Joe." Mr. Smith—or Mr. Marsden—was backing toward the door, smiling nervously. "That was all a long time ago, and—"

"Not so long as all that." Mr. Ormiston got ponderously to his feet, balancing with one hand on a stack of herring barrels so as not to put weight on his bandaged foot. "Not so long as would make the navy forget you, you filthy deserter!"

Mr. Smith disappeared abruptly up the ladder, pushing past two seamen attempting to come down these, handling a third like a side of beef between them. Muttering curses, they dropped him on the deck in front of me with a thud and stood back, gasping. It was Captain Stebbings.

" 'e's not dead," one of them informed me helpfully.

"Oh, good," I said. My tone of voice might have left something to be desired, for the captain opened one eye and glared at me.

"You're leaving me . . . to be butchered . . . by this bitch?" he said hoarsely, between labored gasps. "I'd ra-rather die hon-honorablblbl . . ." The sentiment gurgled off into a bubbling noise that made me rip open his smoke-stained, blood-soaked second-best coat and shirt. Sure enough, there was a neat round hole in his right breast and the nasty wet slurp of a sucking chest wound coming from it.

I said a very bad word, and the two men who had brought him to me shuffled and muttered. I said it again, louder, and, seizing Stebbings's hand, slapped it over the hole.

"Hold that there, if you want a chance at an honorable death," I said to him. "You!" I shouted at one of the men trying to edge away. "Bring me some oil from the galley. Now! And *you*—" My voice caught the other, who jerked guiltily to a halt. "Sailcloth and tar. Fast as you can!"

"Don't talk," I advised Stebbings, who seemed inclined to make remarks. "You have a collapsed lung, and either I get it reinflated or you die like a dog, right here."

"Hg," he said, which I took for assent. His hand was a nice meaty one, and doing a reasonably good job of sealing the hole for the moment. The trouble was that he undoubtedly had not only a hole in his chest but a hole in the lung, too. I had to provide a seal for the external hole so air couldn't get into the chest and keep the lung compressed, but had also to make sure there was a way for air from the pleural space around the lung to make an exit. As it was, every time he exhaled, air from the injured lung went straight into that space, making the problem worse.

He might also be drowning in his own blood, but there wasn't a hell of a lot I could do about that, so I wouldn't worry about it.

"On the good side," I told him, "it was a bullet, and not shrapnel or a splinter. One thing about red-hot iron: it sterilizes the wound. Lift your hand for a moment, please. Breathe out." I grabbed his hand myself and lifted it for the count of two while he exhaled, then slapped it back over the wound. It made a squelching sound, owing to the blood. It was a lot of blood for a hole like that, but he wasn't coughing or spitting blood. . . . Where—oh.

"Is this blood yours or someone else's?" I demanded, pointing at it.

His eyes were half shut, but at this he turned his head and bared his bad teeth at me in a wolf's grin.

"Your . . . husband's," he said in a hoarse whisper.

"Wanker," I said crossly, lifting his hand again. "Breathe out." The men had seen me dealing with Stebbings; there were other casualties from the *Teal* coming or being carried along, but most of them seemed ambulatory. I gave cursory directions to the able-bodied with them, regarding the application of pressure to wounds or the placement of broken limbs so as to avoid further injury.

It seemed an age before the oil and cloth arrived, and I had sufficient time to wonder where Jamie and Ian were, but the first-aid supplies came at last. I ripped off a patch of sailcloth with my knife, tore a longish strip of calico to use as field dressing, then pushed Stebbings's hand away, wiped off the blood with a fold of my petticoat, sloshed lamp oil over his chest and the sailcloth patch, then pressed the cloth down to form a rudimentary seal, putting his hand back over it in such a way that one end of the patch remained free, while I wound the improvised field dressing round his torso.

"All right," I said. "I'll need to stick the patch down with tar for a better seal, but it will take a little time to warm that. You can go and be doing that now," I advised the sailor who had brought the oil, who was once again try-ing to execute a quiet sneak. I scooted round to view the casualties squatting or sprawling on the deck. "Right. Who's dying?"

For a wonder, only two of the men brought in from the *Teal* were dead, one with hideous head wounds from flying splinters and grapeshot, the other exsanguinated as a result of losing half his left leg, probably to a cannonball.

Might have saved that one, I thought, but the moment's regret was subsumed in the needs of the next moment.

Not all that bad, I thought, working my way quickly down the line on my knees, doing a hasty triage and issuing instructions to my unwilling assistants. Splinter wounds, two grazed by musket balls, one with half an ear torn off, one with an embedded ball in the thigh, but nowhere near the femoral artery, thank God ...

Bangings and shufflings were coming from the lower hold, where repairs were being effected. As I worked, I pieced together the actions of the battle from the remarks passed by the wounded men awaiting my attention.

Following a ragged exchange of broadsides, which had brought down the *Teal*'s cracked mainmast and holed the *Asp* above the waterline, the *Teal*— opinions differed on whether Captain Roberts had done it a-purpose or not— had veered sharply toward the *Asp,* scraping the side of the ship and bringing the two vessels railing to railing.

It seemed inconceivable that Stebbings had intended to board the *Asp,* with so few dependable men as he had; if it had been deliberate, he might have meant to ram us. I glanced down, but the captain's eyes were closed, and he was a nasty color. I lifted his hand and heard a small hiss of air, then placed it back on his chest and went on with my work. Plainly he was in no shape to set the record straight regarding his intentions.

Whatever they had been, Captain Hickman had forestalled them, leaping over the *Teal*'s rail with a shriek, followed by a swarm of Asps. They had cut their way across the deck without much resistance, though the men from the *Pitt* had gathered together around Stebbings near the helm and fought ferociously. It was clear that the Asps must win the day, though—and then the *Teal* had struck heavily aground, throwing everyone flat on deck.

Convinced that the ship was about to sink, everyone who could move did, boarders and defenders together going back over the rail onto the *Asp*— which sheered abruptly away, with some benighted defender who remained on the *Teal* sending a last shot or two after her, only to scrape her own bottom on a gravel bar.

"Not to worry, ma'am," one of the men assured me. "She'll swim directly the tide comes in."

The noises from below began to diminish, and I looked over my shoulder every few moments, in hopes of seeing Jamie or Ian.

I was examining one poor fellow who'd taken a splinter in one eyeball, when his other eye suddenly widened in horror, and I turned to find Rollo panting and dripping by my side, enormous teeth exposed in a grin that put Stebbings's feeble attempt to shame.

"Dog!" I cried, delighted. I couldn't hug him—well, I wouldn't, really— but looked quickly round for Ian, who was limping in my direction, sopping wet, too, but with a matching grin.

"We fell into the water," he said hoarsely, squatting on the deck beside me. A small puddle formed under him.

"So I see. Breathe deeply for me," I said to the man with the splinter in his eye. "One . . . yes, that's right . . . two . . . yes . . ." As he exhaled, I took hold of the splinter and pulled, hard. It slid free, followed by a gush of vitreous humor and blood that made me grit my teeth and made Ian retch. Not a lot of blood, though. *If it hasn't gone through the orbit, I might be able to stave off infection by removing the eyeball and packing the socket. That'll have to wait, though.* I slashed a ribbon of cloth from the man's shirttail, folded it hastily into a wad, soaked it in brandy, pressed it to the ruined eye, and made him hold it firmly in place. He did, though he groaned and swayed alarmingly, and I feared he might fall over.

"Where's your uncle?" I asked Ian, with a gnawing sense that I didn't want to hear the answer.

"Right there," Ian said, nodding to one side. I swung round, one hand still bracing the shoulder of the one-eyed man, to see Jamie coming down the ladder, in heated argument with Captain Hickman, who was following him. Jamie's shirt was soaked with blood, and he was holding a wad of something likewise blood-soaked against his shoulder with one hand. Possibly Stebbings hadn't been merely trying to aggravate me. Jamie wasn't falling down, though, and while he was white, he was also furious. I was reasonably sure he wouldn't die while angry and seized another strip of sailcloth to stabilize a compound fracture of the arm.

"Dog!" said Hickman, coming to a stop beside the supine Stebbings. He didn't say it with the same intonation I had used, though, and Stebbings opened one eye.

"Dog, yourself," he said thickly.

"Dog, dog, dog! Fucking dog!" Hickman added for good measure, and aimed a kick at Stebbings's side. I grabbed for his foot and managed to shove him off balance, so that he lurched sideways. Jamie caught him, grunting with pain, but Hickman struggled upright, pushing Jamie away.

"Ye canna murder the man in cold blood!"

"Can, too," Hickman replied promptly. "Watch me!" He drew an enormous horse pistol out of a ratty leather holster and cocked it. Jamie took it by the barrel and plucked it neatly out of his hand, leaving him flexing his fingers and looking surprised.

"Surely, sir," Jamie said, striving for reasonableness, "ye canna mean to kill a wounded enemy—one in uniform, taken under his own flag, and a man who has surrendered himself to ye. That couldna be condoned by any honorable man."

Hickman drew himself up, going puce.

"Are you impugning my honor, sir?"

I saw the muscles in Jamie's neck and shoulders tense, but before he could speak, Ian stepped up beside him, shoulder to shoulder.

"Aye, he is. So am I."

Rollo, his fur still sticking up in wet spikes, growled and rolled back his black lips, showing most of his teeth in token of his support of this opinion.

Hickman glanced from Ian's scowling, tattooed visage, to Rollo's impressive carnassials, and back to Jamie, who had uncocked the pistol and put it in his own belt. He breathed heavily.

"On your head be it, then," he said abruptly, and turned away.

Captain Stebbings was breathing heavily, too, a wet, nasty sound. He was white to the lips, and the lips themselves were blue. Still, he was conscious. His eyes had been fixed on Hickman throughout the conversation and followed him now as he left the cabin. When the door had closed behind Hickman, Stebbings relaxed a little, shifting his gaze to Jamie.

"Might've . . . saved yourself . . . the trouble," he wheezed. "But you have . . . my thanks. For what . . ." He gave a strangled cough, pressed a hand hard against his chest, and shook his head, grimacing. " . . . what they're worth," he managed.

He closed his eyes, breathing slowly and painfully—but still, breathing. I rose stiffly to my feet and at last had a moment to look at my husband.

"No but a wee cut," he assured me, in answer to my look of suspicious inquiry. "I'll do for now."

"Is all of that blood yours?" He glanced down at the shirt pasted to his ribs and lifted the non-wounded shoulder dismissively.

"I've enough left to be going on with." He smiled at me, then glanced around the deck. "I see ye've got matters well in hand here. I'll have Smith bring ye a bit of food, aye? It's going to rain soon."

It was; the smell of the oncoming storm swept through the hold, fresh and tingling with ozone, lifting the hair off my damp neck.

"Possibly not Smith," I said. "And where are you going?" I asked, seeing him turn away.

"I need to speak wi' Captain Hickman and Captain Roberts," he said, with a certain grimness. He glanced upward, and the matted hair behind his ears stirred in the breeze. "I dinna think we're going to Scotland in the *Teal,* but damned if I ken where we *are* going."

THE SHIP EVENTUALLY grew quiet—or as quiet as a large object composed of creaking boards, flapping canvas, and that eerie hum made by taut rigging can get. The tide had come in, and the ship did swim; we were moving north again, under light sail.

I had seen off the last of the casualties; only Captain Stebbings remained, laid on a crude pallet behind a chest of smuggled tea. He was still breathing, and not in terrible discomfort, I thought, but his condition was much too precarious for me to let him out of my sight.

By some miracle, the bullet seemed to have seared its way into his lung, rather than simply severing blood vessels in its wake. That didn't mean he wasn't bleeding into his lung, but if so, it was a slow seep; I would long since have known about it, otherwise. He must have been shot at close range, I thought sleepily. The ball had still been red-hot when it struck him.

I had sent Abram to bed. I should lie down myself, for tiredness dragged at my shoulders and had settled in aching lumps at the base of my spine. Not yet, though.

Jamie had not yet come back. I knew he would come to find me when he'd finished his summit meeting with Hickman and Roberts. And there were a few preparations still to be made, just in case.

In the course of Jamie's earlier rummaging through Hickman's desk in search of food, I'd noticed a bundle of fresh goose quills. I'd sent Abram to beg a couple of these and to bring me the largest sailmaker's needle to be found—and a couple of wing bones discarded from the chicken stew aboard the *Pitt*.

I chopped off the ends of a slender bone, looked to be sure the marrow had all been leached out by cooking, then shaped one end into a careful point, using the ship's carpenter's small sharpening stone for the purpose. The quill was easier; the tip had already been cut to a point for writing; all I had to do was to cut off the barbs, then submerge quill, bone, and needle in a shallow dish of brandy. That would do, then.

The smell of the brandy rose sweet and heavy in the air, competing with the tar, turpentine, tobacco, and the salt-soaked old timbers of the ship. It did at least partially obliterate the scents of blood and fecal matter left by my patients.

I'd discovered a case of bottled Meursault wine in the cargo, and now thoughtfully extracted a bottle, adding it to the half bottle of brandy and a stack of clean calico bandages and dressings. Sitting down on a keg of tar, I leaned back against a big hogshead of tobacco, yawning and wondering idly why it was called that. It did not appear to be shaped like a hog's head, certainly not like the head of any hog *I* knew.

I dismissed that thought and closed my eyes. I could feel my pulse throbbing in fingertips and eyelids. I didn't sleep, but I slowly descended into a sort of half consciousness, dimly aware of the sough of water past the ship's sides, the louder sigh of Stebbings's breath, the unhurried bellows of my own lungs, and the slow, placid thumping of my heart.

It seemed years since the terrors and uproar of the afternoon, and from the distance imposed by fatigue and intensity, my worry that I might have been having a heart attack seemed ridiculous. Was it, though? It wasn't impossible. Surely it had been nothing more than panic and hyperventilation—ridiculous in themselves, but not threatening. Still . . .

I put two fingers on my chest and waited for the pulsing in my fingertips to equalize with the pulsing of my heart. Slowly, almost dreaming, I began to pass through my body, from crown to toes, feeling my way through the long quiet passages of veins, the deep violet color of the sky just before night. Nearby I saw the brightness of arteries, wide and fierce with crimson life. Entered into the chambers of my heart and felt enclosed, the thick walls moving in a solid, comforting, unending, uninterrupted rhythm. No, no damage, not to the heart nor to its valves.

I felt my digestive tract, tightly knotted up under my diaphragm for hours, relax and settle with a grateful gurgle, and a sense of well-being flowed down like warm honey through limbs and spine.

"I dinna ken what ye're doing, Sassenach," a soft voice said nearby. "But ye look well content."

I opened my eyes and sat up. Jamie came down the ladder, moving carefully, and sat down.

He was very pale, and his shoulders were slumped with exhaustion. He smiled faintly at me, though, and his eyes were clear. My heart, solid and re-liable as I just proved it to be, warmed and softened as though it had been made of butter.

"How do you—" I began, but he raised a hand, stopping me.

"I'll do," he said, with a glance at the pallet where the recumbent Stebbings lay, breathing shallowly and audibly. "Is he asleep?"

"I hope so. And you *should* be," I observed. "Let me tend you so you can lie down."

"It's no verra bad," he said, gingerly picking at the wad of crusty fabric tucked inside his shirt. "But it could use a stitch or two, I suppose."

"I suppose so, too," I said, eyeing the brown stains down the right side of his shirt. Given his customary inclination to understatement, he likely had a gaping slash down his breast. At least it would be easy to get at, unlike the awkward wound suffered by one of the *Pitt*'s sailors, who had somehow been struck just behind the scrotum by a pellet of grapeshot. I thought it must have struck something else first and bounced upward, for it luckily hadn't pene-trated deeply, but was flattened as a sixpence when I got it out. I'd given it to him as a souvenir.

Abram had brought a can of fresh hot water just before he left. I put a fin-ger into it and was pleased to find it still warm.

"Right," I said, with a nod at the bottles on the chest. "Do you want brandy, or wine, before we start?"

The corner of his mouth twitched, and he reached for the wine bottle.

"Let me keep the illusion of civilization for a wee bit longer."

"Oh, I think that's reasonably civilized stuff," I said. "I haven't a cork-screw, though."

He read the label, and his eyebrows rose.

"No matter. Is there something to pour it into?"

"Just here." I pulled a small, elegant wooden box out of a nest of straw in-side a packing case and opened it triumphantly to display a Chinese porcelain tea set, gilt-edged and decorated with tiny red and blue turtles, all looking in-scrutably Asiatic, swimming through a forest of gold chrysanthemums.

Jamie laughed—no more than a breath, but definitely laughter—and, scor-ing the neck of the bottle with the point of his dirk, knocked it neatly off against the rim of a tobacco hogshead. He poured the wine carefully into the two cups I'd set out, nodding at the vivid turtles.

"The wee blue one there reminds me of Mr. Willoughby, aye?"

I laughed myself, then glanced guiltily at Stebbings's feet—all that was showing of him at the moment. I'd taken his boots off, and the loose toes of his grimy stockings drooped comically over his feet. The feet didn't twitch, though, and the slow, labored breathing went on as before.

"I haven't thought of Mr. Willoughby in years," I observed, lifting my cup in toast. "Here's to absent friends."

Jamie replied briefly in Chinese and touched the rim of his own cup to mine with a faint *tink*!

"You remember how to speak Chinese?" I asked, intrigued, but he shook his head.

"No much. I havena had occasion to speak it since I last saw him." He breathed in the bouquet of the wine, closing his eyes. "That seems a verra long time ago."

"Long ago and far away." The wine smelled warmly of almonds and apples, and was dry but full-bodied, clinging richly to the palate. Jamaica, to be exact, and more than ten years ago. "Time flies when you're having fun. Do you think he's still alive—Mr. Willoughby?"

He considered that, sipping.

"Aye, I do. A man who escaped from a Chinese emperor and sailed halfway round the world to keep his balls is one wi' a good deal of determination."

He seemed disinclined to reminisce further about auld acquaintance, though, and I let him drink in silence, feeling the night settle comfortably around us with the gentle rise and fall of the ship. After his second cup of wine, I peeled his crusty shirt off and gingerly lifted the blood-caked wad of handkerchief that he'd used to stanch the wound.

Rather to my surprise, he was right: the wound was small, and wouldn't need more than two or three stitches to put right. A blade had gone in deep, just under his collarbone, and ripped a triangular flap of flesh coming out.

"Is this all your blood?" I asked, puzzled, lifting the discarded shirt.

"Nay, I've got a bit left," he said, eyes creasing at me over the teacup. "Not much, mind."

"You know quite well what I mean," I said severely.

"Aye, it's mine." He drained his cup and reached for the bottle.

"But from such a small . . . oh, dear God." I felt slightly faint. I could see the tender blue line of his subclavian vein, passing just under the collarbone and running directly above the clotted gape of the wound.

"Aye, I was surprised," he said casually, cradling the delicate china in both big hands. "When he jerked the blade out, the blood sprayed out like a fountain and soaked us both. I've never seen it do like that before."

"You have probably not had anyone nick your subclavian artery before," I said, with what attempt at calm I could muster. I cast a sideways glance at the wound. It *had* clotted; the edges of the flap had turned blue and the sliced flesh beneath was nearly black with dried blood. No oozing, let alone an arterial spray. The blade had thrust up from below, missing the vein and just piercing the artery behind it.

I took a long, deep breath, trying with no success whatever not to imagine what would have happened had the blade gone the barest fraction of an inch deeper, or what might have happened, had Jamie not had a handkerchief and the knowledge and opportunity to use pressure on the wound.

Belatedly, I realized what he'd said: "*The blood sprayed out like a fountain and soaked us both.*" And when I'd asked Stebbings whether it was his own blood soaking his shirt, he'd leered and said, "*Your husband's.*" I'd thought he was only being unpleasant, but—

"Was it Captain Stebbings who stabbed you?"

"Mmphm." He made a brief affirmative noise as he shifted his weight, leaning back to let me get at the wound. He drained the cup again and set it down, looking resigned. "I was surprised he managed it. I thought I'd dropped him, but he hit the floor and came up wi' a knife in his hand, the wee bugger."

"*You* shot him?"

He blinked at my tone of voice.

"Aye, of course."

I couldn't think of any bad words sufficient as to encompass the situation and, muttering "Jesus H. Roosevelt *Christ*!" under my breath, set about swabbing and suturing.

"Now, listen to me," I said, in my best military surgeon's voice. "So far as I can tell, it was a very small nick, and you managed to stop the bleeding long enough for a clot to form. But that clot is *all* that is keeping you from bleeding to death. Do you understand me?" This was not completely true—or it wouldn't be, once I'd stitched the supporting flesh back into place—but this was no time to give him a loophole.

He looked at me for a long moment, quite expressionless.

"I do."

"That means," I emphasized, stabbing the needle into his flesh with sufficient force that he yelped, "you must *not* use your right arm for at least the next forty-eight hours. You must not haul on ropes, you must not climb rigging, you must not punch people, you must not so much as scratch your arse with your right hand, do you hear me?"

"I expect the whole ship hears ye," he muttered, but glanced down his cheek, trying to see his collarbone. "I generally scratch my arse wi' my left hand, anyway."

Captain Stebbings had definitely heard us; a low chuckle came from behind the tea chest, followed by a rumbling cough and a faint wheeze of amusement.

"And," I continued, drawing the thread through the skin, "you may *not* get angry."

His breath drew in with a hiss.

"Why not?"

"Because it will make your heart beat harder, thus raising your blood pressure, which will—"

"Blow me up like a bottle of beer that's been corked too long?"

"Much the same. Now—"

Whatever I had been going to say vanished from my mind in the next instant as Stebbings's breathing suddenly changed. I dropped the needle and, turning, seized the dish. I shoved the tea chest aside, putting the dish on it, and fell to my knees next to Stebbings's body.

His lips and eyelids were blue, and the rest of his face was the color of putty. He was making a horrid gasping noise, his mouth gaping wide, gulping air that wasn't helping.

There were luckily well-known bad words for *this* situation, and I used a few of them, swiftly turning back the blanket and digging my fingers into his pudgy side in search of ribs. He squirmed and emitted a high, ludicrous *heeheehee*, which made Jamie—the needle still swinging by its thread from his collarbone—give a nervous laugh in response.

"This is no time to be ticklish," I said crossly. "Jamie—take one of those quills and slide the needle inside." While he did this, I rapidly swabbed Stebbings's skin with a brandy-soaked wad of cloth, then took the quill-and-needle in one hand, the brandy bottle in the other, and drove the quill point-first into the second intercostal space, like hammering in a nail. I felt the subterranean *pop* as it went through the cartilage into the pleural space.

He made a high *eeeeee* sound at that, but it wasn't laughter. I'd cut the quill a little shorter than the needle, but the needle had sunk in when I'd hit it. I had a moment of panic, trying to get hold of the needle with my finger-nails to pull it out, but finally managed. Stale-smelling blood and fluid sprayed out through the hollow quill, but only for a moment, then dimin-ished to a faint hiss of air.

"Breathe slowly," I said more quietly. "*Both* of you."

I was watching the quill anxiously, looking for any further drainage of blood—plainly, if he was bleeding heavily into the lung, there was almost nothing I could do—but I was seeing only the light seepage from the punc-ture wound, a red smear on the outside of the quill.

"Sit down," I said to Jamie, who did, ending cross-legged on the floor be-side me.

Stebbings was looking better; the lung had at least partially inflated, and he was white now, his lips pale, but pale pink. The hissing from the hollow quill died to a sigh, and I put my finger over the open end of it.

"Ideally," I said in a conversational tone, "I'd be able to run a length of tubing from your chest into a jar of water. That way the air around your lung could escape, but air couldn't get back in. As I haven't got anything tubelike that's longer than a few inches, that's not going to work." I rose up on my knees, motioning to Jamie.

"Come here and put your finger over the end of this quill. If he starts suf-focating again, take it off for a moment, until the air stops hissing out."

He couldn't conveniently reach Stebbings with his left hand; with a side-long glance at me, he reached slowly out with his right and stoppered the quill with his thumb.

I got to my feet, groaning, and went to rummage the cargo again. It might have to be tar. I'd tacked the oiled patch to his chest on three sides with warm tar, and there was plenty left. Not ideal; I likely couldn't get it out again in a hurry. Would a small plug of wet fabric be better?

In one of Hannah Arnold's chests, though, I found treasure: a small col-lection of dried herbs in jars—including one of powdered gum arabic. The herbs were interesting and useful in themselves, being plainly imported: cin-chona bark—I must try to send that back to North Carolina for Lizzie, if we ever got off this horrible tub—mandrake, and ginger, things that never grew in the Colonies. Having them to hand made me feel suddenly rich. Stebbings groaned behind me, and I heard the scuff of fabric and a soft hiss as Jamie took his thumb away for a moment.

Not even the riches of the fabled East would do Stebbings much good. I opened the jar of gum arabic and, scooping out a bit into the palm of my hand, dribbled water into it and set about fashioning the resultant gooey ball into a roughly cylindrical plug, which I wrapped in a scrap of yellow calico printed with honeybees, finishing it off with a neat twist at the top. This accomplished to my satisfaction, I came back and, without comment, pulled the hollow quill—already showing signs of cracking from the working of Stebbings's rib muscles—out of its hole and wriggled the sturdier—and larger—hollow chicken bone into its place.

He didn't laugh this time, either. I plugged the end of the bone neatly and, kneeling in front of Jamie, resumed my stitching on his collarbone.

I felt perfectly clearheaded—but in that oddly surreal way that is an indication of total exhaustion. I'd done what had to be done, but I knew I couldn't stay upright much longer.

"What does Captain Hickman have to say?" I asked, much more by way of distracting both of us than because I really wanted to know.

"A great number of things, as ye might imagine." He took a deep breath and fixed his eyes on a huge turtle shell that had been wedged in among the boxes. "Discarding the purely personal opinions and a certain amount of excessive language, though . . . we're bound up the Hudson. For Fort Ticonderoga."

"We . . . what?" I frowned at the needle pushed halfway through the skin. "Why?"

His hands were braced on the deck, fingers pressing into the boards so hard the nails were white.

"That's where he was bound when the complications occurred, and that's where he means to go. He's a gentleman of verra fixed views, I find."

A loud snort came from behind the tea chest.

"I did notice something of the sort." I tied the last suture and clipped the thread neatly with my knife. "Did you say something, Captain Stebbings?"

The snort was repeated, more loudly, but without emendation.

"Can't he be convinced to put us ashore?"

Jamie's fingers hovered over the fresh stitching, obviously wanting to rub the stinging site, but I pushed them away.

"Aye, well . . . there are further complications, Sassenach."

"Do tell," I murmured, standing up and stretching. "Oh, God, my back. What *sort* of complications? Do you want some tea?"

"Only if there's a good deal of whisky in it." He leaned his head back against the bulkhead, closing his eyes. There was a hint of color in his cheeks, though his forehead shone with sweat.

"Brandy do you?" I needed tea—minus alcohol—badly myself, and headed for the ladder, not waiting for his nod. I saw him reach for the wine bottle as I set foot on the lowest rung.

There was a brisk wind blowing up above; it swirled the long cloak out around me as I emerged from the depths, and whooshed up my petticoats in a most revivifying fashion. It revivified Mr. Smith—or, rather, Mr. Marsden—too, who blinked and looked hastily away.

"Evening, ma'am," he said politely, when I'd got my assorted garments back under control. "The colonel doing well, I hope?"

"Yes, he's—" I broke off and gave him a sharp look. "The colonel?" I had a slight sinking sensation.

"Yes'm. He's a militia colonel, isn't he?"

"He *was*," I said with emphasis.

Smith's face broke into a smile.

"No *was* about it, ma'am," he said. "He's done us the honor to take command of a company—Fraser's Irregulars, we're to be called."

"How apt," I said. "What the devil—how did this happen?"

He tugged nervously at one of his earrings, seeing that I perhaps wasn't as pleased by the news as might be hoped.

"Ah. Well, to tell the truth, ma'am, I'm afraid it was my fault." He ducked his head, abashed. "One of the hands aboard the *Pitt* recognized me, and when he told the captain who I was . . ."

The revelation of Mr. Marsden's real name—in combination with his adornments—had caused considerable uproar among the motley crew presently on board the *Asp*. Sufficiently so that he had been in some danger of being thrown overboard or set adrift in a boat. After a certain amount of acrimonious discussion, Jamie had suggested that perhaps Mr. Marsden could be persuaded to change his profession and become a soldier—for a number of the hands aboard the *Asp* had already proposed to leave her and join the Continental forces at Ticonderoga, portaging the goods and weapons across to Lake Champlain and then remaining as militia volunteers.

This found general approbation—though a few disgruntled persons were still heard to mutter that a Jonah was a Jonah, didn't matter if he was a sailor or not. "That being why I thought I best make myself scarce below, if you see what I mean, ma'am," Mr. Marsden concluded.

It also solved the problem of what to do with the imprisoned hands from the *Pitt* and the displaced seamen from the *Teal;* those who preferred joining the American militia would be allowed to do so, while those British seamen who preferred the prospect of life as prisoners of war could be accommodated in this desire at Fort Ticonderoga. About half the men from the *Teal* had expressed a decided preference for employment on land, after their recent seagoing adventures, and they also would join the Irregulars.

"I see," I said, rubbing two fingers between my brows. "Well, if you'll excuse me, Mr. . . . Marsden, I must be going and making a cup of tea. With a lot of brandy in it."

THE TEA HEARTENED ME, sufficiently to send Abram—found drowsing by the galley fire in spite of having been ordered to bed—to take some to Jamie and Captain Stebbings while I made the rounds of my other patients. They were mostly as comfortable as might be expected—that is, not very, but stoic about it, and in no need of exigent medical intervention.

The temporary strength lent me by tea and brandy had mostly ebbed by the time I made my way back down the ladder into the hold, though, and my foot slipped off the final rung, causing me to drop heavily onto the deck, with a thump that elicited a startled cry from Stebbings, followed by a groan. Waving away Jamie's raised brow, I hurried over to check the patient.

He was very hot to the touch, his full face flushed, and a nearly full cup of tea lay discarded near him.

"I tried to make him drink, but he said he couldna swallow more than a mouthful." Jamie had followed me, and spoke softly behind me.

I bent and placed my ear near Stebbings's chest, auscultating as best I could through the layer of blubber covering it. The chicken-bone tube, momentarily unplugged, gave only a modest hiss of air and no more than a trace of blood.

"So far as I can tell, the lung's expanded at least partially," I said, addressing Stebbings for form's sake, though he merely stared at me, glassy-eyed. "And I think the bullet must have cauterized a good deal of the damage; otherwise, I think we'd be seeing much more alarming symptoms." Otherwise, he'd be dead by now, but I thought it more tactful not to say so. He might easily be dead soon, in any case, from fever, but I didn't say that, either.

I persuaded him to drink some water and sponged his head and torso with more of it. The hatch cover had been left off, and it was reasonably cool in the hold, though the air didn't move much down below. Still, I saw no benefit in taking him into the wind on deck, and the less he was moved, the better.

"Is that . . . my . . . cloak?" he asked suddenly, opening one eye.

"Er . . . probably," I replied, disconcerted. "Do you want it back?"

He made a brief grimace and shook his head, then lay back, eyes closed, breathing shallowly.

Jamie was propped against the tea chest, head back, eyes closed, and breathing heavily. Feeling me sit down beside him, though, he raised his head and opened his eyes.

"Ye look as though ye're about to fall over, Sassenach," he said softly. "Lie down, aye? I'll mind the captain."

I saw his point. In fact, I saw two of them—and him. I blinked and shook my head, momentarily reuniting the two Jamies, but there was no denying that he was right. I'd lost touch with my body again, but my mind, instead of sticking to the job, had simply wandered off somewhere in a daze. I rubbed my hands hard over my face, but it didn't help appreciably.

"I'll have to sleep," I explained to the men, all four of them now watching me with the perfect wide-eyed attention of barn owls. "If you feel the pressure building up again—and I think it will," I said to Stebbings, "pull the plug out of the tube until it eases, then put it back. If either of you think you're dying, wake me up."

With no further ado, and feeling as though I were watching myself doing it, I eased down onto the planking, put my head on a fold of Stebbings's cloak, and fell asleep.

I WOKE AN UNACCOUNTABLE time later and lay for some minutes lacking coherent thought, my mind rising and falling with the movement of the deck beneath me. At some point, I began to distinguish the murmur of men's voices from the shush and bang of seagoing noises.

I had fallen so deeply into oblivion that the events prior to my falling asleep took a moment to recall, but the voices brought them back. Wounds, the reek of brandy, the rip of sailcloth tearing, rough in my hands, and the smell of the dye in the bright, wet calico. Jamie's bloody shirt. The sucking sound of the hole in Stebbings's chest. The memory of that would have brought me upright at once, but I had stiffened from lying on the boards. A sharp twinge of agony lanced from my right knee to my groin, and the muscles of my back and arms hurt amazingly. Before I could stretch them enough to struggle to my feet, I heard the captain's voice.

"Call Hickman." Stebbings's voice was hoarse and low, but definite. "I'd rather be shot than do this anymore."

I didn't think he was joking. Neither did Jamie.

"I dinna blame ye," he said. His voice was soft but serious, as definite as Stebbings's.

My eyes were beginning to focus again, as the paralyzing ache in my muscles eased a little. From where I lay, I could see Stebbings from the knees down and most of Jamie, sitting beside him, head bowed on his own knees, tall form slumped against the tea chest.

There was a pause, and then Stebbings said, "You don't, eh? Good. Go get Hickman."

"Why?" Jamie asked, after what seemed an equal pause for thought—or perhaps only to gather strength to answer. He didn't lift his head; he sounded almost drugged with fatigue. "Nay need to rouse the man from his bed, is there? If ye want to die, just pull that thing out of your chest."

Stebbings made some sort of noise. It might have started as a laugh, a groan, or an angry retort, but ended in a hiss of air between clenched teeth. My body tensed. Had he actually tried to pull it out?

No. I heard the heavy movement of his body, saw his feet curl briefly as he sought a more comfortable position, and heard Jamie's grunt as he leaned over to help.

"Someone...might as well get...satisfaction from me...dying," he wheezed.

"I put yon hole in ye," Jamie pointed out. He straightened up and stretched with painful care. "It wouldna please me overmuch to watch ye die from it." I thought he must be well past the point of exhaustion, and plainly he was as stiff as I was. I must get up, make him go lie down. But he was still talking to Stebbings, sounding unconcerned, like a man discussing an abstruse point of natural philosophy.

"As for satisfying Captain Hickman—d'ye feel some sense of obligation toward him?"

"I don't." That one came out short and sharp, though succeeded by a deep gasp for air.

"It's a clean death," Stebbings managed after a few more breaths. "Quick."

"Aye, that's what I thought," Jamie said, sounding drowsy. "When it was me."

Stebbings gave a grunt that might have been interrogative. Jamie sighed. After a moment, I heard the rustle of cloth and saw him move his left leg, groaning as he did so, and turn back the cloth of his kilt.

"See that?" His finger ran slowly up the length of his thigh, from just above the knee, almost to the groin.

Stebbings gave a slightly more interested grunt, this one definitely questioning. The drooping toes of his socks moved as his feet twitched.

"Bayonet," Jamie said, casually flipping his kilt back over the twisting, runneled scar. "I lay for two days after, wi' the fever eating me alive. My leg swelled, and it stank. And when the English officer came to blow our brains out, I was pleased enough."

A brief silence.

"Culloden?" Stebbings asked. His voice was still hoarse, and I could hear the fever in it, but there was interest there now, too. "Heard . . . about it."

Jamie said nothing in response but yawned suddenly, not bothering to smother it, and rubbed his hands slowly over his face. I could hear the soft rasp of beard stubble.

Silence, but the quality of it had changed. I could feel Stebbings's anger, his pain and fright—but there was a faint sense of amusement in his labored breath.

"Going to . . . make me . . . ask?"

Jamie shook his head.

"Too long a story, and one I dinna care to tell. Leave it that I wanted him to shoot me, verra badly, and the bastard wouldna do it."

The air in the little hold was stale but uneasy, filled with the shifting scents of blood and luxury, of industry and illness. I breathed in, gently, deep, and could smell the tang of the men's bodies, a sharp copper savage smell, bitter with effort and exhaustion. Women never smelled like that, I thought, even in extremity.

"Revenge, then, is it?" Stebbings asked after a bit. His restless feet had stilled. His dirty stockings drooped and his voice was tired.

Jamie's shoulders moved, slowly, as he sighed, and his own voice was nearly as tired as Stebbings's.

"No," he said, very softly. "Call it payment of a debt."

A debt? I thought. To whom? To the Lord Melton who had declined to kill him, out of honor, who had instead sent him home from Culloden, hidden in a wagon filled with hay? To his sister, who had refused to let him die, who had dragged him back to life by sheer strength of will? Or to those who had died when he had not?

I had stretched myself enough now to be able to rise, but didn't, yet. There was no urgency. The men were silent, their breathing part of the breathing of the ship, the sigh of the sea outside.

It came to me, quiet but sure, that I knew. I had glimpsed the abyss often, over someone's shoulder as they stood on the edge, looking down. But I had looked once, too. I knew the vastness and the lure of it, the offer of surcease.

I knew they were standing now, side by side and each alone, looking down.

PART FOUR

Conjunction

A FLURRY OF SUSPICION

Lord John Grey to Mr. Arthur Norrington
4 February 1777
(Cipher 158)

My dear Norrington,

Pursuant to our conversation, I have made certain discoveries which I think it prudent to confide.

I paid a visit to France at the end of the year and, while there, visited the Baron Amandine. I stayed with the baron for several days, in fact, and had conversation of him on a number of occasions. I have reason to believe that Beauchamp is indeed concerned in the matter we discussed and has formed an attachment to Beaumarchais, who is thus likely similarly involved. I think Amandine is not himself concerned but that Beauchamp may use him as a front of some kind.

I requested an audience with Beaumarchais, but was denied. As he would normally have received me, I think I have poked a stick into some nest. It would be useful to watch that quarter.

Be also alert to any mention in the French correspondence of a company called Rodrigue Hortalez et Cie *(I beg you will speak with the person handling the Spanish correspondence, as well). I cannot discover anything amiss, but neither can I discover anything solid regarding them, such as the names of the directors, and that in itself strikes me as suspicious.*

If your duty allow, I should be pleased to hear of anything you learn concerning these matters.

> *Your servant, sir,*
> *Lord John Grey*

Postscriptum: If you can tell me, who is presently in charge of the American Department, with regard to correspondence?

Lord John Grey to Harold, Duke of Pardloe
4 February 1777
(family cipher)

Hal—

I saw Amandine. Wainwright does live at the manor house—a place called Trois Flèches—and does maintain an unwholesome relationship with the baron. I met the baron's sister, Wainwright's wife. She certainly knows of the link between her brother and her husband, but does not admit it openly. Beyond that, she appears to know nothing whatever. I have seldom met a more stupid woman. She is openly lewd in manner and a very bad cardplayer. So is the baron, by which token I am convinced that he does know something of Wainwright's political machinations; he behaved shiftily when I steered the conversation in that direction, and I am sure he is not schooled in the art of misdirection. He is not stupid, though. Even if he were, he will certainly have told Wainwright of my visit. I have alerted Norrington to watch for any activity on that front.

Knowing what I do of Wainwright's abilities and connexions (or rather, the lack of them), I cannot quite fathom his involvement. Granted, if the French government does have such schemes in mind as he indicated, they would hardly make open communication regarding them, and sending someone like Wainwright to speak to someone like me might be considered sufficiently sub rosa. Certainly such an approach has the benefit of being deniable. And yet something seems wrong in this, in a way I cannot yet define.

I will be with you soon, and hope by then to be in possession of some definite information regarding one Captain Ezekiel Richardson, likewise one Captain Denys Randall-Isaacs. Should you be able to investigate either of these names through your own connexions, you would greatly oblige

> Your most affectionate brother,
> John

Postscriptum: I trust your health is mending.

Harold, Duke of Pardloe, to Lord John Grey
6 March 1777
Bath
(family cipher)

I'm not dead. Wish I were. Bath is vile. I am daily wrapped in canvas and carried off like a parcel to be sunk in boiling water that smells of rotten eggs, then hauled out and forced to drink it, but Minnie says

*she will divorce me by petition in the House of Lords on the grounds of
insanity caused by immoral acts if I don't submit. I doubt this, but here
I am.*

*Denys Randall-Isaacs is the son of a Englishwoman named Mary
Hawkins and a British army officer: one Jonathan Wolverton
Randall, captain of dragoons, deceased, killed at Culloden. The mother
is still alive and married to a Jew named Robert Isaacs, a merchant in
Bristol. He's still alive, too, and has a half interest in a warehouse in
Brest. Denys is one of your damned politicals, got ties to Germain, but I
can't find out more than that without being too overt for your tastes.
Can't find out anything in bloody Bath.*

*Don't know much about Richardson, but will find out directly. Sent
letters to some people in America. Yes, I am discreet, thank you, and so
are they.*

*John Burgoyne is here, taking the cure. Very cock-a-hoop, as Germain
has approved his scheme to invade from Canada. I have mentioned
William to him, as his French and German are good and Burgoyne is
to have a number of Brunswickers. Still, tell Willie to be careful;
Burgoyne seems to think he is to be commander-in-chief of the army in
America—a notion that I daresay will come as rather a surprise both to
Guy Carleton and Dick Howe.*

Trois Flèches. *Three arrows. Who is the third?*

London
March 26, 1777
The Society for the Appreciation of the
English Beefsteak, a Gentleman's Club

"Who is the third?" Grey repeated in astonishment, staring at the note he had just opened.

"The third what?" Harry Quarry handed his sopping cloak to the steward and sank heavily into the chair beside Grey's, sighing with relief as he held his hands out to the fire. "God's teeth, I'm frozen solid. You're going to Southampton in *this?*" He flung one big cold-blanched hand at the window, which framed a dismal prospect of icy sleet, driven almost horizontal by the wind.

"Not 'til tomorrow. It may have cleared by then."

Harry gave the window a look of deep suspicion and shook his head. "Not a chance. Steward!"

Mr. Bodley was already tottering toward them under the weight of a tea tray laden with seedcake, sponge cake, strawberry jam, marmalade, hot buttered crumpets in a basket wrapped in white linen, scones, clotted cream, almond biscuits, sardines on toast, a pot of beans baked with bacon and onion, a plate of sliced ham with gherkins, a bottle of brandy with two glasses, and—perhaps as an afterthought—a steaming teapot with two china cups and saucers alongside.

"Ah!" said Harry, looking happier. "I see you expected me."

Grey smiled. If not on campaign or called away by duty, Harry Quarry invariably entered the Beefsteak at four-thirty on a Wednesday.

"I thought you'd need sustenance, with Hal on the sick list." Harry was one of the two regimental colonels—as distinct from Hal, who was Colonel of the Regiment, it being his own regiment. Not all colonels took an active hand in the operations of their regiments, but Hal did.

"Malingering bugger," Harry said, reaching for the brandy. "How is he?"

"Quite his usual self, to judge from his correspondence." Grey handed Quarry the unfolded letter, which the latter read with a burgeoning grin.

"Aye, Minnie will have him sorted like a hand of whist." He put down the letter, nodding at it as he raised his glass. "Who's Richardson and why do you want to know about him?"

"Ezekiel Richardson, Captain. Lancers, but detached for intelligence work."

"Oh, intelligence laddie, eh? One of your Black Chamber lot?" Quarry wrinkled his nose, though it was not clear whether this was a response to the notion of intelligence laddies or the presence of a dish of grated horseradish accompanying the sardines.

"No, I don't know the man well personally," Grey admitted, and felt the same pang of deep unease that had been afflicting him with increased frequency ever since his receipt of William's letter from Quebec a week before. "I had been introduced to him by Sir George, who knew his father, but we didn't talk much on that occasion. I had heard a few things to his credit—in a quiet sort of way—"

"That being, I suppose, the only way one wants to hear anything about a man in that line of business. Huuuuuh!" Harry drew a tremendous gasp of air through his open mouth and up into his sinuses, by the sound of it, then coughed once or twice, eyes watering, and shook his head in admiration. "Fresh horseradish," he croaked, taking another large spoonful. "Very . . . huuuuuuh . . . fresh."

"Quite. Anyway, I met him again in North Carolina, we talked a bit more, and he asked my permission to approach William with a proposition regarding intelligencing."

Quarry stopped, a slice of sardine-laden toast halfway to his mouth.

"You don't mean to say you've let him lure Willie off into the weeds?"

"That was certainly not my intent," Grey said, nettled. "I had some reason to feel that the suggestion would be good for Willie; for one thing, it would get him out of North Carolina and end with him attached to Howe's staff."

Quarry nodded, masticating with care, and swallowed thickly.

"Aye, right. But now you have doubts?"

"I do. The more so because I can find very few people who actually know Richardson well. Everyone who recommended him to me in the first place did so by reason of someone else's recommendation, it seems. Except for Sir George Stanley, who is presently in Spain with my mother, and old Nigel Bruce, who's rather inconveniently died in the meantime."

"Thoughtless."

"Yes. I imagine I could root out more information, had I time, but I haven't. Dottie and I sail day after tomorrow. Weather permitting," he added, with a glance at the window.

"Ah, this would be where I come in," Harry observed, without animus. "What shall I do with any information I find? Tell Hal, or send it to you?"

"Tell Hal," Grey said with a sigh. "God knows what the post may be like in America, even with the Congress sitting in Philadelphia. If anything seems urgent, Hal can expedite matters here far more easily than I can there."

Quarry nodded and refilled Grey's glass. "You're not eating," he observed.

"I lunched late." Quite late. In fact, he hadn't had luncheon yet. He took a scone and spread it desultorily with jam.

"And Denys Wossname?" Quarry asked, flicking the letter with a pickle fork. "Shall I inquire about him, too?"

"By all means. Though I may make better progress with him on the American end of the matter. That's at least where he was last seen." He took a bite of scone, observing that it had achieved that delicate balance between crumbliness and half-set mortar that is the ideal of every scone, and felt some stirrings of appetite return. He wondered whether he should put Harry onto the worthy Jew with the warehouse in Brest, but decided not. The question of French connections was more than delicate, and while Harry was thorough, he was not subtle.

"Right, then." Harry selected a slice of sponge cake, topped it with two almond biscuits and a dollop of clotted cream, and inserted the whole into his mouth. Where did he put it? Grey wondered. Harry was thickset and burly, but never stout. No doubt he sweated it off during energetic exercise in brothels, that being his favorite sport despite advancing age.

How old was Harry? he wondered suddenly. A few years older than Grey, a few years younger than Hal. He'd never thought about it, no more than he had with reference to Hal. The two of them had always seemed immortal; he had never once contemplated a future lacking either one of them. But the skull beneath Harry's wig was nearly hairless now—he had, in his usual way, removed it to scratch his head at some point and set it casually back without regard to straightness—and the joints of his fingers were swollen, though he handled his teacup with his usual delicacy.

Grey felt of a sudden his own mortality, in the stiffening of a thumb, the twinge of a knee. Most of all, in the fear that he might not be there to protect William, while he was still needed.

"Eh?" said Harry, raising a brow at whatever showed on Grey's face. "What?"

Grey smiled and shook his head, taking up his brandy glass once more.

"*Timor mortis conturbat me,*" he said.

"Ah," said Quarry thoughtfully, and raised his own. "I'll drink to that."

THE PLOT THICKENS

28 February, A.D. 1777
London

Major General John Burgoyne,
to Sir George Germain
. . . I do not conceive any expedition from the sea can be so formidable to the enemy, or so effectual to close the war, as an invasion from Canada by Ticonderoga.

April 4, 1777
on board HMS Tartar

HE'D TOLD DOTTIE that the *Tartar* was only a twenty-eight-gun frigate and that she must therefore be modest in her packing. Even so, he was surprised to see the single trunk—granted, a large one—two portmanteaux, and a bag of needlework that comprised her entire luggage.

"What, not a single flowered mantua?" he teased. "William won't know you."

"Bosh," she replied with her father's talent for succinct clarity. But she smiled a little—she was very pale, and he hoped it wasn't incipient seasickness—and he squeezed her hand and went on holding it all the time until the last dark sliver of England sank into the sea.

He was still amazed that she'd managed it. Hal must be more frail than he'd let on, to be bamboozled into allowing his daughter to take ship for America, even under Grey's protection and for the laudable purpose of nursing her wounded brother. Minnie, of course, would not be parted from Hal for a moment, though naturally worried sick for her son. But that she had uttered no word of protest at this adventure . . .

"Your mother's in on it, is she?" he asked casually, provoking a startled look through a veil of windblown hair.

"On what?" Dottie pawed at the blond spiderweb of her hair, escaped *en masse* from the inconsequent snood in which she'd bound it and dancing over her head like flames. "Oh, help!"

He captured her hair, smoothing it tight to her head with both hands, then gathering it at her neck, where he plaited it expertly, to the admiration of a passing seaman, clubbed it, and tied it up with the velvet ribbon that was all that remained from the wreck of her snood.

"On what, forsooth," he told the back of her head, as he finished the job. "On whatever the dreadful enterprise is on which you've embarked."

She turned round and faced him, her stare direct.

"If you want to describe rescuing Henry as a dreadful enterprise, I agree entirely," she said with dignity. "But my mother would naturally do anything she could to get him back. So would you, presumably, or you wouldn't be here." And without waiting for a reply, she turned smartly on her heel and made for the companionway, leaving him speechless.

One of the first ships of the spring had brought a letter with further word of Henry. He was still alive, thank God, but had been badly wounded: shot in the abdomen, and very ill in consequence through the brutal winter. He had survived, though, and been moved to Philadelphia with a number of other British prisoners. The letter had been written by a fellow officer there, another prisoner, but Henry had managed to scribble a few words of love to his family at the bottom and sign his name; the memory of that straggling scrawl ate at John's heart.

He was encouraged somewhat by the fact that it *was* Philadelphia, though. He had met a prominent Philadelphian while he was in France and had formed an immediate liking for him that he thought was returned; there might be something of use in the acquaintance. He grinned involuntarily, recalling the instant of his meeting with the American gentleman.

He hadn't paused long in Paris, only long enough to make inquiries after Percival Beauchamp, who was not there. Retired to his home in the country for the winter, he was told. The Beauchamp family's main estate, a place called *Trois Flèches,* near Compiègne. And so he had bought a fur-lined hat and a pair of seaboots, wrapped himself in his warmest cloak, hired a horse, and set grimly off into the teeth of a howling gale.

Arriving mud-caked and frozen, he had been greeted with suspicion, but the quality of his accoutrements and his title had gained him entrance, and he had been shown to a well-appointed parlor—with, thank God, an excellent fire—to await the baron's pleasure.

He'd formed an expectation of the Baron Amandine on the basis of Percy's remarks, though he thought Percy had likely been practicing upon him. He also knew how futile it was to theorize in advance of observation, but it was inhuman not to imagine.

In terms of imagining, he'd done a good job of not thinking of Percy during the last . . . was it eighteen years, nineteen? But once it became obvious that thinking of him was now a professional as well as a personal necessity, he was both surprised and disconcerted to find just how much he remembered. He knew what Percy liked and therefore had evolved a mental picture of Amandine in accordance.

The reality was different. The baron was an older man, perhaps a few years Grey's senior, short and rather plump, with an open, pleasant face. Well dressed, but without ostentation. He greeted Grey with great courtesy. But then he took Grey's hand, and a small electric shock ran through the Englishman. The baron's expression was civil, no more—but the eyes held a look of interest and avidity, and despite the baron's unprepossessing appearance, Grey's flesh answered the look.

Of course. Percy had told Amandine about him.

Surprised and wary, he gave the brief explanation he had prepared, only to be informed that, *hélas,* Monsieur Beauchamp was not at home but had gone with Monsieur Beaumarchais to hunt wolves in Alsace. Well, there was one supposition confirmed, Grey thought. But surely his lordship would condescend to accept the hospitality of *Trois Flèches,* for the night at least?

He accepted this invitation with many expressions of unworthy thanks, and having doffed his outer clothes and replaced his seaboots with Dottie's garish carpet slippers—which made Amandine blink, though he at once praised them exceedingly—he was propelled down a long corridor lined with portraits.

"We will take some refreshment in the library," Amandine was saying. "Plainly, you are perishing of cold and inanition. But if you do not mind, allow me to introduce you *en route* to my other guest; we will invite him to join us."

Grey had murmured acquiescence, distracted by the light pressure of Amandine's hand, which rested on his back—slightly lower than was usual.

"He is an American," the baron was saying, as they reached a door toward the end of the corridor, and his voice conveyed considerable in the way of amusement in that word. He had a most unusual voice—soft, warm, and somehow smoky, like oolong tea with a lot of sugar.

"He enjoys to spend some time each day in the solar," the baron went on, pushing open the door and gesturing Grey ahead of him. "He says it keeps him in a state of robust health."

Grey had been looking politely at the baron during this introduction, but now turned to speak to the American guest and so was introduced to Dr. Franklin, reclining comfortably in a padded chair, lit by a flood of sunlight, stark naked.

In the subsequent conversation—conducted with the greatest aplomb on the part of all parties—he learned that it was Dr. Franklin's invariant practice to bathe in air every day when possible, as skin breathed quite as much as did lungs, taking in air and releasing impurities; thus the ability of the body to defend itself from infection was substantially impaired if the skin were constantly suffocated in insanitary clothing.

Throughout the introductions and conversation, Grey was acutely aware of Amandine's eyes upon him, full of speculation and amusement, and of the cumbersome feel of his own insanitary clothing upon his doubtless suffocating skin.

It was an odd feeling, to meet a stranger and know that said stranger was already privy to his deepest secret, that he in fact—if Percy were not altogether lying, and Grey didn't think he had been—shared it. It gave him a feeling of danger and vertigo, as though he leaned out from some sharp precipice. It also bloody excited him, and *that* alarmed him very much.

The American (now speaking pleasantly about an unusual geological formation he had seen on his journey from Paris; had his lordship noticed it?) was an elderly man, and his body, while in fair condition aside from patches of some purplish eczema about the lower limbs, was not an object of sexual consideration. Nonetheless, Grey's flesh was tight on his bones, and not enough of his blood was in his head. He could feel Amandine's eyes on him, frankly evaluating him, and recalled all too clearly the exchange with Percy regarding Percy's wife and his brother-in-law the baron: *Both, on occasion. Together?* Had the baron's sister accompanied her husband, or was she perhaps at home? For one of the few times in his life, Grey wondered seriously whether he might be a pervert.

"Shall we join the good doctor in his beneficial practice, my lord?"

Grey jerked his eyes away from Franklin, to see the baron beginning to peel off his coat. Fortunately, before he could think of anything to say, Franklin rose, remarking that he felt he had had sufficient benefit for the day. "Though of course," he said, meeting Grey's eyes directly, with an expression of the deepest interest—and not a little amusement, too, "you must not allow my departure to prevent your own indulgence, *messieurs.*"

The baron, impeccably polite, at once resumed his coat, and saying he would join them for *un aperitif* in the library, disappeared into the corridor.

Franklin had a silk dressing gown; Grey held it for him, watching the white, slightly sagging—but remarkably firm and unwrinkled—buttocks disappear as the American slowly worked his arms into the sleeves, remarking as he did so upon a touch of arthritis in his shoulder joints.

Turning and tying the sash, he fixed an open gray gaze upon Grey.

"Thank you, my lord," he said. "I take it you were not previously acquainted with Amandine?"

"No. I knew his . . . brother-in-law, Monsieur Beauchamp, some years ago. In England," he added, for no particular reason.

Something flickered in Franklin's eyes at the name "Beauchamp," causing Grey to ask, "You know him?"

"I know the name," Franklin replied equably. "Is Beauchamp an Englishman, then?"

A number of astonishing possibilities had flashed through Grey's mind at that simple remark "*I know the name,*" but an equally rapid evaluation of them decided him upon the truth as safest, and he merely said, "Yes," in a tone indicating that this was simple fact, no more.

Over the next few days, he and Franklin had had a number of interesting conversations, in which the name of Percy Beauchamp was conspicuous by its absence. When Franklin returned to Paris, though, Grey was left both with a genuine liking for the elderly gentleman—who upon learning that Grey was bound for the Colonies in the spring had insisted upon giving him letters of introduction to several friends there—and a conviction that Dr. Franklin knew precisely what Percy Beauchamp was and had been.

"Beg pardon, sir," said one of the *Tartar*'s hands, elbowing Grey ungently out of the way and breaking his reverie. He blinked, coming back to find that his ungloved hands had turned to ice in the wind and his cheeks were numb. Leaving the sailors to their freezing task, he went below, feeling a peculiar small and shameful warmth at the memory of his visit to *Trois Flèches.*

3 May, 1777
New York

Dear Papa,

I have just received your Letter about Cousin Henry, and hope very much that you will be able to discover his Whereabouts and obtain his Release. If I can hear Anything of him, I will do my best to let you know. Is there anyone to whom I should address Letters to you in the Colonies? (If I hear of no Alternative, I shall send them in care of Mr. Sanders in Philadelphia, with a Copy for Safety to Judge O'Keefe in Richmond.)

I hope you will excuse my own sad Delinquency in corresponding. It does not—alas—stem from any press of urgent Activity on my Part, but rather from ennui and lack of anything of Interest about which to write. After a tedious Winter immured in Quebec (though I did considerable Hunting, and shot a very vicious Thing called a Glutton), I finally received my new orders from General Howe's Aide-de-camp in late March, when some of Sir Guy's people came back to the Citadel, and I returned to New York in consequence of them.

I never received any Word from Captain Randall-Isaacs, nor have I been able to hear anything of him since my Return. I fear very much that he may have been lost in the Blizzard. If you know his people, perhaps you would send them a Note with my Hopes for his Survival? I would do so myself, save that I am not sure where to find them, nor how to phrase my Sentiments delicately, in case they are also in Doubt of his Fate, or worse, are not in Doubt. You will know what to say, though; you always do.

I was somewhat luckier in my own Travels, having suffered only minor Shipwreck on my way downriver (we came to Grief during the Portage at Ticonderoga, being fired upon by a Party of American Sharpshooters from the Fort. No one was harmed, but the Canoes were peppered with Shot and some Holes were unfortunately not discovered before we put back into the Water, whereupon two of them sank abruptly), this followed by waist-deep Mud and the reemergence of carnivorous Insects when I took to the Roads. Since my Return, though, we have done little of interest, though there are constant rumors of what we may do. Finding that Inactivity chafes more in what you may call a civilized Setting (though none of the Girls in New York can dance at all), I volunteered to ride Dispatches, and have found some Relief in that.

Yesterday, however, I received Orders sending me back to Canada, there to join General Burgoyne's Staff. Do I detect your fine Italian Hand in this, Papa? If so, thank you!

Also, I have seen Captain Richardson again; he came to my Rooms last Night. I had not seen him for nearly a Year, and was much surprised. He did not ask for an Account of our Journey into Quebec (not surprising, as the Information would be sadly out-of-date by now), and

*when I asked after Randall-Isaacs, only shook his Head and said he did
not know.*

*He had heard I had an Errand to carry special Dispatches to
Virginia, before going to Canada, and while of course Nothing must
delay me in that Errand, had thought of asking me to do a small
Service for him as I returned northward. Somewhat wary as a Result
of my long Sojourn in the frozen North, I asked what this might be,
and was told that it was no more than the Delivery of a cipher Message
to a group of Loyalist gentlemen in Virginia, something that would be
simple for me, owing to my Familiarity with the Terrain; the job would
not delay me more than a Day or two, he assured me.*

*I said I would do it, but more because I should like to see some Parts
of Virginia that I remember with fondness than because I should like to
oblige Captain Richardson. I am somewhat wary of him.*

*Godspeed your travels, Papa, and please give my Love to my precious
Dottie, whom I long to see. (Tell her I trapped forty-two Ermine in
Canada; she shall have a Cloak made of the Skins!)*

> *Your most affectionate Reprobate,*
> *William*

34

PSALMS, 30

October 6, 1980
Lallybroch

BRIANNA'S ARRANGEMENT with the Hydro Electric Board
provided for her working three days a week doing site inspections,
overseeing maintenance and repair operations as required, but allowed
her to stay at home doing reports, forms, and other paperwork the other two
days. She was trying to decipher Rob Cameron's notes regarding the power
feed from the second turbine at Loch Errochty, which appeared to have been
written with grease pencil on the remains of the bag that had held his lunch,
when she became aware of sounds in the laird's study across the hall.

She'd been vaguely conscious of a low humming for some time, but insofar as she'd noticed the sound had put it down to a fly trapped by the window.
The hum had now acquired words, though, and a fly would not have been
singing "*The King of Love my Shepherd is,*" to the tune of "St. Columba."

She froze, realizing that she'd *recognized* the tune. The voice was rough as coarse-grit sandpaper, and it cracked now and then...but it went up and it went down, and it was, it *really* was, a song.

The song stopped abruptly in a fit of coughing, but after some heavy-duty throat-clearing and cautious humming, the voice started up again, this time using an old Scottish tune she thought was called "Crimond."

> *"The Lord's my Shepherd, I'll not want.*
> *He makes me down to lie.*
> *In pastures green; He leadeth me*
> *The quiet waters by."*

"The quiet waters by" was repeated once or twice in different keys, and then, with increased vigor, the hymn went on:

> *"My soul He doth restore again:*
> *And me to walk doth make*
> *Within the paths of righteousness,*
> *Even for His Name's own sake."*

She sat at her desk, shaking, tears running down her cheeks and a handkerchief pressed to her mouth so he wouldn't hear. "Thank you," she whispered into its folds. "Oh, thank you!"

The singing stopped, but the humming resumed, deep and contented. She got herself back under control and wiped the tears hastily away; it was nearly noon—he'd be coming in any time to ask if she was ready for lunch.

Roger had had considerable doubt about the assistant choirmaster's position—doubt he'd tried not to let her see, and doubt she'd shared until he came home to tell her he'd been given the Children's Choir as his main responsibility. Her own doubt had flown then; children were at once totally uninhibited about voicing the sorts of remarks regarding social oddity that their elders never would, and entirely accepting of such oddity, once they got used to it.

"How long did it take them to ask about your scar?" she'd asked, when he'd come home smiling from his first solo practice with the kids.

"I didn't time it, but maybe thirty seconds." He rubbed two fingers lightly over the ragged mark across his throat, but didn't stop smiling. *"Please, Mr. MacKenzie, what's happened to your neck? Was ye hangit?"*

"And what did you tell them?"

"Told them aye, I was hangit in America, but I lived, praise God. And a couple of them had elder siblings who'd seen *High Plains Drifter* and told them about it, so that raised my stock a good bit. I think they expect me to wear my six-guns to the next practice, though, now the secret's out." He gave her a Clint Eastwood one-eyed squint, which had made her burst out laughing.

She laughed now, remembering it, and just in time, for Roger stuck his head in, saying, "How many different versions of the Twenty-third Psalm would ye say there are, set to music?"

"Twenty-three?" she guessed, rising.

"Only six in the Presbyterian hymnal," he admitted, "but there are metrical settings for it—in English, I mean—that go back to 1546. There's one in the *Bay Psalm Book* and another in the old *Scottish Psalter,* and any number of others here and there. I've seen the Hebrew version, too, but I think I'd best not try that one on the St. Stephen's congregation. Do the Catholics have a musical setting?"

"Catholics have a musical setting for everything," she told him, lifting her nose to sniff for indications of lunch from the kitchen. "But psalms we usually sing to a chant setting. I know four different Gregorian chant forms," she informed him loftily, "but there are lots more."

"Yeah? Chant it for me," he demanded, and stopped dead in the corridor, while she hastily tried to recall the words to the Twenty-third Psalm. The simplest chant form came back automatically—she'd sung it so often in childhood that it was part of her bones.

"That's really something," he said, appreciative, when she'd finished. "Go through it a time or two with me later? I'd like to do it for the kids, just for them to hear. I think they could do Gregorian chant really well."

The kitchen door burst open and Mandy scampered out, clutching Mr. Polly, a stuffed creature who had started out life as a bird of some kind, but now resembled a grubby terry-cloth bag with wings.

"Soup, Mama!" she shouted. "Come eat soup!"

And soup they ate, Campbell's Chicken Noodle made from the can, and cheese sandwiches and pickles to fill the cracks. Annie MacDonald was not a fancy cook, but everything she made was edible, and that was saying a good deal, Brianna thought, with memories of other meals eaten around dying fires on soggy mountaintops or scraped as burnt offerings out of an ashy hearth. She cast a glance of deep affection at the gas-fired Aga cooker that kept the kitchen the coziest room in the house.

"Sing me, Daddy!" Mandy, teeth coated in cheese and mustard round her mouth, gave Roger an entreating grin.

Roger coughed on a crumb and cleared his throat.

"Oh, aye? Sing what?"

" 'Free Bly Mice'!"

"All right. Ye'll need to sing with me, though—keep me from getting off." He smiled at Mandy and beat time softly on the table with the handle of his spoon.

"Three blind mice . . ." he sang, and pointed the handle at Mandy, who drew a heroic breath and echoed, "Free, Bly, MICE!" at the top of her lungs—but with perfect rhythm. Roger raised his eyebrows at Bree and continued the song, in the same counterpoint fashion. After five or six rousing repetitions, Mandy tired of it, and, with a brief "M'scuse me," rose from the table and took off like a low-flying bumblebee, caroming off the doorjamb on her way out.

"Well, she's got a definite sense of rhythm," Roger said, wincing as a loud thud echoed back from the corridor, "if not of coordination. Be a little while before we know if she's got any pitch, though. Your da had a great sense of rhythm, but he couldn't hit the same note twice."

"That reminded me a bit of what you used to do on the Ridge," she said, on impulse. "Singing a line of a psalm and having the people answer it back."

His face changed a little at mention of that time. He'd come newly to his vocation then, and the certainty of it had transformed him. She'd never seen him so happy before—or since, and her heart turned over at the flash of longing she saw in his eyes.

He smiled, though, and, reaching out a napkin-covered finger, wiped a smear of mustard from beside her own mouth.

"Old-fashioned," he said. "Though they still do it that way—the line-singing in kirk—on the Isles, and maybe in the remoter bits of the Gaeltacht. The American Presbyterians won't have it, though."

"They won't?"

"*It is proper to sing without parceling out the psalm line by line,*" he quoted. "*The practice of reading the psalm, line by line, was introduced in times of ignorance, when many in the congregation could not read; therefore, it is recommended that it be laid aside, so far as convenient.* That's from the Constitution of the American Presbyterian Church."

Oh, so you did think about being ordained while we were in Boston, she thought but didn't say aloud.

"Times of ignorance," she repeated, instead. "I'd like to know what Hiram Crombie would have had to say to that!"

He laughed, but shook his head.

"Well, it's true enough; most of the folk on the Ridge couldn't read. But I'd disagree with the notion that ye'd only sing the psalms that way because of ignorance, or a lack of books." He paused for thought, idly scraping up a stray noodle and eating it.

"Singing all together, that's grand, no doubt about it. But to do it in that back-and-forth way—I think there's maybe something about it that draws the people closer, makes them feel more involved in what they're singing, what's truly happening. Maybe it's only because they've got to concentrate harder to remember each line." He smiled briefly, and looked away.

Please! she thought passionately, whether to God, the Blessed Virgin, Roger's guardian angel, or all three. *You've got to let him find a way!*

"I . . . meant to ask ye something," he said, suddenly diffident.

"What's that?"

"Well . . . Jemmy. He *can* sing. Would ye—of course he'd go to Mass with you still—but would ye mind if he was to come along with me, as well? Only if he liked," he added hastily. "But I think he might enjoy being in the choir. And I'd . . . like him to see I have a job, too, I suppose," he added, with a half-rueful smile.

"He'd love that," Brianna said, remarking mentally to the heavenly host, *Well, that was fast!* Because she saw at once—and wondered whether Roger had, but she didn't think so—that this offered a graceful way by which she and Mandy could attend the Presbyterian services, as well, without any overt conflict between their two faiths.

"Would you come with us to the early Mass at St. Mary's?" she asked. "Because then we could all just go across to St. Stephen's together and see you and Jem sing."

"Yes, of course."

He stopped, the sandwich halfway to his mouth, and smiled at her, his eyes green as moss.

"It's better, isn't it?" he said.

"Lots," she said.

LATER IN THE AFTERNOON, Roger called her across to the study. There was a map of Scotland laid on his desk, next to the open notebook in which he was compiling the thing they had taken to calling—with a jokiness that barely covered the aversion they felt in even talking about it—"The Hitchhiker's Guide," after the BBC radio comedy.

"Sorry to interrupt," he said. "But I thought we'd best do it before Jem comes home. If ye're going back to Loch Errochty tomorrow . . ." He put the point of his pencil on the blue blotch labeled *L.Errochty.* "You could maybe get an accurate bearing for the tunnel, if ye're not quite sure where it is. Or are you?"

She swallowed, feeling the remains of her cheese sandwich stir uneasily at the memory of the dark tunnel, the rocking of the little train, of passing through . . . it.

"I don't, but I have something better. Wait." She stepped across to her own office and brought back the binder of Loch Errochty's specs.

"Here are the drawings for the tunnel construction," she said, flipping the binder open and laying it on the desk. "I have the blueprints, too, but they're at the main office."

"No, this is great," he assured her, poring over the drawing. "All I really wanted is the compass orientation of the tunnel to the dam." He glanced up at her. "Speaking of that—have ye been all across the dam itself?"

"Not all across," she said slowly. "Just the east side of the servicing bay. But I don't think—I mean, look." She put a finger on the drawing. "I hit it somewhere in the middle of the tunnel, and the tunnel is nearly in a straight line with the dam. If it runs in a line—is that what you think it does?" she added, looking at him curiously. He shrugged.

"It's a place to start. Though I suppose engineers would have a better-sounding word than 'guess'?"

"Working hypothesis," she said dryly. "Anyway, if it *does* run in a line, rather than just existing in random spots, I'd probably have felt it in the dam if it was there at all. But I could go back and check." Even she could hear the reluctance in her voice; he certainly did, and ran a light hand down her back in reassurance.

"No. I'll do it."

"What?"

"I'll do it," he repeated mildly. "We'll see if I feel it, too."

"No!" She straightened up abruptly. "You can't. You don't—I mean, what if something . . . happens? You can't take that kind of risk!"

He looked at her thoughtfully for a moment, and nodded.

"Aye, I suppose there's something of a risk. But small. I've been all over the Highlands, ken, in my younger years. And now and again I've felt something queer pass through me. So have most folk who live here," he added with a smile. "Queerness is part of the place, aye?"

"Yes," she said, with a brief shudder at thought of water horses, *ban-sidhe,* and Nuckelavees. "But you know what sort of queerness this is—and you know damned well it can kill you, Roger!"

"Didn't kill you," he pointed out. "Didn't kill us on Ocracoke." He spoke lightly, but she could see the shadow of that journey on his face with the speaking. It hadn't killed them—but it had come close.

"No. But—" She looked at him and had a deep, wrenching instant in which she experienced at once the feel of his long, warm body next to hers in bed, the sound of his deep, corncrake voice—and the cold silence of his absence. "No," she said, and made it apparent by her tone that she was prepared to be as stubborn as necessary about it. He heard that and gave a mild snort.

"All right," he said. "Let me just put it down, then." Comparing drawing and map, he chose a spot on the map that might correspond roughly with the center of the tunnel and raised one dark eyebrow in question. She nodded, and he made a light pencil mark in the shape of a star.

There was a large, definite star, made in black ink, over the site of the stone circle on Craigh na Dun. Smaller ones in light pencil at the sites of other stone circles. Someday, they might have to visit those circles. But not yet. Not now.

"Ever been to Lewis?" Roger asked—casually, but not as though it were an idle question.

"No, why?" she said warily.

"The Outer Hebrides are part of the Gaeltacht," he said. "They do the line-singing in the *Gàidhlig* on Lewis, and on Harris, too. Don't know about Uist and Barra—they're mostly Catholic—but maybe. I'm thinking I'd like to go and see what it's like these days."

She could see the Isle of Lewis on the map, shaped like a pancreas, off the west coast of Scotland. It was a large map. Large enough for her to see the small legend *Callanish Stones,* on the Isle of Lewis.

She exhaled slowly.

"Fine," she said. "I'll go with you."

"Ye've got work, haven't you?"

"I'll take time off."

They looked at each other in silence for a moment. Brianna broke away first, glancing at the clock on the shelf.

"Jem'll be home soon," she said, the prosaic nature of daily life asserting itself. "I'd better start something for supper. Annie brought us a nice salmon that her husband took. Shall I marinate it and bake it, or would you like it grilled?"

He shook his head and, rising, began to fold the map away.

"I won't be in to supper tonight. It's lodge night."

THE PROVINCIAL GRAND Masonic Lodge of Inverness-shire included a number of local lodges, two of them in Inverness. Roger had joined

Number 6, the Old Inverness Lodge, in his early twenties, but had not set foot inside the building in fifteen years, and did so now with a mingled sense of wariness and anticipation.

It was, though, the Highlands—and home. The first person he saw upon walking in was Barney Gaugh, who had been the burly, smiling station agent when Roger had come to Inverness on the train, aged five, to live with his great-uncle. Mr. Gaugh had shrunk considerably, and his tobacco-stained teeth had long since been replaced by equally tobacco-stained dentures, but he recognized Roger at once and beamed in delight, seizing him by the arm and towing him into a group of other old men, half of whom likewise exclaimed over his return.

It was weird, he thought a bit later, as they settled to the business of the lodge, doing the routine rituals of the Scottish Rite. *Like a time warp,* he thought, and nearly laughed out loud.

There were differences, aye, but they were slight—and the *feeling* of it . . . He could close his eyes and, if he imagined the haze of stubbed-out cigarettes to be the smoke of a hearth, it could be the Crombies' cabin on the Ridge, where the lodge there had met. The close murmur of voices, line and response, and then the relaxation, the shifting of bodies, fetching of tea and coffee, as the evening became purely social.

There were a good many present—many more than he was used to—and he didn't at first notice Lionel Menzies. The headmaster was across the room, frowning in concentration, listening to something a tall bloke in shirtsleeves was saying to him, leaning close. Roger hesitated, not wanting to break in upon their conversation, but the man talking to Menzies glanced up, saw Roger, returned to his conversation—but then stopped abruptly, gaze jerking back to Roger. To his throat, specifically.

Everyone in lodge had stared at the scar, whether openly or covertly. He'd worn an open-collared shirt under his jacket; there was no point in trying to hide it. Better to get it over with. The stranger stared at the scar so openly, though, as almost to be offensive.

Menzies noticed his companion's inattention—he could hardly not—and, turning, saw Roger and broke into a smile.

"Mr. MacKenzie," he said.

"Roger," Roger said, smiling; first names were usual in lodge, when they weren't being formally "brother so-and-so." Menzies nodded and tilted his head, drawing his companion into introduction. "Rob Cameron, Roger MacKenzie. Rob's my cousin—Roger's one of my parents."

"I thought so," Cameron said, shaking him warmly by the hand. "Thought you must be the new choirmaster, I mean. My wee nephew's in your infants' choir—that'll be Bobby Hurragh. He told us all about ye over supper last week."

Roger had seen the private glance exchanged between the men as Menzies introduced him and thought that the headmaster must also have mentioned him to Cameron, likely telling him about his visit to the school following Jem's Gaelic incident. That didn't concern him at the moment, though.

"Rob Cameron," he repeated, giving the man's hand a slightly stronger squeeze than usual before releasing it, this causing him to look startled. "You work for the Hydro, do you?"

"Aye. What—"

"Ye'll ken my wife, I think." Roger bared his teeth in what might—or might not—be taken for a genial smile. "Brianna MacKenzie?"

Cameron's mouth opened, but no sound came out. He realized this and closed it abruptly, coughing.

"I—uh. Yeah. Sure."

Roger had sized the man up automatically as he'd grasped his hand, and knew if it came to a fight it'd be a short one. Evidently, Cameron knew it, too.

"She, uh . . ."

"She told me, aye."

"Hey, it was no but a wee joke, right?" Cameron eyed him warily, in case Roger meant to invite him to step outside.

"Rob?" said Menzies curiously. "What—"

"What's this, what's this?" cried old Barney, bustling up to them. "Nay politics in lodge, lad! Ye want to talk your SNP shite to brother Roger, take it roond to the pub later." Seizing Cameron by the elbow, Barney towed him off to another group across the room, where Cameron at once settled into conversation, with no more than a brief glance back at Roger.

"SNP shite?" Roger asked, brows raised at Menzies. The headmaster lifted one shoulder, smiling.

"Ken what auld Barney said. Nay politics in lodge!" It was a Masonic rule, one of the most basic—no discussion of religion or politics in lodge—and probably the reason Freemasonry had lasted as long as it had, Roger thought. He didn't care much about the Scottish National Party, but he did want to know about Cameron.

"Wouldn't dream of it," Roger said. "Our Rob's a political, though, is he?"

"My apologies, brother Roger," Menzies said. The look of humorous good nature hadn't deserted him, but he did look somewhat apologetic. "I didn't mean to expose your family's business, but I did tell my wife about Jem and Mrs. Glendenning, and women being what they are, and my wife's sister living next door to Rob, Rob got to hear about it. He was interested because of the *Gàidhlig*, aye? And he does get carried away a bit. But I'm sure he didn't mean to be seeming too familiar with your wife."

It dawned on Roger that Menzies had hold of the wrong end of the stick regarding Rob Cameron and Brianna, but he didn't mean to enlighten him. It wasn't only the women; gossip was a way of life in the Highlands, and if word got round about the trick Rob and his mates had played on Bree, it might cause more trouble for her at her work.

"Ah," he said, seeking for a way to steer the conversation away from Brianna. "Of course. The SNP's all for resurrecting the *Gàidhlig*, aren't they? Does Cameron have it himself?"

Menzies shook his head. "His parents were among those who didn't want their kids to speak it. Now, of course, he's keen to learn. Speak of that—" He broke off abruptly, eyeing Roger with his head to one side. "I had a thought. After we spoke the other day."

"Aye?"

"I wondered, just. Would ye maybe think of doing a wee class now and then? Maybe only for Jem's form, maybe a presentation for the school as a whole, if you felt comfortable about it."

"A class? What, in the *Gàidhlig*?"

"Yes. You know, very basic stuff, but maybe with a word or two about the history, maybe a bit of a song—Rob said ye're choirmaster at St. Stephen's?"

"Assistant," Roger corrected. "And I don't know about the singing. But the *Gàidhlig* . . . aye, maybe. I'll think about it."

HE FOUND BRIANNA WAITING up, in his study, a letter from her parents' box in her hand, unopened.

"We don't have to read it tonight," she said, putting it down, rising, and coming to kiss him. "I just felt like I wanted to be close to them. How was lodge?"

"Odd." The business of the lodge was secret, of course, but he could tell her about Menzies and Cameron, and did.

"What's the SNP?" she asked, frowning.

"The Scottish National Party." He skinned out of his coat, and shivered. It was cold, and there was no fire in the study. "Came in during the late thirties, but didn't get really going until quite recently. Elected eleven members to Parliament by 1974, though—respectable. As ye might gather from the name, their goal is Scottish independence."

"Respectable," she repeated, sounding dubious.

"Well, moderately. Like any party, they have their lunatic elements. For what it's worth," he added, "I don't think Rob Cameron's one of them. Just your average arsehole."

That made her laugh, and the sound of it warmed him. So did her body, which she pressed against his, arms round his shoulders.

"That would be Rob," she agreed.

"Menzies says he's interested in the Gaelic, though. If I teach a class, I hope he doesn't turn up in the front row."

"Wait—what? Now you're teaching Gaelic classes?"

"Well, maybe. We'll see about it." He found himself reluctant to think too much about Menzies's suggestion. Maybe it was only the mention of singing. Croaking out a tune to guide the kids was one thing; singing alone in public—even if it was only schoolkids—was something else again.

"That can wait," he said, and kissed her. "Let's read your letter."

June 2, 1777
Fort Ticonderoga

"Fort Ticonderoga?" Bree's voice rose in astonishment, and she all but jerked the letter from Roger's hands. "What on earth are they doing in Fort Ticonderoga?"

"I don't know, but if ye'll settle for a moment, we'll maybe find out."

She didn't reply but came round the desk and leaned over, her chin propped on his shoulder, her hair brushing his cheek as she focused anxiously on the page.

"It's okay," he said, turning to kiss her cheek. "It's your mum, and she's in an especially parenthetical mood. She doesn't normally do that unless she's feeling happy."

"Well, yes," Bree murmured, frowning at the page, "but...Fort Ticonderoga?"

Dear Bree, et al—

As you've doubtless gathered from the heading of this letter, we are not (yet) in Scotland. We had a certain amount of difficulty on our voyage, involving a) the Royal navy, in the person of one Captain Stebbings, who attempted to press your father and your cousin Ian (it didn't work); b) an American privateer (though her captain, one— and one of him is more than enough—Asa Hickman insists upon the more dignified "letter of marque" as the designation of his ship's mission, which is essentially piracy but executed under the authority of the Continental Congress); c) Rollo; and d) the gentleman I mentioned to you earlier, named (I thought) John Smith, but who turns out to be a deserter from the Royal navy named Bill (aka "Jonah," and I begin to think they are right) Marsden.

Without going into the details of the whole blood-soaked farce, I will merely report that Jamie, Ian, the damned dog, and I are all fine. So far. I'm hoping this state of affairs continues for the next forty-two days, that being when your father's short-term militia contract expires. (Don't ask. Essentially, he was saving Mr. Marsden's neck, as well as providing for the welfare of a couple of dozen seamen inadvertently forced into piracy.) Once it does, we propose to leave promptly on whatever transport might be headed in the general direction of Europe, provided only that said transport is not captained by Asa Hickman. We may have to travel overland to Boston in order to do this, but so be it. (I suppose it would be interesting to see what Boston looks like these days. The Back Bay still being water and all, I mean. At least the Common will still be there, if sporting rather more cows than we were used to.)

The fort is under the command of one General Anthony Wayne, and I have the uncomfortable feeling that I have heard Roger mention this man, using the nickname "Mad Anthony." I'm hoping this designation

*either does or will refer to his conduct in battle, rather than in admin-
istration. So far he seems rational, if harried.*

Being harried is *rational, as he is expecting the more or less imminent arrival of the British army. Meanwhile, his chief engineer, a Mr.
Jeduthan Baldwin (you'd like him, I think. Very energetic fellow!), is
building a Great Bridge, to connect the fort with the hill they call
Mount Independence. Your father is commanding a crew of laborers at
work on this bridge; I can see him just now, from my perch on one of the
fort's demilune batteries. He stands out, rather, being not only twice the
size of most of the men but one of the few wearing a shirt. Most of them
in fact work naked, or wearing only a clout, because of the heat and
wet. Given the mosquitoes, I think this is a mistake, but no one asked
me.*

*No one asked my opinion of the hygienic protocols involved in main-
taining a proper sick bay and prisoner accommodations, either (we
brought several British prisoners with us, including the aforementioned
Captain Stebbings who should by all rights be dead, but somehow isn't),
but I told them anyway. I am thus* persona non grata *with Lieutenant
Stactoe, who thinks he is a surgeon but isn't, and therefore am prevented from treating the men under his care, most of whom will be
dead within a month. Fortunately, no one cares if I treat the women,
children, or prisoners, and so I am usefully occupied, there being a lot of
them.*

*I have a distinct notion that Ticonderoga changed hands more than
once, but am not sure how often or when. This last point rather weighs
upon my mind.*

*General Wayne has almost no regular troops. Jamie says the fort is
seriously undermanned—and even I can see this; half the barracks are
vacant—and while the occasional militia company comes in from New
Hampshire or Connecticut, these normally enroll for only two or three
months, as we did. Even so, the men often don't stay their full term;
there is a constant melting away, and General Wayne complains—
publicly—that he is reduced to (and I quote) "Negroes, Indians, and
women." I told him that he could do worse.*

*Jamie says also that the fort lacks half its guns, these having been
abstracted by a fat bookseller named Henry Knox, who took them two
years ago and managed by some feat of persistence and engineering to
get them all the way to Boston (Mr. Knox himself having to be conveyed
in a cart along with them, he weighing in excess of three hundred
pounds. One of the officers here, who accompanied that expedition,
described it, to general hilarity), where they proved very useful indeed
in getting rid of the British.*

*What's somewhat more worrying than these points is the existence of
a small hill, directly across the water from us, and no great distance
away. The Americans named it Mount Defiance when they took
Ticonderoga away from the British (you remember Ethan Allen?
"Surrender in the name of the Great Jehovah and the Continental*

*Congress!" I hear that poor Mr. Allen is presently in England, being
tried for treason, he having rather overreached himself by trying to take
Montreal on the same terms), and that's rather apt—or would be, if the
fort was capable of putting men and artillery on top of it. They aren't,
and I think the fact that Mount Defiance commands the fort and is
within cannon-shot of it probably will not be lost on the British army, if
and when they get here.*

*On the good side, it is almost summer. The fish are jumping, and if
there was any cotton, it would probably reach my waist. It rains frequently, and I've never seen so much vegetation in one place. (The air
is so rich with oxygen, I occasionally think I will pass out, and am
obliged to nip into the barracks for a restorative whiff of dirty laundry
and chamber pots (though the local usage is "thunder-mug," and for
good reason). Your cousin Ian takes foraging parties out every few
days, Jamie and a number of the other men are accomplished fishermen, and we eat extremely well in consequence.*

*I won't go on at great length here, as I'm not sure when or where I'll
be able to dispatch this letter via one or more of Jamie's several routes
(we copy each letter, if there's time, and send multiple copies, since even
normal correspondence is chancy these days). With luck, it will go with
us to Edinburgh. In the meantime, we send you all our love. Jamie
dreams now and then of the children; I wish I did.*

Mama

Roger sat in silence for a moment, to be sure Bree had had time to finish
reading the letter—though in fact she read much faster than he did; he
thought she must be reading it twice. After a moment, she sighed through
her nose in a troubled fashion and straightened up. He put up a hand and
rested it on her waist, and she covered it with her own. Not mechanically; she
gripped his fingers tightly—but absently. She was looking across at the bookshelves.

"Those are new, aren't they?" she asked quietly, lifting her chin toward the
right-hand bay.

"Yeah. I sent to Boston for them. They came in a couple of days ago." The
spines were new and shiny. History texts, dealing with the American
Revolution. *Encyclopedia of the American Revolution,* by Mark M. Boatner
III. *A Narrative of a Revolutionary Soldier,* by Joseph Plumb Martin.

"Do you want to know?" he asked. He nodded at the open box on the
table before them, where a thick sheaf of letters still remained unopened, on
top of the books. He hadn't yet brought himself to admit to Bree that he'd
looked at the books. "I mean—we know they probably made it out of
Ticonderoga all right. There are a lot more letters."

"We know one of them probably did," Bree said, eyeing the letters.
"Unless . . . Ian knows, I mean. He could have . . ."

Roger pulled his hand back and reached with determination into the box.
Bree drew in her breath, but he ignored it, taking a handful of letters from the
box and flipping through them.

"Claire, Claire, Claire, Jamie, Claire, Jamie, Jamie, Claire, Jamie"—he stopped, blinking at a letter addressed in an unfamiliar hand—"maybe you're right about Ian; do you know what his handwriting looks like?"

She shook her head.

"I don't think I ever saw him write anything—though I suppose he *can* write," she added, dubious.

"Well . . ." Roger put down the folded sheet, and looked from the scatter of letters to the bookshelf and thence to her. She was slightly flushed. "What do you want to do?"

She considered, her eyes flicking to and from the bookshelves and the wooden box.

"The books," she said, decided, and strode across to the shelves. "Which one of these will tell us when Ticonderoga fell?"

George III, Rex Britanniae
to Lord George Germain

> . . . *Burgoyne may command the corps to be sent from Canada to Albany* . . .
>
> *As sickness and other contingencies must be expected, I should think not above 7,000 effectives can be spared over Lake Champlain, for it would be highly imprudent to run any risk in Canada . . . Indians must be employed.*

35

TICONDEROGA

June 1, 1777
Fort Ticonderoga

I FOUND JAMIE ASLEEP, lying naked on the pallet in the tiny chamber that had been allotted to us. It was at the top of one of the stone-built barracks buildings, and thus hot as Hades by mid-afternoon. Still, we were rarely in it during the day, Jamie being out on the lake with the bridge builders, and I being in the hospital building or the family quarters—all of those being equally hot, of course.

By the same token, though, the stones held enough heat to keep us warm in the cool evenings—there was no fireplace—and it did have a small window.

There was a good breeze off the water toward sunset, and for a few hours between, say, ten p.m. and two a.m., it was very pleasant. It was about eight now—still light out and still toasty in; sweat shone on Jamie's shoulders and darkened the hair at his temples to a deep bronze.

On the good side, our tiny attic was the only room at the top of the building and thus had some modicum of privacy. On the other hand, there were forty-eight stone steps up to our aerie, and water must be carried up and slops carried down them. I'd just hauled up a large bucket of water, and the half of it that hadn't spilled down the front of my dress weighed a ton. I put it down with a clunk that brought Jamie upright in an instant, blinking in the gloom.

"Oh, sorry," I said. "I didn't mean to wake you."

"No matter, Sassenach," he said, and yawned immensely. He sat up, stretched, then scrubbed his hands through his damp, loose hair. "Have ye had supper?"

"Yes, I ate with the women. Have you?" He normally ate with his crew of laborers when they stopped work, but sometimes was summoned to dine with General St. Clair or the other militia officers, and these quasi-formal occasions took place much later.

"Mmm-hmm." He lay back on the pallet and watched as I poured water into a tin washing bowl and dug out a tiny lump of lye soap. I stripped to my shift and began meticulously scrubbing, though the strong soap stung my already raw skin and the fumes of it were enough to make my eyes water.

I rinsed my hands and arms, tossed the water out the window—pausing briefly to shout, "Gardy-loo!" before doing so—and started over.

"Why are ye doing that?" Jamie asked curiously.

"Mrs. Wellman's little boy has what I'm almost sure is the mumps. Or ought that to be *are* the mumps? I've never been sure whether it's plural or not. In any case, I'm taking no chance on transmitting it to you."

"Is it a terrible thing, mumps? I thought only weans got it."

"Well, normally it *is* a child's disease," I said, wincing at the touch of the soap. "But when an adult gets it—particularly an adult male—it's a more serious matter. It tends to settle in the testicles. And unless you *want* to have balls the size of muskmelons—"

"Are ye sure ye have enough soap there, Sassenach? I could go and find more." He grinned at me, then sat up again and reached for the limp strip of linen that served us as a towel. "Here, *a nighean*, let me dry your hands."

"In a minute." I wriggled out of my stays, dropped my shift, and hung it on the hook by the door, then pulled my "home" shift over my head. It wasn't quite as sanitary as having surgical scrubs to wear to work, but the fort absolutely crawled with diseases, and I'd do whatever I could to avoid bringing them back to Jamie. He'd run into enough of them in the open.

I splashed the last of the water over my face and arms, then sat down on the pallet beside Jamie, giving a small cry as my knee cracked painfully.

"God, your poor hands," he murmured, gently patting them with the towel, then swabbing my face. "And your nose is sunburnt, too, the wee thing."

"What about yours?" Callused as they normally were, his hands were still a mass of nicks, scraped knuckles, splinters, and blisters, but he dismissed that with a brief flick of one hand and lay back down again with a luxurious groan.

"Does your knee still hurt, Sassenach?" he asked, seeing me rub it. It hadn't ever quite recovered from being strained during our adventures on the *Pitt*, and climbing stairs provoked it.

"Oh, just part of the general decline," I said, trying to make a joke of it. I flexed my right arm, gingerly, feeling a twinge in the elbow. "Things don't bend quite so easily as they used to. And other things hurt. Sometimes I think I'm falling apart."

Jamie closed one eye and regarded me.

"I've felt like that since I was about twenty," he observed. "Ye get used to it." He stretched, making his spine give off a series of muffled pops, and held out a hand. "Come to bed, *a nighean*. Nothing hurts when ye love me."

He was right; nothing did.

I FELL BRIEFLY ASLEEP, but woke by instinct a couple of hours later to go and check the few patients who needed an eye kept on them. These included Captain Stebbings, who had—to my surprise—stoutly refused either to die or to be doctored by anyone but me. That hadn't gone over well with Lieutenant Stactoe or the other surgeons, but as Captain Stebbings's demand was backed up by the intimidating presence of Guinea Dick—pointed teeth, tattoos, and all—I remained his personal surgeon.

I found the captain mildly feverish and wheezing audibly, but asleep. Guinea Dick rose from his own pallet at the sound of my step, looking like a particularly fearsome manifestation of someone's nightmare.

"Has he eaten?" I asked softly, laying my hand lightly on Stebbings's wrist. The captain's tubby form had shrunk considerably; even in the gloom, I could easily see the ribs I'd once had to grope for.

"Him has little soup, ma'am," the African whispered, and moved a hand toward a bowl on the floor, covered with a handkerchief to keep out the roaches. "Like you say. I give him more when he wake to piss."

"Good." Stebbings's pulse was a little fast, but not alarming, and when I leaned over him and inhaled deeply, I detected no scent of gangrene. I'd been able to withdraw the tube from his chest two days before, and while there was a slight exudation of pus from the site, I thought it a local infection that would likely clear without assistance. It would have to; I had nothing to assist it.

There was almost no light in the hospital barracks, only a rush-dip near the door and what little illumination came from the fires in the courtyard. I couldn't judge of Stebbings's color, but I saw the flash of white as he half-opened his eyes. He grunted when he saw me, and closed them again.

"Good," I said again, and left him in the tender charge of Mr. Dick.

The Guinea man had been offered the chance to enlist in the Continental army but had refused, choosing to become a prisoner of war with Captain Stebbings, the wounded Mr. Ormiston, and a few other seamen from the *Pitt*.

"I am English, free man," he had said simply. "Prisoner maybe for a little, but free man. Seaman, but free man. American, maybe not free man."

Maybe not.

I left the hospital barracks, called in at the Wellmans' quarters to check on my case of mumps—uncomfortable, but not dangerous—and then strolled slowly across the courtyard under a rising moon. The evening breeze had died down, but the night air had some coolness in it, and moved by impulse, I climbed to the demilune battery that looked across the narrow end of Lake Champlain to Mount Defiance.

There were two guards, but both were fast asleep, reeking of liquor. It wasn't unusual. Morale at the fort was not high, and alcohol was easily available.

I stood by the wall, a hand on one of the guns, its metal still faintly warm from the day's heat. Would we get away, I wondered, before it was hot from being fired? Thirty-two days to go, and they couldn't go fast enough to suit me. Aside from the menace of the British, the fort festered and stank; it was like living in a cesspool, and I could only hope that Jamie, Ian, and I would leave it without having contracted some vile disease or having been assaulted by some drunken idiot.

I heard a faint step behind me and turned to see Ian himself, tall and slender in the glow of the fires below.

"Can I speak to ye, Auntie?"

"Of course," I said, wondering at this unaccustomed formality. I stood aside a little, and he came to stand beside me, looking down.

"Cousin Brianna would have a thing or two to say about that," he said, with a nod through the half-built bridge below. "So has Uncle Jamie."

"I know." Jamie had been saying it for the last two weeks—to the fort's new commander, Arthur St. Clair, to the other militia colonels, to the engineers, to anyone who would listen, and not a few who wouldn't. The folly of expending vast amounts of labor and material in building a bridge that could be easily destroyed by artillery on Mount Defiance was clear to everyone except those in command.

I sighed. It wasn't the first time I'd seen military blindness, and I was very much afraid it wouldn't be the last.

"Well, leaving that aside . . . what did you want to speak to me about, Ian?"

He took a deep breath and turned toward the moonlit vista over the lake.

"D'ye ken the Huron who came to the fort a wee while past?"

I did. Two weeks before, a party of Huron had visited the fort, and Ian had spent an evening smoking with them, listening to their stories. Some of these concerned the English General Burgoyne, whose hospitality they had previously enjoyed.

Burgoyne was actively soliciting the Indians of the Iroquois League, they said, spending a great deal of time and money in wooing them.

"He says his Indians are his secret weapon," one of the Huron had said, laughing. "He will unleash them upon the Americans, to burn like lightning, and strike them all dead."

Knowing what I did of Indians in general, I thought Burgoyne might be a trifle overoptimistic. Still, I preferred not to think what might happen if he *did* succeed in persuading any number of Indians to fight for him.

Ian was still staring at the distant hump of Mount Defiance, lost in thought.

"Be that as it may," I said, calling the meeting to order. "Why are you telling me this, Ian? You should tell Jamie and St. Clair."

"I did." The cry of a loon came across the lake, surprisingly loud and eerie. They sounded like yodeling ghosts, particularly when more than one of them was at it.

"Yes? Well, then," I said, slightly impatient. "What did you want to talk to me about?"

"Babies," he said abruptly, straightening up and turning to face me.

"What?" I said, startled. He'd been quiet and moody ever since the Hurons' visit, and I assumed that something they'd told him had caused it—but I couldn't imagine what they might have said to him regarding babies.

"How they're made," he said doggedly, though his eyes slid away from mine. Had there been more light, I was sure I could have seen him blushing.

"Ian," I said, after a brief pause. "I decline to believe that you don't know how babies are made. What do you *really* want to know?"

He sighed, but at last he looked at me. His lips compressed for a moment, then he blurted, "I want to know why I canna make one."

I rubbed a knuckle across my lips, disconcerted. I knew—Bree had told me—that he had had a stillborn daughter with his Mohawk wife, Emily, and that she had then miscarried at least twice. Also that it was this failure that had led to Ian's leaving the Mohawk at Snaketown and returning to us.

"Why do you think it might be you?" I asked bluntly. "Most men blame the woman when a child is stillborn or miscarried. So do most women, for that matter."

I had blamed both myself and Jamie.

He made a small Scottish noise in his throat, impatient.

"The Mohawk don't. They say when a man lies wi' a woman, his spirit does battle with hers. If he overcomes her, then the child is planted; if not, it doesna happen."

"Hmm," I said. "Well, that's one way of putting it. And I wouldn't say they're wrong, either. It *can* be something to do with either the man or the woman—or it may be something about them together."

"Aye." I heard him swallow before he went on. "One of the women wi' the Huron was Kahnyen'kehaka—a woman from Snaketown, and she kent me, from when I was there. And she said to me that Emily has a child. A live child."

He had been moving restlessly from foot to foot as he talked, cracking his knuckles. Now he stilled. The moon was well up and shone on his face, making hollows of his eyes.

"I've been thinking, Auntie," he said softly. "I've been thinking for a verra long time. About her. Emily. About Yeksa'a. The—my wee bairn." He stopped, big knuckles pressed hard into his thighs, but he gathered himself again and went on, more steadily.

"And just lately I have been thinking something else. If—*when*," he corrected, with a glance over one shoulder, as though expecting Jamie to pop up through a trap, glaring, "we go to Scotland, I dinna ken how things might be. But if I—if I was to wed again, maybe, either there or here . . ." He looked up at me suddenly, his face old with sorrow but heartbreakingly young with hope and doubt.

"I couldna take a lass to wife if I kent that I should never give her live bairns."

He swallowed again, looking down.

"Could ye maybe . . . look at my parts, Auntie? To see if maybe there's aught amiss?" His hand went to his breechclout, and I stopped him with a hasty gesture.

"Perhaps that can wait a bit, Ian. Let me take a history first; then we'll see if I need to do an examination."

"Are ye sure?" He sounded surprised. "Uncle Jamie told me about the sperm ye showed him. I thought maybe mine might not be quite right in some way."

"Well, I'd need a microscope to see, in any case. And while there *are* such things as abnormal sperm, usually when that's the case, conception doesn't take place at all. And as I understand it, that wasn't the difficulty. Tell me—" I didn't want to ask, but there was no way round it. "Your daughter. Did you see her?"

The nuns had given me my stillborn daughter. "*It's better if you see,*" they had said, gently insistent.

He shook his head.

"Not to say so. I mean—I saw the wee bundle they'd made of her, wrapped in rabbit skin. They put it up high in the fork of a red cedar. I went there at night, for some time, just to . . . well. I did think of taking the bundle down, of unwrapping her, just to see her face. But it would ha' troubled Emily, so I didn't."

"I'm sure you're right. But did . . . oh, hell, Ian, I'm so sorry—but did your wife or any of the other women ever say that there was anything visibly wrong with the child? Was she . . . deformed in any way?"

He glanced at me, eyes wide with shock, and his lips moved soundlessly for a moment.

"No," he said at last, and there was both pain and relief in his voice. "No. I asked. Emily didna want to talk about her, about Iseabaìl—that's what I would ha' named her, Iseabaìl—" he explained, "but I asked and wouldna stop until she told me what the baby looked like.

"She was perfect," he said softly, looking down at the bridge, where a chain of lanterns glowed, reflected in the water. "Perfect."

So had Faith been. Perfect.

I put a hand on his forearm, ropy with hard muscle.

"That's good," I said quietly. "Very good. Tell me as much as you can, then, about what happened during the pregnancy. Did your wife have any bleeding between the time you knew she was pregnant and when she gave birth?"

Slowly I led him through the hope and fear, the desolation of each loss, such symptoms as he could remember, and what he knew of Emily's family; had there been stillbirths among her relations? Miscarriages?

The moon passed overhead and started down the sky. At last I stretched and shook myself.

"I can't be positive," I said. "But I think it's at least possible that the trouble was what we call an Rh problem."

"A what?" He was leaning against one of the big guns, and lifted his head at this.

There was no point in trying to explain blood groups, antigens, and antibodies. And it wasn't actually all that different from the Mohawk explanation of the problem, I thought.

"If a woman's blood is Rh-negative, and her husband's blood is Rh-positive," I explained, "then the child will be Rh-positive, because that's dominant—never mind what that means, but the child will be positive like the father. Sometimes the first pregnancy is all right, and you don't see a problem until the next time—sometimes it happens with the first. Essentially, the mother's body produces a substance that kills the child. *But,* if an Rh-negative woman should have a child by an Rh-negative man, then the fetus is always Rh-negative, too, and there's no problem. Since you say Emily has had a live birth, then it's possible that her new husband is Rh-negative, too." I knew absolutely nothing about the prevalence of Rhesus-negative blood type in Native Americans, but the theory did fit the evidence.

"And if that's so," I finished, "then you shouldn't have that problem with another woman—most European women are Rh-positive, though not all."

He stared at me for so long that I wondered whether he had understood what I'd said.

"Call it fate," I said gently, "or call it bad luck. But it wasn't your fault. Or hers." Not mine. Nor Jamie's.

He nodded, slowly, and leaning forward, laid his head on my shoulder for a moment.

"Thank ye, Auntie," he whispered, and lifting his head, kissed my cheek.

The next day, he was gone.

36

THE GREAT DISMAL

June 21, 1777

WILLIAM MARVELED AT THE road. True, there were only a few miles of it, but the miracle of being able to ride straight into the Great Dismal, through a place where he vividly recalled having had to swim his horse on a previous visit, all the while dodging snapping turtles and venomous snakes—the convenience of it was astonishing. The horse seemed of similar mind, picking up its feet in a lighthearted way, outpacing the clouds of tiny yellow horseflies that tried to swarm them, the insects' eyes glinting like tiny rainbows when they drew close.

"Enjoy it while you can," William advised the gelding, with a brief scratch of the mane. "Muddy going up ahead."

The road itself, while clear of the sweet gum saplings and straggling pines that crowded its edge, was muddy enough, in all truth. Nothing like the treacherous bogs and unexpected pools that lurked beyond the scrim of trees, though. He rose a little in the stirrups, peering ahead.

How far? he wondered. Dismal Town stood on the shore of Lake Drummond, which lay in the middle of the swamp. He had never come so far into the Great Dismal as he was now, though, and had no notion of its actual size.

The road didn't go so far as the lake, he knew that. But surely there was a trace to follow; those inhabitants of Dismal Town must come and go on occasion.

"Washington," he repeated under his breath. "Washington, Cartwright, Harrington, Carver." Those were the names he'd been given by Captain Richardson, of the Loyalist gentlemen from Dismal Town; he'd committed them to memory and punctiliously burned the sheet of paper containing them. Having done so, though, he was seized by irrational panic lest he forget the names, and had been repeating them to himself at intervals throughout the morning.

It was well past noon now, and the wispy clouds of the morning had been knitting themselves up into a low sky the color of dirty wool. He breathed in slowly, but the air didn't have that prickling scent of impending downpour—yet. Besides the ripe reek of the swamp, rich with mud and rotting plants, he could smell his own skin, salty and rank. He'd washed his hands and head as he could but hadn't changed nor washed his clothes in two weeks, and the rough hunting shirt and homespun breeches were beginning to itch considerably.

Though perhaps it wasn't just dried sweat and dirt. He clawed viciously at a certain crawling sensation in his breeches. He'd swear he'd picked up a louse in the last tavern.

The louse, if there was one, wisely desisted, and the itch died. Relieved, William breathed deep and noticed that the swamp's scents had grown more pungent, the sap of resinous trees rising in answer to the oncoming rain. The air had suddenly assumed a muffled quality that deadened sound. No birds sang now; it was as though he and the horse rode alone through a world wrapped in cotton wool.

William didn't mind being alone. He'd grown up essentially alone, without brothers or sisters, and was content in his own company. Besides, solitude, he told himself, was good for thinking.

"Washington, Cartwright, Harrington, and Carver," he chanted softly. But beyond the names, there was little to think of with regard to his present errand, and he found his thoughts turn in a more familiar direction.

What he thought of most frequently on the road was women, and he touched the pocket under the tail of his coat, reflective. The pocket would hold one small book; it had been a choice on this journey between the New Testament his grandmother had given him or his treasured copy of *Harris's List of Covent Garden Ladies*. No great contest.

When William was sixteen, his father had caught him and a friend engrossed in the pages of his friend's father's copy of Mr. Harris's notorious guide to the splendors of London's women of pleasure. Lord John had raised an eyebrow and flipped slowly through the book, pausing now and then to raise the other eyebrow. He had then closed the book, taken a deep breath, administered a brief lecture on the necessary respect due to the female sex, then told the boys to fetch their hats.

At a discreet and elegant house at the end of Brydges Street, they took tea with a beautifully gowned Scottish lady, a Mrs. McNab, who appeared to be on the friendliest of terms with his father. At the conclusion of the refreshment, Mrs. McNab had rung a small brass bell, and . . .

William shifted in his saddle, sighing. Her name had been Margery, and he had written a perfervid panegyric to her. Had been madly in love with her.

He'd gone back, after a fevered week of reckoning his accounts, with the fixed intent of proposing marriage. Mrs. McNab had greeted him kindly, listened to his stumbling professions with the most sympathetic attention, then told him that Margery would, she was sure, be pleased with his good opinion but was, alas, occupied just this minute. However, there was a sweet young lass named Peggy, just come from Devonshire, who seemed lonely and would doubtless be so pleased to have a bit of conversation whilst he was waiting to speak with Margery . . .

The realization that Margery was just that minute doing with someone else what she'd done with *him* was such a staggering blow that he'd sat staring openmouthed at Mrs. McNab, rousing only when Peggy came in, fresh-faced, blond, and smiling, and with the most remarkable—

"Ah!" William slapped at the back of his neck, stung by a horsefly, and swore.

The horse had slowed without his noticing, and now that he *did* notice . . .

He swore again, louder. The road had disappeared.

"How the bloody hell did *that* happen?" He'd spoken loudly, but his voice seemed small, muted by the staggered trees. The flies had followed him; one bit the horse, who snorted and shook his head violently.

"Come on, then," William said, more quietly. "Can't be far off, can it? We'll find it."

He reined the horse's head around, riding slowly in what he hoped was a wide semicircle that might cut the road. The ground was damp here, rumpled with tussocks of long, tangled grass, but not boggy. The horse's feet left deep curves where they struck in the mud, and thick flecks of matted mud and grass flew up, sticking to the horse's hocks and sides and William's boots.

He had been heading north–northwest. . . . . He glanced instinctively at the sky, but no help to be found there. The uniform soft gray was altering, here and there a heavy-bellied cloud bulging through the muffling layer, sullen and murmurous. A faint rumble of thunder reached him, and he swore again.

His watch chimed softly, the sound strangely reassuring. He reined up for a moment, not wanting to risk dropping it in the mud, and fumbled it out of his watch pocket. Three o'clock.

"Not so bad," he said to the horse, encouraged. "Plenty of daylight left." Of course, this was a mere technicality, given the atmospheric conditions. It might as well have been the far side of twilight.

He looked up at the gathering clouds, calculating. No doubt about it: it was going to rain, and soon. Well, it wouldn't be the first time he and the horse had gotten wet. He sighed, dismounted, and unrolled his canvas bedsack, part of his army equipment. He got up again and, with the canvas draped round his shoulders, his hat unlaced and pulled well down, resumed a dogged search for the road.

The first drops came pattering down, and a remarkable smell rose from the swamp in response. Earthy, rich, green, and . . . fecund, somehow, as though the swamp stretched itself, opening its body in lazy pleasure to the sky, releasing its scent like the perfume that wafts from an expensive whore's tumbling hair.

William reached by reflex for the book in his pocket, meaning to write down that poetic thought in the margins, but then shook his head, muttering, "Idiot," to himself.

He wasn't really worried. He had, as he'd told Captain Richardson, been in and out of the Great Dismal many times. Granted, he'd not been here by himself; he and his father had come now and then with a hunting party or with some of his father's Indian friends. And some years before. But—

"Shit!" he said. He'd pressed the horse through what he'd hoped was the thicket edging the road, only to find more thicket—dark clumps of hairy-barked juniper, aromatic as a glass of Holland gin in the rain. No room to turn. Muttering, he kneed the horse and pulled back, clicking his tongue.

Uneasily, he saw that the imprints of the horse's hooves were filling slowly with water. Not from the rain; the ground was wet. Very wet. He heard the sucking noise as the horse's back hooves struck bog, and by reflex he leaned forward, urgently kneeing the horse in the ribs.

Caught wrong-footed, the horse stumbled, caught himself—and then the horse's hind legs gave way suddenly, slipping in the mud, and he flung up his head, whinnying in surprise. William, taken equally unaware, bounced over his rolled bed-sack and fell off, landing with a splash.

He rose up like a scalded cat, panicked at the thought of being sucked down into one of the quaking bogs that lurked in the Great Dismal. He'd seen the skeleton of a deer caught in one once, nothing still visible save the antlered skull, half sunk and twisted to one side, its long yellow teeth showing in what he'd imagined to be a scream.

He splashed hastily toward a tussock, sprang atop it, and crouched there like the toad-king, heart hammering. His horse—was it trapped, had the bog got it?

The gelding was down, thrashing in the mud, whinnying in panic, muddy water flying in sheets from its struggles.

"Jesus." He clutched handsful of the rough grass, balanced precariously. Was it bog? Or only a slough?

Gritting his teeth, he stretched one long leg out, gingerly setting foot on the agitated surface. His boot pressed down . . . down . . . He pulled it hastily back, but it came readily, with a *ploop!* of mud and water. Again . . . yes, there was a bottom! All right, now the other . . . He stood up, arms waving storklike for balance, and . . .

"All right!" he said, breathless. A slough—no more, thank God!

He splashed toward the horse and snatched up the canvas bedsack, loosened in the fall. Flinging it over the horse's head, he wrapped it hastily round the animal's eyes. It was what you did for a horse too panicked to leave a burning barn; his father had shown him how when the barn at Mount Josiah had been struck by lightning one year.

Rather to his astonishment, it seemed to help. The horse was shaking its head to and fro but had quit churning its legs. He seized the bridle and blew into the horse's nostrils, talking calming nonsense.

The horse snorted, spraying him with droplets, but seemed to collect itself. He pulled its head up, and it rolled onto its chest with a great swash of muddy water, and in almost the same motion, surged heavily to its feet. It shook itself from head to tail, the canvas flapping loose and mud showering everything within ten feet of the animal.

William was much too happy to care. He seized the end of the canvas and pulled it off, then took hold of the bridle.

"Right," he said, breathless. "Let's get out of this."

The horse was not paying attention; its dish-faced head lifted suddenly, turned to the side.

"What—"

The huge nostrils flared red, and with an explosive grunt, the horse charged past him, jerking the reins from his hands and knocking him flat in the water—again.

"You frigging *bastard*! What the devil—" William stopped short, crouched in the mud. Something long, drab, and extremely fast passed less than two paces from him. Something big.

His head jerked round, but it was already gone, silent in pursuit of the blundering horse, whose panicked flight he could hear receding in the distance, punctuated by the crashing of broken brush and the occasional clang of shed equipment.

He swallowed. They hunted now and then together, he'd heard. Catamounts. In pairs.

The back of his neck prickled, and he turned his head as far as he could manage, afraid to move more for fear of drawing the attention of anything that might be lurking in the dark tangle of gum trees and underbrush behind him. No sound, save the increasing patter of raindrops on the swamp.

An egret burst white from the trees on the far side of the slough, nearly stopping his heart. He froze, breath held until he thought he'd suffocate in the effort to hear, but nothing happened, and at last he breathed and rose to his feet, the skirts of his coat plastered to his thighs, dripping.

He was standing in a peat bog; there was spongy vegetation under his feet, but the water rose up over the tops of his boots. He wasn't sinking, but he couldn't pull the boots out with his feet still in them and was obliged to draw his feet out one at a time, then wrench the boots free and squelch toward higher ground in his stockings, boots in his hands.

The sanctuary of a rotted log reached, he sat down to empty the water out of his boots, grimly reckoning his situation as he put them on again.

He was lost. In a swamp known to have devoured any number of people, both Indian and white. On foot, without food, fire, or any shelter beyond the flimsy protection offered by the canvas bedsack—this the standard army issue, a literal sack made of canvas with a slit in it, meant to be stuffed with straw or dry grass—both these substances conspicuously lacking in his present circumstances. All he possessed otherwise was the contents of his pockets, this consisting of a clasp knife, a lead pencil, a very soggy bit of bread and cheese, a filthy handkerchief, a few coins, his watch, and his book, also doubtless soaked. He reached to check, discovered that the watch had stopped and the book was gone, and swore, loudly.

That seemed to help a bit, so he did it again. The rain was falling heavily now, not that it mattered in the slightest, given his state. The louse in his breeches, evidently waking to discover its habitat flooded, set off on a determined march to discover drier quarters.

Muttering blasphemies, he stood up, draped the empty canvas over his head, and limped off in the direction in which his horse had departed, scratching.

HE NEVER FOUND THE horse. Either the catamount had killed it, somewhere out of sight, or it had escaped to wander alone through the swamp. He did find two items shed from its saddle: a small waxed packet containing tobacco, and a frying pan. Neither of these seemed immediately useful, but he was loath to part with any remnant of civilization.

Soaked to the skin and shivering under the scanty shelter of his canvas, he crouched among the roots of a sweet gum tree, watching lightning split the night sky. Each blue-white flash was blinding, even through closed eyelids, each jolt of thunder shaking air gone sharp as a knife with the acrid smell of lightning and burnt things.

He had grown almost accustomed to the cannonade when a tremendous blast knocked him flat and swept him skidding sideways through mud and rotted leaves. Choking and gasping, he sat up, swiping mud off his face. What the *devil* had happened? A sharp pain in his arm penetrated his confusion, and, looking down, he saw by the light of the lightning's flash that a splinter of wood, perhaps six inches long, was embedded in the flesh of his right forearm.

Glaring wildly round, he saw that the swamp near him was suddenly studded with splinters and chunks of fresh wood, and the smell of sap and heartwood rose, piercing amid the hot, dancing scent of electricity.

There. Another flash, and he saw it. A hundred feet away, he had noted a huge bald cypress, thinking to use it as a landmark come dawn; it was by far the tallest tree within sight. No longer: the lightning showed him empty air where the towering trunk had been, another flash, the ragged spike of what was left.

Quivering and half deafened by the thunder, he pulled the splinter out of his arm and pressed the fabric of his shirt to the wound to stop it bleeding. It wasn't deep, but the shock of the explosion made his hand shake. He pulled his canvas tight round his shoulders against the driving rain, and curled up again among the sweet gum's roots.

Sometime in the night, the storm moved off, and with the cessation of the noise, he lapsed into an uneasy doze, from which he woke to find himself staring into the white nothingness of fog.

A coldness beyond the bone chill of dawn went through him. His childhood had been spent in the Lake District of England, and he'd known from his earliest memories that the coming of fog on the fells was a danger. Sheep were often lost in the fog, falling to their deaths, parted from the flock and killed by dogs or foxes, freezing, or simply disappearing. Men were sometimes lost in the fog, as well.

The dead came down with the fog, Nanny Elspeth said. He could see her, a spare old woman, straight-backed and fearless, standing at the nursery window, looking out at the drifting white. She'd said it quietly, as though to herself; he didn't think she'd realized he was there. When she did, she drew the curtain with a brisk snap and came to make his tea, saying nothing more.

He could do with a cup of hot tea, he thought, preferably with a great deal of whisky in it. Hot tea, hot buttered toast, jam sandwiches, and cake . . .

The thought of nursery teas recalled his wodge of soggy bread and cheese, and he drew this carefully out of his pocket, immeasurably heartened by its presence. He ate it slowly, savoring the tasteless mass as though it were a brandied peach, and felt very much better, despite the clammy touch of the fog on his face, the dripping of water from the ends of his hair, and the fact that he was still wet to the skin; his muscles ached from shivering all night.

He *had* had the presence of mind to set the frying pan out in the rain the night before, and thus had fresh water to drink, tasting deliciously of bacon fat.

"Not so bad," he said aloud, wiping his mouth. "Yet."

His voice sounded strange. Voices always did, in a fog.

He'd been lost in fog twice before, and he had no desire to repeat that experience, though repeat it he did, now and then, in nightmares. Stumbling blind through a white so thick he couldn't see his own feet, hearing the voices of the dead.

He closed his eyes, preferring momentary darkness to the swirl of white, but could still feel its fingers, cold on his face.

He'd heard the voices then. He tried not to listen now.

He got to his feet, determined. He had to move. At the same time, to go wandering blind through bogs and clinging growth would be madness.

He tied the frying pan to his belt and, slinging the wet canvas over his shoulder, put out a hand and began to grope. Juniper wouldn't do; the wood shredded under a knife, and the trees grew in such fashion that no branch ran straight for more than a few inches. Sweet gum or tupelo was better, but an alder would be best.

He found a small stand of alder saplings after an age of sidling cautiously through the mist, planting one foot at a time and waiting to see the effect, pausing whenever he hit a tree to press its leaves to his mouth and nose by way of identification.

Feeling about among the slender trunks, he picked one an inch or so in diameter and, planting his feet solidly, grasped the sapling with both hands and wrenched it up. It came, with a groan of yielding earth and a shower of leaves— and a heavy body slithered suddenly across his boot. He let out a cry and smashed the root end of his sapling down, but the snake had long since fled.

Sweating despite the chill, he undid the frying pan and used it to prod gingerly at the unseen ground. Eliciting no movement, and finding the surface relatively firm, he turned the pan over and sat upon it.

By bringing the wood close to his face, he could make out the movements of his hands sufficiently as to avoid cutting himself and, with a good deal of labor, managed to strip the sapling and trim it to a handy six-foot length. He then set about whittling the end to a sharpened point.

The Great Dismal was dangerous, but it teemed with game. That was the lure that drew hunters into its mysterious depths. William wasn't about to try to kill a bear, or even a deer, with a homemade spear. He was, however, reasonably adept at gigging frogs, or had been. A groom on his grandfather's estate had taught him long ago, he'd done it often with his father in Virginia, and while it wasn't a skill he'd found occasion to practice in the last few years in London, he felt sure that he hadn't forgotten.

He could hear the frogs all round him, cheerfully unimpressed by the fog.

"Brek-ek-ek-ex, co-ax, co-ax," he murmured. "Brek-ek-ek-ex co-ax!" The frogs seemed likewise unimpressed with quotations from Aristophanes.

"Right, you. Just wait," he said to them, testing his point with a thumb. Adequate. A gigging spear ideally would be trident-shaped. . . . Well, why not? He had time.

Biting his tongue with concentration, he set about to carve two additional sharpened twigs and notch them to join the main spear. He briefly considered twisting bits of juniper bark to make a binding, but rejected that notion in favor of unraveling a length of thread from the fringe of his shirt.

The swamp was sodden in the wake of the storm. He'd lost his tinderbox, but he doubted that even one of Jehovah's thunderbolts, such as he'd witnessed the night before, would ignite a fire here. On the other hand, by the time the sun came out and he eventually succeeded in catching a frog, he'd probably be desperate enough to eat it raw.

He paradoxically found this thought comforting. He wasn't going to starve, then, nor would he die of thirst—being in this swamp was like living in a sponge.

He had nothing so definite as a plan. Only the knowledge that the swamp was large but finite. That being so, once he had the sun to guide him and could be assured of not wandering in circles, he proposed to make his way in a straight line until he reached solid ground or the lake. If he found the lake . . . well, Dismal Town was built on its edge. He had only to walk round the circumference, and eventually he would find it.

So, provided that he took care with the quaking bogs, didn't fall prey to some large animal, wasn't bitten by a venomous snake, and didn't take a fever from putrid water or the swamp's miasma, everything would be all right.

He tested the binding, jabbing the spear gently into the mud, and found it secure. Nothing to do but wait, then, for the fog to lift.

The fog showed no disposition to lift. If anything, it was thicker; he could barely make out his fingers, held a few inches from his eyes. Sighing, he gathered his damp coat round him, settled the gig by his side, and wriggled his spine into a precarious rest against the remaining alders. He put his arms round his knees to hoard what little heat his body still held, and closed his eyes to block the whiteness.

The frogs were still at it. Now without distraction, though, he began to hear the other noises of the swamp. Most of the birds were silent, waiting out the fog as he was, but now and then the deep, startling boom of a bittern echoed through the fog. There were scurrying noises and splashings now and then—muskrat? he wondered.

A loud *plunk!* betokened a turtle dropping off a log into water. He preferred those sounds, because he knew what they were. More unnerving were the faint rustlings, which might be the rubbing of branches—though the air was too still, surely, for wind?—or the movement of something hunting. The shrill cry of something small, cut off abruptly. And the creakings and groanings of the swamp itself.

He'd heard the rocks talking to themselves on the fells at Helwater. The Lake District, his maternal grandparents' home. In the fog. He hadn't told anyone that.

He moved a little and felt something just below his jaw. Clapping a hand to the spot, he discovered a leech that had attached itself to his neck. Revolted, he ripped it loose and flung it as hard as he could into the fog. Patting himself all over with trembling hands, he settled back into his crouch, trying to repel the memories that came flooding in with the swirling mist. He'd heard his mother—his real mother—whisper to him, too. That was why he'd gone into the fog. They'd been picnicking on the fells, his grandparents and Mama Isobel and some friends, with a few servants. When the fog came down, sudden as it sometimes did, there was a general scurry to pack up the luncheon things, and he had been left by himself, watching the inexorable white wall roll silently toward him.

And he'd swear he'd heard a woman's whisper, too low to make out words but holding somehow a sense of longing, and he had known she spoke to him.

And he'd walked into the fog. For a few moments, he was fascinated by the movement of the water vapor near the ground, the way it flickered and shimmered and seemed alive. But then the fog grew thicker, and in moments he'd known he was lost.

He'd called out. First to the woman he thought must be his mother. *The dead come down in the fog.* That was nearly all he knew about his mother—that she was dead. She'd been no older than he was now when she died. He'd seen three paintings of her. They said he had her hair and her hand with a horse.

She'd answered him, he'd swear she'd answered him—but in a voice with no words. He'd felt the caress of cool fingers on his face, and he'd wandered on, entranced.

Then he fell, badly, tumbling over rocks into a small hollow, bruising himself and knocking out all his wind. The fog had billowed over him, marching past, urgent in its hurry to engulf things, as he lay stunned and breathless in the bottom of his small declivity. Then he began to hear the rocks murmur all around him, and he'd crawled, then run, as fast as he could, screaming. Fell again, got up and went on running.

Fell down, finally unable to go further, and huddled terrified and blind on the rough grass, surrounded by vast emptiness. Then he heard them calling out for him, voices he knew, and he tried to cry out in reply, but his throat was raw from screaming, and he made no more than desperate rasping noises, running toward where he thought the voices were. But sound moves in a fog, and nothing is as it seems: not sound, not time nor place.

Again and again and again, he ran toward the voices but fell over something, tripped and rolled down a slope, stumbled into rocky outcrops, found himself clinging to the edge of a scarp, the voices now behind him, fading into the fog, leaving him.

Mac had found him. A big hand had suddenly reached down and grabbed him, and the next minute he was lifted up, bruised and scraped and bleeding but clutched tight against the Scottish groom's rough shirt, strong arms holding him as though they'd never let him go.

He swallowed. When he had the nightmare, sometimes he woke with Mac holding him. Sometimes he didn't and woke in a cold sweat, unable to go back to sleep for fear of the waiting fog and the voices.

He froze now, hearing footsteps. Breathed cautiously—and smelled the unmistakable ripe smell of pig shit. He didn't move; wild pigs were dangerous if you startled them.

Snuffling noises, more footsteps, the rustle and shower of water drops as heavy bodies brushed the leaves of holly and yaupon bushes. Several of them, moving slowly but moving nonetheless. He sat up sharp, turning his head to and fro, trying to locate the sound exactly. Nothing could move with purpose in this fog—unless they were following a path.

The swamp was crisscrossed with game paths, made by the deer and used by everything from possums to black bears. These paths wound aimlessly, only two things certain about them: one, that they did lead to drinkable water, and two, that they did not lead into a quaking bog. Which, under the circumstances, was enough for William.

They'd said one other thing about his mother. "*Reckless,*" his grandmother had said sadly, shaking her head. "*She was always so reckless, so impulsive.*" And her eyes had rested then on him, apprehensive. *And you're just like her,* said those anxious eyes. *God help us all.*

"Maybe I am," he said out loud, and, gripping his frog spear, stood up, defiant. "But *I'm* not dead. Not yet."

He knew that much. And that to stand still when lost was a good idea only if someone was looking for you.

37

PURGATORY

A T MIDDAY ON THE third day, he found the lake.
He'd come to it through a cathedral of towering bald cypress, their
great buttressed trunks rising like pillars from the flooded ground.
Half starved, light-headed from a rising fever, he walked slowly through calf-
deep water.

The air was still; so was the water. The only movement was the slow drag
of his feet and the buzzing insects that plagued him. His eyes were swollen
from the bites of mosquitoes, and the louse had company in the form of chig-
gers and sand fleas. The darning needles that darted to and fro didn't bite like
the hundreds of swarming tiny flies, but had their own form of torment—
they made him glance at them, sunlight glinting gold and blue and red from
their gauzy wings and shining bodies, dizzying in the light.

The smooth surface of the water reflected the trees standing in it so perfectly that he could not be sure quite where he himself was, balanced precariously between two looking-glass worlds. He kept losing his sense of up and
down, the dizzying sight through the branches of the towering cypress above
the same as that below. The trees loomed more than eighty feet over him, and
the sight of drifting clouds seeming to sail straight through the gently stirring
branches below gave him the constant queer sense that he was about to fall—
up or down, he couldn't tell.

He'd pulled the cypress splinter from his arm and done his best to bleed
the wound, but there were smaller slivers of wood left behind, trapped under
the skin, and his arm was hot and throbbing. So was his head. The chill and
fog had disappeared as though they had never existed, and he walked slowly
through a world of heat and stillness that shimmered round the edges. The
backs of his eyes burned.

If he kept his eyes fixed on the purling of water away from his boots, the V-
shaped waves broke the disturbing reflection and kept him upright. But
watching the dragonflies . . . That made him sway and lose his bearings, as
they seemed not fixed in either air or water, but part of both.

A strange depression appeared in the water, a few inches from his right calf.
He blinked, then saw the shadow, sensed the weight of the heavy body undulating through the water. An evil, pointed, triangular head.

He gulped air and stopped dead. The moccasin, by great good fortune, did
not.

He watched it swim away, and wondered whether it might be fit to eat. No
matter; he'd broken his frog spear, though he'd caught three frogs before the
fragile binding gave way. Small ones. They hadn't tasted badly, despite the

rubbery feel of the raw flesh. His stomach clenched, gnawing, and he fought the insane impulse to dive after the snake, seize it, and rip the flesh from its bones with his teeth.

Maybe he could catch a fish.

He stood still for several minutes, to be sure the snake had left. Then swallowed and took another step. And walked on, eyes fixed on the small waves his moving feet made, breaking the looking-glass water into fragments around him.

A short time later, though, the surface began to move, hundreds of tiny wavelets lapping against the gray-brown wood of the cypress trees, shimmering so that the dizzy swirl of trees and clouds disappeared. He lifted his head and saw the lake before him.

It was vast. Much bigger than he had thought it would be. Giant bald cypresses stood in the water, the stumps and carcasses of earlier progenitors bleaching in the sun among them. The far shore was dark, thick with tupelo, alder, and hobblebush. And the water itself seemed to stretch for miles before him, brown as tea with the infusions of the trees that grew in it.

Licking his lips, he bent and scooped up a handful of the brown water and drank, then drank again. It was fresh, a little bitter.

He wiped a wet hand across his face; the cool wetness made him shiver with a sudden chill.

"Right, then," he said, feeling breathless. He pushed ahead, the ground sloping away gradually beneath him, until he stood in the open water, the dense growth of the swamp behind him. Chills still swept him, but he ignored them.

Lake Drummond had been named for an early governor of North Carolina. A hunting party, including Governor William Drummond, had gone into the swamp. A week later, Drummond, the sole survivor, had staggered out, half dead from hunger and fever but with news of a huge, unsuspected lake in the midst of the Great Dismal.

William drew a long, shuddering breath. Well, nothing had eaten him yet. And he'd reached the lake. Which way was Dismal Town?

He scanned the shore slowly, looking for any trace of chimney smoke, any break in the dense growth that might betoken a settlement. Nothing.

With a sigh, he reached into his pocket and found a sixpence. He flipped it into the air and nearly missed catching it, fumbling wildly as it bounced off his slow fingers. *Got it, got it!* Tails. Left, then. He turned resolutely and set off.

His leg knocked against something in the water, and he glanced down, just in time to see the white flash of the moccasin's mouth as it rose up in the water and struck at his leg. Reflex alone jerked his foot up, and the snake's fangs stuck briefly in the leather of his boot top.

He yelled and shook his leg violently, dislodging the reptile, which flew off and landed with a splash. Nothing daunted, the thing turned round upon itself almost instantly and arrowed toward him through the water.

William ripped the frying pan from his belt and swung it with all his strength, scooping the snake from the water and lofting it into the air. He didn't wait to see where it landed, but turned and ran, splashing wildly toward the shore.

He rushed up into the growth of gum and juniper and paused, gasping for breath, relieved. The relief was short-lived. He did turn then, to look, and saw the snake, its brown skin gleaming like copper, slither its way up onto the bank in his wake and come undulating determinedly after him across the matted ground.

He let out a yelp and fled.

He ran blindly, feet squelching at every step, ricocheting off trees and through slapping branches, his legs seized by hobblebush and holly, through which he fought his way in a shower of leaves and torn-off twigs. He didn't look back, but wasn't really looking forward, either, and thus ran without warning slap into a man standing in his path.

The man let out a cry and went over backward, William atop him. He pushed himself up and found himself looking down into the face of an astonished Indian. Before he could apologize, someone else grabbed him by the arm and pulled him roughly upright.

It was another Indian, who said something to him, angry and interrogative.

He groped for any stray bit of trade talk, found nothing, and, pointing in the direction of the lake, gasped, "Snake!" The Indians evidently understood the word, though, for their faces changed at once to wariness, and they looked where he was pointing. In support of his story, the annoyed moccasin shot into sight, wriggling through the roots of a sweet gum.

The Indians both let out exclamations, and one of them seized a club from a sling at his back and struck at the snake. He missed, and the snake writhed up at once into a tight coil and struck at him. The snake missed, too, but not by much, and the Indian jerked back, dropping his club.

The other Indian said something in disgust. Taking his own club in hand, he began warily to circle the moccasin. The snake, further enraged by this persecution, spun upon its own contortious coils with a loud hiss and launched itself, spearlike, at the second Indian's foot. He let out a cry and leapt back, though he did keep hold of his club.

William, meanwhile, delighted not to be the focus of the snake's annoyance, had backed out of the way. Seeing the snake momentarily off balance, though—if snakes could be said to have any in the first place—he gripped his frying pan, swung it high, and brought it down, edge-on, with all his force.

Brought it down again, and again and again, his strength driven by panic. At last he stopped, breathing like a blacksmith's bellows, sweat pouring down his face and body. Swallowing, he lifted the frying pan gingerly, expecting to find the snake a bloody mince on the riven ground.

Nothing. He could smell the reptile—a low stench, like that of rotten cucumbers—but could see nothing. He squinted, trying to make sense of the mass of cut-up mud and leaves, then looked up at the Indians.

One of them shrugged. The other pointed off toward the lake and said something. Evidently, the snake had prudently decided that it was outnumbered and returned to its own pursuits.

William stood up awkwardly, frying pan in hand. The men all exchanged nervous smiles.

He was comfortable with Indians, generally; many of them crossed his land, and his father always made them welcome, smoking with them on the veranda, taking supper with them. He couldn't tell which people these two claimed—the faces had the look of some one of the Algonkian tribes, high-cheeked and bold, but surely this was far south of their usual hunting grounds?

The Indians were examining him in turn, and exchanged a glance that set something tingling at the base of his spine. One of them said something to the other, watching him sidelong to see whether he understood. The other smiled broadly at him, showing brown-stained teeth.

"Tobacco?" the Indian asked, extending a hand, palm upward.

William nodded, trying to slow his breathing, and reached slowly into his coat, right-handed, so as not to have to set down the frying pan in his left.

Likely these two knew the way out of the swamp; he should establish friendly relations, and then . . . He was trying to think logically, but his lower faculties were interfering. His lower faculties thought he should get the devil away from here, and now.

Coming out with the waxed parcel of tobacco, he threw it as hard as he could at the foremost Indian, who had started toward him, and ran.

A startled exclamation behind him, and then the sound of grunts and thumping feet. His lower faculties, thoroughly justified in their apprehensions, spurred him on, but he knew he couldn't keep it up for long; being chased by the snake had consumed most of what strength he had—and being obliged to run with an iron frying pan in one hand wasn't helping.

His best chance lay in outdistancing them sufficiently as to find a hiding place. With this thought in mind, he drove himself to greater exertions, dashing over open ground beneath a growth of gum trees, then swerving into a thicket of juniper, popping out again almost immediately onto a game trail. He hesitated for an instant—hide in the thicket?—but the urge to run was overwhelming, and he pounded down the narrow trail, vines and branches snatching at his clothes.

He heard the pigs in time, thank God. Startled snorts and grunts, and a great rustling of brush and sucking sounds, as a number of heavy bodies scrambled to their feet. He smelled warm mud and the reek of pig flesh; there must be a wallow round the curve of the path.

"Shit," he said under his breath, and leapt into the brush off the path. Jupiter, now what? Climb a tree? He was breathing hard, sweat running in his eyes.

All the trees nearby were juniper, some very large but dense and twisted, impossible to climb. He dodged round one and crouched behind it, trying to still his breathing.

His heart was hammering in his ears; he'd never hear pursuit. Something touched his hand, and he swung the frying pan by reflex, leaping to his feet.

The dog let out a surprised yelp as the pan glanced off its shoulder, then bared its teeth and growled at him.

"What the devil are you doing here?" William hissed at it. Bloody hell, the thing was the size of a small horse!

The dog's hackles rose, making it look exactly like a wolf—Jesus, it couldn't *be* a wolf, surely?—and it began to bark.

"Shut up, for God's sake!" But it was too late; he could hear Indian voices, excited and quite near. "Stay," he whispered, putting out a palm toward the dog as he edged backward. "Stay. Good dog."

The dog did not stay, but followed him, continuing to growl and bark. The sound of this further disturbed the pigs; there was a thunder of hooves along the path and a surprised whoop from one of the Indians.

William caught a flicker of movement from the corner of his eye and whirled, weapon at the ready. A very tall Indian blinked at him. Hell, more of them.

"Leave off, dog," said the Indian mildly, in a distinct Scots accent. William blinked in turn.

The dog did cease barking, though it continued to circle him, unnervingly close and growling all the time.

"Who—" William began, but was interrupted by the two original Indians, who at this point appeared suddenly out of the undergrowth. They came to an abrupt halt at sight of the newcomer—and cast a wary eye at the dog, who turned its attention on them, wrinkling back its muzzle and displaying an impressive array of gleaming teeth.

One of the original Indians said something sharp to the newcomer—thank God, they weren't together. The tall Indian replied, in a distinctly unfriendly tone. William had no idea what he'd said, but it didn't sit well with the other two. Their faces darkened, and one put a hand impulsively to his club. The dog made a sort of gurgling noise in its throat, and the hand fell at once.

The original Indians seemed disposed to argue, but the tall Indian cut them off, saying something peremptory and flipped a hand in an unmistakable "Be off with you" gesture. The other two exchanged glances, and William, straightening up, moved to stand by the side of the tall Indian and glowered at them. One of them gave him back the evil look, but his friend looked thoughtfully from the tall Indian to the dog and shook his head, the movement almost imperceptible. Without a further word, the two turned and left.

William's legs were shaking, waves of fever heat passing over him. Despite a disinclination to get any closer to the dog's level than necessary, he sat down on the ground. His fingers had gone stiff, he'd clutched the handle of the frying pan so hard. With some difficulty, he unbent them and set the thing down beside him.

"Thank you," he said, and wiped a sleeve across his sweating jaw. "You—speak English?"

"I've met Englishmen who'd say no, but I think ye'll maybe understand me, at least." The Indian sat down beside him, looking at him curiously.

"Christ," William said, "you aren't an Indian." *That* certainly wasn't an Algonkian face. Seen clearly now, the man was much younger than he'd thought, perhaps only a little older than himself, and plainly white, though his skin was sun-browned and he bore facial tattoos, a double line of dots that looped across his cheekbones. He was dressed in leather shirt and leggings, and wore a most incongruous red-and-black Scotchman's plaid over one shoulder.

"Aye, I am," the man said dryly. He raised his chin, indicating the direction taken by the departing Indians. "Where did ye meet wi' that lot?"

"By the lake. They asked for tobacco, and I—gave it to them. But then they chased me; I don't know why."

The man shrugged.

"They thought to take ye west and sell ye as a slave in the Shawnee lands." He smiled briefly. "They offered me half your price."

William took a deep breath.

"I thank you, then. That is—I suppose you haven't any intention of doing the same thing?"

The man didn't laugh aloud, but gave off a distinct sense of amusement.

"No. I'm no going west."

William began to feel a little easier, though the heat of his endeavors was beginning to give way to chills again. He wrapped his arms about his knees. His right arm was beginning to hurt again.

"You don't—do you suppose they might come back?"

"No," the man said, casually indifferent. "I told them to be gone."

William stared at him.

"And why do you think they'll do as you say?"

"Because they're Mingo," the man replied patiently, "and I'm Kahnyen'kehaka—a Mohawk. They're afraid of me."

William gave him a narrow look, but the man was not practicing upon him. He was nearly as tall as William himself, but thin as a coach whip, his dark-brown hair slicked back with bear grease. He looked competent, but not a person to inspire fear.

The man was studying him with an interest equal to his own. William coughed and cleared his throat, then extended a hand. "Your servant, sir. I'm William Ransom."

"Oh, I ken ye well enough," the man said, a rather odd note in his voice. He put out his own hand and shook William's firmly. "Ian Murray. We've met." His eyes traveled over William's torn, disheveled clothes, his scratched, sweating face, and his mud-caked boots. "Ye look a bit better than the last time I saw ye—but not much."

MURRAY LIFTED THE CAMP kettle off the fire and set it on the ground. He laid the knife in the embers for a moment, then dipped the hot blade into the frying pan, now filled with water. The hot metal hissed and gave off clouds of steam.

"Ready?" he said.

"Yes."

William knelt down by a big poplar log and laid his injured arm flat on the wood. It was visibly swollen, the bulge of a large remnant splinter dark under his skin, the skin around it stretched and transparent with pus, painfully inflamed.

The Mohawk—he couldn't yet think of him as anything else, despite the name and accent—glanced at him across the log, eyebrows raised quizzically.

"Was that you I heard? Screamin', earlier?" He took hold of William's wrist.

"I shouted, yes," William said stiffly. "A snake struck at me."

"Oh." Murray's mouth twitched a little. "Ye scream like a lassie," he said, eyes returning to his work. The knife pressed down.

William made a deeply visceral noise.

"Aye, better," said Murray. He smiled briefly, as though to himself, and with a firm grip on William's wrist sliced cleanly through the skin beside the splinter, laying it open for six inches or so. Turning back the skin with the point of the knife, he flicked out the large splinter, then picked delicately at the smaller slivers the cypress shard had left behind.

Having removed as much as he could, he then wrapped a fold of his ragged plaid round the handle of the camp kettle, picked it up, and poured the steaming water into the open wound.

William made a much more visceral sound, this one accompanied by words.

Murray shook his head, and clicked his tongue in reproof.

"Aye, well. I suppose I'll have to keep ye from dying, because if ye do die, ye're bound to go to hell, usin' language like that."

"I don't propose to die," William said shortly. He was breathing hard, and mopped his brow with his free arm. He lifted the other gingerly and shook blood-tinged water from his fingertips, though the resulting sensation made him light-headed. He sat down on the log, rather suddenly.

"Put your heid atween your knees, if ye're giddy," Murray suggested.

"I am not giddy."

There was no response to this save the sound of chewing. While waiting for the kettle to boil, Murray had waded into the water and pulled several handsful of some strong-smelling herb that grew on the verge. He was in process now of chewing the leaves, spitting the resultant green wads into a square of cloth. Extracting a rather shriveled onion from the haversack he carried, he cut a generous slice from this and eyed it critically, but seemed to think it would pass without mastication. He added it to his packet, folding the cloth neatly over the contents.

This he placed over the wound and wrapped it in place with strips of cloth torn from William's shirttail.

Murray glanced up at him thoughtfully.

"I suppose ye're verra stubborn?"

William stared at the Scot, put out at this remark, though in fact he had been told repeatedly, by friends, relatives, and military superiors, that his intransigence would one day kill him. Surely it didn't show on his face!

"What the devil do you mean by that?"

"It wasna meant as an insult," Murray said mildly, and bent to tighten the knot of the impromptu bandage with his teeth. He turned away and spat out a few threads. "I hope ye are—because it'll be a good distance to find ye help, and if you're sufficiently stubborn as not to die on me, that would be good, I think."

"I said I don't propose to die," William assured him. "And I don't need help. Where—are we anywhere near Dismal Town?"

Murray pursed his lips.

"No," he said, and raised one brow. "Were ye bound there?"

William considered for an instant, but nodded. No harm in telling him that, surely.

Murray raised an eyebrow.

"Why?"

"I—have business with some gentlemen there." As he said this, William's heart gave a lurch. Christ, the book! He'd been so confounded by his various trials and adventures that the true importance of his loss had not even struck him.

Beyond its general entertainment value and its usefulness as palimpsest for his own meditations, the book was vital to his mission. It contained several carefully marked passages whose code gave him the names and locations of those men he was to visit—and, more importantly, what he was to tell them. He could recall a good many of the names, he thought, but for the rest . . .

His dismay was so great that it overshadowed the throbbing in his arm, and he stood up abruptly, seized by the urge to rush back into the Great Dismal and begin combing it, inch by inch, until he should recover the book.

"Are ye all right, man?" Murray had risen, too, and was looking at him with a combination of curiosity and concern.

"I—yes. Just—I thought of something, that's all."

"Well, think about it sitting down, aye? Ye're about to fall into the fire."

In fact, William's vision had gone bright, and pulsating dots of dark and light obscured most of Murray's face, though the look of alarm was still visible.

"I—yes, I will." He sat down even more abruptly than he'd risen, a heavy cold sweat sudden on his face. A hand on his good arm urged him to lie down, and he did, feeling dimly that it was preferable to fainting.

Murray made a Scottish noise of consternation and muttered something incomprehensible. William could feel the other man hovering over him, uncertain.

"I'm fine," he said—without opening his eyes. "I just . . . need to rest a bit."

"Mmphm."

William couldn't tell whether this particular noise was meant as acceptance or dismay, but Murray went away, coming back a moment later with a blanket, with which he covered William without comment. William made a feeble gesture of thanks, unable to speak, as his teeth had begun to chatter with a sudden chill.

His limbs had been aching for some time, but he had ignored it in the need to push on. Now the burden of it fell full on him, a bone-deep ache that made him want to moan aloud. To keep from it, he waited until the chill relaxed enough to let him speak, then called to Murray.

"You are familiar with Dismal Town yourself, sir? You've been there?"

"Now and again, aye." He could see Murray, a dark silhouette crouched by the fire, and hear the chink of metal on stone. "It's verra aptly named."

"Ha," William said weakly. "I daresay. And h-h-have you met a Mr. Washington, by chance?"

"Five or six of them. The general's got a good many cousins, aye?"

"The g-g—"

"General Washington. Ye've heard of him, maybe?" There was a distinct hint of amusement in the Scottish Mohawk's voice.

"I have, yes. But—surely that . . ." This made no sense. His voice trailed off, and he rallied, forcing his drifting thoughts back into coherence. "It is a Mr. Henry Washington. He is kin to the general, too?"

"So far as I ken, anyone named Washington within three hundred miles is kin to the general." Murray stooped to his bag, coming out with a large furry mass, a long, naked tail dangling from it. "Why?"

"I—nothing." The chill had eased, and he drew a grateful breath, the knotted muscles of his belly relaxing. But the faint threads of wariness were making themselves felt through puzzlement and the gathering fog of fever. "Someone told me that Mr. Henry Washington was a prominent Loyalist."

Murray turned toward him in astonishment.

"Who in Bride's name would tell ye that?"

"Plainly someone grossly mistaken." William pressed the heels of his hands against his eyes. His wounded arm hurt. "What is that thing? Possum?"

"Muskrat. Dinna fash; it's fresh. I killed it just before I met ye."

"Oh. Good." He felt obscurely comforted and couldn't think why. Not the muskrat; he'd eaten muskrat often enough and found it tasty, though the fever had stolen his appetite. He felt weak with hunger, but had no desire to eat. Oh. No, it was the "dinna fash." Spoken with just that kindly, matter-of-fact intonation—Mac the groom had used to say that to him, often, whether the trouble was being thrown from his pony or not being allowed to ride into the town with his grandfather. *"Dinna fash; it will be all right."*

The ripping sound of skin parting from the underlying muscle made him momentarily dizzy and he closed his eyes.

"Ye've got a red beard."

Murray's voice came to him, filled with surprise.

"You've only just now noticed that?" William said crossly, and opened his eyes. The color of his beard was an embarrassment to him; while the hair on his head, chest, and limbs was a decent sort of dark chestnut, that on his chin and privates was an unexpectedly vivid shade that mortified him. He shaved fastidiously, even on shipboard or on the road—but his razor, of course, had departed with the horse.

"Well, aye," Murray said mildly. "I expect I was distracted earlier." He fell silent, concentrating on his work, and William tried to relax his mind, hoping to sleep for a time. He was tired enough. Repeated images of the swamp played themselves out before his closed eyes, though, wearying him with visions that he could neither ignore nor dismiss.

Roots like the loops of snares, mud, rank brown dollops of cold pig shit, the turds uneasily humanlike . . . churned dead leaves . . .

Dead leaves floating on water like brown glass, reflections shattering around his shins . . . words in the water, the pages of his book, faint, mocking as they sank away . . .

Looking up, the sky as vertiginous as the lake, feeling that he might fall up as easily as down and drown in the water-clogged air . . . drowning in his sweat . . . a young woman licked the sweat from his cheek, tickling, her body heavy, hot, and cloying, so that he turned and twisted, but could not escape her oppressive attentions . . .

. . . sweat collecting behind his ears, thick and greasy in his hair . . . growing like fat slow pearls in the stubble of his vulgar beard . . . chilling on his skin, his clothes a dripping shroud . . . the woman was still there, dead now, dead weight on his chest, pinning him to the icy ground . . .

Fog and the creeping cold . . . white fingers prying into his eyes, his ears. He must keep his mouth shut or it would reach inside him . . . All white.

He curled into a ball, shaking.

William did at last fall deeper into a fitful sleep, from which he roused some time later, to the rich smell of roasted muskrat, and found the enormous dog lying pressed against him, snoring.

"Jesus," he said, with disconcerting recollections of the young woman in his dreams. He pushed feebly at the dog. "Where did *that* come from?"

"That's Rollo," Murray said reprovingly. "I made him lie wi' ye for a bit of heat; ye've got a shaking ague, if ye hadn't noticed."

"I had noticed that, yes." William struggled upright and made himself eat but was happy to lie down again, at a safe distance from the dog, who was now lying on his back, paws drooping, looking like nothing so much as a giant hairy dead insect. William passed a hand downward over his clammy face, trying to remove *that* disturbing image from his mind before it made its way into his fever dreams.

Night had come well on, and the sky opened overhead, clear and empty and vast, moonless but brilliant with distant stars. He thought of his father's father, dead long before his own birth, but a noted amateur astronomer. His father had often taken him—and sometimes his mother—to lie on the lawns at Helwater, to look up at the stars and name the constellations. It was a cold sight, that blue-black emptiness, and made his fevered blood tremble, but the stars were a comfort, nonetheless.

Murray was looking upward too, a look of distance on his tattooed face.

William lay back, half-propped against the log, trying to think. What was he to do next? He was still trying to absorb the news that Henry Washington and thus, presumably, the rest of his Dismal Town contacts were rebels. Was this odd Scottish Mohawk right in what he'd said? Or did he seek to mislead him, for some purpose of his own?

What would that be, though? Murray could have no notion who William was, beyond his name and his father's name. And Lord John had been a private citizen when they had met years before, on Fraser's Ridge. Murray could not tell, surely, that William was a soldier, let alone an intelligencer, and could not possibly know his mission.

And if he did not wish to mislead him and was correct in what he said . . . William swallowed, his mouth sticky and dry. Then he had had a narrow escape. What might have happened, had he walked into a nest of rebels, in such a remote place as Dismal Town, and blithely revealed himself and his purpose? *They'd hang you from the nearest tree,* his brain said coldly, *and toss your body into the swamp. What else?*

Which led to an even more uncomfortable thought: how could Captain Richardson have been so mistaken in his information?

He shook his head violently, trying to shake his thoughts into order, but the only result was to make him dizzy again. Murray's attention had been attracted by the motion, though; he looked in William's direction, and William spoke, on impulse.

"You are a Mohawk, you said."

"I am."

Seeing that tattooed face, the eyes dark in their sockets, William didn't doubt it.

"How did that come to be?" he asked hurriedly, lest Murray think he was casting aspersions on the other's truthfulness. Murray hesitated visibly, but did answer.

"I married a woman of the Kahnyen'kehaka. I was adopted into the Wolf clan of the people of Snaketown."

"Ah. Your . . . wife is . . . ?"

"I am no longer wed." It wasn't said with any tone of hostility, but with a sort of bleak finality that put paid to any further conversation.

"I'm sorry," William said formally, and fell silent. The chills were coming back, and despite his reluctance, he slid down, drawing the blanket up around his ears, and huddled against the dog, who sighed deeply and released a burst of flatulence but didn't stir.

When the ague finally eased again, he lapsed back into dreams, these now violent and dreadful. His mind had taken hold somehow of Indians, and he was pursued by savages who turned into snakes, snakes who became tree roots that writhed through the crevices of his brain, bursting his skull, liberating further nests of snakes who coiled themselves into nooses . . .

He woke again, drenched in sweat and aching to the bones. He tried to rise but found his arms would not support him. Someone knelt by him—it was the Scot, the Mohawk . . . Murray. He located the name with something like relief, and with even more relief, realized that Murray was holding a canteen to his lips.

It was water from the lake; he recognized its odd, fresh-tasting bitterness, and drank thirstily.

"Thank you," he said hoarsely, and gave back the empty canteen. The water had given him strength enough to sit up. His head still swam with fever, but the dreams had retreated, at least for the moment. He imagined that they lurked just beyond the small ring of light cast by the fire, waiting, and determined that he would not sleep again—not at once.

The pain in his arm was worse: a hot, stretched feeling, and a throbbing that ran from fingertips to the middle of his upper arm. Anxious to keep both the pain and the night at bay, he had another try at conversation.

"I have heard that the Mohawk think it unmanly to show fear—that if captured and tortured by an enemy, they will not show any sign of distress. Is that true?"

"Ye try not to be in that position," Murray said, very dry. "Should it happen, though . . . ye must show your courage, that's all. Ye sing your death song and hope to die well. Is it different for a British soldier, then? Ye dinna want to die as a coward, do ye?"

William watched the flickering patterns behind his closed eyelids, hot and ever-changing, shifting with the fire.

"No," he admitted. "And it's not so different—the hoping to die well if you have to, I mean. But it's more likely to be a matter of just being shot or knocked on the head, isn't it, if you're a soldier—rather than being tortured to death by inches. Save you run afoul of a savage, I suppose. What—have you ever seen someone die like that?" he asked curiously, opening his eyes.

Murray reached out one long arm to turn the spit, not answering at once. The firelight showed his face, unreadable.

"Aye, I have," he said quietly, at last.

"What did they do to him?" He wasn't sure why he'd asked; perhaps only for distraction from the throbbing in his arm.

"Ye dinna want to know." This was said very definitely; Murray was not by any means teasing him into further inquiry. Nonetheless, it had the same effect; William's vague interest sharpened at once.

"Yes, I do."

Murray's lips tightened, but William knew a few things about extracting information by this time and was wise enough to preserve silence, merely keeping his eyes fixed on the other man.

"Skinned him," Murray said at last, and poked at the fire with a stick. "One of them. In bitty pieces. Thrust burning slivers of pitch pine into the raw places. Cut away his privates. Then built up the fire about his feet, to burn him before he could die of the shock. It . . . took some time."

"I daresay." William tried to conjure a picture of the proceedings—and succeeded much too well, turning away his eyes from the blackened muskrat carcass, stripped to bones.

He shut his eyes. His arm continued to throb with each beat of his heart, and he tried not to imagine the sensation of burning slivers being forced into his flesh.

Murray was silent; William couldn't even hear his breathing. But he knew, as surely as if he were inside the other's head, that he, too, was imagining the scene—though in his case, imagination was not necessary. He would be reliving it.

William shifted a little, sending a hot blaze of pain through his arm, and clenched his teeth, not to make any noise.

"Do the men—did *you*, I should say—think how you would do, yourself?" he asked quietly. "If you could stand it?"

"Every man thinks that." Murray got up abruptly and went to the far edge of the clearing. William heard him make water, but it was some minutes longer before he came back.

The dog wakened suddenly, head lifting, and wagged its huge tail slowly to and fro at sight of its master. Murray laughed softly and said something in an odd tongue—Mohawk? Erse?—to the dog, then bent and ripped a haunch from the muskrat's remains, tossing it to the beast. The animal rose like lightning, its teeth snapping shut on the carcass, then trotted happily to the far side of the fire and lay down, licking its prize.

Bereft of his bed companion, William lay down gingerly, head pillowed on his good arm, and watched as Murray cleaned his knife, scrubbing blood and grease from it with handfuls of grass.

"You said you sing your death song. What sort of song is that?"

Murray looked nonplused at that.

"I mean," William fumbled for clearer meaning, "what sort of thing would you—would one—say in a death song?"

"Oh." The Scotsman looked down at his hands, the long knobbed fingers rubbing slowly down the length of the blade. "I've only heard the one, mind. The other two I saw die that way—they were white men and didna have death songs, as such. The Indian—he was an Onondaga—he . . . well, there was a good deal in the beginning about who he was: a warrior of what people, I mean, and his clan, his family. Then quite a bit about how much he despised u—the folk who were about to kill him." Murray cleared his throat.

"A bit about what he'd done: his victories, valiant warriors he'd killed, and how they'd welcome him in death. Then . . . how he proposed to cross the . . ." He groped for a word. " . . . the—it—the way between here and what lies after death. The divide, I suppose ye'd say, though the word means something more like a chasm."

He was quiet for a moment, but not as though he had finished—more as though trying to recall something exactly. He straightened himself suddenly, took a deep breath, and with his eyes closed, began to recite something in what William supposed to be the Mohawk tongue. It was fascinating—a tattoo of "n"s and "r"s and "t"s, steady as a drumbeat.

"Then there was a bit where he went on about the nasty creatures he'd encounter on his way to paradise," Murray said, breaking off abruptly. "Things like flying heads, wi' teeth."

"Ew," said William, and Murray laughed, taken by surprise.

"Aye. I wouldna like to see one, myself."

William considered this for a moment.

"Do you compose your own death song ahead of time—in case of need, I mean? Or just trust to the, um, inspiration of the moment?"

Murray looked a little taken back by that. He blinked and looked aside.

"I . . . well . . . it's no usually talked about, ken? But aye—I did have a friend or two who told me a bit about what they'd thought of, should there ever be need."

"Hmm." William turned on his back, looking up at the stars. "Do you sing a death song only if you're being tortured to death? What if you're only ill but think you might die?"

Murray stopped what he was doing and peered toward him, suspicious.

"Ye're no dying, are ye?"

"No, just wondering," William assured him. He didn't *think* he was dying.

"Mmphm," the Scot said dubiously. "Aye, well. No, ye sing your death song if ye're sure ye're about to die; it doesna matter why."

"The more credit to you, though," William suggested, "if you do it whilst having burning splinters stuck into you?"

The Scot laughed out loud, and suddenly looked much less like an Indian. He rubbed his knuckles across his mouth.

"To be honest . . . the Onondaga . . . I didna think he did it so verra well," Murray blurted. "It doesna seem right to criticize, though. I mean, I canna say I'd do better—in the circumstances."

William laughed, too, but both men fell silent then. William supposed that

Murray was, as he was, imagining himself in such case, tied to a stake, about to suffer appalling torture. He gazed up into the void above, tentatively composing a few lines: *I am William Clarence Henry George Ransom, Earl of* . . . No, he'd never liked his string of names. *I am William* . . . he thought muzzily. *William* . . . *James* . . . James was his secret name; he hadn't thought of it in years. Better than Clarence, though. *I am William.* What else was there to say? Not much, as yet. No, he'd better not die, not until he'd done something worth a proper death song.

Murray was silent, the fire reflected in his somber eyes. Watching him, William thought the Scottish Mohawk had had his own death song ready for some time. Shortly he fell asleep to the crackle of fire and the quiet crunching of bones, burning, but brave.

HE WAS WANDERING through a haze of tortured dreams involving being chased by black serpents across an endless wobbling bridge over a bottomless chasm. Flying yellow heads with rainbow eyes attacked him in swarms, their tiny teeth, sharp as a mouse's, piercing his flesh. He waved an arm to beat them off, and the pain that shot through the arm at the motion roused him.

It was still dark, though the cool, live feel of the air told him the dawn was not far off. The touch of it on his face made him shiver, prompting another chill.

Someone said something that he didn't understand, and still entangled in the miasma of fever dreams, he thought it must be one of the serpents he'd been talking to earlier, before they started chasing him.

A hand touched his forehead, and a large thumb pried up one of his eyelids. An Indian's face floated in his sleep-bleared vision, looking quizzical.

He made an irritable noise and jerked his head away, blinking. The Indian said something, questioning, and a familiar voice replied. Who . . . Murray. The name seemed to have been floating by his elbow, and he recalled dimly that Murray himself had accompanied him in his dream, rebuking the serpents in a stern Scotch burr.

He wasn't speaking English now, though, nor even the peculiar Scotch tongue from the Highlands. William forced his head to turn, though his body was still convulsed with chill.

A number of Indians were crouched round the fire, squatting to keep their backsides from the dew-wet grass. One, two, three . . . six of them. Murray was sitting on the log with one of them, engaged in conversation.

No, seven. Another man, the one who had touched him, leaned over him, peering into his face.

"Think you're going to die?" the man asked, with a faint air of curiosity.

"No," William said between clenched teeth. "Who the devil are you?"

The Indian seemed to think this an amusing question and called to his fellows, apparently repeating it. They all laughed, and Murray glanced in his direction, rising as he saw that William was awake.

"Kahnyen'kehaka," the man looming over him said, and grinned. "Who the devil are *you?*"

"My kinsman," Murray said shortly, before William could reply. He nudged the Indian aside and squatted beside William. "Still alive, then?"

"Evidently." He scowled up at Murray. "Care to introduce me to your . . . friends?"

The first Indian went off into gales of laughter at this and apparently translated it to the two or three others who had come to peer interestedly at him. They thought it funny, too.

Murray seemed substantially less amused.

"My kinsmen," he said dryly. "Some of them. D'ye need water?"

"You have a lot of kinsmen . . . cousin. Yes, if you please."

He struggled upright, one-armed, reluctant to leave the clammy comfort of his dew-wet blanket but obeying an innate urge that told him he wanted to be on his feet. Murray seemed to know these Indians well, but kin or not, there was a certain tenseness to Murray's mouth and shoulders. And it was plain enough that Murray had told them that William was his kinsman because if he hadn't . . .

"Kahnyen'kehaka." That's what the Indian had said when asked who he was. It wasn't his name, William realized suddenly. It was what he was. Murray had used the word yesterday, when he'd sent away the two Mingos.

"*I'm Kahnyen'kehaka,*" he'd said. "*A Mohawk. They're afraid of me.*" He'd said it as a simple statement of fact, and William had not chosen to make an issue of it, circumstances being as they were. Seeing a number of what were plainly Mohawk together, he could appreciate the Mingos' prudence. The Mohawk gave off an air of genial ferocity, this overlying a casual confidence entirely proper to men who were prepared to sing—however badly—whilst being emasculated and burnt alive.

Murray handed him a canteen, and he drank thirstily, then splashed a little water over his face. Feeling a bit better, he went for a piss, then walked to the fire and squatted between two of the braves, who eyed him with open curiosity.

Only the man who had pried his eyelid open seemed to speak English, but the rest nodded to him, reserved but friendly enough. William glanced across the fire and started back, nearly losing his balance. A long, tawny shape lay in the grass beyond the fire, the light gleaming on its flanks.

"It's dead," Murray said dryly, seeing his startlement. The Mohawk all laughed.

"Gathered that," he replied, just as dryly, though his heart was still pounding from the shock. "Serve it right, if it's the one that took my horse." Now he came to look, he perceived other shapes beyond the fire. A small deer, a pig, a spotted cat, and two or three egrets, small white mounds in the dark grass. Well, that explained the Mohawks' presence in the swamp: they'd come for the hunting, like everyone else.

Dawn was coming; the faint wind stirred the damp hair on his neck and brought him the tang of blood and musk from the animals. Both his mind and his tongue felt thick and slow, but he managed a few words of praise for the success of the hunters; he knew how to be polite. Murray, translating for him, looked surprised, though pleased, to discover that William had manners. William didn't feel well enough to take offense.

Conversation became general then, accomplished for the most part in Mohawk. The Indians showed no particular interest in William, though the man beside him handed him a chunk of cold meat in a companionable fashion. He nodded thanks and made himself eat it, though he would as soon have forced down one of his shoe soles. He felt unwell and clammy, and when he had finished the meat, nodded politely to the Indian next him and went to lie down again, hoping he wouldn't vomit.

Seeing this, Murray lifted his chin in William's direction and said something to his friends in Mohawk, ending with a question of some kind.

The English-speaker, a short, thickset fellow in a checked wool shirt and buckskin trousers, shrugged in reply, then got up and came to bend over him again.

"Show me this arm," he said, and without waiting for William to comply, picked up his wrist and pulled up the sleeve of his shirt. William nearly passed out.

When the black spots stopped whirling in front of his eyes, he saw that Murray and two more Indians had come to join the first. All of them were looking at his exposed arm in open consternation. He didn't want to look, but risked a glance. His forearm was grotesquely swollen, nearly twice its normal size, and dark reddish streaks ran from under the tightly bandaged poultice, down his arm toward the wrist.

The English-speaker—what had Murray called him? *Glutton,* he thought, but why?—drew his knife and cut the bandage. Only with the removal of its constriction did William realize how uncomfortable the binding had been. He repressed the urge to rub his arm, feeling the pins and needles of returning circulation. Pins and needles, bloody hell. It felt as though his arm were engulfed by a mass of fire ants, all stinging.

"Shit," he said, through his teeth. All the Indians knew that word, evidently, for they all laughed, save Glutton and Murray, who were squinting at his arm.

Glutton—he didn't look fat, why was he called that?—poked gingerly at the arm, shook his head, and said something to Murray, then pointed off toward the west.

Murray rubbed a hand over his face, then shook his head violently, in the manner of a man shaking off fatigue or worry. Then he shrugged and asked something of the group at large. Nods and shrugs, and several of the men got up and went into the wood.

A number of questions revolved slowly through William's brain, round and bright like the metal globes of his grandfather's orrery in the library of the London house at Jermyn Street.

What are they doing?
What's happening?
Am I dying?
Am I dying like a British soldier?

Why did he...British soldier... His mind caught the tail of that one as it passed, pulling it down to look at more carefully. "*British soldier*"—who had said that? The answer spun slowly into view. Murray. When they'd talked in the night...what had Murray said?

"*Is it different for a British soldier, then? Ye dinna want to die as a coward, do ye?*"

"Not going to die at all," he muttered, but his mind ignored him, intent on tracking this small mystery. What had Murray meant by that? Had he been speaking theoretically? Or had he in fact recognized William *as* a British soldier?

Not possible, surely.

And what the devil had he said in reply? The sun was coming up, the dawning light bright enough to hurt his eyes, soft as it was. He squinted, concentrating.

"*It's not so different—the hoping to die well if you have to,*" he'd said. So he'd answered as though he *was* a British soldier, damn him.

At the moment, he didn't really care whether he died well or like a dog. . . . Where was the—oh, there. Rollo sniffed at his arm, making a small whining noise in the back of his throat, then nosed at the wound and began to lick it. It felt most peculiar: painful, but weirdly soothing, and he made no move to drive the dog away.

What...oh, yes. He had simply replied, not noticing what Murray had said. But what if Murray *did* know who—or what—he was? A small stab of alarm pierced the muddle of his slowing thoughts. Had Murray been following him, before he came into the swamp? Seen him speaking to the man at the wilderness farm near the edge of the swamp, perhaps, and followed, ready to intercept him when the opportunity should offer? But if that were true . . .

What Murray had said about Henry Washington, about Dismal Town—was it a lie?

The stocky Indian knelt down beside him, nudging the dog away. William couldn't ask any of the questions clogging his brain.

"Why do they call you Glutton?" he asked instead, through the haze of hot pain.

The man grinned and pulled open the neck of his shirt, to display a mass of welted scars that covered neck and chest.

"Killed one," he said. "With my hands. My spirit animal now. You have one?"

"No."

The Indian looked reproving at this.

"You need one, you going to live through this. Pick one. Pick a strong one."

Muzzily obedient, William groped through random images of animals: pig...snake...deer...catamount...no, too rank, foul-smelling.

"Bear," he said, settling on that with a sense of certainty. Didn't get any stronger than a bear, did it?

"Bear," the Indian repeated, nodding. "Yes, that's good." He slit William's sleeve with his knife; the fabric would no longer fit easily over the swollen arm. Sunlight washed suddenly over him, glanced silver from the blade of his knife. He looked at William then and laughed.

"You got one red beard, Bear Cub, you know that?"

"I know that," William said, and shut his eyes against the spears of morning's light.

GLUTTON WANTED THE CATAMOUNT'S skin, but Murray, alarmed by William's condition, refused to wait for him to skin it. The upshot of the resulting argument was that William found himself occupying a hastily constructed travois, cheek by jowl with the dead cat, being dragged over rough terrain behind Murray's horse. Their destination, he was given to understand, was a small settlement some ten miles distant, which boasted a doctor.

Glutton and two of the other Mohawk came with them in order to show the way, leaving their other companions to continue hunting.

The catamount had been gutted, which William supposed might be better than not—the day was warm, and getting hot—but the scent of blood drew masses of flies, which feasted at their leisure, as the horse, burdened with the travois, could not go fast enough to outpace them. The flies hummed and buzzed and shrilled about his ears, setting his nerves on edge, and while most were interested in the cat, enough of them cared to try William for taste as sufficed to keep his mind off his arm.

When the Indians paused for urination and water, they hauled William to his feet—a relief, even wobbly as he was. Murray glanced at his fly-bitten, sun-burned features, and reaching into a skin bag slung at his waist, pulled out a battered tin, which turned out to contain a highly malodorous ointment, with which he anointed William liberally.

"It's no but another five or six miles," he assured William, who hadn't asked.

"Oh, good," William said, with what vigor he could muster. "It's not hell after all, then—only purgatory. What's another thousand years?"

That made Murray laugh, though Glutton regarded him in puzzlement.

"Ye'll do," Murray said, clapping him on the shoulder. "Want to walk for a bit?"

"God, yes."

His head swam, his feet refused to point forward, and his knees seemed to bend in unwonted directions, but anything was better than another hour of communing with the flies that blanketed the catamount's glazed eyes and drying tongue. Provided with a stout stick cut from an oak sapling, he plodded doggedly behind the horse, alternately drenched with sweat and shaking with clammy chills, but determined to stay upright until and unless he actually fell down.

The ointment did keep the flies at bay—all the Indians were likewise smeared with it—and when not fighting the shaking, he lapsed into a sort of trance, concerned only with putting one foot before the other.

The Indians and Murray kept an eye on him for a time, but then, satisfied that he could remain upright, returned to their own conversations. He could not understand the two Mohawk-speakers, but Glutton appeared to be cate-chizing Murray closely concerning the nature of purgatory.

Murray was having some difficulty in explaining the concept, apparently owing to the Mohawk having no notion of sin, or of a God concerned with the wickedness of man.

"You're lucky you became Kahnyen'kehaka," Glutton said at last, shaking his head. "A spirit not satisfied with an evil man being dead but that wants to torture him after death? And Christians think we're cruel!"

"Aye, well," Murray replied, "but think. Say a man is a coward and hasna died well. Purgatory gives him a chance to prove his courage after all, no? And once he is proved a proper man, then the bridge is open to him, and he can pass through the clouds of terrible things unhindered to paradise."

"Hmm!" Glutton said, though he seemed still dubious. "I suppose if a man can stand to be tortured for hundreds of years . . . but how does he do this, if no body?"

"D'ye think a man needs a body to be tortured?" Murray asked this with a certain dryness, and Glutton grunted in what might be either agreement or amusement and dropped the subject.

They all walked in silence for some time, surrounded by birdcalls and the loud buzzing of flies. Preoccupied with the effort of remaining upright, William had fixed his attention on the back of Murray's head as a means of not veering off the trail and thus noticed when the Scot, who was leading the horse, slowed his pace a little.

He thought at first that this was on his account and was about to protest that he could keep up—for a little while, at least—but then saw Murray glance swiftly at the other Mohawk, who had drawn ahead, then turn to Glutton and ask something, in a voice too low for William to make out the words.

Glutton hunched his shoulders in reluctance, then let them fall, resigned. "Oh, I see," he said. "She's your purgatory, eh?"

Murray made a sound of reluctant amusement. "Does it matter? I asked if she's well."

Glutton sighed, shrugging one shoulder.

"Yes, well. She has a son. A daughter, too, I think. Her husband . . ."

"Aye?" Murray's voice had hardened in some fashion.

"You know Thayendanegea?"

"I do." Now Murray sounded curious. William was curious himself, in a vague, unfocused sort of way, and waited to hear who Thayendanegea might be and what he had to do with the woman who was—who had been—Murray's paramour? Oh, no.

"I am no longer wed." His wife, then. William felt a faint pang of sympathy, thinking of Margery. He had thought of her only casually, if at all, in the past four years, but suddenly her betrayal seemed tragedy. Images of her swam about him, fractured by a sense of grief. He felt moisture running down his face, didn't know if it was sweat or tears. The thought came to him, slowly, as from a great distance, that he must be off his head, but he had no notion what to do about it.

The flies weren't biting but were still buzzing in his ears. He listened to the hum with great concentration, convinced that the flies were trying to tell him something important. He listened with great attention, but could make out only nonsense syllables. "Shosha." "Nik." "Osonni." No, that was a word, he knew that one! White man, it meant white man—were they talking about him?

He pawed clumsily at his ear, brushing at the flies, and caught that word again: "purgatory."

For a time, he could not place the meaning of the word; it hung in front of him, covered with flies. Dimly, he perceived the horse's hindquarters, gleaming in the sun, the twin lines made in the dust by the—what was it? A thing made of—bed—no, canvas; he shook his head. It was his bedsack, wrapped about two trailing saplings, trailing . . . "travois," that was the word—yes. And the cat, there was a cat there, looking at him with eyes like rough amber, its head turned over its shoulder, openmouthed, its fangs showing.

Now the cat was talking to him, too.

"You mad, you know that?"

"I know that," he murmured. He didn't catch the cat's reply, growled in a Scottish accent.

He leaned closer, to hear. Felt as though he floated down, through air thick as water, toward that open mouth. Suddenly all sense of effort ceased; he was no longer moving but was supported somehow. Couldn't see the cat . . . oh. He was lying facedown on the ground, grass and dirt beneath his cheek.

The cat's voice floated back to him, angry but resigned.

"This purgatory of yours? You think you can get out walking backward?"

Well, no, William thought, feeling peaceful. That made no sense at all.

38

PLAIN SPEECH

THE YOUNG WOMAN SNICKED the blades of her scissors in thoughtful fashion.

"Thee is sure?" she asked. "It seems shame, Friend William. Such a striking color!"

"I should think you'd consider it unseemly, Miss Hunter," William said, smiling. "I had always heard that Quakers think bright colors to be worldly." The only color in her own dress was a small bronzy-colored brooch that held her kerchief together. Everything else was shades of cream and butternut—though he thought these suited her.

She looked reprovingly at him.

"Immodest ornament in dress is hardly the same as grateful acceptance of the gifts God hath given. Do bluebirds pluck out their feathers, or roses fling away their petals?"

"I doubt that roses itch," he said, scratching at his chin. The notion of his beard as a gift of God was novel, but not sufficiently persuasive as to convince him to go about as a whiskeranto. Beyond its unfortunate color, it grew with vigor, but sparsely. He looked disapprovingly at the modest square of looking glass in his hand. He could do nothing about the peeling sunburn that patched his nose and cheeks, or the scabbed scrapes and scratches left by his adventures in the swamp—but the hideous copper curls that sprouted jauntily from his chin and plastered themselves like a disfiguring moss along his jaw—that, at least, could be amended at once.

"If you please?"

Her lips twitched, and she knelt down beside his stool, turning his head with a hand beneath his chin so as to take best advantage of the light from the window.

"Well, then," she said, and laid the scissors cool against his face. "I'll ask Denny to come and shave thee. I daresay I can cut thy beard without wounding thee, but"—her eyes narrowed and she leaned closer, snipping delicately round the curve of his chin—"I've not shaved anything more lively than a dead pig, myself."

"Barber, barber," he murmured, trying not to move his lips, "shave a pig. How ma—"

Her fingers pressed up under his chin, firmly shutting his mouth, but she made the small snorting sound that passed with her for laughter. *Snip, snip, snip.* The blades tickled pleasantly against his face, and the wiry hairs brushed his hands as they fell into the worn linen towel she'd placed across his lap.

He'd had no opportunity to study her face at such close range and took full advantage of the brief opportunity. Her eyes were almost brown and not quite green. He wished suddenly to kiss the end of her nose. He shut his eyes, instead, and breathed. She'd been milking a goat, he could tell.

"I can shave myself," he said, when she lowered the scissors.

She raised her brows and glanced downward at his arm. "I should be surprised if thee can feed thyself yet, let alone shave."

In all truth, he could barely lift his right arm, and she had been feeding him for the last two days. That being so, he thought better of telling her that he was in fact left-handed.

"It's healing well," he said, instead, and turned his arm so the light shone upon it. Dr. Hunter had removed the dressing only that morning, expressing gratification at the results. The wound was still red and puckered, the skin around it unpleasantly white and moist. It was, however, undoubtedly healing; the arm was no longer swollen, and the ominous red streaks had disappeared.

"Well," she said consideringly, "it's a fine scar, I think. Well knit, and rather pretty."

"Pretty?" William echoed, looking skeptically at his arm. He'd heard men now and then describe a scar as "pretty," but most commonly they meant one that had healed straight and clean and did not disfigure the bearer by passing through some significant feature. This one was jagged and sprawling, with a long tail leading toward his wrist. He had—he was told sometime after the fact—narrowly escaped loss of the arm: Dr. Hunter had grasped it and placed his amputation saw just above the wound, only to have the abscess that had formed below it burst in his hand. Seeing this, the doctor had hastily drained the wound, packed it with garlic and comfrey, and prayed—to good effect.

"It looks like an enormous star," Rachel Hunter said approvingly. "One of significance. A great comet, perhaps. Or the Star of Bethlehem, which led the Wise Men to the manger of Christ."

William turned his arm, considering. He thought it looked rather more like a bursting mortar shell, himself, but said merely, "Hmm!" in an encouraging manner. He wished to continue the conversation—she seldom lingered when she fed him, having much other work to do—and so lifted his newly shorn chin and gestured at the brooch she wore.

"That's pretty," he said. "Not too worldly?"

"No," she said tartly, putting a hand to the brooch. "It's made of my mother's hair. She died when I was born."

"Ah. I'm sorry," he said, and with a moment's hesitation added, "So did mine."

She stopped then and looked at him, and for a moment, he saw a flicker of something in her eyes that was more than the matter-of-fact attention she would give to a cow in calf or a dog that had eaten something that disagreed with it.

"I'm sorry, too," she said softly, then turned with decision. "I'll fetch my brother."

Her footsteps went down the narrow stair, quick and light. He picked up the ends of the towel and shook it out the window, scattering the ruddy hair clippings to the four winds, and good riddance. He might have grown a beard as a rudimentary disguise, had it been a decently sober brown. As it was, a full beard of that garish color would rivet the eye of everyone who saw him.

What to do now? he wondered. Surely he would be fit to leave by tomorrow.

His clothes were still wearable, if worse for wear; Miss Hunter had patched the tears in his breeches and coat. But he had no horse, no money save two sixpences that had been in his pocket, and had lost the book with the list of his contacts and their messages. He might recall a few of their names, but without the proper code words and signs . . .

He thought quite suddenly of Henry Washington, and that hazy half-remembered conversation with Ian Murray by the fire, before they had begun to speak of death songs. Washington, Cartwright, Harrington, and Carver. The chanted list returned to him, together with Murray's puzzled reply to his mention of Washington and Dismal Town.

He could not think of any reason why Murray should seek to mislead him on the matter. But if he was correct—was Captain Richardson grossly mistaken in his intelligence? That was possible, certainly. Even in as short a time as he had been in the Colonies, he had learned just how quickly loyalties could shift, with changing news of threat or opportunity.

But . . . said the small, cold voice of reason, and he felt its chilly touch on his neck. *If Captain Richardson was not mistaken . . . then he meant to send you to death or imprisonment.*

The sheer enormity of the idea dried his mouth, and he reached for the cup of herbal tea that Miss Hunter had brought him earlier. It tasted foul, but he scarcely noticed, clutching it as though it might be a talisman against the prospect he imagined.

No, he assured himself. It wasn't possible. His father knew Richardson. Surely if the captain were a traitor—what was he thinking? He gulped the tea, grimacing as he swallowed.

"No," he said aloud, "not possible. Or not likely," he added fairly. "Occam's razor."

The thought calmed him a little. He had learned the basic principles of logic at an early age and had found William of Occam a sound guide before. Was it more likely that Captain Richardson was a hidden traitor who had deliberately sent William into danger—or that the captain had been misinformed or had simply made a mistake?

Come to that—what would be the point of it? William was under no delusions concerning his own importance in the scheme of things. Where would be the benefit to Richardson—or anyone else—in destroying a junior officer engaged in minor intelligencing?

Well, then. He relaxed a bit, and taking an unwary mouthful of the ghastly tea, choked on it and coughed, spraying tea everywhere. He was still wiping up the residue with his towel when Dr. Hunter came trotting briskly up the stair. Denzell Hunter was perhaps ten years his sister's senior, somewhere in his late twenties, small-boned and cheerful as a cock sparrow. He beamed at sight of William, plainly so delighted at his patient's recovery that William smiled warmly back.

"Sissy tells me thee requires to shave," the doctor said, setting down the shaving mug and brush he had brought. "Plainly, thee must be feeling well enough to contemplate a return to society—for the first thing any man does when free of social constraint is to let his beard grow. Has thee moved thy bowels as yet?"

"No, but I propose to do so almost at once," William assured him. "I am not, however, of a mind to venture out in public looking like a bandit—not even to the privy. I shouldn't wish to scandalize your neighbors."

Dr. Hunter laughed, and withdrawing a razor from one pocket and his silver-rimmed spectacles from another, set the latter firmly on his nose and picked up the shaving brush.

"Oh, Sissy and I are already a hissing and a byword," he assured William, leaning close to apply the lather. "Seeing banditti emerging from our privy would merely confirm the neighbors in their opinions."

"Really?" William spoke carefully, twisting his mouth so as to avoid having it inadvertently filled with soap. "Why?" He was surprised to hear this; once regaining his senses, he had asked where he was and learned that Oak Grove was a small Quaker settlement. He had thought Quakers in general to be most united in their religious sentiments—but then, he did not really know any Quakers.

Hunter heaved a deep sigh, and laying down the shaving brush, took up the razor in its stead.

"Oh, politics," he said, in an offhand tone, as of one wishing to dismiss a tiresome but trivial subject. "Tell me, Friend Ransom, is there someone to whom I might send, to tell them of thy mishap and delivery?" He paused in the shaving, to allow William to reply.

"No, I thank you, sir—I shall tell them myself," William said, smiling. "I am sure I will be able to leave by tomorrow—though I assure you that I will not forget your kindness and hospitality when I reach my . . . friends."

Denzell Hunter's brow furrowed a little, and his mouth compressed as he resumed the shaving, but he made no argument.

"I trust thee will forgive my inquisitiveness," he said after a moment, "but where does thee intend to go from here?"

William hesitated, not sure what to reply. He had in fact not decided exactly where to go, given the lamentable state of his finances. The best notion that had occurred to him was that he might head for Mount Josiah, his own plantation. He was not positive but thought he must be within forty or fifty miles of it—if the Hunters might give him a little food, he thought he could reach it within a few days, a week at most. And once there, he could reequip himself with clothes, a decent horse, arms, and money, and thus resume his journey.

It was a tempting prospect. To do that, though, was to reveal his presence in Virginia—and to cause considerable comment, as everyone in the county not only knew him but knew that he was a soldier. To turn up in the neighborhood dressed as he was . . .

"There are a few Catholics at Rosemount," Dr. Hunter observed with diffidence, wiping the razor on the much-abused towel. William glanced at him in surprise.

"Oh?" he said warily. Why the devil was Hunter telling him about Catholics?

"I beg pardon, Friend," the doctor apologized, seeing his reaction. "Thee had mentioned thy friends—I thought . . ."

"You thought I was—" Puzzlement was succeeded by a jolt of realization, and William slapped a hand in reflex against his chest, naturally finding nothing but the much-worn nightshirt he was wearing.

"Here it is." The doctor bent swiftly to open the blanket box at the foot of the bed and stood up, the wooden rosary swinging from one hand. "We had to remove it, of course, when we undressed thee, but Sissy put it safe away to keep for thee."

"We?" William said, seizing on this as a means of delaying inquiry. "You—and Miss Hunter—undressed me?"

"Well, there was no one else," the doctor said apologetically. "We were obliged to lay thee naked in the creek, in hopes of quelling thy fever—thee does not recall?"

He did—vaguely—but had assumed the memory of overwhelming cold and a sense of drowning to be more remnants of his fever dreams. Miss Hunter's presence had fortunately—or perhaps unfortunately—not formed part of those memories.

"I could not carry thee alone," the doctor was explaining earnestly. "And the neighbors—I did provide a towel for the preservation of thy modesty," he assured William hastily.

"What quarrel do your neighbors have with you?" William inquired curiously, reaching out to take the rosary from Hunter's hand. "I am not a Papist myself," he added offhandedly. "It is a . . . memento, given me by a friend."

"Oh." The doctor rubbed a finger across his lip, plainly disconcerted. "I see. I had thought—"

"The neighbors . . . ?" William asked, and suppressing his embarrassment, hung the rosary once more around his neck. Perhaps the mistake over his religion was the basis of the neighbors' animus?

"Well, I daresay they would have helped to carry thee," Dr. Hunter admitted, "had there been time to go and fetch someone. The matter was urgent, though, and the nearest house is a goodly distance."

This left the question of the neighbors' attitude toward the Hunters unanswered, but it seemed unmannerly to press further. William merely nodded and stood up.

The floor tilted abruptly under him and white light flickered at the edge of his vision. He grabbed at the windowsill to keep from falling and came to his senses a moment later, bathed in sweat, with Dr. Hunter's surprisingly strong grip of his arm preventing his tumbling headfirst into the yard below.

"Not quite so fast, Friend Ransom," the doctor said gently, and, hauling him in, turned him back toward the bed. "Another day, perhaps, before thee stands alone. Thee has more phlegm than is useful to thee, I fear."

Mildly nauseated, William sat on the bed and allowed Dr. Hunter to wipe his face with the towel. Evidently he had a bit more time in which to decide where to go.

"How long, do you think, before I can walk a full day?"

Denzell Hunter gave him a considering look.

"Five days, perhaps—four, at the least," he said. "Thee is robust and full-blooded, else I would say a week."

William, feeling puny and pallid, nodded and lay down. The doctor stood frowning at him for a moment, though it did not seem that the frown was directed at him; it seemed rather an expression of some inner concern.

"How . . . far will thy travels take thee?" the doctor asked, choosing his words with apparent care.

"Quite some distance," William replied, with equal wariness. "I am headed . . . toward Canada," he said, suddenly realizing that to say more might imply more than he wished to give away regarding his reasons for travel. True, a man might have business in Canada without necessarily having dealings with the British army who occupied Quebec, but as the doctor had mentioned politics . . . best to be politic about the matter. And certainly he would not mention Mount Josiah. Whatever the Hunters' strained relations with their neighbors, news concerning their visitor might easily spread.

"Canada," the doctor repeated, as though to himself. Then his gaze returned to William. "Yes, that is some considerable distance. Luckily, I have killed a goat this morning; we will have meat. That will help to restore thy strength. I will bleed thee tomorrow, to restore some balance to thy humors, and then we shall see. For the moment . . ." He smiled and extended a hand. "Come. I'll see thee safe to the privy."

39

A MATTER OF CONSCIENCE

THERE WAS A STORM coming; William could feel it in the shifting of the air, see it in the racing cloud shadows that scudded across the worn floorboards. The heat and damp oppression of the summer day had lifted, and the restlessness of the air seemed to stir him, as well. Though still weak, he could not remain abed, and managed to get up, clinging to the washstand until the initial giddiness left him.

Left to himself, he then passed some time in walking from one side of the room to the other—a distance of ten feet or so—one hand pressed against the wall for balance. The effort drained and dizzied him, and now and then he was obliged to sit down on the floor, head hung between his knees, until the spots ceased to dance before his eyes.

It was on one of these occasions, while seated beneath the window, that he heard voices from the yard below. Miss Rachel Hunter's voice, surprised and questioning—a man's reply, low-voiced and husky. A familiar voice—Ian Murray!

He shot to his feet and just as quickly subsided back onto the floor, vision black and head swimming. He clenched his fists and panted, trying to will the blood to return to his head.

"He will live, then?" The voices were distant, half buried in the murmur of the chestnut trees near the house, but he caught that. He struggled up onto his knees and caught hold of the sill, blinking into the cloud-shattered brightness of the day.

Murray's tall figure was visible at the edge of the dooryard, gaunt in buckskins, the huge dog at his side. There was no sign of Glutton or the other Indians, but two horses were cropping grass in the lane behind Murray, reins dangling. Rachel Hunter was gesturing to the house, plainly inviting Murray to come in, but he shook his head. He reached into the bag at his waist and withdrew a small package of some sort, which he handed to the girl.

"Hoy!" William shouted—or tried to shout; he hadn't much breath—and waved his arms. The wind was rising with a shivering rush through the chestnut leaves, but the motion must have caught Murray's eye, for he glanced up, and seeing William in the window, smiled and lifted his own hand in greeting.

He made no move to enter the house, though. Instead, he picked up the reins of one horse and put them into Rachel Hunter's hand. Then, with a wave of farewell toward William's window, he swung himself up onto the other horse with an economical grace and rode away.

William's hands tightened on the sill, disappointment surging through him at seeing Murray vanish into the trees. Wait, though—Murray had left a horse. Rachel Hunter was leading it around the house, her apron and petti-coats aswirl in the rising wind, one hand on her cap to keep it in place.

It must be for him, surely! Did Murray mean to come back for him, then? Or was he to follow? Heart thumping in his ears, William pulled on his patched breeches and the new stockings Rachel had knitted for him, and af-ter a short struggle got his water-stiffened boots on over them. The effort left him trembling, but he stubbornly made his way downstairs, lurching, sweat-ing, and slipping but arriving in the kitchen at the bottom in one piece.

The back door opened with a blast of wind and light, then slammed abruptly, jerked out of Rachel's hand. She turned, saw him, and yelped in startlement.

"Lord save us! What is thee doing down here?" She was panting with exer-tion and fright, and glared at him, tucking wisps of dark hair back under her cap.

"Didn't mean to startle you," William said in apology. "I wanted—I saw Mr. Murray leaving. I thought I might catch him up. Did he say where I was to meet him?"

"He did not. Sit, for heaven's sake, before thee falls down."

He didn't want to. The desire to be out, to go, was overwhelming. But his knees were shaking, and if he didn't sit down shortly . . . Reluctantly, he sat.

"What did he say?" he asked, and realizing suddenly that he was sitting in a lady's presence, gestured at the other stool. "Sit, please. Tell me what he said."

Rachel eyed him but sat, smoothing her windblown clothing back into place. The storm was rising; cloud shadows raced across the floor, across her face, and the air seemed to waver, as though the room were underwater.

"He asked after thy health, and when I told him thee was mending, he gave me the horse, saying it was for thee." She hesitated for an instant, and William pushed.

"He gave you something else, did he not? I saw him give you a package of some kind."

Her lips pressed together for an instant, but she nodded, and reaching into her pocket, handed him a small bundle, loosely wrapped in cloth.

He was eager to see what the packet contained—but not so eager that he did not notice the marks in the cloth, deep lines where string had once been tied round it. And tied very recently. He glanced up at Rachel Hunter, who looked away, chin high, but with color rising in her cheeks. He cocked an eye-brow at her, then bent his attention to the packet.

Opened, it contained a small sheaf of paper continentals; a worn pouch containing the sum of one guinea, three shillings, and tuppence in coin; a much-folded—and refolded, if he was any judge—letter; and another, smaller, bundle, this one still tied. Setting aside this and the money, he opened the letter.

Cousin,

I hope to find you in better health than when last seen. If so, I will leave a horse and some funds to assist your travels. If not, I will leave the money, to pay either for medicine or your burial. The other thing is

*a gift from a friend whom the Indians call Bear-Killer. He hopes that
you will wear it in good health. I wish you luck in your ventures.*

*Your ob't. serv.,
Ian Murray*

"Hmm!" William was baffled by this. Evidently Murray had business of his
own and could not or did not wish to stay until William was able to travel.
Though somewhat disappointed—he would have liked to talk further with
Murray, now that his mind was clear again—he could see that it might be better that Murray did not mean them to travel together.

It dawned upon him that his immediate problem was solved; he now had the
means to resume his mission—or as much of it as he could. He could at least
reach General Howe's headquarters, make a report, and get new instructions.

It was remarkably generous of Murray; the horse had looked sound, and
the money was more than enough to see him comfortably fed and lodged all
the way to New York. He wondered where on earth Murray had got it; by his
looks, the man hadn't a pot to piss in—though he had a good rifle, William
reminded himself—and he was plainly educated, for he made a decent fist of
writing. What could have caused the odd Scottish Indian to take such interest in him, though?

Bemused, he reached for the smaller bundle and untied the string.
Unwrapped, the contents proved to be the claw of a large bear, pierced and
strung on a leather thong. It was old; the edges were worn, and the knot in
the leather had hardened so far that it would plainly never be untied again.

He stroked the claw with a thumb, tested the point. Well, the bear spirit
had stood him in good stead so far. Smiling to himself, he put the thong over
his head, leaving the claw to hang outside his shirt. Rachel Hunter stared at
it, her face unreadable.

"You read my letter, Miss Hunter," William said reprovingly. "Very
naughty of you!"

The flush rose higher in her cheeks, but she met his eye with a directness
he was unaccustomed to find in a woman—with the marked exception of his
paternal grandmother.

"Thy speech is far superior to thy clothes, Friend William—even were they
new. And while thee has been in thy right mind for some days now, thee has
not chosen to say what brought thee to the Great Dismal. It is not a place fre-
quented by gentlemen."

"Oh, indeed it is, Miss Hunter. Many gentlemen of my acquaintance go
there for the hunting, which is unexcelled. But naturally, one does not hunt
wild boar or catamounts in one's best linen."

"Neither does one go hunting armed only with a frying pan, Friend
William," she riposted. "And if thee is a gentleman in truth—where is thy
home, pray?"

He fumbled for an instant, unable to recall at once his alter ego's particulars, and seized instead on the first city to come to his mind.

"Ah—Savannah. In the Carolinas," he added helpfully.

"I know where it is," she snapped. "And have heard men speak who come from there. Thee doesn't."

"Are you calling me a liar?" he said, amazed.

"I am."

"Oh." They sat gazing at each other in the half light of the gathering storm, each calculating. For an instant, he had the illusion that he was playing chess with his grandmother Benedicta.

"I am sorry for reading thy letter," she said abruptly. "It was not vulgar curiosity, I assure thee."

"What, then?" He smiled a little, to indicate that he bore no animus for her trespass. She didn't smile back, but looked at him narrowly—not in suspicion, but as though gauging him in some way. At last she sighed, though, and her shoulders slumped.

"I wished to know a little of thee, and of thy character. The companions who brought thee to us seem dangerous men. And thy cousin? If thee is one like them, then—" Her teeth fixed briefly in her upper lip, but she shook her head, as though to herself, and continued more firmly.

"We must leave here within a few days—my brother and myself. Thee told Denny that thee travels north; I wish that we may travel with thee, at least for a time."

Whatever he'd been expecting, it wasn't that. He blinked and said the first thing that came to his mind.

"Leave here? Why? The . . . er . . . the neighbors?"

She looked surprised at that.

"What?"

"I beg your pardon, ma'am. Your brother seemed to indicate that relations between your family and those who dwell nearby were . . . somewhat strained?"

"Oh." One corner of her mouth tucked back; he could not tell if this betokened distress or amusement—but rather thought it was the latter.

"I see," she said, and drummed her fingers thoughtfully on the table. "Yes, that's true, though it was not what I—well, and yet it has to do with the matter. I see I must tell thee everything, then. What does thee know about the Society of Friends?"

He knew only one family of Quakers, the Unwins. Mr. Unwin was a wealthy merchant who knew his father, and he had met the two daughters at a musicale once, but the conversation had not touched upon philosophy or religion.

"They—er, you—dislike conflict, I believe?" he answered cautiously.

That surprisingly made her laugh, and he felt pleasure at having removed the tiny furrow between her brows, if only temporarily.

"Violence," she corrected. "We thrive upon conflict, if it be verbal. And given the form of our worship—Denny says thee is not a Papist after all, yet I venture to suppose that thee have never attended a Quaker meeting?"

"The opportunity has not so far occurred, no."

"I thought not. Well, then." She eyed him consideringly. "We have preachers who will come to speak at meeting—but anyone may speak at meeting, upon any subject, if the spirit moves him or her to do so."

"Her? Women speak in public, too?"

She gave him a withering look.

"I have a tongue, just as thee does."

"I'd noticed," he said, and smiled at her. "Continue, please."

She leaned forward a little to do so but was interrupted by the crash of a shutter swinging back against the house, this followed by a spatter of rain, dashed hard across the window. Rachel sprang to her feet with a brief exclamation.

"I must get the chickens in! Close the shutters," she ordered him, and dashed out.

Taken aback but amused, he did so, moving slowly. Going upstairs to fasten the upper shutters made him dizzy again, and he paused on the threshold of the bedroom, holding the doorjamb until his balance returned. There were two rooms upstairs: the bedroom at the front of the house, where they had put him, and a smaller room in the rear. The Hunters now shared this room; there was a truckle bed, a washstand with a silver candlestick upon it, and little else, save a row of pegs upon which hung the doctor's spare shirt and breeches, a woolen shawl, and what must be Rachel Hunter's go-to-meeting gown, a sober-looking garment dyed with indigo.

With rain and wind muffled by the shutters, the dim room seemed still now, and peaceful, a harbor from the storm. His heart had slowed from the exertion of climbing the stair, and he stood for a moment, enjoying the slightly illicit sense of trespass. No sound from below; Rachel must be still in pursuit of the chickens.

There was something faintly odd about the room, and it took him only a moment to decide what it was. The shabbiness and sparsity of the Hunters' personal possessions argued poverty—yet these contrasted with the small signs of prosperity evident in the furnishings: the candlestick was silver, not plate or pewter, and the ewer and basin were not earthenware but good china, painted with sprawling blue chrysanthemums.

He lifted the skirt of the blue dress hanging on the peg, examining it curiously. Modesty was one thing; threadbareness was another. The hem was worn nearly white, the indigo faded so that the folds of the skirt showed a fan-shaped pattern of light and dark. The Misses Unwin had dressed quietly, but their clothes were of the highest quality.

On sudden impulse, he brought the cloth to his face, breathing in. It smelled faintly still of indigo, and of grass and live things—and very perceptibly of a woman's body. The musk of it ran through him like the pleasure of good wine.

The sound of the door closing below made him drop the dress as though it had burst into flame, and he made for the stairs, heart hammering.

Rachel Hunter was shaking herself on the hearth, shedding drops of water from her apron, her cap wilted and soggy on her head. Not seeing him, she took this off, wrung it out with a mutter of impatience, and hung it on a nail hammered into the chimney breast.

Her hair fell down her back, wet-tailed and shining, dark against the pale cloth of her jacket.

"The chickens are all safe, I trust?" He spoke, because to watch her unawares with her hair down, the smell of her still vivid in his nose, seemed suddenly to be an unwarrantable intimacy.

She turned round, eyes wary, but made no immediate move to cover her hair.

"All but the one my brother calls the Great Whore of Babylon. No chicken possesses anything resembling intelligence, but that one is perverse beyond the usual."

"Perverse?" Evidently she perceived that he was contemplating the possibilities inherent in this description and finding them entertaining, for she snorted through her nose and bent to open the blanket chest.

"The creature is sitting twenty feet up in a pine tree, in the midst of a rainstorm. Perverse." She pulled out a linen towel and began to dry her hair with it.

The sound of the rain altered suddenly, hail rattling like tossed gravel against the shutters.

"Hmmph," said Rachel, with a dark look at the window. "I expect she will be knocked senseless by the hail and devoured by the first passing fox, and serve her right." She resumed drying her hair. "No great matter. I shall be pleased never to see any of those chickens again."

Seeing him still standing, she sat down, gesturing him to another stool.

"You did say that you and your brother proposed to leave this place and travel north," he reminded her, sitting down. "I collect the chickens will not make the journey with you?"

"No, and the Lord be praised. They are already sold, along with the house." Laying the crumpled towel aside, she groped in her pocket and withdrew a small comb carved from horn. "I did say I would tell thee why."

"I believe we had reached the point of learning that the matter has something to do with your meeting?"

She breathed deeply through her nose and nodded.

"I said that when a person is moved of the spirit, he speaks in meeting? Well, the spirit moved my brother. That is how we came to leave Philadelphia."

A meeting might be formed, she explained, wherever there were sufficient Friends of like mind. But in addition to these small local meetings, there were larger bodies, the Quarterly and Yearly Meetings, at which weighty matters of principle were discussed and actions affecting Quakers in general were decided upon.

"Philadelphia Yearly Meeting is the largest and most influential," she said. "Thee is right: the Friends eschew violence, and seek either to avoid it or to end it. And in this question of rebellion, Philadelphia Yearly Meeting thought and prayed upon the matter, and advised that the path of wisdom and peace plainly lay in reconciliation with the mother country."

"Indeed." William was interested. "So all of the Quakers in the Colonies are now Loyalists, do you mean?"

Her lips compressed for an instant.

"That is the advice of the Yearly Meeting. As I said, though, Friends are led of the spirit, and one must do as one is led to do."

"And your brother was led to speak in favor of rebellion?" William was amused, though wary; Dr. Hunter seemed an unlikely firebrand.

She dipped her head, not quite a nod.

"In favor of independency," she corrected.

"Surely there is something lacking in the logic of that distinction," William observed, raising one brow. "How might independency be achieved without the exercise of violence?"

"If thee thinks the spirit of God is necessarily logical, thee know Him better than I do." She ran a hand through the damp hair, flicking it over her shoulders with impatience.

"Denny said that it was made clear to him that liberty, whether that of the individual or of countries, is a gift of God, and that it was laid upon him that he must join in the fight to gain and preserve it. So we were put out of meeting," she ended abruptly.

It was dark in the room, with the shutters closed, but he could see her face by the dim glow from the smothered hearth. That last statement had moved her strongly; her mouth was pinched, and there was a brightness to her eyes that suggested she might weep, were she not determined not to.

"I collect this is a serious thing, to be put out of meeting?" he asked cautiously.

She nodded, looking away. She picked up the discarded damp towel, smoothed it slowly, and folded it, plainly choosing her words.

"I told thee that my mother died when I was born. My father died three years later—drowned in a flood. We were left with nothing, my brother and I. But the local meeting saw to it that we did not starve, that there was a roof—if one with holes—over our heads. There was a question in meeting, how Denny might be 'prenticed. I know he feared that he must become a drover or a cobbler—he lacks somewhat to be a blacksmith," she added, smiling a little despite her seriousness. "He would have done it, though—to keep me fed."

Luck had intervened, however. One of the Friends had taken it upon himself to try to trace any relatives of the orphaned Hunter children, and after a number of letters to and fro, had discovered a distant cousin, originally from Scotland but presently in London.

"John Hunter, bless his name. He is a famous physician, he and his elder brother, who is *accoucheur* to the Queen herself." Despite her egalitarian principles, Miss Hunter looked somewhat awed, and William nodded respectfully. "He inquired as to Denny's abilities, and hearing good report, made provision for Denny to remove to Philadelphia, to board there with a Quaker family and to go to the new medical college. And then he went so far as to have Denny go to London, to study there with himself!"

"Very good luck, indeed," William observed. "But what about you?"

"Oh. I—was taken in by a woman in the village," she said, with a quick casualness that did not deceive him. "But Denzell came back, and so of course I came to keep his house until he might wed."

She was pleating the towel between her fingers, looking down into her lap. There were small lights in her hair where the fire caught it, a hint of bronze in the dark brown locks.

"The woman—she was a goodly woman. She took care I should learn to keep a house, to cook, to sew. That I should . . . know what is needful for a woman to know." She glanced at him with that odd directness, her face sober.

"I think thee cannot understand," she said, "what it means to be put out of meeting."

"Something like being drummed out of one's regiment, I expect. Disgraceful and distressing."

Her eyes narrowed for a moment, but he had spoken seriously, and she saw that.

"A Friends' meeting is not only a fellowship of worship. It is . . . a community of mind, of heart. A larger family, in a way."

And for a young woman bereft of her own family?

"And to be put out, then . . . yes, I see," he said quietly.

There was a brief silence in the room then, broken only by the sound of the rain. He thought he heard a rooster crow, somewhere far off.

"Thy mother is dead, too, thee said." Rachel looked at him, dark eyes soft. "Does thy father live?"

He shook his head.

"You will think I am exceeding dramatic," he said. "It is the truth, though—my father also died upon the day of my birth."

She blinked at that.

"Truly. He was a good fifty years my mother's senior. When he heard that she was dead in ch—in childbirth, he suffered an apoplexy and died upon the spot." He was annoyed; he seldom stuttered anymore. She had not noticed, though.

"So thee is orphaned, too. I am sorry for thee," she said quietly.

He shrugged, feeling awkward.

"Well. I knew neither of my parents. And in fact, I did have parents. My mother's sister became my mother, in all respects—she's dead now, too—and her husband . . . I have always thought of him as my father, though he is not related to me by blood." It occurred to him that he was treading on dangerous ground here, talking too much about himself. He cleared his throat and endeavored to guide the conversation back to less personal matters.

"Your brother. How does he propose to . . . er . . . to implement this revelation of his?"

She sighed.

"This house—it belonged to a cousin of our mother's. He was a widower, and childless. He had willed the house to Denzell, though when he heard about our being put out of meeting, he wrote to say that he meant to alter his will. By happenstance, though, he caught a bad ague and died before he could do so. But all his neighbors knew, of course—about Denny—which is why . . ."

"I see." It seemed to William that while God might not be logical, He seemed to be taking a most particular interest in Denzell Hunter. He thought it might not be mannerly to say so, though, and inquired in a different direction.

"You said the house was sold. So your brother—"

"He has gone in to the town, to the courthouse, to sign the papers for the sale of the house and make arrangement for the goats, pigs, and chickens. As soon as that is done, we will . . . leave." She swallowed visibly. "Denny means to join the Continental army as a surgeon."

"And you will go with him? As a camp follower?" William spoke with some disapproval; many soldiers' wives—or concubines—did "follow the drum," essentially joining the army with their husbands. He had not seen much of camp followers yet himself, as there had been none on the Long Island campaign—but he'd heard his father speak of such women now and then, mostly with pity. It wasn't a life for a woman of refinement.

She lifted her chin, hearing his disapproval.

"Certainly."

A long wooden pin lay on the table; she must have taken it from her hair when she removed her cap. Now she twisted her damp hair up into a knot and stabbed the pin decisively through it.

"So," she said. "Will thee travel with us? Only so far as thee may be comfortable in doing so," she added quickly.

He had been turning the notion over in the back of his mind all the while they had talked. Plainly, such an arrangement would have advantages for the Hunters—a larger group was always safer, and it was apparent to William that, his revelation notwithstanding, the doctor was not a natural warrior. It would, he thought, have some advantage to himself, as well. The Hunters knew something of the immediate countryside, which he did not, and a man traveling in a group—particularly a group including a woman—was much less noticeable, and much less suspicious, than one alone.

It dawned on him suddenly that if Hunter meant to join the Continental army, there might be excellent opportunity of getting close enough to Washington's forces to gain valuable intelligence of them—something that would go a long way toward compensating for the loss of his book of contacts.

"Yes, certainly," he said, and smiled at Miss Hunter. "An admirable suggestion!"

A flash of lightning stabbed suddenly through the slits of the shutters, and a clap of thunder crashed overhead, almost simultaneously. Both of them started violently at the noise.

William swallowed, feeling his ears still ring. The sharp scent of lightning burned the air.

"I do hope," he said, "that that was a signal of approval."

She didn't laugh.

40

THE BLESSING OF BRIDE
AND OF MICHAEL

THE MOHAWK KNEW HIM as Thayendanegea—Two Wagers. To the English, he was Joseph Brant. Ian had heard much of the man when he dwelt among the Mohawk, by both his names, and had wondered more than once just how well Thayendanegea managed the treacherous ground between two worlds. Was it like the bridge? he thought suddenly. The slender bridge that lay between this world and the next, the air around it assailed by flying heads with rending teeth? Sometime he would like to sit by a fire with Joseph Brant and ask him.

He was going to Brant's house now—but not to speak with Brant. Glutton had told him that Sun Elk had left Snaketown to join Brant and that his wife had gone with him.

"They are in Unadilla," Glutton had said. "Probably still there. Thayendanegea fights with the English, you know. He's talking to the Loyalists up there, trying to get them to join him and his men. He calls them 'Brant's Volunteers.'" He spoke casually; Glutton was not interested in politics, though he would fight now and then, when the spirit moved him.

"Does he?" Ian said, just as casually. "Well, then."

He had no particular idea where Unadilla was, save that it was in the colony of New York, but that was no great difficulty. He set out next day at dawn, heading north.

He had no company save the dog and his thoughts, most of the time. At one point, though, he came to a summer camp of Mohawk and was welcomed there.

He sat with the men, talking. After a time, a young woman brought him a bowl of stew, and he ate it, barely noticing what was in it, though his belly seemed grateful for the warmth and stopped clenching itself.

He couldn't say what drew his eye, but he looked up from the men's talk to see the young woman who had brought him the stew sitting in the shadow just outside the fire, looking at him. She smiled, very slightly.

He chewed more slowly, the taste of the stew suddenly a savor in his mouth. Bear meat, rich with fat. Corn and beans, spiced with onions and garlic. Delicious. She tilted her head to one side; one dark brow rose, elegant, then she rose, too, as though lifted by her question.

Ian set down his bowl and belched politely, then got up and went outside, paying no attention to the knowing looks of the men with whom he'd been eating.

She was waiting, a pale blur in the shadow of a birch. They talked—he felt his mouth form words, felt the tickle of her speech in his ears, but was not really aware of what they said. He held the glow of his anger like a live coal in the palm of his hand, an ember smoking in his heart. He had no thought of her as water to his scorching, nor did he think to kindle her. There were flames behind his eyes, and he was mindless as fire is, devouring where there was fuel, dying where there was not.

He kissed her. She smelled of food, worked skins, and sun-warmed earth. No hint of wood, no tinge of blood. She was tall; he felt her breasts soft and pushing, dropped his hands to the curve of her hips.

She moved against him, solid, willing. Drew back, letting cool air touch his skin where she had been, and took him by the hand to lead him to her long-house. No one glanced at them as she took him into her bed and, in the half-dark warmth, turned to him, naked.

He'd thought it would be better if he couldn't see her face. Anonymous, quick, some pleasure for her, perhaps. Surcease, for him. For the few moments when he lost himself, at least.

But in the dark, she was Emily, and he fled from her bed in shame and anger, leaving astonishment behind.

FOR THE NEXT TWELVE days he walked, the dog by his side, and spoke to no one.

THAYENDANEGEA'S HOUSE STOOD by itself in large grounds, but near enough the village to be still part of it. The village was much as any other, save that many of the houses had two or three grindstones by the step; each woman ground meal for her family, rather than take it to a mill.

There were dogs in the street, dozing in the shadows of wagons and walls. Every one sat up, startled, when Rollo came within scenting distance. A few growled or barked, but none offered to fight.

The men were another matter. There were several men leaning on a fence, watching another with a horse in a field. All of them cast glances at him, half curious, half wary. He didn't know most of them. One of them, though, was a man named Eats Turtles, whom he had known in Snaketown. Another was Sun Elk.

Sun Elk blinked at him, startled as any of the dogs, and then stepped out into the road to face him.

"What are you doing here?"

He considered for a split second telling the truth—but it wasn't a truth that could be told quickly, if at all, and certainly not before strangers.

"None of your business," he answered calmly.

Sun Elk had spoken to him in Mohawk, and he'd answered in the same language. He saw eyebrows rise, and Turtle made to greet him, clearly hoping to avert whatever storm was in the offing by making it clear that Ian was Kahnyen'kehaka himself. He returned Turtle's greeting, and the others drew back a little, puzzled—and interested—but not hostile.

Sun Elk, on the other hand . . . Well, Ian hadn't expected the man to fall on his neck, after all. He'd hoped—insofar as he'd thought about Sun Elk, which was very little—that he'd be elsewhere, but here he was, and Ian smiled wryly to himself, thinking of old Grannie Wilson, who had once described her son-in-law, Hiram, as looking *"like he wouldn't give the road to a bear."*

It was an apt description, and Sun Elk's disposition was not improved either by Ian's reply nor by the subsequent smile.

"What do you want?" Sun Elk demanded.

"Nothing that's yours," Ian replied, as mildly as possible.

Sun Elk's eyes narrowed, but before he could say anything else, Turtle intervened, inviting Ian to come into his house, to eat, to drink.

He should. It wasn't polite to refuse. And he could ask, later, privately, where Emily was. But the need that had brought him over three hundred miles of wilderness acknowledged no requirements of civility. Neither would it brook delay.

Besides, he reflected, readying himself, he'd known it would come to this. No point in putting it off.

"I wish to speak with her who was once my wife," he said. "Where is she?"

Several of the men blinked at that, interested or taken back—but he saw Turtle's eyes flick toward the gates of the large house at the end of the road.

Sun Elk, to his credit, merely drew himself up and planted himself more solidly in the road, ready to defy *two* bears, if necessary. Rollo didn't care for this and lifted his lip in a growl that made one or two of the men step back sharply. Sun Elk, who had better reason than most of them to know just what Rollo was capable of, didn't move an inch.

"Do you mean to set your demon on me?" he asked.

"Of course not. *Sheas, a choin,*" he said quietly to Rollo. The dog stood his ground for a moment longer—just long enough to indicate that it was *his* idea—and then turned aside and lay down, though he kept up a low grumble, like distant thunder.

"I have not come to take her from you," Ian said to Sun Elk. He'd meant to be conciliatory, but he hadn't really expected it to work, and it didn't.

"You think you *could*?"

"If I dinna want to, does it matter?" Ian said testily, lapsing into English.

"She wouldn't go with you, even if you killed me!"

"How many times must I say that I dinna want to take her away from ye?"

Sun Elk stared at him for a minute, his eyes quite black.

"Often enough for your face to say the same thing," he whispered, and clenched his fists.

An interested murmur rose from the other men, but there was an intangible drawing away. They wouldn't interfere in a fight over a woman. That was a blessing, Ian thought vaguely, watching Sun Elk's hands. The man was right-handed, he remembered that. There was a knife on his belt, but his hand wasn't hovering near it.

Ian spread his own hands peaceably.

"I wish only to talk with her."

"Why?" Sun Elk barked. He was close enough for Ian to feel the spray of spittle on his face, but he didn't wipe it away. He didn't back away, either, and dropped his hands.

"That's between me and her," he said quietly. "I daresay she'll tell ye later." The thought of it gave him a pang. The statement didn't seem to reassure Sun Elk, who without warning hit him in the nose.

The crunch echoed through his upper teeth, and Sun Elk's other fist struck him a glancing blow on the cheekbone. He shook his head to clear it, saw the blur of movement through watering eyes, and—more by good fortune than intent—kicked Sun Elk solidly in the crotch.

He stood breathing heavily, dripping blood on the roadway. Six pairs of eyes went from him to Sun Elk, curled in the dust and making small, urgent noises. Rollo got up, walked over to the fallen man, and smelled him with interest. All the eyes came back to Ian.

He made a small motion of the hand that brought Rollo to heel and walked up the road toward Brant's house, six pairs of eyes fixed on his back.

WHEN THE DOOR OPENED, the young white woman who stood there gaped at him, eyes round as pennies. He'd been in the act of wiping his bloody nose with his shirttail. He completed this action and inclined his head civilly.

"Will ye be so good as to ask Wakyo'teyehsnonhsa if she will be pleased to speak wi' Ian Murray?"

The young woman blinked, twice. Then she nodded and swung the door to—pausing with it halfway shut, in order to look at him once more and assure herself that she'd really seen him.

Feeling strange, he stepped down into the garden. It was a formal English garden, with rosebushes and lavender and stone-flagged paths. The smell of it reminded him of Auntie Claire, and he wondered briefly whether Thayendanegea had brought back an English gardener from London.

There were two women at work in the garden, some distance away; one was a white woman, by the color of the hair beneath her cap, and in her middle years by the stoop of her shoulders—perhaps Brant's wife? he wondered. Was the young woman who had answered the door their daughter? The other woman was Indian, with her hair in a plait down her back but streaked with white. Neither one turned to look at him.

When he heard the click of the door latch behind him, he waited a moment before turning around, steeling himself against the disappointment of being told that she was not here—or, worse, that she had refused to see him.

But she was there. Emily. Small and straight, with her breasts showing round in the neck of a blue calico gown, her long hair bound up behind but uncovered. And her face fearful—but eager. Her eyes lit with joy at the sight of him, and she took a step toward him.

He would have crushed her to him had she come to him, made any gesture inviting it. *And what then?* he wondered dimly, but it didn't matter; after that first impulsive movement toward him, she stopped and stood, her hands fluttering for an instant as though they would shape the air between them, but then folding tight before her, hidden in the folds of her skirt.

"Wolf's Brother," she said softly, in Mohawk. "My heart is warm to see you."

"Mine, too," he said in the same language.

"Have you come to speak with Thayendanegea?" she asked, tilting her head back toward the house.

"Perhaps later." Neither of them mentioned his nose, though from the throbbing, it was likely twice its normal size and there was blood all down the front of his shirt. He glanced around; there was a path that led away from the house, and he nodded at that. "Will you walk with me?"

She hesitated for a moment. The flame in her eyes had not gone out, but it burned lower now; there were other things there—caution, mild distress, and what he thought was pride. He was surprised that he should see them so clearly. It was as though she were made of glass.

"I—the children," she blurted, half turning toward the house.

"It doesna matter," he said. "I only—" A dribble of blood from one nostril stopped him, and he paused to wipe the back of his hand across his upper lip. He took the two steps necessary to bring them within touching distance, though he was careful not to touch her.

"I wished to say to you that I am sorry," he said formally, in Mohawk. "That I could not give you children. And that I am glad you have them."

A lovely warm flush rose in her cheeks, and he saw the pride in her overcome the distress.

"May I see them?" he asked, surprising himself as much as her.

She wavered for an instant, but then turned and went into the house. He sat on a stone wall, waiting, and she returned a few moments later with a small boy, maybe five years old, and a girl of three or so in short plaits, who looked gravely at him and sucked her fist.

Blood had run down the back of his throat; it felt raw and tasted of iron.

Now and then on his journey, he'd gone carefully over the explanation Auntie Claire had given him. Not with any notion of telling it to Emily; it could mean nothing to her—he barely understood it himself. Only, maybe, as some shield against this moment, seeing her with the children he could not give her.

"*Call it fate,*" Claire had said, looking at him with a hawk's eye, the one that sees from far above, so far above, maybe, that what seems mercilessness is truly compassion. "*Or call it bad luck. But it wasn't your fault. Or hers.*"

"Come here," he said in Mohawk, putting out a hand to the little boy. The boy glanced at his mother, but then came to him, looking up in curiosity to his face.

"I see you in his face," he said softly to her, speaking English. "And in his hands," he added in Mohawk, taking the child's hands—so amazingly small— in his own. It was true: the boy had her hands, fine-boned and supple; they curled up like sleeping mice in his palms, then the fingers sprang out like a spider's legs and the boy giggled. He laughed, too, closed his own hands swiftly on the boy's, like a bear gulping a pair of trout, making the child shriek, then let go.

"Are you happy?" he asked her.

"Yes," she said softly. She looked down, not meeting his eyes, and he knew it was because she would answer honestly but did not wish to see if her answer hurt him. He put a hand under her chin—her skin was so soft!—and lifted her face to him.

"Are you happy?" he asked again, and smiled a little as he said it.

"Yes," she said again. But then gave a small sigh, and her own hand touched his face at last, light as a moth's wing. "But sometimes I miss you, Ian." There was nothing wrong with her accent, but his Scots name sounded impossibly exotic on her tongue—it always had.

He felt a lump in his throat, but kept the faint smile on his face.

"I see you dinna ask me whether *I'm* happy," he said, and could have kicked himself.

She gave him a quick look, direct as a knife point.

"I have eyes," she said, very simply.

There was a silence between them. He looked away but could feel her there, breathing. Ripe. Soft. He felt her softening further, opening. She had been wise not to go into the garden with him. Here, with her son playing in the dirt near her feet, it was safe. For her, at least.

"Do you mean to stay?" she asked at last, and he shook his head.

"I am going to Scotland," he said.

"You will take a wife among your own people." There was relief in that, but regret, too.

"Are your people no longer my own?" he asked, with a flash of fierceness. "They washed the white blood from my body in the river—you were there."

"I was there."

She looked at him for a long time, searching his face. Likely enough that she would never see him again; did she seek to remember him, or was she looking for something in his features, he wondered?

The latter. She turned abruptly, raising a hand to him to wait, and disappeared into the house.

The little girl ran after her, not wanting to stay with the stranger, but the little boy lingered, interested.

"Are you Wolf's Brother?"

"I am, aye. And you?"

"They call me Digger." It was a child's sort of name, used for convenience until the person's real name should declare itself in some way. Ian nodded, and they remained a few minutes, looking each other over with interest, but with no sense of awkwardness between them.

"She who is mother's mother to my mother," Digger said quite suddenly. "She talked about you. To me."

"She did?" said Ian, startled. That would be Tewaktenyonh. A great woman, head of the Women's Council at Snaketown—and the person who had sent him away.

"Does Tewaktenyonh still live?" he asked, curious.

"Oh, yes. She's older than the mountains," the little boy answered seriously. "She has only two teeth left, but she still eats."

Ian smiled at that.

"Good. What did she say to you of me?"

The boy screwed up his face, recollecting the words.

"She said I was the child of your spirit but I should not say so to my father."

Ian felt the blow of that, harder than any the child's father had dealt him, and couldn't speak for a moment.

"Aye, I dinna think ye should say so, either," he said, when words returned to him. He repeated the sentiment in Mohawk, in case the boy might not have understood English, and the child nodded, tranquil.

"Will I be with you, sometime?" he asked, only vaguely interested in the answer. A lizard had come out onto the stone wall to bask, and his eyes were fixed on it.

Ian forced his own words to be casual.

"If I live."

The boy's eyes were narrowed, watching the lizard, and the tiny right hand twitched, just a little. The distance was too far, though; he knew it, and glanced at Ian, who was closer. Ian cut his eyes at the lizard without moving, then looked back at the boy and agreement sprang up between them. *Don't move,* his eyes warned, and the boy seemed to cease breathing.

It didn't do to think in such situations. Without pausing to draw breath, he snatched, and the lizard was in his hand, astonished and thrashing.

The little boy chortled and hopped up and down, clapping his hands with glee, then held them out for the lizard, which he received with the greatest concentration, folding his hands about it so that it might not escape.

"And what will ye do with him?" Ian asked, smiling.

The boy held the lizard up to his face, peering at it intently, and his brow furrowed in thought.

"I will name him," he said at last. "Then he will be mine and bless me when I see him again." He brought the lizard up, eyeball to eyeball, and each stared unblinking at the other.

"Your name is Bob," the boy declared at last in English, and with great ceremony set the lizard on the ground. Bob leapt from his hands and disappeared under a log.

"A verra good name," Ian said gravely. His bruised ribs hurt with the need not to laugh, but the urge vanished in the next moment, as the distant door opened and Emily came out, a bundle in her arms.

She came up to him and presented him with a child, swaddled and bound to a cradleboard, in much the same way he had presented the lizard to Digger.

"This is my second daughter," she said, shyly proud. "Will you choose her name?"

He was moved, and touched Emily's hand, very lightly, before taking the cradleboard onto his knee and looking searchingly into the tiny face. She could not have given him greater honor, this permanent mark of the feeling she had once held for him—still might hold for him.

But as he looked at the little girl—she regarded him with round, serious eyes, taking in this new manifestation of her personal landscape—a conviction took root in him. He didn't question it; it was simply there, and undeniable.

"Thank you," he said, and smiled at Emily with great affection. He laid his hand—huge, and rough with callus and the nicks of living—on the tiny, perfect, soft-haired head. "I will bless all your children wi' the blessings of Bride and of Michael." He lifted his hand then, and reaching out, drew Digger to him. "But this one is mine to name."

Her face went quite blank with astonishment, and she looked quickly from him to her son and back. She swallowed visibly, unsure—but it didn't matter; *he* was sure.

"Your name is Swiftest of Lizards," he said, in Mohawk. The Swiftest of Lizards thought for a minute, then nodded, pleased, and with a laugh of pure delight, darted away.

41

SHELTER FROM THE STORM

NOT FOR THE FIRST time, William was startled to realize the breadth of his father's acquaintance. In casual conversation as they rode, he had mentioned to Denzell Hunter that his father had once known a Dr. John Hunter—in fact, the association, involving an electric eel, an impromptu duel, and the implications of body-snatching, was part of the situation that had sent Lord John to Canada and the Plains of Abraham. Might this John Hunter perhaps be the beneficent relative that Miss Rachel had mentioned?

Denny Hunter had brightened at once.

"How remarkable! Yes, it must be the same. Particularly since thee mentions body-snatching in connection with him." He coughed, seeming a little embarrassed.

"It was a most . . . educational association," Hunter said. "Though a disturbing one, upon occasion." He glanced back at his sister, but Rachel was well behind them, her mule ambling and Rachel herself half asleep in the saddle, her head nodding like a sunflower's.

"Thee understands, Friend William," Hunter said, lowering his voice, "that in order to become skilled in the arts of surgery, it is necessary to learn how the human body is constructed and to understand its workings. Only so much can be learned from texts—and the texts upon which most medical men rely are . . . well, to be blunt about it, they are wrong."

"Oh, yes?" William was only half attending to the conversation. The other half of his mind was evenly divided among his assessment of the road, a hope that they might reach somewhere habitable in time to procure supper, and an appreciation of the slenderness of Rachel Hunter's neck on the rare occasions when she rode in front of him. He wanted to turn round and look at her again, but couldn't do it so soon, in all decency. Another few minutes . . .

" . . . Galen and Aesculapius. The common conception is—and has been for a very long time—that the ancient Greeks had written down everything known regarding the human body; there was no need to doubt these texts or to create mystery where there was none."

William grunted. "You should hear my uncle go on about ancient military texts. He's all for Caesar, who he says was a very decent general, but he takes leave to doubt that Herodotus ever saw a battlefield."

Hunter glanced at him in surprised interest. "Exactly what John Hunter said—in different terms—regarding Avicenna! 'The man's never seen a pregnant uterus in his life.'" He smacked a fist upon his pommel to emphasize the point, and his horse jerked its head, startled.

"Whoa, whoa," said Hunter, alarmed, sawing on the reins in a way calculated to have the horse rearing and pawing in moments. William leaned over and neatly took the reins out of Denzell's hands, giving them slack.

He was rather glad of the brief distraction, as it kept Hunter from discoursing further about uteruses. William was not at all sure what a uterus was, but if it got pregnant, it must have to do with a woman's privates, and that was not something he wished to discuss within the hearing of Miss Hunter.

"But you said your association with Dr. John Hunter was disturbing," he said, handing Hunter back the reins and hastening to change the subject before the doctor could think of something more embarrassing to mention. "Why was that?"

"Well . . . we—his students—learned the mysteries of the human body from . . . the human body."

William felt a slight clench of the belly.

"Dissection, you mean?"

"Yes." Hunter glanced at him, concerned. "It is a distasteful prospect, I know—and yet, to see the marvelous fashion in which God has ordered things! The intricacies of a kidney, the amazing interior of a lung—William, I cannot tell thee what revelation it is!"

"Well . . . yes, I see it must be," William said guardedly. Now he could reasonably glance back, and did so. Rachel had straightened, stretching her back, head tilted so that her straw hat fell back, the sun on her face, and he smiled. "You . . . er . . . where did you get the bodies to dissect?"

Dr. Hunter sighed.

"That was the disturbing aspect. Many were paupers from the workhouse or the street, and their deaths were most pitiable. But many were the bodies of executed criminals. And while I must be pleased that some good came of their deaths, I could not but be appalled at those deaths."

"Why?" William asked, interested.

"Why?" Hunter blinked at him behind his spectacles, but then shook his head, as though shaking off flies. "But I forget thee is not one of us—your pardon. We do not condone violence, Friend William, and surely not killing."

"Not even criminals? Murderers?"

Denzell's lips compressed, and he looked unhappy, but shook his head.

"No. Let them be imprisoned or put to some useful labor. But for the state to commit murder in its turn is a dreadful violation of God's commandment; it implicates all of us in the commission of this sin. Does thee not see?"

"I see that the state, as you call it, has responsibility for its subjects," William said, rather nettled. "You expect constables and judges to see that you and your property are secure, don't you? If the state has that responsibility, surely it must have the means of carrying it out."

"I do not contest that—imprison criminals, if necessary, as I say. But the state has no right to kill people on my behalf!"

"Has it not?" William said dryly. "Have you any idea of the nature of some of the criminals who are executed? Of their crimes?"

"Has thee?" Hunter gave him a raised brow.

"I have, yes. The Governor of Newgate Prison is an acquaintance— another acquaintance—of my father's; I have sat at table with him and heard stories that would take the curl out of your wig, Dr. Hunter. If you wore one," he added.

Hunter responded to the jest with a fleeting smile.

"Call me by my name," he said. "Thee knows we do not hold by titles. And I admit the truth of what thee says. I have heard—and seen—more terrible things than you have likely heard at your father's table. But justice lies in God's hand. To do violence—to take a life—is to violate God's command and do grievous sin."

"And if you are attacked, injured, you may not fight back?" William demanded. "You may not defend yourselves? Your families?"

"We rely upon the goodness and mercy of God," Denzell said firmly. "And if we are killed, then we die in the firm expectation of God's life and resurrection."

They rode in silence for a moment before William said conversationally, "Or you rely upon the willingness of someone else to commit violence for you."

Denzell drew a deep, instinctive breath, but thought better of whatever he had meant to say. They rode in silence for some time, and when they spoke again, it was of birds.

IT WAS RAINING WHEN they woke next day. Not a quick thundershower, here and gone, but a heavy, remorseless sort of rain that looked set to pour steadily all day. There was no point in staying where they were; the rocky overhang under which they had sheltered for the night lay directly exposed to the wind, and the rain had already dampened the firewood sufficiently as to cause their breakfast fire to yield much more smoke than heat.

Still coughing intermittently, William and Denny loaded the pack mule while Rachel bound up a bundle of the least-damp sticks in canvas. If they found shelter by nightfall, they might at least be able to start a fire to cook their supper, even if the rain continued.

There was little conversation. Even had they been so inclined, the rain beat so heavily upon trees and ground and upon their hats that anything said had to be half shouted to be heard.

In a state of sodden but dogged determination, they rode slowly north by northeast, Denny anxiously consulting his compass when they reached a crossroad.

"What think thee, Friend William?" Denny took off his spectacles and wiped them—to little effect—on the skirt of his coat. "Neither road runs precisely as we might wish, and Friend Lockett did not mention this crossroad in his instruction. That one"—he pointed at the road that crossed the one they were set upon—"appears to run north, while this one is due east. At the moment." He glanced at William, his face oddly naked without his spectacles.

A farmer named Lockett and his wife had been their last contact with humanity, three days before. She had given them supper, sold them bread, eggs, and cheese, and her husband had set them on the road—toward Albany, he said; they should run across an indication of the Continental army somewhere between here and there. But he *hadn't* mentioned a crossroad.

William gave the muddy ground a glance, but the crossroad itself lay in a low spot and was nothing more now than a small lake. No clues to traffic— but the road they were on seemed substantially wider than the smaller one crossing it.

"This one," he said firmly, and nudged his horse squelching through the lake to the other side.

Now it was late afternoon, and he was beginning to be worried about his decision. Had they been upon the right road, they should—said Mr. Lockett—encounter a small hamlet called Johnson's Ford by the end of the day. Of course, the rain had slowed them, he told himself. And while the countryside looked as vacant and writhingly verdant as ever, villages and farmsteads *did* pop up as suddenly as mushrooms after a heavy rain. In which case, they might encounter Johnson's Ford at any moment.

"Maybe the place has dissolved." Rachel leaned out from her saddle to call to him. Rachel had nearly dissolved herself, and he grinned, in spite of his worry. The rain had beaten the brim of her straw hat down, so that it hung limp as a duster around her head; she was obliged to lift the front of it in order to peer out, like a suspicious toad under a harrow. Her clothes were soaked through, as well, and as she was wearing three layers of everything, she resembled nothing so much as a large, untidy bale of wet laundry, forked steaming from the kettle.

Before he could reply to her, though, her brother sat up straight in his saddle, showering water in all directions, and pointed dramatically down the road.

"Look!"

William jerked his head round, assuming that their destination was in sight. It wasn't, but the road was no longer empty. A man was walking briskly toward them through the mud, a split burlap sack shielding his head and shoulders from the rain. In the current state of desolation, anything human was a sight to gladden the eyes, and William spurred up a little to hail the fellow.

"Well met, young sir," said the man, peering up at William from his burlap refuge. "Where ye bound, this dismal day?" He lifted a lip in ingratiation, showing a broken dogtooth, stained with tobacco.

"Johnson's Ford. Are we headed aright?"

The man reared back, as though astonished.

"Johnson's Ford, you say?"

"I do, yes," William said, with a certain amount of testiness. He sympathized with the lack of company in rural parts and the subsequent impulse of the inhabitants to detain travelers as long as possible, but this was not the day for it. "Where is it?"

The man shook his head back and forth in slow dismay.

" 'Fraid ye've missed your turn, sir. Ought to've gone left at the crossroads."

Rachel made a small, pitiable sound at this. The light was already failing, shadow beginning to pool round the horses' feet. It was several hours' ride back to the crossroad; they could not hope to reach it before nightfall, let alone make their way to Johnson's Ford.

The man plainly realized this, as well. He smiled happily at William, revealing a wide expanse of brown gum.

"If so be as you gennelmen'll help me cotch my cow and drive 'er home, the wife'd be pleased to offer ye supper and a bed."

There being no reasonable alternative, William accepted this suggestion with what grace he could, and leaving Rachel sheltering under a tree with the animals, he and Denny Hunter went to assist with the cow-cotching.

The cow in question, a rawboned shaggy beast with a wild eye, proved both elusive and obdurate, and it took the combined talents of all three men to capture it and drag it to the road. Soaked to the skin and thickly plastered with mud, the bedraggled party then followed Mr. Antioch Johnson—for so their host had introduced himself—through the gathering shades of night to a small ramshackle farmhouse.

The rain was still pelting down, though, and any roof was welcome, leaky or not.

Mrs. Johnson proved to be a ragged slattern of uncertain age, with even fewer teeth than her husband and a sullen disposition. She glared at the dripping guests and turned her back rudely upon them, but did produce wooden bowls of a vile, congealed stew—and there was fresh milk from the cow. William noticed that Rachel took but a single bite of the stew, turned pale, removed something from her mouth, and set down her spoon, after which she confined herself to the milk.

He himself was much too hungry either to taste the stew or care what was in it—and, fortunately, it was too dark to examine the contents of his bowl.

Denny was making an effort to be sociable, though he was swaying with weariness, answering Mr. Johnson's unending questions about their origins, journey, destination, connections, news of the road, and opinions and news regarding the war. Rachel attempted a smile now and then, but her eyes kept passing uneasily around their surroundings, returning again and again to their hostess, who sat in the corner, her own eyes hooded, brooding over a fuming clay pipe that hung from a slack lower lip.

Belly full and with dry stockings, William felt the labors of the day begin to catch up to him. There was a decent fire in the hearth, and the leaping flames lulled him into a sort of trance, the voices of Denny and Mr. Johnson fading into a pleasant murmur. He might have fallen asleep right there, had the rustle of Rachel rising to her feet to visit the privy not broken the trance, reminding him that he should check the horses and mules. He'd rubbed them dry as well as he could and paid Mr. Johnson for hay, but there was no real barn to shelter them, only a crude roof of branches perched on spindly poles. He didn't want them standing all night in mud should the shelter be flooded.

It was still raining, but the air outside was clean and fresh, filled with the night scent of trees, grasses, and rushing water. After the fug indoors, William felt nearly light-headed with the fragrance. He ducked through the rain to the shelter, doing his best to keep the small torch he had brought alight, enjoying every breath.

The torch sputtered but kept burning, and he was glad to see that the shelter had not flooded; the horses and mules—and the wild-eyed cow—were all standing on damp straw, but not hock-deep in mud. The privy door creaked, and he saw Rachel's slender dark shape emerge. She saw the torch and came to join him, drawing her shawl about her against the rain.

"Are the beasts all right?" Raindrops sparkled in her damp hair, and he smiled at her.

"I expect their supper was better than ours."

She shuddered in recollection.

"I should much prefer to have eaten hay. Did thee *see* what was in—"

"No," he interrupted, "and I shall be much happier if you don't tell me."

She snorted, but desisted. He had no desire to go back into the fetid house at once, and Rachel seemed similarly disinclined, moving to scratch her mule's drooping ears.

"I do not like the way that woman looks at us," Rachel said after a moment, not looking at him. "She keeps staring at my shoes. As though she wonders whether they would fit her."

William glanced at Rachel's feet himself; her shoes were not in any way fashionable but were sturdy and well made, though also well worn and smeared with dried mud.

Rachel glanced uneasily at the house. "I will be pleased to leave here, even if it should still be raining in the morning."

"We'll leave," he assured her. "Without waiting for breakfast, if you prefer." He leaned against one of the upright poles that supported the shelter, feeling the mist of rain cool on his neck. The drowsiness had left him, though the tiredness had not, and he realized that he shared her sense of unease.

Mr. Johnson seemed amiable, if uncouth, but there was something almost too eager in his manner. He leaned forward avidly in conversation, eyes agleam, and his dirty hands were restless on his knees.

It might be only the natural loneliness of a man who lacked company—for surely the presence of the sullen Mrs. Johnson would be little consolation— but William's father had taught him to pay attention to his instincts, and he therefore did not try to argue himself out of them. Without comment or apology, he rummaged in the saddlebag hanging from the post and found the small dagger that he carried in his boot while riding.

Rachel's eyes followed it as he tucked it into the waist of his breeches and pulled his shirt loose to cover it. Her chin was puckered, but she didn't protest.

The torch was beginning to gutter, almost burned out. He held out his arm, and Rachel took it without protest, drawing close to him. He wanted to put his arm around her but contented himself with drawing in his elbow, finding the distant warmth of her body a comfort.

The bulk of the farmhouse was darker than the night, lacking either door or window at the back. They circled it in silence, rain thumping on their skulls, feet squelching on the sodden ground. Only a flicker of light showed through the shutters, the faintest indication of human tenancy. He heard Rachel swallow, and touched her hand lightly as he opened the door for her.

"Sleep well," he whispered to her. "The dawn will come before you know it."

IT WAS THE STEW that saved his life. He slept almost at once, overcome by weariness, but found his sleep troubled by obnoxious dreams. He was walking down a hallway with a figured Turkey carpet, but realized after a time that what he had taken for twining patterns in the rug were in fact snakes, which raised their heads, swaying, at his approach. The snakes were slow-moving, and he was able to skip over them but lurched from side to side as a result, hitting the walls of the corridor, which seemed to be closing in upon him, narrowing the way.

Then he was enclosed so tightly that he must proceed sideways, the wall behind him scraping his back, the plaster surface before him so close that he could not bend his head to look down. He was worried about the snakes in the carpet, but couldn't see them, and kicked out to the side with his feet, now and then hitting something heavy. Panicked, he felt one twine about his leg, then glide upward, wrapping round his body and burrowing its head through the front of his shirt, prodding him hard and painfully in the abdomen, looking for somewhere to bite.

He woke suddenly, panting and sweating, aware that the pain in his guts was real. It bit with a sharp cramp, and he pulled up his legs and rolled onto his side an instant before the ax struck the floorboards where his head had just been.

He let out a tremendous fart and rolled in blind panic toward the dark figure struggling to free the ax from the wood. He struck Johnson's legs, grabbed them, and yanked. The man fell on him with a curse and grabbed him by the throat. William punched and thrashed at his opponent, but the hands on his throat clung like grim death, and his vision darkened and flashed with colored lights.

There was screaming going on somewhere nearby. More by instinct than plan, William suddenly lunged forward, striking Johnson in the face with his forehead. It hurt, but the death grip on his throat relaxed, and he wrenched loose and rolled over, scrambling to his feet.

The fire had died to embers, and there was no more than a faint glow of light in the room. A heaving mass of bodies in the corner was the source of the screaming, but nothing he could do about that.

Johnson had kicked the ax loose; William saw the dull gleam of its blade in the split second before Johnson seized it and swung it at his head. He ducked, rushed in, and managed to grab Johnson's wrist, pulling hard. The cheek of the falling ax blade struck his knee a paralyzing blow, and he crumpled, pulling Johnson down with him, but got the other knee up in time to keep from being flattened beneath the other man's body.

He jerked to the side, felt sudden heat at his back and the ping of sparks; they had rolled into the edge of the hearth. He reached back and seized a handful of hot embers, which he ground into Johnson's face, ignoring the searing pain in his palm.

Johnson fell back, clutching his face and making short *ah! ah!* noises, as though he had not breath to scream. The ax was dangling from one hand; he sensed William rise and swung it blindly, one-handed.

William grabbed the ax handle, jerked it from Johnson's grasp, took a good two-handed hold upon the throat of the handle, and brought the bit down on Johnson's head with a *choonk* like a kicked pumpkin. The impact vibrated through his hands and arms; he let go and stumbled backward.

His mouth was full of bile; saliva overflowed and he wiped a sleeve across his mouth. He was breathing like a bellows but could not seem to get any air in his lungs.

Johnson reeled toward him, arms outstretched, the ax sticking in his head. The handle quivered, turning to and fro like an insect's feeler. Slowly, horribly, Johnson's hands reached up to take hold of it.

William wanted to scream but didn't have the breath for it. Backing away in panic, he brushed a hand against his breeches and felt wetness there. He glanced down, fearing the worst, but saw instead the cloth dark with blood, and at the same time realized that there was a slight stinging sensation at the top of his thigh.

"Bloody... hell," he muttered, fumbling at his waist. He'd managed to stab himself with his own dagger, but it was still there, thank God. The feel of the hilt steadied him, and he pulled it out, still backing away as Johnson came toward him, making a sort of yowling noise, yanking at the ax handle.

The ax came loose, releasing a gush of blood that rolled down Johnson's face and splattered William's face and arms and chest. Johnson swung the ax with a huff of effort, but his movements were slow and clumsy. William ducked aside, farting with the movement but regaining his nerve.

He tightened his grip on the dagger and looked for a place to stick it. Round the back, his mind suggested. Johnson was dashing one forearm uselessly across his face, trying to clear his eyes, the ax held in the other hand, sweeping to and fro in wide, trembling swaths.

"William!" Surprised by the voice, he glanced aside and was nearly struck by the wavering blade.

"Shut up," he said crossly. "I'm busy."

"Yes, I see that," said Denny Hunter. "Let me help thee." He was white-faced and shaking nearly as much as Johnson, but stepped forward and, with a sudden lunge, seized the ax handle and pulled the implement out of

Johnson's grasp. He stepped back and dropped it on the floor with a *thunk,* looking as though he might be sick at any moment.

"Thank you," said William. He stepped forward and drove the dagger upward under Johnson's ribs, into his heart. Johnson's eyes opened wide with the shock and stared directly into William's. They were gray-blue, with a scattering of gold and yellow flecks near the dark iris. William had never seen anything more beautiful and stood transfixed for an instant, until the feel of the pumping blood over his hand returned him to himself.

He jerked the knife free and stood back, letting the body fall. He was trembling all over and about to shit himself. He turned blindly and headed for the door, brushing past Denny, who said something that he didn't quite hear.

Shuddering and gasping in the privy, though, he thought the doctor had said, "Thee did not have to do that."

Yes, he thought, *I did,* and bowed his head upon his knees, waiting for everything to abate.

WILLIAM EMERGED AT LAST from the privy, feeling clammy and rubber-limbed but less internally volatile. Denny Hunter rushed past him and into the structure, from which explosive noises and loud groans were immediately heard. Moving hastily away, he made his way through a spatter of rain toward the house.

Dawn was some way off, but the air had begun to stir, and the farmhouse stood out against the paling sky, black and skeletal. He entered, feeling very uncertain, to find Rachel, white as bone, standing guard with a broom over Mrs. Johnson, who was wrapped tightly in a filthy sheet, thrashing a bit and making peculiar hissing and spitting noises.

Her husband's remains lay facedown by the hearth in a pool of congealing blood. He didn't want to look at the body, but felt it would be somehow wrong not to, and went and stood by it for a moment, looking down. One of the Hunters had poked up the fire and added wood; there was warmth in the room, but he couldn't feel it.

"He's dead," Rachel said, her voice colorless.

"Yes." He didn't know how he was meant to feel in such a situation and had no real idea how he *did* feel. He turned away, though, with a slight sense of relief, and came to look at the prisoner.

"Did she . . . ?"

"She tried to cut Denny's throat, but she stepped on my hand and woke me. I saw the knife and screamed, and he seized her, and . . ." She pulled a hand through her hair, and he saw that she had lost her cap, and the hair was loose and tangled.

"I sat on her," she said, "and Denny rolled her up in the sheet. I don't think she can speak," Rachel added, as he stooped to look at the woman. "Her tongue is split."

Mrs. Johnson, hearing this, thrust out her tongue in vindictive fashion and waggled the two halves of it independently at him. With the memory of the dream snakes vivid in his mind, he flinched in instinctive revulsion, but saw the look of satisfaction that crossed her face.

"If she can do that with her nasty tongue, she can talk," he said, and, reaching down, took hold of the woman's scrawny throat. "Tell me why I shouldn't kill you, too."

"Iss not my fault!" she said promptly, in such a rasping hiss that he nearly let go of her in shock. "He makess me help him."

William glanced over his shoulder at the body on the hearth.

"Not anymore." He tightened his grip, feeling the beat of her pulse against his thumb. "How many travelers have you killed, the two of you?"

She didn't answer but stroked her upper lip lasciviously with her tongue, first one half and then the other. He let go her throat and slapped her hard across the face. Rachel gasped.

"Thee must not—"

"Oh, yes, I must." He rubbed his hand against the side of his breeches, trying to get rid of the feel of the woman's sweat, her slack skin, her bony throat. His other hand was beginning to throb painfully. He wanted suddenly to pick up the ax and smash her with it, over and over—crush her head, hack her to bits. His body trembled with the urge; she saw it in his eyes and stared back at him, eyes black and glittering.

"You don't want me to kill her?" he asked Rachel.

"Thee must not," she whispered. Very slowly, she reached for his burned hand, and, when he did not pull away, took it into hers. There was a roaring in his ears, and he felt dizzy.

"Thee is hurt," she said softly. "Come outside. I will wash it."

She led him out, half blind and stumbling, and made him sit on the chopping block while she brought a bucket of water from the trough. It had stopped raining, though the world dripped and the dawn air was moist and fresh in his chest.

Rachel bathed his hand in the cold water, and the burning eased a little. She touched his thigh, where the blood had dried in a long patch down his breeches, but let it go when he shook his head.

"I'll bring thee whisky; there is some in Denny's bag." She stood up, but he grabbed her wrist with his good hand, holding hard.

"Rachel." His own voice sounded odd to him, remote, as though someone else was speaking. "I've never killed anyone before. I don't—I don't quite know what to do about it." He looked up at her, searching her face for understanding. "If it had been—I expected it to be in battle. That—I think I'd know how. How to feel, I mean. If it had been like that."

She met his eyes, her face drawn in troubled thought. The light touched her, a pink softer than the sheen of pearls, and after a long time she touched his face, very gently.

"No," she said. "Thee wouldn't."

PART FIVE

To the Precipice

42

CROSSROAD

WILLIAM PARTED FROM the Hunters at a nameless cross-road somewhere in New Jersey. It was not politic for him to go further; their inquiries regarding the position of the Continental army were being greeted with increasing hostility, indicating that they were getting close. Neither rebel sympathizers nor Loyalists who feared reprisal from an army on their doorstep wished to say anything to mysterious travelers who might be spies or worse.

The Quakers would have an easier time of it without him. They were so plainly what they were and Denzell's intent to enlist as a surgeon both so simple and so admirable that, if they were alone, people would help them, he thought. Or at least receive their inquiries more kindly. With William, though . . .

Saying that he was a friend of the Hunters had been sufficient, earlier in the journey. Folk were curious about the little group, but not suspicious. As they drew farther into New Jersey, though, the agitation of the countryside increased markedly. Farms had been raided by foraging parties, both by Hessians from Howe's army, trying to lure Washington into open battle from his lurking place in the Watchung Mountains, and from the Continental army, desperate for supplies.

Farmhouses that would normally have welcomed strangers for the news they bore now repelled them with muskets and harsh words. Food was growing harder to find. Rachel's presence sometimes helped them get close enough to offer money—and William's small store of gold and silver was certainly helpful; Denzell had put most of the money from the sale of their house with a bank in Philadelphia to secure Rachel's future safety, and the paper money issued by the Congress was almost universally rejected.

There was no means by which William could masquerade as a Quaker, though. Beyond his inability to master plain speech, his size and bearing made people nervous—the more so as he, with the memories of Captain Nathan Hale vivid in his mind, would not say that he meant to enlist in the Continental army nor ask any questions that might later be presented as evidence of spying. His silence—perceived as menacing—also made people nervous.

He hadn't spoken to the Hunters regarding their parting, and both Denzell and Rachel had been careful not to ask about his own plans. Everyone knew the time had come, though; he could feel it in the air when he woke that morning. When Rachel handed him a chunk of bread for breakfast, her hand brushed his, and he nearly seized her fingers. She felt the strength of his stifled impulse and looked up, startled, directly into his eyes. More green than brown today, and he would have sent discretion to the devil and kissed her—he thought she would not have objected—had her brother not just then emerged from the bushes, buttoning his flies.

He chose the place, all of a sudden. Naught to be gained by delay, and maybe better to do it without thinking too much. He pulled his horse to a stop in the middle of the crossroad, startling Denzell, whose mare bridled and danced at the jerk on her reins.

"I will leave you here," William said abruptly, and more harshly than he had intended. "My way lies north"—he nodded in that direction, and thank God the sun was up so he could tell which way north was—"while I think that if you continue to the east, you will encounter some representatives of Mr. Washington's army. If . . ." He hesitated, but they should be warned. From what the farmers had said, it was plain that Howe had sent troops into the area.

"If you meet with British troops or Hessian mercenaries—do you speak German, by chance?"

Denzell shook his head, eyes wide behind his spectacles. "Only a little French."

"That's good. Most Hessian officers have good French. If you meet with Hessians who don't and they offer to molest you, say to them, '*Ich verlange, Euren Vorgesetzten zu sehen; ich bin mit seinem Freund bekannt.*' That means, 'I demand to see your officer; I know his friend.' Say the same thing if you meet with British troops. In English, of course," he added awkwardly.

A faint smile crossed Denzell's face.

"I thank thee," he said. "But if they do take us to an officer, and he demands to know the name of this theoretical friend?"

William smiled back.

"It won't really matter. Once you're in front of an officer, you will be safe. But as for a name—Harold Grey, Duke of Pardloe, Colonel of the Forty-sixth Foot." Uncle Hal didn't know everyone, as his own father did, but anyone in the military world would know *him*—or of him, at least.

He could see Denzell's lips move silently, committing this to memory.

"And who is Friend Harold to thee, William?" Rachel had been regarding him narrowly beneath the sagging brim of her hat, and now pushed this back on her head to view him more directly.

He hesitated again, but after all, what did it matter now? He would never see the Hunters again. And while he knew that Quakers would not be impressed by worldly shows of rank and family, he still sat straighter in his saddle.

"Some kin to me," he said casually, and, digging in his pocket, brought out the small purse the Scotsman Murray had given him. "Here. You will need this."

"We will do well enough," Denzell said, waving it away.

"So will I," William said, and tossed the purse toward Rachel, who put up her hands in reflex and caught it, looking as much surprised by the fact that she had done so as by his own action. He smiled at her, too, his heart full.

"Fare thee well," he said gruffly, then wheeled his horse and set off at a brisk trot, not looking back.

―――――

"THEE KNOWS HE is a British soldier?" Denny Hunter said quietly to his sister, watching William ride away. "Likely a deserter."

"And if he is?"

"Violence follows such a man. Thee knows it. To remain long with such a man is a danger—not only to the body. But to the soul, as well."

Rachel sat her mule in silence for a moment, watching the empty road. Insects buzzed loud in the trees.

"I think thee may be a hypocrite, Denzell Hunter," she said evenly, and pulled her mule's head around. "He saved my life *and* thine. Would thee prefer him to have held his hand and see me dead and butchered in that dreadful place?" She shuddered slightly in spite of the heat of the day.

"I would not," her brother said soberly. "And I thank God that he was there to save thee. I am sinner enough to prefer thy life to the welfare of that young man's soul—but not hypocrite enough to deny it, no."

She snorted and, taking off her hat, waved away a gathering cloud of flies.

"I am honored. But as for thy talk of violent men and the danger of being in the vicinity of such men—is thee not taking me to join an army?"

He laughed ruefully.

"I am. Perhaps thee is right and I am a hypocrite. But, Rachel—" He leaned out and caught her mule's bridle, keeping her from turning away. "Thee knows I would have no harm befall thee, either of body or soul. Say the word and I will find thee a place with Friends, where you may stay in safety. I am sure that the Lord has spoken to me, and I must follow my conscience. But there is no need for thee to follow it, too."

She gave him a long, level look.

"And how does thee know that the Lord has not spoken to me, as well?"

His eyes twinkled behind his spectacles.

"I am happy for thee. What did He say?"

"He said, 'Keep thy fat-headed brother from committing suicide, for I will require his blood at thy hand,'" she snapped, slapping his hand away from the bridle. "If we are going to join the army, Denny, let us go and find it."

She kicked the mule viciously in the ribs. Its ears sprang straight up, and with a startled whoop from its rider, it shot down the road as though fired from a cannon.

―――――

WILLIAM RODE FOR some way, back particularly straight, showing excellent form in his horsemanship. After the road curved out of sight of the crossroad, he slowed and relaxed a bit. He was sorry to leave the Hunters, but already beginning to turn his thoughts ahead.

Burgoyne. He'd met General Burgoyne once, at a play. A play written by the general, no less. He didn't recall anything about the play itself, as he'd been engaged in a flirtation of the eyes with a girl in the next box, but afterward he'd gone down with his father to congratulate the successful playwright, who was flushed and handsome with triumph and champagne.

"Gentleman Johnny" they called him in London. A light in London society's firmament, in spite of the fact that he and his wife had some years before been obliged to flee to France to escape arrest for debt. No one held debt against a man, though; it was too common.

William was more puzzled by the fact that his uncle Hal seemed to like John Burgoyne. Uncle Hal had no time for plays, nor for the people who wrote them—though, come to think, he had the complete works of Aphra Behn on his shelves, and William's father had once told him, in deepest secrecy, that his brother Hal had conceived a passionate attachment for Mrs. Behn following the death of his first wife and before his marriage to Aunt Minnie.

"Mrs. Behn was dead, you see," his father had explained. "Safe."

William had nodded, wishing to seem worldly and understanding, though in fact he had no real notion what his father meant by this. Safe? How, safe?

He shook his head. He didn't expect ever to understand Uncle Hal, and chances were that was best for both of them. His grandmother Benedicta was probably the only person who did. Thought of his uncle, though, led him to think of his cousin Henry, and his mouth tightened a little.

Word would have reached Adam, of course, but he likely could do nothing for his brother. Neither could William, whose duty called him north. Between his father and Uncle Hal, though, surely . . .

The horse threw up his head, snorting a little, and William looked ahead to see a man standing by the road, one arm raised to hail him.

He rode slowly, a sharp eye on the wood, lest the man have confederates hidden to waylay unwary travelers. The verge was open here, though, with a thick but spindly growth of saplings behind it; no one could hide in there.

"Good day to you, sir," he said, reining up a safe distance from the old man. For old he was; his face was seamed like a tin mine's slag heap, he leaned on a tall staff, and his hair was pure white, tied back in a plait.

"Well met," the old gentleman said. Gentleman for he stood proud, and his clothes were decent, and now William came to look, there was a good horse, too, hobbled and cropping grass some distance away. William relaxed a little.

"Where do you fare, sir?" he asked politely. The old man shrugged a little, easy.

"That may depend upon what you can tell me, young man." The old man was a Scot, though his English was good. "I am in search of a man called Ian Murray, whom I think you know?"

William was disconcerted by this; how did the old man know that? But he knew Murray; perhaps Murray had mentioned William to him. He replied cautiously, "I know him. But I am afraid I have no idea where he is."

"No?" The old man looked keenly at him. *As though he thinks I might lie to him,* William thought. *Suspicious old sod!*

"No," he repeated firmly. "I met him in the Great Dismal, some weeks ago, in company with some Mohawk. But I do not know where he might have gone since then."

"Mohawk," the old man repeated thoughtfully, and William saw the sunken eyes fasten on his chest, where the great bear claw rested outside his shirt. "Did you get that wee bawbee from the Mohawk, then?"

"No," William replied stiffly, not knowing what a bawbee was, but thinking that it sounded in some way disparaging. "Mr. Murray brought it to me, from a—friend."

"A friend." The old man was frankly studying his face, in a way that made William uncomfortable and therefore angry. "What is your name, young man?"

"None of your business, sir," William said, as courteously as possible, and gathered his reins. "Good day to you!"

The old man's face tightened, as did his hand on the staff, and William turned sharply, lest the old bugger mean to try to strike him with it. He didn't, but William noticed, with a small sense of shock, that two fingers of the hand that grasped the staff were missing.

He thought for a moment that the old man might mount and come after him, but when he glanced back, the man was still standing by the road, looking after him.

It made no real difference, but, moved by some obscure notion of avoiding notice, William put the bear's claw inside his shirt, where it hung safely concealed next to his rosary.

43

COUNTDOWN

Fort Ticonderoga
June 18, 1777

Dear Bree and Roger,

Twenty-three days and counting. I hope we'll be able to leave on schedule. Your cousin Ian left the fort a month ago, saying that he had a wee bit of business to take care of but would be back by the time Jamie's militia enlistment was up. Ian himself declined to enlist, being instead a volunteer forager, so he's not technically AWOL. Not that the fort's commander is really in a position to do anything about deserters, save hang them if they're silly enough to come back, and none of them do. I'm not sure what Ian's doing, but I have some hope that it may be good for him.

Speaking of the fort's commander, we have a new one. Great excitement! Colonel Wayne left a few weeks ago—doubtless sweating with relief as much as with the humidity—but we have come up in the world. The new commander is a major general, no less: one Arthur St. Clair, a genial and very handsome Scot, whose attractiveness is considerably enhanced by the pink sash he affects on formal occasions. (The nice thing about belonging to an ad hoc *army is that one apparently gets to design one's own uniform. None of this stuffy old British convention about regimentals.)*

General St. Clair comes with outriders: no fewer than three *lesser generals, one of them French (your father says General Fermoy is rather fishy, militarily speaking), and about three thousand new recruits. This has substantially heartened everyone (though placing an ungodly strain on the latrine facilities. The lines are fifteen deep in the mornings at the pits, and there is a severe shortage of thunder mugs), and St. Clair made a nice speech, assuring us that the fort cannot possibly be taken now. Your father, who was standing next to the general at the time, said something under his breath in Gaelic at this point, but not very far under, and while I understand the general was born in Thurso, he conveniently affected not to understand.*

The bridge-building between the fort and Mount Independence continues apace . . . and Mount Defiance continues to sit there across the water. An inoffensive little hill, to look at—but a good bit higher than the fort. Jamie had Mr. Marsden row across with a target—a four-foot square of wood, painted white—and set it up near the top of the hill, where it was plainly visible from the fort's batteries. He invited General Fermoy (he does not *get a pink sash, despite being French) to come and try his hand at shooting with one of the new rifles (Jamie having thoughtfully abstracted several of these from the cargo of the* Teal *before patriotically donating the rest to the American cause). They blasted the target to bits, an act whose significance was not lost on General St. Clair, who came along to watch. I think General St. Clair will be almost as pleased as I will be when your father's enlistment is up.*

The new influx has made things busier, of course. Most of the new recruits are reasonably healthy, for a wonder, but there are the usual minor accidents, cases of venereal disease, and summer ague—enough that Major Thacher—he's the chief medical officer—has taken to turning a blind eye when I surreptitiously bind up a wound, though he draws the line at allowing me access to sharp instruments. Fortunately, I have a small knife with which to lance boils.

I am also growing very short of useful herbs, since Ian's defection. He used to bring me things from his foraging expeditions, but it really isn't safe to venture out of the fort save in large bodies. Two men who went out hunting a few days ago were found murdered and scalped.

While my medical kit thus remains a little sparse, I have as some compensation acquired a ghoul. This is a Mrs. Raven from New Hampshire, whose husband is a militia officer. She's relatively young, in her thirties, but has never had children and thus has a lot of emotional energy to expend. She battens on the sick and dying, though I'm sure she considers herself to be sympathetic in the extreme. She revels in ghastly detail, which, while mildly repulsive in itself, does make her a competent aide, since she can be counted on not to faint while I set a compound fracture or amputate (quickly, before Major Thacher or his henchman, Lieutenant Stactoe, notices) a gangrenous digit, for fear of missing something. Granted, she does wail and carry on a bit, and is much given to clutching her rather flat chest and allowing her eyes to bulge while describing these adventures to other people afterward (she nearly prostrated herself from hyperventilation when they brought in the men who were scalped), but one takes what one can get in the way of help.

At the other end of the scale in terms of medical competence, though, the new influx of recruits has brought with it a young Quaker doctor named Denzell Hunter and his sister, Rachel. I haven't yet spoken to him personally, but from what I see, Dr. Hunter really is a doctor, and seems even to have some vague notion of germ theory, owing to his having trained with John Hunter, one of the great men of medicine (on the chance that Roger will be reading this, I will refrain from telling you the manner in which John Hunter discovered how gonorrhea is transmitted—well, no, actually I won't: he stabbed himself in the penis with a lancet covered in pus from an infected victim and was deeply gratified with the results, according to Denny Hunter, who recounted this interesting incident to your father while bandaging his thumb, which got squashed between two rolling logs—don't worry, it isn't broken; just badly bruised). I'd love to see how Mrs. Raven would take this story, but I suppose propriety would prevent young Dr. Hunter telling her.

You are, of course, minding the children's vaccination schedule.

With all my love,
Mama

BRIANNA HAD CLOSED the book, but her hand kept returning involuntarily to the cover, as though she wished to open it again, in case it might say something different.

"What's twenty-three days past June eighteenth?" She should be able to reckon that—she could do things like that in her head—but nervousness had deprived her of the ability to compute.

"Thirty days hath September," Roger chanted quickly under his breath, rolling up his eyes to the ceiling, "April, June—right, June's got thirty days, so twelve days from the eighteenth to the thirtieth, and ten more makes it the tenth of July."

"Oh, dear Lord."

She'd read it three times, looking again wouldn't make a difference; still, she opened the book once more, to the page with John Burgoyne's portrait. A handsome man—"And doesn't he just know it, too!" she said aloud, making Roger frown at her in consternation—as painted by Sir Joshua Reynolds, he was in uniform, his hand resting on the hilt of his sword, standing against a dramatic backdrop of gathering storm clouds. And there it was on the next page, plain in black and white.

On the sixth of July, General Burgoyne attacked Fort Ticonderoga with a force of some 8,000 regulars, plus several German regiments under the Baron von Riedesel, and a number of Indians.

WILLIAM FOUND General Burgoyne and his army somewhat more easily than the Hunters had discovered General Washington's whereabouts. On the other hand, General Burgoyne was making no attempt to hide.

It was a lavish camp, by army standards. Neatly arranged rows of white canvas tents covered three fields and ran off into the woods. Making his way to the commander's tent to report, he spotted a pile of empty wine bottles near the general's tent that rose nearly to his knee. As he had not heard that the general was a notable souse, he assumed this largesse to be the result of an open-handed hospitality and a liking for company. A good sign in a commander, he thought.

A yawning servant was picking off the remnants of the lead seals, tossing the metal into a can, presumably to be melted for bullets. He gave William a sleepy, inquiring eye.

"I've come to report to General Burgoyne," William said, drawing himself up. The servant's eye traveled slowly up the length of his body, lingering with vague curiosity on his face and making him doubt the thoroughness of his morning shave.

"Dinner party with the brigadier and Colonel St. Leger last night," the servant said at last, and belched slightly. "Come back this afternoon. Meanwhile"—he stood slowly, wincing as though the movement hurt his head, and pointed—"the mess tent's over there."

FRIENDS

Fort Ticonderoga
June 22, 1777

MUCH TO MY surprise, I found Captain Stebbings sitting up.
White-faced, bathed in sweat, and swaying like a pendulum—but
upright. Mr. Dick hovered over him, clucking with the tender
anxiety of a hen with one chick.

"I see you're feeling better, Captain," I said, smiling at him. "Have you on
your feet any day now, won't we?"

"Been . . . on my feet," he wheezed. "Think I might die."

"What?"

"Him be *walking*!" Mr. Dick assured me, torn between pride and dismay.
"On my arm, but him walk, sure!"

I was on my knees, listening to lungs and heart through the wooden
stethoscope Jamie had made for me. A pulse fit for an eight-cylinder race car,
and a good bit of gurgling and wheezing, but nothing horribly alarming.

"Congratulations, Captain Stebbings!" I said, lowering the stethoscope
and smiling at him. He still looked dreadful, but his breathing was beginning
to slow. "You probably won't die today. What brought on this burst of ambi-
tion?"

"My . . . bosun," he managed, before a fit of coughing intervened.

"Joe Ormiston," Mr. Dick clarified, with a nod in my direction. "Him foot
stink. The captain go see him."

"Mr. Ormiston. His foot stinks?" That sounded all sorts of alarm bells. For
a wound in this particular setting to smell so notably as to draw attention was
a very bad indication. I rose to my feet but was detained by Stebbings, who
had taken a firm grip of my skirt.

"You—" he said, laboring for air. "You take care of him."

He bared stained teeth at me in a grin.

" 'S an order," he wheezed. "Ma'am."

"Aye, aye, Cap'n," I said tartly, and made off for the hospital building,
where the majority of the sick and wounded were housed.

"Mrs. Fraser! What's amiss?" The eager cry came from Mrs. Raven, who
was coming out of the commissary as I passed. She was tall and lean, with dark
hair that perpetually straggled out from under her cap, which it was doing at
the moment.

"I don't know yet," I said briefly, not stopping. "But it might be serious."

"Oh!" she said, barely refraining from adding, "Goody!" Tucking her basket under her arm, she fell in beside me, firmly set to Do Good.

Invalid British prisoners were housed alongside the American sick in a long stone building lit by narrow, glassless windows and either freezing or stifling, depending on the weather. It was presently hot and humid outdoors—it was mid-afternoon—and entering the building was like being struck in the face with a hot, wet towel. A *dirty* hot, wet towel.

It wasn't hard to find Mr. Ormiston; there was a knot of men standing round his cot. Lieutentant Stactoe was among them—that was bad—arguing with little Dr. Hunter—that was good—with a couple of other surgeons trying to put in their own opinions.

I knew without looking what they were arguing about; clearly Mr. Ormiston's foot had taken a turn for the worse, and they intended to amputate it. In all probability, they were right. The argument would likely be about *where* to amputate, or who was to do it.

Mrs. Raven hung back, nervous at sight of the surgeons.

"Do you really think . . ." she began, but I paid her no attention. There are times for thinking, but this wasn't one of them. Only action, and fast, decisive action at that, would serve. I took in a lungful of the thick air and stepped forward.

"Good afternoon, Dr. Hunter," I said, elbowing my way between the two militia surgeons and smiling at the young Quaker doctor. "Lieutenant Stactoe," I added as an afterthought, not to be overtly rude. I knelt beside the patient's cot, wiped my sweaty hand on my skirt, and took his.

"How are you, Mr. Ormiston? Captain Stebbings has sent me to take care of your foot."

"He *what?*" Lieutenant Stactoe began, in a peeved sort of voice. "Really, Mrs. Fraser, what can you possibly—"

"That's good, ma'am," Mr. Ormiston interrupted. "The captain said as how he'd send you; I was just a-telling these gentlemen here as they needn't be concerned, as I was sure *you'd* know the best way to do it."

And I'm sure they were pleased to hear that, I thought, but smiled at him and squeezed his hand. His pulse was fast and a little light, but regular. His hand, though, was very hot, and I wasn't even faintly surprised to see the reddish streaks of septicemia rising up his leg from the mangled foot.

They had unwrapped the foot, and Mr. Dick had unquestionably been right: him stank.

"Oh, my *God*," said Mrs. Raven behind me, in complete sincerity.

Gangrene had set in; if the smell and tissue crepitation were not enough, the toes had begun to blacken already. I didn't waste time in being angry at Stactoe; given the original condition of the foot, and the treatment available, I might not have been able to save it, either. And the fact that gangrene was so clearly present was actually a help; there couldn't be any question that amputation was necessary. But in that case, I wondered, why were they arguing?

"I take it you agree that amputation is necessary, Mrs. Fraser?" the lieutenant said, with sarcastic courtesy. "As the patient's *physician?*" He had his instruments already laid out on cloth, I saw. Decently kept; not disgustingly filthy—but plainly not sterilized.

"Certainly," I said mildly. "I'm very sorry about it, Mr. Ormiston, but he's right. And you will feel much better with it off. Mrs. Raven, will you go and bring me a pan of boiling water?" I turned to Denzell Hunter, who, I saw, was holding Mr. Ormiston's other hand, plainly counting his pulse.

"Do you not agree, Dr. Hunter?"

"I do, yes," he said mildly. "We are in disagreement regarding the degree of amputation required, not its necessity. What is the boiling water for, Friend . . . Fraser, he said?"

"Claire," I said briefly. "Sterilization of the instruments. To prevent post-operative infection. As much as possible," I added honestly. Stactoe made a very disrespectful noise at this, but I ignored it. "What do you recommend, Dr. Hunter?"

"Denzell," he said, with a fleeting smile. "Friend Stactoe wishes to amputate below the knee—"

"Of course I do!" Stactoe said, furious. "I wish to preserve the knee joint, and there is no need to do it higher!"

"Oddly enough, I'm inclined to agree with you," I told him, but turned back to Denzell Hunter. "But you don't?"

He shook his head and pushed his spectacles up the bridge of his nose.

"We must do a mid-femoral amputation. The man has a popliteal aneurysm. That means—"

"I know what it means." I did, and was already feeling behind Mr. Ormiston's knee. He emitted a high-pitched giggle, stopped abruptly, and went red in the face with embarrassment. I smiled at him.

"Sorry, Mr. Ormiston," I said. "I won't tickle you again."

I wouldn't need to. I could feel the aneurysm plainly; it throbbed gently against my fingers, a big, hard swelling right in the hollow of the joint. He must have had it for some time; a wonder it hadn't burst during the sea battle or the arduous portage to Ticonderoga. In a modern operating room, it might be possible to do the lesser amputation and repair the aneurysm—but not here.

"You're right, Friend Denzell," I said, straightening up. "As soon as Mrs. Raven brings the hot water, we'll—" But the men weren't listening to me. They were staring at something behind me, and I turned to see Guinea Dick, stripped to a breechclout because of the heat and glistening with sweat, *all* his tattoos on display, advancing upon us with a black glass bottle held ceremoniously between his hands.

"Him captain send you grog, Joe," he said to Mr. Ormiston.

"Well, God bless the captain for a good un!" Mr. Ormiston said in heartfelt thanks. He took the bottle of rum, drew the cork with his teeth, and began to swallow with a single-minded determination.

Sloshing and splashing heralded Mrs. Raven's return with the water. Nearly every fire had a kettle on; finding boiling water was no difficulty. She had, bless her, also brought a bucket of cold water so that I could wash my hands without burning myself.

I took one of the short-bladed, brutal amputation knives, preparing to plunge it into the hot water, only to have it snatched from my hand by an outraged Lieutenant Stactoe.

"What are you doing, madam!" he exclaimed. "That is my best blade!"

"Yes, that's why I propose to use it," I said. "*After* I wash it."

Stactoe was a small man with close-cropped, bristly gray hair; he was also two or three inches shorter than I, as I discovered when I stood up and faced him, eyeball to eyeball. His face went a shade or two redder.

"You will ruin the temper of the metal, subjecting it to boiling water!"

"No," I said, keeping my own temper—for the moment. "Hot water will do nothing but clean it. And I will not use a dirty blade on this man."

"Oh, won't you?" Something like satisfaction glimmered in his eyes, and he clutched the blade protectively to his bosom. "Well, then. I suppose you'll have to leave the work to those who can do it, won't you?"

Guinea Dick, who had remained to watch after delivery of the bottle, had been following the progress of the argument with interest and, at this point, leaned over and plucked the knife from Stactoe's hand.

"Him captain says her does for Joe," he said calmly. "Her does."

Stactoe's mouth fell open in outrage at this gross insult to his rank, and he lunged at Dick, grabbing for the blade. Dick, with reflexes honed by tribal warfare and years of British seamanship, swung the blade at Stactoe with the obvious intent of removing his head. He would likely have succeeded, save for Denzell Hunter's equally good reflexes, which sent him leaping for Dick's arm. He missed but succeeded in knocking the big Guineaman into Stactoe. They clutched each other—Dick dropping the knife—and staggered to and fro for an instant before both overbalanced and crashed into Ormiston's cot, sending patient, rum bottle, hot water, Denzell Hunter, and the rest of the instruments sprawling across the stone floor with a clatter that stopped every conversation in the building.

"Oooh!" said Mrs. Raven, deliciously shocked. This was turning out even better than she had expected.

"Denny!" said an equally shocked voice behind me. "What does thee think thee is doing?"

"I am . . . assisting Friend Claire in her surgery," Denzell said with some dignity, sitting up and patting round the floor in search of his spectacles.

Rachel Hunter bent and picked up the errant spectacles, which had slid across the stones, and restored these firmly to her brother's face, while keeping a wary eye on Lieutenant Stactoe, who was slowly rising from the floor, much in the manner of a hot-air balloon, visibly swelling with rage.

"You," he said in a hoarse voice, and pointed a small, trembling finger at Dick. "I shall have you hanged for assaulting an officer. I shall have *you*, sir"—swinging the accusatory digit toward Denzell Hunter—"court-martialed and broke! As for you, *madam*—" He spat the word, but then stopped dead, momentarily unable to think of anything sufficiently terrible with which to threaten me. Then, "I shall ask your husband to beat you!" he said.

"Come 'n' tickle me, darlin'," a slurred voice said from the floor. I looked down, to see a leering Mr. Ormiston. He had kept hold of the rum bottle during the wreck, continued to employ it afterward, and, face suffused with rum, was now making random pawing motions in the vicinity of my knee.

Lieutenant Stactoe made a noise indicating that this was the frozen limit, if not well beyond, and, hastily bundling up his fallen instruments, he marched off, bristling with knives and saws, dropping occasional small objects in his wake.

"Did thee want me, Sissy?" Denzell Hunter had got to his feet by this time and was righting the fallen cot.

"Not so much me as Mrs. Brown," his sister said, a dry note in her voice. "She says it is her time, and she wants thee. Right. Now."

He snorted briefly, and glanced at me.

"Mrs. Brown is an hysteric, in the literal meaning of the term," he said apologetically. "I think she cannot deliver for another month yet, but she suffers false labor on a regular basis."

"I know her," I said, suppressing a smile. "Better you than me, mate." Mrs. Brown *was* an hysteric. Also the wife of a colonel of militia and therefore—she thought—well above the services of a mere midwife. Hearing that Dr. Denzell Hunter had worked with Dr. John Hunter, who was *accoucheur* to the *Queen!*—obviously, my services could be dispensed with.

"She is not bleeding, nor her water broke?" Denzell was asking his sister in a resigned voice. Guinea Dick, totally unperturbed by the recent conflict, had restored the bedding to the cot and now squatted, lifted all fifteen stone of Mr. Ormiston as if he were a feather bed, and deposited him and his bottle gently thereon.

"I think him ready," he announced, after scrutinizing the patient, who was now lying back, eyes closed, happily murmuring, "Just a little lower, dear, aye, that's it, tha's it . . ."

Denzell looked helplessly from Mr. Ormiston to his sister to me.

"I will have to go to Mrs. Brown, though I think it not pressingly urgent. Can thee wait a little while and I will do this for thee?"

"Her does it," said Dick, glowering.

"Yes, her does," I assured him, tying back my hair. "But what her is going to do it *with* is another question. Have you any instruments that I might borrow, Dr.—er, Friend Denzell?"

He rubbed his forehead, thinking.

"I have a decent saw." He smiled briefly. "And I do not mind if thee wishes to boil it. But no heavy blade. Shall I send Rachel to ask one of the other surgeons?"

Rachel's face closed a bit at this suggestion, and I thought that perhaps Dr. Hunter was not all that popular with the other surgeons.

I eyed Mr. Ormiston's very solid leg, estimating the thickness of flesh to be cut, and put a hand through the slit in my skirt to the sheath of my knife. It was a good, sturdy knife, and Jamie had just sharpened it for me. A curved blade would be better, but I thought the length was sufficient . . .

"No, don't trouble. I think this will work. If you would find your brother's saw, Miss—er, Rachel." I smiled at her. "And, Mrs. Raven, I'm afraid the water's gone, would you—"

"Oh, yes!" she cried, and seizing the pan, clattered off, kicking one of Lieutenant Stactoe's oddments on the way.

A number of people had been watching the drama of Mr. Ormiston's foot, fascinated. Now that the lieutenant was gone, they began to sidle nearer, looking fearfully at Guinea Dick, who grinned genially at them.

"Can Mrs. Brown wait a quarter of an hour?" I asked Denzell. "It will be a little easier if I have someone who knows what they're doing to support the leg while I cut. Dick can restrain the patient."

"A quarter of an hour?"

"Well, the actual amputation will take a little less than a minute, if I don't encounter any difficulties. But I'll need a bit of time to prepare, and I could use your help in ligating the severed blood vessels afterward. Where has the rum bottle gone, by the way?"

Denzell's dark brows were almost touching his hairline, but he gestured to Mr. Ormiston, who had gone to sleep and was now snoring loudly, the rum bottle cradled in his arm.

"I don't propose to drink it," I said dryly, answering his expression. I pulled the bottle free and poured a little onto a clean rag, with which I began to swab Mr. Ormiston's hairy thigh. The lieutenant had fortunately left his jar of sutures, and the oddment Mrs. Raven had kicked was a tenaculum. I would need it to seize the ends of severed arteries, which had an annoying tendency to pop back into the flesh and hide, squirting blood all the while.

"Ah," said Denzell, still at a loss but game. "I see. Can I . . . help?"

"If I might borrow your belt for a ligature?"

"Oh, yes," he murmured, and unbuckled it without hesitation, looking interested. "I collect thee has done this before."

"Many times, unfortunately." I bent to check Mr. Ormiston's breathing, which was stertorous but not labored. He'd downed nearly half the bottle within five minutes. That was a dose that would likely kill someone less inured to rum than a British seaman, but his vital signs were reasonably good, fever notwithstanding. Drunkenness was not by any means the equivalent of anesthesia; the patient was stunned, not unconscious, and would certainly come to when I began cutting. It did allay fear, though, and might dull the immediate pain slightly. I wondered whether—and when—I might ever be able to make ether again.

There were two or three small tables in the long room, these heaped with bandages, lint, and other dressing materials. I chose a good supply of relatively clean materials and returned with them to the bedside just as Mrs. Raven—panting and red-faced, anxious lest she had missed anything—arrived, water bucket sloshing. A moment later, Rachel Hunter returned, similarly panting from her hurry, with her brother's saw.

"If you would not mind dousing the saw blade, Friend Denzell?" I said, tying a burlap sack round my waist to serve as an apron. Sweat was running down my back, tickling between my buttocks, and I tied a length of bandaging round my head bandanna-style, to keep the sweat from running into my eyes as I worked. "And scrub the stains there near the handle? Then my knife and that tenaculum, if you don't mind."

Looking bemused, he did, to interested murmurs from the crowd, who had plainly never witnessed such an outlandish proceeding, though Mr. Dick's savage presence was keeping them at a safe distance.

"Does thee suppose the lieutenant would indeed have our friend here hanged?" Denzell whispered to me, with a nod at Dick. "Or could, come to that?"

"I'm sure he'd love to, but I really don't think he can, no. Mr. Dick is an English prisoner. Can he have you court-martialed, do you think?"

"I suppose he might try," Denzell said, seeming not perturbed at the prospect. "I enlisted, after all."

"Did you?" That seemed odd, but he wasn't the only Quaker I'd met on a battlefield, so to speak.

"Oh, yes. I think the army does not have so many surgeons that it can afford to hang one, though. And I doubt that being reduced in rank would much affect my expertise." He smiled cheerfully at me. "Thee has no rank at all, if I am not mistaken, and yet I trust thee will manage."

"God willing," I said, and he nodded gravely.

"God willing," he repeated, and handed me the knife, still hot from the boiling water.

"You might want to stand back a bit," I said to the spectators. "It's going to be messy."

"Oh, dear, oh, dear," said Mrs. Raven, with a tremulous gasp of anticipation. "How perfectly *ghastly!*"

45

THREE ARROWS

Mottville, Pennsylvania
June 10, 1777

GREY SAT UP suddenly, narrowly avoiding cracking his head on the low beam that passed above his bed. His heart was pounding, his neck and temples wet with sweat, and he had no notion for a moment where he was.

"The third arrow," he said aloud, and shook his head, trying to match the words to the extraordinarily vivid dream from which he had so abruptly emerged.

Was it dream, memory, or something partaking of the nature of both? He had been standing in the main salon of *Trois Flèches,* looking at the very fine Stubbs hanging to the right of the baroque mantelpiece. The walls were crowded with pictures—hung above, below, crammed in without regard to subject or merit.

Was that how it had been? He remembered vaguely a sense of oppression at the abundance of ornament, but had the paintings truly crowded in so, portraits leering from above, below, faces in every direction?

In the dream, the Baron Amandine had stood to one side of him, the solid shoulder touching his; they were much of a height. The Baron was speaking of one of the paintings, but Grey could not remember what he was saying— something about the technique employed by the painter, perhaps.

On his other side stood Cecile Beauchamp, the baron's sister, standing equally close, a bare shoulder brushing Grey's. She wore powder in her hair and a perfume of jasmine; the baron, a feral cologne of bergamot and civet. He remembered—for surely dreams had no smell?—the mingling of the thick fragrances with the bitterness of wood ash in the stifling warmth of the room, and the faint feeling of nausea this mingling induced. Someone's hand had cupped one of his buttocks, squeezed it familiarly, and then commenced to stroke it in an insinuating fashion. He didn't know whose hand it was.

That hadn't been part of the dream.

He lay back slowly on his pillow, eyes closed, trying to recapture the images from his sleeping mind. The dream had changed after that to something erotic, someone's mouth on his highly responsive flesh; it was the sensations associated with this, in fact, that wakened him. He didn't know whose mouth it was, either. Dr. Franklin had been somewhere in this dream, as well; Grey recalled the white buttocks, slightly sagging, still firm, as the man walked down a corridor in front of him, long gray hair straggling down a bony back, loose rolls of skin around the waist, talking with complete unconcern about the pictures, which lined the walls of the corridor, as well. It was a vivid recollection, charged with feeling. Surely he hadn't—not with Franklin, even in a dream. But it was something to do with the paintings . . .

He tried to recall some of the paintings but was no longer sure what was real, what emerged from the bourne of dreams. There were landscapes . . . a thing purporting to be an Egyptian scene, though he took leave to doubt that the painter had ever set foot south of the Breton coast. The usual family portraits—

"Yes!" he sat up abruptly and this time *did* smack the crown of his head on the beam, hard enough that he saw stars and emitted a grunt of pain.

"Uncle John?" Dottie's voice came clearly from the other bed, startled, and a rustling of bedclothes from the floor indicated that her maid had likewise wakened. "What's happened?"

"Nothing, nothing. Go back to sleep." He swung his legs out of bed. "Just . . . going to the privy."

"Oh." Flouncings and mutterings from the floor, a sternly rebuking *shush!* from Dottie. He found the chamber door by feel, for the shutters had been put up and the room was black as sin, and made his way downstairs by the dim light from the banked fire in the inn's main room.

The air outside was fresh and cool, scented with something he didn't recognize but that tugged at his memory. It was a relief to let go the struggle with his obstinate dream and submerge himself in this purely sensory remembrance. It brought back long rides in Virginia, muddy roads, fresh leaves, the sense of a horse beneath him, the kick of a gun, the feel of a deer's blood spilling hot over his hand . . . of course, hunting with William.

He felt the immediacy of the wilderness wash over him, that strong, strange sense so peculiar to America: the sense of something waiting among the trees—not inimical, but not welcoming, either. He had loved those few years in Virginia, away from the intrigues of Europe, the constant sociality of London. Valued them mostly, though, for the closeness that had grown between him and his son in those years in the wilderness.

He had not yet seen fireflies on this journey. He glanced into the thick grass as he walked, but it was probably too late; fireflies came out mostly in the early evening. He looked forward to showing them to Dottie. William had been enchanted by his first sight of them when they came to live in Virginia—had caught them in his hand, cupping one gently and exclaiming as it lit the darkened hollow of his palm. Had greeted their return each summer with joy.

Relieved in body and at least superficially soothed in mind, he sat slowly down on the chopping block in the innyard, unwilling to return yet to the frowsy darkness above.

Where was Henry? he wondered. Where did he sleep tonight? Housed in some dungeon? No, the Colonies really had no such thing. Even common houses were remarkably comfortable and airy. Perhaps his nephew was held in a gaol, a barn, some cellar—and yet he had, so far as they knew, survived the winter in spite of what must be a serious wound. He would have had money, though; perhaps he had been able to pay for better housing, perhaps a doctor's care.

God willing, they would find him soon. They were no more than two days' ride from Philadelphia. And he had the letters of introduction Franklin had given him—Franklin again! Damn the man and his air-bathing. Though Grey had joined him in this process once, from curiosity, and found it oddly pleasant, if a little unnerving, to be sitting mother-naked in a room equipped with elegant furniture, potted plants in the corners, paintings on the—

No. No, there were no paintings in the solar at *Trois Flèches*, of course not.

There it was. The tail of his elusive dream, twitching tantalizingly at him from under a rock. He closed his eyes, filled his lungs with the scent of the summer night, and purposely forced his mind to go blank.

Trois Flèches. Three arrows. Who is the third? The words of Hal's letter appeared on the inside of his eyelids, sufficiently startling that he opened his eyes. Used as he was to Hal's oblique thought processes, he hadn't made much of this at the time. Evidently it had taken root in his mind, though, only to emerge in the middle of the night in the middle of nowhere, out of the depths of an absurd dream. Why?

He rubbed gently at the crown of his head, which was sore from his collision with the beam, but not broken. His fingers unconsciously moved down, fingering the spot where Jamie Fraser's wife had covered the trephine hole in his skull with a silver sixpence hammered flat. She had stitched the skin over it quite cleverly and the hair had grown again, but it was easy to feel the small hard curve under it. He seldom noticed or thought of it save in cold weather, when the metal grew markedly cold and sometimes caused headache and made his nose run.

It had been cold, very cold, when he visited *Trois Flèches*. The thought floated through his head like a moth.

There were sounds behind the inn. The clop of hooves on packed dirt, the murmur of voices. He sat very still.

The moon was halfway down; it was late, but hours yet 'til dawn. No one should have business at this hour, save it was a dark business. The sort of business he had no desire to witness—let alone to be seen witnessing.

They were coming, though; he couldn't move without being seen, and instead stilled even his breathing to the barest wisp of air.

Three men, quiet, purposeful, on horseback, one leading a laden mule. They passed no more than two paces from him, but he didn't move, and the horses, if they sensed him, found him no threat. They turned onto the road that led to Philadelphia. Why this secrecy? he wondered—but didn't waste time in much wondering. He had noticed it at once upon his return to North Carolina the year before: a morbid excitement, an uneasiness in the air itself. It was more pronounced here; he had been aware of it since they had landed.

People were wary in a way that they hadn't been. *They don't know who to trust,* he thought. *And so they trust no one.*

The thought of trust conjured an immediate and vivid recollection of Percy Wainwright. *If there is anyone in the world I trust less . . .*

And just like that, he had it. The picture of Percy, dark-eyed and smiling, thumb running over the surface of his wineglass as though he stroked Grey's prick, saying casually, "*I married one of the sisters of the Baron Amandine . . .*"

"*One* of the sisters," Grey whispered aloud, and the dream crystallized in his mind, the sense of cold from the stones of *Trois Flèches* so vivid that he shivered, though the night was not cold at all. Felt the warmth of those two lascivious, vicious bodies pressing on him from either side. And on the wall to one side, disregarded among the careless profusion, a small painting of three children, two girls, one boy, posed with a dog, and the outer wall of *Trois Flèches* recognizable behind them.

The second sister. The third arrow, whom Hal, with his unerring sense of oddity, had never seen but had noticed nonetheless.

The Beauchamps were a noble, ancient family—and like most such families, they referred often, if casually, to themselves. He had heard during his visit of the doings of cousins, uncles, aunts, distant connections . . . but never of the second sister.

She might have died in childhood, of course; such things were common. But in that case, why would Percy have said . . . ?

Now his head *was* beginning to ache. With a sigh, he rose and went inside. He had no notion where or when—but he was going to have to speak to Percy again. He was appalled to find that the prospect did not alarm him.

46

LEY LINES

BRIANNA PAUSED BY the fish-viewing chamber. It wasn't yet the breeding season, when—she'd been told—the great salmon swarmed through the chutes of the fish ladder that allowed them to climb the dam at Pitlochry, but now and then a silvery flash shot into view with heart-stopping suddenness, fighting strongly against the current for a moment before shooting up into the tube that led to the next stage of the ladder. The chamber itself was a small white housing let into the side of the fish ladder, with an algae-clouded window. She'd paused there to gather her thoughts—or, rather, to suppress some of them—before going in to the dam.

It was nonsense to worry about something that had already happened. And she did know that her parents were all right. Or at least, she amended, had made it out of Fort Ticonderoga; there were a good many letters left.

And she could at any moment *read* those letters, too, and find out. That was what made it so ridiculous. She supposed she wasn't really *worried*. Just . . . preoccupied. The letters were wonderful. But at the same time, she was only too aware of how much even the most complete letter must leave out. And according to Roger's book, General Burgoyne had left Canada in early June, his plan being to march south and join General Howe's troops, cutting the Colonies essentially in half. And on July 6, 1777, he had paused to attack Fort Ticonderoga. What—

"*Coimhead air sin!*" said a voice behind her. She jerked round, startled, to find Rob Cameron standing there, gesturing excitedly at the fish-viewing window. She turned back just in time to see a tremendous silver fish, spotted dark over the back, give a great heave against the current before disappearing up the chute.

"*Nach e sin an rud as brèagha a chunnaic thu riamh?*" he said, the wonder of it still showing on his face. Is that not the most beautiful thing you've ever seen?

"*Cha mhór!*" she replied, wary, but unable not to smile in return. Almost.

His own smile remained but became more personal as he focused on her. "Ah, ye do have the *Gàidhlig*! My cousin said, but I didna quite believe it— you with your prah-pah Bah-ston accent," he said, drawling the syllables in what he plainly thought *was* a Boston accent.

"Yeah, pahk yah cah in Hah-vahd Yahd," she said, in a real—but exaggerated—one. He burst out laughing.

"How d'ye do that? Ye don't speak *Gàidhlig* with that sort of accent. I mean—ye've got one, but it's . . . different. More like ye'd hear on the Isles— Barra, maybe, or Uist."

"My da was Scots," she said. "I got it from him."

That made him look at her afresh, as though she were a novel sort of fish he'd just pulled up on his hook.

"Yeah? From around here? What's his name?"

"James Fraser," she replied. Safe enough; there were dozens. "And was. He's . . . gone."

"Ach, too bad," he said sympathetically, and briefly touched her arm. "Lost my dad last year. Tough, eh?"

"Yes," she said briefly, and made to go past him. He turned at once and fell into step beside her.

"Ye've got wee ones, too, Roger said?" He felt her start of surprise, and smiled sideways at her. "Met him in lodge. Nice guy."

"Yes, he is," she said, guarded. Clearly Roger had talked with Rob long enough for Rob to know that Roger was her husband and that they had children. Rob didn't pursue the reference any further, though, instead stretching and throwing back his head.

"Gahhh . . . too nice a day to spend in a dam. Wish I could be on the water." He nodded toward the tumbling river, where half a dozen be-wadered anglers stood among the waves with the predatory intentness of herons. "You or Roger fly-fish at all?"

"I have," she said, and felt the memory of a casting rod whipping in her hands, sending a small thrill up the nerve endings. "You fish, then?"

"Aye, I've got a permission for Rothiemurchus." He looked proud, as though this was something special, so she made approving noises. He glanced sideways at her, caramel-eyed and smiling. "If ever ye want to come out with your rod, just say the word. Boss." He grinned suddenly at her, careless and charming, and went ahead of her into the dam office, whistling.

A ley line is an observed alignment between two geographical features of interest, usually an ancient monument or megalith. There are a number of theories about ley lines and considerable controversy as to whether they actually exist as a phenomenon, and not only as an artifact.

By that I mean that if you choose any two points that have interest for humans, there's very likely to be a path that leads between them, no matter what those points are. There is a major roadway between London and Edinburgh, for instance, because people frequently want to go from one to the other, but this is not normally called a ley line. What people usually have in mind when using this term is an ancient pathway that leads, say, from a standing stone to an ancient abbey, which is itself likely built on a spot of much older worship.

Since there isn't much objective evidence beyond the obvious existence of such lines, there's a lot of guff talked about them. Some people think the lines have a magical or mystical significance. I don't see any grounds for this myself, and neither does your mother, who is a scientist. On the other hand, science changes its mind now and then, and what looks like magic may really have a scientific explanation (NB—put in footnote about Claire and the plant-harvesting).

However, among the theories regarding ley lines, there is one that appears to have at least a possible physical basis. Perhaps you will already know what dowsers are, by the time you come to read this; I will take you out with one as soon as the opportunity occurs. Just in case, though—a dowser is a person who can detect the presence of water or sometimes bodies of metal underground, like the ore in mines. Some of them use a Y-forked stick, a metal rod, or some other object with which to "divine" the water; some merely sense it. The actual basis of this skill is not known; your mother says that Occam's razor would say that such people just recognize the type of geology that is most likely to harbor underground water. I've seen dowsers work, though, and am pretty sure there is more to it than that— especially in view of the theories I'm telling you here.

One theory of how dowsing works is that the water or metal has a magnetic current, to which the dowser is sensitive. Your mother says that the first part of this is true and that, furthermore, there are large bands of geomagnetic force in the earth's crust, which run in opposing directions all round the globe. Further, she tells me that these bands are detectible by objective measures but are not necessarily permanent; indeed, the earth undergoes occasional (every umpty-million years, I think; she didn't know the exact frequency) reversals of its geomagnetic force—nobody knows why, but the usual suspect is sunspots—with the poles exchanging places.

Another interesting bit of information is that homing pigeons (and quite possibly other sorts of birds) demonstrably do sense these geomagnetic lines, and use them to navigate by, though no one yet has figured out quite how they do it.

What we suspect—your mother and I—and I must emphasize that we may easily be wrong in this supposition—is that ley lines do exist, that they are (or correlate with) lines of geomagnetic force, and that where they cross or converge you get a spot where this magnetic force is . . . different, for lack of a better word. We think these convergences—or some of them— may be the places where it is possible for people who are sensitive to such forces (like pigeons, I suppose) to go from one time to another (that would be your mother and me, and you, Jem, and Mandy). If the person reading this is a child (or grandchildren) not yet born, then I don't know whether you will have this sensitivity, ability, what-you-may-call-it, but I assure you that it is real. Your grandmother speculated that it is a genetic trait, much like the ability to roll one's tongue; if you haven't got it, the "how" of it is simply incomprehensible, even though you can observe it in someone who does have the trait. If that's the case for you, I don't know whether to apologize or congratulate you, though I suppose it's no worse than the other things parents give their children, all unknowing, like crooked teeth or shortsightedness. We didn't do it on purpose, either way, please believe that.

Sorry, I've got off the track here. The basic point is that the ability to

time-travel may be dependent on a genetic sensitivity to these . . .
convergences? vortices? . . . of ley lines.

Owing to the peculiar geological history of the British Isles, you find a
lot of ley lines here and, likewise, a great number of archaeological sites
that seem to be linked by those lines. Your mother and I intend to note, so
far as can be done without danger—and make no mistake about this; it is
very dangerous—the occurrence of such sites as might be portals.
Obviously, there's no way of knowing for sure whether a specific site is a
portal or not.*

The observation that sites seem to be "open" on the dates that correspond
to the sun feasts and fire feasts of the ancient world (or at least more open
than at other times) may—if this hypothesis is right—have something to do
with the gravitational pull of the sun and moon. This seems reasonable,
given that those bodies really do affect the behavior of the earth with respect
to tides, weather, and the like—why not time vortices, too, after all?

*Footnote: Your mother says—well, she said quite a bit, in which I picked
out the words "Unified Field Theory," which I gather is something that
doesn't yet exist, but if it did, it would explain a hell of a lot of things, and
among these might be an answer to why a convergence of geomagnetic lines
might affect time in the spot where the convergence occurs. All I personally
got from this explanation is the notion that space and time are
occasionally the same thing, and gravity is somehow involved. This makes
as much sense to me as anything else regarding this phenomenon.

Footnote 2:

"Does that make sense?" Roger asked. "So far, at least?"

"Insofar as anything about it makes sense, yes." Despite the uneasiness that
came over her whenever they discussed it, she couldn't help smiling at him;
he looked so earnest. There was a blotch of ink on his cheek, and his black
hair was ruffled up on one side.

"Professoring must be in the blood," she said, pulling a tissue out of her
pocket, licking it in mother-cat fashion, and applying it to his face. "You
know, there's this wonderful modern invention called a ballpoint . . ."

"Hate them," he said, closing his eyes and suffering himself to be tidied.
"Besides, a fountain pen is a great luxury, compared to a quill."

"Well, that's true. Da always looked like an explosion in an ink factory
when he'd been writing letters." Her eyes returned to the page, and she
snorted briefly at the first footnote, making Roger smile.

"Is that a decent explanation?"

"Considering that this is meant for the kids, more than adequate," she assured him, lowering the page. "What goes in Footnote Two?"

"Ah." He leaned back in his chair, hands linked, looking uneasy. "That."

"Yes, that," she said, instantly alerted. "Is there something like an Exhibit
A that's meant to go there?"

"Well, yes," he said reluctantly, and met her eyes. "Geillis Duncan's notebooks. Mrs. Graham's book would be Exhibit B. Your mother's explanation
of planting superstitions is Footnote Four."

Brianna could feel the blood draining from her head and sat down, just in case.

"You're sure that's a good idea?" she asked, tentative. She didn't herself know where Geillis Duncan's notebooks *were*—and didn't want to. The little book that Fiona Graham, Mrs. Graham's granddaughter, had given them was safely tucked away in a safe-deposit box in the Royal Bank of Scotland in Edinburgh.

Roger blew out his breath and shook his head.

"No, I'm not," he said frankly. "But look. We don't know how old the kids will be when they read this. Which reminds me—we need to make some kind of provision about it. Just in case something happens to us before they're old enough to be told . . . everything."

She felt as though a melting ice cube were sliding slowly down her back. He was right, though. They might both be killed in a car crash, like her mother's parents. Or the house might burn—

"Well, no," she said aloud, looking at the window behind Roger, which was set into a stone wall some eighteen inches thick. "I don't suppose *this* house will burn down."

That made him smile.

"No, not too worried about that. But the notebooks—aye, I know what ye mean. And I did think of maybe just going through them myself and sort of straining out the information—she did have quite a bit about which stone circles seemed to be active, and that's useful. Because reading the rest of it is . . ." He waved a hand in search of the right word.

"Creepy," she supplied.

"I was going to say like watching someone go slowly mad in front of you, but 'creepy' will do." He took the pages from her and tapped them together. "It's just an academic tic, I suppose. I don't feel right in suppressing an original source."

She gave a different snort, one indicating what she thought of Geillis Duncan as an original source of anything bar trouble. Still . . .

"I suppose you're right," she said reluctantly. "Maybe you could do a summary, though, and just mention where the notebooks are, in case someone down the line is *really* curious."

"Not a bad thought." He put the papers inside the notebook and rose, closing it as he did so. "I'll go down and get them, then, maybe when school's out. I could take Jem and show him the city; he's old enough to walk the Royal Mile, and he'd love the castle."

"Do *not* take him to the Edinburgh Dungeon!" she said at once, and he broke into a broad grin.

"What, ye don't think wax figures of people being tortured are educational? It's all historical, aye?"

"It would be a lot less horrible if it wasn't," she said, and, turning, caught sight of the wall clock. "Roger! Aren't you supposed to be doing your Gaelic class at the school at two o'clock?"

He glanced at the clock in disbelief, snatched up the pile of books and papers on his desk, and shot out of the room in a flurry of very eloquent Gaelic.

She went out into the hall to see him hastily kiss Mandy and charge for the door. Mandy stood in the open doorway, waving enthusiastically.

"Bye-bye, Daddy!" she cried. "Bwing me ice cweam!"

"If he forgets, we'll go into the village after supper and get some," Brianna promised, bending down to pick her daughter up. She stood there holding Mandy, watching Roger's ancient orange Morris cough, choke, shudder, and start up with a brief belch of blue smoke. She frowned slightly at the sight, thinking she must get him a set of new spark plugs, but waved as he leaned out at the corner of the drive, smiling back at them.

Mandy snuggled close, murmuring one of Roger's more picturesque Gaelic phrases, which she was obviously committing to memory, and Bree bent her head, inhaling the sweet scent of Johnson's baby shampoo and grubby child. No doubt it was the mention of Geillis Duncan that was making her feel still uneasy. The woman was well and truly dead, but after all . . . she was Roger's multiple great-grandmother. And perhaps the ability to travel through stone circles was not the only thing to be passed down through the blood.

Though surely some things were diluted by time. Roger, for instance, had nothing in common with William Buccleigh MacKenzie, Geillis's son by Dougal MacKenzie—and the man responsible for Roger's being hanged.

"Son of a witch," she said, under her breath. "I hope you rot in hell."

"'At's a bad word, Mummy," Mandy said reprovingly.

IT WENT BETTER than he could have hoped. The schoolroom was crowded, with lots of kids, a number of parents, and even a few grandparents crammed in round the walls. He had that moment of light-headedness—not quite panic or stage fright, but a sense of looking into some vast canyon that he couldn't see the bottom of—that he was used to from his days as a performer. He took a deep breath, put down his stack of books and papers, smiled at them, and said, *"Feasgar math!"*

That's all it ever took; the first words spoken—or sung—and it was like taking hold of a live wire. A current sprang up between him and the audience, and the next words seemed to come from nowhere, flowing through him like the crash of water through one of Bree's giant turbines.

After a word or two of introduction, he started with the notion of Gaelic cursing, knowing why most of the kids had come. A few parents' brows shot up, but small, knowing smiles appeared on the faces of the grandparents.

"We haven't got bad words in the *Gàidhlig,* like there are in the English," he said, and grinned at the feisty-looking towhead in the second row, who had to be the wee Glasscock bugger who'd told Jemmy he was going to hell. "Sorry, Jimmy.

"Which is not to say ye can't give a good, strong opinion of someone," he went on, as soon as the laughter subsided. "But *Gàidhlig* cursing is a matter of art, not crudeness." That got a ripple of laughter from the old people, too, and several of the kids' heads turned toward their grandparents, amazed.

"For example, I once heard a farmer whose pig got into the mash tell her that he hoped her intestines would burst through her belly and be eaten by crows."

An impressed "Oo!" from the kids, and he smiled and went on, giving carefully edited versions of some of the more creative things he'd heard his father-in-law say on occasion. No need to add that, lack of bad words notwithstanding, it is indeed possible to call someone a "daughter of a bitch" when wishing to be seriously nasty. If the kids wanted to know what Jem had really said to Miss Glendenning, they'd have to ask him. If they hadn't already.

From there, he went to a more serious—but quick—description of the Gaeltacht, that area of Scotland where Gaelic was traditionally spoken, and told a few anecdotes of learning the Gaelic on herring boats in the Minch as a teenager—including the entire speech given by a particular Captain Taylor when a storm scoured out his favorite lobster hole and made away with all his pots (this piece of eloquence having been addressed, with shaken fist, to the sea, the heavens, the crew, and the lobsters). That one had them rolling again, and a couple of the old buggers in the back were grinning and muttering to one another, they having obviously encountered similar situations.

"But the *Gàidhlig* is a language," he said, when the laughter had died down once more. "And that means its primary use is for communication—people talking to one another. How many of you have ever heard line singing? Waulking songs?"

Murmurs of interest; some had, some hadn't. So he explained what waulking was: "The women all working together, pushing and pulling and kneading the wet wool cloth to make it tight and waterproof—because they didn't have macs or wellies in the auld days, and folk would need to be out of doors day and night, in all kinds of weather, tending their animals or their crofts." His voice was well warmed by now; he thought he could make it through a brief waulking song and, flipping open the folder, sang them the first verse and refrain, then got them to do it, as well. They got four verses, and then he could feel the strain starting to tell and brought it to a close.

"My gran used to sing that one," one of the mothers blurted impulsively, then blushed red as a beet as everyone looked at her.

"Is your gran still alive?" Roger asked, and at her abashed nod, said, "Well, then, have her teach it to you, and you can teach it to your kids. That kind of thing shouldn't be lost, aye?"

A small murmur of half-surprised agreement, and he smiled again and lifted the battered hymnbook he'd brought.

"Right. I mentioned the line singing, too. Ye'll still hear this of a Sunday in kirk out on the Isles. Go to Stornoway, for instance, and ye'll hear it. It's a way of singing the psalms that goes back to when folk hadn't many books—or maybe not so many of the congregation could read. So there'd be a precentor, whose job it was to sing the psalm, one line at a time, and then the congregation would sing it back to him. This book"—and he raised the hymnal—"belonged to my own father, the Reverend Wakefield; some of you might recall him. But originally it belonged to another clergyman, the Reverend Alexander Carmichael. Now he..." And he went on to tell them about the Reverend Carmichael, who had combed the Highlands and the Isles in the nineteenth century, talking with people, urging them to sing him their songs and tell him their ways, collecting "hymns, charms, and incantations" from the oral tradition wherever he could find them, and had published this great work of scholarship in several volumes, called the *Carmina Gadelica*.

He'd brought one volume of the *Gadelica* with him, and while he passed the ancient hymnal round the room, along with a booklet of waulking songs he'd put together, he read them one of the charms of the new moon, the Cud Chewing Charm, the Indigestion Spell, the Poem of the Beetle, and some bits from "The Speech of Birds."

> Columba went out
> An early mild morning;
> He saw a white swan,
> *"Guile, guile,"*
> Down on the strand,
> *"Guile, guile,"*
> With a dirge of death,
> *"Guile, guile."*
>
> A white swan and she wounded, wounded,
> A white swan and she bruised, bruised,
> The white swan of the two visions,
> *"Guile, guile,"*
> The white swan of the two omens,
> *"Guile, guile,"*
> Life and death,
> *"Guile, guile,"*
> *"Guile, guile."*
>
> When thy journey,
> Swan of mourning?
> Said Columba of love,
> *"Guile, guile,"*
> From Erin my swimming,
> *"Guile, guile,"*
> From the Fiann my wounding,
> *"Guile, guile,"*
> The sharp wound of my death,
> *"Guile, guile,"*
> *"Guile, guile."*
>
> White swan of Erin,
> A friend am I to the needy;
> The eye of Christ be on thy wound,
> *"Guile, guile,"*
> The eye of affection and of mercy,
> *"Guile, guile,"*
> The eye of kindness and of love,
> *"Guile, guile,"*

Making thee whole,
"Guile, guile,"
"Guile, guile."

Swan of Erin,
"Guile, guile,"
No harm shall touch thee,
"Guile, guile,"
Whole be thy wounds,
"Guile, guile."

Lady of the wave,
"Guile, guile,"
Lady of the dirge,
"Guile, guile,"
Lady of the melody,
"Guile, guile."

To Christ the glory,
"Guile, guile,"
To the Son of the Virgin,
"Guile, guile,"
To the great High-King,
"Guile, guile,"
To Him be thy song,
"Guile, guile,"
To Him be thy song,
"Guile, guile,"
"Guile guile!"

His throat hurt almost unbearably from doing the swan calls, from the soft moan of the wounded swan to the triumphant cry of the final words, and his voice cracked with it at the last, but triumphant it was, nonetheless, and the room erupted in applause.

Between soreness and emotion, he couldn't actually speak for a few moments, and instead bowed and smiled and bowed again, mutely handing the stack of books and folders to Jimmy Glasscock to be passed round, while the audience swarmed up to congratulate him.

"Man, that was *great*!" said a half-familiar voice, and he looked up to find that it was Rob Cameron wringing his hand, shining-eyed with enthusiasm. Roger's surprise must have shown on his face, for Rob bobbed his head toward the little boy at his side: Bobby Hurragh, whom Roger knew well from the choir. A heartbreakingly pure soprano, and a wee fiend if not carefully watched.

"I brought wee Bobby," Rob said, keeping—Roger noticed—a tight grip on the kid's hand. "My sister's had to work today and couldn't get off. She's a widow," he added, by way of explanation, both of the mother's absence and his own stepping in.

"Thanks," Roger managed to croak, but Cameron just wrung his hand again, and then gave way to the next well-wisher.

Among the mob was a middle-aged woman whom he didn't know but who recognized him.

"My husband and I saw you sing once, at the Inverness Games," she said, in an educated accent, "though you went by your late father's name then, did you not?"

"I did," he said, in the bullfrog croak that was as far as his voice was prepared to go just now. "Your—you have—a grandchild?" He waved vaguely at the buzzing swarm of kids milling round an elderly lady who, pink with pleasure, was explaining the pronunciation of some of the odd-looking Gaelic words in the storybook.

"Yes," the woman said, but wouldn't be distracted from her focus, which was the scar across his throat. "What happened?" she asked sympathetically. "Is it permanent?"

"Accident," he said. " 'Fraid so."

Distress creased the corners of her eyes and she shook her head.

"Oh, *such* a loss," she said. "Your voice was beautiful. I am so sorry."

"Thanks," he said, because it was all he could say, and she let him go then, to receive the praise of people who'd never heard him sing. Before.

Afterward, he thanked Lionel Menzies, who stood by the door to see people out, beaming like the ringmaster of a successful circus.

"It was wonderful," Menzies said, clasping him warmly by the hand. "Even better than I'd hoped. Tell me, would ye think of doing it again?"

"Again?" He laughed, but broke off coughing in the middle. "I barely made it through this one."

"Ach." Menzies waved that off. "A dram'll see your throat right. Come down the pub with me, why don't you?"

Roger was about to refuse, but Menzies's face shone with such pleasure that he changed his mind. The fact that he was wringing with sweat—performing always raised his body temperature by several degrees—and had a thirst fit for the Gobi Desert had nothing to do with it, of course.

"Just the one, then," he said, and smiled.

As they crossed the parking lot, a battered small blue panel truck pulled up and Rob Cameron leaned out of the window, calling to them.

"Like it, did ye, Rob?" Menzies asked, still beaming.

"Loved it," Cameron said, with every evidence of sincerity. "Two things, Rog—I wanted to ask, maybe, if ye'd let me see some of the old songs ye have; Siegfried MacLeod showed me the ones you did for him."

Roger was a little taken aback, but pleased.

"Aye, sure," he said. "Didn't know you were a fan," he joked.

"I love all the old stuff," Cameron said, serious for once. "Really, I'd appreciate it."

"Okay, then. Come on out to the house, maybe, next weekend?"

Rob grinned and saluted briefly.

"Wait—two things, ye said?" Menzies asked.

"Oh, aye." Cameron reached over and picked up something from the seat between Bobby and him. "This was in with the Gaelic bits ye were handing round. It looked as though it was in there by mistake, though, so I took it out. Writing a novel, are ye?"

He handed out the black notebook, "The Hitchhiker's Guide," and Roger's throat clenched as though he'd been garroted. He took the notebook, nodding speechlessly.

"Maybe ye'll let me read it when it's done," Cameron said casually, putting his truck in gear. "I'm a great one for the science fiction."

The truck pulled away, then stopped suddenly and reversed. Roger took a firmer grip on the notebook, but Rob didn't look at it.

"Hey," he said. "Forgot. Brianna said ye've got an old stone fort or some such on your place?"

Roger nodded, clearing his throat.

"I've got a friend, an archaeologist. Would ye mind, maybe, if he was to come and have a look at it sometime?"

"No," Roger croaked, then cleared his throat again and said more firmly, "No, that'd be fine. Thanks."

Rob grinned cheerfully at him and revved the engine.

"Nay bother, mate," he said.

47

HIGH PLACES

ROB'S ARCHAEOLOGIST friend, Michael Callahan, turned out to be a genial bloke in his fifties with thinning sandy hair, sunburned so badly and so often that his face looked like patchwork, dark freckles blotched among patches of raw pink skin. He ferreted about among the collapsed stones of the old church with every sign of interest, asking Roger's permission to dig a trench along the outside of one wall.

Rob, Brianna, and the kids all came up briefly to watch, but archaeological work is not a spectator sport, and when Jem and Mandy got bored, the lot of them went down to the house to make lunch, leaving Roger and Mike to their poking.

"I don't need you," Callahan said, glancing up at Roger after a bit. "If you've things to do."

There were always things to do—it was a farm, after all, if a small one—but Roger shook his head.

"I'm interested," he said. "If I won't be in your way . . . ?"

"Not a bit of it," Callahan said cheerfully. "Come and help me lift this, then."

Callahan whistled through his teeth as he worked, occasionally muttering to himself, but for the most part made no comment on whatever he was look-ing at. Roger was called on now and then to help clear away rubble or hold an unstable stone while Callahan peered underneath it with a small torch, but for the most part Roger sat on the bit of uncollapsed wall, listening to the wind.

It was quiet on the hilltop, in the way that wild places are quiet, with a con-stant sense of unobtrusive movement, and it struck him odd that this should be so. Normally you didn't get that feeling in places where people had lived, and plainly people had been mucking about on this hilltop for a good long time, judging from the depth of Callahan's trench and the small whistles of interest he gave off now and then, like a marmoset.

Brianna brought them up sandwiches and lemonade and sat down beside Roger on the wall to eat.

"Rob gone off, then?" Roger asked, noticing that the truck was gone from the dooryard.

"Just to run some errands, he said. He said it didn't look as though Mike would be finished anytime soon," she said, with a glance at Callahan's trouser seat, this sticking out from a bush as he burrowed happily beneath it.

"Maybe not," Roger said, smiling, and leaning forward, kissed her lightly. She made a low, contented noise in her throat and stepped back, but kept hold of his hand for a moment.

"Rob asked about the old songs you did up for Sig MacLeod," she said, with a sideways glance down toward the house. "Did you tell him he could see them?"

"Oh, aye, I'd forgot that. Sure. If I'm not down when he comes back, you can show him them. The originals are in my bottom file drawer, in a folder la-beled *Cèolas.*"

She nodded and went down, long sneakered feet sure as a deer's on the stony path, and her hair down her back in a tail the color of the same deer's pelt.

As the afternoon wore on, he found himself dropping into a state not far off trance, his mind moving sluggishly and his body not much faster, coming in leisurely fashion to lend a hand where wanted, exchanging the barest of words with Callahan, who seemed similarly bemused. The drifting haze of the morning had thickened, and the cool shadows amid the stones faded with the light. The air was cool with water on his skin, but there was no hint of rain. You could almost feel the stones rising up around you, he thought, coming back to what they once were.

There were comings and goings at the house below: the slam of doors, Brianna hanging out the family wash, the kids and a couple of wee lads from the next farm over who'd come to spend the night with Jem all racing through the kailyard and outbuildings, playing some kind of tag that involved a good deal of noise, their shrieks high and sharp as the cries of fishing os-preys. Once he glanced down and saw the Farm and Household truck, pre-sumably come to deliver the pump for the cream separator, for Roger saw Brianna shepherding the driver into the barn, he unable to see around the large carton in his arms.

After five, a fresh strong breeze came up, and the haze began to dissipate. As though this was a signal waking Callahan from his dream, the archaeologist straightened, stood a moment looking down at something, then nodded.

"Well, it may be an ancient site," he said, climbing out of his trench and groaning as he leaned to and fro, stretching his back. "The structure's not, though. Likely built sometime in the last couple of hundred years, though whoever built it used much older stones in the construction. Probably brought them from somewhere else, though some may be from an earlier structure built on the spot." He smiled at Roger. "Folk are thrifty in the Highlands; last week I saw a barn with an ancient Pictish stone used in the foundation and a floor made with bricks from a demolished public lavatory in Dornoch."

Callahan looked out to the west, shading his eyes, where the haze now hung low over the distant shore.

"High places," he said, matter-of-factly. "They always chose the high places, the old ones. Whether it was a fort or a place of worship, they always went up."

"The old ones?" Roger asked, and felt a brief prickle of the hair on his nape. "Which old ones?"

Callahan laughed, shaking his head.

"Don't know. Picts, maybe—all we know about them is the bits of stonework they left here and there—or the folk who came before them. Sometimes you see a bit of something that you know was made—or at least placed—by men, but can't fit it into a known culture. The megaliths, for instance—the standing stones. Nobody knows who set those up or what for."

"Don't they," Roger murmured. "Can you tell what sort of ancient site this was? For war or worship, I mean?"

Callahan shook his head.

"Not from what's apparent on the surface, no. Maybe if we excavated the underlying site—but to be honest, I don't see anything that would make any-one really want to do that. There are hundreds of sites like this on high places, all through the British Isles and Brittany, too—old Celtic, many of them, Iron Age, lots much older." He picked up the battered saint's head, stroking it with a sort of affection.

"This lady's much more recent; maybe the thirteenth, fourteenth century. Maybe the family's patron saint, handed down over the years." He gave the head a brief, unself-conscious kiss and handed it gently to Roger.

"For what it's worth, though—and this isn't scientific, just what I think myself, having seen more than a few such places—if the modern structure was a chapel, then the ancient site beneath it was likely a place of worship, too. Folk in the Highlands are set in their ways. They may build a new barn every two or three hundred years—but chances are it'll be right where the last one stood."

Roger laughed.

"True enough. Our barn's still the original one—built in the early 1700s, along with the house. But I found the stones of an earlier croft buried when I dug up the stable floor to put in a new drain."

"The 1700s? Well, you'll not be needing a new roof for at least another hundred years, then."

It was nearly six but still full daylight. The haze had vanished in that mys-terious way it sometimes did, and a pale sun had come out. Roger traced a small cross with his thumb on the statue's forehead and set the head gently in the niche that seemed made for it. They'd finished, but neither man made a move to leave just yet. There was a sense of comfort in each other's company, a sharing of the spell of the high place.

Down below, he saw Rob Cameron's battered truck parked in the door-yard and Rob himself sitting on the back stoop, Mandy, Jem, and Jem's friends leaning in on either side of him, evidently absorbed in the pages he held. What the devil was he doing?

"Is that singing I hear?" Callahan, who had been looking off to the north, turned half round, and as he did so, Roger heard it, too. Faint and sweet, no more than a thread of sound, but enough to pick up the tune of "Crimond."

The strength of the stab of jealousy that went through him took his breath, and he felt his throat close as though some strong hand choked him.

Jealousy is cruel as the grave: the coals thereof are coals of fire.

He closed his eyes for an instant, breathing slow and deep, and with a lit-tle effort, dredged up the first bit of that quotation: *Love is strong as death.*

He felt the choking sensation begin to ease and reason return. Of course Rob Cameron could sing; he was in the men's choir. Only make sense that if he saw the rudimentary musical settings Roger had noted for some of the old songs, he'd try to sing them. And kids—especially his kids—were attracted to music.

"Have you known Rob for long, then?" he asked, and was pleased to hear his voice sound normal.

"Oh, Rob?" Callahan considered. "Fifteen years, maybe . . . No, I tell a lie, more like twenty. He came along as a volunteer on a dig I had going on Shapinsay—that's one of the Orkneys—and he wasn't but a lad then, in his late teens, maybe." He gave Roger a mild, shrewd look. "Why?"

Roger shrugged.

"He works with my wife, for the Hydro Board. I don't know him much myself. Only met him recently, in lodge."

"Ah." Callahan watched the scene below for a moment, silent, then said, not looking at Roger, "He was married, to a French girl. Wife divorced him a couple of years ago, took their son back to France. He's not been happy."

"Ah." That explained Rob's attachment to his widowed sister's family, then, and his enjoyment of Jem and Mandy's company. He breathed once more, freely, and the small flame of jealousy flickered out.

As though this brief exchange had put a period to the day, they picked up the leavings from their lunch and Callahan's rucksack and came down the hill, companionable in silence.

"WHAT'S THIS?" There were two wineglasses set on the counter. "Are we celebrating something?"

"We are," Bree said firmly. "The children going to bed, for one thing."

"Oh, bad, were they?" He felt a small twinge of guilt—not very severe—for having spent the afternoon in the high, cool peace of the ruined chapel with Callahan rather than chivvying small mad things out of the kailyard.

"Just really energetic." She cast a suspicious glance toward the door to the hall, through which the muted roar of a television came from the big front parlor. "I *hope* they'll be too worn out to spend the night jumping on the beds. They've had enough pizza to put six grown men into a coma for a week."

He laughed at that—he'd eaten most of a full-sized pepperoni himself and was beginning to feel comfortably stuporous.

"What else?"

"Oh, what else are we celebrating?" She gave him a cat-in-the-cream look. "Well, as for me . . ."

"Yes?" he said, obliging.

"I've passed the provisional employment period; now I'm permanent, and they can't get rid of me, even if I wear perfume to work. And *you*," she added, reaching into the drawer and placing an envelope in front of him, "are formally invited by the school board to do a reprise of your *Gàidhlig* triumph at five different schools next month!"

He felt a moment's shock, then a warm flood of something he couldn't quite identify, and realized with a greater shock that he was blushing.

"Really?"

"You don't think I'd tease you about something like that?" Not waiting for an answer, she poured the wine, purple-rich and aromatic, and handed him a glass. He clinked it ceremoniously against her own.

"Here's tae us. Wha's like us?"

"Damned few," she replied in broad Scots, "and they're all deid."

THERE WAS A certain amount of crashing upstairs after the children were sent to bed, but a brief appearance by Roger in the persona of Heavy Father put a stop to that, and the slumber party simmered down into storytelling and stifled giggles.

"Are they telling dirty jokes?" Bree asked, when he came back down.

"Very likely. Ought I make Mandy come down, do you think?"

She shook her head.

"She's probably asleep already. And if not, the sort of jokes nine-year-old boys tell won't warp her. She isn't old enough to remember the punch lines."

"That's true." Roger took up his refilled glass and sipped, the wine soft on his tongue and dense with the scents of black currant and black tea. "How old was Jem when he finally learned to tell jokes? You remember how he got the form of jokes but didn't really understand the idea of content?"

"What's the difference between a . . . a . . . a button and a sock?" she mimicked, catching Jem's breathless excitement to a T. "A . . . BUFFALO! HAHAHAHAHA!"

Roger burst out laughing.

"Why are you laughing?" she demanded. Her eyes were growing heavy-lidded, and her lips were stained dark.

"Must be the way you tell it," he said, and lifted his glass to her. "Cheers."

"*Slàinte.*"

He closed his eyes, breathing the wine as much as drinking it. He was beginning to have the pleasant illusion that he could feel the heat of his wife's body, though she sat a few feet away. She seemed to emanate warmth, in slow, pulsing waves.

"What do they call it, how you find distant stars?"

"A telescope," she said. "You can't be drunk on half a bottle of wine, good as it is."

"No, that's not what I mean. There's a term for it—heat signature? Does that sound right?"

She closed one eye, considering, then shrugged.

"Maybe. Why?"

"You've got one."

She looked down at herself, squinting.

"Nope. Two. Definitely two."

He *wasn't* quite drunk, and neither was she, but whatever they were was a lot of fun.

"A heat signature," he said, and, reaching out, took hold of her hand. It was markedly warmer than his, and he was positive he could feel the heat of her fingers throb slowly, increasing and diminishing with her pulse. "I could pick you out of a crowd blindfolded; you glow in the dark."

She put aside her glass and slid out of her chair, coming to a stop kneeling between his knees, her body not quite touching his. She *did* glow. If he closed his eyes, he could just about see it through the white shirt she wore.

He tipped up his glass and drained it.

"Great wine. Where did ye get it?"

"I didn't. Rob brought it—a thank-you, he said, for letting him copy the songs."

"Nice guy," he said generously. At the moment, he actually thought so.

Brianna reached for the wine bottle and poured the last of it into Roger's glass. Then she sat back on her heels and looked at him owl-eyed, the empty bottle clutched to her chest.

"Hey. You owe me."

"Big-time," he assured her gravely, making her giggle.

"No," she said, recovering. "You said if I brought my hard hat home, you'd tell me what you were doing with that champagne bottle. All that hooting, I mean."

"Ah." He considered for a moment—there was a distinct possibility she'd hit him with the wine bottle if he told her, but then, a bargain was a bargain, after all—and the vision of her naked save for the hard hat, radiating heat in all directions, was enough to make a man cast caution to the winds.

"I was trying to see if I could get the exact pitch of the sounds ye make when we're making love and you're just about to...er...to...it's something between a growl and a really deep hum."

Her mouth opened slightly, and her eyes slightly more. The tip of her tongue was a dark, dark red.

"I think it's the F below middle C," he concluded hurriedly. She blinked.

"You're kidding."

"I am not." He picked up his half-full glass and tilted it gently, so the rim touched her lip. She closed her eyes and drank, slowly. He smoothed her hair behind her ear, his finger moving slowly down the length of her neck, watching her throat move as she swallowed, moved his fingertip along the strong arch of her collarbone.

"You're getting warmer," she whispered, not opening her eyes. "The second law of thermodynamics."

"What's that?" he said, his voice dropping, too.

"The entropy of an isolated system that is not in equilibrium tends to increase, reaching a maximum at equilibrium."

"Oh, aye?"

"Mmm-hmm. That's why a warm body loses heat to a colder one, until they're the same temperature."

"I knew there had to be a reason why that happened." All sounds from upstairs had ceased, and his voice sounded loud, even though he was whispering.

Her eyes opened suddenly, an inch from his, and her black-currant breath on his cheek was as warm as his skin. The bottle hit the parlor carpet with a soft thud.

"Want to try for E flat?"

48

HENRY

June 14, 1777

H E HAD FORBIDDEN Dottie to accompany him. He wasn't sure what he might find. In the event, though, he was surprised. The address to which he had been directed was in a modest street in Germantown, but the house was commodious and well kept, though not large.

He knocked at the door and was greeted by a pleasant-faced young African woman in neat calico, whose eyes widened at sight of him. He had thought best not to wear his uniform, though there were men in British uniform here and there in the streets—paroled prisoners, perhaps, or soldiers bearing official communications. Instead, he had put on a good suit of bottle-green, with his best waistcoat, this being gold China silk, embroidered with a number of fanciful butterflies. He smiled, and the woman smiled in turn and put a hand over her mouth to hide it.

"May I help you, sir?"

"Is your master at home?"

She laughed. Softly, and with real amusement.

"Bless you, sir, I have no master. The house is mine."

He blinked, disconcerted.

"Perhaps I have been misdirected. I am in search of a British soldier, Captain Viscount Asher—Henry Grey is his name. A British prisoner of war?"

She lowered her hand and stared at him, eyes wide. Then her smile returned, broad enough to show two gold-stuffed teeth at the back.

"Henry! Well, why didn't you say so, sir? Come in, come in!"

And before he could put down his stick, he was whisked inside, up a narrow staircase, and into a neat small bedroom, where he discovered his nephew Henry, sprawled on his back and naked from the waist up, with a small, beaky-looking man in black poking at his belly—this crisscrossed with a number of violent-looking scars.

"I beg your pardon?" He peered over the beaky man's shoulder and waved gingerly. "How do you do, Henry?"

Henry, whose eyes had been fastened on the ceiling in a tense sort of way, glanced at him, away, back, then sat up abruptly, this movement resulting in an exclamation of protest from the little beaky person and a cry of pain from Henry.

"Oh, God, oh, God, oh, God." Henry doubled over, arms clutching his belly and his face clenched in pain. Grey seized him by the shoulders, seeking to ease him back.

"Henry, my dear. Do forgive me. I didn't mean—"

"And who are you, sir?" the beaky man cried angrily, springing to his feet and facing Grey with clenched fists.

"I am his uncle," Grey informed him shortly. "Who are you, sir? A doctor?"

The little man drew himself up with dignity.

"Why, no, sir. I am a dowser. Joseph Hunnicutt, sir, professional dowser."

Henry was still bent double, gasping, but seemed to be getting a little of his breath back. Grey touched his bare back gently. The flesh was warm, a little sweaty, but didn't seem fevered.

"I am sorry, Henry," he said. "Will you survive, do you think?"

Henry, to his credit, managed a breathless grunt of laughter.

"It'll do," he got out. "Just . . . it takes . . . a minute."

The pleasant-faced black woman was hovering at the door, a sharp eye on Grey.

"This man says he's your uncle, Henry. Is that so?"

Henry nodded, panting a little. "Lord John . . . Grey. May I pre . . . sent Mrs. Mercy Wood . . . cock?"

Grey bowed punctiliously, feeling slightly ridiculous.

"Your servant, madam. And yours, Mr. Hunnicutt," he added politely, bowing again.

"Might I ask," he said, straightening up, "*why* there is a dowser poking you in the abdomen, Henry?"

"Why, to find the bit o' metal what's a-troubling the poor young man, o' course," said Mr. Hunnicutt, looking up his long nose—for he was shorter than Grey by several inches.

"I called for him, sir—your lordship, I mean." Mrs. Woodcock had come into the room by this time, and was looking at him with a faint air of apology. "It's only that the surgeons hadn't any luck, and I was so afraid that they'd kill him next time."

Henry had by now managed to unbend. Grey eased him slowly back until he lay against the pillow, pale and sweating.

"I couldn't bear it again," he said, closing his eyes briefly. "I can't."

With Henry's stomach exposed to view and an opportunity to examine it at leisure, Grey could see the puckered scars of two bullet wounds and the longer, clean-edged scars made by a surgeon digging for metal. Three of them. Grey had five such scars himself, crisscrossing the left side of his chest, and he touched his nephew's hand in sympathy.

"Is it truly necessary to remove the ball—or balls?" he asked, looking up at Mrs. Woodcock. "If he has survived so far, perhaps the ball is lodged in a place where—"

But Mrs. Woodcock shook her head decidedly.

"He can't eat," she said bluntly. "He can't swallow a thing but soup, and none so much of that. He wasn't but skin and bones when they brought him to me," she said, gesturing at Henry. "And you can see, he's not that much more now."

He wasn't. Henry took after his mother rather than Hal, being normally ruddy-cheeked and of a rather stocky build. There was no evidence of either trait at the moment; every rib showed plain, his belly was so sunken that the points of his hip bones poked up sharp through the linen sheet, and his face was approximately the same hue as said sheet, bar deep violet circles under the eyes.

"I see," Grey said slowly. He glanced at Mr. Hunnicutt. "Have you managed to locate anything?"

"Well, I have," the dowser said, and, leaning over Henry's body, laid a long, thin finger gently on the young man's belly. "One, at least. T'other, I'm not so sure of, just yet."

"I told you, Mercy, it's no good." Henry's eyes were still closed, but his hand rose a little and Mrs. Woodcock took it, with a naturalness that made Grey blink. "Even if he was sure—I can't do it again. I'd rather die." Weak as he was, he spoke with an absolute conviction, and Grey recognized the family stubbornness.

Mrs. Woodcock's pretty face was creased in a worried frown. She seemed to feel Grey's eyes upon her, for she looked briefly up at him. He didn't change expression, and she lifted her chin a little, meeting his eyes with something not far from fierceness, still holding Henry's hand.

Oh, like that, is it? Grey thought. *Well, well.*

He coughed, and Henry opened his eyes.

"Be that as it may, Henry," he said, "you will oblige me by not dying before I can bring your sister to bid you farewell."

49

RESERVATIONS

July 1, 1777

T HE INDIANS WORRIED him. General Burgoyne found them enchanting. But General Burgoyne wrote plays.

It is not, William wrote slowly in the letter to his father that he was composing, struggling to find form in words for his reservations, *that I think him a fantasist or suspect that he does not appreciate the essential nature of the Indians he deals with. He appreciates it very much. But I remember talking with Mr. Garrick once in London, and his reference to the playwright as a little god who directs the actions of his creations, exerting absolute control upon them. Mrs. Cowley argued with this, saying that it is delusion to assume that the creator controls his creations and that an attempt to exert such control while ignoring the true nature of those creations is doomed to failure.*

He stopped, biting his quill, feeling that he had come close to the heart of the matter but perhaps not quite reached it.

I think General Burgoyne does not quite apprehend the independence of mind and purpose that . . . No, that wasn't quite it. He drew a line through the sentence and dipped his quill for a fresh try. He turned a phrase over in his mind, rejected it, did the same with another, and at last abandoned the search for eloquence in favor of a simple unburdening of his mind. It was late, he'd walked nearly twenty miles in the course of the day, and he was sleepy.

He believes he can use the Indians as a tool, and I think he is wrong. He stared at the sentence for a bit, shook his head at its bluntness, but could think of nothing better and could waste no more time on the effort; the stub of his candle had almost burned out. Comforting himself with the idea that, after all, his father knew Indians—and probably General Burgoyne—much better than he did, he briskly signed, sanded, blotted, and sealed the letter, then fell into his bed and a dreamless sleep.

The sense of uneasiness regarding the Indians remained with him, though. He had no dislike of Indians; in fact, he enjoyed their company, and hunted now and again with some of them, or shared a companionable evening drinking beer and telling stories round their fires.

"The thing is," he said to Balcarres one evening, as they walked back from a particularly bibulous dinner that the general had held for his staff officers, "they don't read the Bible."

"Who don't? Hold up." Major Alexander Lindsay, Sixth Earl of Balcarres, put out a hand to ward off a passing tree and, clutching it one-handed to keep his balance, groped for his flies.

"Indians."

It was dark, but Sandy turned his head and William could just about see one eye shut slowly in the effort to fix the other on him. There had been a great deal of wine with dinner, and a number of ladies present, which added to the conviviality.

Balcarres concentrated on his pissing, then exhaled with relief and closed both eyes.

"No," he said. "They mostly don't." He seemed content to leave the matter there, but it had occurred to William—himself a little less organized in thought than usual—that perhaps he had failed to express himself completely.

"I mean," he said, swaying just a little as a gust of wind boomed down through the trees, "the centurion. You know, he says go and the fellow goeth. You tell an Indian go and maybe he goeth and maybe he damned well goeth not, depending how the prospect strikes him."

Balcarres was now concentrating on the effort of doing up his flies and didn't answer.

"I mean," William amplified, "they don't take orders."

"Oh. No. They don't."

"You give your Indians orders, though?" He'd meant to make it a statement, but it didn't quite come out that way. Balcarres led a regiment of light infantry but also kept a large group of rangers, many of them Indians; he not infrequently dressed like one himself.

"But then, you're a Scot."

Balcarres had succeeded in doing up his flies and now stood in the center of the path, squinting at William.

"You're drunk, Willie." This was said with no tone of accusation; more with the pleased sense of one who has made a useful deduction.

"Yes. But I'll be sober in the morning and you'll *still* be a Scot." This struck them both as hilarious and they staggered some distance together, repeating the jest at intervals and bumping into each other. By simple chance, they stumbled upon William's tent first, and he invited Balcarres to join him in a glass of negus before bed.

"Sett . . . les the stomach," he said, narrowly avoiding falling headfirst into his campaign chest as he groped for cups and bottles. "Makes you sleep better."

Balcarres had succeeded in lighting the candle and sat holding it, blinking owl-eyed in its glow. He sipped the negus William handed to him carefully, eyes closed as though to savor it, then suddenly opened them.

"What's being a Scot have to do with reading the Bible?" he demanded, this remark having evidently returned suddenly to his cognizance. "You calling me a heathen? My grandmother's Scots and she reads the Bible all the time. I've read it myself. Bits of it," he added, and gulped the rest of his glass.

William frowned, trying to remember what on earth . . .

"Oh," he said. "Not the Bible. Indians. Stubborn buggers. Don't goeth. Scots don't goeth either when you tell them, or not all the time. I thought maybe that was why. Why they listen to you," he added as an afterthought. "Your Indians."

Balcarres thought that funny, too, but when he had at length stopped laughing, he shook his head slowly to and fro.

"It's . . . you know a horse?"

"I know a lot of horses. Which one?"

Balcarres spit a small quantity of negus down his chin, but wiped it away.

"A horse," he repeated, drying his hand on his breeches. "You can't make a horse do anything. You see what he's going to do and then you tell him to do that, and he thinks it's your idea, so next time you tell him something, he's more likely to do what you tell him."

"Oh." William considered this carefully. "Yes." They drank for a bit in silence, mulling over this profundity. At last Balcarres looked up from a long contemplation of his glass.

"Who do you think has better tits?" he asked seriously. "Mrs. Lind or the baroness?"

50

EXODUS

Fort Ticonderoga
June 27, 1777

MRS. RAVEN WAS beginning to worry me. I found her waiting outside the barracks at dawn, looking as though she had slept in her clothes, eyes hollow but gleaming with intensity. She clung to me, close on my heels through the day, talking constantly, and her conversation, usually focused at least nominally on the patients we were seeing and the inescapable logistics of daily life in a fort, began to deviate from the narrow confines of the present.

At first, it was no more than an occasional reminiscence of her early married life in Boston; her first husband had been a fisherman, and she had kept two goats whose milk she sold in the streets. I didn't mind hearing about the goats, named Patsy and Petunia; I had known a few memorable goats myself, noticeably a billy goat named Hiram, whose broken leg I had set.

It wasn't that I was uninterested in her randomly dropped remarks about her first husband; they were, if anything, too interesting. The late Mr. Evans appeared to have been a violent drunkard on shore—which was far from unusual—with a penchant for cutting off the ears or noses of people who displeased him, which was a trifle more individualistic.

"He nailed the ears to the lintel of my goat shed," she said, in the tone one might use to describe one's breakfast. "Up high, so the goats couldn't get at them. They shrivel up in the sun, you know, like dried mushrooms."

"Ah," I said. I thought of remarking that smoking a severed ear prevented that little problem, but thought better of it. I didn't know whether Ian was still carrying a lawyer's ear in his sporran, but I was reasonably sure he wouldn't welcome Mrs. Raven's eager interest in it, if so. Both he and Jamie made off when they saw her coming, as though she had the plague.

"They say the Indians cut pieces off their captives," she said, her voice going low, as one imparting a secret. "The fingers first, one joint at a time."

"How very revolting," I said. "Do please go to the dispensary and get me a bag of fresh lint, would you?"

She went off obediently—she always did—but I thought I heard her talking to herself under her breath as she did so. As the days crept on and tension mounted in the fort, I became convinced of it.

Her conversational swings were getting wider—and wilder. Now she ranged from the distant past of her idealized childhood in Maryland to an equally distant future—a rather grisly one, in which we had all been either killed by the British army or captured by Indians, with consequences ranging from rape to dismemberment—these procedures often accomplished simultaneously, though I told her that most men had neither the necessary concentration nor yet the coordination for it. She was still capable of focusing on something directly in front of her, but not for long.

"Could you speak to her husband, do you think?" I asked Jamie, who had just come in at sunset to tell me that he'd seen her trudging in circles round and round the big cistern near the parade ground, counting under her breath.

"D'ye think he hasn't noticed that his wife's going mad?" he replied. "If he hasn't, I think he'll no appreciate being told. And if he has," he added logically, "what d'ye expect him to do about it?"

There was in fact not much anyone could do about it, bar keep an eye on her and try to soothe her more vivid fancies—or at least keep her from talking about them to the more impressionable patients.

As the days went on, though, Mrs. Raven's eccentricities seemed not much more pronounced than the anxieties of most of the fort's inhabitants, particularly the women, who could do nothing but tend their children, wash the laundry—under heavy guard on the lakeshore, or in small mobs round the steaming cauldrons—and wait.

The woods were not safe; a few days before, two picket guards had been found no more than a mile from the fort, murdered and scalped. This grisly discovery had had the worst effect on Mrs. Raven, but I couldn't say that it did much for my own fortitude. I couldn't look out from the batteries with my earlier sense of pleasure in the endless miles of thick green; the very vigor of the forest itself seemed a threat now. I still wanted clean linen, but my skin tingled and crept whenever I left the fort.

"Thirteen days," I said, running a thumb down the doorpost of our sanctum. Jamie had, with no comment, cut a notch for each day of the enlistment period, slashing through each notch when he came to bed at night. "Did you notch the posts when you were in prison?"

"Not in Fort William or the Bastille," he said, considering. "Ardsmuir . . . aye, we did then. There wasna any sentence to keep track of, but . . . ye lose so much, so fast. It seemed important to keep a hold on something, even if it was only the day of the week."

He came to stand beside me, looking at the doorpost and its long line of neat notches.

"I think I might have been tempted to run," he said, very quietly. "If it weren't for Ian being gone."

It wasn't anything I hadn't thought—or been aware of him thinking. It was becoming more obvious by the second that the fort couldn't stand attack by the size of the force that was—indubitably—on its way. Scouts were coming in more frequently with reports on Burgoyne's army, and while they were whisked instantly into the commandant's office and just as hastily trundled out of the fort again, everyone knew within an hour what news they had brought—precious little so far, but that little, alarming. And yet Arthur St. Clair could not bring himself to order the evacuation of the fort.

"A blot on his record," Jamie said, with an evenness that betrayed his anger. "He canna bear to have it said that he lost Ticonderoga."

"But he will lose it," I said. "He must, mustn't he?"

"He will. But if he fights and loses it, that's one thing. To fight and lose it to a superior force is honorable. To abandon it to the enemy without a fight? He canna reconcile himself to it. Though he's no a wicked man," he added thoughtfully. "I'll talk to him again. We all will."

"All" being the militia officers, who could afford to be outspoken. A number of the regular army officers shared the militia's feelings, but discipline prevented most of them from speaking bluntly to St. Clair.

I didn't think Arthur St. Clair was a wicked man, either—nor yet a stupid one. He knew—must know—what the cost of fighting would be. Or the cost of surrender.

"He's waiting for Whitcomb, ken," Jamie said conversationally. "Hoping he'll tell him Burgoyne hasna got any artillery to speak of." The fort could indeed hold out against standard siege tactics; forage and provisions had been coming in from the surrounding countryside in abundance, and Ticonderoga still had some artillery defenses and the small wooden fort on Mount Independence, as well as a substantial garrison decently supplied with muskets and powder. It could not hold out against major artillery placed on Mount Defiance, though. Jamie had been up there, and told me that the entire interior of the fort was visible—and thus subject to enfiladement at the enemy's discretion.

"He can't really think that, surely?"

"No, but until he knows for sure, he hasna got to make up his mind for sure, either. And none of the scouts has yet brought him anything certain."

I sighed and pressed a hand to my bosom, blotting a tickle of sweat.

"I can't sleep in there," I said abruptly. "It's like sleeping in hell."

That took him by surprise and made him laugh.

"All right for you," I said, rather cross. "You get to go sleep under canvas tomorrow." Half the garrison was being moved to tents outside the fort, the better to be out and maneuverable, ready in case of Burgoyne's approach.

The British were coming; how close they were, how many men they had, and how well armed they were was unknown.

Benjamin Whitcomb had gone to find out. Whitcomb was a lanky, pock-marked man in his thirties, one of the men known as the Long Hunters, men who could—and did—spend weeks in the wilderness, living off the land. Such men were not sociable, having no use for civilization, but they were valuable. Whitcomb was the best of St. Clair's scouts; he had taken five men to go and find Burgoyne's main force. I hoped they would return before the enlistment period was up; Jamie wanted to be gone—so did I, badly—but plainly we couldn't go without Ian.

Jamie moved abruptly, turning and going back into our room.

"What do you need?" He was digging in the small blanket chest that contained our few spare clothes and the other oddments we'd picked up since coming to the fort.

"My kilt. If I'm going to make representations to St. Clair, I'd best be formal about it."

I helped him to dress and brushed and plaited his hair for him. He had no proper coat, but he had clean linen, at least, and his dirk, and even in shirtsleeves he looked impressive.

"I haven't seen you in your kilt in weeks," I said, admiring him. "I'm sure you'll make an impression on the general, even without a pink sash."

He smiled and kissed me.

"It'll do no good," he said, "but it wouldna be right not to try."

I walked with him across the parade ground to St. Clair's house. There were thunderheads rising out on the lake, charcoal black against the blazing sky, and I could smell ozone in the air. It seemed a suitable portent.

SOON. EVERYTHING said, *Soon.* The fragmentary reports and rumors that flew like pigeons through the fort, the closeness of the sultry air, the occasional boom of cannon in the distance, fired for practice—we hoped it was only practice—from the distant picket position called the Old French Lines.

Everyone was restless, unable to sleep in the heat unless drunk. I wasn't drunk, and I was restless. Jamie had been gone for more than two hours, and I wanted him. Not because I cared what St. Clair had had to say to the militia. But between heat and exhaustion, we hadn't made love in more than a week, and I was beginning to suspect that time was growing short. If we were obliged either to fight or to flee in the next few days, heaven only knew how long it might be before we had a private moment again.

I had been strolling round the parade ground, keeping an eye on St. Clair's house, and when at last I saw him come out, I made my way toward him, walking slowly to allow him to take leave of the other officers who had come out with him. They stood for a moment close together, the slump of shoulders and angry tilt of heads telling me that the effect of their protests had been exactly what Jamie had predicted.

He walked slowly away, hands behind him, head bent in thought. I came quietly alongside and tucked my hand into the crook of his elbow, and he looked down at me, surprised but smiling.

"Ye're out late, Sassenach. Is aught amiss?"

"Not at all," I said. "It just seemed like a nice evening for a walk in a garden."

"In a garden," he repeated, giving me a sideways glance.

"The commandant's garden, to be exact," I said, and touched the pocket of my apron. "I, um, have the key." There were a number of small gardens inside the fort, most of them practical plots meant for the production of vegetables. The formal garden behind the commandant's quarters had been designed by the French many years before, though, and while it had since been neglected and overrun by the seeds of airborne weeds, it had one rather interesting aspect—a high wall surrounding it, with a gate that locked. I'd thoughtfully abstracted the key earlier in the day from General St. Clair's cook, who had come to me for a throat wash. I would put it back when I called on him the next day to check his sore throat.

"Ah," said Jamie thoughtfully, and turned obligingly back toward the commandant's house.

The gate was round the back, out of view, and we slipped hastily down the alley that led past the garden wall, while the guard outside St. Clair's house was talking to a passerby. I closed the gate quietly behind us, locked it, and pocketed the key, then went to Jamie's arms.

He kissed me slowly, then raised his head, eyeing me.

"I might need a bit of help, mind."

"That can be arranged," I assured him. I laid a hand on his knee, where the kilt had folded up, exposing flesh. I moved a thumb lightly, liking the soft, wiry feel of the hairs on his leg. "Um . . . did you have any particular sort of help in mind?"

I could smell him in spite of his careful washing, the dried sweat of his labor on his skin spiced with dust and wood chips. He'd taste of it, too, sweet and salt and musk.

I slid my hand up his thigh beneath the kilt, feeling him shift and flex, the sudden groove of muscle smooth beneath my fingers. To my surprise, though, he stopped me, grasping my hand through the fabric.

"Thought you wanted help," I said.

"Touch yourself, *a nighean*," he said softly.

That was a trifle disconcerting, particularly given that we were standing in an overgrown garden no more than twenty feet from an alleyway much patronized by militiamen looking for a place to get quietly drunk. Still . . . I leaned back against the wall and obligingly pulled the shift above my knee. I held it there, gently stroking the skin of my inner thigh—which was, in fact, very soft. I drew the other hand up the line of my stays, to the top, where my breasts swelled out against the thin, damp cotton.

His eyes were heavy; he was still half drunk with fatigue but becoming more alert by the moment. He made a small interrogative sound.

"Ever hear the one about sauce for the gander?" I said, twiddling thoughtfully with the string that held the neckline of my shift.

"What?" That had brought him out of the haze; he was starkly awake, bloodshot eyes wide open.

"You heard me."

"Ye want me to . . . to—"

"I do."

"I couldna do that! In front of you?"

"If I can do it in front of *you*, you can certainly return the favor. Of course, if you'd rather I stopped . . ." I let my hand fall—slowly—from the string. Paused, thumb very lightly ticking to and fro, to and fro, over my breast like the hand of a metronome. I could feel my nipple, round and hard as a musket ball; it must be visible through the fabric, even in this light.

He swallowed; I heard it.

I smiled and let my hand fall farther, taking hold of the hem of my skirt. And paused, one eyebrow raised.

As though hypnotized, he reached down and took hold of the hem of his kilt.

"That's a good lad," I murmured, leaning back on one hand. I raised one knee and set my foot on the wall, letting the skirt fall away, baring my thigh. Reached down.

He said something under his breath in Gaelic. I couldn't tell if it was an observation on the imminent prospect before him or whether he was commending his soul to God. In either case, he lifted his kilt.

"What do you mean, you need help?" I asked, eyeing him.

He made a small, urgent noise indicating that I should continue, so I did.

"What are you thinking?" I asked after a moment, fascinated.

"I'm not thinking."

"Yes, you are; I can see it on your face."

"Ye don't want to know." Sweat was beginning to gleam across his cheekbones, and his eyes had gone to slits.

"Oh, yes, I do—oh, wait. If you're thinking about someone other than me, I *don't* want to know."

He opened his eyes at that, and fixed me with a look that ran straight up between my quivering legs. He didn't stop.

"Oh," I said, a little breathless myself. "Well . . . when you can talk again, I *do* want to know, then."

He went on looking at me, with a gaze that now struck me as markedly akin to that of a wolf eyeing a fat sheep. I shifted a little against the wall and waved away a cloud of gnats. He was breathing fast, and I could smell his sweat, musky and acrid.

"You," he said, and I saw his throat move as he swallowed. He crooked the index finger of his free hand at me. "Come here."

"I—"

"Now."

Mesmerized, I slid away from the wall and took two steps toward him. Before I could say or do anything else, there was a flurry of kilt and a large, hot hand was gripping me by the scruff of the neck. Then I was lying on my back in long grass and wild tobacco, Jamie solidly inside me, and the hand was over my mouth—a good thing, I realized dimly, as there were voices coming toward us along the alley on the other side of the garden wall.

"Play wi' fire' and ye may get singed, Sassenach," he whispered in my ear. He had me pinned like a butterfly and, with a solid grip on my wrists, kept me from moving, even though I was jerking and writhing under him, slippery and desperate. Very slowly, he lowered himself so his full weight rested on me.

"Ye want to know what I was thinking, do ye?" he murmured in my ear.

"Mmp!"

"Well, I'll tell ye, *a nighean,* but—" He paused in order to lick my earlobe. *"NNG!"*

The hand tightened warningly over my mouth. The voices were near enough to make out words now: a small party of young militiamen, half drunk and in search of whores. Jamie's teeth closed delicately on my ear, and he began to nibble thoughtfully, his breath warm and tickling. I wriggled madly, but he wasn't budging.

He gave the same thorough treatment to the other ear before the men had moved out of earshot, then kissed the end of my nose, taking his hand off my mouth at last.

"Ah. Now, where was I? Oh, aye—ye wanted to hear what I was thinking of."

"I've changed my mind." I was panting shallowly, as much from the weight on my chest as from desire. Both were considerable.

He made a Scottish noise indicating deep amusement and tightened his grip on my wrists.

"You started it, Sassenach—but I'll finish it." Whereupon he put his lips to my wet ear and told me in a slow whisper *exactly* what he'd been thinking. Not moving an inch while he did so, save to put his hand back over my mouth when I began to call him names.

Every muscle in my body was jumping like a snapped rubber band when he finally moved. In one sudden motion, he raised himself and slid back, then forward hard.

When I could see and hear again, I realized that he was laughing, still balanced above me.

"Put ye out of your misery, did I, Sassenach?"

"You . . ." I croaked. Words failed me, but two could play at this game. He hadn't moved, in part to torture me—but in equal part because he couldn't; not without ending it at once. I flexed my soft, slick muscles once around him, slowly, gently—then did it three times, fast. He made a gratifying noise and lost it, jerking and groaning, the pulse of it exciting an echo in my own flesh. Very slowly, he lowered himself, sighing like a deflated bladder, and lay beside me, breathing slowly, eyes closed.

"*Now* you can sleep," I said, stroking his hair. He smiled without opening his eyes, breathed deep, and his body relaxed, settling into the earth.

"And next time, you bloody Scot," I whispered in his ear, "I'll tell you what *I* was thinking."

"Oh, God," he said, and laughed without making a sound. "D'ye remember the first time I kissed ye, Sassenach?"

I lay there for some time, feeling the bloom of sweat on my skin and the reassuring weight of him curled asleep in the grass beside me, before I finally remembered.

"I said I was a virgin, not a monk. If I find I need help ... I'll ask."

IAN MURRAY WOKE from a deep and dreamless sleep to the sound of a bugle. Rollo, lying close beside him, lurched upright with a startled, deep *WOOF!*, and glared round for the threat, hackles raised.

Ian scrambled up, as well, one hand on his knife, the other on the dog.

"Hush," he said under his breath, and the dog relaxed fractionally, though he kept up a low, rolling growl, just below the range of human hearing—Ian felt it, a constant vibration in the huge body under his hand.

Now he was awake, he heard them easily. A subterranean stirring through the wood, as submerged—but quite as vibrant—as Rollo's growl. A very large body of men, a camp, beginning to wake at no very great distance. How had he managed not to perceive them the night before? He sniffed, but the wind was wrong; he picked up no scent of smoke—though now he *saw* smoke, thin threads of it rising against the pale dawn sky. A lot of campfires. A very big camp.

He had been rolling up his blanket as he listened. There was nothing more to his own camp, and within seconds he had faded into the brush, blanket tied to his back and his rifle in hand, the dog huge and silent at his heel.

51

THE BRITISH ARE COMING

Three Mile Point, New York Colony
July 3, 1777

THE DARK PATCH of sweat between Brigadier Fraser's broad shoulders had the shape of the Isle of Man on the map in the old schoolroom at home. Lieutenant Greenleaf's coat was entirely soaked with sweat, the body almost black, and only the faded sleeves showing red.

William's own coat was less faded—shamefully new and bright, in fact—but likewise clung to his back and shoulders, heavy with the humid exhalations of his body. His shirt was wringing; it had been stiff with salt when he put it on a few hours before, the constant sweating of the previous days' exertion crystallized in the linen, but the stiffness had washed away as the sun rose, borne on a flood of fresh sweat.

Looking up at the hill the brigadier proposed to climb, he had had some hope of coolness at the summit, but the exertion of the climb had canceled out any benefit of altitude. They had left camp just after dawn, the air then so delicious in its freshness that he'd longed to run naked through the woods like an Indian, catch fish from the lake, and eat a dozen of them for his breakfast, fried in cornmeal, fresh and hot.

This was Three Mile Point, so called because it was three miles south of the fort at Ticonderoga. The brigadier, leading the advance force, had staged his troops here and proposed to climb to a height with Lieutenant Greenleaf, an engineer, to survey the terrain before moving further.

William had been assigned to the brigadier a week earlier, to his pleasure. The brigadier was a friendly, sociable commander, but not in the same way as General Burgoyne. Though William would not have cared had the man been a tartar—he would be in the forward lines; that was all that mattered.

He was carrying some of the engineer's equipment, as well as a couple of canteens of water and the brigadier's dispatch box. He helped to set up the surveying tripod and obligingly held measuring rods at intervals, but at length it was done, everything recorded, and the brigadier, having conferred with Greenleaf at some length, sent the engineer back to camp.

The immediate business concluded, the brigadier seemed disinclined to descend at once, instead walking slowly about, appearing to enjoy the slight breeze, and then settling on a rock, uncorking his canteen with a sigh of pleasure.

"Sit, William," he said, motioning William to his own rock. They sat in silence for a bit, listening to the sounds of the forest.

"I know your father," the brigadier said suddenly, then smiled, a charming smile. "Everyone tells you that, I suppose."

"Well, yes, they do," William admitted. "Or if not him, my uncle."

General Fraser laughed. "A considerable burden of family history to be borne," he commiserated. "But I'm sure you bear it nobly."

William didn't know what to say and made a politely indeterminate noise in response. The brigadier laughed again and passed him the canteen. The water was so warm that he barely felt it pass down his throat, but it smelled fresh and he could feel it slake his thirst.

"We were together at the Plains of Abraham. Your father and I, I mean. Did he ever tell you about that night?"

"Not a great deal," William said, wondering if he was doomed to meet every soldier who had fought on that field with James Wolfe.

"We came down the river at night, you know. All of us petrified. Especially me." The brigadier looked out over the lake, shaking his head a little at the memory. "Such a river, the St. Lawrence. General Burgoyne mentioned that you had been in Canada. Did you see it?"

"Not a great deal, sir. I traveled overland for the most part on the way to Quebec, and then came down the Richelieu. My father told me about the St. Lawrence, though," he felt obliged to add. "He said it was a noble river."

"Did he tell you that I nearly broke his hand? He was next to me in the boat, and as I leaned out to call to the French sentry, hoping that my voice would not break, he gripped my hand to steady me. I felt his bones grinding, but under the circumstances didn't really notice until I let go and heard him gasp."

William saw the brigadier's eyes drift to his own hands and the small ripple across his wide brow, not quite puzzlement but the look of someone trying unconsciously to fit memory to present circumstance. His father had long, slender, elegant hands with fine bones. William's fingers were long, but his hands were vulgarly large, broad of palm and brute-knuckled.

"He—Lord John—he is my stepfather," he blurted, then blushed painfully, embarrassed both by the admission and by whatever freak of mind had made him say it.

"Oh? Oh, yes," the brigadier said vaguely. "Yes, of course."

Had the brigadier thought he spoke from pride, pointing out the ancientness of his own bloodline?

The only comfort was that his face—the brigadier's face, too—was so red from exertion that the blush could not show. The brigadier, as though responding to the thought of heat, struggled out of his coat, then unbuttoned his waistcoat and flapped it, nodding to William that he might do likewise—which he did, sighing with relief.

The conversation turned casually to other campaigns: those the brigadier had fought in, those William had (mostly) heard of. He became gradually aware that the brigadier was gauging him, weighing his experience and his manner. He was uncomfortably aware that the former was inglorious; was General Fraser aware of what had happened during the Battle of Long Island? Word did travel fast in the service.

Eventually, there was a pause in the conversation and they sat companionably in their shirtsleeves for a bit, listening to the soughing of the trees overhead. William wished to say something in his own defense but could think of no way to approach the matter gracefully. But if he did not speak, explain what had happened...well, there was no good explanation. He'd been a booby, that was all.

"General Howe speaks well of your intelligence and boldness, William," the brigadier said, as though continuing their earlier conversation, "though he said he thought you had not had opportunity as yet to show your talent for command."

"Ah...no, sir," William replied, sweating.

The brigadier smiled.

"Well, we must be sure to remedy that lack, must we not?" He stood up, groaning slightly as he stretched and shrugged his way back into his coat. "You'll dine with me later. We shall discuss it with Sir Francis."

CONFLAGRATION

WHITCOMB HAD COME back. With several British scalps, according to popular rumor. Having met Benjamin Whitcomb and one or two of the other Long Hunters, I was prepared to believe this. They spoke civilly enough, and they were far from the only men at the fort who dressed in rough leather and ragged homespun or whose skin shrank tight to raw bones. But they were the only men with the eyes of animals.

The next day, Jamie was called to the commandant's house and didn't come back until after dark.

A man was singing by one of the courtyard fires near St. Clair's quarters, and I was sitting on an empty salt-pork barrel listening, when I saw Jamie pass by on the far side of the fire, heading for our barracks. I rose quickly and caught him up.

"Come away," he said softly, and led me toward the commandant's garden. There was no echo of our last encounter in this garden, though I was terribly aware of his body, of the tension in it and the beating of his heart. Bad news, then.

"What's happened?" I asked, my voice low.

"Whitcomb caught a British regular and brought him in. He wouldna say anything, of course—but St. Clair was canny enough to put Andy Tracy in a cell with the man, saying he was accused of being a spy—that Tracy was a spy, I mean."

"That was bright," I said with approval. Lieutenant Andrew Hodges Tracy was an Irishman, bluff and charming, a born liar—and if anyone could winkle information out of someone without the use of force, Tracy would have been my own first choice. "I take it he found out something?"

"He did. We also had in three British deserters—Germans. St. Clair wanted me to talk to them."

Which he had. The information brought by the deserters might be suspect—save that it correlated with the information tricked from the captured British soldier. The solid information for which St. Clair had been waiting for the last three weeks.

General Carleton had remained in Canada with a small force; it was indeed General John Burgoyne, in charge of a large invasion army, who was heading toward the fort. He was reinforced by General von Riedesel, himself in command of seven Brunswick regiments, *plus* a light infantry battalion and four companies of dragoons. And his vanguard was less than four days' march away.

"Not too good," I observed, taking a deep breath.

"It is not," he agreed. "Worse, Burgoyne has Simon Fraser as brigadier under him. He has the forward command."

"A relative of yours?" That was a rhetorical question; no one with that name could possibly be anything else, and I saw the shadow of a smile cross Jamie's face.

"He is," he said dryly. "A second cousin, I think. And a verra bonny fighter."

"Well, he would be, wouldn't he? Is that the last of the bad news?"

He shook his head.

"Nay. The deserters said Burgoyne's army is short of supplies. The dragoons are on foot, because they canna get fresh horses. Though I dinna ken whether they've eaten them or not."

It was a hot, muggy night, but a shiver raised the hairs on my arms. I touched Jamie's wrist and found the hairs there bristling, as well. *He'll dream of Culloden tonight,* I thought abruptly. I dismissed that for the moment, though.

"I should think that would be good news. Why isn't it?"

His wrist turned and his hand took mine, lacing our fingers tight together.

"Because they havena supplies enough to mount a siege. They'll need to overrun us and take us by force. And they verra likely can."

THREE DAYS LATER, the first British lookouts appeared on Mount Defiance.

THE NEXT DAY, anyone could see—and everyone *did* see—the beginnings of an artillery emplacement being built on Mount Defiance. Arthur St. Clair, bowing at last to the inevitable, gave word to begin the evacuation of Fort Ticonderoga.

Most of the garrison was to move to Mount Independence, taking with them all the most valuable supplies and ordnance. Some of the sheep and cattle must be slaughtered, the rest driven off into the woods. Some militia units were to leave through the woods and find the road to Hubbardton, where they would wait as reinforcements. Women, children, and invalids were to be dispatched down the lake by boat, with a light guard. It began in an orderly manner, with word sent out to bring everything that would float up to the lakeshore after dark, men collecting and checking their equipment, and orders sent out for the systematic destruction of everything that could not be carried away.

This was the usual procedure, to deny the enemy any use of supplies. In this instance, the matter was somewhat more pressing: the deserters had said that Burgoyne's army was running short of supplies already; denying him the facilities of Ticonderoga might bring him to a halt—or at least slow him down perceptibly, as his men would be obliged to forage and live off the country while they waited for supplies from Canada to follow him.

All of this—the packing, the loading, the slaughtering and livestock-driving, the destruction—must be accomplished clandestinely, under the very noses of the British. For if they saw that a retreat was imminent, they would fall on us like wolves, destroying the garrison as they left the safety of the fort.

Tremendous thunderheads boiled up over the lake in the afternoons, towering black things that rose miles high and full of lightning. Sometimes they broke after nightfall, pounding the lake, the mounts, the picket lines, and the fort with water that fell as though dumped from a bottomless bucket. Sometimes they only drifted past, grumbling and ominous.

Tonight the clouds were low and fierce, veined with lightning and blanketing the sky. Heat lightning throbbed through their bodies and crackled between them in bursts of sudden, silent conversation. And now and then a sudden fork shot blue-white and vivid to the ground with a crack of thunder that made everyone jump.

There was very little to pack. Just as well, as there was very little time in which to pack it. I could hear the flurry all through the barracks as I worked: people calling out in search of lost objects, mothers bellowing for lost children, and the shuffle and thunder of feet, steady as echoing rain in the wooden stairwells.

Outside, I could hear the agitated baaing of a number of sheep, disturbed at being turned out of their pens, and a sudden racket of shouting and mooing, as a panicked cow made a break for it. Not surprising; there was a strong smell of fresh blood in the air, from the slaughtering.

I had seen the garrison on parade, of course; I knew how many men there were. But to see three or four thousand people pushing and shoving, trying to accomplish unaccustomed tasks in a tearing hurry, was like watching a kicked-over anthill. I made my own way through the seething mass, clutching a flour sack with spare clothes, my few medical supplies, and a large chunk of ham I had acquired from a grateful patient, wrapped in my extra petticoat.

I would evacuate with the boat brigade, minding a group of invalids—but I didn't mean to go without seeing Jamie.

My heart had been in my mouth for so long that I could barely speak. Not for the first time, I thought how convenient it was to have married a very tall man. It was always easy to pick Jamie out of a crowd, and I saw him within moments, standing on one of the demilune batteries. Some of his militiamen were with him, all looking downward. I assumed that the boat brigade must be forming below; that was heartening.

The prospect, once I reached the edge of the battery and could see, was considerably less heartening. The lakeshore below the fort looked like the return of a particularly disastrous fishing fleet. There *were* boats. All kinds of boats, from canoes and rowboats to dories and crude rafts. Some were dragged up onto the shore, others were evidently floating away, unmanned—

I caught sight during a brief lightning flash of a few heads bobbing in the water as men and boys swam after them to fetch them back. There were few lights on the shore, for fear of giving away the plan of retreat, but here and there a torch burned, showing arguments and fistfights, and beyond the reach of torchlight, the ground seemed to heave and ripple in the dark, like a swarming carcass.

Jamie was shaking hands with Mr. Anderson, one of the *Teal*'s original hands, who had become his *de facto* corporal.

"Go with God," he said. Mr. Anderson nodded and turned away, leading the small knot of militiamen. They passed me as I came up, and one or two nodded to me, their faces invisible in the shadow of their hats.

"Where are they going?" I asked Jamie.

"Toward Hubbardton," he replied, his eyes still on the lakeshore below. "I told them it was their own choice, but I thought best they went sooner rather than later." He lifted his chin toward the humped black shape of Mount Defiance, where the sparks of campfires glowed near the summit. "If they dinna ken what's happening, it's gross incompetence. Were I Simon Fraser, I should be on the march before first light."

"You don't mean to go with your men?" A spark of hope sprang up in my heart.

There was little light on the battery, only the reflected glow from the torches on the stairs and the bigger fires inside the fort. This was enough for me to see his face clearly, though, when he turned to look at me. It was somber, but there was an eagerness in the set of his mouth, and I recognized the look of a soldier ready to surge into action.

"No," he said. "I mean to go with you." He smiled suddenly, and I gripped his hand. "Ye dinna think I mean to leave ye to wander in the wilderness with a parcel o' diseased half-wits? Even if it does mean getting into a boat," he added with a touch of distaste.

I laughed despite myself.

"Not very kind," I said. "But not inaccurate, either, if you mean Mrs. Raven. You haven't seen her anywhere, have you?"

He shook his head. The wind had pulled half his hair loose from its thong, and he removed this now and placed it between his teeth, gathering up his hair in a heavy tail to rebind it.

Someone down the battery said something, sounding startled, and both Jamie and I jerked round to look. Mount Independence was on fire.

"FIRE! FIRE!"

The screams brought people—already flustered and upset—rushing out of the barracks like coveys of flushed quail. The fire was just beneath the summit of Mount Independence, where General Fermoy had established an outpost with his men. A tongue of flame soared upward, steady as a candle taking breath. Then a gust of wind flattened it, and the flame squatted for a moment, as though someone had turned down the gas on a stove, before bursting out again in a much wider conflagration that lit up the mount, showing the tiny black shapes of what looked like hundreds of people in the act of striking tents and loading baggage, all silhouetted against the fire.

"It's Fermoy's quarters on fire," a soldier said beside me, disbelieving. "Isn't it?"

"It is," said Jamie on my other side, sounding grim. "And if we can see the retreat starting from here, Burgoyne's lookouts must surely see it, too."

And as simply as that, the rout began.

Had I ever doubted the existence of something like telepathy, this would have been enough to quell any reservations. The soldiers were already at breaking point from St. Clair's delay and the constant drum of rumors beating on stretched nerves. As the fire on Mount Independence spread, the conviction that the redcoats and the Indians would be upon us at once spread from mind to mind without the necessity for speech. Panic was loose, spreading its broad black wings over the fort, and the confusion at the water's edge was disintegrating into chaos before our eyes.

"Come, then," Jamie said. And before I knew it, I was being hustled down the narrow steps of the battery. A few wooden huts had been set on fire— these on purpose, to deprive the invaders of useful matériel—and the light from the flames lit up a scene from hell. Women dragging half-dressed children, screaming and trailing bedclothes, men throwing furniture from windows. A thunder mug crashed on the stones, sending shards of sharp pottery slicing across the legs of the people nearby.

A voice came breathless behind me. "A golden guinea says the silly French bugger set the house on fire himself."

"I'll gie ye nay odds on that one," Jamie replied briefly. "I only hope he went up with it."

A tremendous flash of lightning lit up the fort like day and screams rose from every part of it, only to be drowned almost instantly by the explosion of thunder. Predictably, half the people thought the wrath of God was about to be visited upon us—this, in spite of the fact that we had been having thunderstorms of similar ferocity for days, I thought crossly—while those of secular mind were still more panicked because the militia units on the outer lines were being lit up as they withdrew, in full sight of the British on Mount Defiance. Either way, it didn't help matters.

"I have to fetch my invalids!" I shouted into Jamie's ear. "You go and get the things from the barracks."

He shook his head. His flying loose hair was lit up by another lightning flash, and he looked like one of the principal demons himself.

"I'm no leaving you," he said, taking a firm clasp of my arm. "I might never find ye again."

"But—" My objection died as I looked. He was right. There were thousands of people running, pushing, or simply standing in place, too stunned to think what to do. If we were separated, he might *not* find me, and the thought of being alone in the woods below the fort—these infested with bloodthirsty Indians as well as redcoats—was not something I wanted to contemplate for more than ten seconds.

"Right," I said. "Come on, then."

The scene inside the hospital barracks was less frantic only because most of the patients were less capable of movement. They were, if anything, more agitated than the people outside, as they'd gleaned only the most fragmentary intelligence from people rushing in and out. Those with families were being dragged bodily from the building with barely enough time to seize their clothes; those without were in the spaces between cots, hopping on one foot to get into their breeches or staggering toward the door.

Captain Stebbings, of course, was not doing any of these things. He lay placidly on his cot, hands folded on his chest, observing the chaos with interest, a rush dip burning placidly on the wall above him.

"Mrs. Fraser!" He greeted me cheerfully. "I suppose I shall be a free man again shortly. Hope the army brings me some food; I think there's not much chance of supper here tonight."

"I suppose you will," I said, unable not to smile back at him. "You'll take care of the other British prisoners, will you? General St. Clair is leaving them behind."

He looked mildly offended at this.

"They're my men," he said.

"So they are." In fact, Guinea Dick, almost invisible against the stone wall in the dim light, was crouching beside the captain's bed, a stout walking stick in his hand—in order to fend off would-be looters, I supposed. Mr. Ormiston was sitting up on his own cot, pale-faced but excited, picking at the binding on his stump.

"They're really coming, are they, ma'am? The army?"

"Yes, they are. Now, you must take good care of your wound and keep it clean. It's healing well, but you mustn't put any strain at all on it for another month at least—and wait at least two months before you have a peg fitted. *Don't* let the army surgeons bleed you—you need all your strength."

He nodded, though I knew he'd be lining up for a fleam and a bleeding-bowl the moment a British surgeon showed up; he believed deeply in the virtues of being let blood and had been slightly mollified only by my having leeched his stump now and then.

I clasped his hand in farewell, and was turning to go when his own grip tightened.

"A moment, ma'am?" He let go my hand, fumbling at his neck, and withdrew something on a string. I could barely see it in the gloom, but he put it into my hand and I felt a metal disc, warm from his body.

"If happen you might see that boy Abram again, ma'am, I should take it kind if you'd give him that. That's my lucky piece, what I've carried for thirty-two years; you tell him it will keep him safe in time o' danger."

Jamie was looming up in the dark beside me, radiating impatience and agitation. He had a small group of invalids in tow, all clutching random possessions. I could hear Mrs. Raven's distinctive high-pitched voice in the distance, wailing. I thought she was calling my name. I ducked my head and put Mr. Ormiston's lucky piece around my neck.

"I'll tell him, Mr. Ormiston. Thank you."

SOMEONE HAD SET fire to Jeduthan Baldwin's elegant bridge. A pile of rubbish smoldered near one end, and I saw black devil shapes running to and fro along the span with chisels and pry bars, ripping up the planks and throwing them into the water.

Jamie shouldered a way through the mob, me behind him and our little band of women, children, and invalids scurrying at my heels like goslings, honking in agitation.

"Fraser! Colonel Fraser!" I turned at the shout, to see Jonah—Bill, I mean—Marsden running down the shore.

"I'll come with you," he said, breathless. "You'll need someone can steer a boat."

Jamie didn't hesitate for more than a fraction of a second. He nodded, jerking his head toward the shore.

"Aye, run. I'll bring them along as fast as I can."

Mr. Marsden vanished into the dark.

"The rest of your men?" I said, coughing from the smoke.

He shrugged, a broad-shouldered silhouette against the black shimmer of the water.

"Gone."

Hysterical screams came from the direction of the Old French Lines. These spread like wildfire through the woods and down the lakeshore, people shouting that the British were coming. Panic beating its wings. It was so strong a thing, that panic, that I felt a scream rise in my own throat. I throttled it and felt irrational anger in its place, displaced from myself to the fools behind me who were shrieking and would have scattered, had they been able to. But we were close upon the shore now, and people were pressing toward the boats in such numbers that they were capsizing some of the craft as they piled in, higgledy-piggledy.

I didn't *think* the British were at hand—but I didn't know. I knew that there had been more than one battle at Fort Ticonderoga ... but when had they occurred? Was one of them going to be tonight? I didn't know, and the sense of urgency propelled me to the shore, helping to support Mr. Wellman, who had contracted the mumps from his son, poor man, and was doing very badly in consequence.

Mr. Marsden, bless him, had commandeered a large canoe, which he had paddled a little way out from shore to prevent its being overrun. When he saw Jamie approaching, he came in, and we succeeded in getting a total of eighteen people—these including the Wellmans and Mrs. Raven, pale and staring as Ophelia—into it.

Jamie glanced quickly back at the fort. The main gates hung wide, and firelight shone out of them. Then he glanced up at the battery where he and I had stood a little while before.

"There are four men by the cannon trained on the bridge," he said, his eyes still fixed on the red-bellied billows of smoke rising from the interior of the fort. "Volunteers. They'll stay behind. The British—or some of them—

will certainly come across the bridge. They can destroy almost everyone on the boom, and then flee—if they can."

He turned away then, and his shoulders bunched and flexed as he dug the paddle hard.

MOUNT INDEPENDENCE

Mid-afternoon, July 6

BRIGADIER FRASER'S MEN advanced upon the picket fort at the top of the mount, the one the Americans ironically called "Independence." William led one of the forward parties and had his men fix their bayonets as they drew close. There was a deep silence, broken only by the snap of branches and shuffle of boots in the thick leaf mold, the stray clack of a cartridge box against musket butt. Was it a waiting silence, though?

The Americans could not fail to know they were coming. Did the rebels lie in ambush, ready to fire upon them from the crude but very solid fortification he could see through the trees?

He motioned to his men to stop some two hundred yards short of the summit, hoping to pick up some indication of the defenders, if defenders there were. His own company halted obediently, but there were men behind, and they began to push into and through his own company without regard, eager to storm the fort.

"Halt!" he shouted, aware as he did so that the sound of his voice presented almost as good a target to an American rifleman as would the sight of his red coat. Some of the men did halt but were at once dislodged by more behind them, and within seconds the whole of the hillside was a mass of red. They could not stop longer; they would be trampled. And if the defenders had meant to fire, they could not ask for a better opportunity—and yet the fort stayed silent.

"On!" William roared, throwing up his arm, and the men burst from the trees in a splendid charge, bayonets held ready.

The gates hung ajar, and the men charged straight in, heedless of danger—but danger there was none. William came in with his men, to find the place deserted. Not only abandoned, but evidently abandoned in an amazing hurry.

The defenders' personal belongings were strewn everywhere, as though dropped in flight: not only heavy things like cooking utensils, but clothes, shoes, books, blankets . . . even money, seemingly cast aside or dropped in panic. Much more to the point, so far as William was concerned, was the fact that the defenders had made no effort to blow up ammunition or powder that could not be carried away; there must be two hundredweight, stacked in kegs! Provisions, too, had been left behind, a welcome sight.

"Why did they not set fire to the place?" Lieutenant Hammond asked him, looking goggle-eyed round at the barracks, still fully furnished with beds, bedding, chamber pots—ready for the conquerors to move straight in to.

"God knows," William replied briefly, then lunged forward as he saw a private soldier come out of one of the rooms, festooned in a lacy shawl and with his arms full of shoes. "You, there! We'll have no looting, none! Do you hear me, sir?"

The private did and, dropping his armful of shoes, made off precipitately, lacy fringes flapping. A good many others were at it, too, though, and it was clear to William that he and Hammond would be unable to stop it. He shouted above the increasing din for an ensign and, seizing the man's dispatch box, scribbled a hasty note.

"Take that to General Fraser," he said thrusting it back at the ensign. "Fast as ever you can go!"

Dawn
July 7, 1777

"I WILL NOT HAVE these horrid irregularities!" General Fraser's face was deeply creased, as much with rage as with fatigue. The small traveling clock in the general's tent showed just before five o'clock in the morning, and William had the oddly dreamy feeling that his head was floating somewhere over his left shoulder. "Looting, theft, rampant undiscipline—I will not have it, I say. Am I understood? All of you?"

The small, tired group of officers gave assent in a chorus of grunts. They had been up all night, chivvying their troops into some form of rough order, keeping back the rank and file from the worst excesses of looting, hurriedly surveying the abandoned outposts at the Old French Lines, and tallying the unexpected bounty of provisions and ammunition left for them by the fort's defenders—four of whom had been found when the fort was stormed, dead drunk by the side of a primed cannon, trained on the bridge below.

"Those men, the ones who were taken. Has anyone been able to talk with them as yet?"

"No, sir," Captain Hayes said, stifling a yawn. "Still dead to the world—very nearly dead for good, the surgeon said, though he thinks they'll survive."

"Shit themselves with fear," Hammond said softly to William. "Waiting all that time for us to come."

"More likely boredom," William murmured back without moving his mouth. Even so, he caught the brigadier's bloodshot eye and straightened up unconsciously.

"Well, it's not as though we need them to tell us much." General Fraser waved a hand to dispel a cloud of smoke that had drifted in, and coughed. William inhaled gently. There was a succulent scent embodied in that smoke, and his stomach coiled in anticipation. Ham? Sausage?

"I've sent word back to General Burgoyne that Ticonderoga is ours—again," the brigadier added, breaking into a grin at the hoarse cheer from the officers. "And to Colonel St. Leger. We shall leave a small garrison to take stock and tidy things up here, but the rest of us . . . Well, there are rebels to be caught, gentlemen. I cannot offer you much respite, but certainly there is time for a hearty breakfast. *Bon appetit!*"

RETURN OF THE NATIVE

Night, July 7

IAN MURRAY PASSED INTO the fort without difficulty. There were rangers and Indians aplenty, mostly lounging against the buildings, many of them drunk, others poking through the deserted barracks, occasionally chased away by harassed-looking soldiers set to guard the fort's unexpected bounty.

There was no sign of slaughter, and he breathed easier. That had been his first fear, but while there was mess—and to spare—there was no blood and no smell of powder smoke. No shot had been fired here in the last day or so.

He had a thought and went toward the hospital barracks, largely ignored, as it held nothing anyone would want. The smells of urine, shit, and old blood had decreased; most of the patients must have gone with the retreating troops. There were a few people there, one in a green coat who he thought must be a surgeon, some plainly orderlies. As he watched, a pair of stretcher-bearers came out through the door, boots scraping as they negotiated the shallow stone steps. He leaned back into the concealment of the doorway, for following the stretcher was the tall form of Guinea Dick, his face split in a cannibal's grin.

Ian smiled himself, seeing it; Captain Stebbings still lived, then—and Guinea Dick was a free man. And here, Jesus, Mary, and Bride be thanked, came Mr. Ormiston behind him, stumping slowly on a pair of crutches, tenderly supported on either side by a pair of orderlies, the puny wee creatures dwarfed by the seaman's bulk. He could tell Auntie Claire, then—she'd be pleased to hear they were all right.

If he found Auntie Claire again—but he wasn't much worried, really.

Uncle Jamie would see her safe, come hell, wildfire, or the entire British army. When or where he'd see them again was another matter, but he and Rollo moved much faster than any army could; he'd catch them up soon enough.

He waited, curious to see whether there was anyone else left in the hospital, but either there was not or they were to be left there for the nonce. Had the Hunters gone with St. Clair's troops? In a way, he hoped they had—even knowing that they would likely fare better with the British than on the run down the Hudson Valley with the refugees from Ticonderoga. As Quakers, he thought they would do well enough; the British probably wouldn't molest them. But he thought he would like to see Rachel Hunter again sometime, and his chance of that was much better if she and her brother had gone with the rebels.

A little more poking about convinced him of two things: that the Hunters had indeed gone, and that the leaving of Ticonderoga had been accomplished in the midst of panic and disorder. Someone had set fire to the bridge below, but it had only partially burned, perhaps put out by a rainstorm. There was a great deal of debris on the lakeshore, suggesting a massive embarkation— automatically he glanced toward the lake, where he could plainly see two large ships, both flying the Union flag. From his current perch on the battery, he could see redcoats swarming over both Mount Defiance and Mount Independence, and knew a small, surprising flare of resentment against them.

"Well, you'll not keep it long," he said under his breath. He spoke in Gaelic, and a good thing, too, for a passing soldier glanced casually at him, as though feeling the stress of his regard. He looked away himself, turning his back on the fort.

There was nothing to do here, no one to wait for. He'd eat and pick up some provisions, then go fetch Rollo and be off. He could—

A shattering *whoom!* close at hand made him jerk round. To his right, one of the cannon was trained downward toward the bridge, and just behind it, openmouthed with shock, was a Huron man, swaying with drink.

There was a lot of shouting from below; the troops thought they were being fired on from the fort, though the shot had gone high, splashing harmlessly into the lake.

The Huron giggled.

"What did you do?" Ian asked, in an Algonkian tongue he thought the man would most likely know. Whether he understood or not, the man simply laughed harder, tears beginning to run down his face. He gestured to a smoking tub nearby; good Christ, the defenders had gone so fast, they had left a tub of slow match burning.

"Boom," said the Huron, and gestured at a length of slow match, pulled from the tub and left draped on the stones like a glowing snake. "Boom," he said again, nodding at the cannon, and laughed until he had to sit down.

Soldiers were running up to the battery, and the shouting from outside was equaled by that inside the fort. It was probably a good time to go.

55

RETREAT

. . . we are pursuing the rebels, a great number of whom have taken to the lake in boats. The two sloops on the lake are following, but I am sending four companies down to the portage point, where I think the chance of capture is good.

—*Brigadier General Simon Fraser, to Major General J. Burgoyne*

July 8, 1777

WILLIAM WISHED HE hadn't accepted the brigadier's invitation to breakfast. If he had contented himself with the lean rations that were a lieutenant's lot, he would have been hungry, but happy. As it was, he was on the spot—blissfully filled to the eyes with fried sausage, buttered toast, and grits with honey, for which the brigadier had developed a fondness—when the message had come from General Burgoyne. He didn't even know what it had said; the brigadier had read it while sipping coffee, frowning slightly, then sighed and called for ink and quill.

"Want a ride this morning, William?" he'd asked, smiling across the table.

Which is how he'd come to be at General Burgoyne's field headquarters when the Indians had come in. Wyandot, one of the soldiers said; he wasn't familiar with them, though he had heard that they had a chief called Leatherlips, and he did wonder how that had come about. Perhaps the man was an indefatigable talker?

There were five of them, lean, wolfish-looking rascals. He couldn't have said what they wore or how they were armed; all his attention was focused on the pole that one of them carried, this decorated with scalps. Fresh scalps. White scalps. A musky smell of blood hung in the air, unpleasantly ripe, and flies moved with the Indians, buzzing loudly. The remains of William's lavish breakfast coagulated in a hard ball just under his ribs.

The Indians were looking for the paymaster; one of them was asking, in a surprisingly melodious English, where the paymaster was. So it was true, then. General Burgoyne had unleashed his Indians, sent them coursing through the woods like hunting dogs to fall upon the rebels and spread terror among them.

He did *not* want to look at the scalps but couldn't help it; his eyes followed them as the pole bobbed through a growing crowd of curious soldiers—some mildly horrified, some cheering. Jesus. Was that a *woman's* scalp? It had to be; a flowing mass of honey-colored hair, longer than any man would wear his hair, and shining as though its owner brushed it a hundred strokes every night, like his cousin Dottie said she did. It was not unlike Dottie's hair, though a little darker—

He turned away abruptly, hoping that he wouldn't be sick, but turned just as abruptly back when he heard the cry. He'd never heard a sound like that before—a shriek of such horror, such grief, that his heart froze in his chest.

"Jane! Jane!" A Welsh lieutenant he knew slightly, called David Jones, was forcing his way through the crowd, beating at the men with fists and elbows, lunging toward the surprised Indians, his face contorted with emotion.

"Oh, God," breathed a soldier near him. "His fiancée's called Jane. He can't mean—"

Jones threw himself at the pole, snatching at the fall of honey-colored hair, shrieking "JANE!" at the top of his lungs. The Indians, looking disconcerted, jerked the pole away. Jones flung himself on one of them, knocking the surprised Indian to the ground and hammering him with the strength of insanity.

Men were pushing forward, grabbing at Jones—but not doing so with any great heart. Appalled looks were being shot at the Indians, who clustered together, eyes narrowed and hands at their tomahawks. The whole sense of the gathering had changed in an instant from approval to outrage, and the Indians plainly sensed it.

An officer William didn't know strode forward, daring the Indians with a hard eye, and tore the blond scalp from the pole. Then stood holding it, disconcerted, the mass of hair seeming alive in his hands, the long strands stirring, waving up around his fingers.

They had finally pulled Jones off the Indian; his friends were patting his shoulders, trying to urge him away, but he stood stock-still, tears rolling down his face and dripping from his chin. "Jane," he mouthed silently. He held out his hands, cupped and begging, and the officer who held the scalp placed it gently into them.

WHILE STILL ALIVE

LIEUTENANT STACTOE WAS standing by one corpse, arrested. Very slowly, he squatted down, his eyes fixed on something, and as though by reflex covered his mouth with one hand.

I really didn't want to look.

He'd heard my footsteps, though, and took his hand away from his mouth. I could see the sweat trickling down his neck, the band of his shirt pasted to his skin, dark with it.

"Do you suppose that was done while he was still alive?" he asked, in an ordinary tone of voice.

Reluctantly, I looked over his shoulder.

"Yes," I said, my voice as unemotional as his. "It was."

"Oh," he said. He stood, contemplated the corpse for a moment, then walked away a few steps and threw up.

"Never mind," I said gently, and took him by the sleeve. "He's dead now. Come and help."

Many of the boats had gone astray, been captured before they reached the end of the lake; many more had been taken by British troops waiting at the portage point. Our canoe and several more had escaped, and we had made our way through the woods for a day and a night and most of another day before meeting with the main body of troops fleeing overland from the fort. I was beginning to think that those who were captured were the lucky ones.

I didn't know how long it had been since the small group we had just discovered was attacked by Indians. The bodies were not fresh.

GUARDS WERE POSTED at night. Those not on watch slept as though poleaxed, exhausted by a day of flight—if anything so cumbrous and labored could be described by such a graceful word. I woke just past dawn from dreams of Snow White trees, gape-mouthed and grasping, to find Jamie crouched beside me, a hand on my arm.

"Ye'd best come, *a nighean*," he said softly.

Mrs. Raven had cut her throat with a penknife.

There wasn't time to dig a grave. I straightened her limbs and closed her eyes, and we piled rocks and branches over her before staggering back to the rut that passed for a road through the wilderness.

AS DARKNESS CAME up through the trees, we began to hear them. High ululating shrieks. Hunting wolves.

"March on, march on! Indians!" one of the militiamen shouted.

As if summoned by the shout, a bloodcurdling shriek wavered through the darkness nearby, and the stumbling retreat turned at once to headlong panic, men dropping their bundles and pushing one another out of the way in their haste to flee.

There were shrieks from the refugees, too, though these were quickly stifled.

"Off the road," Jamie said, low and fierce, and began pushing the slow and bewildered into the woods. "They may not know where we are. Yet."

And then again, they might.

"D'ye have your death song ready, Uncle?" Ian whispered. He had caught us up the day before, and now he and Jamie were pressed close on either side of me, where we had taken cover behind a huge fallen trunk.

"Oh, I'll sing them a death song, if it comes to that," Jamie muttered, half under his breath, and took out one of the pistols from his belt.

"You can't sing," I said. I hadn't meant to be funny—I was so frightened that I said it by reflex, the first thing that came into my mind—and he didn't laugh.

"That's true," he said. "Well, then."

He primed the pistol, closed the pan and thrust it into his belt.

"Dinna be afraid, *a nighean*," Jamie whispered, and I saw his throat work as he swallowed. "I'll not let them take ye. Not alive." He touched the pistol at his belt.

I stared at him, then at the pistol. I hadn't thought it possible to be more afraid.

I felt suddenly as though my spinal cord had snapped; my limbs wouldn't move, and my bowels very literally turned to water. I understood in that moment exactly what had led Mrs. Raven to slash her own throat.

Ian whispered something to Jamie and slid away, silent as a shadow.

It occurred to me, belatedly, that by taking time to shoot me if we should be overrun, Jamie was very likely to fall alive into the hands of the Indians himself. And I was sufficiently terrorized that I couldn't tell him not to do it.

I took hold of my courage with both hands and swallowed hard.

"Go!" I said. "They won't—they probably won't harm women." My outer skirt hung in tatters, as did my jacket, and the whole ensemble was covered in mud, leaves, and the small bloody splotches of slow-moving mosquitoes— but I was still identifiably female.

"The devil I will," he said briefly.

"Uncle." Ian's voice came softly out of the darkness. "It's not Indians."

"What?" I made no sense of this, but Jamie straightened abruptly.

"It's a redcoat, running alongside us, shrieking like an Indian. Driving us."

Jamie swore under his breath. It was almost completely dark by now; I could see only a few vague shapes, presumably those of the people with us. I heard a whimper, almost underfoot, but when I looked, could see no one.

The shrieks came again, now from the other side. If the man was driving us—did he know we were there? If so, where did he mean to drive us? I could feel Jamie's indecision—which way? A second, perhaps two, and he took me by the arm, pulling me deeper into the wood.

We ran slap into a large group of refugees within minutes; they had stopped dead, too terrified to move in any direction. They huddled together, the women clutching their children, hands clasped tight over the little ones' mouths, breathing "Hush!" like the wind.

"Leave them," Jamie said in my ear, and tightened his grip on my arm. I turned to go with him, and suddenly a hand seized my other arm. I screamed, and everyone near erupted in screams by sheer reflex. Suddenly the wood around us was alive with moving forms and shouts.

The soldier—it was a British soldier; from so close I could see the buttons on his uniform and felt the thump of his cartridge box as it swung, striking me in the hip—leaned down to peer at me and grinned, his breath stale and scented with decay.

"Stand still, love," he said. "You're going nowhere now."

My heart was pounding so hard in my ears that it was a full minute before I realized that the grip on my other arm was gone. Jamie had vanished.

WE WERE MARCHED back up the road in a tight group, moving slowly through the night. They let us drink at a stream at daylight but kept us moving until the early afternoon, by which time even the most able-bodied were ready to drop.

We were herded, none too gently, into a field. Farmer's wife that I was, I winced to see the stalks—only weeks away from harvest—being trampled underfoot, the fragile gold of the wheat cut and mangled into black mud. There was a cabin among the trees at the far end of the field; I saw a girl run out onto the porch, clap a hand to her mouth in horror, and disappear back inside.

Three British officers came across the field, heading for the cabin, ignoring the seething mass of invalids, women, and children, all of whom were milling to and fro, with no idea what to do next. I wiped the sweat out of my eyes with the end of my kerchief, tucked it back into my bodice, and looked round for anyone who might be nominally in charge.

None of our own officers or able-bodied men seemed to have been captured; there had been only a couple of surgeons superintending the removal of the invalids, and I hadn't seen either one in two days. Neither one was here. *All right, then,* I thought grimly, and walked up to the nearest British soldier, who was surveying the chaos through narrowed eyes, musket in hand.

"We need water," I said to him without preamble. "There's a stream just beyond those trees. May I take three or four women to fetch back water for the sick and wounded?"

He was sweating, too; the faded red wool of his coat was black under the arms, and melted rice powder from his hair was rimed in the creases of his forehead. He grimaced, indicating that he didn't want to deal with me, but I simply stared at him, as close as I could get. He glanced around, in hopes of finding someone to send me to, but the three officers had disappeared into the cabin. He raised one shoulder in surrender, looking away.

"Aye, go on, then," he muttered, and turned his back, stalwartly guarding the road, along which new prisoners were still being herded.

A quick traverse of the field turned up three buckets and a like number of sensible women, worried but not hysterical. I sent them to the stream and began to quarter the field, making a quick assessment of the situation—as much in order to keep my own worry at bay as because there was no one else to do it.

Would we be kept here long? I wondered. If we would be held here for more than a few hours, sanitation trenches must be dug—but the soldiers would have the same need. I'd leave that for the army to deal with, then. Water was coming; we'd need to run relays to the stream nonstop for a bit. Shelter . . . I glanced at the sky; it was hazy but clear. Those who could move on their own were already helping to drag the desperately sick or wounded into the shade of the trees along one side of the field.

Where was Jamie? Had he got away safe?

Above the calls and anxious conversations, I heard now and then the whisper of distant thunder. The air clung to my skin, thick with humidity. They would have to move us somewhere—to the nearest settlement, wherever that might be—but it might take several days. I had no idea where we were.

Had he been captured, too? If so, would they take him to the same place they'd take the invalids?

Chances were that they would release the women, not wishing to feed them. The women would stay with their sick men, though—or most of them would—sharing whatever food was available.

I was walking slowly across the field, conducting a mental triage—the man on the stretcher there was going to die, probably before nightfall; I could hear the rales of his breathing from six feet away—when I caught sight of movement on the cabin's porch.

The family—two adult women, two teenagers, three children, and a baby in arms—was leaving, clutching baskets, blankets, and such bits of their household as could be carried. One of the officers was with them; he took them across the field and spoke with one of the guards, evidently instructing him to let the women pass. One of the women paused at the edge of the road and looked back—just once. The others went straight on, without a backward glance. Where were their men?

Where are mine?

"Hallo," I said, smiling at a man with a recently amputated leg. I didn't know his name but recognized his face; he was one of the few black men at Ticonderoga, a carpenter. I knelt down beside him. His bandages were awry, and the stump was leaking badly. "Bar the leg, how do you feel?" His skin was pale gray and clammy as a wet sheet, but he gave me a feeble grin in return.

"My left hand doesn't hurt much right now." He lifted it in illustration, but dropped it like a chunk of lead, lacking strength to hold it up.

"That's good," I said, sliding my fingers under his thigh to lift it. "Let me fix this for you—we'll have you some water in a minute."

"That'd be nice," he murmured, and shut his eyes against the sun.

The flapping end of the loose bandage was twisted up like a snake's tongue, stiff with dried blood, and the dressing awry. The dressing itself, a poultice of flaxseed and turpentine, was soggy, pink with leaking blood and lymph. No choice but to reuse it, though.

"What's your name?"

"Walter." His eyes were still closed, his breath coming in shallow gasps. So was mine; the thick, hot air was like a pressure bandage round my chest. "Walter . . . Woodcock."

"Pleased to know you, Walter. My name's Claire Fraser."

"Know you," he murmured. "You're Big Red's lady. He make it out of the fort?"

"Yes," I said, and blotted my face against my shoulder to keep the sweat out of my eyes. "He's all right."

Dear God, let him be all right.

The English officer was coming back toward the cabin, passing within a few feet of me. I glanced up, and my hands froze.

He was tall, slender but broad-shouldered, and I would have known that long stride, that unself-conscious grace, and that arrogant tilt of the head anywhere. He paused, frowning, and turned his head to survey the littered field. His nose was straight as a knife blade, just that tiny bit too long. I closed my eyes for an instant, dizzy, sure I was hallucinating—but opened them again at once, knowing that I wasn't.

"William Ransom?" I blurted, and his head jerked toward me, surprised. Blue eyes, dark blue, Fraser cat-eyes, narrowed to a slant against the sun.

"I, er, beg your pardon." *God, what did you speak to him for?* But I couldn't have helped it. My fingers were pressed against Walter's leg, holding the bandage; I could feel his femoral pulse against my fingertips, bumping as erratically as my own.

"Do I know you, ma'am?" William asked, with the shadow of a bow.

"Well, yes, you do," I said, rather apologetically. "You stayed for a little time with my family, some years ago. A place called Fraser's Ridge."

His face changed at once at the name, and his gaze sharpened, focusing on me with interest.

"Why, yes," he said slowly. "I recall. You are Mrs. Fraser, are you not?" I could see his thoughts working, and was fascinated; he hadn't got Jamie's way of hiding what he thought—or if he did, wasn't using it. I could see him wondering—nice, well-mannered boy that he was—what the proper social response to this awkward situation might be, and—a quick glance over his shoulder at the cabin—how the demands of his duty might conflict with it.

His shoulders stiffened with decision, but before he could say anything, I leapt in.

"Do you think it might be possible to find some buckets for water? And bandages?" Most of the women had already torn strips from their petticoats to serve this function; much longer, and we'd all be half naked.

"Yes," he said slowly, and glanced down at Walter, then toward the road. "Buckets, yes. There's a surgeon with the division behind us; when I have a moment, I'll send someone back with a request for bandages."

"And food?" I asked hopefully. I hadn't eaten more than a handful of half-ripe berries in nearly two days. I wasn't suffering hunger pangs—my stomach was in knots—but I was having bouts of light-headedness, spots passing before my eyes. No one else was in much better case; we were going to lose a number of the invalids to the heat and simple weakness, if we weren't given food and shelter soon.

He hesitated, and I saw his eyes flit over the field, obviously estimating numbers.

"That may be . . . our supply train is—" His lips firmed, and he shook his head. "I'll see what can be done. Your servant, ma'am." He bowed politely and turned away, striding toward the road. I watched him go, fascinated, the soggy dressing limp in my hand.

He was dark-haired, though the sun struck a gleam of red from the crown of his head; he wore no powder. His voice had deepened—well, of course it had; he'd been no more than twelve the last time I met him—and the sheer oddness of hearing Jamie speaking in a cultured English accent made me want to laugh, despite our precarious situation and my worry for Jamie and Ian. I shook my head and returned to the task at hand.

A British private arrived an hour after my conversation with Lieutenant Ransom, bearing four buckets, which he dropped unceremoniously at my side without remark before heading back to the road. Two hours later, a sweating orderly came trundling through the trampled wheat with two large haversacks filled with bandages. Interestingly enough, he headed directly for me, which made me wonder just how William had described me.

"Thank you." I took the sacks of bandages with gratitude. "Do you—do you think we might get some food soon?"

The orderly was looking over the field, grimacing. Of course—the invalids were likely about to become his responsibility. He turned back to me, though, civil but obviously very tired.

"I doubt it, ma'am. The supply train is two days behind us, and the troops are living off what they're carrying or what they find as they go." He nodded toward the road; on the other side, I could see a number of English soldiers making camp. "I'm sorry," he added formally, and turned to go.

"Oh." He stopped, and taking the strap of his canteen off, handed it to me. It was heavy and gurgled enticingly. "Lieutenant Ellesmere said I was to give you this." He smiled briefly, the lines of tiredness easing. "He said you looked hot."

"Lieutenant Ellesmere." That must be William's title, I realized. "Thank you. And please thank the lieutenant, if you see him." He was clearly on the point of departure, but I couldn't help asking, "How did you know who I was?"

His smile deepened as he glanced at my head.

"The lieutenant said you'd be the curly-wig giving orders like a sergeant-major." He looked round the field once more, shaking his head. "Good luck, ma'am."

THREE MEN DIED before sunset. Walter Woodcock was still alive, but barely. We'd moved as many men as we could into the shade of the trees along the edge of the field, and I'd divided the seriously wounded into small groups, each allocated a bucket and two or three women or walking invalids to tend them. I'd also designated a latrine area and done my best to separate the infectious cases from those who were fevered from wounds or malaria. There were three suffering from what I hoped was only "summer ague," and one who I feared might have diphtheria. I sat beside him—a young wheelwright from New Jersey—checking the membranes of his throat at intervals, giving him as much water as he would take. Not from my canteen, though.

William Ransom, bless his soul, had filled his canteen with brandy.

I uncorked it and took a sparing sip. I'd poured out small cupfuls for each small group, adding each cupful to a bucket of water—but had kept a bit for my own use. It wasn't selfishness; for better or worse, I was in charge of the captives for the moment. I had to stay on my feet.

Or my bottom, as the case might be, I thought, leaning back against the bole of an oak tree. My feet ached all the way to my knees, my back and ribs twinged with each breath, and I had to close my eyes now and then to control the dizziness. But I was sitting still, for what seemed like the first time in several days.

The soldiers across the road were cooking their meager rations; my mouth watered and my stomach contracted painfully at the scent of roasting meat and flour. Mrs. Wellman's little boy was whining with hunger, his head laid on his mother's lap. She was stroking his hair mechanically, her eyes fixed on her husband's body, which lay a little way away. We had no sheet or blanket with which to shroud him, but someone had given her a handkerchief to cover his face. The flies were very bad.

The air had cooled, thank God, but was still heavy with the threat of rain; thunder was a constant faint rumble over the horizon and it would probably pour sometime during the night. I plucked the sweat-soaked fabric away from my chest; I doubted it would have time to dry before we were drenched with rain. I eyed the encampment across the road, with its lines of small tents and brush shelters, with envy. There was a slightly larger officers' tent as well, though several officers had taken up temporary quarters in the commandeered cabin.

I ought to go there, I thought. See the most senior officer present, and beg for food for the children, at least. When the shadow of that tall pine sapling touched my foot, I decided. Then I'd go. In the meantime, I uncorked the canteen and took another small swallow.

Movement caught my eye, and I looked up. The unmistakable figure of Lieutenant Ransom stalked out of the tents and came across the road. It lifted my heart a little to see him, though the sight of him renewed my worry for Jamie—and reminded me, with a small sharp pang, of Brianna. At least *she* was safe, I thought. Roger and Jemmy and Amanda, too. I repeated their names to myself as a small refrain of comfort, counting them like coins. Four of them safe.

William had undone his stock, and his hair was untidy, his coat stained with sweat and dirt. Evidently the pursuit was wearing on the British army, too.

He glanced round the field, spotted me, and turned purposefully in my direction. I got my feet under me, struggling upward against the press of gravity like a hippopotamus rising from a swamp.

I'd barely got to my feet and raised a hand to smooth my hair when someone else's hand poked me in the back. I started violently but luckily didn't scream.

"It's me, Auntie," Young Ian whispered from the shadows behind me. "Come with—oh, Jesus."

William had come within ten paces of me and, raising his head, had spied Ian. He leapt forward and grabbed me by the arm, yanking me away from the trees. I yelped, as Ian had an equally firm grip on the other arm and was yanking lustily in that direction.

"Let her go!" William barked.

"The devil I will," Ian replied hotly. "*You* let go!"

Mrs. Wellman's little son was on his feet, staring round-eyed and openmouthed into the forest.

"Mama, Mama! *Indians!*"

Shrieks rose from the women near us, and everyone began a mad scramble away from the forest, leaving the wounded to their own devices.

"Ah, bugger!" Ian said, letting go in disgust. William didn't, jerking me with such force that I crashed into him, whereupon he promptly wrapped his arms about my waist and dragged me a little way into the field.

"Will ye bloody leave go of my auntie?" Ian said crossly, emerging from the trees.

"You!" said William. "What are you—well, never mind that. Your aunt, you say?" He looked down at me. "Are you? His aunt? Wait—no, of course you are."

"I am," I agreed, pushing at his arms. "Let go."

His grasp loosened a little, but he didn't release me.

"How many others are in there?" he demanded, lifting his chin toward the forest.

"If there were any others, ye'd be deid," Ian informed him. "It's just me. Give her to me."

"I can't do that." But there was an uncertain note in William's voice, and I felt his head turn, glancing toward the cabin. So far, no one had come out, but I could see some of the sentries near the road shifting to and fro, wondering what the matter was. The other captives had stopped running, but were quivering with incipient panic, eyes frantically searching the shadows among the trees.

I rapped William sharply on the wrist with my knuckles and he let go and took a step back. My head was spinning again—not least from the very peculiar sensation of being embraced by a total stranger whose body felt so familiar to me. He was thinner than Jamie, but—

"D'ye owe me a life or not?" Not waiting for an answer, Ian jerked a thumb at me. "Aye, then—it's hers."

"Hardly a question of her life," William said, rather crossly, with an awkward nod in my direction, acknowledging that I might have a possible interest in this discussion. "Surely you don't suppose we kill women?"

"No," Ian said evenly. "I dinna suppose it at all. I ken verra well that ye do."

"We do?" William echoed. He looked surprised, but a sudden flush burned in his cheeks.

"You do," I assured him. "General Howe hanged three women at the head of his army in New Jersey, as an example."

He seemed completely nonplused by this.

"Well . . . but—they were spies!"

"You think I don't look like a spy?" I inquired. "I'm much obliged for your good opinion, but I don't know that General Burgoyne would share it." There were, of course, a good many other women who'd died at the hands of the British army, if less officially, but this didn't seem the moment to make an account of them.

"General Burgoyne is a gentleman," William said stiffly. "So am I."

"Good," Ian said briefly. "Turn your back for thirty seconds, and we'll trouble ye nay more."

I don't know whether he would have done it or not, but just then, Indian cries tore the air, coming from the far side of the road. Further frantic screams came from the captives, and I bit my own tongue in order not to scream, too. A tongue of fire shot up into the lavender sky from the top of the officers' tent. As I gaped, two more flaming comets shot across the sky. It looked like the descent of the Holy Ghost, but before I could mention this interesting observation, Ian had seized my arm and jerked me nearly off my feet.

I managed to snatch up the canteen as we passed, on a dead run for the forest. Ian grabbed it from me, almost dragging me in his haste. Gunfire and screams were breaking out behind us, and the skin all down my back contracted in fear.

"This way." I followed him without heed for anything underfoot, stumbling and twisting my ankles in the dusk as we threw ourselves headlong into the brush, expecting every moment to be shot in the back.

Such is the brain's capacity for self-amusement, I was able to imagine in vivid detail my wounding, capture, descent into infection and sepsis, and eventual lingering death—but not before being obliged to witness the capture and execution of both Jamie—I had recognized the source of the Indian screams and flaming arrows without difficulty—and Ian.

It was only as we slowed—perforce; I had such a stitch in my side that I could barely breathe—that I thought of other things. The sick and wounded I had left behind. The young wheelwright with the bright red throat. Walter Woodcock, teetering over the abyss.

You couldn't give any of them more than a hand to hold, I told myself fiercely, limping as I stumbled after Ian. It was true; I knew it was true. But I also knew that now and then a hand in the dark gave a sick man something to cling to, against the rushing wind of the dark angel. Sometimes it was enough; sometimes it wasn't. But the ache of those left behind dragged at me like a sea anchor, and I wasn't sure whether the wetness streaming down my cheeks was sweat or tears.

It was full dark now, and the boiling clouds covered the moon, allowing only fitful glimpses of its brilliant light. Ian had slowed still more, to let me keep up with him, and took my arm now and then to help me over rocks or across creeks.

"How . . . far?" I gasped, stopping once more for breath.

"Not much," Jamie's voice replied softly beside me. "Are ye all right, Sassenach?"

My heart gave a tremendous bump, then settled back in my chest as he groped for my hand, then gathered me briefly against himself. I had a moment of relief so profound that I thought my bones had dissolved.

"Yes," I said, into his chest, and with great effort lifted my head. "You?"

"Well enough now," he said, passing a hand over my head, touching my cheek. "Can ye walk just a bit further?"

I straightened, swaying a little. It had begun to rain; heavy drops plopped into my hair, cold and startling on my scalp.

"Ian—have you got that canteen?"

There was a soft *pop!* and Ian set the canteen in my hand. Very carefully, I tilted it into my mouth.

"Is that brandy?" Jamie said, sounding astonished.

"Mmm-hmm." I swallowed, as slowly as I could, and handed the canteen to him. There were a couple of swallows left.

"Where did ye get it?"

"Your son gave it to me," I said. "Where are we going?"

There was a long pause from the darkness, and then the sound of brandy being drunk.

"South," he said at last, and taking my hand, led me on into the wood, the rain whispering on the leaves all round us.

SOAKED AND SHIVERING, we caught up to a militia unit just before dawn, and were nearly shot in mistake by a nervous sentry. By that point, I didn't really care. Being dead was immensely preferable to the prospect of taking one more step.

Our *bona fides* being established, Jamie disappeared briefly and came back with a blanket and three fresh corn dodgers. I inhaled my share of this ambrosia in four seconds flat, wrapped myself in the blanket, and lay down under a tree where the ground was damp but not soggy and so thick with dead leaves that it gave spongily beneath me.

"I'll be back in a bit, Sassenach," Jamie whispered, squatting beside me. "Dinna go anywhere, aye?"

"Don't worry—I'll be here. If I move a muscle before Christmas, it will be too soon." A faint warmth was already returning to my shivering muscles, and sleep was pulling me down with the inexorability of quicksand.

He gave the breath of a laugh, and reached out a hand, tucking the blanket in around my shoulders. The dawn light showed the deep lines that the night had carved in his face, the smudges of dirt and exhaustion that stained the strong bones. The wide mouth, compressed for so long, had relaxed now in the relief of momentary safety, looking oddly young and vulnerable.

"He looks like you," I whispered. His hand stopped moving, still on my shoulder, and he looked down, long lashes hiding his eyes.

"I know," he said, very softly. "Tell me of him. Later, when there's time."

I heard his footsteps, a rustle in damp leaves, and fell asleep, a prayer for Walter Woodcock half finished in my mind.

THE DESERTER GAME

T HE WHORE GRUNTED through the rag clenched in her teeth.

"Nearly done," I murmured, and ran the backs of my knuckles gently down her calf by way of reassurance before returning to the debridement of the nasty wound in her foot. An officer's horse had stepped on her as they—and a number of other people and animals—had jostled to drink at a creek during the retreat. I could clearly see the print of the horseshoe nails, black in the red puffy flesh of her instep. The edge of the shoe itself, worn paper-thin and sharp as a knife, had made a deep, curved gash that ran across the metatarsals, vanishing between the fourth and fifth toes.

I'd been afraid I was going to have to remove the little toe—it seemed to be dangling by no more than a shred of skin—but when I examined the foot more closely, I discovered that all the bones were miraculously intact—as nearly as I could tell, without access to an X-ray machine.

The horse's hoof had driven her foot into the mud of the stream bank, she'd told me; that had likely saved the bones from being crushed. Now if I could manage to stem the infection and didn't have to amputate the foot, she might just be able to walk again normally. Maybe.

With a degree of cautious hope, I put down the scalpel and reached for a bottle of what I hoped was a penicillin-containing liquid brought with me from the fort. I'd salvaged the barrel optic of Dr. Rawlings's microscope from the house fire and found it very useful indeed for starting fires—but without the eyepiece, staging mechanism, or mirror, it was of limited use in determining the genus of microorganisms. I could be sure that what I'd grown and filtered was bread mold, all right—but beyond that . . .

Suppressing a sigh, I poured the liquid generously over the raw flesh I'd just exposed. It wasn't alcoholic, but the flesh *was* raw. The whore made a high-pitched noise through the cloth and breathed through her nose like a steam engine, but by the time I'd made a compress of lavender and comfrey and bound up the foot, she was calm, if flushed.

"There," I said, with a small pat to her leg. "I think that will do nicely now." I started to say automatically, "Keep it clean," but bit my tongue. She hadn't any shoes or stockings and was either walking daily through a wilderness of rocks, dirt, and streams, or living in a filthy camp littered with piles of dung, both human and animal. The bottoms of her feet were hard as horn and black as sin.

"Come and find me in a day or two," I said instead. *If you can,* I thought. "I'll check it and change the dressing." *If I can,* I thought, with a glance at the knapsack in the corner where I kept my dwindling stocks of medicaments.

"Thank 'ee kindly," the whore said, sitting up and putting her foot gingerly to the ground. Judging from the skin of her legs and feet, she was young, though you couldn't tell from her face. Her skin was weathered, lined with hunger and strain. Her cheekbones were sharp with hunger, and her mouth was drawn in on one side where the teeth were missing—lost to decay or knocked out by a customer or another whore.

"Will 'ee be here for a bit, think?" she asked. "I've a friend, like, got the itch."

"I'll be here for the night, at least," I assured her, suppressing a groan as I rose to my feet. "Send your friend; I'll see what I can do."

Our group of militia had met with others, forming a large body, and within a few days we began to cross paths with other rebel groups. We were running into fragments of General Schuyler's and General Arnold's armies, these also moving south down the Hudson Valley.

We were still moving all day but began to feel secure enough to sleep at night, and with food provided—irregularly, but still food—by the army, my strength began to return. The rain usually came at night, but today it had been raining at dawn, and we had been trudging through mud for hours before some shelter came in sight.

General Arnold's troops had stripped the farmstead and burnt the house. The barn was heavily charred down one side, but the fire had gone out before consuming the building.

A gust of wind blew through the barn, raising eddies of decayed straw and dirt, whipping our petticoats round our legs. The barn had originally had a plank floor; I could see the lines of the boards, embedded in the dirt. The foragers had taken them for firewood, but it had been too much trouble for them to knock down the barn, thank God.

Some of the refugees fleeing Ticonderoga had sought shelter here; more would be along before nightfall. A mother with two small, exhausted children slept curled by the far wall; her husband had settled them here and gone to look for food.

Pray ye that your flight be not in the winter, nor on the Sabbath day...

I followed the whore to the door and stood looking after her. The sun was touching the horizon now; perhaps an hour of light left, but the sunset breeze was already moving in the treetops, night's skirts rustling as she came. I shivered reflexively, though the day was still warm enough. The old barn was chilly.

And what then? said the small, apprehensive voice that lived in the pit of my stomach. *What would it be like when the weather turned truly cold?*

"Then I'll put on another pair of stockings," I muttered to it. "Hush up!"

A truly Christian person would doubtless have given the spare stockings to the barefoot whore, remarked the sanctimonious voice of my conscience.

"You hush up, too," I said. "Plenty of opportunity to be Christian later, if the urge should strike me." Half the people fleeing needed stockings, I dared say.

I wondered what I might be able to do for the whore's friend, if she did come. "The itch" might be anything from eczema or cowpox to gonorrhea—though given the woman's profession, something venereal was the best bet. Back in Boston, it would likely have been a simple yeast infection—oddly enough, I almost never saw those here, and speculated idly that it might be owing to the nearly universal lack of underclothes. So much for the advances of modernity!

I glanced at my knapsack again, calculating what I had left and how I might use it. A fair amount of bandages and lint. A pot of gentian ointment, good for scrapes and minor wounds, which occurred in abundance. A small stock of the most useful herbs for tincture and compress: lavender, comfrey, peppermint, mustard seed. By some miracle, I still had the box of cinchona bark I had acquired in New Bern—I thought of Tom Christie and crossed myself, but dismissed him from mind; there was nothing I could do about him and much too much to think of here. Two scalpels I had taken from Lieutenant Stactoe's body—he had succumbed to a fever on the road—and my silver surgical scissors. Jamie's gold acupuncture needles; those might be used to treat others, save that I had no idea how to place them for anything other than seasickness.

I could hear voices, parties of foragers moving through the trees, here and there someone calling out a name, searching for a friend or family member lost in transit. The refugees were beginning to settle for the night.

Sticks cracked near at hand, and a man came out of the woods. I didn't recognize him. One of the "greasy-stockinged knaves" from one of the militias, no doubt; he had a musket in one hand and a powder horn at his belt. Not much else. And yes, he was barefoot, though his feet were much too big to wear my stockings—a fact that I pointed out to my conscience, in case it should feel compelled to try to prod me into charitable behavior again.

He saw me in the door and raised a hand.

"You the conjure-woman?" he called.

"Yes." I'd given up trying to make people call me a doctor, let alone a physician.

"Met a whore with a mighty fine new bandage on her foot," the man said, giving me a smile. "She said as there's a conjure-woman up to the barn, has some medicines."

"Yes," I said again, giving him a quick once-over. I saw no obvious wound, and he wasn't sick—I could tell that from his color and the upright way he walked. Perhaps he had a wife or child, or a sick comrade.

"Hand 'em over to me now," he said, still smiling, and pointed the muzzle of the musket at me.

"What?" I said, surprised.

"Give me the medicines you've got." He made a small jabbing motion with the gun. "Could just shoot you and take 'em, but I ain't wanting to waste the powder."

I stood still and stared at him for a moment.

"What the devil do you want them for?" I'd been held up once before for drugs—in a Boston emergency room. A young addict, sweating and glassy-eyed, with a gun. I'd handed them over instantly. At the moment, I wasn't inclined.

He snorted and cocked his gun. Before I could even think about being scared, there was a sharp bang and the scent of powder smoke. The man looked terribly surprised, the musket sagging in his hands. Then he fell at my feet.

"Hold that, Sassenach." Jamie thrust the just-fired pistol into my hand, stooped, and took the body by the feet. He dragged it out of the barn into the rain. I swallowed, reached into my bag, and took out the extra stockings. I dropped these in the woman's lap, then went to set down the pistol and my sack by the wall. I was conscious of the eyes of the mother and her children on me—and saw them shift suddenly to the open door. I turned to see Jamie come in, soaked to the skin, his face drawn and set with fatigue.

He crossed the barn and sat down by me, laid his head on his knees, and closed his eyes.

"Thank you, sir," said the woman, very softly. "Ma'am."

I thought for a moment that he had fallen instantly asleep, for he didn't stir. After a moment, though, he said, in an equally soft voice, "Ye're welcome, ma'am."

I WAS MORE THAN pleased to find the Hunters when we reached the next village; they had been in one of the barges that had been captured early, but had succeeded in escaping by the simple expedient of walking into the woods after dark. As the soldiers who had captured them had not bothered to count their captives, no one noticed they had gone.

Overall, things were looking up somewhat. Food was becoming more abundant, and we were among regular Continentals. We were still only a few miles in front of Burgoyne's army, though, and the strain of the long retreat was telling. Desertion was frequent—though no one knew quite how frequent. Organization, discipline, and military structure were being restored as we came under the sway of the Continental army, but there were still men who could melt away unobtrusively.

It was Jamie who thought of the deserter game. Deserters would be welcomed into the British camps, fed, given clothes, and interrogated for information.

"So we'll give it to them, aye?" he said. "And it's only fair we take the same in return, is it not?"

Smiles began to grow on the faces of the officers to whom he was propounding this idea. And within a few days, carefully chosen "deserters" were making their way surreptitiously to the enemy camps and being taken before

British officers, where they poured out the stories with which they'd been carefully prepared. And after a good supper, they would take the first opportunity to re-desert back to the American side—bringing with them useful information about the British forces pursuing us.

Ian dropped in to Indian camps now and then if it seemed safe, but didn't play this particular game; he was memorable. I thought Jamie would have liked to masquerade as a deserter—it would appeal to his sense of drama, as well as his sense of adventure, which was acute. His size and striking appearance put this notion out of consideration, though; the deserters must all be ordinary-looking men who were unlikely to be recognized later.

"Because sooner or later, the British are going to realize what's afoot. They're not fools. And they willna take it kindly when they do realize."

We had found shelter for the night in another barn—this one unburnt and still equipped with a few piles of musty hay, though the stock had long since vanished. We were alone, but probably wouldn't be for long. The interlude in the commandant's garden seemed as though it had taken place in someone else's life, but I laid my head on Jamie's shoulder, relaxing against his solid warmth.

"Do ye think maybe—"

Jamie stopped abruptly, his hand tightening on my leg. An instant later, I heard the stealthy rustling that had alerted him, and my mouth went dry. It might be anything from a prowling wolf to an Indian ambush—but whatever it was was sizable, and I fumbled—as silently as possible—for the pocket in which I had stowed the knife he'd given me.

Not a wolf; something passed the open door, a shadow the height of a man, and vanished. Jamie squeezed my thigh and then was gone, moving crouched through the empty barn without a sound. For an instant, I couldn't see him in the dark, but my eyes were well adapted, and I found him seconds later, a long dark shadow pressed against the wall, just inside the door.

The shadow outside had come back; I saw the brief silhouette of a head against the paler black of the night outside. I got my feet under me, skin prickling with fear. The door was the only egress; perhaps I should throw myself on the floor and roll up against the base of a wall. I might escape detection—or, with luck, be able to grab the ankles of an intruder, or stab him through the foot.

I was just about to implement this strategy when a tremulous whisper came out of the dark.

"Friend—Friend James?" it said, and I let out the breath I had been holding in a gasp.

"Is that you, Denzell?" I said, trying to sound normal.

"Claire!" He burst through the door in relief, promptly tripped over something, and fell headlong with a crash.

"Welcome back, Friend Hunter," Jamie said, the nervous urge to laugh evident in his voice. "Are ye hurt?" The long shadow detached itself from the wall and bent to help our visitor up.

"No. No, I don't think so. Though in fact I scarcely know . . . James, I did it!"

There was a momentary silence.

"How close, *a charaid*?" Jamie asked quietly. "And do they move?"

"No, thank the Lord." Denzell sat down abruptly beside me, and I could feel his trembling. "They're waiting for their wagons to come up. They daren't outrun their supply line too far, and they're having terrible trouble; we've made such a mess of the roads"—the pride in his voice was palpable— "and the rain's helped a great deal, too."

"D'ye ken how long it might be?"

I saw Denzell nod, eager.

"One of the sergeants said it might be two, even three days. He was telling some of the soldiers to be mindful of their flour and beer, as they wouldn't get any more until the wagons came."

Jamie exhaled, and I felt some of the tension leave him. Mine did, too, and I felt a passionate wave of thankfulness. There would be time to sleep. I had just begun to relax a little; now the tension flowed out of me like water, to such an extent that I barely noticed what else Denzell had to confide. I heard Jamie's voice, murmuring congratulations; he clapped Denzell on the shoulder, and slid out of the barn, no doubt to go pass on the information.

Denzell sat still, breathing audibly. I gathered what was left of my concentration and made an effort to be amiable.

"Did they feed you, Denzell?"

"Oh." Denzell's voice changed, and he began to fumble in his pocket. "Here. I brought this away for thee." He pushed something into my hands: a small squashed loaf, rather burnt about the edges—I could tell from the hard crust and the smell of ashes. My mouth began to water uncontrollably.

"Oh, no," I managed to say, trying to give it back. "You should—"

"They fed me," he assured me. "Stew, of a sort. I ate all I could. And I've another loaf in my pocket for my sister. They gave me the food," he assured me earnestly. "I didn't steal it."

"Thank you," I managed to say, and with the greatest self-control, tore the loaf in half and tucked one half in my pocket for Jamie. Then I crammed the remainder in my mouth and ripped at it like a wolf wrenching bloody mouthfuls from a carcass.

Denny's stomach echoed mine, rumbling with a series of great borborygmi.

"I thought you said you ate!" I said, accusing.

"I did. But the stew seems not inclined to lie quiet," he said, with a small, pained laugh. He bent forward, arms folded over his stomach. "I—um, don't s'pose that thee might have a bit of barley water or peppermint to hand, Friend Claire?"

"I do," I said, unspeakably relieved that I still had the remnants in my sack. I hadn't much left, but I did have peppermint. There was no hot water; I gave him a handful to chew, washed down with water from a canteen. He drank thirstily, burped, and then stopped, breathing in a way that told me just what was happening. I guided him hastily to the side and held his head while he vomited, losing peppermint and stew together.

"Food poisoning?" I asked, trying to feel his forehead, but he slid away from me, collapsing onto a heap of straw, his head on his knees.

"He said he'd hang me," he whispered suddenly.

"Who?"

"The English officer. A Captain Bradbury, I think his name was. Said he thought I was a-playing at spies and soldiers, and if I didn't confess at once, he'd hang me."

"But he didn't," I said softly, and put a hand on his arm.

He was trembling all over, and I saw a drop of sweat hanging from the tip of his chin, translucent in the dimness.

"I told him—told him he could, I s'posed. If he pleased. And I truly thought he would. But he didn't." His breath came thick, and I realized that he was crying, silently.

I put my arms around him, held him, making hushing noises, and after a little he stopped. He was quiet for a few minutes.

"I thought—I would be prepared to die," he said softly. "That I would go happy to the Lord, whenever He chose to call me. I am ashamed to find it untrue. I was so much afraid."

I took a long, deep breath, and sat back beside him.

"I always wondered about martyrs," I said. "No one ever said they weren't afraid. It's only that they were willing to go and do whatever they did in spite of it. You went."

"I did not set up to be a martyr," he said after a moment. He sounded so meek, I nearly laughed.

"I doubt very much that many people do," I said. "And I think a person who did would be very obnoxious indeed. It's late, Denzell, and your sister will be worried. And hungry."

IT WAS AN HOUR or more before Jamie came back. I was lying in the hay, my shawl pulled over me, but wasn't asleep. He crawled in beside me and lay down, sighing, putting an arm over me.

"Why him?" I asked after a moment, trying to keep my voice calm. It didn't work; Jamie was acutely sensitive to tones of voice—anyone's, but particularly mine. I saw his head turn sharply toward me, but he paused a moment in turn before answering.

"He wished to go," he said, doing much better with the approximation of calmness than I had. "And I thought he'd do well with it."

"Do *well*? He's no actor! You know he can't lie; he must have been stammering and tripping over his tongue! I'm astonished that they believed him—if they did," I added.

"Oh, they did, aye. D'ye think a real deserter wouldna be terrified, Sassenach?" he said, sounding faintly amused. "I meant him to go in sweating and stammering. Had I tried to give him lines to speak, they'd ha' shot him on the spot."

The thought of it made the bolus of bread rise in my throat. I forced it back down.

"Yes," I said, and took a few breaths, feeling cold sweat prickle over my own face, seeing little Denny Hunter, sweating and stammering before the cold eyes of a British officer.

"Yes," I said again. "But . . . couldn't someone else have done it? It's not just that Denny Hunter is a friend—he's a doctor. He's needed."

Jamie's head turned toward me again. The sky outside was beginning to lighten; I could see the outline of his face.

"Did ye not hear me say he wished to do it, Sassenach?" he asked. "I didna ask him. In fact, I tried to dissuade him—for the very reason ye said. But he wouldna hear it and only asked me to look after his sister, should he not come back."

Rachel. My stomach clenched afresh at mention of her.

"What can he have been *thinking*?"

Jamie sighed deeply and turned onto his back.

"He's a Quaker, Sassenach. But he's a man. If he was the sort of man who'd not fight for what he believes, he'd ha' stayed in his wee village and poulticed horses and looked after his sister. But he's not." He shook his head and looked at me.

"Would ye have had me stay at home, Sassenach? Turn back from the fight?"

"I would," I said, agitation fading into crossness. "In a heartbeat. I just know you aren't bloody *going* to, so what's the point?"

That made him laugh.

"So ye do understand," he said, and took my hand. "It's the same for Denzell Hunter, aye? If he's bound to risk his life, then it's my job to see he gets the most return from his gambling."

"Bearing in mind that the return of most gambling is a big, fat zero," I remarked, trying to repossess the hand. "Hasn't anyone ever told you that the house always wins?" He wasn't letting go, but had begun to run the ball of his thumb gently back and forth over the tips of my fingers.

"Aye, well. Ye reckon the odds and cut the cards, Sassenach. And it's not *all* luck, ken?" The light had grown, in that imperceptible predawn way. Nothing so blatant as a sunbeam; just a gradual emergence of objects as the shadows round them went from black to gray to blue.

His thumb slipped inside my hand, and I curled my fingers involuntarily over it.

"Why isn't there a word that means the opposite of 'fade'?" I asked, watching the lines of his face emerge from night's shadow. I traced the shape of one rough brow with my thumb and felt the springy mat of his short beard against the palm of my hand, changing as I watched it from amorphous smudge to a distinction of tiny curls and wiry springs, a glowing mass of auburn, gold, and silver, vigorous against his weathered skin.

"I dinna suppose ye need one," he said. "If ye mean the light." He looked at me and smiled as I saw his eyes trace the outlines of my face. "If the light is fading, the night's coming on—and when the light grows again, it's the night that's fading, aye?"

It was, too. We should sleep, but the army would be astir around us shortly.

"Why is it that women don't make war, I wonder?"

"Ye're no made for it, Sassenach." His hand cupped my cheek, hard and rough. "And it wouldna be right; you women take so much more with ye, when ye go."

"What do you mean by that?"

He made the small shrugging movement that meant he was looking for a word or a notion, an unconscious movement, as though his coat was too tight, though he wasn't wearing one at the moment.

"When a man dies, it's only him," he said. "And one is much like another. Aye, a family needs a man, to feed them, protect them. But any decent man can do it. A woman . . ." His lips moved against my fingertips, a faint smile. "A woman takes life with her when she goes. A woman is . . . infinite possibility."

"Idiot," I said, very softly. "If you think one man is just like any other."

We lay for a bit, watching the light grow.

"How many times have ye done it, Sassenach?" he asked suddenly. "Sat betwixt the dark and the dawn, and held a man's fear in the palms of your hands?"

"Too many," I said, but it wasn't the truth, and he knew it. I heard his breath come, the faintest sound of humor, and he turned my hand palm up, his big thumb tracing the hills and valleys, joints and calluses, lifeline and heartline, and the smooth fleshy swell of the mount of Venus, where the faint scar of the letter "J" was still barely visible. I'd held him in my hand for the best part of my life.

"Part of the job," I said, meaning no flippancy, and he did not take it that way.

"D'ye think I'm not afraid?" he asked quietly. "When I do my job?"

"Oh, you're afraid," I said. "But you do it anyway. You're a frigging gambler—and the biggest gamble of all is a life, isn't it? Maybe yours—maybe someone else's."

"Aye, well," he said softly. "Ye'd know about that, I suppose.

"I'm the less bothered for myself," he said thoughtfully. "Looking at it all in all, I mean, I've done the odd useful thing here and there. My children are grown; my grandchildren are thriving—that's the most important thing, no?"

"It is," I said. The sun was up; I heard a rooster crow, somewhere in the distance.

"Well, so. I canna say I'm so verra much afraid as I used to be. I shouldna like dying, of course—but there'd maybe be less regret in it. On the other hand"—one side of his mouth turned up as he looked at me—"while I'm maybe less afraid for myself, I'm that wee bit more reluctant to kill young men who've not yet lived their lives." And that, I thought, was as close as I'd get to an apology for Denny Hunter.

"Going to assess the age of the people shooting at you, are you?" I asked, sitting up and beginning to brush hay out of my hair.

"Difficult," he admitted.

"And I sincerely hope that you don't propose to let some whippersnapper kill you, merely because they haven't had such a full life as yours yet."

He sat up, too, and faced me, serious, ends of hay bristling from hair and clothes.

"No," he said. "I'll kill them. I'll just mind it more."

58

INDEPENDENCE DAY

Philadelphia
July 4, 1777

GREY HAD NEVER been to Philadelphia before. Bar the streets, which were execrable, it seemed a pleasant city. Summer had graced the city's trees with huge verdant crowns, and a walk left him lightly dusted with leaf fragments and the soles of his boots sticky with fallen sap. Perhaps it was the febrile temperature of the air that was responsible for Henry's apparent state of mind, he thought darkly.

Not that he blamed his nephew. Mrs. Woodcock was lissome but rounded, with a lovely face and a warm character. *And* she had nursed him away from death's door when the local prison officer had brought him to her, worried lest a potentially lucrative prisoner die before yielding a full harvest. That sort of thing formed a bond, he knew—though he had never, thank God, felt any sort of *tendresse* for any of the women who had attended him in ill health. Except for . . .

"Shit," he said involuntarily, causing a clerical-looking gentleman to glare at him in passing.

He had clapped a mental teacup over the thought that had buzzed through his head like a meddlesome fly. Unable not to look at it, though, he cautiously lifted the cup and found Claire Fraser under it. He relaxed a little.

Certainly not a *tendresse*. On the other hand, he was damned if he could have said what it had been. A most peculiar sort of unsettling intimacy, at least—no doubt the result of her being Jamie Fraser's wife and her knowing what his own feelings for Jamie were. He dismissed Claire Fraser, and went back to worrying about his nephew.

Pleasant Mrs. Woodcock undeniably was, and just as undeniably rather too fond of Henry for a married woman—though her husband was a rebel, Henry had told him, and God knew when or whether he might return. Well enough; there was no danger of Henry losing his head and marrying her, at least. He could imagine the scandal, should Henry bring home a carpenter's widow, and she a sable enchantress, to boot. He grinned at the thought and felt more charitable toward Mercy Woodcock. She had, after all, saved Henry's life.

For now. The unwelcome thought buzzed in before he could clap the teacup over it. He couldn't avoid it for long; it kept coming back.

He understood Henry's reluctance to undergo another surgery. And there was the lingering fear that he might be too weak to withstand it. But at the same time, he could not be allowed to remain in his present state; he would simply dwindle and die, once illness and pain had drained the last of his vitality. Not even the fleshly attractions of Mrs. Woodcock would hold him, once that happened.

No, the surgery must be done, and soon. In Grey's conversations with Dr. Franklin, the old gentleman had made him acquainted with a friend, Dr. Benjamin Rush, who he claimed was a most prodigious medical man. Dr. Franklin urged Grey to visit him, should he ever find himself in the city—had given Grey a letter of introduction, in fact. He was on his way to present this, in hopes that Dr. Rush might either be practiced in surgery or be able to refer him to someone who was. Because, whether Henry wanted it or not, it had to be done. Grey could not take Henry home to England in his present state, and he had promised both Minnie and his brother that he would bring their youngest son back, were he still alive.

His foot slipped on a muddy cobble, and he let out a whoop and pitched sideways, arms pinwheeling for balance. He caught himself and shook his clothes back into order with a good assumption of dignity, ignoring the giggles of two milkmaids who had been watching.

Damn it all, she was back. Claire Fraser. Why? . . . Of course. The ether, as she called it. She'd asked him for a carboy of some sort of acid and had told him that she required it to make ether. Not as in the ethereal realm but a chemical substance that rendered people unconscious, so as to make surgery . . . painless.

He stopped dead in the middle of the street. Jamie had told him about his wife's experiments with the substance, with a full account of the amazing operation she had performed on a young boy, he rendered completely senseless as she opened his abdomen, removed an offending organ, and sewed him back together. After which the child was right as a grig, apparently.

He walked on more slowly, thinking furiously. Would she come? It was a laborious journey to almost anywhere from Fraser's Ridge. Not such a terrible trip from the mountain to the shore, though. It was summer, the weather was good; the journey could be made in less than two weeks. And if she would come to Wilmington, he could arrange for her to be brought to Philadelphia on whatever naval vessel was available—he knew people in the navy.

How long? How long might it take her—if she would come? More sobering thought: how long did Henry have?

He was pulled from these troubling reflections by what appeared to be a small riot proceeding down the street in his direction. A number of people, most of them drunken to judge by their behavior, which involved a good deal of shouting and pushing and waving of handkerchiefs. A young man was beating a drum, with much enthusiasm and no skill, and two children bore between them an outlandish banner, striped red and white but with no legend upon it.

He pressed back against a house, to give them room to pass. They did not pass, however, but instead hauled up before a house on the opposite side of the street and stood there shouting slogans in English and German. He caught the shout of "Liberty," and someone blew a cavalry charge upon a trumpet. And then he caught the shout of "Rush! Rush! Rush!"

Good God, it must be the house he was seeking, that of Dr. Rush. The mob seemed good-humored; he supposed they did not mean to drag the doctor out for a dose of tar and feathers, this being a notable form of public entertainment, or so he had been told. Cautiously, he approached and tapped a young woman on the shoulder.

"I beg your pardon." He had to lean close and shout into her ear to be heard; she whirled and blinked in surprise, then caught sight of his butterfly waistcoat and broke into a broad smile. He smiled back.

"I am seeking Dr. Benjamin Rush," he shouted. "Is this his house?"

"Yes, it is." A young man beside the young woman heard him and turned, his eyebrows shooting up at sight of Grey. "You have business with Dr. Rush?"

"I have a letter of introduction to the doctor from a Dr. Franklin, a mutual—"

The young man's face broke into a huge grin. Before he could say anything, though, the door of the house opened and a slender, well-dressed man in his thirties came out onto the stoop. There was a roar from the crowd, and the man, who must surely be Dr. Rush himself, held out his hands to them, laughing. The noise quieted for a moment, the man leaning out to talk with someone in the crowd. Then he ducked into the house, came out again with his coat on, came down the steps to a roar of applause, and the whole mob moved off again, banging and bugling with renewed fervor.

"Come along!" the young man bellowed in his ear. "There'll be free beer!"

Which is how Lord John Grey found himself in the taproom of a prosperous tavern, celebrating the first anniversary of the publication of the Declaration of Independence. There were political speeches of an impassioned, if not very eloquent, variety, and it was in the course of these that Grey learned that Dr. Rush was not only a wealthy and influential rebel sympathizer but a prominent rebel himself; in fact, as he learned from his newfound friends, both Rush *and* Dr. Franklin turned out to have signed the seditious document in the first place.

Word spread through the people round them that Grey was a friend of Franklin's, and he was much hailed in consequence, eventually being conveyed by insensible degrees through the crowd until he found himself face-to-face with Benjamin Rush.

It wasn't the first time Grey had been in close proximity to a criminal, and he kept his composure. This was plainly not the time to lay his nephew's situation before Rush, and Grey contented himself with shaking the young doctor by the hand and mentioning his connection with Franklin. Rush was most cordial, and shouted over the noise that Grey must come to call at his house when they both should be at leisure, perhaps in the morning.

Grey expressed his great willingness to do so and retired gracefully through the crowd, hoping that the Crown would not manage to hang Rush before he had a chance to examine Henry.

A racket in the street outside put a momentary stop to the festivities. There was considerable shouting and the thump of projectiles striking the front of the building. One of these—which proved to be a large, muddy rock—struck and shattered a pane of the establishment's window, allowing the bellows of "Traitors! Renegados!" to be heard more clearly.

"Shut your face, lickspittle!" shouted someone inside the tavern. Globs of mud and more rocks were hurled, some of these coming through the open door and broken window, along with patriotic shouts of "God Save the King!"

"Geld the Royal Brute!" shouted Grey's earlier acquaintance in reply, and half the tavern rushed out into the street, some pausing to break legs from stools to assist in the political discussion which then ensued.

Grey was somewhat concerned lest Rush be set upon by the Loyalists in the street and attacked before he could be of use to Henry, but Rush and a few others whom he took to be prominent rebels, as well, hung back from the fray and, after taking brief counsel, elected to leave through the tavern's kitchen.

Grey found himself left in the company of a man from Norfolk named Paine, a malnourished, ill-dressed wretch, large of nose and vivid of personality, possessed of strong opinions on the subjects of liberty and democracy and a most remarkable command of epithet regarding the King. Finding conversation difficult, as he could not reasonably express any of his own contrary opinions on these subjects, Grey excused himself with the intention of following Rush and his friends out the back way.

The riot outside, having reached a brief crescendo, had proceeded to its natural conclusion with the flight of the Loyalists, and people now had begun to flow back into the tavern, borne on a tide of righteous indignation and self-congratulation. Among these was a tall, slender, dark man, who looked round from his conversation, met Grey's eye, and stopped dead.

Grey walked up to him, hoping that the beating of his heart was not audible above the fading noise in the street.

"Mr. Beauchamp," he said, and took Perseverance Wainwright by hand and wrist, in what might be taken for cordial greeting but was in reality firm detention. "A private word with you, sir?"

HE WOULD NOT bring Percy to the house he had taken for himself and Dottie. Dottie would not recognize him, for she had not even been born when Percy vanished from Grey's life; it was merely the operation of the instinct which would have prevented him giving a small child a venomous snake to play with.

Percy, whatever his motive, did not suggest taking Grey to *his* lodgings, probably didn't want Grey knowing where he was staying, in case he thought to abscond quietly. After a moment's indecision—for Grey did not yet know the city—Grey agreed to Percy's suggestion that they walk to the common called Southeast Square.

"It's a potter's field," Percy said, leading the way. "Where they bury strangers to the city."

"How appropriate," Grey said, but Percy either didn't hear or affected not to. It was some way, and they didn't talk much, the streets being full of people. Despite the holiday aspects and the striped banners hung here and there—they all seemed to have a field of stars, though he hadn't seen the same arrangement twice, and the stripes varied in size and color, some having red, white, and blue stripes, some only red and white—there was a frenetic air to the gaiety, and an edged sense of danger in the streets. Philadelphia might be the rebels' capital, but it was far from being a stronghold.

The common was quieter, as might be expected of a graveyard. At that, it was surprisingly pleasant. There were only a few wooden grave markers here and there, giving such details as were known about the person interred beneath them; no one would have gone to the expense of placing gravestones, though some charitable soul had erected a large stone cross upon a plinth in the center of the field. Without conference, they headed for this object, following the course of a small creek that ran through the common.

It had occurred to Grey that Percy might have suggested their destination in order to give himself time to think on the way. Well enough—he'd been thinking, too. So when Percy sat down upon the base of the plinth and turned to him with an air of expectation, he didn't bother with observations on the weather.

"Tell me about the Baron Amandine's second sister," he said, standing before Percy.

Percy blinked, startled, but then smiled.

"Really, John, you amaze me. Claude didn't tell you about Amélie, I'm sure."

Grey didn't reply to that, but folded his hands beneath the tail of his coat and waited. Percy thought for a moment, then shrugged.

"All right. She was Claude's older sister; my wife, Cecile, is the younger."

" 'Was,' " Grey repeated. "So she's dead."

"She's been dead for some forty years. Why are you interested in her?" Percy pulled a handkerchief from his sleeve to dab at his temples; the day was hot, and it had been a long walk; Grey's own shirt was damp.

"Where did she die?"

"In a brothel in Paris." That stopped Grey in his tracks. Percy saw it and gave a wry smile. "If you must know, John, I am looking for her son."

Grey stared at him for a moment, then slowly sat down beside him. The gray stone of the plinth was warm under his buttocks.

"All right," he said, after a moment. "Tell me, if you would be so good."

Percy gave him a sideways glance of amusement—full of wariness, but still amused.

"There are things I cannot tell you, John, as you must surely appreciate. By the way, I hear that there is a rather heated discussion taking place between the British secretaries of state as to which of them shall make an approach regarding my previous offer—and to whom, exactly, to make it. I suppose this is your doing? I thank you."

"Don't change the subject. I'm not asking you about your previous offer." *Not yet, anyway.* "I'm asking you about Amélie Beauchamp and her son. I cannot see how they may be connected with the other matter, so I assume they have some personal significance to you. Naturally, there are things you cannot tell me regarding the larger matter"—he bowed slightly—"but this mystery about the baron's sister seems somewhat more personal."

"It is." Percy was turning something over in his mind; Grey could see it working behind his eyes. The eyes were lined and a little pouched but the same as ever; a warm, lively brown, the color of sherry-sack. His fingers drummed briefly on the stone, then stopped, and he turned to Grey with an air of decision.

"Very well. Bulldog that you are, if I *don't* tell you, you will doubtless be following me all over Philadelphia, in an effort to discover my purpose in being here."

This was precisely what Grey intended doing in any case, but he made an indeterminate noise that might be taken as encouragement before asking, "What *is* your purpose in being here?"

"I'm looking for a printer named Fergus Fraser." Grey blinked at that; he hadn't been expecting any concrete answer.

"Who is . . . ?"

Percy held up a hand, folding down the fingers as he spoke.

"He is, first, the son of one James Fraser, a notable ex-Jacobite and current rebel. He is, secondly, a printer, as indicated—and, I suspect, a rebel like his father. And, thirdly, I strongly suspect that he is the son of Amélie Beauchamp."

There were blue and red dragonflies hovering over the creek; Grey felt as though one of these insects had flown suddenly up his nose.

"You are telling me that James Fraser had an illegitimate son by a French whore? Who happened also to be the daughter of an ancient noble family?" Shock did not begin to describe his feelings, but he kept his tone light, and Percy laughed.

"No. The printer *is* Fraser's son, but is adopted. He took the boy from a brothel in Paris more than thirty years ago." A trickle of sweat ran down the side of Percy's neck, and he wiped it away. The warmth of the day had made his cologne blossom on his skin; Grey caught the hint of ambergris and carnation, spice and musk together.

"Amélie was, as I said, Claude's older sister. In her teens she was seduced by a much older man, a married nobleman, and got with child. The normal thing would have been for her simply to be married hastily off to a complaisant husband, but the nobleman's wife died quite suddenly, and Amélie made a fuss, insisting that since he was now free, he must marry *her*."

"He was not so inclined?"

"No. Claude's father was, though. I suppose he thought such a marriage would improve the family fortunes; the comte was a very wealthy man, and while not political, did have a certain . . . standing."

The old Baron Amandine had been willing to keep things quiet in the beginning, but as he began to see the possibilities of the situation, he became bolder and threatened all kinds of things, from a complaint to the King—for old Amandine was active at court, unlike his son—to a lawsuit for damages and an application to the Church for excommunication.

"Could he actually have done that?" Grey asked, fascinated despite his reservations about Percy's veracity. Percy smiled briefly.

"He could have complained to the King. In any case, he didn't get the chance. Amélie disappeared."

The girl had vanished from her home in the middle of one night, taking her jewels. It was thought that perhaps she had intended to run away to her lover, in the hope that he would give in and marry her, but the comte professed complete ignorance of the matter, and no one came forward to say that they had seen her, either leaving *Trois Flèches* or entering the Paris mansion of the Comte St. Germain.

"And you think she somehow ended in a Paris brothel?" Grey said incredulously. "How? And if so, how did you discover this?"

"I found her marriage lines."

"What?"

"A contract of marriage, between Amélie Élise LeVigne Beauchamp and Robert-François Quesnay de St. Germain. Signed by both parties. And a priest. It was in the library at *Trois Flèches,* inside the family Bible. Claude and Cecile are not very religiously inclined, I'm afraid," Percy said, shaking his head.

"And you are?" That made Percy laugh; he knew that Grey knew precisely what his feelings regarding religion were.

"I was bored," he said without apology.

"Life at *Trois Flèches* must have been tedious indeed, if it forced you to read the Bible. Did the sub-gardener quit?"

"Did—oh, Emile." Percy grinned. "No, but he had a terrible bout of *la grippe* that month. Couldn't breathe through his nose at all, poor man."

Grey felt again a treacherous impulse to laugh, but restrained it, and Percy went on without a pause.

"I actually wasn't *reading* it; I have all of the most excessive damnations memorized, after all. I was interested in the cover."

"Heavily bejeweled, was it?" Grey asked dryly, and Percy gave him a look of mild offense.

"It has not *always* got to do with money, John, even for those of us not blessed with such substance as yourself."

"My apologies," said Grey. "Why the Bible, then?"

"I will have you know that I am a bookbinder of no mean repute," Percy said, preening a little. "I took it up in Italy as a means of making a living. After you so gallantly saved my life. Thank you for that, by the way," he said, with a direct look whose sudden seriousness made Grey look down to avoid his eyes.

"You're welcome," he said gruffly, and, bending, carefully induced a small green caterpillar that was inching its way across the polished toe of his boot to inch onto his finger.

"Anyway," Percy went on, not losing a beat, "I discovered this curious document. I had heard of the family scandal, of course, and recognized the names at once."

"You asked the present baron about it?"

"I did. What did you think of Claude, by the way?" Percy had always been like quicksilver, Grey thought, and he hadn't lost any of his mutability with age.

"Bad cardplayer. A wonderful voice, though—does he sing?"

"Indeed he does. And you're right about the cards. He can keep a secret, if he likes, but he can't lie at all. You'd be amazed at how powerful a thing perfect honesty is, in some circumstances," Percy added reflectively. "It almost makes me think there might be something in the Eighth Commandment."

Grey muttered something about "more honored in the breach," but then coughed and begged that Percy might continue.

"He didn't know about the marriage contract, I'm sure of it. He was genuinely staggered. And after a certain amount of hesitation—'bloody, bold, and resolute' may be your watchwords, John, but they are not his—he gave his consent for me to dig into the matter."

Grey ignored the implied flattery—if that's what it was, and he thought it was—and carefully deposited the caterpillar onto the leaves of what looked like an edible bush.

"You looked for the priest," he said with certainty.

Percy laughed with what sounded like genuine pleasure, and it occurred to Grey with a small shock that of course he knew Percy's mind, and Percy his; they had been conversing, through the veils of statecraft and secrecy, for many years. Of course, Percy had likely known to whom he was talking, and Grey hadn't.

"Yes, I did. He was dead—murdered. Killed in the street at night while hurrying to give the last rites to a dying parishioner, such a terrible thing. A week after the disappearance of Amélie Beauchamp."

This was beginning to rouse Grey's professional interest, though the private side of him was still more than wary.

"The next thing would have been the comte—but if he was capable of killing a priest to keep his secrets, it would have been dangerous to approach him directly," Grey said. "His servants, then?"

Percy nodded, mouth quirked at one corner in appreciation of Grey's acuity.

"The comte was dead, too—or he disappeared, at least; he had a reputation as a sorceror, oddly enough—and he died a good ten years after Amélie. But I looked for his old servants, yes. I found a few of them. For some people, it really *is* always about money, and the assistant coachman was one of those. Two days after Amélie disappeared, he delivered a carpet to a brothel near the Rue Fauborg. A very heavy carpet that had about it a smell of opium—which he recognized, because he had at one point transported a troupe of Chinese acrobats who came to entertain at a fete at the mansion."

"And so you went to the brothel. Where money . . ."

"They say water is the universal solvent," Percy said, shaking his head, "but it isn't. You could plunge a man into a barrel of freezing water and leave him for a week, and you would accomplish much less than you might with a modest quantity of gold."

Grey silently noted the adjective "freezing," and nodded to Percy to continue.

"It took some time, repeated visits, different attempts—the madam was a true professional, meaning that whoever had paid her predecessor had done so on a staggering scale, and her doorkeeper, while old enough, had had his tongue torn out at an early age; no help there. And of course none of the whores had been there when the infamous carpet was delivered, that being so long before."

He had, however, patiently traced the families of the present whores—for some occupations run in families—and managed after months of work to discover an old woman who had been employed at the brothel and who recognized the miniature of Amélie that he had brought from *Trois Flèches*.

The girl had indeed been brought to the brothel, in the middle stages of pregnancy. That had not mattered particularly; there were patrons with such tastes. A few months later, she had been delivered of a son. She had survived childbirth but died a year later, during a plague of influenza.

"And I could not *begin* to tell you the difficulties of finding out anything about a child born in a Paris brothel forty-odd years ago, my dear." Percy sighed, employing his handkerchief again.

"But your name is Perseverance," Grey noted with extreme dryness, and Percy glanced sharply at him.

"Do you know," he said lightly, "I believe you are the only person in the world who knows that?" And from the expression in his eyes, that was one too many.

"Your secret is safe with me," Grey said. "That one, at least. What about Denys Randall-Isaacs?"

It worked. Percy's face shimmered like a pool of quicksilver in the sun. In half a heartbeat, he had the perfect blankness back in place—but it was too late.

Grey laughed, though without humor, and stood up.

"Thank you, Perseverance," he said, and walked away through the grassy graves of the nameless poor.

That night, when his household was asleep, he took pen and ink to write to Arthur Norrington, to Harry Quarry, and to his brother. Toward dawn, he began, for the first time in two years, to write to Jamie Fraser.

BATTLE OF BENNINGTON

General Burgoyne's camp
August 11, 1777

THE SMOKE OF burnt and burning fields hung over the camp, had done so for days. The Americans were still withdrawing, destroying the countryside in their wake.

William was with Sandy Lindsay, talking about the best way to cook a turkey—one of Lindsay's scouts having just brought him one—when the letter arrived. It was likely William's imagination that a dreadful silence fell upon the camp, the earth shook, and the veil of the temple was rent in twain. But it was very shortly apparent that something had happened, nonetheless.

There was a definite change in the air, something amiss in the rhythms of speech and movement among the men surrounding them. Balcarres felt it, too, and stopped in his examination of the turkey's outspread wing, looking at William with eyebrows raised.

"What?" said William.

"I don't know, but it isn't good." Balcarres thrust the limp turkey into his orderly's hands and, snatching up his hat, made for Burgoyne's tent, William on his heels.

They found Burgoyne tight-lipped and white with anger, his senior officers in clusters round him, speaking to one another in low, shocked voices.

Captain Sir Francis Clerke, the general's aide-de-camp, emerged from the press, head down and face shadowed. Balcarres caught at his elbow as he passed.

"Francis—what's happened?"

Captain Clerke was looking noticeably agitated. He glanced behind him into the tent, then stepped aside and moved out of earshot, taking Balcarres and William with him.

"Howe," he said. "He's not coming."

"Not coming?" William said stupidly. "But—is he not leaving New York after all?"

"He's leaving," Clerke said, his lips so tight it was a wonder he could speak at all. "To invade Pennsylvania."

"But—" Balcarres darted an appalled look toward the entrance to the tent, then back at Clerke.

"Exactly."

The true proportions of the disaster were revealing themselves to William. General Howe was not merely cocking a snook at General Burgoyne by ignoring his plan, which would be bad enough from Burgoyne's point of view. By choosing to march on Philadelphia rather than coming up the Hudson to join Burgoyne's troops, Howe had left Burgoyne essentially to his own devices, in terms of supply and reinforcement.

In other words, they were on their own, separated from their supply trains, with the disagreeable choice of continuing to pursue the retreating Americans through a wilderness from which all sustenance had been stripped—or turning round and marching ignominiously back to Canada, through a wilderness from which all sustenance had been stripped.

Balcarres had been expostulating along these lines to Sir Francis, who rubbed a hand over his face in frustration, shaking his head.

"I know," he said. "If you'll excuse me, my lords—"

"Where are you going?" William asked, and Clerke glanced at him.

"To tell Mrs. Lind," Clerke said. "I thought I'd best warn her." Mrs. Lind was the wife of the chief commissary officer. She was also General Burgoyne's mistress.

WHETHER MRS. LIND had exerted her undeniable gifts to good effect, or whether the general's natural resiliency of character had asserted itself, the blow of Howe's letter was swiftly encompassed. *Whatever you want to say about him,* William wrote in his weekly letter to Lord John, *he knows the benefit of certain decision and swift action. We have resumed our pursuit of the Americans' chief body of troops with redoubled effort. Most of our horses have been abandoned, stolen, or eaten. I have quite worn through the soles of one pair of boots.*

In the meantime, we receive intelligence from one of the scouts to the effect that the town of Bennington, which is not too far distant, is being used as a gathering place for the American commissary. By report, it is lightly guarded, and so the General is sending Colonel Baum, one of the Hessians, with five hundred troops to capture these much-needed supplies. We leave in the morning.

Whether his drunken conversation with Balcarres was in part responsible, William never knew, but he had discovered that he was now spoken of as being "good with Indians." And whether it was owing to this dubious capacity or to the fact that he could speak basic German, he found himself on the morning of August 12 deputed to accompany Colonel Baum's foraging expedition, this including a number of dismounted Brunswick cavalry, two three-pounder artillery pieces, and a hundred Indians.

By report, the Americans were receiving cattle, funneled out of New England, these being collected in quantity in Bennington, as well as a considerable number of wagons, these full of corn, flour, and other necessaries.

It was, for a wonder, not raining when they set out, and that alone gave the expedition a feeling of optimism. Anticipation of food increased this sense significantly. Rations had been short for what seemed a very long time, though in fact it had been only a week or so. Still, more than a day spent marching without adequate food seems a long time, as William had good cause to know.

Many of the Indians were still mounted; they circled the main body of soldiers, riding ahead a little way to scout the road, coming back to offer guidance through or around places where the road—no more than a trace at the best of times—had given up the fight and been absorbed by the forest or drowned by one of the rain-swollen streams that leapt unexpectedly out of the hills. Bennington was near a river called the Walloomsac, and as they walked, William was discussing in a desultory way with one of the Hessian lieutenants whether it might be possible to load the stores onto rafts for transport to a rendezvous downstream.

This discussion was entirely theoretical, since neither of them knew where the Walloomsac went nor whether it was navigable to any extent, but it gave both men a chance to practice the other's language and so passed the time on a long, hot march.

"My father spent much time in Germany," William told Ober-Leftenant Gruenwald, in his careful, slow German. "He is of the food of Hanover very fond."

Gruenwald, from Hesse-Cassel, allowed himself a derisive twitch of the mustache at mention of Hanover, but contented himself with the observation that even a Hanoverian could roast a cow and perhaps boil some potatoes to accompany it. But his own mother made a dish from the flesh of swine and apples, beswimming in red wine and spiced with nutmeg and cinnamon, that made his mouth water only to remember.

Water was running down Gruenwald's face, sweat making tracks in the dust and dampening the collar of his light-blue coat. He took off his tall grenadier's headdress and wiped his head with a giant spotted kerchief, sodden from many earlier employments.

"I think we will maybe not find cinnamon today," Willie said. "Maybe a pig, though."

"If we do, I will him roast for you," Gruenwald assured him. "As for apples . . ." he tucked a hand into his tunic and withdrew a handful of small red crab apples, which he shared out with William. "I haff a bushel of these. I haff—"

Excited yips from an Indian riding back down the column interrupted him, and William looked up to see the rider throw back an arm, gesturing behind him and shouting, "River!"

The word enlivened the sagging columns, and William saw the cavalry—who had insisted upon wearing their high boots and their broadswords, in spite of their lack of horses, and had suffered in consequence—draw themselves up, clanking loudly with anticipation.

Another shout came from the forward line.

"Cow turds!"

That caused a general cheer and much laughter among the men, who hastened on with a quicker step. William saw Colonel Baum, who did still have a horse, turn out of the column and wait on the roadside, leaning down to speak briefly with the officers as they came past. William saw his aide lean close, pointing up a small hill opposite.

"What do you think—" he said, turning to Gruenwald, and was startled to find the ober-leftenant staring at him blank-faced, his jaw hanging open. The man's hand loosened and fell to his side, and the mitred helmet fell and rolled away in the dust. William blinked and saw a thick worm of red snake its way slowly down from under Gruenwald's dark hair.

Gruenwald sat down quite suddenly and fell backward in the road, his face gone a muddy white.

"Shit!" said William, and jerked suddenly to an awareness of what had just happened. "*Ambush!*" he bellowed at the top of his lungs. *"Das ist ein Überfall!!"*

There were shouts of alarm rising from the column, and the crack of sporadic firing from the woods. William grabbed Gruenwald under the arms and dragged him hastily into the shelter of a group of pine trees. The ober-leftenant was still alive, though his coat was wet with sweat and blood. William made sure the German's pistol was loaded and in his hand before taking his own pistol and dashing toward Baum, who was standing in his stirrups, shrieking directions in high, shrill German.

He caught only a word here and there and looked urgently round, to see whether he could tell what the colonel's orders were from the actions of the Hessians. He caught sight of a little group of scouts, running down the road toward him, and ran to meet them.

"Goddamned lot of rebels," one scout gasped, out of breath, pointing behind him. "Coming."

"Where? How far?" He felt as though he were about to run out of his skin, but forced himself to stand still, speak calmly, breathe.

A mile, maybe two. He did breathe then, and managed to ask how many there were. Maybe two hundred, maybe more. Armed with muskets, but no artillery.

"Right. Go back and keep an eye on them." He turned back toward Colonel Baum, feeling the surface of the road strange under his feet, as though it wasn't quite where he expected it to be.

THEY DUG IN, hastily but efficiently, entrenching themselves behind shallow earthworks and makeshift barricades of fallen trees. The guns were dragged up the small hill and aimed to cover the road. The rebels, of course, ignored the road, and swarmed in from both sides.

There might have been two hundred men in the first wave; it was impossible to count them as they darted through the heavy wood. William could see the flicker of movement and fired at it, but without any great hope of hitting anyone. The wave hesitated, but only for a moment.

Then a strong voice bellowed, somewhere behind the rebel front, "We take them now, or Molly Stark's a widow tonight!"

"What?" said William, disbelieving. Whatever the man shouting had meant, his exhortation had a marked effect, for an enormous number of rebels came boiling out of the trees, headed at a mad run for the guns. The soldiers minding the guns promptly fled, and so did a good many of the others.

The rebels were making short work of the rest, and William had just settled down grimly to do what he could before they got him, when two Indians came springing over the rolling ground, seized him under the arms, and, yanking him to his feet, propelled him rapidly away.

Which was how Lieutenant Ellesmere found himself once more cast in the role of Cassandra, reporting the debacle at Bennington to General Burgoyne. Men killed and wounded, guns lost—and not a single cow to be shown for it.

And I haven't yet killed a single rebel, either, he thought tiredly, making his way slowly back to his tent afterward. He thought he should regret that, but wasn't sure he did.

60

DESERTER GAME, ROUND II

J AMIE HAD BEEN bathing in the river, sluicing sweat and grime from his body, when he heard remarkably odd swearing in French. The words were French, but the sentiments expressed were definitely not. Curious, he clambered out of the water, dressed, and went down the bank a little way, where he discovered a young man waving his arms and gesturing in an agitated attempt to make himself understood to a bemused party of workmen. As half of them were Germans and the rest Americans from Virginia, his efforts to communicate with them in French had so far succeeded only in entertaining them.

Jamie had introduced himself and offered his services as interpreter. Which is how he had come to spend a good bit of each day with the young Polish engineer whose unpronounceable last name had quickly been shortened to "Kos."

He found Kos both intelligent and rather touching in his enthusiasm—and was himself interested in the fortifications Kościuszko (for he prided himself on being able to say it correctly) was building. Kos, for his part, was both grateful for the linguistic assistance and interested in the occasional observations and suggestions that Jamie was able to make, as the result of his conversations with Brianna.

Talking about vectors and stresses made him miss her almost unbearably but at the same time brought her somehow nearer to him, and he found himself spending more and more time with the young Pole, learning bits of his language and allowing Kos to practice what he fondly imagined to be English.

"What is it that brought ye here?" Jamie asked one day. In spite of the lack of pay, a remarkable number of European officers had come to join—or tried to join—the Continental army, evidently feeling that even if the prospects of plunder were limited, they could bamboozle the Congress into granting them rank as generals, which they could then parlay into further occupation back in Europe. Some of these dubious volunteers were actually of use, but he'd heard a good bit of muttering about those who weren't. Thinking of Matthias Fermoy, he was inclined to mutter a bit himself.

Kos wasn't one of these, though.

"Well, first, money," he said frankly, when asked how he had come to be in America. "My brother the manor in Poland has, but family no money, nothing for me. No girl look at me without money." He shrugged. "No place in

Polish army, but I know how to build things, I come where things to build."
He grinned. "Maybe girls, too. Girls with good family, good money."

"If ye came for money and girls, man, ye joined the wrong army," Jamie
said dryly, and Kościuszko laughed.

"I say *first* money," he corrected. "I come to Philadelphia, read there *La
Declaration*." He pronounced it in French, and bared his head in reverence
at the name, clasping his sweat-stained hat to his breast. "This thing, this
writing . . . I am ravish."

So ravished was he by the sentiments expressed in that noble document
that he had at once sought out its author. While probably surprised by the
sudden advent of a passionate young Pole in his midst, Thomas Jefferson had
made him welcome, and the two men had spent most of a day deeply involved
in the discussion of philosophy (in French), from which they had emerged
fast friends.

"Great man," Kos assured Jamie solemnly, crossing himself before putting
his hat back on. "God keep him safe."

"*Dieu accorde-lui la sagesse,*" Jamie replied. *God grant him wisdom.* He
thought that Jefferson would certainly be safe, as he was no soldier.

Kos had wiped a strand of stringy dark hair out of his mouth and shaken
his head.

"Maybe wife, one day, if God wills. This—what we do here—more important than wife."

They returned to work, but Jamie found his mind dwelling with interest
on the conversation. The notion that it was better to spend one's life in pursuit of a noble goal than merely to seek safety—he agreed with that entirely.
But surely such purity of purpose was the province of men without families?
A paradox there: a man who sought his own safety was a coward; a man who
risked his family's safety was a poltroon, if not worse.

That led on to more rambling paths of thought and further interesting para-
doxes: Do women hold back the evolution of such things as freedom and other
social ideals, out of fear for themselves or their children? Or do they in fact inspire such things—and the risks required to reach them—by providing the
things worth fighting for? Not merely fighting to defend, either, but to propel
forward, for a man wanted more for his children than he would ever have.

He would have to ask Claire what she thought of this, though he smiled to
think of some of the things she *might* think of it, particularly the part about
whether women hindered social evolution by their nature. She'd told him
something of her own experiences in the Great War—he couldn't think of it
by any other name, though she told him there was another, earlier one by that
name. She said disparaging things about heroes now and then, but only when
he'd hurt himself; she knew fine what men were for.

Would he be here, in fact, if it weren't for her? Would he do this anyway,
only for the sake of the ideals of the Revolution, if he were not assured of victory? He had to admit that only a madman, an idealist, or a truly desperate
man would be here now. Any sane person who knew anything about armies
would have shaken his head and turned away, appalled. He often felt appalled,
himself.

But he would, in fact, do it—were he alone. A man's life had to have more purpose than only to feed himself each day. And this was a grand purpose— grander, maybe, than anyone else fighting for it knew. And if it took his own life in the doing . . . he wouldn't enjoy it, but he'd be comforted in the dying, knowing he'd helped. After all, it wasn't as though he would be leaving his wife helpless; unlike most wives, Claire would have a place to go if something befell him.

He was once more in the river, floating on his back and thinking along these lines, when he heard the gasp. It was a feminine gasp, and he put his feet down at once and stood up, wet hair streaming over his face. He shoved it back to find Rachel Hunter standing on the bank, both hands pressed over her eyes and every line of her body strained in an eloquence of distress.

"Did ye want me, Rachel?" he asked, wiping water out of his eyes in an effort to locate just where on the riverbank he had left his clothes. She gasped again and turned her face in his direction, hands still over her eyes.

"Friend James! Thy wife said I would find thee here. I beg pardon for— please! Come out at once!" Her anguish broke out and her hands dropped, though she kept her eyes tight shut as she reached out to him, pleading.

"What—"

"Denny! The British have him!"

Cold shot through his veins, much colder than the wind on his exposed wet skin.

"Where? How? Ye can look now," he added, hastily buttoning his breeches.

"He went with another man, posing as deserters." He was up the bank beside her, shirt over his arm, and saw that she had her brother's spectacles in the pocket of her apron; her hand kept going to them, clutching them. "I told him not to, I did!"

"I told him, too," Jamie said grimly. "Are ye sure, lass?"

She nodded, pale as a sheet and her eyes huge in her face, but not—not yet—weeping.

"The other man—he came back, just now, and ran to find me. He—it was ill-luck, he said; they were brought before a major, and it was the same man who had threatened to hang Denny when he did it last time! The other man ran for it and escaped, but they caught Denny, and this time, this time . . ." She was gasping for breath and could barely speak for dread, he saw. He put a hand on her arm.

"Find the other man and send him to my tent, so he can tell me exactly where your brother is. I'll go to fetch Ian and we'll get him back." He squeezed her arm gently to make her look at him, and she did, though so distracted he thought she barely saw him.

"Dinna fash yourself. We'll get him back for ye," he repeated gently. "I swear it, by Christ and His Mother."

"Thee must not swear—oh, the devil with it!" she cried, then clapped a hand over her mouth. She shut her eyes, swallowed, and took it away again. "Thank you," she said.

"Ye're welcome," he said, with an eye to the sinking sun. Did the British prefer to hang people at sunset or at dawn? "We'll get him back," he said once more, firmly. *Dead or alive.*

THE CAMP'S commanding officer had built a gibbet in the center of the camp. It was a crude affair of unbarked logs and rough timber, and from the holes and gouges round its nails, had been disassembled and moved several times. It looked effective, though, and the dangling noose gave Jamie a feeling of ice in his water.

"We've played the deserter game once too often," Jamie whispered to his nephew. "Or maybe three."

"D'ye think he's ever used it?" Ian murmured back, peering down at the sinister thing through their screen of oak saplings.

"He wouldna go to that much work only to scare someone."

It scared *him,* badly. He didn't point out to Ian the spot near the bottom of the main upright, where someone's—or someones'—desperately flailing feet had kicked away chunks of the bark. The makeshift gibbet wasn't high enough for the drop to break a man's neck; a man hanged on it would strangle slowly.

He touched his own neck in reflexive aversion, Roger Mac's mangled throat and its ugly raw scar clear in his mind. Even clearer was the memory of the grief that had overwhelmed him, coming to take down Roger Mac from the tree they'd hanged him on, knowing him dead and the world changed forever. It had been, too, though he hadn't died.

Well, it wasn't going to change for Rachel Hunter. They weren't too late, that was the important thing. He said as much to Ian, who didn't reply but gave him a brief glance of surprise.

How do you know? it said, plain as words. He lifted a shoulder and inclined his head toward a spot a little farther down the hill, where an outcrop of rock covered in moss and bearberry would give them cover. They moved off silently, keeping low, making their movements in the same slow rhythm to which the wood was moving. It was twilight and the world was full of shadows; it was no trick to be two more.

He knew they hadn't hanged Denny Hunter yet, because he'd seen men hanged. Execution left a stain upon the air and marked the souls of those who saw it.

The camp was quiet. Not literally—the soldiers were making considerable racket, and a good thing, too—but in terms of its spirit. There was neither a sense of dread oppression nor the sick excitement that sprang from the same source; you could feel such things. So Denny Hunter was either here, alive— or had been sent elsewhere. If he was here, where would he be?

Confined somehow, and under guard. This wasn't a permanent camp; there was no stockade. It was a big camp, though, and it took them some time to circle it, checking to see whether Hunter might be somewhere in the open, tied to a tree or shackled to a wagon. He was nowhere in sight, though. That left the tents.

There were four large ones, and one of these plainly housed the commissary; it stood apart and had a small cluster of wagons near it. It had also a constant stream of men going in and out, emerging with sacks of flour or dried peas. No meat, though he could smell cooking rabbit and squirrel from some of the campfires. The German deserters had been right, then; the army was living off the land, as well as it could.

"The commander's tent?" Ian whispered softly to him. It was plain to see, with its pennants and the knot of men who stood about just outside its entrance.

"I hope not." Plainly they'd have taken Denny Hunter *to* the commander for interrogation. And if he were still in doubt as to Hunter's *bona fides,* he might have kept the man close at hand for further questioning.

Had he already made up his mind on the matter, though—and Rachel had been convinced of it—he wouldn't keep him. He would have been sent somewhere under guard to await his reckoning. Under guard and out of sight, though Jamie doubted the British commander feared a rescue attempt.

"Eeny-meeny-miney-mo," he muttered under his breath, twitching a finger back and forth between the two remaining tents. A guard with a musket was standing more or less between them; no telling which he was set to guard. "That one." He lifted his chin to the one on the right, but even as he did so felt Ian stiffen beside him.

"Nay," Ian said softly, eyes riveted. "The other."

There was something strange in Ian's voice, and Jamie glanced at him in surprise, then down at the tent.

At first, his only thought was a fleeting sense of confusion. Then the world changed.

It was twilight, but they were by now no more than fifty yards away; there was no mistaking it. He hadn't seen the boy close-to since he was twelve, but he had memorized every moment they'd spent in each other's presence: the way he carried himself, the quick, graceful movement—*that's from his mother,* he thought in a daze of shock, seeing the tall young officer make a gesture of the hand that was Geneva Dunsany to the life—the shape of his back, his head and ears, though the slender shoulders had thickened to a man's. *Mine,* he thought, with a surge of pride that shocked him nearly as much as William's sudden appearance had. *They're mine.*

Jarring as they were, these thoughts took less than half a second to dash through his head and out again. He breathed in, very slowly, and out again. Had Ian remembered William from their meeting seven years earlier? Or was the resemblance so instantly visible to a casual eye?

It didn't matter now. The camp was beginning its supper preparations; within minutes everyone would be engrossed in the meal. It was better to move then, even without the cover of darkness.

"It has to be me, aye?" Ian gripped his wrist, compelling his attention. "D'ye want to make the diversion before or after?"

"After." He'd been thinking, in the back of his mind, all the time they were creeping toward the camp, and now the decision lay ready, as though someone else had made it. "Best if we can get him away quiet. Try, and if things go wrong, screech."

Ian nodded and, with no further conversation, dropped to his belly and began a stealthy worming through the brush. The evening was cool and pleasant after the heat of the day, but Jamie's hands felt cold and he cupped them round the clay belly of the little firepot. He'd carried it from their own camp, feeding it bits of dry stick along the way. It was hissing softly to itself as it fed on a chunk of dried hickory, both the sight and the smell of it safely hidden in the haze of campfire smoke that drifted through the trees, dispelling the gnats and the bloodthirsty mosquitoes, thank God and His mother.

Wondering at his own twitching—it wasn't like him—he touched his sporran, checking yet again that the cork had not come loose from the bottle of turpentine, even though he knew well it hadn't; he'd smell it.

The arrows in his quiver shifted as he shifted his weight, the fletchings rustling. He was in easy bowshot of the commander's tent, could have the canvas well alight in seconds if Ian screeched. If he didn't . . .

He began to move again, eyes flitting over the ground, searching for a patch that would do. Dry grass there was in plenty, but it would go up too fast if that was all there was. He wanted a fast flame but a big one.

The soldiers would have already scavenged the nearby forest for firewood, but he spotted a fallen fir snag, too heavy to carry away. Foragers had snapped the lower branches off, but there were plenty left, thick with dried needles that the wind hadn't taken yet. He moved back slowly, far enough out of sight that he could move quickly again, gathering armfuls of dry grass, bark scraped hasty from a log, anything that would kindle.

Flaming arrows in the commander's tent would compel instant attention, to be sure, but they would also cause widespread alarm; soldiers would boil out of the camp like hornets, looking for attackers. A grass fire, no. Such things were common, and while it would certainly create diversion, no one would be looking further once they'd seen it was nothing.

A few minutes and he had his diversion ready. So busy he'd been, he hadn't even taken thought to look again at his son.

"God damn ye for a liar, Jamie Fraser," he said under his breath, and looked.

William was gone.

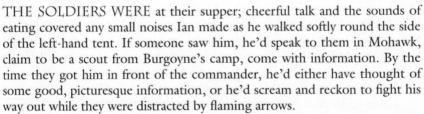

THE SOLDIERS WERE at their supper; cheerful talk and the sounds of eating covered any small noises Ian made as he walked softly round the side of the left-hand tent. If someone saw him, he'd speak to them in Mohawk, claim to be a scout from Burgoyne's camp, come with information. By the time they got him in front of the commander, he'd either have thought of some good, picturesque information, or he'd scream and reckon to fight his way out while they were distracted by flaming arrows.

That wouldn't help Denny Hunter, though, and he was careful. There were pickets posted, but he and Uncle Jamie had watched long enough to see the pattern of them and spy the dead spot where a picket's vision was obstructed by the trees. He knew he couldn't be seen behind the tent, save someone heading for the woods for a piss stumbled over him.

There was a gap at the bottom of the tent and a candlestick lit inside; a spot in the canvas glowed dim in the twilight. He watched the gap and saw no shadow move. Right, then.

He lay down and inserted a cautious hand, feeling along the dirt floor, hoping no one inside stamped on his hand. If he could find a cot, he could squirm in and lie under it. If—something touched his hand and he bit his tongue, hard.

"Is thee a friend?" whispered Denny's voice. Ian could see the Quaker's shadow on the canvas, a squatting blur, and Denny's hand held his hard.

"Aye, it's me," he whispered back. "Keep quiet. Stand back."

Denny moved, and Ian heard the clink of metal. Dammit, the buggers had him in fetters. He compressed his lips and slid under the edge of the tent.

Denny greeted him silently, his face alight with hope and alarm. The little Quaker lifted his hands, nodded to his feet. Full irons. Christ, they *did* mean to hang him.

Ian leaned in close to whisper in Denny's ear.

"I go out before ye. Lie down there, easy as ye can, close as ye can." He jerked his chin at the back wall of the tent. "Dinna move yourself; I'll pull ye through." Then get Denny onto his shoulders like a dead fawn and head for the woods, hooting like an owl to let Uncle Jamie know it was time to set the fire.

It wasn't possible to move a man in chains in total silence, but with any luck at all, the scraping of spoons on mess kits and the soldiers' conversation would cover any stray clinking. He pulled the canvas out as far as he could, reached under, and took firm hold of Denny's shoulders. The wee bugger was heavier than he looked, but Ian got Denny's upper body mostly clear of the tent without too much trouble. Sweating, he scuttled to the side and reached in to take hold of Denny's ankles, wrapping the chain round his own wrist to take up the slack.

There was no sound, but Ian's head jerked up before his mind even told him that the air near him had moved in a way that meant someone was standing there.

"Hush!" he said by reflex, not knowing whether he was talking to Denny or to the tall soldier who had stepped out of the wood behind him.

"What the devil—" the soldier began, sounding startled. He didn't finish the question, but took three paces fast and grabbed Ian by the wrist.

"Who are you and what are you—Good God, where did *you* come from?" William the soldier stared into Ian's face, and Ian thanked God briefly for the fact that his other wrist was immobilized by Denny's chain, for otherwise William would be already dead. And he didn't want to have to tell Uncle Jamie *that*.

"He has come to help me escape, Friend William," Denny Hunter said mildly from the shadows on the ground behind Ian. "I would take it kindly if thee did not hinder him, though I will understand if thy duty compels thee."

William's head jerked, looked wildly round, then down. Had the circumstances been less dire, Ian would have laughed at the expressions—for there were a great number of them, run through in the course of a heartbeat—on it. William closed his eyes for an instant, then opened them again.

"Don't tell me," he said shortly. "I don't want to know." He squatted beside Ian and, between them, they had Denny out in a matter of seconds. Ian took a deep breath, put his hands to his mouth, and hooted, then paused a moment and did it once again. William stared at him in mingled puzzlement and anger. Then Ian ducked the point of his shoulder into Denny's midriff and, with William heaving, got the doctor onto his shoulders with little more than a startled grunt and a slight clanking of fetters.

William's hand closed on Ian's forearm, and his head, a dark oval in the last traces of light, jerked toward the woods.

"Left," he whispered. "There are latrine trenches on the right. Two pickets, a hundred yards out." He squeezed hard and let go.

"May you be held in God's light, Friend William." Denny's whisper came breathless by Ian's ear, but Ian was already going and didn't know whether William had heard. He supposed it didn't matter.

A few moments later, he heard the first shouts of "Fire!" behind him in the camp.

61

NO BETTER COMPANION
THAN THE RIFLE

September 15, 1777

BY EARLY SEPTEMBER, we had reached the main army, encamped on the Hudson near the village of Saratoga. General Horatio Gates was in command, and received the ragtag and bobtail refugees and random militia with pleasure. For once, the army was tolerably well supplied, and we were equipped with clothes, decent food—and the remarkable luxury of a small tent, in honor of Jamie's status as a colonel of militia, in spite of the fact that he had no men.

Knowing Jamie as I did, I was reasonably sure this would be a temporary state of affairs. For my part, I was delighted to have an actual cot to sleep on, a tiny table to eat from—and food to put on it on a fairly regular basis.

"I've brought ye a present, Sassenach." Jamie plumped the bag down on the table with a pleasantly meaty-sounding thump and a waft of fresh blood. My mouth began to water.

"What is it? Birds?" It wasn't ducks or geese; those had a distinctive scent about them, a musk of body oils, feathers, and decaying waterweeds. But partridges, say, or grouse . . . I swallowed heavily at the thought of pigeon pie.

"No, a book." He pulled a small package wrapped in tattered oilcloth from the bulging sack and proudly set it in my hands.

"A book?" I said blankly.

He nodded encouragingly.

"Aye. Words printed on paper, ye'll recall the sort of thing? I ken it's been a long time."

I gave him an eye and, attempting to ignore the rumbling of my stomach, opened the package. It was a well-worn pocket-sized copy of *The Life and Opinions of Tristram Shandy, Gentleman—Vol. I*, and despite my disgruntlement at being presented with literature instead of food, I was interested. It *had* been a long time since I'd had a good book in my hands, and this was a story I'd heard of but never read.

"The owner must have been fond of it," I said, turning the little volume over gently. The spine was nearly worn through, and the edges of the leather cover were rubbed shiny. A rather nasty thought struck me.

"Jamie . . . you didn't . . . take this from a, er, a *body*, did you?" Stripping weapons, equipment, and usable clothing from fallen enemies was not considered looting; it was an unpleasant necessity. Still . . .

He shook his head, though, still rummaging in the bag.

"Nay, I found it at the edge of a wee creek. Dropped in flight, I expect."

Well, that was better, though I was sure the man who had dropped it would regret the loss of this treasured companion. I opened the book at random and squinted at the small type.

"Sassenach."

"Hmm?" I glanced up, jerked out of the text, to see Jamie regarding me with a mixture of sympathy and amusement.

"Ye need spectacles, don't ye?" he said. "I hadna realized."

"Nonsense!" I said, though my heart gave a small jump. "I see perfectly well."

"Oh, aye?" He moved beside me and took the book out of my hand. Opening it to the middle, he held it in front of me. "Read that."

I leaned backward, and he advanced in front of me.

"Stop that!" I said. "How do you expect me to read anything that close?"

"Stand still, then," he said, and moved the book away from my face. "Can ye see the letters clear yet?"

"No," I said crossly. "Farther. Farther. No, bloody farther!"

And at last was obliged to admit that I could not bring the letters into focus at a distance of nearer than about eighteen inches.

"Well, it's *very* small type!" I said, flustered and discomfited. I had, of course, been aware that my eyesight was not so keen as it once had been, but to be so rudely confronted with the evidence that I was, if not blind as a bat, definitely in competition with moles was a trifle upsetting.

"Twelve-point Caslon," Jamie said, giving the text a professional glance. "I will say the leading's terrible," he added critically. "And the gutters are half what they should be. Even so—" He flipped the book shut and looked at me, one eyebrow raised. "Ye need spectacles, *a nighean*," he repeated gently.

"Hmph!" I said. And on impulse picked up the book, opened it, and handed it to him. "So—read it yourself, why don't you?"

Looking surprised and a little wary, he took the book and looked into it. Then extended his arm a little. And a little more. I watched, experiencing that same odd mix of amusement and sympathy, as he finally held the book nearly at arm's length, and read, *"So that the life of a writer, whatever he might fancy to the contrary, was not so much a state of composition, as a state of warfare; and his probation in it, precisely that of any other man militant upon earth— both depending alike, not half so much upon the degrees of his WIT—as his RESISTANCE."*

He closed it and looked at me, the edge of his mouth tucked back.

"Aye, well," he said. "I can still shoot, at least."

"And I can tell one herb from another by smell, I suppose," I said, and laughed. "Just as well. I don't suppose there's a spectacle-maker this side of Philadelphia."

"No, I suppose not," he said ruefully. "When we get to Edinburgh, though, I ken just the man. I'll buy ye a tortoiseshell pair for everyday, Sassenach, and a pair wi' gold rims for Sundays."

"Expect me to read the Bible with them, do you?" I inquired.

"Ah, no," he said, "that's just for show. After all"—he picked up my hand, which smelled of dill weed and coriander, and, lifting it to his mouth, ran the point of his tongue delicately down the lifeline in my palm—"the important things ye do by touch, aye?"

WE WERE INTERRUPTED by a cough from the door of the tent, and I turned to see a large, bearlike man with long gray hair loose upon his shoulders. He had an amiable face with a scar through the upper lip and a mild but keen eye, which went at once to the bag on the table.

I stiffened a little; there were strict prohibitions against the looting of farms, and while Jamie had taken these particular hens scratching in the wild, there was no way of proving that, and this gentleman, while dressed in casual homespun and hunting shirt, bore himself with the unmistakable authority of an officer.

"You'd be Colonel Fraser?" he said, with a nod toward Jamie, and extended a hand. "Daniel Morgan."

I recognized the name, though the only thing I knew about Daniel Morgan—a footnote in Brianna's eighth-grade history book—was that he was a famous rifleman. This wasn't particularly useful; everyone knew that, and the camp had buzzed with interest when he had arrived at the end of August with a number of men.

He now glanced with interest at *me*, and then at the bag of chickens, flecked with incriminating tufts of feather.

"By your leave, ma'am," he said, and without waiting for my leave, picked up the sack and pulled out a dead chicken. The neck flopped limp, showing the large, bloody hole through its head where an eye—well, two eyes—had once been. His scarred mouth pursed in a soundless whistle and he looked sharply up at Jamie.

"You do that a-purpose?" he asked.

"I always shoot them through the eye," Jamie replied politely. "Dinna want to spoil the meat."

A slow grin spread over Colonel Morgan's face, and he nodded. "Come with me, Mr. Fraser. Bring your rifle."

WE ATE THAT night at Daniel Morgan's fire, and the company—filled with chicken stew—raised cups of beer and hooted to toast the addition of a new member to their elite corps. I hadn't had a chance of private conversation with Jamie since Morgan's abduction of him that afternoon, and rather wondered what he made of his apotheosis. But he seemed comfortable with the riflemen, though he glanced now and then at Morgan, with the look that meant he was still making up his mind.

For my part, I was extremely pleased. By their nature, riflemen fought from a distance—and often a distance much greater than a musket's range. They were also valuable, and commanders were not likely to risk them in close combat. No soldier was safe, but some occupations had a much higher rate of mortality—and while I accepted the fact that Jamie was a born gambler, I liked him to have the best odds possible.

Many of the riflemen were Long Hunters, others what they called "over-mountain men," and thus had no wives with them here. Some did, and I made instant acquaintance with the women by the simple expedient of admiring one young woman's baby.

"Mrs. Fraser?" one older lady said, coming to plump down on the log beside me. "Are you the conjure-woman?"

"I am," I said pleasantly. "They call me the White Witch." That reared them back a bit, but the forbidden has its own strong appeal—and after all, what could I do in the middle of military camp, surrounded by their husbands and sons, all armed to the teeth?

Within minutes, I was dispensing advice on everything from menstrual cramps to colic. I caught a glimpse of Jamie, grinning at sight of my popularity, and gave him a discreet wave before turning back to my audience.

The men, of course, continued drinking, with outbreaks of raucous laughter, then the fall of voices as one man took over a story, only to have the cycle repeat. At one point, though, the atmosphere changed, so abruptly that I broke off an intense discussion of diaper rash and looked over toward the fire.

Daniel Morgan was rising laboriously to his feet, and there was a distinct air of anticipation among the watching men. Was he about to make a speech, welcoming Jamie?

"Oh, dear Lord," said Mrs. Graham under her breath beside me. "He's a-doing it again."

I hadn't time to ask her *what* he was a-doing, before he a-did it.

He shambled to the center of the gathering, where he stood swaying like an old bear, his long gray hair wafting in the wind of the fire and his eyes creased with amiability. They were focused on Jamie, though, I saw.

"Got something to show you, Mr. Fraser," he said, loudly enough that the women who had still been talking stopped, every eye going to him. He took hold of the hem of his long woolen hunting shirt and pulled it off over his head. He dropped it on the ground, spread his arms like a ballet dancer, and stumped slowly round.

Everyone gasped, though from Mrs. Graham's remark, most of them must have seen it before. His back was ridged with scars from neck to waist. Old scars, to be sure—but there wasn't a square inch of unmarked skin on his back, massive as it was. Even I was shocked.

"The British did that," he said conversationally, turning back and dropping his arms. "Give me four hundred and ninety-nine lashes. I counted." The gathering erupted in laughter, and he grinned. "Was supposed to give me five hundred, but he missed one. I didn't point it out to him."

More laughter. Obviously, this was a frequent performance, but one that his audience loved. There were cheers and more toasts when he finished and went to sit beside Jamie, still naked to the waist, his shirt wadded casually in his hand.

Jamie's face gave nothing away—but I saw that his shoulders had relaxed. Evidently he had made up his mind about Dan Morgan.

JAMIE LIFTED THE LID of my small iron pot, with an expression somewhere between caution and hope.

"Not food," I informed him, rather unnecessarily, as he was wheezing in the manner of one who has inadvertently inhaled horseradish into the sinuses.

"I should hope not," he said, coughing and wiping his eyes. "Christ, Sassenach, that's worse than usual. D'ye mean to poison someone?"

"Yes, *Plasmodium vivax*. Put the lid back on." I was simmering a decoction of cinchona bark and gallberries, for the treatment of malarial cases.

"Have we *got* any food?" he asked plaintively, dropping the lid back in place.

"In fact we have." I reached into the cloth-covered pail at my feet and triumphantly pulled out a meat pie, its crust golden and shimmering with lard.

His face assumed the expression of an Israelite beholding the promised land, and he held out his hands, receiving the pie with the reverence due a precious object, though this impression was dispelled in the next instant as he took a large bite out of it.

"Where did ye get it?" he asked, after a few moments of blissful mastication. "Are there more?"

"There are. A nice prostitute named Daisy brought them for me."

He paused, examined the pie critically for signs of its provenance, then shrugged and took another bite.

"Do I want to know what it was ye did for her, Sassenach?"

"Well, probably not while you're eating, no. Have you seen Ian?"

"No." The response might have been abbreviated by the exigencies of eating pie, but I caught the slightest shiftiness in his manner and stopped, staring at him.

"Do you *know* where Ian is?"

"More or less." He kept his eyes fixed firmly on the meat pie, thus confirming my suspicions.

"Do I want to know what he's doing?"

"No, ye don't," he said definitely.

"Oh, God."

———

IAN MURRAY, having carefully dressed his hair with bear grease and a pair of turkey feathers, removed his shirt, leaving this rolled up with his tattered plaid under a log, and told Rollo to guard it, then walked across a small stretch of open ground toward the British camp.

"Hold!"

He turned a face of bored impassivity toward the sentry who had hailed him. The sentry, a boy of fifteen or so, was holding a musket whose barrel shook noticeably. Ian hoped the numpty wouldn't shoot him by accident.

"Scout," he said succinctly, and walked past the sentry without a backward glance, though he felt a spider strolling to and fro between his shoulder blades. *Scout,* he thought, and felt a small bubble of laughter rise up. Well, it was the truth, after all.

He strolled through the camp in the same manner, ignoring the occasional stare—though most of those who noticed him merely glanced at him and then away.

Burgoyne's headquarters was easy to spot, a large tent of green canvas that sprouted like a toadstool among the neat aisles of small white tents that housed the soldiers. It was some distance away—and he didn't mean to get any closer just now—but he could glimpse the comings and goings of staff officers, messengers . . . and the occasional scout, though none of these was Indian.

The Indian camps were on the far side of the army encampment, scattered in the forest outside the neat military grid. He was not sure whether he might meet some of Thayendanegea's people, who might in turn recognize him. This wouldn't be a difficulty, as he had said nothing regarding politics during his ill-fated visit to Joseph Brant's house; they would likely accept him on sight without any awkward questions.

If he were to encounter some of the Huron and Oneida that Burgoyne employed to harass the Continentals, that might be a wee bit touchier. He had complete confidence in his ability to impress them with his identity as a Mohawk—but if they were either too suspicious or too impressed, he wouldn't learn much.

He had learned a few things simply from his walk through the camp. Morale was not high; there was rubbish between some of the tents, and most of the washerwomen among the camp followers were sitting in the grass drinking gin, their kettles cold and empty. Still, the atmosphere in general seemed subdued but resolute; some men were dicing and drinking, but more were melting lead and making musket balls, repairing or polishing their weapons.

Food was short; he could sense hunger in the air, even without seeing the line of men waiting outside the baker's tent. None of them looked at him; they were focused on the loaves that emerged—these broken in half before being handed out. Half rations, then; that was good.

None of this was important, though, and as for troop numbers and armament—these were well established by now. Uncle Jamie and Colonel Morgan and General Gates would like to know about the stores of powder and ammunition, but the artillery park and powder magazine would be well guarded, with no conceivable reason for an Indian scout to be nosing round there.

Something tugged at the corner of his vision and he glanced cautiously round, then hastily jerked his eyes forward, forcing himself to walk at the same pace. Jesus, it was the Englishman he'd saved from the swamp—the man who'd helped him get wee Denny free. And—

He clamped down on that thought. He kent it well enough; no one could look like that and *not* be. But he felt it dangerous even to acknowledge the thought to himself, lest it show somehow on his face.

He forced himself to breathe as usual and walk without concern, because a Mohawk scout would have none. Damn. He'd meant to spend the remaining hours of daylight with some of the Indians, picking up what information he could, and then after dark come quietly back into camp, stealing up within earshot of Burgoyne's tent. If yon wee lieutenant was wuthering round, though, it might be too dangerous to try. The last thing he wanted was to meet the man face-to-face.

"Hey!" The shout ran into his flesh like a sharp splinter. He recognized the voice, knew it was aimed at him, but didn't turn round. Six paces, five, four, three . . . He reached the end of an alley of tents and sheared off to the right, out of sight.

"Hey!" The voice was closer, almost behind him, and he broke into a run, heading for the cover of the trees. Only one or two soldiers saw him; one started to his feet but then stood, uncertain what to do, and he pushed past the man and dived into the trees.

"Well, that's torn it," he muttered, crouched behind a brush shelter. The tall lieutenant was questioning the man he'd shoved past. Both of them were looking toward the wood, the soldier shaking his head and shrugging helplessly.

Christ, the wee loon was coming toward him! He turned and stepped silently through the trees, working his way deeper into the wood. He could hear the Englishman behind him, crashing and rustling like a bear just out of its den in the spring.

"Murray!" he was shouting. "Murray—is that you? Wait!"

"Wolf's Brother! Is that you?"

Ian said something very blasphemous under his breath in Gaelic, and turned to see who had addressed him in Mohawk.

"It *is* you! Where's your demon wolf? Did something finally eat it?" His old friend Glutton was beaming at him, adjusting his breechclout after having a piss.

"I hope something eats you," Ian said to his friend, keeping his voice low. "I need to get away. There is an Englishman following me."

Glutton's face changed at once, though it didn't lose either its smile or its eager expression. The wide grin widened further, and he jerked his head behind him, indicating the opening to a trail. Then his face went suddenly slack, and he staggered from one side to the other, lurching in the direction Ian had come.

Ian barely made it out of sight before the Englishman called William came rushing into the clearing, only to run slap into Glutton, who clutched him by the lapels of his coat, gazed up soulfully into his eyes, and said, "Whisky?"

"I haven't any whisky," William said, brusque but not impolite, and tried to detach Glutton. This proved a difficult proposition; Glutton was much more agile than his squat appearance suggested, and the instant a hand was removed from one spot, it clung limpetlike to another. To add to the performance, Glutton began to tell the lieutenant—in Mohawk—the story of the famous hunt that had given him his name, pausing periodically to shout, "WHISHKEE!" and fling his arms about the Englishman's body.

Ian spared no time to admire the Englishman's own facility with language, which was considerable, but made off as fast as possible, circling to the west. He couldn't go back through the camp. He might take refuge in one of the Indian camps, but it was possible that William would look for him there, once he'd escaped from Glutton.

"What the hell does he want with me?" he muttered, no longer bothering with silence but cleaving the brush with a minimum of breakage. William the lieutenant had to know he was a Continental, because of Denny Hunter and the deserter game. Yet he had not raised a general alarm upon seeing him— only called out in surprise, and then as one wanting conversation.

Well, maybe that was a trick. Wee William might be young, but he was not stupid. Couldn't be, considering who his fath—and the man *was* chasing him.

He could hear voices fading behind him—he thought that William had perhaps now recognized Glutton, in spite of the fact that he had been half dead with fever when they met. If so, he would know Glutton was his, Ian's, friend—and instantly detect the ruse. But it didn't matter; he was well into the wood by now. William would never catch him.

The smell of smoke and fresh meat caught his nose, and he turned, going downhill toward the bank of a small stream. There was a Mohawk camp there; he knew it at once.

He paused, though. The scent of it, the knowledge of it, had drawn him like a moth—but he mustn't enter. Not now. If William *had* recognized Glutton, the first place he would look for Ian was the Mohawks' camp. And if she should be there . . .

"You, *again?*" said an unpleasant Mohawk voice. "You don't learn, do you?"

Actually, he did. He'd learned enough to hit first. He turned on his heel and swung from somewhere behind his knees, continuing up with all the power in his body. "*Aim to hit* through *the bugger's face*," Uncle Jamie had instructed him when he began to go about in Edinburgh alone. It was, as usual, good advice.

His knuckles burst with a crunch that shot blue lightning straight up his arm and into his neck and jaw—but Sun Elk flew backward two paces and crashed into a tree.

Ian stood panting and gently touching his knuckles, recalling too late that Uncle Jamie's advice had begun with, "*Hit them in the soft parts if ye can.*" It didn't matter; it was worth it. Sun Elk was moaning softly, his eyelids flutter-ing. Ian was debating the merits of saying something of a dismissive nature and walking grandly away, versus kicking him in the balls again before he could get up, when William the Englishman walked out from the trees.

He looked from Ian, still breathing as though he'd run a mile, to Sun Elk, who had rolled onto his hands and knees but didn't seem to want to get up. Blood was dripping from his face onto the dead leaves. *Splat. Splat.*

"I have no wish to intrude upon a private affair," William said politely. "But I would appreciate a word with you, Mr. Murray." He turned, not wait-ing to see if Ian would come, and walked back into the trees.

Ian nodded, having no notion what to say, and followed the Englishman, cherishing in his heart the last faint *splat!* of Sun Elk's blood.

The Englishman was leaning against a tree, watching the Mohawk camp by the stream below. A woman was stripping meat from a fresh deer's carcass, hanging it to dry on a frame. She wasn't Works With Her Hands.

William switched his dark-blue gaze to Ian, giving him an odd feeling. Ian already felt odd, though, so it didn't really matter.

"I am not going to ask what you were doing in the camp."

"Oh, aye?"

"No. I wished to thank you for the horse and money and to ask you whether you have seen Miss Hunter, since you so kindly left me in the keep-ing of her and her brother."

"I have, aye." The knuckles on his right hand were already puffed to twice their size and starting to throb. He'd go and see Rachel; she'd bandage them for him. The thought was so intoxicating that he didn't at first realize that William was waiting—not all that patiently—for him to expound on his state-ment.

"Ah. Aye, the . . . er . . . the Hunters are wi' the army. The . . . um . . . *other* army," he said, a little awkwardly. "Her brother's an army surgeon."

William's face didn't change but seemed somehow to solidify. Ian watched it in fascination. He'd seen Uncle Jamie's face do the exact same thing, many times, and knew what it meant.

"Here?" William said.

"Aye, here." He inclined his head toward the American camp. "There, I mean."

"I see," William said calmly. "When you see her again, will you give her my kindest regards, then? And her brother, too, of course."

"Oh . . . aye," Ian said, thinking, *Like that, is it? Well, ye're no going to see her yourself, and she'd have nothing to do wi' a soldier anyway, so think again!* "Certainly," he added, belatedly aware that his only value to William at this point lay in his supposed role as messenger to Rachel Hunter, and wondering just how much that was worth.

"Thank you." William's face had lost that look of iron; he was examining Ian carefully, and at last nodded.

"A life for a life, Mr. Murray," he said quietly. "We're quits. Don't let me see you next time. I may not have a choice."

He turned and left, the red of his uniform visible for some time through the trees.

62

ONE JUST MAN

September 19, 1777

THE SUN ROSE invisible, to the sound of drums. Drums on both sides; we could hear the British reveille, and by the same token they must hear ours. The riflemen had had a brief skirmish with British troops two days before, and owing to the work of Ian and the other scouts, General Gates knew very well the size and disposition of Burgoyne's army. Kościuszko had chosen Bemis Heights for a defensive position; it was a high river bluff, with numerous small ravines down to the river, and his crews had labored like madmen for the last week with shovels and axes. The Americans were ready. More or less.

The women were not, of course, admitted to the councils of the generals. Jamie was, though, and thus I heard all about the argument between General Gates, who was in command, and General Arnold, who thought he should be. General Gates, who wanted to sit tight on Bemis Heights and wait for the British attack, versus General Arnold, who argued vehemently that the Americans must make the first move, forcing the British regulars to fight through the thickly wooded ravines, ruining their formations and making them vulnerable to the riflemen's sniper fire, falling back—if necessary—to the breastworks and entrenchments on the Heights.

"Arnold's won," Ian reported, popping briefly up out of the fog to snag a piece of toasted bread. "Uncle Jamie's away wi' the riflemen already. He says he'll see ye this evening, and in the meantime . . ." He bent and gently kissed my cheek, then grinned impudently and vanished.

My own stomach was knotted, though with the pervasive excitement as much as with fear. The Americans were a ragged, motley lot, but they had had time to prepare, they knew what was coming, and they knew what was at stake. This battle would decide the campaign in the north. Either Burgoyne would overcome and march on, trapping George Washington's army near Philadelphia between his forces and General Howe's—or his army of invasion would be brought to a halt and knocked out of the war, in which case Gates's army could move south to reinforce Washington. The men all knew it, and the fog seemed electric with their anticipation.

By the sun, it was near ten o'clock when the fog lifted. The shots had begun some time earlier, brief, distant pings of rifle fire. Daniel Morgan's men were taking out the pickets, I thought—and knew from what Jamie had said the night before that they were meant to aim for the officers, to kill those soldiers wearing silver gorgets. I hadn't slept the night before, envisioning Lieutenant Ransom and the silver gorget at his throat. In fog, in the dust of battle, at a distance . . . I swallowed, but my throat stayed stubbornly closed; I couldn't even drink water.

Jamie had slept, with the stubborn concentration of a soldier, but had waked in the deep hours of the night, his shirt soaked with sweat in spite of the chill, trembling. I didn't ask what he had been dreaming about; I knew. I had got him a dry shirt and made him lie down again with his head in my lap, then stroked his head until he closed his eyes—but I thought he hadn't slept again.

It wasn't chilly now; the fog had burned away, and we heard sustained rattles of gunfire, patchy, but repeated volleys. Faint, distant shouting, but impossible to make out who was shouting what at whom. Then the sudden crash of a British fieldpiece, a resounding boom that struck the camp silent. A lull, and then full-scale battle broke out, shooting and screaming and the intermittent thud of cannon. Women huddled together or set about grimly packing up their belongings, in case we should have to flee.

About midday, a relative silence fell. Was it over? We waited. After a little, children began whining to be fed and a sort of tense normality descended—but nothing happened. We could hear moaning and calls for help from men wounded—but no wounded were brought in.

I was ready. I had a small mule-drawn wagon, equipped with bandages and medical equipment, and a small tent as well, which I could set up in case I needed to perform surgery in the rain. The mule was staked nearby, grazing placidly and ignoring both the tension and the occasional burst of musketry.

In the middle of the afternoon, hostilities broke out again, and this time the camp followers and cook wagons actually began to retreat. There was artillery on both sides, enough of it that the continuous cannonading rolled like thunder, and I saw a huge cloud of black powder smoke rise up from the bluff. It was not quite mushroom-shaped, but made me think nonetheless of Nagasaki and Hiroshima. I sharpened my knife and scalpels for the dozenth time.

IT WAS NEAR evening; the sun sank invisibly, staining the fog with a dull and sullen orange. The evening wind off the river was rising, lifting the fog from the ground and sending it scudding in billows and swirls.

Clouds of black powder smoke lay heavy in the hollows, lifting more slowly than the lighter shreds of mist and lending a suitable stink of brimstone to a scene that was—if not hellish—at least bloody eerie.

Here and there a space would suddenly be cleared, like a curtain pulled back to show the aftermath of battle. Small dark figures moved in the distance, darting and stooping, stopping suddenly, heads uplifted like baboons keeping watch for a leopard. Camp followers; the wives and whores of the soldiers, come like crows to scavenge the dead.

Children, too. Under a bush, a boy of nine or ten straddled the body of a red-coated soldier, smashing at the face with a heavy rock. I stopped, paralyzed at the sight, and saw the boy reach into the gaping, bloodied mouth and wrench out a tooth. He slipped the bloody prize into a bag that hung by his side, groped farther, tugging, and, finding no more teeth loose, picked up his rock in a businesslike way and went back to work.

I felt bile rise in my throat and hurried on, swallowing. I was no stranger to war, to death and wounds. But I had never been so near a battle before; I had never before come on a battlefield where the dead and wounded still lay, before the ministrations of medics and burial details.

There were calls for help and occasional moans or screams, ringing disembodied out of the mist, reminding me uncomfortably of Highland stories of the *urisge*, the doomed spirits of the glen. Like the heroes of such stories, I didn't stop to heed their call but pressed on, stumbling over small rises, slipping on damp grass.

I had seen photographs of the great battlefields, from the American Civil War to the beaches of Normandy. This was nothing like that—no churned earth, no heaps of tangled limbs. It was still, save for the noises of the scattered wounded and the voices of those calling, like me, for a missing friend or husband.

Shattered trees lay toppled by artillery; in this light, I might have thought the bodies turned into logs themselves, dark shapes lying long in the grass— save for the fact that some of them still moved. Here and there, a form stirred feebly, victim of war's sorcery, struggling against the enchantment of death.

I paused and shouted into the mist, calling his name. I heard answering calls, but none in his voice. Ahead of me lay a young man, arms outflung, a look of blank astonishment on his face, blood pooled round his upper body like a great halo. His lower half lay six feet away. I walked between the pieces, keeping my skirts close, nostrils pinched tight against the thick iron smell of blood.

The light was fading now, but I saw Jamie as soon as I came over the edge of the next rise. He was lying on his face in the hollow, one arm flung out, the other curled beneath him. The shoulders of his dark blue coat were nearly black with damp, and his legs thrown wide, booted heels askew.

The breath caught in my throat, and I ran down the slope toward him, heedless of grass clumps, mud, and brambles. As I got close, though, I saw a scuttling figure dart out from behind a nearby bush and dash toward him. It fell to its knees beside him and, without hesitation, grasped his hair and yanked his head to one side. Something glinted in the figure's hand, bright even in the dull light.

"Stop!" I shouted. "Drop it, you bastard!"

Startled, the figure looked up as I flung myself over the last yards of space. Narrow red-rimmed eyes glared up at me out of a round face streaked with soot and grime.

"Get off!" she snarled. "I found 'im first!" It was a knife in her hand; she made little jabbing motions at me, in an effort to drive me away.

I was too furious—and too afraid for Jamie—to be scared for myself.

"Let go of him! Touch him and I'll kill you!" I said. My fists were clenched, and I must have looked as though I meant it, for the woman flinched back, loosing her hold on Jamie's hair.

"He's mine," she said, thrusting her chin pugnaciously at me. "Go find yourself another."

Another form slipped out of the mist and materialized by her side. It was the boy I had seen earlier, filthy and scruffy as the woman herself. He had no knife but clutched a crude metal strip, cut from a canteen. The edge of it was dark, with rust or blood.

He glared at me. "He's ours, Mum said! Get on wi' yer! Scat!"

Not waiting to see whether I would or not, he flung a leg over Jamie's back, sat on him, and began to grope in the side pockets of his coat.

" 'E's still alive, Mum," he advised. "I can feel 'is 'eart beatin'. Best slit his throat quick; I don't think 'e's bad hurt."

I grabbed the boy by the collar and jerked him off Jamie's body, making him drop his weapon. He squealed and flailed at me with arms and elbows, but I kneed him in the rump, hard enough to jar his backbone, then got my elbow locked about his neck in a stranglehold, his skinny wrist vised in my other hand.

"Leave him go!" The woman's eyes narrowed like a weasel's, and her eye-teeth shone in a snarl.

I didn't dare take my eyes away from the woman's long enough to look at Jamie. I could see him, though, at the edge of my vision, head turned to the side, his neck gleaming white, exposed and vulnerable.

"Stand up and step back," I said, "or I'll choke him to death, I swear I will!"

She crouched over Jamie's body, knife in hand, as she measured me, trying to make up her mind whether I meant it. I did.

The boy struggled and twisted in my grasp, his feet hammering against my shins. He was small for his age, and thin as a stick, but strong nonetheless; it was like wrestling an eel. I tightened my hold on his neck; he gurgled and quit struggling. His hair was thick with rancid grease and dirt, the smell of it rank in my nostrils.

Slowly, the woman stood up. She was much smaller than I, and scrawny with it—bony wrists stuck out of the ragged sleeves. I couldn't guess her age—under the filth and the puffiness of malnutrition, she might have been anything from twenty to fifty.

"My man lies yonder, dead on the ground," she said, jerking her head at the fog behind her. " 'E hadn't nothing but his musket, and the sergeant'll take that back."

Her eyes slid toward the distant wood, where the British troops had retreated. "I'll find a man soon, but I've children to feed in the meantime—two besides the boy." She licked her lips, and a coaxing note entered her voice. "You're alone; you can manage better than we can. Let me have this one— there's more over there." She pointed with her chin toward the slope behind me, where the rebel dead and wounded lay.

My grasp must have loosened slightly as I listened, for the boy, who had hung quiescent in my grasp, made a sudden lunge and burst free, diving over Jamie's body to roll at his mother's feet.

He got up beside her, watching me with rat's eyes, beady-bright and watchful. He bent and groped about in the grass, coming up with the makeshift dagger.

"Hold 'er off, Mum," he said, his voice raspy from the choking. "I'll take 'im."

From the corner of my eye, I had caught the gleam of metal, half buried in the grass.

"Wait!" I said, and took a step back. "Don't kill him. Don't." A step to the side, another back. "I'll go, I'll let you have him, but . . ." I lunged to the side and got my hand on the cold metal hilt.

I had picked up Jamie's sword before. It was a cavalry sword, larger and heavier than the usual, but I didn't notice now.

I snatched it up and swung it in a two-handed arc that ripped the air and left the metal ringing in my hands.

Mother and son jumped back, identical looks of ludicrous surprise on their round, grimy faces.

"Get away!" I said.

Her mouth opened, but she didn't say anything.

"I'm sorry for your man," I said. "But my man lies here. Get away, I said!" I raised the sword, and the woman stepped back hastily, dragging the boy by the arm.

She turned and went, muttering curses at me over her shoulder, but I paid no attention to what she said. The boy's eyes stayed fixed on me as he went, dark coals in the dim light. He would know me again—and I him.

They vanished in the mist, and I lowered the sword, which suddenly weighed too much to hold. I dropped it on the grass and fell to my knees beside Jamie.

My own heart was pounding in my ears and my hands were shaking with reaction, as I groped for the pulse in his neck. I turned his head and could see it, throbbing steadily just below his jaw.

"Thank God!" I whispered to myself. "Oh, thank God!"

I ran my hands over him quickly, searching for injury before I moved him. I didn't think the scavengers would come back; I could hear the voices of a group of men, distant on the ridge behind me—a rebel detail coming to fetch the wounded.

There was a large knot on his brow, already turning purple. Nothing else that I could see. The boy had been right, I thought, with gratitude; he wasn't badly hurt. Then I rolled him onto his back and saw his hand.

Highlanders were accustomed to fight with sword in one hand, targe in the other, the small leather shield used to deflect an opponent's blow. He hadn't had a targe.

The blade had struck him between the third and fourth fingers of his right hand and sliced through the hand itself, a deep, ugly wound that split his palm and the body of his hand, halfway to the wrist.

Despite the horrid look of the wound, there wasn't much blood; the hand had been curled under him, his weight acting as a pressure bandage. The front of his shirt was smeared with red, deeply stained over his heart. I ripped open his shirt and felt inside, to be sure that the blood was from his hand, but it was. His chest was cool and damp from the grass but unscathed, his nipples shrunken and stiff with chill.

"That . . . tickles," he said in a drowsy voice. He pawed awkwardly at his chest with his left hand, trying to brush my hand away.

"Sorry," I said, repressing the urge to laugh with the joy of seeing him alive and conscious. I got an arm behind his shoulders and helped him to sit up. He looked drunk, with one eye swollen half shut and grass in his hair. He acted drunk, too, swaying alarmingly from side to side.

"How do you feel?" I asked.

"Sick," he said succinctly. He leaned to the side and threw up.

I eased him back on the grass and wiped his mouth, then set about bandaging his hand.

"Someone will be here soon," I assured him. "We'll get you back to the wagon, and I can take care of this."

"Mmphm." He grunted slightly as I pulled the bandage tight. "What happened?"

"What happened?" I stopped what I was doing and stared at him. "*You're* asking *me?*"

"What happened in the battle, I mean," he said patiently, regarding me with his one good eye. "I know what happened to me—roughly," he added, wincing as he touched his forehead.

"Yes, roughly," I said rudely. "You got yourself chopped like a butchered hog, and your head half caved in. Being a sodding bloody hero again, that's what happened to you!"

"I wasna—" he began, but I interrupted, my relief over seeing him alive being rapidly succeeded by rage.

"You didn't have to go to Ticonderoga! You *shouldn't* have gone! Stick to the writing and the printing, you said. You weren't going to fight unless you had to, you said. Well, you *didn't* have to, but you did it anyway, you vainglorious, pigheaded, grandstanding Scot!"

"Grandstanding?" he inquired.

"You know just what I mean, because it's just what you did! You might have been killed!"

"Aye," he agreed ruefully. "I thought I was, when the dragoon came down on me. I screeched and scairt his horse, though," he added more cheerfully. "It reared up and got me in the face with its knee."

"Don't change the subject!" I snapped.

"Is the subject not that I'm not killed?" he asked, trying to raise one brow and failing, with another wince.

"No! The subject is your stupidity, your bloody selfish stubbornness!"

"Oh, that."

"Yes, that! You—you—oaf! How dare you do that to me? You think I haven't got anything better to do with my life than trot round after you, sticking pieces back on?" I was frankly shrieking at him by this time.

To my increased fury, he grinned at me, his expression made the more rakish by the half-closed eye.

"Ye'd have been a good fishwife, Sassenach," he observed. "Ye've the tongue for it."

"You shut up, you fucking bloody—"

"They'll hear you," he said mildly, with a wave toward the party of Continental soldiers making their way down the slope toward us.

"I don't care who hears me! If you weren't already hurt, I'd—I'd—"

"Be careful, Sassenach," he said, still grinning. "Ye dinna want to knock off any more pieces; ye'll only have to stick them back on, aye?"

"Don't bloody tempt me," I said through my teeth, with a glance at the sword I had dropped.

He saw it and reached for it, but couldn't quite manage. With an explosive snort, I leaned across his body and grabbed the hilt, putting it in his hand. I heard a shout from the men coming down the hill and turned to wave at them.

"Anyone hearing ye just now would likely think ye didna care for me owermuch, Sassenach," he said, behind me.

I turned to look down at him. The impudent grin was gone, but he was still smiling.

"Ye've the tongue of a venemous shrew," he said, "but you're a bonnie wee swordsman, Sassenach."

My mouth opened, but the words that had been so abundant a moment before had all evaporated like the rising mist.

He laid his good hand on my arm. "For now, *a nighean donn*—thank ye for my life."

I closed my mouth. The men had nearly reached us, rustling through the grass, their exclamations and chatter drowning out the ever-fainter moans of the wounded.

"You're welcome," I said.

"HAMBURGER," I SAID under my breath, but not far enough under. He raised an eyebrow at me.

"Chopped meat," I elaborated, and the eyebrow fell.

"Oh, aye, it is. Stopped a sword stroke wi' my hand. Too bad I didna have a targe; I could have turned the stroke, easy."

"Right." I swallowed. It wasn't the worst injury I'd seen, by a long shot, but it still made me slightly sick. The tip of his fourth finger had been sheared off cleanly, at an angle just below the nail. The stroke had sliced a strip of flesh from the inside of the finger and ripped down between the third and fourth fingers.

"You must have caught it near the hilt," I said, trying for calm. "Or it would have taken off the outside half of your hand."

"Mmphm." The hand didn't move as I prodded and poked, but there was sweat on his upper lip, and he couldn't keep back a brief grunt of pain.

"Sorry," I murmured automatically.

"It's all right," he said, just as automatically. He closed his eyes, then opened them.

"Take it off," he said suddenly.

"What?" I drew back and looked at him, startled.

He nodded at his hand.

"The finger. Take it off, Sassenach."

"I can't do that!" Even as I spoke, though, I knew that he was right. Aside from the injuries to the finger itself, the tendon was badly damaged; the chances of his ever being able to move the finger, let alone move it without pain, were infinitesimal.

"It's done me little good in the last twenty years," he said, looking at the mangled stump dispassionately, "and likely to do no better now. I've broken the damned thing half a dozen times, from its sticking out like it does. If ye take it off, it willna trouble me anymore, at least."

I wanted to argue, but there was no time; wounded men were beginning to drift up the slope toward the wagon. The men were militia, not regular army; if there was a regiment near, there might be a surgeon with them, but I was closer.

"Once a frigging hero, always a frigging hero," I muttered under my breath. I thrust a wad of lint into Jamie's bloody palm and wrapped a linen bandage swiftly around the hand. "Yes, I'll have to take it off, but later. Hold still."

"Ouch," he said mildly. "I did say I wasna a hero."

"If you aren't, it isn't for lack of trying," I said, yanking the linen knot tight with my teeth. "There, that will have to do for now; I'll see to it when I have time." I grabbed the wrapped hand and plunged it into the small basin of alcohol and water.

He went white as the alcohol seeped through the cloth and struck raw flesh. He inhaled sharply through his teeth, but didn't say anything more. I pointed peremptorily at the blanket I had spread on the ground, and he lay back obediently, curling up under the shelter of the wagon, bandaged fist cradled against his breast.

I rose from my knees, but hesitated for a moment. Then I knelt again and hastily kissed the back of his neck, brushing aside the queue of his hair, matted with half-dried mud and dead leaves. I could just see the curve of his cheek; it tightened briefly as he smiled and then relaxed.

Word had spread that the hospital wagon was there; there was already a straggling group of walking wounded awaiting attention, and I could see men carrying or half-dragging their injured companions toward the light of my lantern. It was going to be a busy evening.

Colonel Everett had promised me two assistants, but God knew where the colonel was at the moment. I took a moment to survey the gathering crowd and picked out a young man who had just deposited a wounded friend beneath a tree.

"You," I said, tugging on his sleeve. "Are you afraid of blood?"

He looked momentarily startled, then grinned at me through a mask of mud and powder smoke. He was about my height, broad-shouldered and stocky, with a face that might have been called cherubic had it been less filthy.

"Only if it's mine, ma'am, and so far it ain't, Lord be praised."

"Then come with me," I said, smiling back. "You're now a triage aide."

"Say what? Hey, Harry!" he yelled to his friend. "I been promoted. Tell your mama next time you write, Lester done amounted to something, after all!" He swaggered after me, still grinning.

The grin rapidly faded into a look of frowning absorption as I led him quickly among the wounded, pointing out degrees of severity.

"Men pouring blood are the first priority," I told him. I thrust an armful of linen bandages and a sack of lint into his hands. "Give them these—tell their friends to press the lint hard on the wounds or put a tourniquet round the limb above the wound. You know what a tourniquet is?"

"Oh, yes, ma'am," he assured me. "Put one on, too, when a panther clawed up my cousin Jess, down to Caroline County."

"Good. Don't spend time doing it yourself here unless you have to, though—let their friends do it. Now, broken bones can wait a bit—put them over there under that big beech tree. Head injuries and internal injuries that aren't bleeding, back there, by the chestnut tree, if they can be moved. If not, I'll go to them." I pointed behind me, then turned in a half circle, surveying the ground.

"If you see a couple of whole men, send them up to put up the hospital tent; it's to go in that flattish spot, there. And then a couple more, to dig a latrine trench . . . over there, I think."

"Yes, sir! Ma'am, I mean!" Lester bobbed his head and took a firm grip on his sack of lint. "I be right after it, ma'am. Though I wouldn't worry none about the latrines for a while," he added. "Most of these boys already done had the shit scairt out of 'em." He grinned and bobbed once more, then set out on his rounds.

He was right; the faint stink of feces hung in the air as it always did on battlefields, a low note amid the pungencies of blood and smoke.

With Lester sorting the wounded, I settled down to the work of repair, with my medicine box, suture bag, and bowl of alcohol set on the wagon's tailboard and a keg of alcohol for the patients to sit on—provided they could sit.

The worst of the casualties were bayonet wounds; luckily there had been no grapeshot, and the men hit by cannonballs were long past the point where I could help them. As I worked, I listened with half an ear to the conversation of the men awaiting attention.

"Wasn't that the damnedest thing ye ever saw? How many o' the buggers were there?" one man was asking his neighbor.

"Damned if I know," his friend replied, shaking his head. "For a space there, ever'thing I saw was red, and nothin' but. Then a cannon went off right close, and I didn't see nothin' but smoke for a good long time." He rubbed at his face; tears from watering eyes had made long streaks in the black soot that covered him from chest to forehead.

I glanced back at the wagon but couldn't see under it. I hoped shock and fatigue had enabled Jamie to sleep, in spite of his hand, but I doubted it.

Despite the fact that nearly everyone near me was wounded in some fashion, their spirits were high and the general mood was one of exuberant relief and exultation. Farther down the hill, in the mists near the river, I could hear whoops and shouts of victory and the undisciplined racket of fifes and drums, rattling and screeching in random exhilaration.

Among the noise, a nearer voice called out: a uniformed officer, on a bay horse.

"Anybody seen that big redheaded bastard who broke the charge?"

There was a murmur and a general looking around, but no one answered. The horseman dismounted and, wrapping his reins over a branch, made his way through the throng of wounded toward me.

"Whoever he is, I tell you, he's got balls the size of ten-pound shot," remarked the man whose cheek I was stitching.

"And a head of the same consistency," I murmured.

"Eh?" He glanced sideways at me in bewilderment.

"Nothing," I said. "Hold still just a moment longer; I'm nearly done."

IT WAS A HELLISH night. Some of the wounded still lay in the ravines and hollows, as did all the dead. The wolves that came silently out of the wood did not distinguish between them, judging from the distant screams.

It was nearly dawn before I came back to the tent where Jamie lay. I lifted the flap quietly, so as not to disturb him, but he was already awake, lying curled on his side facing the flap, head resting on a folded blanket.

He smiled faintly when he saw me.

"A hard night, Sassenach?" he asked, his voice slightly hoarse from cold air and disuse. Mist seeped under the edge of the flap, tinted yellow by the lantern light.

"I've had worse." I smoothed the hair off his face, looking him over carefully. He was pale but not clammy. His face was drawn with pain, but his skin was cool to the touch—no trace of fever. "You haven't slept, have you? How do you feel?"

"A bit scairt," he said. "And a bit sick. But better now you're here." He gave me a one-sided grimace that was almost a smile.

I put a hand under his jaw, fingers pressed against the pulse in his neck. His heart bumped steadily under my fingertips, and I shivered briefly, remembering the woman in the field.

"You're chilled, Sassenach," he said, feeling it. "And tired, too. Go and sleep, aye? I'll do a bit longer."

I *was* tired. The adrenaline of the battle and the night's work was fading fast; fatigue was creeping down my spine and loosening my joints. But I had a good idea of what the hours of waiting had cost him already.

"It won't take long," I reassured him. "And it will be better to have it over. Then you can sleep easy."

He nodded, though he didn't look noticeably reassured. I unfolded the small worktable I had carried in from the operating tent and set it up in easy reach. Then I took out the precious bottle of laudanum and poured an inch of the dark, odorous liquid into a cup.

"Sip it slowly," I said, putting it into his left hand. I began to lay out the instruments I would need, making sure that everything lay orderly and to hand. I had thought of asking Lester to come and assist me, but he had been asleep on his feet, swaying drunkenly under the dim lanterns in the operating tent, and I had sent him off to find a blanket and a spot by the fire.

A small scalpel, freshly sharpened. The jar of alcohol, with the wet ligatures coiled inside like a nest of tiny vipers, each toothed with a small, curved needle. Another with the waxed dry ligatures for arterial compression. A bouquet of probes, their ends soaking in alcohol. Forceps. Long-handled retractors. The hooked tenaculum, for catching the ends of severed arteries.

The surgical scissors with their short, curved blades and the handles shaped to fit my grasp, made to my order by the silversmith Stephen Moray. Or almost to my order. I had insisted that the scissors be as plain as possible, to make them easy to clean and disinfect. Stephen had obliged with a chaste and elegant design, but had not been able to resist one small flourish—one handle boasted a hooklike extension against which I could brace my little finger in order to exert more force, and this extrusion formed a smooth, lithe curve, flowering at the tip into a slender rosebud against a spray of leaves. The contrast between the heavy, vicious blades at one end and this delicate conceit at the other always made me smile when I lifted the scissors from their case.

Strips of cotton gauze and heavy linen, pads of lint, adhesive plasters stained red with the dragon's-blood juice that made them sticky. An open bowl of alcohol for disinfection as I worked, and the jars of cinchona bark, mashed garlic paste, and yarrow for dressing.

"There we are," I said with satisfaction, checking the array one last time. Everything must be ready, since I was working by myself; if I forgot something, no one would be at hand to fetch it for me.

"It seems a great deal o' preparation, for one measly finger," Jamie observed behind me.

I swung around to find him leaning on one elbow, watching, the cup of laudanum undrunk in his hand.

"Could ye not just whack it off wi' a wee knife and seal the wound with hot iron, like the regimental surgeons do?"

"I could, yes," I said dryly. "But fortunately I don't have to; we have enough time to do the job properly. That's why I made you wait."

"Mmphm." He surveyed the row of gleaming instruments without enthusiasm, and it was clear that he would much rather have had the business over and done with as quickly as possible. I realized that to him this looked like slow and ritualized torture, rather than sophisticated surgery.

"I mean to leave you with a working hand," I told him firmly. "No infection, no suppurating stump, no clumsy mutilation, and—God willing—no pain, once it heals."

His eyebrows went up at that. He had never mentioned it, but I was well aware that his right hand and its troublesome fourth finger had caused him intermittent pain for years, ever since it had been crushed at Wentworth Prison, when he was held prisoner there in the days before the Stuart Rising.

"A bargain's a bargain," I said, with a nod at the cup in his hand. "Drink it."

He lifted the cup and poked a long nose reluctantly over the rim, nostrils twitching at the sickly-sweet scent. He let the dark liquid touch the end of his tongue and made a face.

"It will make me sick."

"It will make you sleep."

"It gives me terrible dreams."

"As long as you don't chase rabbits in your sleep, it won't matter," I assured him. He laughed despite himself, but had one final try.

"It tastes like the stuff ye scrape out of horses' hooves."

"And when was the last time you licked a horse's hoof?" I demanded, hands on my hips. I gave him a medium-intensity glare, suitable for the intimidation of petty bureaucrats and low-level army officials.

He sighed.

"Ye mean it, aye?"

"I do."

"All right, then." With a reproachful look of long-suffering resignation, he threw back his head and tossed the contents of the cup down in one gulp.

A convulsive shudder racked him, and he made small choking noises.

"I did say to sip it," I observed mildly. "Vomit, and I'll make you lick it up off the floor."

Given the scuffled dirt and trampled grass underfoot, this was plainly an idle threat, but he pressed his lips and eyes tight shut and lay back on the pillow, breathing heavily and swallowing convulsively every few seconds. I brought up a low stool and sat down by the camp bed to wait.

"How do you feel?" I asked, a few minutes later.

"Dizzy," he replied. He cracked one eye open and viewed me through the narrow blue slit, then groaned and closed it. "As if I'm falling off a cliff. It's a verra unpleasant sensation, Sassenach."

"Try to think of something else for a minute," I suggested. "Something pleasant, to take your mind off it."

His brow furrowed for a moment, then relaxed.

"Stand up a moment, will ye?" he said. I obligingly stood, wondering what he wanted. He opened his eyes, reached out with his good hand, and took a firm grip of my buttock.

"There," he said. "That's the best thing I can think of. Having a good hold on your arse always makes me feel steady."

I laughed and moved a few inches closer to him, so his forehead pressed against my thighs.

"Well, it's a portable remedy, at least."

He closed his eyes then and held on tight, breathing slowly and deeply. The harsh lines of pain and exhaustion in his face began to soften as the drug took effect.

"Jamie," I said softly, after a minute. "I'm sorry about it."

He opened his eyes, looked upward, and smiled, giving me a slight squeeze.

"Aye, well," he said. His pupils had begun to shrink; his eyes were sea-deep and fathomless, as though he looked into a great distance.

"Tell me, Sassenach," he said, a moment later. "If someone stood a man before ye and told ye that if ye were to cut off your finger, the man would live, and if ye did not, he would die—would ye do it?"

"I don't know," I said, slightly startled. "If that was the choice, and no doubt about it, and he was a good man...yes, I suppose I would. I wouldn't like it a bit, though," I added practically, and his mouth curved in a smile.

"No," he said. His expression was growing soft and dreamy. "Did ye know," he said after a moment, "a colonel came to see me, whilst ye were at work wi' the wounded? Colonel Johnson; Micah Johnson, his name was."

"No; what did he say?"

His grip on my bottom was beginning to slacken; I put my own hand over his, to hold it in place.

"It was his company—in the fight. Part of Morgan's, and the rest of the regiment just over the hill, in the path of the British. If the charge had gone through, they'd ha' lost the company surely, he said, and God knows what might have become o' the rest." His soft Highland burr was growing broader, his eyes fixed on my skirt.

"So you saved them," I said gently. "How many men are there in a company?"

"Fifty," he said. "Though they wouldna all have been killed, I dinna suppose." His hand slipped; he caught it and took a fresh grip, chuckling slightly. I could feel his breath through my skirt, warm on my thighs.

"I was thinking it was like the Bible, aye?"

"Yes?" I pressed his hand against the curve of my hip, keeping it in place.

"That bit where Abraham is bargaining wi' the Lord for the Cities of the Plain. 'Wilt thou not destroy the city,'" he quoted, " 'for the sake of fifty just men?' And then Abraham does Him down, a bit at a time, from fifty to forty, and then to thirty, and twenty and ten."

His eyes were half closed, and his voice peaceful and unconcerned.

"I didna have time to inquire into the moral state of any o' the men in that company. But ye'd think there might be ten just men among them—good men?"

"I'm sure there are." His hand was heavy, his arm gone nearly limp.

"Or five. Or even one. One would be enough."

"I'm sure there's one."

"The apple-faced laddie that helped ye wi' the wounded—he's one?"

"Yes, he's one."

He sighed deeply, his eyes nearly shut.

"Tell him I dinna grudge him the finger, then," he said.

I held his good hand tightly for a minute. He was breathing slowly and deeply, his mouth gone slack in utter relaxation. I rolled him gently onto his back and laid the hand across his chest.

"Bloody man," I whispered. "I knew you'd make me cry."

THE CAMP OUTSIDE lay quiet, in the last moments of slumber before the rising sun should stir the men to movement. I could hear the occasional call of a picket and the murmur of conversation as two foragers passed close by my tent, bound for the woods to hunt. The campfires outside had burned to embers, but I had three lanterns, arranged to cast light without shadow.

I laid a thin square of soft pine across my lap as a working surface. Jamie lay facedown on the camp bed, head turned toward me so I could keep an eye on his color. He was solidly asleep; his breath came slow and he didn't flinch when I pressed the sharp tip of a probe against the back of his hand. All ready.

The hand was swollen, puffy, and discolored, the sword wound a thick black line against the sun-gold skin. I closed my eyes for a moment, holding his wrist, counting his pulse. *One-and-two-and-three-and-four . . .*

I seldom prayed consciously when preparing for surgery, but I did look for something—something I could not describe but always recognized: a certain quietness of soul, the detachment of mind in which I could balance on that knife-edge between ruthlessness and compassion, at once engaged in utmost intimacy with the body under my hands and capable of destroying what I touched in the name of healing.

One-and-two-and-three-and-four . . .

I realized with a start that my own heartbeat had slowed; the pulse in my fingertip matched that in Jamie's wrist, beat for beat, slow and strong. If I was waiting for a sign, I supposed that would do. *Ready, steady, go,* I thought, and picked up the scalpel.

A short horizontal incision over the fourth and fifth knuckles, then down, cutting the skin nearly to the wrist. I undermined the skin carefully with the scissors' tips, then pinned back the loose flap of skin with one of the long steel probes, digging it into the soft wood of the board.

I had a small bulb atomizer filled with a solution of distilled water and alcohol; sterility being impossible, I used this to lay a fine mist over the operating field and wash away the first welling of blood. Not too much; the vasoconstrictor I had given him was working, but the effect wouldn't last long.

I gently nudged apart the muscle fibers—those that were still whole—to expose the bone and its overlying tendon, gleaming silver among the vivid colors of the body. The sword had cut the tendon nearly through, an inch above the carpal bones. I severed the few remaining fibers, and the hand twitched disconcertingly in reflex.

I bit my lip, but it was all right; aside from the hand, he hadn't moved. He felt different; his flesh had more life than that of a man under ether or Pentothal. He was not anesthetized but only drugged into stupor; the feel of his flesh was resilient, not the pliant flaccidity I had been accustomed to in my days at the hospital in my own time. Still, it was a far cry—and an immeasurable relief—from the live and panicked convulsions that I had felt under my hands in the surgeon's tent.

I brushed the cut tendon aside with the forceps. There was the deep branch of the ulnar nerve, a delicate thread of white myelin, with its tiny branches spreading into invisibility, deep in the tissues. Good, it was far enough toward the fifth finger that I could work without damage to the main nerve trunk.

You never knew; textbook illustrations were one thing, but the first thing any surgeon learned was that bodies were unnervingly unique. A stomach would be roughly where you expected it to be, but the nerves and blood vessels that supplied it might be anywhere in the general vicinity, and quite possibly varying in shape and number, as well.

But now I knew the secrets of this hand. I could see the engineering of it, the structures that gave it form and movement. There was the beautiful strong arch of the third metacarpal, and the delicacy of the web of blood vessels that supplied it. Blood welled, slow and vivid: deep red in the tiny pool of the open field; brilliant scarlet where it stained the chopped bone; a dark and royal blue in the tiny vein that pulsed below the joint; a crusty black at the edge of the original wound, where it had clotted.

I had known, without asking myself how, that the fourth metacarpal was shattered. It was; the blade had struck near the proximal end of the bone, splintering its tiny head near the center of the hand.

I would take that, too, then; the free chunks of bone would have to be removed in any case, to prevent them irritating the adjoining tissues. Removing the metacarpal would let the third and fifth fingers lie close together, in effect narrowing the hand and eliminating the awkward gap that would be left by the missing finger.

I pulled hard on the mangled finger, to open the articular space between the joints, then used the tip of the scalpel to sever the ligament. The cartilages separated with a tiny but audible *pop!* and Jamie jerked and groaned, his hand twisting in my grasp.

"Hush," I whispered to him, holding tight. "Hush, it's all right. I'm here, it's all right."

I could do nothing for the boys dying on the field, but here, for him, I could offer magic and know the spell would hold. He heard me, deep in troubled opium dreams; he frowned and muttered something unintelligible, then sighed deeply and relaxed, his wrist going once more limp under my hand.

Somewhere near at hand, a rooster crowed, and I glanced at the wall of the tent. It was noticeably lighter, and a faint dawn wind drifted through the slit behind me, cool on the back of my neck.

Detach the underlying muscle with as little damage as could be managed. Tie off the small digital artery and two other vessels that seemed large enough to bother with, sever the last few fibers and shreds of skin that held the finger, then lift it free, the dangling metacarpal surprisingly white and naked, like a rat's tail.

It was a clean, neat job, but I felt a brief sense of sadness as I set the mangled piece of flesh aside. I had a fleeting vision of him holding newly born Jemmy, counting the tiny fingers and toes, delight and wonder on his face. His father had counted his fingers, too.

"It's all right," I whispered, as much to myself as to him. "It's all right. It will heal."

The rest was quick. Forceps to pluck out the tiny pieces of shattered bone. I debrided the wound as best I could, removing bits of grass and dirt, even a tiny swatch of fabric that had been driven into the flesh. Then no more than a matter of cleaning the ragged edge of the wound, snipping a small excess of skin, and suturing the incisions. A paste of garlic and white-oak leaves, mixed with alcohol and spread thickly over the hand, a padding of lint and gauze, and a tight bandage of linen and adhesive plasters, to reduce the swelling and encourage the third and fifth fingers to draw close together.

The sun was nearly up; the lantern overhead seemed dim and feeble. My eyes were burning from the close work and the smoke of fires. There were voices outside, the voices of officers moving among the men, rousing them to face the day—and the enemy?

I laid Jamie's hand on the cot, near his face. He was pale, but not excessively so, and his lips were a light rosy color, not blue. I dropped the instruments into a bucket of alcohol and water, suddenly too tired to clean them properly. I wrapped the discarded finger in a linen bandage, not quite sure what to do with it, and left it on the table.

"Rise and shine! Rise and shine!" came the sergeants' rhythmic cry from outside, punctuated by witty variations and crude responses from reluctant risers.

I didn't bother to undress; if there was fighting today, I would be roused soon enough. Not Jamie, though. I had nothing to worry about; no matter what happened, he wouldn't fight today.

I unpinned my hair and shook it down over my shoulders, sighing with relief at its looseness. Then I lay down on the cot beside him, close against him. He lay on his stomach; I could see the small, muscular swell of his buttocks, smooth under the blanket that covered him. On impulse, I laid my hand on his rump and squeezed.

"Sweet dreams," I said, and let the tiredness take me.

63

SEPARATED FOREVER FROM
MY FRIENDS AND KIN

LIEUTENANT LORD ELLESMERE had finally killed a rebel. Several, he thought, though he could not be sure of those he'd shot at; some of them fell but might be only wounded. He was sure of the man who had attacked one of the British cannon, with a party of other rebels. He'd hacked that man half through the body with a cavalry saber, and he felt a strange numbness in his sword arm for several days after, this making him flex his left hand every few minutes to be sure he could still use it.

The numbness was not limited to his arm.

The days after the battle in the British camp were spent partially in the orderly retrieval of the wounded, the burial of the dead, and in regathering their forces. What forces remained to be gathered. Desertion was rife; there was a constant small stream of furtive departures—one day a whole company of Brunswickers defected.

He oversaw more than one burial detail, watching with set face as men—and boys—he knew were consigned to the earth. On the first couple of days, they hadn't buried the bodies deep enough, and were obliged to listen all night to the howling and snarling of wolves fighting over the carcasses they had dragged from the shallow graves. They reburied what was left the next day, deeper.

Fires burned every hundred yards around the camp at night, for American sharpshooters came close in the dark, taking out the pickets.

The days were blazingly hot, the nights miserably cold—and no one rested. Burgoyne had issued an order that *no officer nor soldier should ever sleep without his cloaths,* and William had not changed his linen in more than a week. It didn't matter what he smelled like; his own reek was undetectable. The men were obliged to be in the lines, with their arms, an hour before dawn, and to remain there until the sun had burned away the fog, to be sure the fog did not hide Americans ready to attack.

The daily bread allowance was cut. Salt pork and flour were running out, and the sutlers lacked tobacco and brandy, to the disgruntlement of the German troops. On the good side, the British defenses were in splendid order, with two large redoubts built and a thousand men sent out to cut trees to open fields of fire for the artillery. And Burgoyne had announced that General Clinton was expected within ten days, with a supporting force—and food, it was to be hoped. All they had to do was wait.

"The Jews wait the Messiah not more than we wait General Clinton," joked Ober-Leftenant Gruenwald, who had by some miracle survived his wound at Bennington.

"Ha-ha," said William.

THE AMERICAN CAMP was in good spirits, more than ready to finish the job they had started. Unfortunately, while the British camp was short of rations, the Americans were short of ammunition and powder. The result was a period of restless stasis, during which the Americans picked constantly at the periphery of the British camp but could make no real progress.

Ian Murray found this tedious in the extreme, and after a token foray in the fog had resulted in a careless companion's stepping on a discarded gun spike and puncturing his foot, he decided this was adequate excuse to pay a visit to the hospital tent where Rachel Hunter was assisting her brother.

The prospect so animated him, though, that he paid inadequate attention to his own footing in the fog and plunged headfirst into a ravine, striking his head a glancing blow on a rock. Thus it was that the two men limped into camp, supporting each other, and made their halting way to the hospital tent.

It was busy in the tent; this was not where the battle-wounded lay but where those with trivial afflictions came for treatment. Ian's head was not broken, but he was seeing two of everything, and closed one eye in hopes that this might help him spot Rachel.

"Ho ro," someone behind him said in open approval, *"mo nighean donn bhoideach!"* For one head-spinning instant, he thought it was his uncle speaking and blinked stupidly, wondering why Uncle Jamie should be making flirtatious remarks to his aunt while she was working—but Auntie Claire wasn't here at all, his slow wits reminded him, so what . . .

One hand over his eye to keep it from falling out of his head, he turned carefully and saw a man in the opening of the tent.

The morning sun struck sparks from the man's hair, and Ian's mouth fell open, feeling that he had been struck in the pit of the stomach.

It wasn't Uncle Jamie, he could see that at once as the man came in, also helping a limping comrade. The face was wrong: red and weather-beaten, with cheerful, snub features; the hair was ginger, not rufous, and receded sharply from the man's temples. He was solidly built, not terribly tall, but the way he moved . . . like a catamount, even burdened with his friend, and for some reason Ian could not remove the lingering impression of Jamie Fraser.

The red-haired man was kilted; they both were. *Highlanders,* he thought, thoroughly fuddled. But he'd known that from the moment the man spoke.

"*Có thu?*" Ian asked abruptly. *Who are you?*

Hearing the Gaelic, the man looked at him, startled. He gave Ian a quick up-and-down, taking in his Mohawk dress, before answering.

"*Is mise Seaumais Mac Choinnich à Boisdale,*" he answered, courteously enough. "*Có tha faighneachd?*" *I am Hamish MacKenzie, of Boisdale. Who asks?*

"Ian Murray," he replied, trying to focus his addled wits. The name sounded faintly familiar—but why would it not? He knew hundreds of MacKenzies. "My grandmother was a MacKenzie," he offered, in the usual way of establishing relations among strangers. "Ellen MacKenzie, of Leoch."

The man's eyes sprang wide

"Ellen, of Leoch?" cried the man, very excited. "Daughter of him they called Jacob Ruaidh?"

In his excitement, Hamish's grip had tightened on his friend, and the man gave a yelp. This attracted the attention of the young woman—the one Hamish had greeted as "O, beautiful nut-brown maiden"—and she came hurrying to see the matter.

She *was* nut brown, Ian saw; Rachel Hunter, tanned by the sun to the exact soft shade of a hickory nut, what showed of her hair beneath her kerchief the shade of walnut hulls, and he smiled at the thought. She saw him and narrowed her eyes.

"Well, and if thee is able to grin like an ape, thee is not much hurt. Why—" She stopped, astonished at the sight of Ian Murray locked in embrace with a kilted Highlander, who was weeping with joy. Ian was not weeping, but was undeniably pleased.

"Ye'll want to meet my uncle Jamie," he said, adroitly disentangling himself. "*Seaumais Ruaidh,* I think ye called him."

⁂

JAMIE FRASER HAD his eyes shut, cautiously exploring the pain in his hand. It was sharp-edged, strong enough to make him queasy, but with that deep, grinding ache common to broken bones. Still, it was a healing ache.

Claire spoke of bones knitting—and he'd often thought this was more than a metaphor; it sometimes felt that someone was indeed stabbing steel needles into the bone and forcing the shattered ends back into some pattern, heedless of how the flesh around them felt about it.

He should look at his hand, he knew that. He had to get used to it, after all. He'd had the one quick glance, and it had left him dizzy and on the point of vomiting out of sheer confoundment. He could not reconcile the sight, the feel of it, with the strong memory of how his hand *ought* to be.

He'd done it before, though, he reminded himself. He'd got used to the scars and the stiffness. And yet... he could remember how his young hand had felt, had looked, so easy, limber and painless, folded round the handle of a hoe, the hilt of a sword. Clutching a quill—well, no. He smiled ruefully to himself. That hadn't been either easy or limber, even with his fingers at their unmarred best.

Would he be able to write at all with his hand now? he wondered suddenly, and in curiosity flexed his hand a little. The pain made him gasp, but... his eyes were open, fixed on his hand. The disconcerting sight of his little finger pressed close to the middle one did make his belly clench, but... his fingers curled. It hurt like Christ crucified, but it was just pain; there was no pull, no stubborn hindrance from the frozen finger. It... worked.

"I mean to leave you with a working hand." He could hear Claire's voice, breathless but sure.

He smiled a little. It didn't do to argue with the woman over any matter medical.

I CAME INTO the tent to fetch my small cautery iron and found Jamie sitting on the cot, slowly flexing his injured hand and contemplating his severed finger, which lay on a box beside him. I had wrapped it hastily in a plaster bandage, and it looked like a mummified worm.

"Er," I said delicately. "I'll, um, dispose of that, shall I?"

"How?" He put out a tentative forefinger, touched it, then snatched back his hand as though the detached finger had moved suddenly. He made a small, nervous sound that wasn't quite a laugh.

"Burn it?" I suggested. That was the usual method for disposing of amputated limbs on battlefields, though I had never personally done it. The notion of building a funeral pyre for the cremation of a single finger seemed suddenly absurd—though no more so than the idea of simply tossing it into one of the cookfires and hoping no one noticed.

Jamie made a dubious noise in his throat, indicating that he wasn't keen on the idea.

"Well... I suppose you could smoke it," I said, with equal dubiety. "And keep it in your sporran as a souvenir. Like Young Ian did with Neil Forbes's ear. Has he still got that, do you know?"

"Aye, he does." Jamie's color was beginning to come back, as he regained his self-possession. "But, no, I dinna think I want to do that."

"I could pickle it in spirits of wine," I offered. That got the ghost of a smile.

"Ten to one, someone would drink it before the day was out, Sassenach."
I thought that was generous odds, myself. More like a thousand to one. I
managed to keep my medicinal alcohol mostly intact only by virtue of having
one of Ian's more ferocious Indian acquaintances guard it, when I wasn't using it—and sleeping with the keg next to me at night.

"Well, I think that leaves burial as the only other option."

"Mmphm." That sound indicated agreement, but with reservations, and I
glanced up at him.

"What?"

"Aye, well," he said, rather diffidently. "When wee Fergus lost his hand,
we . . . well, it was Jenny's notion. But we held a bit of a funeral, ken?"

I bit my lip. "Well, why not? Will it be a family affair, or shall we invite
everyone?"

Before he could answer this, I heard Ian's voice outside, talking to someone, and an instant later his disheveled head pushed through the flap. One of
his eyes was black and swollen and there was a sizable lump on his head, but
he was grinning from ear to ear.

"Uncle Jamie?" he said. "There's someone here to see ye."

"HOW IS IT that ye come to be here, *a charaid?*" Jamie asked, somewhere
after the third bottle. We had had supper long since, and the campfire was
burning low.

Hamish wiped his mouth and handed the new bottle back.

"Here," he repeated. "Here in the wilderness, d'ye mean? Or here, fighting against the King?" He gave Jamie a direct blue look, so like one of Jamie's
own that Jamie smiled, recognizing it.

"Is the second of those questions the answer to the first?" he said, and
Hamish gave him the shadow of a smile in return.

"Aye, that would be it. Ye were always quick as the hummingbird, *a
Sheaumais.* In body *and* mind." Seeing from my expression that I was perhaps not quite so swift in my perceptions, he turned to me.

"It was the King's troops who killed my uncle, the King's soldiers who
killed the fighting men of the clan, who destroyed the land, who left the
women and the bairns to starve—who battered down my home and exiled
me, who killed half the people left to me with cold and hunger and the
plagues of the wilderness." He spoke quietly, but with a passion that burned
in his eyes.

"I was eleven years old when they came to the castle and put us out. I
turned twelve on the day that they made me swear my oath to the King—they
said I was a man. And by the time we reached Nova Scotia . . . I was."

He turned to Jamie.

"They made ye swear, too, *a Sheaumais?*"

"They did," Jamie said softly. "A forced oath canna bind a man, though,
or keep him from his knowledge of right."

Hamish put out a hand, and Jamie gripped it, though they did not look at
each other.

"No," he said, with certainty. "That it cannot."

Perhaps not; but I knew they were both thinking, as I was, of the language of that oath: *May I lie in an unconsecrated grave, separated forever from my friends and kin.* And both thinking—as I was—how great the odds were that that fate was exactly what would happen to them.

And to me.

I cleared my throat.

"But the others," I said, impelled by the memory of so many I had known in North Carolina, and knowing the same was true of many in Canada. "The Highlanders who are Loyalists?"

"Aye, well," Hamish said softly, and looked into the fire, the lines of his face cut deep by its glow. "They fought bravely, but the heart of them was killed. They want only peace now and to be left alone. But war doesna leave any alone, does it?" He looked suddenly at me, and for a startling instant I saw Dougal MacKenzie looking out of his eyes, that impatient, violent man who had hungered for war. Not waiting for an answer, he shrugged and went on.

"War's found them again; they've nay choice but to fight. But anyone can see what a pitiful rabble the Continental army is—or was." He lifted his head, nodding a little, as though to himself, at sight of the campfires, the tents, the vast cloud of starlit haze that hung above us, full of smoke and dust and the scent of guns and ordure. "They thought the rebels would be crushed, and quickly. Oath notwithstanding, who but a fool would join such risky business?"

A man who had had no chance to fight before, I thought.

He smiled crookedly at Jamie.

"I am surprised we were not crushed," he said, sounding in fact faintly surprised. "Are ye not surprised as well, *a Sheaumais*?"

"Amazed," Jamie said, a faint smile on his own face. "Glad of it, though. And glad of you . . . *a Sheaumais*."

They talked through most of the night. When they lapsed into Gaelic, I got up, put a hand on Jamie's shoulder in token of good night, and crawled into my blankets. Exhausted by the day's work, I drifted into sleep at once, soothed by the sound of their quiet talk, like the sound of bees in the heather. The last thing I saw before sleep took me was Young Ian's face across the fire, rapt at hearing of the Scotland that had vanished just as he himself was born.

64

A GENTLEMAN CALLER

"MRS. FRASER?" A pleasant masculine voice spoke behind me, and I turned to see a stocky, broad-shouldered officer in the doorway of my tent, in shirtsleeves and waistcoat, a box cradled in one arm.

"I am. May I help you?"

He didn't look sick; in fact, he was healthier-looking than most of the army, his face very weathered but well-fleshed and ruddy. He smiled, a sudden, charming smile that quite transformed his big beaky nose and heavy brows.

"I was in hopes that we might transact a little business, Mrs. Fraser." He raised one of the bushy brows and, at my gesture of invitation, came into the tent, ducking only a little.

"I suppose that depends what you're looking for," I said, with a curious look at his box. "If it's whisky, I can't give you that, I'm afraid." There was in fact a small keg of this valuable substance hidden under the table at the moment, along with a larger keg of my raw medicinal alcohol—and the smell of the latter was strong in the air, as I was steeping herbs in it. This gentleman was not the first to have been drawn by the scent—it attracted soldiers of all ranks like flies.

"Oh, no," he assured me, though casting an interested look at the table behind me, where I had several large jars in which I was growing what I hoped was penicillin. "I'm told, though, that you possess a stock of cinchona bark. Is that so?"

"Well, yes. Please, sit." I waved him to my patient stool and sat down myself, knee to knee. "Do you suffer from malaria?" I didn't think so—the whites of his eyes were clear; he wasn't jaundiced.

"No, may the Lord be thanked for His mercy. I have a gentleman in my command—a particular friend—who does, though, very badly, and our surgeon has no Jesuit bark. I hoped that you might be induced, perhaps, to make a trade . . . ?"

He had laid the box on the table beside us, and at this flipped it open. It was divided into small compartments and contained a remarkable assortment of things: lace edging, silk ribbon, a pair of tortoiseshell hair combs, a small bag of salt, a pepperbox, an enameled snuffbox, a pewter brooch in the shape of a lily, several bright hanks of embroidery silk, a bundle of cinnamon sticks, and a number of small jars filled apparently with herbs. And a glass bottle, whose label read . . .

"Laudanum!" I exclaimed, reaching for it involuntarily. I stopped myself, but the officer gestured to me to go ahead, and I pulled it carefully from its resting place, drew the cork, and moved the bottle warily past my nose. The pungent, sickly-sweet scent of opium drifted out, a genie in a bottle. I cleared my throat and put the cork back in.

He was watching me with interest.

"I was not sure what might best suit you," he said, waving at the box's contents. "I used to run a store, you see—a great deal of apothecary's stuff, but luxurious dry goods in general. I learnt in the course of my business that it is always best to give the ladies a good deal of choice; they tend to be much more discriminating than do the gentlemen."

I gave him a sharp glance, but it wasn't flummery; he smiled at me again, and I thought that he was one of those unusual men—like Jamie—who actually liked women, beyond the obvious.

"I imagine we can accommodate each other, then," I said, returning the smile. "I ought not to ask, I suppose—I don't intend to hold you up; I'll give you what you need for your friend—but with thought of possible future trade, have you got more laudanum?"

He continued to smile, but his gaze sharpened—he had rather unusual eyes, that pale gray often described as "spit-colored."

"Why, yes," he said slowly. "I have quite a bit. Do you . . . require it regularly?"

It occurred to me that he was wondering whether I was an addict; it wasn't at all uncommon, in circles where laudanum was easily obtainable.

"I don't use it myself, no," I replied equably. "And I administer it to those in need with considerable caution. But relief of pain is one of the more important things I can offer some of the people who come to me—God knows I can't offer many of them cure."

His brows went up at that. "That's a rather remarkable statement. Most persons in your profession seem to promise cure to nearly everyone."

"How does that saying go? 'If wishes were horses, beggars might ride'?" I smiled, but without much humor. "Everyone wants a cure, and certainly there's no physician who doesn't want to give them one. But there are a lot of things beyond the power of any physician, and while you might not tell a patient that, it's as well to know your own limits."

"You think so?" He tilted his head, regarding me curiously. "Do you not think that the admission of such limits, *a priori*—and I do not mean only in the medical way, but in any arena of endeavor—that such an admission in itself *establishes* limits? That is, might that expectation prevent one from accomplishing all that is possible, because one assumes that something is *not* possible and therefore does not strive with all one's power to achieve it?"

I blinked at him, rather surprised.

"Well . . . yes," I said slowly. "If you put it that way, I rather think I agree with you. After all"—I waved a hand toward the tent flap, indicating the surrounding army—"if I didn't—*we* didn't—believe that one can accomplish things beyond all reasonable expectation, would my husband and I be *here*?"

He laughed at that.

"Brava, ma'am! Yes, an impartial observer would, I think, call this venture sheer madness. And they might be right," he added, with a rueful tilt of the head. "But they'll have to defeat us, nonetheless. We shan't give up."

I heard voices outside: Jamie, talking casually with someone, and in the next moment he had ducked inside the tent.

"Sassenach," he began, "can ye come and—" He stopped dead, seeing my visitor, and drew up a bit, with a formal bow. "Sir."

I glanced back at the visitor, surprised; Jamie's manner made it clear that this was a superior officer of some sort; I'd thought him perhaps a captain or a major. As for the officer himself, he nodded, friendly but reserved.

"Colonel. Your wife and I have been discussing the philosophy of endeavor. What do you say—does a wise man know his limits, or a bold one deny them? And which way do you declare yourself?"

Jamie looked mildly startled and glanced at me; I lifted one shoulder an inch.

"Ah, well," he said, switching his attention back to my visitor. "I've heard it said that a man's reach must exceed his grasp—or what's a heaven for?"

The officer stared at him for an instant, mouth open, then laughed with delight and slapped his knee.

"You and your wife are two of a kind, sir! *My* kind. That's splendid; do you recall where you heard it?"

Jamie did; he'd heard it from me, more than once over the years. He merely smiled and shrugged, though.

"A poet, I believe, but I've forgot the name."

"Well, a perfectly expressed sentiment, nonetheless, and I mean to go and try it on Granny directly—though I imagine he'll just blink stupidly at me through his spectacles and bleat about supplies. *There's* a man who knows his limits," he remarked to me, still good-humored but with a distinct edge in his voice. "Knows his own damnably low limits and won't let anyone else exceed them. A heaven's not for the likes of him."

That last remark went beyond edgy; the smile had faded from his face, and I glimpsed a hot anger at the back of his pale eyes. I had a moment of disquiet; "Granny" could only be General Gates, and this man was plainly a disaffected member of the high command. I sincerely hoped Robert Browning and I hadn't just landed Jamie in the middle of something.

"Well," I said, trying to make light of it, "they can't defeat you if you won't give up."

The shadow that had rested on his brow cleared and he smiled at me, merry-eyed once more.

"Oh, they'll never defeat me, Mrs. Fraser. Trust me!"

"I will," I assured him, turning to open one of my boxes. "Let me get the Jesuit bark for you . . . er . . ." I hesitated, not knowing his rank, and he noticed, clapping a hand to his forehead in apology.

"My apologies, Mrs. Fraser! What can you think of a man who bursts into your presence, rudely demanding medicaments and failing even to introduce himself properly?"

He took the small package of shredded bark from my hand, retaining the hand itself, and bowed low over it, gently kissing my knuckles.

"Major General Benedict Arnold. Your servant, ma'am."

JAMIE LOOKED AFTER the departing general, a slight frown on his face. Then he glanced back at me and the frown disappeared instantly.

"Are ye all right, Sassenach? Ye look as though you're about to fall over."

"I might, at that," I said rather faintly, and groped for my stool. I sat on it and discovered the new bottle of laudanum on the table beside me. I picked it up, finding the solid weight of it a reassurance that I hadn't imagined the gentleman who'd just left us.

"I was mentally prepared to run into George Washington or Benjamin Franklin in person at some point," I said. "Even John Adams. But I didn't really expect *him* ... and I *liked* him," I added ruefully.

Jamie's brows were still up, and he glanced at the bottle in my lap as though wondering whether I'd been having a nip.

"Why should ye not like—oh." His face changed. "Ye know something about him?"

"Yes, I do. And it's not something I want to know." I swallowed, feeling a little ill. "He's not a traitor yet—but he will be."

Jamie glanced back over his shoulder, to be sure we were not overheard, then came and sat on the patient's stool, taking my hands in his.

"Tell me," he said, low-voiced.

There were limits to what I *could* tell him—and, not for the first time, I regretted not having paid more attention to Bree's history homework, as that formed the nucleus of my specific knowledge regarding the American Revolution.

"He fought on our—on the American side for some time, and was a brilliant soldier, though I don't know any of the details of that. But at some point, he became disillusioned, decided to switch sides, and began making overtures to the British, using a man called John André as his go-between—André was captured and hanged, I know that much. But I think Arnold got away to England. For an American *general* to turn his coat ... it was such a spectacular act of treason that the name 'Benedict Arnold' became a synonym for traitor. *Will* become, I mean. If someone commits some horrible act of betrayal, you call them 'a Benedict Arnold.' "

The sick feeling hadn't gone away. Somewhere—right this minute—one Major John André was happily going about his business, presumably without the slightest notion of what lay in his future.

"When?" Jamie's fingers pressing mine drew my attention away from Major André's impending doom and back to the more urgent matter.

"That's the problem," I said helplessly. "I don't know. Not yet—I *think* not yet."

Jamie thought for a moment, brows drawn down.

"I'll watch him, then," he said quietly.

"Don't," I said, by reflex. We stared at each other for a long moment, recalling Charles Stuart. It hadn't escaped either of us that attempting to interfere with history could have serious unintended consequences—if in fact it could be done at all. We had no notion what it was that might turn Arnold from patriot—which he certainly was at the moment—to the traitor he would be. Was his fight with Gates the niggling grain of sand that would form the heart of a treacherous pearl?

"You don't know what small thing might affect someone's mind," I pointed out. "Look at Robert the Bruce and that spider."

That made him smile.

"I'll gang warily, Sassenach," he said. "But I'll watch him."

65

HAT TRICK

October 7, 1777

. . . Well, then, order on Morgan to begin the Game.

General Horatio Gates

ON A QUIET autumn morning, crisp and golden, a British deserter entered the American camp. Burgoyne was sending out a reconnaissance force, he said. Two thousand men, to test the strength of the American right wing.

"Granny Gates's eyes nearly popped through his spectacles," Jamie told me, hastily reloading his cartridge box. "And nay wonder."

General Arnold, present when the news came, urged Gates to send out a strong force against this foray. Gates, true to form, had been cautious, and when Arnold requested permission to go out and see for himself what the British were about, had given his subordinate a cold look and said, "I am afraid to trust you, Arnold."

"Matters rather went downhill from there," Jamie said, grimacing slightly. "The end of it all was that Gates said to him—and I quote ye exactly, Sassenach—'General Arnold, I have nothing for you to do. You have no business here.'"

I felt a chill that had nothing to do with the temperature of the morning air. Was this the moment? The thing that had—or would—turn Benedict Arnold against the cause he had fought for? Jamie saw what I was thinking, for he lifted one shoulder and said simply, "At least it's nothing to do wi' us this time."

"That *is* a comfort," I said, and meant it. "Take care, will you?"

"I will," he said, taking up his rifle.

This time, he was able to kiss me goodbye in person.

THE BRITISH reconnaissance had a double purpose: not only to see exactly where the Americans were—for General Burgoyne had no real idea; American deserters had stopped coming in long since—but also to acquire much-needed forage for the remaining animals. Consequently, the leading companies stopped in a promising wheat field.

William sent his infantrymen to sit down in double rows among the standing grain, while the foragers began cutting the grain and loading it on horses. A lieutenant of dragoons, a black-headed Welshman named Absolute, waved from the other side of the field and called him to a game of hazard in his tent in the evening. He had just taken breath to call back when the man beside him let out a gasp and crumpled to the ground. He never heard the bullet, but ducked to the ground, calling out to his men.

Nothing further happened, though, and after a few moments they rose cautiously and went about their work. They began to see small parties of rebels, though, stealing through the trees, and William became conscious of a growing conviction that they were being surrounded. When he spoke of this to another officer, though, the man assured him that the rebels had decided to remain behind their defenses to be attacked.

They were soon undeceived on this point when, in mid-afternoon, a large body of Americans appeared in the woods on their left and heavy cannon opened up, slamming six- and twelve-pound balls that would have done great damage, were it not for the intervening trees.

The infantrymen scattered like quail, despite the calls of their officers. William caught sight of Absolute, pelting down the field through the wheat after a group of his men, and, turning, seized a corporal of one of his own companies.

"Gather them!" he said, and, not waiting for an answer, grabbed the bridle of one of the foragers' horses, a surprised-looking bay gelding. It was his intent to ride for the main camp for reinforcements, for plainly the Americans were out in force.

He never got there, for as he pulled the horse's head around, the brigadier rode onto the field.

JAMIE FRASER CROUCHED in the grove at the base of the wheat field with a group of Morgan's men, taking aim as he could. It was as hot a battle as he'd seen, and the smoke from the cannon in the wood drifted through the field in heavy, choking clouds. He saw the man on the horse, a high-ranking British officer, to judge from his braid. Two or three others, juniors, were near him, also on horseback, but he had eyes only for the one.

Grasshoppers flew out of the field like hailstones, panicked by the trampling feet; one struck him in the cheek, buzzing, and he slapped at it, heart thumping as though it had been a musket ball.

He knew the man, though only by his general's uniform. He had met Simon Fraser of Balnain two or three times, but when they both were lads in the Highlands—Simon was a few years younger, and Jamie's vague memories of a small, round, cheerful wee lad who trotted after the older boys, waving a shinty stick taller than himself, had nothing in common with the stout, solid man who rose now in his stirrups, calling out and brandishing his sword, attempting to rally his panicked troops by sheer force of personality.

The aides were urging their mounts round his, trying to shield him, plainly urging him to come away, but he ignored them. Jamie caught a white glimpse of a face turned toward the wood, then away—plainly they knew the trees were full of riflemen, or could be, and were trying to keep out of range.

"There he is!" It was Arnold, crashing his small brown mare regardless through the heavy brush, his face alight with savage glee. "The generals!" he bellowed, rising in his own stirrups and throwing out an arm. "Shoot the generals, boys! Five dollars to the man who shoots yon fat bastard from his saddle!"

The random crack of rifle fire answered him at once. Jamie saw Daniel Morgan's head turn sharp, eyes fierce at Arnold's voice, and the rifleman started toward him, moving as fast as his rheumatism-crippled limbs would let him.

"Again! Try again!" Arnold smote a fist on his thigh, caught sight of Jamie watching him. "You—shoot him, can't you?"

Jamie shrugged and, lifting the rifle to his shoulder, aimed deliberately high and wide. The wind had turned and the smoke of the shot stung his eyes, but he saw one of the junior officers near Simon jump and clap a hand to his head, twisting in the saddle to see his hat roll away into the wheat.

He wanted to laugh, though his wame curled a bit, realizing that he had nearly shot the man through the head, entirely by accident. The young man—yes, he was young, tall, and thin—rose in his stirrups and shook a fist at the wood.

"You owe me a hat, sir!" he shouted.

Arnold's high, piercing laugh echoed through the wood, clear over the shouting, and the men with him hooted and screamed like crows.

"Come over here, younker, and I'll buy you two!" Arnold shouted back, then reined his horse in a restless circle, bellowing at the riflemen. "Damn your eyes for a crew of blind men, will nobody kill me that frigging general?"

One or two shots spattered through the branches, but most of the men had seen Daniel Morgan stumping toward Arnold like an animated tree, gnarled and implacable, and held their fire.

Arnold must have seen him, too, but ignored him. He jerked a pistol from his belt and fired sideways across his body at Fraser, though he could not hope to hit anything at that distance, and his horse startled at the noise, ears flat back. Morgan, who had nearly reached him, was obliged to jerk back to avoid being trampled; he stumbled, and fell flat.

Without an instant's hesitation, Arnold leapt off his horse and bent to raise the older man, apologizing with a completely sincere solicitude. Which, Jamie saw, was unappreciated by Morgan. He thought old Dan might just give Arnold one in the stones, rank and rheumatism notwithstanding.

The general's horse was trained to stand, but the unexpected shot over her ears had spooked her; she was dancing nervously, feet a-rattle in the drifts of dead leaves and eyes showing white.

Jamie seized the reins and pulled the mare's nose down, blowing into her nostrils to distract her. She whuffed and shook her head, but ceased to dance. He stroked her neck, clicking his tongue, and her ears rose a bit; his hand was bleeding again, he saw, but it was a slow seep through the bandage, not important. Over the solid curve of the mare's neck, he could see Morgan, upright now and violently rejecting Arnold's efforts to dust the leaf mold from his clothes.

"You are relieved of command, sir! How dare you to order my men?"

"Oh, fuck that for a game of soldiers!" Arnold said, impatient. "I'm a general. He's a general"—he jerked his head toward the distant figure on horseback—"and I want him dead. Time enough for politics when it's over—this is a fight, dammit!" Jamie caught a sudden strong whiff of rum, sweet and fierce under the smell of smoke and trampled wheat. Aye, well, perhaps that had somewhat to do with it—though from what he knew of Arnold, there was little enough to choose between the man stone sober and another raving with drink.

The wind came in gusts, hot past his ears, thick with smoke and random sounds: the rattle of muskets punctuated by the crash of artillery to the left, and through it the shouting of Simon Fraser and his juniors, calling the Hessians and English to rally, the grunts of impact and shrieks of pain from farther away, where the Hessians fought to break through General Enoch Poor's advancing men.

General Ebenezer Learned's column was pressing the Hessians from above; Jamie could see the knot of green German uniforms, struggling amid a surge of Continentals but being forced back from the edge of the field. Some were trying to break away, to head downfield toward General Fraser. A glimpse of motion drew his eye; the young man he had deprived of a hat was galloping up the field, bent low over his horse's neck, saber drawn.

The general had moved a little, away from the wood. He was nearly out of range for most of Morgan's men—but Jamie was well placed; he had a clear shot from here. He glanced down. He had dropped his rifle when he took the horse, but the gun was loaded; he had reloaded by reflex after his first shot. The half-empty cartridge was still folded in the hand that held the reins; priming would take but an instant.

"*Sheas, a nighean,*" he murmured to the horse, and took a deep breath, trying to will himself to calm, will that calmness into the mare, though his hand was throbbing with the rush of his blood. "*Cha chluinn thu an còrr a chuireas eagal ort,*" he said, under his breath. *No more. Ye'll hear nay more to fright ye.*

He had not even thought about it when he'd fired to miss Fraser. He would kill any other man on the field—but not that one. Then he caught sight of the young soldier on the horse, coat bright red among the thrashing sea of green and blue and homespun, laying about him with his saber, and felt his mouth twitch. Not that one, either.

It seemed the young man was having a lucky day. He had cut through Learned's column at the gallop, taking most of the Continentals unaware, and those who saw him were too much occupied with fighting or unable to shoot him because they had discharged their weapons and were fixing bayonets.

Jamie stroked the horse absently, whistling gently through his teeth and watching. The young officer had reached the Hessians, had got the attention of some, and was now fighting his way back down the field, a stream of dark green coats in his wake, Hessians at the trot, making for the narrowing gap as Poor's men rushed in from the left.

Jamie was so much occupied by this entertaining spectacle that he had ignored the shouting match taking place between Dan Morgan and General Arnold. The sound of a whoop from overhead interrupted both.

"I got him, by Jaysus!"

Jamie looked up, startled, and saw Tim Murphy perched in the branches of an oak, grinning like a goblin, the barrel of his rifle snug in a fork. Jamie jerked his head round and saw Simon Fraser, slumped and swaying in his saddle, arms folded round his body.

Arnold let out a matching whoop, and Morgan glanced up at Murphy, nodding grudging approval.

"Good shot," he called.

Simon Fraser was wobbling, about to fall—one of his aides reached for him, shouting desperately for help, another reined his horse to and fro, undecided where to go, what to do. Jamie clenched his fist, felt a jolt of pain shoot through his maimed hand, and stopped, palm flat on the saddle. Was Simon dead?

He couldn't tell. The aides had overcome their panic; two of them rode close on either side, supporting the slumping figure, fighting to keep him in the saddle, heedless of the cheering from the wood.

He glanced up the field, searching for the young man with the saber. He couldn't find him and felt a small stab of loss—then picked him up, engaged in a hand-to-hand with a mounted militia captain. No kind of finesse in that sort of fight; it was as much the horse as the man, and as he watched, the horses were forced apart by the crush of bodies round them. The British officer didn't try to force his mount back; he had a goal in mind and shouted and gestured, urging on the small company of Hessians he had extracted from the melee above. Then he turned back toward the wood and saw what was happening, General Fraser's horse being urged away, the general's swaying body a splotch of red against the trampled wheat.

The young man stood in his stirrups for an instant, dropped, and spurred his horse toward the general, leaving his Hessians to follow as they might.

Jamie was close enough to see the darker crimson of the blood that soaked the middle of Simon Fraser's body. If Simon wasn't dead already, he thought, it wouldn't be long. Grief and fury at the waste of it burned in his throat. Tears from the smoke were already running down his cheeks; he blinked and shook his head violently to clear his eyes.

A hand jerked the reins unceremoniously from his fingers, and Arnold's stocky body brushed him away from the mare in a gust of rum. Arnold swung up into the saddle, face red as the scarlet maple leaves with excitement and victory.

"Follow me, boys!" he shouted, and Jamie saw that the wood was aswarm with militia, companies Arnold had collected on his mad dash for the battlefield. "To the redoubt!"

The men cheered and rushed after him, breaking branches and stumbling in their eagerness.

"Follow that goddamned fool," Morgan said shortly, and Jamie glanced at him in surprise. Morgan scowled at Arnold's back.

"He'll be court-martialed, mark my words," the old rifleman said. "He'd best have a good witness. You're it, James. Go!"

Without a word, Jamie seized his rifle from the ground and set off at a run, leaving the wood with its gentle rain of gold and brown. Following Arnold's broad-shouldered whooping form, his waving hat. Into the wheat.

———

THEY DID FOLLOW him. A bellowing horde, an armed rabble. Arnold was mounted, but his horse found it heavy going, and the men were not hard-pressed to keep up. Jamie saw the back of Arnold's blue coat blotched black with sweat, molded like a rind to the burly shoulders. One shot from the rear, the confusion of battle . . . But it was no more than a passing thought, gone in an instant.

Arnold was gone, too, with a whoop, spurring his mare up and around, past the redoubt. Jamie assumed he must be meaning to ride in from the rear—suicide, as the place was crawling with German grenadiers; he could see their mitred hats poking up above the walls of the redoubt. Perhaps Arnold meant to commit suicide—perhaps only to create a diversion for the men attacking the redoubt from the front, with his own death an acceptable price to be paid for it.

The redoubt itself stood fifteen feet high, a packed earthen wall with a palisade of logs built atop it—and between earth and palisade were abatis, logs sharpened to a point and flung down pointing outward.

Balls were spattering the field before the redoubt, and Jamie ran, dodging bullets he couldn't see.

He scrabbled with his feet, clawing for purchase on the logs of the abatis, got one hand through a gap and onto a log, but lost his grip on the flaking bark and fell back, landing bruisingly on his rifle and knocking out his wind. The man beside him fired up through the gap, and white smoke spurted over him, hiding him momentarily from the Hessian he'd glimpsed above. He rolled over and crawled fast away before the smoke could drift off or the fellow decide to drop a grenade through it.

"Get clear!" he shouted over his shoulder, but the man who'd fired was trying his own luck with a running jump. The grenade fell through the gap just as the man leapt upward. It caught him in the chest and went off.

Jamie rubbed his hand on his shirt, swallowing bile. The skin of his palm stung, scraped and full of bark splinters. Shards of metal and wood chips had exploded outward; something had struck Jamie in the face, and he felt the sting of his sweat and the warmth of blood running down his cheek. He could see the grenadier, a glimpse of green coat through the gap in the abatis. Quick, before he moved.

He grabbed a cartridge from his bag and ripped it with his teeth, counting. He could load a rifle in twelve seconds, he knew it, had timed it. *Nine* . . .

eight . . . What was it Bree taught the weans, counting seconds? Hippopotami, aye. *Six hippopotami . . . five hippopotami . . .* He had an insane urge to laugh, seeing in his mind's eye a group of several hippopotami solemnly watching him and making critical remarks regarding his progress. *Two hippopotami . . .* He wasn't dead yet, so he pressed himself close up under the abatis, aimed the barrel through the gap, and fired at the smear of green that might be a fir tree but wasn't, since it screamed.

He slung the rifle onto his back and once more leaped, fingers digging desperately into the unpeeled log. They slipped, splinters running up under his nails, and pain shot through his hand like lightning but now he had his other hand up, grabbed his right wrist with his sound left hand, and locked his grip round the log. His feet slid on the loose-packed dirt, and for an instant he swung free, like a squirrel hanging from a tree branch. He pulled upward against his weight and felt something tear in his shoulder, but couldn't stop to favor it. A foot, he had his foot braced on the underside of the log now. A wild swing with his free leg and he was clinging like a sloth. Something chunked into the log he clung to; he felt the shiver through the wood.

"Hold on, Red!" someone screamed below him, and he froze. Another chunking sound and something came down on the wood an inch from his fingers—an ax? He didn't have time to be scared; the man below fired past his shoulder—he heard the ball whiz past, buzzing like an angry hornet—and he pulled himself toward the base of the log in a rush, hand over hand as fast as he could, worming his way between the logs, clothes ripping, and his joints, too.

There were two Hessians lying just above his gap, dead or wounded. Another, ten feet away, saw his head pop through and reached into his sack, teeth bared beneath a waxed mustache. A bloodcurdling yell came from behind the Hessian, though, and one of Morgan's men brought down a tomahawk on his skull.

He heard a noise and turned in time to see a corporal step on one of the Hessian bodies, which abruptly came to life, rolling up with musket in hand. The Hessian struck up with all his force, the blade of the bayonet ripping up through the corporal's breeches as he stumbled, tearing free in a spray of blood.

By reflex, Jamie seized his rifle by the barrel and swung it, the motion snapping through his shoulders, arms, and wrists as he tried to drive the butt through the man's head. The jolt of collision wrenched his arms, and he felt the bones of his neck pop and his sight go white. He shook his head to clear it and smeared sweat and blood from his eye sockets with the heel of his hand. Shit, he'd bent the rifle.

The Hessian was dead for good, a look of surprise on what was left of his face. The wounded corporal was crawling away, one leg of his breeches soaked with blood, his musket slung onto his back, his own bayonet blade in his hand. He glanced over his shoulder and, seeing Jamie, shouted, "Rifleman! Your back!"

He didn't turn to see what it was but dived headlong and to the side, rolling into leaves and trampled earth. Several bodies rolled over him in a grunting tangle and crashed against the palisades. He got up slowly, took one of the pistols from his belt, cocked it, and blew out the brains of a grenadier poised to throw one of his grenades over the edge.

A few more shots, groans, and thumps, and as quickly as that, the fight died down. The redoubt was littered with bodies—most of them green-clad. He caught a glimpse of Arnold's little mare, white-eyed and limping, riderless. Arnold was on the ground, struggling to stand.

Jamie felt nearly unable to stand himself; his knees had gone to water and his right hand was paralyzed, but he wobbled over to Arnold and half-fell down beside him. The general had been shot; his leg was all-over blood, and his face was white and clammy, his eyes half-closing from the shock. Jamie reached out and gripped Arnold's hand, calling his name to pull him back, thinking even as he did so that this was madness; he should slip his dirk into the man's ribs and spare both him and the victims of his treachery. But the choice was made and past before he had time to think about it. Arnold's hand tightened on his.

"Where?" Arnold whispered. His lips were blanched. "Where am I hit?"

"It's your leg, sir," Jamie said. "The same where ye were hit before."

Arnold's eyes opened and fixed upon his face.

"I wish it had been my heart," he whispered, and closed them again.

66

DEATHBED

A BRITISH ENSIGN came just after nightfall, under a flag of truce. General Gates sent him to our tent; Brigadier Simon Fraser had learned of Jamie's presence and wished to see him.

"Before it's too late, sir," the ensign said, low-voiced. He was very young and looked shattered. "Will you come?"

Jamie was already rising, though it took him two tries to get up. He wasn't hurt, beyond a number of spectacular bruises and a sprained shoulder, but he hadn't had the strength even to eat when he staggered back after the battle. I'd washed his face for him and given him a glass of beer. He was still holding it, undrunk, and now set it down.

"My wife and I will come," he said hoarsely.

I reached for my cloak—and, just in case, my kit.

I NEEDN'T HAVE bothered with the kit. General Fraser lay on a long dining table in the main room of a large log cabin—the Baroness von Riedesel's house, the little ensign had murmured—and it was apparent from a glance that he was beyond any aid I could offer. His broad face was almost bloodless in the candlelight, and his body was wrapped in bandages, these soaked with blood. Fresh blood, too; I saw the wet patches slowly spreading, darker than the patches of dried blood already there.

Absorbed by the dying man, I'd only dimly registered the presence of several other people in the room and had consciously noticed only two: the surgeons who stood near the bed, bloodstained and white-faced with fatigue. One of them darted a glance at me, then stiffened a little. His eyes narrowed, and he nudged his fellow, who looked up from his contemplation of General Fraser, frowning. He looked at me with no particular comprehension and went back to his fruitless meditation.

I gave the first surgeon a straight look, but without any hint of confrontation. I did not mean to intrude on his territory. There was nothing I could do here, nothing anyone could do, as the surgeons' exhausted attitudes clearly showed. The second man hadn't given up, and I admired him for it, but the scent of putrefaction in the air was unmistakable, and I could hear the general's breathing—long, stertorous sighs, with a nerve-wringing silence between them.

There was nothing I could do for General Fraser as a doctor, and there were people here who could offer better comfort than I could. Jamie, perhaps, among them.

"He hasn't long," I whispered to Jamie. "If there's anything you want to say to him..."

He nodded, swallowing, and went forward. A British colonel at the side of the impromptu deathbed narrowed his eyes but, at a murmur from another officer, stepped back a little so that Jamie could approach.

The room was small and very crowded. I kept back, trying to stay out of the way.

Jamie and the British officer murmured together for a moment. A young officer, no doubt the general's aide, knelt in the shadow on the far side of the table, holding the general's hand, his own head bowed in obvious distress. I pushed the cloak back over my shoulders. Cold as it was outside, the air inside was beastly hot, unhealthy and suffocating, as though the fever that was devouring General Fraser before our eyes had risen from the bed and spread through the cabin, unsatisfied with its meager prey. It was a miasma, thick with decaying bowels, stale sweat, and the taste of black powder that hung in the men's clothes.

Jamie bent, then knelt himself, to come closer to Fraser's ear. The general's eyes were closed, but he was conscious; I saw his face twitch at the sound of Jamie's voice. His head turned and his eyes opened, the dullness in them brightening momentarily in recognition.

"Ciamar a tha thu, a charaid?" Jamie asked softly. *How are you, cousin?*

The general's mouth twitched a little.

"Tha ana-cnàmhadh an Diabhail orm," he replied hoarsely. *"Feumaidh gun do dh'ith mi rudegin nach robh dol leam."* *I have the devil of an indigestion. I must have eaten something that disagreed with me.*

The British officers stirred a little, hearing the Gaelic, and the young officer on the far side of the bed looked up, startled.

Not nearly as startled as I was.

The shadowed room seemed to shift around me, and I half-fell against the wall, pressing my hands against the wood in hopes of finding something solid to hold on to.

Sleeplessness and grief lined his face, and it was still grimed with smoke and blood, smeared racoonlike across his brow and cheekbones by a careless sleeve. None of that made the slightest difference. His hair was dark, his face narrower, but I would have known that long, straight nose and those slanted blue cat-eyes anywhere. He and Jamie knelt on either side of the general's deathbed, no more than five feet apart. Surely, no one could fail to see the resemblance, if . . .

"Ellesmere." A captain of infantry stepped forward and touched the young man's shoulder with a murmured word and a small jerk of the head, plainly telling him to leave the general's side, in order to give General Fraser a moment's privacy, should he desire it.

Don't look up! I thought as fiercely as I could in Jamie's direction. *For God's sake, don't look up!*

He didn't. Whether he had recognized the name or had caught a glimpse of that soot-smeared face across the bed, he kept his own head bent, his features hid in shadow, and leaned nearer, speaking very low to his cousin Simon.

The young man rose to his feet, slow as Dan Morgan on a cold morning. His shadow wavered on the rough-cut logs behind him, tall and spindly. He was paying no attention to Jamie; every fiber of his being was focused on the dying general.

"It is gladness to be seeing you once more on earth, *Seaumais mac Brian*," Fraser whispered, bringing both his hands across with an effort to clasp Jamie's. "I am content to die among my comrades, whom I love. But you will tell this to those of our blood in Scotland? Tell them . . ."

One of the other officers spoke to William, and he turned reluctantly away from the bedside, answering low-voiced. My fingers were damp with sweat, and I could feel beads of perspiration running down my neck. I wanted desperately to take off my cloak but feared to make any movement that might draw William's attention to me and thus toward Jamie.

Jamie was still as a rabbit under a bush. I could see his shoulders tight under the damp-dark coat, his hands gripping the general's, and only the flicker of the firelight on the ruddy crown of his head gave any illusion of movement.

"It shall be as you say, *Shimi mac Shimi*." I could barely hear his whisper. "Lay your wish upon me; I will bear it."

I heard a loud sniff beside me and glanced aside to see a small woman, dainty as a porcelain doll despite the hour and the circumstance. Her eyes shone with unshed tears; she turned her head to dab at them, saw me watching, and gave me a tremulous attempt at a smile.

"I am so glad that your husband is come, madam," she whispered to me in a soft German accent. "It—it is a comfort, perhaps. That our dear friend shall have the solace of a kinsman by his side."

Two of them, I thought, biting my tongue, and by an effort of will didn't look in William's direction. The awful thought came suddenly to me that William might recognize *me,* and make some effort to come and speak with me. Which might well mean disaster, if . . .

The baroness—for she must be von Riedesel's wife—seemed to sway a little, though it might be only an effect of the shifting firelight and the press of bodies. I touched her arm.

"I need air," I whispered to her. "Come outside with me."

The surgeons were drifting back toward the bed, intent as vultures, and the Gaelic murmurings were broken suddenly by a terrible groan from Simon Fraser.

"Bring a candle!" one of the surgeons said sharply, moving quickly toward the bedside.

The baroness's eyes shut tight, and I saw her throat move as she swallowed. I took her hand and led her quickly out.

IT WASN'T LONG but seemed an age before the men came out, heads bowed.

There was a short, sharp argument outside the cabin, conducted in low voices by reason of respect for the dead, but nonetheless heated. Jamie kept to one side, with his hat on, pulled well down, but one of the British officers turned to him now and then, obviously requesting his opinion.

Lieutenant William Ransom, aka Lord Ellesmere, kept to himself, too, as befitted his relatively lowly rank in this company. He didn't join in the argument, seeming too much shocked by the death. I wondered whether he had seen anyone he knew die before—and then realized how idiotic that thought was.

But battlefield deaths, however violent, are not the same as the death of a friend. And from the looks of young William, Simon Fraser had been friend as well as commander to him.

Occupied by these surreptitious observations, I hadn't been paying more than the most cursory attention to the main point of argument—that being the immediate disposition of General Fraser's body—and none at all to the two medical men, who had come out of the cabin and now stood a little apart, murmuring to each other. From the corner of my eye, I saw one reach into his pocket and hand the other a twist of tobacco, wave off the other's thanks, then turn away. What he said, though, seized my attention as effectively as though his head had burst into flame.

"*See you a bit later, then, Dr. Rawlings,*" he'd said.

"Dr. Rawlings?" I said by reflex, and the second doctor turned.

"Yes, ma'am?" he said politely, but with the air of an exhausted man struggling against an overwhelming urge to tell the world to go to hell. I recognized the impulse and sympathized—but having spoken, had no choice but to continue.

"I beg your pardon," I said, flushing a little. "I just caught your name and was struck by it—I used to know a Dr. Rawlings."

The effect of this casual remark was unexpected. His shoulders drew back abuptly and his dull gaze sharpened into eagerness.

"You did? Where?"

"Er . . ." I floundered for a moment, as in fact I had never actually met Daniel Rawlings—though I certainly felt I knew him—and temporized by saying, "His name was Daniel Rawlings. Would that perhaps be a relative of yours?"

His face lighted up and he seized me by the arm.

"Yes! Yes, he is my brother. Pray tell me, ma'am, do you know where he is?"

I had a nasty sinking feeling in the pit of my stomach. I did in fact know exactly where Daniel Rawlings was, but the news wasn't going to be welcome to his brother. There was no choice, though; I had to tell him.

"I'm terribly sorry to have to tell you that he's dead," I said, as gently as I could. I put my own hand over his and squeezed, my throat constricting again as the light in his eyes died.

He stood unmoving for the space of several breaths, his eyes focused somewhere beyond me. Slowly, they refocused on me and he took one more deep breath and firmed his mouth.

"I see. I . . . had feared that. How did he—how did it happen, do you know?"

"I do," I said hurriedly, seeing Colonel Grant shift his weight in a manner indicating imminent departure. "But it's—a long story."

"Ah." He caught the direction of my glance and turned his head. All the men were moving now, straightening their coats, putting on their hats as they exchanged a few final words.

"I'll find you," he said abruptly, turning back to me. "Your husband—he is the tall Scottish rebel, I think they said he is kin to the general?"

I saw his gaze flick momentarily toward something beyond me, and alarm pricked like needles in my skin. Rawlings's brows were slightly knitted, and I knew, as clearly as if he had spoken, that the word "kin" had triggered some connection in his mind—and that he was looking at William.

"Yes. Colonel Fraser," I said hurriedly, grasping him by the sleeve before he could look at Jamie and complete the thought that was forming.

I had been groping in my kit as we spoke and at this point found the folded square of paper I'd been looking for. I pulled it out and, unfolding it quickly, handed it to him. There was still room for doubt, after all.

"Is this your brother's hand?"

He seized the paper from me and devoured the small, neat script with an expression in which eagerness, hope, and despair were mingled. He closed his eyes for an instant, then opened them, reading and rereading the receipt for Bowel-Bind as if it were Holy Writ.

"The page is burnt," he said, touching the singed edge. His voice was husky. "Did Daniel . . . die in a fire?"

"No," I said. There was no time; one of the British officers stood impatiently behind him, waiting. I touched the hand that held the page. "Keep that, please. And if you can manage to cross the lines—I suppose you can now—you'll find me most easily in my tent, near the artillery park. They . . . er . . . they call me the White Witch," I added diffidently. "Ask anyone."

His bloodshot eyes widened at that, then narrowed as he examined me closely. But there was no time for further questions; the officer stepped forward and muttered something in Rawlings's ear, with no more than a cursory glance in my direction.

"Yes," Rawlings said. "Yes, certainly." He bowed to me, deeply. "Your servant, madam. I am very much obliged to you. May I . . . ?" He lifted the paper, and I nodded.

"Yes, of course, please keep it."

The officer had turned, obviously intent on chivvying another errant member of his party, and with a brief glance at his back, Dr. Rawlings stepped close and touched my hand.

"I'll come," he said, low-voiced. "As soon as I may. Thank you." He looked up then at someone behind me, and I realized that Jamie had finished his business and come to fetch me.

He stepped forward and, with a brief nod to the doctor, took my hand.

"Where is your hat, Lieutenant Ransom?" The colonel spoke behind me, quietly reproving, and for the second time in five minutes I felt the hair stand up on the back of my neck. Not at the colonel's words but at the murmured reply.

" . . . rebel whoreson shot it off my head," said a voice. It was an English voice, young, hoarse with suppressed grief, and tinged with anger. Other than that—it was Jamie's voice, and Jamie's hand tightened so abruptly on mine that he nearly crushed my fingers.

We were at the trailhead that led upward from the river; two more steps would see us safely into the shelter of the fog-veiled trees. Instead of taking those two steps, Jamie stopped dead for the space of a heartbeat, then dropped my hand, turned on his heel, and, taking the hat off his head, strode over and thrust it into Lieutenant Ransom's hands.

"I believe I owe ye a hat, sir," he said politely, and turned away at once, leaving the young man blinking at the battered tricorne in his hands. Glancing back, I caught a glimpse of William's baffled face as he looked after Jamie, but Jamie was propelling me up the path as though Red Indians were at our heels, and a stand of fir saplings hid the lieutenant from view within seconds.

I could feel Jamie vibrating like a plucked violin string, and his breath was coming fast.

"Have you quite lost your mind?" I inquired conversationally.

"Very likely."

"What on earth—" I began, but he only shook his head and pulled me along, until we were well out of both sight and hearing of the cabin. A fallen log that had so far escaped the woodcutters lay half across the path, and Jamie sat down suddenly on this and put a shaking hand to his face.

"Are you all right? What on earth is the matter?" I sat beside him and put a hand on his back, beginning to be worried.

"I dinna ken whether to laugh or to weep, Sassenach," he said. He took his hand away from his face, and I saw that, in fact, he appeared to be doing both. His lashes were wet, but the corners of his mouth were twitching.

"I've lost a kinsman and found one, all in the same moment—and a moment later realize that for the second time in his life, I've come within an inch of shooting my son." He looked at me and shook his head, quite helpless between laughter and dismay.

"I shouldna have done it, I ken that. It's only—I thought all at once, *What if I dinna miss, a third time?* And—and I thought I must just . . . speak to him. As a man. In case it should be the only time, aye?"

COLONEL GRANT cast a curious look at the trailhead, where a trembling branch marked the passage of the rebel and his wife, then turned his gaze on the hat in William's hands.

"What the devil was that about?"

William cleared his throat. "Evidently, Colonel Fraser was the, um, rebel whoreson who deprived me of my hat during the battle yesterday," he said, hoping for a tone of dry detachment. "He has . . . recompensed me."

A hint of humor came into Grant's strained face.

"Really? Decent of him." He peered dubiously at the object in question. "Has it got lice, do you think?"

In another man, at another time, this might have been interpreted as calumny. But Grant, while more than ready to denigrate the Colonials' courage, abilities, and dispositions, clearly intended the question only as a practical discovery of fact; most of the English and Hessian troops were crawling with lice, and so were the officers.

William tilted the hat, scrutinizing it as well as the dim light allowed. The thing was warm in his hands, but nothing moved along the seams.

"Don't think so."

"Well, put it on, then, Captain Ransom. We must show a good example to the men, you know."

William had in fact assumed the object, feeling slightly queer at the warmth of it on his head, before properly hearing what Grant had said.

"Captain . . . ?" he said faintly.

"Congratulations," Grant said, the ghost of a smile lightening the exhaustion on his face. "The brigadier . . ." He glanced back at the reeking, silent cabin, and the smile faded. "He wanted you made captain after Ticonderoga— should have been done then, but . . . well." His lips thinned, but then relaxed. "General Burgoyne signed the order last night, after hearing several accounts of the battle. I gather that you distinguished yourself."

William ducked his head awkwardly. His throat was thick and his eyes burned. He couldn't remember what he'd done—only that he'd failed to save the brigadier.

"Thank you," he managed, and could not keep from glancing back himself. They had left the door open. "Do you know—did he—no, it doesn't matter."

"Did he know?" Grant said gently. "I told him. I brought the order."

Unable to speak, William bobbed his head. The hat, for a wonder, fit him, and stayed in place.

"God, it's cold," Grant said softly. He tugged his coat closer, glancing round at the dripping trees and the fog that lay thick among them. The others had gone back to their duties, leaving them alone. "What a desolate place. Terrible time of day, too."

"Yes." William felt a momentary relief at being able to admit his own sense of desolation—though the hour and the place had little to do with it. He swallowed, glancing back at the cabin. The open door bothered him; while the fog lay heavy as a feather bed on the forest, the mist near the cabin was rising, drifting around the windows, and he had the uneasy fancy that it was somehow . . . *coming* for the brigadier.

"I'll just . . . close that door, shall I?" He'd started for the cabin, but was arrested by Grant's gesture.

"No, don't."

William glanced at him in surprise, and the colonel shrugged, trying to make light of it.

"The donor of your hat said we must leave it open. Some Highland fancy—something about the, um, soul requiring an exit," he said delicately. "And at least it's too bloody cold for the flies," he added, with no delicacy at all.

William's shriveled stomach clenched, and he swallowed the bitterness that rose in the back of his throat at the vision of swarming maggots.

"But surely we can't . . . How long?" he demanded.

"Not long," Grant assured him. "We're only waiting for a burial detail."

William stifled the protest that rose to his lips. Of course. What else could be done? And yet the memory of the trenches they had dug by the Heights, the dirt freckling his corporal's cold round cheeks . . . After the last ten days, he would have thought himself beyond sensitivity to such things. But the sounds of the wolves that came to eat the dying and the dead echoed suddenly in the hollow pit of his stomach.

With a muttered excuse, he stepped aside into the wet shrubbery and threw up, as quietly as he could. Wept a little, silent, then wiped his face with a handful of wet leaves and came back.

Grant tactfully affected to believe William had simply gone to relieve himself, and made no inquiries.

"An impressive gentleman," he remarked casually. "The general's kinsman, I mean. Wouldn't think they were related to look at, would you?"

Caught up in dying hope and tearing grief, William had barely noticed Colonel Fraser before the latter had so suddenly given him the hat—and been too startled to notice much about him then. He shook his head in agreement, though, having a vague recollection of a tall figure kneeling down by the bed, the firelight touching the crown of his head briefly with red.

"Looks more like you than like the brigadier," Grant added offhandedly, then laughed, a painful creak. "Sure you haven't a Scottish branch in your family?"

"No, Yorkshiremen back to the Flood on both sides, save one French great-grandmother," William replied, grateful for the momentary distraction of light conversation. "My stepfather's mother is half Scotch—that count, do you think?"

Whatever Grant might have said in reply was lost, as the sound of a doomed soul came down to them through the gloom. Both men froze, listening. The brigadier's piper was coming, with Balcarres and some of his rangers. The burial detail.

The sun had risen but was invisible, blocked by cloud and the canopy of trees. Grant's face was the same color as the fog, pale, sheened with moisture.

The sound seemed to come from a great distance and yet from the forest itself. Then wails and ululating shrieks joined the piper's lament—Balcarres and his Indians. Despite the chilling sounds, William was a little comforted; it would not be just a hasty field burial, undertaken without regard or respect.

"Sound like howling wolves, don't they?" muttered Grant. He ran a hand down his face, then fastidiously wiped his wet palm on his thigh.

"Yes, they do," said William. He took a firm stance and waited to receive the mourners, conscious all the time of the cabin at his back, its door standing silent, open to the mist.

GREASIER THAN GREASE

I HAD ALWAYS assumed that surrender was a fairly simple thing. Hand over your sword, shake hands, and march off—to parole, prison, or the next battle. I was disabused of this simpleminded assumption by Dr. Rawlings, who did indeed make his way across the lines two days later to speak to me about his brother. I'd told him everything I could, expressing my particular attachment to his brother's casebook, through which I felt I'd known Daniel Rawlings. The second Dr. Rawlings—his name was David, he said—was easy to talk to and lingered for a while, the conversation moving on to other subjects.

"Gracious, no," he said, when I'd mentioned my surprise that the ceremony of surrender had not occurred at once. "The terms of surrender must be negotiated first, you know—and that's a prickly business."

"Negotiated?" I said. "Does General Burgoyne have a *choice* in the matter?"

He seemed to find that funny.

"Oh, indeed he does," he assured me. "I happen to have seen the proposals which Major Kingston brought over this morning for General Gates's perusal. They begin with the rather firm statement, that having fought Gates twice, General Burgoyne is quite prepared to do it a third time. He's not, of course," the doctor added, "but it saves his face by allowing him to then note that he has of course noticed the rebels' superiority in numbers and thus feels justified in accepting surrender in order to save the lives of brave men upon honorable terms. By the way, the battle is not officially over yet," he added, with a faint air of apology. "General Burgoyne proposes a cessation of hostilities while negotiations are under way."

"Oh, really," I said, amused. "I wonder if General Gates is disposed to accept this at face value."

"No, he's not," said a dry Scottish voice, and Jamie ducked his head and came into the tent, followed by his cousin Hamish. "He read Burgoyne's proposal, then reached into his pocket and whipped out his own. He demands an unconditional surrender and requires both British and German troops to ground their arms in camp and march out as prisoners. The truce will last 'til sunset, at which time Burgoyne must make his reply. I thought Major Kingston would have an apoplexy on the spot."

"Is he bluffing, do you think?" I asked. Jamie made a small Scottish noise in his throat and cut his eyes at Dr. Rawlings, indicating that he thought this an improper thing to be discussing in front of the enemy. And given Dr. Rawlings's evident access to the British high command, perhaps he was right.

David Rawlings tactfully changed the subject, opening the lid of the case he had brought with him.

"Is this the same as the case you had, Mrs. Fraser?"

"Yes, it is." I had noticed it immediately but hadn't liked to stare at it. It was somewhat more battered than my case, and had a small brass nameplate attached to it, but was otherwise just the same.

"Well, I was in no real doubt as to my brother's fate," he said, with a small sigh, "but that settles the matter entirely. The cases were given to us by our father, himself a physician, when we entered practice."

I glanced at him, startled.

"You don't mean to tell me—were you twins?"

"We were, yes." He looked surprised that I hadn't known that.

"Identical?"

He smiled.

"Our mother could invariably tell us apart, but few other people could."

I stared at him, feeling an unusual warmth—almost embarrassment. I had, of course, built up a mental picture of Daniel Rawlings as I read his casebook entries. Suddenly meeting him face-to-face, as it were, gave me something of a turn.

Jamie was staring at me in bemusement, eyebrows raised. I coughed, blushing, and he shook his head slightly and, with another Scottish noise, picked up the deck of cards he'd come for and led Hamish out.

"I wonder—are you in need of anything particular in the medical line?" David Rawlings asked, blushing in turn. "I am quite short of medicinals, but I do have duplicates of some instruments—and quite a good selection of scalpels. I should be most honored if you would . . ."

"Oh." That was a gallant offer, and my embarrassment was at once submerged in a tide of acquisitiveness. "Would you perhaps have an extra pair of tweezers? Small forceps, I mean?"

"Oh, yes, of course." He pulled out the lower drawer, pushing a clutter of small instruments aside in search of the tweezers. As he did so, I caught sight of something unusual and pointed at it.

"What on earth is that?"

"It is called a jugum penis," Dr. Rawlings explained to me, his color increasing noticeably.

"It looks like a bear trap. What is it—it can't be a device for performing circumcision, surely?" I picked up the object, which caused Dr. Rawlings to gasp, and I eyed him curiously.

"It—er, please, dear lady..." He almost snatched the thing out of my hands, thrusting it back into his chest.

"What on earth is it for?" I asked, more amused than offended by his reaction. "Given the name, obviously—"

"It prevents nocturnal...er...tumescence." His face by this time was a dark, unhealthy sort of red, and he wouldn't meet my eye.

"Yes, I imagine it would do that." The object in question consisted of two concentric circles of metal, the outer one flexible, with overlapping ends, and a sort of key mechanism that enabled it to be tightened. The inner one was sawtoothed—much like a bear trap, as I'd said. Rather obviously, it was meant to be fastened round a limp penis—which would stay in that condition, if it knew what was good for it.

I coughed. "Um... *why*, precisely, is that desirable?"

His embarrassment faded slightly into shock.

"Why...it...the...the loss of the male essence is most debilitating. It drains the vitality and exposes a man to all manner of sickness, as well as grossly impairing his mental and spiritual faculties."

"Just as well no one's thought of mentioning that to my husband," I said.

Rawlings gave me a completely scandalized look, but before the discussion could assume even more improper proportions, we were fortunately interrupted by a stir outside, and he took the opportunity to shut his case and tuck it hastily back under his arm before coming to join me at the tent's entrance.

There was a small parade crossing the camp, a hundred feet away. A British major in dress uniform, blindfolded, and so red in the face I thought he might pop. He was being led by two Continental soldiers, and a fife player was following them at a semi-discreet distance, playing "Yankee Doodle." Bearing in mind what Jamie had said about an apoplexy, I was in no doubt that this was the unfortunate Major Kingston who had been selected to deliver Burgoyne's surrender proposals.

"Dear me," murmured Dr. Rawlings, shaking his head at the sight. "I am afraid this process could take some time."

IT DID. A week later, we were all still sitting there, as letters made their stately way once or twice a day between the two camps. There was a general air of relaxation in the American camp; I thought things were probably still a little tense across the way, but Dr. Rawlings had not come back, so general gossip was the only way of judging the progress—or lack of it—of the surrender negotiations. Evidently General Gates *had* been bluffing, and Burgoyne had been astute enough to realize it.

I was pleased to be in one place long enough to wash my clothes without risk of being shot, scalped, or otherwise molested. Beyond that, there were a good many casualties from the two battles who still required nursing.

I had been aware, in a vague sort of way, of a man lurking round the edges of our encampment. I'd seen him several times, but he had never come close enough to speak to me, and I'd put him down as likely suffering from some embarrassing ailment like clap or piles. It often took such men a good while to muster either the courage or the desperation to ask for help, and once they did, they'd still wait to speak to me privately.

The third or fourth time I noticed him, I tried to catch his eye, to induce him to come close enough so that I could arrange to examine him privately, but each time he slid away, eyes downcast, and disappeared into the anthill of seething militia, Continentals, and camp followers.

He reappeared quite suddenly toward sunset of the next day, while I was making a sort of pottage, using a bone—unidentifiable as to animal, but reasonably fresh, and with shreds of meat still clinging to it—given me by a patient, two wizened yams, a handful of grain, another handful of beans, and some stale bread.

"You are Mrs. Fraser?" he asked, in a surprisingly educated Lowland Scottish accent. Edinburgh, I thought, and had a faint pang at the memory of Tom Christie's similar speech. He had always insisted upon calling me "Mrs. Fraser," spoken in just that clipped, formal way.

Thoughts of Tom Christie vanished in the next instant, though.

"They call you the White Witch, do they not?" the man said, and smiled. It wasn't in any way a pleasant expression.

"Some do. What of it?" I said, taking a good grip on my spurtle and staring him down. He was tall and thin, narrow-faced and dark, dressed in the uniform of a Continental. Why had he not gone to his regimental surgeon, in preference to a witch? I wondered. Did he want a love philter? He scarcely seemed the type.

He laughed a little, and bowed.

"I wished only to be sure I had come to the right place, madam," he said. "I intended no offense."

"None taken." He was not doing anything noticeably threatening, other than perhaps standing too close to me, but I didn't like him. And my heart was beating faster than it ought.

"You evidently know my name," I said, striving for coolness. "What's yours, then?"

He smiled again, looking me over with a careful air that struck me as one inch short of insolence—and a short inch, at that.

"My name doesn't matter. Your husband is James Fraser?"

I had a sudden strong urge to dot him one with the spurtle but didn't; it might annoy him but wouldn't get rid of him. I didn't want to admit to Jamie's name and didn't bother asking myself why not. I simply said, "Excuse me," and, taking the camp kettle off the fire, set it on the ground and walked off.

He hadn't expected that and didn't follow me at once. I walked away fast, whisked round behind a small tent belonging to the New Hampshire militia and into a group of people gathered round another fire—militiamen, some with their wives. One or two looked surprised by my abrupt appearance, but all of them knew me and cordially made room, nodding and murmuring greetings.

I looked back from this refuge and could see the man, silhouetted by the sinking sun, standing by my own abandoned fire, the evening wind lifting wisps of his hair. It was no doubt my imagination that made me think he looked sinister.

"Who's that, Auntie? One of your rejected suitors?" Young Ian spoke by my ear, a grin in his voice.

"Certainly rejected," I said, keeping an eye on the man. I'd thought he might follow me, but he remained where he was, face turned in my direction. His face was a black oval, but I knew he was staring at me. "Where's your uncle, do you know?"

"Oh, aye. He and Cousin Hamish are takin' Colonel Martin's money at loo, over there." He jerked his chin in the direction of the Vermont militia encampment, where Colonel Martin's tent rose, recognizable by a large tear in the top, which had been patched with a piece of yellow calico.

"Is Hamish good at cards?" I asked curiously, glancing toward the tent.

"No, but Uncle Jamie is, and he kens when Hamish will do the wrong thing, which is almost as good as him doing the right thing, aye?"

"I'll take your word for it. Do you know who that man is? The one standing by my fire?"

Ian squinted against the low sun, then suddenly frowned.

"No, but he's just spat in your soup."

"He *what*?!" I spun on my heel, in time to see the anonymous gentleman stalk away, back stiff. "Why, that bloody filthy *arsehole*!"

Ian cleared his throat and nudged me, indicating one of the militia wives, who was viewing me with considerable disapproval. I cleared my own throat, swallowed my further remarks on the subject, and gave her what I hoped was an apologetic smile. We were, after all, probably going to be obliged to beg her hospitality, if we were to get any supper now.

When I looked back at our own fire, the man was gone.

"Shall I tell ye something, Auntie?" Ian said, frowning thoughtfully at the empty shadows lengthening beneath the trees. "He'll be back."

JAMIE AND HAMISH did not return for supper, leading me to suppose that the loo must be going well for them. Things were going reasonably well for me, too; Mrs. Kebbits, the militia wife, did feed Ian and myself, and very hospitably, with fresh corn dodgers and rabbit stew with onions. Best of all, my sinister visitor didn't return.

Ian had gone off about his own business, Rollo at heel, so I banked the fire and prepared to set off for the hospital tents for evening rounds. Most of the severely injured had died within the first two or three days after the battle; of the rest, those who had wives, friends, or relatives to care for them had been taken off to their own camps. There were three dozen or so left, men on their own, with lingering but not immediately life-threatening injuries or illnesses.

I put on a second pair of stockings, wrapped my thick wool cloak around myself, and thanked God for the cold weather. A chill had struck in late September, setting the woods afire with a glory of red and gold, but also helpfully killing off the insects. The relief of camp life without flies was marvelous in itself—no surprise to me that flies had been one of the Ten Plagues of Egypt. The lice, alas, were still with us, but without flies, fleas, and mosquitoes, the threat of epidemic illness was tremendously decreased.

Still, every time I came near the hospital tent, I found myself sniffing the air, alert for the telltale fecal stench that might portend a sudden irruption of cholera, typhus, or the lesser evils of a salmonella outbreak. Tonight, though, I smelled nothing beyond the usual cesspit smell of the latrines, overlaid by the funk of unwashed bodies, filthy linens, and a lingering tang of old blood. Reassuringly familiar.

Three orderlies were playing cards under a canvas lean-to next to the biggest tent, their game lit by a rush dip whose flame rose and flickered in the evening wind. Their shadows swelled and shrank on the pale canvas, and I caught the sound of their laughter as I passed. That meant none of the regimental surgeons was about; just as well.

Most of them were simply grateful for whatever help was offered and thus left me to do what I would. There were always one or two who'd stand on their dignity and insist on their authority, though. Usually no more than a nuisance, but very dangerous in case of emergency.

No emergencies tonight, thank God. There were a number of tin candlesticks and stubs of varying lengths in a bowl outside the tent; I lit a candle from the fire and, ducking inside, made my way through the two large tents, checking vital signs, chatting with the men who were awake, and evaluating their condition.

Nothing very bad, but I had some concern for Corporal Jebediah Shoreditch, who had suffered three separate bayonet wounds during the storming of the great redoubt. By some miracle, none had hit any vital organs, and while the corporal was rather uncomfortable—one thrust having plowed upward through his left buttock—he wasn't displaying any major signs of fever. There was some sign of infection in the buttock wound, though.

"I'm going to irrigate this," I told him, eyeing my half-full bottle of tincture of gentian. This was nearly the last of it, but with luck, there shouldn't be great need again until I was in a position to make more. "Wash it out, I mean, to rid you of the pus. How did it happen?" The irrigation wasn't going to be comfortable; better if he could be distracted a little by telling me the details.

"Wasn't retreatin', ma'am, and don't you think it," he assured me, taking a good grip on the edge of his pallet as I turned back the blanket and peeled away the crusty bits of a tar-and-turpentine dressing. "One o' them sneaky Hessian sons of bitches was a-playin' dead, and when I went to step over him, he come to life and reared up like a copperhead, bay'net in hand."

"Bayonet in *your* hand, you mean, Jeb," joked a friend who lay nearby.

"Nah, that was another un." Shoreditch shrugged off the joke with a casual glance at his right hand, wrapped in bandages. One of the Hessians had pinned his hand to the ground with a bayonet blade, he told me—whereupon Shoreditch had snatched up his fallen knife with his left hand and swiped it murderously across the Hessian's calves, felling him, and then had cut the Hessian's throat—disregarding a third attacker, whose thrust had removed the top part of his left ear.

"Somebody shot that un, Lord be praised, afore he could improve his aim. Speak of hands, Ma'am, is the colonel's hand a-doing well?" His forehead shone with sweat in the lantern light, and the tendons stood out in his forearms, but he spoke courteously.

"I think it must be," I said, pressing slowly on the plunger of my irrigating syringe. "He's been at cards with Colonel Martin since this afternoon—and if his hand was poor, he'd have come back by now."

Shoreditch and his friend both chuckled at this feeble pun, but he let go a long sigh when I took my hands away from the new dressing, and rested his forehead on the pallet for a moment before rolling painfully onto his good side.

"Thank you kindly, ma'am," he said. His eyes passed with apparent casualness over the figures that moved to and fro in the darkness. "If you was to see Friend Hunter or Doc Tolliver, might you ask 'em to stop a moment?"

I raised a brow at this, but nodded and poured him a cup of ale; there was plenty now that the supply lines from the south had caught up, and it would do him no harm.

I did the same for his friend, a man from Pennsylvania named Neph Brewster, who was suffering from dysentery, though I added a small handful of Dr. Rawling's Bowel-Bind mixture before handing over the cup.

"Jeb ain't meanin' no disrespect to you, ma'am," Neph whispered, leaning confidentially close as he took the drink. "It's only as he can't shit 'thout help, and that ain't somethin' he wants to ask a lady. Mr. Denzell or the Doc don't come by soon, I'll help him, though."

"Shall I fetch one of the orderlies?" I asked, surprised. "They're just outside."

"Oh, no, ma'am. Once the sun goes down, they figure as how they're off duty. Won't come in, save there's a fight or the tent catches fire."

"Hmm," I said. Plainly attitudes among medical orderlies weren't that different from one time to another.

"I'll find one of the surgeons," I assured him; Mr. Brewster was thin and yellow, and his hand shook so badly that I had to put my own fingers round his to help him drink. I doubted he could stand long enough to manage his own necessities, let alone help Corporal Shoreditch with his. Mr. Brewster was game, though.

"Shittin' is somethin' I can claim to have some skill at by now," he said, grinning at me. He wiped his face with a trembling hand and paused between swallows to breathe heavily. "Ah . . . might you have a bit o' cooking grease to hand, ma'am? My arsehole's raw as a fresh-skinned rabbit. I can put it on myself—unless you'd *like* to help, o' course."

"I'll mention it to Dr. Hunter," I replied dryly. "I'm sure he'd be delighted."

I finished my rounds quickly—most of the men were asleep—and went in search of Denny Hunter, who I found outside his own tent, bundled up against the cold with a muffler round his neck, dreamily listening to a ballad being sung at a nearby campfire.

"Who?" He came out of his trance at my appearance, though it took him a moment to return fully to earth. "Oh, Friend Jebediah, to be sure. Of course—I'll go at once."

"Have you got any goose or bear grease?"

Denny settled his spectacles more firmly on his nose, giving me a quizzical look.

"Friend Jebediah is not constipated, is he? I understood his difficulty to be more one of engineering than of physiology."

I laughed, and explained.

"Oh. Well. I do *have* some ointment," he said doubtfully. "But it is mentholated—for the treatment of grippe and pleurisy, thee knows. I fear that will do Friend Brewster's arse no favors."

"I fear not," I agreed. "Why don't you go and help Mr. Shoreditch, and I'll find a bit of plain grease and bring it along?"

Grease—any kind of grease—was a staple of cooking, and it took only two inquiries at campfires to procure a cup of it. It was, the donor informed me, rendered possum fat. "Greasier than grease," the lady assured me. "Tasty, too." This last characteristic was unlikely to be of much interest to Mr. Brewster—or at least I hoped not—but I thanked her effusively and set off through the darkness, back toward the small hospital tent.

At least I *intended* to head in that direction. The moon had not yet risen, though, and within a few minutes I found myself on a thickly wooded hillside that I didn't remember, stumbling over roots and fallen branches.

Muttering to myself, I turned left—surely that was . . . No, it wasn't. I stopped, cursing silently. I couldn't be lost; I was in the middle of a campground containing at least half the Continental army, to say nothing of dozens of militia companies. Exactly where I was on said campground, though . . . I could see the glimmer of several fires through the trees, but the configuration of them seemed unfamiliar. Disoriented, I turned the other way, straining my eyes in search of the patched roof of Colonel Martin's large tent, that being the biggest landmark likely to be visible in the darkness.

Something ran over my foot, and I jerked in reflex, slopping liquefied possum fat over my hand. I gritted my teeth and wiped it gingerly on my apron. Possum fat *is* extremely greasy, its major drawback as a general-purpose lubricant being that it smells like dead possum.

My heart was beating fast from the shock and gave a convulsive leap when an owl came out of the copse to my right, a piece of the night taking sudden silent flight a few feet from my face. Then a branch cracked suddenly, and I heard the movements of several men, murmuring together as they pushed through the undergrowth nearby.

I stood quite still, teeth set in my lower lip, and felt a wave of sudden, irrational terror.

It's all right! I told myself, furious. *It's only soldiers looking for a shortcut. No threat, no threat at all!*

Tell that *to the Marines,* my nervous system replied, at the sound of a muffled curse, the scuffle and crunch of dry leaves and breaking branches, and the sudden kicked-melon thump of a solid object meeting someone's head. A cry, the crash of a falling body, and hurried rustling as the thieves rifled their victim's pockets.

I couldn't move. I wanted desperately to run but was rooted to the spot; my legs simply wouldn't respond. It was exactly like a nightmare, with something terrible coming my way but no ability to move.

My mouth was open, and I was exerting all my strength to keep from screaming, while at the same time terrified that I *couldn't* scream. My own breathing was loud, echoing inside my head, and all of a sudden I felt my throat harsh with swallowed blood, my breath labored, nostrils blocked. And the weight on me, heavy, amorphous, crushing me into ground rough with stones and fallen pinecones. I felt hot breath in my ear.

There, now. I'm sorry, Martha, but you got to take it. I got to give it to you. Yeah, there ... oh, Christ, there ... there ...

I didn't remember falling to the ground. I was curled into a ball, face pressed to my knees, shaking with rage and terror. Crashing in the brush nearby, several men passed within a few feet of me, laughing and joking.

And then some small fragment of my sanity spoke up in the recesses of my brain, cool as dammit, dispassionately remarking, *Oh, so that's a flashback. How interesting.*

"I'll show you interesting," I whispered—or thought I did. I don't believe I made a sound. I was fully dressed—swaddled against the cold—I could *feel* the cold on my face, but it made no difference. I was naked, felt cool air on my breasts, my thighs—between my thighs ...

I clamped my legs together as tightly as I could and bit my lip as hard as I could. Now I really did taste blood. But the next thing didn't happen. I remembered it vividly. But it *was* a memory. It didn't happen again.

Very slowly, I came back. My lip hurt, and I was drooling blood; I could feel the gouge, a loose flap of flesh in my inner lip, and taste silver and copper, as though my mouth was filled with pennies.

I was breathing as though I'd run a mile, but I *could* breathe; my nose was clear, my throat soft and open, not bruised, not abraded. I was drenched in sweat, and my muscles hurt from being clenched so hard.

I could hear moaning in the brush to my left. *They didn't kill him, then,* I thought dimly. I supposed I should go and see, help him. I didn't want to, didn't want to touch a man, see a man, be anywhere near one. It didn't matter, though; I couldn't move.

I was no longer frozen in the grip of terror; I knew where I was, that I was safe—safe enough. But I couldn't move. I stayed crouched, sweating and trembling, and listened.

The man groaned a few times, then rolled slowly over, branches rustling.

"Oh, shit," he mumbled. He lay still, breathing heavily, then sat up abruptly, exclaiming, "Oh, *shit*!"—whether at the pain of the movement or the memory of the robbery, I didn't know. There was mumbled cursing, a sigh, silence ... then a shriek of pure terror that hit my spinal cord like a jolt of electricity.

Mad scrambling sounds as the man scuffled to his feet—why, why, what was going on? Crashing and rattling of flight. Terror was infectious; I wanted to run, too, was on my feet, my heart in my mouth, but didn't know where to go. I couldn't hear anything above that idiot's crashing. What was bloody out there?

A faint rustle of dry leaves made me jerk my head round—and saved me by a split second from having a heart attack when Rollo thrust his wet nose into my hand.

"Jesus H. Roosevelt Christ!" I exclaimed, relieved at the sound of my own voice. The sound of rustling footsteps came toward me through the leaves.

"Oh, there ye are, Auntie." A tall presence loomed up, no more than a shadow in the dark, and Young Ian touched my arm. "Are ye all right, Auntie?" There was an anxious tone in his voice, bless him.

"Yes," I said rather faintly, then with more conviction, "Yes. I am. I got turned about, in the dark."

"Oh." The tall figure relaxed. "I thought ye must have lost your way. Denny Hunter came and said ye'd gone off to find some grease but ye'd no come back, and he was worrit for ye. So Rollo and I came to find ye. Who was yon fellow that Rollo scared the bejesus out of?"

"I don't know." The mention of grease made me look for the cup of possum grease. It was on the ground, empty and clean. From the lapping noises, I deduced that Rollo, having finished off what was in the cup, was now tidily licking the dead leaves on which grease had spilled when I dropped it. Under the circumstances, I didn't feel I could really complain.

Ian bent and scooped up the cup.

"Come back to the fire, Auntie. I'll find some more grease."

I made no demur at this and followed him down off the hillside, paying no real attention to my surroundings. I was too occupied in rearranging my mental state, settling my feelings, and trying to regain some kind of equilibrium.

I'd heard the word "flashback" only briefly, in Boston in the sixties. We didn't call it flashback earlier, but I'd heard about it. And I'd seen it. Shell shock, they said in the First World War. Battle fatigue, in the Second. It's what happens when you live through things you shouldn't have been able to live through and can't reconcile that knowledge with the fact that you did.

Well, I did, I said defiantly to myself. *So you can just get used to it.* I wondered for an instant who I was talking to and—quite seriously—whether I was losing my mind.

I certainly remembered what had happened to me during my abduction years before. I'd have strongly preferred not to but knew enough about psychology not to try to suppress the memories. When they showed up, I looked carefully at them, doing deep-breathing exercises, then stuffed them back where they'd come from and went to find Jamie. After a time, I found that only certain details showed up vividly: the cup of a dead ear, purple in the dawn light, looking like an exotic fungus; the brilliant burst of light I'd seen when Harley Boble had broken my nose; the smell of corn on the breath of the teenaged idiot who'd tried to rape me. The soft, heavy weight of the man who did. The rest was a merciful blur.

I had nightmares, too, though Jamie generally woke at once when I began to make whimpering noises and grabbed me hard enough to shatter the dream, holding me against him and stroking my hair, my back, humming to me, half asleep himself, until I sank back into his peace and slept again.

This was different.

———————

IAN WENT FROM fire to fire in search of grease and at length obtained a small tin containing half an inch of goose grease mixed with comfrey. It was more than a bit rancid, but Denny Hunter had told him what it was for, and he didn't suppose the state of it mattered so much.

The state of his aunt concerned him somewhat more. He knew fine well why she sometimes twitched like a wee cricket or moaned in her sleep. He'd seen the state of her when they'd got her back from the bastards, and he knew the sort of things they'd done to her. Blood rose in him and the vessels at his temples swelled at memory of the fight when they'd taken her back.

She hadn't wished to take her own revenge, when they'd rescued her; he thought perhaps that had been a mistake, though he understood the part about her being a healer and sworn not to kill. The thing was, some men needed killing. The Church didn't admit that, save it was war. The Mohawk understood it fine. So did Uncle Jamie.

And the Quakers . . .

He groaned.

Out of the frying pan, into the fire. The instant he'd got the grease, his steps had turned, not toward the hospital tent where Denny almost surely was—but toward the Hunters' tent. He could pretend he was going to the hospital tent; the two were near enough together. But he'd never seen any point in lying to himself.

Not for the first time, he missed Brianna. He could say anything to her, and she to him—more, he thought, than she could sometimes say to Roger Mac.

Mechanically, he crossed himself, muttering, *"Gum biodh iad sabhailte, a Dhia."* That they might be safe, O God.

For that matter, he wondered what Roger Mac might have counseled were he here. He was a quiet man, and a godly one, if a Presbyterian. But he'd been on that night's ride and joined in the work, and not a word said about it after.

Ian spared a moment's contemplation of Roger Mac's future congregation and what they'd think of that picture of their minister, but shook his head and went on. All these wonderings were only means to keep him from thinking what he'd say when he saw her, and that was pointless. He wanted only to say one thing to her, and that was the one thing he couldn't say, ever.

The tent flap was closed, but there was a candle burning within. He coughed politely outside, and Rollo, seeing where they were, wagged his tail and uttered a cordial *woof*!

The flap was thrust back at once, and Rachel stood there, mending in one hand, squinting into the dark but already smiling; she'd heard the dog. She'd taken off her cap, and her hair was messed, coming down from its pins.

"Rollo!" she said, bending down to scratch his ears. "And I see thee've brought thy friend along, too."

Ian smiled, lifting the little tin.

"I brought some grease. My aunt said your brother needed it for his arse-hole." An instant too late, he re-collected himself. "I mean—for *an* arse-hole." Mortification flamed up his chest, but he was speaking to perhaps the only woman in camp who might take arseholes as a common topic of conversation. Well, the only one save his auntie, he amended. Or the whores, maybe.

"Oh, he'll be pleased; I thank thee."

She reached to take the tin from him, and her fingers brushed his. The tin box was smeared with the grease and slippery; it fell and both of them bent to retrieve it. She straightened first; her hair brushed his cheek, warm and smelling of her.

Without even thinking, he put both hands on her face and bent to her. Saw the flash and darkening of her eyes, and had one heartbeat, two, of perfect warm happiness, as his lips rested on hers, as his heart rested in her hands.

Then one of those hands cracked against his cheek, and he staggered back like a drunkard startled out of sleep.

"What does thee do?" she whispered. Her eyes wide as saucers, she had backed away, was pressed against the wall of the tent as though to fall through it. "Thee must not!"

He couldn't find the words to say. His languages boiled in his mind like stew, and he was mute. The first word to surface through the moil in his mind was the *Gàidhlig,* though.

"*Mo chridhe,*" he said, and breathed for the first time since he'd touched her. Mohawk came next, deep and visceral. *I need you.* And tagging belatedly, English, the one best suited to apology. "I—I'm sorry."

She nodded, jerky as a puppet.

"Yes. I—yes."

He should leave; she was afraid. He knew that. But he knew something else, too. It wasn't him she was afraid of. Slowly, slowly, he put out a hand to her, the fingers moving without his will, slowly, as though to guddle a trout.

And by an expected miracle, but miracle nonetheless, her hand stole out toward his, trembling. He touched the tips of her fingers, found them cold. His own were warm, he would warm her. . . . In his mind, he felt the chill of her flesh against his own, noted the nipples hard against the cloth of her dress and felt the small round weight of her breasts, cold in his hands, the press of her thighs, chill and hard against his heat.

He was gripping her hand, drawing her back. And she was coming, bone-less, helpless, drawn to his heat.

"Thee must not," she whispered, barely audible. "We must not."

It came to him dimly that of course he could not simply draw her to him, sink to the earth, push her garments out of the way, and have her, though every fiber of his being demanded that he do just that. Some faint memory of civilization asserted itself, though, and he grabbed for it. At the same time, with a terrible reluctance, he released her hand.

"No, of course," he said, in perfect English. "Of course we mustn't."

"I—thee—" She swallowed and ran the back of her hand across her lips.

Not as though to wipe away his kiss, but in astonishment, he thought. "Does thee know—" She stopped dead, helpless, and stared at him.

"I'm not worried about whether ye love me," he said, and knew he spoke the truth. "Not now. I'm worried about whether ye might die because ye do."

"Thee has a cheek! I didn't say I loved thee."

He looked at her then, and something moved in his chest. It might have been laughter. It might not.

"A great deal better ye don't," he said softly. "I'm no a fool, and neither are you."

She made an impulsive gesture toward him, and he drew back, just a hair.

"I think ye'd best not touch me, lass," he said, still staring intently into her eyes, the color of cress under rushing water. "Because if ye do, I'll take ye, here and now. And then it's too late for us both, isn't it?"

Her hand hung in the air, and while he could see her willing it, she could not draw it back.

He turned from her then and went out into the night, his skin so hot that the night air turned to steam as it touched him.

RACHEL STOOD stock-still for a moment, listening to the pounding of her heart. Another regular sound began to intrude, a soft lapping noise, and she looked down, blinking, to see that Rollo had tidily polished off the last of the goose grease from the tin she had dropped and was now licking the empty tin.

"Oh, Lord," she said, and put a hand over her mouth, afraid that if she laughed, it would erupt into hysterics. The dog looked up at her, his eyes yellow in the candlelight. He licked his lips, long tail waving gently.

"What am I to do?" she asked him. "Well enough for thee; thee can chase about after him all day, and share his bed at night, and not a word said."

She sat down on the stool, her knees feeling weak, and took a grip of the thick fur that ruffed the dog's neck.

"What does he mean?" she asked him. " 'I'm worried about whether ye might die because ye do?' Does he think me one of those fools who pines and swoons and looks pale for love, like Abigail Miller? Not that she'd think of actually dying for anyone's sake, let alone her poor husband's." She looked down at the dog and shook his ruff. "And what does he mean, kissing that chit—forgive my lack of charity, Lord, but there's no good to be done by ignoring the truth—and not three hours later kissing me? Tell me that! What does he *mean* by it?"

She let go of the dog then. He licked her hand politely, then vanished silently through the tent flap, no doubt to convey her question to his annoying master.

She ought to be putting coffee on to boil and getting up some supper; Denny would be back soon from the hospital tent, hungry and cold. She continued to sit, though, staring at the candle flame, wondering whether she would feel it were she to pass her hand through it.

She doubted it. Her whole body had ignited when he'd touched her, sudden as a torch soaked in turpentine, and she was still afire. A wonder her shift did not burst into flames.

She knew what he was. He'd made no secret of it. A man who lived by violence, who carried it within him.

"And I used that when it suited me, didn't I?" she asked the candle. Not the act of a Friend. She had not been content to trust in God's mercy, not willing to accept His will. She'd not only connived at and encouraged violence, she'd put Ian Murray in gross danger of both soul and body. No, no good to be done by ignoring the truth.

"Though if it's truth we're speaking here," she said to the candle, still feeling defiant, "I bear witness that he did it for Denny, as much as for me."

"Who did what?" Her brother's bent head poked into the tent, and he straightened up, blinking at her.

"Will thee pray for me?" she asked abruptly. "I am in great danger."

Her brother stared at her, eyes unblinking behind his spectacles.

"Indeed thee is," he said slowly. "Though I am in doubt that prayer will aid thee much."

"What, has thee no faith left in God?" She spoke sharp, made still more anxious by the thought that her brother might have been overcome by the things he had seen in the last month. She feared they had shaken her own faith considerable but depended upon her brother's faith as she would on shield and buckler. If that were gone . . .

"Oh, endless faith in God," he said, and smiled. "In thee? Not quite so much." He took off his hat and hung it on the nail he had driven into the tent pole, and checked to be sure that the flap was closed and tied fast behind him.

"I heard wolves howling on my walk back," he remarked. "Closer than was comfortable." He sat down and looked directly at her.

"Ian Murray?" he asked bluntly.

"How did thee know that?" Her hands were trembling, and she wiped them irritably on her apron.

"I met his dog just now." He eyed her with interest. "What did he say to thee?"

"I—nothing."

Denny cocked one brow in disbelief, and she relented.

"Not much. He said—I was in love with him."

"Is thee?" Denny asked, sounding not at all surprised.

"How can I be in love with such a man?"

"If thee were not, I do not suppose thee would be asking me to pray for thee," he pointed out logically. "Thee would simply send him away. 'How' is probably not a question I am qualified to answer—though I imagine thee means it rhetorical, in any case."

She laughed, in spite of her agitation.

"No," she said, smoothing the apron over her knees. "I do *not* mean it rhetorical. More . . . well, would thee say that Job was being rhetorical when he asked the Lord what He was thinking? I mean it in that way."

"Questioning the Lord is an awkward business," her brother said thoughtfully. "Thee does get answers, but they are inclined to lead thee to strange places." He smiled at her again, but gently and with a depth of sympathy in his eyes that made her look away.

She sat pleating the cloth of the apron between her fingers, hearing the shouts and drunken singing that marked every night in camp. She wished to say that places didn't get much stranger than this—two Friends, in the midst of an army, and part of it—but it was indeed Denny's questioning of the Lord that had got them here, and she did not wish him to feel that she blamed him for it.

Instead, she looked up and asked earnestly, "Has thee ever been in love, Denny?"

"Oh," he said, and looked at his own hands, cupped on his knees. He still smiled, but it had altered, become inward, as though he saw something inside his head. "Yes. I suppose so."

"In England?"

He nodded. "Yes. It—would not do, though."

"She . . . was not a Friend?"

"No," he said softly. "She was not."

In a way, that was a relief; she had been fearing that he had fallen in love with a woman who would not leave England, but had felt obliged himself to return to America—for her sake. Insofar as her own feelings for Ian Murray were concerned, though, this did not augur well.

"I'm sorry about the grease," she said abruptly.

He blinked.

"Grease?"

"For someone's arsehole, Friend Murray said. The dog ate it."

"The dog ate . . . oh, the dog ate the grease." His mouth twitched, and he rubbed the thumb of his right hand slowly over his fingers. "That's all right; I found some."

"You're hungry," she said abruptly, and stood up. "Wash thy hands and I'll put the coffee on."

"That would be good. I thank thee, Rachel. Rachel . . ." He hesitated, but was not a man to avoid things. "Friend Murray said to thee that thee loves him—but not that he loves thee? That seems—a peculiar way of expression, does it not?"

"It does," she said, in a tone indicating that she didn't wish to discuss Ian Murray's peculiarities. She was not about to try to explain to Denny that Ian Murray had not declared himself to her in words because he hadn't needed to. The air around her still shimmered with the heat of his declaration. Though . . .

"Perhaps he did," she said slowly. "He said *something* to me, but it wasn't in English, and I didn't understand. Does thee know what '*mo cree-ga*' might mean?"

Denny frowned for a moment, then his brow cleared.

"That would be the Highlander's tongue, what they call the *Gàidhlig*, I think. No, I don't know what it means—but I have heard Friend Jamie say that to his wife, in such circumstances as to make it evident that it is a term of deep . . . affection." He coughed.

"Rachel—does thee wish me to speak to him?"

Her skin still burned, and her face felt as though it glowed with fever, but at this, a deep shard of ice seemed to pierce her heart.

"Speak to him," she repeated, and swallowed. "And say . . . what?" She had found the coffeepot and the pouch of roasted acorns and chicory. She poured a handful of the blackened mixture into her mortar and commenced to pound it as though the cup were full of snakes.

Denny shrugged, watching her with interest.

"Thee will break that mortar," he observed. "As to what I should say— why, thee must tell me, Rachel." His eyes were still intent upon her, but serious now, with no hint of humor. "I will tell him to stay away and never to speak to thee again, if thee wishes it. Or if thee prefers, I can assure him that thy affection for him is only that of a friend and that he must refrain from further awkward declarations."

She poured the grounds into the pot and then added water from the canteen she kept hanging on the tent pole.

"Are those the only alternatives you see?" she asked, trying to keep her voice steady.

"Sissy," he said, very gently, "thee cannot wed such a man and remain a Friend. No meeting would accept such a union. Thee knows that." He waited a moment and added, "Thee did ask me to pray for thee."

She didn't answer or look at him but untied the tent flap and went out to put the coffeepot among the coals, pausing to poke up the fire and add more wood. The air glowed near the ground, lit by the smoke and fiery haze of thousands of small fires like hers. But the night above stretched black and clear and infinite, the stars burning with their own cold fire.

When she went back in, he was half under the bed, muttering.

"What?" she demanded, and he backed out, bringing with him the small crate that held their foodstuffs—save that it didn't. Only a scattering of raw acorns and an apple, half-gnawed by mice, remained.

"*What?*" she repeated, shocked. "What has happened to the food?"

Denny was flushed and plainly angry, and rubbed his knuckles hard across his lips before replying.

"Some misbegotten son of a—of Belial . . . has slit the tent and taken it."

The resultant flood of fury at this news was almost welcome, for the distraction that it offered.

"Why, that—that—"

"Doubtless," Denny said, taking a deep breath and seeking to regain control of himself, "he was hungry. Poor soul," he added, with a distinct lack of charitable intonation.

"If so, he might have asked to be fed," she snapped. "He is a thief, plain and simple." She tapped a foot, fuming. "Well. I will go and beg some food myself, then. Watch the coffee."

"Thee need not go on my account," he protested, but it was a halfhearted protest; she knew he had not eaten since morning and was starved, and she said as much to him with a wide-eyed stare in his direction.

"The wolves . . ." he said, but she was already wrapping up her cloak and pulling on her cap.

"I'll take a torch," she assured him. "And it would be an unlucky wolf who made the mistake of crossing me in my present mood, I assure thee!" She seized her gathering bag and went out quickly, before he could ask her where she proposed to go.

SHE MIGHT HAVE gone to a dozen different tents nearby. Puzzlement and suspicion of the Hunters had faded after Denny's adventures as a deserter, and Rachel herself had cordial relations with a number of the militia wives who camped near them.

She might have told herself that she hesitated to disturb these worthy women so late. Or that she wished to hear the latest news regarding the surrender—Friend Jamie was always privy to the negotiations and would tell her what he could. Or that she thought to consult Claire Fraser regarding a small but painful wart upon her great toe and might as well do this while seeking food, for the sake of convenience.

But she was an honest woman and told herself none of these things. She was walking toward the Frasers' camp as though drawn by a magnet, and the magnet's name was Ian Murray. She saw this clearly, thought her own behavior insane—and could no more do otherwise than she could change the color of her eyes.

What she meant to do, say, or even think if she *did* see him was unimaginable, but she walked on nonetheless, steady as though she went to market, the light of her torch a beacon upon the trampled dirt of her path, her own shadow following, huge and strange upon the pale canvas of the tents she passed.

68

DESPOILER

I WAS TENDING the fire when I heard the sound of slow footsteps approaching. I turned, to see a massive shape between me and the moon, coming fast. I tried to run but couldn't make my legs obey me. As in all the best nightmares, I tried to scream, only to find it trapped in my throat. I choked, and it came out as a small, strangled "*eep.*"

The monstrous shape—manlike, but humped and headless, grunting—stopped before me, and there was a short whoosh and a loud thump of something hitting the ground that sent the cold air rushing up under my skirt.

"I brought ye a present, Sassenach," Jamie said, grinning and wiping sweat from his jaw.

"A...present," I said faintly, looking at the enormous heap of... what?...he had dropped on the ground at my feet. Then the smell reached me.

"A buffalo robe!" I exclaimed. "Oh, Jamie! A real buffalo robe?"

Not much doubt of that. It was not—thank God—a fresh one, but the scent of its original owner was still perceptible, even in the cold. I fell to my knees, running my hands over it. It was well-cured, flexible, and relatively clean, the wool of it rough under my hands but free of mud, burrs, clumps of dung, and the other impedimenta that normally attended live buffalo. It was enormous. And warm. Wonderfully warm.

I sank my freezing hands into the depths of it, which still held Jamie's body heat.

"Oh," I breathed. "You won it?"

"I did," he said proudly. "From one of the British officers. A decent man at cards," he added fairly, "but no luck."

"You've been playing with British officers?" I cast an uneasy look in the direction of the British camp, though it wasn't visible from here.

"Just one. A Captain Mansel. He came wi' the latest reply from Burgoyne and was obliged to wait while Granny chews it over. He'll be lucky if he's not skinned to the bone before he goes back," he added callously. "Worse luck wi' cards I never saw."

I paid no attention, engrossed in examining the robe. "This is marvelous, Jamie! It's huge!"

It was. A good eight feet long, and wide enough that two people could lie cradled in its warmth—provided they didn't mind sleeping close. The thought of crawling into that enveloping shelter, warm and cozy, after so many nights shivering under threadbare blankets...

Jamie appeared to have been thinking along similar lines.

"Big enough for the two of us," he said, and touched my breast, very delicately.

"Oh, really?"

He leaned closer, and I caught his own scent above the gamy pong of the buffalo robe—dry leaves, and the bitterness of acorn coffee, laced with sweet brandy, top notes to the deep male scent of his skin.

"I could pick you out of a dozen men in a dark room," I said, closing my eyes and inhaling enjoyably.

"I daresay ye could; I havena bathed in a week." He put his hands on my shoulders and bent his head until our foreheads touched.

"I want to unlace the neck o' your shift," he whispered, "and suckle your breasts until ye curl up like a wee shrimp, wi' your knees in my balls. Then take ye fast and hard, and fall asleep wi' my head pillowed on your naked breasts. Really," he added, straightening up.

"Oh," I said. "What a good idea."

───

IN FAVOR AS I WAS of the suggested program, I could see that Jamie required nourishment before executing anything of a further strenuous nature; I could hear his stomach rumbling from a yard away.

"Playing cards takes it out of you, does it?" I observed, watching him demolish three apples in six bites.

"Aye, it does," he said briefly. "Have we any bread?"

"No, but there's beer."

As though the word had evoked him, Young Ian materialized out of the gloom.

"Beer?" he said hopefully.

"Bread?" Jamie and I said together, sniffing like dogs. Wafting from Ian's clothes was a yeasty, half-burned fragrance, which proved to come from two small loaves in his pockets.

"Where did you get these, Ian?" I asked, handing him a canteen of beer.

He drank deep, then lowered the canteen and stared vacantly at me for a moment.

"Ah?" he said vaguely.

"Are you all right, Ian?" I peered at him in some concern, but he blinked, and intelligence returned momentarily to his face.

"Aye, Auntie, fine. I'll just . . . ah . . . oh, thank ye for the beer." He handed back the empty canteen, smiled at me as though I were a stranger, and wandered off into the darkness.

"Did you see that?" I turned to find Jamie absorbed in dabbing up bread crumbs from his lap with a moistened finger.

"No, what? Here, Sassenach." He handed me the second loaf.

"Ian acting like a half-wit. Here, you have half; you need it more than I do."

He didn't argue.

"He wasna bleeding or staggering, was he? Well, then, I suppose he's fallen in love wi' some poor lass."

"Oh? Well, that would fit the symptoms. But . . ." I nibbled the bread slowly, to make it last; it was crusty and fresh, clearly just out of the ashes. I'd seen young men in love, certainly, and Ian's behavior *did* fit the symptomology. But I hadn't seen it in Ian, not since . . . "I wonder who?"

"God knows. I hope it's no one of the whores." Jamie sighed and rubbed a hand over his face. "Though maybe better that than someone else's wife."

"Oh, he wouldn't—" I began, but then saw the wry look on his face. "Oh, he *didn't*?"

"No, he didn't," Jamie said, "but a near thing—and no credit to the lady involved."

"Who?"

"Colonel Miller's lady."

"Dear me." Abigail Miller was a sprightly young blonde of twenty or so, and twenty or so years younger than her rather stout—and distinctly humorless—husband. "Just . . . *how* near a thing?"

"Near enough," Jamie said grimly. "She had him up against a tree, rubbing up to him like a wee cat in heat. Though I imagine her husband will ha' put a stop to her antics by now."

"He *saw* them?"

"Aye. He and I were walking together, came round a bush, and there they were. It was clear enough to me that it wasna the lad's idea—but he wasna resisting all that much, either."

Colonel Miller had frozen for an instant, then strode forward, gripped his startled wife by the arm, and with a murmured "Good day, sir" to Jamie, had dragged her off, squealing, in the direction of his camp.

"Jesus H.... when did this happen?" I demanded.

Jamie glanced at the rising moon, estimating.

"Oh, maybe five or six hours ago."

"And he's already managed to fall in love with someone *else*?"

He smiled at me.

"Ever heard of *coup de foudre*, Sassenach? It didna take me more than one good look at you."

"Hmm," I said, pleased.

WITH SOME EFFORT, I heaved the heavy buffalo robe over the stack of cut fir branches that formed the foundation of our bed, spread our two blankets over the robe, then folded the whole thing over like a dumpling, creating a large, weatherproof, cozy pocket into which I inserted myself, shivering in my shift.

I left the tent flap open, watching Jamie as he drank coffee and talked with two militiamen who had come by to gossip.

As my feet thawed for the first time in a month, I relaxed into untrammeled bliss. Like most people obliged to live outdoors in the autumn, I normally slept in everything I owned. Women moving with the army would occasionally remove their stays—if it wasn't raining, you saw them hung to air from tree branches in the mornings sometimes, like huge, malodorous birds poised for flight—but most simply loosened the ties and lay down regardless. Stays are quite comfortable to wear while standing up, but leave a lot to be desired in terms of nightwear.

Tonight, with the prospect of warm, waterproof shelter at hand, I had actually gone so far as to take off not only my stays—rolled up under my head as a pillow—but also skirt, blouse, jacket, and kerchief, crawling into bed in nothing save my shift and stockings. I felt absolutely depraved.

I stretched luxuriously and ran my hands down the length of my body, then thoughtfully cupped my breasts, contemplating Jamie's proposed plan of action.

The warmth of the buffalo robe was making me deliciously drowsy. I thought I needn't struggle to stay awake; I could tell that Jamie wasn't in any mood to forbear waking me out of chivalrous regard for my rest.

Had the fortuitous acquisition of the buffalo robe inspired him? I wondered, thumb dreamily circling one nipple. Or had sexual desperation inspired him to bet on the thing? What with his injured hand, it had been...how many days? I was absently totting up the total in my mind when I heard the low murmur of a new voice by the fire, and sighed.

Ian. Not that I wasn't pleased to see him, but...oh, well. At least he hadn't turned up just as we were...

He was sitting on one of the stones near the fire, head bent. He took something from his sporran and rubbed it thoughtfully between his fingers as he talked. His long, homely face was worried—but bore an odd sort of glow.

How peculiar, I thought. I'd seen it before, that look. A sort of intent concentration on something wonderful, a marvelous secret held to himself.

It was a girl, I thought, both amused and touched. He'd looked just that way at Mary, the young prostitute who had been his first. And Emily?

Well, yes . . . I thought so, though in that instance his joy in her had been terribly shadowed by the knowledge of his impending separation from everyone and everything else he loved.

Cuimhnich, Jamie had said to him, laying his own plaid over Ian's shoulders in farewell. *"Remember."* I had thought my heart would break, to leave him—I knew Jamie's had.

He was still wearing the same ragged plaid, pinned to the shoulder of his buckskins.

"Rachel *Hunter?*" Jamie said, loud enough for me to hear, and I jerked upright, startled.

"Rachel *Hunter?*" I echoed. "You're in love with Rachel?"

Ian looked at me, startled by my jack-in-the-box appearance.

"Oh, there ye are, Auntie. I wondered where ye'd got to," he said mildly.

"Rachel Hunter?" I repeated, not intending to let him elude the question.

"Well . . . aye. At least, I . . . well, aye. I am." The admission made the blood rise in his cheeks; I could see it even by firelight.

"The lad is thinking we'd maybe have a word wi' Denzell, Sassenach," Jamie explained. He looked amused, but slightly worried, as well.

"A word? What for?"

Ian looked up and glanced from one to the other of us. "It's only . . . Denny Hunter's no going to like it. But he thinks the world of Auntie Claire, and he respects you, of course, Uncle Jamie."

"Why would he not like it?" I asked. I had by now extracted myself from the robe and, wrapping my shawl round my shoulders, sat down on a rock beside him. My mind was racing. I liked Rachel Hunter very much. And I was *very* pleased—to say nothing of relieved—if Ian had at last found a decent woman to love. But . . .

Ian gave me a look.

"Surely ye've noticed that they're Quaker, Auntie?"

"I did, yes," I said, giving him back the look. "But—"

"And I'm not."

"Yes, I'd noticed that, too. But—"

"She'd be put out of meeting, if she weds me. Most likely they both would. They've been put out once already for Denny's going wi' the army, and that was hard for her."

"Oh," said Jamie, pausing in the act of tearing off a bit of bread. He held it for a moment, frowning. "Aye, I suppose they would." He put the bread into his mouth and chewed slowly, considering.

"Do you think she loves you, too, Ian?" I asked, as gently as possible.

Ian's face was a study, torn between worry, alarm, and that inner glow that kept breaking through the clouds of distress.

"I—well . . . I think so. I hope so."

"You haven't *asked* her?"

"I . . . not exactly. I mean—we didna really *talk,* ken?"

Jamie swallowed his bread and coughed.

"Ian," he said. "Tell me ye havena bedded Rachel Hunter."

Ian gave him a look of affront. Jamie stared at him, brows raised. Ian dropped his gaze back to the object in his hands, rolling it between his palms like a ball of dough.

"No," he muttered. "I wish I had, though."

"What?"

"Well . . . if I had, then she'd have to wed me, no? I wish I'd thought of that—but no, I couldna; she said stop, and I did." He swallowed, hard.

"Very gentlemanly of you," I murmured, though in fact I rather saw his point. "And very intelligent of her."

He sighed. "What am I to do, Uncle Jamie?"

"I don't suppose you could become a Quaker yourself?" I asked hesitantly.

Both Jamie and Ian looked at me. They didn't resemble each other in the slightest, but the look of ironic amusement on both faces was identical.

"I dinna ken very much about myself, Auntie," Ian said, with a painful half smile, "but I think I wasna born to be a Quaker."

"And I suppose you couldn't—no, of course not." The thought of professing a conversion that he didn't mean had plainly never entered his mind.

It struck me quite suddenly that, of all people, Ian would understand exactly what the cost to Rachel would be if her love for him severed her from her people. No wonder he hesitated at the thought of her paying such a price.

Always assuming, I reminded myself, that she *did* love him. I had better have a talk with Rachel first.

Ian was still turning something over in his hands. Looking closer, I saw that it was a small, darkened, leathery-looking object. Surely it wasn't—

"That isn't Neil Forbes's ear, is it?" I blurted.

"Mr. Fraser?"

The voice brought me up standing, hairs prickling at the back of my neck. Bloody hell, not *him* again? Sure enough, it was the Continental soldier, the despoiler of my soup. He came slowly into the circle of firelight, deep-set eyes fixed on Jamie.

"I am James Fraser, aye," Jamie said, setting down his cup and gesturing politely toward a vacant rock. "Will ye take a cup of coffee, sir? Or what passes for it?"

The man shook his head, not speaking. He was looking Jamie over appraisingly, like one about to buy a horse and not sure of its temper.

"Perhaps ye'd prefer a warm cup o' spittle?" Ian said, in an unfriendly tone. Jamie glanced at him, startled.

"Seo mac na muice a thàinig na bu thràithe gad shiubhal," Ian added. He didn't take his eyes off the stranger. *"Chan eil e ag iarraidh math dhut idir uncle."* This is the misbegotten son of a pig who came earlier in search of you. He means you no good, Uncle.

"Tapadh leat Iain. Cha robh fios air a bhith agam," Jamie answered in the same language, keeping his voice pleasantly relaxed. Thank you, Ian. I should never have guessed. "Have ye business with me, sir?" he asked, changing to English.

"I would speak with you, yes. In privacy," the man added, with a dismissive glance at Ian. Apparently I didn't count.

"This is my nephew," Jamie said, still courteous but wary. "Ye may speak in front of him."

"I fear ye may think differently, Mr. Fraser, when you hear what I've to say. And once said, such things cannot be unsaid. Leave, young man," he said, not bothering to look at Ian. "Or you will both regret it."

Both Jamie and Ian stiffened visibly. Then they moved, at nearly the same instant, bodies shifting subtly, their feet coming under them, shoulders squaring. Jamie gazed thoughtfully at the man for a moment, then inclined his head an inch toward Ian. Ian rose without a word and disappeared into the darkness.

The man stood waiting, until the sound of Ian's footsteps had faded and the night settled into silence around the tiny fire. Then he moved round the fire and sat down slowly, opposite Jamie, still maintaining that unnerving air of scrutiny. Well, it unnerved *me;* Jamie merely picked up his cup and drained it, calm as though he were sitting at his own kitchen table.

"If ye've aught to say to me, sir, say it. It's late, and I'm for my bed."

"A bed with your lovely wife in it, I daresay. Lucky man." I was beginning to dislike this gentleman intensely. Jamie ignored both the comment and the mocking tone in which it was spoken, leaning forward to pour the last of the coffee into his cup. I could smell the bitter tang of it, even over the scent the buffalo robe had left on my shift.

"Does the name of Willie Coulter recall itself to you?" the man asked abruptly.

"I've kent several men of that name and that ilk," Jamie replied. "Mostly in Scotland."

"Aye, it was in Scotland. On the day before the great slaughter at Culloden. But you had your own wee slaughter on that day, no?"

I had been racking my memory for any notion of a Willie Coulter. The mention of Culloden struck me like a fist in the stomach.

Jamie had been obliged to kill his uncle Dougal MacKenzie on that day. And there had been one witness to the deed besides me: a MacKenzie clansman named Willie Coulter. I had assumed him long dead, either at Culloden or in the difficulties that followed—and I was sure Jamie had thought likewise.

Our visitor rocked back a little on his rock, smiling sardonically.

"I was once overseer on a sugar plantation of some size, you see, on the island of Jamaica. We'd a dozen black slaves from Africa, but blacks of decent quality grow ever more expensive. And so the master sent me to market one day with a purse of silver, to look over a new crop of indentures—transported criminals, the most of them. From Scotland."

And among the two dozen men the overseer had culled from the ragged, scrawny, lice-ridden ranks was Willie Coulter. Captured after the battle, tried and condemned in quick order, and loaded onto a ship for the Indies within a month, never to see Scotland again.

I could just see the side of Jamie's face and saw a muscle jump in his jaw. Most of his Ardsmuir men had been similarly transported; only the interest of John Grey had saved him from the same fate, and he had distinctly mixed feelings about it, even so many years after the fact. He merely nodded, though, vaguely interested, as though listening to some traveler's tale in an inn.

"They all died within two weeks," the stranger said, his mouth twisting. "And so did the blacks. Bloody pricks brought some filthy fever with them from the ship. Lost me my position. But I did get one thing of value to take away with me. Willie Coulter's last words."

JAMIE HADN'T MOVED appreciably since Mr. X had sat down, but I could sense the tension thrumming through him; he was strung like a bow with the arrow nocked.

"What is it ye want?" he asked calmly, and leaned forward to pick up the tin mug of coffee, wrapped in rags.

"Mmphm." The man made a pleased sound in his throat and sat back a little, nodding.

"I kent ye for a sensible gentleman. I'm a modest man, sir—shall we say a hundred dollars? To show your good faith," he added, with a grin that displayed snaggled teeth discolored by snuff. "And to save ye the trouble of protest, I'll just mention that I ken ye've got it in your pocket. I happened to speak wi' the gentleman ye won it from this afternoon, aye?"

I blinked at that; evidently Jamie had had an extraordinary run of luck. At cards, at least.

"To show good faith," Jamie repeated. He looked at the cup in his hand, then at the Lowlander's grinning face, but evidently decided that the distance was too great to throw it at him. "And to be going on with . . . ?"

"Ah, well. We can be discussing that later. I hear ye're a man of considerable substance, Colonel Fraser."

"And ye propose to batten on me like a leech, do ye?"

"Why, a bit of leeching does a man good, Colonel. Keeps the humors in balance." He leered at me. "I'm sure your good wife kens the wisdom of it."

"And what do you mean by *that,* you slimy little worm?" I said, standing up. Jamie might have decided against throwing a cup of coffee at him, but I was willing to have a try with the pot.

"Manners, woman," he said, giving me a censorious glance before shifting his gaze back to Jamie. "Do ye not beat her, man?"

I could see the tautness in Jamie's body subtly shifting; the bow was being drawn.

"Don't—" I began, turning to Jamie, but never got to finish. I saw the expression change on Jamie's face, saw him leap toward the man—and whirled just in time to see Ian materialize out of the darkness behind the blackmailer and put a sinewy arm round his throat.

I didn't see the knife. I didn't have to; I saw Ian's face, so intent as almost to be expressionless—and I saw the ex-overseer's face. His jaw dropped and the whites of his eyes showed, his back arching up in a futile attempt at escape.

Then Ian let go, and Jamie caught the man as he began to fall, his body gone suddenly and horribly limp.

"Jesus God!"

The exclamation came from directly behind me, and I whirled again, this time to see Colonel Martin and two of his aides, as drop-jawed as Mr. X had been a moment before.

Jamie glanced up at them, startled. Then in the next breath, he turned and said quietly over his shoulder, *"Ruith." Run.*

"Hi! Murder!" one of the aides shouted, springing forward. "Stop, villain!"

Ian had lost no time in taking Jamie's advice; I could see him darting toward the edge of the distant wood, but there was enough light from the many campfires to reveal his flight, and the shouts of Martin and his aides were rousing everyone in hearing; people were jumping up from their firesides, peering into the dark, shouting questions. Jamie dropped the overseer's body by the fire and ran after Ian.

The younger of the aides hurtled past me, legs churning in furious pursuit. Colonel Martin dashed after him, and I managed to stick out a foot and trip him. He went sprawling through the fire, sending a fountain of sparks and ashes into the night.

Leaving the second aide to beat out the flames, I picked up my shift and ran as fast as I could in the direction Ian and Jamie had taken.

The encampment looked like something from Dante's *Inferno*, black figures shouting against the glow of flames, pushing one another amid smoke and confusion, shouts of "Murder! Murder!" ringing from different directions as more people heard and took it up.

I had a stitch in my side but kept running, stumbling over rocks and hollows and trampled ground. Louder shouts from the left—I paused, panting, hand to my side, and saw Jamie's tall form jerking free of a couple of pursuers. He must mean to draw pursuit away from Ian—which meant . . . I turned and ran the other way.

Sure enough, I saw Ian, who had sensibly stopped running as soon as he saw Jamie take off, now walking at a good clip toward the wood.

"Murderer!" a voice shrieked behind me. It was Martin, blast him, somewhat scorched but undaunted. "Stop, Murray! Stop, I say!"

Hearing his name shouted, Ian began to run again, zigzagging around a campfire. As he passed in front of it, I saw the shadow at his heels—Rollo was with him.

Colonel Martin had drawn up even with me, and I saw with alarm that he had his pistol in hand.

"St—" I began, but before the word was out, I crashed headlong into someone and fell flat with them.

It was Rachel Hunter, wide-eyed and openmouthed. She scrambled to her feet and ran toward Ian, who had frozen when he saw her. Colonel Martin cocked his pistol and pointed it at Ian, and a second later Rollo leapt through the air and seized the colonel's arm in his jaws.

The pandemonium grew worse. There were bangs from two or three pistols, and Rollo dropped writhing to the ground with a yelp. Colonel Martin jerked back, cursing and clutching his injured wrist, and Jamie drew back and punched him in the belly. Ian was already rushing toward Rollo; Jamie grabbed the dog by two legs, and, between them, they made off into the darkness, followed by Rachel and me.

We made it to the edge of the wood, heaving and gasping, and I fell at once to my knees beside Rollo, feeling frantically over the huge shaggy body, hunting for the wound, for damage.

"He's not dead," I panted. "Shoulder . . . broken."

"Oh, God," Ian said, and I felt him turn to glance in the direction from which pursuit was surely headed. "Oh, Jesus." I heard tears in his voice, and he reached to his belt for his knife.

"What are you *doing*?!" I exclaimed. "He can be healed!"

"They'll kill him," he said, savage. "If I'm no there to stop them, they'll kill him! Better I do it."

"I—" Jamie began, but Rachel Hunter forestalled him, falling to her knees and grabbing Rollo by the scruff.

"I'll mind thy dog for thee," she said, breathless but certain. "Run!"

He took one last despairing look at her, then at Rollo. And he ran.

TERMS OF SURRENDER

WHEN THE MESSAGE came from General Gates in the morning, Jamie knew what it must be about. Ian had got clean away, and little surprise. He'd be in the wood or perhaps in an Indian camp; either way, no one would find him until he wished to be found.

The lad had been right, too; they *did* want to kill the dog, particularly Colonel Martin, and it had taken not only all Jamie's resources but the young Quaker lass's prostrating herself upon the hound's hairy carcass and declaring that they must kill her first.

That had taken Martin back a bit, but there was still considerable public opinion in favor of dragging her away and doing the dog in. Jamie had prepared himself to step in—but then Rachel's brother had come out of the dark like an avenging angel. Denny stood in front of her and denounced the crowd as cowards, recreants, and inhuman monsters who would seek to revenge themselves upon an innocent animal, to say nothing of their damnable injustice—yes, he'd really said "damnable," with the greatest spirit, and the memory of it made Jamie smile, even in the face of the upcoming interview—in driving a young man to exile and perdition out of their own suspicion and iniquity, and could they not seek to find within their own bowels the slightest spark of the divine compassion that was the God-given life of every man . . .

Jamie's arrival at Gates's headquarters cut short these enjoyable reminiscences, and he straightened himself, assuming the grim demeanor suitable to trying occasions.

Gates looked as though he had been severely tried himself—which he had, in all justice. The bland, round face never looked as though it had any bones, but now it sagged like a soft-boiled egg, and the small eyes behind the wire-rimmed spectacles were huge and bloodshot when they looked at Jamie.

"Sit down, Colonel," Gates said, and pushed a glass and decanter toward him.

Jamie was dumbfounded. He'd had enough grim interviews with high-ranking officers to know that you didn't start them out with a cordial dram. He accepted the drink, though, and sipped it cautiously.

Gates drained his own, much less cautiously, set it down, and sighed heavily.

"I require a favor of you, Colonel."

"I shall be pleased, sir," he replied, with still more caution. What could the fat bugger possibly want of him? If it was Ian's whereabouts or an explanation of the murder, he could whistle for that and must know it. If not . . .

"The surrender negotiations are almost complete." Gates gave a bleak glance to a thick stack of handwritten papers, perhaps drafts of the thing.

"Burgoyne's troops are to march out of camp with the honors of war and ground arms at the bank of the Hudson at the command of their own officers. All officers will retain their swords and equipment, the soldiers, their knapsacks. The army is to march to Boston, where they will be properly fed and sheltered before embarking for England. The only condition imposed is that they are not to serve in North America again during the present war. Generous terms, I think you will agree, Colonel?"

"Verra generous, indeed, sir." Surprisingly so. What had made a general who undeniably held the whip hand to the extent that Gates did offer such extraordinary terms?

Gates smiled sourly.

"I see you are surprised, Colonel. Perhaps you will be less so if I tell you that Sir Henry Clinton is heading north." And Gates was in a rush to conclude the surrender and get rid of Burgoyne in order to have time to prepare for an attack from the south.

"Aye, sir, I see."

"Yes, well." Gates closed his eyes for an instant and sighed again, seeming exhausted. "There is one additional request from Burgoyne before he will accept this arrangement."

"Yes, sir?"

Gates's eyes were open again and passed slowly over him.

"They tell me you are a cousin to Brigadier General Simon Fraser."

"I am."

"Good. Then I am sure you will have no objection to performing a small service for your country."

A small service pertaining to Simon? Surely . . .

"He had at one time expressed a desire to several of his aides that, should he die abroad, they might bury him at once—which they did, in fact; they buried him in the Great Redoubt—but that when convenient, he wished to be taken back to Scotland, that he might lie at peace there."

"Ye want me to take his body to Scotland?" Jamie blurted. He could not have been more astonished had Gates suddenly got up and danced a hornpipe on his desk. The general nodded, his amiability increasing.

"You are very quick, Colonel. Yes. That is Burgoyne's final request. He says that the brigadier was much beloved by his men and that knowing his wish is fulfilled will reconcile them to marching away, as they will not feel they are abandoning his grave."

This sounded thoroughly romantic, and quite like something Burgoyne might do, Jamie reflected. He had a reputation for dramatic gesture. And he was probably not wrong in his estimation of the feelings of the men who had served under Simon—he was a good fellow, Simon.

Only belatedly did it dawn on him that the final result of this request . . .

"Is . . . there some provision to be made for my reaching Scotland with the body, sir?" he asked delicately. "There is a blockade."

"You will be transported—with your wife and servants, if you like—on one of His Majesty's ships, and a sum will be provided you for transporting the coffin once it has come ashore in Scotland. Have I your agreement, Colonel Fraser?"

He was so stunned, he scarcely knew what he said in response, but evidently it was sufficient, for Gates smiled tiredly and dismissed him. He made his way back to his tent with his head in a whirl, wondering whether he could disguise Young Ian as his wife's maid, in the manner of Charles Stuart.

OCTOBER 17, like all the days that had gone before it, dawned dark and foggy. In his tent, General Burgoyne dressed with particular care, in a gorgeous scarlet coat with gold braid and a hat decorated with plumes. William saw him, when he went with the other officers to Burgoyne's tent for their last, anguished meeting.

Baron von Riedesel spoke to them, too; he took all the regimental flags. He would give them to his wife, he said, to be sewn inside a pillow and taken secretly back to Brunswick.

William cared for none of this. He was conscious of deep sorrow, for he had never before left comrades on a battlefield and marched away. Some shame, but not much—the general was right in saying that they could not have mounted another attack without losing most of the army, so wretched was their condition.

They looked wretched now, lining up in silence, and yet when fife and drum began to play, each regiment in its turn followed the flying colors, heads high in their tattered uniforms—or whatever clothing they could find. The enemy had withdrawn on Gates's order, the general said. That was delicate, William thought numbly; the Americans would not be present to witness their humiliation.

Redcoats first, and then the German regiments: dragoons and grenadiers in blue, the green-clad infantry and artillery from Hesse-Cassel.

On the river flats, scores of horses lay dead, the stench adding to the somber horror of the occasion. The artillery parked their cannon here, and the infantry, rank by rank by unending rank, poured out their cartridge boxes and stacked their muskets. Some men were sufficiently furious as to smash the butts of their guns before throwing them on the piles; William saw a drummer put his foot through his drum before turning away. He was not furious, or horrified.

All he wanted now was to see his father again.

THE CONTINENTAL troops and the militia marched to the meeting-house at Saratoga and from there lined up along both sides of the river road. Some women came, watching from a distance. I could have stayed in camp, to see the historic ceremony of surrender between the two generals, but I followed the troops instead.

The sun had risen and the fog had fled, just as it had done every day for the last few weeks. There was a smell of smoke in the air, and the sky was the infinite deep blue of October.

Artillery and infantry stood along the road, evenly spaced, but that spacing was the only uniform thing about them. There was no common dress, and each man's equipment was distinctively his own, in form and how he held it—but each man held his musket, or his rifle, or stood beside his cannon.

They were a motley crew in every sense of the word, festooned with powder horns and shot bags, some wearing outlandish old-fashioned wigs. And they stood in grave silence, each man with his right foot forward, right hands on their guns, to watch the enemy march out, with the honors of war.

I stood in the wood, a little way behind Jamie, and I saw his shoulders stiffen a little. William walked past, tall and straight, his face the face of a man who is not really there. Jamie didn't dip his head or make any effort not to be seen—but I saw his head turn just slightly, following William out of sight in the company of his men. And then his shoulders dropped just a little, as though a burden dropped from them.

Safe, that gesture said, though he still stood straight as the rifle beside him. *Thank God. He is safe.*

70

SANCTUARY

Lallybroch

ROGER COULD NOT have said quite what impelled him to do it, other than the sense of peace that hung about the place, but he had begun to rebuild the old chapel. By hand, and alone, one stone upon another.

He'd tried to explain it to Bree; she'd asked.

"It's *them*," he said at last, helpless. "It's a sort of . . . I feel as though I need to connect with them, back there."

She took one of his hands in her own, spreading his fingers, and ran the ball of her thumb gently over his knuckles, down the length of his fingers, touching the scabs and grazes, the blackened nail where a stone had slipped and bruised it.

"Them," she repeated carefully. "You mean my parents."

"Yes, among other things." Not only with Jamie and Claire but with the life their family had built. With his own sense of himself as a man—protector, provider. And yet it was his bone-deep urge to protect that had led him to abandon all his Christian principles—on the eve of ordination, no less—and set out in pursuit of Stephen Bonnet.

"I suppose I'm hoping I can make sense of . . . things," he'd said, with a wry smile. "How to reconcile what I thought I knew then with what I think I am now."

"It's not Christian to want to save your wife from being raped and sold into slavery?" she inquired, a distinct edge in her voice. "Because if it's not, I'm taking the kids and converting to Judaism or Shinto or something."

His smile had grown more genuine.

"I found something there." He fumbled for words.

"You lost a few things, too," she whispered. Not taking her eyes from his, she reached out, the tips of her fingers cool on his throat. The rope scar had faded somewhat but was still darkly visible; he made no effort to hide it. Sometimes when he spoke with people, he could see their eyes fix on it; given his height, it was not unusual for men to seem to be speaking directly *to* the scar, rather than to himself.

Found a sense of himself as a man, found what he thought was his calling. And that, he supposed, was what he was looking for under those piles of fallen stone, under the eyes of a blind saint.

Was God opening a door, showing him that he should be a teacher now? Was this, the Gaelic thing, what he was meant to do? He had plenty of room to ask questions, room and time and silence. Answers were scarce. He'd been at it most of the aftenoon; he was hot, exhausted, and ready for a beer.

Now his eye caught the edge of a shadow in the doorway, and he turned— Jem or maybe Brianna, come to fetch him home to tea. It was neither of them.

For a moment, he stared at the newcomer, searching his memory. Ragged jeans and sweatshirt, dirty-blond hair hacked off and tousled. Surely he knew the man; the broad-boned, handsome face was familiar, even under a thick layer of light-brown stubble.

"Can I help you?" Roger asked, taking a grip on the shovel he'd been using. The man wasn't threatening but was roughly dressed and dirty—a tramp, perhaps—and there was something indefinable about him that made Roger uneasy.

"It's a church, aye?" the man said, and grinned, though no hint of warmth touched his eyes. "Suppose I've come to claim sanctuary, then." He moved suddenly into the light, and Roger saw his eyes more clearly. Cold, and a deep, striking green.

"Sanctuary," William Buccleigh MacKenzie repeated. "And then, Minister dear, I want ye to tell me who ye are, who *I* am—and what in the name of God almighty *are* we?"

PART SIX

Coming Home

71

A STATE OF CONFLICT

September 10, 1777

JOHN GREY FOUND himself wondering how many horns a dilemma could have. Two, he believed, was the standard number, but supposed that it was theoretically possible to encounter a more exotic form of dilemma—something like the four-horned sheep he had once seen in Spain.

The most pressing of the horns arrayed under him at present concerned Henry.

He'd written to Jamie Fraser, explaining Henry's state and asking whether Mrs. Fraser might see her way to come. He had, as delicately as possible, assured her of his willingness to bear all expenses of the journey, to expedite her travel in both directions by ship (with protection from the exigencies of warfare insofar as the royal navy could provide it), and to provide her with whatever materials and instruments she might require. Had even gone so far as to procure a quantity of vitriol, which he recalled her needing for the composition of her ether.

He had spent a good deal of time with quill suspended over the page, wondering whether to add anything regarding Fergus Fraser, the printer, and the incredible story Percy had told him. On the one hand, this might bring Jamie Fraser belting up from North Carolina to look into the matter, thus improving the chances of Mrs. Fraser coming, as well. On the other... he was more than reluctant to expose any matter having to do with Percy Beauchamp to Jamie Fraser, for assorted reasons, both personal and professional. In the end, he had said nothing of it and made his appeal solely on behalf of Henry.

Grey had waited through an anxious month, watching his nephew suffer from heat and inanition. At the end of the month, the courier he had sent to take his letter to North Carolina returned, sweat-soaked, caked with mud, and with two bullet holes in his coat, to report that the Frasers had left Fraser's Ridge with the declared intent of removing to Scotland, though adding helpfully that this removal was presumed to be only in the nature of a visit, rather than a permanent emigration.

He had fetched a physician to visit Henry, of course, not waiting for Mrs. Fraser's reply. He had succeeded in introducing himself to Benjamin Rush and had that gentleman examine his nephew. Dr. Rush had been grave but encouraging, saying that he believed one of the musket balls, at least, had created scarring, this partially obstructing Henry's intestines and encouraging a localized pocket of sepsis, which caused his persistent fever. He had bled Henry and prescribed a febrifuge, but made the strongest representations to Grey that the situation was delicate and might worsen abruptly; only surgical intervention might effect a cure.

At the same time, he said that he did believe Henry to be strong enough to survive such surgery—though there was, of course, no certainty of a happy outcome. Grey had thanked Dr. Rush but had chosen to wait just a little while, in hopes of hearing from Mrs. Fraser.

He looked out the window of his rented house on Chestnut Street, watching brown and yellow leaves scour to and fro among the cobbles, driven by a random wind.

It was mid-September. The last ships would depart for England at the end of October, just ahead of the Atlantic gales. Ought he to try to get Henry on one of them?

He had made the acquaintance of the local American officer in charge of prisoners of war billeted in Philadelphia and made an application for parole. This had been granted without difficulty; captured officers were normally paroled, save there was something unusual or dangerous about them, and Henry plainly was unlikely to attempt escape, foment rebellion, or support insurrection in his present state.

But he had not yet managed to arrange to have Henry exchanged, which status would permit Grey to move him back to England. Always assuming that Henry's health would stand the journey, and that Henry himself would be willing to go. Which it likely wouldn't, and Henry wasn't, he being so much attached to Mrs. Woodcock. Grey was quite willing to take her to England, too, but she wouldn't consider leaving, as she had heard that her husband had been taken prisoner in New York.

Grey rubbed two fingers between his brows, sighing. Could he force Henry aboard a naval vessel against his will—drugged, perhaps?—thus breaking his parole, ruining his career, and endangering his life, on the supposition that Grey could find a surgeon in England more capable than Dr. Rush of dealing with the situation? The best that could be hoped from such a course of action was that Henry would survive the journey long enough to say good-bye to his parents.

But if he did *not* undertake this drastic step, he was left with the choice of forcing Henry to submit to a horrifying surgery that he feared desperately and which was very likely to kill him—or watching the boy die by inches. Because he *was* dying; Grey saw it plainly. Sheer stubbornness and Mrs. Woodcock's nursing were all that were keeping him alive.

The thought of having to write to Hal and Minnie and tell them . . . No. He stood up abruptly, unable to bear more indecision. He would call upon Dr. Rush at once and make arrangements—

The front door slammed open, admitting a blast of wind, dead leaves, and his niece, pale-faced and round-eyed.

"Dottie!" His first, heart-stopping fear was that she had rushed home to tell him that Henry had died, for she had gone to visit her brother as she usually did every afternoon.

"Soldiers!" she gasped, clutching him by the arm. "There are soldiers in the street. Riders. Someone said Howe's army is coming! Advancing on Philadelphia!"

HOWE MET Washington's army at Brandywine Creek on September 11, some distance south of the city. Washington's troops were driven back, but rallied to make a stand a few days later. A tremendous rainstorm arose in the midst of the battle, though, putting an end to hostilities and allowing Washington's army to escape to Reading Furnace, leaving a small force behind under General Anthony Wayne at Paoli.

One of Howe's commanders, Major General Lord Charles Grey—a distant cousin of Grey's—attacked the Americans at Paoli at night, with orders to his troops to remove the flints from their muskets. This prevented discovery from the accidental discharge of a weapon, but also obliged the men to use bayonets. A number of Americans were bayoneted in their beds, their tents burned, a hundred or so made captive—and Howe marched into the city of Philadelphia, triumphant, on September 21.

Grey watched them, rank upon rank of redcoats, marching to drum music, from the porch of Mrs. Woodcock's house. Dottie had feared that the rebels, forced to abandon the city, might fire the houses or kill their British prisoners outright.

"Nonsense," Grey had said to this. "They are rebel Englishmen, not barbarians." Nonetheless, he had put on his own uniform and his sword, tucked two pistols into his belt, and spent twenty-four hours sitting on the porch of Mrs. Woodcock's house—with a lantern by night—coming down now and then to speak to any officer he knew who passed by, both to glean news of the situation and to ensure that the house remained unmolested.

The next day he returned to his own house, through streets of shuttered windows. Philadelphia was hostile, and so was the surrounding countryside. Still, the occupation of the city was peaceful—or as peaceful as a military occupation well can be. Congress had fled as Howe approached, and so had many of the more prominent rebels, including Dr. Benjamin Rush.

So had Percy Beauchamp.

72

THE FEAST OF ALL SAINTS

Lallybroch
October 20, 1980

B RIANNA PRESSED THE letter to her nose and inhaled deeply. So long after, she was sure it was imagination rather than odor, but still she sensed the faint aromas of smoke in the pages. Maybe it was memory as much as imagination; she knew what the air was like in an ordinary, full of the scents of hearthfire, roasting meat, and tobacco, with a mellow smell of beer beneath it all.

She felt silly smelling the letters in front of Roger but had developed the habit of sniffing them privately, when she read them over by herself. They'd opened this one the night before and had read it several times together, discussing it—but she'd got it out again now, wanting just to hold it privately and be alone with her parents for a bit.

Maybe the scent was really there. She'd noticed that you don't actually remember smells, not the same way you remember something you've seen. It's just that when you smell that smell again, you know what it is—and often it brings back a lot of other memories with it. And she was sitting here on a fall day, surrounded by the ripeness of apples and heather, the dust of ancient wood paneling, and the hollow smell of wet stone—Annie MacDonald had just mopped the hall—but she was seeing the front room of an eighteenth-century ordinary, and smelling smoke.

November 1, 1777
New York

Dear Bree, et al—

Do you remember the high school field trip when your economics class went to Wall Street? I am at the moment sitting in an ordinary at the foot of Wall Street, and neither a bull nor a bear to be seen, let alone a ticker-tape machine. No wall, either. A few goats, though, and a small cluster of men under a big leafless buttonwood tree, smoking pipes and conferring head-to-head. I can't tell whether they're Loyalists complaining, rebels plotting in public (which is, by the way, very much safer than doing it in private, though I do hope you won't need to make use of that bit of special knowledge), or simply merchants and traders—business is being done, I can tell that; hands shaken, bits of paper scribbled and exchanged. It's amazing how business thrives in wartime; I think it's because the normal rules—whatever they normally are—are suspended.

That's true of most human transactions, by the way. Hence the flowering of wartime romances and the founding of great fortunes in the wake of wars. It seems rather paradoxical—though maybe it's only logic (ask Roger whether there is such a thing as a logical paradox, will you?)—that a process so wasteful of lives and substance should then result in an explosion of babies and business.

Since I speak of war—we are all alive, and mostly intact. Your father was slightly wounded during the first battle at Saratoga (there were two, both very bloody), and I was obliged to remove the fourth finger of his right hand—the stiff one; you'll recall it. This was traumatic, of course (as much to me as to him, I think), but not altogether a disaster. It's healed very well, and while the hand is still giving him a good bit of pain, it's much more flexible and I think will be more useful to him overall.

We are—belatedly—about to take ship to Scotland, under rather peculiar circumstances. We are to sail tomorrow, on HMS Ariadne, accompanying the body of Brigadier General Simon Fraser. I met the brigadier very briefly before his death—he was dying at the time—but he was evidently a very good soldier and much beloved by his men. The British commander at Saratoga, John Burgoyne, asked as a sort of footnote to the surrender agreement that your father (he being a kinsman of the brigadier's and knowing where his family place in the Highlands is) take the body to Scotland, in accordance with the brigadier's wishes. This was unexpected, but rather fortuitous, to say the least. I can't think how we should have managed it otherwise, though your father says he would have thought of something.

The logistics of this expedition are a trifle delicate, as you might suppose. Mr. Kościuszko (known as "Kos" to his intimates, which includes your father—well, actually, he's known as "Kos" to everybody, because no one (other than your father) can pronounce his name, or cares to try. Your father's very fond of him and vice versa) offered his services, and with the aid of General Burgoyne's butler (doesn't everyone take their butler to war with them?), who supplied him with a great deal of lead foil from wine bottles (well, you really can't blame General Burgoyne if he's taken to drink, in the circumstances, though my general impression is that everyone on both sides drinks like a fish all of the time, regardless of the military situation of the moment), has produced a miracle of engineering: a lead-lined coffin (very necessary) on detachable wheels (also very necessary; the thing must weigh close to a ton—your father says no, it's only seven or eight hundredweight, but as he hasn't tried to lift it, I don't see how he would know).

General Fraser had been buried for a week or so and had to be exhumed for transport. It wasn't pleasant, but could have been worse. He had a number of Indian rangers, many of whom also esteemed him; some of these came to the unburying with a medicine person (I think it was a man but couldn't be sure; it was short and round and wore a bird mask), who incensed the remains heavily with burning sage and sweetgrass (not much help in terms of olfaction, but the smoke did draw a gentle veil over the more horrid aspects of the situation) and sang over him at some length. I should have liked to ask Ian what was being sung, but owing to an unpleasant set of circumstances that I won't go into here, he wasn't present.

I'll explain it all in a later letter; it's very complicated, and I must finish this before the sailing. The important points, in re Ian, are that he is in love with Rachel Hunter (who is a lovely young woman, and a Quaker, which presents some difficulties) and that he is technically a murderer and thus unable to appear in public in the vicinity of the Continental army. As a side result of the technical murder (a very unpleasant person, and no great loss to humanity, I assure you), Rollo was shot and injured (beyond the superficial bullet wound, he has a broken scapula; he should recover but can't be moved easily. Rachel is keeping him for Ian while we go to Scotland).

As the brigadier was known to be revered by his Indian associates, the Ariadne's *captain was startled, but not overly disturbed, to be informed that the body is being accompanied not only by his close kinsman (and wife) but by a Mohawk who speaks little English (I should be more than surprised if anyone in the royal navy can tell the difference between Gaelic and Mohawk, come to that).*

I hope this attempt is rather less eventful than our first voyage. If so, the next letter should be written in Scotland. Keep your fingers crossed.

All my love,
Mama

P.S. Your father insists upon adding a few words to this. This will be his first try at writing with his altered hand, and I would like to watch to see how it's working, but he instructs me firmly that he requires privacy. I don't know whether this is to do with his subject matter or simply with the fact that he doesn't want anyone to see him struggle. Both, probably.

The third page of the letter was markedly different. The writing was much larger than usual, and more sprawling. Still identifiably her father's hand, but the letters seemed looser, less jagged somehow. She felt her heart twist, not only from the thought of her father's mutilated hand, slowly drawing each letter—but for what he had thought it worth so much effort to write:

My Dearest,

Your Brother is alive, and unwounded. I saw him march out from Saratoga with his Troops, bound for Boston and eventually England. He will not fight again in this War. Deo gratias.

Your most loving Father,
JF

Postscriptum: It is the Feast of All Saints. Pray for me.

The nuns had always told them—and she'd told him. By saying an Our Father, a Hail Mary, and a Glory Be on the Feast of All Saints, you can obtain the release of a soul from purgatory.

"You bloody man," she muttered, sniffing ferociously and fumbling in her desk for a tissue. "I knew you'd make me cry. *Again*."

"BRIANNA?"

Roger's voice came from the kitchen, surprising her. She hadn't expected him to come down from the chapel ruins for another hour or two, and she blew her nose hastily, calling, "Coming!" and hoping that the recent tears didn't show in her voice. It was only as she hit the corridor and saw him holding the green baize door to the kitchen half open that it occurred to her that there had been something odd about his voice, as well.

"What is it?" she said, hastening her step. "The kids—"

"They're fine," he interrupted. "I told Annie to take them down to the post office in the village for an ice cream." He stepped away from the door then and beckoned her to enter.

She stopped dead, just inside the door. A man was leaning back against the old stone sink, arms folded. He straightened up when he saw her and bowed, in a way that struck her as terribly odd and yet familiar. Before she could think why that should be, he straightened again and said, "Your servant, ma'am," in a soft Scottish voice.

She looked straight into eyes that were the twins of Roger's, then glanced wildly *at* Roger, just to be sure. Yes, they were.

"Who—"

"Allow me to introduce William Buccleigh MacKenzie," Roger said, a distinct edge in his voice. "Also known as the Nuckelavee."

For an instant, none of this made any sense whatever. Then things—astonishment, fury, disbelief—came flooding into her mind at such a rate that none of them could make it to her mouth, and she simply gaped at the man.

"I'll ask your pardon, ma'am, for frightening your weans," the man said. "I'd nay notion they were yours, for the one thing. I ken what weans are like, though, and I didna wish to be discovered before I'd made some sense of it all."

"All . . . *what*?" Brianna finally found a couple of words. The man smiled, very slightly.

"Aye, well. As to that, I think you and your husband may know better than I."

Brianna pulled out a chair and sat down rather abruptly, motioning to the man to do the same. As he came forward into the light from the window, she saw that there was a graze on his cheekbone—a prominent cheekbone, and one that with the modeling of his temple and eye socket seemed terribly familiar; the man himself seemed familiar. But of course he was, she thought dazedly.

"Does he know who he is?" she asked, turning to Roger. Who, now that she noticed, was nursing his right hand, which appeared to have blood on the knuckles. He nodded.

"I told him. Not sure he believes me, though."

The kitchen was its usual solid, homely place, peaceful with the autumn sun coming in and the blue-checkered dish towels hung on the Aga. But now it felt like the backside of Jupiter, and when she reached for the sugar bowl, she would not have been at all surprised to see her hand pass through it.

"I should be inclined to believe a good deal more today than I should have been three months ago," the man said, with a dry intonation that held some faint echo of her father's voice.

She shook her head violently, in hopes of clearing it, and said, "Would you like some coffee?" in a polite voice that could have belonged to a sitcom housewife.

His face lightened at that, and he smiled. His teeth were stained and a little crooked. *Well, of course they are,* she thought with remarkable lucidity. *No dentists to speak of in the eighteenth century.* The thought of the eighteenth century sent her surging to her feet.

"You!" she exclaimed. "*You* got Roger hanged!"

"I did," he said, not looking very perturbed. "Not that I meant to. And if he likes to strike me again for it, I'll let him. But—"

"That was for scaring the kids," Roger said with equal dryness. "The hanging . . . we'll maybe talk about that a bit later."

"Fine talk for a minister," the man said, looking faintly amused. "Not that most ministers go about interfering wi' a man's wife."

"I—" Roger began, but she interrupted him.

"*I'll* bloody hit you," Brianna said, glaring at the man. Who, to her annoyance, squinched his eyes shut and leaned forward, features clenched.

"All right," he said, through compressed lips. "Go ahead."

"Not in the face," Roger advised, surveying a bruised knuckle. "Make him stand up and go for his balls."

William Buccleigh's eyes popped open, and he looked reproachfully at Roger. "D'ye think she needs advice?"

"I think *you* need a fat lip," she told him, but sat slowly down again, eyeing him. She took a breath down to her toenails and let it out.

"Right," she said, more or less calmly. "Start talking."

He nodded cautiously and touched the bruise on his cheekbone, wincing a little.

Son of a witch, she thought suddenly. *Does he know that?*

"Did ye not mention coffee?" he asked, sounding a little wistful. "I havena had real coffee in years."

HE WAS FASCINATED by the Aga and pressed his backside against it, fairly shivering with delight.

"Oh, sweet Virgin," he breathed, eyes closed as he reveled in the heat. "Is it not the lovely thing."

The coffee he pronounced good in itself but rather feeble—reasonable, Brianna thought, knowing that such coffee as he was used to was boiled over a fire, often for several hours, rather than gently perked. He apologized for his manners, which were actually fine, saying that he hadn't eaten in some little while.

"How have ye been feeding yourself?" Roger asked, eyeing the steadily diminishing pile of peanut-butter-and-jelly sandwiches.

"Stole from cottages, to begin with," Buccleigh admitted frankly. "After a bit, I found my way to Inverness and was sittin' on the curb of the street, quite dazed by the huge great roaring things goin' by me—I'd seen the cars on the road north, of course, but it's different when they're whizzin' past your shins. Anyway, I'd sat down outside the High Street Church, for I knew that place, at least, and thought I'd go and ask the minister for a bite of bread when I'd got myself a bit more in hand. I was that wee bit rattled, ken," he said, leaning confidentially toward Brianna.

"I suppose so," she murmured, and lifted an eyebrow at Roger. "Old High St. Stephen's?"

"Aye, it was the High Church—meaning on the High Street, not Anglican—before it was Old, or joined congregations with St. Stephen's." He switched his attention to William Buccleigh. "Did ye, then? Speak to the minister? Dr. Weatherspoon?"

Buccleigh nodded, mouth full.

"He saw me sitting there and came out to me, the kind man. Asked was I in need, and when I assured him I was, he told me where to go for food and a bed, and I went there. An aid society, they called it, a charity, and it surely was."

The people who ran the aid society had given him clothes—"for what I had on was little more than rags"—and helped him to find a job doing rough labor for a dairy farm outside the town.

"So why are ye not on the dairy farm?" Roger asked, at the same moment that Brianna asked, "But how did you come to Scotland?" Their words colliding, they stopped, gesturing to each other to continue, but William Buccleigh waved a hand at them both and chewed rapidly for a moment, then swallowed several times and gulped more coffee.

"Mother of God, that stuff's tasty, but it sticks in your craw. Aye, ye want to know why I'm here in your kitchen eating your food and not dead in a creek in North Carolina."

"Since you mention it, yes," said Roger, leaning back in his chair. "Start with North Carolina, why don't you?"

Buccleigh nodded once more, leaned back in turn with his hands linked comfortably over his stomach, and began.

HE'D BEEN STARVED out of Scotland, like so many folk after Culloden, and had scraped together the money to emigrate with his wife and infant son.

"I know," Roger said. "It was me you asked to save them, on the ship. The night the captain put the sick ones over the rail."

Buccleigh looked up, startled, green eyes wide.

"Was it, then? I didna see ye at all, in the dark and me desperate. If I'd kent that . . ." He trailed off, then shook his head. "Well, what's done is done."

"It is," Roger said. "I couldn't see you in the dark, either. I only kent ye later, because of your wife and son, when I met them again at Alaman-k." To his intense annoyance, the last sound caught in his throat with a glottal click. He cleared it and repeated evenly, "At Alamance."

Buccleigh nodded slowly, eyes fastened with interest on Roger's throat. Was that regret in his eyes? Probably not, Roger thought. He hadn't thanked him for saving his wife and child, either.

"Aye. Well, I'd thought to take land and farm it, but . . . well, the long and the short of it was, I wasna much of a farmer. Nor a builder. Didna ken the first thing about the wilderness, not much more about crops. Not a hunter, either. We would ha' starved, surely, had I not taken Morag and Jem—that's my son's name, too, is that not strange?—back down to the piedmont and scraped a little work on a wee turpentine plantation there."

"Stranger than you know," Bree said, half under her breath. And a little louder, "So?"

"So the fellow I worked for turned out for the Regulation, and those of us on the place went, too. I should have left Morag behind, but there was a fellow on the place who had a hot eye for her—he was the blacksmith and had but one leg, so he'd not be coming with us to the fight. I couldna leave her to him, so she and the wean came with me. Where the next fellow she meets is *you*," he said pointedly.

"Did she not tell ye who I was?" Roger asked testily.

"Well, she did, then," Buccleigh admitted. "She'd said about the ship and all, and said that was you. Even so," he added, giving Roger a hard eye, "d'ye go about makin' love to other men's wives regular, or was it just Morag took your fancy?"

"Morag is my five—or maybe only four—times great-grandmother," Roger said evenly. He fixed Buccleigh with a stare equal to the other man's. "And since you asked me who ye are—you're my grandda. Five or six times back. My son's named Jeremiah after my da, who was named for his grandda—who was named for *your* son. I think," he added. "I might be missing one or two Jeremiahs along the way."

Buccleigh stared at him, stubbled face gone quite blank. He blinked once or twice, glanced at Brianna, who nodded, then returned his stare to Roger, carefully scrutinizing his face.

"Look at his eyes," Brianna said helpfully. "Shall I bring you a mirror?"

Buccleigh's mouth opened as though to answer, but he found no words and shook his head as though dislodging flies. He picked up his cup, stared into it for a moment as though astonished to find it empty, and set it down. Then looked at Brianna.

"Ye wouldna have anything in the house stronger than coffee, would ye, *a bhana-mhaighstir?*"

IT TOOK ROGER a little rummaging in his study to find the genealogical table the Reverend had drawn up years before. While he was gone, Bree found the bottle of Oban and poured William Buccleigh a generous glass.

With no hesitation, she poured for herself and Roger, as well, and put a jug of water on the table.

"Do you take a little water?" she asked politely. "Or do you like it neat?"

Rather to her surprise, he reached at once for the water and splashed a little into the whisky. He saw her expression and smiled.

"If it was the rotgut, I'd throw it down. Whisky worth drinking, a little water opens the flavor. But ye ken that, don't ye? Ye're no Scots, though."

"Yes, I am," she said. "On my father's side. His name is—was—James Fraser, of Lallybroch. They called him the Dunbonnet."

He blinked, looked round the kitchen, then back at her.

"Are you . . . another, then?" he said. "Like your husband and me. Another of—whatever it is?"

"Whatever it is," she agreed. "And yes. You knew my father?"

He shook his head, closing his eyes as he sipped, and took a moment to reply while the whisky made its way down.

"Dear Lord, that's good," he breathed, and opened his eyes. "Nay, I was born only a year or so before Culloden. I heard of the Dunbonnet, though, when I was a lad."

"You said you weren't much of a farmer," Bree said curiously. "What did you do in Scotland, before you left?"

He took a deep breath and let it out through his nose, in just the way her father did. *A MacKenzie thing,* she thought, entertained.

"I was a lawyer," he said abruptly, and picked up his glass.

"Well, there's a useful profession," Roger said, coming in in time to hear this. He eyed Buccleigh contemplatively, then shook his head and spread out the MacKenzie family tree on the tabletop.

"There you are," he said, putting a finger on the relevant entry, then moved a finger down the page. "And there I am." Buccleigh blinked at it, then bent closer to study it in silence. Brianna saw his throat move as he swallowed once or twice. His face was pale beneath the stubble when he looked up.

"Aye, those are my parents, my grandparents. And there's wee Jem—my Jem—where he should be, right enough. I've another child, though," he said suddenly, turning to Bree. "Or I think I have. Morag was breeding when I—when I—went."

Roger sat down. His face had lost a little of the angry wariness, and he regarded William Buccleigh with what might be sympathy.

"Tell us that bit," he suggested. "How you went."

Buccleigh pushed across his empty whisky glass but didn't wait for it to be refilled.

The owner of the plantation he'd worked on had been ruined in the wake of Alamance, gaoled for taking part in the Regulation and his property confiscated. The MacKenzies had drifted for a time, having no money and no home, no close kin who might help them.

Brianna exchanged a quick glance with Roger. Had Buccleigh known it, he was within a short distance of close kin—and wealthy kin, at that. Jocasta Cameron was Dougal MacKenzie's sister—this man's aunt. If he knew it.

She raised her brows in silent question to Roger, but he shook his head slightly. Let that wait.

At last, Buccleigh said, they'd made the decision to go back to Scotland. Morag had family there, a brother in Inverness who'd done well for himself, was a prosperous corn chandler. Morag had written to him, and he had urged them to come back, saying he would find a place for William in his business.

"At that point, I should ha' been glad of a place shoveling dung out of the holds of cattle ships," Buccleigh admitted with a sigh. "Ephraim—that's Morag's brother, Ephraim Gunn—said he thought he might have use for a clerk, though. And I *can* write a fair hand and do sums."

The lure of work—work that he was well equipped to do—and a place to live was strong enough to make the little family willing to embark once more on the perilous Atlantic voyage. Ephraim had sent a draft on his bank for their passage, and so they had come back, landing in Edinburgh, and from there had made their slow way north.

"By wagon, for the most part." Buccleigh was on his third glass of whisky, Brianna and Roger not so far behind. He poured a little water into his empty glass and swished it round his mouth before swallowing, to clear his throat, then coughed and went on.

"The wagon broke down—again—near the place they call Craigh na Dun. I'm thinking the two of ye will know it?" He glanced back and forth between them, and they nodded. "Aye. Well, Morag wasna feeling all that peart, and the bairn was peely-wally, too, so they lay down in the grass to sleep a bit whilst the wheel was mending. The drover had a mate and didna need my help, so I set off to stretch my legs."

"And you climbed the hill, to the stones," Brianna said, her own chest feeling tight at the thought.

"Do you know what date it was?" Roger broke in.

"Summer," William Buccleigh said slowly. "Near Midsummer Day, but I couldna swear to the day exactly. Why?"

"The summer solstice," Brianna said, and hiccuped slightly. "It's—we think it's open. The—whatever it is—on the sun feasts and the fire feasts."

The sound of a car coming down the drive came faintly to them, and all three looked up as though surprised in some furtive business.

"Annie and the kids. What are we going to do with him?" she asked Roger.

He glanced with narrowed eyes at Buccleigh for an instant, then made up his mind. "We'll need a bit of thought to explain ye," Roger said, rising. "Just for the moment, though—come with me, aye?"

Buccleigh stood at once and followed Roger into the scullery. She heard Buccleigh's voice rise in momentary astonishment, a brief mutter of explanation from Roger, then the grating noise as they moved the bench that hid the access panel covering the priest's hole.

Moving as if in a trance, Brianna rose hastily to clear and wash the three glasses, to put away the whisky and water. Hearing the knocker go against the front door, she jumped a little. Not the kids, after all. Who could that be?

She swept the family tree off the table and hurried down the hall, pausing to toss it onto Roger's desk as she made her way to the door.

How old is he? she thought abruptly, as she reached for the handle. *He looks to be in his late thirties, maybe, but—*

"Hi," said Rob Cameron, looking faintly alarmed at the look on her face. "Have I come at a bad time, then?"

ROB HAD COME to bring back a book Roger had lent him and to deliver an invitation: would Jem like to come to the pictures with Bobby on the Friday, then have a nice fish supper and spend the night?

"I'm sure he would," Brianna said. "But he's not—oh, there he is." Annie had just driven up, with a clashing of gears that made the engine die in the driveway. Brianna shuddered slightly, pleased that Annie hadn't taken *her* car.

By the time the kids had been extracted from the car, wiped off, and made to shake hands politely with Mr. Cameron, Roger had come out from the back of the house and was at once drawn into a conversation about his efforts on the chapel, which went on to such an extent that it became obvious that it was supper-time, and it would have been rude not to ask him to stay...

And so Brianna found herself scrambling eggs and heating beans and frying potatoes in a sort of daze, thinking of their uninvited guest under the scullery floor, who must be smelling the cooking and dying of hunger—and *what* on earth were they going to do with him?

All the time they ate, making pleasant conversation, herding the kids off to bed while Roger and Rob talked Pictish stones and archaeological excavations in the Orkneys, she found her mind dwelling on William Buccleigh MacKenzie.

The Orkneys, she thought. *Roger said the Nuckelavee is an Orkney ghoulie. Has he been in the Orkneys? When? And why the bloody hell was he hanging round our broch all this time? When he found what had happened, why didn't he just go right back? What is he doing here?*

By the time Rob took his leave—and another book—with profuse thanks for the food and a reminder of the movie date on Friday, she was prepared to haul William Buccleigh out of the priest's hole by the scruff of the neck, drive him straight to Craigh na Dun herself, and stuff him bodily into a stone.

But when he finally clambered out, moving slowly, white-faced and clearly hungry, she found her agitation lessening. Just a little. She made fresh eggs for him, quickly, and sat with him while Roger went round the house, checking doors and windows.

"Though I suppose we needn't worry so much about that," she observed caustically, "since you're *inside* now."

He looked up, tired but wary.

"I did say I was sorry," he said softly. "D'ye want me to go?"

"And where *would* you go, if I said yes?" she asked unkindly.

He turned his face toward the window over the kitchen sink. In the daylight, it looked out on peace, on the kailyard with its worn wooden gate and the pasture beyond. Now there was nothing out there but the black of a moonless Highland night. The sort of night when Christians stayed indoors and put holy water on the doorposts, because the things that walked the moors and the high places were not always holy.

He didn't say anything but swallowed, and she saw the fair hairs on his forearms rise.

"You don't have to go," she said, gruff. "We'll find you a bed. But tomorrow..."

He bobbed his head, not looking at her, and made to rise. She stopped him with a hand on his arm and he looked at her, startled, his eyes dark in the quiet light.

"Just tell me one thing now," she said. "Do you want to go back?"

"Oh, God, yes," he said, and turned his head away, but his voice was thick. "I want Morag. I want my wee lad."

She let go of his wrist and stood up, but another thought had occurred to her.

"How old are you?" she asked abruptly, and he shrugged, brushing the back of his wrist across his eyes.

"Eight and thirty," he said. "Why?"

"Just...curious," she said, and moved to turn the Aga's heat down to its nighttime setting. "Come with me; I'll make you a bed in the parlor. Tomorrow we'll—we'll see."

She led him down the hall past Roger's study, and in her stomach was a ball of ice. The light was on, and the family tree Roger had taken out to show William Buccleigh was still where she'd tossed it, on the desk. Had he seen the date? She thought not—or if he had, he hadn't noticed. The dates of birth and death weren't listed for everyone on that table—but they were for him. William Buccleigh MacKenzie had died, according to that table, at age thirty-eight.

He won't get back, she thought, and the ice rose up around her heart.

LOCH ERROCHTY LAY dull as pewter under a lowering sky. They were standing on the footbridge across Alt Ruighe nan Saorach, the river that fed the loch, looking down to where the man-made loch spread itself between the smooth hills. Buck—he'd said that was what folk called him in America, and he'd got used to it—looked and looked, his face a study in amazement and dismay.

"Down there," he said softly, pointing. "See where that wee burn comes down into it? That's where my auntie Ross's house stood. About a hundred feet below the burn."

About thirty feet below the surface of the loch now.

"I imagine it's something of a wrench," Brianna said, not without sympathy. "To see things so changed."

"It is that." He glanced at her, those eyes, so unsettlingly like Roger's, quick in his face. "It's maybe more that so much *hasna* changed. Up there, aye?" He lifted his chin toward the distant mountains. "Just like they always were. And the wee birds in the grass, and the salmon jumping in the river. I could set foot on yon shore"—he nodded toward the end of the footbridge— "and feel as though I had walked there yesterday. I *did* walk there yesterday! And yet...all the people are gone.

"All of them," he ended softly. "Morag. My children. They're all dead. Unless I can go back."

She hadn't planned to ask him anything; better to wait until she and Roger could talk to him together in the evening after the kids were down. But the opportunity offered itself. Roger had driven Buck around the Highlands near Lallybroch, down the Great Glen along Loch Ness, and finally dropped him off at the Loch Errochty dam, where she was working today; she'd drive him back with her for supper.

They'd argued—in whispers—about it the night before. Not about what to say about him; he'd be Daddy's relative, come for a short visit. That was the truth, after all. But whether to take him into the tunnel. Roger had been in favor of this, she very much against, remembering the shock of the ... timeline? ... cutting through her like a sharpened wire. She still hadn't decided.

But now he'd brought up the subject of going back, on his own.

"When you came to yourself after you ... came through, and realized what had happened," she asked curiously, "why didn't you go back into the circle right then?"

He shrugged.

"I did. Though I canna say that I realized straight off what *had* happened. I didna come to that for some days. But I kent something terrible had happened and the stones were to do wi' it. So I was wary of them, as I imagine ye can understand." He quirked an eyebrow at her, and she nodded reluctantly.

She *could* understand. She wouldn't go within a mile of a standing stone herself, unless it was to save some member of her family from a horrible fate. And even then she might think twice. She dismissed the thought, though, and returned to her interrogation.

"But you did go back, you said. What happened?"

He looked helplessly at her, spreading his hands.

"I dinna ken how to describe it to ye. Nothing like that's ever happened to me before."

"Try," she suggested, hardening her voice, and he sighed.

"Aye. Well, I walked up to the circle, and this time I could hear them—the stones. Talking to themselves, like, buzzing like a hive of bees, and with a sound in it made the hairs stand up on my nape."

He'd wanted to turn and run then, but with thought of Morag and Jemmy in his mind, had determined to push on. He'd walked into the center of the circle, where the sound assailed him from all sides.

"I thought I'd lose my mind from it," he said frankly. "Putting my fingers in my ears did nay good at all; it was inside me, like as if 'twas comin' from my bones. Was it like that for you?" he asked suddenly, peering at her curiously.

"Yes, it was," she answered shortly. "Or close enough. Go on. What did you do then?"

He'd seen the big cleft stone he'd gone through the first time and, taking as deep a breath as he could hold, had lunged through it.

"And ye can skin me for a liar if ye like," he assured her. "I canna for the life of me tell ye what happened next, but after it did, I was lyin' on the grass in the midst of the stones, and I was on fire."

She looked at him, startled.

"Literally? I mean, were your clothes burning, or was it just—"

"I ken what 'literally' means," he said, with an edge in his voice. "I may not be what you are, but I *was* educated."

"Sorry." She made a small apologetic nod and gestured to him to go on.

"Anyway, aye, I was *literally* on fire. My shirt was in flames. Here—" He unzipped his wind-cheater and fumbled with the buttons of Roger's blue cambric shirt, pulling the edges apart to show her the sprawling reddish mark of a healing burn on his chest. He would have buttoned it again at once, but she motioned him not to and bent to look closer. It seemed to be centered on his heart. Was that significant? she wondered.

"Thank you," she said, straightening up. "What—what were you thinking about when you went through?"

He stared at her.

"I was thinking I wanted to get back, what else?"

"Yes, of course. But were you thinking of someone in particular? Of Morag, I mean, or your Jem?"

The most extraordinary expression—shame? embarrassment?—crossed his face, and he looked away.

"I was," he said briefly, and she knew he lied but couldn't think why. He coughed and went on hurriedly.

"Well, so. I rolled upon the grass to put it out, and then I was sick. I lay there for a good while, not having the strength to rise. I dinna ken how long, but a long time. Ye ken what it's like here, close to Midsummer Day? That milky light when ye canna see the sun, but it's not really set?"

"The summer dim," she murmured. "Aye—I mean, yes, I know. So did you try again?"

It *was* shame now. The sun was low and the clouds glowed a dull orange that washed loch and hills and bridge in a sullen flush, but it was still possible to make out the darker flush that spread across his broad cheekbones.

"No," he muttered. "I was afraid."

Despite her distrust of him and her lingering anger over what he'd done to Roger, she felt an involuntary spurt of sympathy at the admission. After all, both she and Roger had *known*, more or less, what they were getting into. He hadn't expected what happened at all and still knew almost nothing.

"I would have been, too," she said. "Did you—"

A shout from behind interrupted her, and she turned to see Rob Cameron bounding along the riverbank. He waved and came up onto the bridge, puffing a little from the run.

"Hi, boss," he said, grinning at her. "Saw ye on my way out. If ye're off the clock, I thought would ye fancy a drink on the way home? And your friend, too, of course," he added, with a friendly nod toward William Buccleigh.

With that, of course, she had no alternative but to introduce them, passing Buck off with their agreed-on story: Roger's relative, staying with them, just in town briefly. She politely declined the offer of a drink, saying that she must get home for the kids' supper.

"Another time, then," Rob said lightly. "Nice to meet ye, pal." He bounded off again, light-footed as a gazelle, and she turned to find William Buccleigh looking after him with narrowed eye.

"What?" she demanded.

"Yon man's got a hot eye for you," he said abruptly, turning to her. "Does your husband know?"

"Don't be ridiculous," she said, just as abruptly. Her heart had sped up at his words, and she didn't like it. "I work with him. He's in the lodge with Roger, and they talk about old songs. That's all."

He made one of those Scottish noises that can convey all manner of indelicate meaning and shook his head.

"I may not be what you are," he repeated, smiling unpleasantly. "But I'm no a fool, either."

ONE EWE LAMB
RETURNS TO THE FOLD

November 24, 1777
Philadelphia

LORD JOHN GREY desperately needed a valet. He had employed a person so described but found the man worse than useless, and a thief to boot. He had discovered the erstwhile valet slipping teaspoons down his breeches and had—after forcibly extracting the spoons—dismissed him. He should, he supposed, have had the man arrested, but really was not sure what the local constable would do if summoned by a British officer.

Most of the British prisoners of war had been taken out of the city as Howe's army advanced, the Americans wishing to keep them for exchange. Henry had not.

He brushed his own uniform, grimly considering. He wore it daily now, as protection for Dottie and Henry. He had not been an actively serving officer for years but, unlike most men in that position, had not resigned his lieutenant-colonel's commission, either. He wasn't sure what Hal would have done had he *tried* to resign, but since it was a commission in Hal's own regiment and Grey didn't need to sell it, the point was moot.

One of the buttons was loose. He took the hussif out of his kit, threaded a needle without squinting, and whipped the button tightly to the coat. The action gave him a small feeling of satisfaction, though acknowledging it made him admit just how little he felt he could control these days—so little that sewing on a button should seem cause for satisfaction.

He frowned at himself in the glass and twitched irritably at the gold lace on his coat, which was tarnished in places. He did know what to do about that, but damned if he was going to sit polishing it up with a lump of urine-soaked bread. Knowing General Sir William Howe as he did, he doubted that his own appearance would affect his reception, even should he roll up to Howe's headquarters in a sedan chair with his head wrapped in a Turkish turban. Howe frequently didn't bathe or change his linen for a month or more—and not only when in the field.

Still. It would have to be an army surgeon, and Grey wanted his pick of them. He grimaced at the thought. He had known too many army surgeons, some of them at unpleasantly close range. But Howe's army had come into the city in late September. It was mid-November now, the occupation was well established, and with it a general animus among the citizenry.

Those physicians of a rebellious bent had either left the city or would have nothing to do with a British officer. Those with Loyalist sympaties would have been more than happy to oblige him—he was invited to many parties given by the wealthy Loyalists of the city and had been introduced to two or three physicians there—but he had found none with any reputation for surgery. One dealt mostly with cases of venereal disease, another was an *accoucheur,* and the third was plainly a quacksalver of the worst sort.

So he was bound for Howe's headquarters, to beg assistance. He couldn't wait any longer; Henry had held his own and even seemed to gain a bit of strength with the cooling of the weather. Better it was done now, to give him a chance to heal a little before the winter came with its chill and the fetid squalor of closed houses.

Ready, he buckled on his sword and stepped out into the street. There was a soldier, half bowed under a heavy rucksack, walking slowly along the street toward him, looking at the houses. He barely glanced at the man as he came down the steps—but a glance was enough. He looked again, incredulous, and then ran down the street, heedless of hat, gold lace, sword, or dignity, and seized the tall young soldier in his arms.

"Willie!"

"Papa!"

His heart overflowed in a most remarkable way; he could seldom remember being so happy but did his best to contain it, not wanting to embarrass Willie with unmanly excesses of emotion. He didn't let go of his son but stood back a little, looking him up and down.

"You're ... dirty," he said, unable to repress a large, foolish grin. "Very dirty indeed." He was. Also tattered and threadbare. He still wore his officer's gorget, but his stock was missing, as were several buttons, and one cuff of his coat was torn quite away.

"I have lice, too," Willie assured him, scratching. "Is there any food?"

"Yes, of course. Come in, come in." He took the rucksack off Willie's shoulder and beckoned him to follow. "Dottie!" he shouted up the stairs as he pushed open the door. "Dottie! Come down!"

"I *am* down," his niece said behind him, coming out of the day parlor, where she was accustomed to breakfast. She had a piece of buttered toast in her hand. "What do you—oh, *Willie!*"

Disregarding questions of filth and lice, William swept her up in his arms, and she dropped the toast on the carpet and squeezed him round the body, laughing and crying, until he protested that she had cracked all his ribs and he should never breathe easy again.

Grey stood watching this with the utmost benevolence, even though they had quite trampled the buttered toast into the rented carpet. They really *did* appear to love each other, he reflected. Maybe he'd been wrong. He coughed politely, which did not disentangle them but did at least make Dottie look blankly over her shoulder at him.

"I'll go and order some breakfast for William, shall I?" he said. "Take him into the parlor, why don't you, my dear, and give him a dish of tea."

"Tea," Willie breathed, his face assuming the beatific air of one beholding—or being told about—some prodigious miracle. "I haven't had tea in weeks. Months!"

Grey went out to the cookhouse, this standing at a little distance behind the house proper so that the latter should not be destroyed when—not if—something caught fire and burned the cookhouse to the ground. Appetizing smells of fried meat and stewed fruit and fresh bread floated out of this ramshackle structure.

He had employed Mrs. Figg, a nearly spherical black woman, as cook, on the assumption that she could not have gained such a figure without having both an appreciation of good food and the ability to cook it. In this assumption he had been proved right, and not even that lady's uncertain temperament and taste for foul language made him regret his decision, though it did make him approach her warily. Hearing his news, though, she obligingly put aside the game pie she was making in order to assemble a tea tray.

He waited to take this back himself, meaning to give William and Dottie a little time alone together. He wanted to hear everything—for of course everyone in Philadelphia knew about Burgoyne's disastrous meeting at Saratoga, but he particularly wanted to find out from William what John Burgoyne had known or understood beforehand. According to some of his military acquaintances, Sir George Germain had assured Burgoyne that his plan had been accepted and that Howe would march north to meet him, cutting the American colonies in half. According to others—several of Howe's staff among them—Howe had never been apprised of this plan in the first place, let alone consented to it.

Was this arrogance and presumptuousness on Burgoyne's part, obstinacy and pride on Howe's, idiocy and incompetence on Germain's—or some combination of all three? If pressed, he'd place his wager on this last possibility, but was curious to know how deeply Germain's office might have been involved. With Percy Beauchamp vanished from Philadelphia, leaving not a wrack behind, his further movements would have to be observed by someone else, and Arthur Norrington was likely to communicate his own findings to Germain rather than to Grey.

He carried the loaded tray carefully back, to find William on the sofa in his shirtsleeves drinking tea, his hair unbound and loose on his shoulders.

Dottie was sitting in the wing chair before the fire, holding her silver comb on her knee, and with a look on her face that nearly made Grey drop the tray.

She turned a startled face on him as he came in, so blank that it was clear she barely saw him. Then something changed and her face altered, like one coming back in a twinkling from somewhere leagues away.

"Here," she said, rising at once and reaching for the tray. "Let me have that."

He did, covertly glancing between the two young people. Sure enough, Willie looked odd, too. Why? he wondered. They had been excited, thrilled, exuberantly affectionate with each other a few moments before. Now she was pale but trembling with an inner excitement that made the cups rattle in their saucers as she began to pour out tea. *He* was flushed where she was pale, but not—Grey was almost sure—with any sort of sexual excitement. He had the look of a man who . . . well, no. It *was* sexual excitement, he thought, intrigued—he had, after all, seen it often and was a keen observer of it in men—but it wasn't focused on Dottie. Not at all.

What the devil are they up to? he thought. He affected to ignore their distraction, though, and sat down to drink tea and hear Willie's experiences.

The telling calmed William a little. Grey watched William's face change as he talked, sometimes haltingly, and felt a deep pang at seeing it. Pride, yes, great pride; William was a man now, a soldier, and a good one. But Grey had also a lurking regret for the disappearance of the last traces of Willie's innocence; the briefest look at his eyes proved that had gone.

The accounts of battle, politics, Indians, all had the opposite effect on Dottie, he saw. Far from being calmed or happy, she grew more visibly agitated by the moment.

"I was about to go to visit Sir William, but I think I'll go see Henry first," Grey said at last, rising and brushing toast crumbs from the skirts of his coat. "Do you want to come with me, Willie? Or the both of you, for that matter? Or would you rather rest?"

They exchanged a look in which complicity and plotting were so evident that he blinked. Willie coughed and stood up, too.

"Yes, Papa. I do want to see Henry, of course. But Dottie has just been telling me how grave his state is—and about your intent to get an army surgeon to deal with it. I was . . . thinking . . . I know an army surgeon. A most excellent fellow. Very knowing, and wonderfully gentle in his manner—but quick as a snake with his blade," he hastened to add. His color had risen remarkably, saying this, and Grey viewed him with fascination.

"Really," Grey said slowly. "He sounds an answer to prayer. What is his name? I could ask Sir William—"

"Oh, he's not with Sir William," Willie said hastily.

"Oh, one of Burgoyne's men?" The paroled soldiers of Burgoyne's defeated army had all—with exceptions like William—marched to Boston, there to embark for England. "Well, I would of course like to have him, but I doubt we can send to Boston for him and have him come in a timely fashion, given the time of year and the likelihood—"

"No, he's not in Boston." Willie exchanged another of those looks with Dottie. She caught Grey watching them this time, went red as the roses on the teacups, and looked sedulously at her toes. Willie cleared his throat.

"In fact, he is a Continental surgeon. But Washington's army has gone into winter quarters at Valley Forge—that's no more than a day's ride. He will come if I go in person to ask him, I am sure of it."

"I see," Grey said, thinking rapidly. He was sure that he didn't see the half of it—whatever "it" was—but on the face of things, this did seem an answer to prayer. It would be a simple matter to ask Howe to arrange an escort and a flag of truce for Willie, as well as a guarantee of safe passage for the surgeon.

"All right," he said, making up his mind on the moment. "I'll speak to Sir William about it this afternoon."

Dottie and Willie gave identical sighs—of relief? *What the devil?* he thought yet again.

"Right, then," he said briskly. "Come to think, you'll wish to wash and change, Willie. I'll go to Howe's headquarters now, and we'll see Henry this afternoon. What is the name of this famous Continental surgeon, that I may have Sir William write a pass for him?"

"Hunter," said Willie, and his sunburned face seemed to glow. "Denzell Hunter. Be sure to tell Sir William to write the pass for two; Dr. Hunter's sister is his nurse—he'll need her to come along and help."

74

TWENTY–TWENTY

December 20, 1777
Edinburgh

T HE PRINT ON THE PAGE sprang into focus, clear and black, and I exclaimed in startlement.

"Ah, close, then?" Mr. Lewis, the spectacle-maker, twinkled at me over his own spectacles. "Try these." He gently removed the trial spectacles from my nose and handed me another pair. I put them on, examined the page of the book before me, then looked up.

"I had no idea," I said, amazed and delighted. It was like being reborn; everything was fresh, new, crisp, and vivid. I had suddenly reentered the half-forgotten world of fine print.

Jamie stood by the shop's window, book in hand and a handsome pair of steel-rimmed square spectacles on his long nose. They gave him a most unaccustomed scholarly air, and he looked for a moment like a distinguished stranger, until he turned to look at me, his eyes slightly magnified behind the lenses. He shifted his gaze over the top of them and smiled at sight of me.

"I like those," he said with approval. "The round ones suit your face, Sassenach."

I had been so taken with the new detail of the world around me that it hadn't even occurred to me to wonder what *I* looked like. Curious, I got up and came to peer into the small looking glass hung on the wall.

"Goodness," I said, recoiling slightly. Jamie laughed, and Mr. Lewis smiled indulgently.

"They are most becoming to you, ma'am," he said.

"Well, possibly," I said, warily examining the stranger's reflection in the glass. "It's just rather a shock." It wasn't really that I'd forgotten what I looked like. It was just that I hadn't thought about it in months, beyond putting on clean linen and not wearing gray, which tended to make me look as though I'd been inexpertly embalmed.

I had on brown today, an open jacket of brown velvet the color of ripe cattails, with a narrow grosgrain ribbon in gold down the edges, over my new gown—this a heavy coffee-colored silk with a close-fitted bodice and three lace-edged petticoats to show at the ankle. We would not be long in Edinburgh, owing to the exigencies of getting the brigadier to his final resting place and Jamie's eagerness to be away to the Highlands—but we did have business to conduct here. Jamie had said firmly that we could not appear as ragamuffins and had sent for a dressmaker and a tailor as soon as we reached our lodgings.

I stood back a little, preening. In all honesty, I was surprised to find how well I looked. During the long months of traveling, of retreat and battle with the Continental army, I had been reduced to my basic essence: survival and function. What I looked like would have been entirely irrelevant, even had I had a mirror.

In fact, I'd subconsciously expected to find a witch in the glass, a worn-looking woman with wild gray hair and a fierce expression. Possibly a long hair or two sprouting from the chin.

Instead . . . well, it was still recognizably me. My hair—uncapped but covered by a small, flat straw hat with a dainty bunch of cloth daisies on it—was tied up behind. But flattering small wisps curled round my temples, and my eyes were a bright clear amber behind the new spectacles, with a surprising look of guileless expectancy.

I had the lines and creases of my age, of course, but on the whole, my face had settled peaceably on my bones, rather than running away in jowls and wattles down my neck. And the bosom, with just a discreet shadow showing the swell of my breasts—the royal navy had fed us lavishly on the sea journey, and I had regained some of the weight I had lost during the long retreat from Ticonderoga.

"Well, not all that bad, really," I said, sounding so surprised that Jamie and Mr. Lewis both laughed. I took off the spectacles with considerable regret—Jamie's spectacles were simple steel-rimmed reading glasses, so could be taken at once, but my own pair would be ready, complete with gold rims, by the next afternoon, Mr. Lewis promised—and we left the shop to embark upon our next errand: Jamie's printing press.

"WHERE'S IAN this morning?" I asked, as we made our way to Princes Street. He'd been gone when I awoke, leaving not a wrack behind, let alone any word of his whereabouts. "You don't suppose he's decided to run for it rather than go home?"

"If he has, I'll track him down and beat him to a pudding, and he kens that perfectly well," Jamie said absently, looking up across the park to the great bulk of the castle on its rock, then putting on his glasses—futilely—to see whether they made a difference. "Nay, I think he's likely gone to the brothel."

"At eleven o'clock in the morning?" I blurted.

"Well, there's nay rule about it," Jamie said mildly, taking off the glasses, wrapping them in his handkerchief, and putting them into his sporran. "I've been known to do it in the morning now and then. Though I doubt he's bent on carnal knowledge just this minute," he added. "I told him to go and see whether Madame Jeanne still owns the place, for if so, she'll be able to tell me more, in a shorter space of time, than anyone else in Edinburgh. If she's there, I'll go and see her in the afternoon."

"Ah," I said, not really liking the notion of his going round for a cozy tête-à-tête with the elegant Frenchwoman who had once been his partner in the whisky-smuggling business but admitting the economy of the proposal. "And where would Andy Bell be at eleven o'clock in the morning, do you suppose?"

"In bed," Jamie said promptly. "Sleeping," he added with a grin, seeing the look on my face. "Printers are sociable creatures, as a rule, and they congregate in taverns of an evening. I've never known one to rise wi' the lark, save he's got bairns wi' the colic."

"You're proposing to roust him out of bed?" I asked, stretching my step to keep up with him.

"No, we'll find him at Mowbray's at dinnertime," he said. "He's a graver—he needs *some* light to work by, so he rises by noon. And he eats at Mowbray's most days. I only want to see whether his shop's burnt down or not. And whether the wee bugger's been using my press."

"You make it sound as though he's been using your wife," I said, amused at the grim tone of this last.

He made a small Scottish noise acknowledging the presumed humor of this remark while simultaneously declining to share in it. I hadn't realized that he felt so strongly about his printing press, but after all, he'd been separated from it for nearly twelve years. Little wonder if his lover's heart was beginning to beat at thought of being reunited with it at last, I thought, privately entertained.

Then again, perhaps he *was* afraid Andy Bell's shop had burned down. It wasn't an idle fear. His own printer's shop *had* burned down twelve years before; such establishments were particularly vulnerable to fire, owing both to the presence of a small open forge for melting and recasting type and to the quantities of paper, ink, and similar flammable substances kept on the premises.

My stomach growled softly at thought of a midday dinner at Mowbray's; I had very pleasant memories of our last—and only—visit there, which had involved some excellent oyster stew and an even better chilled white wine, among other pleasures of the flesh.

It would be a little time 'til dinner, though; laborers might open their dinner pails at noon, but fashionable Edinburgh dined at the civilized hour of three o'clock. Possibly we could acquire a fresh bridie from a street vendor, I thought, hastening in Jamie's wake. Just to tide us over.

Andrew Bell's shop was, luckily, still standing. The door was closed against the draft, but a small bell rang over it to announce our presence, and a middle-aged gentleman in shirtsleeves and apron looked up from a basket of slugs he was sorting.

"A good morning to you, sir. Ma'am," he said cordially, nodding to us, and I saw at once that he was not a Scot. Or, rather, not born in Scotland, for his accent was the soft, slightly drawling English of the Southern colonies. Jamie heard it and smiled.

"Mr. Richard Bell?" he asked.

"I am," said the man, looking rather surprised.

"James Fraser, your servant, sir," Jamie said politely, bowing. "And may I present my wife, Claire."

"Your servant, sir." Mr. Bell bowed in return, looking rather bewildered but with perfect manners.

Jamie reached into the breast of his coat and withdrew a small bundle of letters, tied with a pink ribbon.

"I've brought ye word from your wife and daughters," he said simply, handing them over. "And I've come to see about sending ye home to them."

Mr. Bell's face went blank, and then all the blood drained out of it. I thought he was going to faint for a moment, but he didn't, merely grasping the edge of the counter for support.

"You-you—home?" he gasped. He had clutched the letters to his breast, and now brought them down, looking at them, his eyes welling. "How—how did she . . . My wife. Is she well?" he asked abruptly, jerking up his head to look at Jamie, sudden fear in his eyes. "Are they all right?"

"They were all bonny as doves when I saw them in Wilmington," Jamie assured him. "Verra much desolated by your absence from them, but well in themselves."

Mr. Bell was trying desperately to control his face and his voice, and the effort reduced him to speechlessness. Jamie leaned over the counter and touched him gently on the arm.

"Go and read your letters, man," he suggested. "Our other business will wait."

Mr. Bell's mouth opened once or twice, soundless, then he nodded abruptly and, whirling round, blundered through the door that led to the back room.

I sighed, and Jamie glanced down at me, smiling.

"It's good when something comes right, isn't it?" I said.

"It's no made right yet," he said, "but it will be." He then pulled his new spectacles out of his sporran and, clapping them onto his nose, flipped up the counter flap and strode purposefully through.

"It *is* my press!" he exclaimed accusingly, circling the enormous thing like a hawk hovering over its prey.

"I'll take your word for it, but how can you tell?" I came cautiously after him, keeping back my skirts from the ink-stained press.

"Well, it's got my name on it, for the one thing," he said, stooping and pointing up at something under it. "Some of them, anyway." Leaning upside down and squinting, I made out *Alex. Malcolm* carved on the underside of a small beam.

"Apparently it still works all right," I observed, straightening up and looking round the room at the posters, ballads, and other examples of the printing and engraving arts displayed there.

"Mmphm." He tried the moving parts and examined the press minutely before reluctantly admitting that, in fact, it seemed in good condition. He still glowered, though.

"And I've been *paying* the wee bugger all these years, to keep it for me!" he muttered. He straightened up, looking balefully at the press. I had in the meantime been poking about the tables near the front wall, which held books and pamphlets for sale, and picked up one of the latter, which was titled at the top *Encyclopedia Britannica*, and below this, "Laudanum."

Tincture of opium, or liquid laudanum, otherwise called the thebaic tincture, is made as follows: take of prepared opium two ounces, of cinnamon and cloves, each one drachm, of white wine one pint, infuse them a week without heat, and then filter it through paper.

Opium at present is in great esteem, and is one of the most valuable of all the simple medicines. Applied externally, it is emollient, relaxing, and discutient, and greatly promotes suppuration: if long kept upon the skin, it takes off hair, and always occasions an itching; sometimes it exulcerates it, and raises little blisters, if applied to a tender part: sometimes, on external application, it allays pain, and even occasions sleep: but it must by no means be applied to the head, especially to the sutures of the skull; for it has been known to have the most terrible effects in this application, and even bring death itself. Opium taken internally removes melancholy, eases pain, and disposes of sleep; in many cases removes hemorrhages, provokes sweating.

A moderate dose is commonly under a grain . . .

"Do you know what 'discutient' means?" I asked Jamie, who was reading the type set up in the form on the press, frowning as he did so.

"I do. It means whatever ye're talking about can dissolve something. Why?"

"Ah. Perhaps that's why applying laudanum to the sutures of the skull is a bad idea."

He gave me a baffled look.

"Why would ye do that?"

"I haven't the faintest idea." I returned to the pamphlets, fascinated. One of them, titled "The Womb," had some very good engravings of a dissected female pelvis and internal organs, done from varying angles, as well as depictions of the fetus in various stages of development. If this was Mr. Bell's work, I thought, he was both a superb craftsman and a very diligent observer.

"Have you got a penny? I'd like to buy this."

Jamie dug into his sporran and laid a penny on the counter, glanced at the pamphlet in my hand, and recoiled.

"Mother of God," he said, crossing himself.

"Well, probably not," I said mildly. "Certainly *a* mother, though." Before he could reply to this, Richard Bell came out of the back room, red-eyed but composed, and seized Jamie by the hand.

"You cannot know what you have done for me, Mr. Fraser," he said earnestly. "If you can indeed help me to return to my family, I—I—well, in fact, I do not know what I could possibly do to show my gratitude, but be assured that I will bless your soul forever!"

"I'm much obliged to ye for the thought, sir," Jamie said to him, smiling. "It may be that ye can do me a small service, but if not, I shall still be most thankful for your blessings."

"If there is anything I can do, sir, anything at all!" Bell assured him fervently. Then a faint hesitation came over his face—possibly a recollection of whatever his wife had had to say about Jamie in her letter. "Anything short of . . . of treason, I should say."

"Och, no. Well short of treason," Jamie assured him, and we took our leave.

I TOOK A SPOONFUL of the oyster stew and closed my eyes in ecstasy. We had come a little early, in order to get a seat by the window overlooking the street, but Mowbray's had filled up fast, and the clishmaclaver of cutlery and conversation was almost deafening.

"You're sure he's not here?" I said, leaning across the table to make myself heard. Jamie shook his head, rolling a sip of the cold Moselle around his mouth with an expression of bliss.

"Ye'll ken well enough when he is," he said, swallowing it.

"All right. What sort of not-quite-treasonous thing are you planning to make poor Mr. Bell do in return for passage home?"

"I mean to send him home in charge of my printing press," he replied.

"What, entrust your precious darling to a virtual stranger?" I asked, amused. He gave me a mildly dirty look in return, but finished his bite of buttered roll before answering.

"I dinna expect him to be abusing her. He's no going to print a thousand-run of *Clarissa* on her aboard ship, after all."

"Oh, it's a her, is it?" I said, vastly entertained. "And what, may I ask, is her name?"

He flushed a little and looked away, taking particular care to coax a specially succulent oyster into his spoon, but finally muttered, "Bonnie," before gulping it.

I laughed, but before I could make further inquiries, a new noise intruded on the racket, and people began to put down their spoons and stand up, craning to see out of the windows.

"*That* will be Andy," Jamie told me.

I looked down into the street and saw a small knot of boys and idlers, clapping and cheering. Looking up the street to see what was coming, I beheld one of the biggest horses I had ever seen. It wasn't a draft horse but an enormously tall gelding, close to seventeen hands, so far as my inexpert eye could judge.

On top of it was a very small man, sitting up straight and regally ignoring the cheers of the crowd. He came to a stop directly below us and, turning round, removed a wooden square from the saddle behind him. He shook this out, revealing it to be a folding wooden ladder, and one of the street children ran forward to hold the foot of it while Mr. Bell—for it couldn't be anyone else—descended to the plaudits of passersby. He tossed a coin to the child who'd held the ladder, another to a lad who'd taken his horse's head, and disappeared from view.

A few moments later, he came through the door into the main dining room, taking off his cocked hat and bowing graciously to the calls of greeting from the diners. Jamie raised a hand, calling "Andy Bell!" in a resonant voice that cut through the thrum of talk, and the little man's head jerked in our direction, surprised. I watched with fascination as he came toward us, a slow grin spreading over his face.

I couldn't tell whether he had some form of dwarfism or had merely suffered badly from malnutrition and scoliosis in his youth, but his legs were short in proportion to his upper body, and his shoulders crooked; he barely topped four feet, and only the crown of his head—this covered by a very fashionable wig—showed as he passed between the tables.

These aspects of appearance faded into insignificance, though, as he drew close and I perceived his most striking attribute. Andrew Bell had the biggest nose I had ever seen, and in the course of an eventful life, I had seen a number of prize specimens. It began between his eyebrows, and curved gently down for a short distance as though nature had intended him to have the profile of a Roman emperor. Something had gone amiss in the execution, though, and to this promising beginning, something that looked like a small potato had been affixed. Knobbly and red, it took the eye.

It took quite a few eyes; as he drew close to our table, a young lady nearby saw him, gasped audibly, and then clapped a hand over her mouth, this precaution being quite insufficient to quell her giggles.

Mr. Bell heard her, and without breaking his stride, he reached into his pocket, withdrew an immense papier-mâché nose decorated with purple stars, which he clapped over his own, and, fixing the young woman with an icy stare, passed by.

"My dear," Jamie said to me, grinning as he rose to his feet and extending a hand to the little engraver, "may I name my friend, Mr. Andrew Bell? My wife, Andy. Claire is her name."

"Charmed, madam," he said, removing the false nose and bowing low over my hand. "When did you acquire this rare creature, Jamie? And whatever would such a lovely lass want with a great, vulgar lout such as you, I wonder?"

"I lured her into marriage wi' descriptions of the beauties of my printing press," Jamie said dryly, sitting down and motioning to Andy Bell to join us.

"Ah," said Andy, with a sharp look at Jamie, who raised his brows and widened his eyes. "Hmm. I see ye've been by the shop, then." He nodded at my reticule, from which the top of the pamphlet I'd bought was protruding.

"We have," I said hastily, pulling out the pamphlet. I didn't *think* Jamie proposed to squash Andy Bell like a bug for having made free with his printing press, but his relationship with "Bonnie" was news to me, and I wasn't sure quite how deep his sense of affronted proprietorship went.

"This is remarkably fine work," I said to Mr. Bell, with complete sincerity. "Tell me, how many different specimens did you use?"

He blinked a little but answered readily, and we had a pleasant—if rather gruesome—conversation regarding the difficulties of dissection in warm weather and the effect of saline solution versus alcohol for preservation. This caused the people at the next table to end their meal rather hurriedly, casting veiled looks of horror as they left. Jamie leaned back in his chair, looking pleasant but fixing Andy Bell with an unwavering gaze.

The little engraver betrayed no particular discomfort under this basilisk stare and went on telling me about the response when he had published the bound edition of the *Encyclopedia*—the King had somehow happened to see the plates of the "Womb" section and had ordered those pages to be torn out of the book, the ignorant German blatherskite!—but when the waiter came to take his order, he ordered both a very expensive wine and a large bottle of good whisky.

"What, whisky wi' the stew?" blurted the waiter, astonished.

"No," he said with a sigh, pushing back his wig. "Concubinage. If that's what ye call it when ye rent the services of a man's beloved."

The waiter shifted his look of astonishment to me, then went bright red and, choking slightly, backed away.

Jamie fixed a narrow eye on his friend, now buttering a roll with aplomb.

"It'll take more than whisky, Andy."

Andy Bell sighed and scratched his nose.

"Aye, then," he said. "Say on."

⁂

WE FOUND IAN waiting at the small hotel, chatting with a couple of draymen in the street. Seeing us, he took his leave—and a small package, thrust surreptitiously under his coat—and came in with us. It was teatime, and Jamie ordered it to be brought up to our rooms, for the sake of discretion.

We had lashed out, rather, in the matter of accommodations, and had taken a suite of rooms. The tea was now laid out in the parlor, an appetizing array of grilled finnan haddie, Scotch eggs, toast with marmalade, and scones with jam and clotted cream, accompanying an enormous pot of strong black tea. I inhaled the fragrant steam from the table and sighed with pleasure.

"It's going to be rather a wrench, going back to no tea," I observed, pouring out for everyone. "I don't suppose we'll get any in America for another, what—three or four years?"

"Oh, I wouldna say that," Jamie said judiciously. "Depends where we go back to, aye? Ye can get tea fine in places like Philadelphia or Charleston. Ye only need to ken a good smuggler or two, and if Captain Hickman's no been sunk or hanged by the time we go back..."

I put down my cup and stared at him.

"You don't mean you aren't planning to go ho—to go back to the Ridge?" I had a sudden empty feeling in the pit of my stomach, remembering our plans for the New House, the smell of balsam fir, and the quiet of the mountains. Did he really mean to move to Boston or Philadelphia?

"No," he said, surprised. "Of course we shall go back there. But if I mean to be in the printing trade, Sassenach, we shall need to be in a city for a time, no? Only 'til the war is over," he said, encouraging.

"Oh," I said in a small voice. "Yes. Of course." I drank tea, not tasting it. How could I have been so stupid? I had never once thought that, of course, a printing press would be pointless on Fraser's Ridge. In part, I supposed, I simply hadn't really believed he *would* get his press back, let alone thought ahead to the logical conclusion if he did.

But now he had his Bonnie back, and the future had suddenly acquired a disagreeable solidity. Not that cities didn't have considerable advantages, I told myself stoutly. I could finally acquire a decent set of medical instruments, replenish my medicines—why, I could even make penicillin and ether again! With a little better appetite, I took a Scotch egg.

"Speaking of smugglers," Jamie was saying to Ian, "what is it ye have in your coat? A present for one of the ladies at Madame Jeanne's?"

Ian gave his uncle a cold look and removed the small package from his pocket.

"A wee bit o' French lace. For my mam."

"Good lad," Jamie said with approval.

"What a sweet thought, Ian," I said. "Did you—I mean, was Madame Jeanne still *in situ*?"

He nodded, putting the package back into his coat.

"She is. And verra eager to renew her acquaintance wi' *you*, Uncle," he added, with a slightly malicious grin. "She asked would ye care to come round this evening for a bit of entertainment."

Jamie's nose twitched as he glanced at me.

"Oh, I think not, Ian. I'll send a note saying we shall wait upon her tomorrow morning at eleven. Though ye're free to take up her invitation yourself, of course." It was clear that he was only teasing, but Ian shook his head.

"Nay, I wouldna go wi' a whore. Not 'til it's settled between Rachel and me," he said seriously. "One way or the other. But I shallna take another woman to my bed until she tells me that I must."

We both looked at him in some surprise across the teacups.

"You *do* mean it, then," I said. "You feel...er...betrothed to her?"

"Well, of course he does, Sassenach," Jamie said, reaching for another slice of toast. "He left her his dog."

I ROSE LATE and leisurely next morning, and as Jamie and Ian were likely to be some time about their business, I dressed and went shopping.

Edinburgh being a city of commerce, Jamie had been able to convert our stock of gold—still quite a lot of it left—to bank drafts and cash, as well as to make arrangements for deposition of the cache of letters we had accumulated since Fort Ticonderoga. He had left a fat purse for my use, and I proposed to spend the day shopping, as well as collecting my new spectacles.

It was with these perched proudly on my nose and a bag containing a selection of the best of the herbs and medicines available from Haugh's Apothecary that I returned to Howard's hotel at teatime, with a rare appetite.

My appetite received a slight check, though, when the hotel's majordomo stepped out of his sanctum, wearing a slightly pained expression, and asked if he might have a word, madam?

"We do appreciate the honor of General Fraser's . . . presence," he said apologetically, conducting me to a small, cramped stairwell leading to the basement. "A great man, and a very fine warrior, and of course we are cognizant of the heroic nature of the . . . er . . . the manner of his death. It's only that . . . well, I hesitate to mention it, madam, but a coal-man this morning mentioned a . . . *smell*."

This last word was so discreet that he fairly hissed it into my ear as he ushered me off the stair and into the Howard's coal cellar, where we had made arrangements for the general to repose in dignity until we left for the Highlands. The smell itself was not nearly so discreet, and I snatched a handkerchief from my pocket and clapped it to my nose. There was a small window high up in one wall, from which a dim, smeary light seeped into the basement. Beneath this was a wide chute, under which stood a small mountain of coal.

In solitary dignity, draped with a canvas, the general's coffin stood well apart, lit by a solemn beam from the tiny window. A beam that gleamed from the small puddle beneath the coffin. The general was leaking.

"AND SAW THE skull beneath the skin," I quoted, tying a turpentine-soaked rag about my head, just under my nose, *"and breastless creatures under ground leaned backward with a lipless grin."*

"Apt," said Andy Bell, giving me a sideways glance. "Your own, is it?"

"No, a gentleman named Eliot," I told him. "As you say, though—apt."

Given the agitation of the hotel staff, I thought I had better take steps without waiting for Jamie and Ian to return, and after a moment's thought, had sent the bootboy on the run to inquire if Mr. Bell might like to come and observe something interesting in the medical line?

"The light's wretched," Bell said, standing on tiptoe to peer down into the coffin.

"I've called for a couple of lanterns," I assured him. "And buckets."

"Aye, buckets," he agreed, looking thoughtful. "What d'ye think, though, for what ye might call the longer term? It'll be some days to get him intae the Highlands—maybe weeks, this time o' year."

"If we tidy things up a bit, I thought perhaps you would know a discreet blacksmith who might be able to come and patch the lining." A seam in the lead foil lining the coffin had come apart, probably from the jostling involved in getting it from the ship, but it looked like a fairly simple repair—granted a blacksmith with a strong stomach and a low level of superstition regarding corpses.

"Mmm." He had taken out a sketching block and was making preliminary drawings, light notwithstanding. He scratched his potatolike nose with the end of his silver pencil, thinking. "Could do that, aye. But there are other ways."

"Well, we could boil him down to the bones, yes," I said, a little testily. "Though I hate to think what the hotel would say if I asked for the lend of their laundry cauldrons."

He laughed at that, to the undisguised horror of the footman who had appeared on the stairway, holding two lanterns.

"Ah, dinna fash yoursel', sonny," Andy Bell told him, taking the lanterns. "Naebody here but us ghouls."

He grinned broadly at the sound of the footman taking the stairs three at a time, but then turned and eyed me speculatively.

"It's a thought, aye? I could take him back tae my shop. Get him aff your hands, and naebody the wiser, sae heavy as your box there is. Mean to say, like, no one's going to want to gaze upon the dear departed's face once ye get him where he's going, are they?"

I didn't take offense at the suggestion, but shook my head.

"Putting aside the possibility of one or both of us being taken up as body snatchers, the poor man *is* my husband's kinsman. And he didn't want to be here in the first place."

"Well, nae one does, surely?" Bell said, blinking. "No much help for it, though. *The skull beneath the skin*, as your man Eliot so movingly puts it."

"I meant Edinburgh, not a coffin," I clarified. Fortunately, my purchases from Haugh's had included a large bottle of denatured alcohol, which I had brought down, discreetly wrapped in a rough apron procured from one of the housemaids. "He wanted to be buried in America."

"Really," Bell murmured. "Quaint notion. Ah, well. Two things I can think of, then. Repair the leak, and fill up the box wi' a gallon or twa o' cheap gin—well, it's cheaper than what ye've got there," he said, seeing my look. "Or . . . how long can ye stay in Edinburgh, do ye think?"

"We hadn't meant to stay longer than a week—but we might stretch it a day or two," I said cautiously, unbundling the bale of rags the majordomo had given me. "Why?"

He tilted his head back and forth, contemplating the remains by lantern light. An apt word, "remains."

"Maggots," he said succinctly. "They'll do a nice, clean job of it, but they do take time. Still, if we can take most o' the flesh off—hmm. Got a knife of any sort?" he asked.

I nodded, reaching into my pocket. Jamie had, after all, given me the knife because he thought I'd need it.

"Got maggots?" I said.

I DROPPED THE misshapen ball of lead into a saucer. It clinked and rolled to a stop, and we all looked at it in silence.

"That's what killed him," I said at last. Jamie crossed himself and murmured something in Gaelic, and Ian nodded soberly. "God rest him."

I hadn't eaten much of the excellent tea; the smell of corruption lingered at the back of my throat, in spite of the turpentine and the virtual bath I had taken in alcohol, followed by a real bath in the hotel's tub with soap and water as hot as I could stand.

"So," I said, clearing my throat. "How was Madame Jeanne?"

Jamie looked up from the bullet, his face lightening.

"Oh, verra bonnie," he said, grinning. "She had a good bit to say about the state of things in France. And a certain amount to say about one Percival Beauchamp."

I sat up a little straighter.

"She *knows* him?"

"She does indeed. He calls at her establishment now and then—though not in the way of business. Or rather," he added, with a sidelong glance at Ian, "not in the way of her usual business."

"Smuggling?" I asked. "Or spying?"

"Possibly both, but if it's the latter, she wasna telling me about it. He brings in quite a bit of stuff from France, though. I was thinking that maybe Ian and I would go across, whilst the general's doing whatever he's doing— how long did wee Andy think it would take to make him decent?"

"Anything from three or four days to a week, depending on how, um, active the maggots are." Ian and Jamie both shuddered reflexively. "It's just the same thing that happens underground," I pointed out. "It will happen to all of *us*, eventually."

"Well, aye, it is," Jamie admitted, taking another scone and ladling quantities of cream onto it. "But it's generally done in decent privacy so ye havena got to think about it."

"The general is quite private," I assured him, with a shade of acerbity. "He's covered in a good layer of bran. No one will see a thing, unless they go poking about."

"Well, that's a thought, isn't it?" Ian chipped in, sticking a finger in the jam. "This is Edinburgh. The place has a terrible reputation for body snatching, because of all the doctors wanting them to cut up for study. Had ye best not put a guard on the general, just to be sure he makes it to the Highlands wi' all his pieces?" He stuck the finger in his mouth and raised his brows at me.

"Well, in fact, there *is* a guard," I admitted. "Andy Bell suggested it, for just that reason." I didn't add that Andy had made a bid for the general's body himself—nor that I had told Mr. Bell in no uncertain terms what would happen to him if the general turned up missing.

"Ye said Andy helped ye with the job?" Jamie asked curiously.

"He did. We got on extremely well. In fact . . ." I hadn't been going to mention the subject of our conversation until Jamie had had a pint or so of whisky, but the moment seemed opportune, so I plumped in.

"I was describing various things to him while we worked—interesting surgeries and medical trivia, you'll know the sort of things."

Ian murmured something under his breath about ghoulies of a feather, but I ignored him.

"Aye, so?" Jamie was looking wary; he knew something was coming but not what it was.

"Well," I said, taking a breath, "the long and the short of it is that he suggested I write a book. A medical book."

Jamie's eyebrows had risen slowly, but he nodded at me to go on.

"A sort of manual for regular people, not for doctors. With principles of proper hygiene and nutrition, and guides to the common sorts of illness, how to make up simple medicines, what to do for wounds and bad teeth—that sort of thing."

The brows were still up, but he kept nodding, finishing the last bite of scone. He swallowed.

"Aye, well, it sounds a good sort of book—and surely ye'd be the person to write it. Did he happen to 'suggest' how much he thought it might cost to have such a thing printed and bound?"

"Ah." I let out the breath I'd been holding. "He'll do three hundred copies, a maximum of a hundred fifty pages, buckram binding, *and* distribute them through his shop, in exchange for the twelve years' rent he owes you for your printing press."

Jamie's eyes bulged and his face went red.

"And he's throwing in the maggots for free. *And* the guard," I added hastily, shoving the port in front of him before he could speak. He seized the glass and downed it in a gulp.

"That wee grasper!" he said, when he could speak. "Ye didna sign anything, did ye?" he asked anxiously. I shook my head.

"I did tell him I thought you'd maybe want to bargain with him," I offered meekly.

"Oh." His color began to recede toward normal levels.

"I do want to," I said, looking down at my hands, clasped together in my lap.

"Ye'd never said anything about wanting to write a book before, Auntie," Ian said, curious.

"Well, I hadn't really thought about it," I said defensively. "And it would have been terribly difficult and expensive to do while we were living on the Ridge."

Jamie muttered, "Expensive," and poured another glass of port, which he drank more slowly, making occasional faces at the taste as he thought.

"Ye really want this, Sassenach?" he said at last, and at my nod, set down the glass with a sigh.

"All right," he said with resignation. "But ye're having a leather-bound special edition, too, wi' gilded end pages. And five hundred copies. I mean, ye'll want some to take back to America, won't you?" he added, seeing my stunned look.

"Oh. Yes. I would like that."

"Well, then." He picked up the bell and rang for the maid. "Tell the young woman to take away this wretched stuff and bring some decent whisky. We'll toast your book. And then I'll go and speak to the wicked wee man."

I HAD A FRESH QUIRE of good-quality paper. I had half a dozen sturdy goose quills, a silver penknife with which to sharpen them, and an inkwell provided by the hotel—rather battered but filled, the majordomo had assured me, with the very best iron-gall ink. Jamie and Ian had gone to France for a week, to look into various interesting leads given them by Madame Jeanne, leaving me to mind the general and commence my book. I had all the time and leisure I required.

I took a sheet of paper, pristine and creamy, placed it just so, and dipped my quill, excitement thrumming in my fingers.

I closed my eyes in reflex, then opened them again. Where ought I to begin?

Begin at the beginning and go on till you come to the end: then stop. The line from *Alice's Adventures in Wonderland* drifted through my mind, and I smiled. Good advice, I supposed—but only if you happened to know where the beginning was, and I didn't quite.

I twiddled the quill a bit, thinking.

Perhaps I should have an outline? That seemed sensible—and a little less daunting than starting straight in to write. I lowered the quill and held it poised above the paper for a moment, then picked it up again. An outline would have a beginning, too, wouldn't it?

The ink was beginning to dry on the point. Rather crossly, I wiped it and was just about to dip it again, when the maid scratched discreetly at the door.

"Mrs. Fraser? There's a gentleman downstairs, askin' to see ye," she said. From her air of respect, I supposed it couldn't be Andy Bell. Besides, she likely would have said so if it was; everyone in Edinburgh knew Andy Bell.

"I'll come down," I said, rising. Perhaps my subconscious would come to some kind of conclusion regarding beginnings while I dealt with this gentleman, whomever he was.

Whomever he was, he *was* a gentleman, I saw that at once. He was also Percival Beauchamp.

"Mrs. Fraser," he said, his face lighting with a smile as he turned at the sound of my step. "Your servant, *madame.*"

"Mr. Beauchamp," I said, allowing him to take my hand and raise it to his lips. An elegant person of the time would doubtless have said something like, "*I fear you take me at a disadvantage, sir,*" with anything between haughtiness and flirtation. Not being an elegant person of the time, I merely said, "What are *you* doing here?"

Mr. Beauchamp, on the other hand, had any amount of elegance.

"Looking for you, dear lady," he replied, and gave my hand a slight squeeze before releasing it. I repressed a reflexive urge to wipe it on my dress and nodded toward a pair of armchairs arranged by the window.

"Not that I'm not flattered," I said, arranging my skirts. "But don't you want my husband? Oh!" I said, another thought occurring. "Or did you want to consult me medically?"

His lips twitched as though he thought this an amusing notion, but he shook his head respectfully. "Your husband is in France—or so Jeanne LeGrand tells me. I came to speak to you."

"Why?"

He lifted his smooth dark brows at that but didn't answer at once, instead lifting a finger in a gesture to the hotel clerk to summon refreshment. I didn't know if he was merely being polite or wanted the time to formulate his address, now that he'd seen me again. In any case, he took his time.

"I have a proposition for your husband, *madame*. I would have spoken with him," he said, forestalling my question, "but he had left for France already when I learned he was in Edinburgh, and I, alas, must leave myself before he will return. I thought it better to speak directly with you, though, rather than to explain myself in a letter. There are things it's wiser not to commit to writing, you know," he added, with a sudden smile that made him very appealing.

"All right," I said, settling myself. "Say on."

I LIFTED THE GLASS of brandy and took a sip, then raised it and looked critically through it.

"No, it's just brandy," I said. "Not opium."

"I beg your pardon?" He looked involuntarily into his own glass, just in case, and I laughed.

"I mean," I clarified, "that good as it is, it's not nearly good enough to make me believe a story like that."

He didn't take offense but tilted his head to one side.

"Can you think of any reason why I should invent such a tale?"

"No," I admitted, "but that doesn't mean there isn't one, does it?"

"What I have told you is not impossible, is it?"

I considered that one for a moment.

"Not *technically* impossible," I conceded. "But certainly implausible."

"Have you ever seen an ostrich?" he asked, and, without inquiring, poured more brandy into my glass.

"Yes. Why?"

"You must admit that ostriches are frankly implausible," he said. "But clearly not impossible."

"One to you," I conceded. "But I do think that Fergus being the lost heir to the Comte St. Germain's fortune is slightly more implausible than an ostrich. Particularly if you consider the part about the marriage license. I mean . . . a lost *legitimate* heir? It is France we're talking about, isn't it?"

He laughed at that. His face had flushed with brandy and amusement, and I could see how very attractive he must have been in his youth. He wasn't by any means bad-looking now, come to that.

"Do you mind my asking what you do for a living?" I asked curiously.

He was disconcerted by that and rubbed a hand over his jaw before answering, but met my eyes.

"I sleep with rich women," he said, and his voice held a faint but disturbing trace of bitterness.

"Well, I do hope you aren't regarding me in the light of a business opportunity. The gold-rimmed spectacles notwithstanding, I really haven't got any money."

He smiled and hid it in his brandy glass.

"No, but you would be a great deal more entertaining than the usual woman who does."

"I'm flattered," I said politely. We sipped brandy in silence for a bit, both thinking how to proceed. It was raining—naturally—and the patter of it on the street outside and the hiss of the fire beside us was soothing in the extreme. I felt oddly comfortable with him, but after all, I couldn't spend all day here; I had a book to write.

"All right," I said. "*Why* have you told me this story? Wait—there are two parts to that. One, why tell me rather than Fergus himself? And two, what is your personal interest in the situation, assuming it *is* true?"

"I did try to tell Mr. Fraser—Fergus Fraser, that is," he said slowly. "He declined to speak with me."

"Oh!" I said, recalling something. "Was it you who tried to abduct him, in North Carolina?"

"No, it wasn't," he said promptly, and with every evidence of sincerity. "I did hear about the occasion, but I don't know who his assailant was. More than likely, it was someone he had annoyed with his work." He shrugged that off and continued. "As for my personal interest . . . that runs along with the reason for my telling your husband—because I'm telling *you* only as your husband is unavailable."

"And that would be?"

He glanced quickly round to see that we were not overheard. No one was near us, but he still lowered his voice.

"I—and the interests I represent in France—wish the rebellion in America to succeed."

I didn't know what I'd been expecting, but it wasn't that, and I gawked at him.

"You expect me to believe you're an American patriot?"

"Not at all," he said. "I don't care about politics in the slightest. I'm a man of business." He eyed me assessingly. "Have you ever heard of a company called *Hortalez et Cie*?"

"No."

"It is ostensibly an importing and exporting business, run out of Spain. What it actually is is a facade for the purpose of funneling money to the Americans, without visibly involving the French government. We have so far moved many thousands through it, mostly to buy arms and ammunition. *Madame* LeGrand mentioned the company to your husband but without telling him what it was. She left it to me to decide whether to reveal the true nature of *Hortalez* to him."

"You're a French intelligence agent—is that what you're telling me?" I said, the penny dropping at last.

He bowed.

"But you aren't French, I don't think," I added, looking hard at him. "You're English."

"I was." He looked away. "I am a citizen of France now."

He fell silent, and I leaned back a little in my chair, watching him—and wondering. Wondering both how much of this was true and, in a more distant way, whether he might conceivably be an ancestor of mine. Beauchamp was not an uncommon name, and there was no great physical resemblance between us. His hands were long-fingered and graceful, like mine, but the fingers were shaped differently. The ears? His were somewhat large, though delicately shaped. I really had no idea what my own ears looked like, but assumed that if they were noticeably large, Jamie would have mentioned it at some point.

"What is it that you want?" I asked quietly at last, and he looked up.

"Tell your husband what I have told you, if you please, *madame*," he said, quite serious for once. "And suggest to him that it is not only in the best interests of his foster son to pursue this matter—but very much in the interests of America."

"How is that?"

He lifted one shoulder, slim and elegant.

"The Comte St. Germain had extensive land holdings in a part of America that is currently held by Great Britain. The French part of his estate—currently being squabbled over by a number of claimants—is extremely valuable. If Fergus Fraser can be proved to be Claudel Rakoczy—Rakoczy is the family name, you understand—and the heir to this fortune, he would be able to use it to help in financing the revolution. From what I know of him and his activities—and I know a good deal, by this time—I think he would be amenable to these aims. If the revolution is successful, then those who backed it would have substantial influence over whatever government is formed."

"And you could stop sleeping with rich women for money?"

A wry smile spread over his face.

"Precisely." He rose and bowed deeply to me. "A great pleasure to speak with you, *madame*."

He had almost reached the door when I called after him.

"*Monsieur* Beauchamp!"

"Yes?" He turned and looked back, a dark, slender man whose face was marked with humor—and with pain, I thought.

"Have you any children?"

He looked completely startled at that.

"I really don't think so."

"Oh," I said. "I only wondered. Good day to you, sir."

75

SIC TRANSIT GLORIA MUNDI

The Scottish Highlands

I T WAS A LONG WALK from the farmhouse at Balnain. As it was early January in Scotland, it was also wet and cold. Very wet. And *very* cold. No snow—and I rather wished there had been, as it might have discouraged Hugh Fraser's insane notion—but it had been raining for days, in that dismal way that makes hearths smoke, and even clothes that have not been outside grow damp, and drives the chill so far into your bones that you think you'll never be warm again.

I'd come to this conviction myself some hours ago, but the only alternative to continuing to slog through the rain and mud was to lie down and die, and I hadn't quite reached that extremity. Yet.

The creaking of the wheels stopped abruptly, with that slushing sound that indicated they had sunk once more in the mud. Under his breath, Jamie said something grossly inappropriate to a funeral, and Ian smothered a laugh with a cough—which became real and went hoarsely on and on, sounding like the bark of a large, tired dog.

I took the flask of whisky out from under my cloak—I didn't think something with that kind of alcohol content would freeze, but I wasn't taking any chances—and handed it to Ian. He gulped, wheezed as though he'd been hit by a truck, coughed some more, and then handed the flask back, breathing hard, and nodded thanks. His nose was red and running.

So were all the noses around me. Some of them possibly from grief, though I suspected that either the weather or the catarrh was responsible for most of them. The men had all gathered without comment—they'd had practice—around the coffin and, with concerted heaving, managed to get it out of the ruts and onto a firmer section of road, this covered mostly in rocks.

"How long do you think it's been since Simon Fraser last came home?" I whispered to Jamie, as he came back to take his place beside me toward the end of the funeral procession. He shrugged and wiped his nose with a soggy handkerchief.

"Years. He wouldna really have had cause, would he?"

I supposed not. As a result of the wake held the night before at the farmhouse—a place a little smaller than Lallybroch but constructed on much the same lines—I now knew a great deal more about Simon Fraser's military career and exploits than I had before, but the eulogy hadn't included a timetable. If he'd fought everywhere they said he had, though, he would hardly have had time to change his socks between campaigns, let alone come home to Scotland. And the estate wasn't his, after all; he was the second youngest of nine children. His wife, the tiny *bainisq* trudging at the head of the procession on her brother-in-law Hugh's arm, had no household of her own, I gathered, and lived with Hugh's family, she having no children alive— or nearby, at least—to care for her.

I did wonder whether she was pleased that we'd brought him home. Would it not have been better just to know that he'd died abroad, doing his duty and doing it well, than to be presented with the dismayingly pitiful detritus of her husband, no matter how professionally packaged?

But she had seemed, if not happy, at least somewhat gratified at being the center of such a fuss. Her crumpled face had flushed and seemed to unfold a little during the festivities of the night, and now she walked on with no sign of flagging, doggedly stepping over the ruts made by her husband's coffin.

It was Hugh's fault. Simon's much elder brother and the owner of Balnain, he was a spindly little old man, barely taller than his widowed sister-in-law, and with romantic notions. It was his pronouncement that, instead of planting Simon decently in the family burying ground, the family's most gallant warrior should be interred in a place more suited to his honor and the reverence due him.

Bainisq, pronounced "bann-eeshg," meant a little old lady; was a little old man merely an "eeshg"? I wondered, looking at Hugh's back. I thought I wouldn't ask until we were back at the house—assuming we made it there by nightfall.

At long last, Corrimony hove into sight. According to Jamie, the name meant "a hollow in the moor," and it was. Within the cup-shaped hollow in the grass and heather rose a low dome; as we grew closer, I saw that it was made from thousands and thousands of small river rocks, most the size of a fist, some the size of a person's head. And around this dark gray rain-slicked cairn was a circle of standing stones.

I clutched Jamie's arm by reflex. He glanced at me in surprise, then realized what I was looking at and frowned.

"D'ye hear anything, Sassenach?" he murmured.

"Only the wind." This had been moaning along with the funeral procession, mostly drowning out the old man chanting the *coronach* before the coffin, but as we came out onto the open moor, it picked up speed and rose several tones in pitch, sending cloaks and coats and skirts flapping like ravens' wings.

I kept a cautious eye on the stones but sensed nothing as we drew to a halt before the cairn. It was a passage tomb, of the general kind they called a *clava* cairn; I had no notion what that signified, but Uncle Lamb had had photographs of many such sites. The passage was meant to orient with some astronomical object on some significant date. I glanced up at the leaden, weeping sky and decided that today was probably not the day, anyway.

"We dinna ken who was buried there," Hugh had explained to us the day before. "But clearly a great chieftain of some sort. Must ha' been, the terrible trouble it is to build a cairn like that!"

"Aye, to be sure," Jamie had said, adding delicately. "The great chieftain: he's no buried there anymore?"

"Oh, no," Hugh assured us. "The earth took him, long since. There's no but a wee stain of his bones there now. And ye needna be worrit about there being a curse upon the place, either."

"Oh, good," I murmured, but he paid no attention.

"Some lang nebbit opened the tomb a hundred years ago or more, so if there *was* to be a curse on it, it surely went off attached to him."

This was comforting, and in fact none of the people now standing about the cairn seemed at all put off or bothered by its proximity. Though it might just be that they had lived near it for so long that it had become no more than a feature of the landscape.

There was a certain amount of practical discussion, the men looking at the cairn and shaking their heads dubiously, gesturing in turn toward the open passage that led to the burial chamber, then toward the top of the cairn, where the stones had either been removed or had simply fallen in and been cleared away below. The women gravitated closer together, waiting. We had arrived in a fog of fatigue the day before, and while I had been introduced to all of them, I had trouble keeping the proper name attached to the proper face. In truth, their faces all looked similar—thin, worn, and pale, with a sense of chronic exhaustion about them, a tiredness much deeper than waking the dead would account for.

I had a sudden recollection of Mrs. Bug's funeral. Makeshift and hasty— and yet carried out with dignity and genuine sorrow on the part of the mourners. I thought these people had barely known Simon Fraser.

How much better to have regarded his own last wish as stated and left him on the battlefield with his fallen comrades, I thought. But whoever said funerals were for the benefit of the living had had the right of it.

The sense of failure and futility that had followed the defeat at Saratoga had made his own officers determined to accomplish *something,* to make a proper gesture toward a man they had loved and a warrior they honored. Perhaps they had wanted to send him home, too, because of their desire for their own homes.

The same sense of failure—plus a deadly streak of romanticism—had doubtless made General Burgoyne insist upon the gesture; I thought he likely felt his own honor required it. And then Hugh Fraser, reduced to a hand-to-mouth existence in the wake of Culloden and faced with the unexpected homecoming of his younger brother, unable to produce much in the way of a funeral, but deeply romantic himself . . . and the end of it this strange procession, bringing Simon Fraser to a home no longer his and a wife who was a stranger to him.

And his place will know him no more. The line came to mind as the men made their decision and began to dismount the coffin from its wheels. I had drawn closer, along with the other women, and found I was now standing within a foot or two of one of the standing stones that ringed the cairn. These were smaller than the stones on Craigh na Dun—no more than two or three feet high. Moved by sudden impulse, I reached out and touched it.

I hadn't expected anything to happen, and it very luckily didn't. Though had I suddenly vanished in the midst of the burial, it would have substantially enlivened the event.

No buzzing, no screaming, no sensation at all. It was just a rock. After all, I thought, there was no reason why *all* standing stones should be assumed to mark time portals. Presumably the ancient builders had used stones to mark any place of significance—and surely a cairn like this one must have been significant. I wondered what sort of man—or woman, perhaps?—had lain here, leaving no more than an echo of their bones, so much more fragile than the enduring rocks that sheltered them.

The coffin was lowered to the ground and—with much grunting and puffing—shoved through the passage into the burial chamber in the center of the tomb. There was a large flat slab of stone that lay against the cairn, this incised with strange cup-shaped marks, presumably made by the original builders. Four of the stronger men took hold of this and maneuvered it slowly over the top of the cairn, sealing the hole above the chamber.

It fell with a muffled thud that sent a few small rocks rolling down the sides of the cairn. The men came down then, and we all stood rather awkwardly round it, wondering what to do next.

There was no priest here. The funeral Mass for Simon had been said earlier, in a small, bare stone church, before the procession to this thoroughly pagan burial. Evidently, Hugh's researches hadn't discovered anything regarding rites for such things.

Just when it seemed that we would be obliged simply to turn round and slog our way back to the farmhouse, Ian coughed explosively and stepped forward.

The funeral procession was drab in the extreme, none of the bright tartans that had graced Highland ceremonies in the past. Even Jamie's appearance was subdued, cloaked, and his hair covered with a black slouch hat. The sole exception to the general somberness was Ian.

He had provoked stares when he'd come downstairs this morning, and the staring hadn't stopped. With good reason. He'd shaved most of his head and greased the remaining strip of hair into a stiff ridge down the middle of his scalp, to which he had attached a dangling ornament of turkey feathers with a pierced silver sixpence. He *was* wearing a cloak, but under it had put on his worn buckskins, with the blue-and-white wampum armlet his wife, Emily, had made for him.

Jamie had looked him slowly up and down when he appeared and nodded, one corner of his mouth turning up.

"It willna make a difference, aye?" he'd said quietly to Ian as we headed for the door. "They'll still ken ye for who ye are."

"Will they?" Ian had said, but then ducked out into the downpour without waiting for an answer.

Jamie had undoubtedly been right; the Indian finery was a dress rehearsal in preparation for his arrival at Lallybroch, for we were bound there directly, once Simon's body was decently disposed of and the farewell whisky had been drunk.

It had its uses now, though. Ian slowly removed his cloak and handed it to Jamie, then walked to the entrance of the passage and turned to face the mourners—who watched this apparition, bug-eyed. He spread his hands, palms upward, closed his eyes, put back his head so the rain ran down his face, and began to chant something in Mohawk. He was no singer, and his voice was so hoarse from his cold that many words broke or disappeared, but I caught Simon's name in the beginning. The general's death song. It didn't go on for long, but when he dropped his hands, the congregation uttered a deep, collective sigh.

Ian walked away, not looking back, and without a word the mourners followed. It was finished.

76

BY THE WIND GRIEVED

T HE WEATHER CONTINUED to be terrible, with fitful gusts of snow now added to the rain, and Hugh pressed us to stay, at least for another few days, until the sky should clear.

"It might well be Michaelmas before that happens," Jamie said to him, smiling. "Nay, cousin, we'll be off."

And so we were, bundled in all the clothes we possessed. It took more than two days to reach Lallybroch, and we were obliged to shelter overnight in an abandoned croft, putting the horses in the cow byre next to us. There was no furniture nor peat for the hearth, and half the roof had gone, but the stone walls broke the wind.

"I miss my dog," Ian grumbled, huddling under his cloak and pulling a blanket over his goose-pimpled head.

"Would he sit on your heid?" Jamie inquired, taking a firmer hold on me as the wind roared past our shelter and threatened to rip away the rest of the threadbare thatch overhead. "Ye should have thought about it being January, before ye shaved your scalp."

"Well enough for you," Ian replied, peering balefully out from under his blanket. "Ye've got Auntie Claire to keep warm with."

"Well, ye might get a wife yourself one of these days. Is Rollo going to sleep with the both of ye when ye do?" Jamie inquired.

"Mmphm," Ian said, and pulled the blanket down over his face, shivering.

I shivered, too, in spite of Jamie's warmth, our combined cloaks, three woolen petticoats, and two pairs of stockings. I had been in a number of cold places in my life, but there's something remarkably *penetrating* about the Scottish cold. In spite of my longing for a warm fire and the remembered coziness of Lallybroch, though, I was almost as uneasy about our approaching homecoming as Ian was—and Ian had been growing more like a cat on hot bricks, the farther we got into the Highlands. He twitched and muttered to himself now, thrashing in his blankets in the darkened confines of the shed.

I had wondered when we landed in Edinburgh whether we ought to send word of our arrival to Lallybroch. When I'd suggested this, though, Jamie laughed.

"D'ye think we stand the slightest chance of getting within ten miles o' the place without everyone hearing of it? Never fear, Sassenach," he'd assured me. "The minute we set foot in the Highlands, everyone from Loch Lomond to Inverness will know that Jamie Fraser's comin' home with his English witch, and a red Indian with him, to boot."

"English witch?" I said, not sure whether to be entertained or offended. "Did they call me that? When we were at Lallybroch?"

"Frequently to your face, Sassenach," he said dryly. "But ye didna have enough Gaelic then to know it. They didna mean it as an insult, *a nighean*," he added more gently. "Nor will they now. It's only that Highlanders call a thing as they see it."

"Hmm," I said, a trifle taken back.

"They'll no be wrong, now, will they?" he'd asked, grinning.

"Are you implying that I *look* like a witch?"

"Well, not sae much just this minute," he said, narrowing one eye judiciously. "First thing in the morning, maybe—aye, that's a more fearsome prospect."

I hadn't a looking glass, not having thought to acquire one in Edinburgh. I did still have a comb, though, and snuggling now with my head beneath Jamie's chin, resolved to stop some way short of Lallybroch and employ it thoroughly, rain or no rain. Not, I thought, that it would likely make much difference whether I arrived looking like the Queen of England or like a dandelion gone to seed. It was Ian's homecoming that was important.

On the other hand . . . I wasn't sure quite what my own welcome might be. There was unfinished business, to put it mildly, between myself and Jenny Murray.

We had been good friends once. I hoped we might be again. But she had been the chief engineer of Jamie's marriage to Laoghaire MacKenzie. From the best of motives, no doubt; she'd worried for him, lonely and rootless on his return from captivity in England. And in all justice, she'd thought me dead.

What had she thought, I wondered, when I'd suddenly appeared again? That I had abandoned Jamie before Culloden and then had second thoughts? There hadn't been time for explanations and rapprochement—and there *had* been that very awkward moment when Laoghaire, summoned by Jenny, had showed up at Lallybroch, accompanied by her daughters, taking Jamie and me very much by surprise.

A bubble of laughter rose in my chest at thought of that encounter, though I certainly hadn't laughed at the time. Well, perhaps there would be time to talk now, once Jenny and Ian had recovered from the shock of their youngest son's homecoming.

I became aware, from subtle shiftings behind me, that while the horses were breathing heavily and peacefully in their byre and Ian had finally subsided into phlegm-rattling snores, I wasn't the only one still lying awake thinking of what might await us.

"You aren't asleep, either, are you?" I whispered to Jamie.

"No," he said softly, and shifted his weight again, gathering me more closely against him. "Thinking about the last time I came home. I had such fear—and a verra wee bit of hope. I imagine it's maybe like that for the lad now."

"And for you now?" I asked, folding my own hands over the arm that encircled me, feeling the solid, graceful bones of wrist and forearm, gently touching his maimed right hand. He sighed deeply.

"Dinna ken," he said. "But it'll be all right. You're with me, this time."

THE WIND DROPPED sometime in the night, and the day, by some miracle, dawned clear and bright. Still cold as a polar bear's bottom, but not raining. I thought that a good omen.

Nobody spoke as we cleared the last high pass that led to Lallybroch and saw the house below. I felt a loosening in my chest and only then realized how long I'd been holding my breath.

"It hasn't changed, has it?" I said, my breath white on the cold air.

"There's a new roof on the dovecote," Ian said. "And Mam's sheep pen is bigger." He was doing his best to sound nonchalant, but there was no mistaking the eagerness in his voice. He nudged his horse and pulled a little in front of us, the turkey feathers in his hair lifting on the breeze.

It was early afternoon, and the place was quiet; the morning chores had been done, the evening milking and supper-making not yet started. I didn't see anyone outside save a couple of big, shaggy Highland cattle munching hay in the near pasture, but the chimneys were smoking and the big white-harled farmhouse had its usual hospitable, settled air.

Would Bree and Roger ever go back here? I wondered suddenly. She'd mentioned it, when the notion of their leaving became fact and they had begun to plan.

"It's vacant," she'd said, eyes fixed on the twentieth-century-style shirt she was making. "For sale. Or it was, when Roger went there a few years—ago?" She looked up with a wry smile; it wasn't really possible to discuss time in any customary way. "I'd like the kids to live there, maybe. But we'll just have to see how . . . things work out."

She'd glanced then at Mandy, asleep in her cradle, faintly blue around the lips.

"It will work out fine," I'd said firmly. "Everything will be just fine."

Lord, I prayed now silently, *that they might be safe!*

Ian had swung off his horse and was waiting impatiently for us. As we dismounted, he headed for the door, but our arrival had been noted, and it swung wide before he could touch it.

Jenny stopped dead in the doorway. She blinked, once, and her head tilted slowly back as her eyes traveled up the long, buckskin-covered body, with its roped muscles and small scars, to the crested, feathered head with its tattooed face, so carefully expressionless—save for the eyes, whose hope and fear he could not hide, Mohawk or no.

Jenny's mouth twitched. Once . . . twice . . . then her face broke and she began to utter small, hysterical whoops that turned into unmistakable laughter. She gulped, whooped again, and laughed so hard that she staggered backward into the house and had to sit down on the bench in the hall, where she bent double with her arms wrapped round her middle and laughed until the sound gave out and her breath came in faint, wheezing gasps.

"Ian," she said at last, shaking her head. "Oh, God, Ian. My wee lad."

Ian looked entirely taken aback. He looked at Jamie, who shrugged, his own mouth twitching, then back at his mother.

She gulped for air, her chest heaving, then stood up, went to him, and wrapped her arms about him, her tear-streaked face pressed to his side. His arms went slowly, carefully around her, and he held her to him like something fragile, of immense value.

"Ian," she said again, and I saw her small, taut shoulders suddenly slump. "Oh, Ian. Thank God ye've come in time."

SHE WAS SMALLER than I had remembered, and thinner, her hair with a little more gray in it though still darkly vibrant—but the deep-blue cat-eyes were just the same, as was the natural air of command she shared with her brother.

"Leave the horses," she said briskly, wiping her eyes on the corner of her apron. "I'll have one o' the lads take care of them. Ye'll be frozen and starving—take off your things and come into the parlor." She glanced at me, with a brief look of curiosity and something else that I couldn't interpret—but didn't meet my eyes directly or say more than "Come," as she led the way to the parlor.

The house smelled familiar but strange, steeped in peat smoke and the scent of cooking; someone had just baked bread, and the yeasty smell floated down the hall from the kitchen. The hall itself was nearly as cold as the outdoors; all the rooms had their doors closed tight to keep in the heat from their fires, and a welcome wave of warmth eddied out when she opened the door to the parlor, turning to pull Ian in first.

"Ian," she said, in a tone I'd never heard her use before. "Ian, they've come. Your son's come home."

Ian the elder was sitting in a large armchair close to the fire, a warm rug over his legs. He struggled to his feet at once, a little unsteady on the wooden peg he wore in replacement of a leg lost in battle, and took a few steps toward us.

"Ian," Jamie said, his voice soft with shock. "God, Ian."

"Oh, aye," Ian said, his own voice wry. "Dinna fash; it's still me."

Phthisis, they called it. Or doctors did. It meant "wasting," in the Greek. Laymen called it by the blunter name "consumption," and the reason why was all too apparent. It consumed its victims, ate them alive. A wasting disease, and waste it did. Ate flesh and squandered life, profligate and cannibal.

I'd seen it many times in England of the thirties and forties, much more here in the past. But I'd never seen it carve the living flesh from the bones of someone I loved, and my heart went to water and drained from my chest.

Ian had always been whipcord thin, even in times of plenty. Sinewy and tough, his bones always near the surface of his skin, just as Young Ian's were. Now...

"I may cough, but I won't break," he assured Jamie, and, stepping forward, put his arms round Jamie's neck. Jamie enfolded him very gently, the gingerness of the embrace growing firmer as he found that Ian didn't break—and closed his eyes to keep the tears in check. His arms tightened, trying involuntarily to keep Ian from the abyss that all too plainly yawned at his feet.

I can count all my bones. The Biblical quote came unbidden to my mind. I quite literally *could;* the cloth of his shirt lay over ribs that showed so clearly that I could see the articulations where each one joined the protruding knobs of his backbone.

"How long?" I blurted, turning to Jenny, who was watching the men, her own eyes bright with unshed tears. "How long has he had it?"

She blinked once and swallowed.

"Years," she said, steadily enough. "He came back from the Tolbooth in Edinburgh with the cough, and it never left. It's got worse over the last year, though."

I nodded. A chronic case, then; that was something. The acute form—"galloping consumption," they called it—would have taken him in months.

She gave me back the question I had asked her, but with a different meaning.

"How long?" she said, so softly that I barely heard her.

"I don't know," I said, with equal softness. "But ... not long."

She nodded; she had known this for a long time.

"Just as well ye came in time, then," she said, matter-of-fact.

Young Ian's eyes had been fixed on his father from the moment we entered the room. The shock showed plainly on his face, but he kept himself in hand.

"Da," he said, and his voice was so hoarse that the word emerged in a strangled croak. He cleared it viciously and repeated, "Da," coming forward. The elder Ian looked at his son, and his face lit with a joy so profound that it eclipsed the marks of illness and suffering.

"Oh, Ian," he said, holding out his arms. "My wee lad!"

IT WAS THE Highlands. And it was Ian and Jenny. Which meant that matters that might have been avoided out of confusion or delicacy were instead addressed forthrightly.

"I may die tomorrow, or not for a year," Ian said frankly, over jam bread and tea, hastily magicked out of the kitchen to sustain the weary travelers until supper should be ready. "I'm betting on three months, myself. Five to two, if anyone fancies a wager. Though I dinna ken how I'll collect my winnings." He grinned, the old Ian showing suddenly through his death's-head face.

There was a murmur of something not quite laughter among the adults. There were a great many people crammed into the parlor, for the announcement that had brought forth bread and jam had also caused every inhabitant of Lallybroch to come boiling out of its rooms and recesses, thundering down the stairs in their anxiety to greet and reclaim their prodigal. Young Ian had nearly been knocked flat and trampled by his family's affection, and this, coming on the heels of the shock of seeing his father, had stunned him into muteness, though he kept smiling, quite helpless in the face of a thousand questions and exclamations.

Jenny had rescued him at last from the maelstrom, taking him by the hand and pushing him firmly into the parlor with the elder Ian, then popping back out herself to quell the riot with a flashing eye and a firm word before ushering the rest of them in an orderly fashion.

Young Jamie—Ian and Jenny's eldest, and Jamie's namesake—now lived at Lallybroch with his wife and children, as did his sister, Maggie, and her two children, her husband being a soldier. Young Jamie was out on the estate, but the women came to sit with me. All of the children were clustered round Young Ian, staring and asking so many questions that they collided with one another, and pushed and shoved, arguing as to who asked what and who should be answered first.

The children had paid no attention to the elder Ian's remark. They already knew Grandda was dying, and the fact was of no interest by comparison with the fact of their fascinating new uncle. A tiny girl with her hair in stubby plaits sat in Young Ian's lap, tracing the lines of his tattoos with her fingers, now and then sticking one inadvertently in his mouth as he smiled and made hesitant answers to his inquisitive nieces and nephews.

"Ye could have written," Jamie said to Jenny, with an edge of reproach in his voice.

"I did," she said, with her own edge. "A year ago, when his flesh began to melt away and we kent it was more than a cough. I asked ye to send Young Ian then, if ye could."

"Ah," Jamie said, discomfited. "We must ha' left the Ridge before it came. But did I not write last April, to tell ye we were coming? I sent the letter from New Bern."

"If ye did, I never got it. Nay wonder, with the blockade; we see no more than half what we used to that's sent from America. And if ye left last March, it's been a long voyage, no?"

"A bit longer than I expected, aye," Jamie said dryly. "Things happened along the way."

"So I see." Without the least hesitation, she picked up his right hand and examined the scar and the close-set fingers with interest. She glanced at me, one eyebrow quirked, and I nodded.

"It—he was wounded, at Saratoga," I said, feeling oddly defensive. "I had to."

"It's a good job," she said, gently flexing his fingers. "Does it pain ye much, Jamie?"

"It aches in the cold. Nay bother otherwise, though."

"Whisky!" she exclaimed, sitting bolt upright. "Here ye are, frozen to the bone, and I've not thought—Robbie! Run and fetch down the special bottle from the shelf above the coppers." A gangling boy who had been hovering on the edge of the crowd round Young Ian gave his grandmother a reluctant glance, but then, catching the depth charge of her eye, shot out of the room to do her bidding.

The room was more than warm; with a peat fire simmering on the hearth and so many people talking, laughing, and exuding body heat, it was on the verge of tropical. But there was a deep chill around my heart whenever I looked at Ian.

He lay back in his chair now, still smiling. But exhaustion was evident in the slump of his bony shoulders, the droop of his eyelids, the clear effort it took to keep smiling.

I looked away and found Jenny looking at me. She glanced away at once, but I had seen speculation in her eyes, and doubt. Yes, we'd have to talk.

THEY SLEPT WARM that first night, tired to the point of collapse, close together and enfolded by Lallybroch. But Jamie heard the wind on the edge of waking. It had come back in the night, a cold moan around the eaves of the house.

He sat up in bed in the dark, hands wrapped around his knees, listening. The storm would be coming; he could hear snow in the wind.

Claire lay beside him, half curled in sleep, her hair a dark smudge across the white pillow. He listened to her breathe, thanking God for the sound, feeling guilt at the soft, unhindered flow of it. He'd been hearing Ian's cough all evening and gone to sleep with the sound of that labored breathing in his mind, if not his ears.

He'd managed from sheer exhaustion to put aside the matter of Ian's illness, but it was there with the waking, heavy as a stone in his chest.

Claire shifted in her sleep, turning half onto her back, and desire for her welled up in him like water. He hesitated, aching for Ian, guilty for what Ian had already lost and he still had, reluctant to wake her.

"I feel maybe like you did," he whispered to her, too low to wake her. "When ye came through the stones. Like the world is still there—but it's no the world ye had."

He'd swear she hadn't wakened, but a hand came out from the sheets, groping, and he took it. She sighed, long and sleep-laden, and pulled him down beside her. Took him in her arms and cradled him, warm on her soft breasts.

"You're the world I have," she murmured, and then her breathing changed, and she took him down with her into safety.

77

MEMORARAE

THEY'D BEEN EATING breakfast in the kitchen, just the two Ians, for his father had waked coughing before dawn and fallen back into such a deep sleep afterward that his mother hadn't wanted to waken him, and he himself had been hunting over the hills with his brother and nephews all night. They had stopped on the way back at Kitty's house, and Young Jamie had declared they would stay to eat and sleep a bit, but Ian had been restless, wanting to come home, though he couldn't have said why.

Perhaps for this, he thought, watching his father shake salt over his porridge in the same way he'd seen him do it for fifteen years, before he'd left Scotland. He'd never once thought of it, in all his time away, but now that he saw it again, it was as though he'd never left, as though he'd spent every morning of his life here at this table, watching his father eat porridge.

He was possessed of a sudden desire to memorize this moment, to know and to sense every last thing about it, from the worn-smooth wood under his elbows to the stained granite of the countertop and the way the light fell through the tattered curtains at the window, lighting the bulge of muscle at the corner of his father's jaw as he chewed a bit of sausage.

The elder Ian glanced up suddenly, as though feeling his son's eyes on him.

"Shall we go out on the moor?" he said. "I've a fancy to see if the red deer are calving yet."

He was surprised at his father's strength. They walked for several miles, talking of nothing—and everything. He knew it was so they could grow easy with each other again and say the things that had to be said—but he dreaded the saying.

They stopped at last far up on a high stretch of moorland, where they could see the roll of the great smooth mountains and a few wee lochs, glittering like fish under a pale high sun. They found a saint's spring, a tiny pool with an ancient stone cross, and drank from the water, saying the prayer of respect for the saint, and then sat down to rest a little way beyond.

"It was a place like this where I died the first time," his father said casually, running a wet hand over his sweating face. He looked rosy and healthy, though so thin. That bothered Young Ian, knowing he was dying yet seeing him like this.

"Aye?" he said. "When was that, then?"

"Oh, in France. When I lost my leg." The elder Ian glanced down at his wooden peg, indifferent. "One minute I was standing up to fire my musket, and the next I was lyin' on my back. I didna even ken I'd been hit. Ye'd think ye'd notice being hit by a six-pound iron ball, wouldn't ye?"

His father grinned at him, and he smiled grudgingly back.

"I would. Surely ye thought *something* must ha' happened, though."

"Oh, aye, I did. And after a moment or two, it came to me that I must ha' been shot. But I couldna feel any pain at all."

"Well, that was good," Young Ian said encouragingly.

"I kent then I was dying, aye?" His father's eyes were on him but looked beyond him, at that far-off battlefield. "I wasna really bothered, though. And I wasna alone." His gaze focused then on his son, and he smiled a little. Reaching out, he took hold of Ian's hand—his own wasted to the bone, the joints of it swollen and knobbled, but the span of his grasp still as big as his son's.

"Ian," he said, and paused, his eyes crinkling. "D'ye ken how odd it is, to say someone's name when it's yours, as well? Ian," he repeated, more gently, "dinna fash. I wasna afraid then. I'm not afraid now."

I am, Ian thought, but he couldn't say that.

"Tell me about the dog," his father said then, smiling. And so he told his father about Rollo. About the sea battle where he'd thought Rollo drowned or dead, how it had all come about that they'd gone to Ticonderoga and been at the terrible battles of Saratoga.

And told him, without thinking about it, for thinking would have frozen the words in his throat, about Emily. About Iseabaìl. And about the Swiftest of Lizards.

"I—havena told anyone else about that," he said, suddenly shy. "About the wee lad, I mean."

His father breathed deep, looking happy. Then coughed, whipped out a handkerchief, and coughed some more, but eventually stopped. Ian tried not to look at the handkerchief, in case it should be stained with blood.

"Ye should—" the elder Ian croaked, then cleared his throat and spat into the handkerchief with a muffled grunt. "Ye should tell your mother," he said, his voice clear again. "She'd be happy to ken ye've got a son, no matter the circumstances."

"Aye, well. Maybe I will."

It was early for bugs, but the moor birds were out, poking about, taking flight past their heads and calling out in alarm. He listened to the sounds of home for a bit and then said, "Da. I've got to tell ye something bad."

And sitting by a saint's pool, in the peace of the early spring day, Ian told him what had happened to Murdina Bug.

His father listened with a grave attention, head bowed. Young Ian could see the heavy streaks of gray in his hair and found the sight both moving and paradoxically comforting. *At least he's lived a good life,* he thought. *But maybe Mrs. Bug did, too. Would I feel worse about it if she'd been a young girl?* He thought he would, but he felt badly enough as it was. A little better for the telling, though.

The elder Ian rocked back on his haunches, arms clasped about his good knee, thinking.

"It wasna your fault, of course," he said, with a sidelong look at his son. "D'ye ken that, in your heart?"

"No," Ian admitted. "But I'm trying."

His father smiled at that, but then grew grave again.

"Ye'll manage. If ye've lived with it this long, ye'll be all right in the end. But this matter of old Arch Bug, now. He must be as old as the hills, if he's the same one I kent—a tacksman for Malcolm Grant, he was."

"That's the man. I keep thinking that—he's old, he'll die—but what if he dies and I dinna ken he's dead?" He made a gesture of frustration. "I dinna want to kill the man, but how can I not, and him wandering about, set to do harm to Ra—to my—well, if I should ever have a wife . . ." He was floundering, and his father put a stop to it, grasping his arm.

"Who is she?" he asked, interest bright in his face. "Tell me about her."

And so he told about Rachel. He was surprised that there was so much to tell, in fact, considering that he'd known her only a few weeks and kissed her just the once.

His father sighed—he sighed all the time, it was the only way he got enough breath, but this one was a sigh of happiness.

"Ah, Ian," he said fondly. "I'm happy for ye. I canna say how happy. It's what your mother and I have prayed for, these many years, that ye'd have a good woman to love and a family by her."

"Well, it's soon to be speaking of my family," Young Ian pointed out. "Considering she's a Quaker and likely won't wed me. And considering I'm in Scotland and she's wi' the Continental army in America, probably bein' shot at or infected wi' plague right this minute."

He'd meant it seriously and was somewhat offended when his father laughed. But then the elder Ian leaned forward and said with utter seriousness, "Ye needna wait for me to die. Ye need to go and find your young woman."

"I canna—"

"Aye, ye can. Young Jamie's got Lallybroch, the girls are well wed, and Michael—" He grinned at the thought of Michael. "Michael will do well enough, I think. A man needs a wife, and a good one is the greatest gift God has for a man. I'd go much easier, *a bhailach*, if I kent ye were well fettled in that way."

"Aye, well," Young Ian murmured. "Maybe so. But I'll not go just yet."

78

OLD DEBTS

J AMIE SWALLOWED THE last bite of porridge and took a deep breath, laying down his spoon.

"Jenny?"

"O' course there's more," she said, reaching for his bowl. Then she caught sight of his face and stopped, eyes narrowing. "Or is that not what ye had need of?"

"I wouldna say it's a need, precisely. But . . ." He glanced up at the ceiling to avoid her gaze and commended his soul to God. "What d'ye ken of Laoghaire MacKenzie?"

He risked a quick glance at his sister and saw that her eyes had gone round, bright with interest.

"Laoghaire, is it?" She sat back down and began to tap her fingers thoughtfully on the tabletop. Her hands were good for her age, he thought: work-worn, but the fingers still slim and lively.

"She's not wed," Jenny said. "But ye'll ken that, I imagine."

He nodded shortly.

"What is it ye want to know about her?"

"Well . . . how she fares, I suppose. And . . ."

"And who's sharing her bed?"

He gave his sister a look.

"Ye're a lewd woman, Janet Murray."

"Oh, aye? Well, awa' wi' ye, then, and ask the cat." Blue eyes just like his own glittered at him for an instant, and the dimple showed in her cheek. He knew that look and yielded with what grace was possible.

"D'ye know?"

"No," she said promptly.

He raised one brow in disbelief. "Oh, aye. Pull the other one."

She shook her head and ran a finger round the edge of the honey jar, wiping off a golden bead. "I swear on St. Fouthad's toenails."

He hadn't heard that one since he was ten and laughed out loud, despite the situation.

"Well, then, no more to be said, is there?" He leaned back in his chair, affecting indifference. She made a small huffing noise, got up, and began busily to clear the table. He watched her with narrowed eyes, not sure whether she was messing him about only for the sake of mischief—in which case, she'd yield in a moment—or whether there was something more to it.

"Why is it ye want to know?" she asked suddenly, eyes on the stack of sticky bowls. That brought him up short.

"I didna say I *did* want to know," he pointed out. "But since ye mentioned it—anyone would be curious, no?"

"They would," she agreed. She straightened up and looked at him, a long, searching sort of look that made him wonder whether he'd washed behind his ears.

"I *don't* know," she said at last. "And that's the truth. I only heard from her that once that I wrote ye."

Aye, and just why did ye write me about it? he wondered, but didn't say so out loud.

"Mmphm," he said. "And ye expect me to believe that ye left it there?"

HE REMEMBERED IT. Standing here in his old room at Lallybroch, the one he'd had as a boy, on the morning of his wedding to Laoghaire.

He'd had a new shirt for the occasion. There wasn't money for much beyond the barest essentials, and sometimes not that—but Jenny had contrived him a shirt; he suspected she'd sacrificed the best of her two shifts for it. He remembered shaving in the reflection in his washbasin, seeing the gaunt, stern face of a stranger emerge beneath his razor, thinking that he must remember to smile when he met Laoghaire. He didn't want to frighten her, and what he saw in the water was enough to frighten *him*.

He thought suddenly of sharing her bed. He resolutely put aside the thought of Claire's body—he had a great deal of practice in that—which caused him instead to think suddenly that it had been years—aye, years! He'd lain with a woman only twice in the last fifteen years, and it was five, six, maybe seven years since the last time. . . .

He'd suffered a moment's panic at the thought that he might find himself unable and touched his member gingerly through his kilt, only to find that it had already begun to stiffen at the mere thought of bedding.

He drew a deep breath, somewhat relieved. One less thing to worry over, then.

A brief sound from the door jerked his head round to see Jenny standing there, wearing an unreadable expression. He coughed and took his hand off his cock.

"Ye haven't got to do it, Jamie," she said quietly, eyes fixed on his. "If ye've thought better of it, tell me."

He'd nearly done it. But he could hear the house. There was a sense of bustle in it, a purpose and a happiness it had lacked for a very long time. It wasn't only his own happiness at stake here—it never had been.

"No," he'd said abruptly. "I'm fine." And smiled reassuringly at her.

As he went downstairs to meet Ian at the foot, though, he heard the rain on the windows and felt a sudden sense of drowning—an unwelcome recollection of his first wedding day and how they'd held each other up, he and Claire, both bleeding, both terrified.

"All right, then?" Ian had said to him, leaning in, low-voiced.

"Aye, fine," he replied, and was pleased at how calm his voice was.

Jenny's face appeared briefly round the door to the parlor. She looked worried, but relaxed when she saw him.

"It's all right, *mo nighean,*" Ian had assured her, grinning. "I've got a grip on him, in case he takes it into his head to bolt." Ian was in fact gripping his arm, rather to Jamie's surprise, but he didn't protest.

"Well, drag him in, then," his sister had said, very dry. "The priest's come."

He'd gone in with Ian, taken up his place beside Laoghaire in front of old Father McCarthy. She glanced up at him briefly, then away. Was she frightened? Her hand was cool in his but didn't shake. He squeezed her fingers gently and she turned her head, looking up at him then, directly. No, not fright, and not candle glow or starshine. There was gratitude in her gaze—and trust.

That trust had entered his heart, a small, soft weight that steadied him, restored at least a few of the severed roots that had held him to his place. He'd been grateful, too.

He turned at the sound of footsteps now and saw Claire coming along the hall. He smiled—noting that he'd done so without the slightest thought—and she came to him, taking his hand as she peered into the room.

"Yours, wasn't it? When you were young, I mean."

"Aye, it was."

"I thought Jenny told me so—when we came here the first time, I mean." Her mouth twisted a little. She and Jenny did speak now, of course, but it was a stilted kind of speaking, both of them overcareful, shy of saying too much or the wrong thing. Aye, well, he was afraid of saying too much or the wrong thing himself, but damned if he'd be a woman about it.

"I need to go and see Laoghaire," he said abruptly. "Will ye kill me if I do?"

She looked surprised. And then, damn her, amused.

"Are you asking my permission?"

"I am not," he said, feeling stiff and awkward. "I only—well, I thought I should tell ye, is all."

"Very considerate of you." She was still smiling, but the smile had taken on a certain wariness. "Would you . . . care to tell me *why* you want to go and see her?"

"I didna say I *want* to see her," he said, a noticeable edge in his voice. "I said I need to."

"Would it be presumptuous of me to ask why you need to see her?" Her eyes were just that bit wider and yellower than usual; he'd roused the hawk in her. He hadn't meant to, at all, but he wavered for an instant, suddenly wanting to seek refuge from his own confusion in an almighty row. But he couldn't in conscience do that. Still less could he explain the memory of Laoghaire's face on their wedding day, the look of trust in her eyes, and the nagging feeling that he had betrayed that trust.

"Ye can ask me anything, Sassenach—and ye have," he added pointedly. "I'd answer if I thought I could make sense."

She made a small sniffing noise, not quite "Hmph!" but he took her meaning clear enough.

"If you only want to know who she's sleeping with, there are probably less direct ways of finding out," she said. Her voice was carefully level, but her pupils had dilated.

"I dinna care who she's sleeping with!"

"Oh, yes, you do," she said promptly.

"I don't!"

"Liar, liar, pants on fire," she said, and on the verge of an explosion, he burst out laughing instead. She looked momentarily taken back but then joined him, snorting with it and her nose going pink.

They stopped in seconds, abashed at being hilarious in a house that hadn't known open laughter for too long—but were still smiling at each other.

"Come here," he said softly, and held out a hand to her. She took it at once, her fingers warm and strong on his, and came to put her arms around him.

Her hair smelled different. Still fresh, and full of the scent of live green things, but different. Like the Highlands. Like heather, maybe.

"You do want to know who it is, you know," she said, her voice warm and tickling through the fabric of his shirt. "Do you want me to tell you why?"

"Aye, I do, and no, I don't," he said, tightening his hold. "I ken well enough why, and I'm sure you and Jenny and every other woman in fifty miles think they do, too. But that's not why I need to see her."

She pushed a little way back then and brushed the falling curls out of her eyes to look up at him. She searched his face thoughtfully and nodded.

"Well, do give her my very best regards, then, won't you?"

"Why, ye vengeful wee creature. I'd never ha' thought it of ye!"

"Wouldn't you, indeed?" she said, dry as toast. He smiled down at her and ran a thumb gently down the side of her cheek.

"No," he said. "I wouldn't. Ye're no one to hold a grudge, Sassenach; ye never have been."

"Well, I'm not a Scot," she observed, smoothing back her hair. "It's not a matter of national pride, I mean." She put a hand on his chest before he could answer, and said, quite seriously, "She never made you laugh, did she?"

"I may have smiled once or twice," he said gravely. "But no."

"Well, just you remember that," she said, and with a swish of skirts, was off. He grinned like a fool and followed her.

When he reached the stairs, she was waiting, halfway down.

"One thing," she said, lifting a finger at him.

"Aye?"

"If you find out who she's sleeping with and don't tell me, I *will* kill you."

BALRIGGAN WAS A small place, little more than ten acres, plus the house and outbuildings. Still, it was bonnie, a large gray stone cottage tucked into the curve of a hill, a bittie wee loch glimmering like a looking glass at its foot. The English had burned the fields and the barn during the Rising, but fields came back. Much more easily than the men who tilled them.

He rode slowly past the loch, thinking that this visit was a mistake. It was possible to leave things behind—places, people, memories—at least for a time. But places held tight to the things that had happened in them, and to come again to a place you had once lived was to be brought face-to-face with what you had done there and who you had been.

Balriggan, though . . . it hadn't been a bad place; he had loved the wee loch and the way it mirrored the sky, so still some mornings that you felt you might walk down into the clouds you saw reflected there, feeling their cold mist rise up about you, to wrap you in their drifting peace. Or in the summer evenings, when the surface glimmered in hundreds of overlapping rings as the hatch rose, the rhythm of it broken now and then by the sudden splash of a leaping salmon.

The road took him closer, and he saw the stony shallows where he'd shown wee Joan and Marsali how to guddle fish, all three of them so intent on their business they'd paid no heed to the midgies biting, and gone home wet to the waist and red with bites and sunburn, the wee maids skipping and swinging from his hands, gleeful in the sunset. He smiled just a little—then turned his horse's head away, up the hill to the house.

The place was shabby but in decent repair, he grudgingly noted. There was a saddle mule browsing in the paddock behind the house, elderly but sound-looking. Well enough. Laoghaire wasn't spending his money on follies or a coach-and-four, at least.

He set his hand on the gate and felt a twist go through his wame. The feel of the wood under his hand was eerily familiar; he'd lifted it without thinking, at the spot where it was always inclined to drag on the path. That twist corkscrewed its way up to his mouth as he recalled his last meeting with Ned Gowan, Laoghaire's lawyer. "*What does the bloody woman want, then?*" he'd demanded, exasperated. To which Ned had replied cheerfully, "*Your head, mounted above her gate.*"

With a brief snort, he went through, closing the gate a bit harder than necessary, and glanced up at the house.

Movement took his eye. A man was sitting on the bench outside the cottage, staring at him over a bit of broken harness on his knee.

An ill-favored wee lad, Jamie thought, scrawny and narrow-faced as a ferret, with a walleye and a mouth that hung open as though in astonishment. Still, Jamie greeted the man pleasantly, asking was his mistress to home the day?

The lad—seen closer to, he must be in his thirties—blinked at him, then turned his head to bring his good eye to bear.

"Who're you, then?" he asked, sounding unfriendly.

"Fraser of Broch Tuarach," Jamie replied. It was a formal occasion, after all. "Is Mrs.—" He hesitated, not knowing how to refer to Laoghaire. His sister had said she persisted in calling herself "Mrs. Fraser," despite the scandal. He hadn't felt he could object—the fault of it being his and he being in America in any case—but damned if he'd call her that himself, even to her servant.

"Fetch your mistress, if ye please," he said shortly.

"What d'ye want wi' her?" The straight eye narrowed in suspicion.

He hadn't expected obstruction and was inclined to reply sharply, but reined himself in. The man clearly kent something of him, and it was as well if Laoghaire's servant was concerned for her welfare, even if the man's manner was crude.

"I wish to speak with her, if ye've no great objection," he said, with extreme politeness. "D'ye think ye might make shift to go and tell her so?"

The man made a rude sound in his throat but put aside the harness and stood up. Too late, Jamie saw that his spine was badly twisted and one leg shorter than the other. There was no way to apologize that would not make matters worse, though, and so he only nodded shortly and let the man lurch his way off into the house, thinking that it was just like Laoghaire to keep a lame servant for the express purpose of embarrassing him.

Then he shook himself in irritation, ashamed of his thought. What was it about him that a hapless woman such as Laoghaire MacKenzie should bring out every wicked, shameful trait he possessed? Not that his sister couldn't do it, too, he reflected ruefully. But Jenny would evoke some bit of bad temper or hasty language from him, fan the flames 'til he was roaring, and then extinguish him neatly with a word, as though she'd doused him with cold water.

"*Go see her,*" Jenny had said.

"All right, then," he said belligerently. "I'm here."

"I see that," said a light, dry voice. "Why?"

He swung round to face Laoghaire, who was standing in the doorway, broom in hand, giving him a cool look.

He snatched off his hat and bowed to her.

"Good day to ye. I hope I see ye well the day." Apparently so; her face was slightly flushed beneath a starched white kerch, blue eyes clear.

She looked him over, expressionless save for fair brows arched high.

"I heard ye were come home. Why are ye here?"

"To see how ye fare."

Her brows rose that wee bit higher.

"Well enough. What d'ye want?"

He'd gone through it in his mind a hundred times but should have known that for the waste of effort it was. There were things that could be planned for, but none of them involved women.

"I've come to say sorry to ye," he said bluntly. "I said it before, and ye shot me. D'ye want to listen this time?"

The brows came down. She glanced from him to the broom in her hand, as though estimating its usefulness as a weapon, then looked back at him and shrugged.

"Suit yourself. Will ye come in, then?" She jerked her head toward the house.

"It's a fine day. Shall we walk in the garden?" He had no wish to enter the house, with its memories of tears and silences.

She regarded him for a moment or two, then nodded and turned toward the garden path, leaving him to follow if he would. He noticed that she kept a grip on the broom, though, and was not sure whether to be amused or offended.

They walked in silence through the kailyard and through a gate into the garden. It was a kitchen garden, made for utility, but it had a small orchard at the end of it, and there were flowers growing between the pea vines and onion beds. She'd always liked flowers; he remembered that with a small twist of the heart.

She'd put the broom over her shoulder, like a soldier carrying a rifle, and strolled beside him—in no hurry but not offering him an opening, either. He cleared his throat.

"I said I'd come to apologize."

"So ye did." She didn't turn to look at him but stopped and poked her toe at a curling potato vine.

"When we . . . wed," he said, trying to retrieve the careful speech he'd thought of. "I should not have asked ye. My heart was cold. I'd no right to offer ye a dead thing."

Her nostrils flared briefly, but she didn't look up. Just went on frowning at the potato vine, as though she suspected it might have bugs.

"I knew that," she said at last. "I did hope—" She broke off, lips pressing tight as she swallowed. "I did hope I might be of help to ye, though. Everyone could see ye needed a woman. Just not *me*, I suppose," she added bitterly.

Stung, he said the first thing that came to his tongue.

"I thought ye needed *me*."

She looked up then, her eyes gone bright. Christ, she was going to weep, he knew it. But she didn't.

"I'd weans to feed." Her voice was hard and flat and hit him like a slap on the cheek.

"So ye did," he said, keeping his temper. It was honest, at least. "They've grown now, though." *And* he'd found dowries for both Marsali and Joan, too, but he didn't suppose he'd be given any credit for that.

"So that's it," she said, her voice growing colder. "Ye think ye can talk your way out of paying me now, is that it?"

"No, that is *not* it, for God's sake!"

"Because," she said, ignoring his denial and swinging round to face him, bright-eyed, "ye can't. Ye shamed me before the whole parish, Jamie Fraser, luring me into a sinful match wi' you and then betraying me, laughin' at me behind your hand wi' your Sassenach whore!"

"I didna—"

"And now ye come back from America, fardeled up like an English popin-jay"—her lip curled in scorn at his good ruffled shirt, which he'd worn to show her respect, God damn it!—"flauntin' your wealth and playin' the great yin wi' your ancient hussy foamin' in her silks and satins on your arm, is it? Well, I'll tell ye—" She swung the broom down from her shoulder and drove the handle of it violently into the ground. "Ye dinna understand one thing about me, and ye think ye can awe me into crawlin' away like a dyin' dog and troubling ye no more! Think again, that's all I'll say to ye—just think again!"

He snatched the purse out of his pocket and flung it at the door of the garden shed, where it struck with a boom and bounced off. He had just a moment to regret having brought a chunk of gold, and not coins that would jingle, before his temper flared.

"Aye, ye're right about *that,* at least! I dinna understand one thing about ye! I never have, try as I might!"

"Oh, try as ye might, is it?" she cried, ignoring the purse. "Ye never tried for an instant, Jamie Fraser! In fact—" Her face clenched up like a fist as she fought to keep her voice under control. "Ye never truly *looked* at me. Never—well, no, I suppose ye looked once. When I was sixteen." Her voice trembled on the word, and she looked away, jaw clamped tight. Then she looked back at him, eyes bright and tearless.

"Ye took a beating for me. At Leoch. D'ye recall that?"

For an instant, he didn't. Then he stopped, breathing heavily. His hand went instinctively to his jaw, and against his will he felt the ghost of a smile rise against the anger.

"Oh. Aye. Aye, I do." Angus Mhor had given him an easier time than he might have—but it was a fair beating, nonetheless. His ribs had ached for days.

She nodded, watching him. Her cheeks were splotched with red, but she'd calmed herself.

"I thought ye'd done it because ye loved me. I went on thinking that, ken, until well after we'd wed. But I was wrong, wasn't I?"

Bafflement must have showed on his face, for she made that small "Mph!" in her nose that meant she was aggravated. He knew her well enough to know *that,* at least.

"Ye pitied me," she said flatly. "I didna see that then. Ye pitied me at Leoch, not only later, when ye took me to wife. I thought ye loved me," she repeated, spacing the words as though speaking to a simpleton. "When Dougal made ye wed the Sassenach whore, I thought I'd die. But I thought maybe *you* felt like dyin', too—and it wasna like that at all, was it?"

"Ah . . . no," he said, feeling awkward and foolish. He'd seen nothing of her feelings then. Hadn't seen a thing but Claire. But of course Laoghaire had thought he loved her; she was sixteen. And would have known that his marriage to Claire was a forced one, never realizing that he was willing. Of course she'd thought she and he were star-crossed lovers. Except that he'd never looked at her again. He rubbed a hand over his face, feeling complete helplessness.

"Ye never told me that," he said finally, letting his hand drop.

"What good would it ha' done?" she said.

So there it was. She'd known—she must have known—by the time he married her what the truth of it was. But still, she must have hoped . . . Unable to find anything to say in reply, his mind took refuge in the irrelevant.

"Who was it?" he asked.

"Who?" Her brow furrowed in puzzlement.

"The lad. Your father wanted ye punished for wantonness, no? Who did ye play the loon with, then, when I took the beating for ye? I never thought to ask."

The red splotches on her cheeks grew deeper.

"No, ye never would, would ye?"

A barbed silence of accusation fell between them. He hadn't asked, then; he hadn't cared.

"I'm sorry," he said softly, at last. "Tell me, though. Who was it?" He hadn't cared then in the least but found himself curious now, if only as a way of not thinking of other things—or not saying them. They hadn't had the past she'd thought, but the past lay still between them, forming a tenuous connection.

Her lips thinned and he thought she wouldn't say, but then they parted, reluctant.

"John Robert MacLeod."

He frowned, at a loss for a moment, and then the name dropped into its proper place in memory and he stared at her.

"John Robert? What, him from Killiecrankie?"

"Aye," she said. "Him." Her mouth snapped shut on the word.

He hadn't known the man well at all, but John Robert MacLeod's reputation among young women had been the subject of a good deal of talk among the men-at-arms at Leoch in his brief time there. A sly, good-looking slink of a man, handsome and lean-jawed—and the fact that he'd a wife and weans at home in Killiecrankie seemed to hamper him not at all.

"Jesus!" he said, unable to stop himself. "Ye're lucky ye kept your maidenheid!"

An ugly flush washed darkly over her from stays to cap, and his jaw dropped.

"Laoghaire MacKenzie! Ye werena such a wanton fool to let him take ye virgin to his bed!?"

"I didna ken he was marrit!" she cried, stamping her foot. "And it was after ye wed the Sassenach. I went to him for comfort."

"Oh, and he gave it ye, I'm sure!"

"Hush your gob!" she shrieked, and, picking up a stone watering pot from the bench by the shed, hurled it at his head. He hadn't expected that—Claire threw things at him frequently, but Laoghaire never had—and was nearly brained; it struck him in the shoulder as he ducked aside.

The watering pot was followed by a hail of other objects from the bench and a storm of incoherent language, all manner of unwomanly swearing, punctuated by shrieks like a teakettle. A pan of buttermilk hurtled toward him, missed its aim, but soaked him from chest to knees with curds and whey.

He was half laughing—from shock—when she suddenly seized a mattock from the shed wall and made for him. Seriously alarmed, he ducked and grabbed her wrist, twisting so she dropped the heavy tool with a thump. She let out a screech like a *ban-sidhe* and whipped her other hand across his face, half-blinding him with her nails. He snatched that wrist, too, and pressed her back into the wall of the shed, her still kicking at his shins, struggling and writhing against him like a snake.

"I'm sorry!" He was shouting in her ear to be heard above the noise she was making. "Sorry! D'ye hear me—I'm *sorry*!" The clishmaclaver stopped him hearing anything behind, though, and he had not the slightest warning when something monstrous struck him behind the ear and sent him staggering, lights flashing in his head.

He kept his grip on her wrists as he stumbled and fell, dragging her down atop him. He wrapped his arms tight round her, to keep her from clawing him again, and blinked, trying to clear his watering eyes.

"Free her, *MacIfrinn!*" The mattock chunked into the earth beside his head.

He flung himself over, Laoghaire still clutched to him, rolling madly through the beds. The sound of panting and uneven steps, and the mattock came down again, pinning his sleeve to the ground and scraping the flesh of his arm.

He jerked free, heedless of tearing skin and cloth, rolled away from Laoghaire, and sprang to his feet, then launched himself without pause at the weazened figure of Laoghaire's servant, who was in the act of raising the mattock above his head, narrow face contorted with effort.

He butted the man in the face with a crunch and bore him flat, punching him in the belly before they hit the ground. He scrambled atop the man and went on punching him, the violence some relief. The man was grunting, whimpering, and gurgling, and he'd drawn back his knee to give the bugger one in the balls to settle the matter when he became dimly aware of Laoghaire, screeching and beating at his head.

"Leave him alone!" she was shrieking, crying and slapping at him with her hands. "Leave him, leave him, for the love of Bride, don't hurt him!"

He stopped then, panting, feeling suddenly a terrible fool. Beating a scrawny cripple who meant only to protect his mistress from obvious attack, manhandling a woman like a street ruffian—*Christ,* what was the matter with him? He slid off the man, repressing an impulse to apologize, and got awkwardly to his feet, meaning to give the poor bugger a hand up, at least.

Before he could manage, though, Laoghaire fell to her knees beside the man, weeping and grappling at him, finally getting him partway sitting, his narrow head pressed to her soft round bosom, she heedless of the blood gushing from his smashed nose, petting and stroking him, murmuring his name. Joey, it seemed to be.

Jamie stood swaying a bit, staring at this demonstration. Blood was dripping from his fingers, and his arm was beginning to burn where the mattock had skinned it. He felt something stinging run into his eyes and, wiping it away, found that his forehead was bleeding; Joey the openmouthed had evidently inadvertently bitten him when he'd butted the man. He grimaced with disgust, feeling the tooth marks in his forehead, and groped for a handkerchief with which to stanch the blood.

Meanwhile, foggy as his head felt, matters on the ground in front of him were becoming clearer by the moment. A good mistress might try to comfort a wounded servant, but he'd yet to hear a woman call a servant *mo chridhe.* Let alone kiss him passionately on the mouth, getting her own face smeared with blood and snot in the process.

"Mmphm," he said.

Startled, Laoghaire turned a blood-smeared, tearstained face to him. She'd never looked lovelier.

"*Him?*" Jamie said incredulously, nodding toward the crumpled Joey. "Why, for God's sake?"

Laoghaire glared at him slit-eyed, crouched like a cat about to spring. She considered him for a moment, then slowly straightened her back, gathering Joey's head once more against her breast.

"Because he needs me," she said evenly. "And you, ye bastard, never did."

HE LEFT THE HORSE to graze along the edge of the loch and, stripping off his clothes, walked into the water. The sky was overcast, and the loch was full of clouds.

The rocky bottom fell away and he let the gray cold water take him, his legs trailing loose behind, his small injuries chilling into numbness. He put his face under the water, eyes closed, to wash the cut on his head, and felt the bubbles of his breath soft and tickling over his shoulders.

He raised his head and began to swim, slowly, with no thought at all.

He lay on his back among the clouds, hair afloat like kelp, and stared up into the sky. A spatter of rain dimpled the water around him, then thickened. It was a soft rain, though; no feel of the drops striking him, only a sense of the loch and its clouds bathing his face, his body, washing away the blood and fret of the last little while.

Would he ever come back? he wondered.

The water filled his ears with its own rush, and he was comforted by the realization that, in fact, he had never left.

He turned at last and struck out for the shore, cutting smooth through the water. It was still raining, harder now, the drops a constant tapping on his bare shoulders as he swam. Still, the sinking sun shone under the clouds and lit Balriggan and its hill with a gentle glow.

He felt the bottom rise and put his feet down, then stood for a moment, waist-deep, looking at it for a bit.

"No," he said softly, and felt remorse soften into regret and, at last, the absolution of resignation. "Ye're right—I never did. I'm sorry."

He walked out of the water then, and with a whistle to the horse, pulled the wet plaid over his shoulders and turned his face toward Lallybroch.

79

THE CAVE

USEFUL HERBS, I wrote, and paused—as usual—to consider. Writing with a quill caused one to be both more deliberate and more economical in writing than doing it with ballpoint or typewriter. Still, I thought, I'd best just make a list here and jot down notes regarding each herb as they came to me, then make a clean draft when I'd got it all straight and made sure to include everything, rather than try to do it all in a single run.

Lavender, peppermint, comfrey, I wrote without hesitation. *Calendula, feverfew, foxglove, meadow-sweet.* Then went back to add a large asterisk beside *foxglove* to remind me to add strong cautions about the use, as all parts of the plant were extremely poisonous in any but very small doses. I twiddled the quill, biting my lip in indecision. Ought it to mention that one at all, given that this was meant to be a useful medical guide for the common man, not for medical practitioners with experience in various medicaments? Because, really, you ought not dose *anyone* with foxglove unless you'd been trained . . . Best not. I crossed it out but then had second thoughts. Perhaps I'd better mention it, with a drawing, but also with a severe warning that it should be used *only* by a physician, in case someone had the bright idea of remedying Uncle Tophiger's dropsy permanently. . . .

A shadow fell across the floor in front of me and I looked up. Jamie was standing there with a most peculiar look on his face.

"What?" I said, startled. "Has something happened?"

"No," he said, and advancing into the study, leaned down and put his hands on the desk, bringing his face within a foot of mine.

"Have ye ever been in the slightest doubt that I need ye?" he demanded.

It took roughly half a second of thought to answer this.

"No," I replied promptly. "To the best of my knowledge, you needed me urgently the moment I saw you. And I haven't had reason to think you've got any more self-sufficient since. What on *earth* happened to your forehead? Those look like tooth—" He lunged across the desk and kissed me before I could finish the observation.

"Thank ye," he said fervently, and, un-lunging, whirled and went out, evidently in the highest of spirits.

"What's amiss wi' Uncle Jamie?" Ian demanded, coming in on Jamie's heels. He glanced back toward the open door into the hall, from the depths of which a loud, tuneless humming was coming, like that of a trapped bumblebee. "Is he drunk?"

"I don't think so," I said dubiously, running my tongue across my lips. "He didn't taste of anything alcoholic."

"Aye, well." Ian lifted a shoulder, dismissing his uncle's eccentricities. "I was just up beyond Broch Mordha, and Mr. MacAllister said to me that his wife's mother was taken bad in the night, and would ye maybe think of coming by, if it wasn't a trouble to ye?"

"No trouble at all," I assured him, rising with alacrity. "Just let me get my bag."

FOR ALL IT was spring, a cold, treacherous season, the tenants and neighbors seemed remarkably healthy. With some caution, I had resumed my doctoring, tentatively offering advice and medicine where it might be accepted. After all, I was no longer the lady of Lallybroch, and many of the folk who'd known me before were now dead. Those who weren't seemed generally glad to see me, but there was a wariness in their eyes that hadn't been there before. It saddened me to see it, but I understood it, all too well.

I had left Lallybroch, left Himself. Left *them*. And while they affected to believe the story Jamie put about, about my having thought him dead and fled to France, they couldn't help but feel I had betrayed them by going. *I* felt I had betrayed them.

The easiness that had once existed between us was gone, and so I didn't routinely visit as I once had; I waited to be called. And in the meantime, when I *had* to get out of the house, I went foraging on my own or walked with Jamie—who also had to get out of the house now and then.

One day, when the weather was windy but fine, he took me farther than usual, saying that he would show me his cave, if I liked.

"I would, very much," I said. I put my hand above my eyes to shield them from the sun as I looked up a steep hill. "Is it up there?"

"Aye. Can ye see it?"

I shook my head. Aside from the big white rock the people called Leap o' the Cask, it could have been any Highland hillside, clustered with gorse, broom, and heather, what ground showed in between only rocks.

"Come on, then," Jamie said, and setting foot on an invisible foothold, smiled and reached a hand to help me up.

It was a hard climb, and I was panting and damp with perspiration by the time he pushed aside a screen of gorse to show me the narrow mouth of the cave.

"I WANT TO go in."

"No, ye don't," he assured her. "It's cold and it's dirty."

She gave him an odd look and half a smile.

"I'd never have guessed," she said, very dry. "I still want to go in."

There was no point in arguing with her. He shrugged and took off his coat to save its getting filthy, hanging it on a rowan sapling that had sprouted near the entrance. He put up his hands to the stones on either side of the entrance, but then was unsure; was it there he had always grasped the stone, or not? *Christ, does it matter?* he chided himself, and, taking firm hold of the rock, stepped in and swung down.

It was just as cold as he'd known it would be. It was out of the wind, at least—not a biting cold, but a dank chill that sank through the skin and gnawed at the bone ends.

He turned and reached up his hands, and she leaned to him, tried to climb down, but lost her footing and half-fell, landing in his arms in a fluster of clothes and loose hair. He laughed and turned her round to look, but kept his arms around her. He was loath to surrender the warmth of her and held her like a shield against cold memory.

She was still, leaning back against him, only her head moving as she looked from one end of the cave to the other. It was barely eight feet long, but the far end was lost in shadow. She lifted her chin, seeing the soft black stains that coated the rock to one side by the entrance.

"That's where my fire was—when I dared have one." His voice sounded strange, small and muffled, and he cleared his throat.

"Where was your bed?"

"Just there by your left foot."

"Did you sleep with your head at this end?" She tapped her foot on the graveled dirt of the floor.

"Aye. I could see the stars, if the night was clear. I turned the other way if it rained." She heard the smile in his voice and put her hand along his thigh, squeezing.

"I hoped that," she said, her own voice a little choked. "When we learned about the Dunbonnet, and the cave . . . I thought about you, alone here—and I hoped you could see the stars at night."

"I could," he whispered, and bent his head to put his lips to her hair. The shawl she'd pulled over her head had slipped off, and her hair smelled of lemon balm and what she said was catmint.

She made a small *hmp* noise in her throat and folded her own arms over his, warming him through his shirt.

"I feel as though I've seen it before," she said, sounding a little surprised. "Though I suppose one cave probably looks a good deal like any other cave, unless you have stalactites hanging from the ceiling or mammoths painted on the walls."

"I've never had a talent for decoration," he said, and she *hmp*'ed again, amused. "As for being here . . . ye've been here many nights wi' me, Sassenach. You and the wee lass, both." *Though I didna ken then she was a lassie,* he added silently, remembering with a small odd pang that now and then he had sat there on the flat rock by the entrance, imagining sometimes a daughter warm in his arms, but now and then feeling a tiny son on his knee and pointing out the stars to travel by, explaining to him how the hunting was done and the prayer ye must say when ye killed for food.

But he'd told those things to Brianna later—and to Jem. The knowledge wouldn't be lost. Would it be of use, though? he wondered suddenly.

"Do folk still hunt?" he asked. "Then?"

"Oh, yes," she assured him. "Every fall, we'd have a rash of hunters coming in to the hospital—mostly idiots who'd got drunk and shot each other by mistake, though once I had a gentleman who'd been badly trampled by a deer he thought was dead."

He laughed, both shocked and comforted. The notion of hunting while drunken . . . though he'd seen fools do it. But at least men still did hunt. Jem would hunt.

"I'm sure Roger Mac wouldna let Jem take too much drink before hunting," he said. "Even if the other lads do."

Her head tilted a little to and fro, in the way it did when she was wondering whether to tell him something, and he tightened his arms a little.

"What?"

"I was just imagining a gang of second-graders having a tot of whisky all round before setting off home from school in the rain," she said, snorting briefly. "Children don't drink alcohol then—at all. Or at least they aren't meant to, and it's scandalous child neglect if they're allowed."

"Aye?" That seemed odd; he'd been given ale or beer with his food since . . . well, as far back as he recalled. And certainly a dram of whisky against the cold, or if his liver were chilled or he had the earache or . . . It was true, though, that Brianna made Jem drink milk, even after he was out of smocks.

The rattle of stones on the hillside below startled him, and he let go of Claire, turning toward the entrance. He doubted it was trouble but nonetheless motioned to her to stay, hoisting himself out of the cave mouth and reaching for his coat and the knife in its pocket even before he looked to see who had come.

There was a woman some way below, a tall figure in cloak and shawl, down by the big rock where Fergus had lost his hand. She was looking up, though, and saw him come out of the cave. She waved to him and beckoned, and with a quick glance round that assured him she was alone, he made his way half-sliding down the slope to the trail where she stood.

"Feasgar math," he greeted her, shrugging into the coat. She was fairly young, perhaps in her early twenties, but he didn't know her. Or thought he didn't, until she spoke.

"Ciamar a tha thu, mo athair," she said formally. *How do you do, Father?*

He blinked, startled, but then leaned forward, peering at her.

"Joanie?" he said, incredulous. "Wee Joanie?" Her long, rather solemn face broke into a smile at that, but it was brief.

"Ye know me, then?"

"Aye, I do, now I come to see—" He put out a hand, wanting to embrace her, but she stood a bit away from him, stiff, and he let the hand drop, clearing his throat to cover the moment. "It's been some time, lass. Ye've grown," he added lamely.

"Bairns mostly do," she said, dry. "Is it your wife ye've got with you? The first one, I mean."

"It is," he replied, the shock of her appearance replaced by wariness. He gave her a quick look-over, in case she might be armed, but couldn't tell; her cloak was wrapped round her against the wind.

"Perhaps ye'd summon her down," Joan suggested. "I should like to meet her."

He rather doubted that. Still, she seemed composed, and he could scarcely refuse to let her meet Claire, if she wished it. Claire would be watching; he turned and gestured toward the cave, beckoning her, then turned back to Joan.

"How d'ye come to be here, lass?" he asked, turning back to her. It was a good eight miles to Balriggan from here, and there was nothing near the cave to draw anyone.

"I was coming to Lallybroch to see ye—I missed your visit when ye came to the house," she added, with a brief flash of what might have been amusement. "But I saw you and . . . your wife . . . walking, so I came after ye."

It warmed him, to think she'd wanted to see him. At the same time, he was cautious. It had been twelve years, and she'd been a child when he left. And she'd spent those years with Laoghaire, doubtless hearing no good opinions of him in that time.

He looked searchingly into her face, seeing only the vaguest memory of the childish features he recalled. She was not beautiful, or even pretty, but had a certain dignity about her that was attractive; she met his gaze straight on, not seeming to care what he thought of what he saw. She had the shape of Laoghaire's eyes and nose, though little else from her mother, being tall, dark, and rawboned, heavy-browed, with a long, thin face and a mouth that was not much used to smiling, he thought.

He heard Claire making her way down the slope behind him and turned to help her, though keeping one eye on Joanie, just in case.

"Dinna fash," Joan said calmly behind him. "I dinna mean to shoot her."

"Och? Well, that's good." Discomposed, he tried to remember—had she been in the house when Laoghaire shot him? He thought not, though he'd been in no condition to notice. She'd certainly known about it, though.

Claire took his hand and hopped down onto the trail, not pausing to settle herself but coming forward at once and taking Joan's hands in both her own, smiling.

"I'm happy to meet you," she said, sounding as though she meant it. "Marsali said I was to give you this." And, leaning forward, she kissed Joan on the cheek.

For the first time, he saw the girl taken aback. She flushed and pulled her hands away, turning aside and rubbing a fold of her cloak under her nose as though taken by an itch, lest anyone see her eyes well up.

"I—thank you," she said, with a hasty dab at her eyes. "You—my sister's written of you." She cleared her throat and blinked hard, then stared at Claire with open interest—an interest that was being returned in full.

"Félicité looks like you," Claire said. "So does Henri-Christian, just a bit— but Félicité very much."

"Poor child," Joan murmured, but couldn't repress the smile that had lit her face at this.

Jamie coughed.

"Will ye not come down to the house, Joanie? Ye'd be welcome."

She shook her head.

"Later, maybe. I wanted to speak to ye, *a athair*, where no one could hear. Save your wife," she added, with a glance at Claire. "As she's doubtless something to say on the matter."

That sounded mildly sinister, but then she added, "It's about my dowry."

"Oh, aye? Well, come away out o' the wind, at least." He led them toward the lee of the big rock, wondering what was afoot. Was the lass wanting to wed someone unsuitable and her mother was refusing to give her her dowry? Had something happened to the money? He doubted that; old Ned Gowan had devised the documents, and the money was safe in a bank in Inverness. And whatever he thought of Laoghaire, he was sure she'd never do anything to the hurt of her daughters.

A huge gust of wind came up the track, whirling up the women's petticoats like flying leaves and pelting them all with clouds of dust and dry heather. They darted into the shelter of the rock and stood smiling and laughing a little with the intoxication of the weather, brushing off the dirt and settling their clothes.

"So, then," Jamie said, before the good mood should have a chance to curdle on them, "who is it ye mean to wed?"

"Jesus Christ," Joan replied promptly.

He stared at her for a moment, until he became aware that his mouth was hanging open and closed it.

"You want to be a nun?" Claire's brows were raised with interest. "Really?"

"I do. I've kent for a long time that I've a vocation, but . . ." She hesitated. " . . . it's . . . complicated."

"I daresay it is," Jamie said, recovering himself somewhat. "Have ye spoken to anyone about it, lass? The priest? Your mother?"

Joan's lips pressed into a thin line.

"Both of them," she said shortly.

"And what did they say?" Claire asked. She was plainly fascinated, leaning back against the rock, combing back her hair with her fingers.

Joan snorted. "My mother says," she said precisely, "that I've lost my mind from reading books—and that's all *your* fault," she added pointedly to Jamie, "for giving me the taste for it. She wants me to wed auld Geordie McCann, but I said I'd rather be dead in the ditch."

"How old *is* auld Geordie McCann?" Claire inquired, and Joan blinked at her.

"Five-and-twenty or so," she said. "What's that to do with it?"

"Just curious," Claire murmured, looking entertained. "There's a young Geordie McCann, then?"

"Aye, his nephew. He's three," Joan added, in the interests of strict accuracy. "I dinna want to wed him, either."

"And the priest?" Jamie intervened, before Claire could derail the discussion entirely.

Joan drew breath, seeming to grow taller and sterner with it.

"*He* says that it's my duty to stay to hame and tend to my aged mother."

"Who's swiving Joey the hired man in the goat shed," Jamie added helpfully. "Ye ken that, I suppose?" From the corner of his eye, he saw Claire's face, which entertained him so much that he was obliged to turn away and not look at her. He lifted a hand behind his back, indicating that he'd tell her later.

"Not while I'm in the house, she doesn't," Joan said coldly. "Which is the only reason I *am* in the house, still. D'ye think my conscience will let me leave, knowing what they'll be up to? This is the first time I've gone further than the kailyard in three months, and if it wasna sinful to place wagers, I'd bet ye my best shift they're at it this minute, damning both their souls to hell."

Jamie cleared his throat, trying—and failing—not to think of Joey and Laoghaire, wrapped in passionate embrace on her bed with the blue-and-gray quilt.

"Aye, well." He could feel Claire's eyes boring into the back of his neck and felt the blood rise there. "So. Ye want to go for a nun, but the priest says ye mustn't, your mother willna give ye your dowry for it, and your conscience willna let ye do it anyway. Is that the state o' things, would ye say?"

"Aye, it is," Joan said, pleased with his concise summary.

"And, um, what is it that you'd like Jamie to do about it?" Claire inquired, coming round to stand by him. "Kill Joey?" She shot Jamie a sidelong yellow-eyed glance, full of wicked enjoyment at his discomfiture. He gave her a narrow look, and she grinned at him.

"Of course not!" Joan's heavy brow drew down. "I want them to wed. Then they'd no be in a state of mortal sin every time I turned my back, *and* the priest couldna say I've to stay at home, not if my mother's got a husband to care for her."

Jamie rubbed a finger slowly up and down the bridge of his nose, trying to make out just how he was meant to induce two middle-aged reprobates to wed. By force? Hold a fowling piece on them? He could, he supposed, but . . . well, the more he thought of it, the better he liked the notion . . .

"Does he *want* to marry her, do you think?" Claire asked, surprising him. It hadn't occurred to him to wonder that.

"Aye, he does," Joan said, with obvious disapproval. "He's always moaning on about it to me, how much he looooves her . . ." She rolled her eyes. "Not that I think he shouldna love her," she hastened to add, seeing Jamie's expression. "But he shouldna be telling *me* about it, now, should he?"

"Ah . . . no," he said, feeling mildly dazed. The wind was booming past the rock, and the whine of it in his ears was eating at him, making him feel suddenly as he used to in the cave, living in solitude for weeks, with no voice but the wind's to hear. He shook his head violently to clear it, forcing himself to focus on Joan's face, hear her words above the wind.

"She's willing, I think," Joan was saying, still frowning. "Though she doesna talk to me about it, thank Bride. She's fond of him, though; feeds him the choice bits and that."

"Well, then . . ." He brushed a flying strand of hair out of his mouth, feeling dizzy. "Why do they not marry?"

"Because of you," Claire said, sounding a trifle less amused. "And that's where I come into this, I suppose?"

"Because of—"

"The agreement you made with Laoghaire, when I . . . came back." Her attention was focused on Joan, but she came closer and touched his hand lightly, not looking at him. "You promised to support her—and find dowries for Joan and Marsali—but the support was to stop if she married again. That's it, isn't it?" she said to Joan, who nodded.

"She and Joey might make shift to scrape along," she said. "He does what he can, but . . . ye've seen him. If ye were to stop the money, though, she'd likely have to sell Balriggan to live—and that would break her heart," she added quietly, dropping her eyes for the first time.

An odd pain seized his heart—odd because it was not his own but he recognized it. It was sometime in the first weeks of their marriage, when he'd been digging new beds in the garden. Laoghaire had brought him out a mug of cool beer and stood while he drank it, then thanked him for the digging. He'd been surprised and laughed, saying why should she think to thank him for that?

"Because ye take care for my place," she'd said simply, "but ye don't try to take it from me." Then she'd taken the empty mug from him and gone back to the house.

And once, in bed—and he flushed at the thought, with Claire standing right by him—he'd asked her why she liked Balriggan so much; it wasna a family place, after all, nor remarkable in any way. And she'd sighed a little, pulled the quilt up to her chin, and said, "It's the first place I've felt safe." She wouldn't say more when he asked her, but only turned over and pretended to fall asleep.

"She'd rather lose Joey than Balriggan," Joan was saying to Claire. "But she doesna mean to lose *him,* either. So ye see the difficulty, aye?"

"I do, yes." Claire was looking sympathetic but shot him a glance indicating that this was—naturally—*his* problem. Of course it was, he thought, exasperated.

"I'll . . . do something," he said, having not the slightest notion what, but how could he refuse? God would probably strike him down for interfering with Joan's vocation, if his own sense of guilt didn't finish him off first.

"Oh, Da! *Thank* you!"

Joan's face broke into a sudden, dazzling smile, and she threw herself into his arms—he barely got them up in time to catch her; she was a very solid young woman. But he folded her into the embrace he'd wanted to give her on meeting and felt the odd pain ease, as this strange daughter fitted herself tidily into an empty spot in his heart he hadn't known was there.

The wind was still whipping by, and it might have been a speck of dust that made Claire's eyes glisten as she looked at him, smiling.

"Just the one thing," he said sternly, when Joan had released him and stood back.

"Anything," she said fervently.

"Ye'll pray for me, aye? When ye're a nun?"

"Every day," she assured him, "and twice on Sundays."

THE SUN WAS starting down the sky by now, but there was still some time to supper. I should, I supposed, be there to offer to help with the meal preparations; these were both enormous and laborious, with so many people coming and going, and Lallybroch could no longer afford the luxury of a cook. But even if Jenny was taken up with nursing Ian, Maggie and her young daughters and the two housemaids were more than capable of managing. I would only be in the way. Or so I told myself, well aware that there was always work for a spare pair of hands.

But I clambered down the stony hill behind Jamie and said nothing when he turned away from the trail to Lallybroch. We wandered down toward the little loch, well content.

"Perhaps I *did* have something to do wi' the books, aye?" Jamie said, after a bit. "I mean, I read to the wee maids in the evenings now and again. They'd sit on the settle with me, one on each side, wi' their heads against me, and it was—" He broke off with a glance at me and coughed, evidently worried that I might be offended at the idea that he'd ever enjoyed a moment in Laoghaire's house. I smiled and took his arm.

"I'm sure they loved it. But I really doubt that you read anything to Joan that made her want to become a nun."

"Aye, well," he said dubiously. "I did read to them out of the *Lives of the*

Saints. Oh, and *Fox's Book of the Martyrs,* too, even though there's a good deal of it to do wi' Protestants, and Laoghaire said Protestants couldna be martyrs because they were wicked heretics, and I said bein' a heretic didna preclude being a martyr, and—" He grinned suddenly. "I think that might ha' been the closest thing we had to a decent conversation."

"Poor Laoghaire!" I said. "But putting her aside—and do let's—what do you think of Joan's quandary?"

He shook his head dubiously.

"Well, I can maybe bribe Laoghaire to marry yon wee cripple, but it would take a deal of money, since she'd want more than she gets from me now. I havena got that much left of the gold we brought, so it would need to wait until I can get back to the Ridge and extract some more, take that to a bank, arrange for a draft . . . I hate to think of Joan having to spend a year at home, trying to keep yon lust-crazed weasels apart."

"Lust-crazed weasels?" I said, entertained. "No, really. Did you see them at it?"

"Not exactly," he said, coughing. "Ye could see there was an attraction atween them, though. Here, let's go along the shore; I saw a curlew's nest the other day."

The wind had quieted and the sun was bright and warm—for the moment. I could see clouds lurking over the horizon, and doubtless it would be raining again by nightfall, but for the moment it was a lovely spring day, and we were both disposed to enjoy it. By unspoken consent, we put aside all disagreeable matters and talked of nothing in particular, only enjoying each other's company, until we reached a shallow, grass-covered mound where we could perch and enjoy the sun.

Jamie's mind seemed to return now and then to Laoghaire, though—I supposed he couldn't help it. I didn't really mind, as such comparisons as he made were entirely to my benefit.

"Had she been my first," he said thoughtfully at one point, "I think I might have a much different opinion of women in general."

"Well, you can't define all women in terms of what they're like—or what one of them is like—in bed," I objected. "I've known men who, well . . ."

"Men? Was Frank not your first?" he demanded, surprised.

I put a hand behind my head and regarded him.

"Would it matter if he wasn't?"

"Well . . ." Clearly taken aback by the possibility, he groped for an answer. "I suppose—" He broke off and eyed me, meditatively stroking one finger down the bridge of his nose. One corner of his mouth turned up. "I don't know."

I didn't know, myself. On the one hand, I rather enjoyed his shock at the notion—and at my age, I was not at all averse to feeling mildly wanton, if only in retrospect. On the other hand . . .

"Well, where do you get off, anyway, casting stones?"

"Ye were *my* first," he pointed out, with considerable asperity.

"So you *said,*" I said, teasing. To my amusement, he flushed up like the rosy dawn.

"Ye didna believe me?" he said, his voice rising in spite of himself.

"Well, you did seem rather well informed, for a so-called virgin. To say nothing of . . . imaginative."

"For God's sake, Sassenach, I grew up on a farm! It's a verra straightforward business, after all." He looked me closely up and down, his gaze lingering at certain points of particular interest. "And as for imagining things . . . Christ, I'd spent months—years!—imagining!" A certain light filled his eyes, and I had the distinct impression that he hadn't stopped imagining in the intervening years, not by any means.

"What are you thinking?" I asked, intrigued.

"I'm thinking that the water in the loch's that wee bit chilly, but if it didna shrink my cock straight off, the feel of the heat when I plunged into ye . . . Of course," he added practically, eyeing me as though estimating the effort involved in forcing me into the loch, "we wouldna need to do it *in* the water, unless ye liked; I could just dunk ye a few times, drag ye onto the shore, and— God, your arse looks fine, wi' the wet linen of your shift clinging to it. It goes all transparent, and I can see the weight of your buttocks, like great smooth round melons—"

"I take it back—I don't want to know what you're thinking!"

"You asked," he pointed out logically. "And I can see the sweet wee crease of your arse, too—and once I've got ye pinned under me and ye canna get away . . . d'ye want it lying on your back, Sassenach, or bent over on your knees, wi' me behind? I could take a good hold either way, and—"

"I am not going into a freezing loch in order to gratify your perverted desires!"

"All right," he said, grinning. Stretching himself out beside me, he reached round behind and took a generous handful. "Ye can gratify them here, if ye like, where it's warm."

80

OENOMANCY

LALLYBROCH WAS A working farm. Nothing on a farm can stop for very long, even for grief. Which is how it came to be that I was the only person in the front of the house when the door opened in the middle of the afternoon.

I heard the sound and poked my head out of Ian's study to see who had come in. A strange young man was standing in the foyer, gazing round appraisingly. He heard my step and turned, looking at me curiously.

"Who are *you?*" we said simultaneously, and laughed.

"I'm Michael," he said, in a soft, husky voice with the trace of a French accent. "And ye'll be Uncle Jamie's faery-woman, I suppose."

He was examining me with frank interest, and I felt therefore free to do the same.

"Is that what the family's been calling me?" I asked, looking him over.

He was a slight man, lacking either Young Jamie's burly strength or Young Ian's wiry height. Michael was Janet's twin but did not resemble her at all, either. This was the son who had gone to France, to become a junior partner in Jared Fraser's wine business, Fraser *et Cie*. As he took off his traveling cloak, I saw that he was dressed very fashionably for the Highlands, though his suit was sober in both color and cut—and he wore a black crepe band around his upper arm.

"That, or the witch," he said, smiling faintly. "Depending whether it's Da or Mam who's talking."

"Indeed," I said, with an edge—but couldn't help smiling back. He was quiet but an engaging young man—well, relatively young. He must be near thirty, I thought.

"I'm sorry for your...loss," I said, with a nod toward the crepe band. "May I ask—"

"My wife," he said simply. "She died two weeks ago. I should have come sooner, else."

That took me aback considerably.

"Oh. I . . . see. But your parents, your brothers and sisters—they don't know this yet?"

He shook his head and came forward a little, so the light from the fan-shaped window above the door fell on his face, and I saw the dark circles under his eyes and the marks of the bone-deep exhaustion that is grief's only consolation.

"I am so sorry," I said, and, moved by impulse, put my arms around him. He leaned toward me, under the same impulse. His body yielded for an instant to my touch, and there was an extraordinary moment in which I sensed the deep numbness within him, the unacknowledged war of acknowledgment and denial. He knew what had happened, what was happening—but could not feel it. Not yet.

"Oh, dear," I said, stepping back from the brief embrace. I touched his cheek lightly, and he stared at me, blinking.

"I will be damned," he said mildly. "They're right."

A DOOR OPENED and closed above, I heard a foot on the stair—and an instant later, Lallybroch awoke to the knowledge that the last child had come home.

The swirl of women and children wafted us into the kitchen, where the men appeared, by ones and twos through the back door to embrace Michael or clap him on the shoulder.

There were outpourings of sympathy, the same questions and answers repeated several times—how had Michael's wife, Lillie, died? She had died of the influenza; so had her grandmother; no, he himself had not caught it; her father sent his prayers and concerns for Michael's father—and eventually the preparations for washing and supper and the putting of children to bed began, and Michael slipped out of the maelstrom.

Coming out of the kitchen myself to fetch my shawl from the study, I saw him at the foot of the stair with Jenny, talking quietly. She touched his face, just as I had, asking him something in a low voice. He half-smiled, shook his head, and, squaring his shoulders, went upstairs alone to see Ian, who was feeling too poorly to come down to supper.

ALONE AMONG THE Murrays, Michael had inherited the fugitive gene for red hair, and burned among his darker siblings like a coal. He had inherited an exact copy of his father's soft brown eyes, though. "And a good thing, too," Jenny said to me privately, "else his da would likely be sure I'd been at it wi' the goatherd, for God knows, he doesna look like anyone else in the family."

I'd mentioned this to Jamie, who looked surprised but then smiled.

"Aye. She wouldna ken it, for she never met Colum MacKenzie face-to-face."

"Colum? Are you sure?" I looked over my shoulder.

"Oh, aye. The coloring's different—but allowing for age and good health . . . There was a painting at Leoch, done of Colum when he was maybe fifteen, before his first fall. Recall it, do ye? It hung in the solar on the third floor."

I closed my eyes, frowning in concentration, trying to reconstruct the floor plan of the castle.

"Walk me there," I said. He made a small amused noise in his throat but took my hand, tracing a delicate line on my palm.

"Aye, here's the entrance, wi' the big double door. Ye'd cross the courtyard, once inside, and then . . ."

He walked me unerringly to the exact spot in my mind, and sure enough, there was a painting there of a young man with a thin, clever face and look of far-seeing in his eyes.

"Yes, I think you're right," I said, opening my eyes. "If he *is* as intelligent as Colum, then . . . I have to tell him."

Jamie's eyes, dark with thought, searched my face.

"We couldna change things, earlier," he said, a note of warning in his voice. "Ye likely canna change what's to come in France."

"Maybe not," I said. "But what I knew—what I told you, before Culloden. It didn't stop Charles Stuart, but *you* lived."

"Not on purpose," he said dryly.

"No, but your men lived, too—and that *was* on purpose. So maybe—just maybe—it *might* help. And I can't live with myself if I don't."

He nodded, sober.

"Aye, then. I'll call them."

THE CORK EASED free with a soft *pop!*, and Michael's face eased, too. He sniffed the darkened cork, then passed the bottle delicately under his nose, eyes half closing in appreciation.

"Well, what d'ye say, lad?" his father asked. "Will it poison us or no?"

He opened his eyes and gave his father a mildly dirty look.

"You said it was important, aye? So we'll have the negroamaro. From Apulia," he added, with a note of satisfaction, and turned to me. "Will that do, Aunt?"

"Er . . . certainly," I said, taken back somewhat. "Why ask me? You're the wine expert."

Michael glanced at me, surprised.

"Ian said—" he began, but stopped and smiled at me. "My apologies, Aunt. I must have misunderstood."

Everyone turned and looked at Young Ian, who reddened at this scrutiny.

"What exactly did ye say, Ian?" Young Jamie asked. Young Ian narrowed his eyes at his brother, who seemed to be finding something funny in the situation.

"I said," Young Ian replied, straightening himself defiantly, "that Auntie Claire had something of importance to say to Michael, and that he must listen, because she's a . . . a . . ."

"*Ban-sidhe*, he said," Michael ended helpfully. He didn't grin at me, but a deep humor glowed in his eyes, and for the first time I saw what Jamie had meant by comparing him to Colum MacKenzie. "I wasn't sure whether he meant that, Auntie, or if it's only you're a conjure-woman—or a witch."

Jenny gasped at the word, and even the elder Ian blinked. Both of them turned and looked at Young Ian, who hunched his shoulders defensively.

"Well, I dinna ken *exactly* what she is," he said. "But she's an Auld One, isn't she, Uncle Jamie?"

Something odd seemed to pass through the air of the room; a sudden live, fresh wind moaned down the chimney, exploding the banked fire and showering sparks and embers onto the hearth. Jenny got up with a small exclamation and beat them out with the broom.

Jamie was sitting beside me; he took my hand and fixed Michael with a firm sort of look.

"There's no real word for what she is—but she has knowledge of things that will come to pass. Listen to her."

That settled them all to attention, and I cleared my throat, deeply embarrassed by my role as prophet but obliged to speak nonetheless. For the first time, I had a sudden sense of kinship with some of the more reluctant Old Testament prophets. I thought I knew *just* what Jeremiah felt like when told to go and prophesy the destruction of Nineveh. I just hoped I'd get a better reception; I seemed to recall that the inhabitants of Nineveh had thrown him into a well.

"You'll know more than I do about the politics in France," I said, looking directly at Michael. "I can't tell you anything in terms of specific events for the next ten or fifteen years. But after that . . . things are going to go downhill fast. There's going to be a revolution. Inspired by the one that's happening now in America, but not the same. The King and Queen will be imprisoned with their family, and both of them will be beheaded."

A general gasp went up from the table, and Michael blinked.

"There will be a movement called the Terror, and people will be pulled out of their homes and denounced, all the aristocrats will either be killed or have to flee the country, and it won't be too good for rich people in general. Jared may be dead by then, but you won't be. And if you're half as talented as I think, you *will* be rich."

He snorted a little at that, and there was a breath of laughter in the room, but it didn't last long.

"They'll build a machine called the guillotine—perhaps it already exists, I don't know. It was originally made as a humane method of execution, I think, but it will be used so often that it will be a symbol of the Terror, and of the revolution in general. You *don't* want to be in France when that happens."

"I—how do ye know this?" Michael demanded. He looked pale and half belligerent. Well, here was the rub. I took a firm grip of Jamie's hand under the table and told them how I knew.

There was a dead silence. Only Young Ian didn't look dumbfounded—but he knew already, and more or less believed me. I could tell that most of those around the table didn't. At the same time, they couldn't really call me a liar.

"That's what I know," I said, speaking straight to Michael. "And that's how I know it. You have a few years to get ready. Move the business to Spain, or Portugal. Sell out and emigrate to America. Do anything you like—but don't stay in France for more than ten years more. That's all," I said abruptly. I got up and went out, leaving utter silence in my wake.

I SHOULDN'T HAVE been surprised, but I was. I was in the hen coop, collecting eggs, when I heard the excited squawk and flutter of the hens outside that announced someone had come into their yard. I fixed the last hen with a steely glare that dared her to peck me, snatched an egg out from under her, and came out to see who was there.

It was Jenny, with an apronful of corn. That was odd; I knew the hens had already been fed, for I'd seen one of Maggie's daughters doing it an hour earlier.

She nodded to me and tossed the corn in handfuls. I tucked the last warm egg into my basket and waited. Obviously she wanted to talk to me and had made an excuse to do so in private. I had a deep feeling of foreboding.

Entirely justified, too, for she dropped the last handful of cracked corn and, with it, all pretense.

"I want to beg a favor," she said to me, but she avoided my eye, and I could see the pulse in her temple going like a ticking clock.

"Jenny," I said, helpless either to stop her or to answer her. "I know—"

"Will ye cure Ian?" she blurted, lifting her eyes to mine. I'd been right about what she meant to ask, but wrong about her emotion. Worry and fear lay behind her eyes, but there was no shyness, no embarrassment; she had the eyes of a hawk, and I knew she would rip my flesh like one if I denied her.

"Jenny," I said again. "I can't."

"Ye can't, or ye won't?" she said sharply.

"I *can't*. For God's sake, do you think I wouldn't have done it already if I had the power?"

"Ye might not, for the sake of the grudge ye hold against me. If that's it— I'll say I'm sorry, and I do mean it, though I meant what I did for the best."

"You . . . what?" I was honestly confused, but this seemed to anger her.

"Dinna pretend ye've no notion what I mean! When ye came back before, and I sent for Laoghaire!"

"Oh." I hadn't quite *forgotten* that, but it hadn't seemed important, in light of everything else. "That's . . . all right. I don't hold it against you. Why *did* you send for her, though?" I asked, both out of curiosity and in hopes of diffusing the intensity of her emotion a little. I'd seen a great number of people on the ragged edge of exhaustion, grief, and terror, and she was firmly in the grip of all three.

She made a jerky, impatient motion and seemed as though she would turn away but didn't.

"Jamie hadn't told ye about her, nor her about you. I could see why, maybe, but I kent if I brought her here, he'd have nay choice then but to take the bull by the horns and clear up the matter."

"She nearly cleared *him* up," I said, beginning to get somewhat hot myself. "She *shot* him, for God's sake!"

"Well, I didna give her the gun, did I?" she snapped. "I didna mean him to say whatever he said to her, nor her to take up a pistol and put a ball in him."

"No, but you told me to go away!"

"Why wouldn't I? Ye'd broken his heart once already, and I thought ye'd do it again! And you wi' the nerve to come prancing back here, fine and blooming, when we'd been . . . we'd been—it was that that gave Ian the cough!"

"That—"

"When they took him away and put him in the Tolbooth. But you werena here when that happened! Ye werena here when we starved and froze and feared for the lives of our men and our bairns! Not for any of it! You were in France, warm and safe!"

"I was in Boston, two hundred years from now, thinking Jamie was dead," I said coldly. "And I *can't* help Ian." I struggled to subdue my own feelings, uncorked with a rush by this ripping of scabs off the past, and found compassion in the look of her, her fine-boned face gaunt and harrowed with worry, her hands clenched so hard that the nails bit into the flesh.

"Jenny," I said more quietly. "Please believe me. If I could do anything for Ian, I'd give my soul to do it. But I'm not magic; I haven't any power. Only a little knowledge, and not enough. I'd give my *soul* to do it," I repeated, more strongly, leaning toward her. "But I can't. Jenny . . . I can't."

She stared at me in silence. A silence that lengthened past bearing, and finally I stepped around her and walked toward the house. She didn't turn around, and I didn't look back. But behind me, I heard her whisper.

"You have nay soul."

81

PURGATORY II

W HEN IAN FELT WELL enough, he came out walking with
Jamie. Sometimes only as far as the yard or the barn, to lean on
the fence and make remarks to Jenny's sheep. Sometimes he felt
well enough to walk miles, which amazed—and alarmed—Jamie. Still, he
thought, it was good to walk side by side through the moors and the forest
and down beside the loch, not talking much but side by side. It didn't matter
that they walked slowly; they always had, since Ian had come back from
France with a wooden leg.

"I'm lookin' forward to having back my leg," Ian had remarked casually
once, when they sat in the shelter of the big rock where Fergus had lost his
hand, looking out over the small burn that ran down at the foot of the hill,
watching for the stray flash of a leaping trout.

"Aye, that'll be good," Jamie had said, smiling a little—and a little wry
about it, too, recalling when he'd waked after Culloden and thought his own
leg missing. He'd been upset and tried to comfort himself with the thought
that he'd get it back eventually, if he made it out of purgatory and into
heaven. Of course, he'd thought he was dead, too, but that hadn't seemed
nearly as bad as the imagined loss of his leg.

"I dinna suppose ye'll have to wait," he said idly, and Ian blinked at him.

"Wait for what?"

"Your leg." He realized suddenly that Ian had no notion what he'd been
thinking, and hastened to explain.

"So I was only thinking, ye wouldna spend much time in purgatory—if at
all—so ye'll have it back soon."

Ian grinned at him. "What makes ye sae sure I willna spend a thousand
years in purgatory? I might be a terrible sinner, aye?"

"Well, aye, ye might be," Jamie admitted. "Though if so, ye must think the
devil of a lot of wicked thoughts, because if ye'd been *doing* anything, I'd
know about it."

"Oh, ye think so?" Ian seemed to find this funny. "Ye havena seen me in
years. I might ha' been doing anything, and ye'd never ken a thing about it!"

"Of course I would," Jamie said logically. "Jenny would tell me. And ye
dinna mean to suggest she wouldna ken if ye had a mistress and six bastard
bairns, or ye'd taken to the highways and been robbing folk in a black silk
mask?"

"Well, possibly she would," Ian admitted. "Though come on, man, there's
nothing ye could call a highway within a hundred miles. And I'd freeze to

death long before I came across anyone worth robbin' in one o' the passes."
He paused, eyes narrowed against the wind, contemplating the criminal possibilities open to him.

"I could ha' been stealing cattle," he offered. "Though there're sae few
beasts these days, the whole parish would ken it at once should one go missing. And I doubt I could hide it amongst Jenny's sheep wi' any hope of its not
bein' noticed."

He thought further, chin in hand, then reluctantly shook his head.

"The sad truth is, Jamie, no one's had a thing worth stealin' in the
Highlands these twenty years past. Nay, theft's right out, I'm afraid. So is for-
nication, because Jenny would ha' killed me already. What does that leave?
There's no really anything to covet. . . . I suppose lying and murder is all
that's left, and while I've met the odd man I would ha' *liked* to kill, I never
did." He shook his head regretfully, and Jamie laughed.

"Oh, aye? Ye told me ye killed men in France."

"Well, aye, I did, but that was a matter of war—or business," he added
fairly. "I was bein' paid to kill them; I didna do it out o' spite."

"Well, then, I'm right," Jamie pointed out. "Ye'll sail straight through purgatory like a rising cloud, for I canna think of a single lie ye've ever told me."

Ian smiled with great affection.

"Aye, well, I may ha' told lies now and then, Jamie—but no, not to you."

He looked down at the worn wooden peg stretched before him and
scratched at the knee on that side.

"I wonder, will it feel different?"

"How could it not?"

"Well, the thing is," Ian said, wiggling his sound foot to and fro, "I can still
feel my missing foot. Always have been able to, ever since it went. Not all the
time, mind," he added, looking up. "But I do feel it. A verra strange thing.
Do ye feel your finger?" he asked curiously, raising his chin at Jamie's right
hand.

"Well . . . aye, I do. Not all the time, but now and then—and the nasty
thing is that even though it's gone, it still *hurts* like damnation, which doesna
seem really fair."

He could have bitten his tongue at that, for here Ian was dying, and him
complaining that the loss of his finger wasn't fair. Ian wheezed with amusement, though, and leaned back, shaking his head.

"If life was fair, then what?"

They sat in companionable silence for a while, watching the wind move
through the pines on the hillside opposite. Then Jamie reached into his
sporran and brought out the tiny white-wrapped package. It was a bit grubby
from being in his sporran but had been tidily preserved and tightly wrapped.

Ian eyed the little bundle in his palm.

"What's this?"

"My finger," Jamie said. "I—well . . . I wondered whether ye'd maybe not
mind to have it buried with ye."

Ian looked at him for a moment. Then his shoulders started to shake.

"God, don't laugh!" Jamie said, alarmed. "I didna mean to make ye laugh!
Christ, Jenny will kill me if ye cough up a lung and die out here!"

Ian *was* coughing, fits of it interspersed with long-drawn-out wheezes of laughter. Tears of mirth stood in his eyes, and he pressed both fists into his chest, struggling to breathe. At last, though, he left off and straightened slowly up, making a sound like a bellows. He sniffed deep and casually spat a glob of horrifying scarlet into the rocks.

"I'd rather die out here laughin' at you than in my bed wi' six priests sayin' prayers," he said. "Doubt I'll get the chance, though." He put out a hand, palm up. "Aye, give it here."

Jamie laid the little white-wrapped cylinder in his hand, and Ian tucked the finger casually into his own sporran.

"I'll keep it safe 'til ye catch me up."

HE CAME DOWN through the trees and made his way toward the edge of the moorland that lay below the cave. It was sharply cold, with a stiff breeze blowing, and the light changed over the land like the flicker of a bird's wings as the clouds slid overhead, long and fleeting. He'd picked up a deer trail through the heather earlier in the morning, but it had disappeared in a stony fall near a brae, and now he was coming back toward the house; he was behind the hill on which the broch stood, this side of it thick with a little wood of beech and pine. He'd not seen a deer or even a coney this morning, but wasn't bothered.

With so many in the house, they could use a deer, to be sure—but he was happy only to be out of the house, even if he came back with nothing.

He couldn't look at Ian without wanting to stare at his face, to commit him to memory, to impress these last bits of his brother-in-law upon his mind in the way that he recalled special vivid moments, there to be taken out and lived through again at need. But at the same time, he didn't *want* to remember Ian as he was now; much better to keep what he had of him: firelight on the side of Ian's face, laughing fit to burst as he'd forced Jamie's arm over in a wrestling match, his own wiry strength surprising them both. Ian's long, knob-jointed hands on the gralloch knife, the wrench and the hot metal smell of the blood that smeared his fingers, the look of his brown hair ruffling in the wind off the loch, the narrow back, bent and springy as a bow as he stooped to snatch one of his toddling bairns or grandchildren off their feet and throw them up giggling into the air.

It was good they'd come, he thought. Better than good that they'd brought the lad back in time to speak to his father as a man, to comfort Ian's mind and take his leave properly. But to live in the same house with a beloved brother dying by inches under your nose wore sadly on the nerves.

With so many women in the house, squabbling was inevitable. With so many of the women Frasers, it was like walking through a gunpowder mill with a lit candle. Everyone tried so hard to manage, to keep in countenance, to accommodate—but that only made it worse when some spark finally set the powder keg off. He wasn't only out hunting because they needed meat.

He spared a sympathetic thought for Claire. After Jenny's anguished request, Claire had taken to hiding in their room or in Ian's study—he had invited her to use it, and Jamie thought that aggravated Jenny still more—writing busily, making the book Andy Bell had put in her mind. She had great powers of concentration and could stay inside her mind for hours—but she had to come out to eat. And it was always there, the knowledge that Ian was dying, grinding like a quern, slow but relentless, wearing away the nerves.

Ian's nerves, too.

He and Ian had been walking—slowly—by the side of the loch two days before, when Ian stopped suddenly, curling in on himself like an autumn leaf. Jamie hurried to take him by the arm before he could fall, and he lowered him to the ground, finding a boulder to brace his back, pulling the shawl high around the wasted shoulders, looking for anything, anything at all he could do.

"What is it, *a charaid*?" he said, anxious, crouching beside his brother-in-law, his friend.

Ian was coughing, almost silently, his body shaking with the force of it. At last the spasm eased and he could draw breath, his face bright with the consumptive flush, that terrible illusion of health.

"It hurts, Jamie." The words were spoken simply, but Ian's eyelids were closed, as though he didn't want to look at Jamie while he spoke.

"I'll carry ye back. We'll get ye a bit of laudanum, maybe, and—"

Ian waved a hand, quelling his anxious promises. He breathed shallowly for a moment before shaking his head.

"Aye, my chest feels like there's a knife in it," he said finally. "But that's no what I meant. I'm no bothered so much about dying—but Christ, the slowness of it is killing me." He did open his eyes then, meeting Jamie's, and laughed as silently as he'd coughed, the barest breath of sound as his body shook with it.

"This dying hurts me, Dougal. I'd have it over." The words came into his mind as clearly as if they'd been spoken just now in front of him, rather than thirty years before in a dark church, ruined by cannon fire. Rupert had said that, dying slow. *"You're my chief, man,"* he'd said to Dougal, imploring. *"It's your job."* And Dougal MacKenzie had done what love and duty called for.

He had been holding Ian's hand, clasping hard, trying to force some notion of well-being from his own calloused palm into Ian's thin gray skin. His thumb slid upward now, pressing on the wrist where he had seen Claire grip, searching out the truth of a patient's health.

He felt the skin give, sliding across the bones of Ian's wrist. He thought suddenly of the blood vow given at his marriage, the sting of the blade and Claire's cold wrist pressed to his and the blood slick between them. Ian's wrist was cold, too, but not from fear.

He glanced at his own wrist, but there was no trace of a scar, either from vows or fetters; those wounds were fleeting, long-healed.

"D'ye remember when we gave each other blood for blood?" Ian's eyes were closed, but he smiled. Jamie's hand tightened on the bony wrist, a little startled but not truly surprised that Ian had reached into his mind and caught the echo of his thoughts.

"Aye, of course." He couldn't help a small smile of his own, a painful one. They'd been eight years old, the two of them. Jamie's mother and her bairn had died the day before. The house had been full of mourners, his father dazed with shock. They had slipped out, he and Ian, scrambling up the hill behind the house, trying not to look at the fresh-dug grave by the broch. Into the wood, safe under the trees.

Had slowed then, wandering, come to a stop at last at the top of the high hill, where some old stone building that they called the fort had fallen down long ago. They'd sat on the rubble, wrapped in their plaids against the wind, not talking much.

"I thought I'd have a new brother," he'd said suddenly. "But I don't. It's just Jenny and me, still." In the years since, he'd succeeded in forgetting that small pain, the loss of his hoped-for brother, the boy who might have given him back a little of his love for his older brother, Willie, dead of the smallpox. He'd cherished that pain for a little, a flimsy shield against the enormity of knowing his mother gone forever.

Ian had sat thinking for a bit, then reached into his sporran and got out the wee knife his father had given him on his last birthday.

"I'll be your brother," he'd said, matter-of-fact, and cut across his thumb, hissing a little through his teeth.

He'd handed the knife to Jamie, who'd cut himself, surprised that it hurt so much, and then they'd pressed their thumbs together and sworn to be brothers always. And had been.

He took a deep breath, bracing himself against the nearness of death, the black finality.

"Ian. Shall I . . ." Ian's eyelids lifted, the soft brown of his gaze sharpening into clarity at what he heard in the thickness of Jamie's voice. Jamie cleared his throat hard and looked away, then looked back, feeling obscurely that to look away was cowardly.

"Will ye have me hasten ye?" he asked, very softly. Even as he spoke, the cold part of his mind sought the way. Not by the blade, no; it was quick and clean, a proper man's departure, but it would cause his sister and the weans grief; neither he nor Ian had the right to leave a final memory stained with blood.

Ian's grip neither slackened nor clung, but of a sudden Jamie felt the pulse he had looked for in vain, a small, steady throb against his own palm.

He hadn't looked away, but his eyes blurred, and he bent his head to hide the tears.

Claire . . . She would know how, but he couldn't ask her to do it. Her own vow kept her from it.

"No," Ian said. "Not yet, anyway." He'd smiled, eyes soft. "But I'm glad to ken ye'll do it if I need ye to, *mo brathair.*"

The flicker of a movement stopped him in his tracks and jerked him instantly from his thoughts.

It hadn't seen him, though he was in sight. The wind was toward him, though, and the deer was busy, nibbling among the crusts of dry heather for sheltered bits of grass and softer moor plants. He waited, listening to the wind. Only the deer's head and shoulders were visible behind a gorse bush, though he thought from the size of the neck that it was a male.

He waited, feeling the way of it seep back into him. Hunting red deer on the moor was different from hunting in the forests of North Carolina. A slower thing altogether. The deer moved out a little from behind the gorse bush, intent on its feeding, and he began, by imperceptible degrees, to raise his rifle. He'd had a gunsmith in Edinburgh straighten the barrel for him but hadn't used it since; he hoped it would aim true.

Hadn't used it since he'd clouted the Hessian with it in the redoubt. He had a sudden, vivid recollection of Claire dropping the misshapen bullet that had killed Simon into the china plate, felt the chink and roll of it in his blood.

Another step, two; the deer had found something tasty and was tugging and chewing with great concentration. Like a thing completing itself, the muzzle of the rifle settled gently on its target. A big buck deer, and no more than a hundred yards. He could feel the big solid heart, pumping under his own ribs, pulsing in the tips of his fingers on the metal. The stock snugged hard into the hollow of his shoulder.

He was just beginning to squeeze the trigger when he heard the screams from the wood behind him. The gun went off, the shot went wild, the deer vanished with a crash of breaking heather, and the screams stopped.

He turned and strode fast into the woods, in the direction where he'd heard them, his heart pounding. Who? A woman, but who?

He found Jenny without much difficulty, standing frozen in the small clearing where he and she and Ian came when they were young, to share out stolen treats and play at knights and soldiers.

She'd been a good soldier.

Maybe she'd been waiting for him, having heard his gun. Maybe she just couldn't move. She stood straight-backed but empty-eyed and watched him come, her shawls wrapped like rusty armor round her.

"Are ye all right, lass?" he asked, setting down his rifle by the big pine where she'd read to him and Ian in the long summer nights when the sun barely set from dusk to dawn.

"Aye, fine," she said, her voice colorless.

"Aye, right," he said, sighing. Coming close, he insisted upon taking her hands in his; she didn't give them to him but didn't resist. "I heard ye scream."

"I didna mean anyone to hear."

"Of course ye didn't." He hesitated, wanting to ask again was she all right, but that was foolish. He knew fine well what the trouble was and why she needed to come and scream in the wood, where no one would hear her and ask stupidly was she all right.

"D'ye want me to go away?" he asked instead, and she grimaced, pulling at her hand, but he didn't let go.

"No. What difference does it make? What difference does anything make?" He heard the note of hysteria in her voice.

"At least . . . we brought the lad home in time," he said, for lack of anything else to offer her.

"Aye, ye did," she said, with an effort at self-control that shredded like old silk. "And ye brought your wife back, too."

"Ye blame me for bringing my wife?" he said, shocked. "Why, for God's sake? Should ye no be happy she's come back? Or d'ye—" He choked off the next words fast; he'd been about to demand whether she resented him still having a wife when she was about to lose her husband, and he couldn't say *that*.

But that wasn't what Jenny had meant, at all.

"Aye, she's come back. But for what?" she cried. "What good is a faery-woman too coldhearted to lift a finger to save Ian?"

He was so staggered by this that he couldn't do anything but repeat "Coldhearted? Claire?" in a dazed fashion.

"I asked, and she denied me." His sister's eyes were tearless, frantic with grief and urgency. "Can ye not make her help me, Jamie?"

The life in his sister, always bright and pulsing, thrummed under his fingers like chained lightning now. Better if she let it loose on him, he thought. She couldn't hurt him.

"*A phiuthar,* she'd heal him if she could," he said, as gently as possible without letting go of her. "She told me ye'd asked—and she wept in the telling. She loves Ian as much—"

"Don't ye *dare* be telling me she loves my husband as much as I do!" she shouted, jerking her hands out of his with such violence that he was sure she meant to strike him. She did, slapping his face so hard that his eye watered on that side.

"I wasna going to tell ye that at all," he said, keeping his temper. He touched the side of his face gingerly. "I was *going* to say that she loves him as much—"

He'd intended to say, "*as she loves me,*" but didn't get that far. She kicked him in the shin hard enough to buckle his leg, and he stumbled, flailing to keep his balance, which gave her the opportunity to turn and fly down the hill like a witch on a broomstick, her skirts and shawls whirling out like a storm around her.

82

DISPOSITIONS

C LEANSING OF WOUNDS, I wrote carefully, and paused, marshaling my thoughts. Boiling water, clean rags, removal of foreign matter. Use of maggots on dead flesh (with a note of caution regarding blowfly and screwworm larvae? No, pointless; no one would be able to tell the difference without a magnifying glass). The stitching of wounds (sterilization of needle and thread). Useful poultices. Ought I to put in a separate section on the production and uses of penicillin?

I tapped the quill on the blotter, making tiny stars of ink, but finally decided against it. This was meant to be a useful guide for the common person. The common person was not equipped for the painstaking process of making penicillin, nor yet likely to have an injection apparatus—though I did think briefly of the penis syringe Dr. Fentiman had shown me, with a faint twinge of amusement.

That in turn made me think—briefly but vividly—of David Rawlings and his jugum penis. Did he really use it himself? I wondered, but hastily dismissed the vision conjured up by the thought and flipped over a few sheets, looking for my list of main topics.

Masturbation, I wrote thoughtfully. If some doctors discussed it in a negative light—and they most certainly did—I supposed there was no reason why I shouldn't give the opposing view—discreetly.

I found myself still making inky stars a few moments later, thoroughly distracted by the problem of talking discreetly about the benefits of masturbation. God, what if I said in print that women did it?

"They'd burn the whole printing, and likely Andy Bell's shop, too," I said aloud.

There was a sharp intake of breath, and I glanced up to see a woman standing in the door of the study.

"Oh, are you looking for Ian Murray?" I said, pushing back from the desk. "He's—"

"No, it's you I was looking for." There was a very odd tone to her voice, and I stood up, feeling suddenly defensive without knowing why.

"Ah," I said. "And you are . . . ?"

She stepped out of the shadowed hall into the light.

"Ye'll not know me, then?" Her mouth twitched in an angry half smile. "Laoghaire MacKenzie . . . Fraser," she added, almost reluctantly.

"Oh," I said.

I would have recognized her at once, I thought, save for the incongruity of context. This was the last place I would have expected her to be, and the fact that she was here . . . A recollection of what had happened the last time she had come to Lallybroch made me reach inconspicuously for the letter opener on the desk.

"You were looking for me," I repeated warily. "Not Jamie?"

She made a contemptuous gesture, pushing the thought of Jamie aside, and reached into the pocket at her waist, bringing out a folded letter.

"I've come to ask ye a favor," she said, and for the first time I heard the tremor in her voice. "Read that. If ye will," she added, and pressed her lips tight together.

I looked warily at her pocket, but it was flat; if she'd brought a pistol, she wasn't carrying it there. I picked up the letter and motioned her to the chair on the other side of the desk. If she took it into her head to attack me, I'd have a little warning.

Still, I wasn't really afraid of her. She was upset; that was clear. But very much in control of herself.

I opened the letter, and, with the occasional glance to be sure she stayed where she was, began to read.

15 February 1778
Philadelphia

"Philadelphia?" I said, startled, and looked up at Laoghaire. She nodded.

"They went there in the summer last year, himself thinking 'twould be safer." Her lips twisted a little. "Two months later, the British army came a-marching into the city, and there they've been since."

"Himself," I supposed, was Fergus. I noted the usage with interest; evidently Laoghaire had become reconciled to her older daughter's husband, for she used the word without irony.

> *Dear Mam,*
>
> *I must ask you to do something for love of me and my children. The trouble is with Henri-Christian. Because of his oddness of form, he has always had some trouble in breathing, particularly when suffering from the catarrh, and has snored like a grampus since he was born. Now he has taken to stopping breathing altogether when he sleeps, save he is propped up with cushions in a particular position. Mother Claire had looked in his throat when she and Da saw us in New Bern and said then that his adenoids—this being something in his throat—were over-large and might give trouble in future. (Germain has these, also, and breathes with his mouth open a good deal of the time, but it is not a danger to him as it is to Henri-Christian.)*
>
> *I am in mortal terror that Henri-Christian will stop breathing one night and no one will know in time to save him. We take it in turns to sit up with him, to keep his head just right and to wake him when he stops breathing, but I do not know how long we can contrive to keep it up. Fergus is worn out with the work of the shop and I with the work of the house (I help in the shop, as well, and so of course does Germain. The little girls are great help to me in the house, bless them, and so willing to care for their little brother—but they cannot be left to sit up with him by night alone).*
>
> *I have had a physician to look at Henri-Christian. He agrees that the adenoids are likely to blame for the obstruction of breathing, and he bled the wee lad and gave me medicine to shrink them, but this was of no use at all and only made Henri-Christian cry and vomit. Mother Claire—forgive me for speaking of her to you, for I know your feelings, but I must—had said that it might be necessary to remove Henri-Christian's tonsils and adenoids at some point, to ease his breathing, and plainly this point has been reached. She did this for the Beardsley twins some time ago on the Ridge, and I would trust no one else to attempt such an operation on Henri-Christian.*
>
> *Will you go to see her, Mam? I think she must be at Lallybroch now, and I will write to her there, begging her to come to Philadelphia as soon as possible. But I fear my inability to communicate the horror of our situation.*

As you love me, Mam, please go to her and ask her to come as quickly as may be.

> *Your most affectionate daughter,*
> *Marsali*

I set down the letter. *I fear my inability to communicate the horror of our situation.* No, she'd done that, all right.

Sleep apnea, they called it; the tendency to stop breathing suddenly when asleep. It was common—and much more common in some sorts of dwarfism, where the respiratory airways were constricted by the skeletal abnormalities. Most people who had it would wake themselves, thrashing and snorting as they breathed again. But the enlarged adenoids and tonsils obstructing his throat—probably a hereditary problem, I thought distractedly, for I'd noted them in Germain and to a lesser extent in the girls, as well—would aggravate the difficulty, since even if the reflex that causes a person short of oxygen to breathe kicked in belatedly, Henri-Christian likely couldn't draw the immediate deep breath that would waken him.

The vision of Marsali and Fergus—and probably Germain—taking it in turns to sit up in a dark house, watching the little boy sleep, perhaps nodding off themselves in the cold and quiet, jerking awake in terror lest he have shifted in his sleep and stopped breathing... A sick knot of fear had formed under my ribs, reading the letter.

Laoghaire was watching me, blue eyes direct under her cap. For once, the anger, hysteria, and suspicion with which she had always regarded me was gone.

"If ye'll go," she said, and swallowed, "I'll give up the money."

I stared at her.

"You think that I—" I began incredulously, but stopped. Well, yes, she plainly *did* believe I would require to be bribed. She thought that I had abandoned Jamie after Culloden, returning only when he had become prosperous again. I struggled with the urge to try to tell her... but that was pointless, and quite beside the point now, too. The situation was clear and sharp as broken glass.

She leaned forward abruptly, her hands on the desk, pressed down so hard that her fingernails were white.

"Please," she said. *"Please."*

I was conscious of strong, conflicting urges: on the one hand, to smack her, and on the other, to put a sympathetic hand over hers. I fought down both and forced myself to think calmly for a moment.

I would go, of course; I'd have to. It had nothing to do with Laoghaire, or with what lay between us. If I did not go, and Henri-Christian died—he well *might*—I'd never be able to live with myself. If I came in time, I could save him; no one else could. It was as simple as that.

My heart sank precipitously at the thought of leaving Lallybroch now. How horrible; how could I, knowing that I left Ian for the last time, perhaps leaving them all and the place itself for the last time. But even as I thought these things, the part of my mind that was a surgeon had already grasped the necessity and was setting about the business of planning the quickest way to Philadelphia, contemplating how I should acquire what I needed once there, the possible obstructions and complications that might arise—all the practical analysis of how I should do what had so suddenly been asked of me.

And as my mind clicked through these things, the ruthless logic overwhelming shock, subduing emotion, it began to dawn upon me that this sudden disaster might have other aspects.

Laoghaire was waiting, eyes fixed on me, her mouth firm, willing me to do it.

"All right," I said, leaning back in my chair and fixing her in turn with a level look. "Let's come to terms, then, shall we?"

"SO," I SAID, eyes fixed on the flight of a gray heron as it crossed the loch, "we made a bargain. I'll go to Philadelphia as quickly as I can to take care of Henri-Christian. She'll marry Joey, give up the alimony—and give her permission for Joan to go to the convent. Though I suppose we'd best get it in writing, just in case."

Jamie stared at me, speechless. We were sitting in the long rough grass at the side of the loch, where I'd brought him to tell him what had happened— and what was going to happen.

"She—Laoghaire—has kept Joan's dowry intact; Joan will have that, for traveling and for her entry to the convent," I added. I took a deep breath, hoping to keep my voice steady. "I'm thinking that—well, Michael will be leaving in a few days. Joan and I could go with him to France; I could sail from there on a French ship, and he could see her safely to her convent."

"You—" he began, and I reached to squeeze his hand, to stop him speaking.

"You can't go now, Jamie," I said softly. "I know you can't."

He closed his eyes, grimacing, and his hand tightened on mine in instinctive denial of the obvious. I clung to his fingers just as tightly, in spite of the fact that it was his tender right hand I held. The thought of being parted from him for any amount of time or space—let alone the Atlantic Ocean and the months it might take before we saw each other again—made the bottom of my stomach fall away and filled me with desolation and a sense of vague terror.

He would go with me if I asked—if I even gave him room for doubt about what he must do. I must not.

He needed this so much. Needed what small time remained with Ian; needed even more to be here for Jenny when Ian died, for he could be her comfort in a way that not even her children could be. And if he had needed to go and see Laoghaire out of guilt over the failure of their marriage—how much more acute would be his guilt at abandoning his sister, yet again, and in her most desperate time of need.

"You can't leave," I whispered, urgent. "I *know*, Jamie."

He opened his eyes then and looked at me, eyes dark with anguish.

"I canna let ye go. Not without me."

"It...won't be long," I said, forcing the words past the lump in my throat—a lump that acknowledged both my sorrow in parting from him and the greater sorrow for the reason why our separation wouldn't be a long one.

"I've gone farther by myself, after all," I said, trying to smile. His mouth moved, wanting to respond, but the trouble in his eyes didn't change.

I lifted his crippled hand to my lips and kissed it, pressed my cheek against it, my head turned away—but a tear ran down my cheek and I knew he felt the wetness of it on his hand, for his other hand reached for me and drew me into him, and we sat pressed together for a long, long time, listening to the wind that stirred the grass and touched the water. The heron had set down at the far side of the loch and stood on one leg, waiting patiently amid the tiny ripples.

"We'll need a lawyer," I said at last, not moving. "Is Ned Gowan still alive?"

MUCH TO MY astonishment, Ned Gowan *was* still alive. How old could he possibly be? I wondered, looking at him. Eighty-five? Ninety? He was toothless and wrinkled as a crumpled paper bag, but still jaunty as a cricket, and with his lawyer's bloodlust quite intact.

He had drawn up the agreement of annulment for the marriage between Jamie and Laoghaire, cheerfully arranging the annual payments to Laoghaire, the dowries for Marsali and Joan. He set himself now just as cheerfully to dismantling it.

"Now, the question of Mistress Joan's dowry," he said, thoughtfully licking the point of his quill. "You specified, sir, in the original document, that this amount—may I say, this very *generous* amount—was to be endowed upon the young woman upon the occasion of her marriage and to remain her sole property thereafter, not passing to her husband."

"Aye, that's right," Jamie said, not very patiently. He'd told me privately that he would prefer to be staked out naked on an anthill than to have to deal with a lawyer for more than five minutes, and we had been dealing with the complications of this agreement for a good hour. "So?"

"So she is not marrying," Mr. Gowan explained, with the indulgence due to someone not very bright but still worthy of respect by reason of the fact that he was paying the lawyer's fee. "The question of whether she can receive the dowry under this contract—"

"She *is* marrying," Jamie said. "She's becoming a Bride o' Christ, ye ignorant Protestant."

I glanced at Ned in some surprise, having never heard that he *was* a Protestant, but he made no demur at this. Mr. Gowan, sharp as ever, noticed my surprise and smiled at me, eyes twinkling.

"I have no religion save the law, ma'am," he said. "Observance of one form of ritual over another is irrelevant; God to me is the personification of Justice, and I serve Him in that guise."

Jamie made a Scottish noise deep in his throat in response to this sentiment.

"Aye, and a fat lot o' good that will do ye, and your clients here ever realize ye're no a papist."

Mr. Gowan's small dark eyes did not cease to twinkle as he turned them on Jamie.

"I am sure ye dinna suggest such a low thing as blackmail, sir? Why, I hesitate even to name that honorable Scottish institution, knowing as I do the nobility of your character—and the fact that ye're no going to get this bloody contract done without me."

Jamie sighed deeply and settled into his chair.

"Aye, get on with it. What's to do about the dowry, then?"

"Ah." Mr. Gowan turned with alacrity to the matter at hand. "I have spoken with the young woman regarding her own wishes in the matter. As the original maker of the contract, you may—with the consent of the other signatory, which, I understand, has been given"—he uttered a dry little cough at this oblique mention of Laoghaire—"alter the terms of the original document. *Since,* as I say, Mistress Joan does not propose to wed, do you wish to rescind the dowry altogether, to keep the existing terms, or to alter them in some way?"

"I want to give the money to Joan," Jamie said, with an air of relief at finally being asked something concrete.

"Absolutely?" Mr. Gowan inquired, pen poised. "The word 'absolutely' having a meaning in law other than—"

"Ye said ye talked to Joan. What the devil does *she* want, then?"

Mr. Gowan looked happy, as he usually did upon perceiving a new complication.

"She wishes to accept only a small portion of the original dowry, this to be used to provide for her reception into a convent; such a donation is customary, I believe."

"Aye?" Jamie raised one eyebrow. "And what about the rest?"

"She wishes the residue to be given to her mother, Laoghaire MacKenzie Fraser, but not given absolutely, if you follow me. Given with conditions."

Jamie and I exchanged looks.

"*What* conditions?" he asked carefully.

Mr. Gowan held up a withered hand, folding down the fingers as he enumerated the conditions.

"One, that the money shall *not* be released until a proper record of the marriage of Laoghaire MacKenzie Fraser and Joseph Boswell Murray shall be written in the parish register of Broch Mordha, witnessed and attested by a priest. Two, that a contract be signed, reserving and guaranteeing the estate of Balriggan and all its inclusive goods as the sole property of Laoghaire MacKenzie Fraser until her death, thereafter being willed as the aforesaid Laoghaire MacKenzie Fraser shall so dispose in a proper will. Thirdly, the money shall not be given absolutely, but shall be retained by a trustee and disbursed in the amount of twenty pounds per annum, paid jointly to the aforesaid Laoghaire MacKenzie Fraser and Joseph Boswell Murray. Fourth, that these annual payments shall be used only for matters pertaining to the upkeep and improvement of the estate of Balriggan. Fifth, that payment of each year's disbursement shall be contingent upon the receipt of proper documentation regarding the use of the previous year's disbursement." He folded down his thumb and lowered his closed fist, and held up one finger of his other hand.

"Sixth—and lastly—that one James Alexander Gordon Fraser Murray, of Lallybroch, shall be trustee for these funds. Are these conditions agreeable, sir?"

"They are," Jamie said firmly, rising to his feet. "Make it so, if ye please, Mr. Gowan—and now, if no one minds, I am going away and having a wee dram. Possibly two."

Mr. Gowan capped his inkwell, tidied his notes into a neat pile, and likewise rose, though more slowly.

"I'll join ye in that dram, Jamie. I want to hear about this war of yours in America. It sounds the grandest of adventures!"

83

COUNTING SHEEP

AS THE TIME GREW SHORTER, Ian found it impossible to sleep. The need to go, to find Rachel, burned in him so that he felt hot coals in the pit of his stomach all of the time. Auntie Claire called it heartburn, and it was. She said it was from bolting his food, though, and it wasn't that—he could barely eat.

He spent his days with his father, as much as he could. Sitting in the corner of the speak-a-word room, watching his father and his elder brother go about the business of Lallybroch, he couldn't understand how it would be possible to stand up and walk away, to leave them behind. To leave his father forever behind.

During the days, there were things to be done, folk to be visited, to talk to, and the land to be walked over, the stark beauty of it soothing when his feelings grew too heated to bear. At night, though, the house lay quiet, the creaking silence punctuated by his father's distant cough and his two young nephews' heavy breathing in the room beside him. He began to feel the house itself breathe around him, drawing one ragged, heavy-chested gasp after another, and to feel the weight of it on his own chest, so he sat up in bed, gulping air only to be sure he could. And finally he would slide out of bed, steal downstairs with his boots in his hands, and let himself out of the kitchen door to walk the night under clouds or stars, the clean wind fanning the coals of his heart to open flame, until he should find his tears and peace in which to shed them.

One night he found the door unbolted already. He went out cautiously, looking round, but saw no one. Likely Young Jamie gone to the barn; one of the two cows was due to calf any day. He should go and help, maybe . . . but the burning under his ribs was painful, he needed to walk a bit first. Jamie would have fetched him in any case, had he thought he needed help.

He turned away from the house and its outbuildings and headed up the hill, past the sheep pen, where the sheep lay in somnolent mounds, pale under the moon, now and then emitting a soft, sudden *bah!*, as though startled by some sheep dream.

Such a dream took shape before him suddenly, a dark form moving against the fence, and he uttered a brief cry that made the nearer sheep start and rustle in a chorus of low-pitched *bah*s.

"Hush, *a bhailach*," his mother said softly. "Get this lot started, and ye'll wake the dead."

He could make her out now, a small, slender form, with her unbound hair a soft mass against the paleness of her shift.

"Speak o' the dead," he said rather crossly, forcing his heart down out of his throat. "I thought ye were a ghost. What are ye doing out here, Mam?"

"Counting sheep," she said, a thread of humor in her voice. "That's what ye're meant to do when ye canna sleep, aye?"

"Aye." He came and stood beside her, leaning on the fence. "Does it work?"

"Sometimes."

They stood still for a bit, watching the sheep stir and settle. They smelled sweetly filthy, of chewed grass and sheep shit and greasy wool, and Ian found that it was oddly comforting just to be with them.

"Does it work to count them, when ye ken already how many there are?" he asked, after a short silence. His mother shook her head.

"No, I say their names over. It's like saying the rosary, only ye dinna feel the need to be asking. It wears ye down, asking."

Especially when ye ken the answer's going to be no, Ian thought, and moved by sudden impulse, put his arm around her shoulders. She made a small sound of amused surprise, but then relaxed, laying her head against him. He could feel the small bones of her, light as a bird's, and thought his heart might break.

They stood for a while that way, and then she freed herself, gently, moving away a little and turning to him.

"Sleepy yet?"

"No."

"Aye, well. Come on, then." Not waiting for an answer, she turned and made her way through the dark, away from the house.

There was a moon, half full, and he'd been out more than long enough for his eyes to adjust; it was simple to follow, even through the jumbled grass and stones and heather that grew on the hill behind the house.

Where was she taking him? Or rather, why? For they were heading uphill, toward the old broch—and the burying ground that lay nearby. He felt a chill round his heart—did she mean to show him the site of his father's grave?

But she stopped abruptly and stooped, so he nearly tripped over her. Straightening up, she turned and put a pebble into his hand.

"Over here," she said softly, and led him to a small square stone set in the earth. He thought it was Caitlin's grave—the child who'd come before Young Jenny, the sister who'd lived but one day—but then saw that Caitlin's stone lay a few feet away. This one was the same size and shape, but—he squatted by it, and running his fingers over the shadows of its carving, made out the name.

Yeksa'a.

"Mam," he said, and his voice sounded strange to his own ears.

"Is that right, Ian?" she said, a little anxious. "Your da said he wasna quite certain of the spelling of the Indian name. I had the stone carver put both, though. I thought that was right."

"Both?" But his hand had already moved down and found the other name.

Iseabaìl.

He swallowed hard.

"That was right," he said very softly. His hand rested flat on the stone, cool under his palm.

She squatted down beside him, and reaching, put her own pebble on the stone. It was what you did, he thought, stunned, when you came to visit the dead. You left a pebble to say you'd been there; that you hadn't forgotten.

His own pebble was still in his other hand; he couldn't quite bring himself to lay it down. Tears were running down his face, and his mother's hand was on his arm.

"It's all right, *a duine*," she said softly. "Go to your young woman. Ye'll always be here wi' us."

The steam of his tears rose like the smoke of incense from his heart, and he laid the pebble gently on his daughter's grave. Safe among his family.

It wasn't until many days later, in the middle of the ocean, that he realized his mother had called him a man.

84

THE RIGHT OF IT

IAN DIED JUST after dawn. The night had been hellish; a dozen times, Ian had come close to drowning in his own blood, choking, eyes bulging, then rising up in convulsion, spewing up bits of his lungs. The bed looked like some slaughter had taken place, and the room reeked of the sweat of a desperate, futile struggle, the smell of Death's presence.

In the end, though, he had lain quiet, thin chest barely moving, the sound of his breathing a faint rattle like the scratch of the rose briers at the window.

Jamie had stood back, to give Young Jamie the place at Ian's side as eldest son; Jenny had sat all night on his other side, wiping away the blood, the evil sweat, all the foul liquids that oozed from Ian, dissolving his body before their eyes. But near the end, in the dark, Ian had raised his right hand and whispered, "Jamie." He hadn't opened his eyes to look, but all of them knew which Jamie it was that he wanted, and Young Jamie had made way, stumbling, so that his uncle could come and grasp that seeking hand.

Ian's bony fingers had closed round his with surprising strength. Ian had murmured something, too low to hear, and then let go—not in the involuntary relaxation of death; simply let go, that business done, and let his hand fall back, open, to his children.

He did not speak again but seemed to settle, his body diminishing as life and breath fled from it. When his last breath came, they waited in dull misery, expecting another, and only after a full minute of silence did they begin to look at one another covertly, steal glances at the ravaged bed, the stillness in Ian's face—and realize slowly that it was over at last.

DID JENNY MIND? he wondered. That Ian's last words had been to him? But he thought not; the one mercy to a going such as his brother-in-law's was that there was time to take leave. He had made a time to speak alone with each of his children, Jamie knew. Comfort them as he could, maybe leave them with a bit of advice, at the least the reassurance that he loved them.

He had been standing next to Jenny when Ian died. She had sighed and seemed to slump beside him, as though the iron rod that had run up her back for the last year had suddenly been pulled out through her head. Her face had showed no sorrow, though he knew it was there; for that moment, though, she had only been glad it was over—for Ian's sake, for all their sakes.

So surely they had found time, she and Ian, to say what had to be said between them, in the months since they knew.

What would he say to Claire in such circumstances? he wondered suddenly. Probably what he *had* said to her, in parting. *"I love you. I'll see you again."* He didn't see any way of improving on the sentiment, after all.

He couldn't stay in the house. The women had washed Ian and laid him out in the parlor and were now embarked on an orgy of furious cooking and cleaning, for word had gone out and people were already beginning to come for the wake.

The day had dawned spitting rain, but for the moment, none was falling. He went out through the kailyard and climbed the little slope to the arbor. Jenny was sitting there, and he hesitated for a moment, but then came and sat down beside her. She could send him away if she wanted solitude.

She didn't; she reached up for his hand and he took it, engulfing hers, thinking how fine-boned she was, how frail.

"I want to leave," she said calmly.

"I dinna blame ye," he said, with a glance at the house. The arbor was covered with new leaves, the green of them fresh and soft from the rain, but someone would find them soon. "Shall we walk down by the loch for a bit?"

"No, I mean I want to leave here. Lallybroch. For good."

That took him aback more than a bit.

"Ye dinna mean that, I think," he said at last, cautious. "It's been a shock, after all. Ye shouldna—"

She shook her head and put a hand to her breast.

"Something's broken in me, Jamie," she said softly. "Whatever it was that bound me . . . it binds me nay more."

He didn't know what to say. He'd avoided the sight of the broch and the burying ground at its foot when he came out of the house, unable to bear the dark wet patch of raw ground there—but now he turned his head deliberately and raised his chin to point at it.

"And ye'd leave Ian?" he asked.

She made a small noise in her throat. Her hand lay against her breast still, and at this she pressed it flat, fierce against her heart.

"Ian's with me," she said, and her back straightened in defiance of the fresh-dug grave. "He'll never leave me, nor I him." She turned her head and looked at him then; her eyes were red, but dry.

"He'll never leave ye, either, Jamie," she said. "Ye ken that, as well as I do."

Tears welled in his own eyes then, unexpected, and he turned his head away.

"I ken that, aye," he muttered, and hoped it was true. Just now the place inside him where he was accustomed to find Ian was empty, hollow and echoing as a *bodhran*. Would he come back? Jamie wondered. Or had Ian only moved a bit, to a different part of his heart, a place he hadn't yet looked? He hoped—but he wouldn't go looking just yet awhile and kent it was for fear of finding nothing.

He wanted to change the subject, give her time and space to think. But it was difficult to find anything to say that didn't have to do with Ian being dead. Or with death in general. All loss is one, and one loss becomes all, a single death the key to the gate that bars memory.

"When Da died," he said suddenly, surprising himself as much as her. "Tell me what happened."

He felt her turn to look at him but kept his own eyes on his hands, the fingers of his left hand rubbing slowly over the thick red scar that ran down the back of his right.

"They brought him home," she said at last. "Lying in a wagon. It was Dougal MacKenzie with them. He told me Da had seen ye being whipped, and all of a sudden he'd fallen down, and when they picked him up, one side of his face was drawn up in anguish but the other was slack. He couldna speak, or walk, and so they took him away and brought him home."

She paused, swallowing, her eyes fixed on the broch and the burying ground.

"I had a doctor to him. He bled Da, more than once, and burned things in a wee burner and wafted the smoke under his nose. He tried to give him medicine, but Da couldna really swallow. I put drops of water on his tongue, but that was all." She sighed deeply. "He died the next day, about noon."

"Ah. He . . . never spoke?"

She shook her head. "He couldna speak at all. Only moved his mouth now and then and made wee gurgling sounds." Her chin puckered a little at the memory, but she firmed her lips. "I could see, though, near the end, he was trying to speak. His mouth was trying to shape the words, and his eyes were on mine, trying to make me understand." She glanced at him.

"He did say, 'Jamie,' the once. I ken that much for sure. For I thought he was trying to ask for you, and I told him Dougal said ye were alive and promised that ye'd be all right. That seemed to comfort him a bit, and he died soon after."

He swallowed thickly, the sound of it loud in his ears. It had begun to rain again, lightly, drops pattering on the leaves overhead.

"*Taing*," he said softly at last. "I wondered. I wish I could have said 'Sorry' to him."

"Ye didna need to," she said just as softly. "He'd ha' known it."

He nodded, unable to speak for a moment. Getting himself under control, though, he took her hand again and turned to her.

"I can say 'Sorry' to you, though, *a phiuthar*, and I do."

"For what?" she said, surprised.

"For believing Dougal when he told me . . . well, when he said ye'd become an English soldier's whore. I was a fool." He looked at his maimed hand, not wanting to meet her eyes.

"Aye, well," she said, and laid her hand on his, light and cool as the new leaves that fluttered round them. "Ye needed him. I didn't."

They sat awhile longer, feeling peaceful, holding hands.

"Where d'ye think he is now?" Jenny said suddenly. "Ian, I mean."

He glanced at the house, then at the new grave waiting, but of course that wasn't Ian anymore. He was panicked for a moment, his earlier emptiness returning—but then it came to him, and, without surprise, he knew what it was Ian had said to him.

"*On your right, man.*" On his right. Guarding his weak side.

"He's just here," he said to Jenny, nodding to the spot between them. "Where he belongs."

PART SEVEN

Reap the Whirlwind

85

SON OF A WITCH

W HEN ROGER AND Buccleigh drove up to the house, Amanda rushed out to meet them and returned to her mother, waving a blue plastic pinwheel on a stick.

"Mama! Look what I got, look what *I* got!"

"Oh, how pretty!" Brianna bent to admire it and, blowing, made the toy spin round.

"I do it, I do it!" Amanda grabbed it back, puffing and blowing with great determination but making little headway.

"From the side, *a leannan*, from the side." William Buccleigh came round the car and picked Amanda up, gently turning her hand so the pinwheel was perpendicular to her face. "Now blow." He put his face close to hers and helped blow, and the pinwheel whirred like a June bug.

"Aye, that's fine, isn't it? You have a go, then, on your own." He gave Bree a half-apologetic shrug and carried Amanda up the path, she industriously puffing and blowing. They passed Jem, who stopped to admire the pinwheel. Roger got out of the car with a couple of carrier bags and paused for a private word with Brianna.

"If we had a dog, I wonder if it would like him, too?" she murmured, nodding after their guest, who was now engaged in animated conversation with both children.

"A man may smile, and smile, and be a villain," Roger replied, watching with a narrowed eye. "And the claims of instinct quite aside, I don't think either dogs or children are necessarily good judges of character."

"Mm. Did he tell you anything else while you were out today?" Roger had taken William Buccleigh into Inverness to replenish his wardrobe, as he possessed nothing more than the jeans, T-shirt, and charity-store jacket in which he'd arrived.

"A few things. I asked him how he'd come here—to Lallybroch, I mean—and what was he doing hanging about. He said he'd seen me on the street in Inverness and recognized me, but I'd got in my car and gone before he could make up his mind to talk to me. He saw me once or twice more, though, and asked cautiously round to find out where I lived. He—" He stopped and looked at her, with a half smile. "Bear in mind what he is and when he came from. He thought—and I don't think he was telling me a tale—that I must be an Old One."

"Really?"

"Aye, really. And on the face of it...well, I did survive being hanged, which most people don't." His mouth twisted a little as he touched the scar on his throat. "And I—we—did, obviously, travel safely through the stones. I mean...I could see his point."

Despite her disquiet, she sniffed with amusement.

"Well, yes. You mean he was afraid of you?"

Roger shrugged, helpless. "He was. And I think I believe him—though I will say that if that's the case, he puts up a good front."

"Would you *act* afraid if you were going to confront a powerful supernatural being? Or would you try to play it cool? Being a male of the species, as Mama puts it. Or a proper man, as Da says. You and Da both act like John Wayne if there's anything fishy going on, and this guy is related to both of you."

"Good point," he said, though his mouth twitched at the "powerful supernatural being." Or possibly the "John Wayne" part. "And he admitted that he was reeling a bit at the shock of everything. I could sympathize with *that*."

"Mm. And we *knew* what we were doing. Sort of. He told me what happened when he came through—did he tell you that, too?"

They had been walking slowly but had nearly reached the door; she could hear Annie's voice in the hall, asking something, exclaiming among the children's chatter, and the lower rumble of William Buccleigh's voice in reply.

"Aye, he did. He wanted—wants, and wants badly—to get back to his own time. Clearly I knew how, and he'd have to come and talk to me to find out. But only a fool would walk straight up to a stranger's door, let alone a stranger you'd come close to killing, much less a stranger who might strike you dead on the spot or turn you into a crow." He shrugged again.

"So he left his job and took to lurking about the place, watching. To see if we were tossing human bones out the back door, I suppose. Jem ran into him out by the broch one day, and he told him he was a Nuckelavee—partly to scare him away, but also because if he came back and told me there was a Nuckelavee up the hill, I might come out and do something magical about it. And if I did . . ." He lifted his hands, palms up.

"If you did, you might be dangerous, but he'd also know you had the power to send him back. Like the Wizard of Oz."

He looked at her for a moment.

"Anyone less like Judy Garland than *him*—" he began, but was interrupted by Annie MacDonald demanding to know what they were hanging about being eaten by midgies for, when there was supper on the table? Apologizing, they went inside.

BRIANNA ATE SUPPER without really noticing what was on her plate. Jem was going to spend the night with Bobby again and go out fishing on Saturday with Rob on the Rothiemurchus estate. She felt a small twinge at that; she remembered her father patiently teaching Jem to cast, with the homemade rod and thread line that was all they had. Would he remember?

Still, it was just as well to have him out of the house. She and Roger were going to have to sit down with William Buccleigh and decide how best to get him back to his own time, and best if Jem wasn't lurking around the edges of such a discussion with his ears flapping. Should they consult Fiona? she wondered suddenly.

Fiona Graham was the granddaughter of old Mrs. Graham, who had kept house for Roger's adoptive father, the Reverend Wakefield. The very proper and elderly Mrs. Graham had also been the "caller"—the holder of a very old tradition indeed. On the fire feast of Beltane, the women whose families had passed the tradition down to them met at dawn and, clothed in white, performed a dance that Roger said was an ancient Norse circle dance. And at the end of it, the caller sang out in words that none of them understood anymore, bringing up the sun, so that as it rose above the horizon, the beam of light shot straight through the cleft of the split stone.

Mrs. Graham had died peacefully in her sleep years before—but had left her knowledge, and her role as caller, to her granddaughter, Fiona.

Fiona had helped Roger when he came through the stones to find Brianna—even contributing her own diamond engagement ring to help him, after his first attempt had ended much as William Buccleigh described his own: in flames in the center of the circle.

They could get a gemstone without much trouble, she thought, automatically passing the bowl of salad to Roger. From what they knew so far, it didn't have to be a terribly expensive stone, or even a large one. The garnets in Roger's mother's locket had apparently been enough to keep him from being killed during his first, abortive try.

She thought suddenly of the burn mark on William Buccleigh's chest and, as she did so, realized that she was staring at him—and he was staring back at her. She choked on a chunk of cucumber, and the subsequent hubbub of back-thumping and arm-raising and coughing and water-fetching luckily explained the redness of her face.

Everyone settled back to their food, but she was aware of Roger looking sideways at her. She shot him a brief look under her lashes, with a faint tilt of the head that said, *"Later. Upstairs,"* and he relaxed, resuming a three-way conversation with "Uncle Buck" and Jemmy about trout flies.

She wanted to talk to him about what Buccleigh had said, and decide what to do about him, as soon as possible. She was *not* going to tell him what William Buccleigh had said about Rob Cameron.

ROGER LAY IN BED, watching the moonlight on Brianna's sleeping face. It was quite late, but he found himself wakeful. Odd, for he usually fell asleep in seconds after making love to her. Fortunately, she did, too; she had tonight, curling into him like a large, affectionate shrimp before lapsing into naked, warm inertness in his arms.

It had been wonderful—but that wee bit different. She was almost always willing, even eager, and that had been no different, though she'd made a particular point of dead-bolting the bedroom door. He'd installed the dead bolt because Jem had learned to pick locks at the age of seven. It was still bolted, in fact, and seeing that, he slid carefully out from under the covers to unfasten it. Jem was spending the night with his new best friend, Bobby, but if Mandy needed them in the night, he didn't want the door locked.

The room was cool, but pleasantly so; they'd put in baseboard heaters, which would be barely adequate to the winter temperatures of the Highlands but fine for late autumn.

Bree slept hot; he'd swear her body temperature rose two or three degrees when she slept, and she often threw off the covers. She lay now, bare to the waist, arms flung over her head and snoring faintly. He cupped a hand absently under his balls, wondering idly whether they might have another go. He thought she wouldn't mind, but . . .

But maybe he shouldn't. When he made love to her, he often took his time and, at the last, was filled with a barbarous delight when she yielded her red-thatched quim—willingly, to be sure, but with an instant always of hesitation, just one final breath of something that was not quite resistance. He thought it was a means of assuring herself—if not him—that she had the right to refuse. A stronghold once breached and repaired has stouter defenses. He didn't think she realized consciously that she did this; he'd never mentioned it to her, wanting no ghost to rise between them.

It had been a little different tonight. She'd balked more noticeably, then yielded with something like ferocity, pulling him in and raking her nails down his back. And he . . .

He'd paused for that one instant, but once safely mounted had had the insane urge to pillage ruthlessly, to show himself—if not her—that she was indeed his, and not her own, inviolate.

And she'd egged him on.

He noticed that he hadn't taken his hand away and was now eyeing his wife like a Roman soldier sizing up one of the Sabine women for weight and portabililty. *Raptio* was the Latin word, usually translated as "rape," though in fact it meant kidnapping, or seizing. *Raptio,* raptor, the seizing of prey. He could see it both ways, and noticed at this point that he *still* hadn't actually removed his hand from his genitals, which in the meantime had decided unilaterally that, no, she wouldn't mind at all.

His cerebral cortex, rapidly being overpowered by something a lot older and much lower down, hazarded a last faint notion that it was to do with having a stranger in the house—especially one like William Buccleigh MacKenzie.

"Well, he'll be gone by Samhain," Roger muttered, approaching the bed. The portal in the stones should be wide open then, and with some sort of gem in hand, the bugger ought to be back to his wife in . . .

He slid beneath the sheets, gathered his own wife up with a firm hand on her very warm bottom, and hissed in her ear, "I'll get you—and your little dog, too."

Her body quivered in a soundless subterranean laugh and, eyes closed, she reached down and drew a delicate fingernail up his very sensitive flesh.

"I'm meeeeeeeelllllllting," she murmured.

HE DID FALL ASLEEP after that. But waked again, somewhere in the wee hours, and found himself annoyingly alert.

It must be him, he thought, slithering out of bed again. *I'll not sleep sound until we get rid of him.* He didn't bother being careful; he could tell from the faint rasp of Brianna's snore that she was dead to the world. He pulled his pajamas over his nakedness and stepped out into the upstairs corridor, listening.

Lallybroch talked to itself at night, as all old houses do. He was used to the sudden startling cracks, as wooden beams in the room cooled at night, and even the creaking of the second-floor hallway, as though someone was walking rapidly up and down it. The rattle of windows when the wind was in the west, reminding him comfortably of Brianna's irregular snoring. It was remarkably quiet now, though, wrapped in the somnolence of deep night.

They'd put William Buccleigh at the far end of the hall, having decided without speaking of it that they didn't want him above, on the same floor with the kids. Keep him close; keep an eye on him.

Roger walked quietly down the hall, listening. The crack under Buccleigh's door was dark, and from inside the room, he heard a deep, regular snore, interrupted once as the sleeper turned in bed, muttered something incomprehensible, and dropped back into slumber.

"That's all right, then," Roger muttered to himself, and turned away. His cerebral cortex, interrupted earlier, now patiently resumed its train of thought. Of course it was to do with having a stranger in the house—and such a stranger. Both he and Brianna felt obscurely threatened by his presence.

In his own case, there was a solid substratum of anger under the wariness, and a good bit of confusion, too. He had, from sheer necessity as well as religious conviction, forgiven William Buccleigh for his role in the hanging that had taken his voice. After all, the man had not tried to kill him personally and couldn't have known what would happen.

But it was a damned sight easier to forgive somebody you knew had been dead for two hundred years than it was to maintain that forgiveness with the bastard living under your nose, eating your food, and being charming to your wife and children.

And let us not forget he is *a bastard, too,* Roger thought savagely, making his way down the stairs in the dark. The family tree he'd shown William Buccleigh MacKenzie revealed him as all correct, pinned down on paper, neatly bracketed by parents and son. The chart was a lie, though. William Buccleigh MacKenzie was a changeling: the illegitimate offspring of Dougal MacKenzie, war chief of Clan MacKenzie, and Geillis Duncan, witch. And Roger thought William Buccleigh didn't know it.

Safely at the bottom of the stair, he turned on the light in the lower hall and went to the kitchen to check that the back door was locked.

They'd discussed that one, he and Brianna, but hadn't come to an agreement yet. He was for letting sleeping dogs lie; what good could it do the man to know the truth of his origins? The Highlands that had spawned those two wild souls was gone, both now and in William Buccleigh's rightful time.

Bree had insisted that Buccleigh had some right to know the truth—though, challenged, could not say quite what right that was.

"*You* are who you think you are, and you always have been," she'd said at last, frustrated but trying to explain. "I wasn't. Do you think it would have been better if I'd never *known* who my real father was?"

In all honesty, it might have been, he thought. The knowledge, once revealed, had torn both their lives apart, exposed them both to terrible things. It had taken his voice. Almost taken his life. Had put her in danger, gotten her raped, been responsible for her having killed a man—he hadn't spoken to her about that; he should. He saw the weight of it in her eyes sometimes and knew it for what it was. He carried the same weight.

And yet . . . would he choose *not* to have known what he now knew? Never to have lived in the past, met Jamie Fraser, seen the side of Claire that existed only in Jamie's company?

It wasn't the tree of good and evil in the Garden of Eden, after all; it was the tree of the *knowledge* of good and evil. Knowledge might be a poisoned gift—but it was still a gift, and few people would voluntarily give it back. Which was just as well, he supposed, since they *couldn't* give it back. And that had been *his* point in the discussion.

"We don't know what harm it could do," he'd argued. "But we don't know it *couldn't* do harm, and serious harm. And what would be the benefit to the man, to know his mother was insane, a sorceress, or both, certainly a multiple murderess, and his father an adulterer and at the least an attempted murderer? It was enough of a shock to *me* when your mother told me about Geillis Duncan, and she's seven generations removed from me. And before you ask, yes, I could have lived without knowing that."

She'd bitten her lip at that and nodded, reluctant.

"It's just—I keep thinking about Willie," Bree had said at last, giving up. "Not William Buccleigh, I don't mean—my brother." She flushed a little, as she always did, self-conscious at speaking the word. "I really wanted him to *know*. But Da and Lord John . . . they so *didn't* want him to know, and maybe they were right. He has a life, a good one. And they said he couldn't keep on having that life if I told him."

"They were right," Roger had said bluntly. "To tell him—if he believed it—would force him to live in a state of deceit and denial, which would eat him alive, or to openly acknowledge that he's the bastard son of a Scottish criminal. Which is Just. Not. On. Not in eighteenth-century culture."

"They wouldn't take his title away," Bree had argued. "Da said that by British law, a child born in wedlock is the legal offspring of the husband, no matter whether the husband was the real father or not."

"No, but imagine living with a title ye don't think you're entitled *to*, knowing the blood in your veins isn't the blue ye've always thought it was. Having people call ye 'Lord So-and-So' and knowing what they'd call ye if they knew the truth." He'd shaken her gently, trying to make her see.

"Either way, it would destroy the life he has, as surely as if you'd set him on a keg of gunpowder and lit the fuse. You wouldn't know when the bang would come, but come it would."

"Mmphm," she'd said, and the argument ended there. But it hadn't been a sound of agreement, and he knew the argument wasn't over.

By now he had checked all the doors and windows on the ground floor, ending in his study.

He flipped on the light and came into the room. He was wide awake, nerves on edge. *Why?* he wondered. Was the house trying to tell him something? He snorted a little. Hard not to have fancies, in the middle of the night in an old house, with the wind rattling the windowpanes. And yet he usually felt very comfortable in this room, felt it was his place. What was wrong?

He glanced quickly over the desk, the deep windowsill with the small pot of yellow chrysanthemums that Bree had put there, the shelves—

He stopped dead, heart thumping in his chest. The snake wasn't there. No, no, it was—his roving eye fixed on it. It was in the wrong place, though. It wasn't in front of the wooden box that held Claire and Jamie's letters but sitting in front of the books two shelves below it.

He picked it up, automatically stroking the old polished cherrywood with his thumb. Perhaps Annie MacDonald had moved it? No. She did dust and sweep in the study, but she never moved anything from its place. Never moved anything anywhere, for that matter; he'd seen her pick up a pair of galoshes carelessly left in the middle of the mudroom, sweep carefully under them, and set them back in the same place, mud splashes and all. She would never have moved the snake.

Still less would Brianna have moved it. He knew—without knowing how he knew it—that she felt as he did about it; Willie Fraser's snake guarded his brother's treasure.

He was lifting down the box before his train of conscious thought had reached its logical conclusion.

Alarm bells were going off right and left. The contents of the box had been disturbed; the little books were on top of the letters at one end of the box, not underneath. He took out the letters, cursing himself for never having counted them. How would he know if one was missing?

He sorted them quickly, read and unread, and *thought* the unread pile was about the same; whoever had been in the box hadn't opened them, that was something. But whoever it was had probably wanted to avoid detection, too.

He thumbed hastily through the opened letters and became aware at once that one was missing: the one written on Brianna's handmade paper with the embedded flowers. The first one. Jesus, what had it said? *We are alive.* He remembered that much. And then Claire had told all about the explosion and the burning of the Big House. Had she said in that one they were going to Scotland? Maybe so. But why in bloody hell should—

Two floors above, Mandy sat up in bed and screamed like a *ban-sidhe*.

HE MADE IT TO Amanda's room a half step before Brianna and scooped the child out of her bed, cradling her against his pounding heart.

"Jemmy, Jemmy!" she sobbed. "He's gone, he's gone. He's *GONE!!*" This last was shrieked as she stiffened in Roger's arms, digging her feet hard into his belly.

"Hey, hey," he soothed, trying to rearrange her and pet her into calm. "It's okay, Jemmy's fine. He's *fine,* he's only gone to visit Bobby overnight. He'll be home tomorrow."

"He's *GONE!*" She squirmed like an eel, not trying to get away but merely possessed by a paroxysm of frantic grief. "He's not here, he's not here!"

"Aye, like I said, he's at Bobby's house, he—"

"Not *here,*" she said urgently, and thumped the palm of her hand repeatedly on the top of her head. "Not here wif me!"

"Here, baby, come here," Bree said urgently, taking the tear-streaked child from him.

"Mama, Mama! Jemmy's *GONE!*" She clung to Bree, staring desperately, still thumping her head. "He's not wif me!"

Bree frowned at Mandy, puzzled, a hand running over her, checking for temperature, swollen glands, tender tummy . . .

"Not with you," she repeated, speaking intently, trying to get Mandy out of her panic. "Tell Mummy what you mean, sweetheart."

"Not *here!*" In utter desperation, Mandy lowered her head and butted her mother in the chest.

"Oof!"

The door at the end of the hall opened, and William Buccleigh came out, wearing Roger's woolen dressing gown.

"What in the name of the Blessed Virgin's all this riot?" he inquired.

"He took him, he took him!" Mandy shrieked, and buried her head in Brianna's shoulder.

Despite himself, Roger was feeling infected by Amanda's fear, irrationally convinced that something terrible had happened.

"Do you know where Jem is?" he snapped at Buccleigh.

"I do not." Buccleigh frowned at him. "Is he not in his bed?"

"No, he isn't!" Brianna snapped. "You saw him leave, for heaven's sake." She forced her way between the men. "Quit it right now, both of you! Roger, take Mandy. I'm going to phone Martina Hurragh." She thrust Amanda, moaning around the thumb in her mouth, into his arms and hurried for the stairs, her hastily acquired nightclothes rustling like leaves.

He rocked Amanda, distracted, alarmed, nearly overcome by her sense of panic. She emitted fright and grief like a radio broadcasting tower, and his own breath came short and his hands were wet with sweat where he clutched her Winnie-the-Pooh nightie.

"Hush, *a chuisle,*" he said, pitching his voice as calmly as he could. "Hush, now. We'll fix it. You tell Daddy what waked you up, and I'll fix it, promise."

She obediently tried to stifle her sobs, rubbing chubby fists into her eyes.

"Jemmy," she moaned. "I want Jemmy!"

"We'll get him back straightaway," Roger promised. "Tell me, what made you wake up? Did you have a bad dream?"

"Uh-huh." She clutched him tighter, her face full of fear. "Was big wocks, *big* wocks. They scweamed at me!"

Ice water ran straight through his veins. Jesus, oh, Jesus. Maybe she *did* remember her trip through the stones.

"Aye, I see," he said, patting her as soothingly as he could, for the ferment in his own breast. He *did* see. In memory he saw those stones, felt and heard them again. And, turning a little, saw the pallor of William Buccleigh's face and knew he heard the ring of truth in Mandy's voice, too.

"What happened then, *a leannan*? Did you go close to the big rocks?"

"Not me; Jem! That man took him and the wocks *ate* him!" At this, she collapsed in tears again, sobbing inconsolably.

"That man," Roger said slowly, and turned a little more, so that William Buccleigh was in her field of view. "Do you mean *this* man, sweetheart? Uncle Buck?"

"No, nonononononono, a *other* man!" She straightened up, staring into his face with huge, tear-filled eyes, straining to make him understand. "Bobby's daddy!"

He heard Brianna coming upstairs. Fast, but unevenly; it sounded as though she was bumping against the walls of the staircase, losing her balance as she hurried.

She stumbled into view at the top of the stair, and Roger felt every hair on his body stand up at the sight of her white, staring face.

"He's gone," she said, hoarse. "Martina says he's not with Bobby, she didn't expect him tonight at all. I made her go outside and look—Rob lives three houses down. She says his truck is gone."

ROGER'S HANDS were numb with cold, and the steering wheel was slippery with their sweat. He took the turn off the highway at such speed that the off-wheels lifted slightly and the car tilted. William Buccleigh's head thumped the window.

"Sorry," Roger muttered mechanically, and received a grunt of acceptance in reply.

"Mind yourself," Buccleigh said, rubbing his temple. "Ye'll have us over in a ditch, and then what?"

Then what, indeed. With great effort, he eased his foot back on the gas. It was near moonset, and a wan quarter moon did little to light the landscape, black as pitch around them. The headlights of the little Morris barely dented the darkness, and the frail beams swung to and fro as they bounced crazily on the dirt road that led near Craigh na Dun.

"Why the devil should this *trusdair* take your son?" Buccleigh rolled down his window and stuck his head out, vainly trying to see farther than the view through the dust-coated windshield. "And why, for the sake of all holy, bring him *here*?"

"How do I know?" Roger said through his teeth. "Maybe he thinks he needs blood to open the stones. *Christ*, why did I write that?" He pounded a fist on the wheel in frustration.

Buccleigh blinked, very startled, but his gaze sharpened at once.

"Is that it?" he said, urgent. "*Is* that how ye do it? Blood?"

"No, dammit!" Roger said. "It's the time of year, and gemstones. We think."

"But ye wrote down blood, with a query mark next it."

"Yes, but—what do you mean? Did you read my notebook, too, you cunt?"

"Language, son," said William Buccleigh, grim but cool. "Of course I did. I read everything in your study I could get my hands on—and so would you, in my place."

Roger throttled back the panic that gripped him, enough to manage a curt nod.

"Aye, maybe I would. And if *you'd* taken Jem—I'd kill ye once I found you, but I'd maybe understand why. But *this* fucker! What does he think he's *doing*, for God's sake?"

"Calm yourself," Buccleigh advised him briefly. "Ye'll do your wean no good if ye lose the heid. This Cameron—is he one like us?"

"I don't know. I don't bloody *know.*"

"There are others, though? It's not just in the family?"

"I don't know—I think there are others, but I don't know for sure." Roger struggled to think, struggled to keep the car rolling at a low enough speed to handle the curves of the road, half overgrown with creeping gorse.

He was trying to pray but managing nothing but a terror-stricken, incoherent *Lord, please!* He wished Bree was with him, but they couldn't have brought Mandy anywhere near the rocks, and if they should be in time to catch Cameron . . . if Cameron was even here . . . Buccleigh would help him, he was fairly sure of that.

The back of his mind harbored a forlorn hope that there was some misunderstanding, that Cameron had mistaken the night and, realizing it, was bringing Jem back home, even as Roger and his bloody five times great-grandfather tore over a rocky moor in the dark, headed straight for the most terrible thing either of them knew.

"Cameron—he read the notebook, too," Roger blurted, unable to bear his own thoughts. "By accident. He pretended to think it was all a—a—fiction, something I'd made up for fun. Jesus, what have I *done*?"

"Look out!" Buccleigh threw his arms over his face and Roger stood on the brake, swerving off the road and into a large rock—barely missing the old blue truck that stood on the road, dark and empty.

HE SCRAMBLED UP the hill, scrabbling for handholds in the dark, rocks rolling under his feet, gorse prickles piercing his palms, now and then stabbing under his nails, making him swear. Far below, he could hear William Buccleigh following. Slowly—but following.

He began to hear them long before he reached the crest. It was three days before Samhain, and the stones knew it. The sound that wasn't a sound at all vibrated through the marrow of his bones, made his skull ring and his teeth ache. He gritted his teeth together and kept on. By the time he reached the stones, he was on hands and knees, unable to stand upright.

Dear God, he thought, *God, preserve me! Keep me alive long enough to find him!*

He could barely form thoughts but recalled the flashlight. He'd brought it from the car and now fumbled it out of his pocket, dropping it, having to grope frantically over the short grass in the circle, finding it at last and squeezing the button with a finger that slipped off four times before finally achieving the strength to make the connection.

The beam of light sprang out, and he heard a muffled exclamation of amazement from the dark behind him. Of course, he thought dazedly, William Buccleigh hadn't yet seen a flashlight. The wavering beam passed slowly round the circle, back. What was he looking for? Footprints? Something Jem had dropped, that would show he'd come this way?

There was nothing.

Nothing but the stones. It was getting worse, and he dropped the flashlight, clutching his head with both hands. He had to move . . . had to go . . . go get Jem . . .

He was dragging himself over the grass, white-blind with the pain and nearly mindless, when strong hands grabbed him by the ankles and hauled him backward. He thought there might have been a voice, but if so, it was lost in the piercing scream that echoed inside his head, inside his soul, and he cried out his son's name as loud as he could to hear something besides that noise, felt his throat tear from the effort, but heard nothing.

Then the earth moved beneath him and the world fell away.

FELL AWAY QUITE literally. When he came to some time later, he found that he and William Buccleigh were resting in a shallow declivity in the side of the hill, forty feet below the stone circle. They'd fallen and rolled; he could tell that from the way he felt and the way Buccleigh looked. There was a hint of dawn in the sky, and he could see Buccleigh, scratched and torn, sitting hunched beside him, curled into himself as though his belly hurt.

"What . . . ?" Roger whispered. He cleared his throat and tried again to ask what had happened, but couldn't manage more than a whisper—and even that made his throat burn like fire.

William Buccleigh muttered something under his breath, and Roger realized that he was praying. He tried to sit up and made it, though his head spun.

"Did ye drag me free?" he demanded in his harsh whisper. Buccleigh's eyes were closed and stayed that way until he had finished his prayer. Then he opened them and glanced from Roger to the top of the hill, where the unseen stones still quired their ghastly song of time undone—no more from here, thank goodness, than an eerie whine that set his teeth on edge.

"I did," Buccleigh said. "I didna think ye were going to make it out on your own."

"I wasn't." Roger lowered himself back onto the ground, dizzy and aching. "Thanks," he added a moment later. There was a great void inside him, vast as the fading sky.

"Aye, well. Maybe it'll help to make up for getting ye hanged," Buccleigh said, in an offhand way. "What now?"

Roger stared up at the sky, rotating slowly overhead. It made him dizzier, so he closed his eyes and reached out a hand.

"Now we go home," he croaked. "And think again. Help me up."

86

VALLEY FORGE

W ILLIAM WORE HIS uniform. It was necessary, he told his father.

"Denzell Hunter is a man of great conscience and principle. I cannot engage to winkle him out of the American camp without proper leave of his officer. I think he would not come. But if I can obtain permission—and I think I can—then I believe he will."

But to obtain formal permission for the services of a Continental surgeon, obviously he had to ask formally. Which meant riding into Washington's new winter quarters at Valley Forge in a red coat, no matter what happened next.

Lord John had closed his eyes for a moment, plainly envisioning just what sort of thing *might* happen next, but then opened them and said briskly, "All right, then. Will you take a servant with you?"

"No," William said, surprised. "Why would I need one?"

"To care for the horses, to manage your goods—and to be the eyes in the back of your head," his father said, giving him a look indicating that he should already have been aware of some of this. He therefore did *not* say, *"Horses?"* or *"What goods?"* but merely nodded and said, "Thank you, Papa. Can you find me someone suitable?"

"Suitable" turned out to be one Colenso Baragwanath, a stunted youth from Cornwall who had come with Howe's troops as a stable-boy. He did know horses, William would give him that.

There were four horses and a pack mule, this last laden with sides of pork, four or five fat turkeys, a bag of rough-skinned potatoes, another of turnips, and a large keg of cider.

"If conditions there are half as bad as I think they are," his father had told him, while overseeing the loading of the mule, "the commander would lend you the services of half a battalion in exchange for this, let alone a surgeon."

"Thank you, Papa," he said again, and swung into his saddle, his new captain's gorget about his neck and a white flag of truce folded neatly into his saddlebag.

Valley Forge looked like a gigantic encampment of doomed charcoal-burners. The place was essentially a wood lot, or had been before Washington's soldiers began felling everything in sight. Hacked stumps were everywhere, and the ground was strewn with broken branches. Huge bonfires burned in random spots, and piles of logs were stacked everywhere. They were building huts as fast as possible—and none too soon, for snow had begun falling three or four hours before, and the camp was already blanketed with white.

William hoped they'd be able to *see* the flag of truce.

"Right, up you go and ride ahead of me," he told Colenso, handing the boy the long stick to which he'd tied the flag. The youth's eyes widened in horror.

"What, me?"

"Yes, you," said Willie impatiently. "Up, or I'll kick your arse."

William's back itched between the shoulder blades as they entered the camp, Colenso crouched like a monkey on his horse's back, holding the flag as low as he dared and muttering strange oaths in Cornish. William's left hand itched, too, wanting to go for the hilt of his sword, the handle of his pistol. But he'd come unarmed. If they meant to shoot him, they'd shoot him, armed or not, and to come unarmed was a sign of good faith. So he put back his cloak, in spite of the snow, to show his lack of weapons, and rode slowly into the storm.

THE PRELIMINARIES went well. No one shot him, and he was directed to a Colonel Preston, a tall, ragged man in the remnants of a Continental uniform, who had eyed him askance but listened with surprising courtesy to his request. Permission was granted—but this being the *American* army, the permission granted was not license to take the surgeon away but rather license to *ask* the surgeon if he would go.

Willie left Colenso with the horses and mule, with strict instructions to keep his eyes open, and made his way up the little hill where he had been told Denzell Hunter likely was. His heart was beating fast, and not only from the exertion. In Philadelphia, he had been sure Hunter would come at his request. Now he wasn't quite so sure.

He had fought Americans, knew a great many of them who were in no respect different from the Englishmen they'd been two years previous. But he'd never walked through an American army camp before.

It seemed chaotic, but all camps did in their early stages, and he was able to perceive the rough order that did in fact exist among the piles of debris and butchered tree stumps. But there was something very different about the feel of this camp, something almost exuberant. The men he passed were ragged in the extreme; not one in ten had shoes, despite the weather, and groups of them huddled like beggars around the bonfires, wrapped in blankets, shawls, the remnants of canvas tents and burlap sacks. And yet they didn't huddle in miserable silence. They talked.

Conversed amiably, telling jokes, arguing, getting up to piss in the snow, to stamp round in circles to get the blood going. He'd seen a demoralized camp before, and this one *wasn't*. Which was, all things considered, amazing. He assumed Denzell Hunter must share this spirit. That being so, would he consent to leave his fellows? No way to tell, save by asking.

There was no door to knock on. He came round a stand of leafless oak saplings that had so far escaped the ax and found Hunter crouched on the ground, sewing up a gash in the leg of a man who lay before him on a blanket. Rachel Hunter held the man's shoulders, her capped head bent over him as she spoke encouragingly to him.

"Did I not tell thee he was quick?" she was saying. "No more than thirty seconds, I said, and so it has been. I counted it out, did I not?"

"Thee counts in a most leisurely fashion, Rachel," the doctor said, smiling as he reached for his scissors and clipped the thread. "A man might walk three times around St. Paul's in one of your minutes."

"Stuff," she said mildly. "'Tis done, in any case. Here, sit thee up and take some water. Thee does not—" She had turned toward the bucket that sat beside her and, as she did so, perceived William standing there. Her mouth opened in shock, and then she was up and flying across the clearing to embrace him.

He hadn't expected *that*, but was delighted and returned the embrace with great feeling. She smelled of herself and of smoke, and it made his blood run faster.

"Friend William! I thought never to see thee again," she said, stepping back with glowing face. "What does thee here? For I think thee has not come to enlist," she added, looking him up and down.

"No," he said, rather gruffly. "I have come to beg a favor. From your brother," he added, a little belatedly.

"Oh? Come, then, he is nearly finished." She led him to Denny, still looking up at him in great interest.

"So thee is indeed a British soldier," she remarked. "We thought thee must be but feared thee might be a deserter. I am pleased thee is not."

"Are you?" he asked, smiling. "But surely you would prefer that I abjure my military service and seek peace?"

"Of course I would that thee should seek peace—and find it, too," she said matter-of-factly. "But thee cannot find peace in oath-breaking and illegal flight, knowing thy soul steeped in deceit and fearing for thy life. Denny, look who has come!"

"Yes, I saw. Friend William, well met!" Dr. Hunter helped his freshly bandaged patient to his feet and came toward William, smiling. "Did I hear thee would ask a favor of me? If it is my power to grant it, it is thine."

"I won't hold you to that," William said, smiling and feeling a knot relax at the base of his neck. "But hear me out, and I hope you will see fit to come."

As he had half-expected, Hunter was at first hesitant to leave the camp. There were not many surgeons, and with so much illness due to the cold and the crowded conditions . . . it might be a week or more before he could return to camp . . . but William wisely kept silence, only glancing once at Rachel and then meeting Denzell's eyes straight on.

Would you have her stay here through the winter?

"Thee wishes Rachel to come with me?" Hunter asked, instantly divining his meaning.

"I will come with thee whether he wishes it or not," Rachel pointed out. "And both of you know it perfectly well."

"Yes," said Denzell mildly, "but it seemed mannerly to ask. Besides, it is not only a matter of thy coming. It—"

William didn't hear the end of his sentence, for a large object was thrust suddenly between his legs from behind, and he emitted an unmanly yelp and leaped forward, whirling round to see who had assaulted him in this cowardly fashion.

"Yes, I was forgetting the dog," Rachel said, still composed. "He can walk now, but I doubt he can manage the journey to Philadelphia on foot. Can thee make shift to transport him, does thee think?"

He recognized the dog at once. There couldn't possibly be two like him.

"Surely this is Ian Murray's dog?" he asked, putting out a tentative fist for the enormous beast to sniff. "Where is his master?"

The Hunters exchanged a brief glance, but Rachel answered readily enough.

"Scotland. He has gone to Scotland on an urgent errand, with his uncle, James Fraser. Does thee know Mr. Fraser?" It seemed to William that both Hunters were staring at him rather intently, but he merely nodded and said, "I met him once, many years ago. Why did the dog not go to Scotland with his master?"

Again that glance between them. What was it about Murray? he wondered.

"The dog was injured, just before they took ship. Friend Ian was kind enough to leave his companion in my care," Rachel said calmly. "Can thee procure a wagon, perhaps? I think thy horse may not like Rollo."

LORD JOHN FITTED the leather strap between Henry's teeth. The boy was half unconscious from a dose of laudanum but knew enough still of his surroundings to give his uncle the bare attempt at a grin. Grey could feel the fright pulsing through Henry—and shared it. There was a ball of venomous snakes in his belly, a constant slithering sensation, punctuated by sudden stabs of panic.

Hunter had insisted upon binding Henry's arms and legs to the bed, that there should be no movement during the operation. The day was brilliant; sun coruscated from the frozen snow that rimmed the windows, and the bed had been moved to take best advantage of it.

Dr. Hunter had been told of the dowser but declined courteously to have the man come again, saying that this smacked of divination, and if he were to ask God's help in this endeavor, he thought he could not do so sincerely were there anything of witchcraft about the process. That had rather affronted Mercy Woodcock, who puffed up a bit, but she kept silence, too glad—and too anxious—to argue.

Grey was not superstitious but *was* of a practical turn of mind and had taken a careful note of the dowser's location of the ball he had found. He explained this, and with Hunter's reluctant assent, took out a small ruler and triangulated the spot on Henry's sunken belly, dabbing a bit of candle black on the place to mark it.

"I think we are in readiness," Denzell said, and, coming close to the bed, put his hands on Henry's head and prayed briefly for guidance and support for himself, for endurance and healing for Henry, and ended in acknowledging the presence of God among them. Despite his purely rational sentiments, Grey felt a small lessening of the tension in the room and sat down opposite the surgeon, with the snakes in his belly calmed for the moment.

He took his nephew's limp hand in his and said calmly, "Just hold on, Henry. I won't let go."

IT *WAS* QUICK. Grey had seen army surgeons at work and knew their dispatch, but even by those standards, Denzell Hunter's speed and dexterity were remarkable. Grey had lost all sense of time, absorbed in the erratic clenching of Henry's fingers, the shrill keen of his screaming through the leather gag, and the doctor's movements, quickly brutal, then finicking as he picked delicately, swabbed, and stitched.

As the last stitches went in, Grey breathed, for what seemed the first time in hours, and saw by the carriage clock on the mantel that barely a quarter of an hour had elapsed. William and Rachel Hunter stood by the mantelpiece, out of the way, and he saw with some interest that they were holding hands, their knuckles as white as their faces.

Hunter was checking Henry's breathing, lifting his eyelids to peer at his pupils, wiping the tears and snot from his face, touching the pulse under his jaw—Grey could see this, weak and irregular but still pumping, a tiny blue thread beneath the waxen skin.

"Well enough, well enough, and thanks be to the Lord who has strengthened me," Hunter was murmuring. "Rachel, will thee bring me the dressings?"

Rachel at once detached herself from William and fetched the neat stack of folded gauze pads and torn linen strips, together with a glutinous mass of some sort, soaking green through the cloth that bound it.

"What is *that*?" Grey asked, pointing at it.

"A poultice recommended to me by a colleague, a Mrs. Fraser. I have seen it to have laudable effects upon wounds of all kinds," the doctor assured him.

"Mrs. Fraser?" Grey said, surprised. "Mrs. *James* Fraser? Where the de— I mean, where did you happen to encounter the lady?"

"At Fort Ticonderoga" was the surprising answer. "She and her husband were with the Continental army through the battles at Saratoga."

The snakes in Grey's belly roused abruptly.

"Do you mean to tell me that Mrs. Fraser is now at Valley Forge?"

"Oh, no." Hunter shook his head, concentrated on his dressing. "If thee will please lift him a little, Friend Grey? I require to pass this bandage underneath—ah, yes, exactly right, I thank thee. No," he resumed, straightening up and wiping his forehead, for it was very warm in the room, with so many people and a blazing fire built up in the hearth. "No, the Frasers have gone to Scotland. Though Mr. Fraser's nephew was sufficiently kind as to leave us his dog," he added, as Rollo, made curious by the smell of blood, now rose from his spot in the corner and poked his nose under Grey's elbow. He sniffed interestedly at the splattered sheets, up and down Henry's naked body. He then sneezed explosively, shook his head, and padded back to lie down, where he promptly rolled onto his back and relaxed, paws in the air.

"Someone must remain with him for the next day or so," Hunter was saying, wiping his hands on a rag. "He must not be left alone, lest he cease breathing. Friend William," he said, turning to Willie, "might it be possible to find a place for us to stay? I should be near for several days, so that I may call regularly to see how he progresses."

William assured him that this had already been taken care of: a most respectable inn, and—here he glanced at Rachel—quite near at hand. Might he convey the Hunters there? Or take Miss Rachel, if her brother should be not quite finished?

It was apparent to Grey that Willie would like nothing better than a ride through the snow-sparkling city alone with this comely Quaker, but Mrs. Woodcock put a spoke in that wheel by observing that, in fact, it was Christmas; she had not had time or opportunity to make much of a meal, but would the gentlemen and lady not honor her house and the day by taking a glass of wine, to drink to Lieutenant Grey's recovery?

This was generally agreed to as a capital idea, and Grey volunteered to sit with his nephew while the wine and glasses were being fetched.

With so many people suddenly gone, the room felt much cooler. Nearly cold, in fact, and Grey drew both sheet and coverlet gently up over Henry's bandaged stomach.

"You'll be all right, Henry," he whispered, though his nephew's eyes were closed, and he thought the young man might be asleep—hoped he was.

But he wasn't. Henry's eyes slowly opened, his pupils showing the effect of the opium; his creased lids showed the pain that the opium could not touch.

"No, I won't," he said, in a weak, clear voice. "He got only one. The second ball will kill me."

His eyes closed again, as the sound of Christmas cheer came up the stairs. The dog sighed.

RACHEL HUNTER PUT one hand to her stomach, another to her mouth, and stifled a rising eructation.

"Gluttony is a sin," she said. "But one that carries its own punishment. I think I may vomit."

"All sins do," her brother replied absently, dipping his pen. "But thee is not a glutton. I saw thee eat."

"But I am like to burst!" she protested. "And, besides, I cannot help but think of the poor Christmas those we left at Valley Forge will make, by comparison with the . . . *the . . . decadence* of our meal tonight."

"Well, that is guilt, not gluttony, and false guilt at that. Thee ate no more than would constitute a normal meal; it is only that thee hasn't had one in months. And I think roast goose is perhaps not the uttermost word in decadence, even when stuffed with oysters and chestnuts. Now, had it been a pheasant stuffed with truffles, or a wild boar with a gilded apple in its mouth . . ." He smiled at her over his papers.

"Thee has seen such things?" she asked curiously.

"I have, yes. When I worked in London with John Hunter. He was much in society and would now and then take me with him to attend a case and sometimes to accompany him and his wife to some grand occasion—most kind of him. But we must not judge, thee knows, most particularly by appearance. Even one who seems most frivolous, spendthrift, or light-minded yet has a soul and is valuable before God."

"Yes," she said vaguely, not really attending. She pulled back the curtain from the window, seeing the street outside as a white blur. There was a lantern hung by the inn's door that cast a small circle of light, but the snow was still falling. Her own face floated in the dark glass of the window, thin and big-eyed, and she frowned at it, pushing a straggle of dark hair back under her cap.

"Does thee think he knows?" she asked abruptly. "Friend William?"

"Does he know what?"

"His very striking resemblance to James Fraser," she said, letting the curtain fall. "Surely thee does not think this coincidence?"

"I think it is not our business." Denny resumed scratching with his quill.

She heaved an exasperated sigh. He was right, but that didn't mean she was forbidden to observe and to wonder. She had been happy—more than happy—to see William again, and while his being a British soldier was no less than she had suspected, she had been extremely surprised to find him an officer of high rank. Much more than surprised to learn from his villainous-looking Cornish orderly that he was a lord, though the little creature had been uncertain what kind.

Yet surely no two men could look so alike who did not share blood in some close degree. She had seen James Fraser many times and admired him for his tall, straight dignity, thrilling a bit at the fierceness in his face, always feeling that niggle of recognition when she saw him—but it wasn't until William suddenly stepped out before her at the camp that she realized *why*. Yet how could an English lord be in any way related to a Scottish Jacobite, a pardoned criminal? For Ian had told her something of his own family history—though not enough; not nearly enough.

"Thee is thinking of Ian Murray again," her brother observed, not looking up from his paper. He sounded resigned.

"I thought thee abjured witchcraft," she said tartly. "Or does thee not include mind reading among the arts of divination?"

"I notice thee does not deny it." He looked up then, pushing his spectacles up his nose with a finger, the better to look through them at her.

"No, I don't deny it," she said, lifting her chin at him. "How did thee know, then?"

"Thee looked at the dog and sighed in a manner betokening an emotion not usually shared between a woman and a dog."

"Hmph!" she said, disconcerted. "Well, what if I *do* think of him? Is that not my business, either? To wonder how he does, what his family in Scotland makes of him? Whether he feels he has come home there?"

"Whether he will come back?" Denny took off his spectacles and rubbed a hand over his face. He was tired; she could see the day in his features.

"He will come back," she said evenly. "He would not abandon his dog."

That made her brother laugh, which annoyed her very much.

"Yes, he will likely come back for the dog," he agreed. "And if he comes back with a wife, Sissy?" His voice was gentle now, and she swung round to the window again, to keep him from seeing that the question disturbed her. Not that he needed to see to know that.

"It might be best for thee and for him if he did, Rachel." Denny's voice was still gentle but held a warning note. "Thee knows he is a man of blood."

"What would thee have me do, then?" she snapped, not turning round. "Marry William?"

There was a brief silence from the direction of the desk.

"William?" Denny said, sounding mildly startled. "Does thee feel for him?"

"I—of course I feel friendship for him. And gratitude," she added hastily.

"So do I," her brother observed, "yet the thought of marrying him had not crossed my mind."

"Thee is a most annoying person," she said crossly, turning round and glaring at him. "Can thee not refrain from making fun of me for one day, at least?"

He opened his mouth to answer, but a sound from outside took her attention, and she turned again to the window, pulling back the heavy curtain. Her breath misted the dark glass, and she rubbed it impatiently with her sleeve in time to see a sedan chair below. The door of it opened and a woman stepped out into the swirling snow. She was clad in furs and in a hurry; she handed a purse to one of the chair-bearers and rushed into the inn.

"Well, that is odd," Rachel said, turning to look first at her brother, and then at the small clock that graced their rooms. "Who goes a-visiting at nine o'clock on Christmas night? It cannot be a Friend, surely?" For Friends did not keep Christmas and would find the feast no bar to travel, but the Hunters had no connections—not yet—with the Friends of any Philadelphia meeting.

A thump of footsteps on the staircase prevented Denzell's reply, and an instant later the door of the room burst open. The fur-clad woman stood on the threshold, white as her furs.

"Denny?" she said in a strangled voice.

Her brother stood up as though someone had applied a hot coal to the seat of his breeches, upsetting the ink.

"Dorothea!" he cried, and in one bound had crossed the room and was locked in passionate embrace with the fur-clad woman.

Rachel stood transfixed. The ink was dripping off the table onto the painted canvas rug, and she thought she ought to do something about that, but didn't. Her mouth was hanging open. She thought she ought to close it, and did.

Quite suddenly she understood the impulse that caused men to engage in casual blasphemy.

RACHEL PICKED UP her brother's spectacles from the floor and stood holding them, waiting for him to disentangle himself. *Dorothea,* she thought to herself. *So this is the woman—but surely this is William's cousin?* For William had mentioned his cousin to her as they rode in from Valley Forge. Indeed, the woman had been in the house when Denny performed the operation on— but then, Henry Grey must be this woman's brother! She had hidden in the kitchen when Rachel and Denny came to the house this afternoon. Why . . . Of course: it was not squeamishness or fear but a wish not to come face-to-face with Denny, and him on his way to perform a dangerous operation.

She thought somewhat better of the woman for that, though she was not yet disposed to clasp her to her own bosom and call her sister. She doubted the woman felt so toward her, either—though in fact, she might not even have noticed Rachel yet, let alone have conclusions about her.

Denny let go of the woman and stood back, though from the look on his glowing face, he could hardly bear not to touch her.

"Dorothea," he said. "Whatever does thee—"

But he was forestalled; the young woman—she was very pretty, Rachel saw now—stepped back and dropped her elegant ermine cloak on the floor with a soft thud. Rachel blinked. The young woman was wearing a sack. No other word for it, though now that she looked, she perceived that it had sleeves. It was made of some coarse gray fabric, though, and hung from the young woman's shoulders, barely touching her body elsewhere.

"I will be a Quaker, Denny," she said, lifting her chin a little. "I have made up my mind."

Denny's face twitched, and Rachel thought he could not make up his own mind whether to laugh, cry, or cover his beloved with her cloak again. Not liking to see the lovely thing lie disregarded on the floor, Rachel bent and picked it up herself.

"Thee—Dorothea," he said again, helpless. "Is thee sure of this? I think thee knows nothing of Friends."

"Certainly I do. You—thee, I mean—see God in all men, seek peace in God, abjure violence, and wear dull clothes so as not to distract your minds with the vain things of the world. Is that not right?" Dorothea inquired anxiously. *Lady* Dorothea, Rachel corrected herself. William had said his uncle was a duke.

"Well . . . more or less, yes," Denny said, his lips twitching as he looked her up and down. "Did thee . . . make that garment?"

"Yes, of course. Is something wrong with it?"

"Oh, no," he said, sounding somewhat strangled. Dorothea looked sharply at him, then at Rachel, suddenly seeming to notice her.

"What's wrong with it?" she appealed to Rachel, and Rachel saw the pulse beating in her round white throat.

"Nothing," she said, fighting her own urge to laugh. "Friends are allowed to wear clothes that fit, though. Thee need not purposefully uglify thyself, I mean."

"Oh, I see." Lady Dorothea gazed thoughtfully at Rachel's tidy skirt and jacket, which might be of butternut homespun but most assuredly fit well, and became her, too, if she did say so.

"Well, that's good, then," Lady Dorothea said. "I'll just take it in a bit here and there." Dismissing this, she stepped forward again and took Denny's hands in her own.

"Denny," she said softly. "Oh, Denny. I thought I should never see you again."

"I thought so, too," he said, and Rachel saw a new struggle taking place in his face—one between duty and desire, and her heart ached for him. "Dorothea . . . thee cannot stay here. Thy uncle—"

"He doesn't know I've gone out. I'll go back," Dorothea assured him. "Once we've settled things between us."

"Settled things," he repeated, and, with a noticeable effort, withdrew his hands from hers. "Thee means—"

"Will thee take a little wine?" Rachel broke in, reaching for the decanter the servant had left for them.

"Yes, thank you. He'll have some, too," Dorothea said, smiling at Rachel.

"I expect he will need it," Rachel murmured, with a glance at her brother.

"Dorothea . . ." Denny said helplessly, running a hand through his hair. "I know what thee means. But it is not only a matter of thee becoming a Friend—always assuming that to be . . . to be . . . possible."

She drew herself up, proud as a duchess.

"Do you doubt my conviction, Denzell Hunter?"

"Er . . . not exactly. I just think that perhaps thee has not given the matter sufficient thought."

"That's what you think!" A flush rose in Lady Dorothea's cheeks, and she glared at Denny. "I'll have you—thee, I mean—know that I've done nothing *but* think, ever since you left London. How the devil do you—thee—think I bloody got here?"

"Thee conspired to have thy brother shot in the abdomen?" Denny inquired. "That seems somewhat ruthless, and perhaps not certain of success."

Lady Dorothea drew two or three long breaths in through her nose, eyeing him.

"Now, you see," she said, in a reasonable tone of voice, "was I not quite the perfect Quaker, I would strike you. Thee. But I have not, have I? Thank you, my dear," she said to Rachel, taking a glass of wine. "You are his sister, I collect?"

"Thee has not," Denny admitted warily, ignoring Rachel. "But even allowing, for the sake of argument," he added, with a glimmer of his usual self, "that God has indeed spoken to thee and said that thee must join us, that still leaves the small matter of thy family."

"There is nothing in your principles of faith that requires me to have my father's permission to marry," she snapped. "I asked."

Denny blinked.

"Who?"

"Priscilla Unwin. She's a Quaker I know in London. You know her, too, I think; she said you'd—thee'd? That can't be right—that you'd lanced a boil on her little brother's bum."

At this point, Denny became aware—perhaps because his eyes were sticking out of his head looking at Lady Dorothea, Rachel thought, not altogether amused—that his spectacles were missing. He put out a finger to push them up the bridge of his nose, then stopped and looked about, squinting. With a sigh, Rachel stepped forward and settled them onto his nose. Then she picked up the second glass of wine and handed it to him.

"She's right," she told him. "Thee needs it."

⸻ ⟩⟩⟩⟩⟩ ⸻

"PLAINLY," LADY DOROTHEA said, "we are getting nowhere." She did not look like a woman accustomed to getting nowhere, Rachel thought, but was keeping a fair grip on her temper. On the other hand, she was not even close to giving in to Denny's urging that she must go back to her uncle's house.

"I'm not going back," she said, in a reasonable tone of voice, "because if I do, you'll sneak off to the Continental army in Valley Forge, where you think I won't follow you."

"Thee would not, surely?" Denny said, and Rachel thought she divined a thread of hope in the question, but she wasn't sure what kind of hope it was.

Lady Dorothea fixed him with a wide blue stare.

"I have followed thee across an entire bloody ocean. You—thee—think a damned army can stop me?"

Denny rubbed a knuckle down the bridge of his nose.

"No," he admitted. "I don't. That is why I have not left. I do not wish thee to follow me."

Lady Dorothea swallowed audibly but bravely kept her chin up.

"Why?" she said, and her voice shook only a little. "Why do you not wish me to follow you?"

"Dorothea," he said, as gently as possible. "Putting aside the fact that thy going with me would put thee in rebellion and in conflict with thy family—it is an army. Moreover, it is a very poor army, and one lacking every conceivable comfort, including clothing, bedding, shoes, and food. Beyond that, it is an army on the verge of disaster and defeat. It is no fit place for you."

"And it is a fit place for your sister?"

"Indeed it is not," he said. "But—" He stopped short, obviously realizing that he was on the verge of stepping into a trap.

"But thee can't stop me coming with thee." Rachel sprang it for him, sweetly. She was not quite sure she should help this strange woman, but she did admire the Lady Dorothea's spirit.

"And you can't stop me, either," Dorothea said firmly.

Denny rubbed three fingers hard between his brows, closing his eyes as though in pain.

"Dorothea," he said, dropping his hand and drawing himself up. "I am called to do what I do, and it is the Lord's business and mine. Rachel comes with me not only because she is pigheaded but also because she is my responsibility; she has no other place to go."

"I do, too!" Rachel said hotly. "Thee said thee would find me a place of safety with Friends, if I wanted. I didn't, and I don't."

Before Denny could come back with anything else, Lady Dorothea held out her hand in a dramatic gesture of command, stopping him dead.

"I have an idea," she said.

"I greatly fear to ask what it is," Denny said, sounding entirely sincere.

"I don't," Rachel said. "What?"

Dorothea looked from one to the other. "I have been to a Quaker meeting. Two, in fact. I know how it's done. Let us hold a meeting and ask the Lord to guide us."

Denny's mouth fell open, greatly entertaining Rachel, who was seldom able to dumbfound her brother but was beginning to enjoy seeing Dorothea do it.

"That—" he began, sounding stunned.

"Is an excellent idea," Rachel said, already dragging another chair near to the fire.

Denny could hardly argue. Looking remarkably discombobulated, he sat, though Rachel noticed that he put her between Dorothea and himself. She wasn't sure whether he was afraid to be too close to Dorothea, lest the power of her presence overwhelm him, or whether it was only that sitting across the hearth from her gave him the best view.

They all settled slowly, shifting a bit for comfort, and lapsed into silence. Rachel closed her eyes, seeing the warm redness of the fire inside her lids, feeling the comfort of it on her hands and feet. She gave silent thanks for it, remembering the constant griping of cold in the camp, the nails of her fingers and toes on fire with it, and the continual shivering that lessened but did not stop when she huddled into her blankets at night and left her muscles fatigued and sore. It was no wonder Denny didn't want Dorothea to go with them. She didn't want to go back, would give almost anything not to go—anything but Denny's well-being. She hated being cold and hungry, but it would be much worse to be warm and well-fed and know that he suffered alone.

Did Lady Dorothea have any idea what it would be like? she wondered, and opened her eyes. Dorothea sat quiet but upright, graceful hands folded in her lap. She supposed Denny was imagining, as Rachel was, those hands reddened and marred by chilblains, that lovely face gaunt with hunger and blotched with dirt and cold.

Dorothea's eyes were shadowed by her lids, but Rachel was sure she was looking at Denny. This was a considerable gamble on Dorothea's part, she thought. For what if the Lord spoke to Denny and said it was impossible, that he must send her away? What if the Lord spoke to Dorothea now, she thought suddenly, or what if He had already? Rachel was quite taken back at the thought. It wasn't that Friends thought that the Lord spoke only to them; it was only that they weren't sure other folk listened very often.

Had she been listening herself? In all honesty, she was forced to admit that she had not. And she knew why: out of a disinclination to hear what she was afraid she must—that she must turn away from Ian Murray and abandon the thoughts of him that warmed her body and heated her dreams in the freezing forest, so she woke sometimes sure that if she put out her hand to the falling snow, it would hiss and vanish from her palm.

She swallowed hard and closed her eyes, trying to open herself to the truth but trembling in fear of hearing it.

All she heard, though, was a steady panting noise, and an instant later

Rollo's wet nose nudged her hand. Disconcerted, she scratched his ears. Surely it wasn't seemly to be doing that in meeting, but he would keep nudging her until she complied, she knew. He half-closed his yellow eyes in pleasure and rested his heavy head upon her knee.

The dog loves him, she thought, rubbing gently through the thick, coarse fur. *Can he be a bad man, if that is so?* It wasn't God she heard in reply but her brother, who would certainly say, *"While dogs are worthy creatures, I think they are perhaps no judge of character."*

But I am, she thought to herself. *I know what he is—and I know him for what he might be, too.* She looked at Dorothea, motionless in her gray bag of a dress. Lady Dorothea Grey was prepared to abandon her former life, and very likely her family, to become a Friend, for Denny's sake. Might it not be, she wondered, that Ian Murray could turn from violence for hers?

Well, there is a proud thought, she scolded herself. *What sort of power does thee think thee has, Rachel Mary Hunter? No one has that sort of power, save the Lord.*

But the Lord did have it. And if the Lord should be so inclined, anything was possible. Rollo's tail moved gently, thumping thrice upon the floor.

Denzell Hunter straightened a little on his stool. It was the slightest movement, but coming as it did out of utter stillness, it surprised both the women, who lifted their heads like startled birds.

"I love thee, Dorothea," he said. He spoke very quietly, but his soft eyes burned behind his spectacles, and Rachel felt her chest ache. "Will thee marry me?"

87

SEVERANCE AND REUNION

April 20, 1778

AS TRANSATLANTIC VOYAGES went—and after our adventures with Captains Roberts, Hickman, and Stebbings, I considered myself something of a connoisseur of seagoing disaster—the trip to America was quite dull. We did have a slight brush with an English man-of-war but fortunately outran her, did run into two squalls and a major storm but luckily didn't sink, and while the food was execrable, I was much too distracted to do more than knock weevils out of the biscuit before eating it.

Half my mind was on the future: Marsali and Fergus's precarious situation, the danger of Henri-Christian's condition, and the logistics of dealing with it. The other half—well, to be fair, seven-eighths—was still at Lallybroch with Jamie.

I felt raw and bruised. Severed in some vital part, as always when parted from Jamie for very long, but also as though I had been violently ejected from my home, like a barnacle ripped from its rock and heedlessly tossed into boiling surf.

The greater part of that, I thought, was Ian's impending death. Ian was so much a part of Lallybroch, his presence there so much a constant and a comfort to Jamie all these years, that the sense of his loss was in a way the loss of Lallybroch itself. Oddly enough, Jenny's words, hurtful as they might have been, didn't really trouble me; I knew only too well the frantic grief, the desperation that one turned to rage because it was the only way to stay alive. And in truth, I understood her feelings, too, because I shared them: irrational or not, I felt that I should have been able to help Ian. What good was all my knowledge, all my skill, if I couldn't help when help was truly vital?

But there was a further sense of loss—and a further nagging guilt—in the fact that I could not be there when Ian died, that I had had to leave him for the last time knowing that I would not see him again, unable to offer comfort to him, or to be with Jamie or his family when the blow fell, or even simply to bear witness to his passing.

Young Ian felt this, too, to an even greater degree. I often found him sitting near the stern, staring into the ship's wake with troubled eyes.

"D'ye think he's gone yet?" he asked me abruptly on one occasion when I'd come to sit beside him there. "Da?"

"I don't know," I told him honestly. "I'd think so, on the basis of how ill he was—but people do sometimes hang on amazingly. When is his birthday, do you know?"

He stared at me in bafflement. "It's in May sometime, near Uncle Jamie's. Why?"

I shrugged and pulled my shawl tighter against the chill of the wind.

"Often people who are very ill, but are near their birthday, seem to wait until it's passed before dying. I read a study of it once. For some reason, it's more likely if the person is famous or well known."

That made him laugh, though painfully.

"Da's never been that." He sighed. "Right now I wish I'd stayed for him. I know he said to go—and I wanted to go," he added fairly. "But I feel bad that I did."

I sighed, too. "So do I."

"But you had to go," he protested. "Ye couldna let poor wee Henri-Christian choke. Da would understand that. I know he did."

I smiled at his earnest attempt to make me feel better.

"He understood why you needed to go, too."

"Aye, I know." He was silent for a bit, watching the furrow of the wake; it was a brisk day and the ship was traveling well, though the sea was choppy, dotted with whitecaps. "I wish—" he said suddenly, then stopped and swallowed. "I wish Da could ha' met Rachel," he said, low-voiced. "I wish she could meet him."

I made a sympathetic sound. I remembered all too vividly the years during which I had watched Brianna grow, aching because she would never know her father. And then a miracle had happened—but it wouldn't happen for Ian.

"I know you told your da about Rachel—he told me you had and was so happy to know about her." That made him smile a little. "Did you tell Rachel about your father? Your family?"

"No." He sounded startled. "No, I never did."

"Well, you'll just have to—what's wrong?" His brow had furrowed, and his mouth turned down.

"I—nothing, really. It's only, I just thought—I never told her anything. I mean, we—didna really talk, aye? I mean, I said things to her now and then, and her me, but just in the ordinary way of things. And then we—I kissed her, and . . . well, that was all about it." He made a helpless gesture. "But I never asked her. I was just sure."

"And now you're not?"

He shook his head, brown hair flying in the wind.

"Oh, no, Auntie; I'm as sure of what's between us as I am of . . . of . . ." He looked about in search of some symbol of solidity on the heaving deck, but then gave up. "Well, I'm surer of how I feel than I am that the sun will come up tomorrow."

"I'm sure she knows that."

"Aye, she does," he said, in a softer voice. "I know she does."

We sat for a bit in silence. Then I stood up and said, "Well, in that case— perhaps you ought to say a prayer for your father and then go and sit near the bow."

I HAD BEEN in Philadelphia once or twice in the twentieth century, for medical conferences. I hadn't liked the place then, finding it grubby and un- welcoming. It was different now, but not much more attractive. The roads that weren't cobbled were seas of mud, and streets that would eventually be lined with run-down row houses with yards full of rubbish, broken plastic toys, and motorcycle parts were now edged with ramshackle shanties with yards full of rubbish, discarded oyster shells, and tethered goats. Granted, there were no black-suited feral policemen visible, but the petty criminals were still the same, and still visible, despite the very obvious presence of the British army; red coats swarmed near the taverns, and marching columns went past the wagon, muskets on their shoulders.

It was spring. I'd give it that much. There were trees everywhere, thanks to William Penn's dictum that one acre in five should be left in trees—even the avaricious politicians of the twentieth century hadn't quite succeeded in deforesting the place, though probably only because they couldn't figure out how to make a profit at it without being caught—and many of the trees were in bloom, a confetti of white petals drifting over the horses' backs as the wagon turned into the city proper.

An army patrol was set up on the main road into the city; they had stopped us, demanding passes from the driver and his two male passengers. I had put on a proper cap, didn't meet anyone's eye, and murmured that I was coming in from the country to tend my daughter, who was about to give birth. The soldiers glanced briefly into the large basket of food I had on my lap, but didn't even look at my face before waving the wagon on. Respectability had its uses. I wondered idly how many spymasters had thought of using elderly ladies? You didn't hear about old women as spies—but then again, that might merely indicate how good they were at it.

Fergus's printshop was not in the most fashionable district but not far off, and I was pleased to see that it was a substantial red-brick building, standing in a row of solid, pleasant-looking houses like it. We had not written ahead to say I was coming; I would have arrived as soon as the letter. With a rising heart, I opened the door.

Marsali was standing at the counter, sorting stacks of paper. She glanced up as the bell above the door rang, blinked, then gaped at me.

"How are you, dear?" I said, and, putting down the basket, hurried to put up the flap of the counter and take her in my arms.

She looked like death warmed over, though her eyes lit with a passionate relief upon seeing me. She nearly fell into my arms and burst into uncharacteristic sobs. I patted her back, making soothing sounds and feeling somewhat alarmed. Her clothes hung limp on her bones, and she smelled stale, her hair unwashed for too long.

"It will be all right," I repeated firmly for the dozenth time, and she stopped sobbing and stood back a bit, groping in her pocket for a grubby handkerchief. To my shock, I saw that she was pregnant again.

"Where's Fergus?" I asked.

"I dinna ken."

"He's left you?!" I blurted, horrified. "Why, that wretched little—"

"No, no," she said hurriedly, almost laughing through her tears. "He's not left me, not at all. It's only he's in hiding—he changes his place every few days, and I dinna ken just which one he's in right now. The weans will find him."

"Why is he in hiding? Not that I need to ask, I suppose," I said, with a glance at the squat black printing press that stood behind the counter. "Anything specific, though?"

"Aye, a wee pamphlet for Mr. Paine. He's got a series of them going, ken, called 'The American Crisis.' "

"Mr. Paine—the Common Sense fellow?"

"Aye, that's him," she said, sniffing and dabbing. "He's a nice man, but ye dinna want to drink with him, Fergus says. Ken how some men are sweet and loving when they're drunk, but some get fou' and it's up wi' the bonnets o' bonnie Dundee and them not even Scots for an excuse?"

"Oh, that sort. Yes, I know it well. How far along are you?" I asked, changing the subject back to one of general interest. "Shouldn't you sit down? You oughtn't to be on your feet for a long time."

"How far . . . ?" She looked surprised and put a hand involuntarily where I was looking, to her slightly swollen stomach. Then she laughed. "Oh, that." She burrowed under her apron and removed a bulging leather sack she had tied around her waist.

"For escaping," she explained. "In case they fire the house and I have to make a run for it wi' the weans."

The sack was surprisingly heavy when I took it from her, and I heard a muffled clicking down at the bottom, beneath the layer of papers and children's small toys.

"The Caslon Italic 24?" I asked, and she smiled, shedding at least ten years on the spot.

"All except 'X.' I had to hammer that one back into a lump and trade it to a goldsmith for enough money for food, after Fergus left. There's still an 'X' in there, mind," she said, taking back the bag, "but that one's real lead."

"Did you have to use the Goudy Bold 10?" Jamie and Fergus had cast two full sets of type from gold, these rubbed in soot and covered with ink until they were indistinguishable from the many sets of genuine lead type in the type case that stood demurely against the wall behind the press.

She shook her head and reached to take the bag back again.

"Fergus took that wi' him. He meant to bury it somewhere safe, just in case. Ye look fair fashed wi' travel, Mother Claire," she went on, leaning forward to peer at me. "Will I send Joanie down to the ordinary for a jug o' cider?"

"That would be wonderful," I said, still reeling a little from the revelations of the last few minutes. "Henri-Christian, though—how is he? Is he here?"

"Out back wi' his friend, I think," she said, rising. "I'll call him in. He's that wee bit tired, poor mite, from not sleepin' well, and he's got such a throat he sounds like a costive bullfrog. Doesna dampen him much, though, I'll tell ye that." She smiled, despite her tiredness, and went through the door into the living quarters, calling "Henri-Christian!" as she went.

"In case they fire the house." Who? I wondered, feeling a chill. The British army? Loyalists? And however was she managing, running a business and a family alone, with a husband in hiding and a sick child who couldn't be left alone while he slept? *The horror of our situation,* she'd said in her letter to Laoghaire. And that had been months ago, when Fergus was still at home.

Well, she wasn't alone now. For the first time since I'd left Jamie in Scotland, I felt something more than the pull of grim necessity in my situation. I'd write to him this evening, I decided. He might—I hoped he would— leave Lallybroch before my letter reached him there, but if so, Jenny and the rest of the family would be glad to know what was going on here. And if by chance Ian was still alive . . . but I didn't want to think of that; knowing that his death meant Jamie's release to come to me made me feel like a ghoul, as though I wished for his death to come sooner. Though in all honesty, I thought Ian himself might wish it to be sooner rather than later.

These morbid thoughts were interrupted by Marsali's return, Henri-Christian scampering beside her.

"Grandmère!" he shouted, seeing me, and leapt into my arms, nearly knocking me over. He was a very solid little boy.

He nuzzled me affectionately, and I felt a remarkable rush of warm joy at seeing him. I kissed and hugged him fiercely, feeling the hole left in my heart by Mandy and Jem's departure fill up a bit. Isolated from Marsali's family in Scotland, I had nearly forgotten that I still had four lovely grandchildren left and was grateful to be reminded of it.

"Want to see a trick, *Grandmère?"* Henri-Christian croaked eagerly. Marsali was right; he did sound like a constipated bullfrog. I nodded, though, and, hopping off my lap, he pulled three small leather bags stuffed with bran out of his pocket and began at once to juggle them with amazing dexterity.

"His da taught him," Marsali said, with a certain amount of pride.

"When I'm big like Germain, Da will teach me to pick pockets, too!"

Marsali gasped and clapped a hand over his mouth.

"Henri-Christian, we dinna ever speak o' that," she said sternly. "Not to anybody. D'ye hear?"

He glanced at me, bewildered, but nodded obediently.

The chill I had felt earlier returned. Was Germain picking pockets professionally, so to speak? I looked at Marsali, but she shook her head slightly; we'd talk about it later.

"Open your mouth and stick out your tongue, sweetheart," I suggested to Henri-Christian. "Let Grannie see your sore throat—it sounds very ouchy."

"Owg-owg-owg," he said, grinning widely, but obligingly opened up. A faint putrid smell wafted out of his wide-open mouth, and even lacking a lighted scope, I could see that the swollen tonsils nearly obstructed his throat altogether.

"Goodness gracious," I said, turning his head to and fro to get a better view. "I'm amazed that he can eat, let alone sleep."

"Sometimes he can't," Marsali said, and I heard the strain in her voice. "Often enough, he canna manage to swallow anything but a bit o' milk, and even that's like knives in his throat, poor bairn." She crouched beside me, smoothing the fine dark hair off Henri-Christian's flushed face. "Can ye help, d'ye think, Mother Claire?"

"Oh, yes," I said, with much more confidence than I actually felt. "Absolutely."

I felt the tension drain out of her like water, and, as though it were a literal draining, tears began to run quietly down her face. She pulled Henri-Christian's head into her bosom so he couldn't see her cry, and I reached out to embrace both of them, laying my cheek against her capped head, smelling the stale musky tang of her terror and exhaustion.

"It's all right now," I said softly, rubbing her thin back. "I'm here. You can sleep."

MARSALI SLEPT the rest of the day and all through the night. I was tired from the journey but managed to doze in the big chair by the kitchen fire, Henri-Christian cradled in my lap, snoring heavily. He did stop breathing twice during the night, and while I got him started again with no difficulty, I could see that something had to be done at once. Consequently, I had a brief nap in the morning and, having washed my face and eaten a bit, went out in search of what I'd need.

I had the most rudimentary of medical instruments with me, but the fact was, tonsillectomy and adenoidectomy didn't really require anything complex in that line.

I wished that Ian had come into the city with me; I could have used his help, and so could Marsali. But it was dangerous for a man of his age; he couldn't enter the city openly without being stopped and questioned by British patrols, likely arrested as a suspicious character—which he most assuredly was. Beyond that . . . he'd been afire to look for Rachel Hunter.

The task of finding two people—and a dog—who might be almost anywhere between Canada and Charleston, with no means of communication other than the foot and the spoken word, would have daunted anyone less stubborn than a person of Fraser blood. Agreeable as he might be, though, Ian was as capable as Jamie of pursuing a chosen course, come hell, high water, or reasonable suggestions.

He did, as he'd pointed out, have one advantage. Denny Hunter was presumably still an army surgeon. If so, he was obviously with the Continental army—some part of the Continental army. So Ian's notion was to discover where the closest part of the army might be just now and begin his inquiries there. To which end he proposed to skulk round the edges of Philadelphia, creeping into taverns and shebeens on the outskirts, and, by means of local gossip, discover where some part of the army presently was.

The most I had been able to persuade him to do was to send word to Fergus's printshop telling us where he was bound, once he'd discovered anything that gave him a possible destination.

In the meantime, all I could do was say a quick prayer to his guardian angel—a most overworked being—then have a word with my own (whom I envisioned as a sort of grandmotherly shape with an anxious expression) and set about doing what I'd come to do.

I now walked through the muddy streets, pondering the procedure. I had done a tonsillectomy only once—well, twice, if you counted the Beardsley twins separately—in the last ten years. It was normally a straightforward, quick procedure, but then again, it wasn't normally performed in a gloomy printshop on a dwarf with a constricted airway, a sinus infection, and a peritonsillar abscess.

Still . . . I needn't do it in the printshop, if I could find a better-lighted place. Where would that be? I wondered. A rich person's house, most likely; one where candle wax was squandered profligately. I'd been in many such houses, particularly during our time in Paris, but knew no one even moderately well-to-do in Philadelphia. Neither did Marsali; I'd asked.

Well, one thing at a time. Before I worried any more about an operating theater, I needed to find a blacksmith capable of fine work, to make the wire-loop instrument I required. I could, in a pinch, cut the tonsils with a scalpel, but it would be more than difficult to remove the adenoids, located above the soft palate, that way. And the last thing I wanted was to be slicing and poking round in Henri-Christian's severely inflamed throat in the dark with a sharp instrument. The wire loop would be sharp enough but was unlikely to damage anything it bumped into; only the edge surrounding the tissue to be removed would cut, and then only when I made the forceful scooping motion that would sever a tonsil or adenoid neatly.

I wondered uneasily whether he had a strep infection. His throat was bright red, but other infections could cause that.

No, we'd have to take our chances with the strep, I thought. I *had* set some penicillin bowls to brew, almost the moment I arrived. There was no way of telling whether the extract I might get from them in a few days was active or not—nor, if it was, just *how* active. But it was better than nothing, and so was I.

I did have one undeniably useful thing—or would, if this afternoon's quest was successful. Nearly five years ago, Lord John Grey had sent me a glass bottle of vitriol and the pelican glassware necessary to distill ether using it. He'd procured those items from an apothecary in Philadelphia, I thought, though I couldn't recall the name. But there couldn't *be* many apothecaries in Philadelphia, and I proposed to visit all of them until I found what I was looking for.

Marsali had said there were two large apothecary's shops in town, and only a large one would have what I needed to make ether. What was the name of the gentleman from whom Lord John Grey had acquired my pelican apparatus? Was he in Philadelphia at all? My mind was a blank, either from fatigue or from simple forgetfulness; the time when I had made ether in my surgery on Fraser's Ridge seemed as distant and mythical as Noah's Flood.

I found the first apothecary and got from him some useful items, including a jar of leeches—though I boggled a little at the thought of putting one inside Henri-Christian's mouth; what if he managed to swallow the thing?

On the other hand, I reflected, he was a four-year-old boy with a very imaginative elder brother. He'd probably swallowed much worse things than a leech. With luck, though, I wouldn't need them. I had also got two cautery irons, very small ones. It was a primitive and painful way of stopping bleeding—but, in fact, very effective.

The apothecary had not had any vitriol, though. He had apologized for the lack, saying that such things must be imported from England, and with the war . . . I thanked him and went on to the second place. Where I was informed that they had had some vitriol but had sold it some time previous, to an English lord, though what he wanted with such a thing, the man behind the counter couldn't begin to imagine.

"An English lord?" I said, surprised. Surely it couldn't be Lord John. Though, come to that, it wasn't as though the English aristocracy was flocking to Philadelphia these days, save those members who were soldiers. And the man had said "a lord," not a major or a captain.

Nothing ventured, nothing gained; I asked and was obligingly told that it was a Lord John Grey, and that he had requested the vitriol be delivered to his house on Chestnut Street.

Feeling a little like Alice down the rabbit hole—I was still a bit light-headed from lack of sleep and the fatigues of the journey from Scotland—I asked the way to Chestnut Street.

The door to the house was opened by an extraordinarily beautiful young woman, dressed in a fashion that made it clear she was no servant. We blinked at each other in surprise; she plainly hadn't been expecting me, either, but when I inquired for Lord John, saying I was an old acquaintance, she readily invited me in, saying that her uncle would be back directly, he had only taken a horse to be shod.

"You would think he'd send the boy," the young woman—who gave her name as Lady Dorothea Grey—said apologetically. "Or my cousin. But Uncle John is most particular about his horses."

"Your cousin?" I asked, my slow mind tracing the possible family connections. "You don't mean William Ransom, do you?"

"Ellesmere, yes," she said, looking surprised but pleased. "Do you know him?"

"We've met once or twice," I said. "If you don't mind my asking—how does he come to be in Philadelphia? I . . . er . . . had understood that he was paroled with the rest of Burgoyne's army and had gone to Boston in order to sail home to England."

"Oh, he is!" she said. "Paroled, I mean. He came here, though, first, to see his father—that's Uncle John—and my brother." Her large blue eyes clouded a little at the mention. "Henry's very ill, I'm afraid."

"I'm so sorry to hear it," I said, sincerely but briefly. I was much more interested in William's presence here, but before I could ask anything further, there was a quick, light step on the porch and the front door opened.

"Dottie?" said a familiar voice. "Have you any idea where—oh, I beg your pardon." Lord John Grey had come into the parlor and stopped, seeing me. Then he actually saw me, and his jaw dropped.

"How nice to see you again," I said pleasantly. "But I'm sorry to hear that your nephew is ill."

"Thank you," he said, and, eyeing me rather warily, bowed low over my hand, kissing it gracefully. "I am delighted to see you again, Mrs. Fraser," he added, sounding as though he actually meant it. He hesitated for a moment, but of course couldn't help asking, "Your husband . . . ?"

"He's in Scotland," I said, feeling rather mean at disappointing him. It flickered across his face but was promptly erased—he was a gentleman, and a soldier. In fact, he was wearing an army uniform, which rather surprised me.

"You've returned to active duty, then?" I asked, raising my brows at him.

"Not exactly. Dottie, have you not called for Mrs. Figg yet? I'm sure Mrs. Fraser would like some refreshment."

"I'd only just come," I said hastily, as Dottie leapt up and went out.

"Indeed," he said, courteously repressing the *why?* that showed plainly on his face. He motioned me to a chair and sat down himself, wearing a rather odd expression, as though trying to think how to say something awkward.

"I am delighted to see you," he said again, slowly. "Did you—I do not wish to sound in any way ungracious, Mrs. Fraser, you must excuse me—but . . . did you come to bring me a message from your husband, perhaps?"

He couldn't help the small light that sprang up in his eyes, and I felt almost apologetic as I shook my head.

"I'm sorry," I said, and was surprised to find that I meant it. "I've come to beg a favor. Not on my own behalf—for my grandson."

He blinked at that.

"Your grandson," he repeated blankly. "I thought that your daughter . . . oh! Of course, I was forgetting that your husband's foster son— his family is here? It is one of his children?"

"Yes, that's right." Without more ado, I explained the situation, describing Henri-Christian's state and reminding him of his generosity in sending me the vitriol and glass apparatus more than four years before.

"Mr. Sholto—the apothecary on Walnut Street?—told me that he had sold you a large bottle of vitriol some months ago. I wondered—do you by any chance still have it?" I made no effort to keep the eagerness out of my voice, and his expression softened.

"Yes, I do," he said, and, to my surprise, smiled like the sun coming out from behind a cloud. "I bought it for you, Mrs. Fraser."

A BARGAIN WAS struck at once. He would not only give me the vitriol but also purchase any other medical supplies I might require, if I would consent to perform surgery on his nephew.

"Dr. Hunter removed one of the balls at Christmas," he said, "and that improved Henry's condition somewhat. The other remains embedded, though, and—"

"Dr. Hunter?" I interrupted him. "Not Denzell Hunter, you don't mean?"

"I do mean that," he said, surprised and frowning a little. "He says he knows you?"

"Yes, indeed," I said, smiling. "We worked together often, both at Ticonderoga and at Saratoga with Gates's army. But what is he doing in Philadelphia?"

"He—" he began, but was interrupted by the sound of light footsteps coming down the stair. I had been vaguely conscious of footsteps overhead as we talked but had paid no attention. I looked toward the doorway now, though, and my heart leapt at the sight of Rachel Hunter, who was standing in it, staring at me with her mouth in a perfect "O" of astonishment.

The next moment she was in my arms, hugging me fit to break my ribs.

"Friend Claire!" she said, letting go at last. "I never thought to see—that is, I am so pleased—oh, Claire! Ian. Has he come back with thee?" Her face was alive with eagerness and fear, hope and wariness chasing each other like racing clouds across her features.

"He has," I assured her. "He's not here, though." Her face fell.

"Oh," she said in a small voice. "Where—"

"He's gone to look for you," I said gently, taking her hands.

Joy blazed up in her eyes like a forest fire.

"Oh!" she said, in a completely different voice. "Oh!"

Lord John coughed politely.

"Perhaps it would be unwise for me to know exactly where your nephew is, Mrs. Fraser," he observed. "As I assume he shares your husband's principles? Just so. If you will excuse me, then, I will go and tell Henry of your arrival. I suppose you wish to examine him?"

"Oh," I said, recalled suddenly to the matter at hand. "Yes. Yes, of course. If you wouldn't mind . . ."

He smiled, glancing at Rachel, whose face had gone white at seeing me but who was now the shade of a russet apple with excitement.

"Not at all," he said. "Come upstairs when you are at leisure, Mrs. Fraser. I'll wait for you there."

88

RATHER MESSY

I MISSED BRIANNA all the time, in greater or lesser degree depending upon the circumstance. But I missed her most particularly now. She could, I was sure, have solved the problem of getting light down Henri-Christian's throat.

I had him laid on a table at the front of the printshop now, taking every advantage of such light as came in there. But this was Philadelphia, not New Bern. If the sky wasn't overcast with clouds, it was hazed with smoke from the city's chimneys. And the street was narrow; the buildings opposite blocked most of what light there was.

Not that it mattered that much, I told myself. The room could have been blazing with sun, and I still couldn't have seen a thing in the inner reaches of Henri-Christian's throat. Marsali had a small mirror with which to direct light, and that would perhaps help with the tonsils—the adenoids would have to be done by touch.

I could feel the soft, spongy edge of one adenoid, just behind the soft palate; it took shape in my mind as I carefully fitted the wire loop around it, handling it with great delicacy so as not to let the edge cut either my fingertips or the body of the swollen adenoid. There was going to be a gush of blood when I sliced through it.

I had Henri-Christian braced at an angle, Marsali holding his inert body almost on his side. Denzell Hunter kept his head steady, clamping the pad soaked in ether firmly over his nose. I had no means of suction other than my own mouth; I'd have to turn him quickly after I made the cut and let the blood run out of his mouth before it ran down his throat and choked him. The tiny cautery iron was heating, its spade-shaped tip thrust into a pan of hot coals. That might be the trickiest part, I thought, pausing to steady myself and steady Marsali with a nod. I didn't want to burn his tongue or the inside of his mouth, and it would be slippery. . . .

I twisted the handle sharply and the little body jerked under my hand.

"Hold him tight," I said calmly. "A little more ether, please."

Marsali's breath was coming hard, and her knuckles were white as her face. I felt the adenoid separate cleanly, come adrift, and scooped it between my fingers, pulling it out of his throat before it could slip down into his esophagus. Tilted his head quickly to the side, smelling the sheared-metal smell of hot blood. I dropped the severed bit of tissue into a pan and nodded to Rachel, who pulled the cautery iron from its coals and put it carefully into my hand.

I still had my other hand in his mouth, keeping the tongue and uvula out of the way, a finger on the site of the ex-adenoid, marking my place. The cautery iron seared a white line of pain down my finger as I slid it down his throat, and I let out a small hiss but didn't move my finger. The scorched scent of burning blood and tissue came hot and thick, and Marsali made a small, frantic noise but didn't loosen her hold on her son's body.

"It is well, Friend Marsali," Rachel whispered to her, clasping her shoulder. "He breathes well; he is not in pain. He is held in the light, he will do well."

"Yes, he will," I said. "Take the iron now, Rachel, if you will? Dip the loop in the whisky please, and give me that again. One down, three to go."

"I HAVE NEVER seen anything like it," Denzell Hunter said, for perhaps the fifth time. He looked from the pad of fabric in his hand to Henri-Christian, who was beginning to stir and whimper in his mother's arms. "I should not have believed it, Claire, had I not seen it with my own eyes!"

"Well, I thought you'd better see it," I said, wiping sweat from my face with a handkerchief. A sense of profound well-being filled me. The surgery had been fast, no more than five or six minutes, and Henri-Christian was already coughing and crying, coming out of the ether. Germain, Joanie, and Félicité all watched wide-eyed from the doorway into the kitchen, Germain keeping tight hold of his sisters' hands. "I'll teach you to make it, if you like."

His face, already shining with happiness at the successful surgery, lit up at this.

"Oh, Claire! Such a gift! To be able to cut without giving pain, to keep a patient quite still without restraint. It—it is unimaginable."

"Well, it's a long way from perfect," I warned him. "And it is very dangerous—both to make and to use." I'd distilled the ether the day before, out in the woodshed; it was a very volatile compound, and there was a better than even chance that it would explode and burn the shed down, killing me in the process. All had gone well, though the thought of doing it again made me feel rather hollow and sweaty-palmed.

I lifted the dropping bottle and shook it gently; more than three-quarters full, and I had another, slightly larger bottle as well.

"Will it be enough, does thee think?" Denny asked, realizing what I was thinking.

"It depends what we find." Henri-Christian's surgery, despite the technical difficulties, had been very simple. Henry Grey's wouldn't be. I had examined him, Denzell beside me to explain what he had seen and done during the earlier surgery, which had removed a ball lodged just under the pancreas. It had caused local irritation and scarring but had not actually damaged a vital organ very badly. He hadn't been able to find the other ball, as it was lodged very deeply in the body, somewhere under the liver. He feared that it might lie near the hepatic portal vein and thus hadn't dared to probe hard for it, as a hemorrhage would almost certainly have been fatal.

I was reasonably sure that the ball hadn't damaged the gallbladder or bile duct, though, and given Henry's general state and symptomology, I suspected that the ball had perforated the small intestine but had seared the internal entrance wound shut in its wake; otherwise, the boy would almost surely have died within days, of peritonitis.

It might be encysted in the wall of the intestine; that would be the best situation. It might be lodged actually within the intestine itself, and that wouldn't be good at all, but I couldn't say how bad it might be until I got there.

But we did have ether. And the sharpest scalpels Lord John's money could buy.

THE WINDOW, after what seemed to John Grey to be an excruciatingly prolonged discussion between the two physicians, remained partly open. Dr. Hunter insisted on the benefit of fresh air, and Mrs. Fraser agreed with this because of the ether fumes but kept talking about something she called germs, worrying that these would come in through the window and contaminate her "surgical field." *She speaks as though she views it as a battle-ground,* he thought, but then looked closely at her face and realized that indeed she did.

He had never seen a woman look like that, he thought, fascinated despite his worry for Henry. She had tied back her outrageous hair and wrapped her head carefully in a cloth like a Negro slave woman. With her face so exposed, the delicate bones made stark, the intentness of her expression—with those yellow eyes darting like a hawk's from one thing to another—was the most unwomanly thing he had ever seen. It was the look of a general marshaling his troops for battle, and seeing it, he felt the ball of snakes in his belly relax a little.

She knows what she's doing, he thought.

She looked at him then, and he straightened his shoulders, instinctively awaiting orders—to his utter amazement.

"Do you want to stay?" she asked.

"Yes, of course." He felt a little breathless, but there was no doubt in his voice. She'd told him frankly what Henry's chances were—not good, but there *was* a chance—and he was determined to be with his nephew, no matter what happened. If Henry died, he would at least die with someone who loved him there. Though, in fact, he was quite determined that Henry would not die. Grey would not let him.

"Sit over there, then." She nodded him to a stool on the far side of the bed, and he sat down, giving Henry a reassuring smile as he did so. Henry looked terrified but determined.

"I can't live like this anymore," he'd said the night before, finally making up his mind to allow the operation. *"I just can't."*

Mrs. Woodcock had insisted upon being present, too, and after a close catechism, Mrs. Fraser had declared that she might administer the ether. This mysterious substance sat in a dropping bottle on the bureau, a faint sickly odor drifting from it.

Mrs. Fraser gave Dr. Hunter something that looked like a handkerchief, and raised another to her face. It *was* a handkerchief, Grey saw, but one with strings affixed to its corners. She tied these behind her head, so the cloth covered her nose and mouth, and Hunter obediently followed suit.

Used as Grey was to the swift brutality of army surgeons, Mrs. Fraser's preparations seemed laborious in the extreme: she swabbed Henry's belly repeatedly with an alcoholic solution she had concocted, talking to him through her highwayman's mask in a low, soothing voice. She rinsed her hands—and made Hunter and Mrs. Woodcock do the same—and her instruments, so that the whole room reeked like a distillery of low quality.

Her motions were in fact quite brisk, he realized after a moment. But her hands moved with such sureness and . . . yes, grace, that was the only word . . . that they gave the illusion of gliding like a pair of gulls upon the air. No frantic flapping, only a sure, serene, and almost mystic movement. He found himself quieting as he watched them, becoming entranced and half forgetting the ultimate purpose of this quiet dance of hands.

She moved to the head of the bed, bending low to speak to Henry, smooth the hair away from his brow, and Grey saw the hawk's eyes soften momentarily into gold. Henry's body relaxed slowly under her touch; Grey saw his clenched, rigid hands uncurl. She had yet another mask, he saw, this one a stiff thing made of basket withes lined with layers of soft cotton cloth. She fitted this gently to Henry's face and, saying something inaudible to him, took up her dropping bottle.

The air filled at once with a pungent, sweet aroma that clung to the back of Grey's throat and made his head swim slightly. He blinked, shaking his head to dispel the giddiness, and realized that Mrs. Fraser had said something to him.

"I beg your pardon?" He looked up at her, a great white bird with yellow eyes—and a gleaming talon that sprouted suddenly from her hand.

"I said," she repeated calmly through her mask, "you might want to sit back a little farther. It's going to be rather messy."

WILLIAM, RACHEL, and Dorothea sat on the edge of the porch like birds on a fence rail, Rollo sprawled on the brick walk at their feet, enjoying the spring sun.

"It's bloody quiet up there," William said, glancing uneasily at the window above, where Henry's room lay. "D'you think they've started yet?" He thought, but didn't say, that he would have expected to hear Henry making a certain amount of noise if they had, despite Rachel's description of her brother's account of the marvels of Mrs. Fraser's ether. A man lie quietly asleep while someone cut open his belly with a knife? All stuff, he would have said. But Denzell Hunter wasn't a man who could be easily beguiled—though he supposed Dottie had somehow managed it. He gave his cousin a sideways glance.

"Have you written Uncle Hal yet? About you and Denny, I mean?" He knew she hadn't—she'd told Lord John, perforce, but persuaded him to let her break the news to her father—but wanted to distract her if he could. She was white to the lips, and her hands had bunched the fabric over her knees into nests of creases. He still hadn't got used to seeing her in dove and cream instead of her usual brilliant plumage—though he thought in fact that the quiet colors suited her, particularly as Rachel had assured her that she might still wear silk and muslin if she liked, rather than sacking material.

"No," Dottie said, giving him a look that thanked him for the distraction, even while acknowledging that she knew what he was doing. "Or, yes, but I haven't sent it yet. If all's well with Henry, I'll write at once with the news and add the bit about Denny and me at the bottom, as a postscript. They'll be so overjoyed about Henry that perhaps they won't notice—or at least won't be as upset about it."

"I rather think they'll notice," William said thoughtfully. "Papa did." Lord John had gone quite dangerously quiet when told and had given Denzell Hunter a look suggesting swords at dawn. But the fact was that Denny had saved Henry's life once and was now helping—with luck and Mrs. Fraser—to save it again. And Lord John was, above all, a man of honor. Besides, William thought that his father was actually relieved to finally know what it was that Dottie had been up to. He hadn't said anything directly to William regarding William's own role in her adventure—yet. He would.

"May the Lord hold thy brother in his hand," Rachel said, ignoring William's remark. "And mine and Mrs. Fraser, as well. But what if all should not go as we wish? Thee will still have to tell thy parents, and they may see news of thy impending marriage as adding insult to injury."

"You are the most tactless plain-spoken creature," William told her, rather irritably, seeing Dottie go whiter still at the reminder that Henry might die in the next minutes, hours, or days. "Henry will be fine. I know it. Denny is a great physician, and Mrs. Fraser...she's...er..." In all honesty, he wasn't sure what Mrs. Fraser was, but she scared him a little. "Denny says she knows what she's doing," he ended lamely.

"If Henry dies, nothing will matter," Dottie said softly, looking at the toes of her shoes. "Not to any of us."

Rachel made a small, sympathetic sound and reached to put her arm round Dottie's shoulder. William added his own gruff clearing of the throat and for an instant thought the dog had done the same.

Rollo's intent, though, was not sympathetic. He had lifted his head suddenly, and the hackles half-rose at his neck, a low growl rumbling through his chest. William glanced automatically in the direction the dog was looking and felt a sudden tightening of his muscles.

"Miss Hunter," he said casually. "Do you know that man? The one down there, near the end of the street, talking to the butter-and-egg woman?"

Rachel shaded her eyes with her hand, looking where he nodded, but shook her head.

"No. Why? Is he what's troubling the dog, does thee think?" She prodded Rollo in the side with her toe. "What's amiss, then, Friend Rollo?"

"I don't know," William said honestly. "It might be the cat; one ran across the road just behind the woman. But I've seen that man before; I'm sure of it. I saw him by the roadside, somewhere in New Jersey. He asked me if I knew Ian Murray—and where he might be."

Rachel gave a little gasp at that, making William look sideways at her in surprise.

"What?" he said. "Do you know where Murray is?"

"No," she said sharply. "I have not seen him since the autumn, at Saratoga, and I have no notion where he is. Does thee know this man's name?" she added, frowning. The man had disappeared now, walking off down a side street. "For that matter, is thee sure he is the same?"

"No," William admitted. "But I think so. He had a staff with him, and so did this man. And there's something about the way he stands—a little stooped. The man I met in New Jersey was very old, and this one walks the same way." He didn't mention the missing fingers; no need to remind Dottie of violence and mutilation just this minute, and he couldn't see the man's hand at this distance anyway.

Rollo had left off growling and settled himself with a brief grunt, but his yellow eyes were still watchful.

"When do you mean to be married, Dottie?" William asked, wishing to keep her mind occupied. A strange smell was coming from the window above them; the dog was wrinkling his nose, shaking his head in a confused sort of way, and William didn't blame him. It was a nasty, sickly kind of thing—but he could distinctly smell blood, as well, and the faint stink of shit. It was a battlefield smell, and it made his insides shift uneasily.

"I want to be married before the fighting starts again in earnest," his cousin answered seriously, turning to face him, "so that I can go with Denny—and Rachel," she added, taking her prospective sister-in-law's hand with a smile.

Rachel returned the smile, but briefly.

"What a strange thing," she said to both of them, but her hazel eyes were fixed on William, soft and troubled. "In only a little while we shall be enemies again."

"I have never felt myself your enemy, Miss Hunter," he replied, just as softly. "And I shall always be your friend."

A smile touched her lips, but the trouble stayed in her eyes.

"Thee knows what I mean." Her eyes slid from William to Dottie, on her other side, and it occurred to William with a jolt that his cousin was about to wed a rebel—to become one herself, in fact. That he must in fact soon be directly at war with a part of his own family. The fact that Denny Hunter would not take up arms would not protect him—or Dottie. Or Rachel. All three of them were guilty of treason. Any of them might be killed, captured, imprisoned. What would he do, he thought suddenly, appalled, if he had to see Denny hanged one day? Or even Dottie?

"I know what you mean," he said quietly. But he took Rachel's hand, and she gave it him, and the three of them sat in silence, linked, awaiting the verdict of the future.

89

INK-STAINED WRETCH

I MADE MY WAY TO the printshop, dead tired and in that state of mind in which one feels drunk—euphoric and uncoordinated. I was in truth somewhat physically drunk, too; Lord John had insisted upon plying both Denzell Hunter and myself with his best brandy, seeing how done up we both were in the wake of the surgery. I hadn't said no.

It was one of the most hair-raising pieces of surgery I'd done in the eighteenth century. I'd done only two other abdominal surgeries: the successful removal of Aidan McCallum's appendix, under the influence of ether—and the very unsuccessful cesarean I'd performed with a garden knife upon the murdered body of Malva Christie. The thought of that gave me the usual pang of sadness and regret, but it was oddly tempered. What I remembered now, walking home in the cool evening, was the feeling of the life I'd held in my hands— so brief, so fleeting—but *there,* unmistakable and intoxicant, a brief blue flame.

I'd held Henry Grey's life in my hands two hours before and felt that blaze again. Once more I'd willed all my strength into the burning of that flame— but this time had felt it steady and rise in my palms, like a candle taking hold.

The bullet had entered his intestine but had not encysted. Instead, it remained embedded but mobile, not able to leave the body but moving enough to irritate the lining of the intestine, which was badly ulcerated. After a quick discussion with Denzell Hunter—who was so fascinated with the novelty of examining a person's working insides while they lay unconscious that he could barely keep his mind on the business at hand, exclaiming in awe at the vivid colors and pulsating throb of live organs—I had decided that the ulceration was too extensive. To excise it would narrow the small intestine dramatically and risk scarring—constricting it further and perhaps obstructing it altogether.

We'd done a modest resection instead, and I felt a twinge of something between laughter and dismay at the recollection of Lord John's face when I severed the ulcerated segment of intestine and dropped it with a *splat* on the floor at his feet. I hadn't done it on purpose; I'd simply needed both my hands and Denzell's to control the bleeding, and we'd lacked a nurse to help.

The boy wasn't out of the woods, not by a long chalk. I didn't know whether my penicillin would be effective, or whether he might develop some hideous infection despite it. But he *was* awake, and his vital signs were surprisingly strong—perhaps, I thought, because of Mrs. Woodcock, who had gripped his hand and stroked his face, urging him to wake with a fierce tenderness that left her feelings for him in no doubt whatever.

I did wonder briefly what the future held for her. Struck by her unusual name, I'd inquired cautiously about her husband and was sure that it was he whose amputated leg I'd tended on the retreat from Ticonderoga. I thought it very likely he was dead; if so, what might happen between Mercy Woodcock and Henry Grey? She was a free woman, not a slave. Marriage wasn't unthinkable—not even as unthinkable as such a relationship would be in the United States two hundred years in the future: marriages involving black and mulatto women of good family to white men were, if not common in the Indies, not a matter of public scandal, either. Philadelphia was not the Indies, though, and from what Dottie had told me of her father . . .

I was simply too tired to think about it, and I needn't—Denny Hunter had volunteered to stay with Henry through the night. I dismissed that particular pair from my mind as I wandered down the street, weaving slightly. I hadn't eaten anything since breakfast, and it was nearly dark; the brandy had sunk directly through the walls of my empty stomach and entered my bloodstream, and I hummed gently to myself as I walked. It was the twilight hour, when things float on the air, when curved cobblestones seem insubstantial and the leaves of trees hang heavy as emeralds, glowing with a green whose fragrance enters the blood.

I should walk faster; there was a curfew. Still, who would arrest me? I was too old for patrolling soldiers to molest me, as they would a young girl, and of the wrong sex to be suspicious. Should I meet a patrol, they wouldn't do more than abuse me and tell me to go home—which I was doing, in any case.

It struck me quite suddenly that I could move the things Marsali described circumspectly as "Mr. Smith's job": the written letters circulated by the Sons of Liberty that passed between villages, between towns, that whirled through the colonies like leaves driven by a spring storm, were copied and sent on, sometimes printed and distributed within the towns, if a bold printer could be found to do the work.

There was a loose network through which these things moved, but it was always prone to discovery, with people arrested and imprisoned frequently. Germain carried such papers often, and my heart was in my throat when I thought of it. An agile boy was less noticeable than a young man or a tradesman going about his business—but the British were not fools and would certainly stop him if he looked at all suspicious. Whereas I . . .

Turning the possibilities over in my mind, I reached the shop and went in, to the smell of a savory supper, the greetings of excited children, and something that drove all thought of my potential new career as a spy from my mind: two letters from Jamie.

20 March, A.D. 1778
Lallybroch

My dearest Claire;

Ian is dead. It has been ten days since the Event, and I thought I should now be able to write calmly. Yet to see those Words written on the

Page just now smote me with the most unexpected Grief; Tears are running down the sides of my Nose, and I was forced to stop to mop my Face with a Handkerchief before continuing. It was not an easy Death and I should be relieved that Ian is now at Peace, and glad for his Translation into Heaven. So I am. But I am also desolate, in a Way that I have never been before. Only the Thought of being able to confide in you, my Soul, gives me Comfort.

Young Jamie has the Estate, as he should; Ian's Will has been read out, and Mr. Gowan will see it executed. There is not much beyond the Land and Buildings; only the smallest Bequests to the other Children, these largely of personal Items. My Sister he has confided to my Care (he having inquired before his Death whether I was willing. I told him he knew better than to ask. He said he did, but thought to inquire whether I felt myself also equal to the Task, and laughed like a Loon. Dear God, I shall miss him).

There were some trifling Debts to be paid; I have discharged them, as we agreed I should.

Jenny worries me. I know she grieves Ian with all her Heart, but she does not weep much, but only sits for long Periods, looking at Something that only she sees. There is a Calmness about her that is almost eerie, as though her Soul has flown with Ian, leaving only the Shell of her Body behind. Though since I mention Shells, it occurs to me that perhaps she is like a Chambered Nautilus, like the one that Lawrence Sterne showed us in the Indies. A large, beautiful Shell, made of many Chambers, but all empty, save the innermost one, in which the small Animal hides itself in safety.

Since I speak of her, though—she bids me tell you of her Remorse regarding Things said to you. I told her we had spoken of it between us, and that your Compassion would not hold it against her, realizing the desperate Circumstances in which she spoke.

On the Morning of Ian's Death, she spoke to me with apparent Rationality, and said she thought she would leave Lallybroch, that with his Death, nothing holds her here. I was, as you may suppose, much astonished to hear this, but did not try to question or dissuade her, assuming this to be only the Counsel of a Mind deranged by Sleeplessness and Grief.

She has since repeated this Sentiment to me, though, with firm Assurance that she is indeed in her right Mind. I am going to France for a short Time—both to accomplish some private Transactions that I will not write of here, and to assure myself before departing for America that both Michael and Joan are settled, they having left together, the Day following Ian's Burial. I said to Jenny that she must think carefully whilst I am absent—but that if she is in Fact convinced that this is what she wants, I will bring her to America. Not to stay with us (I smile, imagining your Face, which is transparent, even in my Mind).

She would have a Place, though, with Fergus and Marsali, where she would be of Use, and yet would not be reminded daily of her Loss—and where she would be in a Position to help and support Young Ian, should he require such Help (or at least to know how he does, if he does not).

(It also occurs to me—as it surely has to her—that Young Jamie's Wife will now be the Lady of Lallybroch, and that there is not Room for Two such. She is wise enough to know what the Difficulties of such a Situation would be, and kind enough to wish to avoid them, for the Sake of her Son and his Wife.)

In any Case, I propose to depart for America by the End of this Month, or as near to that as Passage may be obtained. The Prospect of being Reunited with you lightens my Heart and I remain forever

Your Devoted Husband,
Jamie

Paris
1 April

My dearest Wife;

I am returned very late to my new Lodging in Paris tonight. In fact, I found the Door bolted against me on my Return, and was obliged to shout for the Landlady, who was somewhat ill-tempered at being roused from her Bed. I was the more ill-tempered in my Turn, at finding no Fire laid, no Supper kept, and Nothing upon the Bedframe save a moldy Tick and threadbare Blanket which would not serve to shelter the meanest Beggar.

Further Shouts earned me Nothing save Abuse (from behind a safely lock'd Door), and my Pride would not suffer me to offer Bribes even would my Purse do so. I remain thus in my barren Garret, frozen and starving (this pitiful Picture is here drawn for the craven Purpose of soliciting your Sympathy, and to convince you of how poorly I Fare without you).

I am determined to depart this Place as soon as it be Light, and seek whether better Lodging can be found without excessive Damage to my Purse. Meanwhile, I shall endeavor to forget both Cold and Hunger in pleasant Converse with you, hoping that the Effort of writing will summon your Image before me and lend me the Illusion of your Company.

(I have possessed myself of adequate Light by stealing Downstairs in my Stockings and snatching two silver Candlesticks from the front Parlor, whose deceitful Grandeur seduced me into assuming Residence here. I shall return the Candlesticks tomorrow—when Madame returns the extortionate Fee for this miserable Accommodation.)

To more pleasant Subjects: I have seen Joan, now secure in her Convent, and apparently content (why, no, since you ask; I did not attend the Wedding of her Mother to Joseph Murray—who is, it turns out, a second Cousin to Ian. I sent a handsome Present and my good Wishes, which are sincere). I will visit Michael tomorrow; I look forward to seeing Jared again and will give him your kindest Regards.

In the Meantime, I sought Sustenance this Morning in a Coffeehouse in Montmartre, and was there fortunate to encounter Mr. Lyle, whom I had met in Edinburgh. He greeted me most kindly, inquired after my Fortunes, and after some small Conversation of a personal Nature, invited me to attend the Meeting of a certain Society, whose Members include Voltaire, Diderot, and others whose Opinions are heard in the Circles I seek to influence.

I went thus by Appointment at two o'clock to a House, where I was admitted and found all within most grandly appointed, it being the Paris Residence of Monsieur Beaumarchais.

The Company there gathered was mixt indeed; it ran the Gamut from the shabbiest of Coffee-house Philosophers to the most elegant Ornaments of Parisian Society, the Character common to them all being only a love of Talk. Some Pretentions to Reason and Intellect were made, to be sure, but not insisted on. I could not ask a fairer Wind for my maiden Voyage as a political Provocateur—and Wind, you will see, is a most apt Image in considering the Events of the Day.

After some inconsequent Babble over the refreshment Tables (had I been forewarned of Conditions here, I should have taken Care to stuff my Pockets surreptitiously with Cakes, as I saw more than one of my fellow Guests doing), the Company withdrew into a large Room and took Seats, for the Purpose of witnessing a formal Debate between two Parties.

The Matter under Debate was that popular Thesis, Resolved: that the Pen be mightier than the Sword, with Mr. Lyle and his Adherents defending the Proposition, M. Beaumarchais and his friends stoutly averring the Counter. The Talk was lively, with much Allusion to the Works of Rousseau and Montaigne (and not a little personal Disparagement of the Former, owing to his immoral Views on Marriage), but eventually Mr. Lyle's Party prevailed in their arguments. I thought of showing the Society my Right Hand, as Evidence for the Counter-proposition (a Sample of my Penmanship must have proved the Case to the Satisfaction of All), but Forbore, being but an Observer.

I found Opportunity later to approach Monsieur Beaumarchais, and made such an Observation to him in Jest, by way of fixing his Attention. He was most imprest by sight of my missing Digit, and inform'd of the Occasion of it (or rather, what I chose to tell him), became most animated and insistent that I accompany his Party to the house of the Duchess de Chaulnes, whence he was obliged for Supper, as the Duke is known to have a great Interest in Matters pertaining to the Aboriginal Inhabitants of the Colonies.

You will be wondering, no doubt, what Connexion exists between

Aboriginal Savages and your most elegant Surgery? Have Patience for a few Lines longer.

The ducal Residence is placed in a Street with a sweeping Drive upon which I perceived several fine Carriages ahead of M. Beaumarchais's. Imagine my Delight upon being informed that the Gentleman who descended just before us was none other than M. Vergennes, the Foreign Minister.

I congratulated myself upon my good Fortune in so soon encountering so many Persons suited to my Purpose, and did my best to ingratiate myself with them—to this End, telling Tales of my Travels in America, and borrowing in the Process not a few Stories from our Good Friend Myers.

The Company was most gratifyingly astonished, being particularly attentive to the Story of our Meeting with the Bear and with Nacognaweto and his Fellows. I made much of your valiant Efforts with the Fish, which much amused the Party, though the Ladies appeared most Shocked at my Description of your Indian Attire. Mr. Lyle, to the Contrary, was agog to hear more of your Appearance in leather Trouserings—I judged him by this a confirm'd Lecher and a Reprobate, a Judgement verified later in the Evening by a Passage I observ'd in the Hallway between Mr. Lyle and Mademoiselle Erlande, who I perceive to be most wanton in her own Conduct.

In any Case, this Story led Mr. Lyle to draw the Attention of the Company to my Hand, and urge me to tell them the Story which I had unfolded to him in the Afternoon, of how I came to lose my Finger.

Seeing that the Company had reached such a Pitch of Enjoyment— being well lubricated with Champagne, Holland Gin, and large quantities of Hock—that they hung upon my Words, I spared no Pains in weaving them a Tale of Horror calculated to leave them shivering in their Beds.

I had (I said) been taken Captive by the dreadful Iroquois while journeying from Trenton to Albany. I described in great Detail the frightful Appearance and bloodthirsty Habit of these Savages—which required no great Exaggeration, to be sure—and dwelt at Length upon the fearful Tortures which the Iroquois are wont to inflict upon their hapless Victims. La Comtesse Poutoude swooned at my recounting of the grisly Death of Father Alexandre, and the rest of the Party was much affected.

I told them of Two Spears, who I trust will not object to my Slandering his Character in a good Cause, the more so as he will never hear of it. This Chief, I said, being determined to put me to the Torture, caused me to be stripped naked, and most cruelly whip'd. With Thought of our good Friend Daniel, who has turned the same Misfortune to his Advantage, I raised my Shirt and Displayed my Scars. (I felt somewhat the Whore, but it has been my Observation that most Whores pursue this Profession from Necessity, and I comfort myself that it is much the same.) The reaction of my Audience was all that could be hoped, and I continued my Narrative, secure in the Knowledge that from this Point, they would believe Anything.

Thereafter (I said), two of the Indian Braves brought me fainting into the Chief's Presence, and secured me extended flat upon a large Stone, whose Surface bore sinister Witness to previous Sacrifice conducted thereon.

A heathen Priest or Shaman then approached me, uttering hideous Cries and shaking a Stick decorated by many waving Scalps, which caused me to fear that my own Hair might prove of such Attraction by Virtue of its unusual Colour as shortly to be added to his Collection (I had not powder'd my Hair, tho' from lack of Powder, rather than Forethought). This Fear was much enhanced when the Shaman drew forth a large Knife and advanced upon me, Eyes glittering with Malice.

At this Point, the Eyes of my Hearers were glittering as well, being enlarged to the size of Saucers by Reason of their Attention to my Story. Many of the Ladies cried out in Pity for my desperate Situation, and the Gentlemen uttered fierce Execrations of the foul Savages responsible for my Plight.

I told them then how the Shaman had driven his Knife straight through my Hand, causing me to lose Consciousness by Reason of Fear and Pain. I awoke (I continued) to find my fourth Finger sever'd completely, and Blood pouring from my wounded Hand.

But most horrifying of all was the sight of the Iroquois Chief, seated upon the carved Trunk of a giant Tree, tearing the Flesh from the severed Digit with his Teeth, as one might gobble the Meat of a Chicken's Leg.

At this point in my narrative, La Comtesse swooned again, and— not to be outdone—the Honorable Miss Elliott launched into a full-fledg'd fit of the Hysterics, which fortunately saved me from having to invent the Means of my Escape from the Savages. Professing myself undone by the Memories of my Trials, I accepted a Glass of Wine (I was sweating pretty freely by this time), and escaped from the Party instead, assailed by Invitations on all Sides.

I am much pleased by the Effects of my first Foray. I am further uplifted by Reflection that should Age or Injury prevent my making a Livelihood by means of Sword, Plow, or Printing Press, I might still find useful Employment as a scribbler of Romances.

I expect Marsali will wish to know in great Detail the Appearance of the Gowns worn by the Ladies present, but I must beg her Forbearance for the Moment. I do not pretend not to have observ'd the Matter (though I might so protest, if I thought by so doing to relieve your Mind of Apprehensions concerning any supposed Vulnerability to the Wiles of Femininity. Knowing your suspicious and irrational Nature, my Sassenach, I make no such Protestations), but my Hand will not bear the Strain of recounting such Descriptions now. For the Moment, suffice it to say that the Gowns were of very rich Stuff, and the Charms of the Ladies inside them made most apparent by the Style.

My pilfered Candles are burning low, and both my Hand and my Eyes are so fatigued that I have Difficulty in deciphering my own Words, let alone in forming them—I can only hope you will be able to read the last Part of this illegible Epistle. Still, I retire to my inhospitable Bed in good Spirits, encouraged by the day's Events.

Thus I bid you goodnight, with Assurance of my most tender Thoughts, in trust that you will have patience with and abiding Affection for

> *Your Ink-stain'd Wretch and Most Devoted Husband,*
> *James Fraser*

Postscriptum: Ink-stained Wretch, indeed, as I see that I have con-triv'd to cover both my Paper and my Person with unsightly Blots. I flatter myself that the Paper is the more disfigured.

Postscriptum 2: I have been so absorbed in Composition as to forget my original Intent in writing: to say that I have booked Passage on the Euterpe, *sailing from Brest in two Weeks' Time. Should anything tran-spire to prevent this, I will write again.*

Postscriptum 3: I yearn to lie beside you again, and know your Body complicit with mine.

90

ARMED WITH DIAMONDS
AND WITH STEEL

BRIANNA CUT THE brooch apart with a steady hand and a pair of kitchen shears. It was an antique but not a valuable one—an ugly Victorian thing in the shape of a sprawling silver flower surrounded by writhing vines. Its only worth lay in the scatter of small diamonds that deco-rated the leaves like dewdrops.

"I hope they're big enough," she said, and was surprised at how calm her own voice sounded. She had been screaming inside her own head for the last thirty-six hours, which was how long it had taken them to make their plans and preparations.

"I think they'll be fine," Roger said, and she felt the tension under the calm of his own words. He was standing behind her, his hand on her shoul-der, and the warmth of it was comfort and torment. Another hour, and he would be gone. Perhaps forever.

But there was no choice about it, and she went about the necessary things dry-eyed and steady.

Amanda, very weirdly, had fallen asleep quite suddenly after Roger and William Buccleigh had left in pursuit of Rob Cameron. Brianna had laid her in her bed and sat there watching her sleep and worrying until the men had returned near dawn with their horrifying news. But Amanda had waked as usual, sunny as the day, and apparently with no memory of her dream of screaming rocks. Neither was she bothered about Jem's absence; she had asked once, casually, when he would be home and, receiving a noncommittal "Soon," had gone back to her play, apparently contented.

She was with Annie now; they'd gone into Inverness to do a big shopping, with the promise of a toy. They wouldn't be home until mid-afternoon, and by then the men would be gone.

"Why?" William Buccleigh had asked. "Why would he take your lad?"

That was the same question she and Roger had been asking themselves since the moment they discovered Jem's loss—not that the answer was likely to help.

"Only two things it might be," Roger had answered, his voice thick and cracked. "Time travel—or gold."

"Gold?" Buccleigh's dark green eyes had turned to Brianna, puzzled. "What gold?"

"The missing letter," she'd explained, too tired to worry whether it was safe to tell him. Nothing was safe anymore, and nothing mattered. "The post-script my father wrote. Roger said you'd read the letters. *The property of an Italian gentleman*—you remember that?"

"I took no great notice," Buccleigh admitted. "That's gold, is it? Who's the Italian gentleman, then?"

"Charles Stuart." And so they'd explained, in disjoint fashion, about the gold that had come ashore in the last days of the Jacobite Rising—Buccleigh himself would have been about Mandy's age then, Brianna thought, startled by the notion—to be divided for safety among three Scottish gentlemen, trusted tacksmen of their clans: Dougal MacKenzie, Hector Cameron, and Arch Bug, of clan Grant. She watched carefully, but he gave no sign of recognition at the name of Dougal MacKenzie. No, she thought, he doesn't know. But that was not important now, either.

No one knew what had become of the two-thirds of the French gold held by the MacKenzies or the Grants—but Hector Cameron had fled Scotland in the last days of the Rising, the chest of gold under the seat of his carriage, and had brought it with him to the New World, where part of it had bought his plantation, River Run. The rest . . .

"The Spaniard guards it?" Buccleigh said, heavy fair brows knitted. "What the devil does that mean?"

"We don't know," Roger said. He was sitting at the table, head sunk in his hands, staring down at the wood. "Only Jem knows." Then he had raised his head suddenly, looking at Brianna.

"The Orkneys," he said. "Callahan."

"What?"

"Rob Cameron," he'd said urgently. "How old d'ye think he is?"

"I don't know," she'd said, confused. "Mid, late thirties, maybe. Why?"

"Callahan said Cameron went on archaeological digs with him in his early twenties. Is that far enough back—I mean, I only just now thought—" He had to stop to clear his throat and did so angrily before going on. "If he was into the ancient stuff fifteen, eighteen years ago—might he have known Geilie Duncan? Or Gillian Edgars, I suppose she still was then."

"Oh, no," Brianna said, but in denial, not disbelief. "Oh, no. Not another Jacobite nut!"

Roger had almost smiled at that one.

"I doubt it," he'd said dryly. "I don't think the man's insane, let alone a political idealist. But he does belong to the SNP. They aren't insane, either—but what's the odds that Gillian Edgars would have been involved with them?"

There was no telling, not without digging into Cameron's connections and history, and there was no time for that. But it was possible. Gillian—who'd later taken the name of a famous Scottish witch—had certainly been deeply interested both in Scottish antiquity and in Scottish politics. She might have crossed paths with Rob Cameron, easily. And if so . . .

"If so," Roger said grimly, "God only knows what she might have told him, might have left him with." A few of Geillis's notebooks were in his study; if Rob had known her, he would have recognized them.

"And we bloody well know he read your da's postscript," he added. He rubbed his forehead—there was a dark bruise along his hairline—and sighed. "It doesn't matter, does it? The only thing that matters now is Jem."

And so Brianna gave each of them a chunk of silver studded with small diamonds and two peanut butter sandwiches. "For the road," she said, with a ghastly attempt at humor. Warm clothes and stout shoes. She gave Roger her Swiss army knife; Buccleigh took a stainless-steel steak knife from the kitchen, admiring its serrated edge. There wasn't time for much more.

The sun was still high when the blue Mustang bumped along the dirt road that led near the base of Craigh na Dun; she had to be back before Mandy came home. Rob Cameron's blue truck was still there; a shudder went through her at the sight of it.

"Go ahead," Roger said roughly to Buccleigh when she stopped. "I'll be along directly."

William Buccleigh had given Brianna a quick look, direct and disconcerting, with those eyes, so like Roger's, touched her hand briefly, and got out. Roger didn't hesitate; he'd had time on the way to decide what to say—and there was only one thing to say, in any case.

"I love you," he said softly, and took her by the shoulders, holding her together long enough to say the rest. "I'll bring him back. Believe me, Bree—I'll see you again. In *this* world."

"I love you," she'd said, or tried to. It came out as a soundless whisper against his mouth, but he took it, along with her breath, smiled, gripped her shoulders so hard that she would find bruises there later—and opened the door.

She'd watched them—she couldn't help watching them—as they climbed toward the top of the hill, toward the invisible stones, until they disappeared, out of her sight. Perhaps it was imagination; perhaps she really could hear the stones up there: a weird buzzing song that lived in her bones, a memory that would live there forever. Trembling and tear-blinded, she drove home. Carefully, carefully. Because now she was all that Mandy had.

91

FOOTSTEPS

L ATE THAT NIGHT, she made her way to Roger's study. She felt dull and heavy, the horror of the day blunted by fatigue. She sat at his desk, trying to feel his presence, but the room was empty.

Mandy was asleep, surprisingly unworried by the chaos of her parents' feelings. Of course, she was used to Roger's occasional absences, gone to London or to Oxford, lodge nights in Inverness. Would she remember him if he never came back? Brianna thought with a pang.

Unable to bear that thought, she got up and prowled restlessly round the office, seeking the unfindable. She hadn't been able to eat anything and was feeling light-headed and friable.

She took up the little snake, finding a minimal comfort in its smooth sinuosity, its pleasant face. She glanced up at the box, wondering whether she should seek solace in her parents' company—but the thought of reading letters that Roger might never read with her . . . She put the snake down and stared blindly at the books on the lower shelves.

Beside the books on the American Revolution that Roger had ordered were her father's books, the ones from his old office. *Franklin W. Randall,* the neat spines said, and she took one out and sat down, holding it to her chest.

She'd asked him once before for help—to look after Ian's lost daughter. Surely he would look after Jem.

She thumbed the pages, feeling a little soothed by the friction of the paper.

Daddy, she thought, finding no words beyond that, and needing no more. The folded sheet of paper tucked among the leaves came as no surprise at all.

The letter was a draft—she could see that at once from the crossings-out, the marginal additions, words circled with question marks. And being a draft, it had neither date nor salutation but was plainly intended for her.

> *You've just left me, dearest deadeye, after our wonderful afternoon*
> *at Sherman's (the clay pigeon place—will she remember the name?).*
> *My ears are still ringing. Whenever we shoot, I'm torn between*
> *immense pride in your ability, envy of it, and fear. I don't know quite*

*when you will read this, or if you will. Maybe I'll have the courage to
tell you before I die (or I'll do something so unforgivable that your
mother will—no, she won't. I've never met anyone so honorable as
Claire, notwithstanding. She'll keep her word).*

*What a queer feeling it is, writing this. I know that you'll eventually
learn who—and perhaps what—you are. But I have no idea how you'll
come to that knowledge. Am I about to reveal you to yourself, or will
this be old news when you find it? I can only hope that I've succeeded in
saving your life, either way. And that you will find it, sooner or later.*

*I'm sorry, sweetheart, that's terribly melodramatic. And the last
thing I want to do is alarm you. I have all the confidence in the world
in you. But I am your father and thus prey to the fears that afflict all
parents—that something dreadful and unpreventable will happen to
your child, and you powerless to protect them. And the truth is that
through no fault of your own, you are . . .*

Here he had changed his mind several times, writing *a dangerous person,*
amending that to *always in some danger,* then crossing that out in turn,
adding *in a dangerous position,* crossing *that* out, and circling *a dangerous person,* though with a question mark.

"I get the point, Daddy," she muttered. "What are you *talking* about? I—"

A sound froze the words in her throat. Footsteps were coming down the
hall. Slow, confident steps. A man's. Every hair on her body rose.

The light was on in the hall; it darkened briefly as a shape took form in the
door to the study.

She stared at him, dumbfounded.

"What are *you* doing here?" Even as she spoke, she was rising from the
chair, groping for something that might be used as a weapon, her mind lagging far behind her body, not yet able to penetrate the fog of horror that
gripped her.

"I came for you, hen," he said, smiling. "And for the gold." He laid something on the desk: her parents' first letter. *"Tell Jem the Spaniard guards it,"*
Rob Cameron quoted, tapping it. "I thought maybe it's best you tell Jem
that. And tell him to show me where this Spaniard is. If ye'd like to keep him
alive, I mean. Up to you, though." The smile widened. "Boss."

92

INDEPENDENCE DAY, II

Brest

S EEING JENNY DEAL with it all was disturbing his own presence of mind considerably. He could see her heart in her throat the first time she spoke French to a real Frenchman; her pulse fluttered in the hollow of her neck like a trapped hummingbird. But the *boulanger* understood her—Brest was full of foreigners, and her peculiar accent roused no particular interest—and the sheer delight on her face when the man took her penny and handed her a baguette filled with cheese and olives made Jamie want to laugh and cry at the same time.

"He understood me!" she said, clutching him by the arm as they left. "Jamie, he understood me! I spoke *French* to him, and he kent what I said, clear as day!"

"Much more clearly than he would have had ye spoken to him in the *Gaidhlig*," he assured her. He smiled at her excitement, patting her hand. "Well done, *a nighean*."

She was not listening. Her head turned to and fro, taking in the vast array of shops and vendors that filled the crooked street, assessing the possibilities now open to her. Butter, cheese, beans, sausage, cloth, shoes, buttons . . . Her fingers dug into his arm.

"Jamie! I can buy anything! By myself!"

He couldn't help sharing her joy at thus rediscovering her independence, even though it gave him a small twinge. He'd been enjoying the novel sensation of having her rely on him.

"Well, so ye can," he agreed, taking the baguette from her. "Best not to buy a trained squirrel or a longcase clock, though. Be difficult to manage on the ship."

"Ship," she repeated, and swallowed. The pulse in her throat, which had subsided momentarily, resumed its fluttering. "When will we . . . go on the ship?"

"Not yet, *a nighean*," he said gently. "We'll go and ha' a bite to eat first, aye?"

THE *EUTERPE* WAS meant to sail on the evening tide, and they went down to the docks in mid-afternoon to go aboard and settle their things. But the slip at the dock where the *Euterpe* had floated the day before was empty.

"Where the devil is the ship that was here yesterday?" he demanded, seizing a passing boy by one arm.

"What, the *Euterpe?*" The boy looked casually where he was pointing, and shrugged. "Sailed, I suppose."

"You *suppose?*" His tone alarmed the boy, who pulled his arm free and backed off, defensive.

"How would I know, *Monsieur?*" Seeing Jamie's face, he hastily added, "Her master went into the district a few hours ago; probably he is still there."

Jamie saw his sister's chin dimple slightly and realized that she was near to panic. He wasn't so far off it himself, he thought.

"Oh, is he?" he said, very calm. "Aye, well, I'll just be going to fetch him, then. Which house does he go to?"

The boy shrugged helplessly. "All of them, *Monsieur.*"

Leaving Jenny on the dock to guard their baggage, he went back into the streets that adjoined the quay. A broad copper halfpenny secured him the services of one of the urchins who hung about the stalls, hoping for a half-rotten apple or an unguarded purse, and he followed his guide grimly into the filthy alleys, one hand on his purse, the other on the hilt of his dirk.

Brest was a port city, and a bustling port, at that. Which meant, he calculated, that roughly one in three of its female citizenry was a prostitute. Several of the independent sort hailed him as he passed.

It took three hours and several shillings, but he found the master of the *Euterpe* at last, dead drunk. He pushed the whore sleeping with him unceremoniously aside and roused the man roughly, slapping him into semiconsciousness.

"The ship?" The man stared at him blearily, wiping a hand across his stubbled face. "Fuck. Who cares?"

"I do," Jamie said between clenched teeth. "And so will you, ye wee arsewipe. Where is she, and why are ye not on her?"

"The captain threw me off," the man said sullenly. "We had a disagreement. Where is she? On her way to Boston, I suppose." He grinned unpleasantly. "If you swim fast enough, maybe you can catch her."

IT TOOK THE last of his gold and a well-calculated mixture of threats and persuasion, but he found another ship. This one was headed south, to Charleston, but at the moment he would settle for being on the right continent. Once in America, he'd think again.

His sense of grim fury began finally to abate as the *Philomene* reached the open sea. Jenny stood beside him, small and silent, hands braced on the rail.

"What, *a phiuthar?*" He put his hand in the small of her back, rubbing gently with his knuckles. "You're grieving Ian?"

She closed her eyes for a moment, pressing back into his touch, then opened them and turned her face up to him, frowning.

"No, I'm troubled, thinkin' of your wife. She'll be peeved wi' me—about Laoghaire."

He couldn't help a wry smile at thought of Laoghaire.

"Laoghaire? Why?"

"What I did—when ye brought Claire home again to Lallybroch, from Edinburgh. I've never said sorry to ye for that," she added, looking up earnestly into his face.

He laughed.

"I've never said sorry to *you*, have I? For bringing Claire home and being coward enough not to tell her about Laoghaire before we got there."

The frown between her brows eased, and a flicker of light came back into her eyes.

"Well, no," she said. "Ye haven't told me sorry. So we're square, are we?"

He hadn't heard her say that to him since he'd left home at fourteen to foster at Leoch.

"We're square," he said. He put an arm round her shoulders and she slipped her own around his waist, and they stood close together, watching the last of France sink into the sea.

93

A SERIES OF SHORT, SHARP SHOCKS

I WAS IN MARSALI'S kitchen, plaiting Félicité's hair while keeping one eye on the porridge over the fire, when the bell over the printshop door rang. I whipped a ribbon round the end of the plait and, with a quick admonition to the girls to watch the porridge, went out to attend to the customer.

To my surprise, it was Lord John. But a Lord John I had never seen before. He was not so much disheveled as shattered, everything in order save his face.

"What?" I said, deeply alarmed. "What's happened? Is Henry—"

"Not Henry," he said hoarsely. He put a hand flat on the counter, as though to steady himself. "I have—bad news."

"I can see that," I said, a little tartly. "Sit down, for God's sake, before you fall down."

He shook his head like a horse shaking off flies and looked at me. His face was ghastly, shocked and white, and the rims of his eyes showed red. But if it wasn't Henry . . .

"Oh, God," I said, a fist clenching deep in my chest. "Dottie. What's happened to her?"

"Euterpe," he blurted, and I stopped dead, jarred to the backbone.

"What?" I whispered. *"What?"*

"Lost," he said, in a voice that wasn't his own. "Lost. With all hands."

"No," I said, trying for reason. "No, it's not."

He looked at me directly then, for the first time, and seized me by the forearm.

"Listen to me," he said, and the pressure of his fingers terrified me. I tried to jerk away but couldn't.

"Listen," he said again. "I heard it this morning from a naval captain I know. I met him at the coffeehouse, and he was recounting the tragedy. He saw it." His voice trembled, and he stopped for a moment, firming his jaw. "A storm. He had been chasing the ship, meaning to stop and board her, when the storm came upon them both. His own ship survived and limped in, badly damaged, but he saw the *Euterpe* swamped by a broaching wave, he said—I have no notion what that is—" He waved away his own digression, annoyed. "She went down before his eyes. The *Roberts*—his ship—hung about in hopes of picking up survivors." He swallowed. "There were none."

"None," I said blankly. I heard what he said but took no meaning from the words.

"He is dead," Lord John said softly, and let go of my arm. "He is gone."

From the kitchen came the smell of burning porridge.

JOHN GREY STOPPED walking because he had come to the end of the street. He had been walking up and down the length of State Street since sometime before dawn. The sun was high now, and sweat-damp grit irritated the back of his neck, mud and dung splashed his stockings, and each step seemed to drive the nails in his shoe sole into the sole of his foot. He didn't care.

The Delaware River flowed across his view, muddy and fish-smelling, and people jostled past him, crowding toward the end of the dock in hopes of getting on the ferry making its slow way toward them from the other side. Wavelets rose and lapped against the pier with an agitated sound that seemed to provoke the people waiting, for they began to push and shove, and one of the soldiers on the dock took down his musket from his shoulder and used it to shove a woman back.

She stumbled, shrieking, and her husband, a bantam-rooster of a man, bounced forward, fists clenched. The soldier said something, bared his teeth and made a shooing motion with the gun, his fellow, attracted by the disturbance, turned to see, and with no more incitement than that, there was suddenly a heaving knot of people at the end of the dock and shouts and screams ran through the rest, as people toward the rear tried to get away from the violence, men in the crowd tried to press toward it, and someone was pushed into the water.

Grey took three steps back and watched as two little boys rushed out of the crowd, their faces bloated with fright, and ran off up the street. Somewhere in the crowd, he heard a woman's high call, distraught: "Ethan! Johnny! *Joooooohnnny!*"

Some dim instinct said he should step forward, raise his own voice, assert his authority, sort this. He turned and walked away.

He wasn't in uniform, he told himself. They wouldn't listen, would be confused, he might do more harm than good. But he wasn't in the habit of lying to himself, and dropped that line of argument at once.

He'd lost people before. Some of them dearly loved, more than life itself. But now he'd lost himself.

He walked slowly back toward his house in a numb daze. He hadn't slept since the news had come, save in the snatches of complete physical exhaustion, slumped in the chair on Mercy Woodcock's porch, waking disoriented, sticky with sap from the sycamores in her yard and covered with the tiny green caterpillars that swung down from the leaves on invisible strands of silk.

"Lord John." He became aware of an insistent voice, and with it, the realization that whoever was speaking had called his name several times already. He stopped, and turned to find himself facing Captain Richardson. His mind went quite blank. Possibly his face had, too, for Richardson took him by the arm in a most familiar manner and drew him into an ordinary.

"Come with me," Richardson said in a low voice, releasing his arm, but jerking his head toward the stair. Faint stirrings of curiosity and wariness made themselves felt through the haze that wrapped him, but he followed, the sound of his shoes hollow in the wooden stairwell.

Richardson closed the door of the room behind him and began speaking before Grey could gather his wits to begin questioning him regarding the very peculiar circumstances William had recounted.

"Mrs. Fraser," Richardson said without preamble. "How well do you know her?"

Grey was so taken aback by this that he answered.

"She is the wife—the widow"—he corrected himself, feeling as though he had stuck a pin into a raw wound—"of a good friend."

"A good friend," Richardson repeated, with no particular emphasis. The man could scarcely look more nondescript, Grey thought, and had a sudden creeping vision of Hubert Bowles. The most dangerous spies were men whom no one would look at twice.

"A good friend," Grey repeated firmly. "His political loyalties are no longer an issue, are they?"

"Not if he's truly dead, no," Richardson agreed. "You think he is?"

"I am quite sure of it. What is it you wish to know, sir? I have business."

Richardson smiled a little at this patently false statement.

"I propose to arrest the lady as a spy, Lord John, and wished to be certain that there was no . . . personal attachment on your part, before I did so."

Grey sat down, rather abruptly, and braced his hands on the table.

"I—she—what the devil for?" he demanded.

Richardson courteously sat down opposite him.

"She has been passing seditious materials to and fro all over Philadelphia for the last three months—possibly longer. And before you ask, yes, I'm sure. One of my men intercepted some of the material; have a look, if you like." He reached into his coat and withdrew an untidy wad of papers, these looking to have passed through several hands. Grey didn't think Richardson was practicing upon him, but took his time in deliberate examination. He put down the papers, feeling bloodless.

"I heard that the lady had been received at your house, and that she is often at the house where your nephew abides," Richardson said. His eyes rested on Grey's face, intent. "But she is not a . . . friend?"

"She is a physician," Grey said, and had the small satisfaction of seeing Richardson's brows shoot up. "She has been of—of the greatest service to me and my nephew." It occurred to him that it was likely better that Richardson did not know how much esteem he might hold for Mrs. Fraser, as if he thought there *was* a personal interest, he would immediately cease to give Grey information. "That is ended, though," he added, speaking as casually as possible. "I respect the lady, of course, but there is no attachment, no." He rose then, in a decided manner, and took his leave, for to ask more questions would compromise the impression of indifference.

He set off toward Walnut Street, no longer numb. He felt once more himself, strong and determined. There was, after all, one more service he might perform for Jamie Fraser.

"YOU MUST MARRY me," he repeated.

I'd heard him the first time, but it made no more sense upon repetition. I stuck a finger in one ear and wiggled it, then repeated the process with the other.

"You can't possibly have said what I think you said."

"Indeed I did," he said, his normal dry edge returning.

The numbness of shock was beginning to wear off, and something horrible was beginning to crawl out of a small hole in my heart. I couldn't look at that and took refuge in staring at Lord John.

"I know I'm shocked," I told him, "but I'm sure I'm neither delusional nor hearing things. Why the bloody hell are you *saying* that, for God's sake?!" I rose abruptly, wanting to strike him. He saw it and took a smart step back.

"You are going to marry me," he said, a fierce edge in his voice. "Are you aware that you are about to be arrested as a spy?"

"I—no." I sat down again, as abruptly as I'd stood up. "What . . . why?"

"You would know that better than I would," he said coldly.

In fact, I would. I repressed the sudden flutter of panic that threatened to overwhelm me, thinking of the papers I had conveyed secretly from one pair of hands to another in the cover of my basket, feeding the secret network of the Sons of Liberty.

"Even if that were true," I said, struggling to keep my own voice level, "why the bloody hell would I marry you? Let alone why you would want to marry *me*, which I don't believe for an instant."

"Believe it," he advised me briefly. "I will do it because it is the last service I can render Jamie Fraser. I can protect you; as my wife, no one can touch you. And *you* will do it because . . ." He cast a bleak glance behind me, raising his chin, and I looked around to see all four of Fergus's children huddled in the doorway, the girls and Henri-Christian watching me with huge, round eyes. Germain was looking straight at Lord John, fear and defiance plain on his long, handsome face.

"Them, too?" I asked, taking a deep breath and turning to meet his gaze. "You can protect them, too?"

"Yes."

"I—yes. All right." I rested both hands flat on the counter, as though that somehow could keep me from spinning off into space. "When?"

"Now," he said, and took my elbow. "There is no time to lose."

I HAD NO MEMORY whatever of the brief ceremony, conducted in the parlor of Lord John's house. The only memory I retained of the entire day was the sight of William, standing soberly beside his father—his stepfather—as best man. Tall, straight, long-nosed, his slanted cat-eyes resting on me with uncertain compassion.

He can't be dead, I remembered thinking, with unusual lucidity. *There he is.*

I said what I was told to say and then was escorted upstairs to lie down. I fell asleep at once and didn't wake until the next afternoon.

Unfortunately, it was still real when I did.

DOROTHEA WAS THERE, hovering near me with concern. She stayed with me through the day, trying to coax me to eat something, offering me sips of whisky and brandy. Her presence was not exactly a comfort—nothing could be that—but she was at least an innocuous distraction, and I let her talk, the words washing over me like the sound of rushing water.

Toward evening, the men came back—Lord John and Willie. I heard them downstairs. Dottie went down and I heard her talking to them, a slight rise of interest in her voice, and then her steps on the stairs, quick and light.

"Aunt," she said, breathless. "Are you well enough to come down, do you think?"

"I—yes, I suppose so." Slightly taken aback at being called "Aunt," I rose and made vague tidying motions. She took the brush from my hand, twisted up my hair, and, whipping out a ribboned cap, tucked my hair tenderly under it. I let her, and let her convey me gently downstairs, where I found Lord John and William in the parlor, both of them a little flushed.

"Mother Claire." Willie took my hand and gently kissed it. "Come and look. Papa has found something he thinks you will like. Come and see it," he repeated, drawing me gently toward the table.

"It" was a large wooden chest, made of some expensive wood, banded in gold. I blinked at it and put out a hand to touch it. It looked rather like a cutlery safe but much bigger.

"What . . . ?" I looked up to find Lord John standing beside me, looking somewhat abashed.

"A, um, present," he said, deprived for once of his smooth manners. "I thought—I mean, I perceived that you lacked somewhat in the way of . . . equipment. I do not wish you to abandon your profession," he added gently.

"My profession." A chill was beginning to spread up my spine, along the edges of my jaw. Fumbling a little, I tried to raise the lid of the chest, but my fingers were sweating; they slipped, leaving a slick of moisture gleaming on the wood.

"No, no, this way." Lord John bent to show me, turning the chest toward himself. He slipped the hidden catch, lifted the lid, and swung the hinged doors open, then stood back with something of the air of a conjurer.

My scalp prickled with cold sweat, and black spots began to flicker at the corners of my eyes.

Two dozen empty gold-topped bottles. Two shallow drawers below. And above, gleaming in its velvet bed, the pieces of a brass-bound microscope. A medical chest.

My knees gave way and I fainted, welcoming the cool wood of the floor against my cheek.

THE PATHS OF DEATH

L YING IN THE TANGLED HELL of my bed at night, I searched for the way to death. I longed with every fiber of my being to pass from this present existence. Whether what lay on the other side of life was undreamed glory or only merciful oblivion, mystery was infinitely preferable to my present inescapable misery.

I cannot say what it was that kept me from a simple and violent escape. The means, after all, were always to hand. I had my choice of pistol ball or blade, of poisons ranging from swiftness to stupor.

I rummaged through the jars and bottles of the medicine chest like a madwoman, leaving the little drawers ajar, the doors hanging open, seeking, scrabbling in my haste, ransacking knowledge and memory as I did the chest, knocking jars and bottles and bits of the past to the floor in a jumble.

At last I thought I had them all and, with a shaking hand, laid them one by one by one on the tabletop before me.

Aconite. Arsenic . . .

So many kinds of death to choose from. How, then?

The ether. That would be the easiest, if not quite the surest. Lie down, soak a thick pad of cloth in the stuff, put the mask over my nose and mouth, and drift painlessly away. But there was always the chance that someone would find me. Or that, losing consciousness, my head might fall to one side or I'd suffer convulsions that would dislodge the rag, and I would simply wake again to this aching void of existence.

I sat still for a moment, and then, feeling dreamlike, reached out to pick up the knife that lay on the table, where I had carelessly left it after using it to cut flax stems. The knife Jamie had given me. It was sharp; the edge gleamed raw and silver.

It would be sure, and it would be fast.

JAMIE FRASER STOOD on the deck of the *Philomene,* watching the water slide endlessly away, thinking about death. He had at least stopped thinking about it in a personal manner, since the seasickness had—at long, long last—abated. His thoughts now were more abstract.

To Claire, he thought, death was always the Enemy. Something always to be fought, never yielded to. He was as well acquainted with death as she was but had perforce made his peace with it. Or thought he had. Like forgiveness, it was not a thing once learned and then comfortably put aside but a matter of constant practice—to accept the notion of one's own mortality, and yet live fully, was a paradox worthy of Socrates. And that worthy Athenian had embraced exactly that paradox, he reflected, with the ghost of a smile.

He'd come face-to-face with death often enough—and remembered those encounters with sufficient vividness—to realize that there were indeed worse things. Much better to die than be left to mourn.

He had still a dreadful feeling of something worse than sorrow when he looked at his sister, small and solitary, and heard the word "widow" in his mind. It was wrong. She could not be that, couldn't be severed in that brutal way. It was like watching her be cut in pieces, and he helpless to do anything.

He turned from that thought to his memories of Claire, his longing for her, the flame of her his candle in the dark. Her touch a comfort and a warmth beyond that of the body. He remembered the last evening before she'd left, holding hands on the bench outside the broch, feeling her heartbeat in her fingers, his own steadying to that warm, quick pulse.

Odd how the presence of death seemed to bring with it so many attendants, shades long-forgotten, glimpsed briefly in the gathering shadow. The thought of Claire, and how he had sworn to protect her from the first time he held her, brought back to him the nameless girl.

She'd died in France, on the far side of the void in his head that had been made by the blow of an ax. He hadn't thought of her in years, but suddenly she was there again. She'd been in his mind when he'd held Claire at Leoch, and he'd felt that his marriage might be some small atonement. He'd learned—slowly—to forgive himself for what had not been his fault and, in loving Claire, gave the girl's shade some peace, he hoped.

He had felt obscurely that he owed God a life and had paid that debt by taking Claire to wife—though God knew he would have taken her in any case, he thought, and smiled wryly. But he'd kept faith with the promise to protect her. *The protection of my name, my clan—and the protection of my body,* he'd said.

The protection of my body. There was an irony in that that made him squirm, as he glimpsed another face among the shades. Narrow, mocking, long-eyed—so young.

Geneva. One more young woman dead as the result of his lust. Not his fault, precisely—he'd fought that through, in the long days and nights following her death, alone in his cold bed above the stables, taking what comfort he could in the solid, voiceless presence of the horses shifting and champing in their stalls below. But had he not lain with her, she would not have died; that was inescapable.

Did he owe God another life? he wondered. He had thought it was Willie, the life he'd been given to protect with his own, in exchange for Geneva's. But that trust had had to be handed to another.

Well, he had his sister now and assured Ian silently that he would keep her safe. *As long as I live,* he thought. And that should be some time yet. He thought he'd used only five of the deaths the fortune-teller in Paris had promised him.

"You'll die nine times before you rest in your grave," she'd said. Did it take so many tries to get it right? he wondered.

I LET MY HAND fall back, exposing my wrist, and placed the tip of the knife midway up my forearm. I'd seen many unsuccessful suicides, those who slashed their wrists from side to side, the wounds small mouths that cried for help. I'd seen those who meant it. The proper way was to slit the veins lengthwise, deep, sure cuts that would drain me of blood in minutes, assure unconsciousness in seconds.

The mark was still visible on the mound at the base of my thumb. A faint white "J," the mark he'd left on me on the eve of Culloden, when we first faced the stark knowledge of death and separation.

I traced the thin white line with the tip of the knife and felt the seductive whisper of metal on my skin. I'd wanted to die with him then, and he had sent me on with a firm hand. I carried his child; I could not die.

I carried her no longer—but she was still there. Perhaps reachable. I sat motionless for what seemed a long time, then sighed and put the knife back on the table carefully.

Perhaps it was the habit of years, a bent of mind that held life sacred for its own sake, or a superstitious awe of extinguishing a spark kindled by a hand not my own. Perhaps it was obligation. There were those who needed me— or at least to whom I could be useful. Perhaps it was the stubbornness of the body, with its inexorable insistence on never-ending process.

I could slow my heart, slow enough to count the beats . . . slow the flowing of my blood 'til my heart echoed in my ears with the doom of distant drums.

There were pathways in the dark. I knew; I had seen people die. Despite physical decay, there was no dying until the pathway was found. I couldn't— yet—find mine.

95

NUMBNESS

T HE NEW MEDICAL CHEST sat on the table in my room, gleaming softly in the candlelight. Beside it were the gauze bags of dried herbs I had bought during the morning, the fresh bottles of the tinctures I had brewed in the afternoon, much to Mrs. Figg's displeasure at having her kitchen's purity so perverted. Her slitted eyes said that she knew me for a rebel and thought me likely a witch; she'd retreated to the doorway of the cookhouse while I worked but wouldn't leave altogether, instead keeping silent suspicious watch over me and my cauldron.

A large decanter of plum brandy was keeping me company. Over the course of the last week, I had found that a glass of it at night would let me find surcease in sleep, at least for a little. It wasn't working tonight. I heard the clock on the mantelpiece downstairs chime softly, once.

I stooped to pick up a box of dried chamomile that had spilled, sweeping the scattered leaves carefully back into their container. A bottle of syrup of poppies had fallen over, too, lying on its side, the aromatic liquid oozing round the cork. I set it upright, wiped the golden droplets from its neck with my kerchief, blotted up the tiny puddle from the floor. A root, a stone, a leaf. One by one, I picked them up, set them straight, put them away, the accoutrements of my calling, the pieces of my destiny.

The cool glass seemed somehow remote, the gleaming wood an illusion. Heart beating slowly, erratically, I put a hand flat on the box, trying to steady myself, to fix myself in space and time. It was becoming more difficult by the day.

I remembered, with sudden, painful vividness, a day on the retreat from Ticonderoga. We had reached a village, found momentary refuge in a barn. I'd worked all day then, doing what could be done with no supplies, no medicines, no instruments, no bandages save what I made from the sweat-sodden, filthy clothes of the wounded. Feeling the world recede further and further as I worked, hearing my voice as though it belonged to someone else. Seeing the bodies under my hands, only bodies. Limbs. Wounds. Losing touch.

Darkness fell. Someone came, pulled me to my feet, and sent me out of the barn, into the little tavern. It was crowded, overwhelmed with people. Someone—Ian?—said that Jamie had food for me outside.

He was alone there, in the empty woodshed, dimly lit by a distant lantern.

I'd stood in the doorway, swaying. Or perhaps it was the room that swayed.

I could see my fingers dug into the wood of the doorjamb, nails gone white.

A movement in the dimness. He rose fast, seeing me, came toward me. What was his—

"Jamie." I'd felt a distant sense of relief at finding his name.

He'd seized me, drawn me into the shed, and I wondered for an instant whether I was walking or whether he was carrying me; I heard the scrape of the dirt floor under my feet but didn't feel my weight or the shift of it.

He was talking to me, the sound of it soothing. It seemed a dreadful effort to distinguish words. I knew what he must be saying, though, and managed to say, "All right. Just . . . tired," wondering even as I spoke them whether these sounds were words at all, let alone the right ones.

"Will ye sleep, then, lass?" he'd said, worried eyes fixed on me. "Or can ye eat a bit first?" He let go of me, to reach for the bread, and I put out a hand to the wall to support myself, surprised to find it solid.

The sense of cold numbness had returned.

"Bed," I said. My lips felt blue and bloodless. "With you. Right now."

He'd cupped my cheek, calloused palm warm on my skin. Big hand. Solid. Above all, solid.

"Are ye sure, *a nighean?*" he'd said, a note of surprise in his voice. "Ye look as though—"

I'd laid a hand on his arm, half fearing that it would go through his flesh.

"Hard," I'd whispered. "Bruise me."

My glass was empty, the decanter halfway full. I poured another and took hold of the glass carefully, not wanting to spill it, determined to find oblivion, no matter how temporary.

Could I separate entirely? I wondered. Could my soul actually leave my. body without my dying first? Or had it done so already?

I drank the glass slowly, one sip at a time. Another. One sip at a time.

There must have been some sound that made me look up, but I wasn't aware of having raised my head. John Grey was standing in the doorway of my room. His neckcloth was missing and his shirt hung limp on his shoulders, wine spilled down the front of it. His hair was loose and tangled, and his eyes as red as mine.

I stood up, slow, as though I were underwater.

"I will not mourn him alone tonight," he said roughly, and closed the door.

⁂

I WAS SURPRISED to wake up. I hadn't really expected to and lay for a bit trying to fit reality back into place around me. I had only a slight headache, which was almost more surprising than the fact that I was still alive.

Both those things paled in significance beside the fact of the man in bed beside me.

"How long has it been since you last slept with a woman, if you don't mind my asking?"

He didn't appear to mind. He frowned a little and scratched his chest thoughtfully.

"Oh . . . fifteen years? At least that." He glanced at me, his expression altering to one of concern. "Oh. I do apologize."

"You do? For what?" I arched one brow. I could think of a number of things he *might* apologize for, but probably none of those was what he had in mind.

"I am afraid I was perhaps not . . ." he hesitated. "Very gentlemanly."

"Oh, you weren't," I said, rather tartly. "But I assure you that I wasn't being at all ladylike myself."

He looked at me, and his mouth worked a bit, as though trying to frame some response to that, but after a moment or two he shook his head and gave it up.

"Besides, it wasn't me you were making love to," I said, "and both of us know it."

He looked up, startled, his eyes very blue. Then the shadow of a smile crossed his face, and he looked down at the quilted coverlet.

"No," he said softly. "Nor were you, I think, making love to *me*. Were you?"

"No," I said. The grief of the night before had softened, but the weight of it was still there. My voice was low and husky, because my throat was halfway closed, where the hand of sorrow clutched me unawares.

John sat up and reached to the table, where a carafe stood along with a bottle and a glass. He poured something out of the bottle and handed it to me.

"Thank you," I said, and lifted it to my lips. "Good grief, is that *beer*?"

"Yes, and very good beer, too," he said, tilting back the bottle. He took several hearty gulps, eyes half closed, then lowered it with a sigh of satisfaction. "Clears the palate, freshens the breath, and prepares the stomach for digestion."

Despite myself, I was amused—and shocked.

"Do you mean to tell me that you are in the habit of drinking beer for breakfast every day?"

"Of course not. I have food with it."

"I am amazed that you have a single tooth in your head," I said severely— but risked a small sip. It *was* good beer: heavy-bodied and sweet, with just the right sour edge.

At this point, I noticed a certain tenseness in his posture, which the content of the conversation didn't account for. Slow-witted as I was, it took a moment for me to realize what was amiss.

"Oh. If you need to fart," I said, "don't trouble on my account. Go ahead."

He was sufficiently startled by my observation that he did.

"I do beg your pardon, madam!" he said, his fair skin flushing up to the hairline.

I tried not to laugh, but suppressed amusement jiggled the bed, and he went redder still.

"Would you have any hesitation about it were you in bed with a man?" I asked, out of idle curiosity.

He rubbed his knuckles against his mouth, the color fading a bit from his cheeks.

"Ah. Well, that would depend upon the man. By and large, though, no."

The man. I knew that Jamie was the man in his mind—just as he was in mine. At the moment, I wasn't disposed to resent it.

He knew what I was thinking, too.

"He offered me his body once. You knew that?" His voice was dry.

"I take it you didn't accept." I knew he hadn't but was more than curious to hear his side of that encounter.

"No. What I wanted from him was not that—or not entirely that," he added, with honesty. "I wanted all of it—and was young and proud enough to think that if I could not have that, then I would accept no less. And that, of course, he couldn't give me."

I was silent for a time, thinking. The window was open, and the long muslin curtains moved in the breeze.

"Did you regret it?" I asked. "Not taking him up on his offer, I mean?"

"Ten thousand times, at the very least," he assured me, breaking into a rueful grin. "At the same time . . . refusing him was one of the few acts of true nobility to which I would lay claim for myself. It's true, you know," he added, "selflessness does carry its own reward—for if I *had* taken him, that would have destroyed forever what did exist between us.

"To have given him instead the gift of my understanding, hard come by as it was," he added ironically, "left me with his friendship. So I am left with momentary regret on the one hand, but satisfaction on the other. And in the end it was the friendship that I valued most."

After a moment's silence, he turned to me.

"May I . . . You will think me odd."

"Well, you *are* a bit odd, aren't you?" I said tolerantly. "I don't really mind, though. What is it?"

He gave me a look, strongly suggesting that if one of us was indeed odd, he didn't think it was himself. Gentlemanly instincts suppressed any remark he might have made to this effect, though.

"Will you allow me to see you? Ah . . . naked?"

I closed one eye and looked at him.

"This certainly isn't the first time you've slept—I do mean *slept* with—a woman, is it?" I asked. He *had* been married, though I seemed to recall that he had spent much of his married life living separately from his wife.

He pursed his lips thoughtfully, as though trying to recall.

"Well, no. I do think it may be the first time I've done it entirely voluntarily, though."

"Oh, I *am* flattered!"

He glanced at me, smiling slightly.

"So you should be," he said quietly.

I was of an age, after all, where . . . Well, on the other hand, he presumably didn't have the same instinctive reactions that the majority of men did, in terms of feminine attractions. Which rather left open the question . . .

"Why?"

A shy smile touched the corner of his mouth, and he hitched himself up against the pillow.

"I . . . am not quite sure, to tell you the truth. Perhaps it is only an effort to reconcile my memories of last night with the . . . er . . . actuality of the experience?"

I felt a sharp jolt, as though he had punched me in the chest. He couldn't have known my first thoughts on waking and seeing him—that sharp, disorienting flash when I had thought he was Jamie, remembering so acutely Jamie's flesh and weight and ardor, and so urgently wanted him to be Jamie that I had succeeded for an instant in thinking that he was, only to be crushed like a grape at the realization that he wasn't, all my soft insides spurting out.

Had he felt or thought the same things, waking to find me there beside him?

"Or perhaps it is curiosity," he said, smiling a little more broadly. "I have not seen a naked woman in some time, bar Negro slaves at the docks in Charleston."

"How long is some time? Fifteen years, you said?"

"Oh, a good deal longer than that. Isobel—" He stopped abruptly, the smile vanishing. He hadn't mentioned his dead wife before.

"You never saw her naked?" I asked, with more than idle curiosity. He turned his face away a little, eyes cast down.

"Ah . . . no. It wasn't . . . She did not . . . No." He cleared his throat, then raised his eyes, looking into mine with an honesty raw enough to make me want to look away.

"I am naked to you," he said simply, and drew back the sheet.

Thus invited, I could hardly not look at him. And in all truth, I wanted to, out of simple curiosity. He was trim and lightly built, but muscular and solid. A little softness at the waist, but no fat—and softly furred with vigorous blond hair, darkening to brown at his crutch. It was a warrior's body; I was well acquainted with those. One side of his chest was heavily marked with crisscrossing scars, and there were others—a deep one across the top of one thigh, a jagged thing like a lightning bolt down his left forearm.

At least my own scars weren't visible, I thought, and before I could hesitate further, I pulled the sheet away from my own body. He looked at it with deep curiosity, smiling a little.

"You are very lovely," he said politely.

"For a woman of my age?"

His gaze passed over me dispassionately, not with any sense of judgment but rather with the air of a man of educated tastes evaluating what he saw in the light of years of seeing.

"No," he said finally. "Not for a woman of your age; not for a woman at all, I think."

"As what, then?" I asked, fascinated. "An object? A sculpture?" In a way, I could see that. Something like museum sculptures, perhaps: weathered statues, fragments of vanished culture, holding within them some remnant of the original inspiration, this remnant in some odd way magnified by the lens of age, sanctified by antiquity. I had never regarded myself in such a light, but I couldn't think what else he might mean.

"As my friend," he said simply.

"Oh," I said, very touched. "Thank you."

I waited, then drew the sheet up over both of us.

"Since we're friends . . ." I said, somewhat emboldened.

"Yes?"

"I only wondered . . . have you . . . been quite alone all this time? Since your wife died?"

He sighed, but smiled to let me know he didn't mind the question.

"If you really must know, I have for many years enjoyed a physical relationship with my cook."

"With . . . your cook?"

"Not with Mrs. Figg, no," he said hastily, hearing the horror in my voice. "I meant with my cook at Mount Josiah, in Virginia. His name is Manoke."

"Ma—oh!" I recalled Bobby Higgins telling me that Lord John retained an Indian named Manoke to cook for him.

"It is not merely the relief of necessary urges," he added pointedly, turning his head to meet my eyes. "There is true liking between us."

"I'm pleased to hear that," I murmured. "He, er, he's . . ."

"I have no idea whether his preference is solely for men. I rather doubt it— I was somewhat surprised when he made his desires known in re myself—but I am in no position to complain, whatever his tastes may be."

I rubbed a knuckle over my lips, not wanting to seem vulgarly curious— but vulgarly curious, all the same.

"You don't mind, if he . . . takes other lovers? Or he you, come to that?" I had a sudden uneasy apprehension. I did not intend that what had happened the night before should *ever* happen again. In fact, I was still trying to convince myself that it hadn't happened this time. Nor did I mean to go to Virginia with him. But what if I should and Lord John's household then assumed . . . I had visions of a jealous Indian cook poisoning my soup or lying in wait behind the necessary house with a tomahawk.

John himself seemed to be considering the matter, lips pursed. He had a heavy beard, I saw; the blond stubble softened his features and at the same time gave me an odd feeling of strangeness—I had so seldom seen him less than perfectly shaved and groomed.

"No. There is . . . no sense of possession in it," he said finally.

I gave him a look of patent disbelief.

"I assure you," he said, smiling a little. "It—well. Perhaps I can describe it best by analogy. At my plantation—it belongs to William, of course; I refer to it as mine only in the sense of habitation—"

I made a small polite sound in my throat, indicating that he might curtail his inclinations toward complete accuracy in the interests of getting on with it.

"At the plantation," he said, ignoring me, "there is a large open space at the rear of the house. It was a small clearing at first, and over the years I have enlarged it and finally made a lawn of it, but the edge of the clearing runs up to the trees. In the evenings, quite often, deer come out of the forest to feed at the edges of the lawn. Now and then, though, I see a particular deer. It's white, I suppose, but it looks as though it's made of silver. I don't know whether it comes only in the moonlight or whether it's only that I cannot see it save by moonlight—but it is a sight of rare beauty."

His eyes had softened, and I could see that he wasn't looking at the plaster ceiling overhead but at the white deer, coat shining in the moonlight.

"It comes for two nights, three—rarely, four—and then it's gone, and I don't see it again for weeks, sometimes months. And then it comes again, and I am enchanted once more."

He rolled onto his side in a rustle of bedclothes, regarding me.

"Do you see? I do not own this creature—would not, if I could. Its coming is a gift, which I accept with gratitude, but when it's gone, there is no sense of abandonment or deprivation. I'm only glad to have had it for so long as it chose to remain."

"And you're saying that your relationship with Manoke is the same. Does he feel that way about you, do you think?" I asked, fascinated. He glanced at me, clearly startled.

"I have no idea."

"You, um, don't . . . talk in bed?" I said, striving for delicacy.

His mouth twitched, and he looked away.

"No."

We lay in silence for a few moments, examining the ceiling.

"Have you ever?" I blurted.

"Have I what?"

"Had a lover that you talked to."

He cut his eyes at me.

"Yes. Perhaps not quite so frankly as I find myself talking to *you,* but, yes." He opened his mouth as though to say or ask something further, but instead breathed in, shut his mouth firmly, and let the air out slowly through his nose.

I knew—I couldn't not know—that he wanted very much to know what Jamie was like in bed, beyond what I had inadvertently shown him the night before. And I was obliged to admit to myself that I was very tempted to tell him, only in order to bring Jamie back to life for the brief moments while we talked. But I knew that such revelations would have a price: not only a later sense of betrayal of Jamie but a sense of shame at using John—whether he wished such usage or not. But if the memories of what had passed between Jamie and myself in our intimacy were no longer shared—still, they belonged only to that intimacy and were not mine to give away.

It occurred to me—belatedly, as so many things did these days—that John's intimate memories belonged to him, as well.

"I didn't mean to pry," I said apologetically.

He smiled faintly, but with real humor.

"I am flattered, madam, that you should entertain an interest in me. I know many more . . . conventional marriages in which the partners remain by preference in complete ignorance of each other's thoughts and histories."

With considerable startlement, I realized that there was now an intimacy between myself and John—unexpected and uninvited on both our parts, but . . . there it was.

The realization made me shy, and with that realization came a more practical one: to wit, that a person with functional kidneys cannot lie in bed drinking beer forever.

He noticed my slight shifting and rose at once himself, donning his banyan before fetching my own dressing gown—which, I saw with a sense of unease, some kindly hand had hung over a chair to warm before the fire.

"Where did that come from?" I asked, nodding at the silk robe he held for me.

"From your bedroom, I assume." He frowned at me for a moment before discerning what I meant. "Oh. Mrs. Figg brought it in when she built the fire."

"Oh," I said faintly. The thought of Mrs. Figg seeing me in Lord John's bed—doubtless out cold, disheveled, and snoring, if not actually drooling—was hideously mortifying. For that matter, the mere fact of my *being* in his bed was deeply embarrassing, no matter what I had looked like.

"We *are* married," he pointed out, with a slight edge to his voice.

"Er . . . yes. But . . ." A further thought came to me: perhaps this was not so unusual an occurrence for Mrs. Figg as I thought—had he entertained other women in his bed from time to time?

"Do you sleep with women? Er . . . not sleep, I mean, but . . ."

He stared at me, stopped in the act of untangling his hair.

"Not willingly," he said. He paused, then laid down his silver comb. "Is there anything else you would like to ask me," he inquired, with exquisite politeness, "before I allow the bootboy to come in?"

Despite the fire, the room was chilly, but my cheeks bloomed with heat. I drew the silk dressing gown tighter.

"Since you offer . . . I know Brianna told you what—what we are. Do you believe it?"

He considered me for a time without speaking. He didn't have Jamie's ability to mask his feelings, and I could see his mild irritation at my previous question fade into amusement. He gave me a small bow.

"No," he said, "but I give you my word that I will of course behave in all respects as if I did."

I stared at him until I became aware that my mouth was hanging unattractively open. I closed it.

"Fair enough," I said.

The odd little bubble of intimacy in which we had spent the last half hour had burst, and despite the fact that I had been the one asking nosy questions, I felt like a snail suddenly deprived of its shell—not merely naked but fatally exposed, emotionally as well as physically. Thoroughly rattled, I murmured a farewell and made for the door.

"Claire?" he said, a question in his voice.

I stopped, hand on the doorknob, feeling quite queer; he'd never called me by my name before. It took a small effort to look over my shoulder at him, but when I did, I found him smiling.

"Think of the deer," he said gently. "My dear."

I nodded, wordless, and made my escape. Only later, after I had washed—vigorously—dressed, and had a restorative cup of tea with brandy in it, did I make sense of this last remark.

Its coming is a gift, he'd said of the white deer, *which I accept with grati-tude.*

I breathed the fragrant steam and watched the tiny curls of tea leaf drift to the bottom of the cup. For the first time in weeks, I wondered just what the future might hold.

"Fair enough," I whispered, and drained the cup, the shreds of tea leaf strong and bitter on my tongue.

96

FIREFLY

I T WAS DARK. Darker than any place he'd ever been. Night outside wasn't really ever dark, even when the sky was cloudy, but this was darker than the back of Mandy's closet when they played hide 'n seek. There was a crack between the doors, he could feel it with his fingers, but no light came through it at all. It must still be night. Maybe there'd be light through the crack when it got morning.

But maybe Mr. Cameron would come back when it got morning, too. Jem moved a little away from the door, thinking that. He didn't think Mr. Cameron wanted to hurt him, exactly—he *said* he didn't, at least—but he might try to take him back up to the rocks and Jem wasn't going *there*, not for anything.

Thinking about the rocks hurt. Not as much as when Mr. Cameron pushed him against one and it . . . started, but it hurt. There was a scrape on his el-bow where he banged it, fighting back, and he rubbed at it now, because it was lots better to feel that than to think about the rocks. No, he told himself, Mr. Cameron *wouldn't* hurt him, because he'd pulled him back out of the rock when it tried to . . . He swallowed hard, and tried to think about some-thing else.

He sort of thought he knew where he was, only because he remembered Mam telling Da about the joke Mr. Cameron played on her, locking her in the tunnel, and she said the wheels that locked the doors sounded like bones be-ing chewed, and that's *just* what it sounded like when Mr. Cameron shoved him in here and shut the doors.

He was kind of shaking. It was cold in here, even with his jacket on. Not as cold as when he and Grandda got up before dawn and waited in the snow for the deer to come down and drink, but still pretty cold.

The air felt weird. He sniffed, trying to smell what was going on, like Grandda and Uncle Ian could. He could smell rock—but it was just plain old rock, not . . . *them*. Metal, too, and an oily sort of smell, kind of like a gas station. A hot kind of smell he thought was electricity. There was something in the air that wasn't a smell at all, but a kind of hum. That was power, he recognized that. Not quite the same as the big chamber Mam had showed him and Jimmy Glasscock, where the turbines lived, but sort of the same. Machines, then. He felt a little better. Machines felt friendly to him.

Thinking about machines reminded him that Mam said there was a train in here, a little train, and that made him feel lots better. If there was a train in here, it wasn't all just empty dark space. That hum maybe belonged to the train.

He put out his hands and shuffled along until he bumped into a wall. Then he felt around and walked along with one hand on the wall, found out he was going the wrong way when he walked face first into the doors and said, "Ow!"

His own voice made him laugh, but the laughter sounded funny in the big space and he quit and turned around to walk the other way, with his other hand on the wall to steer by.

Where was Mr. Cameron now? He hadn't said where he was going. Just told Jem to wait and he'd come back with some food.

His hand touched something round and smooth, and he jerked it back. It didn't move, though, and he put his hand on it. Power cables, running along the wall. Big ones. He could feel a little hum in them, same as he could when Da turned on the car's motor. It made him think of Mandy. She had that kind of quiet hum when she was sleeping, and a louder one when she was awake.

He wondered suddenly whether Mr. Cameron might have gone to take Mandy, and the thought made him feel scared. Mr. Cameron wanted to know how you got through the stones, and Jem couldn't tell him—but Mandy for sure couldn't be telling him, she was only a baby. The thought made him feel hollow, though, and he reached out, panicked.

There she was, though. Something like a little warm light in his head, and he took a breath. Mandy was OK, then. He was interested to find he could tell that with her far away. He'd never thought to try before, usually she was just right *there*, being a pain in the arse, and when him and his friends went off without her, he wasn't thinking about her.

His foot struck something and he stopped, reaching out with one hand. He didn't find anything and after a minute got up his nerve to let go of the wall and reach out further, then to edge out into the dark. His heart thumped and he started to sweat, even though he was still cold. His fingers stubbed metal and his heart leaped in his chest. The train!

He found the opening, and felt his way in on his hands and knees, and cracked his head on the thing where the controls were, standing up. That made him see colored stars and he said *"Ifrinn!"* out loud. It sounded funny, not so echoey now he was inside the train, and he giggled.

He felt around over the controls. They were like Mam said, just a switch and a little lever, and he pushed the switch. A red light popped into life, and made him jump. It made him feel lots better, though, just to see it. He could feel the electricity coming through the train, and that made him feel better, too. He pushed the lever, just a little, and was thrilled to feel the train move.

Where did it go? He pushed the lever a little more, and air moved past his face. He sniffed at it, but it didn't tell him anything. He was going away from the big doors, though—away from Mr. Cameron.

Maybe Mr. Cameron would go and try to find out about the stones from Mam or Da? Jem hoped he *would*. Da would settle Mr. Cameron's hash, he kent that for sure, and the thought warmed him. Then they'd come and find him and it would be OK. He wondered if Mandy could tell them where he was. She kent him the same way he kent her, and he looked at the little red light on the train. It glowed like Mandy, steady and warm-looking, and he felt good looking at it. He pushed the lever a little farther, and the train went faster into the dark.

97

NEXUS

RACHEL POKED SUSPICIOUSLY at the end of a loaf. The bread-seller, catching sight, turned on her with a growl.

"Here, don't you be touching that! You want it, it's a penny. You don't, go away."

"How old is this bread?" Rachel said, ignoring the young woman's glower. "It smells stale, and if it is as stale as it looks, I would not give thee more than half a penny for a loaf."

"It's no more than a day old!" The young woman pulled back the tray of loaves, indignant. "There'll be no fresh bread 'til Wednesday; my master can't get flour 'til then. Now, d'you want bread or not?"

"Hmm," said Rachel, feigning skepticism. Denny would have fits if he thought she was trying to cheat the woman, but there was a difference between paying a fair price and being robbed, and it was no more fair to allow the woman to cheat her than it was the other way about.

Were those crumbs on the tray? And were those tooth marks in the end of that loaf? She bent close, frowning, and Rollo whined suddenly.

"Does thee think the mice have been at these, dog?" she said to him. "So do I."

Rollo wasn't interested in mice, though. Ignoring both Rachel's question and the bread-seller's indignant reply, he was sniffing the ground with great industry, making an odd, high-pitched noise in his throat.

"Whatever ails thee, dog?" Rachel said, staring at this performance in consternation. She put a hand on his ruff and was startled at the vibration running through the great hairy frame.

Rollo ignored her touch as well as her voice. He was moving—almost running—in small circles, whining, nose to the ground.

"That dog's not gone mad, has he?" the baker's assistant asked, watching this.

"Of course not," Rachel said absently. "Rollo... *Rollo!*"

The dog had suddenly shot out of the shop, nose to the ground, and was heading down the street, half-trotting in his eagerness.

Muttering under her breath, Rachel seized her marketing basket and went after him.

To her alarm, he was already at the next street and vanished round the corner as she watched. She ran, calling after him, the basket bumping against her leg as she went and threatening to spill out the goods she'd already bought.

What was the matter with him? He'd never acted thus before. She ran faster, trying to keep him in sight.

"Wicked dog," she panted. "Serve thee right if I let thee go!" And yet she ran after him, calling. It was one thing for Rollo to leave the inn on his own hunting expeditions—he always returned. But she was well away from the inn and feared his being lost.

"Though if thy sense of smell is so acute as it seems, doubtless you could follow me back!" she panted, and then stopped dead, struck by a thought.

He was following a scent, so much was clear. But what kind of scent would make the dog do that? Surely no cat, no squirrel...

"Ian," she whispered to herself. "Ian."

She picked up her skirts and ran flat out in pursuit of the dog, heart hammering in her ears, even as she tried to restrain the wild hope she felt. The dog was still in sight, nose to the ground and tail held low, intent on his trail. He went into a narrow alley and she followed without hesitation, hopping and lurching in an effort to avoid stepping on the various squashy, nasty things in her path.

Any of these would normally have fascinated any dog, including Rollo— and yet he ignored them all, following his trail.

Seeing this, she realized suddenly what "dogged" really meant, and smiled to herself at the thought.

Could it be Ian? It was surely folly to think so; her hope would be dashed, and yet she could not conquer the conviction that had sprung up in her breast with the possibility. Rollo's tail flicked round the corner, and she dashed after, breathless.

If it was Ian, what could he be doing? The trail was leading them toward the edge of the town—not along the main road but quite out of the settled, prosperous part of the city, into an area of ramshackle houses and the informal camps of the British camp followers. A flock of chickens squawked and scattered at Rollo's approach, but he didn't pause. Now he was circling back, coming round the far side of a shed and out into a narrow street of packed dirt, curling like a tongue between rows of close-packed, ill-built houses.

She had a pain in her side and sweat was pouring down her face, but she, too, knew the meaning of "dogged" and kept on. The dog was drawing away from her, though; she would lose sight of him at any moment—her right shoe had rubbed the skin from her heel, and she felt as though her shoe was filling with blood, though likely this was imagination. She'd seen men with shoes filled with blood...

Rollo vanished at the end of the street, and she dashed madly after him, her stockings falling down and her petticoat drooping so she stepped on the hem and tore it. If she did find Ian, she'd have a thing to say to him, she thought. If she could speak by then.

There was no sign of the dog at the end of the street. She looked round wildly. She was at the back of a tavern; she could smell the hops from the brew tubs, and the stink of the midden, and voices came from the street on the other side of the building. Soldiers' voices—there was no mistaking the way soldiers talked, even if she couldn't make out the words—and she halted, heart in her throat.

But they hadn't caught someone; it was only the usual way men talked, casual, getting ready to do something. She caught the clink and jingle of equipment, the sound of boots on the pavement—

A hand seized her arm, and she swallowed the shriek before it could tear out of her throat, terrified of giving Ian away. But it wasn't Ian who had grabbed her. Hard fingers dug into her upper arm, and a tall, white-haired old man looked down at her with burning eyes.

IAN WAS FAMISHED. He had not eaten in more than twenty-four hours, unwilling to take time either to hunt or to find a farmhouse that might give him food. He had covered the twenty miles from Valley Forge in a daze, hardly noticing the distance.

Rachel was here. By some miracle, *here*, in Philadelphia. It had taken him some time to overcome the suspicion of Washington's soldiers, but at last a rather stout German officer with a big nose and a peering, friendly way had come along and expressed curiosity regarding Ian's bow. A brief demonstration of archery and a conversation in French—for the German officer had only the most rudimentary English—and he was at last able to inquire as to the whereabouts of a surgeon named Hunter.

This at first produced only blank looks, but von Steuben had taken a liking to Ian and sent someone to ask while he found a little bread. At long last, the someone had come back and said that there *was* a surgeon named Hunter, who was usually in camp, but who went now and then to Philadelphia to tend a private patient. Hunter's sister? The someone had shrugged.

But Ian knew the Hunters: where Denzell was, Rachel was. Granted, no one knew *where* in Philadelphia Dr. Hunter's private patient might be—there was some reserve about it, some hostility that Ian didn't understand but was much too impatient to unravel—but they were at least in Philadelphia.

And now so was Ian. He'd crept into the city just before dawn, threading his way silently through the camps that ringed the city, past the sleeping, blanket-wrapped forms and smothered, reeking campfires.

There was food in the city, food in abundance, and he paused for a moment of anticipatory bliss on the edge of the market square, deciding between fish fried in batter or a Cornish pasty. He had just stepped forward, money in hand, to the pasty-seller's stall, when he saw the woman look over his shoulder and her face change to a look of horror.

He whirled round and was knocked flat. There were screams and shouts, but these were lost in the mad slobber of Rollo's tongue licking every inch of his face, including the inside of his nose.

He whooped at that and half-sat up, fending off the ecstatic dog.

"A choin!" he said, and hugged the huge, wriggling creature in delight. He seized the dog's ruff in both hands then, laughing at the lolling tongue.

"Aye, I'm glad to see ye, too," he told Rollo. "But what have ye done wi' Rachel?"

FERGUS'S MISSING HAND itched. It hadn't done that for some time, and he wished it didn't now. He was wearing a bran-stuffed glove pinned to his sleeve rather than his useful hook—he was much too memorable with that—and it was impossible to rub his stump for relief.

Seeking distraction, he came out of the barn where he'd been sleeping and slouched casually toward a nearby campfire. Mrs. Hempstead nodded at him and picked up a tin mug, into which she ladled thin porridge and passed it over. Aye, well, he thought, there was some advantage to the glove, after all— he couldn't grasp the mug with it but could use it to cradle the hot cup against his chest without burning himself. And, he was pleased to discover, the heat killed the itch.

"Bon jour, madame," he said, with a polite bow, and Mrs. Hempstead smiled, despite her bedraggled tiredness. Her husband had been killed at Paoli, and she eked out a bare living for her three children by doing laundry for English officers. Fergus augmented her income in return for food and shelter. Her house had been taken by her husband's brother, but he had graciously allowed her and her family to sleep in the barn—one of three or four such bolt-holes Fergus employed in turn.

"There was a man looking out for you, sir," she said in a low voice, coming to give him a cup of water.

"Aye?" He kept himself from glancing round; if the man was still here, she would have told him. "Did you see this man?"

She shook her head.

"No, sir. 'Twas Mr. Jessop he spoke to, and Jessop told Mrs. Wilkins's youngest, who came by and said to my Mary. Jessop said he was a Scotchman, very tall, a fine-looking man. Thought he might have been a soldier once."

Excitement sprang up in Fergus's breast, hot as the porridge.

"Had he red hair?" he asked, and Mrs. Hempstead looked surprised.

"Well, I don't know as how the young'un said. Let me ask Mary, though."

"Do not trouble yourself, madame. I will ask myself." He swallowed the rest of the porridge, nearly scalding his throat, and handed back the cup.

Small Mary, carefully questioned, did not know whether the tall Scotchman had red hair; she hadn't seen him, and Tommy Wilkins didn't say. He had, however, told her where Mr. Jessop had seen the man, and Fergus, thanking Mary with his best Gallic courtesy—which made her blush—made his way into the city, heart beating fast.

RACHEL JERKED HER arm, but the old man merely tightened his grip, his thumb digging hard into the muscle below her shoulder.

"Let me go, Friend," she said calmly. "Thee has mistaken me for someone else."

"Oh, I think not," he said politely, and she perceived him to be a Scot. "Yon dog is yours, is he not?"

"No," she said, puzzled and beginning to be vaguely alarmed. "I am but minding him for a friend. Why? Has he eaten one of thy chickens? I will be pleased to pay thee for it. . . ." She leaned away, groping with her free hand for her purse, gauging the possibilities of escape.

"Ian Murray is the name of your friend," he said, and she was now genuinely alarmed to see he did not phrase this as a question.

"Let me go," she said, more strongly. "Thee has no right to detain me."

He paid no attention to this but looked intently into her face. His eyes were ancient, red-rimmed, and rheumy—but sharp as razors.

"Where is he?"

"In Scotland," she told him, and saw him blink with surprise. He bent a little to peer directly into her eyes.

"Do you love him?" the old man asked softly—but there was nothing soft about his tone.

"Let go!" She kicked at his shin, but he stepped aside with an adroitness that surprised her. His cloak swung aside as he moved, and she caught the gleam of metal in his belt. It was a small ax, and with the sudden memory of the dreadful house in New Jersey, she jerked back and shrieked out loud.

"Hush!" the old man snapped. "Come with me, lass." He put a large, dirty hand over her mouth and tried to pull her off her feet, but she struggled and kicked and got her mouth free long enough to scream again, as loudly as she could.

Startled exclamations, as well as the sound of heavy boots, came rapidly toward her.

"Rachel!" A familiar bellow reached her ears, and her heart bounded at the sound.

"William! Help me!"

William was running toward her, and some distance behind him were three or four British soldiers, muskets in hand. The old man said something in Gaelic, in tones of absolute amazement, and let go of her so suddenly that she staggered back, tripped on the torn hem of her petticoat, and sat down hard in the road.

The old man was backing away, but William was roused; he charged the old man, ducking his shoulder, clearly meaning to knock him off his feet. The old man had his ax in his hand, though, and Rachel screamed, "William!" at the top of her voice. But it was no good. There was a flash of light on metal and a sickening thud, and William lurched sideways, took two ungainly steps, and fell.

"William, William! Oh, Lord, oh, Lord . . ." She couldn't get to her feet but crawled to him as fast as she could, moaning. The soldiers were shouting, roaring, running after the old man, but she had no attention to spare for them. All she saw was William's face, ghastly pale, his eyes rolled up in his head so the whites of them showed, and the blood running dark, soaking his hair.

———————

I TUCKED WILLIAM up in bed, despite his protests, and bade him stay there. I was reasonably sure the protests were for Rachel's sake, since as soon as I had shooed her out the door, he allowed me to ease him back onto his pillow, his face pale and clammy under the bandage wrapped around his forehead.

"Sleep," I said. "You'll feel perfectly bloody in the morning, but you won't die."

"Thank you, Mother Claire," he murmured, with the faintest of smiles. "You're always such a comfort. Before you go, though . . ." Despite how ill he plainly felt, his hand on my arm was solid and firm.

"What?" I asked warily.

"The man who attacked Rachel. Do you have any idea who he might be?"

"Yes," I said reluctantly. "From her description, he's a man named Arch Bug. He used to live near us in North Carolina."

"Ah." His face was pale and clammy, but the deep blue eyes brightened a little with interest. "Is he mad?"

"Yes, I think so. He . . . lost his wife under very tragic circumstances, and I do believe it turned his wits to some degree." I did in fact think this was true, and the months and months since that winter night on the Ridge, spent alone in the woods, walking endless roads, listening for the vanished voice of his dead wife . . . If he had not been mad to start with, I thought he would be now. At the same time, I wasn't about to tell William the whole story. Not now, and possibly not ever.

"I'll speak to someone," he said, and suddenly gave a massive yawn. "Sorry. I'm . . . awfully sleepy."

"You have a concussion," I told him. "I'll come and wake you every hour. Speak to whom?"

"Officer," he said indistinctly, his eyes already closing. "Have men look for him. Can't let him . . . Rachel." Her name came out on a sigh as the big young body went slowly limp. I watched him for a moment to be sure he was soundly asleep. Then I kissed his forehead gently, thinking—with the same wrench of the heart with which I had kissed his sister at the same age—*God, you are so like him.*

Rachel herself was waiting on the landing, anxious and disheveled, though she'd made some effort to tidy her hair and cap.

"Will he be all right?"

"Yes, I think so. He has a mild concussion—you know what that is? Yes, of course you do. That, and I've put three stitches into his head. He'll have an ungodly headache tomorrow, but it was a glancing wound, nothing serious."

She sighed, slender shoulders drooping suddenly as the tension went out of them.

"Thank the Lord," she said, then glanced at me and smiled. "And thee, too, Friend Claire."

"My pleasure," I said sincerely. "Are you sure that you're all right? You should sit down and have something to drink." She wasn't hurt, but the shock of the experience had plainly marked her. I knew she wouldn't drink tea, as a matter of principle, but a little brandy, or even water . . .

"I'm fine. Better than fine." Relieved of her worry about William, she looked at me now, her face aglow. "Claire—he's here! Ian!"

"What? Where?"

"I don't know!" She glanced at the door to William's room and drew me a little way away, lowering her voice. "The dog—Rollo. He smelled something and went off after it like a shot. I ran after him, and that's when I ran into the poor madman. I know, thee will tell me he might chase anything, and he might—but, Claire, he has not come back! If he had not found Ian, he would have come back."

I caught her sense of excitement, though I was afraid to hope as much as she did. There were other things that could prevent the dog coming back, and none of them was good. One of them was Arch Bug.

Her description of him just now had taken me aback—and yet she was right, I realized. Ever since Mrs. Bug's funeral at Fraser's Ridge, I had seen Arch Bug only as a threat to Ian—and yet, with Rachel's words, I also saw the maimed, arthritic hands fumbling to pin a bird-shaped brooch to his loved wife's shroud. Poor madman, indeed.

And a bloody dangerous one.

"Come downstairs," I said to her, with another glance at William's door. "I need to tell you about Mr. Bug."

"OH, IAN," SHE whispered, when I had finished my account. "Oh, poor man." I didn't know whether this last referred to Mr. Bug or Ian, but she was right, either way. She didn't weep, but her face had gone pale and still.

"Both of them," I agreed. "All three, if you count Mrs. Bug."

She shook her head, in dismay rather than disagreement.

"Then that is why—" she said, but stopped.

"Why what?"

She grimaced a little, but glanced at me and gave a small shrug.

"Why he said to me that he was afraid I might die because I loved him."

"Yes, I expect so."

We sat for a moment over our steaming cups of lemon balm tea, contemplating the situation. At last, she looked up and swallowed.

"Does thee think Ian means to kill him?"

"I—well, I don't know," I said. "Certainly not to begin with; he felt terrible about what happened to Mrs. Bug—"

"About the fact that he killed her, thee means." She gave me a direct look; not one for easy evasions, Rachel Hunter.

"I do. But if he realizes that Arch Bug knows who you are, knows what you mean to Ian, and means you harm—and make no mistake about it, Rachel, he *does* mean you harm"—I took a swallow of hot tea and a deep breath—"yes, I think Ian would try to kill him."

She went absolutely still, the steam from her cup the only movement.

"He must not," she said.

"How do you mean to stop him?" I asked, out of curiosity.

She let out a long, slow breath, eyes fixed on the gently swirling surface of her tea.

"Pray," she said.

98

MISCHIANZA

May 18, 1778
Walnut Grove, Pennsylvania

IT HAD BEEN quite a long time since I'd seen a gilded roast peacock, and I hadn't really expected to see another. Certainly not in Philadelphia. Not that I should have been surprised, I thought, leaning closer to look—yes, it *did* have eyes made of diamonds. Not after the regatta on the Delaware, the three bands of musicians carried on barges, and the seventeen-gun salute from the warships on the river. The evening had been billed as a "mischianza." The word means "medley" in Italian—I was told—and in the current instance appeared to have been interpreted so as to allow the more creative souls in the British army and the Loyalist community free rein in the production of a gala celebration to honor General Howe, who had resigned as commander in chief, to be replaced by Sir Henry Clinton.

"I am sorry, my dear," John murmured at my side.

"For what?" I asked, surprised.

He was surprised in turn; his fair brows went up.

"Why, knowing your loyalties, I must suppose that it would be painful to you, to see so much . . ." He made a discreet motion of the wrist, indicating the lavish displays around us, which were certainly not limited to the peacock. " . . . so much pomp and extravagant expense devoted to—to—"

"Gloating?" I ended dryly. "I might—but I don't. I know what will happen."

He blinked at that, very much taken aback.

"What will happen? To whom?"

The sort of prophecy I possessed was seldom a welcome gift; in these circumstances, though, I took a rather grim pleasure in telling him.

"To you. The British army, I mean, not you personally. They'll lose the war, in three years' time. What price gilded peacocks then, eh?"

His face twitched, and he hid a smile.

"Indeed."

"Yes, indeed," I replied amiably. *"Fuirich agus chi thu."*

"What?" He stared at me.

"Gaelic," I said, with a small, deep twinge. "It means 'Wait and see.'"

"Oh, I shall," he assured me. "In the meantime, allow me to make known Lieutenant-Colonel Banastre Tarleton, of the British Legion." He bowed to a short, wiry young gentleman who had approached us, an officer of dragoons in a bottle-green uniform. "Colonel Tarleton, my wife."

"Lady John." The young man bowed low over my hand, brushing it with very red, very sensual lips. I wanted to wipe my hand on my skirt, but didn't. "Are you enjoying the festivities?"

"I'm looking forward to the fireworks." He had foxy, clever eyes that missed nothing, and his ripe red mouth twisted at this, but he smiled and left it, turning to Lord John. "My cousin Richard bids me give you his best regards, sir."

John's air of pleasant cordiality warmed into genuine pleasure at that.

"Richard Tarleton was my ensign at Crefeld," he explained to me before switching his attention back to the green dragoon. "How does he do these days, sir?"

They lapsed at once into a detailed conversation of commissions, promotions, campaigns, troop movements, and parliamentary politics, and I moved away. Not out of boredom, but rather out of tact. I had not promised John that I would refrain from passing on useful information; he hadn't asked it. But delicacy and a certain sense of obligation required that I at least not acquire such information through him, or directly under his nose.

I drifted slowly through the crowd in the ballroom, admiring the ladies' dresses, many of them imported from Europe, most of the rest modeled on such imports with such materials as could be obtained locally. The brilliant silks and sparkling embroidery were such a contrast to the homespuns and muslins I was accustomed to see that it seemed surreal—as though I'd found myself in a sudden dream. This impression was heightened by the presence among the crowd of a number of knights, dressed in surcoats and tabards, some with helms tucked under their arms—the afternoon's entertainment had included a mock jousting tournament—and a number of people in fantastic masks and extravagant costume, whom I assumed would later be part of some theatrical presentation.

My attention drifted back over the table where the gaudier viands were displayed: the peacock, tail feathers spread in a huge fan, occupied pride of place in the center of the table, but it was flanked by an entire roast boar on a bed of cabbage—this emitting a smell that made my stomach growl—and three enormous game pies, decorated with stuffed songbirds. Those reminded me suddenly of the King of France's dinner with the stuffed nightingales, and my appetite vanished at once in a puff of nausea and grief recalled.

I shifted my gaze hastily back to the peacock, swallowing. I wondered idly how difficult it might be to abstract those diamond eyes and whether someone was keeping an eye on them. Almost certainly so, and I looked to see if

I could spot him. Yes, there he was, a uniformed soldier standing in a nook between the table and the huge mantelpiece, eyes alert.

I didn't need to steal diamonds, though, I thought, and my stomach curled a little. I had them. John had given me a pair of diamond earrings. When the time came for me to leave . . .

"Mother Claire!"

I had been feeling pleasantly invisible and, startled out of this delusion, now glanced across the room to see Willie, his disheveled head sticking out from the red-crossed tabard of a Knight Templar, waving enthusiastically.

"I do wish you could think of something else to call me," I said, reaching his side. "I feel as though I ought to be swishing round in a habit with a rosary at my waist."

He laughed at that, introduced the young lady making goo-goo eyes at him as Miss Chew, and offered to get us both an ice. The temperature in the ballroom was rising eighty, at least, and sweat darkened not a few of the bright silks.

"What an elegant gown," Miss Chew said politely. "Is it from England?"

"Oh," I said, rather taken aback. "I don't know. But thank you," I added, looking down at myself for the first time. I hadn't really noticed the gown, beyond the mechanical necessities of getting into it; dressing was no more than a daily nuisance, and so long as nothing was too tight or chafed, I didn't care what I wore.

John had presented me with the gown this morning, as well as summoning a hairdresser to deal with me from the neck up. I'd shut my eyes, rather shocked at how enjoyable the man's fingers felt in my hair—but still more shocked when he handed me a looking glass and I saw a towering confection of curls and powder, with a tiny ship perched in it. Full-rigged.

I'd waited 'til he left, then hurriedly brushed it all out and pinned it up as simply as I could. John had given me a look, but said nothing. Concerned with my head, though, I hadn't taken any time to look at myself below the neck, and was vaguely pleased now to see how well the cocoa-colored silk fit me. Dark enough that it might not show sweat stains, I thought.

Miss Chew was watching William like a cat eyeing up a fat, handsome mouse, frowning a little as he stopped to flirt with two other young ladies.

"Will Lord Ellesmere be remaining long in Philadelphia?" she asked, eyes still on him. "I believe someone told me that he is not to go with General Howe. I do hope that is the case!"

"That's right," I said. "He surrendered with General Burgoyne; those troops are all on parole and are meant to go back to England, but there's some administrative reason why they can't embark just yet." I knew William was hoping to be exchanged, so that he could fight again, but didn't mention it.

"Really," she said, brightening. "What splendid news! Perhaps he will be here for my ball next month. Naturally, it will not be quite so good as this one"—she arched her neck a little, tilting her head toward the musicians who had begun to play at the far end of the room—"but Major André says he will lend his skill to paint the backdrops so we may have tableaux, so it will be—"

"I'm sorry," I interrupted, "did you say Major André? Major . . . John André?"

She glanced at me in surprise, half-annoyed at my interruption. "Of course. He designed the costumes for the joust today and has written the play they will do later. Look, there he is, speaking with Lady Clinton."

I looked where she pointed with her fan, feeling a sudden chill wash through me, despite the heat in the room.

Major André was the center of a group, men and women both, laughing and gesturing, plainly the focus of everyone's attention. He was a handsome young man in his late twenties, his uniform tailored to perfection and his face vivid, flushed with heat and pleasure.

"He seems . . . very charming," I murmured, wanting to look away from him, but unable to do so.

"Oh, yes!" Miss Chew was enthusiastic. "He and I and Peggy Shippen did almost all of the work for the mischianza together—he's a marvel, always with such good ideas, and he plays the flute just delightful. So sad that Peggy's father would not let her come tonight—quite unfair!" I thought there was an underlying tone of satisfaction to her voice, though; she was quite pleased not to have to share the limelight with her friend.

"Do let me present him to you," she said suddenly, and folding her fan, slipped her arm through mine. I was taken entirely by surprise and couldn't think of a way to extricate myself before I found myself towed into the group around André, with Miss Chew chattering brightly to him, laughing up at him, her hand familiarly on his arm. He smiled at her, then switched his gaze to me, his eyes warm and lively.

"I am enchanted, Lady John," he said, in a soft, husky voice. "Your servant, madame."

"I—yes," I said abruptly, quite forgetting the usual form. "You—yes. Glad to meet you!" I pulled my hand out of his before he could kiss it, disconcerting him, and backed away. He blinked, but Miss Chew reclaimed his attention at once, and I turned away, going to stand near the door where there was at least a little air. I was covered in cold sweat and vibrating in every limb.

"Oh, there you are, Mother Claire!" Willie popped up beside me, two half-melted ices in his hands, sweating freely. "Here."

"Thank you." I took one, noting absently that my fingers were nearly as cold as the misted silver cup.

"Are you quite all right, Mother Claire?" He bent down to look at me, concerned. "You look quite pale. As though you'd seen a ghost." He winced in brief apology at this clumsy reference to death, but I made an effort to smile back. Not a terribly successful effort, because he was right. I had just seen a ghost.

Major John André was the British officer with whom Benedict Arnold—hero of Saratoga and still a legendary patriot—would eventually conspire. And the man who would go to the gallows for his part in that conspiracy, sometime in the next three years.

"Had you better sit down for a bit?" Willie was frowning in concern, and I made an effort to shake off my cold horror. I didn't want him offering to leave the ball to see me home; he was plainly having a good time. I smiled at him, barely feeling my lips.

"No, that's all right," I said. "I think . . . I'll just step outside for some air."

A BUTTERFLY IN A BUTCHER'S YARD

ROLLO LAY UNDER a bush, noisily devouring the remains of a squirrel he'd caught. Ian sat on a rock, contemplating him.

The city of Philadelphia lay just out of sight; he could smell the haze of fire, the stink of thousands of people living cheek by jowl. Could hear the clop and rattle of people going there, on the road that lay only a few hundred yards away. And somewhere, within a mile of him, hidden in that mass of buildings and people, was Rachel Hunter.

He wanted to step out on the road, stride down it into the heart of Philadelphia, and begin taking the place apart, brick by brick, until he found her.

"Where do we begin, *a cù*?" he said to Rollo. "The printshop, I suppose."

He'd not been there, but supposed it would not be hard to find. Fergus and Marsali would give him shelter—and food, he thought, feeling his stomach growl—and perhaps Germain and the girls could help him hunt for Rachel. Perhaps Auntie Claire could . . . Well, he knew she wasn't a witch or a fairy, but there was no doubt at all in his mind that she was something, and perhaps she would be able to find Rachel for him.

He waited for Rollo to finish his meal, then rose, an extraordinary sense of warmth suffusing him, though the day was overcast and cool. Could he find her that way? he wondered. Walk through the streets, playing the children's game of "warmer, colder," growing steadily warmer as he approached her more closely, coming to her at last just before he burst into flame?

"You could help, ye know," he said reproachfully to Rollo. He'd tried getting Rollo to backtrack to her at once when the dog had found him, but the dog had been so berserk with joy at Ian's return that there was no speaking to him. That was a thought, though—if they somehow ran across her trail, Rollo might take it up, now that he was more sober-minded.

He smiled crookedly at that thought; the bulk of the British army was encamped at Germantown, but there were thousands of soldiers quartered in Philadelphia itself. As well ask the dog to follow the scent of a butterfly through a butcher's yard.

"Well, we won't find her, sitting here," he said to Rollo, and stood up. "Come on, dog."

100

LADY IN WAITING

I WAS WAITING FOR THINGS to make sense. Nothing did. I had lived in John Grey's house, with its gracious stair and crystal chandelier, its Turkey rugs and fine china, for nearly a month, and yet I woke each day with no idea where I was, reaching across an empty bed for Jamie.

I could not believe he was dead. *Could* not. I shut my eyes at night and heard him breathing slow and soft in the night beside me. Felt his eyes on me, humorous, lusting, annoyed, alight with love. Turned half a dozen times a day, imagining I heard his step behind me. Opened my mouth to say something to him—and more than once really *had* spoken to him, realizing only when I heard the words dwindle on the empty air that he was not there.

Each realization crushed me anew. And yet none reconciled me to his loss. I had, with shrinking mind, envisioned his death. He would so have hated drowning. Of all ways to die! I could only hope that the sinking of the ship had been violent, and that he had gone unconscious into the water. Because otherwise . . . he couldn't give up, he wouldn't have. He would have swum and kept swimming, endless miles from any shores, alone in the empty deep, swum stubbornly because he could not give up and let himself sink. Swum until that powerful frame was exhausted, until he could not lift a hand again, and then . . .

I rolled over and pressed my face hard into my pillow, heart squeezing with horror.

"What a bloody, bloody *waste*!" I said into the feathers, clenching handfuls of pillow in my fists as hard as I could. If he'd died in battle, at least . . . I rolled back over and shut my eyes, biting my lip until the blood came.

At last my breathing slowed, and I opened my eyes on darkness again, and resumed waiting. Waiting for Jamie.

Some time later, the door opened, and a slice of light from the hallway fell into the room. Lord John came in, setting a candle on the table by the door, and approached the bed. I didn't look at him, but knew he was looking down at me.

I lay on my bed, staring at the ceiling. Or, rather, looking through it to the sky. Dark, full of stars and emptiness. I hadn't bothered to light a candle, but I didn't curse the darkness, either. Only looked into it. Waiting.

"You are very lonely, my dear," he said, with great gentleness, "and I know it. Will you not let me bear you company, for a little time at least?"

I said nothing, but did move over a little and did not resist when he lay down beside me and gathered me carefully into his arms.

I rested my head on his shoulder, grateful for the comfort of simple touch and human warmth, though it didn't reach the depths of my desolation.

Try not to think. Accept what there is; don't think about what there is not.

I lay still, listening to John breathe. He breathed differently than Jamie, shallower, faster. A very slight catch in his breath.

It dawned on me, slowly, that I was not alone in my desolation or my loneliness. And that I knew all too well what had happened last time this state of affairs had become obvious to both of us. Granted, we were not drunk, but I thought he couldn't help but remember it, as well.

"Do you . . . wish me to . . . comfort you?" he said quietly. "I do know how, you know." And, reaching down, he moved a finger very slowly, in such a place and with such exquisite delicacy that I gasped and jerked away.

"I know you do." I did have a moment's curiosity as to how exactly he had learned, but was not about to ask. "It's not that I don't appreciate the thought—I do," I assured him, and felt my cheeks flush hotter. "It's—it's only—"

"That you would feel unfaithful?" he guessed. He smiled a little sadly. "I understand."

There was a long silence then. And a sense of growing awareness.

"You wouldn't?" I asked. He lay quite still, as if asleep, but wasn't.

"A standing cock is quite blind, my dear," he said at last, eyes still shut. "Surely you know that, physician that you are."

"Yes," I said, "I do know that." And taking him gently but firmly in hand, I dealt with him in tender silence, avoiding any thought of whom he might see in his mind's eye.

COLENSO BARAGWANATH ran as though his boot heels were on fire. He burst into the Fox tavern near the foot of State Street, and barreled through the taproom into the cardroom at the back.

"They found him," he panted. "The ol' man. Ax. With the ax."

Captain Lord Ellesmere was already rising to his feet. To Colenso, he looked some eight feet tall, and awful in aspect. The place where the doctor had stitched his head was bristly with new hair, but the black stitching still showed. His eyes might have been shooting flames, but Colenso was afraid to look too closely. His chest heaved from running and he was out of breath, but he couldn't have thought of a thing to say, even so.

"Where?" said the captain. He spoke very softly, but Colenso heard him and backed toward the door, pointing. The captain picked up the pair of pistols he had laid aside, and putting them in his belt, came toward him.

"Show me," he said.

RACHEL SAT ON the tall stool behind the printshop's counter, head on her hand. She'd wakened with a sense of pressure in her head, probably from the impending storm, and it had ripened into a throbbing headache. She would rather have gone back to Friend John's house, to see if Claire might have a tea that would help, but she'd promised Marsali that she would come and mind the shop while her friend took the children to the cobbler to have their shoes mended and Henri-Christian fitted for a pair of boots, for his feet were too short and wide to fit his sisters' outgrown shoes.

At least the shop was quiet. Only one or two folk had come in, and only one of those had spoken to her—asking the way to Slip Alley. She rubbed her stiff neck, sighing, and let her eyes close. Marsali would be back soon. Then she could go and lie down with a wet rag on her head, and—

The bell above the printshop door went *ting!* and she straightened up, a welcoming smile forming on her face. She saw the visitor and the smile died.

"Leave," she said, scrambling off the stool, measuring the distance between her and the door into the house. "Leave this minute." If she could get through, and out the back—

"Stand still," said Arch Bug, in a voice like rusty iron.

"I know what thee means to do," she said, backing up a step. "And I do not blame thee for thy grief, thy rage. But thee must know it is not right what thee intend, the Lord cannot wish thee to—"

"Be quiet, lass," he said, and his eyes rested on her with an odd sort of gentleness. "Not yet. We'll wait for him."

"For . . . him?"

"Aye, him." With that, he lunged across the counter and seized her arm. She screamed and struggled but could not get loose, and he flipped up the flap in the counter and dragged her through, pushing her hard against the table of books so that the stacks wobbled and fell with papery thumps.

"Thee cannot hope to—"

"I have nay hope," he interrupted, quite calm. The ax was in his belt; she saw it, bare and silver. "I need none."

"Thee will surely die," she said, and made no effort to keep her voice from trembling. "The soldiers will take thee."

"Oh, aye, they will." His face softened a little then, surprisingly. "I shall see my wife again."

"I could not counsel suicide," she said, edging as far away as she could get. "But if thee does intend to die in any case, why does thee insist upon—upon staining thy death, thy soul, with violence?"

"Ye think vengeance a stain?" The beetling white brows lifted. "It is a glory, lass. My glory, my duty to my wife."

"Well, certainly not mine," she said heatedly. "Why should I be forced to serve thy beastly vengeance? I have done nothing to thee or thine!"

He wasn't listening. Not to her, at least. He had turned a little, his hand going to his ax, and smiled at the sound of racing footsteps.

"Ian!" she shrieked. "Don't come in!!"

He came in, of course. She grasped a book and flung it at the old man's head, but he dodged it easily and grabbed her by the wrist once more, his ax in hand.

"Let her go," said Ian, hoarse with running. His chest heaved and sweat was running down his face; she could smell him, even above the old man's musty reek. She jerked her hand out of Arch Bug's clasp, speechless with horror.

"Don't kill him," she said, to both of them. Neither of them listened.

"I told ye, did I not?" Arch said to Ian. He sounded reasonable, a teacher pointing out the proof of a theorem. *Quod erat demonstrandum. Q.E.D.*

"Get away from her," Ian said.

His hand hovered above his knife, and Rachel, choking on the words, said, "Ian! Don't. Thee must not. Please!"

Ian gave her a look of furious confusion, but she held his eyes, and his hand dropped away. He took a deep breath and then a quick step to the side. Bug whirled to keep him in range of the ax, and Ian slid fast in front of Rachel, screening her with his body.

"Kill me, then," he said deliberately to Bug. "Do it."

"No!" Rachel said. "That is not what I—no!"

"Come here, lass," Arch said, and put out his good hand, beckoning. "Dinna be afraid. I'll make it fast."

Ian shoved her hard, so she slammed into the wall and knocked her head, and braced himself before her, crouched and waiting. Unarmed, because she'd asked it.

"Ye'll fucking kill me first," he said, in a conversational tone.

"No," said Arch Bug. "Ye'll wait your turn." The old eyes measured him, cold and clever, and the ax moved a little, eager.

Rachel shut her eyes and prayed, finding no words but praying all the same, in a frenzy of fear. She heard a sound and opened them.

A long gray blur shot through the air, and in an instant, Arch Bug was on the ground, Rollo on top of him, snarling and snapping at the old man's throat. Old he might be but still hale, and he had the strength of desperation. His good hand seized the dog's throat, pushing back, holding off the slavering jaws, and a long, sinewy arm flung out, ax gripped in a maimed fist, and rose.

"No!" Ian dove forward, knocking Rollo aside, grappling for the hand that held the ax, but it was too late; the blade came down with a *chunk!* that made Rachel's vision go white, and Ian screamed.

She was moving before she could see, and screamed herself when a hand suddenly seized her shoulder and hurled her backward. She hit the wall and slid down it, landing winded and openmouthed. There was a writhing ball of limbs, fur, clothes, and blood on the floor before her. A random shoe cracked against her ankle and she scuttled away crabwise, staring.

There seemed to be blood everywhere. Spattered against the counter and the wall, smeared on the floor, and the back of Ian's shirt was soaked with red and clinging so she saw the muscles of his back straining beneath it. He was kneeling half atop a struggling Arch Bug, grappling one-handed for the ax, his left arm hanging limp, and Arch was stabbing at his face with stiffened fingers, trying to blind him, while Rollo darted eellike and bristling into the mass of straining limbs, growling and snapping. Fixed on this spectacle, she was only dimly aware of someone standing behind her but looked up, uncomprehending, when his foot touched her bum.

"Is there something about you that attracts men with axes?" William asked crossly. He sighted carefully along his pistol's barrel, and fired.

101

REDIVIVUS

I WAS PINNING up my hair for tea when there was a scratch at the bedroom door.

"Come," John called, in the act of pulling on his boots. The door opened cautiously, revealing the odd little Cornish boy who sometimes served as William's orderly. He said something to John, in what I assumed to be English, and handed him a note. John nodded kindly and dismissed him.

"Could you understand what he said?" I asked curiously, as he broke the seal with his thumb.

"Who? Oh, Colenso? No, not a word," he said absently, and pursed his lips in a soundless whistle at whatever he was reading.

"What is it?" I asked.

"A note from Colonel Graves," he said, carefully refolding it. "I wonder if—"

There was another knock at the door, and John frowned at it.

"Not now," he said. "Come back later."

"Well, I would," said a polite voice in a Scottish accent. "But there's some urgency, ken?"

The door opened, and Jamie stepped in, closing it behind him. He saw me, stood stock-still for an instant, and then I was in his arms, the overwhelming warmth and size of him blotting out in an instant everything around me.

I didn't know where my blood had gone. Every drop had left my head, and flickering lights danced before my eyes—but none of it was supplying my legs, which had abruptly dissolved under me.

Jamie was holding me up and kissing me, tasting of beer and his beard stubble rasping my face, his fingers buried in my hair, and my breasts warmed and swelled against his chest.

"Oh, there it is," I murmured.

"What?" he asked, breaking off for a moment.

"My blood." I touched my tingling lips. "Do that again."

"Oh, I will," he assured me. "But there are a number of English soldiers in the neighborhood, and I think—"

The sound of pounding came from below, and reality snapped back into place like a rubber band. I stared at him and sat down very suddenly, my heart pounding like a drum.

"Why the bloody hell aren't you dead?"

He lifted one shoulder in a brief shrug, the corner of his mouth turning up. He was very thin, brown-faced, and dirty; I could smell his sweat and the grime of long-worn clothes. And the faint whiff of vomit—he'd not been long off a boat.

"Delay for a few seconds longer, Mr. Fraser, and you may well go back to being dead." John had gone to the window, peering down into the street. He turned, and I saw that his face was pale but glowing like a candle.

"Aye? They were a bit faster than I thought, then," Jamie said ruefully, going to look out. He turned from the window and smiled. "It's good to see ye, John—if only for the moment."

John's answering smile lit his eyes. He reached out a hand and touched Jamie's arm, very briefly, as though wishing to assure himself that he was in fact solid.

"Yes," he said, reaching then for the door. "But come. Down the back stair. Or there's a hatchway to the attic—if you can get onto the roof—"

Jamie looked at me, his heart in his eyes.

"I'll come back," he said. "When I can." He lifted a hand toward me but stopped with a grimace, turned abruptly to follow John, and they were gone, the sound of their footsteps nearly drowned by the noises from downstairs. I heard the door open below and a rough male voice demanding entrance. Mrs. Figg, bless her intransigent little heart, was having none of it.

I'd been sitting like Lot's wife, shocked into immobility, but at the sound of Mrs. Figg's rich expletives was galvanized into action.

My mind was so stunned by the events of the last five minutes that it was, paradoxically, quite clear. There was simply no room in it for thoughts, speculations, relief, joy, or even worry—the only mental faculty I still possessed, apparently, was the ability to respond to an emergency. I snatched my cap, crammed it on my head, and started for the door, stuffing my hair up into it as I went. Mrs. Figg and I together could surely delay the soldiers long enough . . .

This scheme would probably have worked, save that, as I rushed out onto the landing, I ran into Willie—literally, as he came bounding up the stair and collided heavily with me.

"Mother Claire! Where's Papa? There are—" He had seized me by the arms as I reeled backward, but his concern for me was superseded by a sound from the hall beyond the landing. He glanced toward the sound—then let go of me, his eyes bulging.

Jamie stood at the end of the hall, some ten feet away; John stood beside him, white as a sheet, and his eyes bulging as much as Willie's were. This resemblance to Willie, striking as it was, was completely overwhelmed by Jamie's own resemblance to the Ninth Earl of Ellesmere. William's face had hardened and matured, losing all trace of childish softness, and from both ends of the short hall, deep blue Fraser cat-eyes stared out of the bold, solid bones of the MacKenzies. And Willie was old enough to shave on a daily basis; he *knew* what he looked like.

Willie's mouth worked, soundless with shock. He looked wildly at me, back at Jamie, back at me—and saw the truth in my face.

"Who are you?" he said hoarsely, wheeling on Jamie.

I saw Jamie draw himself slowly upright, ignoring the noise below.

"James Fraser," he said. His eyes were fixed on William with a burning intensity, as though to absorb every vestige of a sight he would not see again. "Ye kent me once as Alex MacKenzie. At Helwater."

William blinked, blinked again, and his gaze shifted momentarily to John.

"And who—who the *bloody* hell am *I*?" he demanded, the end of the question rising in a squeak.

John opened his mouth, but it was Jamie who answered.

"You are a stinking Papist," he said, very precisely, "and your baptismal name is James." The ghost of regret crossed his face and then was gone. "It was the only name I had a right to give ye," he said quietly, eyes on his son. "I'm sorry."

Willie's left hand slapped at his hip, reflexively looking for a sword. Finding nothing, he slapped at his chest. His hands were shaking so badly that he couldn't manage buttons; he simply seized the fabric and ripped open his shirt, reached in and fumbled for something. He pulled it over his head and, in the same motion, hurled the object at Jamie.

Jamie's reflexes brought his hand up automatically, and the wooden rosary smacked into it, the beads swinging, tangled in his fingers.

"God damn you, sir," Willie said, voice trembling. "God damn you to hell!" He half-turned blindly, then spun on his heel to face John. "And you! You *knew*, didn't you? God damn you, too!"

"William—" John reached out a hand to him, helpless, but before he could say anything more, there was a sound of voices in the hall below and heavy feet on the stair.

"Sassenach—keep him back!" Jamie's voice reached me through the hubbub, sharp and clear. By sheer reflex, I obeyed and seized Willie by the arm. He glanced at me, mouth open, completely nonplused.

"What—" His voice was drowned by the thunder of feet on the stairs and a triumphant whoop from the redcoat in front.

"There he is!"

Suddenly the landing was thronged with bodies pushing and shoving, trying to get past Willie and me into the hallway. I clung like grim death, despite the jostling and despite Willie's own belated efforts to free himself.

All at once the shouting stopped, and the press of bodies relaxed just a bit. My cap had been knocked over my eyes in the struggle, and I let go of Willie's arm with one hand in order to pull it off. I dropped it on the floor. I had a feeling that my status as a respectable woman wasn't going to be important for much longer.

Brushing disheveled hair out of my eyes with a forearm, I resumed my grip on Willie, though this was largely unnecessary, as he seemed turned to stone. The redcoats were shifting on their feet, clearly ready to charge but inhibited by something. I turned a little and saw Jamie, one arm wrapped around John Grey's throat, holding a pistol to John's temple.

"One step more," he said, calmly but loud enough to be easily heard, "and I put a ball through his brain. D'ye think I've anything to lose?"

Actually, given that Willie and myself were standing right in front of him, I rather thought he did—but the soldiers didn't know that, and judging from the expression on Willie's face, he would have torn his tongue out by the roots rather than blurt out the truth. I also thought he didn't particularly care at the moment if Jamie *did* kill John and then die in a fusillade of bullets. His arm was like iron under my grip; he'd have killed them both himself, if he could.

There was a murmur of menace from the men around me and a shifting of bodies, men readying themselves—but no one moved.

Jamie glanced once at me, face unreadable, then moved toward the back stair, half-dragging John with him. They vanished from view, and the corporal next to me sprang into action, turning and gesturing to his men on the stair.

"Round back! Hurry!"

"Hold!" Willie had come abruptly to life. Jerking his arm away from my slackened grip, he turned on the corporal. "Have you men posted at the back of the house?"

The corporal, noticing Willie's uniform for the first time, straightened himself and saluted.

"No, sir. I didn't think—"

"Idiot," Willie said shortly.

"Yes, sir. But we can catch them if we hurry, sir." He was rocking up onto his toes as he spoke, in an agony to be gone.

Willie's fists were clenched, and so were his teeth. I could see the thoughts crossing his face, as clearly as if they'd been printed on his forehead in movable type.

He didn't *think* Jamie would shoot Lord John but wasn't sure of it. If he sent men after them, there was a decent chance that the soldiers would catch up to them—which in turn meant some chance that one or both would die. And if neither died but Jamie was captured—there was no telling what he might say or to whom. Too much risk.

With a faint sense of déjà vu, I saw him make these calculations, then turn to the corporal.

"Return to your commander," he said calmly. "Let him know that Colonel Grey has been taken hostage by . . . by the rebels, and ask him to notify all guard posts. I am to be informed at once of any news."

There was a displeased murmur from the soldiers on the landing but nothing that could actually be called insubordination, and even this died away in the face of William's glare. The corporal's teeth set briefly in his lip, but he saluted.

"Yes, sir." He turned smartly on his heel, with a peremptory gesture that sent the soldiers clumping heavily down the stair.

Willie watched them go. Then, as though suddenly noticing it, he bent and picked up my cap from the floor. Kneading it between his hands, he gave me a long, speculative look. The next little while was going to be interesting, I saw.

I didn't care. While I was quite sure that Jamie wouldn't shoot John under any circumstances, I was under no misapprehensions about the danger to either of them. I could smell it; the scent of sweat and gunpowder hung thick in the air on the landing, and the soles of my feet still vibrated from the slam of the heavy door below. None of it mattered.

He was alive.

So was I.

GREY WAS STILL IN his shirtsleeves; the rain had cut through the cloth to his flesh.

Jamie went to the shed's wall and put his eye to a crack between the boards. He raised a hand, adjuring silence, and John stood waiting, shivering, as the sound of hooves and voices went past. Who might it be? Not soldiers; there was no sound of brass, no jingling spurs or arms. The sounds faded, and Jamie turned back. He frowned, noticing for the first time that Grey was wet through, and, taking the cloak from his shoulders, wrapped it round him.

The cloak was damp, too, but made of wool, and Jamie's body heat lingered in it. Grey closed his eyes for an instant, embraced.

"May I know what it is that you've been doing?" Grey inquired, opening them.

"When?" Jamie gave him a half smile. "Just now, or since I saw ye last?"

"Just now."

"Ah." Jamie sat down on a barrel and leaned back—gingerly—against the wall.

Grey noted with interest that the sound was nearly "ach," and deduced that Fraser had spent much of his time of late with Scots. He also observed that Fraser's lips were pursed in thought. The slanted blue eyes cut in his direction.

"Ye're sure ye want to know? It's likely better if ye don't."

"I put considerable trust in your judgment and discretion, Mr. Fraser," Grey said politely, "but somewhat more in my own. I'm sure you will forgive me."

Fraser appeared to find that funny; the wide mouth twitched, but he nodded and produced a small packet, sewn in oilskin, from inside his shirt.

"I was observed in the act of accepting this from my foster son," he said. "The person who saw me followed me to an ordinary, then went to fetch the nearest company of soldiers whilst I was refreshing myself. Or so I assume. I saw them coming down the street, supposed that it might be myself they sought, and . . . left."

"You are familiar, I suppose, with the trope regarding the guilty who flee when no man pursues? How do you know they were after you to begin with and not merely interested by your abrupt departure?"

The half smile flickered again, this time tinged with rue.

"Call it the instinct of the hunted."

"Indeed. I am surprised that you allowed yourself to be cornered, as it were, your instincts being what they are."

"Aye, well, even foxes grow old, do they not?" Fraser said dryly.

"Why the devil did you come to my house?" Grey demanded, suddenly irritable. "Why did you not run for the edge of town?"

Fraser looked surprised.

"My wife," he said simply, and it occurred to Grey, with a pang, that it had not been inadvertence or lack of caution that had impelled Jamie Fraser to come to his house, even with soldiers on his heels. He'd come for her. For Claire.

Jesus! He thought with sudden panic. *Claire!*

But there was no time to say anything, even could he have thought what to say. Jamie rose and, taking the pistol from his belt, beckoned him to come.

They went down an alleyway, then through the backyard of a pub, squeezing past the open brew tub, its surface pocked by falling rain. Smelling faintly of hops, they emerged into a street and slowed down. Jamie had gripped his wrist throughout this journey, and Lord John felt his hand beginning to go numb but said nothing. They passed two or three groups of soldiers, but he walked with Jamie, matching him stride for stride, keeping his eyes front. There was no conflict of heart and duty here: to shout for help might result in Jamie's death; it almost surely would result in the death of at least one soldier.

Jamie kept his pistol out of sight, half hidden in his coat but in his hand, putting it back into his belt only when they reached the place where he had left his horse. It was a private house; he left Grey by himself on the porch for a moment with a muttered "Stay here," while he disappeared inside.

A strong sense of self-preservation urged Lord John to run, but he didn't and was rewarded when Jamie emerged again and smiled a little, seeing him. *So you weren't sure I'd stay? Fair enough,* Grey thought. He hadn't been sure, either.

"Come on, then," Jamie said, and with a jerk of his head beckoned Grey to follow him to the stable, where he quickly saddled and bridled a second horse, handing the reins to Grey before mounting his own.

"Pro forma," he said politely to Grey, and, drawing the pistol, pointed it at him. "Should anyone ask later. Ye'll come with me, and I *will* shoot you, should ye make any move to give me away before we're out of the city. We are understood, I hope?"

"We are," Grey replied briefly, and swung up into the saddle.

He rode a little ahead of Jamie, conscious of the small round spot between his shoulder blades. *Pro forma* or not, he'd meant it.

He wondered whether Jamie would shoot him in the chest or simply break his neck when he found out. Likely bare hands, he thought. It was a visceral sort of thing, sex.

The idea of concealing the truth hadn't seriously occurred to him. He didn't know Claire Fraser nearly as well as Jamie did—but he knew beyond the shadow of a doubt that she couldn't keep secrets. Not from anyone. And certainly not from Jamie, restored to her from the dead.

Of course, it might be some time before Jamie was able to speak to her again. But he knew Jamie Fraser infinitely better than he knew Claire—and the one thing he was certain of was that nothing whatever would stand long between Jamie and his wife.

The rain had passed, and the sun shone on the puddles as they splashed through the streets. There was a sense of movement all around, agitation in the air. The army was quartered in Germantown, but there were always soldiers in the city, and their knowledge of imminent departure, anticipation of the return to campaigning, infected the city like a plague, a fever passing invisibly from man to man.

A patrol on the road out of the city stopped them but waved them on when

Grey gave his name and rank. His companion he introduced as Mr. Alexander MacKenzie and thought he felt a vibration of humor from said companion. Alex MacKenzie was the name Jamie had used at Helwater—as Grey's prisoner.

Oh, God, Grey thought suddenly, leading the way out of sight of the patrol. *William.* In the shock of the confrontation and their abrupt departure, he hadn't had time to think. If Grey were dead, what would William do?

His thoughts buzzed like a swarm of hiving bees, crawling over one another in a seething mass; impossible to focus on one for more than an instant before it was lost in the deafening hum. Denys Randall-Isaacs. Richardson. With Grey gone, he would almost certainly move to arrest Claire. William would try to stop him, if he knew. But William didn't know what Richardson was. . . . Grey didn't know, either, not for sure. Henry and his Negro lover—Grey knew they were lovers now, had seen it in both their faces—Dottie and her Quaker: if the twin shocks didn't kill Hal, he'd be on a ship bound for America in nothing flat, and *that* would certainly kill him. Percy. Oh, Jesus, Percy.

Jamie was in front of him now, leading the way. There were little groups of people on the road: mostly farmers coming in with wagonloads of supplies for the army. They looked curiously at Jamie, much more so at Grey. But no one stopped or challenged them, and an hour later Jamie led them down a trace off the main road and into a small woodland dripping and steaming from the recent rain. There was a stream; Jamie swung down off his horse and left it to drink, and Grey did likewise, feeling strangely unreal, as though the leather of saddle and reins was foreign to his skin, as though rain-chilled air passed through him, body and bones, rather than around him.

Jamie crouched by the stream and drank, then splashed water over his head and face and stood up, shaking himself like a dog.

"Thank ye, John," he said. "I hadna time to say it earlier. I'm verra grateful to ye."

"Thank me? It was hardly my choice. You abducted me at gunpoint."

Jamie smiled; the tension of the last hour had eased, and with it the lines of his face.

"Not that. For taking care of Claire, I mean."

"Claire," he repeated. "Ah. Yes. That."

"Aye, that," Jamie said patiently, and bent a little to peer at him in concern. "Are ye quite well, John? Ye look a wee bit peaked."

"Peaked," Grey muttered. His heart was beating very erratically; perhaps it would conveniently stop. He waited for a moment to allow it to do this if it liked, but it went on cheerfully thumping away. No help, then. Jamie was still looking quizzically at him. Best to get it over quickly.

He took a deep breath, shut his eyes, and commended his soul to God.

"I have had carnal knowledge of your wife," he blurted.

He had expected to die more or less instantaneously upon this utterance, but everything continued just as usual. Birds continued chirping in the trees, and the rip and slobber of the horses champing grass was the only sound above that of the rushing water. He opened one eye to find Jamie Fraser standing there regarding him, head to one side.

"Oh?" said Jamie curiously. "Why?"

102

BRED IN THE BONE

I ... UH ... IF you'll excuse me for a moment..." I backed slowly to the door of my room and, seizing the knob, whipped inside and shut the door, leaving Willie to recover himself in decent privacy. And not only Willie.

I pressed myself against the door as though pursued by werewolves, my blood thundering in my ears.

"Jesus H. Roosevelt Christ," I whispered. Something like a geyser rose up inside me and burst in my head, the spray of it sparkling with sunlight and diamonds. I was dimly aware that it had come on to rain outside, and dirty gray water was streaking the windowpanes, but that didn't matter a bit to the effervescence inside me.

I stood still for several minutes, eyes closed, not thinking anything, just murmuring, "Thank you, God," over and over, soundlessly.

A tentative rap on the door jarred me out of this trance, and I turned to open it. William stood on the landing.

His shirt still hung open where he'd torn it, and I could see the pulse beat fast in the hollow of his throat. He bowed awkwardly to me, trying to achieve a smile but notably failing in the attempt. He gave it up.

"I am not sure what to call you," he said. "Under the—the circumstances."

"Oh," I said, mildly disconcerted. "Well. I don't think—at least I *hope* that the relationship between you and me hasn't changed." I realized, with a sudden dampening of my euphoria, that it very well might now, and the thought gave me a deep pang. I was very fond of him, for his own sake, as well as for his father's—or fathers', as the case might be.

"Could you bring yourself to go on calling me 'Mother Claire,' do you think? Just until we can think of something more ... appropriate," I added hastily, seeing reluctance narrow his eyes. "After all, I suppose I am still your stepmother. Regardless of the ... er ... the situation."

He turned that over for a moment, then nodded briefly.

"May I come in? I wish to talk to you."

"Yes, I suppose you do."

If I hadn't known both his fathers, I would have marveled at his ability to suppress the rage and confusion he had so clearly exhibited a quarter of an hour ago. Jamie did it by instinct, John by long experience—but both of them had an iron power of will, and whether William's was bred in the bone or acquired by example, he most assuredly had one.

"Shall I send for something?" I asked. "A little brandy? It's good for shock."

He shook his head. He wouldn't sit—I didn't think he could—but leaned against the wall.

"I suppose that you knew? You could scarcely help but notice the resemblance, I suppose," he added bitterly.

"It *is* rather striking," I agreed, with caution. "Yes, I knew. My husband told me"—I groped for some delicate way of putting it—"the, um, circumstances of your birth some years ago."

And just how was *I* going to describe those circumstances?

It hadn't exactly escaped me that there were a few awkward explanations to be made—but caught up in the alarms of Jamie's sudden reappearance and escape and the giddiness of my own subsequent euphoria, it somehow hadn't occurred to me that I would be the person making them.

I'd seen the little shrine he kept in his room, the double portrait of his two mothers—both so heartbreakingly young. If age was good for anything, surely it should have given me the wisdom to deal with this?

How could I tell him that he was the result of an impulsive, self-willed young girl's blackmail? Let alone tell him that he had been the cause of both his legal parents' deaths? And if anyone was going to tell him what his birth had meant to Jamie, it was going to have to *be* Jamie.

"Your mother..." I began, and hesitated. Jamie would have taken the blame solely upon himself rather than blacken Geneva's memory to her son, I knew. I wasn't having that.

"She was reckless," William said, watching me closely. "Everybody says she was reckless. Was it—I suppose I only want to know, was it rape?"

"God, no!" I said, horrified, and saw his fists uncurl a little.

"That's good," he said, and let out the breath he'd been holding. "You're sure he didn't lie to you?"

"I'm sure." He and his father might be able to hide their feelings; I certainly couldn't, and while I would never be able to make a living playing cards, having a glass face was occasionally a good thing. I stood still and let him see that I told the truth.

"Do you think—did he say—" He stopped and swallowed, hard. "Did they love each other, do you think?"

"As much as they could, I think," I said softly. "They hadn't much time, only the one night." I ached for him and would have liked so much to take him in my arms and comfort him. But he was a man, and a young one, fierce about his pain. He'd deal with it as he could, and I thought it would be some years—if ever—before he learned to share it.

"Yes," he said, and pressed his lips together, as though he'd been going to say something else and thought better of it. "Yes, I—I see." It was quite clear from his tone that he didn't but, reeling under the impact of realization, had no idea what to ask next, let alone what to do with the information he had.

"I was born almost exactly nine months after my parents' marriage," he said, giving me a hard look. "Did they deceive my father? Or did my mother play the whore with her groom before she wed?"

"That might be a bit harsh," I began.

"No, it isn't," he snapped. "Which was it?"

"Your fa—Jamie. He'd never deceive another man in his marriage." *Except Frank,* I thought, a little wildly. But, of course, he hadn't known at first that he was doing it . . .

"My father," he said abruptly. "Pa—Lord John, I mean. He knew—knows?"

"Yes." Thin ice again. I didn't think he had any idea that Lord John had married Isobel principally for his sake—and Jamie's—but didn't want him going anywhere near the question of Lord John's motives.

"All of them," I said firmly, "all four of them; they wanted what was best for you."

"Best for me," he repeated bleakly. "Right." His knuckles had gone white again, and he gave me a look through narrowed eyes that I recognized all too well: a Fraser about to go off with a bang. I also knew perfectly well that there was no way of stopping one from detonating but had a try anyway, putting out a hand to him.

"William," I began. "Believe me—"

"I do," he said. "Don't bloody tell me any more. God *damn* it!" And, whirling on his heel, he drove his fist through the paneling with a thud that shook the room, wrenched his hand out of the hole he'd made, and stormed out. I heard crunching and rending as he paused to kick out several of the balusters on the landing and rip a length of the stair railing off, and I made it to the door in time to see him draw back a four-foot chunk of wood over his shoulder, swing, and strike the crystal chandelier that hung over the stairwell in an explosion of shattering glass. For a moment, he teetered on the open edge of the landing and I thought he would fall, or hurl himself off, but he staggered back from the edge and threw the chunk of wood like a javelin at the remnant of the chandelier with a burst of breath that might have been a grunt or a sob.

Then he rushed headlong down the stairs, thumping his wounded fist at intervals against the wall, where it left bloody smudges. He hit the front door with his shoulder, rebounded, jerked it open, and went out like a locomotive.

I stood frozen on the landing in the midst of chaos and destruction, gripping the edge of the broken balustrade. Tiny rainbows danced on walls and ceiling like multicolored dragonflies sprung out of the shattered crystal that littered the floor.

Something moved; a shadow fell across the floor of the hall below. A small, dark figure walked slowly in through the open doorway. Putting back the hood of her cloak, Jenny Fraser Murray looked round at the devastation, then up at me, her face a pale oval glimmering with humor.

"Like father, like son, I see," she remarked. "God help us all."

103

THE HOUR OF THE WOLF

T HE BRITISH ARMY was leaving Philadelphia. The Delaware was choked with ships, and the ferries ran nonstop from the end of State Street across to Cooper's Point. Three thousand Tories were leaving the city, too, afraid to stay without the army's protection; General Clinton had promised them passage, though their baggage made a dreadful mess—stacked on the docks, crammed into the ferries—and occupied a good deal of space on board the ships. Ian and Rachel sat on the riverbank below Philadelphia, under the shade of a drooping sycamore, and watched an artillery emplacement being disassembled, a hundred yards away.

The artillerymen worked in shirtsleeves, their blue coats folded on the grass nearby, removing the guns that had defended the city, preparing them for shipping. They were in no hurry and took no particular notice of spectators; it didn't matter now.

"Does thee know where they are going?" Rachel asked.

"Aye, I do. Fergus says they're going north, to reinforce New York."

"Thee has seen him?" She turned her head, interested, and the leaf shadows flickered over her face.

"Aye, he came home last night; he'll be safe now, wi' the Tories and the army gone."

"Safe," she said, with a skeptical intonation. "As safe as anyone may be, in times like these, thee means." She'd taken off her cap because of the heat and brushed the damp, dark hair back from her cheeks.

He smiled, but said nothing. She knew as well as he did what the illusions of safety were.

"Fergus says the British mean to cut the colonies in half," he remarked. "Separate north from south and deal with them separately."

"Does he? And how does he know this?" she asked, surprised.

"A British officer named Randall-Isaacs; he talks to Fergus."

"He is a spy, thee means? For which side?" Her lips compressed a little. He wasn't sure where spying fell, in terms of Quaker philosophy, but didn't care to ask just now. It was a tender subject, Quaker philosophy.

"I shouldna like to have to guess," he said. "He passes himself off as an American agent, but that may be all moonshine. Ye canna trust anyone in wartime, aye?"

She turned round to look at him at that, hands behind her back as she leaned against the sycamore.

"Can thee not?"

"I trust you," he said. "And your brother."

"And thy dog," she said, with a glance at Rollo, writhing on the ground to scratch his back. "Thy aunt and uncle, too, and Fergus and his wife? That seems a fair number of friends." She leaned toward him, squinting in concern. "Does thy arm pain thee?"

"Och, it's well enough." He shrugged with his good shoulder, smiling. His arm did hurt, but the sling helped. The ax blow had nearly severed his left arm, cutting through the flesh and breaking the bone. His aunt said he had been lucky, in that it had not damaged the tendons. The body is plastic, she said. Muscle would heal, and so would bone.

Rollo's had; there was no trace of stiffness from the gunshot wound, and while his muzzle was growing white, he slid through the bushes like an eel, sniffing industriously.

Rachel sighed and gave him a direct look under dark, level brows.

"Ian, thee is thinking something painful, and I would much prefer thee tells me what it is. Has something happened?"

A great many things had happened, were happening all around them, would continue to happen. How could he tell her . . . ? And yet he couldn't not.

"The world is turning upside down," he blurted. "And you are the only constant thing. The only thing I—that binds me to the earth."

Her eyes softened.

"Am I?"

"Ye ken verra well that you are," he said gruffly. He looked away, his heart pounding. Too late, he thought, with a mixture of dismay and elation. He'd begun to speak; he couldn't stop now, no matter what might come of it.

"I know what I am," he said, awkward but determined. "I would turn Quaker for your sake, Rachel, but I ken I'm not one in my heart; I think I never could be. And I think ye wouldna want me to say words I dinna mean or pretend to be something I canna be."

"No," she said softly. "I would not want that."

He opened his mouth but couldn't find more words to say. He swallowed, dry-mouthed, waiting. She swallowed, too; he saw the slight movement of her throat, soft and brown; the sun had begun to touch her again, the nut-brown maiden ripening from winter's pale bloom.

The artillerymen loaded the last of the cannon into a wagon, hitched their limbers to teams of oxen, and with laughter and raucous talk moved up the road toward the ferry point. When they were gone at last, a silence fell. There were still noises—the sound of the river, the rustle of the sycamore, and far beyond, the bellowings and crashings of an army on the move, the sound of violence impending. But between them, there was silence.

I've lost, he thought, but her head was still bent in thought. Is she maybe praying? Or only trying to think how to send me away?

Whichever it was, she lifted her head and stood up, away from the tree. She pointed at Rollo, who was lying couchant now, motionless but alert, yellow eyes following every movement of a fat robin foraging in the grass.

"That dog is a wolf, is he not?"

"Aye, well, mostly."

A small flash of hazel told him not to quibble.

"And yet he is thy boon companion, a creature of rare courage and affection, and altogether a worthy being?"

"Oh, aye," he said with more confidence. "He is."

She gave him an even look.

"Thee is a wolf, too, and I know it. But thee is my wolf, and best thee know that."

He'd started to burn when she spoke, an ignition swift and fierce as the lighting of one of his cousin's matches. He put out his hand, palm forward, to her, still cautious lest she, too, burst into flame.

"What I said to ye, before . . . that I kent ye loved me—"

She stepped forward and pressed her palm to his, her small, cool fingers linking tight.

"What I say to thee now is that I do love thee. And if thee hunts at night, thee will come home."

Under the sycamore, the dog yawned and laid his muzzle on his paws.

"And sleep at thy feet," Ian whispered, and gathered her in with his one good arm, both of them blazing bright as day.

AUTHOR'S NOTES

Brigadier General Simon Fraser

There are, as anyone who's read my books will already realize, a *lot* of Simon Frasers running around the eighteenth century. The Brigadier who fought gallantly and was killed at Saratoga is not one of the Frasers of Lovat, but a Fraser of Balnain. That is, not a direct descendant of the Old Fox but certainly a relation of the family. He had an illustrious military career, including the famous taking of Quebec with James Wolfe in 1759 (which battle forms a part of a novella entitled "The Custom of the Army," a Lord John Grey story which will be published in March of 2010 as part of an anthology titled *Warriors*—in case you want more details).

My reason for mentioning the Brigadier particularly, though, is the interesting matter of his grave. Most accounts of Saratoga that mention Simon Fraser of Balnain report that he was buried in the evening of the day he died, within the boundaries of the Great Redoubt (not Breymann's Redoubt, which Jamie stormed with Benedict Arnold, but the larger one on the field), at his own request. Some accounts add details, such as the attendance of Balcarres's rangers, or of the Americans firing a minute gun in Fraser's honor when they realized what was taking place, while other accounts consider these romantic but probably apocryphal details and say that he was attended only by the close members of his staff.

Now, it isn't always possible to go in person to a place you're writing about, nor is it always necessary. It *is* usually desirable, though, and luckily, Saratoga is pretty accessible, and the battlefield there is well preserved and curated. I've walked the field there three times over the course of several years since I first decided that I wanted to use this particular battle as a centerpiece of a book, if not the book I happened to be writing at the time. On one of these occasions, I was there alone, there were no other tourists, and I got into conversation with one of the park employees (dressed in period costume and posted at the rebuilt site of the Bemis farm). After he patiently answered a lot of intrusive questions ("Are you wearing underwear?" being one of them, and "No," being the answer. "Long shirttails," being the further explanation for how one avoids chafing while wearing homespun breeches), allowed me to handle his Brown Bess musket and explained the loading and firing of it, we got into a discussion of the battle and its personalities—since I did, at this point, know quite a lot about it.

General Fraser's grave was at that point noted on the Park Service map—but it wasn't in the Great Redoubt; it was located near the river. I'd been down there but found no marker for it, and so inquired where it was—and why wasn't it in the Great Redoubt? I was informed that the Park Service had at one point—I don't know when, but fairly recently—done an archaeological excavation of the Great Redoubt, including the supposed gravesite. To everyone's surprise, General Fraser was *not* buried there, nor was anyone else. There were signs that a grave had once been dug, and a uniform button was found there, but no signs whatever of a body. (And while the body itself would be long since decomposed, you would expect still to see some signs.) There was (the employee told me) an account that said that General Fraser's grave had been moved to a site near the river, and that that was why the map was so marked—but no one knew where the specific place was, or, in fact, whether the General was in *that* one, either, which was why there was no marker there.

Well, novelists are a conscienceless lot. Those of us who deal with history tend to be fairly respectful of such facts as are recorded (always bearing in mind the proviso that just because it's in print, it isn't necessarily *true*). But give us a hole to slide through, an omission in the historic record, one of those mysterious lacunae that occur in even the best-documented life . . . so all in all, I rather thought that perhaps General Fraser had been sent home to Scotland. (Yes, they did send bodies to and fro in the eighteenth century, on occasion. Someone exhumed poor old Tom Paine from his grave in France, intending to ship him back to America so he could be interred there with honor as a prophet of the Revolution. His body was lost in transit, and no one's ever found it. Speaking of interesting lacunae . . .)

Anyway, as it happened, I went to Scotland last year, and while wandering round the countryside in search of a logical place near Balnain in which to plant General Fraser, stumbled over (literally) the large chambered cairn at Corrimony. Such sites are always evocative, and when I read on the sign posted there that there had once been a body in the central chamber, but it had evidently decayed into the soil (there *were* traces of bones left in the earth, even after a thousand years or more), *and* that the tomb had been broken into sometime in the nineteenth century (thus explaining why you won't find anything in the cairn if you happen to go there now) . . . well, hey. (People always ask novelists where they get their ideas. Everywhere!)

Quaker Plain Speech

The Religious Society of Friends was founded around 1647 by George Fox. As part of the Society's belief in the equality of all men before God, they did not use honorific titles (such as "Mr./Mrs.," "General/Colonel," etc.), and used "plain speech" in addressing everyone.

Now, as any of you who know a second language with Latin roots (Spanish, French, etc.) realize, these languages have both a familiar and a formal version of "you." So did English, once upon a time. The "thee" and "thou" forms that most of us recognize as Elizabethan or biblical are in fact the English familiar forms of "you"—with "you" used as both the plural familiar form ("all y'all"), and the formal pronoun (both singular and plural). As English evolved, the familiar forms were dropped, leaving us with the utilitarian "you" to cover all contingencies.

Quakers retained the familiar forms, though, as part of their "plain speech," until the twentieth century. Over the years, though, plain speech also evolved, and while "thee/thy" remained, "thou/thine" largely disappeared, and the verb forms associated with "thee/thy" changed. From about the mid-eighteenth century onward, plain speech used "thee" as the singular form of "you" (the plural form remained "you," even in plain speech), with the same verb forms normally used for third-person singular. For example, "He knows that/Thee knows that." The older verb endings—"knowest," "doth," etc.—were no longer used.

Scots/Scotch/Scottish

As noted elsewhere (*Lord John and the Brotherhood of the Blade,* see Author's Notes), in the eighteenth century (and indeed, well into the mid-twentieth century), the word "Scotch" and its variants (e.g., "Scotchman") were commonly used (by both English people *and* Scots) to describe an inhabitant of Scotland. The terms "Scottish" and "Scots" were also occasionally used, though less common.

Typos and Terminology

There may be an impulse to regard the term "mess-kid" (as used in Part Three of this book) as a typographical error. It's not. A mess-kid was a shallow, circular bucket in which sailors of the eighteenth and nineteenth centuries were served their food. A mess-*kit*, on the other hand, referred to the utensils carried and used by a soldier.

By the same token, while "crotch" is the usual American English term, the older form, "crutch," would have been used in eighteenth-century English-English usage. Which is not to say there aren't any typographical errors in this book (despite the heroic efforts of Ms. Kathy Lord, the copy editor; the alerts of various friends and translators who read the manuscript in chunks; and a fair amount of diligence by myself, these things happen) but these particular terms aren't.

Saratoga

A tremendous amount of historical research goes into a book like this (I am often bemused by letters from people telling me they'd visited a museum, seen some eighteenth-century artifacts, and been struck all a-heap by discov-

ering that I hadn't just made it all up!), and while there isn't room to acknowledge or list even a fraction of the sources I've used, I did want to mention one specific book.

The two battles of Saratoga were historically important, remarkably dramatic, and very complex, both in the logistics of the battles and in the troop
movements and politics that led up to them. I was fortunate to find, early on
in my researches, Richard M. Ketchum's *Saratoga,* which is an amazingly
well-done portrait of the battles, the background, and the plethora of color-
ful individuals who took part. I just wanted to recommend this book to those
of you with a deeper interest in the historical aspects, as these could only be
touched on lightly in the context of a novel.

Loch Errochty and Tunnel Tigers

During the 1950s and '60s, a great hydroelectric scheme was implemented in
the Scottish Highlands. The work of a great many "tunnel tigers" (also
known as "the Hydro boys")—laborers, many of them from Ireland and
Poland—went into digging tunnels through the mountains and building
dams for the creation of man-made lochs. Loch Errochty is in fact one of
these man-made lochs. The tunnel I've drawn as being associated with it
(complete with miniature train) is like those common to the hydroelectric
scheme as a whole, but I don't know that there actually *is* one at Loch
Errochty. On the other hand, the dam, turbine service chamber, and fish-
viewing chamber at Pitlochry are indeed all there. So are the anglers.

ABOUT THE TYPE

This book was set in Galliard, a typeface designed by Matthew Carter for the Merganthaler Linotype Company in 1978. Galliard is based on the sixteenth-century typefaces of Robert Granjon.